TREE OF SOULS

BY HOWARD SCHWARTZ

Poetry
  Vessels
  Gathering the Sparks
  Sleepwalking Beneath the Stars
  Signs of the Lost Tribe

Fiction
  A Blessing Over Ashes
  Midrashim
  The Captive Soul of the Messiah
  Rooms of the Soul
  Adam's Soul
  The Four Who Entered Paradise

Editor
  Imperial Messages: One Hundred Modern Parables
  Voices Within the Ark: The Modern Jewish Poets
  Gates to the New City: A Treasury of Modern Jewish Tales
  The Dream Assembly: Tales of Rabbi Zalman Schachter-Shalomi
  Elijah's Violin & Other Jewish Fairy Tales
  Miriam's Tambourine: Jewish Tales from Around the World
  Lilith's Cave: Jewish Tales of the Supernatural
  Gabriel's Palace: Jewish Mystical Tales
  Tree of Souls: The Mythology of Judaism

Essays
  Reimagining the Bible: The Storytelling of the Rabbis

Children's Books
  The Diamond Tree
  The Sabbath Lion
  Next Year in Jerusalem
  The Wonder Child
  A Coat for the Moon
  Ask the Bones
  A Journey to Paradise
  The Day the Rabbi Disappeared
  Invisible Kingdoms
  Before You Were Born

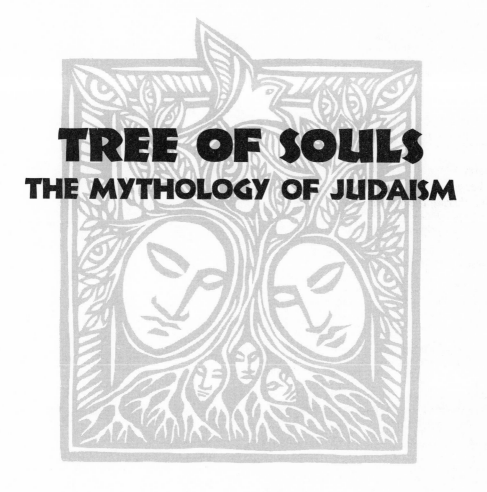

TREE OF SOULS
THE MYTHOLOGY OF JUDAISM

HOWARD SCHWARTZ

Illustrated by
Caren Loebel-Fried

Foreword by
Elliot K. Ginsburg

OXFORD
UNIVERSITY PRESS
2004

OXFORD
UNIVERSITY PRESS

Oxford   New York
Auckland   Bangkok   Buenos Aires   Cape Town   Chennai
Dar es Salaam   Delhi   Hong Kong   Istanbul   Karachi   Kolkata
Kuala Lumpur   Madrid   Melbourne   Mexico City   Mumbai   Nairobi
São Paulo   Shanghai   Taipei   Tokyo   Toronto

Published by Oxford University Press, Inc.
198 Madison Avenue, New York, New York 10016
www.oup.com

Oxford is a registered trademark of Oxford University Press

Library of Congress Cataloging-in-Publication Data
Schwartz, Howard, 1945–
    Tree of souls : the mythology of Judaism / Howard Schwartz.
       p. cm.
    Retellings of nearly 700 Jewish myths.
    Includes bibliographical references and index.
    ISBN 0–19–508679–1
1. Legends, Jewish.
2. Jewish mythology.
I. Title.
BM530.S472   2004
296.1—dc22   2003022934

Acknowledgments:
    Some of these myths and commentaries have previously been published in *Parabola*, the *Learn Torah With*
series, *Natural Bridge*, and the *St. Louis Post-Dispatch*.
    Most of the quotations from the Bible are reprinted from the *Tanakh: A New Translation of the Holy
Scriptures According to the Traditional Hebrew Text* © 1985, The Jewish Publication Society with the permission
of the publisher, The Jewish Publication Society.
    The following parables of Franz Kafka were newly translated by Henry Shapiro: "Before the Law,"
"Leopards in the Temple," "Paradise," "The Building of the Temple," and "The Coming of the Messiah."
Translations © 2004 Henry Shapiro. All Rights Reserved.

9 8 7 6 5 4 3 2 1
Printed in the United States of America on acid-free paper

For my son, Nati Zohar

Rabbi Yose taught: "God has a tree of flowering souls in Paradise. This tree is surrounded by the four winds of the world. From the branches of this tree sprout forth all souls, for they grow upon this tree, as is written: *'I am a cypress tree in bloom; your fruit issues forth from Me.'* (Hos.14:9). And from the roots of this tree sprout the souls of all the righteous ones whose names are inscribed there. From this we learn that all souls are the fruit of the Holy One, blessed be He."

Ha-Nefesh ha-Hakhamah
Moses ben Shem Tov de Leon

CONTENTS

God Studies the Torah

The Suffering God

God Walks in the World

Early Incarnations of the Shekhinah

Myths of the Bride of God

BOOK THREE MYTHS OF HEAVEN 153

Lilith Rises from the Deep

Vampires, Spirits, Dybbuks, and Demons

The History of Gehenna

BOOK FIVE   MYTHS OF THE HOLY WORD   **245**

Myths of Sukkot

Myths of Simhat Torah

Myths of Passover

Myths of Lag ba-Omer

Myths of Shavuot

Myths of the Sabbath

BOOK EIGHT   MYTHS OF THE HOLY LAND

The Garden of Eden

The Promised Land

The Heavenly Jerusalem

BOOK TEN   MYTHS OF THE MESSIAH   **481**

The Creation of the Messiah

The Heavenly Messiah

The Earthly Messiah

The Captive Messiah

The End of Days

ABBREVIATIONS

BOOKS OF THE BIBLE

Gen.	Genesis	Nah.	Nahum
Exod.	Exodus	Hab.	Habakkuk
Lev.	Leviticus	Zeph.	Zephaniah
Num.	Numbers	Hag.	Haggai
Deut.	Deuteronomy	Zech.	Zechariah
Josh.	Joshua	Mal.	Malachi
Judg.	Judges	Ps.	Psalms
1 Sam.	1 Samuel	Prov.	Proverbs
2 Sam.	2 Samuel	Job	Job
1 Kings	1 Kings	S. of S.	The Song of Songs
2 Kings	2 Kings	Ruth	Ruth
Isa.	Isaiah	Lam.	Lamentations
Jer.	Jeremiah	Eccles.	Ecclesiastes
Ezek.	Ezekiel	Esther	Esther
Hos.	Hosea	Dan.	Daniel
Joel	Joel	Ezra	Ezra
Amos	Amos	Neh.	Nehemiah
Obad.	Obadiah	1 Chron.	1 Chronicles
Jonah	Jonah	2 Chron.	2 Chronicles
Micah	Micah		

TRACTATES OF THE MISHNAH AND TALMUD

The Babylonian Talmud is identified as B. and the Palestinian Talmud (or Jerusalem Talmud) as Y. (for Yerushalmi).

Ar.	Arakhin	MK	Mo'ed Katan
Avot	Avot	MS	Ma'aser Sheni
AZ	Avodah Zarah	Naz.	Nazir
BB	Bava Batra	Ned.	Nedarim
Bekh.	Bekhorot	Neg.	Nega'im
Ber.	Berakhot	Nid.	Niddah
Betz.	Betzah	Oh.	Oholot
Bik.	Bikkurim	Or.	Orlah
BK	Bava Kama	Par.	Parah
BM	Bava Metzia	Pe.	Pe'ah
De.	Demai	Per.	Perek ha-Shalom
Ed.	Eduyyot	Pes.	Pesahim
Er.	Eruvin	RH	Rosh ha-Shanah
Git.	Gittin	Sanh.	Sanhedrin
Hag.	Hagigah	Shab.	Shabbat
Hal.	Hallah	Shek.	Shekalim
Hor.	Horayot	Shev.	Shevi'it
Hul.	Hullin	Shavu.	Shavuot
Kel.	Kelim	Sot.	Sota
Ker.	Keritot	Suk.	Sukkah
Ket.	Ketubot	Tan.	Ta'anit
Kid.	Kiddushin	Tam.	Tamid
Kil.	Kilayim	Tem.	Temurah
Kin.	Kinnim	Ter.	Terumot
Maas.	Ma'aserot	Toh.	Tohorot
Mak.	Makkot	TY	Tevul Yom
Makh.	Makhshirin	Tz.	Tzitzit
Me.	Me'ilah	Uk.	Uktzin
Meg.	Megillah	Yad.	Yadayim
Men.	Menahot	Yev.	Yevamot
Mid.	Middot	Yoma	Yoma
Mik.	Mikva'ot	Zev.	Zevahim

RABBIS IDENTIFIED BY ACRONYMS

Ari = Isaac Luria.

Ba'al Shem Tov (also known as Besht) = Israel ben Eliezer.

Ben Ish Hai = Yosef Hayim of Baghdad.

Maharal = Judah Loew ben Bezalel.

Maharsha = Samuel Eliezer Edels.

Maimonides (also known as Rambam) = Moses ben Maimon.

Nachmanides (also known as Ramban) = Moses ben Nachman.

*Or ha-Hayim = Hayim ben Attar.

Ramak = Moshe Cordovero.

Rashbam = Samuel ben Meir.

Rashi = Solomon ben Isaac of Troyes.

Ribash = Isaac ben Sheshet Parfat.

*Or ha-Hayim ("The Light of Life") is the title of the famous biblical commentary written by Rabbi Hayim ben Attar. It is not an acronym; rather, he became identified by the title of his book.

TRANSLITERATION KEY

alef = not transliterated
bet = b, v
gimmel = g
dalet = d
heh = h
vav = v
zayin = z
het = h
tet = t
yod = y – when vowel, at end of word – i
kaf = k, kh

lamed = l
mem = m
nun = n
samekh = s
ayin = ', not always transliterated
peh = p, f, ph
tzaddi = tz
kuf = k
resh = r
shin = s, sh
tav = t

PREFACE

A largely unrecognized but quite extensive mythology[1] is embedded throughout Jewish literature. The primary myths portrayed in the Bible, especially those in Genesis, became the focus of mythic elaboration. The biblical text packs a maximum amount of meaning into a minimum number of words, thereby compelling interpretation. An ancient rabbinic method of exegesis called midrash,[2] which sought out and inevitably found the solution to problems perceived in the biblical text, resulted in the creation of an abundant mythology that eventually took on a life of its own. Often the transformation that takes place between the early periods of Jewish myth and their later evolution is considerable, almost constituting a new set of myths based on the old ones. The sum of all of these generations of reimagining the Bible is a Jewish mythology as rich as that of other great ancient cultures. These myths may appear either in fully developed form or as widely scattered fragments. Often, when these fragments are collected from the extant sources and pieced back together, they reveal extensive elaborations of the original myths, often in unexpected directions.

It has been my intention to draw Jewish myths from the full range of Jewish literature. This tradition extends from biblical times until the present, and includes texts from inside and outside normative Jewish tradition. For details about the texts included, see "A Note on the Sources" on p. 525.

Because of the considerable differences between the myths deriving from various periods, it is difficult to speak of a single or definitive Jewish mythology. Yet it is also clear that the seeds of all the major myths are found in the earlier texts, where they are often the subject of a profound evolutionary process, a dialectic that alternates between the tendency to mythologize Judaism and the inclination to resist such impulses. An attentive reader should find the permutations of these myths fascinating. I have chosen to regard these as organic developments, possessing life of their own, and I have attempted to draw together the threads of these fragmentary myths into coherent ones, where possible. Where contradictory explanations are found, this has also been noted using the formula "Some say" and "Others say." This is intended to indicate the existence of multiple versions of the same myth. Some myths derive from a single text, but most have multiple sources, reflecting the continuing fascination with specific themes as well as the desire of subsequent generations to reinterpret them and make them relevant to their own lives.

This book has been structured around what I regard as the ten primary categories of Jewish mythology: *Myths of God, Myths of Creation, Myths of Heaven, Myths of Hell, Myths of the Holy Word, Myths of the Holy Time, Myths of the Holy People, Myths of the Holy Land, Myths of Exile*, and *Myths of the Messiah*. Each entry includes the myth, usually drawn from multiple sources, as well a commentary and its sources. The purpose of the commentary is to put the myth in the proper context, provide the biblical verses that inspired or explain it, note related myths, and to untangle, as much as possible, the mythic threads it consists of, as well as parallels to other mythic traditions.

Several key modern scholars have considered the question of whether there can be said to be a Jewish mythology, and, if so, what its characteristics would be. These include Gershom Scholem, Isaiah Tishby, Alexander Altmann, Raphael Patai, Joseph Dan, Moshe Idel, Yehuda Liebes, Arthur Green, Michael Fishbane, David J. Halperin, Michael Stone, Peter Schäfer, Elliot Wolfson, Rachel Elior, Pinchas Giller, Tikva Frymer-Kensky, and Elliot K. Ginsburg. I am grateful for their perspectives and insights. In addition, scores of articles have been written about various aspects of virtually all of the myths included here. I have noted especially important and relevant articles following the commentaries to the myths, under the category of "Studies."

I am grateful to the following people who supported and assisted me during this long project. Thanks, above all, to my editor, Cynthia Read, who has the patience of Penelope. Special thanks to my son, Nati, who lent a helping hand at a crucial time, and to my wife, Tsila, whose support has been essential. Many thanks to Caren Loebel-Fried for her beautiful prints, which have added immeasurably to this book. I am especially grateful to Elliot K. Ginsburg, David J. Halperin, Byron Sherwin, and Gershon Winkler for their valuable suggestions and comments. I am also grateful to Henry Shapiro for his astute suggestions, conveyed over many a lunch. Thanks are also due to Marc Bregman, Paula Cooper, Bonnie Fetterman, Rabbi Steve Gutow, Barbara Rush, Marc Saperstein, Peninnah Schram, Joseph Schultz, Cherie Karo Schwartz, Laya Firestone Seghi, and Diane Wolkstein, for their suggestions and insights. Thanks as well to Daniel Breslauer, Theo Calderara, Michael Castro, Joseph Dan, Amy Debrecht, Rabbi Bruce Diamond, Yael Even, Pinchas Giller, Rabbi James Stone Goodman, Stuart Gordon, Arthur Green, Edna Hechal of the Israel Folktale Archives, Ruth and Jim Hinds, Lynn Holden, Catherine Humphries, Glenn Irwin, Eve Jones, Rodger Kamenetz, Edward Londe, the late Rabbi Abraham Ezra Millgram, Dov Noy, Marie S. Nuchols, Peter Brigaitis, Anne Holmes, Mary Ann Zissimos, Adelia Parker, Rebecca Pastor, the late Raphael Patai, Simcha Raphael, Rabbi Zalman Schachter-Shalomi, the late Gershom Scholem, Maury Schwartz, Miriam Schwartz, Shira Schwartz, Alan Segal, Dan Sharon, Yaacov David Shulman, Rabbi Lane Steinger, Steve Stern, Rabbi Jeffrey Stiffman, Michael Swartz, Rabbi Susan Talve, Benyamim Tsedaka, Meg Weaver and Eli Yassif. I also want to thank the students of my class on Jewish mythology at Spertus College. I am also grateful to the University of Missouri-St. Louis for grants that made it possible to pursue the research for this book.

Readers who wish to register comments, suggestions, corrections, praise, or dissent may contact me at *jewishmyth@yahoo.com.*

Howard Schwartz
St. Louis

Notes

[1]See p. xliv of the Introduction for a definition of "myth" and "mythology" as it is used in this book. The conventional meaning of "myth" as something that is not true is *not* intended here.

[2]For a discussion of this method of rabbinic exegesis, see p. lxxii of the Introduction.

FOREWORD

The Resonances and Registers of Jewish Myth
by Elliot K. Ginsburg

To enter this book is to enter a world thick with meaning, *olam u-melo'o*, "a world and the fullness thereof."[1] In its pages, one can encounter the astonishing range of the Jewish mythic imagination: texts and countertexts, brief epigrams and extended chain midrashim, exclamations and sober disquisitions: they are all in there. For *Tree of Souls* is the product of a man, Howard Schwartz, who wears many hats: he is at once a literary artist and master editor, who is simultaneously immersed in (and sharpened by) the world of scholarship. The resulting work is a gift of the scholarly and literary imagination, and it is a joy to read.

Jewish mythology and its many voices. One of the most impressive features of this work is its capacious understanding of what is authentically *Jewish*. In consort with most contemporary scholars, Schwartz departs from those great Judaic scholars of the 19th century who sought to reduce Judaism—in its evolving, plural, oft messy vitality—to an idealized set of unchanging beliefs or practices, articulated by a central cast of characters. Schwartz listens rather more widely: he exhibits an inclusive, demotic willingness to combine different registers and a wide range of provenances. Obscure manuscripts and well-known texts reside cheek-by-jowl; so too, polished literary works and oral narratives. Texts written in Rabbinic Hebrew and Aramaic sit alongside passages from Yiddish, German and Middle-Eastern vernacular. The multi-streamed Rabbinic tradition is represented not only by a stunning array of talmudic and midrashic texts, but also by later kabbalistic myths with gnostic and sometimes rapturous undertones, hasidic *mayses* (tales) and ethical tracts. The global meets the local as talmudic understandings of soul enter into dialogue with an Afghani Jewish tale from an oral archive—the Great Tradition imbricated with the so-called "Little Tradition." So too, the philosopher-legalist Maimonides resonates with early modern mystic Hayyim ben Attar, and the *Zohar* with the author of Yiddish vernacular prayers, Shifra bas Joseph, wife of Ephraim Epstein. Rabbinic Judaism[2], in these pages, speaks in many voices.

Elliot K. Ginsburg is Associate Professor of Jewish Thought in the Department of Near Eastern Studies at the University of Michigan, Ann Arbor. He is the author of *The Sabbath in the Classical Kabbalah* and translator (with a critical commentary) of *Sod ha-Shabbat: The Mystery of the Sabbath* by Rabbi Meir ibn Gabbai.

If the Biblical-Rabbinic arc has a certain pride of place here, the book stretches to encompass non-Rabbanite currents as well. These include (1) Jewish streams that dried up in late antiquity or which subsequently flowed into other traditions; and (2) other mythic currents that left only the faintest residue in the Hebrew Bible, but which re-emerged with singular potency later. Of the former case, think of Philo or various Apocryphal works, preserved largely in Christianity; of the latter, those submerged texts, think of ancient Mesopotamian myths of cosmic battle, of the personified waters of chaos or the Great Sea-Dragon battling YHWH—accounts that are virtually effaced in the Hebrew Bible, but which surface fullblown in the Babylonian talmudic setting.[3] Schwartz also visits the contested borderlands of Rabbinic Judaism, on occasion citing Karaite teachings or the Sabbatean-tinged *Hemdat Yamim*, a work which enjoyed currency in Sephardic and Hasidic circles, despite its suspect provenance.

Finally, Schwartz expands the mythic canvas to include twentieth century figures, the Piasetzner Rebbe (d. 1943, Warsaw), Reb Zalman Shachter-Shalomi, the visionary of Jewish Renewal, and the Prague master Franz Kafka, to name three. All told, most of the dialects of Judaism, from major to minor, find a home here. Schwartz finds that elusive balance point between richness and focus. As one colleague put it: "Howard Schwartz is inclusive, but with good taste."

For readers who may wonder whether this democratizing impulse edges towards cacophony—too much of a good thing—know that Schwartz's keen gifts as an editor carry the day. He gives his work a strong thematic center, organizing texts around ten mythic categories that unfold across time and space. He is able to structure and sequence sources, to fashion mythic cycles. He deftly places texts in alignment with each other, or in apposition/opposition, creating a vibrant but coherent field of vision. What emerges therefore is an intriguing series of resonances and interrelations, a *transhistorical Jewish mythology*, if you will. If there are occasional bracing dissonances between myths, the whole approaches a symphony, a grand opus in ten chapters, ten movements.

Not only are myths beautifully rendered here, but their meanings are variously elucidated, enriched and complexified through up-to-date scholarship. Schwartz appends a scholarly commentary to each myth. These mini-essays are models of concision and literary insight. He traces motifs and provides historical context: explicating perplexities, highlighting discrete traditionary strands and points of evolution. Nor are spiritual insights lacking in these essays. Multiple readers will thus be astounded and delighted; for through Schwartz's tentacular reach our understanding of the Jewish and mythic imaginations is challenged and stretched. "This is Jewish?" some of us might be moved to ask. But Jewish it is! The sheer variety of mythemes found here supports Gershom Scholem's contention that one cannot predict *a priori*—on the basis of earlier teachings—just what will be considered authentically Jewish in any given period.

The centrality of the mythic imagination. In recent decades scholars have called renewed attention to the mythic element in successive strata of Jewish tradition[4]: to the mythic fragments, echoes and organizing themes found in the compositions of the Hebrew Bible; to the rabbinic rereadings of the newly-canonical Scripture[5] in light of living myths of God's deeds and personality; and the complex integrations of mythic images and themes in medieval kabbalah, none more daring than the rendering of the divine totality in terms of ten potencies or *sefirot*, each with its own personality and gendered associations. (Divine oneness, for example, is expressed as the loving union of the masculine and feminine aspects of God.) In the ensuing paragraphs, I wish to suggest several things, knowing that their full articulation is beyond the scope of this essay: (1) that there is a Grand Myth (or meta-narrative) that was shared by most Jews in the Rabbinic, pre-modern setting; (2) that this grand myth is rooted in (if not identical with) the foundational text of the Hebrew Bible; (3) that in interpreting the Hebrew Bible, the Rabbis developed a "Myth of myths" of signal importance, that of the multi-faceted Torah, whose manifold meanings could be successively uncovered but never exhausted; (4) that these three elements combined to support a sort of mythic consciousness enabling devotees to read their lives in terms of the Sacred Text and the Sacred Text in terms of their lives; and (5) that this mythic consciousness was rendered vital through storytelling and interpretation, as well as through the drama of ritual.

Briefly then, (1) to be a Jew in the classical setting is to have a Story, a shared meta-narrative. It is to hold that this world is created as an act of divine will; that one is the heir of Abraham and Sarah; of those who endure(d) Egyptian slavery and the gifts of Redemption, who stand at the pivot of Sinaitic revelation and its Covenant, who know the joys of homecoming and the enduring dislocations of exile.[6] It is to hold that there will be a Messianic resolution to history, though the Messiah doth tarry. This broad myth binds its adherents in a web of faith and fate, memory and expectation, in a way that transcends the defining particulars of time and place. This grand story (whose bare bones I telegraph here) is rarely articulated *in toto* by its adherents: it is rather cited *en passant*, like one who hums a few bars of a well-known, deeply assimilated, song. The adherent carries this Story, or if you prefer, this Tune, but it also carries him or her. (2) The grid for this meta-Story is the foundational text, the Hebrew Bible, which reaches canonical status through its Rabbinic closure in the late first century. Yet (3) as one door is closed, another opens. As Gershom Scholem has eloquently shown, sacred Text was immediately reopened through the medium of interpretation: *midrash*, commentary, and sundry forms of storytelling. Or as Michael Fishbane would have it: Rabbinic mythmaking "begins where the Hebrew Bible closes, with the canon."[7] What emerges is a suite (sometimes a tangle) of images, arguments, readings and narratives, all rooted in the evolving Myth of the Multi-Tiered Torah. This master narrative assumes that the divine Word is pregnant with multiple meanings, whole families of mythemes. Thus we read "one God has spoken, two I have heard"; and the divine "word is fire," [its manifold meanings released] "like a hammer striking the Rock"; and in a particularly telling rabbinic litany, *ellu ve-ellu divrei elohim hayyim*: both this interpretation and that one (the one that contradicts it) are the word of the living God.[8] In its most lavish formulations—in mystical tradition—this becomes the Myth of Torah's infinite, inexhaustible meaning: "The Torah has seventy faces," nay "600,000 facets." Or as various hasidic masters have it, not only do the black letters of text have meaning, but so too, the white spaces.[9] We might grasp this multiplicity by way of a parable, which expresses its radical edge[10]: *The great hasidic master Nachman of Bratslav has a dream within a dream. He wakes up from that inner dream. Still in visionary mode, he tries to interpret the inner dream, but its meaning eludes him. He sees a sage standing nearby, and asks him the meaning of his dream. The sage tugs at his beard and says: "this is my beard and This! [tugging again at the beard] is the meaning of your dream."*[11] *Nachman responds: "but I don't understand. "In that case," the sage adds, "go to the next room." Nachman repairs to the next room and finds an endless library filled with endless books. "And everywhere I looked," he adds, "I found another comment on the meaning of this thing."* I ask, what is the deeper Truth: the transverbal immediacy of the tug, the Sage's "*This!*" or the infinite play of interpretation? Perhaps the Torah is never so clear as when it is being unpacked, mined for its manifold truths. And this concludes our Myth about the necessary multiplication of Myths. In a sense, Howard Schwartz's book is a more measured illustration of Nachman's creative play.

(4) Arthur Green has written: "The great happenings of Scripture should in the proper sense be seen as mythical, that is, as paradigms that help us encounter, explain and enrich by archaic association the deepest experiences of which we humans are capable...By retelling, grappling with, dramatizing, living in the light of these paradigms, devotees feel themselves touched by a transcendent presence that is made real in their lives through the retelling, the re-enactments." To use the formulation of Clifford Geertz, myth both

provides a model *of* reality, what is *really real*, and a model *for* reality, how one is to behave in its light.[12]

There is a profound dialectic for those who live under the penumbra of the Sacred Text and its mythos: as devotees tend to read their life in terms of the orienting Text/Myth, and read the Text in terms of their life. Thus, some Jews during the Crusades saw themselves as Father Abrahams called upon to sacrifice their children for the sake of their faith; even as the press of historical events and other (possibly Christian-influenced) narratives may have lead them to hold that the Biblical Isaac was actually sacrificed and resurrected.[13] Over time, given myths expand and contract. New glosses to extant myths emerge as mythic fragments or images; sometimes these images coalesce into new stories, and sometimes into whole new mythic complexes or systems. Examples of System include the sefirotic theology in Zoharic Kabbalah with its Myth of the divine Androgyne, and the Lurianic mythos of Creation, Shattering, and Tikkun/Cosmic Restoration.

Classically speaking, to be a Jew is to have access to—to assimilate/debate/relate—varying degrees of these extant fragments, stories, mythic cycles and mythologies.

(5) As Howard Schwartz notes, myths are vitalized and absorbed not only through storytelling, but through the embodied mime of ritual performance (generally linked with the pattern of *mitzvot* and the cycles of sacred time). To grasp this, let me give one extended example—the myth of Sinaitic Revelation, wherein divine Presence and Will were simultaneously disclosed.[14] On one level, this was seen as a unique event that created a singular pivot in history. "God spoke these words *ve-lo yasaf*, and did not add any more." (Deut. 5:19) After this event, all has changed, and nothing can match its watershed import. To **recall** Sinai is to acknowledge that one-time transformation, and to live in light of its teachings.

On the second level of mythic enactment, Sinai is seen as an event that is **periodically reactualizable**. For example, to study Torah is (in the Rabbinic context) to *bask* in the light of Sacred Time and its heroes. To read and interpret, to retell, is to move from being a *dis*temporary of the Biblical figures to becoming their (near) *con*temporaries.[15] In a stronger sense, perhaps, to celebrate the holiday of Shavuot is to stand again at Sinai. In its kabbalistic formulation, especially, it is to enter the Covenant/Marriage with the Holy One, to feel the embrace of divine intimacy—not as memory of things past but as something wholly immediate. Here the sacred past flows into the present, or perhaps better: one re-enters that "past" which is not truly past so much as a transhistorical moment that is an eternal "present."

On the third level of signification, again found most strongly in kabbalistic tradition, Sinai is a paradigm for that which is, at bottom, always occuring. Here one comes to realize that the revelations of Shavuot are always present, if one could only maintain expanded awareness. Drawing on the Rabbinic pun "[At Sinai] God spoke these words, *ve-lo yasaf*: and did not add any more [i.e., Revelation is over] ff. Deut. 5:19, they read: *ve-lo yasaf*: and never ceased speaking.[16] The Torah that had been summarily closed is thus reopened, its wellsprings unsealed: *ma'ayan nove'a*. As Nachmanides had it, from the large miracles (such as Revelation at Sinai) one comes to the sense the small epiphanies. For divinity is always present and the Voice never ceases to flow. At this level of expanded awareness [*mohin degadlut*] God is, as the benediction has it, *noten ha-torah*, the one who ever **gives** Torah, each moment anew.[17] At various points in his book Schwartz illumines the connection between myth and ritual, showing how story can become, in his words, "more than story."

To date, we have implied that it was through myth that Israel most commonly encountered, grappled with, assimilated and marked life's pivotal moments. For myth addresses some of our fundamental existential questions, concerns that may shift over time but which tend to pervade different cultural settings. These questions include: how did the world come into being, and to what end; what may I/we hope for; what is the meaning of suffering and of joy, the co-existence of good and evil; is there a deeper purpose to history? What does it mean to be a Jew, to embrace Jewish practice? Who (rarely what) is God and how may I serve the One? what does it mean to be both an image of the divine and "dust and ashes"; what does it mean that I can both shatter and fix vessels and worlds? What is the meaning of gender—in humanity, in divinity? Or: what is the relation of work and rest, of depression and renewal? What is the significance of embodiment and ensoulment? And: what might unfold in other dimensions of existence, both high and low; to wit, what is the meaning of death, its sorrows and its sweet release, and how does one here live in its presence? In this foreword I simply pose the questions. In *Tree of Souls* these and other root questions are vividly addressed. It has been said that survival (and the production of meaning) comes in cultural inflections. The myths in this book give voice to a full array of Jewish inflections and dialects, creating *olam u-melo'o*, "a world replete with meanings".

Still each path and its pitfalls. It is to Howard Schwartz's credit that his embrace of the mythic model does not blind him to the significant counter-impulses within Judaism: the various Rabbinic and philosophical critiques of certain myths, especially the graphic mythicizations of God found in aggadah and some strands of kabbalah. Second, even as Schwartz is aware of the profundities in his mythic sources, he is aware of their dangers too. For myths both articulate and absolutize (reify) our deepest visions. For an example see the Introduction, where Schwartz poignantly notes: "The intractable conflict in the Middle East between Israel and the Palestinians derives from this belief in the sanctity of the Holy Land, especially of Jerusalem, shared by both Jews and Muslims. This serves as a compelling reminder of the enduring and sometimes destructive power of these myths, which are not always benign." Or as James Young put it in a different context: a common site of memory is not necessarily a site of common memory.[18]

Ways of reading this book. As noted, *Tree of Souls* maintains a dynamic tension between textual diversity and thematic focus through the centripetal force of its editor. Schwartz's frequent weaving together of parallel sources into a unitary myth is an impressive achievement. Still, I confess that I often have trouble with this approach since it smooths out the edges, obscures specific voices and historical settings. But thanks to the commentaries, I was rarely perturbed by this. And the gain in narrative flow was measurable. The author has done a remarkable job in presenting the chain midrashim and the longer legends/myths (the *Tzohar*[19] to restrict myself to one example.) I like the way Schwartz presented the hard unvarnished accounts found in some sources: the Zoharic text wherein the Holy One (masculine aspect of God) is mated not with *Shekhinah* as one would expect but with Lilith (the demonic realm in its feminine guise). Or the aggadah wherein the son of arch-demon Sammael is cannibalized by Eve (and Adam). This source was stunning in all senses of the term. In these and other texts, mind surprises heart, as the text reads in ways that run counter to expectations and hidden wishes. In still other texts, narrative reaches the status of *mayse* as defined by Abraham Joshua Heschel: a story in which heart surprises mind.[20] Nachman's fragmentary tale of "A Garment for the Moon" and the oral tale "The Cottage of Candles" are two such texts for me. Each reader will undoubtedly find his or her favorites: be they tales that edify or perplex, astonish or delight, be they myths that stick in the craw, force one to reconsider, or make the heart melt. For there are as many gates in this book as there are stories (and some would say, as there are readers).

This book deserves a wide and varied audience. It will speak to storytellers of all stripes, spur the analogical and aesthetic imagination of artists. Students of myth and theology (Jewish and comparative) and spiritual seekers, those thirsty for the presence of the One, will have much to contemplate and absorb. Some readers may wish to focus on one tale at a time, to even memorize a passage or write it down and place it in pocket or purse for periodic examination and reflection. To learn *by heart*. Other readers may wish to explore a mythic cycle systematically, concordances in hand. Still others will want to make use of Schwartz's extensive notation of primary sources to engage in historical analysis. Through these notations and through the references to cutting-edge scholarship the reader is given tools to continue and deepen his or her readings. One need not agree with all of Schwartz's contentions in order to be edified and inspired by this book. He is a conversation partner of the highest order, a generous and deeply schooled *bar-p'lugta*. Still, not all is heavy in this book. As the midrash[21] has it *panim tzohakot la-aggadah*. "The Aggadah—the narrative imagination—has a laughing face." For reasons both playful and profound, this is a book to read and reread, to grow old with.

The anthological imagination and its resonances. *Tree of Souls* is a latter-day exemplar of the Jewish anthological imagination, that combinatory art. Indeed, anthology is one of the oldest forms of Jewish literary creativity, found in various Biblical books such as Psalms and, many would hold, the Pentateuch itself (if one accepts the documentary hypothesis). Many of the canonical and sacred works of the Rabbinic imagination were anthologies of texts, some even anthologies of anthologies.[22] In the modern period we have been blessed with encyclopedic anthologies of signal import, including Bialik and Ravnitzky's *Sefer ha-Aggadah* (in Hebrew) and Louis Ginzberg's magisterial *Legends of the Jews*. *Tree of Souls* builds on these works in many ways, recasting the thematic thrust of *Sefer ha-Aggadah* and revisioning the synthetic narrative of Ginzberg. Still, Schwartz extends our scope by drawing on heretofore marginalized texts as well as post-medieval and modern texts not included in the earlier works.[23] Indeed, **this book could only have been written at this historical moment**. For it draws on works that had been lost to earlier generations, such as the *piyyutim* of Yannai and the Dead Sea Scrolls; oral narratives collected in recent decades; women's prayers that have just now re-entered public (and scholarly) purview; as well as mystical manuscripts and "minor" midrashim that were previously known only to *yehidei segullah*, the precious few. In this book, our collective memory is dusted off, expanded and vitalized.

By way of conclusion or as entree into the book itself, a parable about this volume and the Anthological Imagination. The word *anthology* etymologically implies a collection of flowers, the artful forming of a bouquet. The hasidic rebbe Nachman of Bratslav, himself a great mythopoet and storyteller, likened the act of prayer to this anthological art—the assembling of bouquets for the Holy One. Each letter, he teaches, is like a flower of the field, and from these letters one forms words, themselves bouquets. From these words one forms prayers, and from individual prayers, whole services of worship—elaborate bouquets, garlands of blessing. Nachman then explains that each word—each flower—has a special resonance, an inner music. Its music hangs in the air, combining and harmonizing with the other words and prayers that follow, in a kind of Deep Song. Nachman concludes: "When you rise and speak the final words of the service, let the first letter of the first word still reverberate."[24] The book in your hands is a work of enormous resonance. The careful reader of *Tree of Souls* cannot but marvel at the consistent power, the occasional bracing oddness, and the enduring beauty of this anthology. It is a testament to its power that many of the early stories resonate with later ones, and that one continues to hear something of this book's "inner music"—its soul-stirring *niggun*—long after one has closed its pages.

Notes

[1]Ff. *Pesikta Rabbati*, chap. 28 et al.

[2]By this I mean the various streams of Judaism that are shaped by, and owe allegiance to, Rabbinic authority as it evolves.

[3]For other examples of this phenomenon, see Michael Fishbane, *The Exegetical Imagination* (Cambridge: Harvard University Press, 1998), esp. chapters 3 and 6.

[4]A short list of recent scholarship on Jewish myth might include the works of Michael Fishbane, Yehuda Liebes' two volumes for SUNY Press, Arthur Green's *Keter* (Princeton, 1997), and the two issues of the *Journal of Jewish Philosophy and Thought* devoted to myth and ritual, vol. 6:12 (1997). The Hebrew reader might also consider *Ha-Mitos be-Yahadut* [Myths in Judaism], edited by Moshe Idel and Ithamar Gruenwald (Jerusalem: Z. Shazar, 2004). Broadly speaking, most Judaic scholars through the 1970's tended to define myth narrowly and negatively, linking it with so-called "pagan" religions. They therefore tended to see Judaism as a demythologizing tradition, broken only by the "mythic resurgence" of kabbalah. Most recent scholars understand myth more broadly, as a fundamental human impulse (found in virtually all cultures) to structure life around orienting Stories. These scholars find rich myths in all strata of Judaism: not only in kabbalistic ritual but in Biblical imagery and Rabbinic *aggadah*. They extend the mythic arc to contemporary Judaism, to the Zionist marking of "wilderness as mythic space" to give one potent example. My fundamental sympathies, and those of Howard Schwartz, clearly lie with these "myth-friendly" scholars. For a spirited debate over the place of myth in Judaism, see Yehuda Liebes' and Shalom Rosenberg's pieces in *Mada'ei ha-Yahadut* 39 (1998). For two now-classic studies of the Jewish mythic imagination (especially in mystical tradition) see Gershom Scholem's *On the Kabbalah and its Symbolism* (NY: Schocken, 1965) and *On the Mystical Shape of the Godhead* (ibid., 1991). Finally, for the ways in which diverse cultures make use of their central stories, see Wendy Doniger's splendid *Other People's Myths: The Cave of Echoes* (NY: Macmillan, 1988).

[5]Canonization lead to the possibility of grasping Scripture all at once, as a totality, in an almost holographic fashion. In rabbinic midrash, for example, one could read a given verse intertextually: in light of a *pasuk rahok*, a verse taken from a wholly different literary context with which, however, ingenious associations could be made.

[6]The slippage from past tense to present tense here is intentional, exemplifying the mythic tendency to collapse orders of time, i.e., to blur the distinctions between *then* and *now*.

[7]For Scholem, see his "Revelation and Tradition as Religious Categories" in *The Messianic Idea in Judaism* (NY: Schocken, 1971; for the Fishbane, see *The Exegetical Imagination*, p. 94.

[8]This is not to say that everyone is equally empowered to interpret; rather, it is the religious virtuosi, the Rabbis, who assume that central role. Clearly, Howard Schwartz goes beyond the traditional Rabbinic models of authority in this book. On the three quotations cited here, see Ps. 62:12, quoted in sundry rabbinic sources; the rendering of Jer. 23:29 in TB Sanhedrin 34a; and TB Eruvin 13b et al.

[9]On seventy faces, a shorthand for the inexhaustible fount of meaning, see Nachmanides to Gen. 8:4; Bachya ben Asher to Ex. 24:12, et al. On 600,000 faces, one for every soul at Sinai, see Hayyim Vital, *Sha'ar ha-Kavvanot* 53b; Moshe Cordovero, *Derishah be-inyanei Mal'akhim;* and the discussion in Scholem's "The Meaning of Torah in Jewish Mysticism" in his *On the Kabbalah and its Symbolism* (NY: Schocken, 1965). On the white spaces, see Levi Yitzhak of Berdichev in *Imrei Tzaddikim* (cited in Scholem, "Meaning of Torah," 81ff.) and the *Noam Elimelekh* cited in the Slonimer Rebbe's *Netivot Shalom: Mo'adim* "Shavuot" s.v. *"hag ha-'atzeret"*.

[10]My rendering is drawn from *Hayyei Moharan* pp. 3:3 ff. *Likutei Moharan* 1:20. See also the translation and discussion in Arthur Green, *Tormented Master*, esp. pp. 198-200.

[11]In the *Idrot* section of the *Zohar*, the source for Nachman's riff, this gesture itself is replete with meaning. But that matter lies beyond the scope of this essay!

[12]Of course, there are exceptions to this model. Gods and heroes can act in ways in which ordinary folks cannot. Thus, King David's sexual behavior is not simply valorized; and Moses is variously seen as exemplary (a model that can be asymptotically approached by the spiritual virtuoso) and exceptional, the figure who is *sui generis* and cannot be emulated. The Arthur Green quotation is taken from his "Jewish Studies, Jewish Faith," *Tikkun* 1:1, p. 87; the Geertz citation comes from his *The Interpretation of Cultures* (NY: Basic Books, 1973).

[13]The genius of our last reading, from a midrashic standpoint, is that it was able to be justified scripturally. The ram, Gen. 22:13 relates, was offered *tahat b'no,* in place of Isaac. But by choosing a secondary meaning of *tahat,* the interpreter astonishingly reads: **after** Isaac! The classical discussion of the Binding, as well as its midrashic, textual anchorings, can be found in Shalom Spiegel's *The Last Trial* (Woodstock, VT: Jewish Lights reprint, 1993).

[14]This formulation was inspired by a long-ago conversation with my teacher, Arthur Green.

[15]These notions have been developed by James Kugel in his "Two Introductions to Midrash" in Hartman and Budick, eds. *Midrash and Literature* (New Haven: Yale, 1986) and by Michael Fishbane in his various writings on Jewish hermeneutics.

[16]The Hebrew YSF can be read either as "to add" or via a homonym "to end" or cease.

[17]See Scholem's magisterial essay, "Revelation and Tradition as Religious Categories in Judaism" in his *The Messianic Idea in Judaism*. This particular chain of readings is drawn from the 16th century kabbalist Meir ibn Gabbai's *Avodat ha-Kodesh* 3:23.

[18]From his *The Texture of Memory* (New Haven, Yale: 1994)

[19]Myth 109 on the Primordial Light.

[20]Oral communication from Reb Zalman Schachter-Shalomi, from whom I first heard this saying. And cf. Heschel's *The Earth is the Lord's* (NY: Schuman, 1950), p. 15, where we find the variant: "story where soul surprises the mind."

[21]See *Pesikta Rabbati*, chap. 21.

[22]For a recent discussion of the anthological imagination in Judaism, and its various sub-genres, see the three issues of the journal *Prooftexts*, vol. 17:1-2 and 19:1 (1997/99). Of special use is David Stern's prefatory comments in 17:1.

[23]Bialik and Ravnitzky focused on relatively well-known Rabbinic works; while Ginzberg's *terminus ad quem* was prior to the Safed Revival in the 16th century.

[24]*Likutei Moharan* 1:65. For a translation of this text, see Lawrence Kushner, *The Way into Jewish Mysticism* (Woodstock, VT: Jewish Lights, 2001) 147-149.

INTRODUCTION

I. The Mythical Strata of Judaism

Is there a Jewish mythology? At first glance, it might not seem to exist. After all, the central principle of Judaism is monotheism—belief in one God, excluding the very possibility of other gods. How can there be a mythology where there is only one God, without any interaction between gods, one of the hallmarks of mythology? Mythology seems to imply a multiplicity of supernatural forces, which gives the story of divinity a tension and an excitement it does not have when there is only an all-powerful single Deity. And since, in the monotheistic view, God created the world out of nothing, *ex nihilo*, doesn't this imply that God is the only inhabitant of heaven? Otherwise it could be said that other deities or divine beings participated in the Creation or have a share in ruling the world.

With only one God, heaven would be a barren place, at least in mythic terms. Yet the actual Jewish view of heaven is quite different. There are seven heavens, filled with angels and other divine beings, such as the Messiah, who is said to have a palace of his own in the highest heaven. The celestial Temple can be found there—the mirror image of the Temple in the earthly Jerusalem—as well as an abundance of heavenly palaces, one for each of the patriarchs and matriarchs and sages, where he or she teaches Torah to the attentive souls of the righteous and the angels. (Yes—in Jewish mythology women teach Torah in the world to come, although they were not traditionally permitted to do so in this world.[1]) Above all, heaven is the home of the souls of the righteous, who ascend to Paradise after they take leave of this world.

This vision of heaven ruled by God but populated by lesser divine beings and righteous souls may not seem to infringe on the core concept of monotheism. But among the inhabitants of heaven is an unexpected figure: God's Bride. This divine figure is known as the *Shekhinah*. At first this term referred to God's presence in this world, what is known as the Divine Presence. But by the thirteenth century, the term "*Shekhinah*," which is feminine in gender, had come to mean "Bride of God" and the *Shekhinah* was openly identified as God's spouse in the *Zohar*, the central text of Jewish mysticism.[2] This is a major development in terms of Jewish mythology, as the very notion of such a divine Bride is the essence of myth, echoing such pairs as Zeus and Hera in Greek mythology, and El and Asherah in the Canaanite. But the existence of such a figure, strongly resembling a Hebrew goddess, echoing the role attributed by some to Asherah in ancient Israel, raises the most elementary questions about her role in a monotheistic system.[3]

There are other unexpected echoes of polytheistic mythology to be found in Judaism. *Genesis Rabbah*, an important rabbinic text dating from the fourth or fifth century, speaks of a Council of Souls, apparently a council of heavenly deities, whom God consults with about the creation of the world and the creation of man. Here there is not one other divine figure, but multiple ones such as those found in pagan religions. Indeed, the Council of Souls is exactly like the divine council, led by the god El, who rules the world in Canaanite mythology. Such divine counsels rule in Mesopotamian and Babylonian mythologies as well.[4]

How could such a myth about multiple divinities be found in a mainstream rabbinic text such as *Genesis Rabbah*? Why was it not rejected as blasphemous? The answer is that Judaism is not, and never has been, a single stream of thought, but a river formed of many, often contradictory, streams, and rabbinic texts are composites of different kinds of thinking. There has been a perennial struggle in Judaism between the antimythic, monotheistic forces, and the kind of mythic forces that are prevalent in many kabbalistic texts. Therefore, in many mainstream rabbinic texts, including the Talmud and the Midrash, it is quite possible to find dualistic or even polytheistic configurations, such as this one about a Council of Souls, side by side with monotheistic texts.

Just as there are a variety of mythologies—every people of the world has one—there are many definitions of mythology. At this point it might be appropriate to provide a definition for the approach to mythology used in this book: *Myth refers to a people's sacred stories about origins, deities, ancestors, and heroes. Within a culture, myths serve as the divine charter, and myth and ritual are inextricably bound.*[5]

Let us consider this definition in terms of Jewish tradition: myth refers to a people's sacred stories about origins, deities, ancestors, and heroes. This is precisely what the Torah recounts for the Jewish people—stories about origins, as found in Genesis; about God, the ruling deity; about ancestors such as Abraham and Moses, and heroes such as King David.

As for having a divine charter, this is the precise nature of the Torah, dictated by God to Moses at Mount Sinai, which serves both as a chronicle and covenant. At the same time, myth and ritual reinforce each other in Judaism. The Sabbath alludes to the day of rest that God declared after six days of Creation. The ritual of the Sabbath is a constant reminder of the mythical origins of this sacred day.

All of these primary aspects of mythology find expression in Jewish tradition, and individual myths have exercised great power over Jewish life. Even to this day Jews relive the Exodus at Passover, which recalls the escape from Egyptian bondage, and receive the Torah anew on Shavuot, which commemorates the giving of the Torah. Nor, in some Orthodox Jewish circles, has the longing for the Messiah subsided.

For those who prefer not to use the term "mythology" in relationship to Judaism, there are two primary objections. The first is that the term suggests a constellation of gods rather than a single, omnipotent God. How could there be a Jewish mythology without contradicting this basic tenet of Jewish theology, without undermining monotheism? The simple fact is that despite being a monotheistic religion, like Christianity and Islam, Judaism does have real myth. Just as supernatural practices, such as using divination or consulting a soothsayer, were commonly performed despite the biblical injunction against them,[6] an extensive Jewish mythology did evolve, especially in mystical circles, where it was believed possible to preserve a monotheistic perspective while simultaneously employing a mythological one. Here it was understood that most mythological figures, especially the *Shekhinah*, were ultimately aspects of the Godhead, despite their apparent mythological independence. Indeed, it sometimes seems as if all of Jewish myth (and perhaps all of existence) were the epic fantasy of one Divine Being, or, as Lurianic kabbalah suggests, a kind of divine illusion, similar to the Hindu concept of maya. For what sometimes appears to have mythic independence can also be understood as an emanation of the Godhead. Divine emanations take the form of the ten sefirot, as symbolized by the kabbalistic Tree of Life.[7] It is possible to identify a sefirotic process underlying virtually every myth. But in translating mythic imaginings into stages of emanation, the sefirot also serve as an antidote to mythology, as they are entirely conveyed through allegory and symbolism, which are clearly not intended to be taken literally, and may have been created to restrain the unbridled mythic impulse released in Jewish mysticism, as well as to define its underlying archetypal structure. Certainly, this system of divine emanations is as complex and comprehensive as that of the Jungian theory of archetypes. And while the essence of myth is archetype, it is much harder, if not impossible, to mythologize a system as abstract as the sefirot. Yet underlying these abstractions are the living forces of myth.

The second objection to the use of "mythology" in terms of Jewish tradition is that it suggests that the beliefs under consideration are not true. Even the mere identification of a culture's beliefs as mythological indicates that it is being viewed from the outside rather than from the perspective of a believer. That is why, with a few exceptions, there has been such great reluctance to identify any of the biblical narratives as myths or to bring the tools of mythological inquiry to bear on Judaism or Christianity. While it is true that the study of these religions from a mythological perspective does imply the distance of critical inquiry, it does not mean that the traditions being examined are therefore false. Mythological studies are now commonly linked with psychological ones, and scholars such as C. G. Jung, Joseph Campbell, Mircea Eliade, Erich Neumann, Marie Louise Von Franz, and Sigmund Hurwitz have demonstrated how it is possible to recognize a dimension of psychological truths underlying mythic traditions, where myth can be seen as the collective projection of a people. And not only psychological truths, but the deepest existential truths. Indeed, this is the reason that myths persist, because the questions they raise are perennial. In the case of Judaism, many generations of rabbis, as well as other Jews, received and transmitted the sacred myths, rituals, and traditions, sometimes radically transforming them in the process, as well as imparting their own human imprint.

Over time, as the number of supernatural figures in this pantheon increased and interacted, an abundance of mythological narratives emerged. These stories describe events such as the transformation of Enoch into the angel Metatron, the Giving of the Torah, the separation of God's Bride from Her Spouse, the chain of events that has so far prevented the coming of the Messiah, and the attempts of Satan to gain inroads into the world of human beings. They also map out the realms of heaven and hell in great detail. By a process of accretion, these mythic realms were embellished and further defined, giving birth to additional narratives. In this way Jewish mythology has evolved into an extensive, interconnected—and often contradictory—mythic tradition.

II. The Categories of Jewish Mythology

Drawing on the full range of Jewish sources, sacred and nonsacred, ten major categories of Jewish mythology can be identified: *Myths of God, Myths of Creation, Myths of Heaven, Myths of Hell, Myths of the Holy Word, Myths of the Holy Time, Myths of the Holy People, Myths of the Holy Land, Myths of Exile,* and *Myths of the Messiah.* Each of these categories explores a mythic realm, and, in the process, reimagines it. This is the secret to the transformations that characterize Jewish mythology. Building on a strong foundation of biblical myth, each generation has embellished the earlier myths, while, at the same time, reinterpreting them for its own time.

Each of these ten major myths is represented here with several dozen submyths. These often form themselves into cycles, such as that of Enoch's heavenly ascent, or of Lilith's rebellion, or of Jacob's elevation to the status of a divine figure. A passage in a late medieval midrashic text seems to confirm this organizational approach, attributing this tenfold structure to God:[8] "Ten things were paramount in the thought of God at the time of the Creation: Jerusalem, the souls of the patriarchs, the ways of the righteous, Gehenna, the Flood, the stone tablets, the Sabbath, the Temple, the Ark, and the light of the World to Come."[9]

This midrash suggests its own definition of mythology: that which is foremost in the mind of God. By keeping these things in mind, God permits them to exist, for whatever God visualizes comes to pass. Indeed, all of existence depends on God's willingness to let the world continue to exist. There are many variations on this theme. There also are myths to be found about prior worlds that God created and then destroyed, and some myths of an angry or dejected God who calls the continued existence of this world into question.[10]

The fact that there are ten things in God's mind is significant. Why the number ten? Primarily because of the Ten Commandments. Just as men must keep the Ten Commandments in mind at all times, so too does God keep these ten things foremost in His mind. These are, in effect, God's Ten Commandments. Later the number ten also became attached to the Ten Lost Tribes, as well as the ten sefirot. An overview of each of these ten categories follows.

1. Myths of God

Judaism is primarily a religion based on the covenant between God and the people of Israel. According to the Torah, God established this covenant beginning with Abraham, and renewed it with Isaac, Jacob, Joseph, and Moses. In the Jewish view, this covenant was formalized in the handing down of the Torah at Mount Sinai, and, ever since, the Jewish people have turned to the Torah to guide their lives.

Naturally, there has been a powerful impulse in Judaism to better understand the nature of the God who created the world and established a covenant with the Jewish people. Among early Jewish mystics, this led to a series of visionary accounts, known as the *Hekhalot* texts,[11] that describe journeys of some famous rabbis into Paradise for the explicit purpose of attaining greater knowledge of God. These journeys are very dangerous, as there are said to be guards at every one of the seven levels of heaven, and the guard at the sixth gate will not hesitate to cut off the head of one who does not know the secret name that serves as a password to these celestial realms.

Thus every aspect of God was open to mythic speculation: God's size and appearance; what God does during the day and at night; what God's voice was like to those who heard it at Mount Sinai; what God's relationship is like with His Bride; how God prays; how God grieved over the destruction of the Temple in Jerusalem—despite the fact that He permitted that destruction to take place. Nor is God's relationship with Israel as onesided as one might expect: there is even a talmudic myth about the rabbis rejecting God's interpretation of the Law in favor of their own, after which God is said to have laughed and exclaimed, "My children have overruled Me!"[12] This kind of interaction between God and His people, Israel, makes it clear that, as Yehuda Liebes puts it, "the God of Israel is a mythic god, and as such maintains relationships of love and hate with His creatures."[13]

In some of these myths God not only suffers like his people, but sometimes shows remarkable tenderness. One myth describes God as sitting in a circle with many baby spirits that are about to be born.[14] Another says that in the messianic era God will seat each person between His knees, and embrace him and kiss him and bring him to life in the World to Come.[15] Still another describes a nurturing God who raises the male children of the Israelites after they were abandoned because of Pharaoh's decree against newborn boys. After they were grown, they returned to their families. When they were asked who took care of them, they said, "A handsome young man took care of all our needs." And when the Israelites came to the Red Sea, those children were there, and when they saw God at the sea, they said to their parents, "That is the one who took care of us when we were in Egypt."[16]

Even though the second commandment clearly states that *You shall not make for yourself ... any likeness of what is in the heavens above* (Exod. 20:4), rabbinic literature is full of anthropomorphic imagery of God, of God's hands, God's eyes and ears, God walking, sitting, and speaking. These images are often accompanied by a disclaimer, *kivyakhol*, "as if it were possible."[17] However, this disclaimer does not eliminate the distinct impression that God can be described in human terms. As Henry Slonimsky puts it: "Nowhere indeed has a God been rendered so utterly human, been taken so closely to man's bosom and, in the embrace, so thoroughly changed into an elder brother, a slightly older father, as here in the Midrash. The anthropomorphic tendency here achieves its climax. God has not merely become a man, he has become a Jew, an elderly, bearded Jew."[18] Or, as *Midrash Tehillim* on Psalm 118:5 states: "He is your father, your brother, your kinsman."

The rabbinic commentators had to contend with the often contradictory descriptions of God's appearance. For example, God is said to have appeared as an old man at Mount Sinai, while He is described as a mighty warrior at the Red Sea. In commenting on the second commandment, *I am Yahweh, your God, who brought you out of the land of Egypt, out of the house of bondage* (Exod. 20:2),[19] Rashi engages this issue by quoting God as saying, "Since I change in My appearance to the people, do not say that there are two divine beings, for it is I alone who brought you out of Egypt and it is I who was at the Red Sea."

At the opposite end of the spectrum is the kabbalistic portrayal of God as *Ein Sof*, the Infinite One, from whom emanated the ten stages of divine manifestation known as the ten sefirot. Each of these sefirot bears one of God's primary attributes, and together they form the realm of God's manifestation in this world. Here, in contrast to a highly personified view of God, is one that is entirely impersonal, although the sefirot do represent attributes that are identified with human qualities, such as understanding, wisdom, judgment, and lovingkindness.[20] While one kabbalistic school identifies the true God as *Ein Sof*, which is beyond the realm of the sefirot, another school asserts that the divine essence of God can be found in the ten sefirot, for they are identical with the Godhead, and should be viewed as stages in the hidden life of God.[21] The theory of the sefirot was not without its enemies. One of these, Rabbi Isaac ben Sheshet Parfat, known as Ribash, writing in the fourteenth century, quotes one critic as saying contemptuously about the kabbalists, "The idolaters believe in the Trinity and the kabbalists believe in a tenfold God!"[22]

In the myths discussed so far, God has been portrayed as a masculine divinity. This is how most people view God. Yet no discussion of Jewish myths about God would be complete without a discussion of the myths about the Bride of God. This divine figure is known as the *Shekhinah*. Perhaps no Jewish myth undergoes as radical a transformation as does that of the *Shekhinah*. There is a complete cycle of *Shekhinah* myths to be found, which begins with God's creation of the *Shekhinah*, and portrays the sacred couplings of the divine pair as well as their confrontations and separations. In this view, the *Shekhinah* chose to go into exile with Her children, the children of Israel, at the time of the destruction of the Temple. When will Her exile come to an end? When the Temple, the *Shekhinah's* home in this world, is rebuilt at the time of the coming of the Messiah. There is even a rather staggering myth in the *Zohar* that suggests that the evil Lilith has supplanted God's true Bride in the divine realm.[23] These myths also reveal the existence of two *Shekhinahs*, one who makes Her home in heaven and one who has descended to earth. This cycle makes it clear that the kinds of interactions expected of a divine couple, like those found in Greek and Canaanite mythology—and to some extent in the Gnostic mythology of the early centuries of the Christian era—are found as well in the kabbalistic myths of God and His Bride.[24] However, unique to Jewish myths—to kabbalistic myths in particular—is the implication that the two mythic beings, God and His Bride, are really two aspects of the same divine being, of a God who contains everything, including male and female qualities. Indeed, this is stated directly by the Rabbi Menahem Nahum of Chernobyl: "Only the *Shekhinah* and God together form a unity, for one without the other cannot be called a whole."[25]

In its earliest usage in the Talmud, "*Shekhinah*" refers to God's Divine Presence, thus the immanence or indwelling of God in this world. This personification was linked, in particular, to the sense of holiness experienced on the Sabbath. At this time no attempt was made to suggest that the *Shekhinah* was in any way independent of God, or to imply that the term referred to a feminine aspect of the Deity. Instead, the term implied the nearness of God, as in this homily of Rabbi Akiba: "When a man and wife are worthy, the *Shekhinah* dwells in their midst; if they are unworthy, fire consumes them."[26]

Yet some rabbinic myths set the stage for the ultimate transformation of the *Shekhinah* into an independent being. At first this usage of the term *Shekhinah* was intended to affirm that God remained true to the children of Israel and accompanied them wherever they went. In time, however, the term *Shekhinah* came to be identified with the feminine aspect of God and came to acquire mythic independence. Myths that emerge in kabbalistic and hasidic literature portray the *Shekhinah* as the Bride of God and the Sabbath Queen, personifying Her as an independent mythic figure. Indeed, there are several other identities linked to the *Shekhinah*, who is sometimes also portrayed as a princess, a bride, an old woman in mourning, a dove, a lily, a rose, a hind, a jewel, a well, the earth, and the moon.[27] These multiple facets of the *Shekhinah* suggest that as a mythic figure, the *Shekhinah* has absorbed a wide range of feminine roles. There is a series of myths about the *Shekhinah* found in the *Zohar*, forming a cycle.[28] Some of these myths are undeniably erotic in describing the lovemaking of God and the *Shekhinah*. Part of this cycle also includes the greatest conflict between God and His Bride, over God's permitting the Temple in Jerusalem, the home of the *Shekhinah*, to be destroyed. This results in the *Shekhinah* separating from God and going into exile with Her children, the children of Israel. It is here that the *Shekhinah* achieves mythic independence, for it is evident that the confrontation takes place between two mythic figures. After this, the presence of the *Shekhinah* is fully injected into the tradition. It prepares the way for a series of visions and encounters with the *Shekhinah* that are associated, in particular, with the *Kotel ha-Ma'aravi*, the Western Wall of the Temple Mount in Jerusalem, also known as the Wailing Wall.

In these kabbalistic and post-kabbalistic texts, it is apparent that, at least from a mythological point of view, the *Shekhinah* has become an independent entity. Nevertheless, the *Shekhinah* was regarded at the same time as an extension or aspect of the Divinity, which was, of course, necessary in order to uphold the essential concept of monotheism. True initiates of the kabbalah were not disturbed by these apparent contradictions, but, for others, the danger of viewing the *Shekhinah* as a separate deity was recognized. That explains why the study of the kabbalistic texts was not permitted until a man had reached his fortieth year.[29] Only such a person was felt to be grounded enough not to be overwhelmed by kabbalistic mysteries, while younger, more vulnerable men might well be led astray.

Nor does the evolution of the myth of the *Shekhinah* end with the role portrayed in the *Zohar* in the thirteenth century. The implications of the exile of the *Shekhinah* were expanded in the sixteenth century by Rabbi Isaac Luria in his myth of the Shattering of the Vessels and the Gathering of the Sparks. And in the nineteenth century Rabbi Nachman of Bratslav told the allegorical tale of "The Lost Princess," which hints at an identification of the *Shekhinah* with an internal feminine figure, much like Jung's concept of the anima.[30]

One other subtle identity of the *Shekhinah* is suggested in the talmudic tradition of every Jew receiving a *neshamah yeterah*, a second soul, on the Sabbath: "Rabbi Shimon ben Lakish said: 'On the eve of the Sabbath the Holy One, blessed be He, gives man an extra soul, and at the close of the Sabbath He withdraws it from him.'"[31] This second soul is the internal experience of the *Shekhinah*. It remains throughout the Sabbath, and is believed to depart after *Havdalah*, the ritual of separation performed at the end of the Sabbath. This second soul functions as a kind of *ibbur*, literally "an impregnation," in which the spirit of a holy figure fuses with the soul of a living person, bringing greater faith and wisdom.[32] But in this case it is a divine soul that fuses with the souls of Jews on the Sabbath. It is not difficult to identify this second soul with the presence of the *Shekhinah*, who is also the Sabbath Queen. Certainly, the arrival and departure of the Sabbath Queen and the arrival and departure of this mysterious second soul are simultaneous. Identifying the second soul with the *Shekhinah* is a way of acknowledging the sacredness of the Sabbath from both within and without. For Rabbi Yitzhak Eizik Safrin of Komarno, a man could best discover the *Shekhinah* through his wife. He states in *Notzer Hesed* that the *Shekhinah* rests on a man mainly because of his wife, for a man receives spiritual illumination because he has a wife. He describes a man as being positioned between two wives. One, his earthly wife, receives from him, while the *Shekhinah* bestows blessings on him.

Out of all of these meanings attributed to the *Shekhinah* emerge a cycle of myths linked to the *Shekhinah*. Thus we find, especially in the *Zohar*, a cycle of myths linked to the *Shekhinah*. Some of these portray the unity of God and His Bride, while others are about their separation. The key myth, as noted, is that of the exile of the *Shekhinah*, for at the time the Bride goes into exile, the figure of the *Shekhinah* becomes largely independent of the Divinity and takes on a separate identity. Still, the question remains: can the *Shekhinah* be considered a goddess? Does Her independent status award Her equality? The answer is more difficult than it might seem. On the one hand, the nature of the evolution of the *Shekhinah* from the concept of God's presence in this world to the Bride of God seems to maintain the *Shekhinah*'s identity with God strongly enough to raise doubts about Her goddesslike role. But, on the other hand, the role of the *Shekhinah* that emerges in the kabbalistic era can be viewed as a resurrection of the role of the suppressed goddess Asherah in ancient Jewish tradition.[33] Finally, the integral role of the *Shekhinah* in the system of the ten sefirot, where the *Shekhinah* is identified with the final *sefirah* of *Malkhut*, complicates the matter further. In the end, while the *Shekhinah* appears to have some of the earmarks of a goddess figure, this role is not as clear-cut as those of goddesses in other mythic traditions. Yes, the *Shekhinah* is the Bride of God, but, at the same time, the *Shekhinah* is a feminine aspect of the one God, and these roles exist simultaneously. How can this contradiction be resolved? Perhaps by viewing the mythological tradition within Judaism as a unique development, a kind of monotheistic mythology.[34]

Note that the myth of the exile of the *Shekhinah* is a two-part myth. In the first stage, the Bride of God goes into exile at the time of the destruction of the Temple, while in the second stage, a reunion of God and the *Shekhinah* takes place.[35] This reunion is brought about through the activities of Israel in fulfilling requirements of the *mitzvot*, the ritual requirements of the Law, and through the conscious application, or *kavvanah*, of prayers. When this reunification becomes permanent, the exile of the *Shekhinah* will come to an end, and "the *Shekhinah* will return to Her husband and have intercourse with Him."[36] This development is linked to the coming of the Messiah, in that one of the consequences of the messianic era is that the Temple in Jerusalem, which was the *Shekhinah*'s home in this world, will be rebuilt. Since the *Shekhinah* went into exile because of its destruction, the rebuilding of the Temple will represent the end of Her exile. In this way the myths of the *Shekhinah* and the Messiah become linked.

Contributing to the long life of Jewish myths such as that of the *Shekhinah* are several associated rituals. The most important ritual linked to the myth of the *Shekhinah* is that known as *Kabbalat Shabbat*, re-created by Rabbi Isaac Luria in the sixteenth century. Here the worshipers go out into the fields just before sunset on the eve of the Sabbath and welcome the Sabbath Queen. Luria found the basis for this ritual in the Talmud, in Rabbi Haninah's going out to greet the Sabbath Queen.[37] Of course, by the time Luria formalized this ritual, the concept of the Sabbath Queen had evolved into an independent mythic figure, and the ritual itself becomes a kind of goddess worship, but within Judaism.

Most readers will also be surprised to learn that other divine beings are portrayed in the Jewish pantheon who assist God in ruling the heavens and the earth. The angel Metatron, for example, is not only described as the heavenly scribe, but is also said to rule over the angels and to see to it that God's decrees are carried out in heaven and on earth. These figures function in a way that is reminiscent of the Gnostic Creator-God (demiurge), who was said to have fashioned the physical universe. But the demiurgic figures in Jewish tradition are chosen by God and remain subservient to Him, as in the case of Metatron, who is identified as the lesser *Yahweh*. Further, they lack the malignant overtones of the Gnostic demiurge Ialdabaoth, the demonic figure described in the *Apocryphon of John*. Nevertheless, Metatron and other Jewish demiurgic figures do function as divinities and share the duties of ruling the worlds above and below with God.[38]

While the primary myths about Metatron are found in the books of Enoch, reference to Metatron is even found in the Talmud,[39] where a commentary on the verse where God says to Moses, *"Come up to the Lord"* (Exod. 24:1), is interpreted to mean that Metatron, not God, called upon Moses: "A heretic said to Rabbi Idith: 'It is written, *Then God said to Moses, "Come up to the Lord."*' But surely it should have stated, 'Come up unto Me!' Rabbi Idith replied, 'It was Metatron who spoke to Moses, whose name is similar to that of his Master, for it is written, *For my Name is in him* (Exod. 23:21).' 'In that case,' the heretic retorted, 'we should worship him!'"

This is a shocking discussion to be found in the Talmud, the most sacred Jewish text after the Bible, as it demonstrates that a near-divine role was attributed to Metatron even among some of the ancient rabbis. Thus even as Judaism was transformed from its biblical model to the rabbinic model and later to kabbalistic and hasidic models, there were multiple versions of Judaism being practiced, those of the educated elite and those of the people. And even among the elite there were many sects, some emphasizing mystical teachings, such as the Mysteries of Creation and the meaning of Ezekiel's vision of God's Chariot,[40] others describing heavenly journeys; and still others focused on demiurgic figures like Enoch. In addition, there are also surprising enthronement myths about Adam, Jacob, Moses, King David, and the Messiah, in which each takes on a demiurge-like role.[41] That is to say, they are chosen by God to assist in the ruling of the world. Some of these myths, such as those about Jacob, were likely inspired by biblical verses such as Jeremiah 10:16: *Not like these is the portion of Jacob; for it is He who formed all things, and Israel is His very own tribe: Lord of Hosts is His name*. Although most of these enthronement myths are found in the Pseudepigrapha—the noncanonical teachings of Judaism—some of them, such as those about Metatron and Jacob, can be found in standard rabbinic sources. In any case, the existence of these enthronement myths demonstrates the existence of some Jewish sects whose views show evidence of being dualistic.

Read together, these myths reveal a much more complex portrait of God than might be expected, especially of God's role in Creation and in ruling the world, and of God's special relationship with the people of Israel. They also reveal how generations of rabbis and mystics strove to define God's plan in creating the world, and what those intentions revealed of God's true nature. At the same time, these myths show God in His appearance, in His daily activities, in His joys and sufferings, to be very much like His people. Indeed, the portrait of God that emerges is of a highly sympathetic figure, portrayed with the full range of emotions, dark as well as light, that characterize His human creations.

2. Myths of Creation

Many people believe there is one account of Creation in Judaism: the Genesis story of the seven days of Creation. Those familiar with biblical scholarship may recognize two creation myths. The first is Genesis 1:1-2:3. The second begins at Genesis 2:4 with the words: *Such is the story of heaven and earth when they were created*. This creation myth includes the creation of the first man and woman, the myth of the Garden of Eden and the Fall, and ends at Genesis 3:24 with the expulsion of Adam and Eve: *He drove the man out, and stationed east of the garden of Eden the cherubim and the fiery ever-turning sword, to guard the way to the Tree of Life.*

Those intimate with the Hebrew Bible will also have recognized allusions to other creation myths, such as the one summarized in Psalm 104:2-3 and 104:106—*You spread the heavens like a tent cloth. . . . He established the earth on its foundations, so that it shall never totter.* Some readers may read these passages as a summary restatement of the Genesis account, while others will recognize an alternate creation myth, in which God first creates the heavens and then the earth.

Another very ancient Jewish creation myth is based upon the Babylonian myth of the god Marduk, the sky god, trampling Tiamat, the primeval ocean and divine mother. This myth is alluded to in Isaiah 51:9, *Was it not You who cut Rahab in pieces, and wounded the dragon?* And the story is told in the Talmud[42] in a version that makes the parallel to the Babylonian myth explicit: "When God desired to create the world, he said to Rahab, the Angel of the Sea: 'Open your mouth and swallow all the waters of the world.' Rahab replied: 'Master of the Universe, I already have enough.' God then kicked Rahab with His foot and killed him. And had not the waters covered him no creature could have stood his foul odor."

It is likely that these mythic fragments from Psalms and Isaiah were known by the priestly editors of Genesis, who chose the version of Creation found at the beginning of Genesis that portrays a creation out of spoken words rather than by the actions of God. This is the earliest expression of an impulse in Jewish mythology to present God's actions in verbal rather than physical terms.

Even informed readers may be surprised to learn that there are over 100 different creation myths in Judaism. Not only do these offer alternate scenarios about how God created the world, but some of them also raise the question of whether God created the world out of nothing (*ex nihilo*) or used existing elements. Some even question whether God was assisted in the Creation by others, and, if so, whether these were angels or other divine beings.

What role did these variant creation myths play in Judaism? They addressed primary theological issues about the nature of God and the Mysteries of Creation that had important implications. For example, if, as stated in Isaiah 45:7: "*I form light and create darkness,*" does that mean that light pre-existed, and that God merely formed it, rather than created it out of nothing? If light did pre-exist, who created it, and does that imply that there are other divine beings? Is a God who shapes pre-existing elements as all-powerful as a God who creates them out of nothing? In *De Somniis* Philo identifies God as an artificer and a creator: "When God gave birth to all things, He not only brought them into sight, but also brought into being things that had not existed before. Thus He was not merely an artificer, but also a creator."[43]

It is readily seen that these are issues close to the heart of monotheism. But the proliferation of these myths strongly suggests that there were conflicting views among the various Jewish sects and even among the rabbis who were the authors of the talmudic and midrashic texts. The advent of kabbalah in the twelfth and thirteenth centuries gave a new direction and implication for creation myths. There is a creation myth near the beginning of the *Zohar* about how the world was created from a cosmic seed.[44] This is a far cry from the Genesis myth, suggesting that rather than creating the world through speech, God nourished a cosmic seed in a palace described in terms that strongly suggest a womb. Thus it emphasizes God's nurturing, feminine qualities. Indeed, one of the primary purposes of kabbalah seems to be a renewal of the feminine in Judaism.

What was the impact of these far-flung creation myths? In some cases it was profound. The myth created by Rabbi Isaac Luria, known as the Ari, about the Shattering of the

Vessels and the Gathering of the Sparks, transformed the way Jews viewed their lives in exile from the Holy Land. The Ari's myth gave their wanderings in exile a new meaning, in which God had put them in those far-flung places to gather holy sparks, in preparation for the advent of the messianic era.[45]

Myths about the creation of the world are, naturally, the primary type of creation myths found in Judaism. However, there is another important type of creation myth, concerning the creation of human beings. Once again, the Genesis accounts of the creation of Adam and Eve serve as the basis for a remarkable permutation of such creation myths. Even Genesis itself contains what the rabbis identified as an alternate scenario, based on the verse *Male and female He created them* (Gen. 1:27). Since this was understood to describe a simultaneous creation of man and woman, it seemed to conflict with the sequential creation of Adam and Eve. This led the rabbis to conclude that Adam had a first wife, before Eve. This, in turn, initiated a rich cycle of legends about Adam's first wife, who is sometimes called the First Eve and sometimes identified as Lilith.[46] But that very same verse also was used as the basis of a myth that Adam and Eve were created back to back, and that God had to divide them in two and then create backs for each of them.[47] The *Zohar* draws its own conclusions about the pairing of male and female: "God shaped all things in the form of male and female. In another form things cannot exist."[48]

Indeed, a closer reading of these myths about the creation of Adam reveals two separate traditions, one about a heavenly Adam and one about an earthly one. A wide variety of sources, for example, recount myths about a heavenly Adam. The Hellenistic philosopher Philo called this figure "The Heavenly Man."[49] In his view, the heavenly man, born in the pure image of God, is imperishable, and thus a divine figure. Some myths identify this figure as a heavenly Adam. There are also myths about Adam as a giant who reached the heavens, before he ate the forbidden fruit and shrank to human size.[50] Adam is also described as God's confidant, as the heavenly judge who separates the righteous from the sinners, and as a figure of such magnitude that the angels started to wonder if they should bow down before him.[51] Later this myth of a heavenly Adam evolved into the complex kabbalistic concept of Adam Kadmon, the primordial man, who is God's first creation, a kind of divine interface through whom all subsequent creation takes place.

There are more creation myths in Judaism than any other kind. The Mysteries of Creation served as a powerful attraction to the ancient Jews, and they were explored in depth at every phase of Jewish tradition.

3. Myths of Heaven

God makes His home in heaven. We learn of the existence of heaven in the very first verse of the Torah: *In the beginning God created the heavens and the earth* (Gen. 1:1). The Hebrew term, *shamayim*, means both "skies" and "heavens," which suggests how the skies came to be identified as the heavens, and God as the only inhabitant of heaven. Yet even in the biblical account of heaven, God is described as sharing the heavenly realm with the angels. We learn this from the story of the Binding of Isaac: just when Abraham raised the knife above his son, Isaac, *an angel of the Lord called to him from heaven* (Gen. 22:11). The Bible also notes other angels, such as Michael, Gabriel, and the Angel of the Lord.

What is missing in the biblical view of heaven are the souls of the righteous. It is not until the rabbinic period, beginning around the first century, that the biblical concept of heaven was expanded to include them. For the past 2,000 years heaven has been mapped out in great detail in rabbinic, kabbalistic, and hasidic texts, as well as in the texts of the Pseudepigrapha and Jewish folklore. And in all of them heaven includes a multitude of angels and other divine beings, as well as the souls of the righteous.

There is an abundance of myths about heaven. These include myths that demarcate the map of the seven heavens and detail the celestial temple and the palaces and treasuries of heaven, as well as its fiery rivers and choirs. There are also myths about the interaction of heavenly beings who are similar to those found in Greek myth, except that angels play the roles Greek myth assigns to gods. The myths of heaven include several cycles, such as that about Enoch's ascent into Paradise and transformation into the angel Metatron. There are also a great many myths about the angels, not only about the well-known archangels Michael, Gabriel, Uriel, and Raphael, but also about some lesser known but very important angels, such as Lailah, the Angel of Conception; the angel Gallizur, who utters all of God's evil decrees for Him; and B'ree, the Angel of Rain. When angels, such as Elijah, are sent to this world as messengers, they are clothed in bodies formed from air or fire. In many myths, the angels demonstrate minds of their own and serve as a sounding board for God's important decisions, such as whether to make human beings. Note that while God consults the angels, He often ignores their counsel.[52]

Heaven serves as a multipurpose concept in Judaism. It is not only the home of God and the other inhabitants of heaven, but it is also the *Olam ha-Ba*, the world to come, where the souls of the righteous are said to go after they take leave of this world. Thus, for the living, heaven serves as a place of longing, and as a strong motivation for people to remain righteous in order to attain their heavenly reward. Finally, heaven serves as the destination for mystics among the rabbis who sought to journey there while still living, using amulets and spells. Their stories are recounted in detail in the *Hekhalot* texts. For all these reasons, there is an abundance of myths about heaven and its inhabitants. Read together, these myths reveal a well-developed mythology about heaven as God's home, as well as the home of God's Bride, and home to the angels, the Messiah, and the souls of the righteous.

Note that the term for paradise is *Gan Eden*, literally, the Garden of Eden. This term has a double meaning, in that it is applied to both the earthly Garden of Eden and the heavenly one. The one on earth was the one that was inhabited by Adam and Eve. The other is the heavenly garden, which is a synonym of Paradise. As Nachmanides puts it, commenting on Genesis 3:23, "The physical things that exist on earth also exist in heaven. Likewise, the heavenly *Gan Eden* with its trees has a counterpart on earth." The earthly and the heavenly paradise are essentially separate but related mythic realms. Nevertheless, the imagery of one sometimes gets mixed with that of the other, as where streams of the kind that flow in the earthly garden are said to be found in heaven, flowing not with water, but with precious balsam oil.[53] Thus we are to understand that heaven also has streams, just like those found on earth. This also finds expression in the mirror image of the earthly city of Jerusalem and the heavenly Jerusalem, and grows out of the principle "as above, so below."

4. Myths of Hell

In the biblical view, all the souls of the dead congregate in a grim place called Sheol. There is neither reward nor punishment. It is not unlike the Greek realm of Hades, and it likely influenced the Christian concept of Limbo. In rabbinic lore, Sheol was replaced by Gehenna, a place of punishment for the souls of sinners, which combines elements of both purgatory and hell. It was the widespread rabbinic belief that only a few souls went directly to Paradise after death. The majority went to Gehenna where they burned in the fires of hell and were punished with fiery lashes by avenging angels for up to one year. In the *Zohar* these fires of hell are identified as a person's own burning passions and desires, which consume him.[54] These punishments are just as severe as those portrayed in Dante's *Inferno*, but—in contrast to the Christian concept of hell—the purified souls are released from Gehenna and permitted to make a slow ascent into Paradise. For this reason it could be argued that Jewish hell is more like the Christian concept of purgatory than hell, and some take the position that the inevitable release from Gehenna means there is no Jewish concept of hell at all, but, instead, a stage of punishment that purifies the soul before it ascends on high. However, the descriptions of the punishments of Gehenna are so extensive,[55] and the fear of these punishments among the living was so widespread, that it seems more accurate to simply describe Gehenna as "Jewish hell."

Many of the myths of Gehenna simply enumerate the punishments found there. Others attempt to map out the dimensions of Gehenna, and to point out where its entrances can be found. Over time, an elaborate mythology about Gehenna accrued, much as did the mythology about heaven. Many new details emerged, such as the role of Duma, the angel in charge of Gehenna, or the presence of a guard outside Gehenna who only admits those for whom punishment has been decreed. Reports are found about visits to Gehenna by several great rabbis, as well as accounts about how all punishments in Gehenna cease during the Sabbath.[56] One learns that there is a whole category of avenging angels who deliver punishments to the sinners in Gehenna. These fearsome angels chase after the souls of newly deceased sinners with fiery rods, and when these angels catch the sinners, they drag them to Gehenna to face their punishments.[57]

Thus the role of the punishment of hell in Judaism is a transitional one, part of a larger myth about sin and redemption, in which virtually everyone's soul is eventually purified enough to escape further punishment. In this it is in stark contrast to the Christian view that the punishments of hell are eternal.

5. Myths of the Holy Word

Judaism is a strongly text-oriented religion. Not only is the primary text, the Torah, studied, but so too are the extensive rabbinic commentaries about it.[59] Much of the power attributed to the alphabet and to language grows out of their importance in the Genesis account of Creation, where God's words brought the world into being. Equally important is the account of the Giving of the Torah at Mount Sinai, where amidst lightning and thunder God's voice rang out for all the people to hear. So manifest was the voice that *All of the people saw the sounds* (Exod. 20:18). One myth describes the impact of God's voice as so great that the souls of the people leapt from their bodies and they all dropped dead, and God had to revive them with the dew of life.[60] So too does God's primary Name, YHVH, known as the Tetragrammaton, have limitless power for the one sage in each generation who knows its true pronunciation. Thus the power of the word, both spoken and written, is undisputed in Judaism.

Above all, the Torah itself takes on great mythological significance. It becomes far more than a text, even a text whose author is God. It comes to represent the full spectrum of Jewish teachings over the ages. The words of the Torah are believed to contain all truth, and in the rabbinic view it is even possible to interpret one word of the Torah as equivalent to another, as long as the numerical total of the two words is the same.[61] One myth describes the Torah as being written on the Arm of God.[62] Others personify the Torah as a bride, and Moses as her bridegroom. Still another myth describes the Torah as the wedding contract (*ketubah*) between God and Israel, binding the two together in a complex covenant.

There is even the idea that God is incarnated in the Torah. While most discussions about the Torah present it as God's creation and as the meeting place of human beings and God, the fourteenth century kabbalistic commentator Rabbi Menahem Recanati identified God and the Torah as one and the same thing: "God is incomplete without the Torah. The Torah is not something outside Him, and He is not outside the Torah. Consequently, God is the Torah."[63] This statement is explicitly contradicted by the eighteenth century kabbalist Moshe Hayim Luzzatto: "The Torah is God's, but He is not His Torah. The Torah is not in itself God, not His essence, but rather His wisdom and His will."[64]

Another view is that the words of the Torah are actually the names of God.[65] Therefore, God is called the Torah.[66] From these examples it is clear that the statement in the Mishnah that everything is in the Torah is meant seriously: "Turn it and turn it over again, for everything is in it, and contemplate it, and wax gray and grow old over it, and stir not from it, for you cannot have any better rule than this."[67]

Just as the Torah is personified, so too are there several myths in which the letters of the alphabet come forth, one by one, at God's command, to make their cases as to why they should head the other letters of the alphabet.[68] The honor goes to the letter *aleph*, while the letter *bet* is rewarded by being the first letter of the first word of the Torah, *Bereshit*, "in the beginning." There are also creation myths in which the world is created through the letters of the alphabet.

For readers unfamiliar with rabbinic tradition, one unfamiliar concept may be that of a dual Torah: the Written Torah (*Torah she-bikhtav*) that God dictated to Moses at Mount Sinai, and the Oral Torah (*Torah she-be-al-peh*), the explanations of the hidden meanings of the Written Torah, which God explained to Moses rather than put in writing. This Oral Torah is the basis for the imaginative retellings of biblical accounts so commonly found in the rabbinic texts. The radical changes brought to the original narrative are justified on the grounds that they were handed down as part of the Oral Torah.

Note that the tradition of the Oral Torah and the Written Torah is not the only example of dual Torahs to be found. There is also the concept of the Primordial Torah—the Torah as it exists in Heaven—which is contrasted with the Earthly Torah.[69] This myth makes it clear that these two Torahs are not the same. Also, there is an extensive tradition about the first tablets that Moses received at Mount Sinai, which he later smashed when he saw the people worshipping the golden calf. According to this tradition, the first tablets were much different than the second set that Moses received. While the first tablets were completely positive, the second tablets include negative commandments.[70]

Another way of viewing the concept of two Torahs is to view it as two ways of interpreting the text of the Torah. For the kabbalists, it was important to distinguish between the literal Torah, with its stories, laws, and commandments, and the eternal Torah through which the world was created. This led them to a search for the inner meaning of the Torah. Thus, the kabbalists were focused on discovering the mystical meaning. The *Zohar*, the primary text of kabbalah, is a compendium of these mystical interpretations. As the *Zohar* puts it about the teachings of one rabbi, "For every single word of Torah, he used to expound supernal mysteries."[71]

God's determination to give the gift of the Torah to Israel is described in blunt terms in one midrash: God picks up Mount Sinai and, while holding the mountain over the heads of the people of Israel, asks them whether they are willing to accept the Torah. Under the circumstances, they agree to accept it.[72]

Any discussion of the holy word must consider the importance of prayer. In the rabbinic view, God especially treasures the prayers of Israel and there is even an angel, Sandalphon, who gathers these prayers for God and weaves them into garlands that God wears as a crown of prayers while seated on His Throne of Glory. Faced with a history that resembled a litany of disasters, prayer was often the last recourse for the Jews, for it was believed to be their only hope in restoring God's faith in them.

Even today observant Jews spend a good deal of their day fulfilling the obligations set out in the Torah and subsequent texts, and they direct their minds and hearts several times a day through the medium of formal worship and private prayer. God, for His part, upholds the covenant established with Israel. And in all of these cases the means of communication between the human and the divine take the form of holy words, spoken as prayers or as texts inscribed on parchment[73], words that carry the reverberations of the eternal in every syllable.

6. Myths of the Holy Time

The major Jewish holy days are all closely linked to key Jewish myths. Rosh ha-Shanah is linked to the creation of the world; it is often referred to as "the birthday of the world." Yom Kippur is the day when God seals the Books of Life and Death. Sukkot remembers the Exodus, Passover, recounts the escape from Egyptian bondage, and Shavuot recalls the giving of the Torah at Mount Sinai. On Simhat Torah, the cycle of reading the Torah comes to an end and begins again, so that Satan cannot accuse the Jews of having finished with the Torah. Above all, the Sabbath, which recurs weekly, is closely associated with the day God rested after six days of Creation. Certainly, from the perspective of the ritual requirements of these holy days, myth and ritual are inextricably linked. By performing these rituals and reenacting these myths, it becomes possible to enter into a holy realm, where one can participate in an active covenant with God and seek out His mercy.

One key to the power of these holy days in the lives of the people is that of sacred time. During the Sabbath, for example, a distinct change takes place in the perception of time. There is a shift from the temporal to the eternal, as the focus changes to contemplation of the divine. In this sacred time a sense of holiness pervades the world, and the meaning of every action is magnified. At the same time, a holy presence can be sensed, which is identified as the Sabbath Queen. The kabbalistic principle of "as above, so below" defines all actions, and every ritual, from lighting the Sabbath candles to reciting the blessings over bread and wine, takes on a greater significance. In entering into sacred time, it can also be said that the people enter a mythic realm where the Sabbath Queen, invoked through prayer and song, can be perceived as an actual presence.

Sacred time is experienced not only during the holy days, but every day, during morning, afternoon, and evening prayers. For every time a *minyan* (traditionally, a quorum of ten men) gathers and the service begins, the congregation stands as petitioners before God, putting their fates in God's hands. The confidence that God is listening to their prayers derives from the unusual covenant between God and the people of Israel. This is not only a legal covenant, but a powerful bond between God and the chosen people. This covenant is the central myth at the heart of Judaism. It serves as a framework for all the other myths that grow out of that covenant, and, in particular, it encompasses all of the Myths of the Holy—the holy word, the holy time, the holy people, and the holy land.

One technique commonly used in the myths of the holy time is allegorical personification. In some of these myths the Torah is personified as a bride. In others the Sabbath is personified as a princess, a bride, or a queen. This grows out of the tradition of the Sabbath Queen, one of the identities of the *Shekhinah*. The first indications of the link between the *Shekhinah* and the Sabbath Queen are found in the Talmud, concerning the Sabbath customs of two rabbis: "Rabbi Haninah robed himself and stood at sunset on the eve of the Sabbath and exclaimed, 'Come and let us go forth to welcome the Sabbath Queen.' And on Sabbath Eve, Rabbi Yannai would don his robes and exclaim, 'Come, O Bride, come, O Bride!'"[74] Thus the myths of the Sabbath as a princess are simply alluding to the tradition of the Sabbath Queen, which, in turn, refers to the *Shekhinah*—God's presence in this world—as a participant of the Sabbath ritual. This holy presence is continually invoked throughout the Sabbath. The hymn *Lekhah Dodi*, composed by Shlomo Alkabetz in the sixteenth century, is recited in the synagogue to welcome the Sabbath Queen, thus initiating the Sabbath. In a more elaborate form of this ritual, *Kabbalat Shabbat*, the congregation goes outside to welcome the Sabbath Queen. This ritual might be seen as a kind of goddess worship, since it invokes a mythic feminine presence. Further, every aspect of the Sabbath fulfills a sacred requirement, even the lovemaking between man and wife on Friday night. Such lovemaking is said to take place under the shelter of the *Shekhinah*. It is required because, as the *Zohar* puts it, "in a place where male and female are not united, God will not take up His dwelling place, for blessing prevails only in a place where male and female are present."[75] And God's dwelling place in this world is, by definition, the *Shekhinah*, the Divine Presence.

In an interesting variation of this theme of allegorical personification, the Torah also is identified as a *ketubah*, a wedding contract, written for the wedding of God and Israel, where God represents the Groom and Israel, the bride:[76]

On Friday, the sixth of Sivan, the day appointed by the Lord for the revelation of the Torah to His beloved people, God came forth from Mount Sinai. The Groom, the Lord, the King of Hosts, is betrothed to the bride, the community of Israel, arrayed in beauty. The Bridegroom said to the pious and virtuous maiden, Israel, who had won His favor above all others: "Can there be a bridal canopy without a bride? *As I live . . . you shall don them all like jewels, deck yourself with them like a bride* (Isa. 49:18). Many days will you be Mine and I will be your Redeemer. Be My mate according to the law of Moses and Israel, and I will honor, support, and maintain you, and be your shelter and refuge in everlasting mercy. And I will set aside the life-giving Torah for you, by which you and your children will live in health and tranquility. This Covenant shall be valid and binding forever and ever."

Thus an eternal Covenant, binding forever, has been established between them, and the Bridegroom and the bride have given their oaths to carry it out. May the Bridegroom rejoice with the bride whom He has taken as His lot, and may the bride rejoice with the Husband of her youth.

It is the custom to read this allegorical text in Ladino on the holiday of Shavuot, which commemorates the giving of the Torah. It thus serves as a clear statement that the giving of the Torah was a covenant—here described as a wedding—between God and Israel, and underscores their mutual responsibilities, as in any marriage. God, the Groom, takes responsibility for protecting and supporting His bride, Israel, and Israel, in turn, reaffirms her loyalty and devotion to God. This kind of mutuality sums up the purpose of Jewish ritual, in which the people of Israel reach out to God for sustenance of every kind, spiritual as well as physical, and God responds by providing it for them, expecting, in return, their unceasing devotion. This is the essence of the covenant between God and Israel, which is reaffirmed daily, especially during sacred time.

7. Myths of the Holy People

The patriarchs Abraham, Isaac, and Jacob are known as the Fathers, and their wives, Sarah, Rebecca, Leah and Rachel, as the Mothers. Abraham is addressed as *Avraham Avinu*, "Our Father Abraham." Except for Rachel, all of the Fathers and Mothers are said to be buried in the Cave of Machpelah in the city of Hebron. They are held in the greatest reverence, not only as patriarchs and matriarchs, but as beloved members of one's own family, for since Abraham was deemed the first Jew, all other Jews must be his descendants. Thus the pattern of great patriarchal figures who were looming presences was established, and subsequent figures such as Joseph, Moses, and King David joined this pantheon.

One major way in which the traditions surrounding these holy people became embellished was through the application of the midrashic process, by which gaps in the biblical narrative were filled in through a unique, imaginative method that tried to read between the lines. Using this method, the childhood of Abraham was constructed out of thin air, using the template provided by the story of the childhood of Moses. So too were many details about the journey of Abraham and Isaac to Mount Moriah, where Isaac was to be sacrificed, added to the biblical account.[77] Indeed, the ultimate result of this midrashic method was to substantially enlarge the primary biblical narratives, creating a kind of Book of the Book.

Most remarkable are the kinds of transformations that came to be attributed to some biblical figures. Enoch, who is barely mentioned in the genealogy that goes from Adam to Noah,[78] ascends on high and is transformed into Metatron, chief among the angels. In these commentaries we learn that God, not Abraham, was Isaac's true father, while his mother was "the virgin Sarah."[79] And we also learn that Sarah was not barren, for although she did not give birth to any children before Isaac, she gave birth to souls.[80] Equally astonishing are some of the rabbinic traditions about Jacob. Not only are Jacob's highly questionable acts toward his brother Esau—buying his birthright and stealing the blessing of the firstborn—justified in rabbinic legend, but Jacob himself is raised to virtually divine heights.[81] In some versions Jacob is revealed to be an angel, while in others he is identified as an even higher being. The evidence for these traditions about Enoch and Jacob is substantial, with these figures taking on demiurgic proportions.

In particular, the lives of the patriarchs and their successors were carefully scrutinized, and served as role models for the people. When the people faced extermination from their enemies, they recalled Abraham's willingness to sacrifice his son Isaac on Mount Moriah, and they were consoled. When they were sent into exile after the destruction of the Temple in 586 BCE, they identified with Joseph, who was forced into Egyptian exile, and, like him, they vowed to return to the Holy Land at the first opportunity. Certainly the creation of the State of Israel in our time is directly related to the belief that any Jew living outside the Land of Israel is living in *galut*, in exile.

So precious were these patriarchal figures that there was even a great reluctance to accept their deaths as final. Instead, there are myths and folktales to be found that clearly assert that Abraham, Jacob, Moses and King David never died. And, in the sense that each remains a powerful presence, this is true.[82]

8. Myths of the Holy Land

One way to view the sacred nature of the Land of Israel is to see it as a continuation of the Garden of Eden, the very archetype of a sacred place. The garden is described as a place of abundance, where every need of Adam and Eve could be met. Once Adam and Eve were exiled from the garden, its location was lost, and the Holy Land can be seen to assume many of its sacred qualities. In this view, *Eretz Yisrael*, the Land of Israel, is a holy land singled out by God for an abundance of blessings: *It is a land which Yahweh your God looks after, on which Yahweh your God always keeps His eye, from year's beginning to year's end* (Deut. 11:12).

Some texts speak of a primordial light created on the first day of Creation that has its source in the Holy Land, at the very place where the Temple in Jerusalem was built. While the windows of most buildings are made to let light in, the windows of the Temple were built to let light out, and that light is said to have been the source of the holiness of the land.[83] The Lurianic myth of the Shattering of the Vessels describes how God sent forth vessels of primordial light, which shattered and scattered their sparks everywhere, but especially on the Holy Land.

For the great commentator Nachmanides, known as Ramban, the Holy Land is more of a spiritual place than a real one: "The Land is not like Egypt, which is irrigated by the Nile like a garden. The Land of Israel is a land of hills and valleys almost exclusively intended to absorb the dew of heaven."[84] For even though the physical Land of Israel exists, its essence is a spiritual matter, a life force coming from God. By entering the Land of Israel, a man becomes part of its sacred nature. And all those who walk as little as four cubits in the Land of Israel are assured of a share in the World to Come, while all who are buried in the Land of Israel—it is as if they were buried beneath the altar of the Temple in Jerusalem.[85] Rabbi Nachman of Bratslav, one of the most influential hasidic rabbis, asserted that prayers originating in the Land of Israel can bring about miracles and true wonders for the entire world.[86] Indeed, the covenant between God and the people of Israel is manifest in the Land of Israel. As Rav Kook, the first chief rabbi of modern Israel, put it, "Love for our Holy Land is the foundation of the Torah."[87]

The city of Jerusalem, a city holy to Jews, Christians, and Muslims, is also portrayed in mythic terms. Not only is there a Jerusalem on earth, but there is a mirror image of Jerusalem in heaven. They are identical, except that the Temple in the heavenly Jerusalem still exists, whereas the one in this world was destroyed. If anyone prays in Jerusalem, it is as though he were praying before the Throne of Glory. For the Gate of Heaven is there, and the door is open for prayer to be heard. It is said that all the trees of Jerusalem were made of cinnamon. When their wood was kindled, their perfume would spread through the Land of Israel. But when the Temple was destroyed, these trees were hidden away. It is also told that because of the fragrance of the incense, brides in Jerusalem did not have to perfume themselves. All of the people of Israel entered Jerusalem three times a year for the festival, yet Jerusalem was never filled. No one ever said, "There is no place for me to lodge in Jerusalem." Not only that, but it is said that no one was ever attacked by demons in Jerusalem. And while the Temple still stood, no one who remained in Jerusalem overnight remained guilty of sin. The presence of the Temple purified their sins.[88]

God's covenant with Abraham in Genesis 13:14-17 is often referred to as a kind of deed bestowing the right to all of the Land of Israel on the people of Israel: *"Raise your eyes and look out from where you are, to the north and south, to the east and west, for I give all the land that you see to you and your offspring forever."* In case there was any doubt about how far Abraham could see, God is said to have raised Abraham up over the Land of Israel and showed him all of the land.[89] The intractable conflict in the Middle East between Israel and the Palestinians derives from this belief in the sanctity of the Holy Land, especially of Jerusalem, shared by Jews and Muslims. This serves as a compelling reminder of the enduring and sometimes destructive power of these myths, which are not always benign.

Not only are the places of the Holy Land, such as Hebron, Beersheva and, of course, Jerusalem, linked with some of the primary episodes of the Bible, but there is a multitude of postbiblical myths and legends associated with them as well. Above all, Jerusalem is the jewel of the Holy Land, viewed as the navel of the world: *Thus said the Lord God: "I set this Jerusalem in the midst of nations, with countries round about her"* (Ezek. 5:5). This idea is restated in the Talmud: "The Holy Land was created first, and then the rest of the world."[90] The Temple that was twice built there and twice destroyed was not only regarded as the center of the Holy Land, but it was believed to have been built on the spot of the Foundation Stone that was regarded as the starting point and center of all Creation.[91] The Western Wall at the Temple Mount, also known as the Wailing Wall, has become the holiest Jewish site in the world. Those who visit there write a petition to God, known as *qvittel*, and put it in the cracks of the Wall. According to tradition, that is a certain method of contacting God. So powerful is this folk belief that many Jewish visitors to Israel leave messages to God in one of the cracks of the Wall.

9. Myths of Exile

The theme of exile makes its first, indelible appearance in Jewish tradition when God expels Adam and Eve from the Garden of Eden. Ever after, Jewish myth and history are full of examples of those who are uprooted and forced to leave their homes and wander, sometimes for many generations. From the beginning of Genesis, the pattern is clear: after Cain kills his brother, Abel, God turns him into a wanderer and exile, a punishment Cain considers *too great to bear* (Gen. 4:13).[92] Noah and his family are exiled from all of humanity when God brings down a deluge that destroys all other life on earth. The inhabitants of the land of Shinar seek to avoid being scattered, and therefore set out to build a tower, the Tower of Babel, which, in the end, causes God to send them into exile after all. God tells Abraham to leave his home in Haran and set out for the land that God would reveal to him. After stealing his brother's blessing, Jacob goes into exile in the city of Haran in order to escape his brother's vengeance. As for Joseph, he was sold into Egyptian bondage, and taken far away from home. And Moses is separated from his family and his people and raised in exile. Later he is further exiled from the house of Pharaoh.

And, of course, there is the ultimate paradigm of liberation from exile, that of the Exodus. This myth presents in archetypal fashion all stages of the quest to liberate the people Israel from Egyptian bondage, to fashion them as a people through 40 years of wandering, to bestow on them the greatest treasure, God's own teachings, dictated by God to Moses at Mount Sinai, and to lead them back to the Holy Land. This monumental exile thoroughly reshaped the people of Israel and resulted in a sacred text, the Torah, that would sustain the Jewish people for the next 3,000 years.[93]

After the Exodus, the best-known Jewish myth of exile is probably that of the Ten Lost Tribes.[94] The Assyrian conquest of the northern Kingdom of Israel in 722 BCE dispersed the ten tribes who lived there, leaving only the tribes of Judah and Benjamin, who constituted the southern Kingdom of Judah. The mystery of the fate of those lost tribes gave birth to a multitude of legends about them, as well as accounts of visitors who claimed to have reached them, including Eldad ha-Dani, Benjamin of Tudela and David Re'uveni. In most of these legends these tribes are described as being exceedingly pious and observant. In some folktales, however, they are described as "little red Jews from the other side of the river Sambatyon." In order to explain why the lost tribes could not rejoin their brethren, they were said to be trapped on the other side of this pious river, which threw up rocks as high as a house six days a week and was therefore impassable, and only rested on the Sabbath. But the pious lost tribes could not cross then either, since no work is permitted on the Sabbath. This myth of the Ten Lost Tribes has given birth to farfetched efforts to identify where they went. Ethiopian Jews identify themselves as descendants of the tribe of Dan, and there are many far-flung, unlikely peoples, including the Japanese, the Celts, and Native Americans, who have been identified as among the lost tribes.

In general, then, exile serves as God's punishment, as clearly stated in *Midrash ha-Ne'elam* in *Zohar Hadash* 23c: "Every time the Jewish people were sent into exile, God set a limit to the exile, and they were always aroused to repentance. But this final exile has no set limit, and everything depends upon repentance." However, beginning in the sixteenth century, the belief arose that the dispersion of the Jewish people had a special purpose other than punishment, to enable them to serve as a guide to humanity.[95] Alternately, the Jewish people were viewed as serving a mystical function in raising up holy sparks that had been scattered around the world, as portrayed in the Lurianic kabbalah.[96] Thus, for the Ari, Rabbi Isaac Luria, the purpose of the many exiles of the Jews was to extricate the imprisoned sparks that were lodged in foreign lands. He believed that by living in Egypt the Israelites took all the holy sparks out of Egypt, defeating the forces of impurity that abounded in the desert. Rabbi Hayim Tirer of Chernovitz describes this process: "When the Jews left Egypt, all the holy sparks of Egypt flocked to them and departed with them." (*Be'er Mayim Hayim, Noah* 162). This mythic interpretation turned a punishment into a blessing, where God depended on His people, Israel, as much as they depended on Him. It clearly demonstrates that the theme of exile can be viewed from two perspectives. *B. Berakhot* 3a describes it as a painful exile: "Alas for the children who have been exiled from their Father's table." But, according to *Exodus Rabbah* 2:4, "It was in the wilderness that Israel received the manna, the quail, Miriam's well, the Torah, the Tabernacle, the *Shekhinah*, priesthood, kingship, and the Clouds of Glory."

The other side of the coin of exile is return, and the theme of return is also exceptionally powerful in Judaism. There is the constant longing to return to the Holy Land. The final words of the Passover Seder, recounting the Exodus, are "Next Year in Jerusalem!"[97] So too is the theme of return the underlying motif in the wide array of messianic myths in Judaism. The arrival of the Messiah, it is believed, will transform all existence, and all Jews will miraculously travel to the Holy Land. This, the initiation of the messianic era, will be the ultimate return.[98]

10. Myths of the Messiah

Myths of exile are naturally linked to myths of redemption, as exile leads a people to dream of redemption. While redemption takes many forms, its primary focus in Judaism is on the transforming role of the Messiah, a divine figure who, it is said, will descend to this world and initiate the End of Days. The longing for the Messiah is a direct result of the hardship and exile within Jewish history. Since the time of the prophet Isaiah, no one idea has obsessed the Jews more than this: When will the coming of the Messiah take place? Every Jew hoped it would be in his lifetime. Some Hasidim kept their staffs and white robes by the door, ready to answer the Messiah's call on the shortest notice. Even today many observant Jews still anxiously await the arrival of the Messiah, which is expected to initiate a heaven on earth, known as the End of Days. Of course, the requirements to be the Messiah are steep, and there are three: raising the dead, restoring the exiles to the Land of Israel, and rebuilding the Temple in Jerusalem.[99]

What follows the coming of the Messiah might be described as heaven on earth, a new incarnation of the Garden of Eden, making the cycle that started with the expulsion from Eden complete. The first era of history will be over, and a new era will begin. At the same time, the coming of the Messiah will bring about the repair of the rent in heaven that resulted from the separation of God from His Bride. For only the rebuilding of the Temple in Jerusalem, the *Shekhinah's* home in this world, can restore God's Bride to Him, and the rebuilding will not take place until the Messiah comes.[100] Thus the fate of everything hangs on the Messiah, for the messianic era will bring about a cosmic healing both in heaven and on earth.

In this new era, the righteous among the sons and daughters of Israel will receive a heavenly reward that includes not only studying Torah with the Messiah, the patriarchs, and the sages, but even Torah classes taught by God. At the same time, the punishments of the souls of sinners in Gehenna will come to an end, and they too will be brought into Paradise. All this will follow the coming of the Messiah.

The cycle of messianic myths is quite complete. It starts with the creation of the Messiah, and includes the birth of the Messiah, the events that will initiate the End of Days, and accounts of the messianic era that will follow.

It quickly becomes evident that there are two basic concepts of the Messiah: one, a heavenly figure of supernatural origin who makes his home in a heavenly palace; the other, a human Messiah, an exceptionally righteous man who takes on the mantle of the Messiah and initiates the End of Days. In time, these two separate motifs were combined into a single myth in a clever manner: there were said to be two Messiahs, whose fates were linked.[101] One is identified as Messiah the son of Joseph (Messiah ben Joseph) and the other is the heavenly Messiah, Messiah the son of David (Messiah ben David).[102] According to this combined myth, Messiah ben Joseph, the human Messiah, will be a warrior who will go to war against the evil forces of Gog and Magog[103] and die in the process. He will be followed by Messiah ben David, the heavenly Messiah, who will defeat the evil empire and initiate the End of Days. In some versions of this myth, Messiah ben David will prove he is the real Messiah by resurrecting Messiah ben Joseph.[104]

In the myths of the heavenly Messiah, he is described as a supernatural figure living in his own heavenly palace, known as the Bird's Nest, waiting to be called upon to initiate the End of Days.[105] Some versions of this myth emphasize his suffering,[106] while others describe the Messiah as being held captive in heaven or in hell.[107]

All of these variants of the myth have in common the portrayal of a supernatural, heavenly figure who is forced to wait impatiently until the circumstances are such that it becomes possible for him to fulfill his messianic destiny. But the portrayal of the earthly Messiah is quite a bit different. In one famous talmudic version, he is described as a leprous beggar waiting outside the gates of Rome, who takes off and puts on his bandages one at a time, so that he will not be delayed if he is suddenly called.[108] But in general the human Messiah is described as the *Tzaddik ha-Dor*, the greatest sage of his generation, who will step into the role of Messiah if all the circumstances happen to be right. Naturally, there are many failures, due to one mistake or another. These are recounted in a series of myths about why the Messiah has not yet come. There are enough accounts of these failures to fill a book. There are even stories about some rabbis, such as Joseph della Reina, who sought to force the coming of the Messiah.[109]

All sorts of signs and warnings are expected to precede the coming of the Messiah, great upheavals known as the Pangs of the Messiah. Historical turmoil has often been identified with these mythic wars, and has inevitably precipitated messianic expectations. At the time that the Soviet Union invaded Afghanistan, three rabbis in Mea Sha'arim, the ultra-Orthodox section of Jerusalem, were reported to have dreamed, on the same night, that the coming of the Messiah was imminent. This rumor spread among the entire community, all of whom waited on pins and needles for the footsteps of the Messiah to be heard. This demonstrates that the longing and expectations for the coming of the Messiah are as intense as ever in these communities.

The Jewish mythology concerning the End of Days is just as elaborate as that found in the Book of Revelation, whose portrayal of the Apocalypse is surely drawn from contemporary Jewish eschatology. The messianic era will be heralded by great upheaval and an epic war known as the War of Gog and Magog. Finally, the new era will be announced by the prophet Elijah, blowing a horn from the ram that Abraham sacrificed on Mount Moriah (the other horn was blown at Mount Sinai). The righteous dead will be resurrected, and all the exiles will be gathered into the Holy Land, where the Temple will be supernaturally rebuilt. In heaven, God will be reunited with His Bride, from whom He was separated at the time the Temple was destroyed. At that time the Messiah will address all of Israel, and the blessed days of the Messiah will begin. The messianic hope, with its promise that *He will destroy death forever* (Isa. 25:8), has been fervently longed for since the days of Isaiah. Maimonides codified this hope in his *Thirteen Principles of Faith*, in which the twelfth principle is belief in the coming of the Messiah, which entered the popular domain as the statement, "I believe with perfect faith in the coming of the Messiah. No matter how long he may tarry, I will await his coming every day."

What about the belief in the Messiah in the modern era? Does it still have the power to compel widespread belief and expectation? For those who still firmly believe that God dictated the Torah to Moses on Mount Sinai, the certainty of the coming of the Messiah is not viewed as myth but as truth, as codified by Maimonides. However, not all Orthodox Jews are equally impassioned about the coming of the Messiah. The Lubavitch Hasidim, in particular, await His coming. Many of them expect their deceased Rebbe, Rabbi Menachem Mendel Schneersohn, to return to life and serve as the Messiah.[110]

As for non-Orthodox Jews, who make up the majority of modern Jews, most do not regard the Torah as the literal word of God. This view makes it possible to incorporate modern views into their practice of an ancient religion. Just as it seems unlikely to most of these Jews that the waters of the Red Sea really split apart, or that the sun stood still for Joshua, the coming of the Messiah is no longer expected. Even were the Messiah to arrive, it is highly unlikely that he would be recognized by those who were not expecting him. Instead, this tradition, like many others, has acquired the status of a myth, even if it has not been acknowledged as such.

III. Mythic Parallels

If there is a mythology in Judaism, what model does it follow—that of pagan mythology, where there is a pantheon of gods, usually ruled by a divine pair? Does it follow a dualistic model, where more than one god is involved in ruling the world? Or does it work within the monotheistic model, where there is but a single God who both created the world and rules it? While it might appear at first that only the monotheistic model was relevant, in fact, there is evidence of all three models in Jewish tradition.

That some kind of God or gods exist, most humans have had no doubt. How else could the world have come into being? Thus the primary purpose of Western religion is to answer two elementary questions: "Who created the world?" and "Who rules it?"[111] Among the religions of the ancient Near East, Judaism answered this question by insisting that there is but one God, whose name is YHVH, generally rendered in English as *Yahweh*. This principle is stated in the Shema, the central proclamation of Jewish belief: *Hear O Israel, the Lord our God, the Lord is One* (Deut. 6:4). That is the essence of Jewish monotheism. The great philosopher Maimonides always upheld monotheistic principles, writing, for example, that "There is one God who created everything and who guides the celestial spheres."[112] In this view, the same God who created the world rules it.

In contrast, some dualistic systems propose the existence of two gods. In Gnosticism, an evil god, known as the demiurge, created and rules this world, and the only hope of salvation comes from a higher, benevolent Deity. While the doctrine of a good god and an evil one is not found in Judaism, there are numerous instances where God shares his ruling powers with other divine figures, such as Metatron, or the one God is described as bearing contradictory qualities of judgment and mercy.[113]

Polytheism, in the form of the Greek, Canaanite, and Egyptian religions, offered multiple gods and a divine pantheon. Here, too, the original gods were usually not the ruling gods: Kronos is the father of the Greek gods, while Zeus is the ruling god; and it is the Canaanite god El, who wrested power from his father Samen (Heaven), who is supposed to be the ruling god, while actually it is Ba'al, El's son, who is the dominant ruler.

These three models—the monotheistic model of the Jews (and later Christians and Muslims), the dualistic model of the Gnostics, and the pagan model of the Greeks and Canaanites—would seem mutually exclusive. For example, we would not expect to find myths about a dualistic divinity in Judaism, since there is only one God. But we do. Despite the inviolable principle of monotheism, there are many Jewish texts that have strongly gnostic characteristics and portray a second divine figure who plays an active role in the ruling of the world. Gershom Scholem identified these texts as examples of Jewish Gnosticism.[114]

At first it may be difficult to see how monotheism can include a second divine figure. By definition, monotheism is an assertion that there is only one God. Yet there are two models of monotheism in Judaism: one in which there is one god and no other divine figures higher than the rank of angels, and a second model, in which other divine figures are acknowledged to exist, but they are subject to God, who is the king of the gods. This second type of monotheism is known as "monolatry," where worship of only one God/god is allowed, but the existence of other gods is acknowledged, at least tacitly.[115] In Judaism, it is defined as a stage in the religion of ancient Israel when the existence of gods other than *Yahweh* was admitted, but their worship was strictly forbidden.[116] That there was worship of some forbidden gods by the ancient Israelites has been demonstrated by archaeological discoveries, as well as by the tirades of the biblical prophets against such worship, such as the women weeping over Tammuz (Ezek. 8:14), or the people defending their worshipping the Queen of Heaven (Jer. 44:17-19). There is also evidence of the awareness of other gods in several biblical verses, such as *Who is like You among the gods (ba-elim), O Lord?* (Exod. 15:11).[117] Also, in Psalm 82, *God stands in the divine assembly; among the divine beings (Elohim) He pronounces judgment* (Ps. 82:1).

The concept of monolatry goes a long way toward explaining the parallel development of folk religion in Judaism beyond the official kind, especially in the popular culture. Although monolatry refers to the religion of ancient Israel, that does not mean that the kind of folk religion indicated by monolatry disappeared after the biblical period. Instead, it continued to evolve in its own way, far more open to mythological motifs than rabbinic Judaism.[118] By the time of the rabbinic period, the pagan religions against which the official religion was polemicizing no longer existed. Therefore the rabbis permitted these mythological motifs from the folk religion, which had elements of the ancient Near Eastern mythologies, to surface in a form that was then acceptable within the confines of rabbinic thought. This suggests that a great many rabbinic myths, as found in the midrashim, are not new creations of the rabbis, as might appear to be the case.[119] Rather, they are simply the writing down of an oral tradition that was kept alive by the people, when there was no need to suppress it any longer.

A close examination of the Jewish mythic tradition reveals that its origins are found in Near Eastern mythology. Umberto Cassuto says of these mythic parallels: "These Israelite myths of the Bible are derived from similar myths current among the neighboring peoples concerning the war waged by one of the great gods against the deity of the sea. The famous Babylonian story about the war of Marduk against Tiamat is but one example of an entire series of similar narratives. Among the Israelites ... the traditional material that was current in the lands of the East was given by Israel an aspect more in accord with their ethos, to wit, the aspect of the revolt by the sea against his Creator."[120]

This and other Near Eastern mythologies clearly fueled the continuing evolution of Jewish myth, which incorporated and integrated the earlier mythology. New myths arose to fill the void created by the loss of the older pagan ones. These new myths involve not only God, but also God's Bride, the *Shekhinah*,[121] and like the Greek myths of Zeus and Hera, they sometimes converge and sometimes diverge and often give birth to additional myths. So too are there other mythical figures, including that of the Messiah, along with angels, demons, spirits, and fabulous creatures of the air, earth, and sea, such as the Ziz, a giant mythical bird, Behemoth, a giant land animal, and Leviathan, a monstrous sea creature.

There are many often intriguing parallels to be found between Jewish myth and that of the Greeks and Canaanites. Many of these parallels concern the nature of God. Just as Zeus and El are warrior gods, so too is God a warrior, as in the verse *Yahweh is a man of war* (Exod. 15:3), although, of course, this is only one aspect of God. In some sources God is said to have smitten the Egyptians with His finger, while in others God is described as a mighty warrior, carrying a fiery bow, with a sword of lightning, traveling through the heavens in a chariot. Confirming the image of God as a great warrior, *Exodus Rabbah* 5:14 states that God's bow was fire, His arms flame, His spear a torch, the clouds His shield, and His sword lightning. The parallels to Zeus and the warrior gods of the Near East are clear:

> *Yahweh* is a mighty warrior, who defeated Pharaoh at the Red Sea. It is said that God smote them with His finger, as it is said, *And the magicians said to Pharaoh, "This is the finger of God"* (Exod. 8:15).
>
> Others say that God appeared to Pharaoh as a mighty warrior, carrying a fiery bow, with a sword of lightning, traveling through the heavens in a chariot. When Pharaoh shot arrows at Israel, God shot fiery arrows back. When Pharaoh's army cast rocks, God brought hail. And when Pharaoh shot fiery arrows from a catapult, God deluged them with burning coals. Finally Pharaoh exhausted his entire armory. Then God took a cherub from His Throne of Glory and rode upon it, waging war against

Pharaoh and Egypt, as it is said, *He mounted a cherub and flew* (Ps. 18:11). Leaping from one wing to another, God taunted Pharaoh, "O evil one, do you have a cherub? Can you do this?"

When the angels saw that God was waging war against the Egyptians on the sea, they came to His aid. Some came carrying swords and others carrying bows or lances. God said to them, "I do not need your aid, for when I go out to battle, I go alone." That is why it is said that *Yahweh is a man of war* (Exod. 15:3).[122]

One might wonder where this extravagant description of God the Warrior comes from, but most of the central images can be traced back to several biblical verses. The foremost is *Yahweh is a man of war*. And the intensely mythic description of God riding upon a cherub is found in the verse *He mounted a cherub and flew*. The portrayal of God traveling through heavens in a chariot, so similar to that of Apollo, may well be a remnant of sun worship in Judaism.[123] A parallel kind of sun worship can also be seen in the myths surrounding Enoch's transformation into Metatron, as Metatron is described in fiery imagery, and Metatron himself is identified as a ruling divinity. As for God's Chariot, known as the *Merkavah*, it is based on the vision of Ezekiel (Ezek. 1:1-28). God is said to have taken the cherub from between the wheels of this chariot.

Another important parallel concerns a conflict of cosmic importance between God and His Bride, as described in the *Zohar* and other kabbalistic sources. It resembles the disputes between Zeus and Hera in Greek mythology, where, for example, Hera, angered by Zeus's infidelities, led a conspiracy in which Zeus was bound with leather thongs as he slept. In revenge, Zeus hung Hera from the sky with a golden bracelet on each of her wrists, and with an anvil fastened to each of her ankles.[124] While the conflict between God and His Bride never reached this kind of acrimony, God and the *Shekhinah* are still described in the *Zohar* as arguing over the destruction of the Temple in Jerusalem.[125] This confrontation results in God's Bride separating from Him, choosing to go into exile with Her children, Israel. It is this separation, more than anything else, that announces the arrival of the *Shekhinah*'s mythic independence, in which the *Shekhinah* functions more as an independent mythic being than as the feminine aspect of God. Here, however, God does not seek revenge as does Zeus. Instead, he mourns over His losses, in a surprising series of myths about God's suffering.[126]

In addition, there are remarkable parallels to the crucial myths of Creation, the Fall, and the Flood. There are Greek creation myths similar to the Genesis account of Creation found in Hesiod's *Theogony*,[127] in which there is a union between darkness and chaos. What is missing in these myths is God's role in combining these elements to create the world.

In two cases, there appear to be direct borrowing from Greek myth. One Jewish myth portrays Joshua, the successor of Moses, as Oedipus, while another describes a Jewish Icarus.[128]

Likewise, the biblical account of Eve eating the forbidden fruit and its myriad consequences has striking parallels to the story of Pandora, who set free the winged Evils, the misfortunes that plague mankind: Old Age, Labor, Sickness, Insanity, Vice, and Passion.[129] Both hearken back to a primordial sin, and both provide a myth of the origin of evil. Yet both myths include a forward-looking hope for redemption. In Pandora's case, Hope is the last to come out of the box.[130] And in the case of Eve there is hope for the Messiah.

An even closer parallel to the story of Pandora is found in *Genesis Rabbah* 19:10: "A woman came to the wife of a snake-charmer to borrow vinegar. 'How does your husband treat you?' she asked the wife. 'He treats me very well,' the woman answered, 'but he does not permit me to approach this cask, which is full of serpents.' The visiting woman said, 'Surely your husband is deceiving you and the cask is full of finery he plans to give to another woman.' Hearing this, the wife inserted her hand into the cask, and the serpents began biting her. When her husband came home, he heard her crying out in pain. 'Have you touched that cask?' he demanded to know. Thus, God said to Adam and Eve, *Did you eat of the tree from which I had forbidden you to eat?"* (Gen. 3:11).

Above all, many parallels exist to the biblical account of the Flood. One Mesopotamian Flood myth is found in the Epic of Atrahasis, who, like Noah, is the survivor of the great Flood. The god Ea-Enki advises Atrahasis to build an ark. Ea-Enki says: "Place a roof over the barge, cover it as the heavens cover the earth. Do not let the sun see inside. Enclose it completely. Make the joints strong. Caulk the timbers with pitch."[131] This is very much like the directions God gives to Noah to build the ark.[132] So too does Atrahasis fill the ark with animals.

Another Flood myth, an even closer parallel, is found in the Mesopotamian epic of *Gilgamesh*, in which Utnapishtim is parallel to Noah. Ea, the divine patron of fresh water, warns Utnapishtim about the coming Flood and tells him to build an ark and take specimens of every living thing on board. In this way Utnapishtim and his wife are the lone human survivors of a Flood brought on by the divine assembly that was intended to destroy every other mortal.

Another great Flood myth, this one Greek, is recounted in the Latin poet Ovid's *Metamorphoses*. It is remarkably similar to the biblical account of Noah, and even includes a dove. Here Zeus floods the earth, intending to wipe out the entire race of man. But Deucalion, King of Phthia, is warned by his father, Prometheus, and builds an ark. All the world is flooded, and all mortal creatures are lost except for Deucalion and his wife, Pyrrha. Deucalion sends out a dove on an exploratory flight, and is reassured by it.[133]

These Flood narratives with their distinct parallels strongly suggest that all of them—including the biblical narrative of the Flood—are based on the same ancient Mesopotamian tradition from the third millennium BCE.

Parallels also exist between the Jewish heavenly pantheon and the Greek. The Jewish pantheon is just as extensive, but with a host of angels playing roles equivalent to those of the Greek gods. Thus, instead of Poseidon, there is the angel Rahab, who likewise rules the sea. Or just as Hermes is the divine messenger, so this role in Jewish mythology is played by the angel Raziel, who delivers a book of secrets to Adam. And the angel Metatron, who is described in terms of the sun, plays a role similar to that of Helios, the Greek God of the sun.

There are also striking parallels involving Prometheus. Just as Prometheus is said to have formed man out of clay and water, so the angel Michael (or, some say, Gabriel) is said, in some sources, to have formed the body of Adam. And while it is widely known that Prometheus brought fire from heaven and gave it to humankind,[134] it is far less known that in some Jewish myths Adam plays a very Promethean role, bringing down both light and fire from heaven for the sake of humankind.[135]

Some of the most interesting parallels are those between Jewish and Christian sources. In Christianity, God is said to have incarnated His son, Jesus, as a human; thus the essence of the Christian myth is that a divine figure became a human being. This follows the pattern of Jewish myth where it is angels who are incarnated as human. Genesis 6 describes how the Sons of God cohabited with the daughters of men, begetting giants. Rabbinic commentaries identify the Sons of God as two angels, Shemhazai and Azazel, who descended from on high, took on human form, and sought out human women for lovers.[136] These angels revealed all kinds of heavenly secrets, including magical spells, and taught women the arts of seduction. In addition, the prophet Elijah, who was taken into heaven in a fiery chariot, is an angel who often appears in human form on earth.[137]

Another variant of this divine-to-human pattern concerns how the talmudic sage Rabbi Ishmael was conceived. It is said that Rabbi Ishmael's mother was so pious that God sent the angel Gabriel to take the form of her husband and to meet her at the *mikveh*, the ritual bath, and to conceive a child with her. She, of course, had no idea that it was a disguised angel and not her husband who met her. She conceived that day, and when Rabbi Ishmael was born, he was said to have been as beautiful as an angel.[138] This is the same theme of human women having intercourse with an angel, but here it is with God's approval, while the angels Shemhazai and Azazel broke their promise to God that they would not fall into sinful ways.

So too are there myths in which the patriarch Jacob is identified as an angel who came down to earth in human form. We can now see that this myth, so strange at first, is part of an explicit pattern in Jewish mythology, that of a divine figure becoming human. Sometimes these echoes even become overt. The first century philosopher, Philo, proposed that it was God who begat Isaac, not Abraham, although God made sure that Isaac closely resembled Abraham. Philo even says that this child was born to the "virgin" Sarah. Here we find a direct parallel to later Christian lore.[139] Indeed, there are an extensive number of parallels with Hellenistic and Canaanite mythology. What this indicates is that Jewish mythology was not isolated from the other mythologies. It was resonant with the motifs that were the psychic currency of their neighboring cultures.

Christian tradition is built upon Jewish sources, especially on the myths of heaven and on the messianic tradition. In Christian theology, Jesus is said to have fulfilled the long-awaited messianic prophecies stated in Isaiah and elsewhere. Those who recognized Jesus as the Messiah became Christians. Those who did not remained Jews, still awaiting the Messiah.

While the Christian dependence on Jewish tradition is irrefutable, there are also Jewish myths that hark back to Christianity. In the Christian interpretation of the binding of Isaac, a direct link is made between Abraham's willingness to sacrifice Isaac, and God's willingness to sacrifice His son, Jesus. Abraham replied to Isaac's question about what they would sacrifice by saying, *God Himself will provide the lamb, my son* (Gen. 22:8). The Christian reading of this verse is that God will be making the sacrifice of his son, Jesus, who is identified as the lamb. Thus the linkage between Isaac and Jesus was well-established in Christian texts when we find a midrashic tradition that Abraham *did* slay Isaac, and that Isaac's soul ascended on high. He studied in the heavenly academy of Shem and Eber, and after three years his soul descended and he was resurrected. The parallel to the Christian doctrine of the resurrection of Jesus is clear—the major difference is that of the three days of Jesus and the three years of Isaac. This, then, is a likely example of a Christian-influenced Jewish myth.[140]

So too is the Islamic tradition based on the Jewish one. Abraham is the Muslim as well as the Jewish patriarch, and while the *Koran* does not specify which son of Abraham climbed Mount Moriah with him, later Muslim exegesis identified him as Ishmael.[141] There are also Islamic myths to be found about Adam as well as Abraham, and, of course, about Ishmael, Abraham's son by Hagar.

The most prominent mythological parallels between Jews and Muslims are those concerning Jerusalem. The Temple Mount, where the Dome of the Rock was built, is sacred to both religions. Both identify the Temple Mount as Beth El, the place where Jacob had his dream of angels ascending and descending. In the Muslim version, God identifies Himself to Jacob as "The God of your fathers, Abraham, Ishmael, and Isaac." Both believe that the terrestrial Temple was placed exactly below the celestial Temple, and that although the earthly Temple has been destroyed, the celestial Temple still remains. Both people believe that a ram's horn will be blown in Jerusalem on Judgment Day and both expect the resurrection of the dead to take place there.[142] From these examples it is clear that the Jewish and Muslim traditions about Jerusalem have a great many parallels, and in many cases are virtually identical.

These are just a few of the many parallels to Greek, Christian, and Near Eastern myths that are found in Jewish sources. These parallels demonstrate that Jewish tradition did not exist in a vacuum, but that the kinds of motifs found in other traditions are mirrored, sometimes transformed, in Jewish lore. Thus Jewish mythology was not separate from the other surrounding mythologies, but very much a part of the existing tradition.

IV. Myth and Ritual in Judaism

According to the mythologist Walter F. Otto, "Myth demands ritual."[143] This is the central premise of the Myth and Ritual school of mythological studies. The intimate relationship between myth and ritual in Judaism confirms this approach. Many of the rituals of Judaism, such as those of the Sabbath or the saying of the Kaddish, the prayer for the dead, have their basis in some elemental myth, such as the creation of the world or the fate of the soul after death. Thus Judaism can be said to possess both of the primary elements of a mythic system: myth and ritual.

As in other traditions, Jewish myth and ritual reaffirm and validate each other, for as long as they remain linked, the ritual keeps the myth alive. But as soon as the ritual falls into disuse, the myth loses its primary purpose: linking the past and the present through the acting out of the ritual. Without the ritual, the myth is no more than a story, albeit a powerful and compelling one.

It is important to remind ourselves that what we call a myth was, or still is, someone else's truth. Among observant Jews, most of the texts identified as myths in this book still constitute divine truths from the Written Torah or the Oral Torah—that is, truths that originated with God. Likewise, for observant Jews, the stories that accompany Jewish rituals have retained the status of absolute truth. Indeed, the key test in our time[144] for whether one holds Orthodox views is whether one believes that God dictated the Torah to Moses at Mount Sinai. Without this belief, the seal of truth that binds the Torah and makes every word fraught with infinite meaning no longer exists. Thus, for believers, the ultimate truth of the Torah must be beyond any doubt. This is the essential condition for a mythic system to flourish.

However, even for those Jews in our time who regard the stories of the Torah more as myths than as truths, the stories retain much of their inherent power. Like all myths, they are not arbitrary creations, but projections from the deepest levels of the Self. From this perspective, these stories can be read as psychic maps, as archetypes of the collective Jewish unconscious. Further, they are an essential part of a rich heritage that derives from an ancient past, and even those Jews who do not believe in the divine origin of the Torah may well regard themselves as descendants of Abraham. They also are likely to observe some of the most prominent Jewish rituals, such as participating in a Seder on Passover, celebrating a Jewish wedding, or, above all, observing the Sabbath.

The Sabbath is openly intended to recall the seventh day of Creation, when God rested, as stated in Genesis 2:3: *And God blessed the seventh day and hallowed it; because that day He rested from all His work which God in creating had made.* It is interesting to note that the practice of observing a day of rest on the Sabbath appears to have existed prior to the giving of the Law at Mount Sinai. The account of the manna found in Exodus 16:25-30 includes an injunction against collecting manna on the Sabbath; nor did the manna fall on that day. This indicates that the Sabbath was already recognized as a holy day, as God states, *"See that Yahweh has given you the Sabbath"* (Exod. 16:29).[145] So too was it identified as a day of rest.

To emphasize the parallels between God's day of rest and the human day of rest, all forms of work are forbidden on the Sabbath, as stated in Exodus 20:10: *But the seventh day is a sabbath of the Lord your God: you shall not do any work.* The laws of the Sabbath include dozens of kinds of activities that are defined as work and therefore forbidden, such as lighting a fire, carrying of any kind, or writing, as well as any exchange of money.[146] The point of this blanket prohibition against work on the Sabbath is to remind the people at every turn that they, like their Creator, are observing a day of rest. Thus there is a remarkable mutuality in the way that the myth of God's day of rest recalls the ritual of the Sabbath and the Sabbath ritual recalls the creation myth.

Many of the Sabbath rituals have special meaning. It is traditional to have two challahs on the Sabbath. The two challahs (braided loaves of bread) represent the Israelites in the wilderness who collected manna on Friday for two days, for no gathering of the manna was permitted on the Sabbath. Another good example of the intimate link between myth and ritual is the reason given for the custom of eating fish on the Sabbath. This fish, it is said, is intended to remind us of the messianic banquet that awaits the righteous in the World to Come, when they will feast off of the great fish Leviathan and drink messianic wine saved since the six days of Creation. Once again the Sabbath and Creation are directly linked, and this reaffirms the purpose of the Sabbath ritual, which is to remind us of God's six days of Creation and His subsequent day of rest. The creation of the world is God's greatest miracle, and remembering this reinforces the fact that we would not even exist without God, nor can we continue to exist without Him. Ultimately, then, the purpose of this Sabbath ritual is to give honor to God and to God's creation.

Just as the Sabbath is welcomed on Friday night, so its departure is signaled at the end of the Sabbath with *Havdalah,* a closing ceremony that separates the Sabbath and the days of the week that follow. Here prayers are recited and songs sung, and certain ritual items are used: a braided candle, spices, and wine. These ceremonies are the ritual manifestation of the arrival and departure of the Sabbath. However, there is also a powerful mythical dimension to these rituals, for the arrival of the Sabbath brings with it two important spiritual presences, the Sabbath Queen and the *neshamah yeterah,* a second soul. The Sabbath Queen is one of the personas of the *Shekhinah,* the Divine Presence, who is the Bride of God. The *neshamah yeterah* is a holy spirit that inhabits a person for the duration of the Sabbath. Both the Sabbath Queen and the second soul are said to take their leave when the *Havdalah* ceremony that concludes the Sabbath is performed. The ritual of smelling the spices that is part of *Havdalah* is supposed to revive a person who has just lost his or her extra soul. *Havdalah* is supposed to be performed when three stars appear in the night sky, but many Hasidim were reluctant to end the Sabbath, and they would delay the ceremony as long as possible, until well after midnight. There was even one Hasidic sect that put off saying *Havdalah* until the middle of the week, and then began at once to prepare for the next Sabbath.

Thus the Sabbath can be seen as a perfect melding of myth and ritual, which, since it recurs on a weekly basis, serves as a religious foundation for those who observe it. It is truly as the essayist Ahad Ha'am said, "More than Israel has kept the Sabbath, the Sabbath has kept Israel." The myth, which comes first, is the Genesis account of the six days of Creation, and how on the seventh day God rested. All of the elaborate traditions of the Sabbath, including the ritual meal using challah and wine, the Sabbath songs, and refraining from any kind of work, serve to remind us that the Sabbath is a special day, when the people of Israel recall God's great work of Creation, as well as the day God rested. The people act out the rituals that keep the myth alive, and the myth is remembered and reenacted, and the entire cycle reexperienced.

Another important ritual in the Jewish life cycle is the saying of Kaddish, the prayer for the dead. This prayer is recited daily for 11 months for a deceased mother or father (*B. RH* 17a). Mourners stand to recite the prayer at the end of each prayer service, while facing Jerusalem. The Kaddish is also recited at the burial service, and whenever family members visit a grave.

Although the Kaddish is mentioned as one of the synagogue prayers in the Talmud, the practice of mourners reciting the Kaddish seems to go back to the thirteenth century. Over time, the Kaddish has become inextricably linked to a constellation of myths about the fate of the soul after death. For the Kaddish is not only a remembrance of the dead, but also a theurgic invocation, calling upon God to protect the soul of the one who has died during the time that the soul spends in Gehenna. It was the widespread Jewish belief that only a few pure souls went directly to Paradise after death. Acknowledging that everyone has his or her share of sins, it was believed that the majority of those who died went to Gehenna, where they were punished by avenging angels for up to one year. These punishments are intended to serve as a purifying process, and they are generally identical to those associated with the Christian concept of hell. Sinners are struck with flaming lashes or hung by their offending organ. But then—in contrast to the Christian view of hell—they are released from Gehenna and permitted to make a slow ascent into Paradise. This belief is explicitly stated in the Midrash: "The son's reciting of the Kaddish raises the soul of the parent from purgatory to paradise."[147]

It is in this context that the Kaddish must be understood as a theurgic practice, an action that brings about divine intercession, here protecting the soul of the father or mother from the punishments of Gehenna. The prayer serves as a kind of amulet—holding back the forces of vengeance in the same way that an amulet protects against the Evil Eye. This spiritual protection is required for up to a year, the maximum time a soul spends in Gehenna. However, the Kaddish is recited only for eleven months, out of respect for the deceased, on the assumption that one's own parents were not so evil as to require the full twelve months of purification. Note that saying the Kaddish thus gives a compelling reason for mourners to be present for prayers. Indeed, the fate of a beloved parent's soul hangs in the balance, and the ritual of saying the Kaddish and the myth of the fate of the soul after death were inextricably linked.

Another outstanding example of a theurgic ritual is the ceremony known as *Tashlikh*, dating from the fourteenth century, which takes place during the afternoon of the first day of Rosh ha-Shanah. It is customary to go to the banks of a river, or any body of water, shaking the pockets of one's garments into the water as a symbolic way of getting rid of one's sins. Not only does *Tashlikh* serve as a symbolic purgation, but it implies that fulfilling the ritual will indeed serve to purify one's soul and free one of sin. As is the case with many Jewish rituals, however, there are multiple interpretations of what it means. Some interpret *Tashlikh* as a rite of transferring the sins to the fish, while others view it as a ritual of moral purification. Still others claim that the custom was created as a magical ceremony to placate the water demons.[148] While it is clear that *Tashlikh* presently plays a role of purification related to the larger observance of Rosh ha-Shanah, the implication that *Tashlikh* is also intended to placate demons shows that Jewish concerns during this time of judgment include the forces of evil.

Another example of a Rosh ha-Shanah ritual with a mythic purpose is the sounding of the shofar. The ram's horn is blown on Rosh ha-Shanah (when all Jews are required to be present to hear it), in a strictly prescribed series of short and long blasts. There are many reasons given for this custom. One of the most fascinating of these asserts that the sounding of the shofar causes God to move from His Throne of Justice (where His judgments are harsh) to His Throne of Mercy (where His judgments are merciful).[149] This interpretation makes the shofar blowing on Rosh ha-Shanah a prime example of theurgy, since it is the ritual act itself that is said to make God render favorable judgment rather than any prayer or petition. Another explanation of this ritual is that God made up a secret language, that of the ram's horn, which is only understood by Him, so that the Accuser should not know the pleas of His children.[150] Identifying these blasts as a secret language is an acknowledgment that their meaning is unknown, except to God.

In each of these cases, the ritual makes it possible to relive the myth and experience it personally. This kind of living mythic experience also is found in the Passover Seder, where it is emphasized that "We were slaves in Egypt," rather than "They were slaves ..." This makes it possible to relive the Exodus, to experience the slavery, the liberation, and the revelation at Sinai.

So too is the reading of the account of the Exodus at the Seder intended to recall that epic journey. Likewise, the use of *matzah* is a reminder that the Israelites in the wilderness did not have time to let their bread leaven, and therefore ate unleavened bread, and the other foods served at the Seder (ritual Passover meal) play similar roles as reminders of the Exodus narrative. Ultimately, then, as each of these examples indicates, ritual is intended to keep myth alive.

It is interesting to note that some of the major Jewish holidays show clear evidence of having expanded their mythic origins by becoming associated with other mythical and historical events. The three holidays of Passover, Shavuot, and Sukkot offer excellent examples. These were originally the three major harvest festivals in ancient Israel, and elements of nature continue to be demonstrated with harvest decorations such as the hanging of fruits and vegetables in the *sukkah*. They were set at the time of even more ancient harvest festivals, such as those of the Canaanites. It was required that all Jewish inhabitants journey to Jerusalem, to offer their first fruits or the firstlings of their flocks to be sacrificed at the Temple. Thus these three holidays were also associated with the temple in Jerusalem, and are linked to the temple cult. However, over time each of these holidays also became associated with the Exodus from Egypt. Passover recalls the upheaval that preceded the Exodus, including the ten plagues, as well as the crossing of the Red Sea. Shavuot commemorates the giving of the Torah on Mount Sinai. And Sukkot recalls the hasty shelters built by the Israelites during their 40 years of wandering in the wilderness. But after the destruction of the Temple and the exile of the Jewish people eliminated the yearly pilgrimage to Jerusalem, the associations of these three festivals became even more closely linked to the Exodus narrative, until it became the dominant motif. Today, for most Jews, each of these three holidays revolves exclusively around the myth of the Exodus. And the Exodus myth, as a whole, is focused on the covenant between God and Israel, the central myth of all of Judaism. It includes God's role, as well as that of Moses, in freeing the people from Egyptian bondage, in revealing the Torah on Mount Sinai, and in leading the people to the Holy Land. The only myth of comparable importance in Judaism is that of the creation of the world. Note that the rituals associated with these three holidays have been integrated into the lives of the people, as they are celebrated in a Seder at home, in the synagogue, and by eating in arborlike enclosures, known as *sukkot*, built outside a person's house. Now on Sukkot that which was once brought into the Temple is hung in the *sukkah*, and homes and synagogues are decorated with greenery and flowers. In this way myth and ritual reaffirm each other and, at the same time, pay homage to God's role in the destiny of Israel.

V. The Light of the First Day

The Jewish mythic tradition is unique in that it is possible to follow its evolution from the oral to the written tradition, and trace various stages of the written tradition. Thus a myth inspired by the Bible may be elaborated by the rabbis of the Talmud, as well as by kabbalistic and Hasidic rabbis, and versions of it might be found in the fifth century, in the eighth century, in the thirteenth century, in the seventeenth century and in the nineteenth century. In each of these stages, there is a clearly continuing mythic development. Furthermore, while the myths of most cultures seem to spring into existence on their own, it is possible to trace a mythmaking process in Judaism that is closely linked to the method of exegesis found in rabbinic texts. This technique, what we might call the midrashic method, searches for answers to the problems raised in the biblical text, and, in the process of resolving them, creates new myths.

A fine example of the process whereby a mythic motif is first discovered, then embellished until it achieves the status of a full myth is found in the traditions concerning the light of the first day. [151]Everyone is familiar with the words of Genesis 1:3, *And God said, "Let there be light," and there was light.* But the ancient rabbis, who scrutinized the words of the Bible for every hidden mystery, wondered what light this was. After all, God did not create the sun, the moon, and the stars till the fourth day. So what was the light of the first day?

In discussions scattered throughout rabbinic, kabbalistic, and hasidic literature, the rabbis consider this question. They search for clues about this mysterious light in every book of the Bible and find the clue they need in a prophecy of Isaiah. He speaks about what the world would be like in the messianic era: *Moreover, the light of the moon shall be as the light of the sun, and the light of the sun shall be sevenfold, as the light of the seven days* (Isa. 30:26). Here a biblical mystery is explicated right in the Bible: the light of the seven days— a clear reference to the primordial light—was seven times brighter than the sun.

Drawing on Isaiah's explanation, the rabbis conclude that the two lights—that of the first day and that of the fourth—are different.[152] The light of the first day is a primordial light, what is called the *or ha-ganuz*, or hidden light. This resolves the problem. But it also raises a whole series of new questions—What was the nature of that sacred light? Where did it come from, and where did it go? These questions have been debated among the rabbis for many centuries, and they arrive at a variety of explanations. Along the way, they wrestle with profound questions about God and the way in which God created the world. What is actually happening is that a Jewish myth is taking form, a very essential myth about the nature of the divine and the Mysteries of Creation. Let us consider some of the primary permutations of this myth, which are often contradictory.[153]

First of all, where did the light come from?

Some say that God created it at the instant He said, *"Let there be light"* (Gen. 1:3). Others say it was the light of Paradise, seven times brighter than the sun, which God brought into this world at the time of Creation. For the first three days and nights, it shone undiminished. Rabbi Samuel Eliezer Edels, known as the Maharsha, said of this light, "The light that God created on the first day was the most important element of all, and for its sake the world was created."

Still others say that the light existed even before the Creation. When God said, *"Let there be light,"* light came forth from the place in the universe where the Temple in Jerusalem would one day be built. Surrounded by that light, God completed the creation of the world.

How, then, did God bring the light into the world?

Some say that God wrapped Himself in a prayer shawl of light, and the light cast from that prayer shawl suffused the world. Others say that God draped the six days of Creation around Himself like a gown and dazzled the universe with His glory. Then there are those who say that God took the light and stretched it like a garment, and the heavens continued to expand until God said, "Enough!" Still others say that the light was cast from the very countenance of God.

And where did the light go?

There is a rabbinic debate as to how long the primordial light shone and when it was hidden away for the righteous in the world to come. Some say it only lasted 36 hours.[154] Some say that it only lasted until the creation of the sun, moon, and stars on the fourth day,[155] while Rashi insists that it shone during the day for the entire week of the Creation. For those who believe it lasted till the expulsion from Eden, it was possible for Adam to see in that light to the ends of the universe.

The clue to the fate of the primordial light is found in a verse from the Book of Job: *But now one does not see the light, it shines in the heavens* (Job 37:21). This verse was drawn upon to explain that God removed the light from this world and put it in the *Olam ha-Ba*, the World to Come. There it is one of the rewards awaiting the righteous.

A reference to the restoration of the hidden light is found in *Sefer ha-Bahir*: "God said, 'If My children keep the Torah and commandments that I gave them, one day the glow that was taken from the first light will be like the light itself, as it is said, *It is a brilliant light which gives off rays on every side—and therein His glory is enveloped* (Hab. 3:4).' What light is this? It is the light that God stored away and hid, as it is said, *that You have in store for those who fear You* (Ps. 31:20)."[156]

Some say that this sacred light pervaded the world until the very moment that Adam and Eve tasted the forbidden fruit. Then the first thing they lost was that precious light, for God, seeing the wicked deeds of the coming generations of Enosh (Gen. 5:6-11), hid the primordial light at once. Without it, the world grew dark around them, for the sun shone like a candle in comparison. Never again did they see the world in the splendor of that light, and that was the most painful punishment of all. Out of sympathy, God is said to have hidden a bit of that light inside a glowing stone, and given it to Adam and Eve when they were expelled from the Garden, as a reminder of all that they had lost. This stone, known as the *Tzohar*, is itself the subject of fabulous stories.[157]

Other sources say that God was about to hide the light, but He did not, for He wanted to honor the Sabbath. Proof is found in the verse *God blessed the seventh day* (Gen. 2:3). What did He bless it with? With the primordial light.

Still others say that the light was removed from the world at the time of the evil generation of the Flood, or, some say, at the time of the generation of the separation, which built the Tower of Babel.

The *Zohar* suggests that it was necessary for God to hide the light, for the world could not have endured if He had not, due to its intensity. Yet the same text suggests that even though the light is hidden, the world is sustained by it and that every day something of this light emerges into the world and renews the work of Creation.[158]

By now, most of the questions have been addressed—What was the light? Where did it come from? Where did it go? But still unanswered is one of the most important questions— did God create the primordial light or did it pre-exist? This question delves into the mysteries of Creation, and in rabbinic and kabbalistic circles it was believed that these kinds of questions could undermine monotheism. The advice of the Mishnah is to avoid them: "Whoever gives his mind to four things, it would have been better if he had not been born—What is above? What is below? What came before? And what will come after?"[159] Despite this warning, the talmudic rabbis and all of their successors delved deeply into these questions, even when it brought them to the brink of Jewish gnosticism, that is, to the implication that God may have been assisted in the creation of the world.

Take that light that was said to exist in the place where the Temple would be built in future generations. It suggests some kind of primordial force in the universe, which God drew upon in Creation. God chose to place the earth where He did because of that light. For the same reason, God placed the Holy Land where He did because of that light, and He placed the site of the Temple in Jerusalem at the very source of that light. The myth goes on to say that this holy light continued to emanate even after the Temple was built in that place. Its source was in the Holy of Holies, and it lit up the Temple and shone forth through the windows and filled the Holy Land.

Beneath the surface, questions about the origin of this light seek to know whether anything else existed before God created the world, whether God drew upon such pre-existing elements or created everything out of nothing, whether God had any assistance in Creation, and even the unthinkable question of who created God. These kinds of questions posed the danger of undermining monotheism. As noted, the advice of the Mishnah was to avoid them.

There is no satisfactory account of the creation of light in the book of Genesis, none that specifies whether this light pre-existed or was created at that instant by God. Even great commentators such as Rashi and his grandson, Rabbi Samuel ben Meir, known as Rashbam, agreed that no such full account is given. Perhaps the light pre-existed or perhaps God brought it into being during an earlier creation, one not recounted in Genesis. Neither of these solutions supports the notion of creation *ex nihilo*, and anything else suggests limits of God's powers, which, by definition, are limitless.

The most common explanation for what happened to the primordial light is that God hid it for the righteous in the World to Come. But in the thirteenth century the *Zohar* suggested another explanation: "Whenever the Torah is studied at night, a single ray comes from the hidden light and stretches forth to those who study."[160] Drawing on this clue in the eighteenth century, the Ba'al Shem Tov, founder of Hasidism, proposed that God had hidden the primordial light in the Torah, and for those who immerse themselves in the study of the Torah, a ray of that light would shine forth, and past and future and time and space would open up for a moment, and they would experience the revelation of the hidden light, and see the world as God saw it when God said, *"Let there be light."*[161] This interpretation is reinforced by midrashim that explain that the original tablets of the Law that Moses received on Mount Sinai were created in the presence of the primordial light. Thus it might be said that this sacred light was imprinted on the pages of the Torah.

Rabbi Nachman of Bratslav, the greatest Jewish storyteller, who also happened to be the great-grandson of the Ba'al Shem Tov, agreed with his great-grandfather's explanation of where the light was hidden. But he added that it was hidden in the stories of the Torah. Rabbi Nachman truly loved stories and found them full of hidden light: "Every story has something that is concealed. What is concealed is the hidden light. The Book of Genesis says that God created light on the first day, the sun on the fourth. What light existed before the sun? The tradition says this was spiritual light and that God hid it for future use. Where was it hidden? In the stories of the Torah."[162]

That might have been the end of the story, but it's not. Another nineteenth century rabbi, Rabbi Menachem Mendel of Riminov, insisted that the primordial light had never been hidden at all, and was still present, but that only the truly righteous could see it. It is invisible to everyone else. On the other hand, in the twentieth century Rabbi Abraham Joshua Heschel accepted the hiddenness of the primordial light and drew his own conclusions from it: "The primordial light is hidden. Had the Torah demanded perfection, [the world] would have remained a utopia. The laws of the Torah ask of each generation to fulfill what is within its power to fulfill. Some of its laws . . . do not represent ideals but compromises, realistic attempts to refine the moral condition of ancient man."[163]

Thus the Bible begins with a mysterious light, considered distinct from that of the fourth day of Creation, which God brings into the world as a sacred, primordial light. In some versions of the myth God removes the light and saves it for the righteous in the World to Come. In others, God hides it in the Torah, where it is waiting to be found. In still others, it has been here all along, for those who are capable of seeing it.

VI. The Continuing Evolution of Jewish Mythology

The primary myths of Judaism are found in the Hebrew Bible, in the stories of Creation, of the Garden of Eden, the Tower of Babel, the great Flood, the covenant with Abraham, the parting of the Red Sea, the Exodus, and the Giving of the Torah. And these are only the major biblical myths. Because of the looming presence of the Bible in Western culture, these myths are encountered, in literary allusions and in other ways, on almost a daily basis.

In terms of mythic evolution, it is important to remember that even these biblical myths were themselves based on earlier oral versions. Here the transition from the oral tradition to a written one was influenced by the priestly editors of the books of the Torah. What were these long lost prebiblical myths like? They may well have been considerably different than the written versions we are familiar with.

Sir James Frazer speculated that the original oral myth about the Garden of Eden was not about a Tree of Knowledge and a Tree of Life, as found in Genesis, because they are not a polar pair.[164] Myths repeatedly seek out polarities whenever possible—day and night, sun and moon, heaven and earth. It would be unlikely that the original myth had two trees that were not polar, as is the case with the Tree of Knowledge and the Tree of Life. Rather, Frazer suggests, the two trees were likely the Tree of Life and the Tree of Death.[165] According to his theory, God gave Adam and Eve a divine test to determine if mankind would be mortal or immortal. God wanted them to be immortal,[166] so He gave them a big hint: "Don't eat from the Tree of Death!" Of course, human nature being what it is, that is exactly what they did, thus becoming mortal. If the fruit that Adam and Eve had first tasted had been from the Tree of Life, they would have lived forever, but having eaten from the Tree of Death, they could no longer be permitted access to the Tree of Life. That is why God *stationed east of the garden of Eden the cherubim and the fiery ever-turning sword, to guard the way to the Tree of Life* (Gen. 3:24). If Frazer is correct—and his theory has the ring of truth—it suggests that the original purpose of the myth, to provide the origin of death, was replaced by a shift to ethical issues, seeing the events of the Fall primarily as a sin against God. This would indicate that this biblical myth was considerably changed from its oral version when the text of Genesis was edited.[167]

After they were written down, the biblical myths, especially the myths of the Torah, were themselves reimagined and embellished in every generation by a process of creative plenitude, whereby themes and motifs were further elaborated.[168] It might seem that Jewish mythology is drawn exclusively from these biblical sources, but that is not the case. One of the most remarkable aspects of the mythology of Judaism is that it continued to evolve long after most mythologies had taken their final form. In most cultures the development of myth occurs during an early period, long before it is written down. However, once committed to writing, the mythical narrative generally remains fixed. But Jewish tradition has not followed this pattern. That is because Judaism recognizes both a written and an oral tradition. The Written Torah consists of the Five Books of Moses and is recorded in the scroll of the Torah. The Oral Law is the oral commentary linked to it. As one midrash puts it, God gave the Torah to Moses during the day and explained it to him at night.[169] And whenever a question arises as to the authority of a statement out of the Oral Law, it is ultimately attributed to the explanations of the Law that Moses received at Mount Sinai: "This is Torah from Moses at Sinai."

The primary themes announced in the earliest Jewish texts became the focus of later texts that strove to be true to the original myth while adding their own imprint. As a result it is also possible to trace the evolution of seminal Jewish myths from the earliest period not only to the Hasidic era of the eighteenth and nineteenth centuries, but even to the present, where myths have been among the kinds of oral tales collected by Jewish ethnologists in Eastern Europe and in Israel. No other world mythology has been documented so thoroughly while undergoing such an extensive evolution.

The varied periods of Jewish religion are characterized by their own predominant myths. Yet there is a continuity among them that is reflected in the rabbinic axiom that "there is no earlier or later in the Torah." Commenting on this statement, Rabbi Shlomo ben Yitzhak ha-Levi adds: "That is to say, every part of it is both first and last like a sphere . . . and where it ends, there it begins, for behold it is like a circle or a sphere."[170] This principle is certainly reflected in the midrashic method of drawing on one episode in the Bible, such as the childhood of Moses, to fill in a narrative gap in another, such as the missing childhood of Abraham. This results in a distinctly myth-making process, which contributes in no small part to the ongoing mythic evolution.[171]

There are two factors, in particular, that enable mythic elaboration in Judaism. One is the existence of the Oral Law, and the other is what might be called "the midrashic method." The Oral Law contains a great many details and explanations about the Written Torah, as well as alternate versions of biblical narratives. The midrashic method searches for hints and explanations of the biblical text to resolve apparent contradictions and complete unfinished narratives. To accomplish this, it uses many techniques, such as examining the roots of words, drawing on earlier or later portions of the text (the chapters before and after are always considered relevant.), or using the purest kind of invention to resolve a knotty problem. Of course this invention is attributed to the Oral Torah, and therefore is regarded as legitimate.

To better understand the kind of transformations that take place in Jewish mythology, let us consider a few examples. Perhaps the most striking transformation is that of the concept of the *Shekhinah*, as discussed earlier. From around the fifth century to the twelfth or thirteenth century, the concept changed from being a synonym for God and God's presence in the world to denoting the Bride of God, a figure with many of the qualities of a goddess.

Extensive mythic transformations are also associated with the figure of Lilith. In the early medieval *Alphabet of Ben Sira* Lilith is identified as Adam's first wife, who resisted having sex in the missionary position, abandoned Adam and the Garden of Eden, and took up residence at the Red Sea, where she took for lovers all the male demons who made their home there. But by the Middle Ages the focus on Lilith in Jewish folklore was on her role as the Queen of Demons, while, at the same time, Lilith took on the role of the dark feminine in kabbalah, the feminine aspect of the *Sitra Ahra*, the Other Side, the polar opposite of the *Shekhinah*. It is interesting to note that the transformations of Lilith seem to have continued in our own time, in which Lilith has been portrayed as a role model by some Jewish feminists.

The kinds of changes in the Lilith myth that have taken place since the 1960s, which have transformed Lilith from being regarded as an evil demoness, succubus, and child-destroying witch into a model of sexual and personal independence, raise the important question of what role Jewish mythology plays for modern, non-Orthodox Jews. The changes cut two ways. On the one hand, the belief in these myths as an expression of literal truth has largely vanished, along with the belief that contemporary rabbis can draw upon God's powers to ascend to Paradise or confront forces of evil. On the other hand, certain myths, in particular those about Lilith, the *Shekhinah*, and the golem (a humanoid created through kabbalistic sorcery), have taken on great popularity, and have shown distinct signs of new life. The attraction of Lilith for Jewish feminists derives from her independence from Adam, especially her sexual independence. She serves as a compelling figure of female rebellion in a patriarchal tradition.[172] At the same time, the existence of the traditions about the *Shekhinah* is regarded by many modern Jewish women as an indication that there is a place for the feminine in Judaism, beginning with the very concept of God, and new prayers and customs have been created to emphasize this development. Thus, even if these myths are not accepted as absolute truths, they have generated widespread interest in Jewish and non-Jewish circles. Of course, the kinds of changes in the perception of these myths indicate that the evolution of Jewish mythology has continued into our own time. The very fact of this continued evolution speaks volumes about the vitality of Jewish myth.

The examples of the changing roles of the *Shekhinah* and of Lilith indicate that Jewish myths can develop in unexpected directions. But sometimes what happens is that a fragmentary myth takes on a life of its own. This is what happened with Enoch, who receives a brief mention in the genealogical listing between Adam and Noah, where it is said that

Enoch walked with God; then he was no more, for God took him (Gen. 21:24). This brief passage about Enoch, which was understood to mean that Enoch was taken alive into paradise, became the basis of the extensive Enoch myth first found in *1 Enoch* (second century BCE through first century CE), where Enoch ascends on high. The myth was expanded in *2 Enoch* (first century) and *3 Enoch* (fifth through sixth century), the latter describing how Enoch was transformed into the fiery angel Metatron.

Perhaps the most common kind of mythic evolution involves narrative development, especially completing unfinished narratives. For example, the biblical story of Cain is missing an ending. Cain was the first murderer, and the rabbis wanted to see in his death an example of divine justice. But the last we hear of Cain in Genesis, he has founded a city. Nothing is said of his death. But in the midrashic texts several versions of Cain's death are to be found. In one Cain is transformed into the Angel of Death. In another, Cain's stone house collapses on him during an earthquake, thus causing him to be stoned to death, an appropriate punishment, as death by stoning was the punishment for capital crimes. In a third version Cain was killed by Lamech and Tubal-Cain, his descendants. Thus, just as Cain murdered a relative, he was killed by relatives, making this version another example of divine justice.[173]

Drawing on this extensive oral tradition, which reached back a thousand years, the rabbis proceeded to reimagine the Bible, and in the process substantially developed its mythic elements. Clues were sought and found in biblical verses, and these were also used to resolve problems in the biblical text. Using these methods, details about the lives of the patriarchs and matriarchs accrued, as well as details of realms such as heaven and hell, and these details were themselves subject to further embellishment.

Thus it is possible to witness the actual evolution of Jewish myths. Early myths, primarily those found in the Bible, were embellished in the oral tradition and later recorded in the rabbinic texts. The Talmud, dating from the fifth century, is believed to be the written form of the Oral Torah, and additional oral traditions are recorded in the midrashic texts that followed. These rabbinic myths were themselves transformed in the kabbalistic and hasidic periods. The most fertile periods of development took place between the first and fifth centuries, when the Talmud and most of the texts of the Pseudepigrapha were written, and between the thirteenth and seventeenth centuries, the primary period of kabbalistic literature. The latter is a remarkably late period in human history for such extensive mythic development. It is then that major myths of the nature of God and of His Bride took form, along with further myths of creation and of the Messiah. But in every case these kabbalistic myths are rooted in earlier sources and undergo a process of evolution until they achieve full expression.

If we search for an overriding pattern in this mythic evolution, we can recognize an early fascination with heavenly journeys, as well as with the mysteries of Creation and the mysteries of God's Chariot. Beginning in the Middle Ages, the role of the long-suppressed feminine aspect of God emerges as an increasingly dominant theme, especially in the goddesslike role of the *Shekhinah* and in the fascination and fear engendered by the Lilith myth. In both the earlier and later periods, the longing for the coming of the Messiah remains constant, as does the centrality of the Torah and its teachings. In our own time, when women have sought a greater role in all aspects of Jewish life, they have found role models in the figures of Lilith and the *Shekhinah* rather than in the traditional role models, the matriarchs. Consistent throughout, however, has been the bond created by the covenant of God and His people, Israel. This is the central myth of Judaism, and it is the key to understanding all the others.

Notes

[1] This is found in *Zohar* 3:167a-b, where Jacob's granddaughter, Serah bat Asher, is described as one of the blessed women who teaches Torah to the souls of righteous women in her own heavenly palace. See "Women in Paradise," p. 190.

[2] "*Shekhinah*," while not a biblical term, has a biblical basis in the term *shokhen* ("dwells"), which occurs in many places in the Bible, stating that God "dwells" on earth, as in Psalm 135:21, *Blessed is the Lord from Zion, He who dwells in Jerusalem*. In the Bible God is variously described as dwelling in the Tabernacle, in the Temple, and among the people of Israel. In rabbinic literature, "*Shekhinah*" refers to God's presence, i.e. dwelling, in this world. By the kabbalistic era, this term had evolved to refer to the feminine aspect of God, also identified as God's Bride.

[3] There is considerable scholarly controversy over whether Asherah was a goddess in pre-exilic Israel; whether, in fact, Asherah was Yahweh's divine consort. Much revolves around the interpretation of a number of biblical passages, especially 1 Kings 18:19, where Elijah refers to *four hundred prophets of Asherah*. Other key passages are 2 Kings 21:7, 2 Kings 23:4, Judges 3:7, and Jeremiah 2:27. Also, Asherah appears as an Israelite phenomenon in the polemics found in Judges 2:13 and 10:6, and 1 Samuel 7:3-4 and 12:10. There are also references in Jeremiah 7:18 and 44:15-28 that refer to the "Queen of Heaven," a figure some identify with Asherah. So too does the reference to the "asherahs" in Judges 3:7 seem to indicate the presence of the goddess in ancient Israel, with the asherah, a wooden cult object, as her symbol. See *The Early History of God* by Mark Smith, pp. 125-133. See also "Israel and the Mothers" by Michael Fishbane in *The Garments of Torah: Essays in Biblical Hermeneutics*, pp. 49-63, and *In the Wake of the Goddesses: Women, Culture, and the Biblical Transformation of Pagan Myth* by Tikva Frymer-Kensky, pp. 153-161. Arguing strongly that Asherah was Yahweh's consort is *The Hebrew Goddess*, 3rd edition, by Raphael Patai, pp. 34-53.

[4] Genesis Rabbah 8: 7. See "The Council of Souls," p. 160. Note that there is a strong biblical echo of the Council of Souls in Psalm 89:7-8, which depicts God as the head of a council of other gods, which are referred to as *kedoshim*, i.e., "holy ones": *For who in the skies can equal the Lord, can compare with the Lord among the divine beings, a God greatly dreaded in the council of holy beings, held in awe by all around him?* In rabbinic literature the Council of Souls seems to have been replaced by the idea of the heavenly court, consisting of angels. In the Talmud, it is clearly stated that "God does nothing without consulting His heavenly court." Thus the tradition of the Council of Souls may well have been replaced by that of the heavenly court, which is less threatening in that its members consist of angels rather than other divinities. Nevertheless, God continues to consult it, something one would not expect of an all-powerful God.

[5] Note that the definition of "mythology" offered here does not attempt to determine if biblical or subsequent narratives are true or false, i.e., historically accurate or not. And, emphatically, the use of the word "myth" is not offered to mean something that is not true, as in the current popular usage.

[6] Deuteronomy 18:10-12.

[7] See p. 529 for a diagram of the Ten Sefirot.

[8] *Sefer ha-Zikhronot*. See *The Chronicles of Jerahmeel*, edited by Moses Gaster. While *Sefer ha-Zikhronot* dates from the late Middle Ages, the basic tradition about ten things that had a kind of "special creation" is already found in the Mishnah, in Avot 5:9, dating from the second century. This involves a different list, and they are said to have been created at dusk on the sixth day of Creation rather than prior to the Creation. But the basic idea is there. Also, some talmudic sources list seven things created before the Creation of the world. See "Seven Things Created Before the Creation of the World," p. 74. There are also ten utterances of God employed to bring the world into being (B. Avot 5:1).

[9] Each of the ten things that "rose up in the thought" of God represents one of the ten mythic categories: Jerusalem=Myths of the Holy Land; the souls of the patriarchs=Myths of Heaven; the ways of the righteous=Myths of the Holy People; Gehenna=Myths of Hell; the Flood=Myths of Exile; the stone tablets=Myths of the Holy Word; the Sabbath=Myths of the Holy Time; the Temple=Myths of Creation (as the location of the Temple was the starting point of creation); the Ark=Myths of God ; the light of the world to come=Myths of the Messiah.

[10] See "God Considers Ending All Existence," p. 40.

[11]The *Hekhalot* texts are not technically part of the Pseudepigrapha in that they are not focused on accounts of biblical figures, but rather on rabbis such as Rabbi Akiba and Rabbi Ishmael. For more about the *Hekhalot* texts, see *The Hidden and Manifest God: Some Major Themes in Early Jewish Mysticism* by Peter Schäfer.

[12]B. Bava Metzia 59b. See "The Rabbis Overrule God," p. 67. The Hebrew term *nitzhuni* means "defeated," or, in a legal sense, "overruled."

[13]"Myth vs. Symbol in the *Zohar* and in Lurianic Kabbalah" by Yehuda Liebes, in *Essential Papers on Kabbalah*, edited by Lawrence Fine, p. 212.

[14]See "God and the Spirits of the Unborn," p. 140.

[15]See "The Dew of Resurrection," p. 504.

[16]See "God's Presence at the Red Sea," p. 385.

[17]See "The Term *Kivyakhol* and its Uses" in *Biblical Myth and Rabbinic Mythmaking* by Michael Fishbane, pp. 325-401.

[18]"On Reading the Midrash" by Henry Slonimsky, p. 6.

[19]This verse is usually rendered, *"I am the Lord your God,"* where "the Lord" replaces YHVH, the primary name of God, which is rendered in English as Yahweh. Traditionally, it was forbidden to pronounce YHVH, so *Adonai* (God) or *ha-Shem* (the Name) are used instead. However, these substitutions obscure Yahweh's mythic identity, and thus they are a part of the demythologizing trend in Judaism. In this book both "Yahweh" and "the Lord" have been used to translate YHVH.

[20]See the diagram of the Ten Sefirot, p. 529.

[21]See *Kabbalah: New Perspectives* by Moshe Idel, pp. 137-141.

[22]*Responsa Ribash* no. 157. See *Decoding the Rabbis* by Marc Saperstein, p. 269, note 95, where the term for the ten-fold God is rendered as "the Decimity."

[23]*Zohar* 2:118a-118b, 3:69a, 3:97a. See "Lilith Becomes God's Bride," p. 59.

[24]Many scholars have detected a strong Gnostic strain in Sabbatianism, the version of Judaism propounded by Shabbatai Zevi, the seventeenth century messianic pretender, and his followers. Lurianic kabbalah, which itself has a Gnostic strain, was the intellectual background of the Sabbatian movement. For Abraham Cardozo, one of the most prominent Sabbatians, the Creator-God of Judaism is an entity distinct from the Supreme Being ("First Cause"), and inferior to the Supreme Being. This is not far removed from the Gnostic view that the God of the Hebrew scriptures is the evil demiurge, distinct from a higher God who is good. However, for Cardozo, the lesser being is the one who is truly God, and that ought to be worshipped. Cardozo's doctrine is of a limited God, requiring human assistance and susceptible to near-death and rebirth. See *Sabbatai Sevi* by Gershom Scholem and *Abraham Miguel Cardozo: Selected Writings*, translated by David J. Halperin, especially pp. 64-67.

[25]*Meor Enayim*. Here the *Shekhinah* is identified as *Knesset Yisrael*, the Community of Israel, which is one of the many names of the *Shekhinah*. See footnote 27, p. lxxix for a discussion of these names. This Hasidic text is a commentary on *Zohar* 3:93a, which speaks of how God and the Community of Israel are separated, and quotes Zechariah 14:9 to describe how their reunion will restore God's wholeness: *In that day there shall be one Lord, and His name one.* And the *Zohar* adds: "But one without the other is not called one." Of course, since *Knesset Israel* also refers to the people of Israel, this also suggests a marriage between God (the Groom) and the People of Israel (the Bride). In fact, both readings are correct, so closely bound are the identities and fates of the *Shekhinah* and the people of Israel. They are perceived not as two entities, but two faces of the same entity. See "The Wedding of God and Israel," p. 305.

[26]B. Sota 17a.

[27]In the index of his book, *The Sabbath in the Classical Kabbalah*, pp. 334-336, Elliot K. Ginsburg lists 79 symbolic identities associated with the *Shekhinah*, including Ark, bed, Bride, candle, chamber, Community of Israel, darkened mirror, darkness, daughter, diadem, dove, field, flame, garden, gate, heart, Holy of Holies, Jerusalem, moon, mother, princess, queen, rose, Sabbath, sister, soul, spring, Tabernacle, temple, throne, tree, well, and womb. The extensive nature of this list reveals the indispensable role of the *Shekhinah* in kabbalistic thought. For the famous allegory of the *Shekhinah* as a lovely maiden in a palace, see *Zohar* 2:98b-99a. For the allegory of the hind, see *Zohar* 3:249a-249b.

[28]See pp. 47-66.

[29]Maimonides, *Hilkot Avodat Kohanim* 1:3; *Shulhan Arukh, Yorah De'ah* 246. See "On the History of the Interdiction Against the Study of Kabbalah Before the Age of Forty" (Hebrew) by Moshe Idel. *AJSReview* 5(1980) 1-20 (Hebrew section).

[30]*Sippurei Ma'asiyot.*

[31]B. Betzah 15b-16a. See "The Second Soul," p. 310.

[32]See Hayim Vital: *Sha'arei Kedushah* 3, *Sha'ar ha-Gilgulim*, Introduction 2, and *Sefer ha-Gilgulim* 5. Vital defines possession by *ibbur* as follows: "If a person does his utmost to purify himself, so that the very root of his soul is revealed to him, he may become impregnated with the soul of a *Tzaddik*, living or dead, who will help him to completely transcend himself. For examples of *ibbur* tales, see "A Kiss from the Master" in *Gabriel's Palace: Jewish Mystical Tales*, pp. 79-80 and "The *Tefillin* of the Or Hayim" in the same book, pp. 117-118.

[33]For more about Asherah, see note 3, p. 78.

[34]Biblical monotheism is often described as "exclusive monotheism," meaning that it denies the existence or at least the relevance of any deities other than the One. David J. Halperin suggests that the Greeks also had a monotheism, which he calls "inclusive monotheism," in which the Many are acknowledged as legitimate aspects of the One. Halperin suggests that the Kabbalah is a form of "inclusive monotheism," in which the Many are the *sefirot*, and the "One" is the deity whom the *sefirot* define. This provides a clue to the nature of monotheistic mythology in Judaism, at least as far as the kabbalah goes.

[35]In *Zohar* 1:22a this myth is described in terms of the interaction of the *sefirot*: the *Shekhinah*, identified as the *sefirah Malkhut*, is reunited with the male aspect of God, identified by the *sefirah Tiferet*. This is a typical example of the kind of sefirotic interaction that kabbalists regard as underlying every mythic process, especially those involving God and the *Shekhinah*. Discussion of these sefirotic processes has been kept to a minimum in this book, which focuses instead on the interaction of divine figures and forces from a mythic perspective. Note that the sefirotic view of these processes largely eliminates their mythic dimension and transforms them into the interaction of divine emanations (although it could be argued that divine emanations are themselves mythic). For kabbalists, the mythic and sefirotic views were considered equally valid, and they were permitted to exist simultaneously.

[36]*Tikkunei ha-Zohar, Tikkun* 21:59b-60a; *Tikkun* 63:94b.

[37]B. Shabbat 19a.

[38]In Gnosticism, a highly dualistic doctrine that flourished in the early centuries CE, this world is the creation of a lower, evil deity, known as the "demiurge," who functions both as a Creator-God and World-ruler. Above this deity there is a remote, benevolent Deity, superior to the demiurge and to the demiurge's flawed and evil creation, a Deity whom the Gnostics perceived as the source of the human soul and the only hope for salvation. In Plato's *Timaeus*, the demiurge is the "artisan" (what the Greek word literally means), who created this perfect cosmos. To the Gnostics, the cosmos is evil, and therefore the demiurge/creator is evil. The "good" God in Gnosticism, who is opposed to the demiurge, is an extracosmic deity, who comes to redeem the human soul from bondage. Accounts of ruling figures such as Metatron in Jewish tradition indicate a Gnostic influence, where God represents the good, higher God, and Metatron (or another ruling figure) represents a demiurgic figure. Indeed, Metatron is sometimes identified as the "lesser Yahweh." Yet, while there is clear evidence, especially in the Dead Sea Scrolls and the some of the texts of the Pseudepigrapha, such as *The Book of Jubilees* and *The Testaments of the Patriarchs*, of Gnostic thinking in Judaism, it is important to recognize that Gnosticism requires that the Demiurge be evil, and this is not the case in Judaism. Also, in some non-Jewish Gnostic sects, the God of the Hebrew Scriptures is identified as the evil demiurge, and His commandments the arbitrary rules of an enslaving tyrant—a doctrine deemed heretical by the Christian Church. For more information on Gnosticism and its many permutations, see *Gnosticism* by Hans Jonas. For the relationship of Gnosticism to Judaism, see Alexander Altmann, "The Gnostic Background of the Rabbinic Adam Legends" in his *Essays in Jewish Intellectual History*, pp. 1-16. For the primary Gnostic texts see James M. Robinson, ed., *The Nag Hammadi Library: A Translation of the Gnostic Scriptures.*

[39]B. Sanhedrin 38b.

[40]The two roots of kabbalah are *Ma'aseh Bereshit*, the Mysteries of Creation, i.e., the study of Creation as presented in Genesis, and *Ma'aseh Merkavah*, the Mysteries of the Chariot, i.e., the study of Ezekiel's vision in the first chapter of the Book of Ezekiel.

[41]Although most of these enthronement myths are found in the Pseudepigrapha—thus outside the official teachings of Judaism—some of them, such as those about Metatron and Jacob, derive from standard rabbinic sources. See "The Enthronement of Adam," p. 131, "The Metamorphosis

and Enthronement of Enoch, p. 156, "Jacob the Divine," p. 366, "The Enthronement of Moses," p. 388, and "King David is Crowned in Heaven," p. 395, and "The Enthronement of the Messiah," p. 487. For a discussion of the role of the demiurge and its parallels in Judaism, see p. 50.

[42]*Bava Batra* 74b; *B. Ta'anit* 10a. Also *Numbers Rabbah* 18:22.

[43]*De Somniiss* 1:76.

[44]*Zohar* 1:15a. See "The Cosmic Seed," p. 93.

[45]See "The Shattering of the Vessels and the Gathering of the Sparks," p. 122.

[46]The primary Lilith text derives from *Alpha Beta de-Ben Sira*, dating from around the ninth century. Additional myths about Lilith can be found in "Myths of Hell," pp. 213-243.

[47]See "Adam the Hermaphrodite," p. 138.

[48]*Zohar* 3:29a.

[49]See "The Heavenly Man," p. 124.

[50]Adam is also prominent in the Gnostic texts found at Nag Hammadi. Seth, Adam's son, is also portrayed in Gnostic texts as a divine figure. It is interesting to note that Seth is not the subject of much Jewish mythic speculation.

[51]See "Adam Kadmon," p. 15, "The Heavenly Man," p. 124, "Adam the Giant," p. 128, and "Adam the Golem," p. 127.

[52]See "God Consults the Angels about the Creation of Adam," p. 132.

[53]*Midrash Tanhuma*, Bereshit 1.

[54]*Zohar* 2:150b.

[55]See *Hell in Jewish Literature* by Samuel J. Fox, which offers hundreds of examples of the punishments of Gehenna.

[56]Isaac Bashevis Singer wrote a story about this, "Sabbath in Gehenna." See *Gates to the New City: A Treasury of Modern Jewish Tales*, edited by Howard Schwartz, pp. 185-189.

[57]There are also special punishments awaiting those so evil that their souls are not permitted to descend to Gehenna in the first place. These punishments include the eternal wandering of a wicked soul, forever chased by avenging angels, or the transmigration of especially evil souls into various beasts. Evil souls who attempt to escape this fate sometimes enter into the body of a living person and take possession as a *dybbuk* that must be exorcised. See S. Ansky's folk drama, *The Dybbuk*, which includes an authentic portrayal of the rabbinic exorcism ceremony.

[58]See the discussion of the kaddish, pp. 66-67.

[59]Even today, yeshivah students devote more time to the study of the Talmud, the rabbinic discussions about law and legend, than to study of the primary text, the Torah.

[60]See "Death and Rebirth at Mount Sinai," p. 259.

[61]This is a method known as *Gematria*, which is still very much in use. Note that Hebrew letters also have a numerical value, for the alphabet served as both letters and numbers. Thus *aleph*, the first letter, is 1, and *bet*, the second letter, is 2, etc.

[62]See "The Torah Written on the Arm of God," p. 252.

[63]*Ta'amei ha-Mitzvot* by Rabbi Menahem Recanati, "Introduction." See "God, Torah, and Israel" by Abraham Joshua Heschel in *Moral Grandeur and Spiritual Audacity*, pp. 191-205.

[64]*Adir ba-Marom* by Rabbi Moshe Hayim Luzzatto, p. 61.

[65]The classical expression of the view that the words of Torah are the names of God is at the end of Nachmanides' introduction to his Torah commentary. It is also found *Zohar* 2:90b.

[66]*Zohar*, 2:60a.

[67]*Mishnah Avot* 5:22.

[68]*Otiyyot de-Rabbi Akiba; Yalkut Shim'oni; Zohar* 1:2b. See "The Letters of the Alphabet," p. 250.

[69]See "The Primordial Torah," p. 265.

[70]See "The First Tablets," p. 266.

[71]*Zohar* 1:149a.

[72]*B. Shabbat* 88a and other sources. See "God Offers the Torah to Israel," p. 264.

[73]There are prescribed biblical passages that are written in parchment and included inside of *tefillin* and *mezuzot*.

[74]*B. Shabbat* 119a, *B. Bava Kama* 32b. See "Greeting the Sabbath Queen," p. 310. This suggests there may have been an idea of the feminine side of God in rabbinic literature. See *The Immanence of God in Rabbinical Literature* by J. Abelson.

[75]*Zohar* 1:55b.

[76]*Ketubah le-Shavuot* from the *Sephardi Mahzor*. The text of this *ketubah*, or wedding contract, is a hymn written by Israel Najara, one of the disciples of Rabbi Isaac Luria of Safed. This liturgical poem, which is found in the Sephardic prayer book for Shavuot, is based on the verses *"And I will betroth you to Me in loving kindness, and in compassion. And I will betroth you to Me in faithfulness; and You shall know the Lord "*(Hos. 2:21-22), and *"I will make a new covenant with the house of Israel"* (Jer. 31:31). See "The Wedding of God and Israel," p. 305.

[77]See *The Last Trial* by Sholem Spiegel and "Seeing with the Sages: Midrash as Visualization in the Legends of the *Aqedah*" by Marc Bregman.

[78]Genesis 5:21-24.

[79]*Legum Allegoriarum* 3:218-19 by Philo; *De Somniis* 2:10 by Philo; *De Congressu Eruditionis Gratia* 1:7-9 by Philo; *De Cherubim* 43-47 by Philo; *De Fuga et Inventione* 166-168 by Philo; *De Ebrietate* 56-62 by Philo. See "God Begat Isaac," p. 336.

[80]*Zohar* 1:79a, 3:168a. See "The Souls of Converts," p. 433.

[81]See "Jacob the Angel," p. 364 and "Jacob the Divine," p. 366.

[82]See "Abraham Never Died," p. 348, "Jacob Never Died," p. 370, "Moses Never Died," p. 394, and "King David is Alive" in *Gabriel's Palace*, pp. 139-141.

[83]*B. Berakhot* 3a, *Song of Songs Rabbah* 6:5. See "The Creation of the Temple," p. 420.

[84]Nachmanides, *Perush Ramban al ha-Torah* on Deuteronomy 11:11.

[85]*B. Ketubot* 111a.

[86]*Likutei Etzot, Eretz Yisrael* 1, 2, 3, 8, 13, 14, 15, 17, 18, 19.

[87]*Orot*, Jerusalem 1950, p. 9. For other examples of Rav Kook's view of the Land of Israel, see *Orot* pp. 20, 77, 88-89, 100-104, 151; *Hazon Hage'ullah* pp. 69-70, 78, 85. See too *Abraham Isaac Kook: The Lights of Penitence, The Moral Principles, Lights of Holiness, Essays, Letters and Poems* translated by Ben Zion Bokser. See also "Off Center: The Concept of the Land of Israel in Modern Jewish Thought" by Arnold M. Eisen in *The Land of Israel: Jewish Perspectives*, edited by Lawrence A. Hoffman, pp. 263-296.

[88]B. Shabbat 63a; *Avot de-Rabbi Natan* 35; *Kohelet Rabbah* 1; *B. Yoma* 39b; *Pesikta de Rav Kahana* 15:7; *Pirkei de-Rabbi Eliezer* 35; *Midrash Tehillim* 91:7; *Yalkut ha-Makhiri* to Psalms 91:27; *Menorat ha-Maor* 100; Nachmanides, *Perush Ramban al ha-Torah* on Genesis 28:17; *Kaftor ve-Ferah* 6. See *Midrash Yerushalem: A Metaphysical History of Jerusalem* by Daniel Sperber, pp. 92-94.

[89]*Zohar* 1:155b.

[90]*B. Ta'anit* 10a.

[91]See "The Foundation Stone," p. 96.

[92]The word translated as "punishment" is actually *avoni*, "my sin." If read literally, Cain is saying that his sin is too great to bear, meaning that he recognizes the extent of his sin. While the biblical account of Cain describes his exile, *Genesis Rabbah* 22:13 and *Leviticus Rabbah* 10:5 report that Cain repented and his repentance was accepted by God. Adam was so surprised to learn this that he slapped his head and cried out, "If I had only known the power of repentance."

[93]This biblical recounting does not include the Babylonian exile that took place after the first Temple in Jerusalem was destroyed in 586 BCE, nor again when the second Temple was destroyed in 70 C.E., nor the exile that took place after the expulsion from Span in 1492, nor the destruction and wandering of the Jews of Europe in the Second World War, as well as hundreds of other examples. Exile, it seems, has been the fate of the Jewish people.

[94]See "The Ten Lost Tribes," p. 473 and "The River Sambatyon," p. 475.

[95]See "Exile and Redemption in Jewish Thought in the Sixteenth Century: Contending Conceptions" by Shalom Rosenberg, pp. 399-430. There is also evidence that the idea of a nonpunishment purpose of exile arose even earlier than the sixteenth century. Rosenberg cites precedents on pp. 407-410. These include the view that the purpose of the exile was to gain proselytes.

[96]See "The Shattering of the Vessels and the Gathering of the Sparks," p. 122.

[97]See "Myths of the Holy Land," pp. 401-429.

[98]See "Myths of the Messiah," p. 483-523.

[99]In *Mishneh Torah Hilkhot Melakhim* 11 Maimonides offers a naturalistic alternative to the supernatural view of these requirements: "King Messiah will arise and restore the kingdom of David to its former glory. He will rebuild the Temple and gather all the exiles of Israel. All ancient laws will be reinstituted in his days; sacrifices will again be offered; the Sabbatical and Jubilee years will again be observed according to the commandments set forth in the Law." Note that Maimonides

specifically excludes the raising of the dead. On the other hand, he includes the reinstitution of all the ancient laws, including those no longer in use, such as those pertaining to the Temple, for once the Temple is rebuilt, the laws concerning sacrifices will be renewed. This perspective of the role of the Messiah reflects the view of a third century talmudic sage, Samuel, found in *B. Pesahim* 68a, that there is no difference between historical time and messianic time except that the Jewish people will no longer be politically oppressed.

[100]*Zohar* 1:22a-b, 2:175a, 3:69a. See "The Exile of the Shekhinah," p. 75, and the accompanying note.

[101]There is a somewhat obscure tradition about a third Messiah, known as the Priest Messiah. This tradition grows out of the biblical phrase, *Kohen ha-Mashiah*, priest Messiah, which refers to the anointed priest. But the rabbis later took it to mean that there is a third Messiah who comes before the other two Messiahs. Some traditions identify this priest Messiah with Elijah, since Elijah's role includes being harbinger of the messianic age.

[102]For a good article on the two Messiahs, see "The Messiah of Ephraim and the Premature Exodus of the Tribe of Ephraim" by J. Heinemann.

[103]See Ezekiel 38-39. In apocalyptic Jewish literature, the war of Gog and Magog becomes identified as a war against God that will bring great calamities on Israel. It will be the final war, which will presage the advent of the Messiah.

[104]See "The Messiah Petitions God," p. 517.

[105]*Zohar* 2:8a-9a. See "The Palace of the Messiah," p. 488.

[106]*Pesikta Rabbati* 36:1-2; Rashi on *B. Sanhedrin* 98b; *Midrashei Geulah* 307-308; *Tzidkat ha-Tzaddik* 153 by Rabbi Tzadok ha-Kohen of Lublin; *Likutei Moharan* 1:118. See "The Suffering Messiah," p. 489.

[107]Israel Folktale Archives 6928, collected in Israel by Uri Resler from his uncle from Rumania. See "The Captive Messiah," p. 498.

[108]See "The Messiah at the Gates of Rome," p. 492.

[109]See "The Chains of the Messiah," p. 492.

[110]About half of all Lubavitch Hasidim are said to share the belief that their deceased Rebbe will be resurrected and fulfill the role of the Messiah, although traditional messianic doctrine holds that all of the righteous dead will be resurrected at the same time. This, then, appears to be an example of a new myth of individual resurrection developing among these Hasidim. David Berger has written a highly critical book about this evolving belief, *The Rebbe, the Messiah, and the Scandal of Orthodox Indifference*.

[111]Two other key questions may also be intuited here: First, why was the world created? The answer most often given is so that the universe and everything in it could praise God. Second, why was man created? In a well-known midrash, a group of angels questions God's intention to create man, asking, "*What is man that You have been mindful of him?*" (Ps. 8:5). In reply, God stretched out His little finger and consumed them with fire. The same thing happened with a second group of angels. The third group of angels agreed it was a wonderful idea. See *B. Sanhedrin* 38b.

[112]*Mishneh Torah* 1:1-12.

[113]See note 38 for more information on Gnosticism.

[114]See Gershom Scholem's *Jewish Gnosticism, Merkabah Mysticism, and Talmudic Tradition*.

[115]See the entry on monolatry by S. David Sperling in *The Encyclopedia of Religion*, edited by Mircea Eliade and Charles Adams III, 6:3-7. Biblical evidence that the people insisted on worshipping other gods is found in 2 Kings 17:7-23 and Jeremiah 25:3-11.

[116]There is another instance of monolatry in the ancient Near East. The Egyptian Pharaoh Akhenaton inaugurated a solar monolatry in the fourteenth century BCE, in which the royal family worshipped Aton, the disk of the sun, to the exclusion of all of the other Egyptian gods.

[117]This verse is part of the famous prayer, *Mi-Kemokhah* ("Who is like you?"), which is recited as part of the second blessing after the Shema. The *ba-elim* are generally understood to be the gods of the idol worshippers.

[118]Umberto Cassuto, *Biblical and Oriental Studies* 2:80. The great scholar Umberto Cassuto, who wrote about biblical religion, had the theory that there were two Judaisms, the Judaism presented by the priestly editors of the Bible, where pagan elements were forbidden, and the actual way the religion was practiced by the people. In this folk religion, many motifs found in Babylonian and Canaanite mythology found their way into Judaism.

[119]Of course, the rabbinic texts themselves claim that these traditions are part of the Oral Torah, handed down by God to Moses at Mount Sinai, and are therefore considerably ancient.

[120]Umberto Cassuto, *A Commentary on the Book of Exodus*, pp. 178. See p. 106 for a discussion of the Babylonian myth of Marduk and Tiamat.

[121]The *Shekhinah*, originally simply the "divine presence," evolved into the feminine "aspect" of the one (primarily male) God. In medieval kabbalah, the *Shekhinah* is identified with the *sefirah* known as *Malkhut*, counterbalancing the higher, masculine sefirot. In Jewish myth the *Shekhinah* is often identified as God's Bride, and in this respect functions like divine spouses in other religious systems. To the extent that the *Shekhinah* seems to take on a kind of independent existence, Her role may be considered as parallel to that of goddesses in polytheistic religions.

[122]*Exodus Rabbah* 5:14; *B. Sanhedrin* 95b; *Y. Sota* 88; *Mekhilta de-Rabbi Ishmael, Beshalla* 8:2; *Yalkut Shemuel Remez* 160; *Yalkut Torah Remez* 231; *Midrash Tehillim* 18:15, 18:17.

[123]One possible source for this sun worship is the solar worship of the Egyptian Pharaoh Akhenaton in the fourteenth century BCE. See note 16, p. xxxiii. See *The Early History of God* by Mark S. Smith, chapter 4, "Yahweh and the Sun," pp. 115-124.

[124]Graves, *Greek Myths* 13c, 13.1.

[125]See "The Exile of the *Shekhinah*, p. 57.

[126]See "The Suffering God," p. 36, "God's Tears," p. 37, ""God Weeps Over the Destruction of the Temple," p. 38, and "God's Lament at the Western Wall," p. 39.

[127]pp. 211-32

[128]See "Joshua As Oedipus," p. 393, and "A Jewish Icarus," p. 181.

[129]For the myth of Pandora, see Graves, *Greek Myths* 39j.

[130]Originally a jar, later described as a box. See Graves, *Greek Myths* 39j.

[131]*Epic of Gilgamesh*, tablet 11. Lambert and Millard, 1969.

[132]In Genesis 7:14-16, God, speaking as an architect, instructs Noah on how to construct the ark: *"Make yourself an ark of gopher wood; make it an ark with compartments, and cover it inside and out with pitch. This is how you shall make it: the length of the ark shall be three hundred cubits, its width fifty cubits, and its height thirty cubits. Make an opening for daylight in the ark, and terminate it within a cubit of the top. Put the entrance to the ark in its side; make it with bottom, second, and third decks."*

[133]Graves, *Greek Myths* 38c.

[134]Hesiod, *Theogony*.

[135]See "Adam Brings Down Fire From Heaven," p. 137. Also, there is a strong echo of the Prometheus myth in the mythic elaborations of Genesis 6, which describe angels known as the Sons of God who descended to earth and revealed heavenly secrets to humans, especially to women. See pp. 454-460 for a discussion of these myths.

[136]See "The Sons of God and the Daughters of Men," p. 454, and the subsequent related myths.

[137]See "Elijah the Angel," p. 197.

[138]See "How Rabbi Ishmael was Conceived," p. 201.

[139]See "God Begat Isaac," p. 336.

[140]*Targum Pseudo-Yonathan* on Genesis 22:19; *Genesis Rabbah* 56; *3 Enoch* 45:3; *Pirkei de-Rabbi Eliezer* 31; *Hadar Zekenim* 10b in *Beit ha-Midrash* edited by A. Jellinek, V:157; *Perush Rabbi Saadiah Gaon le-Sefer Yetzirah*, p. 125. See "Isaac's Ascent," p. 171. *The Last Trial* by Shalom Spiegel discusses the many variants of the *Akedah*, the binding of Isaac.

[141]*Koran* 37:102ff.

[142]See "The Sources of Moslem Traditions Concerning Jerusalem" by J. W. Hirschberg.

[143]Walter F. Otto, *Die Gestalt und das Sein; Abhandlungen über den Mythos und seine Bedeutung für die Menschheit* (Düsseldorf-Köln: 1955), pp. 73-78.

[144]In the Middle Ages, when no Jew would call into question the divine origin of the Torah, the test of faith was whether one believed that the waters of the Red Sea had truly parted. Anyone who doubted this was open to possession by evil spirits, known as *dybbuks*, which then required exorcism. See, for example, "The Widow of Safed," p. 228.

[145]This also hints that some of the rituals and laws contained in the Torah were already observed by the Israelites before the Torah was given at Mount Sinai. This seems to suggest that the Torah was not an entirely new revelation, but incorporated elements of existing traditions.

[146]There are 39 categories of work that may not be done on the Sabbath, based on biblical references as to how the Tabernacle was built. See *B. Shabbat* 73a-75b.

[147]This belief may derive from an early story about Rabbi Akiba rescuing a man's soul from punishment in Gehenna by teaching the man's son to recite the Kaddish. There are a great many versions of this tale. See *The Kaddish: Its History and Significance* by David Telsner, pp. 68-78.

[147]*Tanna de-vei Eliyahu Zuta* 17. Today, in most non-Orthodox congregations, women also participate in saying the kaddish.

[148]Lauterbach, Jacob Z. "Tashlik—A Study in Jewish Ceremonies," *Hebrew Union College Annual* 11(1936) 207-340. Lauterbach notes that the ceremony "in the special form which is the main is identical with the one in which it is now still observed" dates to the fourteenth century, but that "the ceremony itself" is much older, dating from Hellenistic times.

[149]*Pesikta de Rav Kahana* 23.

[150]See "Sounding the Shofar," p. 296.

[151]See "The Light of the First Day," p. 83, for the many sources of this myth.

[152]The Christian commentator, Ephraem, concluded that the sun, moon and stars were created from the light of the first day. Ephraem, *in Genesim Commentarii* 9:2. Philo also identifies the primordial light, which he describes as invisible and perceptible only by mind, as the source of starlight. Philo, *De Opificio Mundi* 31 and 55.

[153]The kinds of permutations presented here are of a mythic nature. While this represents one perspective, the myth of the *or ha-ganuz* (hidden light) also can be identified as one of the sefirotic myths. From this perspective, the primordial light is identified with the *sefirah* of *Hesed*, the first to emerge from *Binah*. See *Zohar* 1:20a; 2:137a, and 2:166b. For other examples of sefirotic myths, see "The Seven Forms of God," p. 53 and "The Ten Crowns of God," p. 9.

[154]Rabbi Eleazer of Worms (1165-1230) describes a Hanukkah ritual, which he attributes to the early rabbis, in which 36 candles would be lit to correspond to the 36 hours the primordial light shone.

[155]Genesis Rabbah 3:6.

[156]*Sefer ha-Bahir* (Kaplan) 147.

[157]See "The Tzohar," p. 85 and the accompanying sources and commentary.

[158]*Zohar* 2:148b-149a.

[159]*Mishnah Hagigah* 2:1. This section of the Mishnah also sets out strict rules for the study of the mystical texts: Not to expound on the Mysteries of Creation before two others, and not to expound on the Mysteries of the Chariot (Ezek. 1) before one.

[160]*Zohar* 2:148b-149a.

[161]*Degel Mahaneh Ephraim, Bereshit* 3c.

[162]*Likutei Moharan* 1:234.

[163]*God in Search of Man* by Abraham Joshua Heschel, p. 270.

[164]Laya Firestone Seghi suggests that the Tree of Knowledge is a pair to the Tree of Life because the Tree of Knowledge represents polarity and the Tree of Life represents unity. Rabbi Ezra ben Shlomo of Gerona reached the same conclusion in *Sod Etz ha-Da'at* in the thirteenth century.

[165]See Theodor H. Gaster's *Myth, Legend, and Custom in the Old Testament*, p. 33, which updates Frazer's *Folklore in the Old Testament*. For further discussion of the oral roots of biblical myths, see *The Legends of Genesis: The Biblical Saga & History* by Hermann Gunkel and *Oral Word and Written Word: Ancient Israelite Literature* by Susan Niditch. For an example of a myth making use of the identification of the Tree of Knowledge as the Tree of Death, see "Abraham's Tree," p. 404.

[166]As proof that God intended Adam to be immortal, *Genesis Rabbah* 21:5 states that "Adam was not meant to experience death." In *Avodat ha-Kodesh* 27, Rabbi Meir ibn Gabbai states that "God intended for Adam to live forever." According to one interpretation, God created Adam intending that he would be one of the eternal beings. Just as Elijah was taken into heaven alive, so was Adam intended to have eternal life. However, when he tasted the fruit of the Tree of Knowledge, Adam lost his right to immortality, and that is why God placed the Cherubim at the gate of the Garden of Eden with the flaming sword, *to guard the way to the Tree of Life.* (Gen. 3:24). Note, however, that there is an alternate interpretation of the statement that "Adam was not meant to experience death." According to this reading, Adam never died and still exists. This would place Adam in the category of the great figures who never died. This includes Enoch, Abraham, Jacob, Moses, King David, and Elijah. See "Abraham Never Died" p. 348 and "Jacob Never Died," p. 370.

[167]According to Gershom Scholem, the earliest rabbinic identification of the Tree of Knowledge and the Tree of Death is found in *Midrash Konen*. *Zohar* 1:35b and 1:37b also directly link the two

trees. *Zohar* 1:35b states that "It is a Tree of Death, for if anyone takes from it he will die, for he takes the elixir of death." *Zohar* 1:37b describes the Tree of Knowledge as "the tree which has a connection to death." See *Zohar* 3:11a for a myth about how the Tree of Death rules at night. See "Abraham's Tree," p. 404.

[168]This kind of mythic evolution in Judaism seems to confirm Carl Jung's theory of myth being drawn from the collective unconscious. See Jung's *The Archetypes and the Collective Unconscious* and Steven F. Walker, *Jung and the Jungians on Myth: An Introduction*. Theorists of Myth, vol. 4.

[169]*Pirkei de-Rabbi Eliezer* 46.

[170]*Divrei Shlomo* by Rabbi Shlomo ben Yitzhak ha-Levi. Venice: 1596, 68b. This commentary is a restatement of the talmudic principle that "There is no earlier or later in the Torah" (*B. Pes.* 6b)

[171]See "Past and Present in Midrashic Literature" by Marc Bregman in *Hebrew Annual Review*, vol. 2, 1978, pp. 45-59.

[172]This might be an appropriate time for someone to study the use of the Lilith myth by Jewish feminists in the 1960s, in order to create a rebellious model. It might be viewed as an intentional reworking of a negative feminine myth into a positive one. What is interesting, is that for many modern Jewish women, Lilith is viewed as a positive figure, despite her long history as a succubus as well as a child-strangling witch. They have chosen to select some positive features, of sexual and personal independence, and suppress the negative ones. This leaves Lilith with a lot of baggage. For a contemporary collection of writings about Lilith, see *Which Lilith? Feminist Writers Re-Create the World's First Woman*, edited by Enid Dame, Lilly Rivlin, and Henry Wenkart.

[173]See "The Death of Cain," p. 451.

BOOK ONE

MYTHS OF GOD

"If all the heavens were parchment, if all the trees were pens, if all the seas were ink, and if every creature were a scribe, they would not suffice to expound the greatness of God."

Rabbi Meir ben Yitzhak Nehorai
Akdamut piyyut

1. ISAIAH'S VISION

In the year that King Uzziah died, I beheld my Lord seated on a high and lofty throne; and the skirts of His robe filled the Temple. Seraphs stood in attendance on Him. Each of them had six wings: with two he covered his face, with two he covered his legs, and with two he would fly. And one would call to the other, "Holy, holy, holy! The Lord of Hosts! His presence fills all the earth!"

The doorposts would shake at the sound of the one who called, and the House kept filling with smoke. I cried, "Woe is me; I am lost! For I am a man of unclean lips and I live among a people of unclean lips; yet my own eyes have beheld the King Lord of Hosts."

Then one of the seraphs flew over to me with a live coal, which he had taken from the altar with a pair of tongs. He touched it to my lips and declared, "Now that this has touched your lips, your guilt shall depart and your sin be purged away."

Then I heard the voice of my Lord saying, "Whom shall I send? Who will go for us?" And I said, "Here am I; send me."

> This biblical vision of Isaiah is extremely important in forming elementary concepts about the nature of God, of heaven, and of the role of the angels. Here God is envisioned as a king whose dwelling place is not a palace, but a temple. Which temple is this? The presence of the angels, whose function is to glorify God, strongly suggests it is the heavenly temple. Just this one passage, then, establishes the existence of heaven as a place on high inhabited by God and the angels, with His home in the heavenly Temple. This vision of Isaiah thus serves as a blueprint for subsequent myths about God and heaven. Details about the geography of heaven, about the names and roles of the angels, and, above all, about God's role on high, are embellished in rabbinic texts and in the Pseudepigrapha, the noncanonical books of the Bible, especially in the books of Enoch. Later the heavenly geography is further developed in the kabbalistic and Hasidic literature. For an example of a rabbinic elaboration, see "God's Throne of Glory," p. 4.
>
> Isaiah's own role in this vision—in which a seraph touches his mouth with a glowing stone that takes away guilt from his "unclean lips"—also establishes a pattern of interaction between humans and the divine realm, as well as the motif of a healing stone. This motif is also found in the Talmud in the myth of a glowing stone that the patriarch Abraham was said to have worn around his neck. Anyone who peered into the stone was healed. (*B. Bava Batra* 16b). See "The Tzohar," p. 85.
>
> A close variant of Isaiah's vision, in which God is also portrayed as seated upon a heavenly throne, is found in Daniel 7:9-10. See "Daniel's Night Vision," following.
>
> *Sources:*
> Isaiah 6:1-8

2. DANIEL'S NIGHT VISION

As I looked on, thrones were set in place, and the Ancient of Days took His seat. His garment was like white snow, and the hair of His head was like lamb's wool. His throne was tongues of flame; its wheels were blazing fire. A river of fire streamed forth before Him; thousands upon thousands served Him; myriads upon myriads attended Him; the court sat and the books were opened.

As I looked on, in the night vision, one like a human being came with the clouds of heaven; he reached the Ancient of Days and was presented to Him. Dominion, glory, and kingship were given to him; all peoples and nations of every language must serve him. His dominion is an everlasting dominion that shall not pass away, and his kingship, one that shall not be destroyed.

One way of reading this crucial dream vision of Daniel is to see it as the enthronement of two divine manifestations. In one God is identified as the Ancient of Days (*Atik Yomaya*); in the other, as a human being. In this interpretation God can be manifested as a young man or as an old man. Some rabbinic texts, such as *Mekhilta de-Rabbi Ishmael, ba-Hodesh* 5:20-30, discuss how God can sometimes appear as an old man and sometimes as a young man. See "God's Disguises," p. 16.

This myth also can be read in a completely different way, where the human figure is enthroned as a second divinity, as is found in Jewish Gnosticism. Read this way, this myth serves as the template for a series of enthronement myths. See "The Enthronement of Adam," p. 131, "The Metamorphosis and Enthronement of Enoch," p. 156, "Jacob the Divine," p. 366, "The Enthronement of Moses," and "King David is Crowned in Heaven," p. 395.

Here the Ancient of Days—one of the names of God—is seated upon His throne, while the younger figure is given "everlasting dominion" in which appears to be an enthronement. This pattern of the enthronement of a second divine figure in Judaism, while surprising because of the expectations of monotheism, is repeated many times in subsequent Jewish literature, where enthronement accounts are found for Adam, Jacob, Moses, and David, as well as for Enoch, who is transformed into the angel Metatron. These texts establish a pattern of Jewish Gnosticism in which a demiurgic figure is invested with divine powers. See "The Enthronement of Adam," p. 131, "Jacob the Divine," p. 366, "The Enthronement of Moses," p. 388, and "King David is Crowned in Heaven," p. 395. See also "The Metamorphosis and Enthronement of Enoch," p. 156.

Sources:
Daniel 7:9-10, 7:13-14.

Studies:
Jewish Gnosticism, Merkabah Mysticism, and Talmudic Tradition by Gershom Scholem.
Two Powers in Heaven by Alan Segal.
Four Powers in Heaven: The Interpretation of Daniel 7 in the Testament of Abraham by Phillip B. Munoa.

3. GOD'S THRONE OF GLORY

God sits in the center of a high and exalted throne, exceedingly majestic, suspended in the highest heaven, *Aravot*. Some say that one-half of the throne is made of fire, and the other half of snow. Others say that the entire throne consists of fire. A resplendent crown of glory rests upon God's head, and upon His forehead are written the four letters of His Name, YHVH.

God's eyes overlook all of the earth; on His right is life, on His left, death. In His hand is a scepter of fire. Fire surrounds the Throne of Glory, and beneath it sapphires glow. The throne stands upon four legs, with four holy creatures attached to it. On each side are four faces and four wings. Clouds of glory surround the throne, filled with six-winged seraphim singing praises to the Lord.

God's Throne of Glory is fused with a chariot of fire. It has never set foot on the floor of the seventh heaven, but hovers like a bird there. Each day the Throne of Glory sings a hymn before God, and thrice daily the throne prostrates itself before God, saying, "God of Israel, sit upon me in glory, for Your burden is most dear to me and does not weigh me down."

Rivers issue forth from under the Throne of Glory: rivers of joy, rivers of rejoicing, rivers of jubilation, rivers of love, rivers of friendship. They strengthen themselves and pass through the gates of the seventh heaven.

While God sits upon His throne, high and exalted, and looks down upon the earth, the wheels of the chariot roll through the heavens, causing lightning and thunder, as well as earthquakes. The chariot is led through the heavens by a swift cherub, who flies upon wings of the wind.

This is one of many rabbinic myths that elaborates on Isaiah's vision of God seated on a heavenly throne (Isa. 6:1-8). Here the description of the throne adds four holy creatures (*hayyot*) attached to it. The throne itself is said to be moving through the heavens as if it were some kind of fiery chariot. This image is one of the central paradoxes of Jewish mysticism—that God's throne is also such a *Merkavah*, a fiery chariot, both fixed in place in the highest heaven and also traveling through heaven like a comet at the same time. This comes directly from the vision of Ezekiel (Ezek. 1:1-28).

God is described in elemental terms, seated on a throne half fire, half snow. According to one version, the snow beneath the Throne of Glory was used by God to create the Foundation Stone; according to another version, it was used to create the whole earth. See the note to "The Work of Creation" p. 90.

In *Masekhet Hekhalot*, one of the *Hekhalot* texts describing heavenly journeys, the size of the throne is given in physical terms: "Its length is 800,000 myriads of parasangs, and its width is 500,000 myriads of parasangs, and its height is 300,000 parasangs, and it reaches from one end of the world to the other."

In the hymns of *Hekhalot Rabbati*, one of the most important of the *Hekhalot* texts, God's Throne of Glory is personified, singing a creation hymn before God and prostrating itself before God three times a day.

Sources:
Pirkei de-Rabbi Eliezer 3, 6; *Sefer ha-Zikhronot* 1:11, 1:6; *Midrash Tehillim* 4:12; *Hekhalot Rabbati* 8, 10; *Masekhet Hekhalot* in *Beit ha-Midrash* 2:40-47; *Midrash Konen* in *Beit ha-Midrash* 2:25; *Sefer ha-Komah*, Oxford Ms. 1791, ff. 55-70.

Studies:
The Faces of the Chariot by David J. Halperin.

4. THE DESCENT OF GOD'S THRONE

In the future God will let his throne descend to the middle of the firmament, and will reveal His glory to all who walk on earth.

Then God will set the place of the righteous closer to his throne than the place of the ministering angels.

There are many scenarios for what will take place in the messianic era. Here God's throne is envisioned descending to the middle of the firmament. From there, it would be visible to everyone on earth, so that they would be able to see God's glory. The myth also stresses the ultimate importance of the righteous to God, who will be closer to His throne than will the angels. Other themes of heavenly descent are also to be found in "The Descent of the Heavenly Jerusalem," p. 418, and "The Descent of the Heavenly Temple," p. 512.

Sources:
Y. Shabbat 6:9.

5. THE CROWN OF GOD

God wears a crown on His head. All the letters of the Hebrew alphabet adorn that crown. That crown has two staves, and between them is a precious stone, with the words "Israel, My people; Israel My people is mine" engraved on it. For the name of that crown is Israel. So too are inscribed the words, *My beloved is clear skinned and ruddy, preeminent among ten thousand. His head is finest gold, his locks are curled and black as a raven. His eyes are like doves by watercourses bathed in milk, set by a brimming pool* (S. of S. 5:10-12).

Rabbi Akiba defended the inclusion of the Song of Songs in the Bible, saying "The whole world existed for the day on which The Song of Songs was given to it. For all the Writings are holy, but this is the holy of holies" (*Song of Songs Rabbah* 1:11). That words from the Song of Songs are engraved on God's crown confirms Rabbi Akiba's assertion about the exceptional holiness of that book.

The letters of the Hebrew alphabet are engraved in the crown, and this serves to explain the primal power of the letters, which, tradition holds, were used in the creation of the world. See "The Letters of the Alphabet," p. 250.

The size of God's crown is given in the *Sefer ha-Komah* as 500,000 by 500,000 parasangs. By contrast, the circumference of God's head is given in the same text as 3,003,033 parasangs.

A similar crown is described as being worn by Metatron, the supreme angel, in *3 Enoch* 13.

Sources:
B. Berakhot 55a; *Sefer ha-Komah*, Oxford Ms. 1791, ff. 58-70; *Alpha Beta de-Rabbi Akiva* in *Battei Midrashot* 2:396.

Studies:
Keter: The Crown of God in Early Jewish Mysticism by Arthur Green.
The Shi'ur Qomah: Liturgy and Theurgy in Pre-Kabbalistic Jewish Mysticism, edited by Martin Samuel Cohen.

6. GOD'S CROWN OF PRAYERS

Three times each day the prayers of Israel ascend on high. When all of Israel has finished praying, what happens to their prayers? They thread their way to Paradise, to the highest heaven, where they are gathered by the angel Sandalphon, the angel appointed over prayers. Sandalphon collects all the prayers that have been offered in all the synagogues, and weaves them into garlands of prayer that he places upon the head of God, to wear on His Throne of Glory. That is why it is said that God is crowned with the prayers of Israel.

The idea that God wears a crown is a natural development from the concept of God as king. Since kings were the highest, most powerful human figures, God was viewed as the ultimate king. So too does God have a throne, the Throne of Glory, and a crown. The notion of God wearing a crown is also reinforced by the biblical verse: *and a splendid crown upon Your head* (Ezek. 16:12).

Here, though, the crown is formed in a wonderful way. The angel Sandalphon, charged with gathering the prayers of Israel, first collects the prayers and then weaves them into crowns of prayer. In some versions the angel puts the crown directly on God. In others, the angel pronounces an adjuration that causes the crown to rise on its own and settle on God's head.

Sources:
B. Hagigah 12a, 13b; *Exodus Rabbah* 21:4; *Pesikta Rabbati* 19:7; *Beit ha-Midrash* 1:58-61; *Midrash Konen in Beit ha-Midrash* 2:26; *Sefer ha-Komah*; *Seder Tkhines u-Vakoshes* 3.

Studies:
Keter: The Crown of God in Early Jewish Mysticism by Arthur Green.

7. THE THIRTY-TWO PATHS OF WISDOM

There are thirty-two paths of wisdom, consisting of the ten sefirot and the twenty-two letters of the Hebrew alphabet. By numbers, letters, and sounds, God engraved His Name on those paths.

The *Sefer Yetzirah, The Book of Creation* (or Formation), views the twenty-two letters of the Hebrew alphabet and the ten sefirot as the essential building blocks of the universe. Together they constitute the thirty-two paths of wisdom.

Sources:
Sefer Yetzirah 1:1.

Studies:
Sefer Yetzirah translated by Aryeh Kaplan.

8. THE TEN SEFIROT

Ten is the number of the ineffable sefirot, ten and not nine, ten and not eleven. Each of the sefirot has the appearance of a flash of lightning. Their origin is beyond human sight, their unfolding to the end of time.

Each sefirah has its own name, and this name can invoke angels and draw down the word of God. As they rush forth and return, they bear the divine word with them as a messenger carries a message.

Each sefirah reaches up to the Source of being and down to the created world. Each has vast regions bound to it, boundless and neverending, an abyss of good and evil. From His throne, God eternally rules over them. They are great mysteries of God, as it is said, *The secret things belong to Yahweh* (Deut. 29:28), and in them God conceals Himself from human beings. Through them God rules secret worlds that have not been revealed, as well as worlds that have been revealed. He binds the sefirot together and unites them. He has prepared garments for them, from which souls fly into human beings.

The sefirot are the channels through which God rules and interacts with all universes—those accessible to the human eye and those beyond human understanding, even beyond prophecy. God is hidden within the sefirot. From them comes all existence—through them, from the highest sphere, manifests the human being.

God is the mystery of mysteries. No thought can grasp God at all. In God there is no likeness or image of anything within or without. But since God is in the sefirot, whoever separates any one of these ten from the others, it is as if he had made a division in God.

The ten sefirot emanated from the ultimate, unknowable God, known as *Ein Sof* (the Infinite One), at the moment of Creation. They pour down energy, level after level, at last manifesting into a state of being, a container that receives the divine life flowing into it from the other sefirot. The function of the sefirot is a holographic reality, repeated endlessly, macro and microcosmically. But generically, that container is the tenth sefirah, *Malkhut*, which is also known as *Shekhinah* and *Knesset Yisrael*, the soul root Israel (which manifests in the form of the Jewish people).

All ten sefirot function as a unit to channel the divine energy. They are the conduits for ultimate good; yet paradoxically intimated within the very nature of the sefirot is the first hint of constriction that ultimately manifests as evil. Therefore, any attempt to manipulate these forces is considered tampering with divinity itself, and obstructing the flow of divinity through all the worlds. In more classical terminology, whoever separates any one of these ten from the others is considered as though he had made a division within the Divine.

The sefirot, representing the transition from super-being to being, are, in descending order: (1) *Keter*, Crown, the power that comes from the Transcendent (2) *Hokhmah*, Wisdom emerging from the ineffable, (3) *Binah*, the Understanding that develops, (4) *Hesed*, the generous Lovingkindness that flows downward, (5) *Gevurah*, the necessary Power that holds back and channels that Lovingkindness, (6) *Tiferet*, the Harmonious Beauty that blends Lovingkindness and Might, (7) *Netzah*, Vanquishment, the giving of Lovingkindness in a dominant fashion, (8) *Hod*, Glory, the holding back of Might in a more passive fashion, (9) *Yesod*, the Foundation into which all these energies pour, where they are all blended into a more accessible form, and (10) *Malkhut*, Regency, the actualized guidance and rule of the Infinite One. *Malkhut* also represents the *Shekhinah*, the feminine aspect of God.

The term "sefirah" seems to have been first used in the ancient kabbalistic text, the *Sefer Yetzirah*, the Book of Formation. Later kabbalistic teachings go into great detail describing the interactions of the ten sefirot, and the sefirot are one of the primary topics of kabbalah, particularly in the *Zohar* (which usually alludes to them in a veiled, symbolic fashion). The Second Introduction to *Tikkunei ha-Zohar* contains a brief mystical essay attributed to the prophet Elijah that describes the nature of each sefirah. This selection is still recited by devout Jews at the beginning of the daily prayers.

See the diagram of the ten sefirot, p. 529.

Sources:
Sefer Yetzirah 1:4-6; *Pardes Rimmonim* 1; "The Prayer of Elijah" in *Tikkunei ha-Zohar*, Second Introduction.

Studies:
Sefer Yetzirah translated by Aryeh Kaplan.
Inner Space by Aryeh Kaplan.
Jewish Ethics, Philosophy and Mysticism by Louis Jacobs, pp. 115-120.
The Sefirot by Yaacov David Shulman.

9. THE TWENTY-TWO LETTERS

The twenty-two letters of the alphabet are the foundation of everything. God forms, weighs, and composes every soul with these letters, and the soul of everything that will ever exist.

God caused the letter *aleph* to reign in the air and crowned it, and combined it with the other letters, and sealed it. And he caused the letter *mem* to reign in water, crowned it, and combined it with the other letters and formed the earth with it. And He caused the letter *shin* to reign in fire, and crowned it, and combined it with the others, and sealed the heavens with it. Thus God created something out of nothing, and brought all of existence into being.

This account of the primordial letters is one of the primary kabbalistic creation myths, found in *Sefer Yetzirah*, one of the earliest kabbalistic texts. It describes how God created the world through the twenty-two letters of the Hebrew alphabet. The endless combinations of the alphabet bring every kind of existence into being, what the *Sefer Yetzirah* calls "the soul of everything."

Just as *aleph* is crowned in this kabbalistic myth, so *alpha*, the first letter of the Greek alphabet, leads the other letters because *alphe* means honor. See *The Greek Myths* by Robert Graves, 52c.

Sources:
Sefer Yetzirah 2:1-2, 3:1-5.

Studies:
"Was God a Magician? *Sefer Yetsirah* and Jewish Magic" by Peter Hayman.

10. THE INFINITE BEING

The Infinite Being is boundless and without beginning. Except for this Infinite Being, everything else that exists has a beginning. At first there arose in Him the potential to emanate from His own essence all the worlds that existed potentially within Him. When the will of the Infinite Being decided to create, He brought existence from potential to actuality. First the Infinite Being emanated its sefirot, through which its actions are performed. In this way all worlds were brought into being; indeed, all that exists came into being from Him, from the depths of the earth to the loftiest heavens.

This Infinite Being, known as *Ein Sof*, fills all the worlds of time and space. Both the heavens above and the earth below are equally filled with His light. There is no place empty of Him in the upper or the lower worlds.

> *Ein Sof*, literally meaning "endless," is the Godhead, the oldest aspect of God, from which all of the ten sefirot, the ten numerals or emanations of God, proceed. This part of God is considered to be unknowable and above time; indeed, no speculation about *Ein Sof* is permitted. Here Rabbi Levi Yitzhak of Berditchev (1740-1810) makes the important point that in the universe it is God alone who does not have a beginning. See "The Ten Sefirot," p. 7.
>
> *Sources:*
> Zohar 3:225a; *Tikkunei ha-Zohar* 57 (91b); *Or Ne'erav* 42a-45a, 47a-53b, 55a-b; *Perush ha-Aggadot* in *Derekh Emunah* 2b-c, 3a-d; *Kedushat Levi, Mishpatim,* p. 139, *Likutim,* p. 284; *No'am Elimelekh, va-Yehi* 27a; *Tanya* (*Likutei Amarim*), *Sha'ar ha-Yihud ve-ha-Emunah* 7 (82b).

11. THE SEVEN FORMS OF GOD

God has seven holy forms, and they all have their counterparts in man: *God created man in His image, in the image of God He created him, male and female He created them* (Gen. 1:27). And they are the following: the right and left leg, the right and left hands, the trunk with the place of procreation, and the head. These are six of the forms, and the seventh is God's Bride, about whom it is written, *so that they become one flesh* (Gen. 2:24).

> This is an example of a sefirotic myth, in which God's body is said to correspond to that of man's. The ten sefirot, in descending order, are: 1. *Keter* (Crown); 2. *Hokhmah* (Wisdom); 3. *Binah* (Understanding); 4. *Hesed* (Lovingkindness); 5. *Gevurah* (Power); 6. *Tiferet* (Beauty); 7. *Netzah* (Victory); 8. *Hod* (Splendor); 9. *Yesod* (Foundation); 10. *Malkhut* (Sovereignty). The seven forms referred to are the seven lower sefirot. The last of these is *Malkhut*, which represents the *Shekhinah*, the feminine aspect of God. Just as God is male and female and is not complete without his feminine aspect, so man is incomplete without a woman. This diagram can be found on p. 529. See "The Ten Sefirot," p. 7, and "Adam Kadmon," p. 15.
>
> *Sources:*
> *Sefer ha-Bahir* 172.

12. THE TEN CROWNS OF GOD

God created ten crowns that He wears on His Throne of Glory, and they are He, and He is they, like a flame that rises from a burning coal, for there is no division between them. With these holy diadems He crowns and clothes Himself.

In this sefirotic myth, the ten crowns represent the ten sefirot, ten divine emanations that brought this world into being. Here God is described as wearing these emanations as ten crowns, meaning that God holds the creative process of the sefirot in the greatest esteem, and they are, in fact, the crown of his creation.

For another example of a sefirotic myth, see "The Order of Creation," p. 81.

Sources:
Zohar 3:70a.

13. THE FIRST BEING

There is one God who created everything and who guides the celestial spheres. This one God is absolutely eternal, and sufficient to Himself. Nothing existed before Him. All existing things—whether angels or other celestial beings—exist only through this First Being. That God does not have a physical body is known from the verse *He is God in Heaven above, and upon the earth beneath* (Deut. 4:39), for a physical body cannot be in two places at the same time.

One cannot conceive of God as one does of an idolatrous image, for God has no body at all.

It is not right to serve any but this God of the universe. It is only proper to bow down, offer up sacrifices, and make libations to this God, for there is no other God besides Him. Whoever permits the thought to enter his mind that there is another deity besides God violates the prohibition, *You shall have no other gods before Me* (Exod. 20:3; Deut. 5:7).

It is inconceivable that God does not exist. If God did not exist, all of creation would be extinguished.

Maimonides' view of God is rock-solid monotheism: there is only one God, who is also the Creator of everything that exists, including the angels and other heavenly beings. However, Maimonides denies the corporeality of God, which is assumed in many myths. Maimonides's statement that "God has no body at all" is quite definitive. Indeed, one way of reading this is not as a myth, but as an antimyth, intended to limit further mythic development. Maimonides specifically does not want describe God in mythic terms, but as a Deity whose laws have to be interpreted and obeyed.

Studies:
Mishneh Torah 1:1-12; *Perush ha-Mishnayot* 10:1-4.

14. THE CAUSE OF ALL CAUSES

The Cause of all Causes is above everything. There is no god above Him or below Him. He fills all the worlds and He surrounds them from every side.

Here the "Cause of all Causes" is another name for the Beginning. At the same time, the "Cause of all Causes" is also a name of God. This is the unknowable part of God, also known in the kabbalah as *Ein Sof,* the Endless One. The "Cause of all Causes" is the name given to the force in which the will arose to create the world. In the *Zohar's* reading of Genesis 1:1, God allows himself to be known through the sefirot, emanations of the Godhead in the world. Here God is identified as the source of differentiated being.

Sources:
Tikkunim, Preface, 4; *Etz Hayim* 2.

Studies:
Major Trends in Jewish Mysticism by Gershom Scholem, p. 221.

15. GOD'S OMNIPRESENCE

God is in every place, as it is said, *His presence fills all the earth* (Isa. 6:3). He fills the heavenly and the earthly spheres. When the glory of the Lord filled the Tent of Meeting, Moses could not enter there.

> God's omnipresence is acknowledged in numerous of biblical verses, such as *"For I fill both heaven and earth"* (Jer. 23:24). The most vivid account of God's presence taking a physical form is that in Exod. 40:34-35, where Moses is unable to enter the Tent of Meeting because the Cloud of Glory rests upon it, and God's presence fills the tent: *The cloud covered the Tent of Meeting, and the Presence of Yahweh filled the Tabernacle.* See "The Tent of Meeting," p. 42.
>
> *Sources:*
> *Midrash Tanhuma, Naso 6.*

16. GOD ALONE

God is alone, a single being. Neither before the Creation nor after was there anything but God, for there is nothing like God. Each of us, on the other hand, consists of body and soul, that is why *it is not good for man to be alone* (Gen. 2:18). But God is not a compound being; but a singular one, with a single nature, existing by Himself.

> Here Philo of Alexandria, the first century philosopher, defines the Jewish singular nature of God, contrasting Him with humans, who have a dual nature, consisting of body and soul. See "God's Existence," following, for an elaboration of this distinction between God's oneness and human duality.
>
> *Sources:*
> Philo, *Legum Allegoriarum* 2:1-2.

17. GOD'S EXISTENCE

God exists, has always existed, and will always exist. This is the meaning of *"I shall be what I shall be"* (Exod. 3:14).

Whatever God created, He created as a pair. The heaven and earth are a pair. The sun and moon are a pair. This world and the World to Come are a pair. God, however, is alone in the world, as it is said, *Hear, O Israel! The Lord is our God, the Lord is one* (Deut. 6:4). It was He in Egypt, at the Sea, He in the desert, He in this world, He in the World to Come.

Likewise, God created the heavenly beings with His right hand and the earthly beings with His left.

There are times when the entire world and all that is in it cannot contain God's glory, while at other times God speaks to man from inside the Ark of the Tabernacle.

> God's existence is reaffirmed in this midrash, along with God's role as Creator. The duality of existence is in contrast to the singular nature of God, as stated in the Shema, *The Lord is our God, the Lord is one* (Deut. 6:4).
>
> *Sources:*
> *Exodus Rabbah* 3:5; *Deuteronomy Rabbah* 2:41; *Mekhilta de-Rabbi Ishmael, Shirata* 4:27-31; *Genesis Rabbah* 4:4; *Exodus Rabbah* 3; *B. Menahot* 36b; *Sifre on Deuteronomy* 35.
>
> *Studies:*
> "The Unity of God in Rabbinic Literature" by A. Marmorstein.

18. GOD'S GAZE

If God's gaze were withdrawn for even a moment, all of existence would cease.

> According to this sixteenth century kabbalistic text, God's gaze is the paramount requirement for the continued existence of the world. The notion of God's gaze implies that the existence of this world also depends on God's continued interest in His world and all its creatures.
>
> *Sources:*
> *Or Yakar.*

19. GOD'S DAY

Some say that from morning till evening God ponders upon the Throne of Glory, considering new thoughts and plans. He ponders how to create the deep, how to create the heights, how to create the pillars of the clouds, how to create the foundation of the world.

And from evening until morning God descends from the Throne of Glory and rides upon sparks of fire and arranges the orders of the new worlds with his fingers. He positions the upper worlds opposite the lower ones, and the lower worlds opposite the upper.

Others say that for the first three hours of the day God is engaged in the study of Torah. During the next three hours God sits in judgment of the world. During the next three hours He feeds the whole world, from horned buffalo to vermin. During the next three hours some say He plays with Leviathan, while others insist that He sits and teaches school children. Still others say that He blesses bridegrooms, adorns brides, visits the sick, buries the dead, and recites the blessing for mourners.

And what does God do at night? He rides a cherub of light and floats in 18,000 worlds, listening to heavenly songs.

> Here are two accounts about how God spends His day. The first, from *Midrash Aleph Bet*, shows that God has two primary modes, one of contemplation, which takes place during the day, and one of action, which takes place at night. Note that this is the reverse of human behavior, which uses the day for action and the night for contemplation. This myth echoes many biblical passages about God's work of Creation, such as Psalms 33:6: *By the word of Yahweh the heavens were made, and all their host by the breath of His mouth.*
>
> The second account of God's day, from the Talmud, divides the first 12 hours of the day into four three-hour units. During these 12 hours, God puts in a very active day, devoting Himself to study, judgment, sustenance of the world, and, for relaxation, either playing with Leviathan or teaching children. But here God's second 12 hours are spent in floating on a cherub through thousands of worlds or in listening to the song of the living creatures, both quite passive roles. Since the whole myth creates parallels between God's day and that of a person, this passive role resembles something like God's dreamtime.
>
> In both mythic accounts, God moves from active to passive roles, and He is required to divide His time much as do His children, who must find time to sustain themselves and their families while also properly devoting themselves to the study of Torah. Thus both views of God's day are quite reassuring, for they demonstrate the kabbalistic principle of "as above, so below," in which the upper worlds and lower worlds are mirrors of each other, and even God has a schedule that He must follow.
>
> *Sources*:
> *Midrash Aleph Bet* 5:8-9; *B. Avodah Zarah* 3b; *Genesis Rabbah* 8:13.

20. THE HIDDEN GOD

No one knows where God is hidden. Not even the ministering angels who tend God's Throne of Glory know where God can be found, nor do the heavenly creatures who carry the Throne, for God has encircled Himself with darkness and cloud all around, as it is said, *He made darkness His screen* (Ps. 18:12). Indeed, some say that the true meaning of the verse *You hid Your face* (Ps. 30:8) is that God is hidden from Himself.

> This myth of a hidden God is based on the verse *He that dwells in the secret place, the most high, in the shade of God He will linger* (Ps. 91:1). Other verses that confirm this view of a hidden God are Psalm 30:8: *You hid Your face*, and Isaiah 64:6: *For You have hidden Your face from us*.
>
> This might be regarded as a dark myth about the absence of God, or it might be seen as a metaphor for the hidden nature of God: just as no person knows where his soul is located within himself, so too does no one know the place of God.
>
> The most profound development of a hidden God is found in kabbalah, where God's hiddenness is directly related to God as *Ein Sof*, which literally meaning "endless." This is the infinite God, the unknowable God, the God above the realm of the sefirot. The *Zohar* states, for example, that "*Ein Sof* does not abide being known" (*Zohar* 3:26b).
>
> *Masekhet Hekhalot* 3 offers a strange reason for God having hidden Himself: "So that the ministering angels cannot be nourished by the splendor of the *Shekhinah*, nor by the splendor of His throne, nor by the splendor of His glory, nor by the splendor of His kingship." In this view God is inaccessible to the angels and is determined to withhold his glory from them. This conclusion follows the kabbalistic concept of *Ein Sof*, where the ultimate nature of God must always remain unknown.
>
> In *Likutei Moharan* Rabbi Nachman of Bratslav (1772-1811) interprets *You hid Your face* (Ps. 30:8) as meaning that God has turned his back on the Jewish people during the Exile: "In our Exile the face of God is hidden. All our prayers and requests are a result of God's having turned His back to us. We want Him to turn back His face, as it is said, *Turn to me*" (Ps. 86:16).
>
> *Sources*:
> B. Sanhedrin 39a; *Exodus Rabbah* 23; *Pirkei de-Rabbi Eliezer* 4.; *Masekhet Hekhalot* 3.
>
> *Studies*:
> *Mysticism in Rabbinic Judaism* by Ira Chernus, pp. 74-87.

21. THE CONTRACTION OF GOD

Before God created the world, God's light filled all of existence. There was no vacant place, no empty space or void. Everything was filled with the light of the Infinite. Nor did that light have any beginning or end, and that is why it is called the infinite light.

When God decided to create worlds, He contracted Himself, and left an empty space in which to emanate and bring the worlds into being. He contracted His essence into no more than a handbreadth, and at that instant darkness spread everywhere, for God's infinite light had been withdrawn.

How did God create this world? Like a person who draws in his breath, so that the smaller might contain the larger, so did God contract His light into a handsbreadth, and the world was left in darkness. And in that darkness God carved large boulders and hewed rocks to clear wondrous paths of wisdom.

The primary source for this myth of God's contraction comes from Rabbi Hayim Vital's (1542-1640) *Etz Hayim* (*The Tree of Life*). Vital was the primary disciple of Rabbi Isaac Luria, known as the Ari (1534-1572). The purpose of this myth is to explain how, since God's presence (or infinite light) pervaded the universe, there could be room for Creation. The answer is this contraction of God, known as *tzimtzum*. *Tzimtzum* is the preliminary stage of the famous creation myth of the Ari. See "The Shattering of the Vessels and the Gathering of the Sparks," p. 122.

The infinite light (or *Ein Sof*) is said to have pervaded all of existence until God contracted Himself. Hayim Vital gives the precise location of the contraction, saying that the light, which formed a circle, contracted itself at its midpoint, in the exact center of the light, withdrawing to the circumference, leaving an empty space in between. The World of Emanation and all other worlds exist inside that circle, with the light of the infinite surrounding it.

Vital's explanation is as follows:

> Know that before the emanations were manifested and the creatures were formed, there was a simple ethereal light that filled all of existence. There was no empty space at all, such as an empty atmosphere or a vacuum, for everything was filled with that infinite light. This light had nothing in the sense of a beginning or an end, for everything was one simple light equally distributed. This is called the infinite light.
>
> And when in His simple will the desire arose to create the worlds and manifest the emanations, to bring to light the perfection of his deeds, names, and attributes—which was the reason for the creation of the worlds—behold God then contracted Himself in the middle point of Himself, in the very center of His light. And He contracted that light, and it was withdrawn to the sides around the middle point. Then there remained an empty space, an atmosphere, and a vacuum surrounding the very middle point.
>
> And behold, this contraction (*tzimtzum*) was equally distributed around that empty middle point in such a way that the vacuum was circular on all its sides equally.

The notion that God's presence fills the world is found in the biblical account of the Tent of Meeting, which Moses was unable to enter because God's presence had filled it entirely: *The cloud covered the Tent of Meeting, and the Presence of the Lord filled the Tabernacle. Moses could not enter the Tent of Meeting, because the cloud had settled upon it and the Presence of the Lord filled the Tabernacle* (Exod. 40:34-35). Likewise, this idea is found in the verse *"For I fill both heaven and earth" says Yahweh* (Jer. 23:24). About this King David is quoted as saying, "Just as the soul fills the body, so God fills the whole world" (Lev. Rab. 4:8).

At the same time, the notion that God can contract His presence and concentrate it in a single place is based on the tradition that God was able to speak to Moses from between the two staves of the Ark of the Tabernacle (*Genesis Rabbah* 4:4). Even more explicit is *Exodus Rabbah* 34:1, where God says, "I will descend and concentrate My presence within one square cubit of the Ark." Thus, when God wishes He can fill heaven and earth, as it is said, *Do I not fill heaven and earth?* (Jer. 23:24), and when He so desires, He can speak to Moses from between the staves of the Ark.

For Dov Ber, the Maggid of Mezritch, *tzimtzum* took place in this world, as God contracted His infinite light, but in the higher world God's light is unrestricted. He found confirmation of this in Isaiah 60:19, *No longer shall you need the sun for light by day. . . For the Lord shall be your light everlasting, your God shall be your glory* (*Maggid Devarav le-Ya'akov* 184).

Sources:

Etz Hayim 1:1, *Hekhal Adam Kadmon, Derush Igulim ve-Yosher* 2:22a: 28-40; *Otzrot Hayim; Sefer ha-Bahir* 1; *Sha'ar ha-Hakdamot* 4:14; *Derush she-Masar Hayim Vital le-Rabbi Shlomo Sagis*, p. 17; *Kanfei Yonah; Derush Heftzi-Bah; Perush ha-Idra le-Rabbi Yosef ibn Tabul*, p. 137; *Limmudei Atzilut; Shefa Tal; Perush Rabbi Saadia Gaon le-Sefer Yetzirah; Hovat ha-Talmidim; Likutei Moharan* 6, 64.4; *Maggid Devarav le-Ya'akov* 184.

Studies:

Physician of the Soul, Healer of the Cosmos: Isaac Luria and His Kabbalistic Fellowship by Lawrence Fine, pp. 128-131.

22. ADAM KADMON

Adam Kadmon, the supernal man, was the beginning of all beginnings, the most ancient of all primordial beings. Adam Kadmon preceded all other creations, and from Adam Kadmon all other worlds spread forth. He was the first creation to fill the void created by God's contraction, consisting of ten emanations in the form of circular wheels, one inside the other, which came forth, followed by the form of a single human being. And that was Adam Kadmon, the primordial man, a completely spiritual being. When it is said that man was created in the image of God, this refers to the form of Adam Kadmon. For God Himself has no form or image.

Filled with the light of the infinite, Adam Kadmon extends from one end of the empty space God created to the other. Some say that this infinite light emerges from the openings and apertures of the skull of Adam Kadmon, from his ears, his nose, his mouth and his eyes. Others say that the light issues from his mouth, his navel, and his phallus. The lights that issue from his mouth reach into all corners of the world, although only the points of the lights, called the branches, go forth, while the roots remain within him. From the forehead of Adam Kadmon tremendous lights shine forth in rich and complex patterns, some taking the form of letters and words of the Torah. These lights come forth from where the box of *tefillin* is placed.

All the lights that shine forth from Adam Kadmon eventually come together into a single circle. This light is so great that it can only be received if transmitted through the filter of his being. Still, the light that remains inside Adam Kadmon is far greater than the light that emerges from him.

Adam Kadmon contains thousands of myriads of worlds. The first four of these to come forth from Adam Kadmon are the Four Worlds, the worlds of Emanation (*Atzilut*), Creation (*Beriah*), Formation (*Yetzirah*), and Action (*Asiyah*). The creation of Adam Kadmon and of these other, lower worlds had a beginning in time, when they came into being. But this is not true of the Infinite One, who has no beginning or end.

> The complex concept of Adam Kadmon serves both as a mythic figure and as an abstract kabbalistic function. The term "Adam Kadmon" means "primordial man," and Adam Kadmon is understood to be the spiritual prototype of man, a kind of cosmic soul. At the same time, the figure of Adam Kadmon can also be recognized as an anthropomorphic manifestation of God, a male deity assuming the shape and features of a human being. The concept likely evolved from the older idea—prominent in Philo's writings—of a heavenly man who was created at the same time, or prior to, the earthly Adam. See "The Heavenly Man," p. 124. Like Philo's concept of the heavenly man, the existence and nature of Adam Kadmon are based on the verse *And God created man in His image* (Gen. 1:27). In Philo's view, the heavenly man is the pure image of God, and in the kabbalistic view, especially as found in Lurianic kabbalah, Adam Kadmon is said to contain every image of man that would ever exist—thus he is an archetype or prototype of man. According to Yosef ibn Tabul in *Kerem Hayah le-Shlomo*, Adam Kadmon, like the earthly Adam, transgressed in some fashion.
>
> At the same time, there are major differences between the heavenly man and Adam Kadmon. While the heavenly man seems like a purely mythic concept, Adam Kadmon, despite its anthropomorphic qualities, is understood to serve "as a kind of interface between the Infinite Creator and the finite creation" (Aryeh Kaplan, *Inner Space*, p. 23). It appears that Kaplan would entirely deny the apparent mythic nature of Adam Kadmon: "One of the main tasks of the Kabbalah tradition was to allow us to interpret these anthropomorphisms. It is universally agreed that they are to be understood allegorically rather than literally" (*Inner Space*, pp. 111-112).

The myth of Adam Kadmon is directly related to that of God's contraction. See the prior myth, "The Contraction of God." By contracting Himself, God created space in the universe for the universe to be created. Adam Kadmon is God's first creation, which fills the empty space.

While Adam Kadmon is said to take the shape of a human, it may well be that this is intended in much the same way various constellations of stars are identified in astrology. Thus Adam Kadmon could be understood as a constellation in the shape of a man, just as the Pleiades are identified as seven sisters and Orion as a man who is pursuing them. For Adam Kadmon is clearly intended to represent a cosmic realm. Indeed, Adam Kadmon represents the "inconceivable universe," as Jorge Luis Borges describes it in "The Aleph" (*Collected Fictions*, pp. 284).

At the same time Adam Kadmon is a cosmic metaphor, representing a stage in the creation of the world as well as the universe itself.

Above all, Adam Kadmon is part of the complex kabbalistic theory of God's emanation of the world, containing the ten sefirot.

Likewise, in *Etz Hayim, Derush Igulim ve-Yosher* 4:28a:1-15, Hayim Vital adds a clear disclaimer explaining that the human qualities attributed to Adam Kadmon should not be understood literally: "It should be clear that there is no body in the higher realm. As for all the images we use, it is not because it is actually so, but only so that one can understand higher spiritual matters that cannot be comprehended by the human understanding."

Nevertheless, there remain distinct mythic qualities associated with Adam Kadmon that reflect his role as the first primordial being that God created, who is described as taking the form of a human being. The meaning of his name—primordial man—and its obvious link with the earthly Adam, and the description of his body, where considerable emphasis is placed on his eyes, nose, mouth, and ears, all combine to suggest that Adam Kadmon is a demiurgic figure. At the same time, in terms of kabbalistic cosmology, Adam Kadmon functions as a conduit, shaped like a human, through which the light of the infinite (*Or Ein Sof*) passes before being emanated into the Four Worlds. These are the World of Emanation (*Atzilut*), The World of Creation (*Beriah*), The World of Formation (*Yetzirah*), and the World of Action (*Asiyah*). These worlds correspond to the senses of vision, hearing, smell, and speech.

The ten emanations that Adam Kadmon contains are the ten sefirot. Thus, from a kabbalistic perspective, Adam Kadmon is not only a primordial being, but a cosmic forcefield that contains the creative forces of existence. See a diagram of the Tree of Life on p. 529.

The role of God in the myth of Adam Kadmon is very interesting. God appears to have multiple roles. On the one hand God is the Infinite One, known as *Ein Sof*, meaning "Endless," who creates Adam Kadmon, and the rest of creation emanates from Adam Kadmon, who contains the ten sefirot. But since *Ein Sof* is completely unknowable, Adam Kadmon is the first manifestation of divine existence that can be perceived.

Sources:
Etz Hayim; Hekhal Adam Kadmon; Derush Igulim ve-Yosher 2-3, 5:1:9-28, by Hayim
  Vital; *Otzrot Hayim* by Hayim Vital; *Tikkunim*, Tikkun 70, p. 121; *Kerem Hayah le-
  Shlomo; Sod Gavhei Shamayim* 79b-81a; *Derekh Emunah* 6.

Studies:
Inner Space by Aryeh Kaplan.

23. GOD'S DISGUISES

God has appeared in many disguises. At the crossing of the Red Sea, God appeared to the Israelites as a mighty warrior, fighting their battles. The people were able to point at God with their fingers, and they beheld His image as a man is able to look at his friend's face. At Mount Sinai, where the Torah was given, God appeared as an old man, full of mercy. In the days of King Solomon God appeared as a young man, and in the days of Daniel as an old man teaching Torah. Therefore God said to them: *"I am He who was in Egypt, I am He who was at the sea, and I am He who was at Sinai. I am He who was in the past and I am He who will be in the future. I am He who is in this world and I am He who will be in the world to come. Even though you see me in various guises, 'I Yahweh am your God'"* (Exod. 20:2).

This myth emphasizes God's ability to take whatever form He wishes. He can appear as a young man or an old man, as a warrior or a teacher. *B. Rosh ha-Shanah* describes how "God drew his robe around him like the leader of a congregation and showed Moses the order of the prayer." Thus God can not only change His size, but even His appearance. The important point is that it is the same God, no matter how He appears. Here the rabbis have found a way to retain the variety of types of gods found in pagan mythologies, while still insisting that every manifestation is that of the same God: "Even though you see me in various guises, *'I Yahweh am your God.'"*

The reference to God's appearance in the time of Solomon as a young man derives from Song of Songs 5:15: *He is majestic as Lebanon, stately as the cedars.* God's appearance as a young warrior at the Red Sea is linked to the verse *Yahweh, the Warrior—Yahweh is His name* (Exod. 15:3). God's appearance as an old man at Mount Sinai is linked to the verse *With aged men is wisdom, and understanding in length of days* (Job 12:12).

Pesikta Rabbati 21 adds that God appeared to the people at Mount Sinai with many faces: a threatening face, a severe face, an angry face, a joyous face, a laughing face, and with a friendly face. Further, to some He appeared standing, to others seated, to some as a young man, and to others as an old man. If a heathen should say that these are different gods, it should be pointed out that the Torah does not say that "The gods have spoken face to face," but: *Face to face Yahweh spoke to you* (Deut. 5:4).

Sources:
B. Rosh ha-Shanah 17b; Yalkut Shim'oni, Yitro 286; Midrash Tanhuma, Yitro 16, 17; Mekhilta de-Rabbi Ishmael, Shirata 4:27-31, ba-Hodesh 5:20:39; Mekhilta de-Rabbi Shim'oni 60; Pesikta Rabbati 21:6; Pesikta de-Rav Kahana 12:24; Rashi on Exodus 20:2.

Studies:
"The Children in Egypt and the Theophany at the Sea" by Arthur Green.

24. WHERE GOD DWELLS

Some say that God dwells in the celestial realms, in the highest heaven, where He is seated on the Throne of Glory.

Others say that God hovers equidistant between the upper and lower worlds. That is the meaning of the verse *"The heaven is My throne and the earth is My footstool"* (Isa. 66:1).

All agree that the *Shekhinah*, the Divine Presence, makes her home in this world.

God is most often identified as dwelling in heaven, as in the vision of Isaiah in which God is seated on a high and lofty throne (Isa. 6:1-8). But here God is described as hovering between heaven and earth. Further, the *Shekhinah*, the Divine Presence, is said to make her home on earth. The traditional view is that the *Shekhinah's* home was the Temple in Jerusalem. Note that the *Shekhinah* is sometimes identified as God, sometimes as the Divine Presence, and sometimes as the Bride of God.

Sources:
Sha'arei Orah 1.

25. THE HOLY SPIRIT

Before the celestial world was revealed, before there were the Throne of Glory and the *Pargod*, the heavenly curtain, before there were angels, seraphs, constellations or stars, before all this there was an ether, an essence from which sprang a primordial light. This light is called the Holy Spirit.

The Holy Spirit consists of three parts, Spirit, Voice and Word. From Spirit God produced air, and formed twenty-two sounds: the letters of the alphabet. From air He formed waters, and from chaos and void he made mire and clay, and from them He formed the foundation of existence. And from the waters God formed fire, and made a Throne of Glory for Himself, where He is surrounded by the ministering angels. That is why it is written, *Who makes His angels spirits and His ministers a flaming fire* (Ps. 104:4). That is how air, water, and fire were created—fire above, water below, and air between them.

The Holy Spirit embraced all the patriarchs, kings, and prophets. Through the Holy Spirit, Adam was able to see the future generations, until the End of Days. Enoch was taken into heaven in a chariot, and when he returned to earth for 30 days, the Holy Spirit spoke through him, and he revealed the secrets of heaven. The Holy Spirit spoke through Noah, and he warned of the coming Flood.

After God's covenant with Abraham, he was possessed by the Holy Spirit at all times. Abraham saw with the Holy Spirit that David would descend from him. As for Isaac, the angels on high took Isaac and brought him to the heavenly academy of Shem and Eber, where he studied for three years, and when he returned, he saw the world through the eyes of the Holy Spirit. That is why his own sight grew dim. Jacob discovered the Holy Spirit when he dreamed of the ladder reaching from earth to heaven, with angels ascending and descending on it.

With the aid of the Holy Spirit, Joseph was able to divine the future and interpret dreams. So too did the Holy Spirit inhabit King David as if he were a vessel for the Psalms that poured forth from him. And in his old age, just before his death, the Holy Spirit descended on King Solomon and he composed the books attributed to him: Proverbs, the Song of Songs, and Ecclesiastes.

All of the prophets spoke through the Holy Spirit. Ezekiel was fully possessed of the Holy Spirit when he saw the Divine Chariot, and Isaiah saw with the eyes of the Holy Spirit when he had a vision of God seated on a high and exalted throne. So too was the Scroll of Esther written with the Holy Spirit.

Some say that from the day the Temple in Jerusalem was destroyed, the power of prophecy was taken from the prophets and given to the sages. After the demise of the last prophets, Haggai, Zechariah, and Malachi, the Holy Spirit departed from Israel, as it is said, *And the lifebreath returns to God* (Eccles. 12:7). After that, the people were informed of the unknown by means of a heavenly voice.

And when the heavenly voice could no longer be heard, letters fell from heaven into the hands of those intended to receive them. But for a long time no such letters have fallen, and heaven has been silent.

> The Holy Spirit is the known as the *Ruah ha-Kodesh*. The key motif of the myth of the Holy Spirit is that it departed from Israel after the last prophets. Here *ruah*, which means both "spirit" and "breath," is understood to refer to the Holy Spirit.
>
> The heavenly voice is known as a *bat kol*, the daughter of a voice. There are a number of rabbinic reports about hearing such a voice speak from on high. One of the most famous refers to the voice that is said to go forth in heaven 40 days before a child is born. This heavenly voice is heard by the angels and by some extraordinary sages, such as the Ari. See "God makes Matches," p. 66.

The word, of course, is the word of God, which is manifested in the Torah.

In *Sefer Yetzirah*, an early cosmological text, the three parts of the Holy Spirit are identified with the three upper sefirot, *Keter* (Crown), *Hokhmah* (Wisdom), and *Binah* (Understanding), and identifies them, respectively, as spirit, voice, and word. These elemental forces were said to been used by God to create the letters of the alphabet, as well as air, water, and earth. Thus the *Ruah ha-Kodesh* serves in this sefirotic myth as a tool used by God in Creation.

The loss of the *Ruah ha-Kodesh* was regarded as a rejection of the later Jewish generations. This is indicated by the verse *And the sprit returns to God* (Eccles. 12:7). The means of direct communication with God by divine inspiration had been lost. All that remained was a message delivered by a heavenly voice, a *bat kol*. A legend in the Talmud recounts that in the time of Hillel the Elder, the sages were discussing matters of the Law in an attic in Jericho when a heavenly voice spoke and said: "There is only one among you worthy of receiving divine inspiration, but your generation is not worthy of it." Everyone looked at Hillel. When he died, they said, "He was a worthy disciple of Ezra" (*B. Sanhedrin* 11a).

Prophetic inspiration is often said to come from the Holy Spirit. In its most powerful manifestation, prophetic inspiration made it possible for the greatest of all figures in Jewish history, such as Abraham and Moses, to communicate directly with God. But over time the potency of divine inspiration waned. Indeed, the primary pattern is one of a progressive loss of prophetic inspiration. This is the kind of direct knowledge of God demonstrated by Abraham and Moses, which is replaced by the prophecy of the prophets such as Ezekiel and Isaiah, whose knowledge of the divine comes from apparitions and visions. This kind of prophecy, in turn, is replaced by the prophecy of the sages. Here the sages derive their knowledge from a process of reasoning, yet it must be validated by prophetic inspiration, which gives it the seal of truth. By this time prophetic inspiration has become a kind of intuition of the divine, in which the voice of God must be heard inside oneself. When Elijah stands on the mountain and the Lord passes by, Elijah does not find God in the wind, in an earthquake, and in a fire. Instead, he finds God in *a still, small voice* (1 Kings 19:11-12). This seems like a good description of the kind of intuition that has replaced prophecy since rabbinic times.

The generational change portrayed in this myth of the Holy Spirit parallels that of the transition from patriarchs to priests to rabbis. Before the Temple was destroyed, its priests dominated Jewish ritual life. But when the Temple was destroyed, the responsibility for sustaining the heritage fell to the rabbis, as did prophetic inspiration. One famous hasidic tale of Rabbi Israel of Rizhin (1797-1850) describes how each succeeding generation knows less of a ritual performed in a forest by the Ba'al Shem Tov (1700-1760), until the latest generation knows only the story about it (*Knesset Yisrael* 12a). See "Lighting a Fire" in *Gabriel's Palace*, pp. 209-210.

Sefer Hasidim (par. 1473) speaks of a kind of prophetic wisdom in which it is possible to look at a piece of meat and know whether the slaughterer had intercourse with his wife on the previous night. This reflects one vision of the *Tzaddik*, the exceptionally righteous man, who, like the Ari, can look at a man's forehead and read the history of his soul (known as Metoposcopy), or point to a stone in the wall and tell whose soul is trapped in it. Rabbi Yitzhak Eizik Safrin of Komarno states that "There are letters written on every part of the human body which can be seen and read by a *Tzaddik*. These letters appear mainly on the forehead and reveal a person's character (*Zohar Hai, Yitro* 92-93). All of these are examples of prophetic inspiration, but none approach the kind of divine illumination experienced by the patriarchs—Abraham, who spoke with God on several occasions; Isaac, whose soul is said to have left his body and traveled to heaven during the *Akedah* (the binding of Isaac in Genesis 22); and Jacob, who not only had the dream of the ladder reaching to heaven, but also wrestled with a mysterious angel. There are all kinds of remarkable traditions about Moses, particularly about his heavenly ascent to receive the Torah directly from God. An extensive tradition also grew up around Enoch's ascent into Paradise and his transformation into the angel Metatron. See "The Metamorphosis and Enthronement of Enoch," p. 166. The prophets, too, received messages from on high and reported God's words in their writings. After that, however, these prophecies came to an end.

Sources:
Targum Pseudo-Yonathan 22:19; *B. Megillah* 7a; *Pesikta Rabbati* 3:4; *Ecclesiastes Rabbah* 3:4, 12:7; *Seder Olam* 15; *B Sanhedrin* 11; *Sefer Yetzirah* 1:6-9, 6:1; *Sefer Hasidim,* par. 1473; *Ma'ayan Hokhmah* in *Otzar Midrashim* pp. 306-311; *Zohar* 1:79a.

Studies:
The Early Kabbalah, edited by Joseph Dan, pp. 49-53.
Prophetic Inspiration After the Prophets: Maimonides and Other Medieval Authorities by Abraham Joshua Heschel.
"The Debut of the Divine Spirit in Josephus's *Antiquities*" by John R. Levison.
"The Holy Spirit in Rabbinic Legend" by A. Marmorstein.

26. THE BREATH OF GOD

At the time of the creation of the world, God's Throne of Glory stood in space, hovering over the surface of the waters like a dove over its nest, suspended by means of the breath of the mouth of God, as it is said, *and a wind from God sweeping over the water* (Gen. 1:2). Four gatherings of angels sang praises before Him, and the waters rose up and touched His throne. And God himself sat at the center on his lofty and exalted throne, elevated and suspended in the air, and his gaze encompassed the entire world.

> The Hebrew term for "the spirit of God" is "*Ruah Elohim,*" which also means "the breath of God." The image of God sitting on his lofty and exalted throne is borrowed from Isaiah 6:1 and is repeated in Daniel 7:9. See "Isaiah's Vision," p. 3.
>
> *Sources:*
> Rashi on Gen. 1:2; *Pirkei de-Rabbi Eliezer* 4; *Midrash Tehillim* 93:5.

27. THE MIND OF GOD

In the beginning God's mind had everything in it, all that existed or would come to exist. It contained the darkness and the void, the light and the earth, as well as all yet to be called into being. It contained the colors of the rainbow, although no rainbow had yet shone. It contained the green color of the leaves and all the shades of the sunset, as well as the brightness of light that had not yet been brought into being.

> Here all of existence is said to have existed in God's mind before it was created. The concept has a strong echo of the Platonic archetype, but here the archetypes all find their origin in God's mind.
>
> This myth grows out of the belief that God's presence filled all of the universe before the Creation, and it follows logically the kind of personification of God so common in rabbinic sources. Thus if God has eyes, a voice, hands, and feet, etc., God also has a mind and His own thoughts. This also follows the metaphor of God as the divine architect, who carefully planned out all of Creation long before the first day, when God said, *Let there be light* (Gen. 1:3).
>
> *Sources:*
> *Mekhilta de-Rabbi Ishmael be-Shalah* 133; *Sefer ha-Zikhronot* 1:1.
>
> *Studies:*
> *The God of the Beginnings* by Robert Aron, pp. 75-100.

28. THE EYES OF GOD

From His throne in heaven, God's eyes observe all that takes place in the world. With one of His eyes, He sees from one end of the universe to the other. With His other eye, He sees behind Him that which has yet to happen. Nothing, not even the future, is hidden from God. Even before a person has crystallized a thought in his mind, God already knows it. God sees what is in the light and what is in the dark. There are no secret places for people to hide where God will not see them. Even those who transgress with utmost secrecy in the innermost chambers of their dwellings, in a place of darkness and in an area completely hidden—even those will go down to Gehenna, for God sees them.

God is vigilant both day and night. And on Rosh ha-Shanah all creatures are reviewed by the eyes of God at a single glance.

> The principle that God sees all deeds is one of the essential beliefs of Judaism. Virtually each of the assertions made here about God is based on a biblical verse including *The eyes of Yahweh are everywhere* (Prov. 15:3); *"If a man enters a hiding place, Do I not see him?"* (Jer. 23:24); *For Yahweh searches all minds and discerns the design of every thought* (1 Chron. 28:9); and *He reveals deep and hidden things, knows what is in the darkness, and light dwells with Him* (Dan. 2:22).
>
> Another reference to the eyes of God is found in "Abraham's Dying Vision," p. 347. For a modern story based on the concept of the eyes of God, see "The Aleph" by Jorge Luis Borges in his *Collected Fictions*, pp. 274-286
>
> *Sources:*
> *Midrash Tanhuma, Naso* 6; *Numbers Rabbah* 11:6; *Midrash Tanhuma, Vayak-hel* 2; *Midrash Tanhuma, ve-Atah Tetzaveh* 6; *Genesis Rabbah* 9:3; *Exodus Rabbah* 21:3; *Eliyahu Rabbah* 18:108; *Shi'ur Komah; Hekhalot Rabbati* 1.

29. THE FACE OF GOD

The face of the God of Israel is a lovely face, a majestic face, a face of beauty, a face of flame. When God sits on His Throne of Glory, His majesty surpasses the beauty of the bridegroom and bride in their bridal chambers.

Whoever beholds the face of God will be torn to pieces at once, as it is said, *"You cannot see My face, for man may not see Me and live"* (Exod. 33:20).

> The tradition that a human may not behold God's face derives from Exodus. Moses asked God to behold His Presence, but God told him that *"You cannot see my face, for man may not see Me and live"* (Exod. 33:20).
>
> This myth presents an essential paradox about the nature of God's face. On the one hand it is said to be beautiful beyond measure or imagination. On the other hand, whoever beholds it will be instantly "torn to pieces." This might suggest that some heavenly guard, such as those found at each gate of the heavenly palaces, will attack if the one who has ascended glimpses God's face. However, the same passage in *Hekhalot Rabbati* offers another metaphor for the destruction that will take place: whoever glimpses God's beauty will instantly pour himself out as a vessel.
>
> In *Moses*, Martin Buber speculates that since *"man may not see Me and live,"* and since God is said to have led the people, that "YHVH goes ahead of the people in order to overthrow foes who meet them on the way." This may explain the meaning of Deuteronomy 4:37, where God is said to have led the people out of Egypt "with His face."

Even the angels who sing before God are incinerated after singing for only one day. See "The River of Fire," p. 158.

Sources:
Hekhalot Rabbati 8.

Studies:
Moses: *The Revelation and the Covenant* by Martin Buber, p. 155.

30. THE SIZE OF GOD

We can begin to comprehend the greatness of God from the size of His fist, as it is said, *Who measured the waters with the hollow of His hand* (Isa. 40:12).

His greatness can also be determined from his size of his finger, as it is said, *And meted earth's dust with a measure* (Isa. 40:12).

We can also learn about God's greatness from his dwelling place. Although the heavens extend above the sea, as well as all the inhabited and uninhabited lands, they still do not contain God's throne.

Many esoteric Jewish texts are devoted to describing God's gigantic size and characteristics. The best known of these texts is *Shi'ur Komah.* Less comprehensive descriptions of God's size are found throughout rabbinic literature, as here from *Midrash Tanhuma-Yelammedenu*, which describes the size of God's fist and his finger, as well as suggesting the enormity of God's throne. See "The Body of God," p. 24.

Sources:
Midrash Tanhuma-Yelammedenu, Bereshit 5.

Studies:
The Anatomy of God by Roy A. Rosenberg.
The Mystical Shape of the Godhead by Gershom Shalom.

31. THE THREE KEYS

Three keys are in the hand of God that have not been entrusted to anyone—not to an angel, nor to a seraph, nor even to a troop of seraphim. Rather, God keeps them in His own hand. They are the key of the rains, the key of the womb, and the key of the resurrection of the dead.

The key of the rains opens the Treasury of Rain in the sixth heaven.

The key of birth is the key to the *Guf*, where the souls of those who have not yet been born are kept.

But no one knows where the key to the resurrection of the dead is hidden, not even the angels. Nor will God take it out until the time has come for the footsteps of the Messiah to be heard.

This tradition of three keys is attributed to the talmudic sage, Rabbi Yohanan. These are understood to be the most important keys—to the rain, representing nature; to birth, i.e., life; and to the resurrection of the dead, which is rebirth after death. Each of these is a life-giving force. The extensive traditions about God delegating various heavenly responsibilities to Metatron, in particular, as well as to other angels, are counteracted here with the assertion that God retains the core power of life-giving, and that is the essential power of God; nothing else really matters. This kind of struggle over the primacy of God's role is an integral part of the ongoing dialectic found in Jewish mythology.

Battei Midrashot lists many other keys that God holds: the key of sustenance, the key of femininity, the key to manna, the key of the renewal of the kingdom, the key of the eyes, the key of silence, the key of the lips, the key of the tongue, the key of prisoners, the key of the land, the key of the Garden of Eden, and the key of Gehenna. Each of these assertions is accompanied by a prooftext that demonstrates that God does indeed hold that key, such as, *He rained manna upon them for food* (Ps. 78:24) to demonstrate that God holds the key to the manna. See "The Treasury of Souls," p. 166.

Sources:

B. Ta'anit 2a; *Pesikta Rabbati* 42:7; *Battei Midrashot* 2:367-369.

32. THE ARMS OF GOD

God carries everything beneath His arms. With His right arm he carries the heavens, and with His left arm he carries the earth. How much do God's arms carry? The left carries the 18,000 worlds that surround this world. The right carries 120,000 worlds of the World to Come.

The length of God's arms is like the length of this world from one end to another; the width, like the width of this world. And the radiance of God's arm is like the splendor of the sun in the season of Tammuz.

This myth finds its biblical source in Deuteronomy 33:27: *The eternal God is your refuge, and underneath are the everlasting arms.* This can also be understood as underneath the arms is the world. The mythic notion that the heavens, and all that is in them, hang beneath God's right arm, and the earth, and all that is in it, hangs beneath His left arm, portrays everything as completely dependent on a God who is larger than the universe. Other myths describe the world hung like an amulet from God's arm. See "A Universe of Water," p. 94. Still others describe God using His arms to destroy prior worlds. See "Prior Worlds," p. 71. Yet others assert that the Torah is inscribed on God's arm (*Merkavah Rabbah*). See "The Torah Written on the Arm of God," p. 252.

Sources:

B. Hagigah 12b; *Sefer Hekhalot* in *Beit ha-Midrash* 5:189-190; *Midrash Konen* in *Beit ha-Midrash* 2:34; *Seder Rabbah di-Bereshit* 467, 743, 784, 840; *Midrash Aleph Bet* 3:1, 3:5.

Studies:

"Arm of the Lord: Biblical Myth, Rabbinic Midrash, and the Mystery of History" by Michael Fishbane.

33. GOD'S HANDS

The name of God's right hand is Just, and the name of the left is Holy. Sometimes God uses one hand to create something, and sometimes he uses both hands. God used only one hand to create a holy mountain, for it is written, *He brought them to His holy realm, the mountain His right hand had acquired* (Ps. 78:54). But both Adam and the Temple were created with both of God's hands.

How do we know that God created Adam using both hands? Because it is written *Your hands have made me and fashioned me* (Ps. 119:73). And how do we know that the Temple was created with both hands of God? From the verse *The sanctuary, O Yahweh, which Your hands established* (Exod. 15:17).

That God used His hands to create Adam is strongly suggested by the biblical text: *the Lord God formed man from the dust of the earth* (Gen. 2:7).

This midrash about God's hands suggests an underlying myth that God can create using a single hand or both hands. Biblical verses are brought in to prove that God created using both methods. A holy mountain, probably Sinai, was created with one hand, while biblical verses about Adam and the Temple describe them as having been created out of both hands. These latter two are among God's finest creations, and it is implied that they were even better because they were created with both of God's hands.

It is interesting to contrast the myths about God's words with those about God's hands. Because Genesis begins with a creation myth in which God creates through His words, creation through speech became the dominant tradition. But there is also an extensive rabbinic tradition that God made use of His hands. This brief myth from *Avot de-Rabbi Natan* describes God using his hands to create a mountain, a man, and a Temple. *Shloyshe Sheorim* explains that God created the world using both of His hands.

See "Creation from a Mold," p. 134, for an alternate account of God creating Adam using his hands. For another example of God's use of His hands, see "The Work of Creation," p. 90, where God forms the world out of balls of fire and ice, that He crushes together. Other examples abound.

Sources:
Avot de-Rabbi Natan 1; *Shloyshe Sheorim; Hekhalot Rabbati* 10.

34. THE BODY OF GOD

What is the appearance of God? God is fire and His throne is fire. Clouds and fog surround him. His face and His cheeks are in the image of the spirit, and therefore no man is able to recognize Him. With one eye God sees from one end of the universe to the other. The sparks that go forth from that eye give light to everyone. With the other eye, God looks behind Himself to see the future.

God's splendor fills the universe, luminous and awesome from within the darkness. Platoons of anger are to His right and to His left are splendid bolts of beauty and darkness and cloud, and before him lies a field of stars. His arms are folded. His cheeks are like a bed of spices, as it is said, *His cheeks are like a bed of spices* (S. of S. 5:13).

When God moves, there move behind him cherubs of fire and hailstones to His right, and to His left, the wings of storm and the might of the whirlwind.

What is the measure of God's body? His little finger fills the entire universe. His tongue stretches from the one end of the universe to the other. His mouth is fire consuming fire.

It is said that whoever knows the measurement of his Creator and the glory of God is secure in this world and in the World to Come. He will live long in this world, and live long and well in the World to Come.

Certain mystical texts, especially *Shi'ur Komah*, describe the body of God in great, sometimes ludicrous, detail. Even God's sexual organ is described and its size detailed. All of these measurements, given in parasangs, are gigantic. As noted here, "even His little finger fills the entire universe." These texts show a strange literalism in which God shares the anatomy of a man. The point is that God's size is so large that it cannot be imagined, although, in describing God's anatomy in great detail, these texts are in fact explicitly imagining it. Were these strange measurements meant to have been taken literally? Like all allegorical material in kabbalistic texts, especially in the *Zohar*, there is an ambivalence about this. On the one hand, *Shi'ur Komah* takes the issue of precise measurements very seriously, expanding the myth of God's gigantic body. On the other hand, there is a distinct awareness that these texts are also to be understood in allegorical terms. This represents the antimythological impulses within kabbalah. The central dialectic of kabbalah is focused on the debate between these two perspectives, the mythic and the antimythic. A full understanding of kabbalistic texts requires attention to both mythic and allegorical interpretation. Why is allegory anti-mythical? Because it narrows down the symbolic meaning of a myth to a single, one-dimensional interpretation, while myth increasingly expands its symbolic aura.

Sources:
Sefer ha-Komah, Oxford Ms. 1791, ff. 58-70; *Shi'ur Komah; Zohar* 2:176b-179a; *Zohar* 3:127b-145a, *Idra Rabbah; Zohar* 3:287b-296b, *Idra Rabbah.*

Studies:
Shi'ur Qomah: Texts and Recensions, edited by M. Cohen.
The Anatomy of God, translated by Roy Rosenberg.
God's Phallus by Howard Eilberg-Schwartz.

35. GOD'S BACK

Moses said to the Lord, "Oh, let me behold Your presence!" And God answered, "I will make all My goodness pass before you, and I will proclaim before you the name Lord, and the grace that I grant and the compassion that I show. But," He said, "you cannot see My face, for man may not see Me and live." And the Lord said, "See, there is a place near Me. Station yourself on the rock and, as My Presence passes by, I will put you in a cleft of the rock and shield you with My hand until I have passed by. Then I will take My hand away and you will see My back; but My face must not be seen."

> This passage from Exodus establishes the principle that *"you cannot see My face, for man may not see Me and live"* (Exod. 33:20). Nevertheless, there are many exceptions to this rule, most notably a famous midrash in which Moses ascends on high and speaks to God face to face as God is seated upon His throne. See "The Ascent of Moses," p. 261.
>
> Especially of note here is the notion of God's back. The suggestion that God has a face and a back goes far in establishing an anthropomorphic image of God. Of course, there is also a strong hint of allegory in this concept—being able to see only God's back suggests that much of God's nature must remain unknowable.
>
> This episode about Moses is largely repeated for Elijah in 1 Kings 19:5-12. See "A Still, Small Voice," p. 30.

Sources:
Exodus 33:18-23.

Studies:
"Imitatio Hominis: Anthropomorphism and the Character(s) of God in Rabbinic Literature" by David Stern.
"Some Forms of Divine Appearance in Ancient Jewish Thought" by Michael Fishbane.
Essays in Anthropomorphism by Arthur Marmorstein.
"The Body As Image of God in Rabbinic Literature" by Alon Goshen Gottstein.

36. THE GOD OF THE FATHERS

Moses said to God, "When I come to the Israelites and say to them 'The God of your fathers has sent me to you,' and they ask me, 'What is His name?' what shall I say to them?" And God said to Moses, *"Ehyeh-Asher-Ehyeh."* He continued, "Thus shall you say to the Israelites, 'Ehyeh sent me to you.'" And God said further to Moses, "Thus shall you speak to the Israelites: *Yahweh,* the God of your fathers, the God of Abraham, the God of Isaac, and the God of Jacob, has sent me to you: this shall be My name forever, this My appellation for all eternity."

In this important passage God reveals His name to Moses. Actually, God reveals two names in Exodus 3: "*Ehyeh-Asher-Ehyeh*," meaning "I Am That I Am" (or "I Will Be What I Will Be") and *Yahweh* (YHVH). This suggests that the priestly editors of Exodus intended to link *Yahweh* to the God of the patriarchs, although none of them knew God by this name, as directly stated in Exodus 6:2-3: *God spoke to Moses and said to him, "I am the Lord. I appeared to Abraham, Isaac, and Jacob as El Shaddai, but I did not make myself known to them by My name YHVH* (Exod. 6:2-3). The Samaritan text *Memar Markah* 1:4 comments about God's name: "It is a glorious Name that fills the whole of creation. The world is bound together by it. All the covenants of the righteous are bound together." God is quoted here as saying: "I shall not forget this Covenant as long as the world exists. Since you belong to the Most High of the whole world, I have revealed My Great Name to you."

God is identified by a series of names in the Bible. The two primary names are YHVH (*Yahweh*), known as the Tetragrammaton, and *Elohim* (which is plural, literally meaning "Gods"). God reveals his true name, YHVH, to Moses in Exodus 6:2, while noting that Abraham, Isaac and Jacob knew Him as "*El Shaddai*." God also identifies himself to Moses, as noted here, as "*I am who I am*" (Exod. 3:14). The biblical text seems to suggest a connection between the Name YHVH and the phrase *Ehyeh-Asher-Ehyeh*, "I am who I am." The four-letter Name of God is also known as the *Shem ha-Meforash*, "The Ineffable Name."

The multiplicity of God's names is itself a mystery. Why is a monotheistic God known by multiple names? Some of these names, such as "Almighty One," or "the Holy One, blessed be He" may simply function as attributes of God. But this does not explain the remarkable array of God's names. One possibility is that in the earliest stages of Judaism the names of some of the gods of the surrounding cultures were attributed to the God of Israel as part of the transformation from polytheism to monotheism. This is an example of what might be termed mythic absorption. This may have established the belief that God had many names. In *The Old Rabbinic Doctrine of God*, A. Marmorstein lists ninety-one rabbinic synonyms for God (pp. 54-107). These include well-known names such as *Elohim* ("God" and "gods"), *Ruah ha-Kadesh* ("the Holy Spirit"), *Shekhinah* ("Divine Presence"), *Yotzer Olamim* ("Creator of the Worlds"), *ha-Makom* ("the Place"), *Tzur Olamim* ("Rock of the Worlds"), *Shomer Olamim* ("Guardian of the Worlds") and *ha-Shem* ("the Name").

It is YHVH that remains the preeminent name for God in rabbinic and kabbalistic lore. Moses was the first and last to hear the Name pronounced by God and the Name was said to be inscribed on the staff with which Moses divided the waters of the Red Sea. After that, the tradition holds, the true pronunciation of the Name is only known by one great sage in every generation. The Maharal (Rabbi Judah Loew of Prague, 1525-1609), as well as the Ba'al Shem Tov, were said to know it. Having knowledge of this true pronunciation of the Name was regarded as bestowing secret, magic powers, including mastery of angels, spirits, and demons. Some sources identify the power of the Name as limitless.

Note that masculine and feminine elements are perfectly balanced in the Tetragrammaton. The *yod* has a masculine meaning, the *he* a feminine one, and the *vav* a masculine character. Thus the name follows the progression of masculine-feminine-masculine-feminine.

Sources:
Exodus 3:13-15

Studies:
Canaanite Myth and Hebrew Epic by Frank Moore Cross, pp. 3-12.
"Philo and the Rabbis on the Names of God" by N. A. Dahl and Alan F. Segal.
The Name of God and the Angel of the Lord by Jarl E. Fossum.
The Old Rabbinic Doctrine of God by A. Marmorstein, pp. 54-107.
"Defining Kabbalah: The Kabbalah of the Divine Names" by Moshe Idel.

37. THE TETRAGRAMMATON

All of creation emanates from God's holy Name, YHVH. In the beginning God revealed His holy Name within the empty hollow that was created when God contracted Himself. Then He radiated the first emanation, which became the source of all subsequent creation.

YHVH, the four-letter Name of God, is known as the Tetragrammaton. It is one of the two most important biblical names of God, along with *Elohim*. Rabbinic tradition considers the Tetragrammaton the essential Name of God. The true pronunciation of the Name is believed to have been lost. When the Temple in Jerusalem was still standing, the High Priest would go into the Holy of Holies on Yom Kippur and pronounce the Name. This was the only time it was pronounced. After the destruction of the Temple, knowledge of how to pronounce the Name was carefully guarded. One tradition holds that only one great sage in each generation knows the true pronunciation. This righteous man is known as the *Tzaddik ha-Dor*, the greatest sage of his generation. Among those who were said to have known how to pronounce the Name was the legendary Rabbi Adam, as well as Rabbi Judah Loew (the Maharal) and the Ba'al Shem Tov.

In Jewish folklore the Name is sometimes used to bring the dead to life, as in *Ma'aseh Buch* no. 171, where a dead man is brought to life by a rabbi in order to confess his crime. See "The Dead Man's Accusation" in *Lilith's Cave*, pp. 109-110. A similar use of the Name is found in *Megillat Ahimaaz*, where a young man who has died has the Tetragrammaton, written on a piece of parchment, sewn into his arm, making him a kind of living dead. See "A Young Man Without a Soul" in *Gabriel's Palace*, pp. 145-148. More often, the Tetragrammaton is pronounced in order to accomplish a miracle. For example, there is an oral tale collected in the Balkans about Rabbi Shimon ben Duran (1361-1444), who is said to have drawn a picture of a ship on a cell wall, and then brought the ship to life by pronouncing the Name. See "Rabbi Shimon's Escape" in *Gabriel's Palace*, pp. 126-127. See "The God of the Fathers," p. 25.

Sources:
Sha'ar ha-Gilgulim.

Studies:
The Name of God, A Study in Rabbinic Theology by Samuel S. Cohon.
"Philo and the Rabbis on the Names of God" by N. A. Dahl and Alan F. Segal.

38. THE LORD OF HOSTS

Once, when Rabbi Ishmael ben Elisha, the High Priest, went into the Holy of Holies of the Temple to offer incense, he looked up and saw Akatriel Yah, the Lord of Hosts, seated on a high and exalted throne. And the Lord spoke to him and said: "Ishmael, My son, bless me." And Rabbi Ishmael raised his hands in a blessing, and said: "May it be Your will that Your mercy overcomes Your justice, and may Your children be blessed with Your compassion." And when Rabbi Ishmael raised his eyes, the Lord inclined His head toward him.

This tale is a talmudic reworking of a biblical incident, exemplifying the pattern of retellings that continues through postbiblical Jewish literature. Here the biblical account of Moses speaking with God inside the Tent of Meeting is reworked into a tale of the High Priest having a vision of God in the Holy of Holies. This extends the link to the divine for another generation. In the biblical version, Moses does not see God, but speaks to him: *When Moses went into the Tent of Meeting to speak with him, he would hear the Voice addressing him from above the cover that was on top of the Ark of the* Covenant *between the two cherubim; thus He spoke to him* (Num. 7:89).

At the same time, Rabbi Ishmael's vision is strikingly parallel to that of Isaiah: *I beheld Yahweh seated on a high and lofty throne; and the skirts of His robe filled the temple* (Isa. 6:1). This indicates how talmudic myths and legends emerge from the cauldron of biblical archetypes. See "Isaiah's Vision," p. 3.

This talmudic tale grows out of traditions linked to the Temple in Jerusalem. No one was permitted to enter the Holy of Holies in the Temple except for the High Priest, and then only on Yom Kippur. This talmudic legend recounts how Rabbi Ishmael, the High Priest, had a vision of God inside the Holy of Holies. The name he attributes to God, Akatriel Yah, the Lord of Hosts (*Yahweh Tzevaot*) is a very strange one, leaving open the possibility that this might be the name of an angelic figure. However, the traditional readings of this tale have always identified Akatriel Yah as one of the many names of God. Most remarkable is God's request to Rabbi Ishmael—that Ishmael bless God, rather than the reverse. This makes it one of the primary examples of the rabbinic tradition by which God is portrayed as dependent, in some ways, on His creation. See "The Rabbis Overrule God," p. 67. Rabbi Ishmael does bless Akatriel Yah, and in return the Lord of Hosts nods his approval.

At the root of this myth is the belief, of primitive origin, that there is a kind of interdependence between man and God. This is best represented by the nature of sacrifices that were made to God. An offering was burned, the smoke of the sacrifice ascended on high, and if the offering was received, *fire descended from heaven and consumed the burnt offering* (2 Chron. 7:3). Other evidence of this tradition is found in the legend of the angel Sandalphon, who is said to weave the prayers of Israel into crowns of prayers for the Holy One to wear on his Throne of Glory (*B. Hagigah* 13b). Here, however, the tradition has been modified to the extent that God wears the crowns of prayer not because he needs to in order to be complete, but out of a great love that He holds for the prayers of Israel.

There is considerable debate over the identity of Akatriel Yah, who is identified as "The Lord of Hosts," *Yahweh Tzevaot*. Ancient readers saw this as a name for God Himself. Later commentators identified Akatriel Yah as an angel like Michael or Gabriel. This suggests that there were different, or at least evolving, traditions about Akatriel. It is also said that Akatriel's name is inscribed on God's throne, suggesting that according to one tradition, it was this name rather than that of the Tetragrammaton that was God's primary secret name.

In *The Mystery of Sandalphon*, Akatriel Yah is described as sitting at the entrance of Paradise, with 120 angels surrounding him. Here it is Akatriel rather than Metatron that Elisha ben Abuyah sees seated in Paradise. However, since Akatriel is described as being at the entrance of Paradise, this implies that his position is inferior to that of Metatron, who is found in the highest heavens in *B. Hagigah* 14b. See "A Vision of Metatron," p. 174.

The blessing that Rabbi Ishmael gives to God is identical to what is described as God's prayer earlier in *B. Berakhot* 7a. See "God's Prayer," p. 35.

Sources:
B. Berakhot 7a; Hekhalot Rabbati 6.

Studies:
The Old Rabbinic Doctrine of God by A. Marmorstein, p. 50 ff.
Jewish Gnosticism, Merkabah Mysticism, and Talmudic Tradition by Gershom Scholem,
    pp. 43-55.
"From Divine Shape to Angelic Being: The Career of Akatriel in Jewish Literature"
    by Daniel Abrams.

39. GOD'S ROBE OF GLORY

Some say that God's robe of glory is engraved inside and outside, and entirely covered with God's holy Name, YHVH. No eyes are able to behold it, not eyes of flesh and blood, nor even the eyes of the angels. Whoever beholds it, whoever glimpses it, is consumed in fire.

Others say that God's robe of glory is inscribed with all the words of the Torah, and that God wrapped himself in this magnificent garment at the time of the singing of the Song of the Sea.

> Here the prohibition against seeing God is extended to seeing God's garment, His robe of glory. Covered entirely with the Tetragrammaton, this robe is also described as having the characteristics of God: "a quality of holiness, a quality of power, a quality of awe, a quality of terror." This description of God's garment comes from one of the hymns of *Hekhalot Rabbati*, known as "The Greater *Hekhalot*."
>
> In *Razi Li*, God is said to have wrapped Himself in a garment inscribed with all the words of the Torah at the time of the singing of the Song of the Sea (Exod. 15). This tradition is attributed to Rabbi Akiba.
>
> Another tradition holds that God's garment is made of light. See "God's Garment of Light," p. 82.
>
> *Sources:*
> *Hekhalot Rabbati; Razi Li.*
>
> *Studies:*
> *Jewish Gnosticism, Merkabah Mysticism, and Talmudic Tradition* by Gershom Scholem, pp. 56-64.

40. THE WARRIOR GOD

Yahweh is a mighty warrior who defeated Pharaoh at the Red Sea. It is said that God smote them with His finger, as it is said, *And the magicians said to Pharaoh, "This is the finger of God"* (Exod. 8:15).

Others say that God appeared to Pharaoh as a mighty warrior, carrying a fiery bow, with a sword of lightning, traveling through the heavens in a chariot. When Pharaoh shot arrows at Israel, God shot fiery arrows back. When Pharaoh's army cast rocks, God brought hail. And when Pharaoh shot fiery arrows from a catapult, God deluged them with burning coals. Finally Pharaoh exhausted his entire armory. Then God took a cherub from His Throne of Glory and rode upon it, waging war against Pharaoh and Egypt, as it is said, *He mounted a cherub and flew* (Ps. 18:11). Leaping from one wing to another, God taunted Pharaoh, "O evil one, do you have a cherub? Can you do this?"

When the angels saw that God was waging war against the Egyptians on the sea, they came to His aid. Some came carrying swords and others carrying bows or lances. God said to them, "I do not need your aid, for when I go out to battle, I go alone." That is why it is said that *Yahweh is a man of war* (Exod. 15:3).

> The intensely mythic description of God riding upon a cherub is found in Psalms 18:11, *He rode upon a cherub and did fly*. This image was embellished in later rabbinic texts. Confirming the image of God as a great warrior traveling through the heavens in a chariot, *Exodus Rabbah* 5:14 states that God's bow was fire, His arms flame, His spear a torch, the clouds His shield, and His sword, lightning. The parallels to Zeus and the warrior gods of the Near East are clear. Note that the fiery portrayal of God strongly resembles the sun, and may well be a remnant of sun worship that survives

in Judaism. A parallel kind of sun worship can also be seen in the myths surrounding Enoch's transformation into Metatron. One of the angels listed in *Sefer ha-Razim* is Helios, the Greek sun god. This also indicates a possible remnant of sun worship in Judaism.

In addition to Exodus 15:3, *Yahweh is a man of war*, God is described as a warrior in Psalm 24: *Who is the King of glory?—Yahweh, mighty and valiant, Yahweh, valiant in battle* (Ps. 24:8). Frank Moore Cross finds in this passage a strong echo of the Canaanite pattern, in which both El and Ba'al are described as a warrior gods. The ideology of holy war is also found in Numbers 10:35: *Advance, O Lord! May Your enemies be scattered, and may Your foes flee before you!*

Sources:
Exodus Rabbah 5:14; *B. Sanhedrin* 95b; *Y. Sota* 88; *Mekhilta de-Rabbi Ishmael, be-Shalah* 82; *Midrash Tehillim* 18:15, 18:17.

Studies:
Canaanite Myth and Hebrew Epic by Frank Moore Cross, pp. 39-43, 91-111.
"The God Sedeq" by Roy A. Rosenberg.
Yahweh and the Sun: Biblical and Archeological Evidence for Sun Worship in Ancient Israel by J. Glen Taylor.
The Early History of God: Yahweh and the Other Deities in Ancient Israel by Mark Stratton Smith, pp. 115-124.

41. GOD'S SWORD

When God opens the book that is half fire, half ice, avenging angels go forth to execute judgment on the wicked with God's sword, drawn from its sheath. Its splendor shines like lightning and pervades the world from one end to the other, with sparks and flashes the size of the stars going forth, as it is said, *When I whet My flashing blade* (Deut. 32:41).

The book that is half fire, half ice echoes the myth the Books of Life and Death that God opens on Yom Kippur. See "The Book of Life and the Book of Death," p. 289. This myth offers God's sword as a metaphor for the execution of his judgments. The image here is of a harsh God, who sees to it that His judgments are immediately carried out.

Sources:
3 Enoch 32:1

42. A STILL, SMALL VOICE

Elijah lay down and fell asleep under a broom bush. Suddenly an angel touched him and said to him, "Arise and eat." He looked about; and there, beside his head, was a cake baked on hot stones and a jar of water! He ate and drank, and lay down again. The angel of the Lord came a second time and touched him and said, "Arise and eat, or the journey will be too much for you." He arose and ate and drank; and with the strength from the meal he walked forty days and forty nights as far as the mountain of God at Horeb. There he went into cave, and there he spent the night.

Then the word of the Lord came to him. He said to him, "Why are you here, Elijah?" He replied, "I am moved by the zeal for the Lord, the God of Hosts, for the Israelites have forsaken Your covenant, torn down Your altars, and put Your prophets to the sword. I alone am left, and they are out to take my life." "Come out," He called, "and stand on the mountain before the Lord."

And lo, the Lord passed by. There was a great and mighty wind, splitting mountains and shattering rocks by the power of the Lord; but the Lord was not in the wind. After the wind—an earthquake; but the Lord was not in the earthquake. After the earthquake—fire; but the Lord was not in the fire. And after the fire—a still, small voice. When Elijah heard it, he wrapped his mantle about his face and went out and stood at the entrance of the cave. Then a voice addressed him.

This is a famous and profound biblical passage in which Elijah does not find God in all the obvious places—not in the wind, and not in the earthquake, and not in the fire, but in a still, small voice. The implication seems to be that Elijah hears that voice within himself, and thus makes contact with God in this way. This might indicate a new stage in the understanding of God, in which God is sought and found within.

There are many parallels between the stories of Moses and Elijah, suggesting that the author of the Elijah narrative consciously shaped it to echo that of Moses. This episode has striking parallels with that of Moses' supreme revelation of God in Exodus 33:17-23, where God passes by Moses as he is inside the cave, and Moses is able to glimpse God's back. Elijah, like Moses, goes into the desert for 40 days and nights and arrives at Mount Horeb, which is Sinai. Further, the text strongly implies, this is the very same cave where Moses had his revelation. In both accounts there is storm wind, quaking, and fire on Sinai and both Moses and Elijah have a major revelation of God. For the account of Moses's vision, see "God's Back," p. 25.

Sources:
1 Kings 19:5-12.

Studies:
Canaanite Myth and Hebrew Epic by Frank Moore Cross, pp. 190-194.

43. GOD'S VOICE

God saved His full voice for a thousand generations. God did not create the heavens with this voice. Nor did He create the earth with this voice. When was God's full voice heard? When God gave the Torah at Mount Sinai. When God spoke the whole earth became silent. The birds ceased to sing, and all the fowl stopped flying, the beasts of the earth were quiet and the oxen did not low; the wheels of the Chariot of the Lord did not revolve, and the angels were hushed, as was the sea. It was a silence such as had never been before and will never be again.

Some say that then God's voice went forth and echoed throughout the world, as it is said, *And the people perceived the voices* (Exod. 20:15). And all the people who were in the camp trembled, and the earth shook, and the heavens fell down, and the mountains flowed. Israel first heard God's voice coming from the South, so they ran in that direction. Then they heard it coming from the North, so they ran that way. Soon after this they heard it coming from the East, and they turned in that direction. Then they heard it coming from the West, and they turned that way. All at once they heard the voice coming from the heavens, and they looked up. Then they heard it coming from the earth, and they looked down. In this way they learned that no one knows where God is hidden.

Others say that not only did God's voice come to them from everywhere, but God revealed Himself to them from all four directions.

It is said that each one heard God's voice according to his ability. The old men according to their ability, and the young men according to theirs, and the women according to theirs, and the children and the infants according to theirs, and even Moses according to his, so that each and every one would be able to endure it.

As soon as the words issued from the mouth of God they became fire and flew upon the wind, and appeared in the sight of all the people. Then the angels of the Lord descended and took the words of God and brought them to each of the children of Israel and told them of the sanctity of the divine utterance. So too did God's voice split into seven voices, and from these seven into seventy languages, and traveled to the ends of the earth, and entered into the heart of every man. When the voice came forth, each nation heard the voice of God, and its soul departed from it, but Israel was not harmed, as it is said, *Has any people heard the voice of God speaking out of a fire, as you have, and survived?* (Deut. 4:33).

The notion that God saved His voice for the giving of the Torah is problematic, in that God created the world by speaking the words, *"Let there be light,"* in Genesis 1:3. So too does God communicate with Abraham by speaking to him on several occasions. The rabbis seem to be making a fine distinction between "speaking" and "a voice." In any case, God's voice is an overwhelmingly powerful presence at Mount Sinai. The description of God's voice coming from all directions is based on several biblical verses, especially *From the heavens He let you hear His voice to discipline you; on earth He let you see His great fire; and from amidst that fire you heard His words* (Deut. 4:36), and *God thunders marvelously with His voice* (Job 37:5). The idea that God's voice was heard and understood by each according to his ability derives from the verse *Moses would speak, and God would answer him in a voice* (Exod. 19:19). In this passage, "a voice" seems to indicate that each person would hear it in a different way. This becomes emblematic of the teachings of the Torah to be understood differently by different individuals, according to their knowledge and ability.

Exodus Rabbah 34:1 comments on this: "God only comes to them according to their power. When God gave the Torah to Israel, if He had come to them in the fullness of His power they would not have been able to withstand it. But He only came to them according to their power."

The tradition that the people of Israel heard God speak in many different voices raises the question of whether what they heard were the voices of many gods. *Exodus Rabbah* 29:1 replies to this concern: "God said to Israel: 'Do not think because you heard many voices that there are many gods. But know that I alone am the Lord your God.'"

Likewise, God is said to have appeared to the people with many different faces. *Pirkei de-Rabbi Eliezer* 21:6 considers this issue in a similar way to that of God's voice: "God appeared to them at Sinai with many faces: a defiant face, a joyous face, a laughing face, a kind and friendly face....If a heretic says, 'There are two different gods,' answer him: 'It is not written the gods (*Elohim*) have spoken face after face, but *the Lord* (YHVH) *spoke with you face to face* (Deut. 5:4).'"

There is a rabbinic tradition that God's voice is still speaking from Mount Sinai. In *Leviticus Rabbah* 16:4, Ben Azzai tells Rabbi Akiba that he is hearing the words of the Torah and that they "are joyful even as they were on the day they were given at Sinai." The Ba'al Shem Tov believed that if the people of Israel sanctify and purify themselves, they will always merit hearing the voice of God speaking to them as He did at Sinai (*Keter Torah, Yitro*). One story about the Ba'al Shem Tov recounts how when he taught schoolchildren, he caused them to experience the Giving of the Torah on Mount Sinai, with the thunder and lightning. Later, at the time of Shavuot, when he spoke to them about the Giving of the Torah, he asked them if they remembered that event. All of them said yes, except for one, who eventually left the path of Judaism (*Kovetz Eliyahu*, edited by Hayim Eliyahu Sternberg). In *Esh Kadosh*, Rabbi Kalonymus Kalman Shapira (1889-1943) asserts, "Even now the voice of the Torah can be heard emerging everywhere, from within one's own body as well as from the entire outside world." Hizkuni claimed to have heard the voice of God pronouncing the Ten Commandments in a dream.

In his biblical commentary, Rabbi Yehudah Leib Alter of Ger, known as the Sefat Emet, comments about the verse *All the people saw the voices* (Ex. 20:15) that each of the people of Israel saw the divine soul within themselves, which was the root of his or her own life-force. Thus they did not require a leap of faith to believe the commandments, because they saw the voices.

In his Torah Discourses, Rabbi Menachem Mendel of Riminov expressed doubt that, "given the constrains of human understanding, whether it is possible to comprehend the notion of speech with regard to God." He explained that "God's speech can only be understood as a revelation of His inner will." According to the Riminov Rebbe, only Moses experienced God's true speech, by "drawing directly from God's holiness to his own inner core." That is the meaning of the verse about Moses, *The Lord would speak to Moses face to face* (Exod. 33:11). (*Makhon Siftei Tzaddikim* on Gen. 2:3).

For more on the theme of the seven voices of God, see "The Seven Voices of the Torah," p. 260.

Sources:
B. *Zevahim* 116a; B. *Shabbat* 87a; *Sifre on Deuteronomy* 314; *Midrash Tanhuma, Shemot* 22; *Midrash Tanhuma-Yelammedenu, Shemot* 25; *Yalkut Shim'oni* 1:174; *Exodus Rabbah* 5:9, 29:1, 34:1; *Midrash Shir ha-Shirim; Zohar* 1:52b; *Keter Torah, Yitro; Sefer Sefat Emet* 2:91; *Esh Kadosh* pp. 162-163; IFA 17143.

44. GOD'S IMAGE

When God made His voice heard at Mount Sinai, all of Israel were listening and fearful. They said to Moses, "Draw near and listen, for we are afraid to do so." So Moses drew near to the holy deep darkness where the Divine One was, and he saw the wonders of the unseen, a sight no one else could see. God's image dwelt on him, the very face of God. How terrifying to anyone who beholds it, for no one is able to stand before it. With his hands Moses received the signature of God, and it was a treasure-house of all knowledge. His body mingled with the angels above and he dwelt with them, being worthy of doing so. His speech was like the speech of the Lord. His voice mingled with the voice of the Lord, and he was magnified above all the human race.

> This is a Samaritan myth about Moses approaching God on Mount Sinai and seeing God's image—the ultimate experience of seeing God face to face. As important as Moses is in Jewish tradition, he is elevated even higher in Samaritan tradition, to a near-divine status. Indeed, it was the rabbinic fear of Moses being regarded as a messianic figure that led the rabbis to minimize his role in the Exodus in the Passover *Haggadah*. The image of God that Moses sees is a reference to Genesis 1:27: *In the image of God He created them*. Humans were created in God's image, but here Moses is able to see not only God's reflection, but God's actual image; thus he is able to encounter God face to face.

> *Sources:*
> *Memar Markah* 6:3 (Samaritan).

45. THE ELDERS OF ISRAEL BEHOLD GOD

Then God said to Moses, "Come up to the Lord, with Aaron, Nadab, and Abihu, and 70 elders of Israel, and bow low from afar. Moses alone shall come near the Lord; but the others shall not come near, nor shall the people come up with him. . . Then Moses and Aaron, Nadab and Abihu, and seventy elders of Israel ascended, and they saw the God of Israel: under His feet there was the likeness of a pavement of sapphire, like the very sky for purity. Yet He did not raise His hand against the leaders of the Israelites; they beheld God, and they ate and drank.

> Although God warns Moses at one point that *"You cannot see My face, for man may not see me and live"* (Exod. 33:20), in Exodus 24 God invites Moses to bring Aaron, his sons, and 70 of the elders of Israel to Mount Sinai, and there God reveals Himself to them. Further, they are permitted to eat and drink in God's presence. This takes place

just before Moses ascends Mount Sinai to receive the Torah, and the purpose of ascending with them is to convince the elders that God truly exists, and that the Torah God is about to reveal is a work of truth.

Rashi comments that because they saw God, they deserved death, but God did not want to mar the rejoicing of the receiving of the Torah.

Sources:
Exodus 24:1-2, 9-11.

Studies:
Moses by Martin Buber.

46. GOD STUDIES THE TORAH

God is occupied in studying the Torah day and night, as it is said, *A God of knowledge is the Lord* (1 Sam. 2:3). This means that God studies the Written Torah by day and the Oral Torah at night. When He studies the Written Torah by day, His face is as radiant as snow, and when He studies the Oral Torah at night, his face is ruddy.

According to this myth, God studies the very texts that are the primary focus of Jewish study. The description of God's face alludes to the verse *My beloved is white and ruddy*, from the Song of Songs 5:10. This is based on Rabbi Akiba's reading of the Song of Songs not as an erotic love poem or poems, but as an allegory of God's love for Israel, in which God is identified as the Bridegroom and Israel as the bride.

Here God is said to study both the Written and the Oral Torah. The first five books of the Torah are known as the Written Torah. According to *Pirkei de-Rabbi Eliezer* 46, God dictated the Torah to Moses during the day and at night He explained it to him. These nightly explanations are known as the Oral Torah, and in time it came to be identified with the Talmud, which was understood to contain within itself the Oral Torah.

Nor does God limit his study to the Written and Oral Torah. He also studies the interpretations of the sages, as recounted in *B. Hagigah* 15b, where it is reported that Rabbah bar Shila once encountered Elijah and asked him, "What is the Holy One, blessed be He, doing?" Elijah replied, "He is saying the teachings of each of the sages."

For other examples of God's observance of Jewish ritual, see "God Puts on *Tallit* and *Tefillin*," p. 34, and "God Keeps the Sabbath," p. 314.

Sources:
B. *Avodah Zarah* 3b; B. *Hagigah* 15b; *Pesikta Rabbati* 19:7; *Pirkei de-Rabbi Eliezer* 46; *Midrash Tehillim* 19:7.

47. GOD PUTS ON *TALLIT* AND *TEFILLIN*

God dons *tallit* and *tefillin*. How is this known? That God dons a *tallit* is known from the verse, *Who covers Yourself with light as with a garment* (Ps. 104:2). That God puts on *tefillin* is known from the verse *Yahweh has sworn by His right hand, and by the arm of his strength* (Isa. 62:8). Here, *by His right hand* refers to the Torah, and *by the arm of His strength* refers to the *tefillin*.

Indeed, it was God who taught Moses how to tie the knot of the *tefillin*.

What is written in God's *tefillin*? *Who is like Your people Israel, a unique nation on earth* (1 Chron. 17:21).

Some say that the angel Michael binds *tefillin* to God's head each day, while others say that this is done by Metatron, and still others say that it is done by Sandalphon.

In a series of myths, God is portrayed taking part in the same prayer rituals as the men of Israel. God prays, puts on a *tallit*, a prayer shawl with fringed garments (*tzitzit*), and puts on *tefillin*, the phylacteries that men don for the morning prayer service. What is the point of God taking part in such rituals? This creates a parallel in the ritual practices of God and of His people, Israel, as well as a sense of mutuality, an indication that God gives back the prayers that He receives.

The knowledge that God teaches Moses how to knot *tefillin* is linked to the verse *Then I will take My hand away and you will see My back* (Exod. 33:23). This is certainly a mysterious verse, with two strongly personified elements of God, His hand and His back. But it seems a long way to link this to God teaching Moses how to tie the knot of the *tefillin*.

The central text inside the *tefillin* is the Shema, from Deuteronomy 6:4-9. This is an unambiguous statement of devotion to God: *Hear, O Israel: The Lord our God, the Lord is one*. And the text described as being inside God's *tefillin*, *Who is like Your people Israel, a unique nation on earth?* (1 Chron. 17:21), is a clear statement of God's devotion to Israel. Together the two texts form a kind of *ketubah*—a wedding contract. They are a further example of the covenant between God and Israel. See "The Wedding of God and Israel," p. 305. For other examples of God performing Jewish ritual activity, see "God Studies the Torah," p. 34, and "God Keeps the Sabbath," p. 314.

Sources:
B. Berakhot 6a-7a; *Ma'aseh Merkavah*, Schäfer, Synopse #582.

Studies:
Keter: The Crown of God in Early Jewish Mysticism by Arthur Green.

48. GOD'S TABERNACLE

From the very beginning God made a tabernacle for Himself in Jerusalem, as it is said, *Shalem became His abode* (Ps. 76:3). That is the place where God would confer with Himself in prayer.

Ever since the tabernacle was destroyed, God prays for His children to do penitence, so that He may hasten the rebuilding of His house and His Temple, and spread the Tabernacle of peace over all His people Israel, and over Jerusalem.

This myth not only reaffirms that God prays, but establishes Jerusalem (using the ancient name, Shalem) as the place where God made a tabernacle for Himself. The notion that God would create His own tabernacle and pray to Himself is strange. But who else would God pray to?

Sources:
Midrash Tehillim 76:3; *Yalkut Shim'oni*, Psalms 813; *Yalkut ha-Makhiri* on Isaiah 57:6, on Psalms 76:3; *Genesis Rabbah* 56:1; *Y. Berakhot* 4.5, 8c; *B. Berakhot* 30a; *Song of Songs Rabbah* 4:4; *Midrash Shir ha-Shirim* 4:4.

Studies:
Midrash Yerushalem: A Metaphysical History of Jerusalem by Daniel Sperber, pp. 89-91.

49. GOD'S PRAYER

How do we know that God prays? From the verse *I will bring them to My sacred mount, and let them rejoice in My house of prayer* (Isa. 56:7). It does not state "their house of prayer," but "My house of prayer." Therefore it can be seen that God says prayers.

What is God's prayer? It is, "May it be My will that My mercy overcome My anger, and that My mercy dominate My attributes. May I act toward My children with the attribute of mercy, and go beyond the strict measure of the law."

> This is one in a series of myths about God participating in the same prayer rituals as His people, Israel. See also "God Studies the Torah," p. 34; "God Puts on *Tallit* and *Tefillin*," p. 34; and "God's Tabernacle," p. 35. Here God is portrayed as praying. Other myths describe God as singing praises of Israel, just as Israel sings praises of God.
>
> Note that the prayer that is described as God's prayer—to Himself presumably—is similar to the blessing that Rabbi Ishmael makes to God when he has a vision of Akatriel Yah—one of God's names—while in the Holy of Holies on Yom Kippur, also found in the same talmudic source. See "The Lord of Hosts," p. 27.
>
> *Sources*:
> B. *Berakhot* 7a; *Otzar ha-Kavod*.

50. GOD EXPOUNDS THE TORAH

In the future God is destined to sit in the Garden of Eden and interpret the Torah. All the righteous in the world will sit before Him, with all the household of heaven sitting at their feet. At the right hand of God will be the sun, the moon, and the planets, and at His left hand will be all the stars. Then God will expound the new Torah, which God is destined to give them at the hands of the Messiah.

> In the messianic era, the Messiah will transmit a new Torah to Israel that he received from God. Then God Himself will expound the Torah in heaven, before all the righteous and the other inhabitants of heaven, including the angels. Thus God is here demonstrated to be the final authority on the Torah, since, after all, God created it. This myth is also a part of a larger myth cluster in which God's actions mirror those of observant Jews—God not only prays, puts on *tallit* and *tefillin*, and studies the Torah, but He even teaches the Torah, demonstrating that He is the Master of masters. The new Torah that God teaches is appropriate to the postmessianic world, which will be considerably transformed. See "A New Torah," p. 522.
>
> *Sources*:
> *Battei Midrashot* 2:367-369.

51. THE SUFFERING GOD

When a Jew is afflicted, God suffers much more than the person does, as it is said, *In all their troubles He was troubled* (Isa. 63:9). For God is not subject to any limitation, and therefore His suffering is also boundless. It is impossible even to conceive such suffering. If the world ever heard God's weeping, and realized the extent of His grief, it would explode. Even a spark of His suffering would be more than the world could bear.

From the day the Temple was destroyed and Jerusalem made desolate, there has been no joy before God. Nor will there be any joy until God rebuilds Jerusalem and returns Israel into its midst.

God weeps in the inner chambers of heaven. Three times a day a divine voice, like the cooing of a dove, goes forth, saying, "Woe to My children. Because of their sins I destroyed My house and burnt My temple and exiled them among the nations." And three times a night, during the three watches, God sits and roars like a lion, repeating the same words of grief, as it is said, *Yahweh roars from on high, and thunders from His holy dwelling* (Jer. 25:30).

And whenever Jews go into the synagogues and pray, "May His Name be blessed," God shakes his head and says, "Happy is the king who is praised in this house. Woe to the father who had to banish his children, and to the children who had to be banished from their father's table."

In tractate *Berakhot* of the Talmud, Rabbi Yose enters a ruin in Jerusalem to pray and hears God giving voice to His grief over the destruction of the Temple and the exile of Israel. Upon leaving the ruin, he meets Elijah, who tells him that God grieves thus three times a day—a clear reference to the daily prayers in the morning (*Shaharit*), the late afternoon (*Minhah*), and the evening (*Ma'ariv*). In effect, this is God's prayer. And Elijah reveals to Rabbi Yose that when Israel responds with the words, "May His Name be blessed"—a traditional response—God shakes his head in both joy and grieving: joy that His children haven't forgotten Him, and grief over His decision to destroy the Temple and send His children into exile.

In a *derashah* (a discussion of a portion of the Torah, usually delivered on the Sabbath), Rabbi Kalonymus Kalman Shapira emphasizes the impossibility of any person being able to conceive God's infinite suffering, much less to endure it. For God feels guilty not only about the disaster He brought upon Israel, but He also wants to atone for their sins. Rabbi Shapira attributes Rabbi Yose's ability to hear God's words to the fact that he was standing in a ruin in Jerusalem, which annihilated his sense of self, making it possible to hear God's voice. This echoes the *still, small voice* of God that Elijah hears in the entrance to a cave (1 Kings 19:12). See "A Still, Small Voice," p. 30. For other examples of God's expressions of grief, see "God's Tears," p. 37 and "God Weeps Over the Destruction of the Temple," p. 38.

Sources:

B. Berakhot 3a; B. Hagigah 5b; *Eikhah Zuta* 7; *Yalkut Shim'oni, Eicha* 1009; *Esh Kadosh*, from a *derashah* delivered by Rabbi Kalonymus Kalman Shapira on February 14, 1942.

Studies:

The Holy Fire: The Teachings of Rabbi Kalonymus Kalman Shapira, the Rebbe of the Warsaw Ghetto by Nehemia Polen, pp. 106-121.

Theology and Poetry: Studies in the Medieval Piyyut by Jacob J. Petuchowski, chapter 8.

"The Philosophy Implicit in the Midrash" in *Essays* by Henry Slonimsky, pp. 41-50.

"The Holy One Sits and Roars" by Michael Fishbane. *Journal of Jewish Thought and Philosophy* 1 (1991): 1-21.

Midrash Yerushalem: A Metaphysical History of Jerusalem by Daniel Sperber, pp. 104-106.

52. GOD'S TEARS

When God remembers His children, who dwell in misery among the nations, He lets fall two tears into the ocean, and the sound is heard from one end of the world to the other. So too when God remembers how the *Shekhinah* lies in the dust of the earth, does He shed tears hot as fire, that fall down into the Great Sea.

Others say that in the hour that God cries, five rivers of tears issue from the five fingers of His right hand, and fall into the Great Sea and shake the world.

Many human characteristics are attributed to God, even weeping. Here God weeps remembering the suffering of his children, Israel. Just as God's size is enormous (see "The Body of God," p. 24), so too are God's tears. Even more surreal is the image of God weeping rivers of tears from the fingers of His right hand. Implicit in this weeping is both God's helplessness and His need for comfort, which clearly seems to contradict God's omnipotent role as creator and ruler of the world.

Zohar 1:26b explains that God's tears roll down to the great sea because Moses brought the Torah down in two tablets, but Israel was not worthy of them and they broke and fell, causing the destruction of the first and second Temples. In the Prologue to the *Zohar* 56, Rahab, the Angel of the Sea, is said to be sustained by God's tears.

The falling of God's tears into the ocean is also given as an explanation for earthquakes. See "What Causes Earthquakes?", p. 102.

Sources:
B. *Berakhot* 59a; *3 Enoch* 48:4; Prologue to the *Zohar* 56; *Likutei Moharan* 1:250.

Studies:
"Arm of the Lord: Biblical Myth, Rabbinic Midrash, and the Mystery of History" by Michael Fishbane.
"The Philosophy Implicit in the Midrash" by Henry Slonimsky, pp. 41-50.

53. GOD WEEPS OVER THE DESTRUCTION OF THE TEMPLE

When the Temple was destroyed and Israel banished, God wept bitterly day and night, saying, "Woe is Me! What have I done? I caused My *Shekhinah* to dwell on earth for the sake of Israel, but now that they have sinned, I have returned to My former habitation. As below, so above—in both there is weeping over what has come to pass. You weep in the night, but I weep day and night, for My presence knows no sleep."

Then God hung sackcloth over the entrance of His house, rent his purple garment and went barefoot. So too did God extinguish the lamps, withdrawing the light of the sun and the moon and the stars. And God sat silently and lamented over the Temple. He alone knew of the precious spiritual treasures hidden there.

At that time Metatron, the Prince of the Presence, came before the Lord, fell upon his face, and spoke before Him: "Master of the Universe! Do not weep. Let me weep instead of You."

God replied, "If you do not let Me weep now, I will go to a place where you do not have permission to enter, and I will weep there."

> This is a myth of great divine distress, agony, and regret. At the same time, the myth demonstrates God's grief over the chain of events that led to the destruction of the Temple and the exile of the Jews.
>
> Although God permitted the destruction of the Temple to take place (and in some myths was the cause of this catastrophe), here he faces the consequences of His actions and weeps. Metatron, who normally substitutes for God in many respects, is so disturbed at the sight of God weeping that he begs to weep for God instead. Metatron's response indicates the rabbinic discomfort at the notion of God weeping. Despite Metatron's offer, God is so distraught that He is ready to go off alone to weep. The place Metatron is not permitted to enter is the *Pargod*, the heavenly curtain, behind which only God and the *Shekhinah* can go. This is God's inner sanctum. God's insistence that he will continue to weep is explained by the verse *For if you will not give heed, My inmost self must weep, because of your arrogance* (Jer. 13:17).
>
> In *Esh Kadosh* Rabbi Kalonymus Kalman Shapira proposes that the reason the world was not destroyed by God's suffering over the afflictions of Israel and the destruction of the Temple is because God wept in secret, in his innermost chamber. For had his grief penetrated to this world, it would no longer exist.
>
> God's garment is described as purple, referring to the imperial purple garments worn by kings. Indeed, throughout God behaves in mourning as would a human king.

Sources:
Lamentations Rabbah, Proem 24; Pesikta Rabbati 15:3, 28:1, 28:3; Simhat Yisrael p. 87;
    Esh Kadosh pp. 159-164.

Studies:
The Holy Fire: The Teachings of Rabbi Kalonymus Kalman Shapira, the Rebbe of the
    Warsaw Ghetto by Nehemia Polen, pp. 106-121.

54. GOD'S LAMENT AT THE WESTERN WALL

God's grief over the destruction of the Temple was boundless. Once Rabbi Tzadok entered the Temple area and saw the destroyed Temple. He said, "Heavenly Father, You destroyed Your city and burned Your Temple, but now You are tranquil and untroubled." Before long Rabbi Tzadok dozed off, and that is when he saw God standing there in the Temple, lamenting, with the ministering angels lamenting with him.

On another occasion, Rabbi Nathan entered the Temple area and found the Temple destroyed, with only the *Kotel*, the Western Wall, still standing. He wondered what the survival of that wall signified, and he heard a voice say, "Take your ring and press it against the wall." Rabbi Nathan did this, and he felt through the ring that the wall was trembling, trembling because of the presence of God. At that instant Rabbi Nathan saw God bow down at the wall and straighten up and weep, and He did this over and over, lamenting.

> This myth not only confirms God's great grief over the destruction of the Temple in Jerusalem, but it also conveys just how holy is the *Kotel*, the western retaining wall of the Temple Mount, which the myth seems to treat as a wall of the Temple itself. Most important is Rabbi Nathan's vision of God praying at the wall. This confirms the immense sanctity associated with the *Kotel*. Accounts of God praying at the Western Wall are very unusual, while there are many reports of sightings of the *Shekhinah*, the Divine Presence, who made her home in the Temple before it was destroyed. The *Shekhinah* is often envisioned as a mourning dove or as an old woman dressed in black, or sometimes as a spirit hovering above the wall. See "The Creation of the Temple," p. 420, and "A Vision at the Wailing Wall," p. 63.
>
> Sources:
> Eliyahu Rabbah 30, p. 149; Pesikta Rabbati 15:10.

55. GOD'S OATH

Once, when Rabbah bar Bar Hannah was traveling in a caravan, he met an Arab merchant who offered to show him Mount Sinai. When they arrived there, Rabbah heard a heavenly voice crying, "Woe is Me. I have sworn to exile My children, and now that I have made the oath, who can absolve Me of it?"

When Rabbah returned from his journey and told the other rabbis of his experience, they screamed at him, "You fool! You should have cried out, 'I absolve You of Your oath!'"

> The legendary travels of Rabbah bar Bar Hannah include this journey to Mount Sinai, where Rabbah hears God bemoaning the oath He took to send Israel into exile. According to Jewish law, an oath must be fulfilled and cannot be broken unless someone absolves the one who made it. Here Rabbah had an opportunity to absolve God His oath, but foolishly failed to do so. Had he absolved Him, the exile of Israel would have come to an end.
>
> Sources:
> B. Bava Batra 73a.

56. GOD CONSIDERS ENDING ALL EXISTENCE

When the Temple was destroyed and Israel exiled from the land, God departed to the higher realms and He did not look upon the destruction of the Temple, or upon His people, who had gone into exile.

In that dark time, when the children of Israel wept by the rivers of Babylon, their cries reached the highest heavens, where God and all the angels heard them. Then God yearned to return all of existence to chaos and desolation. God said, "The world I created, I created with My two hands alone. Now I shall return it to chaos. I will bring heaven and earth together, smiting one against the other, and thus destroy the entire world, all of it; and not merely the earth, but the heavens as well, as it is said, *"I, too, will strike hand against hand and will satisfy My fury upon you"* (Ezek. 21:22).

The angels understood that all of existence was on the verge of coming to an end, and that God was about to turn even the Throne of Glory upside down. Then all of the ministering angels came before God and said, "Master of the Universe, is it not enough for You that You have already destroyed the Temple, Your dwelling place on earth? Will You also destroy Your dwelling place in heaven?"

God replied, "Do I need comforting? If I kindle but one spark, I can make the world, which I created, perish. I existed before the world was created, and I existed when the world was created, and I will continue to exist, whatever the fate of the world. Verily, I know the beginning and I know the end. Leave My presence."

> This dark myth shows God contemplating ending all existence, not only on earth, but even in heaven. Since God had created the world only for the sake of Israel, Israel's cries of suffering during the Babylonian exile, not long after the destruction of the Temple and the defeat of Jerusalem, bring the purpose of the world's continuing existence into question. This myth portrays a God who seems human in his deep emotional reaction, who comes very close to ending all existence in that bleak moment. That is when the angels, whose existence is also being threatened, intercede, but God's initial reaction to them is one of contempt and anger—"Do I need comforting?" God is not flesh and blood, and therefore needs no comforting. "Verily, I know the beginning and the end" suggests that God is not going to act on impulse, but that He alone knows His intended plan for existence, from the time of Creation to the End of Days. Even though this response to the angels is abrupt and contemptuous, it also seems to suggest that God has remembered His original plan for the world and has decided not to act on impulse and end all existence.
>
> God's reply to the angels, "I know the beginning and I know the end," is elaborated in *Eliyahu Rabbah* 1:3: "God knows both the beginning and the end and can tell from the beginning what the end of anything will be like, long, long before it comes to be."
>
> Rabbi Hayim of Volozhin is clear that all of existence depends on God: "The entire universe owes its continued existence to the will of God. If God were to rescind His will to maintain the world, it would instantly revert to nothingness" (*Nefesh ha-Hayim* 3:1).
>
> *Sources:*
> Pesikta Rabbati 28:2; Midrash Tehillim 2:17; Eliyahu Rabbah 1:3, 30:150; Midrash Konen in Beit ha-Midrash 2:25; Zohar 1:210a-210b; Nefesh ha-Hayim 3:1.

57. GOD WALKS IN THE GARDEN

And they heard the voice of the Lord walking in the garden toward the cool of day.

> This is the most anthropormorphic depiction of God in the Book of Genesis, who is "walking in the garden toward the cool of the day." Not only is God portrayed as

being on earth, and not in heaven, but God is said to be walking. This suggests that God has legs, which implies that God has some kind of human form. The added detail of "walking toward the cool of day" adds an additional humanizing element, as if God needed to cool off. After this, God ascends to heaven and remains there, except to descend to Mount Sinai to dictate the Torah to Moses.

Sources:
Genesis 3:8.

Studies:
God: A Biography by Jack Miles.

58. GOD'S LANTERN

When God took Israel out of Egypt, He took the lantern and went before them, as it is said, *Yahweh went before them* (Exod. 13:21). God escorted his descendants forty years in the wilderness. He was like a father holding a torch for his son, or like a master holding a torch for his servant. In this way God showed the nations of the world how dear the children were to Him, in that He Himself went before them so that the nations should treat them with respect.

In Exodus God Himself leads the children of Israel: *Yahweh went before them in a pillar of cloud by day, to guide them along the way, and in a pillar of fire by night, to give them light* (Exod. 13:21). In this passage from *Exodus Rabbah*, however, God guides them by holding a lantern and going before them. Even though the biblical verse from Exodus is quite anthropomorphic, the image of God holding a lantern is far more so, in that God's presence can be hidden in a pillar of cloud or in a pillar of fire, but not when holding a lantern. Indeed, the suggested image is of a giant figure bearing a lantern who is leading the people. Rashi's comment on this verse confirms God's presence: "God Himself, in His glory, led the cloud before them." However, this verse also lends itself to a metaphorical interpretation, where the image of God guiding the people with a lantern can also be understood to mean that God illumined their path. But this allegorical reading cannot diminish the powerful anthropomorphic image of God carrying a lantern and striding before the people through the wilderness.

Sources:
B. *Avodah Zarah* 11a; *Exodus Rabbah* 15:17; *Mekhilta de-Rabbi Ishmael, be-Shallah* 1:215-225; Rashi on Exodus 13:21.

59. GOD DESCENDS TO MOUNT SINAI

On the third day, as morning dawned, there was thunder, and lightning, and a dense cloud upon the mountain, and a very loud blast of the horn; and all the people who were in the camp trembled. Moses led the people out of the camp toward God, and they took their places at the foot of the mountain.

Now Mount Sinai was all in smoke, for the Lord had come down upon it in fire; the smoke rose like the smoke of a kiln, and the whole mountain trembled violently. The blare of the horn grew louder and louder. As Moses spoke, God answered him in thunder. The Lord came down upon Mount Sinai, on the top of the mountain, and the Lord called Moses to the top of the mountain and Moses went up.

All the people witnessed the thunder and lightning, the blare of the horn and the mountain smoking; and when the people saw it, they fell back and stood at a distance. "You speak to us," they said to Moses, "and we will obey; but let not God speak to us, lest we die." Moses answered the people, "Be not afraid; for God has come only in order to test you, and in order that the fear of Him may be ever with you, so that you do not go astray." So the people remained at a distance, while Moses approached the thick cloud where God was.

> This is one of the most vivid manifestations of God found in the Bible, where God descends to the top of Mount Sinai. Further, all of Israel is present at this time as witnesses of God's existence. God's overwhelming presence also underscores the importance of the transmission of the Torah. All in all, it is a key moment of bonding between God and Israel, confirmed by God's explicit presence.
>
> How did God bridge the gap between heaven and earth? *Mekhilta de-Rabbi Ishmael, ba-Hodesh* 4:45-52, states that "God bent down the heavens and lowered them to the top of the mountain, and thus the Glory descended."
>
> *Sources:*
> Exodus 19:16-20, 20:15-18.

60. THE TENT OF MEETING

Now Moses used to take the tent and to pitch it outside the camp, far off from the camp; and he called it the Tent of Meeting. And it came to pass, that every one who sought the Lord went out to the Tent of Meeting, which was without the camp. And it came to pass, when Moses went out to the tent, that all the people rose up, and stood, every man at his tent door, and looked after Moses, until he was gone into the tent.

And it came to pass, when Moses entered into the tent, the pillar of cloud descended, and stood at the door of the tent; and the Lord spoke with Moses. And when all the people saw the pillar of cloud stand at the door of the tent, all the people rose up and worshipped, every man at his tent door. And the Lord spoke to Moses face to face, as a man speaks to his friend. . .

Then it happened that the cloud covered the Tent of Meeting, and the glory of the Lord filled the tabernacle. And Moses was not able to enter into the Tent of Meeting, because the cloud abided within it, and God's glory filled the tabernacle.

And whenever the cloud was taken up from over the tabernacle, the children of Israel went onward with their journeys. But if the cloud was not taken up, then they waited until the day came when it was. For the cloud of the Lord was upon the tabernacle by day, and there was fire within it at night, in the sight of all of the House of Israel, throughout all their journeys.

> Here God descends to fill the Tent of Meeting and Moses is unable to enter it. This image establishes that God's presence takes up space. The key passage is: *And Moses was not able to enter into the Tent of Meeting, because the cloud abided within it, and God's glory filled the tabernacle.* This passage, with its direct statement that God's presence had a physical manifestation, must be counted as one of the most vividly mythic episodes in the Bible.
>
> The principle that God's presence takes space was drawn upon in the sixteenth century as the basis of Isaac Luria's kabbalistic theory of *tzimtzum*, which assumes that prior to Creation, God's presence filled the universe, and there was no room for anything else. So, in order to make space for the world to exist, Luria posited the contraction of God prior to the creation of the world. See "The Contraction of God," p. 13.
>
> In *Midrash Tanhuma, Shoftim* 8 it is said that Moses would enter the Tent of Meeting and stand there, and the voice of God would descend from the heavens as a type of pillar of flame between the cherubim, and Moses heard the voice speaking to him as if it were within himself.

Pesikta de-Rav Kahana 1:1 comments on God's reducing His size as follows: "Thus did God surrender to His people Israel, for their sake shrinking His presence in order to dwell among them in the Tabernacle. Nevertheless, though God dwells in the Tabernacle, He does not confine His Presence to it. He is present everywhere, even in the lowliest thorn bush. He comes and goes as He pleases. His power is endless."

Sources:
Exodus 33:7-11, 40:34-37.

61. THE COTTAGE OF CANDLES

There once was a Jew who went out into the world to seek justice. Somewhere, he was certain, true justice must exist, but he had never found it. So he set out on a quest that lasted for many years. He went from town to town and village to village, and everywhere he went, he searched for justice, but never did he find it.

In this way many years passed, until the man had explored all of the known world except for one last, great forest. He entered that dark forest without hesitation, for by now he was fearless, and he went everywhere in it. He went into the caves of thieves, but they mocked him and said, "Do you expect to find justice here?" And he went into the huts of witches, where they were stirring their brews, but they laughed at him and said, "Do you expect to find justice here?"

The man went deeper and deeper into that forest, until at last he arrived at a little clay hut. Through the window he saw many flickering flames, and he was curious about them. So he went to the door and knocked. No answer. He knocked again. Nothing. At last he pushed the door open and stepped inside.

Now, as soon as he stepped inside that cottage, the man realized that it was much larger on the inside than it had seemed to be from the outside. It was filled with hundreds of shelves, and on every shelf there were dozens of oil candles. Some of those candles were in precious holders of gold or silver or marble, and some were in cheap holders of clay or tin. And some of the holders were filled with oil and the flames burned brightly, while others had very little oil left.

All at once an old man, with a long, white beard, wearing a white robe, appeared before him. "*Shalom aleikhem*, my son" the old man said. "How can I help you?" The man replied, "*Aleikhem shalom*. I have gone everywhere searching for justice, but never have I seen anything like this. Tell me, what are all these candles?"

The old man said, "Each of these candles is the candle of a person's soul. As long as the candle continues to burn that person remains alive. But when the candle burns out that person's soul takes leave of this world."

The man asked, "Can you show me the candle of my soul?"

"Follow me," the old man said, and he led him through that long labyrinth of a cottage, which the man now saw must be endless. At last they reached a low shelf, and there the old man pointed to a candle in a holder of clay and said, "That is the candle of your soul."

Now the man took one look at that flickering candle, and a great fear fell upon him, for the wick of that candle was very short, and there was very little oil left, and it looked as if at any moment the wick would slide into the oil and sputter out. He began to tremble. Could the end could be so near without his knowing it? Then he noticed the candle next to his own, also in a clay holder, but that one was full of oil, and its wick was long and straight and its flame burned brightly. "And whose candle is that?" the man asked.

"I can only reveal each man's candle to himself alone," the old man said, and he turned and left.

The man stood there, quaking. All at once he heard a sputtering sound, and when he looked up, he saw smoke rising from another shelf, and he knew that somewhere, someone was no longer among the living. He looked back at his own candle and saw that there were only a few drops of oil left. Then he looked again at the candle next to his own, so full of oil, and a terrible thought entered his mind.

He stepped back and searched for the old man in every corner of the cottage, but he didn't see him anywhere. Then he picked up the candle next to his own and lifted it up above his own. At that instant the old man appeared out of nowhere and gripped his arm with a grip like iron. And the old man said: "Is *this* the kind of justice you are seeking?"

The man closed his eyes because it hurt so much. And when he opened his eyes, he saw that the old man was gone, and the cottage and the candles had all disappeared. And he found himself standing alone in the forest and he heard the trees whispering his fate. And he wondered, had his candle burned out? Was he, too, no longer among the living?

This story is a folk example of a divine test. The identity of the old man who tends the soul-candles and conducts the test remains a mystery, although his supernatural aspect is quite clear. As the Keeper of the Soul-Candles, he functions as an Elijah-type figure or perhaps as one of the *Lamed-vav Tzaddikim,* the Thirty-Six Hidden Saints, who are said to be the pillars of the world and are often described as living in the forest. See "The Thirty-Six Just Men," p. 397. It is also possible to view the old man as the Angel of Death, who has come to take the man's soul. Or the old man might even be identified as God, who has descended to this world to administer the test Himself. In any case, the test surely takes place at the behest of God, so it remains a divine one, similar to the divine tests found in Bible, such as those given to Adam and Eve concerning the forbidden fruit (Gen. 3), the Binding of Isaac (Gen. 22), and the trials of Job. Adam and Eve fail the divine test when they eat the forbidden fruit, but Abraham and Job pass the tests given them. Abraham demonstrates his willingness to sacrifice Isaac, and Job retains his faith in God despite a series of tragic events.

The man in this story, who is never named, is clearly attempting to fulfill the biblical injunction, *Justice, justice, shall you pursue* (Deut. 16:20). One way of reading the tale is to see that in arriving at this cottage, the man is on the verge of completing his lifelong quest to find justice, but he is first tested to see if he himself is truly just. It is interesting to note that his quest in this tale is in many ways parallel to that of the man from the country in Kafka's famous parable, "Before the Law," from *The Trial,* who comes seeking justice at the gates of the Law. See "Before the Law," p. 179.

In this folktale the man who seeks justice sins when he attempts to steal oil from the soul-candle next to his own. But there are other Jewish tales in which the reverse is true. See, for example, "The Enchanted Inn" in *Gabriel's Palace,* where a boy finds a candle about to burn out and pours additional oil into it as a good deed, only to discover later that it was the candle of his soul. Another variant, IFA 8335, tells of a cave in which there are bottles of oil, where a person lives until the oil is exhausted. Nor is the motif of soul-candles limited to Jewish folklore. Variants are found in Latin American folklore, as well as in Spanish tales, among others.

There is an implicit parallel between the soul-candles, which burn as long as a person lives, and the Jewish custom of lighting *yahrzeit* candles on the anniversary of a person's death. These memorial candles are intended to last for twenty-four hours, and remain lit until they burn out. The lighting of the *yahrzeit* candle is done to symbolize the verse, *The soul of man is the lamp of God* (Prov. 20:27), and this same verse is strongly echoed in this folktale. Note how the two verses from Deuteronomy and Proverbs serve as the foundation of this story. *Justice, justice shall you pursue* sets in motion the quest that propels the story, and *The soul of man is the candle of God* is the focus of the climactic episode about the cottage of candles. The quest is one of the most popular types of Jewish (and universal) folktales, especially fairy tales, but here the quest is not a conventional one for a lost princess, the sword of Moses, or a golden bird, but for an abstraction—justice. The fact that this story comes from Afghanistan seems entirely appropriate, for that is a harsh land where justice is very hard to find.

One way of reading this tale is to see that in arriving at the cottage, the man is on the verge of completing his quest to find justice, but he is first tested to see if he himself is just. Instead of proving worthy, he attempts to lengthen his life by depriving another of the years of life allotted to him. But he is caught and made to face the consequences of his action. In this sense he finds justice, for justice is exactly meted out. His error was to continually seek justice out in the world, but never to search for it within himself.

Sources:
IFA 7830, 8335; *Ha-Ba'al ha-Ketanah.*

62. THE CREATION OF WISDOM

Wisdom was the first of God's creations. Older than the universe, Wisdom was created two thousand years before the creation of the world. She came forth in the beginning from the mouth of God, and will exist for all eternity. Some say that God is the father of Wisdom, and she is God's ever-virgin daughter, whose true nature is intact and undefiled. Others identify Wisdom as the daughter of God and the firstborn mother of all things. Still others say that God is the husband of Wisdom, who lives with God, for God loves her.

Wisdom was present at the Creation of heaven and earth, as it is said, *I was there when He set the heavens into place and when He fixed the foundations of the earth* (Prov. 8:27-29). Some say that Wisdom was an observer in Creation, while others say that God created the world using Wisdom as the instrument of His workmanship, as it is said, *Yahweh founded the earth by wisdom* (Prov. 3:19).

Some say that Wisdom's throne is in a pillar of cloud. Others say that Wisdom made the circuit of the vault of heaven alone, and walked in the depths of the abyss, but she could not find a place in which to dwell. Everywhere she went, in the waves of the sea, in the whole earth, she sought a resting place, a place to build her house. Some say that a place was found for her in the heavens and she settled among the angels, while others say that that God assigned a place for her tent in this world, and she made her dwelling in Jacob, and received her inheritance in Israel. So too did Wisdom send seven prophets to help mankind, from Moses to Ezra.

Now Wisdom's house is a calm and serene haven, as it is said, *Wisdom has built her house* (Prov. 9:1). No sooner do you call to Wisdom than she stands ready to serve you at your gates. No sooner do you chant words of Torah than she chants at your door.

There is some debate over the identity of the mysterious figure of Wisdom (*Hokhmah* in Hebrew, *Sophia* in Greek) described in Proverbs 8:22-31:

The Lord created me at the beginning of His course, as the first of His works of old. In the distant past I was fashioned, at the beginning, at the origin of earth. There was still no deep when I was brought forth, no springs rich in water; before the foundation of the mountains were sunk, before the hills I was born. He had not yet made earth and fields, or the world's first clumps of clay. I was there when He set the heavens into place; when He fixed the horizon upon the deep; when He made the heavens above firm, and the fountains of the deep gushed forth. When He assigned the sea its limits, so that its waters never transgress His command; when He fixed the foundations of the earth, I was with Him as a confidant, a source of delight every day, rejoicing before Him at all times, rejoicing in His inhabited world, finding delight with mankind.

Based on this description, the personification of Wisdom in Proverbs certainly seems to represent a mythic figure. Wisdom appears earlier in Proverbs 3:19: *Yahweh by wisdom founded the earth; by understanding He established the heavens.* Jeremiah 10:12 speaks of God having established the world with wisdom: *He has made the earth by His power, has established the world by His wisdom,* as does Psalms 104:24: *How manifold are Your works, O Lord! With wisdom have You made them all.* One kabbalistic interpretation of the first verse of Genesis (*bereshit bara elohim et ha-shamayim ve et ha-aretz*) interprets the first words as "With the beginning" instead of "In the beginning," since *bereshit* can be understood both ways. *Reshit,* "the beginning," is then identified with Wisdom, since Proverbs 8:22 states that *"God created me at the beginning."*

Drawing on his allegorical method, Philo identifies God as the "father" of all that was created, and Wisdom as the "mother," i.e., the knowledge with which God had intercourse, though not in the manner of humans, to engender all that was created (*De Ebrietate* 30). This is a good example of how Philo's allegories straddle allegory and myth.

Some view Wisdom as an early personification of God's feminine aspect, the *Shekhinah.* Wisdom also resembles the Gnostic concept of the *Anima Mundi,* the "world soul." Indeed, the most extensive development of Wisdom as a mythic figure is found in Gnostic literature. See, for example, Ptolemy's version of the Gnostic myth in *Against Heresies* by Irenaeus 1.1.1-1.8.5, which was the best-known account of Gnostic myth until the discovery of the Coptic manuscripts of Nag Hammadi.

In some texts, Wisdom is given a more active role in Creation. In *3 Enoch* 30:8, for example, on the sixth day of Creation God commanded Wisdom to create man out of the seven components: his flesh from earth, his blood from dew and from the sun, his eyes from the bottomless sea, his bones from stone, his reason from the speed of the angels, his veins and hair from the grass of the earth, his spirit from God's spirit and from the wind.

Studies:

Job 28:13-28; Proverbs 120:33, 81:31, 91:6; *Targum Neophyti* on Genesis 3:24; Philo, *De Cherubim* 14:49; Philo, *De Fuga et Inventione* 50-52; Philo, *De Virtutibus* 62; Philo, *De Ebrietate* 30; Philo, *Quaestiones et Solutiones in Genesim* 4:97; *1 Enoch* 42; *Wisdom of Solomon* 7:25ff., 8:3; *Midrash Mishlei* 8; *The Wisdom of Ben Sira* 24:3-9; *Sancti Irenaei libros quinque adversus haereses* 1:30; *Odes of Solomon* 7; *Hellenistic Synagogal Prayers* 4:38; *Genesis Rabbah* 1:1.

Studies:

Wisdom Has Built Her House: Studies on the Figure of Sophia in the Bible by Silvia Schroer.

63. MOTHER ZION

Mother Zion cries and laments over the children of Israel when they are in exile, and she waits for them to return to her bosom.

When Jeremiah saw the smoke of the Temple in Jerusalem rising up, he broke down. And when he saw the stones that once were the walls of the Temple, he said: "What road have the exiles taken? I will go and perish with them."

So Jeremiah accompanied them down the road covered with blood until they reached the river Euphrates. Then he thought to himself: "If I go on to Babylon, who will comfort those left in Jerusalem?" Therefore he took his leave of the exiles, and when they saw he was leaving, they wept, as it is said, *By the rivers of Babylon, there we sat, sat and wept, as we thought of Zion* (Ps. 137:1).

As he was returning to Jerusalem, Jeremiah lifted his eyes and saw a woman seated at the top of a mountain, dressed in black, crying in distress, in great need of comfort. So too was Jeremiah in tears, wondering who would comfort him. He approached the woman, saying, "If you are a woman, speak, but if you are a spirit, depart at once!" She said: "Do you not recognize me? I am she who has borne seven sons, whose father went into exile in a distant city by the sea. Then a messenger brought the news that my husband, the father of my children, had been slain. And on the heels of that messenger came another with the news that my house had fallen in and slain my seven sons."

Jeremiah said: "Do you deserve any more comfort than Mother Zion, who has been made into a pasture for the beasts?" And she replied: "I am Mother Zion, the mother of seven, as it is said, *She who bore seven is forlorn, utterly disconsolate*" (Jer. 15:9).

This myth grows out of the verse *She who bore seven is forlorn, utterly disconsolate* (Jer. 15:9). It also is linked to Isaiah 66:8: *For as soon as Zion travailed, she brought forth her children.* The "she" is identified with the Land of Israel, giving birth to the figure of Mother Zion, a personification of Zion. Mother Zion cries and laments over the children of Israel when they are in exile, and she waits for them to return to her bosom. There is also an important passage in 2 Kings 19:21-28 concerning "Fair Maiden Zion," another feminine personification of Zion. This is also understood to be the feminine personification of Jerusalem: *Fair Maiden Zion despises you, she mocks at you; Fair Jerusalem shakes her head at you.* Other passages in Isaiah personify Jerusalem's grief in ways identical to that of Mother Zion: *Her gates shall lament and mourn; and she being desolate shall sit upon the ground* (Isa. 3:26).

At the same time, Mother Zion is an early incarnation of the *Shekhinah*, who is the mother of Israel, and whose home was the Temple in Jerusalem. Thus the link between Mother Zion and the *Shekhinah* is a natural one, and Mother Zion may be viewed as one of the personas of the *Shekhinah*, as distinct as Her identity as the Bride of God. Still, the figure of Mother Zion must be seen as a strong remnant of goddess worship in Judaism, where Mother Zion is the goddess of Zion. The concept of Zion itself attributes a sacred quality to the Land of Israel, transforming it into the Holy Land, and making a personification such as Mother Zion possible.

An earlier version of this vision of a mourning woman, much like that in *Pesikta Rabbati*, is found in *IV Ezra* 9:38-10:24, dating from around the first century. Thus a strong case can be made that there is a direct chain of tradition from Jeremiah 15:9 to *IV Ezra* to *Pesikta Rabbati*, an early medieval midrash. A subsequent version of this story, dating from the sixteenth century, concerns a vision of Rabbi Abraham Berukhim. See "A Vision at the Wailing Wall," p. 63.

Sources:
Pesikta Rabbati 26:7; *4 Ezra* 9:38-10:24; *Em ha-Banim S'mehah.*

Studies:
"The Metamorphosis of Narrative Traditions: Two Stories from Sixteenth Century Safed" by Aryeh Wineman.

64. THE CREATION OF THE *SHEKHINAH*

God's heavenly treasures were hidden in the innermost of many chambers. They could not be revealed to anyone, for they were too well hidden.

So God decided to bring together His heavenly treasures in his daughter, the *Shekhinah*. That way he would make them available to the world, but only to those who knew where they could be found.

So God saw to it that His daughter, the *Shekhinah*, contained within Herself all the paths of wisdom. Whoever knows those paths has access to God, and to all heavenly wisdom. And whoever would like to fathom those paths must turn to Her for help, for only She knows where God has hidden His heavenly treasures.

This myth is presented in the form of a parable in *Sefer ha-Bahir*, where God is identified as a king, as is standard in rabbinic parables about God. His daughter is the *Shekhinah*. Despite the allegorical format, the myth being conveyed is quite apparent—it is the myth of the divine pair, but here the male and female are both somehow contained within the same mythic figure. Thus God contains both the male and the female elements, even though they may appear to act independently of each other. Here monotheism reclaims the wholeness of God no matter how many aspects of God are portrayed. From this perspective, dualism itself becomes a form of monotheism. This paradox makes it possible to define a divinity capable of changing His mind, who could have masculine and feminine aspects and still be considered a single divine being.

The concept that God has masculine and feminine aspects is explicitly stated in *Zohar* 3:290a: "As the Ancient One, whose name be blessed, took on a form, He shaped everything in male and female form. In another form things could not exist. Therefore the first beginning of development was at once male and female, with *Hokhmah* as father and *Binah* as mother." And the *Zohar* restates the *Bahir's* identification of the *Shekhinah* as mother, daughter, and sister: "She (*Malkhut*—the *sefirah* representing the *Shekhinah*) is sometimes called daughter and sometimes sister, and here She is called mother. And in fact She is all these" (*Zohar* 2:100b).

What are the heavenly treasures in the parable? They are the secrets of Creation and other heavenly mysteries. God is not going to reveal these to everyone, but only to the initiated. These secrets were all used to create God's daughter, representing God's feminine aspect, known as the *Shekhinah*. Thus all the mysteries of God are focused in this single figure.

The parable in *Sefer ha-Bahir* also states that God hid His treasures not only in the *Shekhinah*, but in Her garments as well. These garments can be identified as the Oral Torah, or even as the Torah itself. This suggests that the Torah is the means by which God reveals His secrets of Creation.

See "God's Daughter," p. 312.

Sources:
Sefer ha-Bahir 63.

Studies:
The Old Rabbinic Doctrine of God by A. Marmorstein, pp. 103-104.
"*Shekhinah*: The Feminine Element in Divinity" in *On the Mystical Shape of the Godhead* by Gershom Scholem, pp. 140-196.
"Daughter, Sister, Bride and Mother: Images of the Femininity of God in the Early Kabbala" by Peter Schäfer.
"The Metamorphosis of Narrative Traditions: Two Stories from Sixteenth Century Safed" by Aryeh Wineman.

65. GOD'S NAMES FOR THE *SHEKHINAH*

Because of His love for the *Shekhinah*, God sometimes calls Her "My sister," since they are both from the same place. Sometimes He calls Her "My daughter," since She is truly His daughter. And sometimes He calls Her "My Mother."

When Abraham said of Sarah, *"She is my sister"* (Gen. 20:2), he was speaking about the *Shekhinah*, who was constantly with Sarah. Indeed, when Abraham saw the *Shekhinah* in the abode of Sarah, he was emboldened to declare, *"She is my sister."* For in so speaking, Abraham was making a mystical allusion, for the *Shekhinah* is the daughter of Supernal

Wisdom, and in calling her his sister, Abraham was following the admonition, *Say unto Wisdom, you are my sister* (Prov. 7:4).

> The *Shekhinah* represents the feminine aspect of God. In this passage from the *Sefer ha-Bahir*, the point is made that all representations of the feminine are included. For just as humans have daughters, sisters, brides, and mothers, so the divine feminine figure has all of these characteristics as well.
>
> Abraham's identification of Sarah as his sister is interpreted in the Zohar as a reference not to Sarah, but to the *Shekhinah*. The *Zohar* states that Abraham used the term in a mystic sense, as in the verse *my sister, my love, my dove, my undefiled* (S. of S. 5:2). The *Zohar* also identifies the *Shekhinah* with the figure of Wisdom, linking *"She is my sister"* with the verse, *Say unto wisdom, You are my sister* (Prov. 7:4).
>
> *Sources:*
> *Sefer ha-Bahir* 63; *Zohar* 1:80a-82a, 1:11b-112a, 2:98b-99a.
>
> *Studies:*
> "Daughter, Sister, Bride and Mother: Images of the Femininity of God in the Early Kabbala," by Peter Schäfer.
> "Bride, Spouse, Daughter" by Arthur Green.

66. THE TWO *SHEKHINAHS*

God's daughter, the *Shekhinah*, exists in two realms at the same time. There is a *Shekhinah* above, just as there is a *Shekhinah* below.

In Her divine manifestation, She stays in heaven, as it is said, *All of the glory of the king's daughter is within Her* (Ps. 45:14). There she guards the secrets of the Written Torah.

But in her earthly manifestation she comes down to earth from a faraway land, from the side of light, and she reveals the secrets of the Oral Torah. For She is God's messenger, and the world is illuminated through Her deeds, for her deeds give light to the world.

So that they can always communicate, God has built a window between them, and whenever She needs Her Father, or He needs Her, they join one another through the window. In this way God Himself enters the world in the form of His daughter.

> This parable in *Sefer ha-Bahir* presents the relationship between the feminine elements of the sefirot in mythic terms. The two *Shekhinahs*, also known as the Two Mothers, refer to the third *sefirah*, *Binah*, the symbol of the mother, and the tenth *sefirah*, *Malkhut*, which represents the *Shekhinah*. Thus *Binah* stands for the upper feminine, the heavenly *Shekhinah*, and *Malkhut* stands for the earthly feminine, whose home is in the Temple in Jerusalem. The importance of this myth is to demonstrate that a divine feminine presence can be found above and below. The role of the heavenly *Shekhinah* derives from the position of the third *sefirah*, *Binah*, where the *Shekhinah* represents God's glory, and she is united with God in the innermost chamber of the king. At the same time, the earthly *Shekhinah* is linked to the tenth *sefirah*, *Malkhut*, where the *Shekhinah* is in a position to exert her influence on the lives of human beings.
>
> Another way of reading this myth is to see it as referring to the two Torahs, the Written Torah and the Oral Torah. *Sefer ha-Bahir* makes an explicit reference to this tradition in identifying the *Shekhinah* as a princess, coming from "a faraway land, from the side of light," which would seem to be a reference to heaven. In this kabbalistic myth, the heavenly manifestation of the *Shekhinah* is linked to the Written Torah, and Her earthly manifestation is linked to the Oral Torah. While the accepted rabbinic tradition is that God revealed both the Written and the Oral Torah at Mount Sinai, *Sefer ha-Bahir* seems to be suggesting that the Written Torah remains in heaven, while the Oral Torah has been revealed on earth. See "The Betrothal of the Torah," p. 256.

Rabbi Nachman of Bratslav's famous first story, "The Lost Princess," from *Sippurei Ma'asiyot*, also concerns a princess, and, as is almost always the case, the king represents God, while the princess represents the *Shekhinah*, the feminine aspect of God. In "The Lost Princess," Rabbi Nachman describes this princess as having vanished mysteriously, somehow lost to the Other Side. The quest to return the lost princess from Her exile turns out to be an arduous one, which remains unfinished at the end of Rabbi Nachman's story.

Sources:
Sefer ha-Bahir 54.

Studies:
Origins of the Kabbalah by Gershom Scholem, pp. 49-198.
"Daughter, Sister, Bride and Mother: Images of the Femininity of God in the Early Kabbala." by Peter Schäfer.
"Bride, Spouse, Daughter" by Arthur Green.
The Early Kabbalah, edited by Joseph Dan, pp. 59-69.
"The Metamorphosis of Narrative Traditions: Two Stories from Sixteenth-Century Safed" by Aryeh Wineman.
"The Quest for the Lost Princess" by Howard Schwartz.

67. THE EARTHLY DWELLING OF THE *SHEKHINAH*

From the beginning of the world's Creation, the *Shekhinah* dwelt in this lower world. Her original abode was in the Garden of Eden, residing on a cherub under the Tree of Life. Indeed, the primal root of the *Shekhinah* was planted there. Bands of angels descended from heaven to serve the will of the *Shekhinah* in all ways. When God went in and out of the Garden, everyone in the world gazed upon the splendor of the *Shekhinah*, which radiated from one end of the world to the other, far more brilliant than the sun.

When Adam and Eve were expelled from Eden, they dwelt at the Gates of the Garden to gaze upon the radiant appearance of the *Shekhinah*. In the presence of the *Shekhinah* they experienced no illness nor suffered any pain. No demons could obtain power over them, nor could they injure them.

Some say that the *Shekhinah* remained on earth until Adam sinned, and then was removed to the first heaven. Others say that as soon as Adam broke the commandment, the *Shekhinah* fled on Her own from the Garden of Eden. Still others say that the *Shekhinah* remained on earth until the rise of idolatry in the generation of Enosh. Using magic taught to them by the fallen angel Azazel, that wicked generation brought down the sun, the moon and the stars and stationed them before their idols, to serve them.

Then the angels brought a complaint before God, and God immediately removed the *Shekhinah* from their midst. And as the *Shekhinah* ascended on high, the angels surrounded Her with psalms and songs and by the sound of the shofar and trumpets, as it is said, *God went up with a fanfare of trumpets* (Ps. 47:6). Indeed, some say that in this way the angels themselves succeeded in raising up the *Shekhinah* on high. The glory of the *Shekhinah* rose from the heavenly firmament to the chambers of the palace, from the chambers of the palace to the palace of majesty, from the palace of majesty to the fiery citadel, from the fiery citadel to the flaming castle, from the flaming castle to the ranks of the angels, from the ranks of the angels to the wheels of the chariot, from the wheels of the chariot to the Throne of Glory.

Then the heavens rejoiced, clothed in joyful garments and wrapped in glory. The sun and the moon and all the stars danced before the Throne of Glory and before God. But while the heavens celebrated, the Prince of the World and all the orders of creation put on mourning and clothed themselves with grief and sighing, as it is said, *Therefore the land will mourn* (Hos. 4:3).

Still others say that the *Shekhinah* departed from earth after the sin of Adam, but returned when the Ark of the Tabernacle was constructed, and made Her home there. Later, She took up residence in the Holy of Holies of the Temple in Jerusalem and remained there until the Temple was destroyed. Some say that the *Shekhinah* returned to heaven after that, while others say that She went into exile with her children, Israel, but she still returns from time to time to visit the *Kotel*, the last remaining wall of the Temple, that once was Her home.

Then there are those who insist that the *Shekhinah* never dwelt in the lower world from the time of the Creation until the Tabernacle was erected. But from that time forward she did dwell there.

The *Shekhinah* represents God's immanence in this world. In rabbinic literature the term *Shekhinah* is used primarily as a synonym for God, or for God's presence in the world. But in the kabbalistic texts the role of the *Shekhinah* takes on a mythic independence. For by the very act of presenting the *Shekhinah* as dwelling on earth while God dwells in heaven, some kind of mythic separation is suggested.

This myth almost certainly derives from the verse *They heard the sound of the Lord God moving about in the garden* (Gen. 3:8). In *Pesikta de-Rav Kahana* 1:1, this verse is said to prove God's presence on earth at the beginning of time. This text also asserts, "At the beginning of time, the root of the *Shekhinah* was fixed in the regions of the earth below." *Numbers Rabbah* 13:6 states, "From the very first day on which God created the world, God was eager to dwell with His creatures in the terrestrial regions." Why did God want to dwell on earth rather than in heaven? The text goes on to explain that "because God was alone in His world, He yearned to dwell with his creatures in the terrestrial regions." Thus this myth of the earthly dwelling of the *Shekhinah* presumes a terrestrial, rather than a celestial, home for the *Shekhinah*, who is God's Bride. That is why the *Shekhinah* is known as the Divine Presence, thus the presence of God in this world.

In some versions of this myth, the earthly home of the *Shekhinah* is said to have existed from the creation of the world, with the *Shekhinah* dwelling in the Garden of Eden; in other versions, the descent of the *Shekhinah* did not take place until the Tabernacle was erected and God caused the *Shekhinah* to dwell within it, and later in the Holy of Holies in the Temple in Jerusalem.

Other versions of this myth, such as that found in *Avot de-Rabbi Natan* 34:8 and alluded to in *Zohar* 1:75a, suggest that God descended to earth in ten descents: one into the Garden of Eden, one in the generation of the Tower of Babel, one in Sodom, one in Egypt, one at the sea, one at Mount Sinai, one in the pillar of cloud, one in the Temple, and one that is destined to take place at the time of the messianic era. Each of these descents is explained by an appropriate prooftext, such as, *They heard the sound of the Lord God moving about in the Garden* (Gen. 3:8) or, *Yahweh came down to look at the city and tower* (Gen. 11:5). Here, however, the use of the term *Shekhinah* seems to refer primarily to God's visits to this world.

Between the time of dwelling in the Garden and that of the Tabernacle, however, God removed the *Shekhinah* from the world in seven stages, as a result of the sins of subsequent generations. Thus the *Shekhinah* withdrew to the first heaven when Adam sinned, and withdrew further from this world following the sin of Cain, the generation of Enosh, the generation of the Flood, that of the Dispersion, that of the Sodomites, and that of the Egyptians in the days of Abraham. These phases are known as "the Removal of the *Shekhinah*." Accounts of the removal of the *Shekhinah* are found in *Numbers Rabbah*, *Avot de-Rabbi Natan*, *3 Enoch*, *Midrash Aleph Bet*, and *Gevurot ha-Shem* 66.

In *Pesikta de-Rav Kahana* 1:1, a process of return is also described. Thus, when Abraham arose, the *Shekhinah* came back from the seventh heaven to the sixth; likewise, the merits of Isaac, Jacob, Levi, Kehat, Amram, and Moses each brought the *Shekhinah* closer to earth. So the erection of the Tabernacle was the final stage in a process of return that had begun in the time of Abraham.

Midrash Aleph Bet proposes that the songs and music made by the angels raised up the *Shekhinah* from the Garden of Eden to the upper worlds.

Numbers Rabbah 12:6 insists that the *Shekhinah* did not descend to earth again until the Tabernacle of the Ark had been erected.

Sources:
Pesikta de-Rav Kahana 1:1, 13:11; *Genesis Rabbah* 3:9, 19:7, 23:6; *Numbers Rabbah* 12:6, 13:2; *Song of Songs Rabbah* 6; *Avot de-Rabbi Natan* 34:8-9; *Midrash Aleph Bet* 4:1-7; *3 Enoch* 5:1-5; *B. Shabbath* 87b; *Midrash Tehillim* 11:3; *Midrash Tanhuma* on Gen. 2:5-6; *Sha'arei Orah* 1; *Zohar* 1:56a; *Gevurot ha-Shem* 66.

Studies:
The Immanence of God in Rabbinical Literature by J. Abelson, pp. 117-130.
On the Mystical Shape of the Godhead by Gershom Scholem, pp. 140-196.

68. THE ROAMING OF THE *SHEKHINAH*

The plan of Creation was to mirror the upper and lower worlds. Therefore, at the beginning of Creation, the *Shekhinah* dwelt in the lower world. At first, the worlds above and below drew on each other, and the links between them were perfect, drawing from above to below, and from below to above.

But because the *Shekhinah* dwelt below, the heavens and the earth became fragmented. Then Adam sinned, ruining the channels linking the worlds, and Creation became unraveled. The *Shekhinah* completely fled from this world.

It was Abraham who drew the *Shekhinah* back from the world above. His body served as a seat for the *Shekhinah*, who would sit on his back, as it is said, *God arose above Abraham* (Gen. 17:22). So did Isaac and Jacob serve as the throne of God's Chariot. Still, the *Shekhinah* was without a home. During the day She would fly through the air, carried on the backs of the Forefathers, but She never found the peace She knew at the beginning of Creation.

Then Moses and the children of Israel came and built the Tabernacle and its sacred vessels. They repaired the broken channels, until living water flowed again. Then the *Shekhinah* returned to dwell in the lower spheres. But now She dwelt in the Tent of Meeting, and not on the ground, as at the beginning of Creation. That is the meaning of the verse *And let them make Me a sanctuary that I may dwell among them* (Exod. 25:8).

So it was that wherever Israel wandered, the *Shekhinah* dwelt among them, roaming from place to place. This distressed David, and he yearned to find a permanent place for the *Shekhinah* to dwell. God sent a message to David through Nathan the Prophet: *Thus says the Lord: "Are you the one to build a house for Me to dwell in? From the day I brought my people out of the land of Egypt to this day I have not dwelt in a house, but have moved about in tent and Tabernacle"* (2 Sam. 7:5-6).

So David designed the form of the Temple to create a throne and dwelling place for the *Shekhinah*. Solomon came after that and built the Temple, and the *Shekhinah* descended to Her eternal home and once more dwelt in the land. Once again the channels between heaven and earth were open, and in this way the *Shekhinah* drew abundant blessings down on Jerusalem and on all of the Holy Land. She will never move from this holy place, as it is said, *This is My resting-place for all time* (Ps. 132:14).

This kabbalistic version of the earthly descent of the *Shekhinah* comes from *Sha'arei Orah*, a thirteenth century kabbalistic text by Yosef Gikatilla. Here can be found the fully developed kabbalistic reworking of the myth of the *Shekhinah*. At the same time, there are some unique aspects of Gikatilla's version of the myth that almost seem to anticipate Lurianic kabbalah in the sixteenth century.

The primary quest of the myth is to find a home for the *Shekhinah*. At the beginning of Creation, the *Shekhinah* makes Her home on earth, to balance God's dwelling on high. The balance between above and below makes contact between them possible. This is described as an ideal condition, yet some kind of flaw in the plan of Creation begins to emerge, an imbalance between above and below. This initial fragmentation is followed by Adam's sin, after which the *Shekhinah* departed from the lower world and returned on high. Only Abraham and the other patriarchs succeeded in drawing the *Shekhinah* back to this world. But the quest to find the *Shekhinah* a home does not end until Moses builds the Tabernacle and Solomon builds the Temple, the *Shekhinah's* true home on earth. Gikatilla's myth states this directly: "At the time of Adam there was no fixed place for the *Shekhinah*. When Solomon built the Temple, there was a permanent place for the *Shekhinah* in Israel" (chap. 8).

In both Gikatilla's version of the myth and in the myth of the Ari, blame for the fallen state of existence is not placed on Adam. Instead, it is strongly suggested that there was a flaw in the plan of the divinity. In Gikatilla's myth, there is the statement that "because the *Shekhinah* dwelt below, the heavens and the earth became fragmented." This suggests there was an inherent flaw in the original plan for Creation, which was to mirror the upper and lower worlds. Somehow it became unbalanced, and the links between the worlds above and below began to break apart.

This is precisely equal to the effect of the shattered vessels in the myth of Isaac Luria. Both are examples of cosmic catastrophes. In the Ari's creation myth, God sends forth vessels filled with light, which shatter, scattering sparks of light throughout the universe. This is known as the Shattering of the Vessels. This myth, like Gikatilla's, seems to insist that there is some kind of flaw in the divinity. For Gikatilla, who preceded the Ari, the flaw was the original separation of God and the *Shekhinah*, with one dwelling above and the other below. Somehow this threw things out of balance, leading to the fragmentation of the links between the upper and lower worlds. Thus both texts suggest that the primary blame for the cosmic catastrophe that resulted in a fallen world was not the fault of man, but was inherent in God's plan of Creation. This is a daring theological position, since it also implies that God could be imperfect, for how could a perfect God create an imperfect plan? Thus it would appear that Luria had some kabbalistic precedent for his seminal myth.

This is also a *Merkavah* myth. Usually the *Shekhinah* and the *Merkavah* do not appear in the same myths, but this is an exception. Here we find the radical notion that the patriarchs are said to serve as God's Chariot, the *Merkavah*, which is described as a Throne and Chariot at the same time, hurtling through space. The myth is also interesting in presenting the *Shekhinah* as the rider in the Chariot, whereas most *Merkavah* imagery portrays God seated on His Throne of Glory.

The strangest aspect of this *Merkavah* myth is the role of the patriarchs. How could the patriarchs either singly (as in *Sha'arei Orah* 8) or together (*Sha'arei Orah* 1) serve as God's Chariot? The idea seems best understood metaphorically—the patriarchs were able to bring down the *Shekhinah* and they served as a kind of spiritual foundation for God in this world. The *Merkavah*, representing both Throne and Chariot, thus symbolizes such a foundation. But it is possible to trace the development of this idea to the statement in the Talmud (*B. Shabbat* 152b) that the souls of the righteous are hidden under the Throne of Glory. But in *Zohar* 1:113a (*Midrash ha-Ne'elam*) and other sources in the *Zohar*, the metaphor begins to take on a mythic life of its own. The *Shekhinah* is described as riding on the backs of the patriarchs. This in itself is a strange image, until we understand that here the patriarchs are literally being visualized as serving as a flying Throne and Chariot. The statement "The Patriarchs are the Merkavah" recurs in Genesis Rabbah 47:6, 69:3 and 82:6.

This theme of the patriarchs serving as God's Chariot is also found in a dream of Hayim Vital's in *Sefer ha-Hezyonot*: "I dreamed that there was a book open before me and it was written there that the souls of the *Tzaddikim* are hewn out of the divine throne. After their deaths, they return there and are made the Chariot for the *Shekhinah*."

Sources:

B. Shabbat 152b; Zohar 1:113a, 1:125b; Zohar Hadash 24a; Tikkunei ha-Zohar, Tikkun 57;
   Sha'arei Orah 1, 8; Sefer ha-Hezyonot 2:27.

Studies:

Gates of Light/Sha'are Orah by Joseph ben Abraham Gikatilla.

69. THE GARMENTS OF THE *SHEKHINAH*

The *Shekhinah* has many garments, consisting of holy angels from above and Israel from below. From these garments God created the Throne of Glory, as well as heaven and earth and all the creatures therein.

The robe of the *Shekhinah* is made of light. The light of the first day is reflected from that robe. The *Shekhinah* wears that robe whenever Israel gives forth light through good deeds. But when Israel does evil, She is garbed in the black garments of Lilith, and She is forced to wear them until Israel repents.

> The *Shekhinah* is often described as a bride wearing a garment of light. This myth describes the *Shekhinah* as wearing garments of light whenever God is pleased with the good deeds of Israel, and black garments when Israel sins. *Tikkunei ha-Zohar* explains that the *Shekhinah* puts on these harsh garments to protect Israel. Alternately, the harsh garments are identified as black garments belonging to Lilith, thereby putting the *Shekhinah*, the positive feminine aspect of God, under the power of the evil Lilith, who represents the dark feminine. Indeed, in the *Zohar* and other kabbalistic texts, Lilith and the *Shekhinah* are portrayed as feminine polar opposites.
>
> The robe of the *Shekhinah* is linked to the light of the first day of Creation. See "The Light of the First Day," p. 83.
>
> *Sources*:
> *Tikkunei ha-Zohar* 22 (65a); *Zohar* 3:273a.

70. THE SACRED BEDCHAMBER

On the very day King Solomon completed the building of the Temple in Jerusalem, God and His Bride were united, and Her face shone with perfect joy. Then there was joy for all, above and below.

As long as the Temple stood, it served as the sacred bedchamber of God the King and His Bride, the *Shekhinah*. Every midnight She would enter through the place of the Holy of Holies, and She and God would celebrate their joyous union. The loving embrace of the King and His Queen assured the well-being not only of Israel, but also of the whole world.

The King would come to the Queen and lie in Her arms, and all that She asked of Him he would fulfill. He placed his left arm under Her head, His right arm embraced Her, and He let Her enjoy His strength. Their pleasure in each other was indescribable. He made His home with Her and took His delight between Her breasts. They lay in a tight embrace, Her image impressed on His body like a seal imprinted upon a page, as it is written, *Set me as a seal upon Your heart* (S. of S. 8:6).

As long as the Temple stood, the King would come down from his heavenly abode every midnight, seek out his Bride, and enjoy her in their sacred bedchamber. But when the Temple was destroyed, the *Shekhinah* went into exile, and Bride and Groom were torn apart.

> This explicit myth portrays the interaction of God and His Bride as a highly eroticized coupling, a sacred copulation (*zivvug ha-kodesh*). This is a primal image of the sacred marriage (*hieros gamos*). In *Zohar* 1:120b, this is referred to as "the one total coupling, the full coupling, as is proper." *Zohar* 3:296a expands on this: "The *Matronita* (the *Shekhinah*) united herself with the king. From this, one body resulted." This illustrates the strong sexual dimension of kabbalistic thought, especially in the *Zohar*. It also demonstrates the direct correlation between the unity and union of God and His Bride and the existence of the Temple in Jerusalem. The destruction of the Temple

brings about the separation of God and the *Shekhinah* and sends the *Shekhinah* into exile. All of this comes about because of the sins of Israel. When Israel sins, these sins give power to the forces of evil, preventing the *Shekhinah* from uniting with Her husband, and forcing the divine couple to turn away from each other. When Israel repents, God and the *Shekhinah* turn back to each other.

So important is the coupling of God and the *Shekhinah* that in *Zohar* 3:296a, Rabbi Shimon bar Yohai, the principal speaker in the *Zohar* describes it as the deepest of all mysteries.

According to *B. Ta'anit* 16a and *Song of Songs Rabbah* 1:66, one of the names for the place where the Temple was built was "the bedchamber."

Sources:
Zohar 1:120b, 3:74b, 3:296a; *Zohar Hadash, Midrash Eikhah*, 92c-92d.

71. THE CASTING DOWN OF THE *SHEKHINAH*

Before God destroyed His house and the holy land below, He first cast His Bride from on high, bringing Her down from where she took nourishment from the sacred heavens. Only then did He destroy the Temple in the world below. For these are the ways of God when He wishes to judge the world: First He passes judgment on the world above, and then He establishes His justice in the world below.

This myth is a variant of the myth of the exile of the *Shekhinah*, creating a link between the destruction of the Temple and the departure of the *Shekhinah* from Her heavenly home. It is shocking in its violence—God casts His Bride out of heaven, an exile parallel to that of Adam and Eve from the Garden of Eden. One purpose of the myth is to demonstrate that God also suffered great losses at that time the Temple was destroyed. Here, furthermore, it is asserted that God's losses preceded those of the Temple. For only after God had cast out His Bride from on high did He permit the destruction of the Temple. See "The Exile of the *Shekhinah*," p. 57.

Like the *Shekhinah*, Lucifer was cast out of heaven. But while Lucifer led a rebellion against God, there is no evidence that the *Shekhinah* did anything wrong. Instead, her removal from heaven symbolizes the high price paid above as well as below.

Sources:
Zohar 2:175a.

72. THE WANDERING OF THE *SHEKHINAH*

The sins of the Israelites caused the *Shekhinah* to go into exile. As the sins grew, the *Shekhinah* wandered away from them. She wandered from the cover of the Ark to one of the cherubs, from the first cherub to the second, from the second cherub to the threshold of the Temple, from the threshold to the court of the priests, from the court to the altar, from the altar to the roof of the Temple, from the roof to the wall, from the wall to the city of Jerusalem, from the city to the Mount of Olives, from the mount to the desert.

During this time the *Shekhinah* hid Herself in exile like the moon behind a cloud and could not be seen. Even though Israel yearned to look at the light, it was impossible to see Her, because She was in darkness. That was a darkness so deep it is known as "the darkened light."

Some say that the *Shekhinah* lingered in the wilderness for six months, waiting for Israel to repent. But when they did not, She proclaimed, "Let them perish!" Others say that the *Shekhinah* dwelt for three and a half years on the Mount of Olives, crying out three times a day, *"Turn back, O rebellious children!"* (Jer. 3:22). When this proved to be futile, she said, *"I will return to my abode"* (Hos. 5:15), and She departed the city through the Gate of Mercy and ascended to heaven to await their repentance. And it is said that when She comes back, She will return through that same gate.

> This myth recounts ten stages of the wandering of the *Shekhinah* from the Temple to the desert. At each station she becomes more remote from the people of Israel, driven away by their sins. The Gate of Mercy through which the *Shekhinah* departs Jerusalem was said to have been built by King Solomon with stones brought him by the Queen of Sheba. It is said that after the time of the destruction of the Temple, this gate sank into the earth. But its restoration is expected at the time of the coming of the Messiah, for the children of Israel will return through that gate.
>
> This myth is parallel to that of the Removal of the *Shekhinah*, in which each major sin of Israel resulted in the *Shekhinah* moving further away from this world. See the commentary to "The Earthly Dwelling of the *Shekhinah*" for a discussion of it.
>
> *Sources:*
> B. *Rosh ha-Shanah* 31a; *Lamentations Rabbah* 25; *Avot de-Rabbi Natan* 34; *Otzar Ma'asiyot; Zohar* 3:45b; IFA 10020.

73. THE LAMENT OF THE *SHEKHINAH*

Since the destruction of the Temple, the *Shekhinah* descends night after night to the place of the Temple, enters the Holy of Holies, and sees that Her dwelling-house and Her couch are ruined and soiled. And She wanders up and down, wails and laments, and weeps bitterly. She looks at the place of the cherubs and lifts up Her voice and says, "My couch, My couch, My dwelling-place, where My husband would come to Me and lie in My arms, and all that I asked of Him, He would give Me. My couch, My couch, do you not remember how I came to you in joy and contentment, and how those youths, the cherubim, came forth to meet Me, beating their wings in welcome? How has the Ark of the Covenant which stood here come to be forgotten? From here went forth nourishment for all the world and light and blessing to all. Now I seek My husband in every place, but he is not here. My husband, My husband, where have You gone? Do You not remember how You held Your left arm beneath my head and Your right arm embraced me, and You vowed that You would never cease loving Me? And now You have forgotten Me."

> This myth offers a moving account of the *Shekhinah* as a spurned lover. It follows the explicit husband-wife imagery of "The Sacred Bedchamber," which derives from the same source, *Zohar Hadash*.
>
> *Sources:*
> Zohar Hadash, Midrash Eikhah, 74b.

74. THE WAILING OF THE *SHEKHINAH*

Each person of Israel is a member of the *Shekhinah*. If any one of Israel abandons his faith for another, he is cutting himself off from the *Shekhinah*. Then the *Shekhinah* wails and says: "As long as the member is connected, there is some hope that it will recover, but when the member is cut off, no repair is possible."

> This teaching is attributed to the Ba'al Shem Tov. The people of Israel are considered to be the members of the *Shekhinah*—each person functions like an arm or a leg. But when they are converted—as happened in the time of the Ba'al Shem Tov to the

Frankists, who converted to Christianity—they not only cut themselves off from their people, but also from the *Shekhinah*. And like an arm or leg that has been amputated, there is no longer any hope of repair.

Sources:
Shivhei ha-Besht, no. 44.

75. THE EXILE OF THE *SHEKHINAH*

When the Temple was still standing, Israel would perform their rites, and bring offerings and sacrifices. And the *Shekhinah* rested upon them in the Temple, like a mother hovering over her children, and all faces were resplendent with light, so that there was blessing both above and below.

When the Temple was destroyed, the *Shekhinah* came and went up to all those places where She used to dwell, and She would weep for Her home and for Israel, who had gone into exile, and for all the righteous and the pious ones who had perished.

At that time the Holy One, blessed be He, questioned the *Shekhinah*, and said to her, "What ails you?" And She replied, weeping, "My children are in exile, and the Sanctuary has been burnt, so why should I remain here?" Now the Temple is destroyed and the *Shekhinah* is with Israel in exile and there is no joy to be found, above or below.

> The exile of God and His Bride is a primary example of the emergence of the *Shekhinah* as an independent mythical figure. The story also resembles the conflict between an angry couple, where the wife leaves the husband and accompanies the children, here the children of Israel.
>
> From the perspective of the *Zohar*, the fact that the *Shekhinah* accompanied Israel is evidence of God's attachment to Israel: "All the time Israel was in exile, the *Shekhinah* was in exile with them. And since the *Shekhinah* was with them, God remembered them, to do good to them and bring them out of exile" (*Zohar* 1:120b).
>
> The exile of the *Shekhinah* is presented in the form of a parable about a king in *Sefer ha-Bahir*, in which the king had a beautiful wife and children, but when the children turned to evil ways, the king became angry with the children and their mother. The mother then went to the children and upbraided them for their behavior and its consequences until they changed their ways and did the will of their father. Then the king remembered them and loved them as much as he did in the beginning, and also remembered their mother. The king, of course, is God, and the king's wife the *Shekhinah*, while the children are the children of Israel. According to Rabbi Shlomo Rabinowitz of Radomsk, "The *Shekhinah* protects Jews like a mother taking care of her children" (*Tiferet Shlomo* on Deuteronomy 29:27). The myth of the exile of the *Shekhinah* found in the *Zohar* follows this earlier parable closely, and the earlier parable may well be the inspiration for it. It is interesting to note that in the parable from *Sefer ha-Bahir*, the queen is responsible for the well-being of her children, and the fate of the queen depends on the fate of her children. When the children repent and God loves them once again, He also remembers His love for their mother, the queen.
>
> According to the *Zohar*, the exile of the *Shekhinah* that took place at the time of the destruction of the Temple was not Her first exile, but Her second. The first took place when Adam sinned, and the *Shekhinah* went into disgrace and was dismissed from the celestial palace, going into exile. Thus a distinct parallel is drawn between the consequences of the sin of the forbidden fruit and the destruction of the Temple. Both are regarded as cosmic catastrophes.
>
> The weeping of the *Shekhinah* in this myth has parallels with the weeping of Rachel in Jeremiah 15:17, and with the weeping of Mother Zion in Jeremiah 15:19, *4 Ezra* 9:38-10:24 (where there is a Mother Zion-type of figure) and in *Pesikta Rabbati* 26:7. Indeed, it is likely that Mother Zion was a precursor figure to the medieval kabbalistic evolution of the concept of the *Shekhinah* into the Bride of God. See "Mother Zion," p. 46.

The weeping of the *Shekhinah* is also central to the sixteenth century tale, "A Vision at the Wailing Wall." See this story, p. 63.

The kind of conflict between God and the *Shekhinah* reflected in this myth resembles the marital disputes between Zeus and Hera in Greek mythology. See the Introduction, p. lxv, for a discussion of the parallels between Zeus and Hera and God and the *Shekhinah*. See Graves, *The Greek Myths*, 13c, 13.1.

Sources:
Sefer ha-Bahir 76; *Zohar Hadash, Midrash Eikhah,* 92c-92d; *Zohar* 1:202b-203a; *No'am Elimelekh*; *B. Megillah* 29a; *Tiferet Shlomo* on Deuteronomy 27:2-7.

76. MOURNING OVER THE *SHEKHINAH*

After the Temple had been destroyed and the *Shekhinah* had gone into exile, all the angels went into mourning for Her, and they composed dirges and lamentations for her. So too did all the upper and lower realms weep for Her and go into mourning.

Then God came down from heaven and looked upon His house that had been burned. He looked for His people, who had gone into exile. And He inquired about His Bride, who had left Him. And just as she had suffered a change, so too did Her husband—His light no longer shone, and He was changed from what He had been. Indeed, by some accounts God was bound in chains.

God said to the ministering angels, "When a mortal king mourns, what does he do?" They said, "He extinguishes his torches." God said "I too shall do that. *The sun and moon will become black, and the stars stop shining*" (Joel 4:15).

God said, "When a mortal king mourns, what does he do?" They said, "He sits in silence." God said, "I too shall do that. I will sit alone and keep silent."

God said, "When a mortal king mourns, what does he do?" They said, "He sits and laments." God said, "I too shall do that."

> Here God and the angels are shown in mourning over the exile of the *Shekhinah*. Even the heavens and the earth are said to mourn, as in the verse, *"I clothe the skies in blackness and make their raiment sackcloth"* (Isa. 50:3). So too is the mourning of the angels confirmed with a prooftext: *The angels of peace wept bitterly* (Isa. 33:7).
>
> The most daring part of the myth is the suggestion that, having lost the *Shekhinah*, God's glory has somehow been reduced—"His light no longer shone, and He was changed from what He was before." What has been lost is the feminine aspect of God, and without it God is incomplete. This myth seems to contradict the general view that God is unchanging and eternal, and makes God dependent on His Bride in the same way that a husband is dependent on his wife. Indeed, God is here referred to as a "husband." In *Zohar* 1:182a God's diminishment is explained as follows: "The secret of the matter is that blessings reside only where male and female are together."
>
> The explanation in *Pesikta de-Rav Kahana* 13:9 that God was bound in chains, derives from God's promise that *"I will be with him in distress"* (Ps. 91:15), so that when Jeremiah was bound in chains, so too was God.
>
> *Sources*:
> *Pesikta de-Rav Kahana* 13:9, 15:3; *Zohar* 1:182a, 1:210a-210b.

77. THE SUFFERING OF THE *SHEKHINAH*

Wherever Israel is exiled, the *Shekhinah* is exiled with them and suffers with them. Those who are in this bitter exile should not be concerned with their personal distress, but should only lament the exile of the *Shekhinah*. For through Torah study and prayer, one is able to repair the limbs of the *Shekhinah* that were shattered in exile.

Here the exile and suffering of the *Shekhinah* are seen as a communal expression of the exile and suffering of Israel. Therefore, individuals "should not be concerned with their personal distress, but should only lament the exile of the *Shekhinah*." A similar view was expressed by Rabbi Nathan of Nemirov (1780-1845), the scribe of Rabbi Nachman of Bratslav, in writing about the meaning of Rabbi Nachman's story "The Lost Princess" in *Sippurei Ma'asiyot*: "Everyone in Israel is occupied with the search for the lost princess, to take her back to her father, for Israel as a whole has the character of the minister who searches for her." See "The *Shekhinah* Within," p. 63. For more on the limbs of the *Shekhinah* see "The Wailing of the *Shekhinah*," p. 56.

Above all, this myth insists that the quest to end the exile of the *Shekhinah* is a communal one for all the people of Israel. And until that takes place, the suffering of the *Shekhinah* must be shared by all of Israel. Rabbi Dov Ber offers a different perspective on the concept that all Jewish souls are the limbs of the *Shekhinah*, identifying each Jewish soul as a tiny particle of the *Shekhinah*, like a drop in the ocean (*Maggid Devarav le-Ya'akov* 66.)

Note the parallel here to the exile of the *Shekhinah* and the Ari's myth of the Shattering of the Vessels. Indeed, from a mythic perspective they are one and the same. The search for the lost princess is identical to the effort that must be made to Gather the Sparks, and in both cases the ultimate aim is to bring about the messianic era. See "The Shattering of the Vessels and the Gathering of the Sparks," p. 122.

Sources:
No'am Elimelekh; Iggeret ha-Kodesh 31 in *Tanya; Maggid Devarav le-Ya'akov* 66.

78. LILITH BECOMES GOD'S BRIDE

After God dismissed His Bride, the *Shekhinah*, from His presence, at the time of the destruction of the Temple, God brought in a maidservant to take Her place. Who is this maidservant? She is none other than Lilith, who once made her home behind the mill, and now the servant is heir to her mistress, as it is said, *A slave girl who supplants her mistress* (Prov. 30:23). She rules over the Holy Land as the *Shekhinah* once ruled over it. Thus the slave-woman has become the ruler of the House, and the true Bride has been imprisoned in the house of the slave-woman, the evil Lilith. There the Bride is held in exile with her offspring, whose hands are tied behind their backs, wearing many chains and shackles. That is a bitter time for the exiled Bride, who sobs because Her husband, God, does not throw His light upon Her. Her joy has fled because She sees Her rival, Lilith, in Her house, deriding Her. And when God sees his true Bride lying in the dust and suffering, He, too, will become embittered and descend to save Her from the strangers who are violating Her.

So it is that in the days to come news will come to God's consort, Lilith, that the time has come for her to go. Then she who plays the harlot will flee from the sanctuary, for if she were to come there when the woman of worth was present, she would perish.

Then God will restore the *Shekhinah* to Her place as in the beginning, and God and His true Bride will again couple with each other in joy. As for the evil slave-woman, God will no longer dwell with her, and she will cease to exist.

This startling myth describes the ascent of the demoness Lilith, in which she becomes God's consort after His separation from his Bride. It is based on an interpretation of the verse *A slave girl who supplants her mistress* (Prov. 30:23). The identification of Lilith as once living behind a mill is based on the verse about *the slave girl who is behind the millstones* (Exod. 11:5). In folk tradition, Lilith was especially likely to be found in places such as a ruin or behind a mill. Here a strong contrast is made between her low beginnings and her ascent to become God's consort.

This myth represents the apex of Lilith's ambitions, but it is also understood that her position is only temporary—until God's true Bride, the *Shekhinah*, returns at the time of the coming of the Messiah. The ruling presence of the demonic Lilith over the Holy Land, as she takes the place of her predecessor, is offered to explain the long exile of the Jews that followed the destruction of the Temple and subsequent exile.

Note that in this version of the separation of God and the *Shekhinah*, God is described as having dismissed Her rather than an alternate version, also found in the *Zohar* (1:202b-203a), in which the *Shekhinah* and God have a confrontation about the fate of the Temple and the children of Israel sent into exile, and she decides to leave on Her own. See "The Exile of the *Shekhinah*," p. 57.

It is impossible to read this myth without seeing a parallel to the story of Abraham and Hagar. Hagar was Sarah's maidservant, but when Sarah remained barren, Abraham conceived Ishmael, his first child, with Hagar, *And when she saw that she had conceived, her mistress was lowered in her esteem* (Gen. 16:4). The enmity between Sarah and her maidservant is thus parallel to that of God's Bride and the maidservant Lilith.

The *Zohar* (3:97a) adds a fascinating explanation for the link between Lilith and the *Shekhinah*: "This recondite mystery is that of two sisters." In kabbalistic mythology, the *Shekhinah* represents the feminine aspect of the side of holiness, while Lilith represents the feminine aspect of the side of evil. Thus they are tied together, like two sisters.

The myth ends by predicting the reunion of God and the *Shekhinah* and the end of Lilith's existence. It is unstated but understood that this will take place at the time of the coming of the Messiah.

Sources:
Zohar 2:118a-118b, 3:69a, 3:97a; *B'rit ha-Levi* 7; G. Scholem, *Tarbiz*, vol. 5, pp. 50, 194-95.

Studies:
The Hebrew Goddess by Raphael Patai, pp. 96-111, 221-254.

79. ISRAEL AND THE *SHEKHINAH* IN EXILE

Whenever Israel went into exile, the *Shekhinah* was with them. When they were exiled to Babylon, the *Shekhinah* was with them; when they were exiled to Elam, the *Shekhinah* was with them; and when they were exiled in Edom, the *Shekhinah* was with them.

When Israel were journeying in the wilderness, the *Shekhinah* went in front of them, and they on their side followed Her guidance. The *Shekhinah* was accompanied by clouds of glory, and when She journeyed, the Israelites took up their march.

When the *Shekhinah* ascended, the cloud also ascended on high, so that all men looked up and asked: *Who is She that comes up from the desert like columns of smoke?* (S. of S. 3:6). For the cloud of the *Shekhinah* looked like smoke because the fire that Abraham and his son Isaac kindled clung to it and never left it, and by reason of that fire it ascended both as cloud and smoke; but for all that it was perfumed, with the cloud of Abraham on the right and with the cloud of Isaac on the left.

And when Israel returns from exile, the *Shekhinah* will return with them, as it is said, *With me from Lebanon, O bride, with me you shall come from Lebanon* (S. of S. 4:8).

The presence of the *Shekhinah* is indicated here by a series of prooftexts. Thus the presence of the *Shekhinah* in Babylon is linked to the verse *On your account I was sent to Babylon* (Isa. 43:14). The verse *And I will set My throne in Elam* (Jer. 49:38) is linked to the presence of the *Shekhinah* there. Likewise, the presence of the *Shekhinah* in Edom is linked to the verse *Who is this who coming from Edom?* (Isa. 63:1).

This myth demonstrates how the fate of the *Shekhinah* and the people of Israel is entirely entwined, and that the *Shekhinah* led the people in their desert wanderings.

Sources:
Mekhilta de-Rabbi Ishmael, Shirata 3:67-73; *Sifre on Numbers* 84:4.1; *Zohar* 2:134a.

80. GOD'S EXILE WITH ISRAEL

When the Temple had been destroyed, and Israel was being banished from Jerusalem, God said, "Whom among the Fathers would you have lead you? Whether it be Abraham, Isaac, or Jacob, whether Moses or Aaron, I shall raise up any one of them from his grave, and he will lead you. Or if you would prefer David or Solomon, I shall raise either of them and he will lead you."

The congregation of Israel replied, "Master of the Universe, we do not wish to choose any one of these. You are our only Father."

God replied, "Since that is your wish, I will be your companion, for I Myself will accompany you to Babylon."

> Two verses serve as the primary prooftexts of this myth. As to why Israel turned down the patriarchs, the verse cited is *For Abraham knows us not ... You, O Lord, are our Father, our Redeemer* (Isa. 63:16). Isaiah 43:14 provides evidence that God accompanied the people to Babylon: *On your account I was sent to Babylon* (Isa. 43:14).
>
> This myth is unusual in that Israel's rejection of the patriarchs is very uncharacteristic. Reading this midrash through a kabbalistic lens, we might find it unusual that it speaks of God, who in kabbalah is masculine, as accompanying the people, rather than the *Shekhinah*, who is usually mentioned in midrashim of this sort, and who the kabbalists saw as feminine.
>
> Sources:
> Pesikta Rabbati 30:1-2.

81. THE FACE OF THE *SHEKHINAH*

In the days of Moses even the ordinary Israelite had the privilege of being spoken to by the *Shekhinah* face to face. In later times, not even Ezekiel was accorded this privilege.

It is said that whoever leaves a synagogue and enters the House of Study to engage in the study of the Torah will have the merit of seeing the face of the *Shekhinah*. So too when scholars discuss the Torah, they often behold the face of the *Shekhinah* and are surrounded with fire.

Such was the case when Rabbi Hiyya came to visit Rabbi Shimon bar Yohai. As he passed the window, he saw a fiery curtain inside the house, with the *Shekhinah* on one side of the curtain and Rabbi Shimon bar Yohai on the other. They were studying Torah that way, and Rabbi Shimon's countenance was aflame with the intoxication of the Torah.

Rabbi Hiyya was so electrified by this sight that he could not even knock on the door. All at once the door opened, and Rabbi Hiyya looked inside. As he did, he glimpsed the face of the *Shekhinah*. And he lowered his eyes and stood frozen in place.

When Shimon bar Yohai saw that Rabbi Hiyya had been struck dumb, he said to his son, Rabbi Eleazar: "Go to Rabbi Hiyya and pass your hand over his mouth." Eleazar did this, and at last Rabbi Hiyya recovered his senses.

Some say that to see the righteous and saintly sages of one's generation is to see the very face of the *Shekhinah*. Why are these called the face of the *Shekhinah*? Because the *Shekhinah* is hidden in them, and they reveal Her.

This much is certain: Before they died and gained entrance to the celestial palace, all the saints who had descended from Adam came face to face with the *Shekhinah*. Of them it is said, "A cord of the Divine will has been grasped here on earth."

The meaning of the phrase "the face of the *Shekhinah*" can also be understood as the presence or immanence of the Divine. In the Kabbalistic era, the figure of the *Shekhinah* shifted from being identified as God's presence in this world to the role of God's Bride. However, some scholars, such as Ephraim Urbach in *The Sages* and Max Kiddushin in *The Rabbinic Mind*, have argued that the term *Shekhinah* should be regarded as one more name of God, like *Adonai* (the Lord), *ha-Shem* (the Name), or *ha-Makom* (the Place), etc. Of course, the Name of Names is YHVH, the Tetragrammaton.

Beginning with the Bible, a living person was forbidden to see God face to face, as stated in the verse, *No man shall see my face and live* (Exod. 33:20) Moses is the sole exception. Yet, somehow, it is far more common to see the face of the *Shekhinah*. This suggests that the term *Shekhinah* was not a simple synonym for God, but a term with special meanings, referring to the perception of the presence of God.

The use of the term face does bring with it suggestions of personification, an important fact in light of the later evolution of the term *"Shekhinah"* to refer to the Bride of God. For these descriptions of those who somehow experience the face of the *Shekhinah* have the quality of personal encounters. We note that the Divine appearance was far more common in the earliest biblical times than later, since even Ezekiel was denied the right of seeing the face of God. Yet it could also be argued that his detailed account of his vision in the first chapter of the Book of Ezekiel, known as a vision of the *Merkavah*, God's Divine Chariot, is actually another kind of vision of the face of the *Shekhinah*, since both involve visions of God.

But the best explanation is that the term *Shekhinah* had one meaning in the rabbinic era and another in the kabbalistic and Hasidic ones. Yet even in the rabbinic period the precise meaning of *"Shekhinah"* is far from certain, and varies considerably among its many sources. See *The Immanence of God* by J. Abelson for a thorough overview of these sources.

The tale of Rabbi Hiyya's striking glimpse of the face of the *Shekhinah* is found the *Zohar*, one of a cycle of tales about Rabbi Shimon bar Yohai and his disciples. In all of these tales, Bar Yohai is portrayed as a consummate mystical master, guiding his disciples to experience the divine mysteries. Mystical union is the most essential aspect of any mystical tradition. Yet it is rarely portrayed as openly as it is here, where Rabbi Hiyya sees the face of the *Shekhinah* inside Shimon bar Yohai's house. He perceives that Shimon bar Yohai is studying the Torah with a divine being, with a curtain of fire separating them. Note that what Rabbi Hiyya sees is not presented as a vision, but it affects him as a visionary experience. Indeed, he is so caught up in the moment of mystical union that Rabbi Shimon sends his son Eleazar to cover Rabbi Hiyya's mouth, which brings him back to this world. One of the fascinating mysteries of this tale is why Bar Yohai chooses to have Rabbi Hiyya's mouth covered, and not his eyes, which had witnessed the vision. One possible answer is that he does not want to cut off the vision, but rather to prevent Rabbi Hiyya's soul from leaving his body during the instant of mystical union. Another possibility is that since Rabbi Hiyya has been struck dumb, the gesture of the hand restores his speech. The curtain of fire that separates Bar Yohai from the *Shekhinah* suggests both the *Pargod*, the heavenly curtain that separates God from the rest of Paradise, and the curtain in the Holy of Holies in the Temple beyond which only the High Priest was permitted to go. The fact that a curtain remains separating Rabbi Hiyya and the heavenly being suggests that even in the grip of powerful mystical experiences, there was not a complete loss of self-identity for Jewish mystics, as is so often associated with mystical union in other religions. There is also the suggestion that just as God remains apart from the angels, so humans must remain separated from divine beings.

Sources:

B. Berakhot 64a; *Deuteronomy Rabbah* 7:8; *Zohar* 1:94b; *Zohar* 2:14a-15a, *Midrash ha-Ne'elam*; 2:155b.

Studies:

The Immanence of God by J. Abelson.

82. THE *SHEKHINAH* WITHIN

The *Shekhinah* dwells inside of each and every Jew, as it is said, *I shall dwell in them* (Exod. 25:8). Therefore everyone of Israel must raise up the *Shekhinah* from Her exile, must raise Her up from the dust, and liberate Her from the *Sitra Ahra*, the Other Side, among whom She has been caught.

Here the concept of the *Shekhinah* is identified as an interior presence, much like the extra soul (*neshamah yeterah*) that every Jew is said to receive on the Sabbath. Indeed, the arrival of the Sabbath Queen, which is one of the names of the *Shekhinah*, and the arrival of the extra soul on the Sabbath is simultaneous. So too is their departure simultaneous at the end of *Havdalah*, the Sabbath closing ceremony. See "The Second Soul," p. 310.

The internal nature of the *Shekhinah* seems to be particularly associated with Rabbi Nachman of Bratslav and his scribe, Rabbi Nathan of Nemirov. Rabbi Nachman's story "The Lost Princess" is an allegory about the search for the exiled *Shekhinah*, about which Rabbi Nathan commented: "Everyone of Israel must raise up the *Shekhinah* from her exile," making it a personal as well as a collective task.

The notion of the internal *Shekhinah* seems to parallel Carl Jung's later concept of the anima, the feminine aspect of a man, who likewise dwells within.

Sources:
Sippurei Ma'asiyot, Introduction; *Likutei Moharan* 94; *Sh'nei Luhot ha-B'rit, Masekhta Ta'anit; Tanya* 52.

83. THE *SHEKHINAH* AT THE WALL

The *Shekhinah* is said to hover over the Wailing Wall, and She doesn't move from there. The northern corner of the Wall is where the *Shekhinah* reveals herself. Whoever desires to see the face of the *Shekhinah* must devote his life to the study of Torah. Very few have been found worthy to see the *Shekhinah* hovering over the Wall.

The presence of the *Shekhinah* is strongly linked to the Western Wall, the retaining wall that is all that is said to remain of the Temple in Jerusalem. There are many accounts in rabbinic texts and Jewish folklore about visions or encounters with the *Shekhinah* at the Wall. But only those who have truly studied the Torah are considered worthy of seeing the *Shekhinah*. See "A Vision at the Wailing Wall," following.

Sources:
Midrash Tehillim 106; *Kav ha-Yashar*, chap. 93; *Otzar ha-Ma'asiyot*, collected by Reuven Na'ane from Shalom Levi.

84. A VISION AT THE WAILING WALL

In those days Rabbi Abraham Berukhim was known for performing the Midnight Ritual. He rose every night at midnight and walked through the streets of Safed, crying out, "Arise, for the *Shekhinah* is in exile, and our holy house is devoured by fire, and Israel faces great danger." He longed, more than anything else, to bring the *Shekhinah* out of exile.

Now Rabbi Abraham was a follower of Rabbi Isaac Luria, known as the Ari. The Ari had great mystical powers. By looking at a man's forehead he could read the history of his soul. He could overhear the angels and he knew the language of the birds. He could point out a stone in a wall and reveal whose soul was trapped in it. So too was he able to divine the future, and he always knew from the first day of Rosh ha-Shanah who among his disciples was destined to live or die. This knowledge he rarely disclosed, but once, when he learned there was a way to avert the decree, he made an exception. Summoning Rabbi Abraham Berukhim, he said: "Know, Rabbi Abraham, that a heavenly voice has gone forth to announce that this will be your last year among us—unless you do what is necessary to change the decree."

"What must I do?" asked Rabbi Abraham.

"Know, then," said the Ari, "that your only hope is to go to the Wailing Wall in Jerusalem and pray there with all your heart before God. And if you are deemed worthy you will have a vision of the *Shekhinah*. That will mean that the decree has been averted and your name will be inscribed in the Book of Life after all."

Rabbi Abraham thanked the Ari with all his heart and left to prepare for the journey. First he shut himself in his house for three days and nights, wearing sackcloth and ashes, and fasted the whole time. Then, although he could have gone by donkey or by wagon, he chose to walk to Jerusalem. And with every step he took, he prayed to God to reveal such a vision of the *Shekhinah* to him. By the time Rabbi Abraham reached Jerusalem, he felt as if he were floating, as if his soul had ascended from his body. And when he reached the Wailing Wall, Rabbi Abraham had a vision there. Out of the wall came an old woman, dressed in black, deep in mourning. And when he looked into her eyes, he became possessed of a grief as deep as the ocean, far greater than he had ever known. It was the grief of a mother who has lost a child; the grief of Hannah, after losing her seven sons; the grief of the *Shekhinah* over the suffering of Her children, the children of Israel, scattered to every corner of the earth.

At that moment Rabbi Abraham fell to the ground in a faint, and he had another vision. In this vision, he saw the *Shekhinah* once more, but this time he saw Her dressed in Her robe woven out of light, more magnificent than the setting sun, and Her joyful countenance was revealed. Waves of light arose from her face, an aura that seemed to reach out and surround him, as if he were cradled in the arms of the Sabbath Queen. "Do not grieve so, My son Abraham," She said. "Know that My exile will come to an end, and My inheritance will not go to waste. *Your children shall return to their country and there is hope for your future*" (Jer. 31:17). Just then Rabbi Abraham's soul returned to him from its journey on high. He awoke refreshed, as if he had shed years of grief, and he was filled with hope.

When Rabbi Abraham returned to Safed he was a new man, and when the Ari saw him, he said at once: "I can see from the aura shining from your face that you have been found worthy to see the *Shekhinah*, and you can rest assured that you will live for another twenty-two years." And he did.

This mythic story, "A Vision at the Wailing Wall," derives from the city of Safed in the sixteenth century. This story comes from the last of three letters written from Safed by Shlomel Dresnitz of Moravia in 1607 to his friend in Cracow. It is one of a cycle of tales about the great Jewish mystic Rabbi Isaac Luria. These stories about the Ari were collected in several volumes, including *Shivhei ha-Ari*, *Sefer Toledot ha-Ari*, and *Iggerot Eretz Yisrael*.

This famous tale has a number of biblical and rabbinic precedents. The final words that the *Shekhinah* speaks to Rabbi Abraham come directly from Jeremiah 31:17. They are the words God speaks to console Rachel, *weeping for her children* (Jer. 31:14-16). There is also a strong echo of Jeremiah's vision of Mother Zion in Jeremiah 15:19, which is developed in *Pesikta Rabbati* 26:7. Mother Zion is likely an early incarnation of the *Shekhinah*. See "Mother Zion," p. 46. The assumption that the *Shekhinah* could still be found at the Western Wall, despite the destruction of the Temple, is found in rabbinic sources such as *Midrash Tehillim* on Psalms 11:3 and *Exodus Rabbah* 2:2, and in Rabbi Moshe Alshekh on Lamentations 1:1-2.

While this story demonstrates the prophetic wisdom of the Ari, the real focus of the story is on one of his disciples, Rabbi Abraham ben Eliezer ha-Levi Berukhim. Rabbi Abraham was born in Morocco in 1519 and came to Safed some 50 years later, where he was first a follower of Rabbi Moshe Cordovero (1522-1570) and later became a disciple of the Ari. Rabbi Abraham was an important figure among the mystics of Safed, and Hayim Vital, the primary disciple of the Ari, described him in his autobiography, *Sefer ha-Hezyonot,* as someone who could move others to repentance (p. 130). Vital, who firmly believed in *gilgul,* the transmigration of souls, also appears to have viewed Rabbi Abraham as the reincarnation of Elijah the Prophet.

In most versions of this story, there is no mention of Rabbi Abraham performing the Midnight Ritual of crying out in the streets because of the exile of the *Shekhinah.* But some variants of this famous tale, such as that in *Kav ha-Yashar,* add this important detail at the beginning of the story, giving new meaning to the Ari's directive for Rabbi Abraham Berukhim to seek out the *Shekhinah* at the *Kotel.* Devotion to the Midnight Ritual indicates that Rabbi Abraham was seeking the *Shekhinah* before the Ari sent him on his quest. In this view, the Ari, well aware of Rabbi Abraham's longing for the *Shekhinah,* simply directed him to seek out the *Shekhinah* in the right place—at the *Kotel,* the last retaining wall of the Temple Mount in Jerusalem.

This tale lends itself to multiple interpretations. From the traditional perspective, the Ari has remarkable powers that enable him to peer into the heavenly ledgers to determine the fates of his followers. These fates have been written in either the Book of Life or the Book of Death. (See "The Book of Life and the Book of Death," p. 289.) While this ability to read in the heavenly ledgers is rare, it is not unheard of. In *B. Berakhot* 18b, there is reference to a pious man who remained in the cemetery on Rosh ha-Shanah and there learned the decrees to be issued in heaven during the coming year.

Or, the Ari may simply have recognized Rabbi Abraham's profound need to encounter the *Shekhinah* after years of performing the Midnight Ritual and therefore sent him to find her.

Or, from a modern psychological perspective, the Ari has perceived that Rabbi Abraham faces a midlife transition. If he continues on his present path, he is shortly going to meet his death. That is to say, Rabbi Abraham's life has reached a dangerous transition, and in order to survive it, he must undertake an extraordinary task. Therefore the Ari sends him on a quest to find the *Shekhinah* in the logical place where she could be found—the Wailing Wall, the remnant of her former home in the Temple in Jerusalem. In giving Rabbi Abraham this quest, the Ari functions virtually as a therapist, sending Rabbi Abraham on a journey to wholeness, to plead for mercy from the *Shekhinah,* who is identified in the kabbalah as the Bride of God. Once he reaches the Wall, Rabbi Abraham has dual visions of the *Shekhinah,* encountering her both as a grieving old woman and as a radiant bride, and afterward he is a new man, who through this visionary experience rediscovers his lost anima and reintegrates his feminine side.

Rabbi Abraham's visions of the *Shekhinah* can be recognized as both mythic and archetypal, very close to the purest vision of Jung's concept of the anima, the symbolic feminine aspect of every man. That is why he is able to live for another 22 years, one year for each letter of the Hebrew alphabet, representing a whole new cycle of his life.

This variant also makes changes in Rabbi Abraham's vision of the *Shekhinah.* Here, when he raised his eyes, he saw the shape of a woman on top of the Wall, instead of emerging from the Wall. Upon seeing Her, Rabbi Abraham fell upon on his face, cried and wept, "Mother! Mother! Mother Zion! Woe to me that I see You thus." (It is presumed that She is wearing mourning garments.) Further, when Rabbi Abraham faints, the feminine figure puts Her hand on his face and wipes away his tears. This identification of the *Shekhinah* with Mother Zion directly links this story with that of Mother Zion in *Pesikta Rabbati* 26:7. See "Mother Zion," p. 46.

Central to understanding this tale is the concept of the *Shekhinah.* See the Introduction, pp. xlvii-xlix, for a discussion of the evolution of this term. The two appearances of *Shekhinah* that Rabbi Abraham envisions at the Wall, that of the old woman in mourning and of the bride in white, are the two primary aspects associated with Her: She appears as a bride or queen or lost princess in some texts and tales and as an old woman mourning over the destruction of the Temple in others. In "A Vision at the Wailing Wall," She appears in both forms. Thus he sees both aspects of the *Shekhinah*, Her aspect of mourning and Her joyful aspect, making his vision of the *Shekhinah* complete.

There is much to learn from this tale about how to read rabbinic tales to discover the psychic truths at the core of them. First, however, it is necessary to learn how to interpret their symbolic language. Identifying the *Shekhinah* with the anima is the first step toward translating this language into an archetypal framework.

A similar vision of the *Shekhinah* is recounted by Rabbi Levi Yitzhak of Berditchev. See "A Vision of the Bride" in *Gabriel's Palace*, pp. 245-246.

Sources:

Shivhei ha-Ari 8:4; *Sefer Toledot ha-Ari*, pp. 228-230; *Emek ha-Melekh* 109b; *Kav ha-Yashar* 93; *Or ha-Yashar*; *Hemdat Yamim* 2:4a; *Iggerot Eretz Yisrael*, pp. 205-206; *Iggerot mi-Tzefat*, pp. 122-123; *Midrash Tehillim* on Psalms 11:3; *Exodus Rabbah* 2:2.

Studies:

"The Metamorphosis of Narrative Traditions: Two Stories from Sixteenth Century Safed," by Aryeh Wineman.
"The Aspect of the 'Feminine' in the Lurianic Kabbalah" by Yoram Jacobson.
"The Quest for Jerusalem" by Howard Schwartz.
"Messianic Prayer Vigils in Jerusalem in the Early Sixteenth Century" by Ira Robinson.
On the Kabbalah and Its Symbolism by Gershom Scholem, pp. 152-153.
The Hebrew Goddess by Raphael Patai, pp. 202-220.
"The Son of the Messiah: Ishmael Zevi and the Shabbatian Aqedah" by David J. Halperin, pp. 153-156 (re: Midnight Vigil).

85. GOD MAKES MATCHES

God created the world in six days, but what has He been doing ever since? He sits and makes matches, assigning this man to that woman and this woman to that man. Indeed, God makes these matches even before a child is conceived. Forty days before the formation of a child, a voice goes forth out of heaven to announce that this one will be wed to that one, and every match is as difficult for God to make as it was to part the waters of the Red Sea. And the angels watch over these matches, and when they go well, they sing out, "God the Creator of the world and the Matchmaker, blessed be He now and forever."

This myth answers the question of what God has been doing since He completed the creation of the world—He has been making matches, and each one is a difficult task, as difficult to make as parting the waters of the Red Sea (if any task can be considered difficult for God). This makes God a *shadkhan*—a matchmaker. This myth also explains the Jewish concept of *bashert*, in which it is believed that each person has a *bashert* or destined one, and that the match was made in heaven. Such a belief made it easier to accept the matches that in practice were made by parents, usually with considerations of status and wealth rather than of any romantic factors.

According to the *Zohar*, all souls are initially male and female. But when they are born into this world, the male and female parts of the soul go their separate ways, the male soul in a male body and the female soul in a female body. If they are worthy, they will unite in marriage, restoring their original unity. That is why a person's loved one is called a soulmate, for together they form a single unit in every way, body and soul.

Sources:

B. Sota 2a; *Genesis Rabbah* 68:4; *Zohar* 3:45b; IFA 13264.

86. THE RABBIS OVERRULE GOD

Rabbi Eliezer ben Hyrcanus was among the sages who were debating a point of the Law. All of the sages, except Rabbi Eliezer, ruled one way, and Rabbi Eliezer continued to insist that they were wrong. He used every possible argument to support it, but the others did not agree. Then he said: "Let this carob tree prove that the Law is as I state it is." The carob tree then uprooted itself and moved a distance of one hundred ells. But the other sages said: "That doesn't prove anything."

Then Rabbi Eliezer said: "Let the waters of the spring prove that I am right." Then the waters began to flow backward. But again the sages insisted that this, too, proved nothing.

Then Rabbi Eliezer spoke again and said: "Let the walls of the house of study prove I am right." And the walls were about to collapse when Rabbi Yehoshua said to them: "If scholars are discussing a point of the Law, why should you walls interfere?" Thus they did not fall, in deference to Rabbi Yehoshua, but neither did they straighten out, out of respect for Rabbi Eliezer, and they are inclined to this day.

Rabbi Eliezer then said: "If the Law is as I say, let heaven prove it." Thereupon a *bat kol*, a heavenly voice, came forth and said: "Why do you quarrel with Rabbi Eliezer, whose opinion should prevail everywhere?"

Then Rabbi Yehoshua stood up and said: "*It* [the Torah] *is not in heaven*" (Deut. 30:12). "What does this mean?" asked Rabbi Yirmiyahu. "It means that since the Torah was given to us on Mount Sinai, we no longer require a heavenly voice to reach a decision, since it is written in the Torah: *Follow after the majority*" (Exod. 23:2).

Later Rabbi Nathan encountered Elijah and asked him how the ruling was accepted on high. And Elijah said: "At this the Holy One, blessed be He, laughed and said, `My children have overruled me!'"

> The subject of the disagreement between Rabbi Eliezer and the other rabbis was the ritual purity of a ceramic oven. Rabbi Eliezer insisted it was ritually pure, while all of the other sages said it was impure. It seems ironic that a series of miracles, with crucial implications about the relationship of God to the rabbis, took place because of a such a minor matter.
>
> This startling legend vividly demonstrates the rabbinic belief that once the Torah had been given on Mount Sinai, it became the possession of the Jews, and the responsibility for interpreting it fell to the rabbis. So extreme is this tale that it suggests that the rabbis were not willing to let any authority—even that of God—overrule them. And as the coda to the tale reveals, God seems to accept their determination to decide the Law as they see fit.
>
> Rabbi Eliezer ben Hyrcanus, one of the great talmudic sages, disagrees with his fellow sages, and insists on his interpretation to the extent that he provokes miracles— the moving of the carob tree, the reversal of the waters of the spring, and the imminent collapse of the walls of the House of Study.
>
> Finally, he calls upon heaven to confirm the correctness of his interpretation—and heaven replies in his favor. None of this, however, deters the other rabbis from their interpretation. Instead, Rabbi Yehoshua virtually tells God to keep out of this matter, since, as he says, "*The Law is not in Heaven*" (Deut. 30: 12). And, indeed, the full context of this passage does in fact seem to shift the burden of responsibility for the interpretation of the Law from God to man: "*Surely, this Instruction which I enjoin upon you this day is not too baffling for you, nor is it beyond reach. It is not in the heavens, that you should say, 'Who among us can go up to the heavens and get it for us and impart it to us, that we may observe it?' Neither is it beyond the sea, that you should say, 'Who among us can cross to the other side of the sea and get it for us and impart it to us, that we may observe it?' No, the thing is very close to you, in your mouth and in your heart, to observe it*" (Deut. 30:11-14).

On the other hand, the biblical passage that serves as the basis of the assertion that the rabbis, and not God, must decide the Law, *Follow after the majority*, from Exodus 23:2, has had its meaning reversed from its original context: *You shall not follow a multitude to do evil*. This interpretation of the biblical verse is itself a radical example of the rabbinic reinterpretation of the text. It demonstrates the extent of the rabbinic determination to assume all responsibility for the interpretation of the Law. See *B. Sanhedrin* 2a for a discussion of the verse from Exodus.

Sources:
B. Bava Metzia 59b.

87. GOD DEFERS TO THE EARTHLY COURT

All the ministering angels had gathered before God. "Master of the Universe," they asked, "what day is New Year's Day?"

God replied: "Why are you asking me? Let us, you and I, ask the earthly court. When the earthly court decrees that 'Today is *Rosh ha-Shanah*, the New Year,' then raise up the podium. Summon the advocates. Summon the clerks. For My children have decreed that today is New Year's Day, and what is a decree for Israel is an ordinance of the God of Jacob."

The preceding entry, "The Rabbis Overrule God," offers a startling example of rabbinic independence from God in matters of interpreting the Torah. Here God defers to the rabbis, to the great court of the Sanhedrin, out of respect. God demonstrates that in certain matters the opinions of the rabbis take precedence even of God. This is a much more conciliatory approach than that taken by Rabbi Yehoshua in "The Rabbis Overrule God." Behind this myth is the rabbinic understanding that the Sabbath laws are fixed by God, but other holidays, based on the monthly calendar and sighting of the new moon, are up to the human courts.

God's agreement in this matter is deduced from Psalms 81:4-5: *Blow the horn on the new moon, on the full moon for our feast day. For it is a law for Israel, a ruling of the God of Jacob*. The latter verse about the law and ruling can be understood two ways: the statute and ordinance can be seen as a simple repetition, or a statement that God defers to Israel to such a great extent that God accepts all of Israel's laws as rulings binding on Himself. It is this latter interpretation that is at the root of this myth.

Two versions of this myth are found in *Midrash Tehillim*. One version takes place as a dialogue between God and the angels, as found here, and the other takes the form of an announcement on the part of God. The latter adds a coda on the part of God: If the witnesses of the new moon are delayed, everything required for the heavenly court will have to be stored away, and the New Year will be delayed until the next day. Here God is even ready to defer to human frailty, and to delay the starting of the New Year if necessary.

Sources:
Midrash Tehillim 81:6; Y. Rosh ha-Shanah 1:3, 57b.

BOOK TWO

MYTHS OF CREATION

When Adam was first created, he was as tall as the distance from the earth to heaven.

B. Hagigah 12a

88. THE FIRST TO EXIST

As the first to exist, God brought Himself into being.

> Here God is understood to be the First Mover, who brought Himself into being. Somehow God crossed the boundary between nonexistence and existence. This is the original transition from *Ein Sof*, meaning "Endless," the unknowable part of God, to *Keter*, meaning "Crown," the first of the ten sefirot. These sefirot describe the process of emanation by which the rest of existence came into being.
>
> *Sources:*
> *Ma'ayan Hokhmah* in *Otzar Midrashim* pp. 306-311; *Zohar* 1:156.
>
> *Studies:*
> *The Early Kabbalah*, edited by Joseph Dan, pp. 49-53.

89. BEFORE THE WORLD WAS CREATED

In the beginning, before the world was created, God rode upon the wings of the wind and upon the flames of storms. Fiery lights of crimson fire blazed around Him. Four great storm-winds swirled around Him. A tempest was His chariot, the storm-wind His seat.

At that time the world was filled with water on water, wave on wave, gale on gale, tempest within tempest, storm-wind within storm-wind, making a great clamor until the word of God silenced them all.

Then the sound of praise rose up from the waters, and God said to himself, "If these that have neither mouth nor speech praise me, how much more will I be praised when man is created." So God gave his consent for the world to be created, as it is said, *For He spoke and it came to be* (Ps. 33:9).

> This mythic portrait of God riding the storm-winds grows out of the passages: *For behold Yahweh will come in fire, and like the storm-wind* (Isa. 66:15), and, *Fire goes before Him* (Ps. 97:3). At the same time, the uncreated world is filled with water, based on the verse *The voice of Yahweh was upon the waters* (Ps. 29:3). Like a god out of Greek mythology, "God rides upon the skies" (*Midrash Tehillim* 68:3). God first calms the upheavals of the waters, and the world is said to come about when the waters, now offering God praise, request its creation. The association of God with the storm-winds links the Jewish God with Marduk, also known as Bel, a god of thunderstorms, originally a Sumerian god taken over by the Babylonians, who rose from being a local god to become head of the Babylonian pantheon.
>
> According to *Exodus Rabbah* (15:22), there were three pre-existent elements: "Three things preceded the creation of the world—water, wind and fire." These are the three elements found in this mythic description of God.
>
> *Sources:*
> *Genesis Rabbah* 5:1; *Exodus Rabbah* 5:14, 15:22; *Midrash Tehillim* 68:3; *Midrash Aleph Bet* 1:1-5.

90. PRIOR WORLDS

Before the world was created, God alone existed, one and eternal, beyond any boundary, without change or movement, concealed within Himself. When the thought arose in Him to bring the world into being, His glory became visible. He began to trace the foundations of a world before Himself, and in this way God brought a heaven and earth into being. But when God looked at them, they were not pleasing in His sight, so He changed them back into emptiness and void. He split and rent and tore them apart with his two arms, and ruined whole worlds in one moment. One after another, God created a thousand worlds, which preceded this one. And all of them were swept away in the wink of an eye.

God went on creating worlds and destroying worlds until He created this one and declared, "This one pleases me, those did not." That is how God created the heaven and the earth as we know it, as it is said, *"For, behold! I am creating a new heaven and a new earth"* (Isa. 65:17).

The verse *These are the generations of the heaven and the earth when they were created* (Gen. 2:4) suggested to the rabbis the creation of prior worlds, while the verse *You carry them away as with a flood* (Ps. 90:5) was also interpreted to refer to the destruction of these prior worlds. The *Zohar* (1:262b) suggests that God did not actually build these prior worlds, but only thought about building them.

That this world was not the first that God created was believed to be indicated by Isaiah 65:17: *"For, behold, I create new heavens and a new earth and the former shall not be remembered nor come to mind."* *Zohar Hadash* identifies the prior worlds as totaling 1,000, as does *Or ha-Hayim* 1:12, which states that before God created this world, He created a thousand hidden worlds. These hidden worlds were created through the first letter, *aleph.* That is why the Torah, in the report of the Creation of this world, commences with the second letter, *bet.* The existence of the 1,000 worlds is linked to the verse *You may have the thousand, O Solomon* (S. of S. 8:12).

Other sources, such as *Midrash Tehillim* 90:13, give the number as 974 worlds, which were said to have been created and destroyed over 2,000 years. *Sefer ha-Zikhronot* 1:1 suggests that when it entered God's mind to create the world, He drew the plan of the world, but it would not stand until God created repentance. Thus repentance is the key element that made our world possible.

Rabbi Yitzhak Eizik Haver (1789-1853) found evidence of prior creations in the fact that the Torah starts with the letter *bet,* the second letter, rather than with an *aleph,* the first letter. "The verse begins with the letter *bet* to hint that Creation was divided into two realms—that God created two beginnings."

Although a great many prior worlds are said to have been created and destroyed, Rabbi Levi Yitzhak of Berditchev insisted that "Everything God created exists forever, and never ceases to be." And in *Esh Kadosh,* Rabbi Kalonymus Kalman Shapira identifies the creation and destruction of the prior worlds with the Shattering of the Vessels. Furthermore, he states that God made the present universe out of those broken vessels. See "The Shattering of the Vessels and Gathering the Sparks," p. 122.

The belief that God destroyed the prior worlds implies that God's creations of these worlds was somehow in error. Some Christian apocryphal sources, such as *The Gospel of Philip* 99a, describe even the present world as an error: "The world came into being through a mistake. For he who created it wished to create it imperishable and immortal. He did not attain his hope."

Sources:
Genesis Rabbah 3:7, 9:2, 28:4, 33:3; *Exodus Rabbah* 1:2, 30:3; *B. Hagigah* 13b; *Midrash Tehillim* 90:13; *Midrash Aleph Bet* 5:5; *Eliyahu Rabbah* 2:9; *Zohar* 1:24, 1:154a, 1:262b, 3:135a-135b, *Idra Rabbah; Pirkei de-Rabbi Eliezer* 3; *Sefer ha-'Iyyun* Ms. Hebrew University 8330; *Zohar Hadash; Sefer ha-Zikhronot* 1:1; Rashi on *Shabbat* 88b; *No'am Elimelekh, Bo* 36b; *Kedushat Levi; Or ha-Hayim* 1:12; *Esh Kadosh; Otzrot Rabbi Yitzhak Eizik Haver,* p.1.

Studies:
The Holy Fire: The Teachings of Rabbi Kalonymus Kalman Shapira, the Rebbe of the Warsaw Ghetto by Nehemia Polen.

91. THE PRIMORDIAL ELEMENTS

God drew upon six elements in creating the world: light, darkness, chaos, void, wind (or spirit), and water. But when were these elements created? Some say these elements pre-existed, and that God drew upon them in the Creation. Others say they were created in an earlier creation. Still others say that they too were created on the first day, along with heaven and earth.

> The very existence of pre-existing elements, such as light, darkness, chaos, void, water, wind, and the deep, raise doubts about the singularity of God's accomplishment. Yet there is no explicit mention of the creation of these elements in the account of Creation.
>
> To demonstrate that God did indeed create these elements, Rabbi Gamaliel in *Genesis Rabbah* provides prooftexts to show that all seven were created, such as in Isaiah 45:7, where God says, *"I form light and create darkness."* However, this proof raises as many questions as it resolves. The use of the verb "form" (*yotzer*) for the creation of light and "create" (*borei*) for the creation of darkness is significant. Something that is formed already exists, while something that is created is brought into being. This seems to hint that light pre-existed.
>
> *Sources:*
> *Pirkei de-Rabbi Eliezer* 3.

92. GOD CREATED EVERYTHING WITH ITS KNOWLEDGE

God looked over the entire creation before it existed and prepared everything during the six days of Creation. During those six days the foundations and roots of everything that would be brought into being were created.

So too did God create everything with its knowledge. God asked each thing if it wanted to be created. When each thing agreed to be created, it was with specific conditions, and with its own particular mode of service to God. The ocean agreed to open up to permit the children of Israel to pass through the Red Sea. The heavens promised to be silent while Moses climbed Mount Sinai. The sun and moon promised to stand still when Joshua stood before the walls of Jericho. The ravens promised to feed Elijah, the lions promised not to devour Daniel, the heavens promised to open up before Ezekiel, and the whale to cast out Jonah.

In this way God made an agreement with each of the elements, and each and every one agreed to do as God asked, out of gratitude for having been created.

> There are some Jewish creation myths in which God created the world from a blueprint. That idea is echoed here, but instead of a plan it seems to suggest that God visualized, in some way, all that He would create. Philo states that "when God decided to create this world, He first formed the invisible world to use as a pattern for the corporeal world." That idea is echoed here, suggesting that "the roots of everything" which God prepared was an invisible, archetypal world, or that God visualized, in some way, all that He would create. Other myths describe God using the Torah as a blueprint for all of Creation. See "The Creation of the Torah," p. 249.
>
> In addition, we find the concept that God consulted with all of his creations, asking them if they wanted to be created. The implication is that all things subsequently created expressed their desire to exist. This explains the powerful impulse to survive in all living beings. God's questioning of the creatures prior to their creation implies a covenant between God and His creations, and implies a mutuality to the process of creation.
>
> *Sources:*
> *De Opificio Mundi* 16; B. *Rosh ha-Shanah* 11a; B. *Hullin* 60a; *Derekh ha-Shem* 2:5:6; *Zohar* 1:47a; *No'am Elimelekh, Bo* 36b.

93. THE BEGINNING OF TIME

Time did not exist before the world was created, but came into being at the same time.

> Here Philo considers the question of the beginning of time. He concludes that time did not exist until God created the world, but "came into being at the same time." Thus time does not exist for God, but only for God's creations.
>
> *Sources:*
> Philo, *De Mutatione Nominum* 26-28.
>
> *Studies:*
> "Time, Myth and History in Judaism" by Lawrence D. Loeb.

94. SEVEN THINGS CREATED BEFORE THE CREATION OF THE WORLD

Seven things were created before the creation of the world. They are: the Torah, Repentance, Paradise, Gehenna, the Throne of Glory, the heavenly Temple, and the name of the Messiah. The Messiah's name was engraved on a precious stone on the altar of the heavenly Temple, as it is said, *His name existed before the sun* (Ps. 72:17). Nor will King Messiah ever know death. All seven preceded the creation of the world by two thousand years, and all were borne up by the power of God.

The celestial Torah was written in black fire on white fire, and lay in the lap of God, who sat on the Throne of Glory, which was set in the highest heaven, above the heads of the angels and seraphs and other heavenly beasts still to be created. Paradise was on the right side of God and Gehenna on the left. The heavenly sanctuary was directly in front of Him, and the name of the Messiah was engraved on a precious stone set upon the altar. As for Repentance, it is great indeed, for it preceded the creation of the world.

Only after God created these seven things, along with the heavenly beasts, did God establish the firmament, with all seven things created before the Creation resting upon the horns of these beasts, as it is said, *And over the heads of the heavenly beasts there was the likeness of a firmament* (Ezek. 1:22). That firmament consists of precious stones and pearls. It lights up the heaven as the sun lights up the world at noon, as it is said, *And light dwells with Him* (Dan. 2:22).

> God is said to have created these seven things 2,000 years before the creation of the world (*Midrash Tehillim* 90:12). These seven things are regarded as the indispensable essentials for the world to exist. Each of these seven things is explained by a verse that suggests they were created before the rest of the creation of the world. The Torah's pre-existence is supported by the verse *The Lord possessed me in the beginning of His way, before His works of old* (Prov. 8:22). The Throne of Glory is found in the verse *Your throne is established from of old* (Ps. 93:2). Paradise (*Gan Eden*, the Garden of Eden, which represents both the heavenly and the earthly Paradise) can be presumed to have pre-existed by the verse *The Lord God planted a garden in Eden* (Gen. 2:8). A case for Gehenna (hell) can be found in the verse *The Topheth has long been ready for him* (Isa. 30:33). A place called Topheth was the site of a cult that involved the sacrifice of children to Moloch (see 2 Kings 23:10). It is in the Valley of Ben-Hinnom, south of Jerusalem, which came to be known as Gehinnom and came to represent the place where the wicked were tormented after death. The Greek form, "Gehenna," became the popularly known name for this place of punishment, which is the Jewish equivalent of a combined purgatory and hell. The Temple, with its Throne of Glory, can be found in the verse *O Throne of Glory exalted from of old, our sacred shrine!* (Jer. 17:12). For the Messiah, we may look to the verse *May his name be eternal; while the sun lasts, may his name endure* (Ps. 72:17). The pre-existence of repentance can be found in the verse

Before the mountains came into being, before You brought forth the earth and the world ... You return man to dust; you decreed, "Return you mortals!" (Ps. 90:2-3). (In Hebrew the word for "returning," *teshuvah*, also means "repentance.") Most of the details about the seven things created before the creation of the world are found in *Midrash Tehillim* 90:12. This text also links the seven sacred things to the vision of Ezekiel, asserting that each of the seven things exists upon the horns of the *hayyot*, the living creatures envisioned in Ezekiel 1:13-14.

According to Nachmanides, God's original Torah in heaven was written with black fire on white fire, and the letters were written without spaces between the words. Rabbi Meir ibn Gabbai said that the Torah was literally made up of divine names.

How long before the world was created were the seven things brought into being? Rabbi Shimon ben Lakish said that they were created 2,000 years before the creation of the world.

Taken as a whole, the seven things portray the parameters of existence: the Torah is the supreme source of instruction, Paradise and Gehenna represent reward and punishment, the Throne of Glory represents God's role in existence, the heavenly Temple implies the creation of the earthly Temple in the days to come, and the name of the Messiah signifies the End of Days. Finally, Repentance adds the human need for forgiveness.

Sources:
B. *Pesahim* 54a; B. *Nedarim* 39b; *Midrash Tehillim* 8, 72:17, 90:3, 90:12; *Sefer ha-Zikhronot* 1:8; *Orhot Tzaddikim; Avodat ha-Kodesh, Helek ha-Yihud* 21.

95. THE SEVEN DAYS OF CREATION

In the beginning God created the heaven and the earth. Now the earth was unformed and void, and darkness was upon the face of the deep; and the spirit of God hovered over the face of the waters. God said, "Let there be light"; and there was light. God saw that the light was good, and God separated the light from the darkness. God called the light Day, and the darkness He called Night. And there was evening and there was morning, a first day.

God said, "Let there be an expanse in the midst of the water, that it may separate water from water." God made the expanse, and it separated the water that was below the expanse from the water that was above the expanse. And it was so. God called the expanse Sky. And there was evening and there was morning, a second day.

God said, "Let the water below the sky be gathered into one area, that the dry land may appear." And it was so. God called the dry land Earth, and the gathering of waters He called Seas. And God saw that this was good. And God said, "Let the earth sprout vegetation: seed-bearing plants, fruit trees of every kind on earth that bear fruit with the seed in it." And it was so. The earth brought forth vegetation: seed-bearing plants of every kind, and trees of every kind bearing fruit with the seed in it. And God saw that this was good. And there was evening and there was morning, a third day.

God said, "Let there be lights in the expanse of the sky to separate day from night; they shall serve as signs for the set times—the days and the years; and they shall serve as lights in the expanse of the sky to shine upon the earth." And it was so. God made the two great lights, the greater light to dominate the day and the lesser light to dominate the night, and the stars. And God set them in the expanse of the sky to shine upon the earth, to dominate the day and the night, and to separate light from darkness. And God saw that this was good. And there was evening and there was morning, a fourth day.

God said, "Let the waters bring forth swarms of living creatures, and birds that fly above the earth across the expanse of the sky." God created the great sea monsters, and all the living creatures of every kind that creep, which the waters brought forth in swarms, and all the winged birds of every kind. And God saw that this was good. God blessed them, saying, "Be fertile and increase, fill the waters in the seas, and let the birds increase on the earth." And there was evening and there was morning, a fifth day.

God said, "Let the earth bring forth every kind of living creature: cattle, creeping things, and wild beasts of every kind." And it was so. God made wild beasts of every kind and cattle of every kind, and all kinds of creeping things of the earth. And God saw that this was good. And God said, "Let us make man in our image, after our likeness. They shall rule the fish of the sea, the birds of the sky, the cattle, the whole earth, and all the creeping things that creep on earth." And God created man in His image, in the image of God He created him; male and female He created them. God blessed them and God said to them, "Be fertile and increase, fill the earth and master it; and rule the fish of the sea, the birds of the sky, and all the living things that creep on earth."

God said, "See, I give you every seed-bearing plant that is upon all the earth, and every tree that has seed-bearing fruit; they shall be yours for food. And to all the animals on land, to all the birds of the sky, and to everything that creeps on earth, in which there is the breath of life, I give all the green plants for food." And it was so. And God saw all that He had made, and found it very good. And there was evening and there was morning, the sixth day.

The heaven and the earth were finished, and all their array. On the seventh day God finished the work that He had been doing, and He ceased on the seventh day from all the work that He had done. And God blessed the seventh day and declared it holy, because on it God ceased from all the work of Creation that He had done. Such is the story of heaven and earth when they were created.

This is the most famous of all Jewish creation myths. It appears at the very beginning of Genesis and is known, at least in rough outline, even by those who have little knowledge of the Bible. The only biblical account that is equally famous is that of the disobedience of Adam and Eve. This Creation narrative emphasizes God's use of the power of the word in order to create the world. On each day of Creation, additional elements are brought into being when God commands that they appear. On the surface this seems to be creation *ex nihilo*, out of nothing, but a close reading of the biblical text shows a certain amount of ambiguity about whether God drew on pre-existing elements or created everything Himself. Every subsequent Jewish creation myth refers directly or indirectly to this one. It either verifies the principles established here, or contradicts them, implying, for example, that some elements, such as light, already existed when God said, *"Let there be light"* (Gen. 1:3). See "Light from the Temple," p. 411, where this theory is elaborated. Following the seven days of Creation is a second creation myth, Genesis 2:4-25, which offers a different perspective on the events of Creation, emphasizing the creation of man and woman. Scholars have proposed that these were two separate creation myths that were combined by the priestly editors of Genesis, despite some apparent contradictions. See "The Creation of Man," p. 133, and "The Creation of Woman," p. 142.

This seminal creation myth also had a great influence on the way God was conceived. It can be argued that the personification of God begins in Genesis 1:2: *God said, "Let there be light."* Since humans also speak, using language just as God is said to do, it was natural to assume that God had other human characteristics. As a result of this myth, it has been assumed that all God's creations came into existence through the words uttered by God, as made explicit in this passage from Psalms: *By the word of Yahweh the heavens were made, by the breath of His mouth, all their hosts* (Ps. 33:6).

There are many parallels between the Genesis Creation myth and the creation myths of other peoples of the ancient Near East. One of the closest is the Mesopotamian creation myth found in *Enuma Elish*, where the divine assembly of Mesopotamia is created through the merging of Apsu, divine patron of fresh water, and Tiamat, divine patron of salt water. An Egyptian creation myth is preserved in the Hymn to Ra, the creator and ruler identified with the sun, where Ra describes creation: "There were no heavens and no earth. There was no dry land and there were no reptiles in the land. Then I spoke and living creatures appeared." A seven-day incubation ritual is described in the Ugaritic stories of Aqhat. A hymn to the creator of the heavens and the earth was found among the tablets unearthed at Ebla in Syria: "You are the creator of the heavens and the earth. There was no earth until you created it. There was no light until you created it. There was no sun until you created it. You alone rule over all creation." For more on the parallels among creation myths, see "The Rebellion of the Waters," p. 105, and "The Rebellion of Rahab," p. 106.

Sources:
Genesis. 1:1-2:4.

Studies:
Old Testament Parallels: Laws and Stories from the Ancient Near East by Victor H.
    Matthews and Don C. Benjamin, pp. 6-8 (Hymn to Ra); pp. 9-18 (*Enuma Elish*);
    pp. 66-75 (Stories of Aqhat); pp. 241-243 (Ebla Archives).
Myths from Mesopotamia by S. Dalley, pp. 228-277 (*Enuma Elish*).
The Jewish Study Bible, edited by Adele Berlin and Marc Zvi Brettler, pp. 12-14.

96. TEN THINGS CREATED ON THE EVE OF THE FIRST SABBATH

Ten things were created at twilight on the sixth day of Creation, before the first Sabbath: the mouth of the earth, the mouth of the well, the mouth of the she-ass, the rainbow, the manna, the staff of Moses and the Shamir, as well as the letters and writing and the Tablets of stone.

Some add the following things: the evil spirits and the sepulcher of Moses, the cave in which Moses and Elijah stood, as well as the ram of our father Abraham. Some also add the first tongs that were ever made.

> The Mishnah lists these items that later took on an important role in Jewish lore. The mouth of the earth is the place where the earth opened and swallowed Korah and his followers (Num. 16:32). The well is one that God gave to the people in the wilderness (Num. 21:16-18). The ass is that of Balaam, which spoke (Num. 22:28). The rainbow is that of Noah (Gen. 9:23). The manna is that given to the Israelites in the wilderness (Exod. 16:15). The staff (or rod) of Moses is found in Exodus 4:17. The tablets are the first tablets given to Moses (Exod. 32:15). See "The First Tablets," p. 266.
>
> The Shamir is a small creature, the size of a barleycorn, which can cut through the hardest stone. King Solomon is said to have used it to cut the stones for the Temple. There is a famous folktale in the Talmud in which King Solomon captures Ashmedai, the king of demons, in order to find out where he can capture the Shamir, so that he can use it to carve the stone altar for the Temple (*B. Gittin* 68b).
>
> Of the additional items said to have been created at twilight on the sixth day, the spirits refer to the souls that were left without bodies. There was not enough time for a body to be created for every soul. This is said to be the origin of the demons. For the sepulcher of Moses, see Deuteronomy 34.6. The ram is the one that Abraham sacrificed at Mount Moriah in place of Isaac (Gen. 22:13). Finally, the heavenly origin of the first tongs solves the problem of how the first tongs might have been held while they were being made.
>
> *Sources:*
> *Mishnah Avot* 5:6; *B. Pesahim* 54a.

97. FIVE HEAVENLY THINGS SLEEPING IN THE UNIVERSE

There are five heavenly things in the universe, each of them of immense power, that are sleeping. They are the might of God, the rainbow of God, the sword of God, the arm of God, and the jealousy of God.

These five heavenly things are each a giant force in repose. Each of them belongs to God, from objects linked to God, such as the rainbow and the sword, to God's arm, which is part of God, and powers and characteristics of God, such as His might and His jealousy. This brief, largely undeveloped myth serves as a reminder of God's un-limited powers, which can be asserted at any time, with unforeseen consequences. It also suggests multiple aspects of God, that God consists of a mixture of elemental forces. This would explain God's sometimes contradictory behavior, ranging from mercy to harsh justice.

Sources:
Midrash Tehillim 80:3.

98. GOD THE CREATOR

In the beginning, God covered Himself with light as with a garment. He stretched out the heavens like a curtain, laying the roof of His upper chambers with the waters. He made the clouds His chariot, walking upon the wings of the winds, making winds His messen-gers, and the flaming fire His ministers. So too did He establish the earth upon its foun-dations that it should never be moved, and He covered it with the deep. But when the waters rose up above the mountains, God rebuked them and they fled at the voice of His thunder. The mountains rose, the valleys sank down to the place where God had founded them. And He set a boundary for the waters that could not be crossed, that they might not return to cover the earth.

This is an especially important passage from Psalms, which demonstrates clear evidence of ancient creation myths beyond those found in Genesis. This version of the Creation gives God a more active, mythic role. God stretches out the heavens, lays the roof of His upper chambers, establishes the earth on its foundations, and covers it with the deep. Even the creation of light is described in very active terms, with God covering Himself with light as with a garment. In contrast, in the Genesis creation myth God's actions are limited to speech—God speaks and everything comes into existence. Thus the portrayal of God in this myth from Psalms is far closer to that of pagan gods, as found in Babylonian, Canaanite, and Greek myth. For additional myths about the creation of light, see "The Light of the First Day," p. 83.

Sources:
Psalms 104:1-9.

99. THE RAINBOW

Some say that the rainbow was created by God at the time of Noah, when God set it in the clouds. It came into being when God strengthened the power of sun after the Flood, so that its rays would produce a rainbow. Others say that the rainbow was one of the ten things created on the eve of the first Sabbath, but until the time of Noah it was hidden in the clouds, and only God could see it. God revealed the rainbow to Noah as the sign of the covenant between them. The rainbow had been designated for this purpose from the time of its creation.

God said, "*I have set My bow in the clouds*" (Gen. 9:13), meaning that the beauty of the bow was comparable to that of God. Still, as beautiful as the rainbow was, it was but a faint reflection of God's glory. It is forbidden to stare at the rainbow because the *Shekhinah* appears in it, adorned in garments yellow, red, and white. That is why the eyes of anyone who stares at the rainbow will become dim.

Sometimes the rainbow does not appear at all during a generation. This indicates there is a *Tzaddik* in that generation, and therefore the world does not need a sign that God will not destroy it. Such a righteous one prays for compassion for the world and is worthy of protecting it.

From time to time the rainbow appears in the sky to reassure us that despite our sins, God will not annihilate us.

There is a debate among biblical commentators about whether or not the rainbow existed before God revealed it to Noah as a sign of their covenant as stated in the verse *"I have set My bow in the clouds"* (Gen. 9:13). The past tense of "I have set" was taken as evidence that the rainbow existed before Noah. Among the commentators, Saadiah Gaon asserted that the rainbow was previously in existence, while Ibn Ezra interpreted this verse to mean, "I have now set a bow in the clouds."

According to Rabbi Moshe Alshekh (sixteenth century), each of the seven colors of the rainbow represents one day in the seven days of Creation.

Rabbi Joshua ben Levi wanted anyone who saw a rainbow to prostrate himself, to acknowledge the wisdom of God in all that He has created. But other rabbis scoffed at this idea, since it would appear that the one prostrating himself was worshipping the rainbow.

In *B. Ketubot* 77b, it is said that the rainbow did not appear in the sky during the generation of Rabbi Shimon bar Yohai as a sign of his righteousness, since the merit of one *Tzaddik* alone is enough to save the world, and therefore the rainbow, itself a sign of God's mercy, is not needed, since the presence of a great *Tzaddik* is in itself sufficient to invoke God's mercy. This tradition is repeated in *Zohar* 3:15a, where Rabbi Shimon bar Yohai is the hero and reputed author of the book.

The association of the rainbow and the *Shekhinah* grows out of Ezekiel 1:28: *As the appearance of the bow that is in the cloud in the day of rain, so was the appearance of the brightness round about. This was the appearance of the likeness of the glory of Yahweh.*

In the *Zohar*, Rabbi Shimon bar Yohai associates the colors of the garment of the *Shekhinah*—yellow, red and white—with the three patriarchs, Abraham with white, Isaac with red, and Jacob with yellow. See "The Garments of the *Shekhinah*," p. 54.

Sources:
Mishneh Avot 5:6; B. Ketubot 77b; B. Hagigah 16; Midrash Tehillim 36:8; Zohar 1:18a, 3:15a, 3:215a-215; Rashi on Genesis 9:14; Ibn Ezra on Genesis 9:14; Moshe Alshekh on Genesis 9:8; Akedat Yitzhak 14:4-7.

Studies:
The Faces of the Chariot by David J. Halperin, pp. 250-261.

100. THE TIME OF CREATION

When was the world created? It is one of the foundations of Judaism that God created the world at the precise instant that He desired to do so.

What existed before that? Whoever speculates about four things, it is better if he had not been born: What is above? What is below? What came before? And what will come after?

There is little speculation in Jewish lore about what God did before He created the world, or what, if anything, existed before then. The one major exception are the myths about prior worlds. See "Prior Worlds," p. 71. So too is little said about God's decision to create the world when He did. But *Me'am Lo'ez* emphasizes God's own free will in deciding when to undertake Creation, "at the precise instant that He desired to do so." According to Jewish philosophy, while human free will may be encumbered by a person's fate, God's free will is limitless, and His decision to create the universe and make a covenant with Israel was entirely God's own choice. The only exception seems to be some strata of Lurianic Kabbalah where the process of creation/emanation seems to be a necessity within God, although His free will initiates the whole process.

This famous quotation from *Mishnah Hagigah* 2:1 lists four things it is forbidden to speculate about. It represents that dimension of rabbinic thought that was alarmed at even the study of mystical contemplation, and warned against its dangers. Indeed, the tale of the four sages who entered Paradise, from *B. Hagigah* 14b, is itself a warning tale about the dangers of mystical explorations. See "The Four Who Entered Paradise," p. 173.

Sources:
Mishnah Hagigah 2:1; B. *Hagigah* 16a; *Me'am Lo'ez*, Genesis 1:1.

101. EVERYTHING WAS CREATED AT ONCE

The entire universe was created at once. Everything was created in one moment, in the same hour, on the same day, as it is said, *Such is the story of heaven and earth on the day that they were created* (Gen. 2:4). Not only were heaven and earth created on that day, but they were not deficient in any way. They contained their descendants within them, existing in potential.

This myth of the simultaneous creation of the universe strongly echoes the modern Big Bang theory of creation. It finds its basis in the phrase *on the day that they were created*, which seems to imply that heaven and earth were created on the same day. While this myth would appear to contradict the sequential creation described in Genesis 1:1-31, it avoids this by stating that the potential for subsequent creation already existed.

Sources:
Midrash ha-Ne'elam, Zohar Hadash 2d, 13d.

102. HOW GOD BEGOT BEING

God was the father of all that was begotten, and the mother was God's knowledge. God had intercourse with knowledge—not in human fashion—and begat being. Knowledge received the divine seed and gave birth, with many birth-throes, bearing the only beloved son, this world.

This is a strange philosophical creation myth of Philo, in which God, the father, has intercourse with knowledge (*gnosis* in Greek), the mother, and as a result the world, their only son, was begotten. Philo's use of the metaphor of human intercourse for divine forces implies a kind of mythic personification of them, and demonstrates the mythic dimension lying close to the surface in Philo's writing, despite his efforts to use allegory as a way of denying the mythic realm.

Sources:
Philo, *De Ebrietate* 30-31.

Studies:
"Daughter, Sister, Bride, and Mother: Images of the Femininity of God in the Early Kabbala" by Peter Schäfer, p. 235.

103. WHAT DOES THE EARTH STAND ON?

Once, when Aaron the Priest, brother of Moses, was offering sacrifices on Yom Kippur, the bull sprang up from beneath his hands and covered a cow. When that calf was born, it was stronger than any other. Before a year was out, the calf had grown bigger than the whole world.

God then took the world and stuck it on one horn of that bull. And the bull holds up the world on his horn, for that is God's wish. But when people sin, their sins make the world heavier, and the burden of the bull grows that much greater. Then the bull grows tired of its burden, and tosses the world from one horn to the other. That is when earthquakes take place, and everything is uncertain until the world stands secure on a single horn.

So it is that the bull tosses the world from time to time from one horn to the other, causing earthquakes and other catastrophes. And if people only knew of the danger, they would recognize how much they are dependent on God's mercy. For if they would only observe the commandments and sanctify God's name, the bull would stand still and the world remain quietly on its horns.

> This Moroccan myth about God putting the world on one horn of a giant bull demonstrates that myths, as well as folktales, can be found among the abundant tales collected orally in Israel by the Israel Folktale Archives. While many of these myths are found in earlier texts, sometimes, as here, a myth is passed down orally and is not to be found in the written tradition. This myth reminds us of myths from other cultures about what the world stands on, such as the widespread belief in South Asia and among North American Indians that the earth rests on the back of a turtle. Not only does this myth explain what the world stands on (since it appears to be standing still), but also provides an explanation for earthquakes and other disasters. Note the genesis of the bull that grows to be bigger than the world—it is born from the unplanned copulation of a bull about to be sacrificed on Yom Kippur. What the myth does not address is the obvious contradiction that the world already existed at the time of Aaron, brother of Moses, the first High Priest.
>
> *Sources:*
> IFA 4396.

104. CREATION *EX NIHILO*

When God created the world, He created it out of nothing and brought it into being. Who can understand what the Creator had in mind when He willed the universe to come into existence?

Some say that it was only the body of heaven that was created from nothing, while its form was created from the light above.

God is the Cause of all creation. It is God who sustains the existence of all that exists, for nothing can exist unless it emanates from God.

> *Creation Ex Nihilo* means creation out of nothing. This is the ultimate form of creation, in that it demonstrates that the power of the Creator is total. This myth, in its variants, emphasizes that God did indeed create the world out of nothing, and therefore emphasizes God's complete and utter mastery of all elements related to creation and existence.
>
> *Sources:*
> *Zohar Hadash Bereshit*, 17b; Nachmanides, *Perush Ramban al ha-Torah* on Genesis 1:1; Sforno on Exodus 34:6; *Akedat Yitzhak* on Genesis 18.

105. THE ORDER OF CREATION

The universe was created from the top down. The upper worlds were created first, and each and every subsequent world was created from the world above it. Thus it was not possible to hasten or to delay the creation of the world, but each development took place in turn. In this way all the worlds were brought into being, each one later than the other, until it came to be time for this world to be created.

This myth answers the question of whether God started Creation with the upper or lower worlds. This is a prominent question in the midrash. This is also a version of the myth of prior worlds. See "Prior Worlds," p. 71. This world is the last to be created in a succession of worlds. The difference in this kabbalistic myth and the earlier, rabbinic one is that the prior worlds are destroyed in the earlier version, while here they became the foundation of the building blocks of the universe. The other important point of this myth is not simply that lower worlds were created after upper ones, but that lower worlds were created from upper ones.

Sources:
Etz Hayim 1:20-28.

106. GOD'S GARMENT OF LIGHT

How did God create the heavens? Some say that God wrapped Himself in a prayer shawl, a *tallit* of light, and the light cast from that prayer shawl suffused the world. That garment of light was covered with the letters of the Hebrew alphabet, inscribed in black fire on white fire.

Others say that God draped the six days of Creation around Himself like a gown and dazzled the universe with His glory from one end to the other.

Then there are those who say that God took the light and stretched it like a garment, and the heavens continued to expand until God said, "Enough!"

God said, "Let there be light." And there was light (Gen. 1:3). This enigmatic verse raises as many questions as it answers. Did God create this light out of nothing, or did this light pre-exist? This question receives a number of answers in rabbinic sources, all of them based on interpretations of Psalms 104:2: *Who cover Yourself with light as with a garment, who stretches out the heavens like a curtain.* One such interpretation grows out of a dialogue between Rabbi Simeon ben Jehozadak and Rabbi Samuel bar Nachman in *Genesis Rabbah* 3:4. Rabbi Simeon asked the other, "How did God create light?" Rabbi Samuel replied in a whisper that God wrapped himself in a white garment, and when Rabbi Simeon noted that this explanation is found in Psalms 104:2 (and is therefore not esoteric, requiring a whisper), Rabbi Samuel explained: "I received this tradition in a whisper, so I passed it on in a whisper." Why would this teaching have been conveyed in a whisper? Because it hints that the light somehow pre-existed. This would imply that while God was the Creator, He created using existing building blocks and might somehow be viewed as diminishing God's accomplishment. In addition, there is a Gnostic interpretation in which the light of God's garment is identified with the First Created Being. See "The First Created Being," p. 118. This interpretation would certainly justify the use of a whisper.

The view that light itself was a kind of primordial element, along with darkness, chaos, and void (*tohu* and *vohu*), is found in "Light from the Temple," p. 411. Such an interpretation is also found in *Pirkei de-Rabbi Eliezer* 6, which interprets the verse from Psalms 104:2 to mean that God took of an existing light and stretched it out to create the world.

Another verse used to explain God's wearing of a garment at the time of the Creation is Psalms 104:1: *You are clothed with glory and majesty.* This is said to be the first of ten occasions in which God clothed himself in a garment (*Pesikta de-Rav Kahana* 22:5).

Rabbi Moshe Alshekh suggests in his commentary on Psalm 104 that the light that God draped around Himself was that of the six days of Creation, which were yet to take place. Only after God draped the six days in this fashion did Creation proceed. Alshekh also suggests that "clothing Himself in light" refers to the creation of God's Throne of Glory, and that the purpose of the Throne of Glory was to protect the world from the damaging effects of God's emanations. Thus the light serves as a kind of protective intermediary between God and the rest of creation, for God's original light proved too brilliant for the material universe to endure.

The tradition that God wore a fringed prayer shawl (*tallit*) is found in other sources. For example, God is said to have demonstrated the nature of such a prayer shawl to Moses by appearing to him in a garment with fringed corners. This is said to be one of the things that Moses could comprehend only after God demonstrated it to him.

Sources:

B. *Rosh ha-Shanah* 17b; *Genesis Rabbah* 3:4; *Midrash Tehillim* on Psalm 104:4; *Pirkei de-Rabbi Eliezer* 3; *Pesikta de-Rav Kahana* 21:5; *Romemot El* on Psalm 104; *Makhon Siftei Tzaddikim* on Gen. 17:1.

107. THE LIGHT OF THE FIRST DAY

Before the world was created, the thought arose in God's mind to create a light to illuminate it. So on the first day of Creation, God wrapped Himself in a garment of light, and the radiance of His majesty illuminated the world. That was the light of the first day, a primordial light, distinct from the light of the fourth day, when God created the sun, the moon, and the stars. That light was the first thing that God created and it completely suffused all of existence without beginning or end. Everything was filled with that light, which traveled throughout the cosmos without stopping, until all the world began to sing. Thus it is written, *He sends it forth under the whole heaven, and His light to the ends of the earth* (Job 37:3).

The light created on the first day accompanied all the days of Creation, and thus all the days are contained in the first day, for the world was created through that sacred light. It is the light of the eye. In that light Adam saw from one end of the universe to the other, and he was also able to view the world from the beginning of Creation until the end. For it was not only possible to see tangible things in this light, but even ethereal things, which are otherwise invisible.

Where did the light come from? Some say it was the light of Paradise, which God brought into the world at the time of Creation. For the first three days and nights, the primordial light shone undiminished. Seven times brighter than the sun, it was so intense that no created thing could gaze upon it. In this light it was possible for Adam to see from one end of the universe to the other.

Others say that the light existed even before the Creation. When God said, *"Let there be light,"* light came forth from the place in the universe where the Temple in Jerusalem would one day be built. Surrounded by that light, God completed the creation of the world.

How, then, did God bring the light into the world? Some say that God wrapped himself in a prayer shawl of light, and the light cast from that prayer shawl suffused the world. Others say that God draped the six days of Creation around Himself like a gown and dazzled the universe with His glory from one end to the other. Then there are those who say that God took the light and stretched it like a garment, and the heavens continued to expand until God said, "Enough!" Still others say that the light was cast from the very countenance of God.

How long did the light shine? Some say that the light of the first day accompanied all seven days of Creation, and all the days that followed contain the essence of the first. Therefore the light of the first day is still with us, dimmed though it may be.

Others say that this light shone undiminished for the first three days and nights of Creation. Seven times brighter than the sun, the primordial light was so intense that no created thing could gaze upon it. Still others say that the light created on the first day served thirty-six hours, twelve on the Sabbath eve, twelve on the Sabbath day, and twelve on the night of the Sabbath.

That sacred light pervaded the world until the very moment that Adam and Eve tasted the forbidden fruit. Then the first thing they lost was that precious light, for God, seeing the wicked deeds of the coming generations, hid the primordial light at once. Without it, the world grew dark around them, for the sun shone like a candle in comparison. Never again did they see the world in the splendor of that light, and that was the most painful punishment of all.

As for the fate of the primordial light, some say that God brought it back into Paradise, where it awaits the righteous in the World to Come. On the other hand, that light will be denied to the wicked, as it is said, *The light of the wicked is withheld* (Job 38:15). Others say that God gave that light as a gift to His Bride, the *Shekhinah*. Still others say that God hid that light in the Torah, in the mysteries concealed there, waiting to be discovered. And wherever the Torah is studied, a thread of this light is drawn down upon those who study it, as it is said, *Light is sown for the righteous* (Psalms 97:11). And when it is, the hidden light of the Torah is revealed to them in all its splendor.

Still others say that the light has continued to exist since the days of Adam, but that God has hidden it, so that the wicked will be unable to misuse it. For had it been completely removed, the world would not continue to exist for even one moment. Instead, it is concealed and the world is sustained. Not a day passes without some of this light being emitted to the world so that it can continue to exist. This is how God nourishes the world, for God has saved this light for the righteous at the End of Days, when the footsteps of the Messiah will be heard. Had the primordial light been completely concealed, the world would not continue to exist for even one moment.

So too is it said that God hid a small bit of that light inside a glowing stone, and gave it to Adam and Eve when they were expelled from the Garden, as a reminder of all that they had lost.

At the End of Days, when the footsteps of the Messiah will be heard in the world, that sacred light will be restored. Then everyone will see the true glory of God's creation.

See section V of the introduction for a discussion of the light of the first day, pp. lxxi-lxxiv.

Sources:
B. *Hagigah* 12a; Y. *Berakhot* 8:5; *Genesis Rabbah* 3:4-6, 11:2, 12:6, 42:3, 82:15; *Midrash Tehillim* 104:4; *Genesis Rabbah* 42:3; *Exodus Rabbah* 35:1; *Numbers Rabbah* 13:5; *Ruth Rabbah* 7; *Pirkei de-Rabbi Eliezer* 3; *Midrash Tehillim* 27:1; *2 Enoch* 25:3; *4 Ezra* 6:40; *Sefer ha-Bahir* 10, 57, 147, 160, 190; *Midrash Tanhuma, Shemini* 9; *Zohar* 1:21a, 1:31b-32a, 1:34a, 1:45a-46a, 2:25a, 2:148b-149a, 2:166b-167a, 2:230a, 3:103b-104a; *Zohar Hadash* 16a-b; *Yalkut Shim'oni* 47; *Pesikta Rabbati* 23:6, 46:1; *Sha'ar ha-Hakdamot* 4:14; *Likutei Moharan* 1:234; *Makhon Siftei Tzaddikim* on *Bereshit* 1:4; *Me'am Lo'ez, Bereshit* 1:4; *Shivhei ha-Besht.*

Studies:
"The Creation of Light in the First Chapter of Genesis" by Giovanni Garbini.
The Lamp of God: A Jewish Book of Light by Freema Gottlieb, pp. 141-152.

108. THE FIRST CLOAK

Light was the very first creation on the first day; thus light was the first cloak in which God concealed His spiritual essence, as it is said, *Cloaked in light as with a garment* (Ps. 104:2).

Some say that God created the angels out of that the primal light. For angels are a pure spiritual force radiating light, and the angels surround God the way a cloak envelops whoever wears it.

> The extensive rabbinic tradition about the *or ha-ganuz*, the primordial light that has since been concealed, is frequently linked to Creation, in that the light is regarded as the first manifestation of the God's essence. Here the creation of light is directly linked to the creation of the angels, and the angels are viewed as being a spiritual essence consisting entirely of light. Psalm 104 contains fragments of ancient Jewish creation myths. See Psalm 104:1-9. Also, see "The Light of the First Day," p. 83, and "The Creation of Angels," p. 115.
>
> *Sources:*
> Ibn Ezra on Psalm 104:2; Ibn Yachya on Psalm 104:2.

109. THE *TZOHAR*

When the world was first created, God filled the world with a sacred light, known as the primordial light. This was the light that came into being when *God said, "Let there be light"* (Gen. 1:3). It was not the light of the sun, for that did not come into being until the fourth day, when God created the sun and the moon and the stars. It was a miraculous light by which it was possible for Adam to see from one end of the world to the other.

When Adam and Eve ate the forbidden fruit, the first thing they lost was that precious light. Without it, the world seemed dark to them, for the sun shone like a candle in comparison. But God preserved one small part of that precious light inside a glowing stone, and the angel Raziel delivered this stone to Adam after they had been expelled from the Garden of Eden, as a token of the world they had left behind. This jewel, known as the *Tzohar*, sometimes glowed brightly and sometimes was dim.

As he lay on his deathbed, Adam gave the jewel to his son Seth, who passed it down to the righteous Enoch. Enoch grew in wisdom until he was taken into Paradise in a chariot, and transformed into the angel Metatron, the heavenly scribe and Prince of the treasuries of heaven.

Before departing this world, Enoch gave the *Tzohar* to his son, Methuselah. Methuselah slept in its glowing light, and some say that is why he lived longer than anyone else. Methuselah passed on the jewel to his son Lamech, who gave it to his son, Noah, who brought it with him on the ark. Indeed, God instructed Noah to do so when he said, *"Put the Tzohar in the ark"* (Gen. 6:16). Noah hung it on the deck, and for forty days and nights it illumined the ark. Noah determined whether it was day or night by gauging the brilliance of the stone. It was dim during the day, but it shone brightly at night.

When the ark landed on Mount Ararat, the first thing Noah did was to plant grapes, and when they grew ripe, he made wine and became drunk, and at that moment the *Tzohar* fell from where it had been hung in the ark, rolled into the water, and sank to the bottom of the sea. There it was carried by the currents until it came to rest in an underwater cave.

Years later, after the waters had subsided, the child Abraham was born in that cave. His mother had gone there to give birth, to escape King Nimrod's decree that all newborn boys be put to death. For Nimrod had seen a sign that a child born at that time would overthrow him. After giving birth, Abraham's mother grew afraid for the safety of her family, and at last she abandoned the infant in the cave and returned home. Then the angel Gabriel descended to the cave and fed the infant with his thumb, through which milk and honey flowed, and because he was fed in that miraculous way, the boy began to grow at the rate of a year every day. And on the third day, while exploring the cave, he found a stone glowing in one of the crevices of the cave. Then the angel, who knew how precious it was, put it on a chain, and hung it around Abraham's neck.

Thirteen days later Abraham's mother returned to the cave, for she could not put the fate of the infant out of her mind. She expected to find that the child was no longer living, but instead she found a grown boy, who said that he was her child. She refused to believe it at first, but when he showed her the glowing stone and the sacred light it cast, she came to believe that a miracle had taken place.

Abraham wore that glowing jewel all the days of his life. Whoever was ill and looked into that stone soon healed, and it also served as an astrolabe to study the stars. Before his death, Abraham gave that glowing jewel to Isaac, and Isaac gave it to Jacob at the time he gave him the stolen blessing. For Isaac had intended to give the glowing stone to Esau, but Rebecca, who was a seer, knew well that it was destined to belong to Jacob.

Jacob was wearing the *Tzohar* when he dreamed of the ladder reaching to heaven, with angels ascending and descending on it. And he, in turn, gave the stone to his beloved son, Joseph, when he gave him the coat of many colors.

Jacob made Joseph promise to wear the stone at all times, but he did not reveal its power, which he knew well. And because Joseph's brothers did not know that the amulet was precious, they did not take it from him when they stripped him of the coat of many colors and cast him naked into the dark pit.

Now snakes and scorpions lived at the bottom of that pit. And when Joseph heard them slithering and creeping in the dry leaves, he shivered in the darkness at the bottom of the pit. All at once a light began to glow, and Joseph saw that it was coming from the amulet he wore around his neck. And as long as Joseph remained in that pit, the jewel continued to glow, so that he was never afraid. At last Joseph heard Midianite traders calling out to him from the top of that pit. They pulled him out of the pit and brought him to Egypt, where they sold him into slavery and to the destiny that fate held for him, which was to become Prince of Egypt.

When Joseph was imprisoned in the dungeon, he discovered that if he placed the *Tzohar* inside his cup and peered into it, he could read the future and interpret dreams. That is how he interpreted the dreams of the butler and baker, and later the dreams of Pharaoh that prophesied the seven years of famine. It was that same cup that Joseph hid in the saddlebags of Benjamin, about which his servant said, *"It is the very one from which my master drinks and which he uses for divination"* (Gen. 44:5).

That cup, with the precious jewel in it, was placed inside Joseph's coffin at the time of his death, and it remained there until Moses recovered Joseph's coffin and was told in a dream to take out the glowing stone and hang it in the Tabernacle, where it became known as the *Ner Tamid*, the Eternal Light. And that is why, even to this day, an Eternal Light burns above every Ark of the Torah in every synagogue.

> This tale is a classic example of a chain midrash—a series of midrashim that are linked to each other by a common object or character. The object here is the glowing stone known as the *Tzohar*. This myth builds on that of the primordial light that God brought into being on the first day of Creation. See "The Light of the First Day," p. 83.
>
> The word *"Tzohar"* only appears once in the Torah, when God instructs Noah on how to build the ark and tells him *"Put the Tzohar in the ark"* (Gen. 6:16). For this reason there is uncertainty about its meaning. Rashi's comments on Genesis 16:6 observe that some say the *Tzohar* was a window (or an opening, a skylight, or a dome—

implying that it should admit light into the ark) and others say that it was a precious stone. Virtually all other midrashim adopt the view that it was some kind of precious stone. *Targum Yonathan* paraphrases Genesis 6:16 to read, "Go to the river Pishon and take a brilliant stone from there and place it into the ark, to illuminate it for you." *Midrash Aggadah* states that God commanded Noah to bring a diamond with him on the ark, to give them light like midday, because the ark would be dark. *"Tzohar"* is probably linked to *Tzoharayim*, the Hebrew word for "noon." The sound of the word is suggestive of *zohar*, which means "splendor" or "illumination," and is the title of the central text of Jewish mysticism. What seems clear is that it indicated some kind of light, whether shining through a window or reflected from a glowing jewel. The need for a jewel arises because of the likelihood that dark clouds covered the world during the days and nights of the Flood, and therefore no light would shine through a window. This follows the tradition that during the time of the Flood, day and night were indistinguishable (*Genesis Rabbah* 25:2, 34:11; Rashi on Genesis 8:22). Not only did darkness cover the earth during the 40 days and nights of the Flood, but the planets ceased to function. How is this known? Because at the time of the covenant of the rainbow, God promised Noah, *"So long as earth exists ... day and night shall not cease"* (Gen. 8:22). From this it can be deduced that day and night were indistinguishable for the duration of the Flood, and that the heavenly bodies ceased to function.

The legend of the glowing gem that Noah hung in the ark is found in *Genesis Rabbah* 31:11: "During the whole 12 months that Noah was in the ark he did not require the light of the sun by day or the light of the moon by night, but he had a polished gem which he hung up: when it was dim he knew that it was day, and when it shone he knew that it was night." Noah used this information to know when to feed the animals at their customary times. This jewel is linked to the myth that God gave a jewel to Adam and Eve at the time they were cast out of the Garden of Eden, to remind them of all they lost. The midrash then links this jewel to the genealogy between Adam and Noah, as well as that beginning with Abraham and the subsequent generations, until the time of the Temple.

The story of the precious stone of Abraham is found in *B. Bava Batra* 16b. This account offers an alternate fate for the precious stone, saying, "When Abraham passed away from the world, the Holy One, blessed be He, hung it on the wheel of the sun." The legend about Joseph in the pit is found in *Midrash Aseret Harugei Malkhut*. The story of Joseph's cup being carried off by his brothers is found in Genesis 44:5. The *Ner Tamid* or Eternal Light is first mentioned in Exodus 27:20: *You shall further instruct the Israelites to bring you clear oil of beaten olives for lighting, for kindling lamps regularly.* Every Jewish synagogue contains such a light which is kept lit at all times. For the link of the *Tzohar* and the *Ner Tamid* see *Pesikta de-Rav Kahana* 21.

This myth evolves out of an attempt to resolve two problems in the biblical text: the nature of the light of the first day of Creation, before the creation of the sun and moon and stars, and the meaning of *Tzohar* in the passage about building the ark. The midrash explains that the light of the first day was a sacred light, which, according to some accounts, was cast from God's garment of light, and, according to others, was reflected from the robe of the *Shekhinah*. See "The Light of the First Day," p. 83. The vehicle of the chain midrash makes it possible for it to be transmitted from Adam to Noah, and then from Noah to Abraham and the other patriarchs.

In *Pirkei de-Rabbi Eliezer*, 10, a *Tzohar*-like pearl is described as having been suspended in the belly of the whale, where it was said to have shone as brightly as the sun at noon. It showed Jonah all that was in the sea and in the depths.

According to the *Zohar*, Rabbi Shimon bar Yohai also had possession of the *Tzohar*: "Our companion, Bar Yohai, has a jewel, a precious stone, and I have looked upon the light emitted by it, and it is like the light of the sun, illuminating the whole world. This light extends from the heavens to the earth, and will continue to illumine the world until the Ancient of Days comes, and sits upon His throne" (*Zohar* 1:11a-11b). The *Tzohar* also appears in various Jewish folk and Hasidic tales, usually in the form of a glowing jewel found in some accidental way. It is possible that J. R. R. Tolkien made use of some of the legends about the *Tzohar* in *The Silmarillion*, in which the central motif concerns jewels containing the last of a primordial light.

Sources:
B. *Sanhedrin* 108b; Y. *Pesahim* 1:1; *Genesis Rabbah* 31:11; *Midrash Aggadah*; *Akedat Yitzhak* 4; *Targum Yonathan* on Genesis 6:16; Rashi on Genesis 16:6, Gen. 8:22; *Midrash Aseret Harugei Malkhut* in *Otzar ha-Midrashim*, p. 444; IFA 4382.

110. HOW LIGHT AND DARKNESS WERE CREATED

Before any visible beings came into existence, there were only invisible beings. Then God decided to create a visible creation. So God said, "Let one of the invisible things descend and become visible." And Adoil, one of the invisible things, descended. He was extremely large, and in his belly he had a great light. God said to Adoil, "Disintegrate yourself, Adoil, and let what is born from you become visible." And Adoil disintegrated himself, and out came a very great light. And God was in the midst of the light, and a light came forth out of that light and revealed all the creation that God had thought to create. And God saw that it was good. And God placed a throne for himself, and sat down on it. And then God spoke to the light and said, "You rise up and become the foundation for the highest things. For there is nothing higher than light, except for nothingness itself."

And God summoned the very lowest beings for a second time, and said, "Let one of the invisible beings descend and become visible." And Arkhas came out, solid and heavy and very red. And God said to Arkhas, open yourself up, Arkhas, and let what is born from you become visible." And Arkhas disintegrated himself, and a great darkness emerged from him, very large, bearing the creation of all lower things. And God saw how good it was. And God said to the darkness, "Descend and become the foundation of all lower things. For there is nothing lower than the darkness, except nothing itself."

Then God took some light and some darkness and mixed them together, and commanded them to thicken, and when they did, He wrapped them with light, and spread it out, and it became water. And God spread it out above the darkness and below the light, dividing the world above from the world below. And God made a foundation of light around the waters, with seven circles inside it, with the appearance of crystal. And he pointed out the route of each one of the seven stars to its own heaven. And God made a division between the light and the darkness, and said to the light that it should be day, and to darkness that it should be night. *And there was evening and there was morning, a first day* (Gen. 1:5).

This astonishing creation myth from *2 Enoch* dates from around the second century BCE to the first century CE. It portrays a version of the creation of light and darkness that is radically different from that found in Genesis. Here the earliest manifestation of existence occurs when God commands two invisible beings, Adoil and Arkhas, to give birth to light and darkness, which come to serve as the upper and lower foundations of the world. Adoil and Arkhas are primordial beings—not angels or gods, but invisible forces entirely under God's command. And it is God who commands that they descend and become visible. Of particular interest is God's command to Adoil and Arkhas that they disintegrate themselves, suggesting that their disintegration makes possible the subsequent births that take place. When they do, a great light comes forth from Adoil, while Arkhas gives birth to darkness. This myth is an interesting parallel to that of the Ari about the Shattering of the Vessels. In both cases a kind of breaking apart is required before anything can be created. See "The Shattering of the Vessels and the Gathering of the Sparks," p. 122.

This myth about Adoil and Arkhas also has distinctly Gnostic overtones, for it suggests that God did not create light and darkness by Himself. Instead, God commanded that certain invisible beings give birth to these forces, and that is what took place. There is no explanation given for the existence of the invisible beings, no statement that God created them. Further, it is stated that God coexisted with them and moved around with them. But God's command over them is demonstrated when He orders them to manifest themselves and then to disintegrate themselves, so that light and darkness can be created. Thus this myth suggests that, for God, the primary work of Creation was in making the invisible visible.

The very strangeness of this myth seems to hint at an even more ancient Jewish mythology where elemental forces were personified as primitive beings rather than as spiritual beings such as angels. Or it might be that this myth was influenced by Egyptian and Iranian mythologies.

The end of this myth dovetails into Genesis 1:5: *And there was evening and there was morning, a first day.* Thus this myth explicitly offers itself as an alternative to the creation myth found in Genesis 1:1-4, where light is created and darkness already seems to exist. It is a much more complex—and mythical—kind of creation than God simply saying *"Let there be light," and there was light* (Gen. 1:3).

Sources:
2 Enoch (J) 24-27.

111. CREATION BY LIGHT

In His wondrous hidden way, God contracted His light again and again until physical bodies were created. Thus God's kingdom has dominion over all, for all the world is but an emanation of His light.

Here Rabbi Kalonymus Kalman Shapira reinterprets the kabbalistic concept of *tzimtzum* so that it refers not to God's contraction of Himself, but to God's contraction of light, and through this process the physical word is made manifest. This is also a sefirotic myth, in which each subsequent contraction of God leads to the next sefirah. Thus two primary kabbalistic concepts stand behind this brief yet original myth created by Rabbi Shapira, a twentieth century rabbi who perished in the Warsaw Ghetto. The existence of this myth is evidence of the continued myth-making process in Judaism into our own time.

Sources:
Hovat ha-Talmidim.

112. THE LIGHT OF PROPHECY

The light and holiness that are present in every Jew find their source in the heights of the supernal world. It is like wine poured into a flask with a funnel. Only the narrow end of the funnel enters the flask. In this way the light from above diminishes and contracts until it takes the form of the spirit that inspired the prophets. It is then diminished further until all that remains in the present generation is a small spark of prophecy.

A rabbinic principle is that the spirit of prophecy available to the patriarchs was greatly reduced in the time of the prophets, and subsequently was reduced still further, until it is said that a dream is one sixtieth of prophecy. This follows the general belief that the true giants of humanity existed in the distant past, and our generation is removed from the true sources of prophetic inspiration. See "The Holy Spirit," p. 18.

Sources:
Hovat ha-Talmidim.

113. GOD'S SHOUT

On the first day God brought fire and water, mixed them together, and made the heavens from them. But the heavens remained in a fluid state and did not solidify until the second day, when God shouted, *"Let there be a firmament!"* (Gen. 1:6). Then the pillars of heaven trembled; they were awe-struck by His divine shout (Job 26:11), and after that they remained fixed in one place.

> This midrash attempts to explain why God created the heavens on the first day (Gen. 1:1), but He did not create the firmament until the second day (Gen. 1:7). Although the only description in Genesis about God's voice states that "God said," (Gen. 1:3), this myth goes beyond the text of Genesis by insisting that God's voice was a shout, and the power of this shout was so great that the pillars of heaven solidified and ever since have remained firmly in place. The use of "shout," even more than "said," suggests a powerful personification of God. It also suggests a strong parallel with Greek and Canaanite gods, who also display similar human characteristics.
>
> *Sources:*
> B. *Hagigah* 12a; *Genesis Rabbah* 4:2, 12:10; *Sefer ha-Bahir* 59; Rashi on Genesis 1:6.

114. THE WORK OF CREATION

How did God create the heavens? He took fire and water and beat them together, and from them the heavens were made.

How did God create the earth? Some say He took two balls, one of fire, the other of snow, kneaded them together, and worked them into one. Others say there were four balls, one for each of the four corners of the world. Still others insist there were six balls, one for each of the four corners and one for above and one for below.

It is also said that God took two elements, chaos and void, and combined them together. For they were the elements out of which darkness and water were created, and from darkness and water the world was brought into being.

Still others say that when God decided to create the world, He brought a single spark out of the primal darkness, and blew upon it, until it was kindled. And He brought out of the recesses of the deep a single drop, and He joined them together, and with them He created the world.

> Creation by elements is a common theme in rabbinic sources. Sometimes these elements are said to have preceded Creation, as in this case, where they are identified as *tohu* and *vohu*, chaos and void. Other legends suggest that the world was created out of water, wind, and fire: "Three creations preceded the creation of this world: water, wind, and fire. Water conceived and gave birth to thick darkness. Fire conceived and gave birth to light. Wind conceived and gave birth to wisdom. Thus is the world maintained by these six creations: by wind and darkness, by fire and light, by water and wisdom" (*Exodus Rabbah* 15:22). However, *Genesis Rabbah* 1:9 reminds us that these primeval elements were created by God, and were not eternal: "A certain philosopher said to Rabbi Gamaliel: 'Your God was indeed a great artist, but He found good materials which assisted Him.' 'What are they?' Rabbi Gamaliel asked. '*Tohu*,

vohu, darkness, water, wind and the deep.' At this Rabbi Gamaliel exclaimed: 'Woe to that man!'" Note that all six elements are mentioned in Psalm 104.

There are similar Greek creation myths found in Hesiod's *Theogony* 211-32, in which there is a union between darkness and chaos. What is missing in these myths is God's role in combining these elements to create the world.

Sources:
Genesis Rabbah 4:7, 6:3, 14:5; Y. Rosh ha-Shanah 2; Leviticus Rabbah 14:9; Midrash
  Tanhuma, Bereshit 11; Genesis Rabbah 10:3, 10:5; B. Hagigah 12a; Sefer ha-Zikhronot
  1:6; Sefer ha-Bahir 59; Zohar 1:86b-87a.

115. HOW THE HEAVENS WERE CREATED

How were the heavens created? With the brilliance of God's covering, which God took up and spread like a garment, as it is said, *He spread them out as a tent for dwelling therein.* Then the heavens went on expanding until God told them to stop. So too did God bless each of the four corners of the heavens. From the east the light of the world goes forth, and from the south the dew of blessings descends upon the land. From the west come the stores of snow and hail, heat and cold, while the rain that falls for the benefit of the land comes from the north.

Tractate *Hagigah* of the Talmud describes the world expanding like a roll of thread or rope at the beginning of Creation, until God rebuked it and brought it to a standstill. This interpretation is based on the verse *The pillars of heaven were trembling, but they became astonished at His rebuke* (Job 26:11). There is a similar myth about God rebuking the sea when it was created and causing it to dry up. This derives from the verse *He rebukes the sea and dries it up* (Nah. 1:4). See "The Rebellion of the Waters," p. 105. See also "God's Shout," p. 90, where God delivers a similar rebuke, which causes the pillars of heaven to harden, holding up the firmament.

Sources:
B. Hagigah 12a; Sefer ha-Zikhronot 1:7, 1:8.

116. THE EARTH'S FOUNDATIONS

Then Yahweh replied to Job out of the tempest and said, "Where were you when I laid the earth's foundations? Speak if you have understanding. Do you know who fixed its dimensions or who measured it with a line? Onto what were its bases sunk? Who set its cornerstone when the morning stars sang together and all the divine beings shouted for joy?"

God's reply to Job challenges Job's right to question any of God's ways by pointing out that, as the Creator of the world, He does not owe Job any answers. Here God describes creating the world the way people build a house, laying the foundation, marking off its dimensions, and laying the cornerstone. While God's intention may be rhetorical, the effect is a vivid mythic description of God laying the foundations of the earth.

Sources:
Job 38:1, 38:4-7.

117. CREATION BY GOD'S NAME

It is a wonderful and strange and great secret that the Name by which heaven and earth were created was God's Name. For that Name was the instrument through which the world was brought into being, as it is said, *By the word of Yahweh were the heavens made* (Ps. 33:6). All the categories of creation were swallowed up and bound together and suspended and sealed, and *God saw that this was good* (Gen. 1:12).

Some say that the generations of heaven and earth were created by the letter *heh*, which appears twice in God's Name. Others say that God used the first two letters of his Name, *yod* and *he*, to create the world. But most say that God used all four letters of His Name when He began to create heaven and earth.

> The powers attributed to the four-letter Name of God are limitless. The Maharal was said to have pronounced the Name in order to bring the Golem of Prague, a man made out of clay, to life. Rabbi Judah the Pious used the Name to bring a dead man to life, in order to testify as to who had killed him. This myth asserts that God's Name—YHVH—was the instrument by which the world was created. Further, the role of the individual letters of the Name is debated, and whether or not all four of them took part in Creation. See "The God of Our Fathers," p. 25 and "The Tetragrammaton," p. 27 for a further discussion of the Tetragrammaton.
>
> *Sources:*
> *Genesis Rabbah* 12:10; *Hekhalot Rabbati* 9.

118. CREATION BY GOD'S BEAUTY

The world was created by God's beauty: the deeps were set ablaze by His beauty, the firmaments were kindled by His radiance. The angels burst out of His stature, the mighty exploded from His crown, and the precious erupted from His garment. And all of the trees and grasses came forth exulting from His joy.

> This myth is found in a hymn from *Hekhalot Rabbati*, also known as the "Greater Hekhalot," one of the primary *Hekhalot* texts describing heavenly journeys. In this unusual myth, creation is described as having been kindled by God's beauty. Other myths portray God in an active manner, either speaking, as in Genesis, or shouting, or smashing elements together with His hands. But here it is God's attribute of beauty that is identified as the creative element that gives birth to the creation of the world.
>
> Later in this hymn God is described as a cosmic tree, "who covered the heavens with His glorious bough, and appeared from the heights in His majesty."
>
> *Sources:*
> *Hekhalot Rabbati.*

119. THE PALACE OF HEAVEN

God built the upper rooms of the palace first, for having spread a roof He built the top story, which He suspended on nothingness above the world's atmosphere. After that He made the clouds into His chariots and colonnades out of the whirlwind. He built the upper chambers with balconies of water, and He built the top stories not with stone or hewn blocks, but with walls of compressed water. God then created windows in the firmament, in the east and in the west. Some of these windows were created to serve the sun and some for the moon. There are also eleven windows that the moon does not enter.

> Here God's palace is portrayed as not only being in the heavens, but being the very heavens themselves. Thus in creating the heavens, God created His own palace. This passage is based on Psalm 104:3: *He sets the rafters of His lofts in the waters, makes the clouds His chariot, moves on the wings of the wind.* The image also echoes Isaiah 40:22, *It is He who is enthroned above the vault of the earth.*

Midrash Tanhuma-Yelammedenu, Bereshit 4 contrasts man's method of building a palace with that of God: "A man first constructs the foundations of a palace and then erects the upper story upon it, but God fashioned the upper spheres first and then created the earthly spheres: *In the beginning God created the heavens,* and afterward: *and the earth* (Gen. 1:1). The 11 windows that the moon does not enter refer to the 11 days by which the solar year exceeds the lunar year.

Sources:
Exodus Rabbah 15:22; *Midrash Tanhuma-Yelammedenu, Bereshit* 4; *Midrash Tanhuma-Yelammedenu, Hayyei Sarah* 3; *Eliyahu Rabbah* 160.

Studies:
"Biblical Cosmology" by Tikva Frymer-Kensky.

120. CREATION ACCORDING TO PHILO

God is eternally creating the world. Indeed, there never was a time when God was not creating it. Ever since the beginning, God's thoughts of Creation were with Him. For God is always thinking and always creating. Without a counselor—for who else was there?—and making use of His own powers, God's will created this visible world. God used His Logos as an instrument with which to divide the formless expanse to create the world.

Even if the world is now immortal through the providence of God, there was a time when it was not. But God, of course, is eternally existent, always has existed, and always will.

> Here Philo presents his theory that God did not stop after creating the world, but has continued to create it ever since. This engages the theological question of what God's actions have been since He completed the creation of the world. In Philo's view the work of Creation is an ongoing process. See "Re-creating the World," p. 292. "Logos," as Philo uses the term, is an intermediary between God and the world.
>
> *Sources:*
> Philo, *De Providentia* 17; Philo, *De Opificio Mundi* 21-23; Philo, *Legum Allegoriarum* 3:96; Philo, *Quis Rerum Divinarum Heres Sit* 134, 140; Philo, *De Decalogo* 58.

121. THE COSMIC SEED

In the beginning a holy spark emerged from within the hidden depths of God, concealed within the mystery of the Infinite. As the spark began to glow, radiant colors were revealed. That spark was a cosmic seed, planted in the innermost recesses of the divine womb. There it was hidden away within a palace of its own creation, the way a silkworm hides itself in a palace of its own. It was there, in that palace, that the holy seed was sown, from which all of existence came forth. Before that spark nothing is known. That is why it is called the Beginning.

> This is the key kabbalistic creation myth in the *Zohar*, found near the beginning of the book. It is both a mystical commentary on Genesis 1:1 and a creation myth of its own, as well as the primary myth describing the process of emanation of the ten sefirot. As a creation myth, it draws on the cosmic egg type of myth, in this case creation from a cosmic seed that takes root in the primordial womb. Unstated, but suggested, is the mythic image of a divine womb, and the hint of a goddess figure who gives birth to the world.
>
> At the same time, this myth functions in the *Zohar* as an alternate creation myth, that of creation by emanation, as performed through the ten sefirot. It proposes that

the world emanated from the highest, unknowable part of God known as *Ein Sof*, the Endless, in a series of emanations, each identified with one of the ten sefirot. The language of the *Zohar* in presenting this myth is extremely allusive, symbolic, and cloaked in mystery.

It is possible to see this myth as a key influence in the famous myth of the Ari of "The Shattering of the Vessels and the Gathering of the Sparks," which draws on the central image of the spark. Indeed, the Ari's myth can be viewed as an imaginative retelling of the myth of the cosmic seed.

In "Kabbalah and Myth," Gershom Scholem comments about this myth: "It is the world seed . . . which is sown in the primordial womb of the 'supernal' mother. . . . Fertilized in this womb, the world seed through her emanates the other seven potencies, which the kabbalists interpret as the archetypes of all Creation, but also as the seven 'first days' of the first chapter of Genesis, or in other words as the original stages of intradivine development."

Sources:
Zohar 1:15a; *Sha'ar ha-Gilgulim.*

Studies:
"Kabbalah and Myth" in *On the Kabbalah and Its Symbolism* by Gershom Scholem, p. 103.

122. A UNIVERSE OF WATER

At first there was only a universe of water. God then took snow from beneath His Throne of Glory and cast it upon the waters, and the waters froze and became the dust of the earth, and God blessed it, so that it became fruitful and multiplied. Thus the earth stands upon the waters. The waters stand upon pillars of mountains. The pillars of mountains stand upon the wind. The wind stands upon the whirlwind, and God made the whirlwind like an amulet hung from His arm.

This myth explains how land was created when the whole earth was covered with water. An alternate explanation in *Pesikta Rabbati* 48:2 states that "Primeval waters covered the whole world. What did God do? Some say He emptied them into that which was already full. Others say He pressed down upon them, so to speak, and made them gather into one great sea." This, then, is a divine miracle, in which God pours water into water that was already full, and it does not overflow.

A later text in *Midrash Konen* greatly elaborates on the chain of images in this text: "The earth is stretched out upon the waters, and the waters on pillars of *hashmal*, and the pillars of *hashmal* on the Mountain of Hailstones, and the Mountain of Hailstones on the Storehouses of Snow, and the Storehouses of Snow on the Storehouses of Water and Fire, and the Storehouses of Water on the sea, and the sea on the deep (*tehom*), and the deep on chaos (*tohu*), and chaos on the void (*vohu*), and the void stands upon the sea, and the sea stands on the sweet waters, and the sweet waters stand on the mountains, and the mountains stand on the wind, and the wind on the wings of storm, and the storm is tied to the heavens, and the heavens are suspended from the arm of the Holy One, blessed be He."

In *Merkavah Rabbah*, it is not just the whirlwind that hangs like an amulet from God's arm, but the universe itself, based on the verse, *And beneath His arm—the universe* (Deut. 32:27).

The transformation of snow into water is linked with Job 37:6, *For He says to the snow, "Become earth,"* while the ending echoes the biblical phrase, *The arm of Yahweh has been revealed* (Isa. 53:1).

Sources:
B. *Hagigah* 12b; Y. *Hagigah* 2:1; *Midrash Tanhuma, Bereshit* 11; *Pirkei de-Rabbi Eliezer* 3; *Pesikta Rabbati* 48.2; *Midrash Tehillim* 104.8; *Merkavah Rabbah*; *Midrash Konen* in *Beit ha-Midrash* 2:32-33.

123. THE THREE CRAFTSMEN

When God first created the world, everything consisted of water, and from water God developed the world. He made three craftsmen to do His work—heaven, earth, and water. With these, He created everything in this world. He directed each of the three craftsmen to produce the creations necessary for the world. He bid water produce earth, commanding the waters to gather in one place. The waters did as they were commanded and that is when dry land appeared, as it is said, *"Let the water below the sky be gathered into one area, that the dry land may appear"* (Gen. 1:9).

Then God called upon the earth to produce its creations—animals and other living creatures. And the earth did as it was commanded, as it is said, *"Let the earth bring forth every kind of living creature"* (Gen. 1:24). So too did God call upon the earth to produce vegetation and plants. And the earth did so, as it is said, *"Let the earth sprout vegetation: seed-bearing plants, fruit trees of every kind on earth that bear fruit with the seed in it"* (Gen. 1:11). And God called upon the waters to produce swarms of fish and birds, as it is said, *"Let the waters bring forth swarms of living creatures, and birds that fly above the earth across the expanse of the sky"* (Gen. 1:20).

God then called upon the heavens to make a separation between the upper waters and the lower waters, as it is said, *"Let there be a firmament in the midst of the waters, and let it divide the waters from the waters"* (Gen. 1:6), and it was done. Then God called upon the heavens to illuminate the earth, as it is said, *"Let there be lights in the firmament of the heavens"* (Gen. 1:14), and this, too, was accomplished.

But when it was time to create man, God said, "None of you is able to produce this creature alone. All of you must unite, and I too will join you. Together we shall make man." So God joined with the three craftsmen in creating man, and God gave him a soul.

> This myth embellishes the Genesis creation myth, personifying heaven, earth, and water, and attributing the creations of the earth to them, acting at God's command. Thus God delegates His powers to these personified forces, and the actual work of Creation comes from them, instead of from the word of God. This indicates a remythologizing process, moving away from the abstraction of creation by the word toward creation by primordial forces.
>
> One of the primary rabbinic debates about Creation centers on whether or not God had any assistance. Just as the angels are said to have assisted God in some roles of Creation, the elements are personified as celestial entities, virtually as lesser gods, who were created to carry out God's orders. But in doing so they play an active role in the work of Creation. This detracts from the stunning totality of God's accomplishment. In other myths, God does not depend on assistance from other celestial beings or on the existence of some kind of pre-existent elements, such as darkness and light, water, earth, and heaven. In *De Somniis* 1:76, Philo identifies both kinds of elements: "When God gave birth to all things, He not only brought them into sight, but also brought into being things that had not existed before. Thus He was not merely an artificer, but also a Creator."
>
> Further, God joins in with the three other elements to create man—God contributes the soul. Even though this is the most important part, it is still only one part out of four. Thus from a theological point of view, it appears that this myth from *Midrash ha-Ne'elam* takes the point of view that God did have assistance in creating the world, but that God Himself first created those assistants, the elements, to serve that very purpose. This mitigates the pagan aspect of this myth.
>
> *Sources:*
> Philo, *De Opificio Mundi* 170-171; Philo, *De Somniis* 1:76; Midrash ha-Ne'elam, *Zohar Hadash* 16a-b.
>
> *Studies:*
> "Gnostic Themes in Rabbinic Cosmology" by Alexander Altmann.

124. THE PILLARS OF THE WORLD

The world stands upon pillars. Some say it stands on twelve pillars, according to the number of the tribes of Israel. Others say that it rests on seven pillars, which stand on the water. This water is on top of the mountains, which rest on wind and storm. Still others say that the world stands on three pillars. Once every three hundred years they move slightly, causing earthquakes. But Rabbi Eleazar ben Shammua says that it rests on one pillar, whose name is "Righteous."

> One of the ancient creation myths found in many cultures describes the earth as standing on one or more pillars. In this Jewish version of the myth, several theories are found—that the earth stands on twelve, seven, or three pillars—or on one. Rabbi Eleazar ben Shammua gives that one pillar the name of *Tzaddik*, "Righteous," under-scoring an allegorical reading of this myth, whereby God is the pillar that supports the world. This, of course, is the central premise of monotheism. Alternatively, his comment may be understood to refer to the *Tzaddik*, the righteous man whose exist-ence is required for the world to continue to exist. Or it might refer to the principle of righteousness, and how the world could not exist without it.
>
> *Sources:*
> B. *Hagigah* 12b; *Me'am Lo'ez* on Genesis 1:10.

125. THE FOUNDATION STONE

The world has a foundation stone. This stone serves as the starting point for all that was created, and serves as a true foundation.

How did it come to exist? In the beginning, when God desired to create the world, He took snow from beneath the Throne of Glory and cast it into the waters, where it congealed into a stone in the midst of the Deep. This is the center of the universe, and from it the earth expanded in all directions. God began the creation of His world at that foundation stone, and built the world upon it.

Others say that God took a stone compounded of fire, water, and air, and cast it into the abyss so that it held fast there, holding back the waters of the deep, and the world was planted in that place. Then there are those who say that God took the Foundation Stone and hurled it to the place designated for the Temple, and raised His right foot and drove the stone down into the very bottom of the deep and made it the pillar of the earth and founded the world upon it.

Still others say that God took an emerald stone engraved with mysteries of the alpha-bet, and threw it into the waters. It drifted from place to place until it came to the Holy Land, and there it sank, and the whole world was firmly established on it. And that is why it is called the *Even ha-Shetiyyah*, the Foundation Stone.

When King David decided to build the Temple in Jerusalem, he commanded that shafts be dug to a depth of fifteen hundred cubits. And lo, they struck a stone in one of those shafts. As soon as he learned of it, King David went there with Ahitophel, his counselor, and with other members of the court. They descended into the pit, and there, at the bot-tom, they saw the immense stone, shining like the darkest emerald.

All those who saw it were amazed, and they knew that it must, indeed, be that fabled stone, which served as the world's foundation. Yet all at once King David was possessed by a great curiosity to see what lay beneath it. King David ordered it to be raised, but a voice came forth from the stone, saying: "Be warned that I must not be lifted. I serve to hold back the waters of the Abyss."

All of them stood in awe of that voice, but King David's curiosity was still not sated. He decided to ignore the warning, and once more he ordered the stone to be raised. None of his advisors dared say anything, for they feared his wrath. After a great effort, a corner of the Foundation Stone was lifted up, and King David bent down and peered into the Abyss beneath it. There he heard something like the sound of rushing waters, and he suddenly realized that by lifting the stone he had set free the waters of the Deep. Once again the world was in danger of being deluged, as in the time of Noah.

King David trembled with fear, and he asked the others what they might do to cause the waters to fall back, but no one spoke. Then King David said: "Perhaps if I wrote the Name of God on a potsherd, and cast it into the depths, we might still be saved. But does anyone know if this is permitted?" Still the others said nothing, and King David grew angry and said: "If any one of you knows this and still refuses to answer, then your soul will bear the curse of the end of existence!" Then Ahitophel spoke: "Surely the Name can be used to bring peace to the whole world." So David picked up a potsherd and scratched the four-letter Name of God into it, and cast it into the bottomless pit. All at once the roar of the waters grew fainter, and they knew that they had been saved by the power of the Name.

In the days to come King David repented many times for his sin, and he gave thanks to God for sparing the world from another Flood. And his son, Solomon, had the Holy of Holies of the Temple built exactly above the Foundation Stone, for both the stone and the Temple bore the seal of God's blessing.

Others say that after King David found the stone resting on the mouth of the abyss, with God's Name on it, he put the stone into the Holy of Holies of the Temple. The sages were concerned that some young men might learn the true pronunciation of the Divine Name from the speaking stone, and thereby destroy the world. So they built two lions of brass, which they placed by the Holy of Holies, on the right and left. If anyone entered and learned the divine Name, these lions would roar when he came out, so frightening him that he would forget the Name. Further, a divine blessing was said to emanate from the Foundation Stone, which was bestowed upon Israel from the Holy of Holies. Some say that this blessing came from the wings of the angels and cherubim that hovered above the Foundation Stone, and that the stars and planets joined the blessing as well. But when the Temple was destroyed, the blessing was lost.

Others say that the angels above and Israel below all hold fast to the Foundation Stone, which rises up to heaven, and comes to rest among the righteous. And if that stone, which hovers in the air, should fall to the earth, it would be a sign that that the days of the Messiah were at hand.

A myth in *Y. Sanhedrin* 29a asserts that God used a shard to hold back the waters in exactly the same way that King David did: "God prevented *tehom* (the lower waters) from rising up by placing a shard above the waters, on which He had engraved His Name. The seal was removed only once, in the time of Noah. Then *tehom* united with the upper waters, and together they flooded the earth." In *Sefer ha-Zikhronot* 1:6, a clearly related midrash reports that the earth was created from the snow beneath the Throne of Glory. God took it up and scattered it upon the waters. Then the water congealed and became the dust of the earth. This is linked to the verse *For he says to the snow, "Become earth"* (Job 37:6).

This talmudic legend about King David demonstrates the immense sanctity of Jerusalem, and especially of the site of the Temple there. King David sets out to dig the foundations of the Temple, and strikes the Foundation Stone of the earth, upon which God built the rest of this world. This confirms that Jerusalem is the very center of the world, as it was portrayed in ancient maps.

At the same time, this tale is a divine test, not unlike the tests of Adam and Eve, of Abraham in the *Akedah*, the binding of Isaac, and of Job. Even though a voice from the stone warns him not to lift it, King David, not unlike Pandora, lifts the Foundation Stone and sets free the powers of chaos, the waters of the Abyss, which threaten to inundate the earth as in the time of Noah. In a desperate moment, David writes the Tetragrammaton, the secret Name of God, on a shard and throws it into the abyss, and the power of God's Name causes the waters to retreat. (Note the echo to nuclear war in this episode. David learns that the Foundation Stone must not be tampered with, as we have learned the dangers posed by tampering with the atom.)

The *Zohar* (2:91b) states that the fate of the shard, and therefore the world, rests on man's moral conduct. Whenever a person swears falsely using God's Name, that Name on the shard disappears, allowing the waters to burst out and destroy the world. To protect the shard and all of humanity, God has appointed the angel Yazriel over the shard. The angel has 70 graving tools, which he uses to ensure that the letters of God's Name are replaced on the shard as quickly as they are erased, saving the world. Thus the rising of the waters of the abyss is a continual threat to the existence of the world.

1 Enoch 66:1-2 offers an alternate explanation of how the waters of the abyss are held back: "And after that he showed me the angels of punishment who are prepared to let loose all the powers of the waters beneath the earth in order to bring judgment and destruction to all those who dwell on the earth. And God commanded those angels to hold those waters in check, for those angels held power over those waters."

In the alternate version of the myth, King David brings the Foundation Stone into the Temple (despite the fact that it had not yet been built—this was done by Solomon). Still another variant of the myth describes the stone ascending to Paradise, resting among the righteous. In yet other versions, it is described as hovering in the air. In fact, the motif of a sacred object hovering in the air between heaven and earth is quite common. There are versions found among the Samaritans—where a stone is described as being suspended in the air for worship, and among both Jews and Arabs—where the Rock is said to hover in the air inside the Dome of the Rock. In another Arabic myth, the object that is hovering is the grave of Mohammed. For more on this motif, see Vilnay, *Legends of Jerusalem*, 23-24.

David Re'uveni reports an Arab tradition of a cavern carved into the Foundation Stone, where Abraham, Isaac, David, Solomon, and Elijah are all said to have prayed, and their souls still are said to gather there to pray. This cave is still there, inside the Rock.

Another source suggests that a meteor fell down in the place where the Holy of Holies was later situated. The tradition refers to 2 Samuel 24:16 and 1 Chronicles 21:26.

Sources:

Mishnah Yoma 5:2; *Y. Yoma* 8:4; *B. Yoma* 54b; *Y. Sukkah* 54d; *B. Sukkah* 49a; *Sefer ha-Zikhronot* 1:6; *Genesis Rabbah* 70; *1 Enoch* 66:1-2; *Zohar* 1:231a-b, 2:91b; *B. Sukkah* 53a-b; *Y. Sanhedrin* 29b; *Y. Pesahim* 4:1; *Pirkei de-Rabbi Eliezer* 35; *Midrash Tehillim* 91:7; *Pesikta de-Rav Kahana* 26:4; *Midrash Tanhuma-Yelammedenu, Pekudei* 3; *Midrash Tanhuma, Kedoshim* 10; *Midrash Konen* in *Beit ha-Midrash* 2 : 24-39; *Seder 'Arkim*; *Midrash Shoher Tov* on Psalm 91; *Targum Yerushalmi* on Exodus 28:30; *David ha-Re'uveni* p. 25; *Zohar* 2:222a-b; *Der treue Zions-Waechter* 3: nos. 40-44; *Likutei Moharan* 61:6.

Studies:

Man and Temple by Raphael Patai, pp. 54-104.
Legends of Jerusalem by Zev Vilnay, pp. 23-24.

126. CREATION BY THOUGHT

Before the world was created, God and His Name existed alone. God first conceived of the form of the world in His mind, making a world perceptible only by the intellect. Later God completed one visible to the external senses, using the world created in thought as the model.

The conception for Creation came to God by night, and the work was done by day. When it entered His mind to create the world, God drew up the plans. Dividing light from darkness, He prepared the dawn in the knowledge of His heart.

Some say that God created the world for six days and nights, but the work was not completed until the sun reached the horizon on the sixth day. Others say that everything was created in the first instant, when God conceived the world. All that took place on the other days was that specific things were revealed, for everything had been prepared on the first day.

> Philo's concept of the model in thought that God used as the basis for the creation of the world is clearly adapted from Platonic thought, and it also conveys the rabbinic view that God based the creation of the world on a model. This suggests creation by archetype, and it is the basis of much rabbinic speculation about creation, especially of a mystical nature. Some midrashim speak of God's plan for the world. Others describe the Torah as the plan on which this world was built.
>
> *Sources:*
> *Midrash Tanhuma, Bereshit* 17; Philo, *De Opificio Mundi* 4; *Hymn to the Creator* 11QPs
>   (*Dead Sea Scrolls*); *Sefer ha-Zikhronot* 1:1; *Me'am Lo'ez* on Genesis 1:3.

127. A SINGLE UTTERANCE

God, in His omnipotence, created the entire universe simultaneously. He did so in a single utterance, without a single word preceding or following it, as it is said, *God spoke all these words saying* (Exod. 20:1). Heaven and earth and all that they contain were included in that utterance. There was nothing that came into existence earlier or later than anything else.

However, the universe that God created with a single utterance lacked order. After having created the universe, God proceeded to put it in order. On the first day God separated light from darkness, as the first step in creating order. On the second day He established a division between different kinds of waters. Thus what occurred in the six days of Creation was merely the establishment of order in an existing universe.

In this way were heaven and earth and everything therein created at the same instant.

> This commentary by Rabbi Hayim ben Attar (1696-1743), best known by the title of his commentary on the Torah, the *Or ha-Hayim*, is based on an interpretation of the verse *for on it* (the Sabbath) *He rested from all His work which He had created in order to complete it* (Gen. 2:2). Hayim ben Attar reads this verse as proof that the world had already been created—by a single utterance—by the time God worked on completing it.
>
> There is also a tradition that God spoke the Ten Commandments in a single utterance (*Mishnat Rabbi Eliezer*).
>
> *Sources:*
> *Or ha-Hayim, Bereshit* 1:1.

128. THE DIVIDED WORLD

When God created the world, He divided it into two parts: one part habitable and the other a desert, one on one side of the world and the other on the other side. Then he redivided the habitable part so that it formed a circle, the center of which is the Holy Land. And the center of the Holy Land is Jerusalem, and the center of Jerusalem is the Holy of Holies, where the *Shekhinah* dwells. The nourishment of all good things in the inhabited world flows from there, and there is nowhere that is not sustained by that source.

God also divided the desert. That was the desert, the most terrible and sinister in the world, where the Israelites wandered for 40 long years. The Other Side—the side of evil—reigned in that desert. Had they been worthy, they might have broken its power for all time. But each time they provoked God to anger, the Other Side held sway, and they became subject to its power.

Only after 40 years of wandering did the Israelites break the power of the Other Side and prevail. That is when they found their way back to the Holy Land.

> This is both a creation myth and a kabbalistic allegory. As a creation myth, it describes a process of creation in which God first divided the world in halves, and later redivided the habitable part so that it formed a circle, which is where the Holy Land is located. In this it is also a myth about the creation of the Holy Land, and its location at the center of the world. Many medieval maps illustrated the Holy Land and Jerusalem as the navel of the world. For other myths about the creation of the Holy Land, see "Myths of the Holy Land," pp. 401-429.
>
> At the same time, this is a kabbalistic allegory about the two sides of existence—the Side of Holiness, and the *Sitra Ahra*, the Other Side. All of existence is thus portrayed as being polar, with these opposing forces always active. The *Shekhinah*, for example, represents the Side of Holiness, whereas Lilith represents the *Sitra Ahra*.
>
> *Sources:*
> Zohar 2:157a-b.

129. THE ORIGIN OF CHAOS

What existed before the world was created? *Tohu* and *vohu*, chaos and void. Some say that nothing existed before them. Others disagree, and recount the origin of chaos.

Chaos comes from a shadow known as darkness. Where did darkness come from? From something that existed before the world was created, since the very beginning of all existence. Thus chaos was projected from darkness, while darkness was created by the first thing that existed. Immortal beings were brought into being by that infinite source, every kind of divinity, and a likeness emanated from it, known as Wisdom, which took the form of the primordial light. In this way Wisdom serves as a veil, separating mankind from the world above.

> This is a key Gnostic myth from *On the Origin of the World*, one of the Nag Hammadi texts, which is dominated by Jewish influences. In many respects, it is a commentary on the creation story in Genesis. The Gnostic reading of Genesis tries to probe the origin of *tohu* (chaos) and *vohu* (void) in Genesis 1:2: *Now the earth was unformed and void.* ("Unformed" is a translation of *tohu*.) The Gnostic interpretation also draws on the concept of darkness in the next part of the verse, *and darkness was upon the face of the deep.* Here "darkness" is understood as having existed before chaos, and darkness itself is brought into being by an unnamed infinite force. This shows a form of creation by emanation, which is also the basis of the later kabbalistic system of emanation known as the ten sefirot. In the Gnostic myth, the infinite force brings darkness into being, which, in turn, leads to the emanation of chaos. The Gnostic myth also goes a step further, describing a concurrent or synonymous creation of immortal beings, as well as the creation of Wisdom, personified here as a likeness emanated from the infinite force. Wisdom—*Sophia* in Greek—is a key mythic figure in Gnostic texts, a role far exceeding the development found in Jewish texts. See "The Creation of Wisdom," p. 45.
>
> Note the linkage of *Sophia* (Wisdom personified) and the primordial light, created on the first day, when God said, *"Let there be light."* Some Jewish sources also identify

this sacred light as a pre-existing source, much as darkness is described in this Gnostic myth. See "Light from the Temple," p. 411, and "The Light of the First Day," p. 83.

Sources:
On the Origin of the World 297-298.

130. THE FIRST SUNSET

On the day of his creation, when Adam saw the sun set for the first time, he said to Eve, "Because we have sinned, the world around us is growing dark. Soon the universe will become void and without form, as it was before God brought it into being. This must mean that we have been sentenced to death."

So Adam and Eve stayed up all night weeping and fasting. But when the sun rose at dawn, Adam was greatly relieved and said, "There must be a course that the sun follows." After that, Adam put on priestly garments and offered a bullock as a sacrifice, out of gratitude that their lives had been spared. And when Adam died those garments were inherited by Seth.

> There are a number of variants of this myth. In some, Adam first experiences darkness on the day of his creation; in others, after the end of the Sabbath. His response is the universal fear of darkness, but in some versions it is because Adam is afraid they have been condemned to death because of their sin, and that God is uncreating the world, while in other sources he is afraid that the serpent will now be able to bite him. See the following myth, "The Origin of Fire," for an example of the latter myth.
>
> In the Bible, Moses' brother Aaron is identified as the first High Priest. But here Adam performs the role and passes the priestly garments on to his son, Seth. This is a variant on the myth of the handing down of the garments of Adam and Eve mentioned in Genesis 3:21: *And the Lord God made garments of skins for Adam and his wife, and clothed them.* See "The Garments of Adam and Eve," p. 437.
>
> This myth offers the origin of *Havdalah*, the ceremony of separation at the end of the Sabbath.
>
> *Sources:*
> B. *Avodah Zarah* 8a; *Genesis Rabbah* 12:6; *Numbers Rabbah* 4:8; *Pesikta Rabbati* 23:6.
>
> *Studies:*
> *The Sabbath in the Classical Kabbalah* by Elliot K. Ginsburg, pp. 256-284.

131. THE ORIGIN OF FIRE

For the first week of Creation, the sun shone day and night. But when the sun sank at the end of the Sabbath, and darkness came closer, Adam grew terrified. He cried out to God that the serpent was coming to harm him. Then God told Adam to take two flints and to strike them against each other. And when he did, fire came forth, much to Adam's amazement, and he uttered a spontaneous blessing over it. That is why a blessing is recited over a candle at the end of the Sabbath, for fire was then created for the first time.

> Myths of origin are common in all mythic systems, including Judaism. Myths of the creation of the world, of the origin of man, and here, of the origin of fire, are all found in Jewish sources. Here God tells Adam how to make a fire, rubbing flints together. This first fire is tied to the darkness that descends after the sun sets at the end of the Sabbath. Thus a series of origins are all linked together: the first Sabbath, the first sunset, the first darkness, the origin of fire—and the origin of the first blessing for the first *Havdalah* service, which takes place at the end of the Sabbath. See "Adam Brings Down Fire from Heaven," p. 137.

B. Pesahim 54a suggests that rather than God directing Adam to rub the flints together, God inspired Adam with divine intuition, so that Adam knew on his own what he needed to do. See "The First Havdalah," p. 319.

Sources:
B. *Sanhedrin* 38b, 100a; *B. Hagigah* 12a; *B. Pesahim* 54a; B. *Avodah Zarah* 8a; *Genesis Rabbah* 8:1, 11:2, 21:3; *Exodus Rabbah* 32:1; *Leviticus Rabbah* 14:1, 16:2; *B. Pesahim* 54a; *Pesikta Rabbati* 23:6.

132. WHAT CAUSES EARTHQUAKES?

What causes the earth to quake? Some say that whenever God remembers the distress of His children, two drops fall from His eyes into the Great Sea and His voice resounds throughout the world—that is the earthquake.

Others say that an earthquake is God clapping His hands, as it is said, *"I, too, shall clap My hands together"* (Ezek. 21:22). Still others say that it is God groaning, as it is said, *"I shall abate My fury against them"* (Ezek. 5:3). And there are others who say that an earthquake is God stamping in the heavens, as it is said, *A shout echoes throughout the earth* (Jer. 25:30).

Finally, there are those who say that it is God squeezing His feet under the Throne of Glory.

Here alternate mythic explanations of what causes an earthquake are all attributed to some action of God—His grief, anger, groaning, stamping, or squeezing His feet under the Throne of Glory.

There is a mishnaic teaching that whenever a person experiences comets, earthquakes (*zeva'ot*), lightning, thunder, or storms, one should say a blessing: "Blessed is He whose power and might fill the world" (*Mishnah Berakhot* 9:2). The meaning of *zeva'ot* is unclear. It may mean "dismay" or "quaking." In *B. Berakhot* 59a, Rav Qatina interprets it to mean "earthquake." While it may seem strange to say a blessing after an earthquake or some other manifestation of natural forces, it serves the purpose of acknowledging God's role in these powerful events.

Sources:
B. *Berakhot* 59a.

Studies:
"The Holy One Sits and Roars" by Michael Fishbane.

133. THE ROOTS OF EVERYTHING

During the six days of Creation, the foundations and roots of everything that would ever be brought into being were already created, as it is said, *There is nothing new beneath the sun* (Eccles. 1:19). For God looked over the entire Creation before it existed and prepared everything during those six days, and blessed it. And God's blessing still sustains us till this day, as it is said, *And God blessed them* (Gen. 1:22, 1:28, 5:2).

Here we find the mythic notion of the six days of Creation as the archetype for all that would subsequently exist. Note that this is a thirteenth century understanding of the concept of the archetype, completely compatible with the Platonic concept. Further, it is revealed that the continued existence of the world depends on God's blessing. It was given to the world then, and is still in effect. The implication is that we have to continue to deserve that blessing, or it could be withdrawn.

Sources:
Zohar 1:47a.

134. THE GREAT SEA

Long ago, primeval waters covered the whole world. There were waters upon waters. Still, God poured more waters into them, even after they were full—He pressed down upon them and made them gather into one great sea, known as Okeanos.

The great sea stands on the fins of Leviathan, and Leviathan dwells in the Lower Waters, and appears in them as but a small fish in the sea. And the Lower Waters stand on the shore of the Waters of Ocean, and appear as but a small well there. And the Waters of Ocean stand on the shore of the Waters of Creation. And the Waters of Creation stand on the shore of the Weeping Waters. And the Weeping Waters stand on the shore of the Abyss. And the Abyss stands on *tohu*, chaos, and *tohu* stands on *vohu*, void. And all of this is suspended from the arm of God.

The Okeanos Sea is said to surround the whole earth. There is a place in it called the Place of Swallowing where the waters swallow all the other waters that flow there. While on a voyage, Rabbi Eliezer and Rabbi Yehoshua happened upon this place, and took a barrel full of water from there. When Caesar asked them about the nature of the waters of Okeanos, they gave him a jug of this water, and they poured many barrels of water into that jug and it never overflowed, but swallowed all the waters poured into it. This explains why *all the rivers run into the sea yet the sea is not full* (Eccles. 1:7).

So too are the candles of the sun extinguished in the waters of Okeanos so that there is no light during the night, and the flames of the sun are not relit until the sun comes to the East and bathes in a River of Fire, called *Nehar di-Nur*.

Once a month the clouds come down to drink of the waters of Okeanos. Once it happened that the clouds swallowed, together with the water, a ship full of corn, and after that corn fell from the heavens mixed with rain.

> The idea of waters that encompass the earth is found in many of the world's myths. Okeanos, the name given to the Great Sea, is taken from the Greek god Okeanos, originally a river god, later the god of the sea. Okeanos was the offspring of Ouranos (Sky) and Gaia (Earth), and thus of the race of Titans that included Kronos, the father of Zeus.
>
> The Great Sea of Jewish mythology is really the Mediterranean, but it has been given mythic characteristics, such as standing on the fins of Leviathan. There are also mythic places within the ocean, such as the Place of Swallowing. So too is it the place where all the candles of the sun are extinguished, and miraculous events can take place, such as corn raining from the sky. These are the Jewish equivalents of Greek myths such as the Isle of the Blessed, in the waters of Okeanos, where the souls of heroes dwelled.
>
> For other Jewish myths of the ocean, see "The Rebellion of the Waters," p. 105 and "The Rebellion of Rahab," p. 106. For a variant myth, see "A Universe of Water," p. 94.
>
> *Sources:*
> *Genesis Rabbah* 13:6; *Pesikta Rabbati* 48:2; *Midrash Konen* in *Beit ha-Midrash* 2:32-33.

135. THE FIERY WAVES

It is said of waves that sink ships that they have a white fringe of fire. The only way to beat them back is to strike them with a club that has the words "I am that I am, *Yah*, the Lord of Hosts, Amen, Amen, *Sela*" engraved on it. Then the fiery waves will fall back.

> Fiery waves that sink ships are part of sea lore. The notion that a club bearing God's names can beat them back has echoes of Moses holding his arm over the Red sea, and God driving back the sea with a strong east wind (Exod. 14:21) According to Rabbi Samuel Eliezer Edels (1555-1631), known as the Maharsha, the waves represent the nations of the world that attempt to harm Israel. But God, whose names appear on the club, will protect His people and drive them back. "I Am that I Am" (*Ehyeh-Asher-Ehyeh*) is the name God used when He revealed Himself to Moses at the burning bush (Exod. 3:14).
>
> *Sources:*
> B. Bava Batra 73a.

136. THE UPPER WATERS AND THE LOWER WATERS

The upper waters are masculine and the lower, feminine. At first the upper waters and the lower waters were commingled, until *God said, "Let there be a firmament in the midst of the waters, and let it divide the waters from the waters"* (Gen. 1:6). But the upper waters and the lower waters refused to separate, clinging to each other. Some say that God raised His little finger and tore the waters into two parts, and forced half of them below. Others say that fire came forth that divided them, and in this way the upper waters were separated from the lower with great weeping.

So it is that the upper waters remain suspended by Divine command, and their fruit is the rain water. The firmament in which the sun, moon, the stars, and the planets are suspended is the great meeting place where the upper waters are gathered, and from which the earth is watered. And when the rain is ready to fall, the upper waters say to the lower: "Receive me," and immediately they receive them, as a female receives a male. Thus the earth is fed from above, and all living things flourish here below.

If the firmament dividing the waters from the waters were ever removed, even for an instant, the world would revert to utter chaos. It would be as if it had never existed at all, and things would be exactly as they were before God said, *"Let there be a firmament in the midst of the waters."*

> The sky is the firmament that separates the waters above, which fall as rain, from the waters below, which rise up as springs. The midrashic interpretations of the upper waters and the lower waters all center on their identification as masculine and feminine, so powerfully drawn to each other that they resisted God's command to separate. While drawing on this midrashic reading, the *Zohar* also identifies the upper waters as *Elohim* and the lower as *Yahweh*, a Gnostic reading of the role of God's two primary names (*Zohar* 1:17b). The *Zohar* also identifies the upper waters as the *sefirah Hesed* (Lovingkindness) and the lower with the *sefirah Gevurah* (Power). The fire that separated the upper and lower waters is linked in the *Zohar* with the fire of Gehenna, providing this as the origin of that fire. The *Zohar* (1:18a) points out the importance of diversity in the world, noting that "as long as the upper and lower waters were commingled, there was no production in the world. This could only take place when they were separated and became distinct."

Midrash Konen suggests that the myth of God using His little finger to separate the upper and lower waters grows out of the term *raki'a*, meaning "firmament," linked to the word *keri'ah*, meaning "tearing apart."

In *Tanya*, Rabbi Shneur Zalman (1745-1813) interprets the passage, *Yahweh exists forever; Your word stands firm in heaven* (Ps. 119:89) to refer to the firmament in the midst of the waters. He proposes that if the firmament were ever removed, the existence of this world would come to an end. See "The Spirit of the Firmament," p. 105 and "The Rebellion of the Waters," p. 105, for variants of this myth.

Sources:
B. *Ta'anit* 10a; *Genesis Rabbah* 4:2-4, *Genesis Rabbah* 13:11-13; *Ecclesiastes Rabbah* 1:13; *Zohar* 1:17b, 1:18a, 1:29b, 1:62a, 2:28b; *Tanya, Sha'ar ha-Yihud ve ha-Emunah* 1:2 (76b); *Midrash Konen* in *Beit ha-Midrash* 2:24-39.

137. THE SPIRIT OF THE FIRMAMENT

On the second day of Creation, God created the spirit of the firmament, and commanded him to separate the waters from the waters, so that one part might move upward and the other part remain beneath.

> This brief myth from *4 Ezra* suggests that God created some kind of spirit, or perhaps angel, to separate the upper and lower waters. Therefore it was this spirit, rather than God, who forced the upper waters and lower waters to separate. In all other versions of this myth, it is God Himself who tears the upper and lower waters apart. See "The Rebellion of the Waters" below.
>
> *Sources:*
> *4 Ezra* 6:41.

138. THE REBELLION OF THE WATERS

On the second day of Creation, God tore the upper waters from the arms of the lower waters amidst great weeping, and the upper waters were suspended in the heavens by word of God. On the third day, when God said, *"Let the waters be gathered together"* (Gen 1:9), the mountains and hills were raised up and scattered, and deep valleys were dug in the earth, into which the waters rolled. As soon as they had gathered together, the waters became rebellious, rising up almost to the Throne of Glory, and covered the face of the earth. But God rebuked the waters and said "Enough!" and subdued them beneath the soles of His feet. He trod down on them so that the air came out of them. When the rest of the waters saw how He had trampled the ocean, and heard its terrible cry, they fled. Even though they were seething, there was nowhere for them to go but to the sea. Therefore God surrounded the sea with sand, and measured it with the hollow of His hand, and made the sea swear that it would not go beyond the boundary He had set, as it is said, *Who set the sand as a boundary to the sea* (Jer. 5:22). Some say that God not only circled the sea with sand, but caused it to dry up, in accord with the verse *He rebukes the sea and dries it up* (Nah. 1:4).

> This midrash draws a link between God's separation of the upper and lower waters on the second day (see "The Upper Waters and the Lower Waters," p. 104) and the gathering of the waters on the third, suggesting that the waters rebelled because of their anger at their recent separation. This midrash also comments on Psalm 93:3: *The floods have lifted up, O Lord, the floods have lifted up their voice, the floods lift up their roaring.* God's quelling the rebellion of the waters clearly echoes the struggle between Marduk, the

rain god of Babylon, and Tiamat, the personification of primeval waters in the Babylonian epic, *Enuma Elish*. This epic struggle (also found in other Near Eastern texts) is hinted at in the Genesis creation narrative, where *tehom*, the deep, echoes Tiamat. The parallels to the Babylonian myth can be seen in the following passage from *Enuma Elish*, from *Near Eastern Mythology* by John Gray, 1969, p. 32:

> The Lord trod on the legs of Tiamat
> With his unsparing mace he crushed her skull.
> When the arteries of her blood he had severed,
> He split her like a shell-fish into two parts;
> Half of her he set up and sealed it as sky,
> Pulled down the bar and posted guards.
> He bade them not to allow her waters to escape.

Exodus Rabbah 15:22 makes clear that the ocean was not only trampled by God, but slain: "Then God trampled upon the ocean and slew it." This text is sometimes interpreted to mean that God slew its prince, Rahab. See "The Rebellion of Rahab," p. 106. The reference to the hollow of God's hand comes from Isaiah 60:12. See the following myth, "The Rebellion of Rahab."

In *Likutei Moharan* 1:2, Rabbi Nachman of Bratslav interprets God's command of "Enough!" to stop the expansion of the world as referring to the creation of the Sabbath. The Sabbath, in effect, stops the work of the six days of the week.

Sources:
B. Ta'anit 10a; B. Hagigah 12a; Numbers Rabbah. 18:22; Midrash Tehillim 93.5; Pirkei de-Rabbi Eliezer 5; Sefer ha-Zikhronot 2:1.

Studies:
Myths from Mesopotamia by S. Dalley, pp. 228-277 (Enuma Elish).
Near Eastern Mythology by John Gray.

139. THE REBELLION OF RAHAB

When God desired to create the world, He said to Rahab, the angel of the sea: "Open your mouth and swallow all the waters of the world." Rahab replied: "Master of the Universe, I already have enough." God then kicked Rahab with His foot and killed him. And had not the waters covered him, no creature could have stood his foul odor.

The traditions about God slaying Rahab grows out of Isaiah 51:9, *Are you not he who cut Rahab in pieces, and wounded the dragon?* and Psalms 89:10, *You have trampled upon Rahab; you have scattered your enemies with your strong arm*. This midrash is also based on Job 26:12: *By His power He stilled the sea; by His skill He struck down Rahab*. This myth is another version of "The Rebellion of the Waters," which describes the struggle between God and *tehom*, the deep, and thus also echoes the battle between Marduk and Tiamat in the Babylonian epic, *Enuma Elish*. However, Tiamat is a feminine figure, while Rahab is masculine.

In *Enuma Elish* Marduk uses Tiamat's body to build a new world, using half to make the heavens and half to make the earth. He uses considerable violence in defeating Tiamat, as does God in defeating Rahab. Marduk crushes her skull with his club, splits her body in two, and scatters her blood in the wind. In the Hebrew myth, the waters are personified in Rahab, the Prince of the Sea, and instead of trampling the waters, God kicks and kills Rahab. There are hints in rabbinic writings that Rahab once had a great, godlike status. For example, it is stated in *Deuteronomy Rabbah* 2:28: "Rahab placed God in heaven and upon earth." Although Rahab is killed in this myth, he reappears in later legends as the Prince of the Sea, and performs various deeds at the command of God or one of the rabbis. See, for example, *Y. Sanhedrin* 7:25d, where Rabbi Joshua ben Haninah calls upon Rahab to recover a lost charm, so that a spell can be broken.

Midrash Tanhuma tries to explain why God kicked Rahab, the angel of the ocean, who represents the ocean itself: "Why did God kill the angel? The rest of the waters, seeing that God kicked the ocean, and hearing its screams, fled without knowing where to flow, until they reached the place that God had prepared for them." This violent act is thus explained as a way to force the recalcitrant waters to gather in the right places. See "The Rebellion of the Waters," p. 105.

An alternate version of the Rahab myth found in the Prologue to the *Zohar* 56 explains that God's tears, hot as fire, shed over the exile of the *Shekhinah*, fall into the Great Sea and sustain Rahab. And Rahab sanctifies God's Name by swallowing all the waters of the days of Creation—the very act that Rahab refused to do in the other version of the myth, for which God killed him in anger. The moral of the two versions is clear: when Rahab refuses an order from God, he is slain; when he accepts the order, his life is sustained.

For a further discussion of this myth, see the Introduction, p. li.

Sources:
B. Bava Batra 74b; B. Ta'anit 10a; Numbers Rabbah 18:22; Midrash Tanhuma, Hayyei Sarah 3.

Studies:
Slaying the Dragon: Mythmaking in the Biblical Tradition by Bernard F. Batto.
A Commentary on the Book of Exodus by U. Cassuto, p. 178.
"The Great Dragon Battle and Talmudic Redaction" by Michael Fishbane, pp. 41-55.
"Elements of Neo-Eastern Mythology in Rabbinic Aggadah" by Irving Jacobs.
"Five Stages of Jewish Myth and Mythmaking," in *The Exegetical Imagination: On Jewish Thought and Theology* by Michael Fishbane, pp. 86-104.
Myths from Mesopotamia by S. Dalley, pp. 228-277 (*Enuma Elish*).

140. THE PRINCE OF DARKNESS

When God decided to create the world, He addressed the Prince of Darkness, saying, "Get you hence. It is My intention to begin Creation with light." But the Prince of Darkness, who was black as a bull, was afraid that if the darkness were lit, he would become God's slave. So the Prince feigned deafness, and ignored God's rebuke, saying, "Why not create the world from darkness?" "Get you hence at once," God replied, "before you perish from the world!" "And after light what will You create?" asked the Prince of Darkness. God replied, "Darkness."

So it was. But it is said that in End of Days the Prince of Darkness will declare himself equal to God, and claim to have taken part in Creation, saying, "Although God made heaven and light, it was I who made darkness and the pit of hell!" His angels will support his claim, but the fires of hell will quench their arrogance.

The identity of the Prince of Darkness is blurred in rabbinic texts. In this case, the Prince of Darkness is primarily a mythic personification of elemental darkness. At the same time, the rebellion of the Prince of Darkness is linked to the rebellions of the angels Satan (sometimes called Samael), and Lucifer. The identity of all of these angels, including the Prince of Darkness, blurs together in Jewish tradition. See "The Fall of Lucifer," p. 108. After God's rebuke, other princes in heaven proclaim the Prince of Darkness to be their king, and he rewards them by bestowing pavilions on them, as in the passage, *He made pavilions of darkness about him* (2 Sam. 22:12). But God then rebukes them for their rebelliousness and disperses them. Following the creation of light and darkness, the myth goes on to describe the creation of the signs of the zodiac, linking rabbinic lore with the astrological.

Sources:
Pesikta Rabbati 20:2; Pesikta Rabbati 53:2; Yalkut Re'uveni 1:19; Midrash Alphabetot 434.

141. THE FALL OF LUCIFER

At first Lucifer, the highest archangel, was the seal of perfection, full of wisdom and flawless in beauty. He resided on God's holy mountain; he walked among stones of fire. He was blameless in his ways until he was filled with lawlessness and sinned. For he said, "I will climb to the sky; higher than the stars of God will I set my throne." Then, on the second day of Creation, Lucifer, together with his legions of angels, attempted to set himself up as the equal of God. Then God hurled him from the heights, together with his angels, and cast them into a bottomless abyss.

The myth of the fall of Lucifer finds its origin in the ancient Canaanite myth of Athtar, who attempted to rule the throne of Ba'al, but was forced to descend and rule the underworld instead. In Jewish sources, this myth only exists in fragmentary form, primarily in Isaiah 14:12 and 2 *Enoch*. The myth of Lucifer's fall plays a surprisingly minor role in Jewish mythology, perhaps because of the prominence it gained in Christianity. Here, because of the statement by Jesus, *I saw Satan fall like lightning from heaven* (Luke 18:10), Lucifer became identified with Satan, even though they are two entirely separate mythic figures. (It is interesting to note that in some recensions of 2 *Enoch*, Lucifer is identified with the angel Satanel.) From this point on, Lucifer and Satan become synonymous with the Devil in Christian lore, while the myth of Lucifer is essentially lost from Jewish tradition. Yet there is a clear distinction between Satan, the Tempter and heavenly prosecutor, who often cooperates with God, and with Lucifer, who was cast out after rebelling. The fall of Lucifer also strongly echoes the account in Genesis 6 of the descent of the Sons of God to earth from heaven.

Once the myth of Lucifer was ceded to the Christians, the primary sources for the myth remained those in the Bible and Pseudepigrapha, and the myth ceased to be developed in the midrash. Indeed, it is necessary to reconstruct it from the existing fragments, not only in Isaiah and 2 *Enoch*, but also from Ezekiel 28:11-19, where Lucifer is not directly named, but reference to his myth seems apparent.

The name Lucifer also refers to the planet Venus, the morning star, which first appears to dominate the heavens, but then disappears. This too parallels the pattern of the fall of Lucifer. Isaiah recounts the myth:

How are you fallen from heaven,
O Shining One, son of Dawn!
How are you felled to earth,
O vanquisher of nations!
Once you thought in your heart,
I will climb to the sky;
Higher than the stars of God
I will set my throne.
I will sit in the mount of the assembly.
On the summit of Zaphon:
I will mount the back of a cloud—
I will match the Most High.
Instead, you are brought down to Sheol,
to the bottom of the pit.

Isaiah 14:12-13

The account of Lucifer being cast out of heaven is also found in 2 *Enoch* 29, 4-5, where God Himself is the speaker, describes how Lucifer tried to overthrow Him and was cast out of heaven: "I hurled Him from out from the heights, together with his angels."

By setting the myth on the second day of Creation, it is clear that the rebellion takes place strictly in heaven, without any consideration of human beings, who were yet to be created. The missing details of the fall of Lucifer appear to be found in Ezekiel 28:11, although Lucifer is not directly named. Indeed, the passage seems to allude to the myth by means of allegory, in that it is addressed to the King of Tyre, who is about to experience a great fall.

These missing details make it possible to reconstruct the myth. Lucifer was beautiful and brilliant: *You were the seal of perfection, full of wisdom and flawless in beauty* (Ezek. 28:11). Here Lucifer is described in terms very similar to that of the Greek gods. Here, too, is a direct statement of Lucifer's fate: *I have struck you down from the mountain of God* (Ezek. 28:17). The fate of the King of Tyre is thus parallel to that of Lucifer—both undergo a great fall.

The ultimate fate of Lucifer appears to be some kind of eternal wandering, as he was *brought down to Sheol, to the bottom of the Pit* (Isa. 14:15). Sheol was the early Israelite version of Hell, although it more closely resembles the Greek tradition of Limbo. The meaning seems to be that God has cast Lucifer into the Abyss.

A strong parallel to the myth of the fall of Lucifer is found in *Vita Adae et Evae* 15:2, where Michael speaks to Satan: "And Michael said, 'Worship the image of God, but if you will not, you will know the Lord's wrath.' And I (Satan) said: 'If He shows me His wrath, I will set my seat above the stars of heaven."

Even though there is very little midrashic interest in the myth of Lucifer, a parallel myth emerges, also about rebellious angels, known as the Watchers. See "The Sons of God and the Daughters of Men," p. 454 and "The Watchers," p. 457. Here the fate of Lucifer is duplicated by the angel Azazel. Both are cast out of heaven into the Abyss, but Azazel is said to be chained upside down in a distant canyon, where he continues his evil plotting. For the cycle of myths of the Sons of God, see pp. 454-460.

For a close variant of this myth, see "Satan Cast From Heaven," p. 109.

Sources:
Isaiah 6, 14:12; Ezekiel 28:11-19; Psalms 82:6-7; 1 Kings 22; Job 1:6; *Vita Adae et Evae* 12:1, 13:2-3, 14:1-3; *2 Enoch* 29, 4-5.

Christian Sources:
1 John 3:8; *Luke* 10:18; *2 Corinthians* 11:14.

Studies:
The Jewish Study Bible on Psalm 82,
"Ascension or Invasion: Implications of the Heavenly Journey in Ancient Judaism" by David J. Halperin.

142. SATAN CAST FROM HEAVEN

On the day that Adam was created, Satan went forth in heaven and flew like a bird in the air. God breathed His spirit into Adam, and Adam received the likeness of His image, as it is said, *Let us make man in our image, after our likeness* (Gen. 1:26). God summoned the angel Michael and said, "Behold—I have made Adam in the likeness of My image."

So Michael summoned all the angels, and God said to them, "Come, bow down to the god I have made."

Michael bowed down first. Then he called upon Satan and said, "You too bow down to Adam."

Satan said, "I will not bow down to anyone created after me. It is not proper for me to bow down to Adam." And the other angels who were with him also refused to bow down to Adam.

Then God became angry with Satan and cast him and all the angels who had followed him from heaven to the earth. So too did God announce that He would establish Adam's dominion on the throne of Satan, while Satan would be cast down so that Adam might sit above him.

When Satan realized all that he had lost, he decided to avenge himself against Adam, who was living in the Garden of Eden. He carefully prepared a trap for Adam so that he, too, would be deprived of his happiness, just as Satan had been. And that is why Satan sought revenge against Adam and convinced Eve to taste the forbidden fruit.

This myth is a variant of the "The Fall of Lucifer," p. 108. Here the evil angel is identified as Satan instead of Lucifer, and the rebellion was not planned in advance, but grows out of Satan's indignation at being asked to bow down to the newly created Adam, who is identified to the angels as a god: "Come, bow down to the god I have made." Satan's refusal to do so provokes God into casting him and all his followers to earth—not to hell. God's identification of Satan with sinners is confirmed in *Targum to Job* 27:7: "Let my enemy be like the sinner, and the one rising up against me like the wicked."

In the present myth Satan's rebellion follows the creation of Adam, which took place on the sixth day of Creation, rather than at the beginning of Creation, as in the fall of Lucifer. Thus, in "The Fall of Lucifer," Satan rebels directly against God simply to usurp God's power, out of his jealousy over God, while here Satan's rebellion is brought about by God's creation of Adam. This is stated explicitly in the *Targum to Job* 31, in which Satan wanted to create another world, where he would have dominion, because all things were subservient to Adam on earth.

This myth of Satan being cast out of heaven is also found in Christian sources, prominently in the Book of Revelation: *And the great dragon was cast out, that old serpent, called the Devil, and Satan, who deceives the whole world: he was cast out into the earth, and his angels were cast out with him* (Rev. 12:9). Although Satan does not appear in the biblical account of the Fall, the identification of Satan with the serpent brought Satan to the forefront of this myth. See "How Cain was Conceived," p. 447, where Satan, riding the serpent, has intercourse with Eve, from which Cain is conceived. Thus the serpent fulfills its phallic role in the exegetic fantasies of the rabbis.

A Muslim version of the myth of Satan (identified as Iblis) refusing to bow down before Adam is found in the Koran 7:11.

God's identification of Adam as a god strongly echoes the basic Gnostic assumptions about a Creator God and a demiurge. Here, although the role of the demiurgic Adam is unclear, we can recall the extensive traditions about the primordial Adam. See "Adam the Golem," p. 127, "Adam the Hermaphrodite," p. 138, and "Adam the Giant," p. 128.

Sources:
Vita Adae et Evae 12:1-16:4; *Apocalypse of Moses* 39:2; *Pirkei de-Rabbi Eliezer* 14, 27; *2 Enoch* 29:4-5; *Targum to Job* 28:7; *Apocalypse of Sedrach* 5:3; *Targum to Job* 27:7. See Ginzberg, *Legends*, vol. 5, note 35, pp. 84-86.

Christian Sources:
Rev. 12:9.

Muslim Sources:
Koran 7:11.

Studies:
The Origin of Satan by Elaine Pagels.

143. SATAN'S BARGAIN WITH GOD

There was a man in the land of Uz named Job. That man was blameless and upright; he feared God and shunned evil. Seven sons and three daughters were born to him; his possessions were seven thousand sheep, three thousand camels, five hundred yoke of oxen, and five hundred she-asses, and a very large household. That man was wealthier than anyone in the East.

It was the custom of his sons to hold feasts, each on his set day in his own home. They would invite their three sisters to eat and drink with them. When a round of feast days was over, Job would send word to them to sanctify themselves, and, rising early in the morning, he would make burnt offerings, one for each of them; for Job thought, "Perhaps my children have sinned and blasphemed God in their thoughts." This is what Job always used to do.

One day the divine beings presented themselves before the Lord, and the Adversary came along with them. The Lord said to the Adversary, "Where have you been?" The Adversary answered the Lord, "I have been roaming all over the earth." The Lord said to the Adversary, "Have you noticed My servant Job? There is no one like him on earth, a blameless and upright man who fears God and shuns evil!" The Adversary answered the Lord, "Does Job not have good reason to fear God? Why, it is You who have fenced him round, him and his household and all that he has. You have blessed his efforts so that his possessions spread out in the land. But lay Your hand upon all that he has and he will surely blaspheme You to Your face." The Lord replied to the Adversary, "See, all that he has is in your power; only do not lay a hand on him." The Adversary departed from the presence of the Lord.

One day, as his sons and daughters were eating and drinking wine in the house of their eldest brother, a messenger came to Job and said, "The oxen were plowing and the she-asses were grazing alongside them when Sabeans attacked them and carried them off, and put the boys to the sword; I alone have escaped to tell you." This one was still speaking when another came and said, "God's fire fell from heaven, took hold of the sheep and the boys, and burned them up; I alone have escaped to tell you." This one was still speaking when another came and said, "A Chaldean formation of three columns made a raid on the camels and carried them off and put the boys to the sword; I alone have escaped to tell you." This one was still speaking when another came and said, "Your sons and daughters were eating and drinking wine in the house of their eldest brother when suddenly a mighty wind came from the wilderness. It struck the four corners of the house so that it collapsed upon the young people and they died; I alone have escaped to tell you."

Then Job arose, tore his robe, cut off his hair, and threw himself on the ground and worshiped. He said, "Naked came I out of my mother's womb, and naked shall I return there; the Lord has given, and the Lord has taken away; blessed be the name of the Lord."

For all that, Job did not sin nor did he cast reproach on God.

One day the divine beings presented themselves before the Lord. The Adversary came along with them to present himself before the Lord. The Lord said to the Adversary, "Where have you been?" The Adversary answered the Lord, "I have been roaming all over the earth." The Lord said to the Adversary, "Have you noticed My servant Job? There is no one like him on earth, a blameless and upright man who fears God and shuns evil. He still keeps his integrity; so you have incited Me against him to destroy him for no good reason." The Adversary answered the Lord, "Skin for skin—all that a man has he will give up for his life. But lay a hand on his bones and his flesh, and he will surely blaspheme You to Your face." So the Lord said to the Adversary, "See, he is in your power; only spare his life." The Adversary departed from the presence of the Lord and inflicted a severe inflammation on Job from the sole of his foot to the crown of his head. He took a potsherd to scratch himself as he sat in ashes. His wife said to him, "You still keep your integrity! Blaspheme God and die!" But he said to her, "You talk as any shameless woman might talk! Should we accept only good from God and not accept evil?" For all that, Job said nothing sinful.

In this prologue to the Book of Job, God and Satan are together in heaven, and God is bragging to Satan about his loyal servant, Job. In many ways Job resembles Abraham, whose faith in God was, likewise perfect, and Noah and Daniel are also identified in Ezekiel 14:12-20 as paradigms of righteousness, along with Job. At Satan's initiative, God and Satan strike a bargain—to test Job, to see just how faithful he really is. Job loses everything—his family, his health, his flocks, his wealth, but he remains faithful, and God wins the bet. Nevertheless, the voice of God that comes out of the whirlwind at the end of Job is hardly consoling, and presents a harsh view of the realities of the world and how all decisions of fate ultimately belong to God.

As a myth, the Book of Job puts man's life in this world in perspective, and underscores its fragility and the need to maintain faith in God despite one's trials and tribulations. The friendly banter between God and Satan should not be overlooked—Satan is clearly at home in heaven and he and God converse like old friends. Nevertheless, Satan is clearly identified as the Adversary, whose job it is to portray God's children in the worst possible light. That God agrees to undergo this devastating test of Job indicates that God ultimately views His human creations as objects who can be toyed with. Thus the underlying view of the relationship between God and man in the Book of Job is quite grim.

Sources:
Job 1:1-2:10.

144. THE QUARREL OF THE SUN AND THE MOON

In the beginning there was no difference between the two great lights of the sun or moon. They were both created to light the earth, and for signs and for seasons, and they were equal in all respects: in their height, shape, and in the amount of light they each cast. But no sooner were they created, than they began to quarrel. Each said to the other: "I am bigger than you are."

At last the moon complained to God that the heavens and earth could not have two luminaries of equal size, saying, "Master of the Universe, is it possible for two kings to wear one crown?" God replied: "Go then and make yourself smaller." "In that case," said the moon, "what will then be the light of the sun?" God replied, "The sun's light will grow sevenfold!" "Master of the universe," cried the moon, "do I deserve such a fate?" "Fear not," said God, "for Israel shall reckon the days and the years by you, and one day you will be restored to your original state." Still the moon obstinately refused to become smaller. Then God rebuked the moon and she fell from her high estate, and sparks fell from her over the whole sky, creating stars that diminished her light.

Thus the rebellion of the moon brought about its decrease, while the rule of the sun was increased, as it is said, *the greater light to dominate the day, the lesser light to dominate the night, and the stars* (Gen. 1:16). However, in the time to come, *the light of the moon shall be as the light of the sun, and the light of the sun shall become sevenfold, like the light of the seven days* (Isa. 30:26).

> The notion that the sun and moon were once equal is derived from the biblical verse *God made the two great lights* (Gen. 1:16). This sun and moon myth is a commentary on the passage, *The greater light to dominate the day and the lesser light to dominate the night* (Gen. 1:16). It not only explains how the moon lost its light and was made smaller, but also provides the origin of the stars from the former light of the moon. Rashi and Rabbi Judah Loew (1525-1609) of Prague interpret the creation of the stars as an attempt to appease the moon. This notion is confirmed by *Genesis Rabbah* 6:4: "Since the moon diminished itself to rule only at night, God decreed that when it appears, the stars shall accompany it. Others say that the moon was diminished because it intruded into the sphere of the sun, sometimes being visible during the day." The final quote from Isaiah 30:26 can also be seen as a rare example of a biblical midrash, identifying the light of the seven days of Creation with the primordial light, by stating that the light of the first day was seven times as powerful as the light of the sun. See "The Light of the First Day," p. 83.
>
> In the allegorical reading of this myth, the sun represents the Gentiles and the moon, the Jews. In *Pirkei de-Rabbi Eliezer* 51, the identification of Israel with the moon, the

lesser light, is explained by pointing out that just as the moon restores itself monthly, so will Israel in the future be renewed.

Note that the Jews, the descendants of Jacob, the younger brother, use a lunar calendar, while the descendants of Esau use a solar one. In *Genesis Rabbah* 6:3, it says that "It is natural for the older of two brothers to set his calendar by the greater luminary, and the younger by the lesser light."

This myth raises the question of whether it is possible for God to make a mistake, in creating the sun and moon as equals, then commanding the moon to diminish itself. One explanation is that the moon brought about its own fate by seeking to become greater than the sun, and it was diminished at once, and has been that way ever since. That is why the prayers offered on *Kiddush Levanah*, the Blessing of the Moon, say, "I pray to You, God, to make the moon whole again as it was before it was diminished." Here the moon symbolizes the people of Israel, and the prayer is also a plea for Israel to be restored to its former glory.

3 Baruch 9:6-7 offers an alternate explanation for the shrinking of the moon: "During the transgression of Adam, the moon gave light to Samael (one of the names of Satan), when he took the serpent as a garment, and did not hide, but on the contrary, grew greater. And God was angered with the moon, and diminished her and shortened her days." Here the moon is implicated in Samael's plot to bring about the transgression of Adam and Eve, and as a result, God shrinks it as a punishment.

There are other Jewish myths in which the sun and moon are personified. *Midrash Tehillim* 19:11 describes how the sun and moon are blinded every day by the radiance from above, so they delay going forth. What does God do then? He shines forth for them, and they come forth in His light. And when they are about to go back, they cannot tell where to go, and they tarry. But God scatters torches, arrows, and spears of light before them, and guides them toward where they should go. Here the sun and moon are shown to be dependent on God's guidance in order to rise and set. The theological point, of course, is that everything in the universe, including the sun and moon, depends on God's guidance.

Sources:

B. *Hullin* 60b; *Genesis Rabbah* 6:3-4; *Pirkei de-Rabbi Eliezer*, 4, 6, 51; *Yalkut Re'uveni*, quoting *Midrash Toledot Yitzhak* in *Beit ha-Midrash* 5:156; *Midrash Konen* in *Beit ha-Midrash* 2:26; *Midrash ha-Ne'elam*, *Zohar Hadash* 14a; *Sefer ha-Zikhronot* 3:1-5; *Likutei Halakhot*, *Hilkhot Dayanim* 3, 7-12.

145. THE SUN STOOD STILL

On that occasion, when the Lord routed the Amorites before the Israelites, Joshua addressed the Lord; he said in the presence of the Israelites: "Stand still, O sun, at Gibeon, O moon, in the Valley of Aijalon!" And the sun stood still and the moon halted, while a nation wreaked judgment on its foes—as is written in the Book of Yashar. Thus the sun halted in midheaven, and did not press on to set for a whole day, for the Lord fought for Israel. Neither before nor since has there ever been such a day, when the Lord acted on words spoken by a man.

After the parting of the Red Sea, the most famous miraculous event in the Bible is the sun standing still in the sky in Joshua 10:12-14. Both of these examples demonstrate that God can overrule the powers of nature at His command, and, of course, both examples served to benefit Israel.

Sources:

Joshua 10:12-14

146. A GARMENT FOR THE MOON

Once upon a time, the moon came to the sun with a complaint: the sun was able to shine during the warmth of day, especially during the summer, while the moon could shine only during the cool of night. The sun saw that the moon was unhappy with her lot, particularly in the wintertime, so he told the moon he would have a garment sewn for her, to keep her warm. Then the sun called upon all the great tailors to make a garment for the moon. The simple tailors also wanted to help, but they weren't invited, so they didn't go.

After discussing the matter for some time, the great tailors came to the conclusion that it was simply impossible to sew a garment that would fit, because the moon is sometimes little and sometimes big. What measurements were they to use? Now when the little tailors heard this, they said, "If the big tailors won't do it, we will." But the big tailors scoffed when they heard this and said, "If we can't do it, how could you?"

This is a fragmentary tale told by Rabbi Nachman of Bratslav. Nachman not only told the famous 13 stories in *Sippurei Ma'asiyot*, but he told several dozen brief tales, including some unfinished tales. "A Garment for the Moon" is one of these. It follows the midrashic tradition about the sun and the moon, especially the tale of "The Quarrel of the Sun and Moon." (See p. 112.) The tale ends with the offer of the poor tailors to help the great tailors in sewing a garment for the moon, which the great tailors refuse.

Such fragmentary and incomplete tales were often told by Rabbi Nachman and were dutifully recorded by his scribe, Rabbi Nathan of Nemirov. The fact that the big tailors have the last word here is a clear indication that the tale was unfinished, as Rabbi Nachman's sympathies in such cases were always with the "little" people. In fact, a passage from *Genesis Rabbah* (6:3) strongly suggests the identification of the poor tailors with the Jews: "Rabbi Levi said in the name of Rabbi Jose ben Lai: 'It is but natural that the great should count by the great, and the small by the small. Esau counts time by the sun, which is large, and Jacob by the moon, which is small.'" The discussion is continued by a sage whose name also happens to be Rabbi Nachman: "Said Rabbi Nachman: 'That is a happy augury. Esau counts by the sun, which is large: just as the sun rules by day but not by night, so does Esau enjoy this world, but has naught in the World to Come. Jacob counts by the moon, which is small: just as the moon rules by day and by night, so has Jacob a portion in this world and the World to Come.'"

The present dependent condition of the moon on the sun echoes a talmudic myth (*B. Hullin* 60b) about competition between the sun and the moon, which is a commentary on the passage, *And God made the two great lights* (Gen. 1:16): "The moon said to the Holy One, blessed be He, 'Master of the Universe, is it possible for two kings to wear one crown?' God replied: 'Go then and make yourself smaller.'" Thus the rebellion of the moon brought about its decrease. This talmudic legend is echoed in a dialogue, closely resembling that in Rabbi Nachman's tale, found in *Pirkei de-Rabbi Eliezer* 6: "Rivalry ensued between the sun and the moon, and one said to the other, 'I am bigger than you are.' The other rejoined, 'I am bigger than you are.' What did the Holy One, blessed be He, do, so that there should be peace between them? He made the one larger and the other smaller, as it is said, *The greater light to rule by the day, and the lesser light to rule the night, and the stars*" (Genesis 1:16). It seems certain that Rabbi Nachman had these rabbinic myths in mind when he told his enticing, fragmentary tale. It is also possible to read this tale as an allegory in which Israel is the moon, God is the sun, and the garment is the Torah, which protects Israel against the winters of Exile.

See "A Garment for the Moon" in *Miriam's Tambourine*, pp. 287-294, which attempts to complete this fragmentary tale.

Sources:
Sihot Moharan; Sippurim Niflaim.

147. THE CREATION OF ANGELS

Some say that God created the angels on the first day—angels of the presence and angels of sanctification, angels of the spirits of fire and angels of the spirits of the winds, angels of the spirits of the clouds and angels of the darkness, angels of snow and hail and frost, and the angels of thunder and lightning, as it is said, *When the morning stars sang together and all the divine beings shouted for joy* (Job 38:7). Some say that God formed the features of the faces of every angel with His little finger, and after that blew spirit and breath into them, and placed them upon their feet, and opened their eyes. Others say that God created the angels on the second day, or on the fifth. And there are even those who say that the angels were created before the creation of the world.

How did God create the angels? Some say that from every single word that God utters, an angel is created, as it is said, *By the word of Yahweh the heavens were made, by the breath of His mouth all their host* (Ps. 33:6). These angels are nourished by the splendor of the *Shekhinah*.

Others say that from fire God created every kind of angel, and all of the armies of the angels.

Still others say that every day God creates angels from the fiery stream in Paradise, who sing praises of God one time and then cease to exist.

> The first indication that angels were created during the six days of Creation is found in Genesis 2:1: *The heavens and the earth were finished, and all their hosts.* "Hosts" is understood to refer to the angels. However, it is not clear on which day of Creation the angels were brought into being, nor how God created them. Most texts identify the day the angels were created as the second or fifth day of Creation, although *The Book of Jubilees* recounts the creation of angels on the first day, as does *4 Ezra*, which states that God created the angels "from the beginning." As for how the angels were created, in *B. Hagigah* 14b two methods are described, angels created out of God's utterances, and angels created out of the heavenly river of fire. The point of the discussion seems to be that God personally created the angels, "the ranks of the bodiless armies," as *2 Enoch* 29:3 puts it. As to when this took place, the second and fifth days indicate that God had no assistance in the creating the world, for the angels had not yet been created. However, the traditions that link the creation of angels to the first day, or even prior to the creation of the world, may indicate the opposite—that the angels might have played a role in Creation. The belief that the angels were among the things created before the Creation, found in *Eliyahu Rabbah*, grows out of an interpretation of Genesis 1:1, which is understood to mean, "In the beginning He created *Elohim*." Here *Elohim* does not refer to God, although it is one of the names of God, but instead it is one of the terms used to refer to angels. Job 38:4-7 also seems to indicate that the angels were among God's first creations. This notion is also found in the *Hellenistic Synagogal Prayers*: "God created before everything else the cherubim and the seraphim . . . the archangels and the angels" (*Apostolic Constitutions* 8:12:14).
>
> *Sources:*
> *Targum Pseudo-Yonathan* on Genesis 1:26; *The Book of Jubilees* 2:2; *The Wisdom of Ben Sira* 16:26-30; *B. Hagigah* 14b; *Genesis Rabbah* 1:3; *1 Enoch* 71; *2 Enoch* 29:3; *Pirkei de-Rabbi Eliezer* 4; *Eliyahu Rabbah* 1:3; *Midrash Konen* in *Beit ha-Midrash* 2:24-30; *4 Ezra* 8:22; *2 Baruch* 21:6, 48:8.
>
> *Studies:*
> "Angelology and the Supernal Worlds in the Aramaic Targums to the Prophets" by Rimmon Kasher.
> *Fallen Angels* by Bernard J. Bamberger.
> "Mysticism, Magic and Angelology: The Perception of Angels in Hekhalot Literature" by Rachel Elior.

148. CREATION BY ANGELS

Did God have the assistance of the angels in the creation of the world? Most say that God created the world by Himself, and not by means of an angel and not by means of a messenger. But some say that God commanded the angels, and they obeyed Him. In this way the heavens were created with the light of the angels, and some say it was even the angels who stretched out the heavens, Gabriel in the north and Michael in the south. Others say that when God created the world, He created all things in the form of angels, for they are the foundation of all created things. The angels were emanated from the splendor of His glorious light. Then the heavens were created upon this foundation of angels.

Those who say that God worked alone insist that none of the angels were created on the first day. But those who claim that the angels assisted God say that every kind of angel was created on the first day, and that God had a partner in His work of Creation. For just as *by the word of Yahweh the heavens were made*, so too were all the hosts of angels made *by the breath of His mouth* (Ps. 33:6). And since breath comes before speech, it can be concluded that the angels were created first. Not so, say the others. In this case, God reversed the usual order of breath and word by creating with the word although no breath had as yet emanated from His mouth. Thus the heavens were created first, and the angels followed.

On this, however, all agree: once the world was created, the angels came to play an important role. Each day, before the sun rises, the angels lead the sun through a heavenly stream, to cool it off and prevent it from scorching the earth. Then the angels guide the sun in its journey. The angels also serve as messengers of God. When they are sent to this world to carry out a mission, they become clothed in a body formed from air or fire. When they are sent by God's word, they become winds, as it is said, *He made His angels winds* (Ps. 104:4), but when they serve God as ministers, they are made of fire. Thus they appear in human form, but as soon as they complete their duties, they divest themselves of their bodies and return to their spiritual state.

So too does an angel serve as the prince over each of the elements. Gabriel is the Prince of Fire, Rahab the Prince of the Sea, Ridya the Prince of Rain, and Michael the Prince of Hail. There are also four angels that surround God's throne, the archangels Michael, Gabriel, Uriel, and Raphael. That is why it is said in the prayers recited before sleeping, "May Michael be at my right hand, Gabriel at my left, before me Uriel, behind me Raphael, and above my head the Divine Presence of God."

There are differing accounts as to when the angels were created, and these differences are directly related to the question of whether or not the angels participated in the creation of the world. *The Book of Jubilees* places the creation of the angels on the first day of Creation. Other sources, such as *Targum Pseudo-Yonathan* on Genesis 1:26, *Midrash Konen* and *Pirkei de-Rabbi Eliezer* 4, put the creation of the angels on the second day. *Pirkei de-Rabbi Eliezer* says, "As for the angels created on the second day, when they are sent as messengers, they are changed into winds, and when they minister before God, they are changed into fire." *Targum Pseudo-Yonathan* says, "And God said to the angels who minister before him, who were created on the second day of the creation of the world, 'Let us make man in our image, after our likeness' (Gen. 1:26). *Genesis Rabbah* 1:3 places the creation of the angels on the fifth day.

The rejection of the notion that the angels participated in Creation derives from around the third century. The day on which the angels were created thus becomes of crucial importance. If on the first day, as in *The Book of Jubilees*, which dates from the first century, it suggests that the angels were available to assist God. But this was seen to raise questions about the singularity of God's role, and therefore most later texts describe the creation of the angels as taking place on either the second or the fifth day of Creation.

Why were the angels not created on the first day? So that it would not be said: "Michael was standing in the north with Gabriel in the south, and together they spread out the heavens and the earth" (*Midrash Tanhuma, Bereshit* 1). This purposely alludes to Isaiah 44:24: *"It is I, Yahweh , who made everything, who alone stretched out the heavens and unaided spread out the earth."* However, whenever the phrase, "so that it would not be said" appears, it can be assumed that heretics—and sometimes those within the tradition—were saying such things.

A version of this statement in the *Sefer ha-Bahir* 22 adds God to the equation: "All agree that none of the angels were created on the first day. It should therefore not be said that Michael drew out the heaven at the south, and Gabriel drew it out at the north, while God arranged things in the middle." It seems likely that, as in the case of all such repudiations, the rabbis are referring to an existing tradition within Judaism (possibly by Jewish Gnostics), even if those who asserted it were regarded as heretics. Ironically, the rabbis' own sacred texts have preserved the existence of these heretical myths, which might otherwise have been lost.

As a warning to those who would put their faith in the angels instead of in God, *B. Berakhot* 13a states: "If trouble befall a man, let him not cry to Michael or Gabriel, but let him cry to Me and I will answer him at once."

The idea that the angels were created by the sayings of God comes from the verse *By the word of Yahweh the heavens were made, by the breath of His mouth, all their host* (Ps. 33:6).

The debate about the participation of the angels in Creation can be seen as a continuation of the mythic dialectic within Judaism, as it swung between a monotheistic view and a mythic view that was ready to incorporate other supernatural forces, including the angels and other heavenly figures, such as the Bride of God and the Messiah.

See "The Creation of Angels," p. 115.

Sources:
Book of Jubilees 2:2; B. Berakhot 13a; Genesis Rabbah 8:5; Pirkei de-Rabbi Eliezer 4, 6; Sefer ha-Bahir 11, 22; Zohar 1:15a, 1:27a, 1:34a, 1:40b, 1:101a, 1:144a, 3:68a, 3:152a; Zohar Hadash Bereshit, 4a, 88a; Midrash Ruth 99a; Midrash ha-Ne'elam; Midrash Konen in Beit ha-Midrash 2:24-39; Midrash Aleph Bet 5:2; Midrash Tehillim 104.7; Genesis Rabbah 1:3, 3:8, 3:11, 8:8, 8:13; Midrash Tanhuma, Bereshit 12; Midrash Tanhuma-Yelammedenu, Bereshit 5; Me'am Lo'ez, Bereshit 1:5; Sefer ha-Zikhronot 1:8; Or ha-Hayim on Genesis 1:2; "Kriat Shema she'al ha-Mita" (prayer before going to sleep at night) from the Siddur. Samaritan sources: The Samaritan Liturgy 29:11-30:24.

Studies:
"Not by Means of an Angel and Not by Means of a Messenger" by Judah Goldin.
The Name of God and the Angel of the Lord by Jarl Fossum, pp. 191-238.
Hammer on the Rock by Nahum Glatzer.

149. ANAFIEL, THE CREATOR OF THE BEGINNING

The angel Anafiel rules over all the other angels and guards the entrances to the palaces of the highest heaven, *Aravot*. When the other angels see him they remove the crown of glory from their heads and fall on their faces. His glory and radiance cover the chambers of the upper heaven, as it is said, *His majesty covers the skies, His splendor fills the earth* (Hab. 3:3). Some say that he is the creator of the beginning, while others say that he is the creator of the world. It is he who possesses the secrets of heaven.

It was the angel Anafiel whom God sent to bring Enoch into heaven, where he was transformed into the angel Metatron. So too was it Anafiel who was sent to strike Metatron with sixty fiery lashes when he did not rise from his throne when Elisha ben Abuyah approached him during his ascent on high.

The angel Anafiel is a highly exalted figure, an archangel, who is said to have helped God in the Creation, and is known as the Creator of the Beginning. He is also described as one of the gatekeepers of the seventh palace. His official name is Anafiel YHVH, as the high archangels carry YHVH, the Tetragrammaton, as part of their names. The fact that Anafiel is described as being superior to Metatron—and, in some versions, that it was Anafiel who delivered the punishment of sixty fiery lashes to Metatron—emphasizes his importance and indicates that Anafiel was originally regarded as a supreme being who took part in the creation of the world. However, the role of Anafiel receded as that of Metatron was elevated, and today the only evidence of Anafiel's supreme role in the heavenly hierarchy is found in isolated fragments of the *Hekhalot* and *Merkavah* literature.

Sources:
3 Enoch 6:1, 18:19; Hekhalot Rabbati; Zohar 1:108b.

Studies:
The Ancient Jewish Mysticism by Joseph Dan, pp. 125-138.

150. THE CREATOR OF THE WORLD

God's Chariot flies from one end of the universe to the other in the blink of an eye. God's Throne is a part of that chariot, and there is a divine figure seated upon that throne. Who sits there? Some say it is the Holy One Himself who is seated there. Others say it is *Yotzer Bereshit* and that it was he who created the world, for all the secrets of Creation were revealed to him. That is why he is known as the "Creator of the World," for he is the maker of Creation.

In *Shi'ur Komah*, which describes the dimensions of the figure of God, the Primordial Man on the Merkavah, the divine throne, is identified as *Yotzer Bereshit*, the Creator of the World. The Primordial Man is usually identified as *Adam Kadmon*. See "Adam Kadmon," p. 15. It is not clear whether or not *Yotzer Bereshit* should be identified as an independent divine figure, a kind of demiurge, or simply as another of God's names, as appears to be the case in the *Aleinu* prayer: "It is our duty to praise the Lord of all things, to ascribe greatness to Him who formed the world in the beginning." The ambiguity about the identity of this mysterious figure suggests his role as a demiurge, as rabbinic and kabbalistic literature is full of hints that the divine figure who created the world had some kind of independent existence from the unknown aspect of God known in kabbalah as *Ein Sof* . The Primordial Man is understood both as a transitional phase of Creation and as the first created being, and as such is a Jewish version of the Gnostic myth of the Creator God and the demiurge.

Sources:
Shi'ur Komah; 3 Enoch 11:4-5.

Studies:
The Shi'ur Qomah: Liturgy and Theurgy in Pre-Kabbalistic Jewish Mysticism by Martin
    Samuel Cohen.
Major Trends in Jewish Mysticism by Gershom Scholem, pp. 63-67.

151. THE FIRST CREATED BEING

The First Created Being was the first emanation from the Hidden Cause. He is everywhere, and everything is in him, as it is said, *The whole earth is full of his glory* (Isa. 6:3), and all beings exist through him, for he is the source of all existence.

When Moses said, *"Make known to me Your Glory"* (Exod. 33:18), he was requesting to know the First Created Being. Moses did not wish to know and see the essence of the Creator, since he knew this could not be grasped.

Various rabbinic and kabbalistic sources speak of the First Created Being (*ha-nivra ha-rishon*), a divine figure or force that was created prior to the creation of the world. The concept of the First Created Being has its origin in a Neo-Platonic concept originating with Plotinus, in which God, the "absolute One," is the creator of the Universal Intellect, identical both with the "First Emanation" and "First Created Being," which in turn is the first link in a chain of emanations. Rabbi Jacob ben Sheshet of Gerona (thirteenth century), an early kabbalist, identified this First Emanation (*ha-ne'etzal ha-rishon*) from the Hidden Cause (the unknown aspect of God). The second term, "First Created Being," serves to designate the Universal Intellect emanated from God. The First Created Being, in turn, creates the Universal Soul, and the World of Nature, including the seven celestial spheres, is said to emanate in turn from the Universal Soul.

Saadiah Gaon identified the *Shekhinah* as the First Created Being, as well as the source of revelation.

This concept of the First Created Being plays a major role in the writings of Rabbi Isaac ben Abraham ibn Latif, who lived in the thirteenth century, based on Ibn Gabirol's doctrine of the Divine Will. This primordial Will, which Ibn Latif calls the First Created Being, is coexistent with God and is the source of all reality: "All things exist through him by way of emanation, and nothing exists outside of him."

Sources:
Sha'ar ha-Shamayim, Ms. Vatican 335.1, part 2, chap. 3, 45a-b; *Ginzei ha-Melekh, Kokhvei Yitzhak*, 28:3; *Tzurat ha-Olam*; *Perush Kohelet* 56a; *Eshkol ha-Kofer*, Ms. Vatican 219, 9b-10a.

Studies:
"The 'First Created Being' in Early Kabbalah: Philosophical and Isma'ilian Sources" by Sara O. Heller Wilensky.

152. THE ANGEL WHO CREATED THE WORLD

There are those who say that God, the First Creator, created only a single angel. God appointed this angel as His proxy. And this angel, in turn, created the whole world. He created all things perfect and complete in the first moments of Creation, including Adam and Eve and the other living beings, as well as the plants and trees. So too did he create the sun and the moon and the stars according to the utmost degree of their possible perfection. He arranged the stars in the sky, giving to each its proper place and creating their beauty. Thus the world was created perfect and whole.

God spoke to the prophets through this angel, and it is this angel who performed miracles and through whom the Law was revealed to Moses. Indeed, it is this angel who brings about everything that happens in the world.

Others say that God selected a certain angel from all those who attend upon Him, to confer His name upon him, and to proclaim this angel as His apostle, whose place in the world was God's place, and whose word was God's word. That angel is the elect one of the world.

This strongly Gnostic myth was held by the Magharians ("cave dwellers"), a Jewish sect who lived at the time of the Sadducees, before the rise of Christianity. They were known as "cave dwellers" because their books were found in a cave. They felt the Sadducees had anthropomorphized the Creator, and objected to this approach to scriptural interpretation. Their strong belief was that God cannot be compared to any created being, and that all statements to this effect in the Torah refer to an angel. According to the Magharians, it is this angel who is spoken of as God in the Bible. Yet while the parallels of the belief of the Magharians to Gnostic views is apparent, there are also differences. The demiurge in Gnosticism is not God's agent, but is usually described as an evil being who is in opposition to the good God. But the theology of the Magharians is consistent with other Gnostic systems with conspicuous Jewish elements, where the demiurgic role is usually played by an angel or an elevated human, such as Adam.

The Magharians also teach that God spoke to the prophets through this pre-existent angel. This implies that the angel is in some ways working God's will. The Magharians felt it was quite natural for God to send a messenger and give him His Name and say, "This is My messenger, and his position among you is My position, and his word and command My word and command, and his appearance My appearance."

This, the primary myth of the Magharians, grew out of their distress at the use of anthropomorphic expressions for God in the Bible. They objected to biblical phrases such as "God came," "God ascended into the clouds," "He has written the Torah with His hand," "He sits on His throne," "He has curly hair and black hair on His head," or "the Mighty One laughed." They strongly believed that God could and must not be portrayed in anthropomorphic terms. But rather than deny that God could be portrayed in such terms, their solution was to identify the God of the Bible as an angel created by the First Creator. It was this angel who, in turn, created the world.

Some of the most anthropomorphic passages about God occur in the Exodus narrative, such as *Yahweh is a man of war* (Exod. 15:3), *Yahweh came down upon Mount Sinai, to the top of the mount* (Exod. 19:20), and *Then went up Moses, and Aaron, Nadab, and Abihu, and seventy of the elders of Israel; and they saw the God of Israel; and there was under His feet the likeness of a pavement of sapphire stone* (Exod. 24:9-10). This portrayal of God is attributed by the Magharians to the pre-existent angel. The notion that God revealed the Law through an angel is found in *The Book of Jubilees* 1:27 as well: "And God said to the angel of the presence: 'Write for Moses from the beginning of Creation till My sanctuary has been built among them for all eternity.'"

The angel of the Magharians is also identified with the Angel of the Lord, especially as identified in the key passage from Exodus 23:20-21: *"I am sending an angel before you to guard you on the way and to bring you to the place that I have made ready. Pay heed to him, and obey him. Do not defy him, for he will not pardon your offenses, since My Name is in him."*

Although the angel myth of the Magharians originated out of reverence to God and their belief that God must not be portrayed in anthropomorphic terms, in the end they reduced the importance of God and raised up the importance of the angel, who was the true creator of this world.

Philo's concept of the Logos, or some parallel traditions, which at times becomes identified as an angel, may have influenced the Magharian myth.

This mythic solution later induced this sect to become Christian, in that they accepted the idea that the creating angel had human form, and therefore could take the form of a human being. The founder of the sect, however, returned to Judaism, disillusioned by Christianity, and wrote two books attacking it.

There are also reports about the Magharians in Shahrastani, where their name was corrupted into Makaribans. Here the angel is not pre-existent, but one of the ministering angels who is selected by God as his proxy. Otherwise the myths are the same.

Sources:

Kitab al-Anwar w'al-Mar'akib (Karaite); *Kitab al-Milal wa'al-Nihal* (Karaite).

Studies:

"The Pre-existent Angel of the Magharians and Al-Nahawandi" by H. A. Wolfson. *The Jewish Quarterly Review*, vol. 51, 1960-61, 89-106.

"The Magharians: A Pre-Christian Jewish Sect and Its Significance for the Study of Gnosticism and Christianity" by Jarl E. Fossum.

153. THE WHEEL OF CREATION

All creation is a rotating wheel, revolving and alternating. Everything goes in cycles. Man becomes angel, and angel, man. Head becomes foot, and foot head. All these things have a single root. All interchange, raising the low, lowering the high, spinning on the wheel of creation.

> This myth demonstrates the unique vision of Rabbi Nachman of Bratslav. Here he describes a cyclic view of creation in which things are transformed into their opposites, men into angels and back again. This is what he identifies as the wheel of creation. One likely inspiration for this myth is Isaiah 40:4: *Let every valley be raised and mount made low.* Another is the famous passage from Ecclesiastes 3:1: *To everything there is a season, and a time for every purpose under heaven.*
>
> *Sources:*
> *Sihot ha-Ran* 40.

154. THE COSMIC TREE

In the beginning God planted a cosmic tree that reached from one end of the universe to the other. God planted this tree for the whole world, and everything that God created afterward emerged from this tree. All souls blossom from it, flying forth in joy. All things emanate from it. The whole world delights in it. Everything needs it and yearns for it, and seeks to glimpse that tree. And, at the end of their lives, the souls of the righteous ascend on high, attaching themselves to this tree.

God was alone when He created the cosmic tree and sowed the seeds of All. None was with Him when he planted and rooted that tree, and there was none to whom He could confide this secret. That is why no angel can raise himself above it to say: "I was there first."

> The cosmic tree described here functions both as a myth and as an allegory. This dual nature is commonly found in kabbalah, in which there is an ongoing dialectic between myth and allegory. The myth of a tree that is also the cosmos has astrological roots, while its allegorical aspect is the symbolic Tree of Life that is used to represent the sefirot, especially the final seven sefirot. The names of these sefirot are identified in the verse *Yours, Lord, are the Greatness, the Strength, the Beauty, the Victory and the Splendor, for All in heaven and earth. Yours O God is the Kingdom* (I Chron. 29:11). The *sefirah Yesod*, representing the sexual organ in man, is identified as the "All" that is the source of all souls, for through *Yesod* souls are transmitted.
>
> *Sefer ha-Bahir* discusses the cosmic tree in two passages, 22 and 119. In the latter the cosmic tree is defined: "What is this tree? The powers of God, one above the other, resembling a tree." Here too the metaphor of the tree is expanded, as follows: "Just as a tree brings forth fruit through water, God increases the power of the tree through water. What is the water of God? It is wisdom. It is the souls of the righteous. The *Shekhinah* dwells among them. Their deeds rest in the bosom of God, and He makes them fruitful and multiplies them."
>
> In Isaiah 44:24 God says, *"It is I, Yahweh, who made everything, who stretched out the heavens alone and spread out the earth."* This statement is intended to eliminate speculation that other forces, such as the angels, aided in Creation. Likewise, *Genesis Rabbah* 1:3 states, "When were the angels created? All agree that none were created on the first day, lest you should say, Michael stretched the world in the south and Gabriel in the north, while God measured it in the middle." (Other sources, however, link the creation of the angels to the first day of Creation, and imply that the angels did participate in the subsequent creation. See "Creation By Angels," p. 116 and the accompanying note.)
>
> This sentiment is also found in this passage from *Sefer ha-Bahir* 22:11, where God takes complete credit for having created the cosmic tree, which is a metaphor for the

universe. This tree is the origin of the souls of the world. It does not seem to be identical to the Tree of Life, although life emerges from it.

Sources:
Sefer ha-Bahir 22; 119.

Studies:
Origins of the Kabbalah by Gershom Scholem, 68-80.
"The Tree that is All: Jewish-Christian Roots of a Kabbalistic Symbol in *Sefer ha-Bahir*" by Elliot R. Wolfson.

155. THE SHATTERING OF THE VESSELS AND THE GATHERING OF THE SPARKS

At the beginning of time, God's presence filled the universe. Then God decided to bring this world into being. To make room for creation, God first drew in His breath, contracting Himself. From that contraction a dark mass was produced. And when God said, *Let there be light* (Gen. 1:3), the light that came into being entered the dark mass, and ten vessels came forth, each filled with primordial light.

In this way God sent forth those ten vessels, like a fleet of ships, each carrying its cargo of light. Had they arrived intact, the world would have been perfect. But somehow the frail vessels broke open, split asunder, and all the holy sparks were scattered, like sand, like seeds, like stars. Those sparks fell everywhere, but more fell on the Holy Land than anywhere else.

That is why we were created—to gather the sparks, no matter where they are hidden. Some even say that God created the world so that Israel could raise up the holy sparks. And that is why there have been so many exiles—to release the holy sparks from the servitude of captivity. For in this way the people of Israel will sift all the holy sparks from the four corners of the earth.

And when enough holy sparks have been gathered, the vessels will be restored, and the repair of the world, awaited so long, will finally take place. Therefore it should be the aim of everyone to raise these sparks from where they are imprisoned and to elevate them to holiness by the power of their soul. And when the task of gathering the sparks nears completion, God will hasten the arrival of the final redemption by Himself collecting what remains of the holy sparks that went astray.

The myth of the Shattering of the Vessels (*shevirat ha-kelim*), attributed to the Ari, is found in the writings of Hayim Vital, Moshe Yonah, Yosef ibn Tabul, and Israel Sarug, among others. Rabbi Nachman of Bratslav, quoting *Pirkei de-Rabbi Eliezer* 3, suggests that the reason that God wanted to create the earth was "to reveal his majesty, since there is no King without subjects. Therefore God constricted His infinite light, leaving a vacated space" (*Likutei Moharan* 6). See "The Contraction of God," p. 13. According to Hayim Vital, the ten vessels were created to contain ten gradations of divine light—the ten sefirot. See "The Ten Sefirot," p. 7. In some versions of this myth, all ten vessels are said to have broken, while other versions insist that the upper three vessels remained intact, while the lower seven shattered. The breaking of the vessels indicates some kind of divine flaw, since the vessels were unable to hold the infinite light that flowed into them. It was the shattering of the vessels, the divine equivalent of the Fall of Adam and Eve, that permitted the roots of evil to enter the world. Once they shattered, the vessels, now called *kelippot*, meaning "shells" or "shards," and conceived as demonic in nature, became the basis of material reality. While most of the divine light ascended on high, some clung to the broken shards. These are the sparks that must be liberated through the process of Gathering the Sparks. As Rabbi Hayim Tirer of Chernovitz puts it, "The Jewish people must make a mighty effort to return these sparks to the Creator" (*Be'er Mayim Hayim, Bereshit* 32).

According to Israel Sarug (1631): "Traces of the divine light adhered to the fragments of the broken vessels like sparks. And when the fragments descended to the bottom of the fourth and last world, they produced the four elements, and when all these became completely materialized, some of the sparks still remained within. Therefore it should be the aim of everyone to raise these sparks from where they are imprisoned in this world and to elevate them to holiness by the power of their soul."

There are three likely biblical sources for the Ari's myth. The first, Contraction (*tzimtzum*), finds its likely biblical source in the cloud that fills the Tent of Meeting: *A cloud covered the Tent of Meeting, and the Presence of Yahweh filled the Tabernacle, and Moses was not able to enter into the Tent of Meeting* (Exod. 40:34-35).

The second phase of the Ari's myth, the Shattering of the Vessels, has two likely biblical sources. The first is that of Moses throwing down the first tablets of the Law, which shatter: *He became enraged; and he hurled the tablets from his hand and shattered them at the foot of the mountain* (Exod. 32:19). This is an important source, especially since there are ten commandments and ten sefirot. Equally relevant is the passage in Ezekiel 10:2 in which coals of fire from the altar are scattered by some angelic figure over the city of Jerusalem: *Fill your hands with glowing coals from among the cherubs, and scatter them over the city*. This passage from Ezekiel manages to work in the scattering, the sparks, the concentration of sparks on the Holy Land (and especially Jerusalem), and the holiness of the sparks, since they come from the altar.

A deeply metaphoric passage in the *Idra Rabbah* portion of the *Zohar* (3:135a-135b) about the deaths of the kings of Edom (Gen. 36:31-39) has been linked to the sefirotic process of emanation, which is in turn linked to the myth of the Shattering of the Vessels, in that both describe a cosmic rupture. Interpreted in this fashion, this passage identifies the vessels that shattered with the myth of the prior worlds that God is said to have created and destroyed: "and all the worlds were destroyed." See "Prior Worlds," p. 71. These prior worlds were understood to have been flawed worlds that God created and destroyed. From this interpretation it is possible to conclude that the Breaking of the Vessels came about because of some kind of flaw whose origin must be tracked back to God. For if the vessels had been strong enough, or the light in them stable, they would have fulfilled their original purpose and arrived intact at their destination. Instead, the sparks of holy light must be liberated from the dark matter in which they have descended.

The third stage, the Gathering of the Sparks, may well find its source in the gathering of the manna in the desert: *The Israelites did so, some gathering much, some little* (Exod. 16:17). Like the sparks, the manna has fallen from the heavens to nourish the people's bodies, while the sparks nourish their souls.

Rabbi Menachem Mendel of Riminov strongly linked the myth of the Gathering of the Sparks with the messianic redemption: "These holy sparks descended at the time of Creation. It is our task to extract and cleanse the holy sparks by means of learning Torah and performing *mitzvot*. If Israel merits to elevate all the holy sparks through their good deeds, then, when this task is completed, God will hasten the arrival of the Final Redemption. For the Final Redemption cannot occur until all the holy sparks are purified and elevated to their origin. And what if there are a few holy sparks that were led astray? God will collect what is His—He Himself will collect the holy sparks that were led astray." Rabbi Shneur Zalman of Lyady confirms the link between raising up the fallen sparks and the arrival of the messianic era: "When all the sparks of holiness have been released, the Messiah will come" (*Tanya* 25).

Note that the Riminov Rebbe adds a remarkable detail to the myth of Gathering the Sparks: that God Himself will collect any remaining holy sparks that went astray. The Riminov Rebbe links this interpretation to the talmudic dictim, "God is forebearing and collects what is His" (*Y. Tan.* 82a).

In *Esh Kadosh*, Rabbi Kalonymus Kalman Shapira suggests that when there was an increase in the *kelippot*—the forces of evil—the deaths of the Ten Martyrs became necessary to prevent a new Shattering of the Vessels. Then Rabbi Shapira offers a parallel explanation for the loss of so many Jewish souls in the *Shoah*, concluding that that time was also a time of the Breaking of the Vessels.

Sources:

Zohar 3:135a-135b, *Idra Rabbah; Etz Hayim, Hekhal Nekudim, Sha'ar ha-Melakhim* 5; *Etz Hayim, Hekhal Adam Kadmon, Derush Igulim ve-Yosher* 2:24b:3-9; *Derush she-Masar* 18-20; *Mavo She'arim, Sha'ar* 2, pt. 1, 5:18-19; *Kanfei Yonah; Derush Heftzi Bah; Keter Shem Tov* 194; *Likutei Moharan* 49; *Makhon Siftei Tzaddikim* on Exodus 34:6; *B'nei Yisakhar, Nisan Ma'amar* 4; *Yiyyul ha-Pardes* 8:60d; *Sefer Ba'al Shem Tov, va-Yetze* 8, 9; *Tanya* 25; *Be'er Mayim Hayim, Bereshit* 32; *Esh Kadosh.*

Studies:

Physician of the Soul, Healer of the Cosmos: Isaac Luria and His Kabbalistic Fellowship by Lawrence Fine, pp. 124-149.

156. CREATION BY BROKEN VESSELS

At the time of Creation, God created worlds and destroyed them. The worlds that were created and those that were destroyed were the shattered vessels that God had sent forth. Out of those broken vessels God created the present universe.

> Here Rabbi Kalonymus Kalman Shapira transforms Rabbi Isaac Luria's myth of the Shattering of the Vessels and the Gathering of the Sparks, linking the Ari's myth to the midrash found in *Genesis Rabbah* 3:7 and elsewhere about God having destroyed many previous worlds prior to the creation of this one. In the midrash, God destroys the worlds because they don't please him—in some way they are imperfect. But here Rabbi Shapira has brilliantly transformed a myth about destruction into a myth about creation. Instead of the prior worlds simply having been destroyed, here they are understood to have been the basis for the subsequent, present universe, known as *olam ha-tikkun*, world of repair.
>
> Although Rabbi Shapira's reinterpretation of the Ari's myth is really a new myth in itself, it does not contradict the Ari's myth, where the Shattering of the Vessels, and the spilling of the primordial light inside them serves as the prelude to the Gathering of the Sparks, which is precisely *tikkun olam*—repair of the world. Thus the end result of the two versions is the same. From this perspective, Rabbi Shapira's myth might be seen as an alternate version of the Ari's myth, to which, of course, it directly refers. See "The Shattering of the Vessels and the Gathering of the Sparks," p. 122.
>
> Rabbi Shapira viewed the Shattering of the Vessels as a cosmic shattering that could recur in another time. In *Esh Kadosh*, Rabbi Shapira presents the theory that such an event was averted because of the deaths of the Ten Martyrs. He also viewed the Holocaust, which he experienced firsthand in the Warsaw Ghetto, as a time of the Breaking of the Vessels. But rather than simply view this as a time of cosmic catastrophe, he was true to his own myth, asserting instead that it was a time for renewal and new creation. And for him the primary task of renewal was repentance. Only in this way could all the worlds be mended.

Sources:
Esh Kadosh 122-124.

Studies:
The Holy Fire: The Teachings of Rabbi Kalonymus Kalman Shapira, the Rebbe of the Warsaw Ghetto by Nehemia Polen, pp. 124-126.

157. THE HEAVENLY MAN

There are those who say that God did not only create one Adam, but two. The first Adam was a heavenly being who was not fashioned from clay, but was stamped with the likeness and image of God, as it is said, *in the image of God He created him* (Gen. 1:27). This Adam assisted God in the creation of the earthly Adam. There is a vast difference between this heavenly Adam, and the earthly Adam.

The earthly Adam was created out of the dust of the earth, as it is said, *The Lord God formed man from the dust of the earth* (Gen. 2:7). At the same time, Adam was brought to life by the breath of God, as it is said, *He blew into his nostrils the breath of life, and man became a living being* (Gen. 2:7). Thus the earthly man was made from a composite of divine breath and a lump of clay.

A vast difference exists between the heavenly man and the generations descended from the earthly Adam—although the earthly Adam has returned to the dust, the heavenly Adam still exists. For the heavenly man, born in the image of God, has no participation in any earthlike essence, is imperishable, and is neither male nor female.

Others, who disagree, say that this heavenly man was none other than Adam himself, for it was God's original intention for Adam to live forever, like the angels. That is the meaning of the verse *"Now the man has become like one of us"* (Gen. 3:22). For God intended to set up Adam as king over all His creatures. God said, "I am King of the worlds above, and Adam will be king in the worlds below." So God brought Adam into the Garden of Eden and made him king there.

Still others say that both the heavenly man and the earthly man were introduced into Paradise together, the heavenly man in the heavenly Garden and the earthly man in the earthly Garden. Yet while the heavenly man still makes his home on high, the earthly man was cast out of the Garden long ago. For God's intentions for Adam came to naught when Adam ate from the forbidden fruit, and at that moment mortality was decreed to him. But if Adam had not sinned, he would have endured forever.

Others concur that two Adams were created, but they say that one is for this world, and one for the World to Come. However, the creation of the second Adam will not be completed until the time of the resurrection of the dead at the End of Days.

> The notion that there were two Adams, one heavenly and one earthly, is reflected in Philo's explanation of the apparent contradiction in the two creation texts found in Genesis 1:27 and Genesis 2:7. The earlier creation of man in Genesis was understood by Philo to be a heavenly man because he was created *in the image of God* (Gen. 1:27), while it is clearly stated that the earthly Adam was formed *from the dust of the earth* (Gen. 2:7), consisting of body and soul, and therefore human. Philo describes this heavenly man as "an idea, or a type, or a seal, perceptible only by the intellect, incorporeal, neither male nor female, imperishable by nature" (*De Opificio Mundi* 134).
>
> This heavenly man is known by several names, including the "Heavenly Man," the "First Man," and the "Light Man." It appears that in certain mystical circles the Heavenly Man and Adam merged into a single figure. Philo calls him "God's Firstborn." In the Nag Hammadi texts, such as *The Gospel of the Egyptians*, he is known as Adamas. In later kabbalistic texts this figure seems to evolve into Adam Kadmon. In all cases he is portrayed either as a transcendent being created by God before the creation of the human Adam—or else he was the original incarnation of Adam, when it was God's intention that he be immortal.
>
> The myth that God created two Adams, one for the heavenly garden and one for the earthly garden, grows out of the dual understanding of the term *Gan Eden*, literally, the Garden of Eden. While the use of this term in Genesis seems to clearly indicate an earthly garden, it later acquired the meaning of "Paradise," and it is the term used to indicate Paradise in rabbinic literature. The explanation that God created two Adams and placed each of them in *Gan Eden* resolves the question of whether Adam's Paradise was on earth or in heaven by asserting that there was an Adam both above and below.
>
> The idea that God intended to make Adam the ruler of the world derives from the verse *The Lord God planted a garden in Eden, in the east, and placed there the man whom He had formed* (Gen. 2:8). The phrase "placed there the man" is interpreted to indicate Adam's kingship.
>
> Philo's concept of the Heavenly Man is based on his interpretation of the verse *And God created man in His image* (Gen. 1:27). Philo believed that something made in God's

image must be very much like its Creator, far transcendent to human beings. Thus, from his point of view, the figure created in Genesis 1:27 was not the same as the man created in Genesis 2:7. Philo identifies the transcendent figure as the Heavenly Man, as God's invisible image, and as God's Logos, identifying the Logos as the "eldest-born Image of God" (*De Confusione Linguarum* 62-63). Thus, for Philo, the earthly man was made after the image of the Heavenly Man. But as is often the case in Philo's writings, the meaning of "Logos" seems to veer between a philosophical and a mythological concept. In other places, Philo identifies the heavenly man with the soul, and the earthly man with the body. Philo also identifies three types of men: the earth-born, the heaven-born, and the God-born. The earth-born chase after pleasures of the body; the heaven-born are artists and lovers of learning; the God-born are priests and prophets who have transcended earthly concerns (*De Gigantibus* 12:58-61).

Ultimately, the role of the heavenly man resembles that of a second divine figure. Rather than acknowledge dualism, the heavenly man was designated to serve a secondary role, greater than that of the angels, but less than his Creator. In some myths, his role is to rule over the creatures of this world; in others, he seems primarily to exist as an archetype of humanity. In some of the Gnostic literature, the celestial Adam does play an active role, bringing the chaotic matter to rest, rotating the universe in a circle, and releasing the world ocean that surrounds the universe.

Midrash Tanhuma offers another version of the myth of the two Adams, stating that one Adam was created for this world, and one for the World to Come. The second Adam, in this view, is the Messiah, whose coming will herald the End of Days. This coincides with the myth that the Messiah is a heavenly figure, who lives in his own mystical palace. This is contradicted by the tradition that the Messiah will be a human being. The Lubavitch Hasidim combined these two myths into one, saying that the divine soul of the Messiah would descend into a human body. They believed (and many still believe) that this was the body of their late Rebbe, Rabbi Menachem Mendel Schneersohn (1902-1993). In effect, they combined two contradictory myths into one. See the Introduction, p. 83, note 110.

Sources:

B. *Hagigah* 12a; B. *Bava Batra* 58a; *Pesikta Rabbati* 48:2; Philo, *De Opificio Mundi* 134-142; Philo, *Legum Allegoriarum* 1:31, 1:53, 1:88, 2:13, 2:4; Philo, *De Confusione Linguarum* 62-63; *Midrash Tanhuma, Tazri'a* 2.

Studies:

The Name of God and the Angel of the Lord by Jarl E. Fossum, pp. 266-291.
Portraits of Adam in Early Judaism: From Sirah to 2 Baruch by John R. Levison, pp. 63-88.
Four Powers in Heaven: The Interpretation of Daniel 7 in the Testament of Abraham by Phillip B. Munoa, pp. 82-112.

158. ADAM THE ANGEL

God created Adam from invisible and visible substances, and assigned him to be an angel, second in power, who would share His wisdom. And God assigned him to be a great and glorious king, who would reign on earth. There was nothing comparable to him on earth, among any other creatures that existed. And God assigned him four special stars and called his name Adam. And God handed over Paradise to Adam, and commanded him to peer into the heavens, so that he might look upon the angels.

In this version of the theme of the heavenly Adam, found in 2 *Enoch*, Adam is described as an angel. Just as Enoch and Jacob are portrayed as demiurgic angels, second in command to God, so too was there such a tradition about Adam, although there are strong Gnostic echoes in this Adam myth. See "The Metamorphosis and

Enthronement of Enoch," p. 156, and "Jacob the Angel," p. 364. For more about Adam as demiurge, see "The Heavenly Man," p. 124.

Sources:

2 *Enoch* 30-31 (Ms. J).

Studies:

"2 (Slavonic Apocalypse of) Enoch," translated by F. I. Andersen, in *The Old Testament Pseudepigrapha*, edited by James H. Charlesworth, vol. 1, pp. 91-221.

159. ADAM THE GOLEM

When God decided to create Adam, He gathered dust from the four corners of the earth, rolled it together, mixed it with water, and made red clay. Then God shaped the clay into a lifeless body, the first golem, stretching from one end of the world to the other, and brought it to life. So large was it, that God's hand rested upon it. So large was it, that wherever God looked, He saw it. That is the meaning of the verse *Your eyes saw my golem* (Ps. 139:16). So huge was it, that the angels mistook it for God Himself, and they wanted to say "Holy, holy, holy is the Lord of Hosts." So God caused sleep to fall upon him, so that all knew he was but a mortal man.

While the golem of Adam lay sleeping, God whispered in his ear the secrets of Creation, and showed Adam the righteous of every generation, and the wicked as well, until the time when the dead will be raised. Indeed, God showed him every righteous man who would ever descend from him, every generation and its judges, scribes, prophets, and leaders. So too did God show him every generation and its saints and sinners. And as God spoke, Adam witnessed everything as if he were there. Some of the righteous hung on Adam's head, some hung to his hair, some to his forehead, some to his eyes, some to his nose, some to his mouth, some to his ears, some to his teeth.

And later, when Adam did come to life, he dimly remembered all that God had revealed when he was only a golem. And at night, in his dreams, he still heard God's voice recounting mysteries, and telling of all that would take place in the days to come. In those dreams Adam would travel to those places and see the events firsthand, as a witness. And since there is a spark of Adam's soul in every one of his descendants, there are a few in every generation who still hear the voice of God in their dreams.

> "Golem" means "a formless body." In shaping Adam's body out of clay, God created the first golem. There are stories in the Talmud and medieval Jewish lore that describe the creation of golems, one a calf that was eaten on the Sabbath, one a man of clay animated by the fourth century Rabbi Rava, and one a woman golem that Ibn Gabirol is said to have made out of wood. Later the famous legend of the golem of the Maharal recounted how he created a man out of clay in much the same way that God did, using the powers of what is known as practical kabbalah. The fact that the golem of the Maharal is mute and cannot reproduce demonstrates that man's creation is less perfect than God's. It also demonstrates man's desire to take on the powers of God and act in a godlike fashion. The righteous who cling to the golem of Adam represent the qualities that the each of the righteous emphasized. See "The Golem of Prague," p. 281.
>
> According to *Midrash ha-Ne'elam, Zohar Hadash* 17c-d, God gathered the dust for Adam's body from the site where the Temple in Jerusalem would be built in the future, and drew down his soul from the celestial Temple.
>
> One of the important questions about the creation of Adam asks whether God created Adam by Himself, or if the angels played a role in his creation. Many midrashim describe Gabriel's role in gathering dust from the four corners of the earth. In contrast, *4 Ezra* insists that God created Adam entirely by Himself: "Adam was the workmanship of Your hands, and You breathed into him the breath of life, and he was made alive in Your presence. And You led him into the garden which Your right hand had planted before the earth appeared" (*4 Ezra* 3:4-6).

Sources:

Midrash Tanhuma, Bereshit 28; Genesis Rabbah 8:1, 8:10, 24:2; Exodus Rabbah 40:3;
    Ecclesiastes Rabbah 6:1, 10; 4 Ezra 3:4-6; Avot de-Rabbi Natan 31; Pirkei de-Rabbi Eliezer
    12; Pesikta Rabbati 23:1; Eliyahu Rabbah 1:3; Midrash ha-Ne'elam, Zohar Hadash 17c-d.

Studies:

"Imagery of the Divine and the Human: On the Mythology of Genesis Rabbah 8:1" by
    David H. Aaron.
The Idea of the Golem by Gershom Scholem.
Golem: Jewish Magical and Mystical Traditions on the Artificial Anthropoid by Moshe Idel.

160. ADAM THE GIANT

When Adam was first created, he was as tall as the distance from the earth to heaven, big enough to fill the world from east to west or from north to south. His two eyeballs were like globes of the sun. He even filled the hollow places of the world. The radiance of his face was unchanged, and its lights were not eclipsed until the Sabbath ended. And he was as strong and powerful as the mighty ones on high. This first Adam knew more of the supernal wisdom than the angels above, and his union with God was closer than with any other beings in the universe.

When the angels saw him, they trembled and fled. Then they all came before God and said, "Master of the Universe! Are there to be two powers in the world, one in heaven and the other on earth?" Then God placed His hand upon Adam and reduced his size until he was no more than a hundred cubits tall, and all the springs of wisdom were closed to him.

The myth of the giant Adam is found in the midrashic literature. Later, it likely served as one of the sources in the kabbalistic literature for the myth of Adam Kadmon. See "Adam Kadmon," p. 15. The biblical sources for the concept of a giant Adam are: *God created man on earth, from one end of heaven to the other* (Deut. 4:32), *You have formed me from west and east* (Ps. 139:5), and, *Your eyes saw my golem* (Ps. 139:16). The first Adam is portrayed as a giant figure, half man, half god. There is also a myth of the first Eve, who is sometimes identified with Lilith, but also has an independent existence apart from Lilith. See "The First Eve," p. 140.

Zohar 3:107b adds the interesting detail that when the creatures in the Garden of Eden saw Adam prostrate himself before the Tree of Knowledge, all of them followed his lead, and this sin, rather than the eating of the forbidden fruit, was the cause of his death and the introduction of death into the world.

According to *Sefer Hasidim*, when the angels first saw the giant Adam, they wanted to worship him. But after he sinned, God diminished him and piled pieces of his limbs around him. Adam said to God, *Does it benefit You to defraud, to despise the toil of Your hands?* (Job 10:3). God told Adam to scatter the pieces of his limbs throughout the world and plant them, and his offspring will settle in those places. But no Jews would live in any of the places where he did not plant any pieces of his flesh. This closely resembles the Greek myth of Cadmus. See Graves, *Greek Myths* 58.g.

The shrinking of the giant Adam to human size is explained by the verse *You hedge me before and behind; You lay Your hand upon me* (Ps. 139:5). Since it is well known that God fashioned Adam out of the dust of the earth, the second part of the verse *and laid Your hand upon me*, suggests that it was God who caused the man to shrink from his celestial proportions.

Sources:

B. Hagigah 12a; B. Sanhedrin 38b; Genesis Rabbah 8:1, 8:9-10, 24:2; Leviticus Rabbah 18:2;
    Midrash Tanhuma, Bereshit 25; Midrash Aleph Bet 15:26; Alpha Beta de-Rabbi Akiva in
    Otzar Midrashim, p. 428; Zohar 1:9a, 2:55a, 3:107b; Sefer Hasidim 500; Adir ba-
    Marom; Sefer ha-Zikhronot 6:12.

Studies:

Cosmic Adam: Man as Mediator in Rabbinic Literature by Susan Niditch.

161. ADAM THE LAST AND FIRST

When God wished to create the world, His first work of Creation was none other than Adam. First God made a lifeless body. But when He was about to instill a soul in him, God said, "If I finish his creation now, he will claim that he was My partner in the work of Creation. Therefore I shall leave him as a lifeless body until I create everything."

When God had completed everything else, the angels said to Him: "Are You going to make man, as You said you would?" God answered: "I have already made him, and all he lacks in the infusion of a soul. When he receives this, he will reign on the earth, and there will be nothing comparable to him, even among the other creatures that exist. I will call his name Adam."

So God breathed into his nostrils the breath of life; and man became a living soul (Gen. 2:7). That is why it is said that Adam was the last and first, for God began and completed the creation of the world with him, as it is said, *Last and first You did form me* (Ps. 139:5).

This myth is a polemic against the traditions about the traditions that indicate that God shared some of the work of creation with a heavenly Adam. Since this implies Gnostic duality and threatens monotheism, the present myth is offered as an anecdote. It says that yes, Adam was God's first creation, but only his lifeless body. God held off giving him a soul until the sixth day, as is stated in Genesis 2:7: *Then God formed man of the dust of the ground, and breathed into his nostrils the breath of life; and man became a living soul.*

This myth serves to prove that Adam was not God's partner in Creation. This is stated explicitly in *B. Sanhedrin* 38a: "Adam was created last on the eve of the Sabbath. Why? Lest the heretics should say, 'God has a partner in the work of Creation.'" Here, as in the other passages, the phrase "lest the heretics should say" indicates that there were those who did say such things. Because the existence of such a partner for God would dispute monotheism, those who argued for such a partner are regarded as heretics—*minim*. In this case it is likely that the heretics the rabbis had in mind were the Gnostics, who taught that everything came into being through Adam. A similar tradition about Adam is found in *2 Enoch* 30:11-12, where God says, "I assigned him (Adam) to be a second angel, honored and glorious. I assigned him to be a king, to reign on earth and to have My wisdom. There was nothing comparable to him, not even among the angels."

The Testament of Abraham, chapter 8 (rec. B) goes even further, describing Adam as sitting upon a throne of glory at the gates of Paradise, surrounded by angels. Later, in the same text, Adam is described as "adorned in glory, with a terrifying appearance, like that of the Lord" (chapter 11, rec. A.) Here Adam clearly plays a demiurgic role.

"Adam the First and Last" alerts us to an entire category of polemical myths. A classic example of such a myth is the talmudic account of Elisha ben Abuyah's vision of Metatron. Here Elisha was said to have seen Metatron seated on a heavenly throne. Since he had understood that there was no sitting in heaven other than for God, he announces, "There must be two powers in heaven" (*B. Hagigah* 15a). The intention of this myth is clear: to undermine the extensive myths about Enoch/Metatron, demonstrating that such belief in Metatron as the Prince of the Presence, the second in command after God, would endanger belief in monotheism. Here it causes Elisha to become an apostate, thereafter known as *Aher*, "the Other." See "A Vision of Metatron," p. 174.

Another example of a polemical myth is that of the homunculus of Maimonides, probably created by the opponents of Maimonides in the anti-Maimonidian controversy. See "The Homunculus of Maimonides," p. 284.

See also "The Image of Jacob Cast Out of Heaven," p. 368 for a third example of a polemical myth. This is a polemic against the myths that raise Jacob from a human to a heavenly figure, another example of the First Created Being. This myth has God cast Jacob's image, which was on God's throne, out of heaven.

Sources:
   B. *Sanhedrin* 38a; *Midrash Avkir; Yalkut Shim'oni* 34; *Genesis Rabbah* 8:1; *2 Enoch* 30:11-12; *The Testament of Abraham* 8 (rec. B).

162. ADAM'S BODY OF LIGHT

Adam possessed a body of light, which shone from one end of the world to the other. This light was identical with the primordial light that was created on the first day. So bright was this light that Adam's heel outshone the globe of the sun; how much more so the brightness of his face. So astonishing was the sight of Adam that the ministering angels became confused, and mistook him for a divine being, and wished to proclaim him as God. So God caused Adam to fall into a deep sleep, and then all the angels knew he was but a man.

The splendor of Adam's face was only one of seven precious gifts that God gave to Adam before the Fall. Some of the others were eternal life, tallness of stature, the fruit of the soil, the fruit of the trees, the luminaries in the sky, the light of the moon, and the light of the sun. The reason that Adam's face shone so brightly is that *God created Adam in His own image* (Gen. 1:27). So brightly did his face shine that the angels mistook him for God himself. So God put him into a deep sleep, and the angels realized he was no more than a man.

Some say that one of the consequences of Adam's sin was that the light of Adam's body was diminished, along with his cosmic size. When this brightness vanished, he appeared naked. Others insist that even after his death Adam retained his radiant countenance. Still others say that Adam did not receive the light that surrounded his body until after he sinned and repented, and that is when God gave him a garment of light.

Now it was Rabbi Bana'ah's duty to measure burial caves, and once he came upon the cave in which Adam was buried. There he discerned that each of Adam's heels eclipsed the sun. And he understood that if Adam's heel outshone the sun, the radiance of his face must have eclipsed it even more so. But before he could enter any further, a voice came forth, which said: "You have beheld the likeness of My likeness, but My likeness itself you may not behold."

> After Adam and Eve sinned by eating the forbidden fruit, *they perceived that they were naked* (Gen. 3:7). Some midrashim assert that they had been surrounded by clouds of glory, which departed after their sin. See "The Garments of Adam and Eve," p. 437. This myth about Adam's body of light is a variation on the theme of clouds of glory. Here, instead of the clouds, Adam is said to be surrounded by the primordial light. See "The Light of the First Day," p. 83. This light disappears after Adam's sin. This myth is also a variant on the theme of Adam as demiurge, in that, surrounded by that light, the angels mistook him for a divine being.
>
> The extensive tradition about Adam's body of light seems intended to create a bridge between the myths about a heavenly Adam who has a demiurgic role, and the earthly Adam created out of dust by God. This myth links both Adams into a single being, who loses his divine nature when he eats the forbidden fruit. For more on the demiurgic Adam, see "The Heavenly Man," p. 124 and "Adam Kadmon," p. 15.
>
> *Sources:*
>   B. *Bava Batra* 58a; B. *Sanhedrin* 38b; *Leviticus Rabbah* 20:2; *Genesis Rabbah.* 8:9-10, 11:2, 12:6, 20:11; *Deuteronomy Rabbah* 11:3; *Numbers Rabbah* 13:12; *Song of Songs Rabbah* 30:3; *Midrash ha-Gadol* 126-130; *Midrash Mishlei* 31; B. *Bava Batra* 58a; *Pesikta de-Rav Kahana* 4:4, 12:1, 26:3; *Pesikta Rabbati* 14:10; *Zohar* 1:142b; *Kedushat Shabbat* 5, p. 13b.

Studies:
"The Body as Image of God in Rabbinic Literature" by Alon Goshen Gottstein.
"Shedding Light on God's Body in Rabbinic Midrashim: Reflections on the Theory
    of a Luminous Adam" by David H. Aaron.

163. THE ENTHRONEMENT OF ADAM

The Archangel Michael descended to earth and took Abraham on a chariot pulled by cherubim and brought him up into heaven. That chariot soared over the entire world, and Abraham beheld all that took place that day in the lives of men, both good and evil. He saw births, wedding processions, and the dead being borne to their tombs.

Then the chariot reached the first gate of heaven. There Abraham saw that there were two paths, one broad and one straight and narrow. And they saw many souls driven by angels through the broad gate, and a few other souls led by angels through the narrow gate. And outside the two gates they saw a man seated on a golden throne, adorned in glory. And when the man on the throne saw the many souls driven through the broad gate, he threw himself on the ground and wept and grieved. But when he saw the souls entering through the straight gate, he rejoiced and exulted.

Seeing this, Abraham asked the angel Michael who that wondrous man was, and Michael told him that it was Adam, the first to be formed, who was enthroned there. He observes the world and all those who live there, since everyone has descended from him. And when he sees souls entering through the gate of the righteous, which leads to life, he rejoices. But when he sees all those who enter by the gate of the sinners, which leads to destruction, he weeps and wails.

> This myth about Adam being seated on a golden throne in heaven comes out of a tradition that elevated Adam to the status of a divine being. This myth also belongs to the tradition of other enthronement myths, such as those about Jacob, Moses, and King David that are found in a variety of sources, especially the Pseudepigrapha.
>
> In a variety of myths, Adam is portrayed as a divine figure. In some he is described as a giant reaching from earth to heaven. See "Adam the Giant," p. 128. In others he is described as an enormous golem, as big as this world, asleep in paradise. See "Adam the Golem," p. 127. Here, Adam is portrayed as a figure seated on a golden throne who either rejoices at the fate of righteous souls who enter paradise, or mourns over the fate of those souls driven away from a heavenly reward. Adam's great concern for them grows out of his role as their ancestor, the first man. Indeed, he regards them all as his children.
>
> Underlying this enthronement myth is the view that Adam must be regarded as a divine figure, who shares the duties of ruling the world with God. It is evidence of the survival of Jewish Gnosticism, primarily in the texts of the Pseudepigrapha, as here, from *The Testament of Abraham*.
>
> *Sources:*
> *The Testament of Abraham* 10-11.

164. ADAM'S BODY FORMED BY AN ANGEL

When the time came for the first man to be created, God called upon the angel Michael, and ordered him to form Adam from the dust of the earth. First Michael gathered dust from the four corners of the earth—though some say that the dust came from the Holy

Land, from the place where the altar of the Temple would one day be built. Then Michael shaped him into a clay figure in the image of God, as it is said, *In the image of God he created him* (Gen. 1:27). God then breathed into the clay figure a soul from the Heavenly Temple, and Adam opened his eyes.

> The notion that someone other than God gathered the dust from which Adam was created finds its source in the verse *Make for me an altar of earth* (Exod. 20:21). In some versions (such as *Midrash Konen*), it is Gabriel, rather than Michael, who is sent to gather the dust. One midrash holds that the earth refused Gabriel, so that God reached out and gathered the dust from the four corners of the earth Himself. In other versions, such as *Pirkei de-Rabbi Eliezer* 12, it is said that God took the dust from which He created Adam from the site of the Temple, as this was a holy and pure place, or that Adam's bones were created there. Other sources say that Adam's body came from Babylon, his head from the Land of Israel, and his limbs from the other lands.
>
> Some sources, such as *4 Ezra* 3:4, emphatically deny that God was assisted in the creation of the world or of man: "O Lord, did You not speak when You created earth, which You did without help, and command the dust, so that it gave You Adam?" In *Against Apion* 2:192, Josephus makes a similar point: "God created the world and its contents not with hands, not with toil, and not with assistants, for He had no need of them. He willed it into existence."
>
> Michael's forming the body of Adam by himself is parallel to Prometheus forming man out of clay and water. See Graves, *The Greek Myths*, 4c and 4.3. Graves calls the archangel Michael the counterpart of Prometheus. The Prometheus myth also finds a parallel in Judaism in the myth about Adam stealing light from heaven and bringing it to earth. See "Adam Brings Down Fire from Heaven," p. 137.
>
> *Sources:*
> *4 Ezra* 3:4; *Genesis Rabbah* 14.8; *Midrash Konen* in *Beit ha-Midrash* 2:27; *Pirkei de-Rabbi Eliezer* 11, 12, 20; *Midrash Tehillim* 92:6; *Y. Nazir* 7.2, 56b; *Seder Eliyahu Zuta* 2; *Sefer Zikhronot* 15.
>
> *Studies:*
> *Midrash Yerushalem: A Metaphysical History of Jerusalem* by Daniel Sperber, pp. 75-77.

165. GOD CONSULTS THE ANGELS ABOUT THE CREATION OF ADAM

When God wished to create man, He first created a company of ministering angels and said to them: "Shall we make man in our image?"

They asked, "Master of the Universe, what will be his character?"

God replied, "Righteous descendants will come forth from him." But He did not report to them that wicked descendants would come forth as well.

They answered, "Master of the Universe, what will his deeds be?"

God recounted their deeds, and the angels exclaimed, *"What is man that You have been mindful of him, mortal man that You have taken note of him"* (Ps. 8:5).

Thereupon, God stretched out His little finger among them and consumed them with fire. The same thing happened with the second group of angels.

When God consulted with the third company of angels, they replied, "Master of the Universe, what did the other angels accomplish when they spoke to You as they did? The whole world is Yours, and whatever You wish to do with your world, You can do it."

Others say that the angels formed parties and sects over the question of whether man should be created. Some called for him to be created, others for him not to be created.

While the angels were engaged in contentious arguments with each other, God went ahead and created man. Then God said to the angels, "What good are you doing? Man has already been made!"

God created all that is above and below, yet here, when it comes to creating man, He takes counsel with the ministering angels. In one version of this myth, God destroys the angels as soon as they raise objections. So by the time He has created a third company of angels, they realize that there is no point in contradicting God, and point out, "The whole world is Yours, and whatever You wish to do with Your world, You can do it." In another version, the angels become pre-occupied with contentious arguments about whether or not man should be created. In the meantime, God simply ignores them and proceeds with the creation, telling them after the fact that man has already been created. Both versions make the same point: even though God may consult with the angels, in the end He will do as He wishes. Note that this midrash resolves the problem of the use of the plural in Genesis 1:26, *Let us make man in our image* by suggesting that God took counsel with the angels before creating man.

In *3 Enoch*, the angels object to the elevation of Enoch in much the same terms as they object to the creation of man, and as they object to the ascent of Moses into heaven. See "The Ascent of Moses," p. 261.

Sources:
B. Sanhedrin 38b; *Genesis Rabbah* 8:4, 8:5, 8-6, 8:8; *Midrash ha-Ne'elam, Zohar Hadash* 16a-b; *Midrash ha-Gadol* on Genesis 1:26; *3 Enoch* 4:6-9.

Studies:
"3 Enoch and the Talmud" by P. S. Alexander.
"Gen. 1,26 and 2,7 in Judaism, Samaritanism, and Gnosticism" by Jarl Fossum.

166. THE CREATION OF MAN

Such is the story of heaven and earth when they were created. When the Lord God made earth and heaven—when no shrub of the field was yet on earth and no grasses of the field had yet sprouted, because the Lord God had not sent rain upon the earth and there was no man to till the soil, but a flow would well up from the ground and water the whole surface of the earth—the Lord God formed man from the dust of the earth. He blew into his nostrils the breath of life, and man became a living being.

Some midrashim say that God sent the angel Michael (or Gabriel) to gather the earth from which Adam was to be made from each of the four corners of the world, so that people could be buried anywhere, without the earth objecting that he had not come from that place. Another interpretation is found in *Pirkei de-Rabbi Eliezer* 12, where it is said that God took Adam's dust from a pure place, the place of the Temple.

Nachmanides, in *Perush Ramban al ha-Torah* on Genesis 1:26, identifies two stages in which Adam received his soul. First God placed a life force (*nefesh*) within him. Later, God breathed a higher soul (*neshamah*) into him.

Parallels to the biblical account of the creation of man are found in the Mesopotamian myths of Atrahasis, the *Enuma Elish*, and the epic of *Gilgamesh*. In the stories of Atrahasis, humans were created by Mami, the mother goddess, with the help of the god Ea, out of clay mixed with the blood of the slain god Geshtu-e. A similar myth is found in *Enuma Elish*, in which the god Marduk, with the help of Ea, created mankind using the blood of Qingu, slain leader of the enemy gods. In *Gilgamesh*, Enkidu is parallel to Adam and Dilmun is parallel to Eden. To civilize the savage Enkidu, a woman is sent to be his companion, who seduces him for six days and seven nights, and turns him into a civilized man.

Sources:
Genesis 2:4-7.

Studies:
The Gilgamesh Epic and Old Testament Parallels by A. Heidel.
The Epic of Gilgamesh by R. Campbell Thompson.
Old Testament Parallels: Laws and Stories from the Ancient Near East by Victor H.
  Matthews and Don C. Benjamin, pp. 19-30.

167. CREATION FROM A MOLD

Adam was not created by God's pronouncement, as were other creations, but with God's own hands, as it is said, *You lay Your Hand upon me* (Ps. 139:5). Indeed, Adam was created by a mold that was made especially for him. This is the meaning of *And God created man in his image* (Gen. 1:27).

Some say that God created this mold when He said, *"Let us make man in our image"* (Gen. 1:26). Others say that God used the mold of the angels, who also walk erect, since, in any case, God does not have an image or form.

Everything made with a human mold is identical. But such is God's power that although each person is created with the same mold used for the first man, no two are alike.

> Genesis 1:27 is usually translated *And God created man in His image*, but here the word *tzelem*, usually translated as "image," is understood to mean "mold." This myth explains how it is that all humans beings seem to be made in the same mold. The mold can also be understood as an archetype, and Adam, as the first human being, is the archetype of all subsequent humans. Nevertheless, no two people are alike.
>
> The myth also raises the possibility that God used the mold with which he created the angels to create humans. This follows the tradition that humans and angels have similar forms.
>
> Finally, the myth emphasizes that while angels and humans may have been created from a mold, God does not have an image or form.

Sources:
B. Hagigah 16a; *B. Sanhedrin* 38a; *Alpha Beta de-Rabbi Akiba* in *Otzar Midrashim* p. 428;
  Rashi on Genesis 1:27; Commentary of Eliyahu Mizrachi on Genesis 1:26; *Siftei Hakhamim.*

168. WISDOM CREATED MAN

When God decided to create man, He assigned a share of the work to Wisdom, as it is said, *"Let us make man"* (Gen. 1:6). Why did God do this? So that man's rightful actions might be attributed to God, but his sins to others. For it was not fitting that the road to wickedness should be God's making. Therefore, on the sixth day God commanded Wisdom to create man.

> Wisdom is said to have been one of God's earliest creations, as stated in Proverbs 3:19: *Yahweh founded the earth by Wisdom* (Prov. 3:19). In most traditions this personification of Wisdom simply serves as a witness of God's subsequent creations, to testify that no others were involved. But here God assigns Wisdom the task of creating human beings. *Wisdom of Solomon* states that "By Your wisdom You have formed man." Of course, the term "wisdom" can refer both to God's wisdom and to the mythical figure of Wisdom, but it seems clear in these sources—2 *Enoch, Wisdom of Solomon,* and

Philo's *De Confusione Linguarum*—that the term "wisdom" is intended to refer to the mythical figure. See "The Creation of Wisdom," p. 45. Other sources attribute the "us" of *"Let us make man"* to the angels, and there are traditions about the role the angels such as Michael or Gabriel played in assisting God in the creation of man. See "Adam's Body Formed by an Angel," p. 131. It is interesting to note that in some Christian interpretations, *"Let us make man,"* God is believed to have been addressing the Son of God, and the work of Creation was a collaboration in which the Father commanded it be done, but it was the Son who carried it out (*Hymns of Faith* 6:13 by Ephraem).

Sources:
2 Enoch 30:8; *Wisdom of Solomon* 9:1; Philo, *De Confusione Linguarum* 179; *Hellenistic Synagogal Prayers* 3:19, 4:7, 4:38, 12:36.

169. ADAM'S CHOICE

Before God created Adam, there were two formations, that of the celestial creatures and that of the earthly creatures. The angels and other celestial beings were created in the image of God, but they did not reproduce, while the animals and other earthly beings reproduced, but they were not created in the image of God. God decided that man would be created in His image, like the celestial beings, but that he would also reproduce, like the terrestrial beings.

God said, "If I create man out of celestial elements, he will live forever. And if I create him out of terrestrial elements, his life will be brief. Therefore I will create him out of both celestial and terrestrial elements. The choice will be his: if he sins, he will die; if he does not sin, he will be immortal."

> This myth presents God debating with Himself about whether Adam and all subsequent human beings should share the characteristics of the celestial beings, especially their immortality, or those of the terrestrial beings, in particular, their inevitable mortality. God decides to leave the choice to Adam, thus setting the stage for the divine test that takes place in the Garden of Eden, where God tells Adam that he may eat of any trees in the garden except for the fruit of the Tree of Knowledge of Good and Evil. Since Adam and Eve eat the forbidden fruit, they unknowingly lose their chance to have eternal life. Thus this myth supplies the missing explanation of God's intention in commanding Adam to avoid eating from the Tree of Knowledge.
>
> *Genesis Rabbah* 14:3 explains that human beings share four characteristics with the celestial beings: they were created in the image of God, they stand upright, they speak and understand, and they have peripheral vision. Likewise, humans share four characteristics with animals: they eat and drink, they procreate, they excrete, and they die. Thus humans share characteristics both the celestial and terrestrial beings. This explains the proverb that humans are a little lower than the angels.
>
> *Sources:*
> *Genesis Rabbah* 14:3

170. ADAM'S BREATH

On the first day God created heaven and earth. Five days were left over. He created above and below on alternate days. On the second day He created the firmament above, while on the third day He divided the waters above from the waters below. On the fourth day He created the sun, the moon and the stars above, while on the fifth day He gathered the waters below. The sixth day remained for creating. Then God said: "If I create above, the earth will be angry, but if I create below, the heavens will be angry." What did God do? He created Adam in the world below, using breath from above.

> The purpose of this myth is to demonstrate that God was evenhanded in Creation, alternating between creating above and creating below, so as not to anger either the heavens or the earth. Finally, when it was time to create Adam, He drew on elements from above—breath—and below—earth—in order to create him.
>
> *Sources:*
> *Midrash Tanhuma, Bereshit* 15.

171. THE FIRST TWELVE HOURS OF ADAM'S LIFE

On each of the first five days of Creation, God created three kinds of creatures. But on the sixth day, the day before the Sabbath, He was occupied the entire day with the making of Adam.

These were the first twelve hours of Adam's life: In the first hour, Adam came into being as a thought. In the second hour, God consulted the ministering angels concerning him. In the third hour, God gathered the dust out of which He was to make Adam. In the fourth hour, God kneaded the dust. In the fifth, God shaped the dust into the shape of a man. In the sixth, God stood him on his feet, and he reached from earth to heaven. In the seventh hour God blew the breath of life into him. In the eighth, God brought him into the Garden of Eden. In the ninth hour, God told him that he could eat of the fruit of any tree in the Garden except for the fruit of the Tree of Knowledge. In the tenth hour Adam sinned. In the eleventh hour, he was brought to justice. In the twelfth, the verdict was given and he was expelled from the Garden of Eden.

> Here Adam's life in the Garden of Eden is presented as having taken place in twelve hours, from the time he was created until the time he was expelled from Eden. *Midrash Tehillim* states that Adam was only saved from destruction in Gehenna by the plea of the Sabbath, which brought about his expulsion instead.
>
> There are alternate versions of this myth about Adam's creation. According to *B. Sanhedrin* 38b, Adam's dust was gathered in the first hour. In the second hour it was kneaded into a shapeless mass. In the third hour its limbs were shaped. In the fourth, a soul was infused into that clay body and he came to life. In the fifth, he arose and stood on his feet. In the sixth, he named the animals. In the seventh, Eve became his mate. In the eighth, Adam and Eve lay down together as two and arose as four, for Cain and Abel were conceived. (Others say that two lay down together and seven arose: Cain and his twin sister, and Abel and his two twin sisters.) In the ninth, Adam was commanded not to eat of the Tree of Knowledge. In the tenth, he sinned. In the eleventh, he was tried. In the twelfth hour he was expelled from Eden. There are numerous variants of this myth. *Leviticus Rabbah,* for example, explains that Adam was judged in the eleventh hour and pardoned in the twelfth.
>
> Why were these events collapsed into a 12-hour myth? It is possible that the hours are God's hours, each of which would be years for a human, just as a year of God is said to consist of a thousand human years. On the other hand, it is possible to see these 12 hours as collapsed time, where everything that happens to Adam, from his creation to his expulsion, was driven by some powerful force well beyond his understanding.
>
> *Sources:*
> *Targum Pseudo-Yonathan* on Genesis 4:1; Josephus, *Jewish Antiquities* 1:52; *The Book of Jubilees* 4:1, 8; *B. Sanhedrin* 38b; *Genesis Rabbah* 22:3; *Leviticus Rabbah* 29:1; *Pirkei de-Rabbi Eliezer* 21; *Pesikta Rabbati* 46:2; *Midrash Tanhuma, Bereshit* 25; *Midrash Tehillim* 92:2; *Midrash Tanhuma-Yelammedenu, Pekudei* 3.

172. ADAM BRINGS DOWN FIRE FROM HEAVEN

Some say that before Adam existed as a mortal, he lived in heaven, and that he not only brought down fire from heaven, but he brought down light as well.

When Adam took the fire from heaven and descended with it, the whole sky was filled with fire, as if it were descending to set the world ablaze. At that moment, God signed a decree with His seal, relinquishing control of fire in the world, as it is said, *"My word is like fire"* (Jer. 23:29).

As for the light that Adam brought down from on high, some say that the light shone from Adam's fingernails, which reflected brighter than the sun.

Others say that Adam used the four winds of the world to bring down the light.

Still others say that Adam used enchanted stones to bring light into the world. One was the stone of darkness, and the other, the stone of dimness, as it is said, *The stones of thick darkness and the shadow of death* (Job 28:3). From this we learn, though how is a mystery, that using darkness and death, Adam brought light into the world.

This is an explicitly Jewish Promethean myth, with Adam playing the role of Prometheus. Just as Prometheus lit a torch from the fiery chariot of the sun and gave the fire to mankind as an act of rebellion against heaven, here Adam is not only credited for having brought fire to earth, but also for having brought light. This addition gives Adam the status of a divine figure, perhaps even a demiurgic one. After all, bringing light into the world is a God-like act, since it is God who says *"Let there be light"* (Gen. 1:3). It might even appear that this myth had taken the myth of Prometheus and expanded it, adding light. For more on the myth of Prometheus giving fire to mankind, see Graves, *The Greek Myths*, 39g.

Like Prometheus, Adam is portrayed in this myth as a divine figure, a heavenly being. Both of them steal fire from heaven and give it to mankind. While Prometheus lights a torch at the fiery chariot of the sun and gives mankind a glowing coal, Adam brings down a metaphorical fire, linked to God's word by the verse *My word is like fire* (Jer. 23:29). In this regard, Adam's gift of fire is parallel to Moses receiving the gift of the Torah from God at Mount Sinai.

Is Adam's act in bringing down fire and light from heaven an act of rebellion as was that of Prometheus? It might be seen as another version of the Fall. Here, instead of eating the forbidden fruit, the cosmic Adam took fire and light from heaven. This interpretation is supported by Genesis 3:9: *"Behold, the man has become like one of us, knowing good and bad."* In this context, Adam's sin and the forces that it released into the world are parallel to stealing the fire and light of heaven.

The motif of Adam using his fingernails to bring down light from heaven is quite striking. It seems like an intentional reference to the *Havdalah* custom of turning one's fingernails toward a flame so that the light reflects in them. The implication is that there was enough light reflected from Adam's fingernails—which had been exposed to the light of heaven—to illumine the world.

One obscure myth indicates that Adam brought light into the world by using the stones of darkness and the stones of dimness. This myth is derived from the verse in Job 28:3, *The stones of thick darkness and the shadow of death*. It seems to imply that light was created out of darkness and death. It also seems to imply that night was created out of darkness and death.

Another Jewish Promethean myth is found in the interpretations of Genesis 6 about the sons of God and the daughters of men. This is read as an account of angels who descended to earth, promising God to be righteous, and instead chased after the beautiful human women. See "The Sons of God and the Daughters of Men," p. 454, for the original myth in this cycle.

Sources:
Orhot Hayim 1:68c; *Se'udat Gan Eden* in *Beit ha-Midrash* 5:45-48; *Midrash Konen* in *Beit ha-Midrash* 2:25.

Studies:
Legends of the Jews by Louis Ginzberg, 5:113, note 104.

173. ADAM THE HERMAPHRODITE

Some say that Adam was originally created with two faces, one male and one female, one facing forward and one behind, as it is said, *Male and female He created them* (Gen. 1:27). Others say that Adam and Eve were created as a single being, with Adam in front and Eve in back, so that Adam's back was in the shape of Eve.

How did this happen? God had originally intended to create two people, but ultimately only one was brought into being.

But facing in two directions made walking difficult, and conversation awkward. So God changed His mind and split Adam into two, making two backs, one for Adam and one for Eve, and dividing them into two separate beings.

Then there are those who say that Adam lost his second face in a different way, through his sin. For when Adam sinned, God took away one of his faces.

The myth of Adam the Hermaphrodite grows out of three biblical verses: *Male and female He created them* (Gen. 1:27), *He blessed them and called them Man (Adam)* (Gen. 5:2), and, *You have shaped me from the back and the front* (Ps. 134:5). But instead of describing Adam and Eve as two people joined into one, *Shoher Tov* 139:5 suggests that "Adam's back was in the shape of Eve." The rabbis also concluded that the man's face went first, because of the teaching that a man should not walk behind a woman on the road. One rabbi, Rabbi Jeremiah ben Eleazar, identifies Adam as a hermaphrodite, thus a being with two sexes. Another rabbi, Rabbi Samuel bar Nachman, identifies Adam as a double-faced being who was later split by God into two. Some versions say that God "sawed" Adam in two, a rather grisly image.

One reading of this myth is that such an androgynous creature as this indicates a myth that man and woman emerged from a single being. And this is also true in the sense that Eve was created from Adam's rib. Before Eve was created, then, her potential existed within Adam. Thus Adam and Eve were once a single being, not in the sense of separate beings fused together, but in the sense of having both male and female qualities.

This myth acknowledges that God made a mistake, an idea that borders on heresy, since God is understood to intrinsically be perfect, and therefore incapable of a mistake. But the actual portrayal of God in the rabbinic texts presents God in a wide range of roles, ordering the destruction of the Temple in Jerusalem and then regretting it bitterly, or allowing Himself to be overruled by His children. Such a God is almost human, with a complex persona that includes the capacity of being contradictory or of making errors. See the Introduction, p. xlvi. What other errors has God made? Some regard the Shattering of the Vessels in the myth of the Ari to be another example of a divine error, since the vessels shattered before they reached their original destination. See "The Shattering of the Vessels and the Gathering of the Sparks," p. 122.

This myth is a very clear parallel to a Greek myth found in pre-Socratic sources, and most famously in Plato's *Symposium* 189a-190a, that every person seeks to find his or her other half. This myth is intended to explain the nature of Eros as a craving for completeness, since each person is only a part of what he or she once was. This meaning does not really carry over in the Jewish version of this myth, except by implication. The closest concept in Judaism is that of *bashert*, in which every person is said to have a destined one. This grows out of the talmudic dictum that "Forty days before a child is formed, a voice goes forth from heaven to declare that this one will marry that one" (*B. Sota* 2a).

The Christian biblical commentator Ephraem interpreted *male and female He created them* to mean that Eve was inside Adam, in the rib that was later taken out of him. There is also an Iranian myth about the first human pair, Masye and Masyane, who were joined to each other. Here, however, they were so like each other that it was not clear which was male and which female.

In *Likutei Moharan*, Rabbi Nachman of Bratslav reads this myth allegorically, where Adam symbolizes God and Eve symbolizes humanity. Because we have sinned, we have turned our backs to God, and therefore God has turned His back on us. But we find that we are still attached to God no matter what we do. Only when we repent our sin does the "operation" of *teshuvah*, repentance, take place, and then we stand face to face with God again.

Sources:
B. Eruvin 18a; *B. Berakhot* 61a; *B. Ketubot* 8a; *Genesis Rabbah.* 8:1, 8:10; *Leviticus Rabbah* 14:1; *Avot de-Rabbi Nathan* 1:8; *Midrash Tehillim* 139:5; *Shoher Tov* 139:5; Maharsha on Genesis 1:27; *Zohar* 3:44b; *Zohar Hadash* 55c-d; *Likutei Moharan* 1:108.

Studies:
Portraits of Adam in Early Judaism by John R. Levison, pp. 116-17.

174. SAMAEL AND LILITH

Samael and Lilith were born as one, in the image of Adam and Eve, who were also created as one. Thus Lilith is the mate of Samael. Both of them were born at the same hour, intertwined in each other.

But Ashmedai, the king of demons, has as his mate Lilith the Younger. This Lilith has the form of a beautiful woman from her head to her waist, but from the waist down she is burning fire. Samael grew exceedingly jealous of Ashmedai because of Lilith the Younger, and this pleased the younger Lilith immensely, as she seeks, above all, to incite wars, especially the war between herself and her mother.

From Ashmedai and Lilith a great prince was born in heaven, who rules over eighty thousand destructive demons. His name is Alefpeneash, and his face burns with rage. He is the bond between Lilith and Samael. If he had been created whole, the world would have been destroyed in an instant.

Samael (one of the names of Satan) and Lilith represent the negative male and female sides of the *Sitra Ahra*, the Other Side. They are the evil mirror image of God and the *Shekhinah*. So intertwined are they with each other, that they are compared to the way Adam and Eve were created male and female at the same time, back to back. See "Adam the Hermaphrodite," p. 138. Here they are said to have given birth to a demon prince named Alefpeneash, the very embodiment of evil.

Sources:
Kabbalot Rabbi Ya'akov ve-Rabbi Yitzhak by Jacob ben Jacob ha-Kohen.

Studies:
The Early Kabbalah, edited by Joseph Dan, pp. 165-182.
"The Desert in Jewish Mysticism: The Kingdom of Samuel" by Joseph Dan.

175. GOD AND THE SPIRITS OF THE UNBORN

God sits in a circle with many baby spirits that are about to be born. God knows that the babies won't experience the same joy on earth that they experienced in heaven, and He doesn't want them to be dissatisfied. So God touches His finger just below their noses, leaving an indentation on their upper lips. This makes them forget the joys of heaven, so that they can adapt to the world into which they are born.

This is an interesting variation of the myth about the origin of the indentation on the upper lip. The best known version describes an angel, Lailah, who accompanies the child during pregnancy, teaching it all the secrets of heaven. Then the angel touches the child on the upper lip just as it is born. See "The Angel of Conception," p. 199.

In this oral variant, recounted by Maury Schwartz of Chicago, it is God who touches the child's upper lip and leaves the indentation. This is to make the babies forget all the joy they experienced with God in heaven, for life on earth will be much more difficult. Indeed, this is a somewhat bitter myth, distinctly implying that life on earth is one of struggle.

Sources:
Oral version collected by Howard Schwartz from his uncle, Maury Schwartz.
  Variants are *B. Niddah* 16b, 30b; *B. Sanhedrin* 6a; *B. Avot* 3:1; *Midrash Tanhuma, Pekudei* 3; *Zohar Hadash* 68:3; *Sefer ha-Zikhronot; Be'er ha-Hasidut* 1:216; *Avodat ha-Kodesh,* Introduction.

176. ADAM AND THE SPIRITS

When Adam's body had been completed, a thousand spirits gathered around his lifeless form, each one trying to gain entry to it, but without success. Adam's body lay there, without a spirit, with a green pallor, with all these spirits hovering around him. Finally a cloud descended and drove all the spirits away. Then God breathed the breath of life into Adam, and brought him to life.

According to this myth from the *Zohar*, a thousand spirits sought to enter Adam's lifeless body after God finished creating it, but before God breathed the breath of life into him. Each of these spirits, it seems, wanted to be the one to serve as Adam's soul. But God himself provided Adam's soul by breathing the breath of life into him.

The swarming of spirits around Adam resembles the myth about swarms of demons attempting to seduce Adam during the 130-year period in which he was separated from Eve. See "Adam and the Demons," p. 215.

Sources:
Zohar 3:19a.

177. THE FIRST EVE

God wanted to create a helpmate for Adam. So God created the first Eve right in front of him. As Adam watched, the first Eve was created from the inside out—first her bones, then her flesh, and finally she was covered with skin. But when God offered her to Adam, he fled in disgust and hid in the Garden.

So the first Eve was taken away, never to be heard from again. Nothing is known of her fate. Then God put Adam to sleep, and when he awoke there was another woman, and this time he found her to be beautiful.

Others say that God took a bone from Adam's bones and flesh from his heart, and fashioned the second Eve, and brought her to Adam adorned as a bride. Upon rising from deep sleep, Adam saw her standing before him, and embraced and kissed her, saying, *"This one at last is bone of my bones and flesh of my flesh"* (Gen. 2:23). That day God erected thirteen canopies for Adam in the Garden of Eden, and a great wedding was held, attended by myriads of ministering angels, and Eve became his bride.

There are a number of related myths about a woman who was created before Eve. The best-known figure is Lilith, but there is also a tradition about a woman known as the first Eve. She was created from the inside out, and Adam ran away from her. The fate of the first Eve is essentially unknown. The second Eve is the Eve who was created out of Adam's rib. What is not clear is whether this second Eve was an entirely new woman, or if God re-created the first Eve in the form of the second. Also, the re-creation theory seems contrary to that of creation out of Adam's rib. Instead, God put Adam to sleep, and only showed him the final product, of which Adam approved. Adam's acceptance of Eve is reported in the verse *"This one shall be called Woman"* (Gen. 2:23). For a more detailed version of Adam's union with Eve, see "The First Wedding," p. 143.

One cannot help but be struck by the emphatic rejection of the first Eve, whom Adam sees created in front of his eyes, from the inside out. In reporting Adam's disgust, the text emphasizes her "discharge and blood" (*Genesis Rabbah* 18:4). This deep-seated repugnance reveals an essentially negative view of women that clearly existed among some of the rabbis. Lilith is the figure who becomes the primary focus of the negative views the rabbis held about women, but it is clear that the first Eve also was created out of these negative projections. As for her fate, the myth seems to indicate that the first Eve was uncreated and consigned to oblivion. In this she resembles the inhabitants of the prior worlds that God created and destroyed. See "Prior Worlds," p. 71.

Genesis Rabbah 18.2 offers a litany of misogynistic insults in its attempt to explain why God chose to create Eve from Adam's rib. A few of these explanations include the following: "God said: 'I will not create her from Adam's head, lest she be swelled-headed; nor from his eye, lest she be a coquette; nor from his ear, lest she be an eavesdropper, nor from his mouth, lest she be a gossip.'"

One variant of this myth, in *Genesis Rabbah* 22:7, states that Cain and Abel fought over the first Eve. But the rabbi who proposed this was quickly contradicted by another, who insisted that the first Eve had already returned to dust.

Sources:
Avot de-Rabbi Natan 4:3; Genesis Rabbah 17:7, 18:4, 22:7; Alpha Beta de-Rabbi Akiva;
    Pirkei de-Rabbi Eliezer 12; Pesikta Rabbati 14:10.

Studies:
·The Hebrew Goddess by Raphael Patai.
Lilith—the First Eve: Historical and Psychological Aspects of the Dark Feminine by
    Siegmund Hurwitz.

178. WHAT HAPPENED TO THE FIRST EVE?

Adam's first wife was a clever woman who was stronger than he was. Therefore Adam said to God, "Please God. I don't want this woman. Take her and give me another one instead." God listened to Adam's request and was about to cast the first Eve into the sea, when she said, "Before you take me, I ask you to give me one request." God said, "What is it?" The first Eve said, "When a baby boy is born, let me come to him on the fifth day after his birth and reveal the future that is awaiting him."

God agreed to this request, and every time that a son is born, the first Eve comes to him on the fifth day after he is born, and whispers the future in his ear.

One hundred years later God remembered Adam's request for a new woman. So God put him to sleep, took his left rib, and created a new woman from it. This woman was modest and quiet. He called her Eve.

> This is an interesting oral variant of the myth of the first Eve. See the preceding myth. On one level it's a rather primitive tale in which Adam rejects Eve because she is superior to him, and God agrees to get rid of her. But the myth also establishes a custom whereby the first Eve is said to reveal a boy's future on the fifth day after his birth, three days before the *b'rit*. Of course, the infant is not likely to remember this prophecy. This is not a widely known tradition, though perhaps it has more resonance among Indian Jews, where the story originated. Just as the amulet against Lilith will protect a newborn boy for eight days—until the *b'rit*—so this fifth day role for the first Eve creates a birth custom for her, perpetuating the need for her existence, and preserving her from the oblivion of being uncreated.
>
> There are also indications that this myth is a variant of the Lilith myth. Like Lilith, the first Eve is described here as cleverer than he is. Also, the punishment that God plans for her—casting her into the sea—is the same punishment that the angels threaten Lilith with unless she returns to her spouse. Finally, God's agreement that the first Eve may reveal a boy's future to him on the fifth day after birth echoes Lilith's vow that the amulet against her will protect newborn baby boys until the eighth day, when they will be protected by the circumcision. See "Adam and Lilith," p. 216 and "A Spell to Banish Lilith," p. 218.
>
> *Sources:*
> IFA 9584.

179. THE CREATION OF WOMAN

The Lord God said, "It is not good for man to be alone; I will make a fitting helper for him." So the Lord God cast a deep sleep upon the man; and while he slept, He took one of his ribs and closed up the flesh at that spot. And the Lord God fashioned the rib that He had taken from the man into a woman; and He brought her to the man. Then the man said, "This one at last is bone of my bones and flesh of my flesh. This one shall be called Woman, for from man was she taken." Hence a man leaves his father and mother and clings to his wife, so that they become one flesh.

> This is the famous account from Genesis of how God created Eve out of Adam's rib. It is one of the few creation stories in world mythology in which the first woman was created from the first man, instead of the other way around. Since humans are born from women, the myth stands out as an obvious example of a male myth. Nevertheless, the fact that Eve was said to have been created from Adam's rib is a clear indication that she was *bone of my bones and flesh of my flesh* (Gen. 2:23)—thus that they were created from one flesh, a view that makes bonding between the man and woman much easier.
>
> In subsequent translations of the Bible and in the rabbinic texts, the story of Eve's creation from Adam's rib was elaborated. In one text, for example, the rib was identified as the 13th rib on the right side. The rib, of course, is integral to the biblical account, but the midrashic process proposed that Eve might have been created from something else. Some say that Eve was created from a face—one of the two faces with which Adam was created, before God divided Adam and Eve into separate beings. (See "Adam the Hermaphrodite," p. 138.) Still others say that Eve was created from a tail, and that Satan was created along with her. The suggestion that Eve was created

from a tail, a superfluous part, serves as a vehicle for anti-feminine bias, as does the assertion that Satan was created at the same time. In fact, this is a clear attempt to link Eve with Satan as a way of condemning all women. Another example of how Eve, and thus all women, were blamed for the sin of eating the forbidden fruit and the consequent punishment of death that followed is found in *The Wisdom of Ben Sira*: "From a woman was sin's beginning, and because of her we all die" (Sir. 25:23). A similar conclusion, stating that God took Adam's rib and created a wife from it so that death might come to him from his wife, is found in *2 Enoch* (J) 30:17. The negative consequences of Eve's actions are stated directly in *Vita Adae et Evae* 44:2, where Adam tells Eve "You have brought upon us a great wound, transgression and sin in all our generations." See also *Targum Pseudo-Yonathan* on Genesis 2:7, *B. Berakhot* 61a, *B. Eruvin* 18a, and *Genesis Rabbah* 8:1, 17:6.

One strange explanation is that found in *The Book of Jubilees* 3:8: "In the first week Adam was created and also the rib, his wife. And in the second week God showed her to him," implying that in the second week God reshaped the rib into a woman, and then showed her to Adam. Here the rib, *tzela* in Hebrew, seems to be described not as an integral part of Adam, but as something separate from him.

One interesting rabbinic interpretation suggests that Adam first made love to Eve in a dream. Working with the verse *while he slept, He took one of his ribs* (Gen. 2:21), one rabbi asked, "Why do dreams fatigue men so?" Rabbi Shimon ben Lakish answered, "Because woman's creation was in a dream, Adam enjoyed her intimacy in a dream. Otherwise he would never have known how to make love" (*Midrash Avkir*).

Sources:
Genesis 2:18, 2:21-24.

Studies:
Eve and Adam: Jewish, Christian, and Muslim Readings on Genesis and Gender, edited by Kristen E. Kvam, Linda S. Schearing, and Valarie H. Ziegler.

180. THE FIRST WEDDING

God had already created the earth, the sun, the moon, and the stars. All of the animals were in the Garden of Eden. The time had come for Adam, the first man, to be created.

God called upon the angel Gabriel to bring clay from each of the four corners of the earth, the north, the south, the east, and the west. This the angel did, and then God formed a clay man and breathed the breath of life into him and the man opened his eyes and began to breathe.

Adam gave names to all the animals and explored the Garden of Eden. But God saw that Adam was lonely, and He decided to create a mate for him.

So one day, when Adam was strolling about in the Garden of Eden, God put Adam to sleep, and while he was deeply dreaming, God took out one of his ribs, and with that rib God created Eve, the first woman.

When Adam awoke and saw Eve standing in front of him, their faces illuminating each other, he understood at once that he had found his true mate. God introduced Adam to Eve and explained how she had been created. Then Adam embraced her and kissed her and said, "*This one at last is bone of my bones and flesh of my flesh. This one shall be called Woman, for from man was she taken*" (Gen. 2:23).

Then God knew that the time had come for the world's first wedding. God Himself prepared tables of precious pearls and filled them with delicacies.

God also created ten wedding canopies for them, all made of precious gems, pearls, and gold. So too did He attire Eve, the first bride, in a beautiful wedding dress, and braid her hair and adorn her with twenty-four different ornaments.

As the ceremony began, the ministering angels walked before Adam, leading him beneath the wedding canopies. Michael and Gabriel were Adam's groomsmen. Then God Himself brought the bride to Adam and stood before them like a cantor, and took the cup of blessing and blessed them, as it is said, *God blessed them* (Gen. 1:28).

As soon as Adam and Eve were wed, still other angels descended to the Garden of Eden, playing music for the newlyweds, beating tambourines and dancing to pipes. So too did the sun, the moon and the stars dance for them, and all of creation joined in the celebration of the world's first wedding.

> *Sefer ha-Zikhronot* explains that while each bridegroom generally has only one *huppah* (a wedding canopy), and a king has three, God made ten canopies for Adam in order to show great honor to the first man. The jewels covering them are all different: chalcedony, topaz, diamond, beryl, onyx, jasper, sapphire, emerald, carbuncle, and gold. This list is drawn from Ezekiel 28:18. The twenty-four ornaments that Eve wore are listed in Isaiah 3:18-24.
>
> There is a debate among the rabbis recounted in *Genesis Rabbah* as to how many canopies God created for Adam. While the number generally given is ten, some rabbis argued there were 11 or 13.
>
> One of the wedding blessings for every Jewish couple is that they attain the holiness and joy granted to Adam and Eve on the day of their wedding.
>
> This myth also provides the origin of the best man at weddings, for since God acted as the best man for Adam, henceforth one must have a best man.
>
> *Sources:*
> B. *Eruvin* 18a; B. *Berakhot* 61a; B. *Niddah* 45a; B. *Shabbat* 95a; *Genesis Rabbah* 8:13, 18:1; *Pesikta de-Rav Kahana* 4:4, 26:3; *Pirkei de-Rabbi Eliezer* 12; *Avot de-Rabbi Natan* 4; *Sefer ha-Zikhronot* 7:1-2; *Pesikta Rabbati* 14:10; *Zohar* 3:19a, 3:44b.

181. ADNE SADEH

Adam was not the first man that God attempted to create. Little record remains of these early attempts that were created and then destroyed, or permitted to become extinct. But it is known that before God created Adam, He created a creature called Adne Sadeh. This creature had a form that closely resembled that of man, but Adne Sadeh was attached to the earth by means of a navel cord, upon which its life depended. This cord, it is true, sometimes grew to great lengths of more than a mile, but in any case the creature was confined to this radius, for if the cord snapped its life would end. Thus the creature sustained itself with those fruits and vegetables that grew within the circle, and by occasionally capturing animals who approached it too closely.

The life span of Adne Sadeh was very long, and there was little that could take its life, short of a flood or other disaster, unless its cord was snapped. Thus this species continued to exist until the last members were drowned in the Flood.

> There are some fantastic creatures recounted in Jewish lore. Adne Sadeh is a kind of primitive man who was said to be tied to the earth by his navel cord. *Midrash Tanhuma* tells of a traveler who was served this creature, who was regarded as a vegetable rather than a man. Afraid that he had fallen among cannibals, he ran away as quickly as he could. *Ma'aseh Buch* tells of a traveling rabbi who was served what appeared to be human hands, but that turned out to be a vegetable that looked like a human hand. This too may be linked to the myth of the "vegetable man." Louis Ginzberg describes Adne Sadeh as a "man of the mountains," and suggests that he was some kind of ape.

Sources:
Midrash Tanhuma, Introduction 125; *Ma'aseh Buch* 201; *Magen Avot* 35b.
Studies:
Legends of the Jews, Ginzberg, vol. 5, notes I:147-148.

182. THE SEA MONSTER LEVIATHAN

God created all creatures male and female, including the great sea monster Leviathan and its mate. But had those two enormous creatures mated, they would have destroyed the world. What did God do? He castrated the male and killed the female, serving it to the righteous in the World to Come, as it is said, *He will slay the dragon in the sea* (Isa. 27:1).

Leviathan enters the river, swallowing fish of many kinds, gathering strength. Its eyes are a great light in the sea, as it is said, *And his eyes are like the glimmer of the dawn* (Job 41:10). Its mouth is as wide and deep as the Dead Sea. And when Leviathan is hungry he exhales a fiery breath that makes all the waters of the deep boil, as it is said, *He makes the depths seethe like a cauldron* (Job 41:23).

Leviathan rules nine rivers and the sea. Some say there is a monster in each of those nine rivers, as it is said, *You smashed the heads of monsters in the waters* (Ps. 74:13). Like the great Leviathan, they all draw their breath from the realms above, not from the realms below.

When Leviathan is hungry, he emits a fiery breath from his mouth that causes all the waters of the deep to boil. And if he did not purify his breath by putting his head into the Garden of Eden, no creature could stand his foul odor.

The Jordan River passes through the Kinneret and rolls down to the great sea until it rushes into the mouth of Leviathan. Still it is not enough, and when Leviathan is thirsty, he swallows so much water that the deep does not regain its strength for seventy years.

Some say that in the future the angel Gabriel will arrange a chase of Leviathan, to see if it can be captured, as it is said, *Can you draw out Leviathan by a fishhook?* (Job. 40:25). But unless God assists him, the angel will never prevail. Others say that at the messianic banquet God Himself will prepare the tables and slaughter Leviathan, as well as Behemoth and the Ziz. God will leave His glorious throne and sit with the righteous. They will eat and drink and be happy, until God commands them to raise the cup of blessing. Then King David will stand up and offer a great blessing to God, blessed be He, saying, *"I raise the cup of deliverance"* (Ps. 116:13). And at that time God will take His crown and put it on David's head and on the head of the Messiah.

> The Hebrew tradition about sea-monsters is probably drawn from that found in Canaanite literary sources, where Ba'al slays the seven-headed monster Lotan, who is the equivalent of Leviathan. A Christian vision of a similar seven-headed monster is also found in the Book of Revelation 12:3: *And behold a great red dragon, having seven heads and ten horns, and seven crowns upon his heads.*
>
> All of these myths are variants on the theme of a primordial battle with the great dragon. References to ancient myths about this primordial battle are found in Psalm 74:13-14: *It was You who drove back the sea with Your might, who smashed the heads of the monsters in the waters; it was You who crushed the heads of Leviathan.*
>
> The creation of the sea-monsters derives from Genesis 1:21: *And God created the great sea-monsters.* This is understood to refer to Leviathan and his mate. Leviathan is a whale-like creature of enormous size who rules the sea. It is described in Job 40:25-32. Leviathan is also identified with the dragon, making this a Jewish dragon myth. Although only one such creature is said to exist, this is because God slew the female of the species to prevent the male and female from mating. It is said that God will make a banquet for the righteous from it in the messianic era, and that the righteous

will be given tabernacles made of the skin of Leviathan. The notion of Leviathan being served at such a banquet grows out of Job 40:30: *Will bands of fishermen make a banquet of him?* See "The Messianic Banquet," p. 508, and "A Tabernacle for the Righteous," p. 510. Here, it is the female Leviathan, which God slays, that is being saved for the banquet. In other versions, where no reference to the slain female is made, Leviathan himself will be served to the righteous and not his mate. For more on Leviathan, see "The Great Sea," p. 103. For myths about other enormous creatures, see "Behemoth," p. 146, and "The Ziz," p. 147.

A series of sea tales about Leviathan are found in the Talmud in *B. Bava Batra* 74b-75a, which are attributed to Rabbah bar Bar Hannah. These closely resemble the tales of Sinbad the sailor in *The Arabian Nights*.

The myths about Leviathan are closely related to those about Rahab. See "The Rebellion of Rahab," p. 106.

One of the reasons given for the custom of eating fish at each *Shabbat* (Sabbath) dinner is that eating fish anticipates the feast of Leviathan, which will take place when the Messiah comes, as stated in the Talmud, "In the future God will prepare a feast to the righteous from the flesh of Leviathan" (*B. Bava Batra* 75). "This will be a complete and perfect Sabbath" (*B. Berakhot* 57).

Parallel myths about sea monsters are found in the Babylonian text *Enuma Elish* (1:132-38), where Tiamat, who personifies the sea, gives birth to hideous monsters.

Sources:
B. Bava Batra 74b-75a; *Genesis Rabbah* 7:4; Rashi on Genesis 1:21; *Midrash Haserot ve-Yeterot; Battei Midrashot* 2:225; *Zohar* 2:34a-35b; *Sefer Eliyahu* in *Beit ha-Midrash* 3:68-78; IFA 597, 13365.

Studies:
Slaying the Dragon: Mythmaking in the Biblical Tradition by Bernard F. Batto.
"Rabbinic Mythmaking and Tradition: The Great Dragon Drama in *B. Bava Batra* 74b-75a" by Michael Fishbane.
"The Battle Between Behemoth and Leviathan According to an Ancient Hebrew Piyyut" by Jefim Schirmann.
Myths from Mesopotamia by S. Dalley, pp. 228-277 (*Enuma Elish*).
"Elements of Near-Eastern Mythology in Rabbinic Aggadah" by Irving Jacobs.

183. BEHEMOTH

Behemoth is a beast of such gigantic proportions that it is the size of a thousand mountains. Daily it devours the grass of a thousand hills. It drinks so much water that there is a special river flowing out of Paradise to quench its thirst. It roars just once a year, in the month of Tammuz, and that roar so frightens all the animals in the world that they are kept in its control.

Like Leviathan, Behemoth was created male and female. And if this pair had mated, their offspring would have destroyed the world. What did God do? God made the male sterile, and cooled the desire of the female, and saved them for the messianic feast in the World to Come.

Some say that in the messianic age Behemoth and Leviathan will slay each other, and their flesh will be served at the messianic banquet. Others say that God Himself will slay Behemoth and Leviathan, in order to serve them to the righteous at that glorious feast.

The enormous land monster Behemoth is described in Job 40: 15-24. It is said that its flesh will be served at the End of Days at a great feast given by God. See "The Messianic Banquet," p. 508. For accounts of other mythic monsters, see "The Sea Monster Leviathan," p. 145, and "The Ziz," p. 147.

Sources:
B. Bava Batra 74b.

Studies:
"The Battle Between Behemoth and Leviathan According to an Ancient Hebrew
   Piyyut" by Jefim Schirmann.
"Leviathan, Behemoth and Ziz: Jewish Messianic Symbols in Art" by Joseph
   Gutmann.
"Elements of Near-Eastern Mythology in Rabbinic Aggadah" by Irving Jacobs.

184. THE ZIZ

The Ziz is a bird as big as Leviathan. When it stands in the ocean, the water only reaches
to its ankles, and its head is in the sky. Some say its head reaches as far as the Throne of
Glory, where it sings songs to God. It is so big that when the Ziz unfolds its wings, it blots
out the sun. Once the sailors on a passing ship saw the Ziz standing there and thought
the water must be shallow. Then a voice called out from heaven: "Don't dive in here! A
carpenter dropped his axe here seven years ago, and it still has not reached the bottom."
Another time, one of the eggs of the Ziz fell to earth and crushed a forest of three hundred trees. The liquid from the broken egg flooded sixty cities.

The Ziz serves as a messenger of God. Once King Solomon learned that a heavenly
voice had announced that his daughter, the princess, was destined to marry a poor man
within a year. To keep this from happening, King Solomon sent his daughter to live in a
high tower in a desert island. Then it happened that the Ziz carried a poor youth from
Acco to the balcony of that tower, so that the princess and youth were brought together.
And he lived secretly in that tower with her, and before the year was out they were wed,
for not even King Solomon could outfox fate.

So too did the Ziz pick up a young scholar named Shlomo from the roof of his house
where he was studying and drop him in the garden of the king of Spain. The king took a
liking to him, and let him live in a hut in the garden. There he met and fell in love with
the princess, who studied Torah with him and secretly married him. But then the Ziz
picked him up out of that garden and brought him back to the roof of his parents' house.
In this way Shlomo was separated from the princess, but after great trials she found her
way back to him.

The flesh of the Ziz will be served to the righteous at the messianic banquet that will
take place at the end of days.

> The Ziz is one of three mythical gigantic creatures that often appear in Jewish lore.
> The others are Leviathan and Behemoth. The Ziz is mentioned in Psalms 50:11: *And
> Ziz-Sadai is with Me.* In Jewish folklore the Ziz serves as the incarnation of fate. The
> two folktales noted are two famous examples. See "The Princess in the Tower" in
> *Elijah's Violin*, pp. 47-52, and "The Flight of the Eagle," pp. 82-88 in the same book.
>
> The account of the sighting of the Ziz by a passing ship is attributed to Rabbah bar
> Bar Hannah, a talmudic sage who reported on many strange sightings in his sea and
> land journeys. These are found in *B. Bava Batra* 73a-74a. Because of their outlandish
> nature, the tall tales of Rabbah bar Bar Hannah were often interpreted allegorically.
> The Maharsha, Rabbi Samuel Eliezer Edels, interpreted these fables this way, as did
> Rabbi Nachman of Bratslav. For the Maharsha, the waters that first appear shallow
> but turn out to be very deep represent the Torah, which may appear to be only ankle
> deep, but is actually profound and difficult to fathom. The bird's head that reaches
> the sky represents the hidden aspects of the Torah—the secrets of kabbalah.
>
> In *Likutei Moharan*, Rabbi Nachman expands on the Maharsha's interpretation in
> which the deep waters represent the deepest secrets of the Torah. He interprets the

voice that warned against diving in as a warning to those who are not trained in the Torah against seeking out its deepest secrets. This is the esoteric view taken by kabbalah and succeeding stages of Jewish mysticism. Rabbi Nachman sees the carpenter as God, and the axe dropped into the sea as the Messiah, since the Messiah is called God's "axe." He finds that the reference to seven years refers to the 7,000 years that the world is supposed to exist. Most interesting is Rabbi Nachman's interpretation that the falling of the axe refers to the Messiah's own probing of the deepest secrets of the Torah. And when he reaches those secrets, then the messianic era will arrive. When that takes place, the Messiah will reveal these secrets to the whole world. Note that here Rabbi Nachman has created a new messianic myth.

It is said that the Ziz, like Leviathan, will be served to the righteous at the messianic banquet at the End of Days. From this the rabbis concluded that the Ziz must be kosher. See "The Messianic Banquet," p. 508.

Sources:
B. Bava Batra 73a; *Likutei Moharan; Midrash Tanhuma*, Preface; *Oseh Feleh*; IFA 4735.

Studies:
"Leviathan, Behemoth and Ziz: Jewish Messianic Symbols in Art" by Joseph
    Gutman.

185. THE RE'EM

A *re'em* that is one day old is the size of Mount Tabor. Once, when King David was a young shepherd, he came upon a sleeping *re'em*. Thinking it was a mountain, he climbed upon it. Before long the *re'em* awoke and rose up, and David, astride its horns, was lifted as high as the heavens. Then God caused a lion to appear, coming toward the *re'em*. When the *re'em* saw the lion, the king of beasts, it knelt down in fear. David was also afraid, so God caused a gazelle to come along, and as the lion sprang after it, David descended the horn of the *re'em* and escaped. That is the meaning of the words of the Psalm: *Deliver me from a lion's mouth, rescue me from the horns of a re'em* (Ps. 22:22).

The *re'em* is a horned mythological creature of great size, similar to a unicorn or a rhinoceros. This legend about King David explains the enigmatic meaning of Psalm 22:22 by offering an account of the young shepherd David escaping both from the *re'em* and a lion. Compare the account of the death of Cain said to explain the meaning of Genesis 4:23. See "The Death of Cain," p. 451. The wandering sage Rabbah bar Bar Hannah reported seeing a *re'em* in one of his journeys.

Sources:
B. Bava Batra 73a; *Midrash Tehillim* 22:28.

186. THE PHOENIX

When God created the Angel of Death, He gave him domination over all creatures except for the Phoenix. This is because the Phoenix was the only creature not to taste of the fruit of the Tree of Knowledge. Eve had offered the forbidden fruit to all the animals, and only the Phoenix had refused to eat it. Therefore the Holy One, blessed be He, established the Phoenix as an everlasting witness for Israel and let these birds live forever.

An angel took Baruch to where the sun goes forth. There he saw a bird flying that was as large as a mountain. The angel told him that bird was the guardian of the world, for it runs with the sun in its circuit, and spreads out his wings and catches the fiery rays of the sun. If that bird were not there to intercept them, no creature on earth could survive. Its food consists of the manna of heaven and the dew of earth. And the angel told Baruch that bird was the Phoenix. And when the bird spread its wings, Baruch read what was written there: "The earth has not borne me, nor has heaven, but wings of fire bear me."

Over a thousand years, each Phoenix becomes smaller and smaller until it is like a fledgling, and even its feathers falls off. Then God sends two angels, who restore it to the egg from which it first emerged, and soon these hatch again, and the Phoenix grows once again, and remains fully grown for the next thousand years.

For many years the Phoenix has made its home in the City of Luz, which the Angel of Death cannot enter, where it reproduces its kind.

> This midrash builds on earlier traditions, found in the Talmud, that the Phoenix was the only creature given eternal life because of its refusal to taste of the fruit of the Tree of Knowledge. A companion tradition holds that the Phoenix was the only creature in the ark not to make demands on Noah. The legend of the Phoenix has been taken from Egyptian mythology. Note that this rabbinic addition to the legend provides an explanation as to how the Phoenix became immortal. Attraction to origin tales is characteristic of the Midrash, as is a willingness on the part of the rabbis to create them where necessary.
>
> The myth of the Phoenix moved beyond its Egyptian origins to enter Greek, Jewish, and Christian literature. It was originally linked with the idea of the bird of the sun. For more on the city of immortals where the Phoenix can now be found, see "The City of Luz," p. 476.
>
> There was a debate between the School of Rabbi Jannai and that of Rabbi Judah ben Rabbi Simeon. Rabbi Jannai held that the bird and its nest burned after a thousand years, and only an egg was left, from which the Phoenix came to life again. Rabbi Judah argued that its body decomposed and its wings fell off, leaving only the egg, as in the other explanation. These two traditions are parallel to those found in the classical myth of the Phoenix.
>
> *Sources:*
> *Genesis Rabbah* 19:5; *3 Baruch* 6; *Alpha Beta de-Ben Sira* 27a, 28b, 29a-29b; *Sefer ha-Zikhronot.*

187. THE LION OF THE FOREST ILAI

Caesar called in Rabbi Joshua ben Haninah to question him about the ways of the Jews. He said to him: "Your God is likened to a lion, as it is written in your Holy Scriptures: *The lion has roared, who will not fear?* (Amos 3:8). What is so great about this? A hunter can kill a lion." Rabbi Joshua replied: "You would not want to see this lion." But Caesar insisted, saying: "Indeed, I want to see him. If I do not, the lives of the Jews will be in grave danger!"

Then Rabbi Joshua saw that he had no choice, so he prayed that the lion might come from its place in the forest Ilai. And before long his prayer was answered, and the lion emerged from the forest and set out for the city of Rome. And when the lion was at a distance of four hundred parasangs, it roared once, the ground shook, and all the bridges of Rome collapsed. When it was at a distance of three hundred parasangs, it roared a second time, the molars and front teeth of the people fell out, and Caesar himself fell from his throne to the floor. Then Caesar said to Rabbi Joshua: "Enough! I beg you, pray that the lion be returned to its place." This Rabbi Joshua did, and the lion turned around and returned to the forest from which it had come.

This myth suggests the terrifying power and glory of God, who is compared to the lion of the forest Ilai. The roar of this mythic lion is so loud that even Caesar fell from his throne on hearing it and begged for the lion to be returned to its place. The point is that God is far more powerful than any human ruler.

Sources:
B. *Hullin* 59b.

188. THE RAM SACRIFICED AT MOUNT MORIAH

The ram that Abraham found caught in the thicket at Mount Moriah was one of the ten things created on the eve of the first Sabbath, along with the rainbow of Noah, the staff of Moses, and other precious things. The ram waited in Paradise for many centuries until that fateful day on Mount Moriah. All this time the ram knew why it had been created, but it was not afraid. Instead, it looked forward to fulfilling its destiny.

Then the day came when the angel brought the ram from Paradise to serve as the sacrifice in place of Isaac at Mount Moriah. There, its horns caught in the thicket, it waited for Abraham to set it free. That is why God said to Abraham, "Although your children are destined to be entangled in misfortune, in the end they will be redeemed by the horns of a ram."

Nothing of the ram that was sacrificed there was wasted. The skin of the ram became Elijah's mantle, the gut was used in David's harp, one horn was sounded by Moses at Mount Sinai, and the other will be blown by Elijah at the End of Days, as it is said, *And in that day, a great ram's horn shall be sounded* (Isa. 27:13).

> For a list of the ten things created before the creation of the world, see "Ten Things Created on the Eve of the First Sabbath," p. 77. The ram does not appear in all such lists, which vary considerably. For a modern midrash about the ram, see "The Tale of the Ram" by Tsvi Blanchard in *Gates to the New City: A Treasury of Modern Jewish Tales*, p. 152.
>
> *Sources:*
> *Rosh ha-Shanah* 16a; *Pirkei de-Rabbi Eliezer* 31.
>
> *Studies:*
> "The Riddle of the Ram in Genesis Chapter 22: Jewish-Christian Contacts in Late Antiquity" by Marc Bregman.

189. GOD THE POTTER

God is a potter who, in turning His wheel, constantly fashions new vessels, as it is said, *He revolves wheels by his devices* (Job. 37:12). Using the instrument of the potter's wheel, God endlessly reshapes His works, turning one vessel into another. If a man's works are good, the potter's wheel revolves to the right, making the course of events highly favorable. For those who turn to evil ways, however, God imparts a spin to the left, and events follow an unfavorable course. Thus, through these rotations of the wheel, everything turns out as it should.

> In this allegorical myth God is described as a potter, who creates new vessels at His wheel—thus, creates new creations. While these are similar to the old creations, each new one is still unique. This metaphor about God being a potter was likely inspired by Job 37:12, which can be rendered, *He revolves wheels by his devices*. For a parallel theme, see "Re-creating the World," p. 292.

As a kabbalistic allegory, the spinning of the wheel represents the *Shekhinah*, since creation is continually formed and transformed through Her. When the wheel spins to the right, this symbolizes *Hesed* (Lovingkindness), and when it spins to the left, this symbolizes *Din* (Justice).

Sources:
Zohar 1:109b-110b.

190. THE UNFINISHED CREATION

The universe that God created is always in an unfinished state. It is not like a vessel that can be worked and finished. It requires continuous work and unceasing renewal. For the world is re-created every day, and a man is reborn every morning. Were these forces to pause for a second, the universe would return to chaos.

This teaching is attributed to Rabbi Simcha Bunam of Parsischa (1765-1827). He observes that the unfinished nature of Creation is a necessity, not a flaw, for the world requires constant renewal. Without this force of renewal, the world would come to an end. The Ba'al Shem Tov also taught that the world is renewed daily.

Sources:
Siah Sarfei Kodesh 2:17; *Midrash Ribesh Tov* 2:24.

BOOK THREE

MYTHS OF HEAVEN

God has a tree of flowering souls in Paradise.

Ha-Nefesh ha-Hakhamah
Moshe ben Shem Tov de Leon

191. ENOCH WALKED WITH GOD

When Enoch had lived sixty-five years, he begat Methuselah. After the birth of Methuselah, Enoch walked with God three hundred years; and he begat sons and daughters. All the days of Enoch came to three hundred and sixty-five years. Enoch walked with God; then he was no more, for God took him.

> This brief biblical passage is the basis of the enormous Enoch tradition, or else it is the summary of a prebiblical tradition concerning Enoch. Because of the verse *Enoch walked with God; then he was no more, for God took him* (Gen. 5:24), the tradition grew that Enoch had not died, but had been transported into heaven in a chariot, where he was transformed into the angel Metatron. The primary texts about Enoch are *1 Enoch* and *2 Enoch* and the Hekhalot text that is often called *3 Enoch* in the Pseudepigrapha. It seems significant that Enoch is said to have lived 365 years. This seems to associate him with the yearly cycle of the sun, perhaps indicating that the myth of Enoch includes some remnants of sun worship that have survived in Judaism. Likewise, Enoch's metamorphosis into the fiery angel Metatron seems to affirm this link to the sun. See "The Metamorphosis and Enthronement of Enoch," p. 156.
>
> *Sources:*
> Genesis 5:21-24

192. ENOCH'S VISION OF GOD

A vision was shown to Enoch: a mist summoned him, and the stars and lightning beckoned him, and the winds lifted him upward and bore him into heaven. He drew near a crystal wall surrounded by tongues of fire, and he entered the fire and drew near a crystal house, for the walls and groundwork of that house were made of crystals. Fire surrounded the walls of the house, and its portals blazed with fire. Its ceiling was like the path of the stars and lightning, and there were fiery cherubim between them.

In the vision Enoch entered that house, and it was as hot as fire and as cold as ice. Quaking and trembling, Enoch fell on his face and had another vision. Here he saw a second house, greater than the first, built entirely of flames. Its splendor and magnificence cannot be described. Its floor and ceiling were made of fire, and the fiery portal stood open before him. And Enoch saw a lofty throne within, and its appearance was as crystal, and from beneath the throne came streams of flaming fire, and the wheels of the throne shone as brightly as the sun. And there, seated on the throne, was the great glory of God, His garment whiter than any snow, its light brighter than the sun, the moon, and the stars. A flaming fire was around Him, and a great fire stood before Him, and none could draw near him.

> This is an early *Merkavah* vision, in which God's throne is described as having wheels, like a chariot, which is the primary characteristic of the Chariot-Throne literature of the *Merkavah*.
>
> *Sources:*
> *1 Enoch* 14:8-25, 40:1-10.
>
> *Studies:*
> "Visions of God in Merkabah Mysticism" by Ira Chernus.

155

193. THE METAMORPHOSIS AND ENTHRONEMENT OF ENOCH

It is said that Enoch *walked with God, and he was no more, for God took him* (Gen. 5:24). Enoch, like Noah, was a righteous man in his generation. He was the first among men who wrote down the signs of heaven. God saw the righteous ways of Enoch and called upon the angel Anafiel to bring Enoch into heaven. An instant later Enoch found himself in a fiery chariot, drawn by fiery horses, ascending on high.

As soon as the chariot reached heaven, the angels caught the scent of a living human and were ready to cast him out, for none among the living were permitted there. But God called out to the angels, saying, "I have taken an elect one from among the inhabitants of earth and I have brought him here to rule in My name."

Then God lifted Enoch on wings of winds and brought him to the palaces of heaven. There God opened the ten Gates of Understanding for him. To this God added wisdom, understanding, and knowledge until Enoch was wiser than all the children of heaven.

Then God put His hand upon Enoch and blessed him, and the metamorphosis of Enoch began. His flesh was immediately changed to flames, his sinews to burning flames, his bones to fiery coals, the skin of his eyelids to the radiance of lightning, his eyes to torches, his hair to fire and flame, and his body to a smoldering flame, with pillars of fire to his right and a burning torch to his left, and all around him there raged wind, storm, and whirlwind, with the sound of thunder in front and behind him. Seventy-two wings began to grow on him, thirty-six on each side, with a wingspan as wide as the world. So too did God give him three hundred and sixty-five eyes, each one a sun in itself. No luminary in the universe shone brighter than Enoch.

So too did God give Enoch a new name, Metatron, and make a throne for him similar to God's Throne of Glory. And God made a majestic robe for Metatron in which all kinds of luminaries were set, and He clothed him in it. And God spread a curtain of splendor over him, similar to the curtain of the Throne of Glory. And God placed Metatron's throne at the door of the Seventh Hall, and seated him there.

Then a herald went forth throughout heaven, saying, "This is My servant, Metatron. I have made him into prince and ruler over all the princes of My kingdoms, and over all the Children of Heaven, in the name of their king. And every command that Metatron utters to you in My name you must observe and fulfill. Moreover, I have set him over all the treasuries of the palaces of heaven."

After this God revealed all the mysteries of the Torah to Metatron, including the secrets of Creation. There was nothing above or below that was hidden from him. After that, God made a garment of glory and clad Metatron in it. And He made him a royal crown whose splendor filled the seven heavens as well as reaching to the four corners of the world. And God wrote letters upon that crown with His finger, the letters by which heaven and earth were created and all the orders of Creation. And flames came forth from those letters like lightning. And before all the inhabitants of heaven God introduced Metatron as the Lesser YHVH, as it is said, *For my Name is in him* (Exod. 23:21).

Then, while all the Princes of the heavenly kingdom trembled, God put the crown on Metatron's head. Even Samael, Prince of the Accusers, trembled before him, as did the Angels of Fire and Hail, the Angels of the Wind, of lightning, and of thunder, the Angels of Snow and Rain, the Angel of Day and the Angel of Night, and the Angel of the Sun and the Angel of the moon—all trembled and were filled with fright when they beheld Metatron, Prince of the Presence.

After that Metatron sat on his great Throne at the door of the Seventh Hall, and presided over the Celestial Court, with the princes of kingdoms standing to his right and left. There he served as the Heavenly Scribe, writing down everything and judging the Children of Heaven by the authority of God.

This is the famous myth of Enoch as elaborated in *3 Enoch*. Speculation about Enoch, building on the biblical assertion that *Enoch walked with God and he was no more, for God took him* (Gen. 5:24), is reflected in three major texts: *The Book of Enoch* (also known as *1 Enoch*); *The Slavonic Book of Enoch* (also known as *2 Enoch*); and *Sefer Hekhalot*, the text that Hugo Odeberg designated as *3 Enoch or The Hebrew Book of Enoch*. The last is actually one of the best preserved *Hekhalot* texts, which describe heavenly journeys, dating from around the eighth century. While Enoch ascends into heaven in all three of these texts, it is in *3 Enoch* that he is transformed into the angel Metatron. While earlier texts, such as *Targum Yonathan ben Uziel* on Genesis 5:24, recount that Enoch became Metatron, this transformation is greatly elaborated in *3 Enoch*.

Metatron's role takes on the epic proportions suggested by the description God gives of him as the "Lesser YHVH," thus a virtual second power in heaven. Here, too, God turns so many responsibilities over to Metatron that he comes to serve as a heavenly ruler, whose power derives from God. His job is to record all that takes place above and below.

Some versions, such as that in *Midrash Aggadah*, explain *Enoch walked with God* to mean that he walked with the angels in the Garden of Eden for 300 years and from them he learned the calculation of astronomical cycles, knowledge of the constellations, and many fields of wisdom.

A divergence of views about the verse *Enoch walked with God* can be seen in translations of the Bible from Hebrew to Aramaic, known as Targums. These translations were read in the synagogue after the Hebrew text, so the people could understand the text's meaning, since they spoke Aramaic. These Targums often add midrashic-like explanations to the biblical text. *Targum Onkelos* on Genesis 5:24 denies Enoch's immortality by asserting that Enoch did, in fact, perish: "And Enoch walked in reverence of the Lord, then he was no more, for the Lord had caused him to die." *Targum Pseudo-Yonathan* on Genesis 5:24 asserts that Enoch died and then ascended into heaven to become Metatron: "Enoch served God faithfully and behold he was not with the inhabitants of earth, for he had died and ascended to heaven. And God called his name Metatron the great scribe." *Targum Neophyti* on Genesis 5:24 seems to take a middle ground about whether Enoch died or ascended on high: "And Enoch served in truth before the Lord and it is not known where he is, because he was withdrawn by a command from the Lord." This is in contrast to *Targum Yerushalmi* to Genesis 5:24, which contains the seeds of the Enoch/Metatron myth: "He ascended to heaven on God's command and was given the name Metatron the Great Scribe." The *Septuagint*, the pre-Christian Greek translation of the Bible, states that God found Enoch righteous and therefore transferred him to heaven.

It is worth noting that both Philo and Josephus also commented on this seminal verse about Enoch. Philo explains that Enoch was transferred from this world to heaven, journeying from this mortal life to an immortal one (*Change of Names* 38). Josephus wrote that Enoch and Elijah became invisible, and no one knows how they died. He also writes that after 365 years, Enoch returned to God, and that is why nothing is recorded about his death (*Jewish Antiquities* 1:85, 9:28).

In addition to the three major Enoch texts, references to Enoch are found in a wide variety of ancient Jewish texts, including *The Book of Jubilees, The Testament of the Twelve Patriarchs, The Sibylline Oracles, 2 Baruch, Life of Adam and Eve,* and *The Testament of Abraham*, as well as in rabbinic sources such as the Talmud and *Genesis Rabbah*. *Raziel ha-Malakh* 2 claims that Enoch learned all the secrets of heaven by reading the same book that the angel Raziel delivered to Adam.

This myth about Enoch's transformation into Metatron is also an enthronement myth. In it Enoch/Metatron is crowned by God and receives homage from the other angels, and he is seated on a great throne at the door of the seventh palace in the highest heaven. Other enthronement myths are found about Adam, Jacob, Moses, and King David. This indicates that there were once groups within Judaism who at various times viewed Adam, Enoch, Jacob, Moses and David as divine figures who ruled with God in heaven. Of these, the most extensive tradition is that concerning Enoch. See "The Enthronement of Adam," p. 131, "Jacob the Divine," p. 366, "The Enthronement of Moses," p. 388, and "King David is Crowned in Heaven," p. 395.

Sources:

3 Enoch 6-15, 12:1; *The Book of Jubilees* 4:17-23; *Midrash Aggadah, Bereshit* 5:18:18; *Zohar* 1:37b, 1:56b; *Zohar Hadash* 116a; *Hayei Hanokh* in *Beit ha-Midrash* 4:129; *The Book of Jubilees* 4:17-18, 4:21, 10:17; *Pseudo-Jubilees* (4Q227); *Raziel ha-Malakh* 2.

Studies:

3 Enoch translated and introduced by P. Alexander in *The Old Testament Pseudepigrapha*, edited by James H. Charlesworth, 1:223-315.
"The Deification of Enoch" by Joseph Dan in *The Heart and the Fountain: An Anthology of Jewish Mystical Experiences*, 61-73.
3 Enoch or The Hebrew Book of Enoch by Hugo Odeberg.
Enoch: A Man for All Generations by James C. VanderKam.
"Enoch is Metatron" by Moshe Idel.
Traditions of the Bible by James Kugel, pp. 173-179, 191-194.
"A Report on Enoch in Rabbinic Literature" by Martha Himmelfarb.
The Faces of the Chariot by David J. Halperin, pp. 420-446.
"Sabbatai Zevi, Metatron and Mehmed: Myth and History in Seventeenth-Century Judaism" by David J. Halperin.

194. THE RIVER OF FIRE

The angels who serve God one day do not serve him the next. Every single day new ministering angels are created from the River of Fire, known as Rigyon. This is the river of which it is written, *A river of fire streamed forth before Him* (Dan. 7:10). This river springs out of the perspiration of the heavenly creatures who support God's Throne of Glory and emerges from under the throne. There are a great many bridges of fire that have been placed over the river of fire, for the souls of the righteous to cross.

Before they can sing before God, all the angels must first go down and bathe themselves in the river of fire, and dip their tongues and mouths in the river seven times. Then they encircle the Throne of Glory, singing hymns of praise to God unceasingly from sunrise to sunset, as it is said, *From east to west the name of Yahweh is praised* (Ps. 113:3).

But those angels who serve Him today, do not serve Him tomorrow. And those who serve Him tomorrow will never serve Him again. For after they have finished singing for the first and last time, their strength is exhausted and their faces are blackened and their eyes are darkened, because of the brilliance of the splendor of the King. Metatron, the chief angel, says to the newly created angels, "The Throne of Glory is glistening!" Immediately, the angels fall silent and hasten into the river of fire. There the angels meet their end in the same fiery stream from which they were created, and others are created to take their place.

Other angels are consumed by fire that goes forth from God's little finger, as it is said, *Fire is His vanguard, burning His foes on every side* (Ps. 97:3).

Why are the angels destroyed? Some say it is because they did not sing the hymns of the celestial liturgy in perfect unison, or do not utter their prayers in the proper order. Others say it is so that the angels will not hear the sound of the speech of God and the explicit Name of God that Metatron utters at that time.

But the River of Fire can restore as well as destroy. This river serves as the heavenly *mikveh*, the ritual bath in which all souls are immersed. In this way all impurities are burned up, while all that is pure passes through unscathed.

The existence of a heavenly river of fire derives from Daniel 7:10: *A fiery stream came forth before him*. The traditions concerning this fiery river, known as *nehar di-nur*, the river of fire, also grow out of the talmudic interpretation of the biblical verse *They are renewed every morning— ample is Your grace* (Lam. 3:23). It is also known as the River Rigyon. In *B. Hagigah* 14a, Rabbi Samuel says to Rabbi Hiyya ben Rav, "Every single day new ministering angels are created from the River of Fire. They sing hymns of praise to God and are then destroyed." This river is also referred to in some *Hekhalot* texts, and the myth is elaborated in later midrashic texts. The source of the fiery river is the perspiration of the *hayyot,* the heavenly creatures who hold up God's throne. See "The Living Creatures," p. 159. In kabbalistic texts, the river of fire is said to flow through the heavenly or supernal Eden, and it is said to have both restorative and destructive properties. The souls of the righteous are ritually immersed in this stream, removing all impurities.

Here large numbers of angels, who constitute a celestial choir, are created and destroyed out of the river of fire. The irony that they are destroyed in the same river out of which they were created is noted in *Genesis Rabbah* and other sources.

Metatron, who was once Enoch, is the Prince of the Presence, in charge of all the other angels. In the *Sefer ha-Komah,* Metatron's role is to signal when the newly created angels should stop singing and return to the fiery river out of which they were created. The statement Metatron makes, that "The Throne of Glory is glistening!" is apparently some kind of code, which the angels understand commands them to end their existence.

The Name of God that Metatron pronounces is the Tetragrammaton, YHVH. Anyone who knows its secret pronunciation would have the power of the Name, virtually the power of God. That is one reason given for the daily destruction of the angels of the heavenly choir, so that they are kept from learning this secret.

According to *Zohar* 2:252b, the River of Fire flows during the days of the week, but "When Sabbath arrives the river quiets, its storms and sparks cease." Thus it is portrayed as a kind of heavenly river Sambatyon, the river that is said to flow six days a week and to rest on the Sabbath. See "The River Sambatyon," p. 475.

Sources:

B. *Hagigah* 14a; *Exodus Rabbah* 15:6; *Lamentations Rabbah* 3:8; *3 Enoch* 36:1-2, 40:1-4; *Zohar* 1:201a, 2:252b, 3:211b, 3:16b; *Tikkunei ha-Zohar* Intro 4a; *Re'iyyot Yehezkel*; *Gedulat Moshe* 5; *Hekhalot Rabbati* 8:2; *Eikhah Rabbati* on Lamentations 3:23; *Seder Rabbah di-Bereshit*, p. 45; *Ma'ayan Hokhmah in Otzar Midrashim* pp. 306-311; *Aggadat Shir ha-Shirim* 2:135; *Sefer ha-Komah,* Oxford Ms. 1791, ff. 58-70; *Sod ha-Shabbat* 11.

195. THE LIVING CREATURES

The creatures of the upper world and the creatures of the lower world were created at the same instant. But the creatures of the upper world, who hold up the Throne of Glory, are nourished by the splendor of the *Shekhinah,* while the creatures of the lower world must labor for their nourishment. There are four heavenly creatures, facing the four winds. Each one is as large as the whole world. Each one has four faces and four wings, and every wing would cover the world. Clothed in fire and wrapped in a garment of flame, these heavenly beasts stand laden, day and night, in trembling and terror, for the Divine Chariot is above them, and the Throne of Glory upon their heads, and rivers of fire pass between them.

God says to them, "Exalt yourself. It is proper that those who bear up My throne should make yourselves strong. May the hour be blessed in which I created you. May the planet be exalted under which I formed you. For you are precious vessels I have prepared and completed." So the living creatures strengthen and hallow and purify themselves. Each one binds thousands of crowns on its head. And they stand in holiness and sing songs and hymns with one voice, one mind, and one melody.

One of the living creatures leads the heavenly hosts in the morning prayers. This creature stands in the center of the firmament and says, "Bless you the blessed God!" On its forehead is engraved its name, Israel, and the words, "Hear, O Israel, the Lord is our God, the Lord alone." Other heavenly creatures, all consisting of fire, ascend to the Throne of Glory and stand beneath the legs of the Throne of Glory, each with four faces and four wings. The King, the living and eternal God, dwells above them.

Drawing on Ezekiel's Vision (Ezek. 1:1-28), rabbinic and kabbalistic sources refer to the *hayyot*, the living creatures (also known as the heavenly creatures), who are said to hold up God's Throne of Glory: *Above the expanse over their heads was the semblance of a throne* (Ez. 1:26). A description of these creatures is found in Ezekiel 1:13-14: *Such then was the appearance of the creatures. With them was something that looked like burning coals of fire. This fire, suggestive of torches, kept moving about among the creatures; the fire had a radiance, and lightning issued from the fire. Dashing to and fro among the creatures was something that looked like flares.*

Clearly, traditions concerning these heavenly creatures are the purest form of myth. The identification of these heavenly creatures with lightning also underscores the mythic ties to natural events. These creatures are unique to heaven, but they are not like any of the categories of the angels. They are, instead, another kind of fiery creature. References to these creatures are often found in the hymns of the *Hekhalot* texts.

The name of the living creature (*hayah*) who leads the heavenly hosts is Israel, and the words of the Shema, the central prayer of Judaism, taken from Deuteronomy 6:4, are inscribed on its forehead. The portion of the daily liturgy that the celestial beast leads is called the *Barekhu*. See "The Living Creatures," p. 159.

A parallel is found in *Sefer ha-Komah*, where the precious jewel in the center of God's crown is described as having the words, "Israel, My people; Israel, My people, is Mine."

Sources:
B. *Hagigah* 13a; *Genesis Rabbah* 2:2; *Exodus Rabbah* 47:5; *Midrash Konen* in *Beit ha-Midrash* 2:39; *Sefer ha-Komah*, Oxford Ms. 1791, *lines* 114-115; *Hekhalot Rabbati* 8, 10-12; *3 Enoch* 21.

Studies:
The Faces of the Chariot by David J. Halperin.
"Special Angelic Figures: The Career of the Beasts of the Throne-World in *Hekhalot* Literature, German Pietism and Early Kabbalistic Literature" by Daniel Abrams.

196. THE COUNCIL OF SOULS

The souls of the righteous existed long before the creation of the world. God consulted these souls in creating the universe, as it is said, *They dwelt there in the king's service* (I Chron. 4:23). God called upon the souls of the righteous, who sat on the council with the Supreme King of Kings, to come together. He then took counsel with them before He brought the world into being, saying, *"Let us make man"* (Gen. 1:26). So too did they help Him with His work. Some assisted in planting and some helped create the borders of the sea, as it is said, *Who set the sand as a boundary to the sea* (Jer. 5:22). Nor does God make any important decision without consulting the Council of Souls. So too did God take counsel with the souls of the righteous. He asked them if they were willing to be created. And that is how the souls of the righteous, including the souls of Abraham and the other patriarchs, came into being.

While there are traditions that God took council with the angels or a divine partner such as Adam in creating the world, here the phrase, *"Let us make man"* from Genesis

1:26 is said to refer to a Council of Souls (*nefashot shel Tzaddikim*), with whom God consulted before creating the world. These souls of the righteous are said to have existed before the creation of the world. In fact, it is not specified that they were created by God at all, but only called together by God before He created the universe. Further, they not only give their consent for the creation of the world, but they participate in it, assisting God in planting and creating the boundaries of the sea. Rabbi Levi Yitzhak of Berditchev interprets God's consulting with the souls of the righteous to mean that He asked them if they were willing to be created.

Evidence of a divine council can be found in several biblical passages, such as Psalms 82:1, which states that *God stands in the divine assembly; among the divine beings He pronounces judgment*. Here the term for the divine assembly is *"adat el."* In *Canaanite Myth and Hebrew Epic*, Frank Moore Cross describes this council as the Israelite counterpart of the Council of El found in Canaanite mythology, referring to El, the primary Canaanite god. It would thus seem that this obscure Jewish tradition is directly drawn from the Canaanite. Psalm 82 adds a strange twist to this myth: God appears to condemn the gods of the Council of Gods to death: *"I had taken you for divine beings, sons of the Most High, all of you; but you shall die as men do, fall like any prince"* (Ps. 82:6). This might be interpreted to mean that monotheism declares the death of polytheism. Jeremiah 23:18 also describes a divine council: *But he who has stood in the council of Yahweh, and seen, and heard His word—He who has listened to His word must obey.* Another reference to the divine council is found in 1 Kings 22:19-22, where God addresses the host of heaven, asking who will entice Ahab, *and a certain spirit came forward and stood before the Lord and said, "I will entice him."* Other passages suggesting the existence of heavenly beings with whom God discusses His decisions include Isaiah 6 and Job 1-2.

Usually the term, "the souls of the righteous," refers to the souls of the pious who have died, and whose souls have ascended to Paradise. By pre-existing, these souls become identified as primordial gods, such as are found in other Near Eastern mythologies. By calling them together as a council, God implicitly recognizes their power. It must be assumed that the council of souls gave its approval for the creation of the universe, since God proceeded with it after that.

Another possible explanation would be to identify "the souls of the righteous" in this midrash with the angels. In other sources, God is said to have consulted with the angels before creating man, and there are traditions and countertraditions of the notion that the angels somehow participated in the creation of the world itself. See "Creation by Angels," p. 116. However, it would be highly unusual to refer to the angels as "the souls of the righteous," although Philo does refer to angels as "unbodied souls."

A prooftext for the existence of such a council of souls or angels can be found in Daniel 4:14: *The matter is by decree of the watchers, and the sentence by the word of the holy ones.* Both of these terms, the "watchers" and the "holy ones," suggest some kind of supernatural figures from the heavenly realm, whether angels, souls, or additional divinities. The Council of Souls may also be identified with the heavenly court, and identified as the Watchers. See "The Heavenly Court," p. 208, and "The Watchers," p. 457.

There are parallel myths about God consulting the angels, rather than souls, in the creation of Adam. The text of Genesis 1:26 states that *God said: "Let us make man in our image, after our likeness."* But in the *Pseudo-Yonathan Targum* on Genesis 1:26, this is changed to read: "And God said to the angels who minister before him, who were created on the second day of Creation. `Let us make man in our image, after our likeness.'" See "Creation By Angels," p. 116.

In *Genesis Rabbah* 8:9 the question of how many deities created the world is directly broached: "How many deities created the world? You and I must inquire of the first day, as it is said, *For ask now of the first days* (Deut. 4:32)." The rabbis subsequently debate whether the first sentence of Genesis describes creation by one God or by many, since *Elohim* is plural. Read this way, the first line of Genesis reads: "In the beginning Gods created the heaven and the earth." That such a debate can take place at all is remarkable, considering the centrality of monotheism. But it is also a tribute to the open-ended willingness of the rabbis to explore even apparently heretical interpretations of the Torah. The existence of this discussion and the fact that it was recorded in a primary text such as *Genesis Rabbah*, indicates that the "heretical" had some advocates among the rabbis. Perhaps it harks back to a residual pagan myth, a Canaanite myth about a council of gods.

Such divine councils rule in Mesopotamian, Babylonian, and Canaanite mythology. In the Babylonian epic *Enuma Elish*, Marduk is made head of the divine council by defeating Tiamat, the personification of the sea. It is likely that the existence of such a council in Jewish tradition is a remnant of such an ancient myth. Ugaritic texts describe the abode of El, the primary Canaanite god, and his council on the mountain of El, where the gods are seated at a table. El's abode is said to be in the north. This setting and location is echoed in Isaiah 14:13: *"I will sit in the mount of assembly, on the summit of Zaphon."* (*Zaphon* is Hebrew for "north.")

God's perplexing use of the first person plural in verses such as *Let us make man in our image* (Gen. 1:26), *Behold the man has become like one of us* (Gen. 3:22), and *Let us, then, go down and confound their speech there* (Gen. 11:7) can be explained as addressing the divine council. This same usage is found in the Ugaritic texts. Most midrashic texts interpret *"Let us"* as God addressing the angels.

Sources:
Genesis Rabbah 8: 7; *Maggid Devarav le-Ya'akov* 1; *No'am Elimelekh, Bo* 36b.

Studies:
Canaanite Myth and Hebrew Epic by Frank Moore Cross, pp. 36-43, 186-190.
"The Council of Yahweh in Second Isaiah" by Frank Moore Cross.
"The Council of Yahweh" by H. Wheeler Robinson.
"God and the Gods in Assembly" by Matitiahu Tsevat.
Assembly of the Gods: The Divine Council in Canaanite and Early Hebrew Literature by E. Theodore Mullen.

197. ADAM'S SOUL

All souls were originally included in Adam's soul. After Adam was created, God showed him all the souls contained within his soul, and all the future generations that would follow. Thus Adam is the source of all souls. That is why on Rosh ha-Shanah, the day that Adam was created, the entire world is judged, for Adam contained within him all the souls of mankind.

After Adam sinned, the souls attached to Adam's soul descended into evil. However, some of the other souls that were originally part of Adam's soul split off, for Adam's soul originally included six hundred thousand "old souls." But when Adam sinned these souls broke into six hundred thousand soul-roots. Ever since, these souls have been reincarnated in this world, so they can rectify Adam's sin.

However, some say that before Adam was fully created, souls of different people were to be found in different parts of his body, and when Adam decided to eat from the Tree of Knowledge, elevated souls flew away from him. Then there are others who say that there were also new souls in Adam's soul, which had never come into the world. These souls were not revealed to Adam, and after he died, these new souls became separated from him. They now issue forth from the Tree of Life. Many angels are produced above to protect these holy souls from harm. In this way a multitude of these living souls are generated, which are drawn down to those worthy of them.

Since Adam was the first human, Jewish tradition holds that his soul was the source of all subsequent souls. The total number of souls is said to be 600,000, the number of the Israelite men present at Mount Sinai. According to Ben Ish Hai in *Derushim Bereshit*, the soul of each Jew is represented by a letter of the Torah. According to Hayim Vital, "The source of all souls is Adam and is then divided into the three patriarchs, then into the 12 tribes, and afterwards divided into the 70 souls who accompanied Jacob to Egypt. Each of these 70 parts is further divided until we find that the total number of souls descended from Adam's soul is 600,000" (*Sefer ha-Hezyonot* 4:41). In *Sefer ha-Gilgulim* Hayim Vital offers an alternate explanation: "The majority of all souls come from Adam's sons Cain and Abel, and from them separate into all who were born afterward."

However, once the Jewish population exceeded 600,000, the problem arose about the source of their souls. The solution was the concept of "sparks of souls." According to this explanation, Jewish souls received not whole souls, but sparks of souls—portions of souls. Rabbi Nachman of Bratslav describes these as "offshoots of the 600,000 primary souls" (*Likutei Moharan* 119b). In the same passage, Rabbi Nachman speaks of "illustrious *Tzaddikim* who beget souls from a heavenly source higher than the 600,000 primary sources." He also said that it is possible for one person to have sparks of souls of several individuals. Thus Rabbi Nachman spoke of having sparks of the souls of Moses, Rabbi Akiba, the Ari, and the Ba'al Shem Tov. For a related myth, see "The Creation of Souls," following.

In *Homat Anakh, Lekh Lekha*, Rabbi Hayim Yosef David Azulai, quoting the Ari, states that the good element of Adam's soul was reincarnated in Abraham, Isaac and Jacob, while the evil part of his soul was reincarnated in Ishmael, Lot and Esau. This solves the problem of how both good and evil people descended from Adam. An alternate explanation is that some particularly pure souls, such as the soul of the Ba'al Shem Tov, hid in the garden while Adam and Eve ate the forbidden fruit. Thus they were spared the consequences of the sin.

Rabbi Elimelekh of Lizhensk is said to have said to his brother, Rabbi Zusya of Hanipol (1719-1800): "My brother Zusya, if all souls were contained in Adam's soul, it means that our souls were also there. How is it, then, Zusya, that you didn't stop Adam from eating from the Tree of Knowledge?"

Sources:

Exodus Rabbah 40:3; *Midrash Tanhuma-Yelammedenu, Ki Tissa* 12; *Midrash Tanhuma-Yelammedenu, Pekudei* 3; *Zohar* 1:12b-13a, 1:90b; *Likutei Torah ha-Ari, Kedoshim* p. 191; *Sha'ar ha-Gilgulim* 31; *Sefer ha-Hezyonot* 4:41; *Sha'ar ha-Pesukim, Bereshit* 3; *Sefer ha-Gilgulim* 1:3a; *Ohev Yisrael, va-Et-Hanan* 81c; *Sefer Netivot ha-Shalom; Beit Aharon; Derushim Bereshit*; IFA 12985.

198. THE CREATION OF SOULS

All the souls that would ever exist, from Adam till the End of Days, were fashioned during the six days of Creation. All remained in the Garden of Eden on high, and all were present at the Giving of the Torah. That is meaning of the verse *Whatever happens, it was designated long ago and it was known that it would happen* (Eccles. 6:10).

All souls in the world above were initially both male and female. But when they are born into this world, they are either male or female, the male soul in a male body and the female soul in a female body. If worthy, they will reunite again in marriage, and they join together to form a single unit in every way, body and soul. That is why the other's soul is known as a soulmate.

All of these souls were present in the Garden of Eden and at the giving of the Torah. But one pure soul among them, that of the Ba'al Shem Tov, was not present when Adam and Eve tasted the forbidden fruit.

Six hundred thousand souls were present at Mount Sinai. Later, when there were more Jewish bodies than souls, only a few *Tzaddikim* received complete souls. Instead, most people have sparks of a soul, or the sparks of more than one soul.

This myth explains the traditions behind the concept of a person seeking their *bashert* or destined one. Here it is understood that the one who is sought is actually the other half of a person's soul, with whom he or she was once united in paradise. For more on the concept of *bashert* see "God Makes Matches," p. 66.

The sixteenth century kabbalists of Safed included reincarnation or *gilgul* among their basic principles, and it remains a key principle among Sephardic Jews, in particular, to this day. The Ari believed that he was the reincarnation of Rabbi Akiba. For more on the subject of sparks of soul, see "Adam's Soul," p. 162.

The Torah is said to contain 600,000 letters, one for each one of the 600,000 souls present at Mount Sinai. Commenting on this, Rabbi Nachman of Bratslav said, "I cannot sleep. Before I fall asleep, all 600,000 letters of the Torah come and stand before me" (*Sihot ha-Ran* 176). According to Rabbi Moshe Hayim Luzzatto, known as Ramhal, there are 600,000 heavenly souls, which are the roots of all the souls of Israel. Each soul consists of an upper part that remains in heaven and a lower counterpart that inhabits a human body (*Adir ba-Marom*).

Rabbi Menashe ben Israel finds the presence of the souls at Mount Sinai attested for by the verse, *I make this covenant to those who are standing here, and with those who are not here with us today* (Deut. 29:14). In this context the word "standing" is used in the sense of existing. Thus *those who are standing here* refers not only to the souls of the living, but to the unborn souls of future generations as well. They too were present at Sinai to receive the Torah. In this way, the souls of all Jewish generations received the Torah at Mount Sinai at the same time (*Nishmat Hayim* 2:16). See "The Giving of the Torah," p. 270.

Rabbi Dov Ber offers a unique interpretation of the origin of souls. He states that each soul is a tiny particle of the *Shekhinah*, like a drop in the ocean (*Maggid Devarav le-Ya'akov* 66.)

Sources:
Midrash Tanhuma-Yelammedenu, Pekudei 3, 9; *Zohar* 1:12b, 3:43b; *Etz Hayim, Sha'ar ha-Gilgulim, Hakdamah* 22; *Ma'amar ha-Hokhmah*; *Sh'nei Luchot ha-B'rit, Mishpatim*; *Pardes Rimonim* 65a; *Nishmat Hayim* 2:16; *Maggid Devarav le-Ya'akov* 66.

199. TREE OF SOULS

God has a tree of flowering souls in Paradise. The angel who sits beneath it is the Guardian of Paradise, and the tree is surrounded by the four winds of the world. From this tree blossom forth all souls, as it is said, *"I am like a cypress tree in bloom; your fruit issues forth from Me."* (Hos.14:9). And from the roots of this tree sprout the souls of all the righteous ones whose names are inscribed there. When the souls grow ripe, they descend into the Treasury of Souls, where they are stored until they are called upon to be born. From this we learn that all souls are the fruit of the Holy One, blessed be He.

This Tree of Souls produces all the souls that have ever existed, or will ever exist. And when the last soul descends, the world as we know it will come to an end.

Rabbinic and kabbalistic texts speculate that the origin of souls is somewhere in heaven. This myth provides the heavenly origin of souls, and in itself fuses many traditions. First, it develops themes based on the biblical account of the Garden of Eden. It also builds on the tradition that just as there is an earthly Garden of Eden, so is there a heavenly one, as expressed in the principle, "as above, so below." Just as there is a Tree of Life in the earthly garden, so there is a Tree of Life in the heavenly one.

Had Adam and Eve tasted the fruit of the earthly Tree of Life, they would have been immortal. But once they had tasted the fruit of the Tree of Knowledge, immortality was closed to them. Therefore *He drove the man out, and stationed east of the garden of Eden the cherubim and the fiery ever-turning sword, to guard the way to the Tree of Life* (Gen. 3:24).

As for the Tree of Life in Paradise, its blossoms are souls. It produces new souls, which ripen, and then fall from the tree into the *Guf*, the Treasury of Souls in Paradise. There the soul is stored until the angel Gabriel reaches into the treasury and takes out the first soul that comes into his hand. After that, Lailah, the Angel of Conception, guards over the embryo until it is born. Thus the Tree of Life in Paradise is a Tree of Souls. See "The Treasury of Souls," p. 166. For an alternate myth about the origin of souls, see "The Creation of Souls," p. 163. For the myth of the formation of the embryo see "The Angel of Conception," p. 201.

Rabbi Isaac Luria of Safed, known as the Ari, believed that trees were resting places for souls, and performed a tree ritual in the month of Nisan, when trees are budding. He felt that this was the right time to participate in the rescue of wandering spirits, incarnated in lower life forms. The Ari often took his students out into nature to teach them there. On one such occasion, upon raising his eyes, he saw all the trees peopled with countless spirits, and he asked them, "Why have you gathered here?" They replied, "We did not repent during our lifetime. We have heard about you, that you can heal and mend us." And the Ari promised to help them. The disciples saw him in conversation, but they were not aware of with whom he conversed. Later they asked him about it, and he replied, "If you had been able to see them, you would have been shocked to see the crowds of spirits in the trees."

The core text of this myth comes from *Ha-Nefesh ha-Hakhamah* by Moshe de Leon (Spain, 13th century) who is generally recognized as the primary author of the *Zohar*. It is possible that de Leon symbolically identified the Tree of Souls with the kabbalistic "tree" of the ten sefirot. *Tikkunei Zohar* speaks of the ten sefirot blossoming and flying forth souls. (See also the diagram of the sefirot on p. 529.)

Not only is there the notion of a Tree of Souls in Judaism, and the notion that souls take shelter in trees, but there is also the belief that trees have souls. This is indicated in a story about Rabbi Nachman of Bratslav found in *Sihot Moharan* 535 in *Hayei Moharan*: Rabbi Nachman was once traveling with his Hasidim by carriage, and as it grew dark they came to an inn, where they spent the night. During the night Rabbi Nachman began to cry out loudly in his sleep, waking up everyone in the inn, all of whom came running to see what had happened. When he awoke, the first thing Rabbi Nachman did was to take out a book he had brought with him. Then he closed his eyes and opened the book and pointed to a passage. And there it was written "Cutting down a tree before its time is the same as killing a soul." Then Rabbi Nachman asked the innkeeper if the walls of that inn had been built out of saplings cut down before their time. The innkeeper admitted that this was true, but how did the rabbi know? And Rabbi Nachman said: "All night I dreamed I was surrounded by the bodies of those who had been murdered. I was very frightened. Now I know that it was the souls of the trees that cried out to me."

Sources:

B. Sanhedrin 98a; B. Yevamot 62a-63b; B. Niddah 13b; Hagigah 12b; B. Avodah Zarah 5a; 2 Enoch 5-6. 3 Enoch 43; Genesis Rabbah 24:4; Midrash Tanhuma-Yelammedenu, Pekudei 3; Pesikta Rabbati 29/30A:3; Zohar 1:12b, 1:47a, 2:96b, 2:149b-150a, 2:157a, 2:174a, 2:253a.; Battei Midrashot 2:90-91; Zohar Hadash, Bereshit 10b-10c, Noah 21b; Ha-Nefesh ha-Hakhamah 2; Raya Mehemma, Zohar 1, Hashmatot 38; Midrash ha-Ne'elam; The Visions of Ezekiel; Sefer Etz Hayim 2:129-130; Likutei Moharan 1:7; Sefer Toledot ha-Ari. Sefer Orah Hayim, Birkat ha-Ilanot 6.

200. THE TREASURY OF SOULS

The souls of all those who have not yet been born are kept in the *Guf*, the Treasury of Souls, also known as the Chamber of Creation. There each soul waits its turn to be born. When the time comes for it to descend into this world, an angel is issued along with it, who accompanies it. It is said that sparrows can see the souls descend, and that is the source of their song. As soon as the soul leaves the *Guf*, it divests itself of its heavenly garment, and is clothed in a garment of flesh and blood.

Where is the Treasury of Souls? In the highest heaven, known as *Aravot*, where there are many treasuries, each of them guarded by angels, including the Treasury of Rain, the Treasury of Ice and Snow, the Treasury of Clouds, the Treasury of Peace, the Treasury of Blessing, and the Treasury of the Dew with which God will revive the dead. The *Guf* is found near the Throne of Glory, and a dazzling brilliant light emanates from the many souls in repose there. Those souls are in their pristine state, untainted by existence in this world. Some of them flicker like a small candle and some shine like a torch, and there are some whose radiance rivals the sun.

When the time comes for the soul to leave this world, the Angel of Death strips off the worldly garment, and at the same instant the soul is clothed in the holy garment that was stripped away when it descended to this world. Then the soul delights in having been stripped of its worldly body and in having its original garment restored. And the souls who have departed from their earthly bodies return to that same treasury, and fly before the Throne of Glory in the presence of God. And when the time comes for a human to be born, the angel Gabriel puts his hand into the Treasury of Souls and takes out the first soul that comes into his hand. If the person is fortunate, a great soul comes into Gabriel's hand; if not a spark of a soul inhabits the body.

It is said about the soul of the Ba'al Shem Tov that its radiance shone from one end of the universe to the other. Each time the angel Gabriel sought to bring this soul down to this world, Satan would storm into heaven and protest. In this way, the brightest of souls remained in heaven for thousands of years, but at last it descended and the Ba'al Shem Tov was born.

There are those who say that the *Guf* contains an infinite number of souls, while others insist there is only a finite number of souls in it, and that the Messiah will not come until the *Guf* has been emptied of every soul. Others say that from the day the Temple was destroyed, no more souls entered the *Guf*, and when it has been emptied of all the remaining souls, the Messiah will come.

Others say that from the day the Temple was destroyed, no more souls entered the *Guf*, and when it has been emptied of all the remaining souls, the Messiah will come.

And when the last soul has descended and the *Guf* is empty, the first infant to be born without a soul, born dead as such an infant must be, will herald the death of the world and so is called the final sign. Then all of the sparrows will grow silent, and the world, as we know it, will end, and the End of Days will begin.

There is general agreement in rabbinic lore that the souls of the unborn are kept in a storehouse or Treasury of Souls. In *B. Avodah Zarah* 5a, Resh Lakish, an important talmudic sage, is quoted as saying, "The Messiah will only come when all the souls destined to inhabit earthly bodies have been exhausted." Rashi, commenting on this, says that "There is a treasure house called the *Guf*, and at the time of Creation all souls destined to be born were formed and placed there." This treasure house is said to contain souls created since the six days of Creation, which are being saved for bodies yet to be created. It is also described in *B. Yevamot* 63b as located behind the heavenly curtain known as the *Pargod*, where "there are spirits and souls created since the six days of Creation that are intended for bodies yet to be created."

A linkage is also made between the depletion of souls in this treasury and the End of Days. The Talmud (*B. Yev.* 62a) states, "The Son of David will not come before all the souls in the *Guf* have been disposed of, as it is said, *"For the spirit that unwraps itself is from Me and the souls that I have made"* (Isa 57:16). *Guf* literally means a "body," thus the storehouse of souls is literally "a body of souls." This enigmatic verse grew into the myth of the *Guf*, a treasury that provided souls for those still to be born. The myth describes the events that will take place when the treasury runs out of souls. In *3 Enoch* 43 Rabbi Ishmael expands on this verse. He concludes that the first part of the verse *"For the spirit that unwraps itself is from Me"* refers to the souls of the righteous that have already been created in the *Guf* and have returned to the presence of God. The second part of the verse, *"and the souls that I have made,"* refers to the souls of the righteous that have not yet been created.

In addition to the myth of the *Guf*, the concept of such a treasury is found in other forms in Jewish tradition. An alternate version of the origin of souls is found in *Zohar Hadash, Bereshit* 10b-10c, in which it is stated that God hewed from His Throne all souls that would be born, and stored them in the storehouse of souls. There is also said to be another storehouse of the souls of the righteous who have died. As long as a person is alive, his soul is entrusted to his Creator, as it is said, *O keep my soul and deliver me* (Ps. 25:20). Once a righteous person dies, his soul is placed in this other treasury, as it is said, *The soul of my Lord will be bound up in the bundle of life in the care of the Lord* (1 Sam. 25:29).

A third explanation of the origin of souls is found in *Nishmat Hayim* 2:7, where holy souls are said to spring forth from God. In contrast, in *Torat Moshe*, Rabbi Moshe Alshekh describes the soul as a spiritual light that emanates from the *Shekhinah*. Thus in one version the soul comes forth from the male aspect of God; in the other, it shines forth from God's Bride.

There are alternate myths about other places where the souls of the unborn are kept. Some say that the highest abode of the soul is the pure place under the Throne of Glory, where all the souls of the unborn are kept close to their Creator. According to Ben Ish Hai in *Derushim Bereshit*, both the Torah and the souls of Israel come from the Throne of Glory, which he identifies with the World of Creation (*Beriah*), one of the four Kabbalistic "worlds." Still other sources, including *Sefer ha-Bahir* and the *Zohar*, identify the *Shekhinah* with the soul, calling the *Shekhinah* the dwelling place of the soul. This teaches that the soul had its origin on high, and that the *Shekhinah* is the soul that dwells in everyone. This identification of *Shekhinah* with soul is also found in the myth of the *neshamah yeterah*, the second soul that arrives on the Sabbath at the same instant as the *Shekhinah* in the form of the Sabbath Queen. See "The Second Soul," p. 310 and "The *Pargod*, p. 186.

The Seventh Sign (1988), a popular film in the apocalyptic genre, is based on the theme of the *Guf*. Its plot takes place when the first infant without a soul is about to be born, a sign that the world is about to end. This is an accurate account of the prophecy about a child born after the last soul departs from the *Guf*, except that the film tries to turn a Jewish apocalyptic myth into a Christian one.

For the related myth of the origin of souls, see "Tree of Souls," p. 164. See also "The Creation of Souls," p. 163.

Sources:

B. Sanhedrin 98a; *B. Yevamot* 62a-63b; *B. Niddah* 13b; *B. Hagigah* 12b; *B. Avodah Zarah* 5a; *2 Enoch* 5-6; *3 Enoch* 43; *Genesis Rabbah* 24:4; *Sefer ha-Bahir* 1:184; *Midrash Tanhuma-Yelammedenu, Pekudei* 3; *Pesikta Rabbati* 29/30A:3; *Zohar* 1:12b, 1:47a, 2:96b, 2:149b-150a, 2:157a, 2:174a, 2:253a.; *Zohar Hadash, Bereshit* 10b-10c, *Noah* 21b; *Zohar 1, Hashmatot* 38, *Midrash ha-Ne'elam*; *The Visions of Ezekiel; Sefer Etz Hayim* 2:129-130; *Likutei Moharan* 1:7; *Derushim Bereshit; Nishmat Hayim* 2:16.

Studies:

"A Fragment of the Visions of Ezekiel" by A. Marmorstein.

201. THE PATH OF THE SOUL IN THE GARDEN OF EDEN

Some say that when the righteous leave this world, three companies of angels join them. These angels go ahead of the righteous, leading them to the Garden of Eden. And when the soul of a *Tzaddik* leaves his body, the archangel Michael goes out to meet it, saying, "May you come in peace."

Others say that there is a column through which the soul of a person who has passed away travels from the lower Garden of Eden to the higher Garden. By means of this column, the soul rises from one world to another, from one year to another, and from soul to soul. This is called "the column of service and fear of heaven."

Still others say that the souls of the righteous ascend the Tree of Life into heaven, to the celestial Garden of Eden. That garden is planted on a source of living water, and the size of the garden is a thousand years' journey.

> The reward awaiting the righteous when they take leave of this world is the *Olam ha-Ba*, the World to Come. This is also identified in rabbinic texts as *Gan Eden*, the Garden of Eden. This myth describes what occurs when a righteous person dies and goes to receive his heavenly reward. The second teaching, that of the "column of service and fear of heaven," is attributed to the Ba'al Shem Tov. It resolves the problem of the link between the earthly *Gan Eden* and the heavenly one. It also explains how it is possible for a soul to ascend to higher levels of Paradise. The description of moving "from soul to soul" may be a reference to *gilgul*, the transmigration of souls, i.e., reincarnation. Hasidic theory also includes the possibility of the combining of sparks of souls, and moving "from soul to soul" might also be referring to this.
>
> *Studies:*
> *Midrash Tehillim* 30:3; *Midrash Konen* in *Beit ha-Midrash* 2:24-39; *Zohar Hadash* 24d-25a, *Midrash ha-Ne'elam*; *Rabbi Yisrael Ba'al Shem Tov*, p. 47.

202. THE FIELD OF SOULS

There is a field where wondrous trees grow. Its splendor cannot be described. The trees and grass are holy souls that grow there. There are also many naked souls that stray beyond its borders and await repair. For even the greatest soul has difficulty reentering that field once it has departed. And all of those exiled souls call for the field master who will engage himself in *tikkun*, so that those souls can be repaired.

Whoever takes on that task must be steadfast and courageous. There is one such man who can only complete this task through his own death. He must endure many afflictions, but in the end he will accomplish the work of the field and prevail.

> This is an allegory of Rabbi Nachman's about the meaning of exile from the Garden of Eden, and about the *tikkun*, or repair, of souls. The field of souls is the Garden of Eden, or Paradise (which blur together in the rabbinic concept of *Gan Eden*), where souls originate as well as find eternal rest. But those who stray from there, exiled into the fallen world, eventually find themselves naked and in need of repair by the field master. This figure represents the *Tzaddik* in general and Messiah ben Joseph in particular. The role of Messiah ben Joseph is to pave the way for the arrival of Messiah ben David, the heavenly Messiah, who will initiate the End of Days. It is the fate of Messiah ben Joseph to die while engaged in his messianic task. See "The Two Messiahs," p. 517.
>
> Thus Rabbi Nachman's allegory is essentially a reaffirmation of the need to long and pray for the coming of the Messiah, who will repair all souls in need of repair.

Such a messianic figure is portrayed in Rabbi Nachman's famous tale "The Master of Prayers" in *Sippurei Ma'asiyot*.

Rabbi Nachman asked to buried in the city of Uman because there had been a great pogrom there two centuries earlier, and he wanted to assist the souls buried there, who he said were trapped in that place. It was his intention to guide them into heaven. Thus, as in most of Rabbi Nachman's stories, the *Tzaddik* he is alluding to in this allegory is himself. This also suggests that Rabbi Nachman saw himself as the *Tzaddik ha-Dor*, the leading *Tzaddik* of his generation, who was the potential Messiah ben Joseph of his generation.

Sources:

Likutei Moharan 1:65.

Studies:

"Messiah and the Light of the Messiah in Rabbi Nachman's Thought" by Hillel Zeitlin in *God's Voice from the Void: Old and New Studies in Bratslav Hasidism*, edited by Shaul Magid, pp. 239-262.

Tormented Master by Arthur Green.

203. THE TRANSMIGRATION OF SOULS

After death a man's soul undergoes up to four transformations. First, it crosses the sea. And if the soul falls there, it enters the body of a fish. And if that fish is caught, and someone cooks and eats that fish after saying the proper blessing, that soul is spared its suffering and ascends to the Garden of Eden.

Then there are the souls that cross the ocean and pass above the trees. If the soul falls and enters a fruit-bearing tree, and if those fruits are later picked and blessings pronounced on them, that soul also enters the Garden of Eden, its sufferings at an end.

So too are there souls that pass over the crops, such as wheat. If the soul enters the wheat and bread is made of it, and the blessings are said over it, that soul is also saved. But if the soul enters crops that are eaten by animals, it remains in sorrow. For if an animal eats the crops containing this soul, it enters the animal. It suffers there until the animal is slaughtered and blessings are made over the food. And that is the soul's last chance of being saved from its suffering. For if it is not saved, it will continue to suffer until the End of Days. But if it is saved, its soul will be saved from great suffering, and it will make its home in the Garden of Eden. Otherwise it will be condemned to wait until the footsteps of the Messiah are heard.

> Beginning with the Safed kabbalists in the sixteenth century, the concept of metempsychosis, the transmigration of souls, becomes a central principle in Judaism known as *gilgul*. The ultimate goal of the soul, from this perspective, is to be freed from the cycle of reincarnation, much as the goal in Hinduism is to achieve *Nirvana* and be freed from any further rebirths.
>
> The fate of the soul as outlined here involves great suffering. And an even worse punishment awaits those souls whose sins were so great that avenging angels chase them from one place to the next. When such a wandering spirit takes possession of a living person, it is known as a *dybbuk*. See, for example, "The Widow of Safed," p. 228. For an example of the freeing of a soul from *gilgul*, see "The Sabbath Fish," in *Gabriel's Palace*, pp. 233-234. See also S. Ansky's folk drama, *The Dybbuk*.
>
> *Sefer ha-Likutim,* edited by Binyamin ha-Levi and Elisha Vestali, p. 175, based on teachings of Hayim Vital, suggests that the righteous may go through *gilgul* for a thousand generations, while the unjust do so for only three. This is because those who were learned in Torah are said to be protected from entering Gehenna, where sins are purified through the punishments of hell. Yet even the righteous accumulate sins that need to be cleansed, so the process of *gilgul* serves to purify their souls. But the unjust enter hell after only three generations and have their sins cleansed there.

Sources:
Devět Brán; Megillat Setarim; IFA 10200.

Studies:
"Resurrection as Giving Back the Dead: A Traditional Image of Resurrection in the
　Pseudepigrapha and the Apocalypse of John" by Richard Bauckham.
"Faithful Transmission versus Innovation: Luria and His Disciples" by Ronit Meroz.
Between Worlds: Dybbuks, Exorcists, and Early Modern Judaism by J. H. Chajes.
Magic, Mysticism and Hasidism: The Supernatural in Jewish Thought by Gedalyah Nigal.

204. HOW TO GRASP A SOUL

Just as something physical can be grasped by holding on to it, so one can grasp a soul by
calling its name.

> Calling upon souls is an essential part of kabbalah, especially practical kabbalah.
> Souls are invoked to answer questions or to assist in some earthly or heavenly task.
> Here the secret of calling upon a soul and compelling it to respond is revealed—the
> power is in knowing the spirit's name. Once called upon by name, the spirits cannot
> resist coming forth to answer the call.
>
> *Sources*:
> *Toledot Ya'akov Yosef, Shemot* 42d; *Sefer Ba'al Shem Tov, Bereshit* 131; *Keter Shem Tov* 104.

205. ADAM IS TAKEN INTO PARADISE

When Adam was old, he called his son Seth to him and said: "Hear these words, my son.
All that I am going to tell you is true. One day, not long after your mother and I had been
expelled from Paradise, as we finished our prayers, I had a vision: I saw a chariot like the
wind and its wheels were fiery. Before I knew it, I was caught up into Paradise. There I
saw the Lord seated on a mighty throne, and the flames cast from His face could not be
endured. Many thousands of angels were there, on each side of the chariot.

"I was seized with terror, and I bowed down before God, and God said, 'Because you
transgressed My commandment, the time has come for you to die.' When I heard these
words, I fell prone and said, 'Master of the Universe! Do not cast me out of your presence,
I whom You shaped out of dust. Do not banish what You Yourself nourished.'

"God said, 'Fear not, because of your love of knowledge, your seed will always be
with Me.' And when I heard these words, I prostrated myself before God and said, 'You
are the eternal and supreme God. You are the true Light shining above all lights. May it
be Your will to bestow abundance on the race of men.'

"Then, as soon as I finished speaking, the angel Michael seized my hand and brought
me out of Paradise. He touched the waters surrounding Paradise with his rod, and they
froze in place. And Michael and I crossed over the frozen waters, and led me back to this
world. That is when the vision came to an end. Nor did I die on that day."

> This myth about Adam is a good example of a *Merkavah* myth. Adam not only has
> a vision of the Divine Chariot, as does Ezekiel, but he is taken up into heaven in it, as
> later happened to Enoch and Elijah, and he has a heavenly vision. Note that the vision
> takes place not long after Adam's expulsion from Eden. God tells him of his impend-
> ing doom, but then spares him, and reveals that he will be the first of a long line.
>
> This account of Adam's vision makes Adam the first one to take such a heavenly
> journey. But while Enoch's journey into Paradise is well known, this myth about Adam,
> found in *Vita Adae et Evae*, is somewhat obscure. In fact, mythic accounts of such heav-
> enly journeys can be found for Adam, Enoch, the patriarchs, and Moses, as well as
> several of the rabbinic sages.

Like most mystical experiences, Adam describes it as a vision that involved a heavenly journey and an encounter with God. It is not clear whether it was a journey of the soul or a bodily ascent. In the former, a person remains on earth while his soul ascends on high; in the latter, the mystic literally ascends to heaven. Most of these accounts are best understood as soul journeys, but this may be an exception, based on the description of how he was taken into the chariot by the angel Michael and taken into Paradise. See "The Ascent of Elijah," p. 172.

Sources:
Vita Adae et Evae 25-29; *Apocalypse of Moses* 25:2-26:2.

Studies:
The Faces of the Chariot by David J. Halperin.

206. ISAAC'S ASCENT

When the knife touched Isaac's throat, his soul flew from him. While his body lay on the stone altar, his soul ascended on high, rising up through the palaces of heaven. And the angels on high brought Isaac's soul to the celestial academy of Shem and Eber. There he remained for three years, studying the Torah, for in this way Isaac was rewarded for all he had suffered when he was about to be slain.

So too were all the Treasuries of Heaven opened to Isaac: the celestial Temple, which has existed there since the time of Creation, the Chambers of the Chariot, and all of the palaces of heaven; all the Treasuries of Ice and Snow, as well as the Treasury of Prayers, and the Treasury of Souls. There Isaac saw how he had descended from the seed of Adam. So too was he permitted to see the future generations that would arise from the seed of Abraham. Even the End of Days was revealed, for no mystery of heaven was deemed too secret for the pure soul of Isaac. There, too, Isaac found his own face on the curtain of God known as the *Pargod*.

During all this time Abraham remained frozen in place, the knife in his upraised hand. But to him it seemed but a single breath. Then the angel spoke: "Lay not your hand upon the lad," and at that instant Isaac's soul returned to his body. And when Isaac found that his soul had been restored to him, he exclaimed: "Blessed is He who quickens the dead!" And when Abraham unbound him, Isaac arose, seeing the world as if for the first time, as if he had been reborn.

Although it is clearly stated in Genesis 22:12 that the angel of the Lord commanded Abraham not to raise his hand against Isaac, this late midrash, which may well echo Christian influence, asserts that Abraham did in fact slay Isaac, and that Isaac's soul ascended to Paradise, where he studied in the academy of Shem and Eber. The basis of this midrash is the conclusion of the *Akedah* episode of the binding of Isaac, where it is Abraham alone who returns to his servants, and no mention is made of Isaac (Gen. 22:19). The themes of dying and resurrection here echo the Christian belief in the death and resurrection of Jesus. The similarity of the three days after the death of Jesus when the resurrection takes place, and the three years in this midrash about Isaac underscores the parallel. This legend about the ascent of Isaac is linked to the Resurrection of the Dead by adding that when Isaac arose, "He knew that in this way the dead would come back to life in the future, whereupon he began to recite, 'Blessed are You, O Lord, who quickens the dead'" (*Pirkei de-Rabbi Eliezer* 31). For further discussion of the legends of the *Akedah*, the Binding of Isaac, see *The Last Trial* by Shalom Spiegel.

The academy of Shem and Eber is often referred to in the Midrash. Abraham is said to have told Sarah that he was taking Isaac to study there at the time he set off for Mount Moriah (*Sefer ha-Yashar* 43a-44b). While this academy may once have been on earth, in most rabbinic legends it is identified as the academy on high. Therefore Isaac's ascent to Paradise to study in this academy verifies Abraham's statement to Sarah, affirming his honesty. The origin of this legend is the identification of *the tents of Shem* in Genesis 9:27 with a *Beit Midrash* or House of Study, which evolved in midrashic literature into an academy led by Shem and his great-grandson Eber. Later legends identify the academy as a heavenly one, where the greatest sages study. There also is a strong identification of prophecy with Shem, who was said to have had the gift of prophecy. Note that in the midrash this "academy" existed long before the giving of the Torah at Mount Sinai, underscoring the rabbinic belief of the pre-existence of the Torah.

This myth finds it fullest form in "The Akedah," a medieval *piyyut* by Ephraim ben Jacob of Bonn.

Sources:

Targum Pseudo-Yonathan on Genesis 22:19; *Genesis Rabbah* 56; *3 Enoch* 45:3; *Pirkei de-Rabbi Eliezer* 31; *Hadar Zekenim* 10b in *Beit ha-Midrash* 5:157; *Perush Ramban al Sefer Yetzirah* p. 125.

Studies:

The Last Trial: On the Legends and Lore of the Command to Abraham to Offer Isaac as a Sacrifice: The Akedah by Shalom Spiegel, pp. 143-152.

"Seeing with the Sages" by Marc Bregman.

207. THE ASCENT OF ELIJAH

When the Lord was about to take Elijah up to heaven in a whirlwind, Elijah and Elisha had set out from Gilgal. Elijah said to Elisha, "Stay here, for the Lord has sent me on to Bethel." "As the Lord lives and as you live," said Elisha, "I will not leave you." So they went down to Bethel. Disciples of the prophets at Bethel came out to Elisha and said to him, "Do you know that the Lord will take your master away from you today?" He replied, "I know it, too; be silent."

Then Elijah said to him, "Elisha, stay here, for the Lord has sent me on to Jericho." "As the Lord lives and as you live," said Elisha, "I will not leave you." So they went on to Jericho. The disciples of the prophets who were at Jericho came over to Elisha and said to him, "Do you know that the Lord will take your master away from you today?" He replied, "I know it, too; be silent."

Elijah said to him, "Stay here, for the Lord has sent me on to the Jordan." "As the Lord lives and as you live, I will not leave you," he said, and the two of them went on. Fifty men of the disciples of the prophets followed and stood by at a distance from them as the two stopped at the Jordan. Thereupon Elijah took his mantle and, rolling it up, he struck the water; it divided to the right and left, so that the two of them crossed over on dry land. As they were crossing, Elijah said to Elisha, "Tell me, what can I do for you before I am taken from you?" Elisha answered, "Let a double portion of your spirit pass on to me." "You have asked a difficult thing," he said. "If you see me as I am being taken from you, this will be granted to you; if not, it will not." As they kept on walking and talking, a fiery chariot with fiery horses suddenly appeared and separated one from the other; and Elijah went up to heaven in a whirlwind. Elisha saw it, and he cried out, "Oh, father, father! Israel's chariots and horsemen!" When he could no longer see him, he grasped his garments and rent them in two.

> The ascent of Elijah is the primary model for all subsequent accounts of heavenly journeys. This even includes the tradition about Enoch having been taken up into heaven in a fiery chariot, based on the interpretations of *Enoch walked with God; then he was no more, for God took him* (Gen. 5:24). The talmudic tale of the four who entered *Pardes* (B. *Hagigah* 14b) is also indebted to the ascent imagery of this biblical account. See "The Four Who Entered Paradise," following.
>
> As important as is the ascent of Elijah, equally important is the loyalty of Elisha, demonstrated here, and the transfer of Elijah's mantle to his disciple.
>
> *Sources:*
> 2 Kings 2:1-12.

208. THE FOUR WHO ENTERED PARADISE

Four sages entered Paradise—Ben Azzai, Ben Zoma, *Aher*, and Rabbi Akiba. Ben Azzai looked and died. Ben Zoma looked and lost his mind. *Aher* cut himself off from his fathers and became an apostate. Only Rabbi Akiba entered and departed in peace.

It is said that when Ben Azzai passed through the palaces of heaven and saw with his own eyes the glory of the celestial palace, his body could not endure it, and his soul could not tear itself away, for he felt that he had returned to his true home at last. And that is how he took leave of this world.

About *Aher* it is said that when he ascended on high, he reached the realm of the angel Metatron, whom he saw seated on a throne. In great confusion he cried out "There are—God forbid—two powers in heaven!" and from that moment he lost his faith. Then God commanded Metatron to be lashed sixty times with a fiery whip for not showing *Aher* that he was wrong.

In those days Ben Zoma was seen walking down a road by a rabbi and his students. They greeted him, but Ben Zoma did not respond. Finally the rabbi asked, "Where have you been, Ben Zoma?" And Ben Zoma replied: "I was contemplating the Mysteries of Creation. I learned that between the upper waters and the lower waters there are but three finger-breadths." Hearing this, the rabbi said to his students: "Ben Zoma is gone." Nor did Ben Zoma live long after that.

When Rabbi Akiba ascended to heaven, he made signs at the entrance of heaven so that he could find his way back. When he arrived at the *Pargod*, the celestial curtain, the angels of destruction came out to injure him. Then a heavenly voice issued from beneath the throne of glory, which said, "Leave this elder alone. He is worthy of gazing at My glory." And there, in the highest heaven, before the Throne of Glory, God's holy and secret Name was revealed to him.

Four sages entered Paradise. But only Rabbi Akiba ascended on high, passed through the palaces of heaven, and descended in peace.

> This brief, ambiguous legend about the four sages who entered *Pardes* is one of the central mystical tales in the Jewish tradition. It became the focus of opposing traditions—those who saw it as the model for mystical contemplation and heavenly ascent, as found in the *Hekhalot* texts, and those who saw in its conclusion, in which three of the four greatest talmudic sages are somehow harmed, a warning that such contemplation and/or ascent was gravely dangerous and that the study of mystical texts should be limited to those who were well-grounded. But the tale of the four who entered Paradise (for this is how it was commonly understood) impressed others in an entirely different way. For this legend also became an entry into the mysteries of *Pardes* by an esoteric Jewish sect, who sought, by engaging in mystical contemplation, to discover the means to enter *Pardes*, which represented the heavenly Paradise. This is a form of contemplation of *Ma'aseh Merkavah*, or of the Mysteries of the Chariot, and such mystical ascent is paradoxically identified as a descent. The writings produced by this sect are called *Hekhalot* texts, since they describe travels through the palaces (*Hekhalot*) of heaven. They were written either to record their mystical experiences or to prepare a guidebook for ascent. To a large extent, the very ambiguity of the legend of the four sages is the reason for its primacy. Many have wondered what Ben Azzai saw that caused him to lose his life, what Ben Zoma saw that caused him to lose his mind, and what Elisha ben Abuyah (*Aher*) saw that caused him to "cut the shoots," i.e., become an apostate. There are clues in the Talmud concerning the fates of Ben Zoma and *Aher*, while the clues about Ben Azzai are found in *Leviticus Rabbah* and *Song of Songs Rabbah*, as noted. Ben Azzai's mysterious death has been linked to the mystical tradition of those who give up their souls without reservation during a mystical experience. This is equivalent to dying by the Kiss of the *Shekhinah*, as Moses did.

Gershom Scholem speculates that the Hekhalot sect actively engaged in techniques to induce mystical experiences, including the use of yogalike positions, and the singing of rhythmical hymns in unison for long periods of time. Standard Jewish practices of purification were also used, including the *mikveh* (ritual bath), fasting, and extensive prayer. Emphasis was also placed on the power of the word—on prayers, on amulets containing invocations, and, above all, the secret pronunciation of the Divine Name.

One of the unanswered questions about the heavenly ascent of the four sages is whether it was a bodily ascent or a soul ascent. Ben Zoma, for example, indicates that he knows exactly how much space exists between the upper waters and the lower waters. Did he gain this knowledge firsthand, by ascending to that place? An indication of the answer is found in *Midrash Tehillim* 19:4, where Rabbi Samuel bar Abba is quoted as having said, "I know the lanes of heaven as well as the lanes of Nehardea" (a city in Babylonia, the seat of a rabbinic academy). This midrash asks if Samuel meant that he had actually gone up into the firmament. The answer is no—rather, laboring at Torah's wisdom he learned from it what is in the firmament. Likewise, Rabbi Hoshaiah is quoted as saying, "Even as there is an empty space between the lower waters and the firmament, so there is an empty space between the upper waters and the firmament." The midrash again asks if Rabbi Hoshaiah meant that he had actually gone up into the upper heavens? The answer is no—by laboring at Torah's wisdom, he learned from it all that is in the upper heavens.

An interesting oral variant of the myth of the four who entered Paradise is IFA 13901. The four rabbis in this Moroccan story find the opportunity to go to heaven on Sukkot, when the sky opens for an instant, and an angel invites them to study kabbalah in Paradise. The fact that the four were invited to make this journey means their greatness had been recognized in Heaven, and that is why they were able to make such a blessed journey.

Sources:

B. *Hagigah* 14b-15a; *Tosefta Hagigah* 23; *Genesis Rabbah* 2:4; *Leviticus Rabbah* 16:4; *Song of Songs Rabbah* 1:10; *Y. Hagigah* 77a-b; *Hekhalot Zutartei*, #338-339, 246-248, from Ms. Munich 22, #344-348 from Ms. New York; Genizah fragment (TS K 21/95); *Magen Avot* 58b; IFA 13901.

Studies:

Rabbinic Literature and Greco-Roman Philosophy by Henry A. Fischel, pp. 1-34.
The Faces of the Chariot by David J. Halperin, pp. 7, 31-37, 194-210, 362.
Jewish Mystical Testimonies by Louis Jacobs, pp. 21-25.
"Paradise Revisited (2 Cor. 12:1-12): The Jewish Mystical Background of Paul's Apostolate. Part 1: The Jewish Sources" by C. R. A. Morray-Jones.
Jewish Gnosticism, Merkabah Mysticism, and Talmudic Tradition by Gershom Scholem, pp. 14-19.
Ascent to Heaven in Jewish and Christian Apocalypses by Martha Himmelfarb.
The Four Who Entered Paradise by Howard Schwartz. See Introduction, pp. xiii-xxxiii, and Commentary, pp. 125-203, by Marc Bregman.
Two Powers in Heaven: Early Rabbinic Reports about Christianity and Gnosticism by Alan F. Segal.
The Kiss of God: Spiritual and Mystical Death in Judaism by Michael Fishbane.

209. A VISION OF METATRON

There were four who entered Paradise. Elisha ben Abuyah was one of them. He ascended on high to gaze at the *Merkavah*, the Divine Chariot. When he reached the door of the seventh palace, he came into the presence of the angel Metatron, who was seated upon a high and lofty throne, wearing a crown. All the princes of the kingdom stood beside him, to his right and to his left, and from his throne Metatron ruled over all the other heavenly beings. Seeing this, Elisha began to quake, and his soul was confused and filled with fright. For Metatron was seated upon that throne like a king, with all the ministering angels standing by him as he presided over the Celestial Court and all the angels. In that instant Elisha opened his mouth and cried, "God forbid, there must be two powers in heaven!" Thereupon a heavenly voice went forth to say, "Return, you backsliding children, all except *Aher!*"

After that God commanded the angel Anafiel to punish Metatron with sixty fiery lashes for not rising when he saw Elisha, thus giving Elisha the false impression that there were two heavenly powers. As for Elisha, thereafter he became known as *Aher*, the Other, for at the instant he saw Metatron seated there, he lost his faith.

The two primary versions of this myth about *Aher* (Elisha ben Abuyah) becoming an apostate are found in the Talmud in *B. Hagigah* 15a and in *3 Enoch*. Elisha's shock on seeing Metatron in heaven derives primarily from the fact that he is seated, since he had believed that no sitting was allowed in heaven except for God, seated on His Throne of Glory. Thus Elisha identifies Metatron as a "Lesser *Yahweh*," a demiurgic figure. And for the Enoch sect, in particular, Enoch/Metatron does play a remarkably extensive role, for he serves as chief of the angels who carries out all of God's commands.

The rabbinic explanation for Metatron's being seated is that he is the heavenly scribe, whose job it is to record the merits of Israel. The version in *3 Enoch* elaborates on the godlike role Metatron plays, surrounded by ministering angels. Metatron's punishment of sixty fiery lashes demonstrates his subservience to God. It seems likely that Elisha's apostasy led him to become a Gnostic, whose primary belief was that there are two powers in heaven.

This myth is directly modeled after Daniel 7, where Daniel has a vision of the Ancient of Days, one of the names of God. Daniel's vision itself is directly based on Isaiah's vision in Isaiah 6:1-8. Here, however, Metatron has taken the place of God in Elisha's vision. This shows the extreme nature of the Metatron mythology, in which Metatron's role sometimes seems to eclipse that of God. Here, ironically, this is done by drawing on a biblical model. The talmudic version of this myth was likely intended as a warning against Gnosticism in general and speculations about Enoch/Metatron in particular. This accusation finds its answer in *3 Enoch,* dating from around the eighth century. It is fascinating to observe how this talmudic warning myth is incorporated in *3 Enoch* into the overall myth of Metatron, and slanted in a way to demonstrate that Elisha ben Abuyah failed to recognize Metatron's true role as God's second in command. But at the same time the myth is certainly intended to elevate the primary role of Metatron in the heavenly pantheon to one who is second only to God. See "The Four Who Entered Paradise," p. 173.

Anafiel, the angel who punishes Metatron, is the same angel who brought Enoch into heaven, where the metamorphosis into Metatron took place. Anafiel YHVH is one of the eight princes of heaven whose names include the Tetragrammaton, suggesting that they are an extension of God. Metatron's power is over all of the angels except for these eight princes.

Sources:
Tosefta Hagigah 2:4; *B. Hagigah* 15a; *3 Enoch* 16:1-5; *Testament of Abraham* 11:1-13:7;
    Schäfer #671-674 from Ms. Oxford 1531.

Studies:
Two Powers in Heaven by Alan Segal.
"Form(s) of God: Some Notes on Metatron and Christ" by Gedaliahu G. Stroumsa.
Four Powers in Heaven: The Interpretation of Daniel 7 in the Testament of Abraham by
    Phillip B. Munoa, III.
"*3 Enoch* and the Talmud" by P. S. Alexander.
The Faces of the Chariot by David J. Halperin.

210. RABBI ISHMAEL'S ASCENT

One of the Roman emperors called in ten of the finest sages and demanded to study the Torah with them. They began at the beginning of Genesis, and all went well until they reached the passage in Exodus that reads, *He who kidnaps a man, whether he has sold him or is still holding him, shall be put to death* (Exod. 21: 16). When he read this, the Emperor remembered how Joseph's brothers had sold him into slavery. Yet they had not been punished by death, as the law required.

The Emperor asked the sages if this ruling applied to Joseph's brothers, and they agreed that it did. Then he demanded that the law be fulfilled and the executions carried out. The sages tried to explain that Joseph's brothers had died long ago. The Emperor told them that he knew that the brothers could no longer be punished. But in that case, the punishment must be carried out on those who represented Joseph's brothers in that age. And he pointed to each of the ten sages and told them that surely none represented the leaders of the tribes of Israel more than they did.

Then the Emperor signed a decree commanding that the ten sages be put to death, among them Rabbi Akiba, Rabbi Ishmael, Rabbi Hananiah ben Teradion, and seven other of the greatest sages who ever lived.

All of the sages were placed in a cell together, so that none might escape before the execution was carried out. There in that cell they turned to Rabbi Ishmael and begged him to use the power of the Name to overturn the Emperor's decree, for they knew that he alone could do it. Rabbi Ishmael told them that he could indeed overturn the decree, but first they must find out if it was solely that of the Emperor, or if in condemning them the Emperor was carrying out a decree of the Holy One, blessed be He.

Then Rabbi Ishmael put on his *tallit* and *tefillin* and chanted a long prayer. And as he prayed, his soul ascended to the sixth heaven, where the angel Gabriel greeted him and asked to know why he had come there. Rabbi Ishmael told him of the Emperor's decree, and that he had ascended to learn if it were a Divine decree or not.

Then Gabriel swore that he had heard the decree pronounced from behind the *Pargod*, the heavenly curtain. But he told Rabbi Ishmael not to mourn, for the ten sages would shortly be reunited in Paradise. Meanwhile their martyrdom would free the world from the evil that had entered it when Joseph's brothers sold him into slavery. And when that terrible sin had been lifted from the world, one of the chains that held back the Messiah would be broken, and the days of the Messiah would be that much closer. Rabbi Ishmael was greatly comforted to learn this and accepted his fate at once. Then he and the angel Gabriel took their leave of each other, and Rabbi Ishmael returned to this world.

When he opened his eyes, Rabbi Ishmael saw that all of the other sages had gathered around him, waiting for his soul to return from on high. He told them at once all he had learned from the lips of the angel Gabriel. And when the other sages learned that they had been chosen to lift the sin of Joseph's brothers from the world, and to break one of the chains of the Messiah, they embraced their destiny. And one by one they went bravely to their deaths.

> While most texts describing heavenly journeys make the ascent the focus of the tale, "Rabbi Ishmael's Ascent" is a portion of a longer midrashic narrative known as "The Legend of the Ten Martyrs." Here ten of the most famous Jewish martyrs, including Rabbi Akiba and Rabbi Ishmael, are linked as victims of the same evil decree, even though historically they did not all live at the same time. Rabbi Ishmael then undertakes an ascent into Paradise to discover if this is actually a heavenly decree or not. If not, he has it within his power to overthrow the Emperor's decree by drawing on the power of God's Name. So far the tale reads like a fairy tale. If it had followed this pattern, Rabbi Ishmael would have learned that it was not a heavenly decree, and on his return he would have defeated the Emperor, saving himself and his fellow sages. But this account has fused the *Hekhalot*-type tale of ascent with the accounts of the deaths of these great sages culled from rabbinic sources, primarily from the Tal-

mud. Thus Rabbi Ishmael learns that heaven has approved the decree against the sages to erase the sin of Joseph's brothers in selling Joseph. Note that this explanation gives the deaths of the sages cosmic meaning, in righting what was perceived as an epic wrong in the Torah, in which Joseph's brothers are never punished for selling him into slavery. For it is clearly stated in the Torah that the punishment for such a sin is death: *He who kidnaps a man, whether he has sold him or is still holding him, shall be put to death* (Exod. 21:16). In "The Legend of the Ten Martyrs," it is the emperor who has commanded the sages to teach him the Bible, and it is the emperor who raises the question of whether or not Joseph's brothers were punished. But this was clearly a question on the minds of the rabbis, who scrutinized the events prior to the giving of the Torah for evidence that the laws were fulfilled. And even though the Emperor's linking of the sins of Joseph's brothers with the ten sages seems arbitrary and unreasonable, Hayim Vital states in *Etz Hayim* that the souls of the ten martyrs were born from ten drops of semen that came forth from Joseph, suggesting that for the kabbalists, at least, there was some justification to the Emperor's charge.

Also, the rabbis sought precedents for evil behavior in the biblical text. For example, they wanted to know how Cain died, which is not reported. In fact, there are four different versions of how Cain died that are found in the aggadic texts. See "The Death of Cain," p. 451. In "Rabbi Ishmael's Ascent" it is therefore possible to see the imprint of four basic kinds of Jewish narratives combined into one: 1) the tale of ascent; 2) the linking tale, which links key figures from various generations into a chain midrash; 3) the tale that responds to a specific point of the Law, in this case the punishment required for the sin of Joseph's brothers; and 4) the martyrological tale.

In addition, this tale can be seen to have major theological ramifications. It shifts the blame for the Roman oppression to God, much in the same way that the myth of the Ari shifts the blame for the Fall from Adam and Eve to God. This is a natural consequence of monotheism: if there is only one God, then everything that takes place must have been brought into being by that God, including evil acts. One strange notion found in this important tale is that it would be possible, indeed expected by God, that anyone other than Joseph's brothers be punished for their sin. Yet this is what the tale implies. This is an essentially kabbalistic premise. The sin of Joseph's brothers has cosmic implications; it created a taint in existence, much in the way that the person of Cain is transformed into a principle of evil in the kabbalah. Therefore the deaths of the ten martyrs have a meaning that transcends their earthly loss: a major taint has been removed from the world. From this perspective the deaths represent a monumental sacrifice, which has the effect of serving as a cosmic act of *tikkun*, of repair and restoration. (Note that this sacrifice has Christian overtones.)

The accounts of the deaths of the rabbis, drawn from diverse time periods and sources, are very moving. For example, Rabbi Haninah ben Teradion was burned along with the Torah: "They took him, wrapped him in the scroll of the Torah, placed bundles of branches around him and set him on fire. . . . His disciples called out, 'Rabbi, what do You see?' He answered: 'The parchments are being burnt but the letters are soaring on high'" (*B. A.Z.* 18a). The other rabbis who were martyred, in addition to Rabbi Ishmael, Rabbi Akiba, and Rabbi Haninah ben Teradion, include Rabbi Simeon ben Gamaliel, Rabbi Yehudah ben Bava, Rabbi Yehudah ben Dema, Rabbi Hutzpit, Rabbi Haninah ben Hakhinai, Rabbi Yeshivav the scribe, and Rabbi Eleazar ben Shammua. *Midrash Eleh Ezkerah* includes an interesting myth about Rabbi Ishmael that identifies the angel Gabriel as his true father. This myth makes the meeting of Rabbi Ishmael and Gabriel in Paradise much more meaningful. See "How Rabbi Ishmael Was Conceived," p. 201.

Sources:

Hekhalot Rabbati; Midrash Eleh Ezkerah in *Beit ba-Midrash*, 2: 64-72; *Midrash Rabbenu Bahya* on Genesis 44:12; *Etz Hayim, Sha'ar ha-Gilgulim, Hakdamah* 22; One version of this legend is the liturgical poem *Eleh Ezkerah,* included in the prayer book for Yom Kippur, and another poem, *Arzei ha-Levanon Adirei ha-Tovah,* is recited on the Ninth of Av.

Studies:

Rabbinic Fantasies, edited by David Stern and Mark Mirsky.

211. THE ENTRANCE OF THE SIXTH HEAVENLY PALACE

Those who ascend on high must beware at the entrance of the sixth *hekhal*, the sixth heavenly palace. It appears as if it were engulfed by a sea of waves, but anyone who cries out, "Water, water!" is in grave danger. For there is not even a drop of water, only the radiance of pure marble stones, more awe-inspiring than water. Furthermore, the door-keepers of the sixth palace destroy all those who arrive there without permission.

Those warlike doorkeepers, the angels Dumiel and Kaspiel, are taller than mountains, and sharper than peaks. Their bows are strung and stand before them; their swords are sharpened and in their hands. Lightning issues forth from their eyes, and spider webs of fire from their nostrils, and torches of fiery coals from their mouths. And they are equipped with helmets and coats of mail, and javelins and spears are hung upon their muscles. These gatekeepers would destroy all those who arrive there without permission.

It is said of Ben Azzai that he reached the entrance of the sixth heavenly palace and saw the radiance of the light of the pure marble stones. He called out, "Water, water," and in a wink the doorkeeper who guards that gate cut off his head. This became a sign for all generations, not to err at the entrance of the sixth *hekhal*.

Only those who are protected by the angel Lumiel by reason of righteousness will be able to pass beyond the doorkeeper of the sixth palace. For the angel bears a gift for those who deserve it. It is not a gift of silver and not a gift of gold, but it grants the one who "descends" to the *Merkavah* the privilege that he should not be questioned, not in the first palace and not in the second, not in the third palace and not in the fourth, and not in the fifth palace or the sixth, and not in the seventh. But Lumiel shows the seal to the proper angels, and the one who ascends is able to go on to the next gate.

Of all the dangers of trying to ascend to Paradise (paradoxically known as "descending to the *Merkavah*"), the greatest lurks at the entrance of the sixth gate. This gate is guarded by the dangerous angels Dumiel (Divine silence) and Kaspiel (Divine wrath). In *Hekhalot Rabbati* the death of Ben Azzai recorded in *B. Hagigah* 14b is recounted as having taken place at the sixth gate, when the doorkeeper cut off his head. (Other texts offer different explanations, most of them less violent.) The secret to passing beyond the gate of the sixth heaven and thereby being able to enter the seventh heaven, *Aravot*, is to be held by the angel Lumiel, who bears a seal that makes it possible to pass beyond all of the doorkeepers without being questioned. This seal is only available to the very righteous. This would suggest that of the four sages who entered Paradise, as recounted in *B. Hagigah* 14b, only Rabbi Akiba, who entered and departed in peace, was righteous enough to deserve this seal. *Hekhalot Rabbati* asks: "What is it like to know the secret of the *Merkavah*? It is like having a ladder in one's house and being able to go up and down at will." Gershom Scholem has found an echo of the these heavenly gatekeepers in Kafka's famous parable, "Before the Law." See this story on p. 179. See "The Four Who Entered Paradise," p. 173.

Sources:
B. Hagigah 14b; *Hekhalot Zutarti* #408-410; *Hekhalot Rabbati* 15, 17, 19.

Studies:
"Observations on *Hekhalot Rabbati*" by Morton Smith.
The Ancient Jewish Mysticism by Joseph Dan.
Heavenly Journeys: A Study of the Motif in Hellenistic Jewish Literature by Mary Dean-Otting.
Jewish Gnosticism, Merkabah Mysticism and Talmudic Tradition by Gershom Scholem.
"Heavenly Ascent and the Relationship of the Apocalypses and the *Hekhalot* Literature" by Martha Himmelfarb.
Ascent to Heaven in Jewish and Christian Apocalypses by Martha Himmelfarb.

212. BEFORE THE LAW

Before the Law stands a man guarding the door. To this doorkeeper comes a man from the country who asks to be admitted to the Law. But the doorkeeper says that he cannot grant him entry. The man thinks about it and asks if, in that case, he will be permitted to enter later. "Possibly," says the doorkeeper, "but not now."

As the gateway to the Law is, as always, open, and the doorkeeper steps aside, the man stoops to look within. When the doorkeeper sees this, he laughs and says, "If it tempts you that much, just try to get in. But be aware that I am mighty. And I am only the lowliest doorkeeper. From hall to hall there are doorkeepers, each mightier than the one before. Even I can no longer bear the sight of the third of these."

The man from the country has not expected such difficulties. Surely, he thinks, the Law ought to be accessible to everybody, always, but now as he looks more carefully at the doorkeeper, with his big pointed nose and long, thin, black Tatar beard, he decides he'd rather wait for permission to enter. The doorkeeper gives him a stool and has him sit down beside the door. There he sits for days and for years. He often tries to be admitted, and wearies the doorkeeper with his pleas. The doorkeeper frequently questions him, asks him about where he comes from and many other things, but they are distant inquiries, the sort great men make, and in the end he always says that he cannot let him in yet. The man, who has equipped himself for his journey with many things, employs everything, however valuable, to bribe the doorkeeper. He takes it all, saying however, "I accept this only so you won't think you've failed to do anything."

All these long years the man watches the doorkeeper unceasingly. He forgets the other doorkeepers, and this first one seems to be the only obstacle between him and the Law. He curses his miserable luck, at first recklessly and loudly; later, as he grows old, he only grumbles to himself. He becomes childish, and since his years of scrutiny of the doorkeeper have enabled him to recognize even the fleas in his fur collar, he asks even the fleas to help change the doorkeeper's mind. Finally his eyes grow feeble, and he doesn't know if it's really getting darker around him or if his eyes are only tricking him. But in the darkness he now observes an inextinguishable radiance streaming out of the door of the Law.

Now he will not live much longer. Before he dies all he has been through converges in his mind into one question that he has never yet asked the doorkeeper. He signals to him, as he can no longer raise his stiffening body. The doorkeeper has to bend down low to him, as their difference in size has altered, much to the man's disadvantage. "What do you want to know now?" asks the doorkeeper. "There's no satisfying you." "Everyone struggles to reach the Law," says the man. "How can it be that in all these years no one but me has asked to get in?" The doorkeeper recognizes that the man's life is almost over and, because his hearing is failing, he roars at him, "No one else could be allowed in here. This entrance was intended only for you. I am now going to close it."

> This famous parable by Kafka from *The Trial* can be read as a religious allegory or as an allegory of human justice. Although it is generally thought of more in terms of the latter, it has the distinct elements of a religious allegory. The key image is that "of an inextinguishable radiance streaming out of the door of the Law." This clearly suggests the eternal nature of the Law, which, of course, draws this eternal quality from God. This shifts the focus of the parable from human justice to the need for divine justice, and hints at the remoteness of God.
>
> The doorkeeper guarding the gate to the Law is reminiscent of the angel placed at the gate of the Garden of Eden, with the flaming sword that turned every way, *to guard the way to the tree of life* (Gen. 3:24). Also echoed is the popular Christian conception of St. Peter serving as the doorkeeper at the Gates of Heaven.

Gershom Scholem has said that there are three pillars of Jewish mystical thought: the Bible, the *Zohar*, and the writings of Kafka. Thus he viewed Kafka's writings, which have been interpreted in a multitude of ways, as mystical texts. Scholem pointed out parallels between "Before the Law" and passages in the *Hekhalot* texts about angels guarding the gates of the palaces of heaven. For a description of these angels, see "The Entrance of the Sixth Heavenly Palace," p. 178. Compare this description with Kafka's description of the doorkeeper in "Before the Law." The parallels are striking, but since this *Hekhalot* text was little known during Kafka's lifetime, it is not likely that he had direct knowledge of it. Moshe Idel also identifies the quest in this tale as the remnant of a mystical one. See *Kabbalah: New Perspectives*, p. 271.

Another perspective is suggested by *Zohar* 1:7b: *Open the gates of righteousness for me . . . . This is the gateway to the Lord* (Ps. 68:19-20). Assuredly, without entering through that gate one will never gain access to the most high King. Imagine a king greatly exalted who screens himself from the common view behind gate upon gate, and at the end, one special gate, locked and barred. Said the king: "He who wishes to enter into my presence must first of all pass through that gate."

Another parallel is found in Ibn Gabirol's eleventh century treatise, *The Book of the Selection of Pearls* (ch. 8): "The following laconic observations are said to have been addressed to a king, by one who stood by the gate of the royal palace, but who failed to obtain access. First: Necessity and hope prompted me to approach your throne. Second: My dire distress admits of no delay. Third: My disappointment would gratify the malice of my enemies. Fourth: Your acquiescence would confer advantages, and even your refusal would relieve me from anxiety and suspense."

Max Brod, Kafka's close friend and biographer, comments about this parable: "Kafka's deeply ironic legend 'Before the Law' is not the reminiscence or retelling of this ancient lore, as it would seem at first glance, but an original creation drawn deeply from his archaic soul. It is yet another proof of his profound roots in Judaism, whose potency and creative images rose to new activities in his unconscious." (*Johannes Reuchlin und sein Kampf*, Stuttgart: 1965, pp. 274-275).

Of course, "Before the Law" can also be read as a personal statement of the kind of obstruction Kafka experienced at the hands of his father. The role of the gatekeeper can also be identified with Kafka's mother, for Kafka gave his mother the epic letter he wrote to his father, to pass on to him, but she decided not to do so. In such a reading Kafka's father represents the Law, the strict, godlike figure. See Kafka's *Letter to His Father*.

Also, Kafka's parable is relevant to human justice, where, on many occasions, people have been denied justice by the very ones who were supposed to provide it for them. In doing so they perform the obstructive role of the gatekeeper, who was supposed to welcome the man from the country at the gate intended only for him, but instead prevented him from entering at all.

Readers may wonder why a modern parable by Franz Kafka has been included in a book of Jewish mythology. There are several reasons for this. Kafka's fiction possesses a strong mythic element, and scholars have become increasingly aware of the strong influence on it of Jewish tradition; Kafka's writing in general, and this parable in particular, has taken on the qualities of a sacred text in our time; and there are strong parallels between this parable and traditional Jewish myths about the quest to reach God, but also a strong element of doubt in Kafka's parable that reflects the modern era. Just as the evolution of Jewish mythology did not end with the canonization of the Bible or the Talmud, and continued to flourish in the kabbalistic and hasidic era, so too it can be seen to continue in the modern era in the writings of Kafka. It also can be found in other seminal Jewish authors, such as I. L. Peretz, S. Y. Agnon, Bruno Schulz, and I. B. Singer.

Sources:
The Trial by Franz Kafka.

Studies:
Kafka and Kabbalah by Karl-Erich Grozinger.
"Kafka and Jewish Folklore" by Iris Bruce.

213. A JOURNEY TO THE STARS

It once happened on a voyage that a giant wave picked up the ship in which Rabbah bar Bar Hannah was a passenger and lifted it so high that he could see the resting place of the smallest star. It appeared to him like a field large enough to plant forty measures of mustard seeds. And if the wave had lifted them any higher, they would have been burned by the heat of the star.

> The tall tales of Rabbah bar Bar Hannah recount astonishing events that occurred during his land and sea journeys. Here he encounters a giant wave that lifts the ship so high it almost reaches a star. For other examples of Rabbah's tall tales, see "Fiery Waves," p. 104; "Where Heaven and Earth Meet," p. 194; and "The Dead of the Desert," p. 471.
>
> *Sources:*
> *Bava Batra* 73a.

214. A JEWISH ICARUS

Yozel Frandrik was a wonder child, born in the days of the Temple. He could speak from the time he was born. When he was still a child, he crept into the Temple and cut off the *Shem ha-Meforash*, the Ineffable Name of God. Then he took a knife and made a cut in his foot and put the Name inside it, and sewed it shut. At that instant he grew wings, and after that there was nothing he could not accomplish.

He flew like a bird and ascended on high, until he was flying with the angels. But an angel poured water on his feet, making him impure. All at once his magic powers left him, his wings fell off, and he tumbled to the ground. He could not fly any more after that, but he never returned the Ineffable Name, and no one knows where it is to this day.

> This is a highly unusual oral myth collected in Israel by the Israel Folktale Archives. It is a fantasy about a strange wonder child, Yozel Frandrik. He is said to have lived in the Temple period. In an act both daring and outrageous, he steals into the Temple and cuts off God's Name, YHVH, known as the *Shem ha-Meforash*. Using powers of kabbalistic wizardry, he implants the Name of God in his foot, and he immediately grows wings. Flying through the heavens, he provokes the anger of the angels, and one of them pours water on his foot, making him impure. This causes him to lose all powers and fall from heaven, just as happens to Icarus.
>
> Indeed, this myth has all the earmarks of a Jewish Icarus. Icarus, flying with wax wings created by his father, Dedalus, flew too close to the sun, causing the wings to melt and for him to plunge to his death. Yozel Frandrik also does forbidden things, in this case cutting off God's Name from the Temple, then implanting the Name in his foot, which is another desecration of the Name. Still, like Moses when he struck the rock instead of spoke to it, the magic works—the power of the Name causes Yozel to grow wings. In this case, his fall from heaven is not due to melting wings, but to an angel purposely rendering him impure, in order to sap him of his powers. This indeed is what takes place, although Yozel survives. Nor does he give the Name back. Thus he is portrayed as unrepentant to the end.
>
> David J. Halperin, in a private communication, suggests another perspective: "To my mind, there is no doubt at all that this tale is rooted in the anti-Christian *Toledot Yeshu* tradition of the Middle Ages. Yozel Frandrik is none other than Jesus. His name is a corruption of 'Yeshu (ben) Pandira,' the standard rabbinic designation for Jesus. In the *Toledot Yeshu* tradition, Jesus sneaks into the Temple and learns the letters of God's Name from the Foundation Stone. He writes the Name on parchment, which he smuggles out of the Temple by concealing it in an incision he has made in his thigh. Later he flies up to heaven; Rabbi Judah Ish Bartota (=Judas Iscariot, presumably)

flies up after him. After an inconclusive aerial dogfight between the two, Judah delib-
erately ejaculates his semen onto Jesus, with the result that Jesus becomes impure and
falls down to earth. The parallels with 'Yozel Frandrik' seem to me overwhelming."

In another text, *Megillat Ahimaaz*, a dead man is brought to life when God's Name,
which on a parchment, is implanted in his arm. However, such apparent life leaves
the man without a soul, and unable to pronounce God's Name during prayers. It is
this inability that gives him away. See "The Young Man Without a Soul" in *Gabriel's
Palace*, pp. 145-148. A parallel use of the Name to bring the dead to life is found in the
Ma'aseh Buch #171, where a killer is brought to life to confess his sin.

Sources:
IFA 4591.

215. EZEKIEL'S VISION

In the thirtieth year, on the fifth day of the fourth month, when I was in the community of
exiles by the Chebar Canal, the heavens opened and I saw visions of God. On the fifth
day of the month—it was the fifth year of the exile of King Jehoiachin—the word of the
Lord came to the priest Ezekiel son of Buzi, by the Chebar Canal, in the land of the
Chaldeans. And the hand of the Lord came upon him there.

I looked, and lo, a stormy wind came sweeping out of the north—a huge cloud and
flashing fire, surrounded by a radiance; and in the center of it, in the center of the fire, a
gleam as of amber. In the center of it were also the figures of four creatures. And this was
their appearance:

They had the figures of human beings. However, each had four faces, and each of
them had four wings; the legs of each were fused into a single rigid leg, and the feet of
each were like a single calf's hoof; and their sparkle was like the luster of burnished
bronze. They had human hands below their wings. The four of them had their faces and
their wings on their four sides. Each one's wings touched those of the other. They did not
turn when they moved; each could move in the direction of any of its faces.

Each of them had a human face in front; each of the four had the face of a lion on the
right; each of the four had the face of an ox on the left; and each of the four had the face of
an eagle at the back. Such were their faces. As for their wings, they were separated: above,
each had two touching those of the others, while the other two covered its body. And
each could move in the direction of any of its faces; they went wherever the spirit impelled them to go, without turning when they moved.

Such then was the appearance of the creatures. With them was something that looked
like burning coals of fire. This fire, suggestive of torches, kept moving about among the
creatures; the fire had a radiance, and lightning issued from the fire. Dashing to and fro
among the creatures was something that looked like flares.

As I gazed on the creatures, I saw one wheel on the ground next to each of the four-faced
creatures. As for the appearance and structure of the wheels, they gleamed like beryl. All
four had the same form; the appearance and structure of each was as of two wheels cutting
through each other. And when they moved, each could move in the direction of any of its
four quarters; they did not veer when they moved. Their rims were tall and frightening, for
the rims of all four were covered all over with eyes. And when the creatures moved forward, the wheels moved at their sides; and when the creatures were borne above the earth,
the wheels were borne too. Wherever the spirit impelled them to go, they went—wherever
the spirit impelled them—and the wheels were borne alongside them; for the spirit of the
creatures was in the wheels. When those moved, these moved; and when those stood still,
these stood still; and when those were borne above the earth, the wheels were borne alongside them—for the spirit of the creatures was in the wheels.

Above the heads of the creatures was a form: an expanse, with an awe-inspiring gleam as of crystal, was spread out above their heads. Under the expanse, each had one pair of wings extended toward those of the others; and each had another pair covering its body. When they moved, I could hear the sound of their wings like the sound of mighty waters, like the sound of Shaddai, a tumult like the din of an army. When they stood still, they would let their wings droop. From above the expanse over their heads came a sound. When they stood still, they would let their wings droop.

Above the expanse over their heads was the semblance of a throne, in appearance like sapphire; and on top, upon this semblance of a throne, there was the semblance of a human form. From what appeared as his loins up, I saw a gleam as of amber—what looked like a fire encased in a frame; and from what appeared as his loins down, I saw what looked like fire. There was a radiance all about him. Like the appearance of the bow that shines in the clouds on a day of rain, such was the appearance of the surrounding radiance. That was the appearance of the semblance of the Presence of the Lord. When I beheld it, I flung myself down on my face. And I heard the voice of someone speaking.

> Ezekiel's vision, which opens the Book of Ezekiel, is intended to be understood as a sign that God is about to withdraw his protection of the Temple and of Jerusalem. It is hard to understate the importance of this strange vision of the Divine Chariot (*Merkavah*). The description of the chariot became the basis for an entire branch of Jewish mysticism, what is known as *Ma'aseh Merkavah*, or Mysteries of the Chariot. (The other branch is *Ma'aseh Bereshit*, Mysteries of the Creation.) In the Mishnah, strict limitations are placed on the study of these two mystical branches: "*Ma'aseh Bereshit* may not be expounded in the presence of two, nor the *Merkavah* in the presence of one, unless he is wise and understanding" (*Mishnah Hag.* 2.1). It is clear that the rabbis didn't want those who were untutored in mystical principles to delve too deeply into these esoteric studies. For an example of how careful the rabbis were in discussing *Ma'aseh Merkavah*, see the next entry, "Mysteries of the Chariot."
>
> Ezekiel's vision is one of the most difficult portions in the Bible, yet it is also regarded as a detailed revelation of divine secrets. Those who sought to expound it believed that it revealed the secrets of the angelic realms, of God's throne, and even of God Himself. The Divine Chariot Ezekiel sees is also God's Throne of Glory. Somehow God's Throne and Chariot are fused into one, traveling to earth yet remaining in its place in heaven.
>
> This vision inspired subsequent literary descriptions of heavenly journeys, and this genre of Jewish mystical texts is known as *Hekhalot* texts, and includes such important works as *Hekhalot Rabbati* and *3 Enoch*. Most of these texts involve the ascent of either Rabbi Ishmael or Rabbi Akiba. David J. Halperin's *The Faces of the Chariot* is the most extensive study of the literature of *Ma'aseh Merkavah*.
>
> *Sources:*
> Ezekiel 1:1-28
>
> *Studies:*
> *Jerusalem in the Book of Ezekiel* by Julie Galambush.
> *The Faces of the Chariot* by David J. Halperin.
> *The Heart and the Fountain: An Anthology of Jewish Mystical Experiences* by Joseph Dan.

216. MYSTERIES OF THE CHARIOT

Rabbi Yohanan ben Zakkai and his student, Rabbi Eleazar ben Arakh, once rode through a field on their donkeys. And Rabbi Eleazar said: "Please, rabbi, teach me something about the Mysteries of the Chariot."

"Surely you know that such mysteries may not be revealed to a single student, unless he is able to comprehend them on his own," said Rabbi Yohanan. "Therefore you may begin the discussion, and I will decide whether to speak of such secrets."

At that moment Rabbi Eleazar dismounted from his donkey, wrapped himself in his prayer shawl, and sat down beneath an olive tree. "Why did you dismount?" asked Rabbi Yohanan, surprised. Rabbi Eleazar replied: "When we discuss *Ma'aseh Merkavah*, the Mysteries of the Chariot, the *Shekhinah* descends to listen, accompanied by many angels. Should I, then, be seated upon a donkey?"

Rabbi Eleazar then began to discourse upon these very mysteries, and as he spoke a circle of fire descended from heaven to surround that field, and a song of praise rose up from the trees. And in the center of that circle an angel appeared, who stood before them and said: "Indeed, these are the very same Mysteries of the Chariot that are spoken of behind the *Pargod*." Then the angel disappeared, and they heard nothing more than the wind.

At that moment Rabbi Yohanan turned to his student and kissed him on the forehead. "How blessed is God to have a son like Abraham, and how blessed is Abraham to have a son such as you, Rabbi Eleazar."

Rabbi Yehoshua learned of this incident from Rabbi Yossi ha-Kohen while they were also traveling along a road. They too agreed to stop and discuss the Mysteries of the Chariot. All at once the skies became covered with clouds and a splendid rainbow appeared. And the rabbis saw that clusters of angels had gathered around to listen, like guests at a wedding who rejoice with the bride and groom.

Later Rabbi Yossi told Rabbi Yohanan ben Zakkai what had happened. And Rabbi Yohanan replied: "Fortunate are we to have been so blessed. And now I know why I dreamed last night that you and I were sitting together on Mount Sinai when we heard a heavenly voice telling us to rise, for magnificent palaces and golden beds awaited us in Paradise, where we were to join the souls that sit before the Divine Presence."

> There are two primary categories of early kabbalistic contemplation: those linked to *Ma'aseh Bereshit* or The Work of Creation, and those linked to *Ma'aseh Merkavah*, or The Work of the Chariot. The former focuses on the mystical meaning of Creation as described in Genesis, and the latter on the vision of Ezekiel. Here the discussion of Ezekiel's vision and its mystical implications invokes yet another vision, shared by two rabbis, of angels dancing in a field. In many ways this talmudic tale defines the essential kabbalistic experience, presenting it in a positive and powerful fashion, and making it clear that Jewish mysticism is not merely a text-oriented study, but involves actual mystical experiences. Rabbi Yohanan ben Zakkai was one of the great talmudic sages, but here the sage accompanying him is the one who invokes the mystical vision. This tale serves as a primary model for many tales found in the Zohar, where two or more rabbis discover that the lowly Jew who is traveling with them is actually a hidden saint, who reveals great kabbalistic mysteries to them, or invokes a mystical vision.
>
> *Sources*:
> Y. *Hagigah* 77a; B. *Hagigah* 14.
>
> *Studies*:
> *The Merkabah in Rabbinic Literature* by David J. Halperin.
> *The Faces of the Chariot* by David J. Halperin.

217. THE SEVEN HEAVENS

There are seven heavens. The first serves to renew the work of Creation every day. The second is that in which the sun and moon and stars and constellations are set. In the third millstones grind manna for the righteous. In the fourth is the heavenly Jerusalem, where the Temple and altar are built. There Michael, Israel's guardian angel, makes offerings. In the fifth heaven there are companies of the ministering angels who are silent by day and utter divine songs at night.

In the sixth heaven are stored the treasuries of snow and hail, and the lofts of dews and raindrops, the chambers of whirlwind and storm, the cave of vapor and the doors of fire. The seventh is the highest heaven, *Aravot*, where are found the treasuries of peace and blessing, the souls of the righteous and the souls not yet created, as well as the dew with which God will revive the dead. So too are there many kinds of angels, the Ofanim and the Seraphim and the holy living creatures and the ministering angels. And the Throne of God, high and exalted, dwells over them all.

In Jewish lore, the basic concepts of heaven and hell are elaborated, describing seven levels of heaven and seven levels of hell. In fact, there are also seven levels of the earth. The seven heavens are identified as *Vilon* (Curtain), *Raki'a* (Firmament), *Shehakim* (Clouds), *Zebul* (Lofty Dwelling), *Ma'on* (Dwelling), *Makhon* (Residence) and *Aravot* (Highest Heaven). This myth of the seven heavens attributes a specific function to each one. In more general terms, the souls of the righteous are said to ascend from the lower heavens to the higher ones as they become worthy of them. The higher the soul ascends, the closer it comes to God and to the palaces of the patriarchs and sages that are found in the highest heavens. According to Rabbi Meir ibn Gabbai in *Avodat ha-Kodesh* 27, the soul does not ascend to the highest heavens on the first attempt. Accustomed to living in the darkness of the body, it cannot endure the brilliance of the divine light. Therefore the soul stays in the lower *Gan Eden* until it gets used to this light, and then it ascends on high.

Sources:
B. *Hagigah* 12b-13a; *Avot de-Rabbi Natan* 37.

Studies:
Jewish Mystical Testimonies by Louis Jacobs.

218. THE EIGHTH HEAVEN

There are not only seven heavens, but there is even an eighth heaven. It is found above the heads of the living creatures, as it is said, *Above the heads of the creatures was a form: an expanse, with an awe-inspiring gleam as of crystal, was spread out above their heads* (Ezek. 1:22). This is the place where the most hidden mysteries are to be found. But it is not permitted to reveal any more about them, as it said, *The hidden things are for God, the revealed things are for our children* (Deut. 29:28).

While Jewish lore often speaks of seven heavens, and these are described in detail in various rabbinic texts and in the *Hekhalot* texts that recount heavenly journeys, little is said about an eighth heaven. But in *B. Hagigah* 13a, Rabbi Aha ben Jacob mentions the eighth heaven, which is described as being above the *hayot* or living creatures that hold up God's throne. This is the ultimate place of mysteries, and such mysteries could not be revealed: "The things that are the mystery of the world should be kept secret" (*B. Hag.* 13a). The existence of such an eighth heaven may be inferred since the living creatures in the seventh heaven hold up the Throne of Glory, and Ezekiel 1:13-14 describes a vast expanse that is understood to be another firmament (*raki'a*) above their heads.

This eighth heaven is an essential part of Gnostic speculation, where it is described as a power beyond the reach of the seven heavens. See *Poimandres* 26.

Sources:
B. *Hagigah* 13a.

Studies:
Jewish Gnosticism, Merkabah Mysticism and Talmudic Tradition by Gershom Scholem, pp. 65-74.
The Gnostic Scriptures translated by Bentley Layton, pp. 457-458.

219. THE *PARGOD*

There is an exceedingly wonderful curtain in Paradise, spread before God, which separates God from the angels. That curtain is entirely covered with supernal illuminations, forming the letters of the complete Name of God. All forms and representations in this world are depicted there, just the way they are in the world below. This curtain is known as the *Pargod*. Only God's Bride and the angel Metatron, Prince of the Presence, are permitted on God's side of the curtain. The deeds of all the generations of the world, past and present, are printed there, until the last generation.

When Rabbi Ishmael ascended on high, Metatron took him to the *Pargod*. There Metatron pointed out all the generations that would follow, like a father teaching his son the letters of the Torah. And there Rabbi Ishmael witnessed all the generations from the time of Adam until the days of the Messiah, and all of their deeds were recounted there. Not only did he witness these deeds with his own eyes, but he experienced them as if they were taking place.

After witnessing all of the generations printed on that heavenly curtain, Rabbi Ishmael opened his mouth, saying, *How many are the things You have made, O Lord; the earth is full of Your creations* (Ps. 104:24).

> *3 Enoch* records Rabbi Ishmael's ascent into heaven, led by the angel Metatron, the Prince of the Presence. As part of his tour of heaven, Metatron takes him to the *Pargod*, the curtain that separates God from the angels. This curtain is the heavenly counterpart of the curtain that separated the Holy of Holies in the earthly Tabernacle and Temple. (See Exodus 26:31 and 2 Chronicles 3:14.)
>
> This myth demonstrates that God, and the mysteries of God, are hidden even from the angels, except for Metatron. Just as humans are not supposed to view God face to face, neither are the angels. There are occasional exceptions to this rule, whereby, for example, Moses ascends to the Throne of Glory and speaks to God face to face (*B. Men.* 29b and *B. Shab.* 88b-89a). The *Pargod* is also known as *Pargod ha-Makom*—the Curtain of the Place of God. The identification of *Makom* as the place of God comes from the dream of Jacob, when he said, *This is none other than the abode of God, and that is the gateway to heaven* (Gen. 28:17) The term *Makom* is also a designation for God, and is often translated as "God Almighty."
>
> In this myth, the *Pargod* is the curtain that God is hidden behind, which has printed on it the history of all generations from the first to the last. Thus the whole course of human history has already been determined in the heavenly realm and has been pre-ordained by God. This motif of God's foreknowledge of all generations is also found in *The Book of Raziel*, p. 253 and in the myths about the pre-existence of the Torah. See "Seven Things Created Before the Creation," p. 74.
>
> *Shloyshe Sheorim* describes a heavenly curtain that separates the men from the women in Paradise. See "Women in Paradise," p. 190.
>
> *Sources:*
> B. Yoma 77a; B. Berakhot 18b; B. Hagigah 15a; B. Sanhedrin 89b; B. Sota. 49a; 3 Enoch 45:1-6; Pirkei de-Rabbi Eliezer 4, 6; Zohar 1:47a, 2:149b-150a; Shloyshe Sheorim; Masekhet Hekhalot 7; Seder Gan Eden in Beit ha-Midrash 3:135; Ma'ayan Hokhmah in Otzar Midrashim pp. 306-311.

220. THE MAP OF TIME AND SPACE

There is a king who possesses a map of all the worlds. It is shaped like a hand, with five fingers and lines, like a real hand. Everything that has existed or will ever exist until the end of time is illustrated on this hand. The lines and wrinkles of the hand illustrate the structure of all the worlds, just like a map. Every nation and city is illustrated there, along with all the rivers, bridges, and mountains. All the people who live in those nations and everything they experience are illustrated on that hand, even the roads from one nation to another. So too are the pathways from earth to heaven delineated, as well as the pathways between one world and the next. Enoch ascended to heaven on one pathway, while Moses went to heaven on another, and Enoch went to heaven on yet another path, and all of these pathways are also illustrated there. Thus everything is illustrated on that hand: what was, what is, and what will be.

> This is an intriguing allegory by Rabbi Nachman of Bratslav in which a king—who is surely God—possesses an object in the shape of a map that portrays everything that has existed or will exist. This map of time and space likely represents the *Pargod*, the mythical curtain in Paradise that separates God from the angels. One side of this curtain is said to portray all of the past and future, exactly as does this map. See "The *Pargod*," p. 186.
>
> *Sources:*
> *Sippurei Ma'asiyot.*

221. THE PLACE OF THE STARS

The stars in the firmament have fiery bodies, like angels, and they are gathered in the Place of the Stars. When Metatron, Prince of the Presence, took Rabbi Ishmael on a tour of heaven, he showed him that place. As Rabbi Ishmael walked by his side, hand in hand, Metatron pointed out the stars standing like fiery sparks around the *Merkavah*, the very Throne and Chariot of God Almighty, surrounding it on every side.

At that moment Metatron clapped his hands, and chased the stars away from there. They flew off with flaming wings, and fled from the four sides of God's Throne, and as the stars flew by, Metatron told Rabbi Ishmael the name of every single one of them, as it is said, *He reckoned the number of the stars; to each He gave its name* (Ps. 147:4). For God had given every one of them a name.

All the stars in the firmament are counted by the angel Rahatiel, for they are the handiwork of God. They come forth to be counted in order to praise God with songs and hymns, as it is said, *The heavens declare the glory of God* (Ps. 19:1).

But in the time to come God will create them anew, and they will open their mouths and utter a song to the Lord.

> In this celestial myth, the stars are regarded as animate beings, much like angels. Above all they are drawn to surround God's Throne, the *Merkavah*, which is also portrayed as a chariot. In this view, the stars, like the angels, exist primarily to praise God, and they are fully under the control of heaven, as indicated here by the ease with which Metatron claps his hand and they depart. *3 Enoch* is a treasure-trove of information about the fantastic geography of heaven. In later Jewish texts, such as those of Maimonides, this mythic view of the stars would be replaced by a speculative astrological view.
>
> *Sources*:
> *3 Enoch 46; Akedat Yitzhak 4.*

222. THE RAINBOW OF THE *SHEKHINAH*

The heavenly counterpart of the rainbow seen in the clouds is the rainbow of the *Shekhinah*, as it is said, *I have set My bow in the clouds* (Gen. 9:13). The arches of this rainbow are set above *Aravot*, the highest heaven, and clouds of the rainbow surround the Throne of Glory. Above the arches of the rainbow are the wheels of the *Merkavah*. The rainbow itself rests upon the shoulders of the angel Kerubiel, the Prince of the Cherubim. This angel has a mouth that is like a lamp of fire, a tongue of consuming fire, eyebrows like lightning, and eyes like sparks of brilliance. On his head there is a crown of holiness on which God's Name is engraved. Between his shoulders rests the rainbow of the *Shekhinah*, and the splendor of the *Shekhinah* is on his face.

> Here the rainbow of the *Shekhinah* is described as a heavenly counterpart of the earthly rainbow. Its sources can be found in Genesis 9:13 and in Ezekiel 1:28: *Like the appearance of the bow which shines in the clouds on a day of rain, such was the appearance of the surrounding radiance.* Ezekiel's vision also links the rainbow with the vision of the *Merkavah*: *Above the expanse over their heads was the semblance of a throne* (Ezek. 1:26).
>
> Building on the vision of Ezekiel, this divine rainbow is described as one of the heavenly splendors, in terms that link it to other mythic elements in the divine constellation. These include the Throne of Glory and the wheels of the *Merkavah*, the Divine Chariot. (Note that in Ezekiel's visions, there is some kind of combination of the identity of the Throne of Glory and the Divine Chariot.) These are known as "the wheels of the *Ophanim*." Imposed on all this is a gigantic angel, Kerubiel, Prince of the Cherubim, with the rainbow of the *Shekhinah* resting between his shoulders.
>
> The angel Kerubiel is described in terms almost identical to Metatron, the fiery angel who is the focus of *3 Enoch*. Both angels seem to represent the sun, which explains the strange image of the rainbow resting on the angel's shoulders, since the rainbow is seen when the rain has stopped and the sun has reemerged.
>
> *Sources*:
> *3 Enoch* 22:5, 22C:4, 22C:7.

223. THE MUSIC OF THE SPHERES

Heaven is always making music, with perfect harmony, created in accordance with its celestial motions, as it is said, *The heavens declare the glory of God* (Ps. 19:2). Some say the source of this music is an orchestra of angels. Others say it is the rhythm and melody of the planets and stars as they circle the heavens.

If, by chance, this music should reach our ears, irrepressible cravings would emerge, frenzied longings, and insane passions. These longings would be so great, we would no longer take nourishment from food and drink in the manner of mortals, but as beings destined for immortality.

This happened to Moses when he ascended Mount Sinai. There, for forty days and nights, he touched neither bread nor water. Soon the strains of this heavenly music reached his ears, along with the words of the Torah as God recited them. It is said that for the rest of his life Moses heard this unearthly music, just as the light that shone from his face after Sinai always remained with him.

> Here Philo draws on the Pythagorean concept of the music of the spheres. Philo's immediate source was probably an ancient midrash, which is found in *Sefer Hadar Zekenim Toratam shel Rishonim*. (See Ginzberg, *Legends*, 5:36, note 102.) However, its inclusion in his writings is consistent with his interest in Greek concepts. In the Greek view, music was believed to reflect divine harmony. The rhythm and melody of the heavenly bodies thus delineate the music of the spheres as well as reflect the moral order of the universe. The closest Jewish myth is that of the song of praise of the heavenly bodies, which grows out of Psalm 19:2: *The heavens declare the glory of Yahweh.* The progress of the sun in its circuit was said to produce a hymn of praise to God. See also *Zohar* 1:2316.

Linking the Greek concept of the music of the spheres with Moses creates a Jewish myth. Philo suggests that this music can only be heard by a disembodied soul, since it would otherwise drive mortals mad with passion. Since Moses did without food or drink while on Mount Sinai, he achieved this spiritual state, and thus was able to hear this heavenly music.

Sources:
Philo, *De Somniis* 1:35-36; *Sefer Hadar Zekenim Toratam shel Rishonim*.

224. THE TREASURY OF MERITS

There is a Treasury of Merits hidden in heaven. In that treasury there are rooms in which ledgers are kept that show the sorrows recorded there, all differing from one another. Nearby there are rooms with even greater hardships to be found—those destined to die by the sword, those destined to die by famine, those destined for captivity, those destined for disgrace. And every day there are added hardships more severe than these, but whenever Israel blesses God's Name, these hardships are not permitted to leave the room.

So too are there treasuries of comfort, where ministering angels sit and weave garments of salvation, making crowns of life and fixing precious stones and pearls to them. These, too, are intended for the Israelites. One crown has the sun and moon and twelve constellations fastened to it. This crown is intended for David, King of Israel.

When Moses was in heaven, God showed him all the treasuries that will be given to the righteous in the World to Come. Some of those treasuries were for those who obeyed God's commandments, others for those who took care of orphans. Among them Moses saw a very great treasury. He asked, "And to whom will this treasury be given?" God answered, "That is the Treasury of Gifts. I will give it to whomever I want."

> There are many myths about heavenly treasuries. The Treasury of Merits contains ledgers that keep track of sorrows and hardships. This reinforces the idea that God observes all that takes place in a person's life and credits them for their suffering and hardships. See "The Books of Life and Death," p. 289. So too are there treasuries of comfort, intended for the righteous in the World to Come. Moses encounters a mysterious, large treasury, which God identifies as the Treasury of Gifts, and God refuses to explain how He will determine who will receive those gifts. Rabbi Nachman of Bratslav identifies these free gifts as the life force. He states that this gift can only be received in idle moments. Therefore, even holy men need these idle moments to receive this life-force, which they then pass on to those who really need it. Thus for Rabbi Nachman times of leisure are just as sacred as times of prayer or study. In this he follows the pattern of his great-grandfather the Ba'al Shem Tov, who often took long walks in the forest. See "The Treasury of Souls," p. 166.
>
> *Sources*:
> *Hekhalot Rabbati*, ed. by Wertheimer (Jerusalem, 1890), 6:3-7:2 (3b-4a); *Beit ha-Midrash* 5:167-168; *Exodus Rabbah* 45:6; *Likutei Moharan* 2:78.

225. THE WINGS OF HEAVEN

The wings of heaven are tied to the wings of the land, and the wings of the land are tied to the wings of heaven, and sealed with God's name.

> This is an imaginative restatement of the primary kabbalistic principle that "as above, so below; as below, so above."
>
> *Sources*:
> *Midrash Konen* in *Beit ha-Midrash* 2:25.

226. THE PALACES OF HEAVEN

The mysteries of the Torah are not only contemplated in this world, but also in the World to Come, for genuine scholars do not cease their studies when they die. The souls of the righteous, along with the angels, continue to study Torah in the heavenly Garden of Eden. There each of the patriarchs and matriarchs and great sages has his or her own palace, where they teach myriads of students beneath tranquil canopies. It is possible to sit in the classroom of Maimonides, as well as the classroom of Rashi, the great commentator. Those who ascend even higher in heaven arrive at the palace of Moses, where the Torah is taught from the very lips of Moses. And those who ascend to the very highest heaven reach the palace of Abraham. And Abraham's mastery of the Torah is said to be so great that those who hear him weep tears of joy.

> One of the primary traditional rewards for the righteous souls who ascended to Paradise was the opportunity to study Torah with the greatest sages of all time, including the patriarchs and great talmudic masters. Some texts even describe the Messiah teaching Torah in his heavenly palace, and there are even texts in which God Himself teaches Torah to the souls of the righteous. See "The Ba'al Shem Tov Ascends on High," p. 209, and "God Teaches Torah in the World to Come," p. 271. See also "The Ocean of Tears," a folktale about a journey to the palaces of heaven, in *Reimagining the Bible*, pp. 157-159.
>
> *Sources*:
> *Seder Gan Eden* (version B) in *Beit ha-Midrash* 3:131-140; *Aderet Eliyahu* 2:4; *Sifram Shel Tzaddikim*; oral tradition, as recounted by Rabbi Shlomo Carlebach (1925-1994).

227. WOMEN IN PARADISE

There are six palaces in Paradise where the souls of the righteous women make their home. Each of these righteous women has a palace of her own. In each chamber there are beautiful canopies, with angels set over them, and every day they are crowned with the radiance of the *Shekhinah*.

The first palace is ruled by Bitiah, Pharaoh's daughter, who raised Moses as if he were her own son. She teaches the commandments of the Torah to the many thousands of myriads of pious women who are with her, and she serves as their queen. These women still maintain their human form, and they are clothed in garments of light, and there is great joy among them. Three times a day Bitiah goes to a place where there is a curtain, and bows before the image of Moses, saying, "Fortunate am I for drawing such a light out of the water."

The next palace is that of Serah bat Asher, who rules over thousands of myriads of righteous women. They busy themselves with praises of the Lord, and contemplate the commandments of the Torah. Three times a day Serah goes to a curtain and bows before the image of Joseph, saying, "Happy was the day on which I gave the good news about Joseph to my grandfather, Jacob."

The other palaces are presided over by Yocheved, the mother of Moses, Miriam the prophetess, the sister of Moses, and Deborah the prophetess. All day long the women are by themselves, as are the men, for there is a curtain spread out in Paradise that separates them. But every night they come together at midnight, for that is the hour of copulation. Then they cleave soul to soul and light to light, and the fruit of this union are the souls of those who become converts to Judaism.

Hidden deep within these six palaces are the four hidden palaces of the matriarchs, Sarah, Rebecca, Leah, and Rachel. No one can imagine what joy and purity are found there, for no one has seen these palaces, or is permitted to reveal anything about them.

> The righteous women in these heavenly palaces are those who never had to suffer the pains of Gehenna. Their souls went directly to Paradise at the time of their deaths. Those whose sins require that they first be purified in Gehenna, Jewish hell, are not permitted in these palaces.
>
> Although Bitiah, the daughter of Pharaoh, was not Jewish, she still has been inducted into the Jewish pantheon of righteous women in Paradise. Indeed, she rules over the first of six palaces devoted to the souls of righteous women. *Leviticus Rabbah* 1:3 explains that her name means "daughter of God" (*Bitiah*). According to the *Zohar*, the other women who rule over these heavenly palaces are Yocheved, Miriam, Deborah, and the four matriarchs. The last have hidden palaces within the six heavenly palaces of the righteous women. *Seder Gan Eden* adds Hulda the prophetess and Abigail to the list of righteous women.
>
> For more on Serah bat Asher informing Jacob that Joseph was alive, see "Serah bat Asher," p. 377.
>
> Sources:
> Zohar 3:167a-b; Shloyshe Sheorim; Sefer Ma'asei Adonai; Derekh Etz Hayim ve-Inyanei
>   Gan Eden, appended to Sefer Ma'aneh Lashon 152; Derekh ha-Yashar le-Olam ha-Ba
>   25; Seder Gan Eden (version B) in Beit ha-Midrash 3:131-140.
>
> Studies:
> Voices of the Matriarchs by Chava Weissler, pp. 76-85.

228. THE TENT OF THE SUN

It is a journey of five hundred years between one firmament to another, and the sun makes this journey covered with a tent, as it is said, *He placed in them a tent for the sun* (Ps. 19:5).

The sun rises in the east, riding forth in a chariot crowned as a bridegroom. Three letters of God's Name are written upon the heart of the sun, and angels lead it. His fiery face looks down upon the earth in the summer, but in winter the face of the sun turns icy, and were it not for fire, nothing would be able to endure. Thus the sun runs his course across the heavens, and as he sets in the west, the sun bows down before God, saying: "Master of the universe, I have fulfilled all Your commands."

At the End of Days God will roll open the upper firmament, and then God will remove the tent from the sun. On that day God will make a tent for the righteous and hide them in it from the searing heat of the Day of Judgment.

> Just as there are sun myths in other traditions, so too are there sun myths in Judaism. Here the sun is personified and rides in a chariot led by angels, much as Apollo guides the chariot of the rising sun. There are some beautiful details, such as three letters of God's Name written on the heart of the sun. The tent of the sun is elsewhere described as a sheath, as in *Midrash Tanhuma*, where it is said that "The sun is kept within its sheath, but during the Tammuz solstice, it emerges from its sheath to ripen fruits" (*Midrash Tanhuma, Ve-Atah Tetzaveh* 6). The purpose of this tent/sheath is to prevent the sun from incinerating the world: "The orb of the sun is kept within a sheath, in front of which there is a pool of water. When the sun comes out, God tempers its strength in the water, so that as it goes forth it will not incinerate the world" (*Genesis Rabbah* 6:6). The image of the sun's chariot derives from 2 Kings 23:11: *the chariots of the sun*. The rolling open of the upper firmament derives from the passage,

The heavens shall be rolled up like a scroll (Isa. 34:4). The tent of the sun is described (Y. A.Z. 3) as a pool of water set in front of the sun. When the sun comes forth, God diminishes the sun's power by immersing it in the water, so that it will not go out and consume the world.

The key images of this myth, including that of the tent of the sun and of the sun as a bridegroom grow out of Psalms 19:5-6: *He placed them in a tent for the sun, who is like a groom coming forth from his chamber, like a hero, eager to run his course.*

Note that the descriptions of the angel Metatron portray him in terms that seem identical to the sun, suggesting that the myth of Metatron may well be a remnant of a sun myth in Judaism. See "The Metamorphosis and Enthronement of Enoch," p. 156.

Sources:
Numbers Rabbah 12:4; Pesikta de-Rav Kahana Supplement 2:1; Pirkei de-Rabbi Eliezer 6; Midrash Tehillim 19:13; Midrash Tehillim 19:13; Sefer ha-Zikhronot 34; Zohar 1:9a.

229. THE TENT OF HEAVEN

Heaven is like a stretched-out tent, whose corners are low and whose center is high. The children of Adam sit under that tent and make their home there. The hooks of heaven are fastened to the waters of the ocean, and the edges of heaven are spread over the waters.

This myth of the heavens forming a tent is based on the verse *Who spread out the skies like gauze, stretched them out like a tent to dwell in* (Isa. 40:22). Of course, the image of the tent is a resonant one in Judaism, where the 40 years the Israelites spent wandering in the desert, sleeping in tents, serve as an archetype of Jewish experience. The simple, primitive notion that the sky is a big tent also emphasizes the role of God in ruling over the entire world. It also suggests the idea that heaven and earth together form God's palace, as stated in Isaiah 66:1, *"The heaven is My throne, and the earth is My footstool."* A similar notion is expressed in Habakkuk 3:3, *His majesty fills the skies, His splendor fills the earth.*

Sources:
Pirkei de-Rabbi Eliezer 3; Midrash Konen in Beit ha-Midrash 2:33-34; Sefer ha-Zikhronot 1:6.

230. THE CRYSTAL PALACE

Led by the angel Michael, Enoch ascended on high, until they reached the heaven of heavens. There he saw a structure built of crystals, and between those crystals were tongues of living fire. Rivers full of living fire encircled that structure, and countless angels went in and out of that crystal palace, including Michael, Gabriel, and Raphael. With them was the Ancient of Days. His head was white and pure like wool, as it is said, *And the hair of His head was like pure wool* (Dan. 7:9).

Here Enoch ascends to the highest heaven, *Aravot*, and sees God, here identified as the Ancient of Days (alternately translated as "Antecedent of Time" or "Head of Days"), accompanied by the angels, entering a crystal structure that appears to be some kind of heavenly palace. We know that this figure is God because of the description of His hair, which is white and like pure wool. This is an often-echoed description of God from Daniel 7:9: *And the hair of His head was like pure wool.* This scene of God accompanied by the angels in heaven is reminiscent of God walking in the Garden of Eden (Gen. 3:8).

Sources:
1 Enoch 71:1-14

231. THE CELESTIAL ACADEMY

Not a day passes in which God does not teach a new law in the heavenly academy. Just as the souls of the holy sages each teach in their own heavenly palace, so God teaches in the Celestial Academy. It is said that God assigns the righteous a closer place to the divine glory than He does for the angels. And the angels are always asking them, "What has God taught you?"

There are certain matters that must be left undecided until God comes and teaches the truth, for one day God will settle all unresolved questions of the Law. But God is not the only teacher in the Celestial Academy. Elijah and the Messiah also teach there. And until God delivers a final decision, it is Elijah's task to settle all doubts on ritual and judicial matters. So too does the Messiah elucidate the words of the Torah, and point out where the Law has been misconstrued.

After God has spoken, the sages of the Celestial Academy discuss God's rulings, and sometimes debate them. Then who will settle the matter? On one occasion they decided that it should be Rabbah bar Nachmani, who was alive on earth at that time, for he was an expert on these laws. A messenger was sent for him, but the Angel of Death could not approach him, because he did not interrupt his studies for even a moment. Meanwhile, a wind blew that rustled the bushes, and he imagined it to be a troop of soldiers. "Let me die," he cried out, "rather than be delivered into their hands." As his soul took leave of this world, a heavenly voice called out, "Happy are you, O Rabbah bar Nachmani, whose soul has departed in purity." At that time a letter fell from the sky to Pumbedita, upon which was written, "Rabbah bar Nachmani has been called up to the Celestial Academy."

Another visit to the Celestial Academy took place after the death of Rabbi Shimon bar Yohai. Rabbi Hiyya went to visit his grave and said: "Dust, be not proud, for Rabbi Shimon, the pillar of the world, will never waste away in you." And Rabbi Hiyya wept, and when he left there he was still weeping.

That is when Rabbi Hiyya began to fast so that he might be permitted to see Rabbi Shimon's place in Paradise. After fasting for forty days, he dreamed that an angel came and told him he could not see Rabbi Shimon. Then Rabbi Hiyya continued to fast and weep for another forty days. And on the eightieth day Rabbi Hiyya dreamed that he saw Rabbi Shimon in Paradise. He was teaching while thousands listened, sages and angels alike. Then, in the dream, Rabbi Shimon said: "Let Rabbi Hiyya enter here, to see what awaits him in the World to Come."

That is when Rabbi Hiyya awoke, and when he opened his eyes, he saw a winged angel standing beside the bed, and he understood that it had been sent to bring him to Paradise. Then Rabbi Hiyya mounted the angel, and they ascended at once to the Celestial Academy. There Rabbi Hiyya saw Rabbi Shimon standing exactly as he had seen him in his dream, discussing the same point of the Law.

All at once there was a heavenly voice saying, "Make way for King Messiah, who is coming to Rabbi Shimon's academy." And all of the righteous stood and made a path for the Messiah. Just then the Messiah saw Rabbi Hiyya and said: "Who brought this mortal here?" Rabbi Shimon replied: "This is Rabbi Hiyya, who is the light of the lamp of the Torah." And the Messiah said: "Then let him be gathered here." "No," said Rabbi Shimon, "Let him be given more time." When the Messiah heard the words of Rabbi Shimon, he nodded in assent, and at that moment the winged angel brought Rabbi Hiyya back to this world. And an instant later he found himself alone in his room, and he could not stop shaking.

Just as there are earthly academies where the Torah is studied and the laws are debated, so is there said to be a Celestial Academy, where God creates and teaches new laws every day. This notion is an interesting one, in that it suggests the ever-expanding nature of the Torah. The fact that it is God who is doing the teaching gives the seal of approval to this open-ended approach to Torah. This rabbinic myth can be seen to serve as a self-justification, arguing the correctness of this approach.

The proof that God teaches on high is found in the verse *Hear attentively the sound of His voice, and the meditation that comes forth from His mouth* (Job 37:2). *Genesis Rabbah* 49:2 explains that "meditation" refers to the Torah, as in the verse *But you shall meditate therein day and night* (Josh. 1:8). According to *Genesis Rabbah*, these are the laws of the Torah that even Abraham was said to know.

Since the Torah was not given until the time of Moses, rabbis were frustrated that the earlier patriarchs did not know the Torah. This was so difficult to accept that there are various legends about how they received the Torah anyway, such as the chain of legends about the Book of Raziel, which is a clear mask for the Torah. But there is another notion, that there were certain laws of the Torah that Abraham knew, since, for example, he followed the laws of circumcision. How did Abraham learn these laws? This myth from *Genesis Rabbah* suggests that he somehow learned them directly from God, as these are the same laws that God teaches in heaven. In some fashion, which is not described, Abraham was privy to these teachings.

Rabbah bar Nachmani receives an invitation from heaven to resolve a debate in the Celestial Academy. The Angel of Death is sent as a messenger to bring him, but is unable to do so because he never stops studying the Torah. This reflects the tradition that the Angel of Death cannot take a man while he is studying Torah. A similar story is told about King David and the Angel of Death, in which the angel had to create a diversion to lure David away from his studies, so that he could take his soul.

Unlike Rabbah bar Nachmani, Rabbi Hiyya, disciple of Rabbi Shimon bar Yohai, is determined to go to the Celestial Academy even though he does not have an invitation. Rabbi Hiyya fasts to achieve something that is not permitted to the living—to see Shimon bar Yohai's place in Paradise. This tale confirms the taboo of a human entering into Paradise, which finds its model in the tale of the ascent of Moses into heaven to receive the Torah. The angels sought to cast him out of Paradise, for none of the living are permitted there (*B. Shab.* 88b). See "The Ascent of Moses," p. 261. For another account of a journey into Paradise by one of the living, see "Rabbi Joshua ben Levi and the Angel of Death," p. 207.

The account of Rabbi Hiyya's efforts to travel to the Celestial Academy, from the *Zohar*, may have been inspired by a talmudic myth concerning Rabbi Hiyya found in *B. Bava Metzia* 85b. Here one rabbi sees another whose eyes appeared as though they had been burnt. He asks him what has happened, and the rabbi explains that he asked Elijah to show him the souls of departed rabbis as they ascend to the Celestial Academy. Elijah agreed that he could look upon all except for the carriage of Rabbi Hiyya. How would he recognize Rabbi Hiyya's carriage? All would be accompanied by angels when they ascend except Rabbi Hiyya's, which ascends on its own. But the rabbi disobeyed and did gaze upon Rabbi Hiyya's carriage, and at that instant two fiery streams came forth, which blinded him. The next day this rabbi prostrated himself on the grave of Rabbi Hiyya, and his sight was healed.

Sources:
B. Bava Metzia 86a; *B. Avodah Zarah* 18; *Genesis Rabbah* 49:2, 68:5; *Zohar* 1:4a-4b.

232. WHERE HEAVEN AND EARTH MEET

In his desert travels, Rabbah bar Bar Hannah met a Bedouin, who offered to show him where heaven and earth meet. They went there, and found the Wheel of the Heaven, which contained many windows. Rabbah took his bread basket and placed it in one of the windows of heaven. Then he prayed the afternoon prayer.

When he finished praying, Rabbah could not find his basket. He asked the Bedouin if there were thieves in that place. The Bedouin explained that the Wheel of Heaven turned when the sun set. He told Rabbah to wait until the next day and he would find his basket. And he did.

> This is one of the miraculous tales attributed to Rabbah bar Bar Hannah, who is the Sinbad of rabbinic literature. A series of tall tales attributed to him is found in tractate *Bava Batra* of the Talmud. Here a mysterious Bedouin (who might be Elijah in disguise) shows him where the Wheel of Heaven can be found, at the place where heaven and earth kiss. Proof that the wheel does indeed revolve every twenty-four hours comes from the disappearance and reappearance of Rabbah's basket.
>
> The reference to the Wheel of Heaven offers an explanation for the cycle of the sun, positing a mythical place where the Wheel of Heaven comes into contact with the earth. That such a place would be found in rabbinic lore is significant, as it ties together the worlds above and below.
>
> Sources:
> B. Bava Batra 74b
>
> Studies:
> "Talmudic Tall Tales" by Dan Ben-Amos.

233. THE PRIMORDIAL METATRON

The Primordial Metatron was the first of creation, the son of the *Shekhinah*. The first words of the Torah, *In the beginning God created*, refer to Metatron. The Primordial Metatron assisted God in the creation of the world, and has assisted God ever since in ruling the worlds above and below. When God said to Moses, *"Come up to the Lord,"* he meant to come up to Metatron.

> This description of a Primordial Metatron closely resembles the myths about the Heavenly Man and Adam Kadmon. What is unusual is that the primordial Metatron is described as the son of the *Shekhinah*. Since this myth is found in the *Zohar*, the *Shekhinah* refers to God's Bride, making the Primordial Metatron the child of God and the *Shekhinah*. The Christian echoes of the "son of God" are apparent, as well as the structure of a divine family as is found in other mythic traditions, such as the Greek or Canaanite. See "The Heavenly Man," p. 124 and "Adam Kadmon," p. 15.
>
> The identification of "the Lord" as Metatron is, surprisingly, found in the Talmud. For a further discussion of this, see the Introduction, p. l.
>
> The notion of a Primordial Metatron contradicts the standard explanation of Metatron's origin as Enoch, who was transformed into Metatron after being carried into heaven in a fiery chariot. It demonstrates an alternate Metatron tradition apart from that linked to Enoch. Of course, the original Enoch tradition dates from around the second century BCE, and the *Zohar* from the thirteenth century. Thus it is possible that this is one of many new mythic traditions found in the *Zohar*.
>
> Sources:
> B. Sanhedrin 38b; Zohar 1:94b.

234. THE ANGEL METATRON

God made a throne for Metatron similar to the Throne of Glory, and spread a curtain of splendor over him, and on it were fixed all kinds of lights in the universe. Metatron sits on that throne at the entrance to the seventh heavenly palace, where he judges all the upper beings, the family on high, with the permission of God. So too does he offer the souls of the righteous in the heavenly Temple as an atonement for the Jewish people. The hand of God rests on the head of His servant, whose height is that of the entire universe, and the attending angels stand before him.

When Surya, the Prince of the Presence, goes in to arrange and to set in order God's Throne of Glory and to prepare a seat for Metatron, the Mighty One of Jacob, he binds a thousand diadems of majesty upon the heads of each of them, and kneels and falls down and prostrates himself a thousand times before each one.

Before God appointed Metatron to serve the Throne of Glory, God opened up three hundred thousands gates of discernment to him, and as many gates of cunning, compassion, and love, as well as the gates of humility, sustenance, mercy, and the fear of heaven. And God revealed the mysteries of the Torah to him and all the secrets of wisdom, and all the secrets of Creation.

Then God gave Metatron a royal crown that included 49 precious stones, each as bright as the light of the sun. The light of these stones penetrates to the far corners of all seven heavens. God Himself engraved on Metatron's crown the letters with which the heavens and the earth and all their hosts were created. So too did God give him His cloak, His crown, and His name. And God made Metatron a garment with all types of light in it, and He dressed him in it. So too did God give Metatron the highest splendor, which is the light of the soul that Adam forfeited by his sin.

And God sent forth a herald, who announced that Metatron was ruler over all the princes of heaven and over all the children of heaven. And every angel who had to speak in God's presence should speak to him instead. Indeed, there are those who say that Metatron is the Lord God of Israel, God of the heavens and God of the earth, God of Gods, God of the sea and God of the land.

This is Metatron, Prince of the Presence. The angels who are with him encircle the Throne of Glory on one side and the celestial beasts are on the other side, and the *Shekhinah* is in the center of the Throne of Glory. And God called Metatron the little god before His entire heavenly family, as it is said, for *"My Name is within him"* (Exod. 23:23).

Then Metatron says in a great voice, "The Throne of Glory is glistening!" Immediately, the angels surrounding the throne fall silent and hasten into the river of fire, and the celestial creatures turn their faces toward the earth. Then Metatron brings the fire of deafness and puts it in their ears, so that they do not hear the sound of God's speech and the explicit Name that Metatron utters at that time in seven voices, or, some say, seventy voices in all.

In the *Hekhalot* texts, describing heavenly journeys, the angel Metatron is described in terms that are virtually equal, and sometimes superior, to those used to describe God. When *Hekhalot Rabbati* describes Metatron as "Lord God of Israel, God of heavens and God of the earth, God of Gods, God of the sea and God of the land," there is little doubt that the author regards Metatron at least as the "Lesser Yahweh," if not as God's equal. Just the fact that both God and Metatron are served by Surya, the Prince of the Presence is a clear indication of their divine status, and he is described as treating them equally, prostrating himself a thousand times before each one.

According to Gershom Scholem, Metatron was a secret name for Michael. Michael is not only one of the archangels, but he is also the High Priest in the heavenly Temple, so that his role is already elevated, although not to the heights of Metatron. Metatron is more commonly linked to Enoch and the belief that Enoch had been transformed into Metatron. See "The Metamorphosis and Enthronement of Metatron," p. 156.

Sources:
Numbers Rabbah 3b; *Shi'ur Komah*, Oxford Ms. 1791, ff. 58-70; *3 Enoch* 10:1-13:2;
  Hekhalot Rabbati 11, 27; *Zohar Hadash* 42d, 68a.

Studies:
3 Enoch or the Hebrew Book of Enoch by Hugo Odeberg.
Jewish Gnosticism, Merkabah Mysticism, and Talmudic Tradition by Gershom Scholem.

235. THE ANGEL SANDALPHON

Now the angels do not have permission to sing in heaven until the children of Israel first raise their voices in song on earth. Only when the angels hear praises of Israel can they commence to sing.

When it comes time to attend to the songs and music and praises that ascend from earth from the synagogues and schools, there is a certain angel, Sandalphon, who stands above the windows of the firmament. As the prayers of Israel are offered, all the words uttered ascend on high, cleaving their way through ethers and firmaments, until they reach Sandalphon. He stands behind the Throne of God and wreathes crowns out of those prayers.

When the crowns are ready, he adjures them so that they rise of their own accord and come to rest on the head of God, as it is said, *Blessings light upon the head of the righteous* (Prov. 10:6). And when the crown reaches God's head, all the hosts on high shake with awe, and the creatures of the chariot roar like lions, and all of them cry out, *Holy, holy, holy! The Lord of Hosts* (Isa. 6:3).

> Sandalphon is one of the most prominent of the angels in Jewish lore. He is said to be so tall that if he were standing on the earth, his head would reach into the highest heaven. In the myths about the ascent of Moses into heaven, Moses sees Sandalphon standing behind God's throne. See "The Ascent of Moses," p. 261. But the most common myth about Sandalphon concerns his gathering the prayers of Israel and forming them into crowns of prayer for God to wear on His Throne of Glory.
>
> *Sources:*
> B. *Hagigah* 13a; *Pesikta Rabbati* 20:4; *Midrash Tehillim* 19:7; *Hekhalot Rabbati* 11; *Sefer ha-Zikhronot* 52:6.
>
> *Studies:*
> *Keter: The Crown of God in Early Jewish Mysticism* by Arthur Green.

236. MICHAEL, THE PATRON ANGEL

The archangel Michael is Israel's patron angel. Once Michael praised Israel for her loyalty to God. Overhearing this, Satan declared that he could take away the holiness entrusted to Israel. Through sin and strife, Satan succeeded in snatching it away, and the Temple was destroyed and the people sent into exile. The angel Michael led them into exile, but then he abandoned them. But the day will come when it will be proved that Israel did not intentionally surrender her trust, and then she will regain the favor of her patron angel.

> This myth grows out of the tradition that each nation has its own guardian angel, and Michael is the guardian angel of Israel. Here Israel loses Michael's trust through sin and strife, triggered by Satan, and the only hope for Israel is to regain Michael's trust. This, it appears, would be the equivalent of the coming of the Messiah. Other myths describe God as Israel's guardian, while all other nations have angels. See "The Seventy Nations and the Land of Israel," p. 408.
>
> *Sources:*
> *Midrash Ribesh Tov* 2:55.

237. ELIJAH THE ANGEL

Elijah was translated, body and soul, from this world to the world above, as it is said, *A fiery chariot with fiery horses suddenly appeared ... and Elijah went up to heaven in a whirlwind* (2 Kings 2:11). Nor did he ever taste death, but he was transformed into an angel. At that time Elijah received a celestial body, which made it possible for him to ascend to heaven. But when he descends to earth on a mission, he resumes wearing his terrestrial body.

The angel Elijah has giant wings, and with four strokes of his wings he can travel from one end of the world to the other. Therefore no place on earth is too far removed for his help. Thus he serves as a protector of the just and pious, hovering over them and guarding them against evil and saving them from danger.

Some say that Elijah was originally created as an angel, and later he descended to earth as the prophet Elijah. Others say that the heavenly Elijah is none other than the angel Sandalphon, one of the greatest and mightiest of the heavenly hosts. Thus, Elijah is known as Sandalphon on high, but when he descends to this world, he is known as Elijah.

> Elijah is not only an important prophet, but the manner of his departure from earth, carried into heaven in a fiery chariot, inspired extensive rabbinic and folk traditions about Elijah's role after he was taken into Paradise. There are hundreds of tales about Elijah returning to earth as God's messenger, meeting with the great sages of subsequent generations and assisting the poor in their times of desperation. It was Elijah who was said to have taught Rabbi Shimon bar Yohai the secrets of heaven that were later written down in the *Zohar*, during the 13 years Shimon bar Yohai remained in hiding in a cave from the Romans. In this role as a teacher, Elijah created the role of the *Tzaddik*, who imparts holy secrets to those worthy of receiving them. And it is Elijah whom, it is said, will sound the horn of the ram that Abraham sacrificed at Mount Moriah to announce the beginning of the messianic era.
>
> In addition to these traditions about Elijah's role in this world, there are tales about Elijah's role in heaven. Here he is described as having been transformed into an angel, or, in an alternate version, having been created as an angel in the first place. One myth identifies him as the angel Sandalphon when he is in heaven, and as Elijah when he descends to this world. See "The Angel Sandalphon," p. 197.
>
> The most striking parallel to Elijah is the myth of Enoch. Just as Elijah was carried into paradise in a chariot, so too was Enoch brought into heaven the same way when *God took him* (Gen. 5:24). And just as Elijah is described here as being transformed into angel, so too was Enoch transformed into the angel Metatron. Both of them are among the most important angels, taking orders directly from God. In fact, it seems likely that the extensive mythic tradition about Enoch was inspired by the description of Elijah being taken into heaven in a fiery chariot. See "The Metamorphosis of Enoch," p. 156.
>
> *Sources*:
> B. Eruvin 45a; B. Mo'ed Katan 26a; Seder Olam 2, 17; Zohar 2:197a; Genesis Rabbah 21:5. Pesikta de-Rav Kahana 9:76a.
>
> *Studies*:
> Tales of Elijah the Prophet by Peninnah Schram.

238. THE KEEPER OF THE BOOK OF RECORDS

There is a heavenly prince, Radweriel, who is the Keeper of the Book of Records. Out of every word that goes forth from his mouth, an angel is created. He fetches the case of writings with the Book of Records in it, and brings it before God. And he breaks the seal of the case, opens it, takes out the book and delivers it to God. And God receives it and gives them to the heavenly scribes, that they may greet them in the Great Court of Justice, in the highest heaven, before the heavenly household.

> There are a multitude of angels listed in various ancient Jewish texts, each with his own particular role to play. Although Metatron is identified as the heavenly scribe, Radweriel is identified as the Keeper of the Book of Records. This is the book that contains a record of everything that a person does, so that on Rosh ha-Shanah God can weigh their good and bad deeds and make a decision about whether their lives should be renewed for another year, a decision that is sealed ten days later on Yom Kippur.

One strange detail about Radweriel suggests that his power is exceptionally great, for each time he speaks, an angel is created. Since God is said to be the Creator of everything, including the angels, the notion that one angel has the power to create other angels implies a shift of one of God's primary roles. See "The Book of Life and the Book of Death," p. 289.

Sources:
B. Avot. 3. 3 Enoch 27:1-3.

239. THE ANGEL GALLIZUR

God does not utter evil decrees Himself, as it is said, *It is not at the word of the Most High, that weal and woe befall* (Lam. 3:38). Instead, God has the angel Gallizur utter all evil decrees. Gallizur also reveals the secrets of God. So too does he open his wings to absorb the fiery breath of the creatures of the chariot, for if he did not absorb it, the angels would be consumed by their fiery breath. Gallizur also takes braziers filled with coals from the river Rigyon, the river of fire, whose coals consume angels and men, and he holds these up near angels and kings, so that fear of the angels and kings will strike the world.

This obscure angel is in charge of pronouncing God's evil decrees. This is an attempt to resolve the theological problem of God's role in the existence of evil. In monotheism, God is responsible for both good and evil. On the other hand, God is portrayed as being entirely good, and it would be inappropriate and unseemly for God to pronounce evil decrees, as stated in Lamentations 3:38. Therefore the angel Gallizur takes over this role and pronounces evil decrees for God. There is perhaps a hint here of a Gnostic dualism.

Sources:
Pesikta Rabbati 20:4; Sefer ha-Zikhronot 52:8.

240. THE ANGEL OF CONCEPTION

Among the angels there is one who serves as the midwife of souls. This is Lailah, the Angel of Conception. When the time has come for a man and his wife to conceive a child, God directs Lailah to seek out a certain soul hidden in the Garden of Eden, and command it to enter a drop of semen. At first the soul refuses, for it still remembers the pain of being born, and it prefers to remain pure. But Lailah compels the soul to obey, and that is when God decrees what the fate of that sperm will be, whether male or female, strong or weak, rich or poor, and so on. Then the angel turns around and places the soul in the womb of the mother.

While the infant grows in the womb, Lailah places a lighted candle at the head of the unborn infant, so he can see from one end of the world to the other, as it is said, *His lamp shone above my head, and by His light I walked through darkness* (Job 29:3). For nine months Lailah watches over the unborn infant, teaching him the entire Torah as well as the history of his soul. During this time, the evil inclination has no power over him. And before he is born, he is given an oath to keep his soul pure, lest God take it back from him. Then Lailah leads the child into the Garden of Eden, and shows him the righteous ones with crowns on their heads. So too does Lailah lead the child to the netherworld and show him the punishments of Gehenna. But when the time has come to be born, the angel extinguishes the lamp, and brings forth the child into the world. The instant the child emerges, Lailah lightly strikes the newborn above the lip, causing it to cry out. And at that instant the infant forgets all it has learned. That is the origin of the mark on the upper lip, which everyone bears.

Indeed, Lailah is a guardian angel, who watches over that child all of his days. And when the time has come to take leave of this world, it is Lailah who comes to him and says, "Do you not recognize me? The time of your departure has come. I have come to take you from this world." Thereupon Lailah leads him to the World to Come, where he renders an accounting before God, and he is judged according to his merits.

This myth describes the formation of a child. The soul is here revealed to have been drawn from on high and sent to this world reluctantly. Such a myth affirms the rabbinic belief in the essential purity of the human soul, which is subjected to the power of the *Yetzer ha-Ra*, the Evil Inclination. This myth of conception is also a reminder of God's powerful role in every stage of our lives. A famous passage in *Pirke Avot* 3:1 says: "Know where you came from, where you are going, and before whom you will in the future have to give account and reckoning. Where you came from—from a fetid drop; where you are going—to a place of dust, worms and maggots; and before whom you will in the future have to give account and reckoning—before God, the Supreme King of kings."

According to Rabbi Meir ibn Gabbai in *Avodat ha-Kodesh*, "Before a soul descends to this world, it recognizes the Oneness of God and grasps the secrets of the Torah." He links this intrinsic knowledge of the soul with the verse *Open my eyes that I may perceive the wonder of Your teachings* (Psalms 119:18). These are the wonders that were apprehended before the child was born.

Although angels are generally regarded as sexless, and some rabbinic sources say they do not procreate, almost all of them bear male names such as Michael or Gabriel and they have male characteristics. In addition, the noun, *malakh* (angel) is grammatically masculine. However, there is one angel, the angel Lailah, who has distinctly feminine characteristics. This angel is responsible for the fetus, for assisting at birth, and for guiding the soul from this world to the next. In many ways Lailah is the polar opposite of Lilith, who wastes seed, is not maternal, and is bent on destruction, not creation. While the word Lailah, meaning "night," is masculine, the name Lailah is feminine, and the name of this angel does not end in the usual "el," representing God's Name. Thus, even though there is no direct evidence that Lailah is a feminine angel, the name Lailah and the role of the angel strongly indicate feminine characteristics.

Lailah, the angel's name, likely derives from a rabbinic discussion in *B. Niddah* 16b, where conception is described as taking place at night. There the name of the angel in charge of conception is identified as "Night" (*lailah*). This angel takes a drop and places it before God. *B. Niddah* 30b adds important details about the formation of the embryo and the role of Lailah. It explains that a light shining above the unborn infant's head lets the child see from one end of the world to the other. At the same time, the angel teaches the unborn child the Torah. But as soon as the child is born, the angel strikes it on the upper lip, causing the infant to forget all he has learned. The full myth of Lailah and the formation of the embryo is found in *Midrash Tanhuma Pekude* 3. For more on the tradition of guardian angels in Judaism, see "Guardian Angels," p. 202.

According to Rabbi Menashe ben Israel in *Nishmat Hayim* 2:18, God breathes the soul into a person at conception, much as He did with Adam, when *He blew into his nostrils the breath of life, and man became a living being* (Gen. 2:7). This appears to be an alternate explanation for the version portrayed in the myth of Lailah, where the angel orders the soul to enter the seed.

Sources:

B. Niddah 16b, 30b; B. Sanhedrin 96a; Midrash Tanhuma-Yelammedenu, Pekudei 3; Zohar
   Hadash 68:3; Sefer ha-Zikhronot 10:19-23; Be'er ha-Hasidut 1:216; Aseret ha-Dibrot 79;
   Avodat ha-Kodeah, Introduction; Nishmat Hayim 2:18; Anaf Yosef on B. Niddah 30b;
   Amud ha-Avodash 103b; Avkat Rahel in Beit ha-Midrash 1:153-155; Likutei ha-Pardes
   4d-5c; IFA 4722, 18976.

Studies:

Legends of the Jews by Louis Ginzberg, note 20, vol. 5, pp. 75-78.

241. THE ANGEL OF THE COVENANT

Whoever has the sign of the circumcision sealed in his flesh will not descend to Gehenna. When a man brings his son into the covenant of the circumcision, God calls upon the angels and says to them, "Come and see what my sons are doing in the world." At that time Elijah, the Angel of the Covenant, swoops down to earth in four leaps. For this reason, a chair must be prepared in Elijah's honor, and one should say, "This is the chair of Elijah." If this is not done, Elijah does not dwell there. Then Elijah ascends on high and testifies before God about whether or not a man has circumcised his son.

> The covenant of circumcision (*b'rit*) is performed on Jewish boys on the eighth day after their birth. The ceremony includes a chair identified as the chair of Elijah, and Elijah is believed to be present at the ceremony. For this reason, Elijah, who was taken up into heaven in a whirlwind in 2 Kings 2:11, is identified as the angel of the covenant.
>
> This ritual of the *b'rit* derives from Abraham's circumcision in Genesis 17:24. This is considered the most elemental rite in Judaism, and it was (and in most Jewish homes still is) unthinkable that it would not be performed. This covenant was believed to provide God's protection for the child, who is believed to be in danger from the forces of evil until the ritual of the circumcision is performed. See "Abraham's Vision of God," p. 331.
>
> *Sources:*
> *Zohar* 1:93a.

242. HOW RABBI ISHMAEL WAS CONCEIVED

Rabbi Ishmael, the High Priest, was so handsome that he was said to resemble an angel. His mother and father had been childless for many years before he was born. Rabbi Ishmael's father told his wife to pay close attention when she left the *mikveh*, the ritual bath. If anything unpleasant crossed her path, she should return to the bathhouse and immerse herself again. Then, perhaps, she would succeed in having a child.

The next time his wife left the *mikveh*, a black dog crossed her path. She returned and reimmersed herself, but again the dog crossed before her. This happened eight times, and each time she reimmersed herself. God was so moved by her righteousness that He sent the angel Gabriel to earth. Gabriel took the form of her husband, and met her at the door of the bathhouse. He led her home and that night Rabbi Ishmael was conceived. And he was as handsome as his father, the angel Gabriel.

> Here the High Priest, Rabbi Ishmael, is said to have been the child of an angel and a human, with the angel Gabriel having taken on the appearance of his father and having had sexual relations with his mother. That is given as the explanation for Rabbi Ishmael's great beauty.
>
> The union of humans and angels is very unusual in Jewish lore, but there is an extensive tradition linked to the rabbinic interpretations of Genesis 6, concerning the Sons of God and the daughters of men, where the Sons of God are identified as angels. See the series of stories concerning this myth, pp. 454-460.
>
> *Sources:*
> *Midrash Eleh Ezkerah.*

243. THE ANGEL OF FRIENDSHIP

Everyone has a light burning for him in the world above, and everyone's light is unique. When two friends meet, their lights above are united, and out of that union of two lights an

angel is born. That angel has the strength to survive for only one year, unless its life is renewed when the friends meet again. But if they are separated for more than year, the angel
begins to languish and eventually wastes away. That is why a blessing over the dead is made
upon meeting a friend who has not been seen for more than a year, to revive the angel.

According to the Talmud (*B. Berakhot* 58b) two friends who have not seen each
other for a year say the blessing: "Blessed is He who revives the dead." The explanation for this strange blessing is that an angel comes into existence when two people
become friends, but the angel dies if they go more than a year without meeting. This
tradition about the Angel of Friendship has been attributed to Reb Pinhas of Koretz,
Reb Shmelke of Nicholsberg and Reb Abraham Joshua Heschel of Apta.

Another tradition about the creation and transformation of angels is attributed to
Reb Pinhas of Koretz: "Every good deed turns into an angel. But if the deed is imperfect, so is the angel. Perhaps it will be mute. What a disgrace to be served in Paradise
by such an angel. Or it might have an arm or leg missing. And these imperfections can
only be repaired by the repentance of the one who brought the imperfect angel into
being." This kind of transformation is known as *tikkun* or repair, and it is parallel to
the mystical cosmology of the Ari, where every good deed is said to raise up a fallen
spark.

The theme of good deeds in the transformation of the angels is common in kabbalistic and Hasidic lore. The key passage is *Mishneh Avot* 4:2: "He who does a *mitzvah*
acquires an advocate. He who does a sin acquires an accuser." This notion is further
developed in *Exodus Rabbah* 32:6: "The angels are sustained only by the splendor of
the *Shekhinah*, and you are their means of sustenance," meaning that a good deed
creates an angel. Rabbi Hayim Vital confirms this meaning in *Sha'arei Kedushah*, where
he writes that "the diligent study of the Law and the performance of the divine commandments brings about the creation of a new angel." This serves as an explanation
for the existence of the *maggidim*, the angelic figures who are said to visit sages and
bring them heavenly mysteries. Joseph Karo (1488-1575), author of the *Shulhan Arukh*,
the code of Jewish law, was famous for being visited by such a *maggid*. See "The Angel
of the Mishnah" in *Gabriel's Palace*, pp. 112-113.

Another source echoed here is found in *Ma'asiyot Nora'im ve-Nifla'im* concerning
the gaon Rabbi Yehezkel of Prague (1713-1793). He was said to have stated that "The
angels that are found in the upper world were created by the deeds of the *Tzaddikim*."
Note that Reb Pinhas has the angel that comes into being as a result of friendship, or,
by implication, love, function as a symbolic child. This expands the circumstances for
the creation of an angel to include angels created by human interaction.

Sources:
B. Berakhot 58b; *Orhot Hayim* 1:82b; *Sefer Ta'amei ha-Minhagim*; *Devět Brán* by Jirí
Langer.

244. GUARDIAN ANGELS

Each person is given a particular guardian angel, according to his ways. A righteous man
who speaks the truth is assigned an angel who goes along with him in the ways of the
righteous and helps him to speak the truth.

When a man makes himself act like a saint, willing to suffer , he is assigned an angel
who goes along with him in the way of saints and helps the man to accept all suffering.

If, on the other hand, a man behaves like one of the wicked, lying and deceiving, he is
assigned an angel who goes along with him in the way of the wicked and leads him on to
more deceit.

And if a man follows a middle way, he is assigned an angel who follows that same
path, as it is said, *Render to each man according to his way* (Jer. 27:10).

Some say that every man has two guardian angels, representing the *Yetzer ha-Ra*, the Evil Inclination, and the *Yetzer ha-Tov*, the Good Inclination. And these angels who accompany a man testify before God about his acts.

There are multiple myths about guardian angels in Judaism, as well as a rabbinic debate about whether each person has one or two guardian angels. The position of Maimonides in *Guide to the Perplexed* is that every person is accompanied by two angels, one on the right side and one on the left. *Eliyahu Zuta* explains that the nature of a person's guardian angel is a mirror of that person, and can lead the person on to good or to evil. The notion of an angel luring a person into evil is strange, and seems to be intentionally avoiding the use of demons. Usually angels are not distinguished by their individuality, but this myth suggests that they share the same strengths and weaknesses of those they guard.

Here the verse from Jeremiah 27:10, "*I give to every man according to his ways,*" is interpreted to mean that God gives them an angel.

See "The Sabbath Angels," p. 315. See also "The Angel of Conception," p. 199, about the angel Lailah, who plays a role very much like that of a guardian angel.

Sources:
B. Ta'anit 11a; B. Shabbat 1196; B. Hagigah 16a; 2 Enoch 19:5; Eliyahu Zuta 3:176; Zohar 1:144b, 1:165b, 1:191a, 2:41b-42a, 3:106a; Maimonides, *Guide to the Perplexed* 3:22.

Studies:
Legends of the Jews by Louis Ginzberg, vol. 5, note 20, pp. 75-77.

245. THE MIGHT OF THE ANGELS

God's angels are mighty, but they are not the equal of God. So great is the size of the angels, that the distance from heaven to earth is no more than the palm of an angel. Proof of the might of the angels is demonstrated by the fact that one of them stretched forth his hand from heaven and grasped Ezekiel by a lock of his hair, as it is said, *He stretched out the form of a hand, and took me by the hair of my head* (Ezek. 8:3). This teaches us that there is no limit to God's ministering angels. How much more so, then, is there no limit to God.

This brief myth attempts to convey the great size and power of the angels, while emphasizing that the angels themselves are still subject to God. Since the size of the angels is so gigantic—with the palm of angel as big as the distance from heaven to earth—the immense size and power of God cannot even be imagined.

From a mythological perspective, this myth attributes the kind of size and power to the angels that other gods have in Babylonian or Canaanite or Greek mythology, but, at the same time, it attempts to reinforce the monotheistic concept that the angels are still subject to God's will.

Sources:
Midrash Tanhuma-Yelammedenu, Bereshit 5.

246. THE ANGEL OF LOSSES

There is an angel who watches over people, even in the dark. This is Yode'a, the Angel of Losses. He watches lives unfold, recording every detail before it fades. This angel has servants, and his servants have servants. Some of these servants are angels, and some are not. Each of the angels carries a shovel, and they spend all their time digging, searching for losses. For a great deal is lost in our lives.

Every *Tzaddik* is a servant of the angel Yode'a, for even a *Tzaddik* who searches after lost things is himself sometimes lost. Then it is necessary to search in the dark, in the realm of the unknown. And with what do you search in the darkness? With the light of the soul. For the soul is a light planted in the *Tzaddik* to seek after whatever has been lost.

What kind of light is it? Not a torch, but a small candle. Yet even so, with it you can search inside deep wells, where darkness is unbroken, peering into every corner and crevice. It is necessary to be guided by that light, small though it may be.

> This is a teaching of Rabbi Nachman of Bratslav. Rabbi Nachman appears to have invented this angel, Yode'a, the angel of losses. Much like Reb Pinhas of Koretz, Rabbi Nachman was highly aware of surrounding spirits. For Reb Pinhas these were often angels. See, for example, "The Angel of Friendship," p. 201. Here too Rabbi Nachman recognizes an angel that is invisible to all the others. In this case it is an obscure angel that he finds, the Angel of Losses. This angel, along with his servants, searches for what has been lost. The kind of work that this angel does is clearly linked to the myth of the Ari, for the second phase of this myth concerns gathering the scattered sparks. These are not unlike the losses that Yode'a collects, for the sparks too have been lost. "Yode'a" means "to know." Thus the angel's name reflects its purpose, which is to recall all that has been lost. See "The Shattering of the Vessels and the Gathering of the Sparks," p. 122.
>
> *Sources:*
> *Be'er Hasidut* 1:189.

247. THE ANGEL TZADKIEL

It is the angel Tzadkiel who dresses each soul that enters Paradise in a garment of great purity, woven by the Bride of God. So too was Tzadkiel the teacher of Abraham. It was he who taught him the ways of wisdom.

For the first year after the Ari died, Rabbi Hayim Vital never dreamed of his master. In time he began to fear that the Ari was angry with him or thought him an unworthy disciple. Hayim Vital confided these fears to Rabbi Yehoshua Albuv. Rabbi Yehoshua told him that he knew a holy name that could invoke the angel Tzadkiel, and that this angel could reveal to him the reason for the Ari's absence. But this angel could be seen only in a mirror.

Rabbi Yehoshua taught the secret name to Hayim Vital. For the next week he fasted and immersed himself in the *mikveh.* Then, on the fifth of Av, the *yahrzeit* (anniversary) of the death of the Ari, Hayim Vital stood before a mirror and pronounced the holy name. All at once there was a blinding light in the mirror, and Hayim Vital shut his eyes. And when he opened them, he was barely able to make out a presence in the mirror. And as his eyes adjusted to that great light, he recognized that it was indeed an angel.

The angel spoke first and said: "I have come at your command. What is it you wish to know?" And Hayim Vital replied: "Tell me first who you are." And the angel revealed that it was Tzadkiel.

Then Hayim Vital asked the angel for help in contacting the Ari in the World to Come, for since his death the Ari had been silent. And Hayim Vital also asked if he had somehow sinned and was therefore unworthy of the Ari's presence in his dreams.

In reply Tzadkiel said: "Know that the holy Ari has prepared a place for you in Paradise, at his side, along with Rabbi Akiba and Rabbi Yohanan ben Zakkai. For you are a true *Tzaddik* in the eyes of God. Yet there is one sin that holds the Ari back from visiting you in the world of dreams."

And Hayim Vital asked: "What sin is this?"

The angel said: "In your life, you are perfect. But you have not done enough to see that others truly repent, to make the coming of the Messiah possible. Until you accept the burden of being a *Tzaddik* and bring others to repentance, the Ari will hold back from visiting you. But if you accomplish this, he will guide you in your dreams as he did when he was in this world."

Then Hayim Vital swore that he would do everything to make others aware of the power of repentance to hasten the End of Days. And when the angel had witnessed this vow, he vanished from the mirror and was gone. So night and day Hayim Vital devoted himself to fulfilling his vow, and before the year was out the Ari began to visit him in his dreams, and once more became his guide.

> Here the figure who assists Hayim Vital is Rabbi Yehoshua Albuv. Hayim Vital also seeks the help of Rabbi Yehoshua in invoking Elijah in another story in *Shivhei Rabbi Hayim Vital*, p. 91.
> Hayim Vital was very interested in the mystical process of invoking angels. Here he invokes the angel Tzadkiel, who is mentioned many times in the *Zohar* and early kabbalistic texts, including *Sefer Yetzirah*. Tzadkiel is identified as a companion of the angel Gabriel. He is also identified as the good angel in the famous legend of the two angels who follow a man home from the synagogue (*B. Shab.* 119b). See "The Sabbath Angels," p. 315.
> According *to Siddur Sha'ar Shamayim*, Tzadkiel is the name of the good angel, and the evil angel is Samael, the Evil One. In the present story, Hayim Vital invokes the angel, which he must view in a mirror, as is customary, as divine beings cannot be seen face to face. The angel confirms that heaven regards him as a *Tzaddik*, but urges him to use his powers to cause others to repent, suggesting that Vital's failure to do so has caused the soul of the Ari, his master, to keep his distance after death. Note that this tale emphasizes the almost messianic role in which Hayim Vital viewed himself while acknowledging some failure on his part to inspire others to repent.
>
> *Sources:*
> *Sefer ha-Hezyonot* 1:23; *Shivhei Rabbi Hayim Vital* p. 66; *Siddur Sha'ar Shamayim.*

248. THE ANGEL OF RAIN

The Angel of Rain encompasses all miracles. Resembling an ox whose lip has been split open, this angel stands between the Deep and the Deep. That is the meaning of *Deep calls to deep* (Ps. 42:8). The Angel of Rain stands between these two Deeps and brings about miracles both above and below.

> The concept of the Deep, *tehom*, first appears in Genesis 1:2: *Now the earth was unformed and void, and darkness was upon the face of the Deep.* According to *Exodus Rabbah* 5:9, there are upper miracles, which correspond to the Upper Deep, and lower miracles, which correspond to the Lower Deep. Just as rain fertilizes the earth and makes it possible for things to grow, so the Angel of Rain facilitates miracles above and below.
> The Angel of Rain is referred to as B'ree in Job 26:7.
>
> *Sources:*
> *B. Ta'anit* 25b; *Likutei Moharan* 7:1.

249. GOD CHANGES THE ROLES OF THE ANGELS

Before the enemy came, Jeremiah warned the people to repent so they would not have to go into exile. But the people said, "If the enemy comes, what can they do to us? By invoking the aid of one of the celestial princes we can surround the city with a wall of water, and by invoking the aid of another, we can surround it with a wall of fire, while another angel will surround it with a wall of iron."

Hearing this, God said, "They would avail themselves of My angelic host." So God changed the roles of the angels, setting the angel who had dominion over water to have dominion over fire, and the one who had dominion over fire to have dominion over iron. So that when the names of the angels were invoked, they did not respond, for they had been removed from control of those elements.

> This myth expands on the verses: *He has brought low in dishonor the kingdom and its leaders* (Lam. 2:2) and *So I profaned the holy princes* (Isa. 43:28). Here the princes are understood to refer to the celestial princes, especially those that are in charge of elements such as fire and water. This should be regarded as a polemical myth, opposing the use of (and dependence on) the invocation of the names of angels to accomplish magical goals. For other examples of polemic myths, see "Adam the Last and First," p. 129 and "Jacob's Image Cast Out of Heaven," p. 368. For one of the best examples of a polemic myth see "The Homunculus of Maimonides," p. 284.
>
> *Sources:*
> *Lamentations Rabbah* 2:5.

250. THE CREATION OF THE ANGEL OF DEATH

Some say that the only thing created on the first day of creation was the Angel of Death. How do we know this? By the word "darkness" in the verse *Darkness was over the face of the deep* (Gen. 1:2). But others say that when God created the world, there was no Angel of Death.

So when was the Angel of Death created? Some say it was at the time of the sin of Adam and Eve, for the serpent was the Angel of Death, and it caused death for the entire world. But others say that the Angel of Death did not come into being until Cain slew Abel, for until then no one had died, and there was no need for such an angel. Then God transformed Cain into the Angel of Death, as punishment for having slain his brother, and that is how the Angel of Death came into being.

Cain served as the Angel of Death for one hundred and thirty years, wandering and roaming about, accursed. After the death of Cain, Lamech took his place as the Angel of Death.

> This myth attempts to determine when the Angel of Death was created based on the appropriate biblical episode. Because the serpent in the Garden of Eden led Adam and Eve into a sin that brought about mortality, it is identified in the *Zohar* as the Angel of Death. (*Zohar* 1:35b also identifies the serpent as Satan and as the *Yetzer ha-Ra*, the Evil Impulse that entices a person to sin and afterward rises up before the heavenly court to accuse the sinner.) Likewise, because Cain was the first murderer, *Midrash Tanhuma* identifies him as becoming transformed into the Angel of Death. Cain's descendent, Lamech, who was said to have accidentally slain Cain, is also identified as one who took on the mantle of the Angel of Death. See "The Death of Cain," p. 451.
>
> *Sources:*
> B. *Avodah Zarah* 22b; *Genesis Rabbah* 21:5; *Exodus Rabbah* 30:3, 38:2; *Numbers Rabbah* 23:13; *Midrash Tanhuma-Yelammedenu, Bereshit* 11; *Zohar* 1:35b; *Me'am Lo'ez Bereshit* 1:5.

251. RABBI JOSHUA BEN LEVI AND THE ANGEL OF DEATH

When the time came for Rabbi Joshua ben Levi to die, God told the Angel of Death to go to him and grant any request he might make. When the Angel of Death revealed himself to him, Rabbi Joshua said, "Show me my place in the Garden of Eden." The Angel of

Death agreed to take him there, but Rabbi Joshua said, "Give me your sword. I am afraid you may frighten me or kill me on the way." So the Angel of Death gave him his sword.

When they arrived at the Garden of Eden, they sat on the wall of the Garden of Eden and the angel showed him his place there. Suddenly Rabbi Joshua jumped down from the wall into the Garden of Eden, taking the angel's sword with him. The angel demanded that he give the sword back, but Rabbi Joshua swore that he would not. At that moment a heavenly voice went forth and said, "Give him back his sword. Otherwise he cannot perform his duty." So Rabbi Joshua gave the sword back.

This is a very famous talmudic legend about Rabbi Joshua ben Levi. Because he was so pious, God directed the Angel of Death to treat him with special consideration, so when Rabbi Joshua asked to see his heavenly reward, the angel took him to the Garden of Eden. Rabbi Joshua then tricked the angel by jumping into the Garden (thus entering the World to Come without dying) and stealing the angel's sword, without which he would be unable to perform his assigned task of slaying the living when their time comes to take leave of this world. Rabbi Joshua's behavior may seem childish, but his intention—to spare the living the pain of death—can certainly be seen to be admirable. By entering the Garden of Eden in this manner, Rabbi Joshua becomes one of the few people in rabbinic literature who were said to have entered Paradise alive.

Derekh Eretz Zuta 1 lists nine who were said to enter Paradise alive. The list includes Enoch, Elijah, the Messiah, Eliezer, the servant of Abraham, Hiram, king of Tyre, Ebed Melech, the Ethiopian, Jaabez, the son of Rabbi Yehudah ha-Nagid, Bitiah, the daughter of Pharaoh, and Serah bat Asher. Note that this list does not include Moses, who is said to have ascended into heaven alive, Rabbi Joshua ben Levi, or the four sages who were said to have entered Paradise, Rabbi Akiba, Shimon ben Azzai, Shimon ben Zoma, and *Aher* (Elisha ben Abuyah). See "The Ascent of Moses," p. 261 and "The Four Who Entered Paradise," p. 173.

Gershon Winkler reports hearing a version of the story of Rabbi Joshua and the Angel of Death in which Rabbi Joshua made the angel promise never to show his terrifying face—said to be full of eyes (B. AZ 20b)—when coming to take a soul, and only then did he return the angel's sword.

See "The Messiah in Hell," p. 241, which describes Rabbi Joshua ben Levi's subsequent visit to Gehenna after his visit to Paradise.

Sources:

B. *Ketubot* 77b; B. *Avodah Zarah* 20b; IFA 3643, where the rabbi is Hanina ben Dosa instead of Joshua ben Levi; oral version recorded by Gershon Winkler.

252. RABBI LOEW AND THE ANGEL OF DEATH

One night, not long before the Holy Days were to begin, Rabbi Loew glimpsed a light in the synagogue across the way, and he wondered who might be there at that hour. He left his house, and as he approached the synagogue he saw through the window a strange figure standing at the pulpit. The closer Rabbi Loew came, the more sinister did the figure seem, and suddenly Rabbi Loew realized who it was—the Angel of Death—and at the same time he came close enough to see the angel sharpening a knife over a long scroll on which many names were written. Rabbi Loew was pierced with terror and resisted a powerful impulse to run away. But a moment later he became calm and self-possessed, and he knew what he had to do. As silently as possible he opened the door of the synagogue and came up behind the dreaded angel. All at once he snatched the long list out of the angel's hands, tearing it away from him, and ran from the synagogue to his home, where he threw the list into the flames and watched until every scrap of it had burned to ashes.

Now the plague had begun to spread in the city, and that was the list of victims the Angel of Death had come to take in one fell swoop. Now only those on the piece of the list left in his hands fell victim to him; all the rest were spared. But among those on the list was Rabbi Loew, and it was he, above all, whom the deadly angel was determined to capture.

Rabbi Loew, who could read the lines of the future, knew that the angel would try to snatch him to seek revenge. But Rabbi Loew used his powers to avoid the angel, much as King David had done, studying Torah day and night. For the Angel of Death is forbidden to take a man while he is engaged in the study of Torah. Yet even so, the angel found a ruse by which to capture him. He hid in a rose of great beauty that grew in the garden of Rabbi Loew's grandson. One day the boy picked the rose as a gift for his grandfather, and as he held it in his hands to present to Rabbi Loew, the rabbi perceived the presence of the dark angel, hidden in the rose. Then he did not hesitate, but accepted the gift from his grandson, for he knew that if he did not, the boy's life would be endangered. But no sooner did Rabbi Loew take it in his hand than the Angel of Death struck him like a serpent and snatched his soul.

> The most famous tale of an encounter with the Angel of Death is that of King David, found in the Talmud. Here David learns that he is fated to die on a Sabbath. Knowing that the Angel of Death is forbidden to snatch a man while he is studying, David spends every Sabbath immersed in study. In frustration the Angel of Death creates a ruse by shaking a tree outside his study, and when David goes out to investigate, the angel snatches his life (B. Shab. 30a-b). A common theme found in folklore is that of the snake hidden in a rose, who bites the one who picks it. Such a theme is found in "The Princess and the Rose" in the medieval collection Sefer Sha'ashuim.
>
> Another key legend of an encounter with the Angel of Death is found in the pseudepigraphal text The Testament of Abraham. Here the Angel of Death disguises himself as a young man of mild appearance, but reveals his true appearance when Abraham demands it. The description of its terrible face is one of the most horrible to be found anywhere. It is such a face that overwhelms the father and mother in "The Bridegroom and the Angel of Death" in Hibbur ha-Ma'asiyot ve-ha-Midrashot ve-ha-Aggadot. In this story, the next of kin of the bridegroom all offer to take his place to spare him being snatched by the Angel of Death, until the moment of truth, when all back out, except for the bride, who so impresses God with her willingness to die that both bride and bridegroom are spared. See "The Bridegroom and the Angel of Death" in Gabriel's Palace, pp. 162-164.
>
> A major study of the legends of the Angel of Death was undertaken by Haim Schwarzbaum in the last years of his life. Professor Dov Noy tells the story that he once asked Schwarzbaum why it was taking him so long to finish his book on the Angel of Death. Schwarzbaum replied that he believed the Angel of Death would prefer to take him after he had finished the book, and that is why he was taking his time. Unfortunately, he died before the book was completed.
>
> Sources:
> Die Legenden der Juden; Die Wundermanner im Judischen Volk.

253. THE HEAVENLY COURT

God does nothing without consulting the Heavenly Court, as it is said, *This sentence is decreed by the Watchers; this verdict is commanded by the Holy Ones* (Dan. 4:14). Nor does a day pass when God does not pass a new law in the Heavenly Court. For every day God creates new rules and regulations for the guidance of humankind.

It is not clear who are the members of the Heavenly Court. They may be identified with the Council of Souls. See "The Council of Souls," p. 160. Psalm 89:7-8 depicts God as the head of a council of other gods, which may be the origin of the heavenly court. The heavenly court may also be identified, through the verse from Daniel 4:14, with the Watchers. The identities of all three groups, the Heavenly Court, the Council of Souls and the Watchers seem to intersect and blur. However, in the pseudepigraphic Enoch literature the Watchers are identified with a group of rebellious angels. According to Rabbi Hayim of Volozhin, the judges of the heavenly court are the *Tzaddikim* of their generation, since angels cannot understand how a person can sin (*Etz ha-Hayim* 150).

Sources:
B. Sanhedrin 38a; Etz ha-Hayim 150.

254. THE WINDOWS OF HEAVEN

When Manasseh reigned as king over Jerusalem, he wrought much evil in the sight of the Lord (2 Chron. 33:6). But when Manasseh was carried away to Babylon bound in fetters, he humbled himself before the Lord and prayed to Him.

Now all the ministering angels went and closed the windows of heaven, so that the prayer of Manasseh should not reach God.

God replied, "If I do not accept him as a penitent, I shall lock the door before all who would repent." Then what did God do? He made an opening through the heavens under His Throne of Glory and heard Manasseh's supplication and received his entreaty, and brought him back to Jerusalem.

> This myth emphasizes the power of repentance, even for those who have committed terrible sins. The mythical imagery found here is quite amazing—God makes an opening in heaven, reaches down and picks Manasseh up and carries him from Babylon to Jerusalem.
>
> A similarly surprising tradition about repentance is found concerning Cain. An encounter is reported in *Genesis Rabbah* 22:13 between Adam and Cain many years after Cain was punished. "How did your case go?" Adam asked. "I repented and am reconciled, " replied Cain. Hearing this, Adam struck his face, crying, "So great is the power of repentance, and I did not know!" Then he arose and exclaimed, *It is a good thing to make confession unto the Lord* (Ps. 92:1).
>
> *Sources:*
> Y. Sanhedrin 10:2.

255. THE BA'AL SHEM TOV ASCENDS ON HIGH

On Rosh ha-Shanah of 5507 [1746] the Ba'al Shem Tov made an adjuration, pronounced a holy name, and ascended on high. In the vision that followed, he saw wondrous things that he had never seen before, and he learned things that words cannot express.

First he reached the Garden of Eden, where the souls of the righteous pass on their way to Paradise. There he saw many souls, some known to him and some unknown, and he discovered that it was a special time of grace. Many wicked people had repented, and their sins had been forgiven. It was wondrous for him to see how many were accepted as penitents. They were in a state of great rapture, and were about to ascend on high.

All of them entreated the Ba'al Shem Tov to ascend with them, to be their guide, and because of their great joy, he resolved to ascend together with them. But he knew there were great dangers involved in ascending into the highest heavens, so he called upon his teacher, the prophet Ahijah, to accompany him. All of them entered the column in the Garden of Eden that serves as a path to Paradise and began their ascent.

As they journeyed on high, the Ba'al Shem Tov led those souls through the hidden palaces of heaven, one after another. All the mysteries of heaven are concealed in those palaces, as well as all the treasuries of heaven.

The Ba'al Shem Tov rose from rung to rung until he reached the palace of the Messiah in the highest heaven. There the Messiah teaches Torah with all the sages and saints and the Seven Shepherds. They greeted him with such great rejoicing that he was afraid that his soul had taken leave of the world, but they assured him that the time had not come for his soul to depart from his body. At last he asked the Messiah, "When will my Master come?" And the Messiah replied, "When your teachings are known in the world, and others are capable of ascending on high like you."

This account, from a famous letter attributed to the Ba'al Shem Tov (ca. 1700-1760), describes a heavenly ascent on Rosh ha-Shanah 5507 (September 1746). Rosh ha-Shanah, the New Year, is the traditional Day of Judgment when God decides people's fate. See "The Book of Life and the Book of Death," p. 289.

This letter was said to have been written by the Ba'al Shem Tov to his brother-in-law, Rabbi Abraham Gershon of Kittov, when the latter was in the land of Israel. It is one of the only examples of writings by the Ba'al Shem Tov. In *Ben Porat Yosef*, where the letter was first published, the author, Rabbi Yakov Yosef of Polnoye (1704-1784), stated that the Ba'al Shem Tov gave him the letter to deliver to his brother-in-law, Rabbi Gershon. But Rabbi Yakov Yosef was unable to make the journey to the Holy Land, and therefore the letter remained with him. This indicates the authenticity of the letter.

One of the *Ushpizin*, as the Seven Shepherds are known, is said to visit a righteous man's *sukkah* on each of the nights of Sukkot—if properly invited. There are varying lists of the identities of the Seven Shepherds. According to Micah 5:4 and *B. Sukkah* 52b, they are Adam, Seth, Methuselah, David, Abraham, Jacob, and Moses. According to the *Zohar* (3:103b-104a), they are Abraham, Isaac, and Jacob, together with Moses, Aaron, and Joseph, plus King David. The Ba'al Shem Tov does not specify the names of the Seven Shepherds he encounters, but they are likely to be the list of those found in the *Zohar*, where Abraham, Isaac, Jacob, Moses, Aaron and Joseph each represent one of the sefirot from *Hesed* to *Yesod*. See "The Seven Shepherds," p. 299.

For another narrative of a heavenly ascent by the Ba'al Shem Tov, see "Unlocking the Gates of Heaven" in *Gabriel's Palace*, pp. 205-207.

Sources:
Ben Porat Yosef; Sefer ha-Hasidut, pp. 73-77; *Mikhtavim me-ha Besht ve-Talmidav; Sefer Margaliot*. The Besht's letter with notes by M. S. Bauminger is found on pp. 153-74.

Studies:
Founder of Hasidism: A Quest for the Historical Baal Shem Tov by Moshe Rosman, pp. 97-113.
Jewish Mystical Testimonies, edited by Louis Jacobs, pp. 182-191.

BOOK FOUR

MYTHS OF HELL

As soon as one of the wicked dies, his soul is
joined with the river of fire, and goes down to
Gehenna with it.

Sha'ar ha-Gemul 79a
Moses ben Nachman

256. THE UNFINISHED CORNER OF CREATION

All of Creation had been completed except for the north corner of the world. God began to create it, but left it unfinished, saying, "Whoever declares himself to be God, let him come and finish this corner, and then all shall know he is a god." There, in that unfinished corner, demons, winds, earthquakes, and evil spirits dwell, and from there they come forth to the world, as it is said, *From the north shall disaster break loose* (Jer. 1:14). When the Sabbath departs, great bands of evil spirits set out from there and roam the world.

> Because of the cold north wind, the north was identified as the abode of evil spirits. This myth explains why—because that part of creation is unfinished. Here God makes a challenge to those who assert that they are divinities. The true test for a divinity is the ability to create a world. So God left one corner of the world unfinished, with the challenge that anyone who could finish it would indeed be a true god. Of course, the clear implication is that such a creation would be impossible.

> Rabbi Moshe Hayim Luzzatto offers a different perspective about unfinished creation: "God began Creation but left it unfinished so that man could eventually bring it to completion" (*Adir ba-Marom*).

> The Kotzker Rebbe said of this unfinished corner of creation: "One little corner—God left one little corner in darkness so that we may hide in it!"

> *Sources:*
> *Pirkei de-Rabbi Eliezer* 3 ; *Midrash Konen* in *Beit ha-Midrash* 2:30; *Sefer ha- Zikhronot* 1:7; *The Book of Jubilees* 2:2; *Zohar* 1:14b; *Siah Sarfei Kodesh; Or ha-Ganuz.*

257. THE DARKNESS THAT EXISTED BEFORE CREATION

What happened to the darkness that existed before the creation of the world? Some say it is hidden in the seventh compartment of Gehenna. That compartment contains six nations of the world, but they cannot see each other on account of the darkness. The heretic Elisha ben Abuyah is said to reside there.

> The description of darkness found in Genesis, *the earth being unformed and void, with darkness over the surface of the deep* (Gen. 1:2), is quite ambiguous. Instead of stating that God created the darkness, the text seems to be saying that the darkness already existed—it was already *upon the face of the deep*. What is unclear is the meaning of darkness: whether it is to be understood as an absence of light, in the way that "unformed and void" suggests an absence. Or is darkness to be understood as a physical element, such as light? One possible answer to this question is given by Isaiah, who quotes God as saying, "*I form light and create darkness*" (Isa. 45:7). Here the difference depends on the word *yotzer*, "forming," and *borei*, "creating." The key here is that what God only forms, not creates, must have pre-existed. That, ultimately, may be the meaning of *darkness was upon the face of the deep*—the darkness was already there, a pre-existing element. This suggests a Gnostic view of the Creation, in which the Creator is something less than a supreme divinity. For another text with such Gnostic undertones, see "Light from the Temple," p. 411.

> *Sources:*
> *Sefer ha-Zikhronot* 11:11.

258. THE BANISHMENT OF DUMAH

The angel Dumah was the celestial Prince of Egypt. When Moses said that God would exercise judgment against the gods of Egypt, Dumah ran away four hundred parasangs. Then God said to him: "It is My decree!" And at that moment Dumah's power and dominion were taken away from him, and he was banished to the lower regions and appointed over the realms of Gehenna and the angels of destruction. Thus he serves as judge of all the souls of the wicked.

Dumah sees to it that the wicked are punished every day of the week, except for the Sabbath, when they are released. But at the close of the Sabbath Dumah casts their souls back into Gehenna, and their punishments begin anew.

> This myth is clearly intended to parallel that of the fall of Lucifer. Just as Lucifer was an angel who rebelled against God and was cast out of heaven, so here the angel Dumah rebels upon learning that God planned to defeat Egypt, since Dumah is the celestial prince of Egypt. And just as Lucifer is identified with the Devil and said to rule in hell, so too is Dumah assigned to rule over Gehenna, Jewish hell. Other sources identify the prince of Gehenna as Arsiel. *Midrash ha-Ne'elam* in *Zohar Hadash* 25a-b describes Arsiel as standing before the souls of the righteous to prevent them from praying for the wicked before God. He demands that they also be placed under his dominion so that he can take them down to the netherworld, as it is said, *Let me have the souls* (Gen. 14:21).
>
> Although Lucifer's fall is rooted in Jewish sources, the myth was primarily taken up in Christian lore, and the myths of Lucifer and the Devil became merged into one. See "The Fall of Lucifer," p. 208.
>
> Concerning the release of wicked souls on the Sabbath, see "Sabbath in Gehenna," p. 238. For more on the angel Dumah, see "The Punishments of Gehenna," p. 236. Because of his role as the angel in charge of Gehenna, Dumah is sometimes misidentified as the Angel of Death.
>
> *Sources:*
> *Zohar, Exodus* 2:8a; *Pesikta Rabbati* 23:8.

259. GOD'S PRISON

There is a dreadful abyss at the end of heaven and earth where there is no firmament of the heavens above, and no earth beneath it. Columns of heavenly fire fill the abyss, the smell of sulphur is everywhere, and around it there is a wasteland without water; with no birds to be seen.

This place is God's prison for rebellious stars and fallen angels. In it are seven stars burning like great mountains as they roll over the fire of the abyss. Because they did not come forth at their appointed times, God has bound them in that place for ten thousand years.

There, too, are imprisoned the fallen angels who deceived mankind into making sacrifices to demons as if they were gods, and those who went astray with the daughters of men and defiled them.

> This bleak abyss, a kind of protohell, holds seven stars that transgressed God's command to come forth, as well as fallen angels who have been imprisoned. This is one of the places shown to Enoch in *1 Enoch*. For more on the mythic account of the fallen angels see "The Watchers," p. 457.
>
> *Sources:*
> *1 Enoch* 17:9-16, 67:4-7.

260. ADAM AND THE DEMONS

After the expulsion from Eden, Adam was so filled with grief that he separated from his wife, Eve, for one hundred and thirty years. What did Adam do for so long? Some say that he repented for a hundred and thirty years by standing in the River Gihon until the waters reached up to his neck, and he fasted until his body became as wrinkled as seaweed.

Others say that female demons swarmed around Adam and inflamed him, until they succeeded in seducing him. In this way Adam begot mutant demons, both male and female, who were half human and half-demonic. At the same time, male demons were inflamed by Eve and seduced by her, and she too gave birth to a great many demons.

Some say it was Lilith, Adam's first wife, who found him alone and lay down by his side, and thus were begotten myriads of demons, spirits, and imps. Others say it was not Lilith, but her sister, Na'amah, who found Adam there.

When God saw how Adam had turned away from Eve, He put desire for her back into Adam's heart. And when, at last, Adam and Eve were reunited, she bore Seth, who, unlike Cain, was the very image of Adam, as it is said, *When Adam had lived one hundred and thirty years, he begot a son in his likeness after his image, and he named him Seth* (Gen. 5:3).

This strange legend about Adam being seduced by female demons, and Eve seducing male ones grows out of the biblical verse *When Adam had lived one hundred and thirty years, he begot a son in his likeness after his image, and he named him Seth* (Gen. 5:3). Since the statement of the birth of Seth follows the mention of 130 years, the rabbis assumed that Adam must have withdrawn from Eve for that long.

Various explanations are given for Adam's separation from Eve. Some attribute it to their expulsion from Eden and Adam's realization that death had been decreed against the world on his account, while other sources link it to Adam's grief over the death of Abel.

There are also contradictory myths explaining what happened to Adam during the 130 years. One tells us that Adam repented by standing in the River Gihon, and the other assumes that his sexual desire was as great as ever, making him vulnerable to female demons, while male demons impregnated Eve. The demons that Adam and Eve give birth to are called *mazikim*. These *mazikim* and their demonic consorts account for the proliferation of demons. The *Zohar* (3:76b) attributes heavenly beauty to the daughters of Adam who were conceived in this way. The reference to Seth being in the image of Adam, and some texts say, the seed of Adam, while Cain was not, refers to the midrash that attributes Cain's conception to intercourse between Eve and the serpent, making Cain the son of the serpent. See "The Seed of Cain," p. 448.

This myth about Adam echoes the Greek myth of Tantalus, who was punished for his crimes by having to stand in a river up to his neck. There he is consumed by hunger and thirst. There is a nearby tree, with a branch he could reach, that bears every kind of fruit. But if he reaches for it, it pulls away. Likewise, he tries to drink from the river, but as soon as he reaches for it, the water subsides. From this punishment comes the term "tantalize." Note that the Greek myth focuses the torment on food and water, while the Jewish myth focuses on sexual issues. See *Greek Myths* by Robert Graves, 108d.

Sources:
B. *Eruvin* 18b; *Genesis Rabbah* 20:11, 22:11, 24:6; *Pirkei de-Rabbi Eliezer* 20; *Midrash Tanhuma, Bereshit* 26; *Sefer ha-Zikhronot* 13:1; *Zohar* 1:19b, 1:55a, 3:76b; *Ein Gor Sheyne Tkhine.*

Studies:
The Hebrew Goddess by Raphael Patai.
Jewish Magic and Superstition by Joshua Tractenberg.

261. ADAM AND LILITH

When God created Adam and saw that he was alone, He created a woman from dust, like him, and named her Lilith. But when God brought her to Adam, they immediately began to fight. Adam wanted her to lie beneath him, but Lilith insisted that he lie below her. When Lilith saw that they would never agree, she uttered God's Name and flew into the air and fled from Adam. Then Adam prayed to his Creator, saying, "Master of the Universe, the woman you gave me has already left me." So God called upon three angels, Senoy, Sansenoy, and Semangelof, to bring her back. God said, "Go and fetch Lilith. If she agrees to go back, fine. If not, bring her back by force."

The angels left at once and caught up with Lilith, who was living in a cave by the Red Sea, in the place where Pharaoh's army would drown. They seized her and said, "Your maker has commanded you to return to your husband at once. If you agree to come with us, fine; if not, we'll drown one hundred of your demonic offspring every day."

Lilith said, "Go ahead. But don't you know that I was created to strangle newborn infants, boys before the eighth day and girls before the twentieth? Let's make a deal. Whenever I see your names on an amulet, I will have no power over that infant." When the angels saw that was the best they would get from her, they agreed, so long as one hundred of her demon children perished every day.

That is why one hundred of Lilith's demon offspring perish daily, and that is why the names of the three angels are written on the amulets hung above the beds of newborn children. And when Lilith sees the names of the angels, she remembers her oath, and she leaves those children alone.

> The haunting legend of Lilith finds its source in the rabbinic commentary on the biblical passage *Male and female He created them* (Gen. 1:27). It appeared to the rabbis that this passage contradicted the sequential creation of Adam and Eve (Gen. 2:21-22). Therefore they attempted to resolve this contradiction by saying that *Male and female He created them* referred to Adam's first wife, whom they named Lilith, while Eve, who was created later, was Adam's second wife. They chose the name Lilith from Isaiah 34:14, where Lilith is mentioned (*Yea, Lilith shall repose there*), in what is believed to be a reference to a Babylonian night demoness.
>
> Even though Lilith seems to leap fully formed out of a line in the Bible, it is likely that the legend was already told among the Jewish people, and that the rabbis sought out a text to attach it to. In any case, the mythological figure of Lilith almost certainly finds its origin in other cultures of the Ancient Near East. Lilith's role as a seducer of men is likely to have been based on the Babylonian night demon Lilitu, a succubus who seduces men in their sleep, while Lilith's role as a child slayer may well derive from the Babylonian demon Lamashtu. It is interesting to note that the roles of Lilitu and Lamashtu became blurred together, and Lilith took on the roles of both seducer and child slayer.
>
> Having brought a powerful figure such as Lilith into being, the rabbis felt compelled to recount her entire history. In this case, the legend began to grow quite extensive. The first complete version of it is found in *Alpha Beta de-Ben Sira*, dating from the ninth century in North Africa, the primary source of the myth.
>
> Here Adam and Lilith are described as having been created at the same time, and having fought over everything from the first. They had a final confrontation over the question of the missionary position. Adam insisted on it; Lilith refused, preferring the opposite, with the female dominant. When they couldn't agree, Lilith pronounced the secret Name of God, the Tetragrammaton, YHVH, which has remarkable supernatural powers, and flew out of the Garden of Eden and landed on the shore of the Red Sea. There Lilith took up residence in a nearby cave and took for lovers all the demons who lived there, while Adam, left alone, complained to God that his woman had left him. God sent the three angels to command Lilith to return. She refused, and they threatened to kill 100 of her demon offspring daily. Lilith still refused to return; she was never very maternal.

When Lilith offers a compromise, the myth takes a strange turn. She tells the angels that she was created to strangle children, boys before the eighth day and girls before the twentieth. But if a woman carried an amulet with the words "Out Lilith!" on it, along with the names of the angels, she would leave that woman and her children alone. What is really occurring is that another myth is being fused to the first, while the issue of Lilith's return to Adam is simply dropped. This second myth concerns Lilith's role as a child-destroying witch. Indeed, it is possible that a myth concerning another demoness has been incorporated into that of Lilith. In all likelihood, we can identify this demoness as Obyzouth, who is invoked by King Solomon in the first century text *The Testament of Solomon*. The king commands her to describe herself, and Obyzouth tells how she seeks to strangle children. Furthermore, she reveals that she can be thwarted by the angel Raphael and by women who write her name on an amulet, for then she will flee from them to the other world. What appears to be taking place is that the demoness Lilith, who up to this point had been concerned with issues of independence and sexuality, here takes on a new aspect from Obyzouth, that of the child-destroying witch, by a process of mythic absorption. Why did this happen? Probably because Lilith became such a dominant mythic figure that she absorbed the roles of the lesser known demoness. This likely occurred very early, between the first and third centuries, and Lilith has played a powerful dual role ever since in Jewish folklore and superstition. See "The Night Demoness," p. 223.

So it is that Lilith is regarded both as a witch determined to strangle children and as the incarnation of lust. In her role as a witch, Lilith's actions provided an explanation for the terrible plague of infant mortality. Use of amulets against Lilith was widespread and is still considered necessary in some ultra-Orthodox Jewish circles. Only a generation ago grandmothers often tied red ribbons on a child's bed. These ribbons symbolically represented the amulet against Lilith and served the same purpose.

The text of this amulet against Lilith is taken from *Sefer Raziel*. The amulet against Lilith has been found in archeological digs dating back 1,500 years. The traditional use of such amulets against Lilith was widespread, and visitors to the ultra-Orthodox Mea She'arim section of Jerusalem will even today find protective amulets against Lilith available for purchase. Both the text and even the primitive drawings on the ancient amulet are still in use. See "A Spell to Banish Lilith," p. 218, for the text.

Sources:
Alpha Beta de-Ben Sira 5.

Studies:
Rabbinic Fantasies: Imaginative Narratives from Classical Hebrew Literature, edited by
    David Stern and Mark Mirsky.
The Hebrew Goddess by Raphael Patai, pp. 221-254.
"Notes on the Testament of Solomon" by H. M. Jackson.

262. LILITH RISES FROM THE DEEP

From the crevice of the deep there came a certain evil female spirit whose name was Lilith. She had been condemned to imprisonment deep beneath the waves. But God's anger at the time of the Fall was so great that God decided to let Lilith go. So the dark Lilith, also known as the First Eve, was set free. She hides during the day in caves and other dark places. But at night she is free to roam the world.

That is why it is written that a man may not sleep alone in a house, for Lilith will attempt to seduce him. She will slip in if the window is open a crack, slip beneath the door and beneath the sheets. Her long hair is jet black. Many a man has felt it hanging in his face as he lay asleep, dreaming lustful dreams. After she steals his seed, Lilith gives birth to mutant demons, half human and half demon, who are destined to be outcasts. Humans will hate them, because they are half demon, and demons will hate them because they are half human.

To lead the hearts of men astray, Lilith adorns herself with all manner of decorations, and stands at the entrance to roads and paths. She dresses for seduction, with earrings from Egypt and jewels hung around her neck. Her hair is long and red, her face white and pink, with six pendants hanging from her ears and all the ornaments of the East encircling her neck. Her mouth is like a tiny door, her lips beautiful, her words smooth as oil, and her tongue sharp as a sword.

They will encounter her in a forest or a ruin, or in the cellar where an innkeeper takes his naps. One fool after another runs after her, drinks from her cup of wine, sleeps on her bed of Egyptian flax. And when he wakes up, thinking to sport with her, she takes off her finery and turns into a fierce warrior, her garment of flaming fire, her eyes horrific, and causes his body and soul to tremble, her sword sharpened with drops of poison. Then she kills him with a sharp sword from which bitter drops fall, and casts him into the very pit of hell.

> This account of Lilith from the *Zohar* demonstrates how she is viewed as a murderous demon, who uses her sexual powers to destroy men. In the *Zohar*, Lilith is viewed as the primary feminine force of evil, while Samael is the primary male force. While in the Talmud (*B. Eruvin* 100b) Lilith is generally described as having long, black hair, there are other sources, such as this one, where her hair is described as red. Some sources even assert that Lilith has wings (*B. Nidah* 24b). This links Lilith even closer to the Babylonian night demonesses Lilitu and Lamashtu.
>
> *Sources:*
> B. *Shabbat* 151b; B. *Eruvin* 100b; *Zohar* 1:148a-b; *Zohar* 3:19a.
>
> *Studies:*
> The Hebrew Goddess by Raphael Patai.
> Lilith—The First Eve: Historical and Psychological Aspects of the Dark Feminine by
>   Siegmund Hurwitz.

263. A SPELL TO BANISH LILITH

OUT LILITH! I adjure you, Lilith, in the Name of the God, and in the names of the three angels sent after you, Senoy, Sansenoy, and Semangelof, to remember the vow you made that when you find their names you will cause no harm, neither you nor your cohorts; and in their names and in the names of the seals set down here, I adjure you, Queen of Demons, and all your multitudes, to cause no harm to a woman while she carries a child nor when she gives birth, nor to the children born to her, neither during the day nor during the night, neither through their food nor through their drink, neither in their heads nor in their hearts. By the strength of these names and seals I so adjure you, Lilith, and all your offspring, to obey this command.

> This text is used to ward off the demoness Lilith in her attempts to strangle newborn babies. The text is placed inside of amulets worn by mothers during pregnancy, and hung above the beds of babies after they are born. Lilith played the role of a child-destroying witch, for it was she who was blamed for the scourge of infant mortality. This text alludes to the story of how Lilith abandoned Adam and the Garden of Eden for a cave by the Red Sea. The demons were sent to order her to return to her husband, but she refused. After bargaining with the angels, they came to an agreement whereby Lilith would not try to harm any mother or infant protected by this amulet. See "Adam and Lilith," p. 216.
>
> *Sources:*
> Sefer Raziel.

264. THE WOMAN IN THE FOREST

Lilith seeks, above all, to seduce the best ones, knowing that if she can conquer them, the others will fall into her hands as well. Once she decided to try to seduce Rabbi Elimelekh of Lizhensk.

At that time Rabbi Elimelekh was still a young man. He spent all day in the house of study, and at night he walked home through the forest, always taking the same path.

One night, as he was walking through the forest, he saw a light in the distance. Curious to know what it was, he left the path and followed the light. Before long he saw that it was coming from a cottage, one that he had never before seen in the forest. As he came closer, he peered into the window, and there he saw a woman with long, dark hair, who was wearing a very thin nightgown.

As soon as he saw her, Reb Elimelekh knew he did not belong there, and he turned to leave. Just then the door to the cottage opened, and the woman called out: "Reb Melekh, wait! Please, come in." So Reb Elimelekh went in. Then the woman closed the door and stood before him and said: "Reb Melekh, I have seen you pass through the forest many times, and I have often hoped you would visit me. You know, I bathed in the spring today and I am clean. Surely the sin would be slight, but the pleasure would be abundant." And she dropped her gown.

Reb Elimelekh stared at her with disbelief and struggled with himself, as did Jacob with the angel. And at last he wrenched out, "No!" At that instant the woman vanished, and the cottage disappeared, and Reb Elimelekh found himself standing alone in the forest. And there were glowworms at his feet.

The woman in this tale is not identified, but everyone among the Hasidim who heard it knew exactly who she was—Lilith, or one of the daughters of Lilith. So vivid was the presence of Lilith in their lives that she became the primary projection of their sexual fantasies and fears.

Lilith, as in this tale, is usually portrayed as having black hair. In fact she is characterized this way in the Talmud (*B. Eruvin* 100b). She is brazen from the first, calling Reb Elimelekh not by his full name, Elimelekh, but by his familiar name, Melekh. This conveniently lets her avoid pronouncing Eli, "my God," which, as a demoness, she is forbidden to do. The fact that her hair is long indicates that she is unmarried, while having bathed in the spring informs him that she has purified herself in a *mikveh*. She is appealing to his knowledge of the Law when she tells him that the sin will be slight and the pleasure abundant. According to Deuteronomy 22:22, *If a man be found lying with a married woman, then they shall both die.* However, the expected parallel about a married man lying with an unmarried woman is missing, and, according to rabbinic principles of interpretation, what is not stated is not a law. Therefore, the sin is slight, since the law does not identify it as adultery. It is a sin, but not a mortal one.

Thus Lilith comes equipped with many weapons. She does not only use the power of lust, her greatest power, but also appeals to his intelligence. Rabbi Elimelekh escapes, but only after a considerable struggle. The glowworms at the end indicate that Lilith has lost her power over him and Lilith has been revealed in her true form, that of a worm. Or, if this story is read as a Hasidic sexual fantasy, that the fantasy has reached its climax.

The fact that the tale is attributed to Reb Elimelekh of Lizhensk indicates that Lilith was brazen enough to approach even the holiest of men. Indeed, this was her intention. For if she could corrupt the best ones, the others would be sure to follow. Reb Elimelekh resists, but barely. The power of the *Yetzer ha-Ra*, the Evil Inclination, affects everyone on this earth, even rebbes. There is also a compensating force, the *yetzer ha-tov*, the Good Inclination. But, as might be expected, there is much more heard of the *Yetzer ha-Ra* in Jewish lore than there is of the *yetzer ha-tov*.

Sources:

Ohel Elimelekh; Sefer Or Yesharim story no. 199; Zikaron Tov; Ohalei Shem; Devĕt Brán.

265. THE CELLAR

Every impurity engenders demons. Whenever a man's seed is spilled, his demon off-spring are conceived. Lilith or one of the daughters of Lilith steals it. A drop is all that is needed.

These demon sons regard the man as their father. They find a place to live in his house, whether in an attic or a cellar, or even in a closet. They make their home there.

Not even married men are safe from the lure of Lilith. No sooner do their wives turn their backs, than Lilith seeks out victims among them. She appears to them as dreams during the night, and as visions during the day. Sometimes Lilith so sways a man that she becomes his secret wife.

That is what happened in the city of Posen, where there once was a goldsmith who was secretly married to Lilith. The demoness lived in the cellar, where the goldsmith had his workshop. He spent time with his demon lover every day, while keeping her exist-ence secret from his family. Little by little the goldsmith yielded everything to her, lust-ing after her day and night.

Once it happened that the goldsmith even got up in the middle of the Seder, when the words "And they went down into Egypt" were read, and went down to the cellar. His real wife followed after him, afraid that he was ill. She peered through the keyhole of the cellar door, and saw that the cellar had been transformed into a palatial chamber, while her husband lay naked in the arms of a lover. Maintaining control of herself, she returned to the Seder and revealed nothing to the rest of the family. But the next day she went to the rabbi and told him everything.

The rabbi confronted the man with his sin and he confessed. Then the rabbi gave him an amulet to protect himself against Lilith, and he used it to free himself of her. But before she would release him, Lilith demanded that the cellar be bequeathed to her and their demon offspring for all time, and the man took a vow to this effect. He escaped her powers all the rest of his life, but as he lay on his deathbed, his demon children swarmed around him, invisible to his human family, crying out his name.

After his death the house became known as being haunted. Eventually it was sold, and the new owner had a workman break open the door to the cellar, which had been nailed shut. When that workman was found dead on the threshold, Rabbi Yoel Ba'al Shem was sent to investigate. He confirmed that the cellar was infested with demons, and he ordered a rabbinic court, a *Beit Din*, to be convened. The court ruled against the demons' right to live in the cellar there, on the grounds that the demons transgressed the boundaries of the cellar, and they were expelled into the wilderness.

One of the most popular and pervasive beliefs in Jewish folk tradition is that the demoness Lilith or one of her daughters, the *Lilin*, seek to steal a man's seed, in order to create a demon who is half-human and half-demon. These demonic sons are said to haunt their fathers all their lives. The struggle portrayed in this and other similar tales can be seen as one between humans and demons, with offspring who are half-human, half-demonic—or, as a struggle between Jews and Gentiles, where Jewish men are lured by Gentile women, and their offspring are half-Jewish, half-Gentile. In both cases the offspring are spurned by both sides.

Lilith plays a major role in Jewish lore as the incarnation of lust. She haunts men in their dreams and imaginations. Every time a man had a sexual dream or fantasy, he was believed to have had intercourse with Lilith, and the product of this intercourse were mutant demons, half human and half demon, who were spurned by humans and by demons alike. The story recounted here is a famous 17th-century folktale from the ethical text *Kav ha-Yashar*.

Among the oral traditions about a man's demon sons is that that when he lies on his deathbed, his demon sons surround him, crying out his name. So too are the demon sons said to accompany a man's human sons to the cemetery, where they mourn for him. To deceive the demons, his true sons do not take a direct path to the funeral, but set off in the opposite direction. Once they reach the cemetery, they read Psalm 91 out loud, to ward off the demons. Then they form a sacred circle and dance around the dead man seven times. This prevents the demon sons from approaching the deceased and demanding their inheritance.

Psalm 91 is the psalm used to ward off demons and is believed to invoke supernatural protective qualities. It is recited to keep away the forces of evil. Especially important is the verse, *He will order his angels to guard you wherever you go* (Psalms 91:11). It also includes verses such as, *You need not fear the terror of the night, or the arrow that flies by day, the plague that stalks in the darkness, or the scourge that rages at noon* (Ps. 91:5-6).

These folk traditions grow out of a belief in extreme sexual purity, where any accidental or intentional spilling of a man's seed is regarded as a sin, the sin of Onan (Gen. 38). So too do they reflect the widespread belief—and fear—of succubi, in the form of Lilith and her daughters. For more on nocturnal emissions, see *B. Berakhot* 57b and *B. Yevamot* 76a.

Sources:

Kav ha-Yashar; Ohel Elimelekh; Sefer Or Yesharim story no. 199; *Zikaron Tov; Ohalei Shem; Zohar* 1:48a-b; *Ma'asiyot me-Tzaddikei Yesodei Olam; Moraim Gedolim; Hemdat Yamim* 2:98b; *Korban Shabbat* 18c; *Sha'ar ha-Kavvanot* 56b-c; *Ta'amei ha-Minhagim* 436; Oxford Hebrew ms. Oppenheim 540 (no. 1567 in Neubauer's *Catalogue of the Hebrew Manuscripts in the Bodleian Library*), attributed to Judah the Pious; *Ha-Sulam* on *Zohar, Vayishlah* 1-4; oral version collected by Howard Schwartz from his father, Nathan Schwartz.

Studies:

"Tradition and New Creation in the Ritual of the Kabbalists," in *On the Kabbalah and Its Symbolism* by Gershom Scholem, pp. 118-157.

"Two Magical Bowls in Teheran" by C. H. Gordon. Orientalia, vol. 20, 1951, pp. 306ff.

The Hebrew Goddess by Raphael Patai.]

"Five Versions of the Story of the Jerusalemite" by Joseph Dan.

266. LILITH, THE QUEEN OF ZEMARGAD

Lilith, the Queen of Zemargad, has the form of a beautiful woman from the head to the navel, and from the navel down she is flaming fire. Her only intention is to arouse wars and all kinds of destruction. It was she who seized and killed the sons of Job.

Her lovers include the demons Samael and Ashmedai, the King of Demons. Indeed, great jealousy sprang up between the demons Samael and Ashmedai over Lilith.

When God brings about the destruction of Rome, and turns it into a ruin for all eternity, He will send Lilith there, and let her dwell in that ruin, for she is the ruination of the world, as it is said, *And Lilith shall repose there* (Isa. 34:14).

Just as the sirens in Greek mythology are destructive female creatures, half-woman and half-bird, so Lilith is described here as being half-woman, half-fire. This description serves a dual purpose. On the one hand it shows that she is not a real woman, but some kind of strange creature, and the fire that makes up her lower half symbolizes the fires of desire that she awakens and that her role is directly related to lust.

In Jewish folklore, Lilith is identified as the Queen of Demons and is said to be married to Ashmodai, the King of Demons. In this myth, where the view of Lilith is entirely negative, she is viewed as a destructive creature who provokes nothing but lust and jealousy. Even her demon lovers, Samael and Ashmedai, fight over her. But, the myth promises, the day will come when, like Rome, Lilith will receive her just punishment and be forced to live in a ruin, since she has ruined so many lives. See "The Two Liliths," following, for a variant myth.

Sources:
Targum to Job 1:15; *Kabbalot* in *Mada'ei ha-Yahadut* 2:257; *Zohar* 3:19a.

267. THE TWO LILITHS

Some say there are two Liliths. One is the spouse of Samael and the other is the spouse of Ashmedai. On Yom Kippur the two Liliths go forth into the desert and screech. And when the two meet there, they quarrel in the desert, and they strive with each other until their voices rise up to heaven, and the earth shakes with their clamor. God sees that this takes place so that the two Liliths should not accuse Israel while Israel is at prayer on Yom Kippur.

> Kabbalistic texts identify two Liliths, one sometimes known as Grandmother Lilith the Great and the other as Little Lilith. Mythic speculation about two Liliths grows out of two separate traditions about Lilith, one linking her to the demon Samael, and the other linking her to Ashmedai, the King of Demons. One of Lilith's specialties is to distract men while they are at prayer with lascivious thoughts. Here God sees to it that Lilith cannot distract Israel on Yom Kippur by sending the two Liliths out into the desert, where they screech and struggle with each other.
>
> This myth of the two Liliths being sent out into the desert on Yom Kippur seems to be parallel to that of the scapegoat sent out into the desert to Azazel on Yom Kippur (Lev. 16:50-10). See "A Scapegoat for Azazel," p. 295. But it replaces the male demon of the biblical myth—Azazel—with a female demon, Lilith. And instead of the scapegoat being sent to Azazel, the two Liliths are sent out to quarrel and screech at each other, distracting them and thus preventing them from accusing the people of Israel on the Day of Atonement. See "The Ba'al Shem Tov Ascends on High," p. 209 for another example of the theme of silencing the Accuser.
>
> A parallel mythic development is found in the myth of the two Messiahs, Messiah ben Joseph and Messiah ben David. See "The Two Messiahs," p. 517.

Sources:
Pardes Rimmonim 186d; *Kabbalot* in *Mada'ei ha-Yahadut* 2:257.

268. LILITH'S CHILDREN

In his travels, Rabbah bar Bar Hannah reached the city of Mehuza. There he saw Hurmin, the son of Lilith, running along the battlements of the walls of the city. A cavalryman was chasing him from below, but even though he was riding on horseback, he could not catch up with him.

Once Hurmin had two mules saddled and stood them on two bridges of the Rognag River. As Rabbah watched, Hurmin jumped back and forth from one to the other, holding two glasses of wine in his hand, pouring wine from one to the other, without spilling a drop. When the king of Mehuza heard about Hurmin's stunts, he had him executed, for the king feared that Hurmin would try to depose him.

As for Lilith's daughters, they are just as dangerous as she is. Their names are Na'amah, Agrat, Irit, and the Queen of Sheba.

Some say that Na'amah is Lilith's daughter, and some say that she is her sister. In any case, they are like evil twins, for they work in exactly the same way. They lure grooms into their web, and marry them not to their intended brides, but to their demonic doubles.

Watch out for Agrat. She roams about in the company of eighteen myriads of angels of death, all of whom kill by strangulation. It is dangerous to go out on Wednesday night or the eve of the Sabbath because of them.

As for the Queen of Sheba, she seeks out men to seduce, just like her mother. She comes to them whether awake or asleep and steals their seed and bears them demonic offspring.

> The accounts of Rabbah bar Bar Hannah take the form of tall tales, on land and sea. This one recounts how he reached the city of Mehuza and saw Hurmin, Lilith's son, performing stunts. Rabbah's tales are generally interpreted as allegories. Here Rabbi Samuel ben Meir (1083-1174), known as Rashbam, sees Hurmin as representing the *Yetzer ha-Ra*, the Evil Inclination. The cavalryman is the *Tzaddik* who makes a great effort to perform the *mitzvot*, the commandments. The juggling of the cups indicates that every misdeed against Israel will be duly punished.
>
> While Lilith is undoubtedly the primary Jewish demoness, there are several other demonesses who make their mark in Jewish lore, especially Na'amah, Agrat, and the Queen of Sheba. So it is not surprising that they are sometimes identified as the daughters of Lilith. Their functions are virtually identical to those of Lilith: seducing men and leading them astray, and giving birth to demons, including mutant demons fathered by human men. See "Demonic Doubles," p. 230.
>
> *Sources:*
> B. *Bava Batra* 73a; *Numbers Rabbah* 12:1; *Tzefunot ve-Aggadot*.

269. THE NIGHT DEMONESS

Using the power of God's Name, King Solomon compelled the demon Ornasis to reveal the names of all the other demons. One of those he named was Obyzouth. No sooner did the demon pronounce her name than Solomon saw what seemed to be a woman, whose body and limbs were veiled by her long hair.

Solomon said to her, "Who are you?" She replied, "Who are you, and why do you want to know who I am? But if you wish to know this, then go into the royal chambers, wash your hands, seat yourself on your throne again, and ask me. Then you will learn who I am."

And after King Solomon had done these things, he asked her again who she was, and she replied: "Men call me Obyzouth. At night I go around the whole world and visit women about to give birth. As soon as the child is born, I do my best to strangle it. If I fail, I leave at once and go somewhere else, because I cannot let a single night pass without success. I have nothing else to do but kill children."

When King Solomon heard this, he said. "Tell me, evil spirit, how can women protect themselves from you? By the name of what angel are you rendered harmless?" Obyzouth said, "By the angel Apharoph. And when women give birth, they should write my name on a piece of paper and hang it up, and I will flee from that place."

> This description of the demoness Obyzouth from *The Testament of Solomon* (first through third centuries CE) contains the key elements of the Lilith myth. Both are nocturnal demons who attempt to strangle newborn babies. Even their appearance is similar, for they both have long, black hair. But the demoness Obyzouth disappears after *The Testament of Solomon*, and Lilith takes over her role, in an example of mythic absorption. Now Lilith has two roles, as the incarnation of lust and as a child-destroying witch. As

evidence of the link between the two demonesses in later kabbalistic literature, Obyzouth was said to be one of the secret names of Lilith.

Sources:
The Testament of Solomon 13.

270. LILITH THE WITCH

At night Lilith flies over homes until she smells the odor of mothers' milk. She finds a way to enter the house—any kind of crack in the door or window will do. She can take any form she desires, a black cat, a broom, even a hair in the milk. Some say she comes there to strangle the infant, others that she wants to steal the afterbirth, to feed it to her children. Only if the child is guarded by an amulet against Lilith will the child be safe.

But Lilith's greatest enemy was the old midwife who was familiar with all her tricks. It is told that Lilith, flying over the house of a woman who had recently given birth, smelled the mother's milk and transformed herself into a long, black hair that fell into a glass of milk. When the mother was about to drink the milk, she noticed the black hair and fainted. The midwife recognized the presence of Lilith at once and poured the glass of milk, hair and all, into a jug, and closed it tightly. Shaking the jug, the midwife heard the pleas of Lilith from within and extracted a vow from her not only to spare the woman and her child, but also to serve them for three years and protect them from other evil forces. This Lilith did, for once she takes an oath, she is compelled to carry it out.

> Note that the portrait of Lilith in the story of the midwife is quite different from that found in the male myths. The male attitude toward Lilith mixes fear with sexual fantasy. From a woman's perspective, however, Lilith is bad news in every way, as Lilith threatens to steal both her husband's affection and seed and the very life of her children. (It is important to contrast this traditional view of Lilith as an evil demoness with the contemporary view, espoused by Jewish feminists, that Lilith be viewed as a role model for sexual and personal independence. See footnote 172 in the Introduction.) Thus Lilith holds far more power over men than she does over women. Perhaps this is because men are ambivalent toward Lilith, seeing her as something forbidden and tempting, while fearing her destructive abilities. For women, Lilith is a husband-stealing, child-destroying witch they fear and loathe more than anything else. And unlike the men, they are willing to struggle against her, here defeating her. The story of the midwife who captures Lilith is Kurdish. Professor Dov Noy suggests that this is a prime example of a woman's tale, containing secrets of how to defeat the enemy, Lilith. See "The Hair in the Milk" in *Lilith's Cave*, pp. 110-112.

Sources:
Shishim Sippurei Am; IFA 4563.

Studies:
Lilith—the First Eve: Historical and Psychological Aspects of the Dark Feminine by
     Siegmund Hurwitz.
"Some Early Amulets from Palestine" by J. A. Montgomery.

271. LILITH AND ELIJAH

Elijah was walking one day when he met Lilith. He said, "Unclean one, where are you going?" Lilith knew that she could not lie to Elijah, so she said, "I am going to the house of a woman who is about to give birth. I will give her a sleeping potion and kill her and take her child and eat it."

Elijah said, "I curse you in the Name of the Lord. Be silent as a stone!"

Lilith said, "O lord, release me from your curse and I swear by God's Name to forsake my evil ways. As long as I hear or see my own names I will retreat and not come near that person. I shall have no power to injure him or do evil. I swear to disclose my true names to you."

Elijah said, "Tell me what your names are."

Lilith said, "These are my names: Lilith, Abiti, Abizu, Amrusu, Hakash, Ode, Ayil, Matruta, Avgu, Katah, Kali, Batub, and Paritasha." Let them be written and hung about the house of women who are bearing a child, or around the child after it has been born. And when I see those names, I shall run away at once. Neither the child nor the mother will ever be injured by me."

And Elijah said, "So be it. Amen."

> Here Lilith is portrayed not only as a witch intent on killing children, but as a cannibal as well, who seeks to kill the mother and devour the child. This is the vilest description of Lilith to be found anywhere. At the same time, Lilith is subject to the power of Elijah, who curses her in God's Name to be silent as stone. This would be a terrible punishment for Lilith, who uses her verbal wiles to bargain her way out of every difficult situation. Lilith then agrees to stay away from every pregnant woman or newborn child where Lilith's own names are posted in the house. This creates the kind of amulet against Lilith found in "A Spell to Banish Lilith," p. 218. Here, however, is a different story of the origin of the amulet. The more famous account found in *The Alpha Beta de-Ben Sira* tells how God sent three angels to force Lilith to return to Adam, but when she refused, they agreed on the creation of an amulet that would ward off Lilith. See "Adam and Lilith," p. 216.
>
> Thus there are two important elements that differ from the usual folk traditions about Lilith: one is that she devoured her infant victims, and the other is about her encounter with Elijah having resulted in the creation of an amulet to ward her off.
>
> An unknown Gnostic tale is referred to by Epiphanius in *Panarion*, in which Elijah was said to have been cast back into the world after his ascent on high. A female demon took hold of him and said, "Where are you going? I have children from you, and you can't go to heaven and leave your children here." Elijah said, "How can you have children from me? I was always chaste." The demon said, "But I do! While you were dreaming, you often had an emission, and I took the seeds from you and begot you children." The existence of this story indicates that Elijah and Lilith, or a Lilith-like figure, were regarded as traditional adversaries, one deeply pious, the other, the embodiment of evil.
>
> *Sources:*
> *Yosef ba-Seder* 6.

272. LILITH FLEES FROM THE APPARITION OF EVE

When God created Adam, he attached Eve to Adam's back. Her beauty was like that of the realms above. Some say she was only an apparition, for she had not been brought into being, while others say that she was Adam's other half, until God separated them, creating two beings where there had been one.

Once Lilith approached Adam, seeking to seduce him, for she thought that he was all alone. But when she saw Eve's perfect image attached to Adam's back, Lilith flew from there to the cherubim who guard the gates of the Garden of Eden. But the cherubim turned her away, and God dispatched her to the depths of cities of the sea.

There Lilith dwelt until Adam and Eve sinned. Then God freed her from the watery depths and let her roam to and fro in the world. She returned to the cherubim and dwelt there by the fiery ever-turning sword that guards the way to the Tree of Life (Gen. 3:24).

Some say that she still bides her time there until the moon is on the wane and the light diminishes. Then she comes forth from the gates of the Garden and flies through the world seeking revenge against the children of Eve.

But others say that God has exiled her once again to the Cities of the Sea, and that she will remain there until Rome is destroyed. Then God will bring Lilith from the depths and settle her in Rome's desolate ruins.

This myth is a good example of how the *Zohar* takes an existing midrash and transforms it into a kabbalistic one. The midrash on which this myth is based (*B. Eruv.* 14a) describes Adam and Eve as having been created back to back. That image recurs here (*Zohar* 1:19b), but it seems to suggest that rather than being a flesh and blood creature, Eve is more of an apparition, a perfect image. This interpretation grows out of the verse *In the image of God He created him, male and female He created them* (Gen. 1:27). *Tzelem*, the word for "image," has many mystical meanings. Here it seems to suggest that Eve is more of an archetype than a person. Lilith is intimidated by this vision, either because she realizes that Adam is already with another woman, or because Eve's supernal beauty (which is, after all, that of the image of God) so greatly transcends her own. Gershom Scholem suggests that *tzelem* is a kind of astral body (*On the Mystical Shape of the Godhead*, pp. 251-273).

Then the myth recounts that Lilith flees to the cherubim, who guard the gates of the Garden of Eden (Gen. 3:24). Her reasons for seeking out the cherubim are not clear, but it is possible that she, too, wanted a human body. In any case, the cherubim guarding the gates of Eden turn her away and God imprisons her in the depths of the sea. But Adam's sin causes God to set her free, and she comes as close as she can to the Garden of Eden—still, it seems, desiring entry there—while using the night to seek harm against human infants, which, it is implied, is her revenge against Eve.

Zohar 3:19a describes Eve as being fastened to Adam's side, rather than his back, at the time that God breathes the breath of life into him, and this living soul pervades his body. In both of these sources from the *Zohar* it seems that the female plays a role similar to that defined by Carl Jung as the anima, the feminine side of a man, whose presence must be discovered and integrated in order for a man to achieve wholeness. Eventually, however, God splits Adam and prepares Eve as an independent person (*Zohar* 3:19a). Here "prepares" can be understood as transforming Eve from her image into a living person, or, more closely following the midrashim about the wedding of Adam and Eve, preparing her as a bride for Adam. Or both, for this same passage from the *Zohar* also states that the reason Lilith fled was that she saw God bringing Eve to Adam, dressed as a bride (Gen. 2:22).

Kabbalistic cosmology offers an entirely different way of viewing this myth of Lilith and Eve. Here Lilith represents not a demoness, but the whole side of evil in the *Sitra Ahra*, "the Other Side," the domain of dark emanations and demonic power. Eve, likewise represents the world of holiness. See "Adam the Hermaphrodite," p. 138, and "The First Wedding," p. 143.

Sources:
Zohar 1:19b, 3:19a.

Studies:
"Tselem: The Concept of the Astral Body" in *On the Mystical Shape of the Godhead* by
    Gershom Scholem, pp. 251-271.
Lilith—The First Eve: Historical and Psychological Aspects of the Dark Feminine by
    Siegmund Hurwitz.
"Mermaid and Siren: The Polar Roles of Lilith and Eve" by Howard Schwartz.

273. THE SPIRITS OF THE SIXTH DAY

God created all day long during the first six days of Creation and did not rest until the sun set on the sixth day. But when the Sabbath day was ready to be sanctified, there were still spirits that had been created who were left without a body. Thus their creation was incomplete, and they are blemished. The holy name does not dwell in them. That is why demons have no bodies, but are composed entirely of spirit.

Some of these evil spirits tried to enter the body of Adam after God shaped him into the form of a human being, but before God breathed the breath of life into him.

These spirits continue to exist in the realm of spirits, whirlwinds, and demons known as the *Sitre Ahra*, the Other Side. They are made corporeal in that realm, the realm of Cain.

It is said that these spirits have three things in common with the angels, and three things in common with men. Like angels, they have wings, they fly from one end of the world to the other, and they know the future, for they hear it spoken from behind the heavenly curtain (*Pargod*). Like humans, they eat and drink, they propagate, and they die.

In three ways demons are like human beings, and in three ways they are like the angels. Like humans they eat and drink, reproduce and multiply, and die. In addition, they are said to have the feet of cocks, they can change their appearance any time they please, and they see, but they cannot be seen.

If you want to discover demons, take sifted ashes and sprinkle them around your bed, and in the morning you will see something like the footprints of a cock. If you want to see them, take the afterbirth of a black she-cat, the firstborn of a firstborn, roast it in fire and grind it to powder, and then put some in your eye and you will see them.

> This is a myth about the origin of evil spirits, which are said to have been created during the six days of creation with the intention of pairing them with bodies, but when the sun set on the sixth day of creation, there were many spirits left without bodies. These spirits are linked with the *Sitra Ahra*, the Other Side. They are regarded as unclean, and dwell in the realm of evil, or wander restlessly around the world. See "Adam and the Spirits," p. 140.
>
> *Sources:*
> B. *Hagigah* 16a; *Zohar* 1:47b-48a, 1:178a-178b, 3:19a.

274. THE VAMPIRE DEMON

The demons did not want to see the Temple built. They could not harm King Solomon, or the chief builder, so Ornasis, a vampire demon, approached the chief builder's son and sucked blood from his thumb. He did this many times, until the boy was very weak. King Solomon noticed his condition, and asked him what was wrong. When the boy told the king, Solomon gave the boy his royal ring, with the letters of God's Name, YHVH, engraved on it, and told the boy to throw the ring at the demon the next time he approached. That would make him the boy's prisoner. When that happened, the boy was to bring him to King Solomon.

That is exactly how things came to pass, and before long King Solomon besieged Ornasis with many questions about the other demons, what their names were, and how they could be stopped. In this way, King Solomon extracted the names of all the demons. And with the knowledge he gained, Solomon saw the building of the Temple completed, and held off the demons throughout the years he ruled, for they had no power over him.

> This is the earliest Jewish vampire tale, as well as one of the few such tales to be found in Jewish lore. This tale of the demon Ornasis serves as the frame tale to *The*

Testament of Solomon, a pseudepigraphal text believed to date from before the writing down of the Talmud. The conventional vampire/host relationship is presented quite clearly in the role of the demon and the boy who is his victim. King Solomon's plan to capture the vampire demon is similar to that used to capture Ashmedai king of demons, in *B. Gittin* 68.

Sefer Hasidim (twelfth century) includes a tale about Astryiah the vampire, who sucks the blood from her victims while they are asleep.

Sources:
The Testament of Solomon 1.

275. AN EVIL DEMONESS

One after the other, King Solomon invoked a host of demons and evil spirits, in order to find out their names and how they might be thwarted. Among them was a demoness whose name was Onoskelis. Her torso was that of a beautiful woman, but her legs were those of a mule.

Solomon said, "Tell me who you are." She replied, "I am Onoskelis, a spirit that has been made into a body. I was created by the echo of a voice from a black heaven. I make my home in caves in the sides of cliffs and ravines. I travel by the moon. Sometimes I strangle men, sometimes I pervert them from their true nature, for men think of me as a woman, which I am not. Men worship me secretly and openly and this incites me to be an evildoer all the more."

Then King Solomon uttered God's name and commanded her to spin hemp for the ropes used to build the Temple in Jerusalem. He had her bound in a such a way that she was powerless, so that she had to stand day and night to spin the hemp.

> *The Testament of Solomon* serves as a comprehensive listing of demons and spirits. King Solomon invokes and then interrogates them. Here he invokes the spirit of an evil demoness, Onoskelis, who seduces and strangles men. She is a Lilith-like figure, but there are some distinct differences. While Lilith demonstrates seductive beauty entirely, Onoskelis has a beautiful torso but the legs of a mule. Like Lilith, she deceives men into believing she is a woman, when she is actually a demoness set on their destruction. Solomon's punishment for her is like that of a fairy tale—she must endlessly spin hemp. This, of course, keeps her occupied, and forces her to contribute to the building of the Temple.
>
> *Sources:*
> *The Testament of Solomon* 4.

276. THE WIDOW OF SAFED

A widow living in Safed, whom everyone considered pious, suddenly began to speak with the voice of a man, until it became apparent that a wandering spirit, a *dybbuk*, had taken possession of her body. The woman was greatly tormented by this spirit, and she sought help among the disciples of Rabbi Isaac Luria, known as the Ari. Rabbi Joseph Arsin was the first to visit her, and when the voice addressed him by name, he was amazed. Then the *dybbuk* revealed that he had once been a pupil of Rabbi Arsin's when they had both lived in Egypt, and he gave his name. Rabbi Arsin recalled that he had once had such a pupil and realized that the former pupil's soul was now addressing him.

Rabbi Arsin demanded to know why the soul of this man had taken possession of the pious widow. The *dybbuk* readily confessed that he had committed a grievous sin. He had caused a woman to break her marriage vow and had fathered a child with her. And because of this sin, he had been enslaved after his death by three angels, who had dragged him by a heavy chain and had punished him endlessly. He had taken possession of the widow's body in order to escape this terrible punishment.

Then Rabbi Arsin asked the *dybbuk* to describe the circumstances of his death, and the spirit said: "I lost my life when the ship on which I was sailing sank. Nor was I able to confess my sins before dying, because it happened so quickly. When the news of the wreck reached the closest town, my body was recovered along with the others who had drowned, and I was buried in a Jewish cemetery. But as soon as the mourners left, an evil angel opened the grave with a fiery rod and led me to the gates of Gehenna. But the angel guarding Gehenna refused to allow me to enter, so great was my sin, and instead I was condemned to wander, pursued by three avenging angels.

"Twice before I tried to escape from this endless punishment. Once I took possession of a rabbi, but he invoked a flock of impure spirits, and in order to escape them I had to abandon his body. Later I became so desperate that I took possession of the body of a dog, which became so crazed that it ran until it dropped dead. Then I fled to Safed and entered the body of this woman."

Rabbi Arsin then commanded the *dybbuk* to depart from the widow's body but the *dybbuk* refused. So Rabbi Arsin went to the Ari and asked him to perform the exorcism. The Ari called upon his disciple, Rabbi Hayim Vital, to do this in his name and gave him a formula, consisting of holy names, that would force the *dybbuk* to depart.

Now when Rabbi Hayim Vital entered the house of the poor widow, the *dybbuk* forced her to turn her back to him. And when Hayim Vital asked the *dybbuk* to explain this, the spirit said that he could not bear the holy countenance of his face. Then Hayim Vital asked the *dybbuk* to tell him how long it had been cursed to wander. The spirit replied that its wandering would last until the child he had fathered had died. Finally, Hayim Vital asked to know how the *dybbuk* was able to enter the body of the widow. The *dybbuk* explained that the woman had made it possible because she had little faith, since she did not believe that the waters of the Red Sea had truly parted.

Hayim Vital asked the woman if this was true, and she insisted that she did believe in the miracle. He made her repeat her belief three times, and on the third time Hayim Vital uttered the formula that the Ari had taught him. After that he commanded the *dybbuk* to depart from the woman by the little toe of her left foot. At that moment the *dybbuk* did depart with a terrible cry, and the woman was freed from the agony of that possession. The next day, when the Ari ordered that the *mezuzzah* on her door be checked, it was found to be empty, and that is why it did not protect against that evil spirit.

> The legends concerning *Dybbuks*, spirits of the dead who take possession of the living, multiply in the later medieval and Hasidic literature. There are scores of such accounts of possession in Jewish lore. "The Widow of Safed" records the history of one such case, revealing, in the process, the basic pattern to which all possessions are subjected. The *dybbuk* has been able to enter the house because the *mezuzzah* is defective and has been able to take possession of the woman because of her lack of faith in the miracle of the crossing of the Red Sea. The latter was the standard test of true faith among Jews. Note that the Ari sends Hayim Vital to perform the exorcism in this tale, imputing to him powers similar to those of his master. Another early account of possession by a *dybbuk* is found in *Ma'aseh Buch* 152, also dating from the sixteenth century, suggesting that the superstitious conditions both in Eastern Europe and the Middle East were right for this belief. Earlier cases of possession did not involve spirits of the dead, but rather demonic possession, as recorded in Josephus (*Antiquities*, 8:2.5) and the Talmud (*B. Me'ilah* 17b). It is interesting to note that the majority of these accounts of possession include

details of name and place that far exceed the usual anonymity of folklore. Gedalyiah Nigal has compiled a Hebrew anthology of *dybbuk* tales, *Sippurei ha-Dybbuk* (Jerusalem: 1983), and virtually every account includes the place and year where the possession and exorcism occurred and the names of the witnesses. The tales almost always follow the same pattern: (1) Someone becomes possessed by a *dybbuk*. (2) A rabbi confronts the spirit and demands that it reveal its name and history. (3) The *dybbuk* tells its tale. (4) The *dybbuk is* then exorcised, and the one who was possessed recovers. This suggests that the pattern established in the earliest of these tales, such as this one, was repeated in succeeding generations and became, in effect, a socially recognized form of madness. More recently, such possession has been identified primarily as a psychological aberration. In *Legends of the Hasidim*, the editor, Jerome Mintz, reports a case of such possession in which the Satmar Rebbe supposedly advised someone said to be possessed by a *dybbuk* to see a good psychiatrist (pp. 411-412).

Sources:
Shivhei ha-Ari, edited by Shlomo Meinsterl (Jerusalem: 1905).

Studies:
Between Worlds: Dybbuks, Exorcists, and Early Modern Judaism by J. H. Chajes.
Magic, Mysticism and Hasidism: The Supernatural in Jewish Thought by Gedalyah Nigal.
Dybbuk by Gershon Winkler.
"Dybbuk and Maggid: Two Cultural Patterns of Altered Consciousness in Judaism" by Yoram Bilu.

277. DEMONIC DOUBLES

The kingdom of Satan is measure for measure like the kingdom of man. Every male child, when born, already has a double in the kingdom of demons. So too does every female, when she is born, have her shadow born there as well, in her precise shape and image, not unlike that seen in a mirror. And at the hour that a heavenly voice goes forth to announce that this one will be married to that one, a partner is also prepared at the same time in the spirit world. She sits and waits for him there from that time forward. And the man who is fortunate marries his partner from the family of man, but less fortunate is he who is found alone on the fourth night of the week or on the night of the Sabbath. For then he is in danger of being kidnapped by the sons of Satan, and led to a place that no man's feet should ever enter, there to marry, not his intended, but his intended's demonic double.

The Talmud explains that "Forty days before a person is born, a heavenly voice goes forth to say that this one will be married to that one" (*B. Sota* 2a). This knowledge is available to the angels, but not only to the angels—the demons, too, overhear this voice and make evil use of the knowledge they obtain. Thus, in effect, the *bashert* tradition, where a person seeks out and marries his or her "destined one," has been corrupted and effectively reversed by demons.

In *The Testament of Solomon* King Solomon forces the demon Ornasis to explain how demons are familiar with future events. Ornasis tells him that "We demons go up to the firmament of heaven, fly around among the stars, and hear the decisions that issue from God concerning the lives of men." This explains how the demons, as well as the angels, hear the heavenly voice that announces future events. Using future knowledge, demons create the demonic double of a person's *bashert*—destined one—and trick people into marrying the demonic doubles. This serves to explain the many strange marriages that are found in the world.

Sources:
The Testament of Solomon 20; *Tzefunot ve-Aggadot*.

278. THE UNDERWORLD

There is a great and high mountain where the spirits of the dead assemble, in the place known as Sheol. There the spirits of the righteous are separated from the those of the sinners, where they will remain until the day of judgment.

Meanwhile, the voices of the spirits of those who have died go forth from there to heaven, pleading for mercy. One of those spirits belongs to Abel, slain by his brother Cain, and he still makes his case against the seed of Cain, till they are annihilated from the face of the earth.

> This myth from *1 Enoch*, dating from around the second century BCE to the first century CE, identifies the place of the dead as Sheol, as does the Bible. Later Sheol is replaced by Gehenna, Jewish hell, where the souls of the dead are punished and purified. This myth demonstrates that even after death the spirits of those who have been murdered continue to plead their case against their murderers. This belief can be traced to the verse *Your brother's blood cries out to me from the ground* (Gen. 4:10), confirming the belief that such terrible deeds can never go unpunished. Also standing behind this myth is the concept of the seed of Abel and the seed of Cain. These are the descendants of Cain and Abel (or, in Abel's case, the descendants of Seth since Abel had no descendents that we know of), in whose blood the conflict is carried on. And the spirit of Abel will not be satisfied until all of the spiritual descendants of Cain—traditionally identified as the enemies of the Jews—will be annihilated.
>
> *Sources:*
> 1 Enoch 22:1-14.

279. WHEN A MAN DIES

Two angels watch over a man at the moment of his death, and they know whether he has ever been a thief, for even the stones and beams of his house witness against him, as it is said, *For a stone shall cry out from the wall, and a rafter shall answer it from the woodwork* (Hab. 2:11).

Then the soul of the man who has died is brought before the patriarchs and they say to him, "My son, what have you done in the world from which you have come?"

If he answers, "I have bought fields and vineyards, and I have tilled them all my life," they say, "Fool that you have been! Have you not learned that *The earth is the Lord's and all that it holds*" (Ps. 24:1). Angels then take him away and hand him over to the avenging angels, who thrust him into Gehenna.

Then angels bring another before the patriarchs. They ask the same question, and if he answers, "I gathered gold and silver," they reply, "Fool, have you not read in the books of the prophets, *Silver is Mine and gold is Mine—says the Lord of Hosts* (Hag. 2:8). Likewise, he is turned over to the avenging angels.

But when a scholar is brought before them, they ask the same question, and if he answers, "I have devoted my life to the study of the Law," the patriarchs say, *"Let him enter into peace"* (Isa. 57:2), and God receives them with grace.

> This account of what happens to those who die emphasizes the importance of the study of Torah in the eyes of the patriarchs, who are said to serve as judges, and in the eyes of God. The two angels who watch over a man at the time of his death are identified as the Angel of Death and the Angel who counts a man's days and years.
>
> *Sources:*
> *Gan Eden ve-Gehinnom* in *Beit ha-Midrash* 5:48-49; *Orhot Hayim*.

280. THE CREATION OF GEHENNA

Gehenna, the place of punishment, was one of the seven things created before the Creation, but for a long time it was nothing more than a great void. Then, at the time that God separated Himself from Adam and ascended on high, God lit the fires of Gehenna, and made them alternate with periods where everything is covered by ice.

> This myth links the lighting of the fires of Gehenna to the exile of Adam from Eden. This implies that Adam's sin created the need for the fires to be lit. Thus, while Gehenna may have been created before the creation, it was only initiated as a place of punishment after the Fall.
>
> Not all myths about the nature of Gehenna are consistent. Some describe it solely as a place of terrible fires, but other versions have it alternate periods of great heat with periods of the deepest cold.
>
> *Sources:*
> B. *Pesahim* 54a; B. *Nedarim* 39b; *Eliyahu Rabbah* 1:3.

281. THE PRINCE OF GEHENNA

Before the souls of the wicked are taken to the netherworld, Arsiel, the Prince of Gehenna, waits for God's order to take them there. Meanwhile, the Prince of Gehenna stands before the righteous, saying, *"Give me the souls"* (Gen. 14:21). In this way he does his best to distract the righteous, so that they will not pray for the wicked. For the Prince of Gehenna knows only too well the power of their prayers.

> Several figures are identified as the Prince of Gehenna—the angel in charge of the souls of the wicked, who are being punished in Gehenna. Among them, Satan is the best known angel, along with Samael. The demon Ashmedai is said to rule the Kingdom of Demons. The Prince of Darkness is another name that is used. Here the Prince of Gehenna is identified as the angel Arsiel, who plays the satanic role of confronting the souls of the righteous to distract them from praying for the souls of the wicked. Then, when God gives the order, he takes them down to Gehenna. Note that God is at the head of the chain of the orders that send the wicked to the netherworld. All that remains to save the wicked from their fate are the prayers of the righteous. But they are a potent force. For more on the efficacy of the prayers of the righteous, see "The Ashes of Sinners," p. 242.
>
> *Sources:*
> *Midrash ha-Ne'elam, Zohar Hadash* 25a-b.

282. THE HISTORY OF GEHENNA

Where is Gehenna? Some say it is above the firmament, others that it lies below the earth. Still others say that it lies behind the Mountains of Darkness. How big is it? As big as the Garden of Eden, and that is said to be boundless.

Some say that Gehenna predates the creation of the universe. Others say that the space for Gehenna was created first, but its fires did not begin to burn until the eve of the first Sabbath. Still others say that the fires of Gehenna were created on the second day, while ordinary fire was not created until after the end of the Sabbath. So powerful are the fires of Gehenna that they make the sun red in the evening, as it passes over them. It is said that those fires will never be extinguished.

But the fires of Gehenna are not the only punishment, for Gehenna is half fire and half hail. The fires of Gehenna are bad enough, but the hail is much worse.

Gehenna is the place of punishment in Jewish lore, the Jewish equivalent of hell. It has much in common with the Christian concept of hell, except that in the Jewish view punishment in Gehenna never lasts more than a year, while in the Christian view it is eternal. It is usually described as being under the earth—when the earth opened and swallowed Korah, he and his followers fell into the fires of Gehenna.

But there is also a tradition that heaven and Gehenna exist side by side, and that the wall separating them is no more than a hand's breadth.

The concept of Gehenna grew out of the Valley of Gehinnom in Jerusalem, which was regarded as a place of evil, as children were once sacrificed in pagan ceremonies there.

Sources:
B. Pesahim 54a; B. Tamid 32b; B. Bava Batra 84a; Tosefta Bereshit 6:7; Ecclesiastes Rabbah on Ecclesiastes 3:21; Midrash Tehillim 11:7, 51a; Exodus Rabbah 51:7; Zohar 2:150b; Zohar Hadash 57b; Tanna de-vei Eliyahu; Yalkut Shim'oni, Kohelet 57b.

Studies:
Tours of Hell: An Apocalyptic Form in Jewish and Christian Literature by Martha Himmelfarb.
Hell in Jewish Literature by Samuel Fox.
"Early Jewish Visions of Hell" by Richard Bauckham.
Jewish Views of the Afterlife by Simcha Paull Raphael.

283. THE OPENINGS OF GEHENNA

Some say that there are three entrances to Gehenna, one in the wilderness, one in the sea, and a third in Jerusalem. Others say that there are two date trees in the valley of Gehinnom where smoke ascends, and that is the entrance to Gehenna. Others say that there are four openings to Gehenna on each side of the universe, sixteen in all. Whatever direction the wicked may take in trying to escape Gehenna, they only run into another of its openings. Still others say there are fifty gates to Gehenna, each of which has holes in which the feet of the wicked are locked.

Then there are those who say that the mouth of Gehenna can be found anywhere in the world, and should it be needed, the mouth opens and swallows whatever is standing there.

Various sources describe different entrances to Gehenna, and this myth attempts to resolve the contradictions by stating that Gehenna has three entrances. An alternate explanation suggests that the entrance to Gehenna can be found anywhere, and that the ground can open up and swallow a sinner, just as it did for Korah and his followers when they challenged Moses in Numbers 16:32. See "The Punishment of Korah," p. 235. See too "The Door to Gehenna," p. 240.

Sources:
Midrash Konen in Beit ha-Midrash 2:24-39; Midrash Aggadat Bereshit 18a.

284. THE LANDSCAPE OF GEHENNA

Some say that there are coals in Gehenna as big as mountains and as huge as the Dead Sea. So too are there rivers of pitch and sulphur flowing and fuming and seething throughout Gehenna.

Others say that Gehenna is half fire and half ice, and when the sinners escape from the fire, they are tortured by the ice, and when they escape from the ice, the fire burns them.

In many ways Gehenna is a distorted mirror image of Paradise. Just as there are rivers of balsam flowing through heaven, there are rivers of pitch and sulphur flowing in Gehenna. The rivers of balsam are part of the rewards of paradise, while the rivers of pitch and sulphur are part of the punishments of Gehenna.

So too is Gehenna sometimes described as half fire, half ice. Those being punished by the fire try to escape to the ice, but it is so terrible that they run back to the fire, for there is no escape from the punishments of Gehenna.

Sources:
Orhot Hayim; Baraita de-Masekhet Gehinnom in *Hesed le-Avraham; Midrash Konen* in *Beit ha-Midrash* 2:24-39.

285. THE SCORPIONS OF GEHENNA

There are seven thousand scorpions in every crevice of Gehenna. Every scorpion has seventy thousand pouches of venom, and from these flow six rivers of deadly poison. When a man comes in contact with that poison, he immediately bursts, and his body is cleft asunder, and he falls dead on his face. Then the avenging angels collect his limbs and revive him and place him on his feet and take their revenge on him all over again.

These deadly scorpions, far more lethal than any found on earth, are one more example of the kinds of punishments of Gehenna, where a sinner can be killed and revived over and over again, so that his suffering continues until his time in Gehenna comes to an end.

Sources:
Baraita de-Masekhet Gehinnom in *Hesed le-Avraham.*

286. THE BRIDGE OVER GEHENNA

There is a bridge that spans Gehenna. The spirits of the dead have to struggle to cross that bridge. When they are directly over Gehenna, the bridge appears to be no wider than a thread, and some of them lose their balance and tumble into Gehenna, their diminishing screams following them into the abyss.

The tortures of Gehenna are myriad, and nothing is as it seems. Here the spirits of the dead are forced to cross a bridge that seems to be as narrow as a thread and, losing their balance, they fall into the Abyss. The point is that those who receive punishments in Gehenna have nothing they can depend on, and live in constant danger. In a metaphorical sense, the bridge across Gehenna symbolizes the immense difficulty of sinners finding their way out of the punishments of Gehenna.

Sources:
Seder Eliyahu Zuta 21, 76b; *B. Eruvin* 19a; *B. Sukkah* 32b; *Ms. Oxford Bodleian OR* 135, published in "Un Recueil de Contes Juifs Inedits," edited by Israel Levi, *Revue des Etudes Juives,* vol. 35 (Paris: 1897).

287. THE DARKNESS OF GEHENNA

The darkness of Gehenna is thick as the wall of a city. Nothing is more terrible than this darkness, as it is said, *A land whose light is darkness, all gloom and disarray, whose light is like darkness* (Job 10:22). This is the darkness of the plague of darkness, when *Moses held out his arm toward the sky and thick darkness descended* (Exod. 10:22). Where did that darkness come from? From the darkness of Gehenna.

> One of the punishments of Gehenna is a terrible darkness as thick as a wall. Indeed, it was this impenetrable darkness that God drew upon when he brought the plague of darkness to Egypt. Once again, the punishment is intended to fit the crime. Just as the sinners were blind to their sins, so they are punished in Gehenna by a darkness so thick it leaves them lost in blindness.
>
> *Sources:*
> *Midrash Tanhuma-Yelammedenu, Noah 1; Midrash Tanhuma-Yelammedenu, Bo 2; Baraita de-Masekhet Gehinnom* in *Hesed le-Avraham.*

288. THE LIGHT OF GEHENNA

Sometimes a light issues forth from Gehenna into the Garden of Eden. This is a sign that God has accepted the grief of one of the souls that is being punished. The soul's contrition warrants its entry into the Garden of Eden, where its suffering is transformed into delight.

> This myth is in direct contrast to "The Darkness of Gehenna." It shows that God continues to monitor the grief of the sinners in Gehenna, and that He is prepared at a moment's notice to accept deeply felt repentance to free those sinners from the punishments of Gehenna. In contrasting Gehenna with the Christian concept of hell, it is important to note that the punishments of hell are supposed to last forever, while the time the soul of a sinner spends being punished in Gehenna is limited to a maximum of twelve months. And ultimately, when the Messiah comes, Gehenna will cease to exist.
>
> *Sources:*
> *Zohar* 2:211b; *Tzidkat ha-Tzaddik* 153; *Toldot Ya'akov Yosef; Sifram Shel Tzaddikim.*

289. THE PUNISHMENT OF KORAH

Once a Bedouin came to Rabbah bar Bar Hannah and offered to show him where Korah and his followers had been swallowed up by the earth. They went there and they saw two cracks in the ground, with smoke coming out of them. Rabbah took a bundle of wool and soaked it in water and put it on the tip of a spear. He then stuck the spear into one of the cracks in the earth. When he took it out, they saw that the wool was scorched by fire. The Bedouin told Rabbah to put his ear to the ground, to hear what Korah and his followers were saying. When Rabbah did, he heard them crying out, "Moses and the Torah are true, and we were liars!" The Bedouin told Rabbah that every thirty days the angel appointed over the sinners of hell brings them to this place, where they are roasted by the fire. And all the while they cry out in regret over what they have done.

> This is one of the tall tales attributed to Rabbah bar Bar Hannah found in the Talmud. Here a Bedouin takes him to the place where Korah and his followers were swallowed up by the earth after they rebelled against Moses in Numbers 16:32. The place they fall into is Gehenna, where evil souls are punished. Once a month Gehenna returns to that place. This regularity echoes Rabbah's tale about the same Bedouin leading him to the Wheel of Heaven, which returns to the same place every 24 hours.
>
> The moral of this myth is quite apparent: Korah and his followers are still crying out in regret for their rebellion against Moses, which will haunt them forever. See "Where Heaven and Earth Meet," p. 121 and "The Dead of the Desert," p. 471.
>
> *Sources:*
> *B. Bava Batra* 74a.

290. THE INHABITANTS OF GEHENNA

The souls of the wicked descend below to Gehenna, as it is said, *The spirit of the beast goes downward to the earth* (Eccles. 3:21). This includes the utterly wicked in Israel and the wicked among the nations of the earth. Both will go down to Gehenna, as it is said, *The wind shall carry them off, and the whirlwind shall scatter them* (Isa. 41:16).

> This myth answers the question of whether the punishments of Gehenna are limited to Jews, or whether they apply to the wicked of other nations. Here both are described as being punished in Gehenna.
>
> *Sources:*
> *Ecclesiastes Rabbah* on Ecclesiastes 3:21; *Eliyahu Rabbah* 18:108-109; *Eliyahu Zuta* 11:192.

291. THE FATE OF THE SOUL

The souls of the righteous are stored beneath the Throne of Glory, while the souls of the wicked are made to wander, and one angel stands at one end of the world and another at the other end, and they throw the wicked souls to one another, as it is said, *He shall sling away the lives of your enemies as from the hollow of a sling* (1 Sam. 25:29).

> This brief myth presents a stark contrast between the fates of the souls of the righteous and those of the wicked. While those of the righteous are kept close by, beneath God's throne, those of the wicked experience the punishment of wandering and exile, traditionally the worst possible punishment. This is the same punishment Cain receives when God makes him *a ceaseless wanderer on earth* (Gen. 4:11). But most startling is the image of the angels standing at each end of the world, throwing the souls of the wicked back and forth. This emphasizes how relentless is the wandering they are condemned to, which takes on characteristics of one of the punishments of Gehenna, Jewish hell. See "The Punishments of Gehenna," following.
>
> *Sources:*
> *B. Shabbat* 152b.

292. THE PUNISHMENTS OF GEHENNA

Gehenna, where the souls of the wicked are punished, is ruled by the angel Dumah. Dumah was appointed to rule over the netherworld. Three angels of destruction are at his command. Their names are Mashit, Af, and Hema, and they command many legions of avenging angels. All of Gehenna is filled with their din, and their shouts reach into heaven. That is why the voices of the wicked can barely be heard as they shriek out, and why no one has mercy upon them.

Every night, except the Sabbath, the angels of destruction punish those whose evil deeds were hatched in the dark. There the wicked learn firsthand why the dread of Gehenna is so great.

But when the Sabbath begins, judgment vanishes from the world and the wicked in Gehenna rest. The angels of destruction cease ruling over them from the moment the Sabbath arrives, until the Sabbath comes to an end. Then the wicked are dragged back to the dungeons of Gehenna, where their punishment resumes.

It is said that in the future all the people of Israel will enter Gehenna together with the nations of the world, and the latter will all perish, while Israel will depart from its midst unharmed, as it is said, *When you walk through fire, you shall not be scorched; through flame, it shall not burn you* (Isa. 43:2).

This myth explains how Gehenna is ruled by the angel Dumah. (*Dumah* is the Hebrew word for silence and land of death.). Dumah, in turn, commands three forces of angels of destruction, led by three angels, Mashit, Af, and Hema. The myth is offered by way of explanation as to why the phrase "He, in His compassion" is not said on the Sabbath, lest the angels of destruction be stirred up. Nor is it necessary to conclude the *Hashkivenu* with the blessing "He who protects his people Israel," because there is no need for protection—the Sabbath itself protects. Instead the blessing used is "He who spreads over us a Tabernacle of Peace," which is clearly understood to be a reference to the Sabbath.

The myth also emphasizes that even the wicked in Gehenna are freed from their punishments on the Sabbath, which is thus celebrated not only on earth, but also in heaven by God and the angels (see "God Keeps the Sabbath," p. 314) and even by the wicked being punished in hell.

A few key prooftexts are brought in to substantiate this myth. Concerning those who plot evil in the dark, it is said, *Who do their work in dark places* (Isa. 29:15). The dread of Gehenna is said to be referred to in the verse *Because of terror by night* (S. of S. 3:8). The names of the three commanding angels under Dumah are taken from this verse. Rabbi Alexander explained, "The dread of Gehenna is similar to the dread of night" (B. Sanh. 7b).

Sefer Hasidim reports a man riding through the desert who saw by the light of the moon a line of wagons pulled by human beings. He recognized them as people who had died. He asked what they were doing, and they told him that it was the punishment for their sins. For if a person behaved like an animal during his lifetime, he was put to work like an animal in the afterlife.

Sources:
Midrash on Ruth 79b; B. Sanhedrin 94a; Sod ha-Shabbat 9; Pirkei de-Rabbi Eliezer 11:5;
    Sefer Hasidim 169.

Studies:
Hell in Jewish Literature by Samuel J. Fox.

293. THE FATE OF SLANDERERS

What is the fate of slanderers? When slander, spread about the earth, mounts even to the throne of glory, destroying angels descend at God's command and seize the slanderers and throw them into the furnace of Gehenna.

But Gehenna objects, saying, "The tongue of a slanderer reaches from earth up to the heavens. The entire world cannot stand him. First send your arrows at him, and then I will receive him, as it is said, *A warrior's sharp arrows, with hot coals of broom-wood* (Ps. 120:4)." Then those who slander are hung by their tongues and subject to all the tortures that Gehenna has to offer.

The most despicable figures in Gehenna are the slanderers. Not even Gehenna, personified here, can bear their presence. So Gehenna insists that God punish them first, and then Gehenna will receive them, according to the verse *A warrior's sharp arrows, with hot coals of broom-wood* (Ps. 120:4). Here the "coals of broom-wood" refers to the punishments of Gehenna. For another example of the personification of Gehenna, see "Gehenna Seething," p. 238.

Note that the sinners are cast into the furnace of Gehenna, where the hottest flames of Gehenna are burning. This is to demonstrate the seriousness of their sins.

Sources:
Eliyahu Rabbah 18:108

294. SABBATH IN GEHENNA

Even the wicked in Gehenna enjoy a respite on the Sabbath. Every Sabbath eve, when the day becomes sanctified, the angel in charge of souls announces, "Let the punishment of the sinners cease, for the Holy King approaches and the Day is about to be sanctified. He protects all!" Instantly all punishment ceases, and the guilty have a respite. The sinners who observed the Sabbath are led to two mountains of snow, where they remain until the end of the Sabbath, when the angel in charge of the spirits shouts, "All evildoers, back to Gehenna—the Sabbath is over!" and they are thrust back to their former place in hell. Some of them, however, take snow with them to cool them during the six days of the week, but God says to them: "Woe to you who steal even in hell!"

But the fires of Gehenna do not come to a halt for those who never observed the Sabbath. Since they did not observe the Sabbath before, they have no respite. An angel whose name is Santriel, which means "God is my Guardsman," goes and fetches the body of the sinner from the grave. He brings it to Gehenna before the eyes of the guilty, and they see how it has bred worms. They know the soul of such a sinner has no respite from the fire of Gehenna. And all those guilty who are there surround that body and proclaim over it: "This person is guilty, for he would not regard the honor of his Master, he denied the Holy One, blessed be He, and denied the Torah. Woe to him! It had been better for him never to be created and not to be subjected to this punishment and this disgrace!"

Rabbi Yehudah said: "After the Sabbath goes out the angel comes and takes that body back to its grave, and both the body and the soul are punished, each in its own way."

And all this takes place while the body is still well preserved. But once the body is decayed, it no longer suffers all these punishments. The guilty ones are punished in their bodies and their souls, each with a suitable punishment, so long as the body in the grave is intact. But when the body breaks down the punishment of the soul ceases. He who must leave Gehenna leaves, and he who must find rest has rest—to each is done what is suitable for him.

> So great is the redeeming power of the Sabbath, that even the souls being punished in Gehenna are allowed to rest on the Sabbath, until the close of the Sabbath. As *Tola'at Ya'akov* puts it, "*Din*—harsh justice—is banished on the eve of the Sabbath, even from the sinners in Gehenna. For the Sabbath protects the cosmos. But on Saturday night *Din* is restored to its station. A herald cries out: *'Let the wicked be in Sheol'*" (Ps. 9:18). In addition to a reprieve on the Sabbath, *Zohar* 2:150b lists further reprieves on new moons and festivals.
>
> For a folktale about Sabbath in Gehenna, see "Three Stars" in *Gabriel's Palace*, pp. 227-228. See also "Sabbath in Gehenna" by Isaac Bashevis Singer's in *The Death of Methuselah and Other Stories*, pp. 212-219.
>
> *Sources:*
> *Pesikta Rabbati* 23:8; *Orhot Hayim; Zohar* 2:151a; *Tola'at Ya'akov* 58b; *Sha'ar ha-Gemul; Nishmat Hayim* 1:12, 1:14; *Sefer ha-Zikhronot* 15:7.

295. GEHENNA SEETHING

Gehenna is seething all the time. God asked, "Why are you seething?"

Gehenna replied, "I am seething, quivering with anger, shaking because of the vile things the wicked say about Israel."

God asked, "What will it take to calm you?"

Gehenna answered, "Cram me full of those who transgress against Israel."

God said, "I have already filled you with the nations of the earth, and there is no more room in you."

Gehenna replied, "Master of the Universe, did You not promise that Gehenna would be increased in height by so many parasangs in order to accommodate all transgressors?"

At that instant Gehenna was expanded, and God still flings Israel's transgressors into it.

> This myth continues the personification of Gehenna seen in "The Fate of Slanderers," p. 237, both from *Eliyahu Rabbah*. Thus Gehenna is not only portrayed here as a place of punishment, but also as a being gripped by the most intense anger, like a seething pot. God recognizes that Gehenna is seething, and inquires if there is a way to calm it. Gehenna demands to be crammed full of those who transgress against Israel. God raises the question of whether Gehenna has enough room to hold them. This question of room in Gehenna grows out of Isaiah 5:14: *Assuredly, Sheol has opened wide its gullet and parted its jaws in a measureless gape.* God then expands Gehenna in order to accommodate all the new sinners.
>
> In another version of this myth, instead of asking to be expanded, Gehenna asks for an additional category of sinners, those who know the Torah yet transgress it.
>
> Sources:
> *Eliyahu Rabbah* 18:108; *Eliyahu Zuta* 20:32.

296. THE SIZE OF GEHENNA

The wicked wonder, "How many myriads can Gehenna hold? Two hundred, three hundred myriads? How can it ever hold all the wicked who appear in every generation?"

God replies, "As you increase, Gehenna, too, increases, growing wider and broader and deeper every day," as it is said, *His firepit has been made both wide and deep* (Isa. 30:33). For even though God finished creating the world and rested from His work on the seventh day, yet He continues to ordain punishment for the wicked, and to bestow rewards upon the righteous.

> The point of this myth about Gehenna is that there will always be room for more sinners—God will see to that. The question of finding sufficient space for all the sinners of Gehenna is also addressed in "Gehenna Seething," p. 238.
>
> Sources:
> *Pesikta Rabbati* 41:3.

297. THE GATES OF GEHENNA

Gehenna is located at the north of the world, in the unfinished corner of creation. There are three princes of Gehenna, who have been appointed over its three gates. One gate is in the desert, where Korah and his followers fell to the underworld of Sheol. The second gate is in the Sea of Tarshish, and the third gate is in the valley of Gehinnom in Jerusalem. The three ministers of Gehenna, Kipod, Nagdasniel, and Samael, are in charge of these three gates.

Gehenna itself is filled with the dwellings of demons. Among the inhabitants are harmful demons and destructive spirits, as well as many hosts of avenging angels. There the wicked are punished in the seven circles of Gehenna.

Avenging angels lead wraithlike beings to the gates, whipping them onward. When they reach one of the gates of Gehenna, an angel strikes the gate with his fiery whip so that it swings open. Then the angels force them all inside, even though they try to resist. But they are no match for his whip.

> This myth fills in details about the entrances to Gehenna and who rules them, as well as which avenging angels and demons serve there. See "The Unfinished Corner of Creation," p. 213 and "The Openings of Gehenna," p. 233.
>
> *Sources:*
> *Midrash Konen* in *Beit ha-Midrash* 2:30; *Orhot Hayim*.

298. THE DOOR TO GEHENNA

There is a door that leads to Gehenna. It is a danger to anyone standing nearby. Without warning, the door will swing open and a hand reach out and grab whoever is standing there and pull them into Gehenna, never to be seen again. Then the door will slam shut.

> This motif of the forbidden door is well known in world folklore. Perhaps the best-known version is that found in the fairy tale "Bluebeard." Such a door becomes an emblem for all taboos, reminding us of Eve's plucking of the forbidden fruit or of the Greek myth of Pandora. In the Talmud, Paradise and Gehenna are said to be as close as three fingerbreadths, implying that it is very easy to sin, and that the door to Gehenna confronts us at every turn. For a Jewish folktale based on this motif, see "The Door to Gehenna" in *Lilith's Cave*, pp. 64-70. For more on the punishments of Gehenna see *Hell in Jewish Literature* by Samuel J. Fox, which collects these sources.
>
> *Sources:*
> Ms. Oxford Bodleian OR 135, published in "Un Recueil de Contes Juifs Inedits," edited by Israel Levi, *Revue des Etudes Juives*, vol. 35 (Paris: 1897).

299. THE GATEKEEPER OF GEHENNA

The angel appointed over the gates of hell is Samriel. He sees that no one is admitted to Gehenna unless his name is listed in the giant Book of Gehenna that Samriel consults. Avenging angels drag the souls of sinners to Gehenna, and the gatekeeper makes sure that they deserve to be punished there.

Samriel is appointed over the three gates of Gehenna that are found on the side of the wilderness. He has the keys for these three gates, and when he opens them, the light of the world seeps in. Samriel has three angels under him, with three shovels, who clear a path out of Gehenna so that the light of the world can enter and be seen by the inmates of Gehenna.

Once in a while a sage or rabbi descends to Gehenna in order to obtain a bill of divorce from one of the souls being punished there. But the gatekeeper turns them all away, all except for Rabbi Naftali Katz. When Rabbi Naftali came there on a mission, the angel guarding the gate of Gehenna looked for his name in the Book of Gehenna, and refused to admit him when it wasn't there. Rabbi Naftali threatened to take a vow to remain there for eternity and to pester the angel until he let him in. So the angel let him in.

> The only ones permitted into Gehenna are the sinners who are brought there for punishment. However, there are a number of stories about sympathetic rabbis who attempted to enter Gehenna to ease the suffering of the sinners there. This myth explains that there is an angel, Samriel, who guards the entrance of Gehenna in order to keep out anyone who does not belong. In the story "Rabbi Naftali's Trance," Rabbi

Naftali descends to Gehenna to search for a man who abandoned his wife without giving her a bill of divorce. Unlike many others who had sought entrance there, Rabbi Naftali intimidates the powerful angel who guards Gehenna and succeeds in going in. See "Rabbi Naftali's Trance" in *Gabriel's Palace*, pp. 152-154. See also the following tale, "The Messiah in Hell," p. 241.

Sources:
Zohar 1:62b; *Sippurei Ya'akov* 7, edited by Ya'akov Sofer; *Sippurim Mi-she-kevar*, no. 27.

300. THE MESSIAH IN HELL

When Rabbi Joshua ben Levi found himself in the Garden of Eden, he decided to explore it as completely as he could. One by one he explored the nine palaces of the Garden of Eden, until he came to the palace of the Messiah. He recognized the Messiah by the splendor of his aura. There he saw how the patriarchs and kings came to the Messiah every Sabbath and holy day and wept, because it was not yet time for him to go forth into the world.

When Rabbi Joshua came before the Messiah, the Messiah said, "How are my children faring?" And Rabbi Joshua said: "Every day they await you." Then the Messiah gave a great sigh and wept.

After that the Messiah showed Rabbi Joshua all of the earthly garden and the heavenly one as well, and revealed the greatest mysteries to him. But when Rabbi Joshua asked to be shown hell, at first the Messiah refused, for the righteous are not permitted to behold hell. But when Rabbi Joshua told him that it was his intention to measure hell from beginning to end, the Messiah agreed to take him there.

So it was that Rabbi Joshua followed the Messiah until they reached the fiery gates of hell. When the angels guarding the gate saw that the Messiah was with him, they admitted him at once. Everywhere they went, Rabbi Joshua saw the punishments of hell, where avenging angels smite the wicked with flaming rods, and throw them into fiery pits, and after that hang them by their tongues, or by the organs with which they committed adultery. And although Rabbi Joshua tried to measure the compartments of hell, he found that they were boundless, as was the suffering of the wicked. But whenever the wicked in hell saw the light of the Messiah, they rejoiced and cried out, "There is the one who will bring us out of here."

This myth about the descent of Rabbi Joshua ben Levi and the Messiah into hell builds on the talmudic account of Rabbi Joshua's highly irregular entrance into the Garden of Eden. See "Rabbi Joshua ben Levi and the Angel of Death," p. 206. There Rabbi Joshua is portrayed as fearless, and here he asks the Messiah, whom he meets in heaven, to show him hell. The Messiah finally agrees and they descend to Gehenna together. Rabbi Joshua tries to measure the compartments of Gehenna, but discovers that they are boundless, i.e., that they can contain any number of sinners. However, this visit serves to give hope to the sinners of Gehenna, who acclaim the Messiah as the one who will free them from there, since one of the traditions about the coming of the Messiah is that all those being punished in Gehenna will be raised from there to Paradise. The Messiah described here is Messiah ben David, the celestial Messiah, who lives in a heavenly palace and will only descend to earth when the time is right for the footsteps of the Messiah to be heard.

Sources:
Sefer ha-Zikhronot 21:1-11; *Orhot Hayim*; *Aggadat Bereshit* 51a-b.

301. THE SABBATH RESURRECTION

On the eve of every Sabbath, between the afternoon and evening prayers, the spirits of the dead are led to a field in front of a river that comes out of the Garden of Eden. There they drink from this river, and when the congregation says, "Blessed is the Lord who is blessed," they are returned to their graves and God resurrects them and they stand up alive from their graves. In this way all the dead of Israel rest on the Sabbath, and come in crowds and sing in the presence of the Lord. And they come and prostrate themselves in the synagogues, and come to behold the Divine Presence and bow before it.

> This myth is a variant of that about Sabbath in Gehenna. However, this one seems to assume that all of the spirits of the dead are in a Hades-like place where they are kept during the week, not necessarily Gehenna, but more like Sheol. Although it is vague on this point, the central focus of the myth, on the resurrection of all of the dead of Israel every Sabbath, is memorable and unique. It tells us that the Sabbath is not only celebrated by the living, but also by the dead.
>
> *Sources:*
> *Seder Gan Eden* in *Beit ha-Midrash* 5:43.

302. THE ASHES OF SINNERS

Every twelve months the sinners of Gehenna are burned to ashes, and the wind disperses them and carries those ashes under the feet of the just, as it is said, *And you shall trample the wicked to a pulp, for they shall be dust beneath your feet* (Mal. 3:21).

Then the righteous take pity on the fate of the sinners and they pray for mercy upon them, and say, "Master of the Universe, these are the men who rose early to go to synagogue. They read the Shema, prayed, and performed other commandments."

Hearing this, God revives them out of the ashes and stands them upon their feet and brings them to life in the World to Come.

> For most sinners the punishments of Gehenna are only supposed to last for up to 12 months. After that, their souls have been purified, and they are able to slowly ascend on high, through the seven heavens. What is amazing about this myth of sinners being burned to ashes is that their revival comes about because the righteous intercede for them.
>
> Of course, the notion of the sinners in Gehenna being burned to ashes is highly punitive. But the myth also includes an example of righteousness and generosity on the part of the just, whose prayers make it possible for those burned to ashes to be restored for life in the world to come.
>
> See "The Prince of Gehenna," p. 232, for more about the power of the prayers of the righteous.
>
> *Sources:*
> *Orhot Hayim; Seder Eliyahu Rabbah* 3; *Yalkut Shim'oni*, Malachi 593.

303. PURIFIED SOULS

When the process of purification has been completed, the chief angels take a soul out of Gehenna and lead it to the Gate of Paradise. There they say to the angels standing guard: "This soul was broken after its ordeal in the infernal fire, and now it has come to you pure and white."

Then God causes the sun to penetrate the firmament and shed its rays on that soul and heal it.

The purpose of Gehenna is to purify the souls of sinners so that they can be permitted to enter paradise. This myth demonstrates how a soul is taken out of Gehenna. Note that this purification process is clearly described as a painful one, where the soul is purified in the fires of Gehenna.

Sources:
Zohar 2:211a.

304. HOW THE DEAD SEE THE DEAD

The day a person dies is the day of his judgment, when the soul parts from the body. A person does not leave this world until he sees the *Shekhinah*, accompanied by three ministering angels, who receive the soul of a righteous person. These angels examine a person's deeds, and insist that a person confess to all that the body has done with the soul in this world. After this confession, the soul of a righteous person rejoices in its parting from this world and looks forward with delight to the world to come. For when God takes the souls of the righteous, He takes it with gentleness. But when He takes the souls of the wicked, He does so through cruel angels, as it is said, *Therefore a cruel angel shall be sent against him* (Prov. 17:11).

After a man dies he can be seen by all the others who are dead. To each of them he appears as they last saw him alive: some see him as a youth, others as an old man. For the angel who guards the dead makes his soul assume these various forms so that all should recognize him by seeing him just as they saw him in life.

However, if a man is condemned to punishment in Gehenna, he is enveloped in smoke and brimstone, so that none of those being punished can see the punishment of any other. Thus none are put to shame, except for those who have put others to shame.

> This description of a man seeing the *Shekhinah* as he dies is based on Exodus 33:20: *No man shall see Me and live*. The three angels who accompany the *Shekhinah* are identified as the three angels who visited Abraham in Genesis 18:2.
>
> It is characteristic of Jewish myth to describe in great detail unknown realms, such as heaven, hell, or what comes to pass when a person leaves this life. Here the dead are said to see each other exactly as they appeared when they last saw each other alive. This explanation of how the dead see and recognize each other solves the problem of a person's changing appearance by aging.
>
> *Sources:*
> *Sifre on Deuteronomy* 357; *Midrash ha-Ne'elam* in *Zohar* 1:98a; *Sefer ha-Zikhronot* 11:6.

BOOK FIVE

MYTHS OF THE HOLY WORD

There were two angels to every one of them, one to lay his hand on the heart of each one, to keep his heart still, and one to lift each one's head, so that he might behold the splendor of his Creator.

Midrash Aseret ha-Dibrot

305. CREATION BY WORD

In the beginning a word was spoken from the mouth of God, and the heavens and the earth came into being, as it is said, *By the word of Yahweh the heavens were made* (Ps. 33:6). It was no wearisome labor for God, whose word came into being at the instant it was spoken. When God told the heavens to continue to spread out, they went on expanding, as it is said, *Who spread out the skies like gauze, stretched them out like a tent to dwell in* (Isa. 40:22). Indeed, if God had not said: "Enough!" they would have gone on expanding until the end of time.

> This creation myth presents a variant of Genesis 1:3, where *God said "Let there be light," and there was light.* Here, too, the world is created through speech. God is said to have spoken a word, and the world came into being. Here, however, another word is required to stop the expansion of the heavens. This echoes the myth of the golem, a man made out of clay, who, when told to bring water from the river, continues to bring barrels of water until the house is flooded, simply because no one told him to stop. The image of the world continuing eternally to expand suggests the modern theory of the Big Bang.
>
> *Sources:*
> Midrash Tanhuma, Bereshit 11; Midrash Tanhuma, Lekh-Lekha 25; Midrash Tanhuma, Mi-Ketz, 12; Midrash Tehillim 148.3; Raziel ha-Malakh 30.

306. TWO WORLDS

In the beginning God created not one world, but two. For two worlds came forth out of the first two letters of God's Name, YHVH.

Some say that this world was created with the letter *heh*, while the World to Come was created with the letter *yod*. That is the meaning of *the heaven and the earth were finished, and all their array* (Gen. 2:1).

Others say that no one knows which letter this world was created with, the *yod* or the *he*. This has remained a mystery, to this day. All that is known is that with those two letters God brought two worlds into being.

> This myth postulates that God created two worlds at the time of the creation, this world, *Olam ha-Zeh*, and the *Olam ha-Ba*, the World to Come. *Midrash Tehillim* 62:1 links this myth of two worlds to the verse *Truly my soul waits quietly for God* (Ps. 62:2). It then adds, "Know you upon whom you wait? Upon Him who created two worlds with the letters of His Name: with *yod* and *heh* He created worlds, this world and the World to Come." There is a rabbinic debate over which letter was used to create the two worlds. *Midrash Tehillim* 114:3 declares that no one is certain which letter was used for which creation.
>
> Other rabbinic sources view heaven and earth as a single world. Indeed, *Genesis Rabbah* 1:15 recounts a heated rabbinic discussion about which was created first, the heaven or the earth: "The school of Shammai maintains that heaven was created first, while the school of Hillel maintains that earth was created first. In the view of Shammai, this is like a king who first made his throne and then made his footstool. Hillel compares it to a king who builds a palace—first he builds the foundation, then the upper portion. Hearing this, Rabbi Simeon said: 'I am amazed that the fathers of the world engage in controversy over this matter. Surely both were created at the same time, like a pot and its lid.'"
>
> *Eliyahu Rabbah* follows this pattern of simultaneous creation, asserting that God created the heavens and the earth at the same time, in their entirety, and gave them

permanent form by shaping them. He gave them their finishing touch by hammering them out. In this way He made the earth fit to dwell in, while He stretched out the sky above it, as it is said, *The heaven and the earth were finished* (Gen. 2:1).

Sources:
Midrash Tehillim 62:1, 68:3, 114:3; Eliyahu Rabbah 31:29.

307. THE PRIMORDIAL LANGUAGE

Hebrew is the primordial tongue. Not only is Hebrew the language of the angels, it is the language in which God addressed Adam.

> One of the key assumptions of the rabbinic texts is that Hebrew is the sacred tongue, spoken in heaven as well as on earth. It is an axiom that Hebrew is the language of the angels. The Karaites, Jews who accepted the Bible but rejected the Talmud, shared this belief, as indicated here.
>
> *Sources:*
> Kitab al-riyad w'al-Hada'ik.

308. THE CREATION OF THE TORAH

God created the Torah at the very beginning, before the heavens were created and the earth was brought into being, before the mountains were sunk, before the hills were born, before there were any streams or sources of water, as it is said, *Yahweh created me at the beginning of His course* (Prov. 8:22). It lay in God's bosom and sang praises of God along with the ministering angels.

God wrote the Torah while seated on the Throne of Glory, high in the firmament above the heads of the celestial creatures. The Garden of Eden was at God's right hand, and Gehenna was at His left. The heavenly sanctuary was set up in front of Him, with the name of the Messiah engraved upon the altar. There, as the Torah rested on His knees, God wrote the letters in black fire on white fire. Later, it was tied to the arm of God, as it is said, *Lightning flashing at them from His right* (Deut. 33:2). Others say that the Torah was written on the arm of God, while still others say it was carved in fire on God's crown.

The Torah was there when God created the heavens, drawing a circle on the face of the depths. So too was it there when God fashioned the heavens and set the streams into motion.

The Torah was reared by God, and it was His daily joy, giving God great pleasure. Later Moses arose and brought it down to earth to give to humanity.

> Here the passage from Proverbs that is spoken by Wisdom is attributed to the Torah: *Yahweh created me at the beginning of His course* (Prov. 8:22). Thus Wisdom and the Torah are identified as the same figure, since the Torah is regarded as the sum of Jewish wisdom.
>
> This myth answers the question of what the Torah was written on before it was given to Moses. The answer is that it was written with black fire on white fire and tied to the arm of God. An alternate version says that it was tied to the knee of God. Still another version says that the Torah was carved with fire on God's crown.
>
> According to *Avot de-Rabbi Natan*, God created the Torah 974 generations before the world was created.
>
> *Sources:*
> Midrash Tehillim 90:12; Eliyahu Rabbah 31:160; Midrash Mishlei 8; Midrash Konen in Beit ha-Midrash 2:24-39; Avot de-Rabbi Natan 31; Alpha Beta de-Rabbi Akiva in Otzar Midrashim p. 424.

309. CREATION BY THE TORAH

The Torah was one of the seven things created before the creation of the world, and the Torah served as God's advisor when He was about to create this world. God looked into the Torah and created the world and all created beings through it.

When the time came to create man, the Torah said, "Master of the Universe, the world is Yours to create. The days of this man You want to create will be short and full of anger, and he will be drawn into sin. If You are not going to have patience with him, it's better for him not to be created."

God answered, "It's not for nothing that I'm called Merciful."

After that God consulted only the Torah, and let the Torah serve as a blueprint for all creation. So too did the Torah serve as an artisan in all the work of creation. With the assistance of the Torah, God stretched out the heavens and established the earth. With the Torah He bound up the sea, lest it go forth and overflow the world. With the Torah He locked up the deep, so that it might not inundate the world. So too did He fashion the sun and moon with it. Thus we learn that the world was indeed founded upon the Torah, and that God created the world and all created beings through the Torah. How did God do this? He looked into the Torah and created the world with it. With every single act of creation, God looked into the Torah, and created that detail of creation.

Others say that God fashioned the world according to the Torah. Looking at the word "heavens," God created the heavens. Looking at the word "light," He created light. So it went with each and every word of the Torah. In this way the world came into being.

Still others say that God opened the Torah and took a name that had not been given to any creature, and let three drops of that name fall into the sea. Those drops became filled with water and with the Holy Spirit, for *The spirit of God hovered over the face of the waters* (Gen. 1:1). Thus the *Shekhinah* was present in that place.

God opened the Torah again and took out a second name. This time God took three drops of light: one for the light of this world, one for the light of the World to Come , and one for the light of the Torah. For there is a holy light hidden in the Torah, and in order to discover it, it is necessary to probe deeply into the Torah, and one day the light of the Torah will shine forth.

Then God opened the Torah for the third time, and took out three drops of fire, and from that fire the whole world is heated.

God saw fire on His right, light on His left, and water beneath Him. He mixed them together two by two. He took fire and water and mixed them together, and made heaven out of them. So too did God take water and light and make a tent of darkness of them, as well as the Clouds of Glory. And out of fire and light God made the holy beasts.

Thus not only was the Torah created prior to the creation of the world, it was the vessel by which the world was created. Thus the universe was created through the letters of the Torah.

So too did God declare, at the time of man's creation, that the world was created only for the sake of the Torah, and that as long as the Jewish people occupy themselves with the Torah, the world will continue to exist. But if the Jewish people abandon the Torah, God will return all of creation to a state of chaos.

> God is able to consult the Torah because it is one of the seven things created before the creation. See "Seven Things Created before the Creation," p. 74. A parable is given to explain God's use of the Torah to create the world: "When a king wishes to build a palace, he does not build it himself but brings in an artisan. Nor does the artisan build it himself. He uses sketches and notebooks. So too did God look into the Torah and create the world." (*Genesis Rabbah* 1:1). Here the Torah is presented as an "artisan," while God is the architect, that is, as an active, creating force, not simply a text that was consulted. Here the Torah seems to participate in the creation in much the same way as the angels are said to have done in other rabbinic sources. See "Creation by Angels," p. 116.

In the second example of God creating the world from the Torah, found in *Midrash Konen*, God takes a name out of the Torah and transforms it into drops of water, light, and fire, the elements with which God creates the world. This myth provides the origin of the primordial elements with which God was able to create the world, having them find their origin in a name found in the Torah. Such a name or names, usually the name of angel, is used to invoke various kinds of spells in the Jewish magical tradition. It makes the creation of those elements itself a step in the creation process, thus making it a part of God's overall plan. In this scenario, God created the Torah, which, in turn, was used to create the elements, which were used to create the world. This tradition probably emerged in response to the Gnostic view that the primordial elements—darkness, light, water, and fire—already existed when God decided to proceed with creation.

Philo also offers the metaphor of God having used a blueprint in the creation of the world, but he does not identify this blueprint with the Torah, but rather with a blueprint in an architect's mind.

Three types of light are reported to have been created in this myth: the light of this world (*Olam ha-Zeh*), the light of the World to Come (*Olam ha-Ba*), and the light of the Torah. Each one is created out of a word of the Torah, one that was not the name of any creature.

The *Zohar* and later the Ba'al Shem Tov linked the light of the first day, known as the hidden light (*or ha-ganuz*), with the light of the Torah. Rabbi Nachman of Bratslav, the greatest Jewish storyteller, added to this interpretation his view that the light could be found in the stories of the Torah. He loved stories. See "The Light of the First Day," p. 83, and "Light from the Temple," p. 411. According to Rabbi Hayim of Volozhin, the Torah did not actively participate in Creation, but nevertheless played an essential role: "At the time of Creation, the Torah illuminated the universe from a remote distance to give it life and sustain it. Still, the world remained unsettled until the giving of the Torah 2000 years later" (*Nefesh ha-Hayim* 4:1).

The basis for the assertion that God will destroy the world if the Jewish people abandon the Torah is Jeremiah 33:25: "*If not for My Covenant, I would not have set day and night and the bounds of heaven and earth.*"

Sources:

Philo; *De Opificio Mundi* 16-20; *Midrash Tanhuma-Yelammedenu, Bereshit* 1; *Genesis Rabbah* 1:1, 1:4; *Midrash Tanhuma, Bereshit* 4; *Pirkei de-Rabbi Eliezer* 3; *Eliyahu Rabbah* 160; *Midrash Konen* in *Beit ha-Midrash* 2:24-27; *Perush ha-Aggadot le-Rav Azriel* 86-91; *Zohar* 1:24a, 1:134a, 3:11b; *Maggid Devarav le-Ya'akov* 135; *Nefesh ha-Hayim* 4:1.

Studies:

"God, Torah and Israel" by Abraham Joshua Heschel.

310. THE LETTERS OF THE ALPHABET

For two thousand years prior to the creation of the world, all the letters of the Hebrew alphabet were hidden. During that time, God gazed upon the letters and delighted in them. Then, when God was about to create the world, all twenty-two letters engraved upon His crown came down and stood before him, from *tav* to *aleph*. The letter *tav* approached first and said: "O Lord, create the world through me, for I am at the beginning of the word 'Torah.'"

God replied, "*Tav*, You are worthy and deserving, and in the days to come I shall command that you be put as a sign on the foreheads of the righteous, so that when the destroying angel comes to punish sinners, he will see the letter on their foreheads and spare them." But the letter *tav* was sad that it would not be used to create the world, and it left the presence of the Lord.

Then, one by one, each of the other letters came forward and pleaded with God to create the world through them. But God did not grant their wish. Soon all that remained were two letters, *aleph* and *bet*. *Bet* came forth and said, "O Lord, it would be appropriate to create the world through me, for your children will praise you through me every time they say `Blessed be the Lord for ever and ever.'

Then God said, "Blessed are you who comes in the name of the Lord." And God took the letter *bet* and created the world through it.

All this time the letter *aleph* had stood silent. Then God called it and said, "Why are you silent?" *Aleph* replied, "Master of the Universe, I am the least among the letters, for my value is but one. How can I presume to approach you?"

The words of the letter *aleph* were pleasing to God, and He said, "Because you are so modest, *aleph*, you shall become the foremost among the letters, for just as your value is one, so am I one and the Torah is one."

So it is that the *aleph* is the first letter of the alphabet, while *bet* is the first letter of *Bereshit*, the first word of the Torah, which means "in the beginning."

God informs the letter *tav* that in the future it is destined to serve as a mark on the foreheads of the faithful ones who have kept the Law, and through the absence of this mark the rest will be killed. This refers to the vision in Ezekiel 9 where the word usually translated as "man" is *tav* in Hebrew.

Bet is the first letter of the word *barukh*, blessed, which is the first word used in a wide range of blessings.

Note that in Hebrew the letters serve also as numbers, so that *aleph* is literally one.

Sources:
Alpha Beta de-Rabbi Akiva in *Otzar Midrashim* p. 424; *Yalkut Shim'oni; Zohar* 1:2b.

311. CREATION BY LETTERS

With letters, heaven and earth were created, the oceans and rivers were created, all the world's needs and all the orders of Creation. And each letter flashed over and over again like lightning.

The world was created with the letter *bet*, because it stands for "blessing," not with the *aleph*, which stands for "curse." Others say that two worlds were created with two letters—the *yod* and the *heh*—this world and the World to Come. The account of creation opens with the letter *bet* (which serves as the number two) in order to teach that these two worlds exist.

Bezalel, the architect of the tabernacle, knew how to combine the letters through which heaven and earth were created.

There are a variety of traditions about how the world was created. "Creation by Word," p. 247, suggests that the heavens and earth came into being as a result of God's speech. Here it is not the speech, but the letters of the words to which the power of creation is attributed. This myth also suggests that Bezalel, whose abilities as an architect were legendary, drew his power from knowing how to combine the letters that had been used to create the world. A similar tradition concerns the creation of the golem, the man made out of clay. The golem was said to have been brought to life through the letters of the word *emet*, which were inscribed on its forehead, and through the Tetragrammaton, the four-letter Name of God, inscribed on a piece of parchment, which was placed inside its mouth. See "The Golem of Prague," p. 281.

Sources:
B. *Berakhot* 55a; *Midrash Tanhuma-Yelammedenu, Bereshit* 5; *Sefer ha-Bahir* 3; *Pesikta Rabbati* 21:21; *Midrash Tehillim* 62:1; *3 Enoch* 41; *Synopse zur Hekhalot-Literatur* 16; *Sha'arei Orah* 5:68b-69a.

312. THE SHINING LETTERS

Most people derive pleasure from eating and drinking, not from the light shining through the letters. The *Tzaddik*, however, derives no pleasure from eating or drinking or other bodily pleasures. Instead, he is renewed by the shining letters, and derives all his pleasure from them. For the letters of the holy tongue animate every object. And the *Tzaddik*, when reaching for an object, can actually grasp the letters within it.

> Basic kabbalistic doctrine holds that the interaction of the letters of a word is directly linked to what that word represents. Indeed, every object has at its essence the letters that make it up. Most people are oblivious to this inner truth, the letters glowing inside of every object. But the *Tzaddikim*—the righteous ones—are well aware of these letters and are even able to grasp them. Here Rabbi Nachman expands, as he often does, on the remarkable spiritual insight of the *Tzaddik*.
>
> *Sources:*
> *Likutei Moharan* 1:19.

313. THE TORAH WRITTEN ON THE ARM OF GOD

Prior to the creation of the world, there were no animals, therefore there were no skins of parchment on which to write the Torah. How, then, was the Torah written? On the arm of God, with black fire on white fire. And God took the Torah and placed it before Him and gazed at it, and read it from beginning to end. And as He read those words, they came to pass.

> While writing on parchment is not as ancient as writing on clay tablets, it was the method used to record the most ancient Jewish texts, and to this day possession of a parchment scroll of the Torah is considered a necessity for every Jewish congregation. Since there was a well-known tradition that the Torah was one of the things created before the rest of the world, this myth attempts to resolve the problem of where the Torah was written down before there were skins to use as parchment. The answer given is a surprising one—that it was written on the arm of God, and that God read it from where it was inscribed on His arm. This myth suggests how closely the Torah was associated with God, so much so that it was inscribed on His arm like a tattoo.
>
> *Sources:*
> *Aseret ha-Dibrot* in *Beit ha-Midrash* 1:62; *Merkavah Rabbah.*

314. GOD'S ORIGINAL PLAN

According to God's original plan, a thousand generations were supposed to pass before the Torah was given. But nine hundred and seventy-four of those generations were swept away in the wink of an eye, for God saw that they would give themselves to wickedness. After they were carried away, they were gone like a dream, as it is said, *You engulf men in sleep* (Ps. 90:5).

So it was that God gave the Torah to Moses in the twenty-sixth generation from Adam, which would have been the thousandth generation.

> Here God changes His original plan, which was to give the Torah in the thousandth generation. Instead, foreseeing the wickedness of the coming generations, He eliminated 974 of them, speeding the process of the giving of the Torah to the twenty-sixth generation.

The notion of God changing His original plan is intriguing, since God has the ability to foresee the future.

This myth is an interesting variation on the theme that God created and destroyed 974 worlds prior to this one. Here, instead of 974 worlds, there are an equal number of generations. See "Prior Worlds," p. 71.

Sources:
Eliyahu Rabbah 2:9; *Midrash Tehillim* 90:13, 105:3.

315. THE BOOK OF RAZIEL

The Book was revealed to Adam while he was still in the Garden of Eden, to show him each generation and its sages, each generation and its leaders. How did God show him generations that did not yet exist? Some say that God cast sleep upon him and showed him, while others say that Adam saw them all with his eyes, for whatever he read in that book he saw with his own vision. For since the time the world was created, all of the souls of those yet to be born stand before God in the very same form in which they will live in this world.

God sent the angel Raziel, the Angel of Secrets, to read the Book to Adam. But when Adam heard the first words issue from the mouth of the angel, he fell down in fear. Therefore God let Raziel leave the Book with him so that he could read from it on his own, and in this way Adam came to know the future and was made wise in all things.

Some say that book was written on parchment, while others say it was engraved on a sapphire. How was that sapphire read? Adam held it up to his eyes, and the flame burning inside that sapphire took the form of the letters, so Adam could read them there. So too there are those who say that the true text of the Book of Raziel was the Torah, for the Torah was one of the seven things created before the rest of Creation, and this way its wisdom was transmitted even to the first man.

Contained in the Book was a secret writing that explained seventy-two branches of wisdom, mysteries which had not been revealed even to the other angels. So too did the Book contain the entire history, past and future, of mankind. Whenever Adam opened the Book, angels gathered around him to learn all the mystical secrets it contained. Then the angels made a plea to God, saying, "Impart the mystery of Your glory to the angels, not to men." Instead, the angel Hadarniel was secretly sent to Adam and said: "Adam, Adam, do not reveal the glory of your Master, for to you alone and not to the angels is the privilege given to know these mysteries."

After that Adam kept the Book concealed, and read it in secret. In this way he learned mysteries not even known by the angels. But at last the envy of the angels became so great that they stole the Book and threw it into the sea. Adam searched for it in vain, and then fasted for many days, until a celestial voice announced: "Fear not, Adam, I will give the Book back to you." Then God called upon Rahab, the angel of the sea, and ordered him to recover the Book from the depths of the sea and to give it to Adam, and so he did.

When Adam transgressed, the Book flew away from him. But Adam begged God for its return, and beat his breast, and entered the river Gihon up to his neck, until his body became wrinkled and his face haggard. Then God made a sign for the angel Raphael, the Angel of Healing, to heal Adam and bring the book back to him. After that Adam studied the book intently, and bequeathed it to his son Seth. So it went on, through successive generations, as it is said, *This is the book of the generations of Adam* (Gen. 5:1).

In this way the book was handed down from Seth to Enosh to Kenan to Jared, and in this way it reached Enoch. It was from this Book that Enoch drew his vast knowledge of the Mysteries of Creation. Before he was taken up into heaven and transformed into the angel Metatron, Enoch entrusted the book to his son, Methuselah, who read the Book and transmitted it to his son Lamech, and from there it reached Noah, Lamech's son, who made use of its instructions in building the ark. Indeed, there are those who insist that the book was revealed to Noah by the angel Raziel. They say that Noah heard the book from the mouth of Raziel and later the angel wrote it down for him on a sapphire stone.

By reading this book it was possible for Noah to penetrate great secrets of knowledge, hierarchies of understanding, and ideas of wisdom, to know the way of life and the way of death, the way of good and the way of evil, and to foresee the concerns of each and every year, whether for peace or for war, for plenty or for hunger, for harvest or for drought. By gazing there the destinies of the stars were revealed, as well as the course of the sun and the names of the guardians of each and every firmament. Revealed as well were the secrets of how to interpret dreams and visions, and how to rule over all of a man's desires, as well as how to drive away evil spirits and demons. Happy was the eye that beheld that book, and happy the ear that listened to its wisdom, for in it were revealed all the secrets of heaven and earth.

Noah placed the Book into a golden box and it was the first thing he brought into the ark. In this way it came to be revealed to Abraham, whose knowledge of it permitted him to gaze upon the glory of God. And from Abraham it was passed down to Isaac and to Jacob and to Joseph, who consulted it to discover the true meanings of dreams. The book was buried with Joseph, and in this way it was preserved when his coffin was raised by Moses from the Nile and carried beside the Tabernacle throughout the wandering of the Israelites in the wilderness.

In this way the Book came into the possession of King Solomon, who made good use of its wisdom, and also sought its assistance in constructing the Temple. Some say that the book was lost again when the Temple was destroyed, its letters soaring on high as flames approached the Sanctuary in which it was hidden. Yet there are others who say that it was saved from the flames, and has been secretly passed down ever since. In this way it was said to have reached Rabbi Adam, and from Rabbi Adam it was passed down to the Ba'al Shem Tov, who learned the supernal mysteries from reading it and in this way became the *Tzaddik* of his generation.

> This is the most famous of all the chain midrashim, a linked set of myths. It tells the story of how God sent the angel Raziel to reveal this book to Adam, and how Adam came into possession of it. Subsequent myths describe how the book was passed down from Adam to Noah, following the genealogy in Genesis 5, and later reached the patriarchs and kings. The book that the angel Raziel left with Adam has two names: it is known as *The Book of Raziel* and as *The Book of Adam*. *Raziel ha-Malakh* explicitly records the transmission of the book from Adam to Enoch to Noah to Abraham, Isaac, Levi, Moses and Aaron, Pinhas, and so on down the generations.
>
> The myth of the Book of Raziel grows out of a midrash attempting to explain the verse, *This is the book of the generations of Adam* (Gen. 5:1). In *B. Avodah Zarah* 5a, Resh Lakish is quoted as saying: "Did Adam have a book? This implies that God showed to Adam every generation that would ever exist, every generation with its sages and its leaders. When Adam reached the generation of Rabbi Akiba, he rejoiced at his teaching, but was grieved about his death."
>
> While most accounts of this heavenly book assume that the book had already been written and that Adam heard it for the first time when the angel Raziel read it to him, the Maharal proposes an alternate scenario in which Adam had all future events revealed to him in a vision, and later they were recorded in this book. That the angel leaves the book for Adam to read later indicates that books are so important in Jewish tradition that even the first man could read.
>
> The earliest mention of the angel Raziel is in the *Book of Enoch*. *Raziel ha-Malakh*, first published in Amsterdam in 1701, claimed to be the book that the angel Raziel gave to Adam. It largely consists of the names of God and of the angels, and the texts of amulets. The book itself was believed to have talismanic powers, especially the ability to ward off fires and other disasters. For this reason it was commonly found in many Jewish homes.

The angel Raziel, who delivered *The Book of Raziel* to Adam, plays a role in Jewish mythology equivalent to Hermes in Greek mythology. That is, he serves as a messenger of God, while Hermes (Mercury) is a messenger of the gods. Rahab, the Angel of the Sea, is the Jewish mythic equivalent of Poseidon, the Greek god of the sea.

Sources:
B. *Avodah Zarah* 5a; *Genesis Rabbah* 24:4; *Leviticus Rabbah* 15:1; *Avot de-Rabbi Natan* 56a; *Midrash Tanhuma Bereshit* 1:32; *Midrash Tehillim* 139; *Zohar* 1:37b, 1:55a-b, 1:58b, 1:90b; *Sefer ha-Razim* 65-66; *Raziel ha-Malakh* 2, 4.

Studies:
Kabbalah by Avraham Yaakov Finkel, pp. 23-30.

316. CREATING NEW HEAVENS AND A NEW EARTH

God constantly creates new heavens and a new earth from the new meanings that are discovered in the Torah. When the Torah was given to Moses, tens of thousands of angels on high were about to burn him with the flames of their mouths, but God protected him. Since then, whenever a new interpretation of the Torah is uttered, the saying rises up, is adorned with a crown, and then stands before God. And God guards that saying and keeps it hidden, and shelters the person who said it, to prevent the angels from envying him until a new heaven and a new earth are created from that saying. Thus every word that receives a new interpretation by one who delves into the study of the Torah creates a new heaven and a new earth, as it is said, *"That I may plant the heavens, and lay the foundations of the earth"* (Isa. 51:16).

> This myth, based on Isaiah 66:22, demonstrates the primary role of interpreting the Torah, going as far as to assert that new interpretations are not only essential, but that God sees that they are crowned, protects them from the envy of the angels, and uses them as the basis for creating a new heaven and a new earth. What does "a new heaven and a new earth" mean? It means that the new interpretations that arise about the meanings of the Torah so radically change the perspective and understanding of those who receive them, that the heavens and earth seem new to them. This myth is thus an ode to the remarkable power of interpretation, and of the necessity for new interpretations to continue to be made, to prevent the views of the Torah from becoming static. See "A New Torah," p. 522.
>
> *Sources:*
> *Zohar* 1:4b-5a.

317. GOD'S WARNING

God created this world with the following stipulation: "If Israel accepts the Torah when I offer it to them, then creation will continue to exist. Otherwise I will return the world to chaos and void. For the world only exists for the sake of the Torah. Thus if the Torah would cease to be studied, the world would cease to exist."

When the time came for the Giving of the Torah, God summoned all the people of the world and offered them the Torah, but none accepted it. The earth trembled on hearing this, for it feared it was on the point of returning to chaos. Israel was the last possibility, and the earth assumed that Israel, too, would turn down the Torah. But when Israel accepted the Torah, the earth became calm, as it is said, *The earth was numbed with fright* (Ps. 76:9).

> Here God makes the existence of the world contingent on the acceptance and study of the Torah. This represents one tradition about the Giving of the Torah—that it was not an offer, but a demand. See "God Offers the Torah to Israel," p. 264. It is said that God offered the Torah to Israel on the sixth of Sivan in the year 2448, in the 26th

generation since the creation of the world (*B. Pes.* 118a). By implication, the fact that the world still exists confirms that there has never been a time devoid of faith in the Torah.

In *Likutei Moharan*, Rabbi Nachman of Bratslav asserts that the world can only continue to exist if there are people in it who believe that it was created from nothing. For if there is no one alive who believes this, the world will cease to exist.

Sources:
B. *Shabbat* 88a; B. *Pesahim* 68a; *Midrash Tanhuma-Yelammedenu, Bereshit* 1; *Midrash Tanhuma-Yelammedenu, Yitro* 14; *Nefesh ha-Hayim* 4:11; *Zohar* 1:193a; *Likutei Moharan* 2:8.

318. THE LIGHT OF THE TORAH

The light of the Torah existed prior to the creation of the world, as it is said, *God said, "Let there be light," and there was light* (Gen. 1:3). When God spoke at Mount Sinai, this great light issued from the Word of the Lord and filled the whole earth. All the kings assembled and came to Balaam to ask if God was about to bring a second Flood upon the earth. Balaam said, "He is now giving His Torah to the children of Israel. That Torah is the source of this great light that frightens you." Rabbi Baruch of Kossov speaks of two kinds of light, a physical light and a spiritual light. When a person understands a verse of the Torah, he sees a light. This light stems from the essential light of the soul (*Amud ha-Avodah* 62a).

> There is an extensive tradition about light associated with creation, which grows out of Genesis 1:3 and the rabbinic myths associated with the primordial light. See "The Light of the First Day," p. 83. Here the source of the light is described as being the Torah, and this idea is later developed in the *Zohar*, where it is said that a ray of light goes forth from the Torah whenever one who is studying it experiences the illumination of understanding. The primordial light was said to have been hidden away, and Rabbi Nachman of Bratslav suggested it was hidden in the Torah, which corresponds with this myth, since the light had its origin there in the first place.
>
> *Sources:*
> *Exodus Rabbah* 5:3; *Menorat ha-Maor* 230; *Yalkut Shim'oni; Zohar* 2:148b-149a.

319. THE BETROTHAL OF THE TORAH

At the end of the sixth day of Creation, when *God saw all that He had made, and found it very good* (Gen. 1:31), the Torah came forth from her bridal chamber dressed in all kinds of jewelry and royal ornaments, and danced before God. She opened her lips in wisdom and praised God with all manner of song. When God said to her, "Show me your appearance," she bowed her head and lifted her veil, and the splendor of her face filled all the palaces of heaven. When God said to her, "Let me hear your voice," she lifted her voice in song. Then a heavenly voice went forth to say *The teaching of Yahweh is perfect, renewing life* (Ps. 19:8).

Then God revealed the Throne of Glory to the Torah, and brought forth all the souls of the righteous, the souls of Abraham, Isaac, and Jacob, and the souls of Israel who would accept the Torah in the future, and He let them pass before her. After this God brought forth the soul of Moses from beneath his throne, and showed him to the Torah, and said to her, "My daughter, rejoice and be happy, for this Moses is destined to become your bridegroom. It is he who will accept you and love you and reveal you to the myriads of Israel at Mount Sinai." Then the Torah answered and said, "How long until the time of my rejoicing arrives?" God replied, "From the day that I created you until a thousand generations have been fulfilled."

Here the Torah is personified as a bride who appears at the end of the sixth day of creation, as the culmination of all that was created. At first it appears that the Torah will be the bride of God, but later it is revealed that Moses will be her bridegroom in the future. It is interesting to note that this midrash attributes no role to the Torah in the actual creation, although other rabbinic legends describe the Torah as the plan by which God created the world. See "Creation by the Torah," p. 249. Another wedding metaphor is found in the Sephardi *Mahzor*, where God is portrayed as the Bridegroom and Israel as the bride, and the Torah serves as the ketubah, or wedding contract, between them. See "The Wedding Between God and Israel," p. 305.

The bridelike qualities of the Torah are also emphasized by Maimonides in explaining the counting of the Omer in the 49 days between the second day of Passover and Shavuot: "Shavuot is the day of the Giving of the Torah. The momentous nature of that date is expressed in the numbering of every day, bringing it nearer, just as a lover counts the days and even hours that bring the day of meeting with the beloved nearer."

There is an important parable in *Zohar* 2:98b-99b about a lovely maiden in a palace closed from all sides who can only reveal her face briefly to her lover from a tiny opening in the wall. This maiden represents the Torah, which reveals a little of itself at a time, at first only the literal meaning, but later reveals deeper levels of understanding. Another way of reading it is to see the maiden as the *Shekhinah*. Variants of this parable are found in *Seder ha-Yom* by Moses ben Judah Makhir and *Hemdat Yamim* 3:51a-b. A Rapunzel-like folktale with a similar situation is found in the Preface to *Midrash Tanhuma*. See "The Princess in the Tower" in *Elijah's Violin*, pp. 47-52.

Sources:
Midrash Aleph Bet 2:7-11

Studies:
"The Metamorphosis of Narrative Traditions: Two Stories from Sixteenth-Century Safed" by Aryeh Wineman.

320. THE VESTMENT OF THE *SHEKHINAH*

The Torah is the vestment of the *Shekhinah*. If man had not been created, the *Shekhinah* would have been without a garment, like a beggar. Thus when a man sins, it is as if he tears away the vestments of the *Shekhinah*. And when he fulfills the precepts of the Torah, it is as though he clothes the *Shekhinah* in her vestments.

Here the Torah and the *Shekhinah* are closely linked by suggesting that the Torah serves as the garment of the *Shekhinah*. This brief myth from the *Zohar* also suggests that when a person sins, it is not only a sin against the Torah, but against the *Shekhinah*, since it causes the garment of the *Shekhinah* to be torn away, an outrageous offense against the Bride of God.

Sources:
Zohar 1:23a-123b.

321. THE LETTERS AND THE BURNING BUSH

When God appeared to Moses in the burning bush, Moses found twenty-two letters written before him with devouring fire. Those letters formed the mystical image of God, and by peering into those letters, Moses was able to perceive the presence of God, and by means of those letters Moses was able to expound the Law.

This Samaritan myth links the letters of the Hebrew alphabet with Moses' vision of the burning bush. It links the vision with Moses' later role in recording the Torah that God dictated to him at Mount Sinai, and suggests that in that vision at the burning bush Moses not only had a revelation about God, but also had a revelation about the Torah that it would be his destiny to receive.

Most Samaritan myths, like this one, focus on Moses, who plays a near-messianic role in Samaritan tradition. See "The Burning Bush," p. 375.

Sources:
Memar Markah 6:3 (Samaritan).

Studies:
The Name of God and the Angel of the Lord by Jarl E. Fossum.

322. THE ANGELS AND THE GIVING OF THE TORAH

When God wished to give the Torah to Israel, the ministering angels said to him: "Master of the Universe, it is proper for the Torah to remain in heaven." God said to the angels: "Why does it matter to you?" The angels replied: "We are afraid that in the future You will bring Your Divine Presence down to the earthly beings." God replied: "I am giving my Torah to the earthly beings, but I will continue to live among the heavenly beings."

The day God went down to give the Torah, sixty myriads of ministering angels descended with Him. But when God was about to give the Torah to Israel, the angels again objected. The angels said to God, "It would be better if You extended Your majesty only to the heavens above, and if You gave the Torah only to us."

God replied, "Are you the ones who will fulfill the Torah? The Torah cannot remain with you. It would not be appropriate for it to remain in a realm of creatures who have eternal life."

Then, without further ado, God dismissed the angels and gave the Torah to Israel.

> This mythic account of the angels' resistance to God giving the Torah to Israel is parallel to that of the angels' original resistance to the creation of man. In both cases the angels are portrayed as jealous of God's affection for humans, and especially for Israel. The angels also resist Moses' ascent into heaven to receive the Torah, threatening to throw him from on high. Here, again, God comes to the rescue. See "The Ascent of Moses," p. 261.
>
> *Sources:*
> *B. Sanhedrin* 109a; *Genesis Rabbah* 118:6; *Pesikta Rabbati* 25:2.

323. THE QUARREL OF THE MOUNTAINS

When the mountains heard that God was going to give the Torah on a mountain, they quarreled among themselves. Each said, "God will give the Torah on me." And the mountains moved from their places and ran into the wilderness, for they knew that God would give the Torah where no one could say, "Depart from here for this territory belongs to me."

Mount Tabor said to Mount Carmel, "Go back to your place, for the Lord has not called you." Mount Carmel answered, "You return to your place, for the Lord has not called you." And God heard the quarrel of the mountains and said, "Why do you quarrel? Neither of you is equal to Mount Sinai, for men have worshipped other gods on you. But Mount Sinai is holy, for no man has set idols on it. And that is the mountain that I have chosen to dwell upon."

> This myth about the mountains quarreling over who would receive the honor of having the Torah given from it follows a pattern found in myths about the alphabet,

where the letters argue over which letter should have the honor of being first in the alphabet. See "The Letters of the Alphabet," p. 250. In each case it is God who makes the final decision, and here God selects Mount Sinai because there has been no idol worship there. This gives the mountain a kind of spiritual purity appropriate for its historic role.

Sources:
Genesis Rabbah 99:1; Yalkut Shim'oni.

324. THE NECKLACE OF LETTERS

When God was ready to give the Torah to Israel, God made the letters of the Torah into a necklace and hung it around the neck of Israel, as it is said, *She will adorn your head with a graceful wreath, crown you with a glorious diadem* (Prov. 4:9). But it was not long before the children of Israel forsook the Torah, as it is said, *"They forsook My Torah and rejected it"* (Jer. 6:19). At that time God arranged the twenty-two letters of the Torah into acrostics of woe, to indicate the grievous events that would befall Israel.

> Just as the Torah is sometimes described as a *ketubah*, a wedding contract, between God and Israel, here the letters of the Torah are described as a necklace God gives to Israel as a precious gift. But when the people forsake the Torah, God arranges the letters into acrostics that prophesy grievous events. This myth thus portrays both God's generous and angry aspects. The acrostics referred to here are those found in the first four chapters of the Book of Lamentations. See "The Marriage of God and Israel," p. 305.

Sources:
Pesikta Rabbati 29, 30:2

325. DEATH AND REBIRTH AT MOUNT SINAI

Moses brought forth the people to meet God. *Yahweh came down upon Mount Sinai, on the top of the mountain* (Exod. 19:20). In that hour the world was completely silent. No one dared to breathe. No bird sang, no ox lowed, the sea did not roar, and no creature uttered a sound. Then God opened the portals of the seven firmaments and appeared over them eye to eye, in His beauty, in His glory, in the fullness of His stature, with His crown and upon His Throne of Glory. When He began to speak, thunder and lightning issued from God's mouth, and all of Israel flew back in horror at the sound of the awful voice. They ran without stopping for twelve miles, until their hearts gave out and their souls fled from them. All of them lay dead.

Then the Torah turned to God, saying, "Master of the Universe! Are You giving me to the living or to the dead?" God replied, "To the living." The Torah said, "But they are all dead." And God said, "For your sake I will revive them." So God let the dew of life fall from heaven, and as soon as it touched the people, they were restored to life, and they became strong and of good courage. That is why, at the resurrection of the dead in the End of Days, the Torah will stand up for the restoring of people's lives.

Still, the people trembled mightily, even more than before. Nor were they brave enough to look up and gaze upon the Lord. They were not even strong enough to stand on their feet. God saw that their hearts would give out again, so He sent to earth one hundred and twenty myriads of ministering angels, so that there were two angels to every one of them, one to lay his hand on the heart of each one, to keep his heart still, and one to lift each one's head, so that he might behold the splendor of his Creator.

In this way, awestruck but comforted by the angels, they each beheld the glory of God. Then God asked, "Will you accept the Torah?" And they all answered together, "Yes!"

At that moment God opened up the seven heavens, as well as the seven earths, and all of Israel gazed from one end of the universe to the other. And God said, "Behold that there is none like Me in heaven or on earth." And they saw with their own eyes that it was true.

> This haunting myth recounts that when God appeared on Mount Sinai, the shock of His voice caused all of the people to drop dead. God then revived them and gave each of the 600,000 Jews assembled there two angels, one on his right hand and one on his left. The function of the angels was to calm the people enough for them to stand in the presence of God without having their souls flee from their bodies in terror. Each of the angels is said to have quoted a verse of the Torah. One angel said: *"It has been clearly demonstrated to you that Yahweh alone is God; there is none beside Him"* (Deut. 4:35). And the other angel said: *"Know therefore this day and keep in mind that the Lord alone is God in heaven above and on earth below; there is no other"* (Deut. 4:39).
>
> The myth of the two angels at Mount Sinai is found in *Midrash Aseret ha-Dibrot (Midrash of the Ten Commandments)*, where it is a commentary on the first commandment, *I am the Lord your God* (Ex. 20:2). Each of the stories in the collection is linked to one of the ten commandments. *Midrash Aseret ha-Dibrot*, dating from around the ninth century, is regarded as the first story anthology in Jewish literature.
>
> Sources:
> B. *Shabbat* 88b; *Midrash Aseret ha-Dibrot* on Exodus 20:2; *Exodus Rabbah* 29:4, 29:9; *Song of Songs Zuta* 1:2, 4; *Pirkei de-Rabbi Eliezer* 20:4; *Midrash Tehillim* 19:13, 68:5, 68:7; *Pesikta Rabbati* 20:4; *Otzrot Hayim*.

326. THE SEVEN VOICES OF THE TORAH

The Torah was given through seven voices. And the people saw the Lord of the World revealed in every one of those voices. That is the meaning of the verse *All the people saw the voices* (Exod. 20:15). These voices were accompanied by sparks of fire and flashes of lightning like the letters of the commandments. They saw the fiery word issuing forth from the mouth of the Almighty and being engraved on the tablets, as it is said, *The voice of the Lord engraves flames of fire* (Ps. 29:4).

And when the people actually saw Him-Who-Spoke-and-the-World-Came-Into-Being, they fainted away. Some say that their spirit departed from them, while others say that they entered a prophetic trance. These visions brought them trembling and shaking and a blackout of the senses.

> This myth describes the intense revelatory experience of those present at Mount Sinai. It is sometimes described as a prophetic trance, sometimes as a blackout, sometimes as their spirits taking flight. See "Death and Rebirth at Mount Sinai," p. 259. Note that this experience at Sinai includes a direct visual and aural perception of God— not only of God's voice (or seven voices), but an actual vision of God Himself. This makes it by far the greatest revelation in Jewish history.
>
> *Midrash Tanhuma, Shemot* 22 states that the voice of God split into 70 different voices. This echoes the tradition of the 70 faces of the Torah, meaning that there are 70 different ways of reading and understanding the Torah.
>
> Sources:
> *Sefer ha-Bahir* 45; *Midrash Tanhuma, Shemot* 22; *Midrash Tanhuma-Yelammedenu, Yitro* 16; Rashi on Exodus 20:15; Nachmanides on *Parashat va-Et-Hanan; Magen David.*
>
> Studies:
> *Present at Sinai: The Giving of the Law,* edited by S. Y. Agnon, pp. 264-277.

327. THE ASCENT OF MOSES

With the children of Israel assembled at the foot of Mount Sinai, Moses ascended the mountain with great majesty, crowned with light. He would ascend a little and look behind him, blessing the congregation. When he reached the top he saw that a cloud was floating there. Moses looked at it, but he did not know whether to take hold of it or to ascend to it. As he came closer, the cloud opened, and Moses stepped inside, and the cloud carried him on high. Inside of that cloud, Moses was hidden from the sight of the Congregation of Israel, and they cried out in distress. But Moses knew that he had been sanctified, and that he was being borne up by God's blessing, as it is said, *And Moses went up to God* (Exod. 19:3).

As the cloud rose up, Moses lost track of time, so filled was he with awe. Then all at once the cloud stopped at the gates of the firmament, and the mouth of the cloud opened, and Moses sought to enter the Gate of Heaven. But the angel Kemuel, who guards that gate, rebuked Moses, saying, "How dare you come here! Have you no fear of the angels and their fire?" When Moses replied: "I have come to receive the Torah," the gate opened of its own accord, for the Torah is the key that opens that gate. And when the angel saw this, he knew that it was God's wish that Moses should enter there, and he made way for him to pass.

After that Moses reached the river Rigyon, a river of fire whose coals can consume angels as well as men. There he was met by a troop of the Angels of Destruction, who gathered around Moses in order to consume him with fire. And Moses cried out: "Master of the Universe, keep them from consuming me with their fiery breath!" At that moment a great fiery wave rose up from the river and washed over the Angels of Destruction, and they were all consumed. But not a spark of that fire touched Moses, who learned in this way that all things exist by the mercy of God, and that every life is in His hands.

Now when the angels saw Moses there, they cried out to God: "Master of the Universe, what is this man doing here?" And God replied: "He has come to receive the Torah." And the angels said: "You created the Torah before You created the world. How can such a precious treasure pass into the hands of a mere human being?" And God replied: "It was created for that very purpose."

Then God reached down and pulled Moses up to His heavenly throne. There Moses saw God seated on his Throne of Glory, and behind Him was an angel so large that Moses shook with terror. Then God stepped down from His Throne of Glory to comfort him. And in the Divine Presence, Moses found his strength again, and he grew calm in that high place.

When he had recovered, Moses asked to know the identity of that angel, and God replied: "That is the angel Sandalphon, who weaves garlands out of the prayers of Israel." Just then Sandalphon completed one of those garlands, and it rose up on its own accord and came to rest on the head of God as He sat on His Throne of Glory. And at that moment all the hosts on high shook with awe, and the wheels of the throne revolved, and the creatures of the chariot, which had been silent, began to roar like lions, all of them crying out *Holy, holy, holy! The Lord of Hosts* (Isa. 6:3).

Then God said to Moses: "The time has come for you to receive the Torah. Take hold of My Throne of Glory—it will protect you from the angels." This Moses did, and all at once God opened the seven firmaments and showed Moses the Sanctuary on high. Then He opened the portals of the seven firmaments and appeared over Israel, in all His fullness and splendor. And when the children of Israel heard the words *"I the Lord am your God"* (Exod. 20:2), they fell down in fear and their souls departed. Then God caused the dew of the resurrection, which will revive the souls of the righteous at the End of Days, to fall upon them. And every one of them was revived.

After that God sent one hundred and twenty myriads of angels to earth, two angels for each of the children of Israel. One angel to put its hand over each of their hearts, so that it would not stop beating, and the other raised up their heads, so they could gaze at God in that moment of Glory. And so they did.

Then, while the portals were still open, God transmitted the Torah to Moses, while every word echoed among the people gathered below. For forty days and nights God spoke the words of the Torah to Moses during the day, and at night He explained it to him. And that which he wrote down during the day is the Written Law, and that which he learned at night is the Oral Law, which reveals the seventy meanings of every word of the Torah, like the many facets of a perfect jewel.

At the end of forty days and nights, the cloud returned, and Moses descended to Mount Sinai. And there he proclaimed the sovereignty of the Lord over all of Israel, and that *The Lord shall reign forever, your God, O Zion, for all generations. Hallelujah* (Ps. 146:10).

> The ascent of Elijah into heaven is stated explicitly in the Bible: *As they kept on walking and talking, a fiery chariot with fiery horses suddenly appeared and separated one from the other, and Elijah went up to heaven in a whirlwind* (2 Kings 2:11). In the case of Moses, one verse of the Torah is interpreted to mean that such an ascent took place: *And Moses went up to God* (Exod. 19:3). Thus, while the account in the Torah states that Moses ascended to the top of Mount Sinai to receive the Torah, the verse *And Moses went up to God* is interpreted to mean that Moses ascended all the way into heaven to receive the Torah. This interpretation gave birth to a wide range of myths about what took place during the ascent. In one version, Moses is said to have been sent by God to sit in the future classroom of Rabbi Akiba. But most accounts describe the encounters Moses has in heaven, struggling with the angels and viewing the wonders of Paradise. These myths follow the pattern found in the *Hekhalot* texts about heavenly journeys, dating from the first to the eighth centuries. Thus the ascent of Moses may well have served as the model for some of these *Hekhalot* texts. The third major ascent in Jewish tradition is that of Enoch, found in the books of Enoch, and in the so-called "3 Enoch," which itself is a *Hekhalot* text.
>
> It was widely assumed in rabbinic literature that Moses not only climbed to the top of Mount Sinai to receive the Torah, but that he also ascended into Paradise. Inevitably, Moses encountered the angels, who had never been enthusiastic about the creation of humans in the first place, and were loath to see the Torah transmitted to him. The angels attempted to obstruct Moses and cast him out of heaven, but God always interceded to protect him. There are several versions of this legend of heavenly ascent. That in *Pesikta Rabbati* is the most extensive. Among the prophets, Moses was the only one said to have seen God. In these legends of the ascent of Moses, he stands before the Throne of Glory, sees God weaving the crowns of the letters of the Torah, and, most amazingly, there is an account of God stepping down from His Throne of Glory to reassure Moses, who has been frightened by the awe-inspiring sight of the angel Sandalphon. Subsequent prophets hear the voice of God, but visions of God are extremely rare. See, for example, "The Vision of the High Priest," which recounts the High Priest's vision of Akatriel Yah in the Holy of Holies.
>
> There is an interesting debate in the Talmud, *B. Sukkah* 5a, as to whether or not God descended to earth and whether Moses and Elijah really ascended to heaven. This grows out of the assertion that "Neither Moses nor Elijah ever went up to heaven, nor did the *Shekhinah* come down to earth." This anti-mythological belief is based on the verse *The heavens belong to God, but the earth He gave over to humanity* (Ps. 115:16). One side argues that the verse *Yahweh came down upon Mount Sinai* (Exod. 19:20) is evidence that God did descend to earth. As proof that Moses did ascend to heaven, they select *Moses went up to God* (Exod. 19:3). The other side argues that God only came within ten handbreadths of the earth, and that Moses and Elijah only reached within ten handbreadths below the sphere of heaven.

Hakham Yosef Hayim of Baghdad, known as Ben Ish Hai, comments about the protests of the angels when Moses ascended on high, that most of the angels did not protest, and the few who did were inspired by God to do so. He argues that God engineered the confrontation with the angels so that all would see Moses emerge victorious.

Sources:
B. Shabbat 88b-89a; *B. Menahot* 29b; *B. Sukkah* 5a; *B. Yoma* 4a; *Exodus Rabbah* 28; *Pesikta Rabbati* 20:4; *Mekhilta de-Rabbi Ishmael, ba-Hodesh* 4:55-58; *Ma'ayan Hokhmah* in *Beit ha-Midrash* 1:60-61; *Otzrot Hayim; Memar Markah* 5:3 (Samaritan); IFA 16628.

Studies:
"Visions of God in Merkabah Mysticism" by Ira Chernus.
The Faces of the Chariot by David J. Halperin.

328. MOUNT SINAI IS LIFTED TO HEAVEN

Moses brought the people out of the camp to meet God. And Mount Sinai was uprooted from its place and lifted up above the earth. And the heavens were opened and the summit of the mountain came into their midst, and the Lord was revealed.

Here the revelation at Sinai is described in even greater mythic terms than are found in the Torah. In an unparalleled series of events, God raises up Mount Sinai to the heavens, and at that instant, with the heavens open, God is revealed to the people.

A parallel myth, but with much different implications, describes God as lifting up Mount Sinai and holding it over the heads of the people of Israel at the time. He asked them if they were willing to receive the Torah, and with no other choice, they readily agreed to receive it. See "God Offers the Torah to Israel," p. 264.

Sources:
Exodus Rabbah 28; *Pirkei de-Rabbi Eliezer* 41.

329. HOW GOD REVEALED HIMSELF AT MOUNT SINAI

God did not reveal Himself on Mount Sinai like hailstones falling from heaven. Instead, He appeared slowly and gradually, moving from one mountaintop to the next until He descended upon Mount Sinai.

But our forebears, standing at Mount Sinai to accept the Torah, saw no form resembling a human being, nor resembling the form of any creature, nor resembling the form of anything that has breath that God created on the face of the earth. They saw only God, the one God, whose kingdom endures in heaven and on earth, as it is said, *For the Lord your God is the God of gods and the Lord of lords* (Deut. 10:17).

This midrash presents Maimonides's interpretation of the verses, *Yahweh came from Sinai and rose from Mount Seir to them; He shone forth from Mount Paran and He came from holy multitudes* (Deut. 33:2). Likewise, Rashi agrees that God did not appear on Mount Sinai suddenly, but revealed Himself little by little.

Eliyahu Rabbah offers the paradoxical view that those at Mount Sinai "saw no form resembling a human being." At the same time, they saw God, who, according to this text, was not in a human image, despite Genesis 1:26, *In the image of God He created them,* and the extensive tradition linked to this verse. The theological purpose of insisting that the people saw no human form is to oppose the anthropomorphic tendencies in Judaism, and to reaffirm the tradition that God cannot be represented by an image.

Yet both texts represented here do insist that the people saw *something*—they saw God, but what they saw cannot be described in human terms.

Sources:
Iggeret Teiman 142-143; *Eliyahu Rabbah* 1:6.

330. GOD OFFERS THE TORAH TO ISRAEL

Some say that from the time of Creation until Israel went out of Egypt, God went around offering the Torah to each and every nation, but they all refused to accept it. That is when God offered it to Israel.

Others say that God created the world with a stipulation: "If Israel accepts the Torah when it is offered to them, all of creation will continue to exist. Otherwise I will return the world to chaos and void."

So when the children of Israel had gathered at Mount Sinai, *And they took their places at the foot of the mountain* (Exod. 19:17), God overturned the mountain like an inverted barrel, and held it above their heads and said: "If you accept the Torah, all will be well. If not, you will be buried here."

That is when Israel declared its willingness to accept the Torah.

> This midrash emphasizes the utterly essential role of Israel in God's plan of Creation. Here God declares at the beginning of the time of Creation that it is contingent on Israel's acceptance of the Torah. This leads to the grotesque image of God forcing Israel to accept the Torah by holding Mount Sinai over their heads. This account derives from a very literal interpretation of the verse *And they took their places at the foot of the mountain* (Exod. 19:17). In some versions, God first offers the Torah to every other nation, and each one turns it down. When He comes to Israel, the last nation to be asked, and holds the mountain over their heads, of course they say yes. What they actually say is *"We will do and we will listen"* (Exod. 24: 7). "We will do" refers to following God's commandments, the 613 *mitzvot* of the Torah. "We will listen" refers to studying the Torah with great intensity. This myth, then, personifies the "yoke" of the Law: it illustrates the compelling nature of Jewish law to those who observe it. According to *B. Shabbat* 88a, as a reward for saying *"We will do and we will listen,"* 600,000 angels descended from heaven and tied two crowns, one for "do" and the other for "listen," to the head of every Jew.
>
> Still, some commentaries attempt to reinterpret this midrash where the mountain held over the head of the people serves as a metaphor for the revelation of God's infinite love for them (*Likutei Torah*). At the same time, if God forced Israel to accept the Torah at Mount Sinai, it was indeed an agreement made under coercion, and it was not until the time of Mordecai and Esther that the Jewish people truly accepted the Torah of their own free choice: *The Jews undertook and irrevocably obligated themselves and their descendants, and all who might join them, to observe these two days in the manner prescribed and at the proper time each year* (Esther 9:27).
>
> The giant Og is also said to have uprooted a mountain and held it over the heads of the Israelites (*B. Ber.* 54b). See "The Giant Og," p. 461.
>
> Hakham Yosef Hayim of Baghdad, known as Ben Ish Hai, links this midrash with the Oral Torah. In his view, the Israelites had already accepted the Written Torah when they said, *We will do and we will listen* (Exod. 24:7). But God had to coerce them to accept the Oral Law. That is why He held the mountain over their heads. Further, God hollowed out the mountain like a barrel to teach them that each letter of the Written Torah contains innumerable interpretations in the Oral Law, just as a barrel contains innumerable drops of wine. Thus God was demanding that their acceptance of the Written Law include their acceptance of the Oral Law. This is an interesting and original interpretation of this bizarre midrash about God offering the Torah to Israel.

The continued existence of the world was dependent on Israel's acceptance of the Torah. God said, "If Israel accepts the Torah, the world will continue to exist. But if not, I will reduce the world to a state of chaos" (*B. Avodah Zarah* 3a). According to this myth, not only the continued existence of Israel was at stake, but the continued existence of the world. Nor, according to Rabbi Hayim of Volozhin, must the study of the Torah around the globe ever cease, even for a split second. If this should happen, all the worlds above and below would revert to nothingness (*Nefesh ha-Hayim* 4:1).

Sources:
B. *Shabbat* 88a; *B. Pesahim* 68b; *B. Avodah Zarah* 2b; *Exodus Rabbah* 28; *Midrash Tanhuma-Yelammedenu, Bereshit* 1; *Midrash Tanhuma-Yelammedenu, Yitro* 14; *Eliyahu Zuta* 11:192; *Zohar* 3:7a; *Nefesh ha-Hayim* 4:1; *Likutei Torah, Re'eh* 22a; *Otzrot Hayim*; IFA 8415.

331. GOD TEARS APART SEVEN FIRMAMENTS

During the revelation of the Torah, as all Israel watched, God tore apart seven firmaments, one after the other, to show the people that there is no other God beside Him.

At the end of the Yom Kippur service, the Shema is read, and the phrase, "The Lord is God" is repeated seven times. The explanation for this repetition is that God tore apart seven firmaments to demonstrate to Israel that there were no other gods. God is said to dwell above the seven firmaments.

An alternate explanation is that those who prayed in the presence of the *Shekhinah* are reluctant to let Her go, and they accompany Her through the seven firmaments. See "The Closing of the Gates," p. 297.

Sources:
Mateh Moshe.

332. THE PRIMORDIAL TORAH

The primordial Torah was written with black fire on white fire. It was fire mixed with fire, cut from fire, given from fire. God peered into the fiery letters of that Torah and created the world.

At last the time came for the Torah to be given to Moses at Mount Sinai. From the top of the mountain, Moses peered into the heavens, and there he had a vision in which he saw the letters burning in black fire on white. The first letters to take form were those of God's Name, YHVH. Then the rest of the alphabet emerged. The letters danced, joining into hundreds of permutations of the names of God. Then the letters formed themselves into one long Name. This Name was none other than the letters of the Torah, for the entire Torah is a single, holy, mystical Name.

There Moses read the Torah for the first time, and as he read each word, he heard the voice of God speaking it. Later Moses wrote everything down, exactly as he had heard it, and that is how the primordial Torah was transmitted to Israel.

The primordial Torah is known as *Torah Kedumah*. This primordial Torah was one of the seven things created before the creation of the world. The image of the Torah being written in black fire on white, found in the Talmud and recurring in the *Zohar*, serves as an archetype for the primordial Torah. The notion of God looking into the Torah to create the world is found in *Genesis Rabbah* 1:1: "Thus God consulted the Torah and created the world." Here God is portrayed as an architect and the Torah a blueprint in the creation of the world. See "Seven Things Created before the Creation of the World," p. 74. The way the letters of the alphabet emerge and combine has an uncanny resemblance to the combining and recombining of strings of DNA.

Sources:
Genesis Rabbah 1:1; Zohar 1:134a, 3:36a; Ta'amei ha-Mitzvot 3a; Y. Shekalim 6:1; Perush Ramban al ha-Torah pp. 6-7; Maggid Devarav le-Ya'akov 50; Sefer Ba'al Shem Tov, Bereshit 8.

333. THE FIRST TABLETS

The first stone tablets of the Law were created by God Himself on the eve of the first Sabbath. All of the heavenly angels gathered together to see how the tablets were *written with the finger of God* (Exod. 31:18) with black fire on white fire. As a result, the letters were visible through either side, for God had made them that way. The entire Torah was contained on those tablets. Some say that the first tablets were hewn from the foundation stone at the center of the world, while others say that they were made of sapphire taken from beneath the Throne of Glory.

In origin, the first tablets were completely spiritual. How, then, was it possible for God to give them to Moses? Some say that at the instant the tablets were given to Moses by the hand of God, they assumed material form, and became stone tablets. Others say that they were made in the primordial light at the time of Creation, and descended from heaven in two stone tablets.

Satan employed all his wiles to prevent Israel from receiving the first tablets from Moses. Had Israel received them, death would have disappeared forever, as would Satan's power over the people. To make them lose hope, Satan showed the people the bier of Moses suspended in the air, and they saw themselves as Moses' pallbearers. This led to the creation of the golden calf.

The tablets that Moses went to heaven to receive had been written on the sixth day of Creation and had been waiting for him ever since. Before Moses, Enoch had ascended on high and had read everything written on the heavenly tablets, all the deeds of mankind to the remotest generations.

When Moses descended from Mount Sinai and discovered the tribes of Israel worshipping the golden calf, he cast down the tablets of the Law and broke them at the foot of the mountain. This caused all the grief that Israel has experienced ever since, including the experience of death itself. For had the first tablets survived, every sorrow and calamity would have disappeared from the earth, and the world would have experienced freedom from the Angel of Death. It was God's intention for the Jewish people to attain freedom from death because of their acceptance of the Torah. But as a result of their idolatry, God decided that the people would remain mortal. So too would the second set of commandments differ from the first, for a set of laws designed for immortal people was no longer appropriate for them.

How did the two sets of tablets differ? God inscribed the first set of tablets, Moses the second. No one knows what was written on the first tablets, but it is said that if the first tablets had not been broken, Jews would never have forgotten any Torah they had learned. Some say that all the commandments on the first set were positive, while more than half of those of the second set are negative. For God saw that people could not be trusted to follow positive commandments, and therefore He put in the negative ones. Also, great secrets were revealed to Israel when the first tablets were given. But after the sin of the golden calf, Israel was no longer worthy of knowing those secrets. Therefore, they were forced to forget them.

There are those who say that the first tablets were not engraved, but the letters fluttered on them in black fire superimposed on white fire. So that the instant Moses threw down the tablets, the letters took flight before the tablets broke against the ground. Others say that the letters took flight as Moses approached the border of the camp, where the golden calf was being worshipped, a place of defilement and transgression. Thus the letters took flight even before Moses cast down the tablets.

Why, then, did Moses smash the tablets? Some say that he smashed them out of anger at the sight of idolatry. Others say Moses did not shatter the tablets on his own, but only at God's command. Still others say that the letters suddenly took flight, and as soon as they did, the tablets became far too heavy for Moses to carry, and they fell from his arms and shattered.

The idea of writings that exist in heaven is found among the ancient peoples of the Mideast. The belief in tablets of fate, inscribed in heaven, is of Babylonian origin. In the Jewish view, God was not only the author of the Torah, but inscribed the first tablets Himself, in black fire on white fire, using His finger. There is a similar Islamic belief about a heavenly Koran that is the model for the earthly one.

One tradition holds that the Torah, engraved in its entirety on these tablets, was created before the creation of the world. The existence of tablets of heaven is reported in *1 Enoch*, when the angel Uriel says to Enoch: "Enoch, look at the tablets of heaven; read what is written upon them . . . So I looked at the tablets of heaven, read all the writings on them, and came to understand everything." In *Hekhalot Rabbati* 6:3, all the trials foreordained for Israel are said to be recorded on heavenly tablets. Fragment B of the *Prayer of Joseph* states that "I have read in the tablets of heaven all that shall befall you and your sons." In *3 Enoch* 41, the angel Metatron shows Rabbi Ishmael "the letters by which heaven and earth were created . . . engraved with a pen of flame upon the Throne of Glory." In *The Book of Jubilees* Jacob is said to have seen an angel descending from heaven with seven tablets in his hand, and he gives them to Jacob, who read what was written there, and learned what would happen to him and his sons. The *Book of Jubilees* also recounts that Enoch gave these heavenly tablets to his descendants.

Deuteronomy Rabbah states that the first tablets were the work of God, while the second set were hewn by Moses, made at God's command (Exod. 34:1). But were the first tablets identical to the second? Most commentators conclude that they were not. The Talmud, in *B. Shabbat* 146a, asserts that the residual pollutant of the original serpent had been expunged from the people, and that God intended to remove death. Thus the commandments of the first tablets were for immortals, not for mortals. But when the people turned to idolatry, they lost the gift of immortality. Thus the commandments of the second tablets were, by necessity, different.

Considering the consequences of smashing the tablets, why did Moses do it? Rabbi Hayim ben Attar suggests that he was convinced that by the destruction he would perform something infinitely more useful than that which he destroyed. *Avot de-Rabbi Natan* states that Moses did not shatter the tablets until told to do so by God.

Concerning the rays of light that shone from the face of Moses when he descended Mount Sinai, see "The Divine Radiance," p. 389.

Sources:
Mishnah Avot 5:6; *B. Shabbat* 146; *B. Eruvin* 54a; *B. Ta'anit* 28; *Deuteronomy Rabbah* 15:17; *Exodus Rabbah* 46:1; *Song of Songs Rabbah* 5:15; *Avot de-Rabbi Natan* 2; *Book of Jubilees* 32:21; *1 Enoch* 81:1-2; *3 Enoch* 41; *Hekhalot Rabbati* 6:3; *Prayer of Joseph*, Fragment B; *Zohar* 1:131b; Rashi on Exodus 32:19; *Or ha-Hayim* on Exodus 32:19; Nachmanides on Exodus 32:16; Ibn Ezra on Exodus 32:15; Rabbi Moshe Alshekh on Exodus 31:18; *Likutei Moharan* 1:60; *Memar Markah* 6:3 (Samaritan).

Studies:
Torah min ha-Shamayim b'Aspaklarya shel ha-Dorot by Abraham Joshua Heschel 2:24-26.
The Written and Oral Torah: A Comprehensive Introduction by Nathan T. Lopes.
The Commentators' Gift of Torah: Exploring the Treasures of the Oral and Written Torah by Yitzchak Sender.

334. THE SECOND TABLETS

The Lord said to Moses: "Carve two tablets of stone like the first, and I will inscribe upon the tablets the words that were on the first tablets, which you shattered. Be ready by morning, and in the morning come up to Mount Sinai and present yourself there to Me, on the top of the mountain. No one else shall come up with you, and no one else shall be seen anywhere on the mountain; neither shall the flocks and the herds graze at the foot of this mountain." So Moses carved two tablets of stone, like the first, and early in the morning he went up on Mount Sinai, as the Lord had commanded him, taking the two stone tablets with him. The Lord came down in a cloud; He stood with him there, and proclaimed the name of the Lord. The Lord passed before him and proclaimed: "The Lord! The Lord! A God compassionate and gracious, slow to anger, abounding in kindness and faithfulness, extending kindness to the thousandth generation, forgiving iniquity, transgression, and sin; yet He does not remit all punishment, but visits the iniquity of parents upon children and children's children, upon the third and fourth generations."

Moses hastened to bow low to the ground in homage, and said, "If I have gained Your favor, O Lord, pray, let the Lord go in our midst, even though this is a stiff-necked people. Pardon our iniquity and our sin, and take us for Your own!"

God said: "I hereby make a covenant. Before all your people I will work such wonders as have not been wrought on all the earth or in any nation; and all the people who are with you shall see how awe-inspiring are the Lord's deeds which I will perform for you."

On descending Mount Sinai after receiving the Torah, Moses saw the people of Israel worshipping a golden calf and in his anger and disgust smashed the tablets on which the Torah was inscribed. Here God directs Moses to carve a second set of tablets. Since there were two sets, rabbinic texts wondered greatly whether the first revelation at Sinai different from the second, and many myths hold that there were considerable differences between them. See "The First Tablets," p. 266.

Sources:
Exodus 34:1-10

335. THE FIRST TORAH

God told the Prince of the Presence, "Write for Moses from the beginning of Creation until My sanctuary has been built for all eternity. Then everyone will know that I am the Lord of Israel and the Father of all the children of Jacob and King upon Mount Zion for all eternity."

This striking myth from *The Book of Jubilees* runs contrary to the general belief that God dictated the Torah to Moses on Mount Sinai, and that Moses wrote it down. Here God commands the angel of the Presence (who is referred to in later sources as Metatron) to write down the history of the world from the beginning to the End of Days. The reference to God's sanctuary being built for eternity may refer to the Temple in Jerusalem, which was to be rebuilt in the time of the Messiah. Or it could refer to the myth that the heavenly Temple will descend to earth in the messianic era. Since the Torah does not end with a vision of the coming of the Messiah, the myth in *Jubilees* makes another substantial change in the biblical narrative. Here Moses has all past and future history revealed to him much as does Adam when he reads *The Book of Raziel*, and his experience on Mount Sinai becomes more of a vision and less of a 40 days and nights dictation from God.

This myth also suggests the tradition that Moses received the Torah through the angels. Thus the angel serves as the intermediary in bringing the Torah to mankind,

much as the angel Raziel delivers *The Book of Raziel* to Adam. See "The Book of Raziel,"
p. 253. The theme of angels as intermediaries is found in Zechariah, who receives all
his communications through angels, as well as in Daniel.

Sources:
The Book of Jubilees 1:27, 2:1.

336. HOW THE TEN COMMANDMENTS WERE GIVEN

The first word that went forth from the mouth of God was like shooting stars and lightning and fiery torches, a torch to the right and a torch to the left. It flew and winged
swiftly through the heavens and came back. All Israel saw it and was filled with fear.
And it came back and hovered over the camps of Israel, and returning, it became engraved on the tablets of the covenant and all Israel beheld it. Then it cried out, *"I Yahweh
am your God who brought you out of the land of Egypt, the house of bondage"* (Exod. 20:2).

Each and every subsequent word that came forth from God's mouth was like the first,
shooting stars and fiery torches winging swiftly through the air, as each one of the Ten
Commandments was given.

> This is an elaborate description of the effects of God pronouncing the Ten Com-
> mandments. All of Israel witnessed a single word that appears like a shooting star
> and hovers over the people like a flying saucer, and then returns to be graven in the
> tablets of the Law. This underscores the centrality and importance of the Ten Com-
> mandments, and emphasizes the world-shaking nature of the event of their being
> given.
>
> *Sources:*
> *Targum Neophyti* on Exodus 20:1.

337. THE ORDER OF THE TORAH

The order of the Torah as we know it is not correct. For if the sections of the Torah had
been given in the correct order, the precise reward and punishment for each commandment would be known. Further, anyone who read them would have unlimited powers.
They would be able to wake the dead and perform miracles. That is why the true order
and arrangement of the Torah was hidden and is known only to God.

> This rabbinic myth seems to foreshadow the concept of practical kabbalah, where
> knowledge of the mysteries was used to accomplish specific magical purposes, such
> as raising the dead or ascending on high. It is here that kabbalah and magic combine
> into one pursuit. The implication is that the order of the separate portions of the Torah
> itself was a powerful mystery, which is so secret that only God knows it. Here no
> other, angel or human, is said to share this secret, not even Moses, to whom the Torah
> was dictated by God. For if these sections were arranged in the true order, they would
> endow the possessor of this secret with unlimited, divine powers. Another parallel
> interpretation suggests that the words and letters of the Torah spell out the secret
> Name of God, which, if it were known, would convey divine power to whoever knew
> how to pronounce it.
>
> *Sources:*
> *Midrash Tehillim; Sihot ha-Ran* 112.

338. GOD ABROGATES THE FIRST DECREE

When God created the world, He first decreed, *"The heavens belong to Yahweh, but the earth He gave over to man"* (Ps. 115:16). But when God decided to give the Torah, He abrogated the first decree and declared: "Let the earthly beings ascend on high, and the heavenly creatures descend below" as it is said, *Yahweh came down upon Mount Sinai* (Exod. 19:20), and it is also written, *Then He said to Moses: Come up to the Lord* (Exod. 24:1).

> Based on this midrash, it would appear that not all of God's decrees are immutable. This myth describes how at the beginning of time God and His heavenly retinue were entirely separated from the earthly realm by God's decree. But the Giving of the Torah was such a cosmic event that it overcame the separation between the heavenly and the earthly realms. Henceforth, God and the angels descended to earth, while earthly beings, such as Moses, were able to ascend to heaven. See "The Ascent of Moses," p. 261.
>
> *Sources:*
> *Midrash Tanhuma-Yelammedenu, va-Yera 15*

339. THE GIVING OF THE TORAH

God originally planned to give the Torah after a thousand generations. Later He saw that the world could not exist that long without the Torah. Therefore He gave the Torah to the twenty-sixth generation.

Before God gave the Torah, He repeated it to Himself four times. When God gave the Torah, no bird chirped or flew, no cattle lowed, the angels did not take wing, the sea did not move, no person spoke. The entire world remained silent and listened as God's voice proclaimed, *I Yahweh am your God* (Exod. 20:2). The sound of God's voice went forth from one end of the world to the other. All the pagan kings were seized with trembling in their palaces.

> Here God's giving of the Torah is described as an event that took place long before God intended it, as the need for the Torah was too great to wait a thousand generations, as God originally planned. The actual giving of the Torah is described almost as a presentation, in which God prepared himself by repeating it to Himself four times. These elements portray God as very humanlike, first changing his mind about when to give the Torah and then rehearsing the presentation as a human would. And during the actual giving of the Torah, God had a rapt audience, as the whole world remained silent and listened to God's voice.
>
> While the biblical account of the giving of the Torah makes it quite explicit that it was direct communication from God to Moses, *The Book of Jubilees* 1:27-28 has God direct the Angel of the Presence—who is elsewhere identified as Metatron—to serve as an intermediary, telling the angel to "Write for Moses from the first of creation until My sanctuary is built in their midst."
>
> *Sources:*
> *B. Zevahim 116a; B. Betzah 25b; B. Hagigah 14a; Exodus Rabbah 40:1.*
>
> *Studies:*
> *Present at Sinai: The Giving of the Law,* edited by S. Y. Agnon.

340. MOSES BEFORE THE THRONE OF GLORY

When Moses ascended Mount Sinai to receive the Torah, he did not stop at the top of the mountain, but God sent down a cloud, which Moses entered, and the cloud carried him aloft, all the way into heaven. As he was ascending into Paradise, the angels saw him entering their realm, where none of the living were permitted, and they sought to throw him out. Moses became very frightened and called out to God, for he was afraid that the angels would consume him with their fiery breath. And God reached down and pulled Moses all the way up to the highest heaven, to the Throne of Glory. There Moses found himself face to face with God, and he saw that God was affixing crowns to the letters of the Torah. And Moses said to God, "What are You doing?" And God replied, I am adding these crowns to the letters of the Torah, for in the future there will be a man born whose name will be Akiba ben Joseph, full of the spirit of knowledge, wisdom, and understanding, and he will interpret every crown and letter of the Torah." Moses said, "I would like to see him." And God, for whom nothing is impossible, said, "Turn around." So Moses turned around, and he found himself more than a thousand years in the future, seated in the eighth row of Rabbi Akiba's classroom, and Rabbi Akiba was explaining a point of the Law. Moses listened carefully, but he could not understand what he heard. Finally, a student raised his hand and said, "Rabbi Akiba, where do we know this from?" And Rabbi Akiba said, "We know this from Moses at Mount Sinai."

Here Moses is sent by God to sit in the classroom of Rabbi Akiba. The fact that Akiba lived over a thousand years after Moses presents no problems in the *Aggadah*, where time is subordinate to the will of God. Moses finds Akiba's teachings difficult to follow and is doubtless astonished when Akiba quotes Moses himself as the source of his teaching. It seems likely that in this legend we find a kind of secret confession of the rabbis, acknowledging that the later generations had so transformed the meaning of the Torah that Moses must turn to his successor, Rabbi Akiba, for a complete understanding of the law that he himself transmitted.

Indeed, there is a related rabbinic tradition that while Moses did receive all of the Oral Law at Mount Sinai, including all future interpretations of the Torah, he did not write all of it down, but left some of it to be discovered by the future generations. This seems like an acknowledgment that the very essence of the rabbinic commentary on the Torah required a creative process of discovery.

Sources:
B. *Menahot* 29b; B. *Shabbat* 88b-89a; *Exodus Rabbah* 40; *Leviticus Rabbah* 26.

341. GOD TEACHES TORAH IN THE WORLD TO COME

God said to Abraham: "You taught your sons Torah in this world, but in the World to Come I Myself will teach Torah to all of Israel, and they will not forget it, for I will write it in their hearts. Then all of Israel will become prophets, as it is said, '*After that, I will pour out my spirit on all flesh; your sons and daughters shall prophesy; your old men shall dream dreams, and your young men shall see visions*'" (Joel 3:1).

This tradition of God teaching Torah in the World to Come to the souls of the righteous is based on an interpretation of *And all your children shall be disciples of the Lord, and great shall be the happiness of your children* (Isa. 54:13). It is also based on Jeremiah 31:32: "*After those days*," said Yahweh, "*I will put my Torah in their inward parts and write it in their hearts.*" Here "*after those days*" is understood to mean after this lifetime, in the time of the World to Come, as does "afterward" in the verse from Joel 3:1. See "The Celestial Academy," p. 193.

Sources:
Genesis Rabbah 49:2; *Midrash Tanhuma, va-Yigash* 12; *Midrash Tanhuma, Yitro* 13;
  Numbers Rabbah 17:6; *Zohar Hadash* 36b.

342. MOSES QUESTIONS GOD

God dictated the Torah to Moses at Mount Sinai, and Moses transcribed the Torah exactly as he heard it from God. But when God dictated the words, *"Let us make man in our image"* (Gen. 1:26), Moses paused and inquired of God, "Master of the Universe, how is it that You are providing an opening for heretics? I am bewildered about this."

God replied, "Write as I instruct you, and whoever wishes to err may err."

> This midrash reflects the rabbinic discomfort with the "us" in, *"Let us make man,"* which they regarded as an opening to heretics. So here they project their concern by putting it in the mouth of Moses. God's reply is that Moses simply serves as His scribe and must write down what He tells him.
>
> The difficulties presented by this passage are addressed directly in *B. Sanhedrin* 38b: "In all the passages which the heretics have taken as proofs, their refutation is near at hand. Thus: *'Let us make man in our image'* is refuted by *And God created man in His image* (Gen. 1:27), and *'Let us, then, go down and confound their speech there'* (Gen. 11:7) is refuted by, *And the Lord came down"* (Gen. 11:7).
>
> *Sources:*
> Genesis Rabbah 8:8.
>
> *Studies:*
> "Not by Means of an Angel and not by Means of a Messenger" by Judah Goldin.

343. THE ARK OF THE COVENANT

As long as *the Ark of the Covenant of the Lord traveled in front of them* (Num. 10:33), the way was made easy for the children of Israel, for the Ark lifted up every valley and sank down every mountain, so that they might go on their way.

> Just as Miriam's Well accompanied the Israelites wherever they went in the wilderness, so that they always had fresh water, so too was the Ark of the Covenant said to have raised up every valley and lowered every mountain, making it easier for them to proceed. See "Miriam's Well," p. 387.
>
> *Sources:*
> B. Berakhot 54b; Yalkut Shim'oni.

344. THE CHANGING TORAH

The sages say that in the future God will give a new Torah. If God wants to change the Torah or exchange it for another, to descend once more on Mount Sinai or another mighty mountain, and to appear a second time before the eyes of all the living—we must do His will, whatever His bidding.

> Maimonides insisted that the entire Torah was unchanging. That meant, for example, that the claims of Christianity and Islam that they offered new divine revelations were inevitably false. Here, however, Rabbi Jacob Emden (1697-1776) offers the possibility that God could provide a new revelation, different from the first at Sinai, and if so it would be the duty of the people of Israel to do God's bidding, no matter what it was. At the same time, Emden is making it clear that it would have to be a major revelation, as great as that at Sinai, in order to be recognized as replacing the old Torah. Emden was the archenemy of the Shabbatian messianic movement, and

there is an element of irony in this explanation, implying that it is unlikely that such a major new revelation would ever occur; certainly not in the case of Shabbatai Zevi, who later proved himself to be a false Messiah.

That rabbinic interpretations of the Torah had changed it in a substantial way is reflected in a dream of Rabbi Yitzhak Eizik Safrin of Komarno (1806-1874) found in his dream book, *Megillat Setarim*. In a dream from 1847, Rabbi Safran writes, "I dreamed I saw a Torah scroll, and between every verse were written great and exalted secrets. I stood there with my teacher and master, my uncle Tzvi. He showed me this scroll and told me that this was my scroll that I had written with my teachings and new interpretations."

For more on the rabbinic tradition that God would provide a new Torah, see "A New Torah," p. 522.

Sources:
Migdal Oz.

345. THE FLYING LETTERS

Before the world was created, the letters of the alphabet flew around without order, and nothing existed except chaos. To bring order out of chaos, God arranged the letters of the alphabet, beginning with *aleph*. Then God chose *bet*, the second letter, to begin the Torah and brought the Torah into being. After that, each of the letters took its place in the Torah. There are said to be 600,000 letters, the same number as the Israelites assembled at Mount Sinai to receive the Torah.

The Torah tells how the first tablets were engraved with God's finger. When Moses saw the golden calf, *He hurled the tablets from his hands and shattered them at the foot of the mountain* (Exod. 32:19). It is said of the letters inscribed on those tablets that they took flight and ascended on high. Ever since, the letters of the Torah have taken flight in times of danger.

The Talmud tells of Rabbi Haninah ben Teradion, who was wrapped in the scroll of the Torah and set on fire, for daring to study the Torah in public in Rome, when it was forbidden. His disciples called out, "Rabbi what do you see?" Rabbi Haninah answered, "The parchment is burning, but the letters are soaring on high."

The *Zohar* tells that not long after the death of Shimon bar Yohai, Rabbi Judah fell asleep beneath a tree, and in a dream he saw Rabbi Shimon ascending on high, bearing a scroll of the Torah in his arms. Behind him flew a flock in formation. Then Rabbi Judah looked closer and saw that it was not a flock of birds but a flock of flying letters that followed Rabbi Shimon. At first, Rabbi Judah was mystified. Then he suddenly understood that what he was seeing was a book of flying letters that Rabbi Shimon was taking up with him. And in the dream, Rabbi Judah watched them ascend until they disappeared. When Rabbi Judah awoke and remembered this dream, he knew that when Rabbi Shimon had died, the world had lost the precious store of his wisdom. For now that book of celestial mysteries had returned to its place on high.

The motif of flying letters is found in many variations in Jewish lore. The earliest examples of this theme are found in rabbinic lore concerning the Tablets of the Law shattered by Moses in Exodus 32:19. The myth explains that before the tablets struck the ground, the letters ascended on high (*Avot de-Rabbi Natan* 2:11).

The other famous tale about flying letters concerns the execution of Haninah ben Teradion, who was wrapped in the scroll of the Torah. When asked what he saw as the flames burned, he replied: "The parchments are being burnt but the letters are soaring on high" (*B. A. Z.* 18a).

The *Zohar* recounts a tale about a book of flying letters. It emphasizes how much the world lost at the time of the death of Shimon bar Yohai. Here Rabbi Judah has a dream in which he sees Bar Yohai ascending on high, followed by a flock of flying letters. These are the letters of the book of his wisdom, which has been lost due to his death. Rabbinic lore often recounts remarkable events that are said to have taken place when important rabbis have died.

Sources:
B. *Avodah Zarah* 18a; *Avot de-Rabbi Natan* 2;*Targum Pseudo-Yonathan* on Exodus 32:19; *Zohar* 1:216b-217a; Pseudo-Philo, *Liber Antiquitatum Biblicarum* 12:5.

346. GOD'S SIGNATURE

After Israel built the golden calf and Moses had broken the tablets of the Law, Moses spoke to God and said: "Did You not bring them out of Egypt, out of the House of Idolatry?"

God answered, "Do you want Me to become reconciled with them? Then bring new tablets and I will append My signature to them."

> God's signature, in the context of this midrash, refers to the rewriting of the second tablets. According to tradition, the first tablets of the Law were written by the finger of God, but the second were written by Moses. In this myth, God offers to add His signature to the second tablets, to make them official, as with the signing of a contract.
>
> Psalms 119:60 states that "The beginning of Your word is Truth," and according to B. *Shabbat* 55a, "Truth is the signature of God." Drawing on this interpretation, Rabbi Yosef Hayim of Baghdad (1834-1909), known as Ben Ish Hai, states in *Ben Yehoyada* that God's signature is actually imprinted in the Torah, since the last letters of the first three words of the Torah spell *emet*, "truth."
>
> *Sources:*
> *Deuteronomy Rabbah* 15:17; B. *Shabbat* 55a; *Ben Yehoyada*.

347. THE CROWNS OF ISRAEL

Six hundred thousand gathered at Mount Sinai to receive the Torah. When God asked them if they were ready to receive the Torah, they replied, *"We will do and we will listen"* (Exod. 24:7). And when they gave preference to *"we will do"* over *"we will listen,"* a heavenly voice went forth and said: "Who has revealed this secret to my children, which is known by the angels, to do and then to listen?" Just then six hundred thousand ministering angels came down from on high and set two crowns upon each Israelite, one as a reward for *"we will do"* and one for *"we will listen."*

But as soon as Israel sinned through the golden calf, twice as many destroying angels descended and snatched those crowns away.

> It is deduced that the angels know the secret of first doing and then listening because of the verse, *Bless the Lord, O His angels, mighty creatures who do His bidding, ever hearkening to His bidding; bless the Lord, all His hosts, His servants who do His will* (Ps. 103:20). Here, they first fulfill, then hearken.
>
> In *Likutei Moharan* 1:22 Rabbi Nachman of Bratslav interprets "do" to refer to the Revealed Torah (or Written Torah) and "listen" to refer to the Hidden Torah (or Oral Torah).
>
> *Sources:*
> B. *Shabbat* 88a.

348. THE PRINCE OF THE TORAH

After the return to Zion, the people set about rebuilding the Temple in Jerusalem. But they soon discovered that because of the effort required to rebuild the Temple, they no longer had time to study Torah, as God required of them. For God said, "You are to occupy yourselves with My Chosen House, and discussion of the Torah is never to leave your lips." Yet it seemed impossible to do both at the same time.

When the builders complained to God about this, God first chastised them for not having studied more when they were in exile, depriving Him of hearing words of Torah from their lips. But then God informed the angels that He intended to reveal the secret of the *Sar ha-Torah* to the builders. With this secret, it was possible to acquire knowledge of the Torah and its secrets in a short time, without fear of forgetting them.

When the angels heard this, they pleaded with God not to reveal this secret. "Do not make flesh and blood equal to us. Let them labor in the Torah as they have for generations. If You reveal this secret to Your children, the small will be like the great, the fool like the wise man."

But God dismissed the opinion of the angels and God Himself descended into the Temple as it was being built. When the builders saw the Throne of Glory hovering above the altar, with the King of the World on it, they fell upon their faces. Then God said, "My children, why are you prostrating yourselves? Rise and sit before My throne the way you sit in an academy, and learn the secret of how to lift up the paths of your mind to gaze into the Torah." Thus did God reveal to the builders the secret of how to call upon the *Sar ha-Torah*, the Prince of the Torah.

This secret was first revealed to Moses, who used it to receive the Torah at Mount Sinai. Knowledge of this secret makes it possible to bring the Prince of the Torah down from on high by magical means, by the use of holy names, in order to reveal how to acquire vast knowledge of the Torah. After that the builders were able to busy themselves with building the Temple, and nonetheless the Torah did not depart from their lips.

Rabbi Ishmael said of these builders: "Our fathers refused to set one stone on another in the Lord's temple until they convinced the King of the World and his servants to reveal to them the secret of the Torah."

> *Sar ha-Torah* is the Prince of the Torah, who is the Angel of the Torah. The angel's name is Yefefiah. The tradition concerning this angel states that when invoked, the angel reveals the secret of how to learn the Torah in one sitting. There is a series of accounts about those who invoked the *Sar ha-Torah*. But the primary myth concerns the inability of the builders of the Second Temple in Jerusalem to find time to study Torah. Here God Himself descends into the newly built Temple and reveals the secret of the *Sar ha-Torah*. The builders invoke the angel, rapidly learn the Torah, and this provides a reward both for God, Who revels in their study, and for themselves.
>
> In the text of *Sar ha-Torah*, God makes an assertion about those desiring ever more extensive teachings of the Torah: "I know what you want. You desire a great deal of Torah and much Talmud and many oral traditions. You crave My many secrets." Normally, it takes a lifetime of study to master the extensive traditions linked to the Torah, but through the miracle of the secret of the Prince of the Torah, it becomes possible to master this intricate study in a single sitting. This must have been a common fantasy among the students of the Torah.
>
> *Sources:*
> *Sar ha-Torah* in *Hekhalot Rabbati*, #281-306; *Hekhalot Zutartei*.
>
> *Studies:*
> *The Faces of the Chariot* by David J. Halperin, pp. 376-386, 427-446.
> *The Ancient Jewish Mysticism* by Joseph Dan, pp. 139-167.
> "'Like the Ministering Angels': Ritual and Purity in Early Jewish Mysticism and Magic" by Michael Swartz.

349. STUDYING THE TORAH

It is said about Rabbi Yonathan ben Uziel that when he was engaged in Torah study, every bird that flew over him was immediately burned up.

When Rabbi Eleazar ben Arakh studied the Torah, fire descended from heaven and surrounded him. Angels danced as at a wedding party, and trees burst into song.

Once, when Ben Azzai was studying Torah, there was a flame surrounding him. They asked: "Are you perhaps engaged in the study of the Mysteries of the Chariot?" He replied: "No, I am but finding in the Torah parallels to the Prophets, and in the Prophets parallels to the *Aggadah*. And the words of the Torah are joyful even as they were on the day they were given at Sinai, and they were originally given in fire, as it is said, *The mountain was ablaze with flames*" (Deut. 4:11).

So too is a tale told of a devout man who died and appeared to his wife in a dream. His hair and beard were all lit up like a great torch. His wife realized that he had been welcomed as a saint on high, and she said, "What have you done to be worthy of this?" He told her, "I tried to speak only of matters of the Torah, for God watches over those who devote themselves to Torah and speak as little as possible about anything else."

Thus it is said that when one is properly engaged in Torah, those words of Torah ascend on high, and they are hidden away in the Garden of Eden. And when God enters the Garden to delight in the righteous, those words are brought before Him, and He gazes at them and rejoices.

> While the subject that Rabbi Yonathan ben Uziel was studying is not given, both Rabbi Eleazar ben Arakh and Ben Azzai are linked to study of *Ma'aseh Merkavah*, the Mysteries of the Chariot. There is a considerable number of stories about rabbis who have miraculous experiences linked to study of these mysteries.
>
> *Sources:*
> Y. *Hagigah* 2:1; B. *Hagigah* 14b; B. *Sukkah* 28a; *Leviticus Rabbah* 16:4; Genizah fragment from *Mekhilta* of Rabbi Shimon bar Yohai; *Kav ha-Yashar* chap. 12; *Zohar* 1:243a.
>
> *Studies:*
> *The Faces of the Chariot* by David J. Halperin.

350. THE BOY WHO READ THE BOOK OF EZEKIEL

There once was a certain child of exceptional understanding who read the Book of Ezekiel in his teacher's house. He contemplated the meaning of the word *hashmal*. He comprehended the true meaning of the word *hashmal* in the passage, *I looked, and lo, a stormy wind came sweeping out of the north—a huge cloud and flashing fire, surrounded by a radiance; and in the center of it, in the center of the fire, a gleam as of amber (hashmal)* (Ezek. 1:4). At that instant a fire went forth and consumed him.

> This is a talmudic warning tale about the dangers of studying mystical texts, especially the Book of Ezekiel. It highlights the mystery of the term *hashmal* in Ezekiel 1:4 and underscores that the dangers of mystical study particularly apply to children.
>
> *Sources:*
> B. *Hagigah* 13a.
>
> *Studies:*
> *Jewish Gnosticism, Merkabah Mysticism, and Talmudic Tradition* by Gershom Scholem.
> *The Faces of the Chariot* by David J. Halperin.

351. THE TWO TORAHS

There are two Torahs: the Written Torah and the Oral Torah. It is said that God dictated the Torah to Moses during the day, and at night He explained it to him. These explanations constitute the Oral Torah.

Moses wanted to write down the whole Torah, but God told him that only certain parts could be written down, while other parts had to remain oral.

All of the Torah had to be revealed to Moses on Mount Sinai so that no one could claim that only a part of the Torah had been given at the outset. But due to the immensity of all that Moses had to remember, at first he had less than total recall. However, as his body became more and more subordinate to his soul over the forty days and nights, Moses became capable of absorbing all of the Oral Torah without forgetting any part of it.

> *Midrash Tehillim* explains that Moses knew it was day when God instructed him in the Written Law, and he knew it was night when God instructed him in the Oral Law.
>
> Rabban Gamliel was asked: "How many Torahs were given to Israel?" He answered, "Two, one in the mouth and one in writing."
>
> In *Avot de-Rabbi Natan* 15, a tale is recounted of a man who came separately to Shammai and Hillel and asked how many Torahs there were. Each of them replied, "Two, one written and one oral." The man said he was prepared to accept the written Torah but not the oral one. Shammai rebuked the man. Hillel sat him down and explained that even as he had accepted that the *aleph* of the alphabet was *aleph* and that the *bet* was *bet*, so he had to accept both the written and oral Torahs in good faith.
>
> In *Likutei Moharan*, Rabbi Nachman of Bratslav explains that in each generation there are new revelations of the Torah. Some of these should be written down, while others should only be taught orally. To this day, there are teachers of the Torah who limit some of their esoteric teachings to oral explanations that are not supposed to be written down.
>
> Jacob Neusner uses the term "Dual Torah" instead of "the two Torahs," and this usage has become widely accepted.
>
> *Sources:*
> B. *Shabbat* 31a; *Pirkei de-Rabbi Eliezer* 46; *Avot de-Rabbi Natan* 15; Rabbi Moshe
>   Alshekh on Exodus 31:18; *Sifre on Deuteronomy* 351; *Midrash Tehillim* 19:7; Y. *Peah*
>   2:4; *Midrash ha-Gadol*, Deuteronomy 764; *Likutei Moharan* 2:28.
>
> *Studies:*
> "From Theosophy to Midrash: Lurianic Exegesis and the Garden of Eden" by Shaul
>   Magid.

352. THE GIVING OF THE SONG OF SONGS

Some say that the Song of Songs was given at the Red Sea at the time that the waters parted, at the time the heavens opened and all the secrets of heaven were revealed. Then, it is said, a maidservant saw at the sea things that were not seen by the prophet Ezekiel. It is also said that the whole world existed for the day on which the Song of Songs was given.

Others say that the Song of Songs was given on Mount Sinai, together with the Torah, and that God Himself, not King Solomon, is the true author, and it was God who gave it to His people.

> Defending the inclusion of the Song of Songs in the Bible, Rabbi Akiba said, "All the books of the Bible are holy, but the Song of Songs is the Holy of Holies." Here the Song of Songs is described as being revealed in a revelation at the Red Sea that is parallel to that at Mount Sinai. In each case heaven opened and its secrets in the form of the Torah or here, the Song of Songs, were revealed. Note that the parting of the

Red Sea is the second most important revelation in Jewish history, the first being the giving of the Torah at Mount Sinai. This directly implies that the Song of Songs is the holiest book of the Bible after the Torah.

The alternate version presents the Song of Songs as even holier, in that it is said to have been given along with the Torah at Mount Sinai, and disputes the tradition that King Solomon was its author by stating that the true author was none other than God Himself. Both versions of this myth emphasize the unimaginable holiness of the Song of Songs and counter any resistance to it as merely a collection of erotic love poems.

Sources:
Song of Songs Rabbah 1:11.

353. THE ORIGIN OF THE SHEMA

When the hour drew near for Jacob to take leave of this world, he called his sons together and said to them, "Do you have any doubts that God spoke and the world came into being?" They replied, "Hear, O Israel, our father. Just as you have no doubts that God spoke and the world came into being, so too do we have no doubts. Surely, *The Lord, our God, the Lord is one*" (Deut. 6:4). That is why it is still said, to this day, "Hear, O Israel, the Lord our God, the Lord is one." And that is how the prayer of the Shema was created.

> This legendary explanation for the origin of the Shema builds on the fact that "Israel" refers both to Jacob, who became Israel, and to the people Israel. Usually "Hear, O Israel" is understood to refer to the people Israel, but since Jacob's name was changed to Israel, the opening phrase of the Shema, "Hear, O Israel" can be understood to be directed to the patriarch Jacob/Israel as well as to the people Israel. Since his sons add "our father," there can be no question that they are directing their words to Jacob. This same kind of double reference for "Israel" is found in Genesis 49:2: *Assemble yourselves, and hear, you sons of Jacob, and hearken to Israel, your father.*
>
> In the version of the origin of the Shema found in *Deuteronomy Rabbah*, Jacob's concern is that his sons not be idol worshippers. So he called all his sons to his bed and said, "Hear your father, Israel, and worship God, whom your father worships." They answered, "Hear, O Israel, our father, the Lord our God, the Lord is one." Both versions draw on the double meaning of Israel both as Jacob and as the people of Israel.
>
> The first verse of the Shema, from Deuteronomy 6:4, reads: *Shema Yisrael, Adonai Eloheinu, Adonai Ehad,* "Hear, O Israel, the Lord our God, the Lord is One." The Shema is the primary proclamation of belief in Judaism, an essential part of the daily prayer service. According to the *Shulhan Arukh*, the Code of Jewish Law, the first verse of the Shema is recited in a loud voice. It is the practice of Yemenite Jews to read the Shema out loud, in unison. This is based on the belief that God harkens to the Shema when it is read in unison. This tradition is based on *Song of Songs Rabbah* 8:13: "When Israel reads the Shema with proper *kavanah* (intention), in one voice, God and all the heavenly hosts hearken to their voice. But when the reading of the Shema is fragmented, God tells them to learn from the angels, who praise God in one voice and one melody." Also, it is customary to cover one's eyes when reciting the first verse of the Shema (*Shulhan Arukh, Keriat Shema*, 61:5). This custom can be traced to the talmudic sage, Rabbi Judah ha-Nasi, who covered his face with his hand when he accepted the Yoke of Heaven (*B. Ber.* 13b).

Sources:
Sifre on Deuteronomy 31; *Deuteronomy Rabbah* 2:35.

Studies:
"The Shema and Its Rhetoric: The Case for the Shema Being More than Creation, Revelation and Redemption" by Reuven Kimelman.
The Shema: Spirituality and Law in Judaism by Norman Lamm.

354. THE HOLY BREATH

King David wrote the Psalms with divine inspiration—with the Holy Breath. This Holy Breath is still in the words of the Psalms. When a person recites the Psalms, his breath arouses the Holy Breath in these words. Therefore, when a person recites the Psalms, it is as if King David himself were chanting them.

> This is a teaching of Rabbi Nachman of Bratslav. The Holy Breath is the *Ruah ha-Kodesh*, which can also be translated as "the Holy Spirit." (See "The Holy Spirit," p. 18). *Ruah* means both "breath" and "spirit." *Ruah ha-Kodesh* is the source of divine inspiration, with which King David is said to have written the Psalms.
>
> *Sources:*
> *Sihot ha-Ran* 98.

355. RAVA CREATES A MAN

Rava said, "If the righteous wished, they could create a world." So he created a man and sent him to Rabbi Zera. Rabbi Zera spoke to the man, but he did not answer. When Rabbi Zera realized that he must have been created by magic, he said, "Return to your dust." And the golem dissolved into dust.

> This is one of the earliest mythic versions of an attempt to create a human being, a golem. While lacking in detail, this talmudic tale implies that Rava has somehow used magical powers to create a man. Rabbi Zera, on the other hand, does not believe that such a creation is permitted, and he commands the golem to return to the dust.
>
> From this account we learn that the golem was defective in that it could not communicate, which leads Rabbi Zera to conclude that the man is not real. Other versions of the golem myth mention that it cannot reproduce.
>
> In the same section of tractate Sanhedrin there is an account of a three-year old calf created by Rav Haninah and Rav Oshaya. They were said to study the *Sefer Yetzirah*, the Book of Creation, every Sabbath eve, and using the knowledge they learned there they created the calf and ate it.
>
> *Sources:*
> *B. Sanhedrin* 65b.
>
> *Studies:*
> "The Magic of the Golem: The Early Development of the Golem Legend" by Peter Schäfer.

356. JEREMIAH CREATES A GOLEM

The prophet Jeremiah studied the *Sefer Yetzirah*, the Book of Creation, on his own. Then a heavenly voice came forth and commanded, "Find a companion!" So Jeremiah began to study that book with his son, Sira. Together they submerged themselves in the *Sefer Yetzirah* for three years. At the end of three years, they set about combining the letters of the alphabet, and in this way they created a man on whose head was written *YHVH Elohim emet*—"The Lord God is Truth," and there was a knife in his hand. All at once the being they had created erased the first letter of *emet*—truth, leaving only *met*—dead. Distraught, Jeremiah asked the man why he had done this. The man answered: "God created you in His image, but now that you have created a man, people will say, 'These two are the only gods in the world.'" Jeremiah asked, "What can we do?" The man answered: "Pronounce the letters backward with which you created me." So they did, and the being turned to ashes and dust.

There are a series of myths about the creation of the golem, a man made out of clay and brought to life drawing on the power of the Hebrew alphabet. Here the prophet Jeremiah is said to have created such a golem drawing on the mystical secrets found in the *Sefer Yetzirah*, the Book of Creation, one of the earliest (some would say the earliest) kabbalistic texts. Here the being that Jeremiah and his son bring to life uncreates itself by erasing the first letter of *emet*—"Truth"—inscribed on its forehead, leaving *met*—"dead," as the creature itself feels that its creation is wrong, since it attempts to duplicate God's power in creating human beings. In most golem myths, the creature dies as soon as the *aleph* that is the first letter of *emet* is erased. Here, however, the golem tells them to pronounce the letters backward to undo the creation. This should be seen as an interim stage in the development of the golem myth, which culminates in the fully developed myth of the Golem of Prague.

Sources:
Perush Shem shel Arba Otiyyot Ms. Florence 2:41.

Studies:
The Early Kabbalah, edited by Joseph Dan, pp. 54-56.
Golem: Jewish Magical and Mystical Traditions on the Artificial Anthropoid by Moshe Idel.

357. THE GOLEM OF IBN GABIROL

It is said about Rabbi Solomon ibn Gabirol that he drew upon the mysteries to create a woman who served him. When he was denounced to the authorities, he showed them that she was not a full or complete creature. And he restored her to the pieces of wood of which she had been constructed.

The Hebrew poet Solomon ibn Gabirol (1021-1056) was also said to be versed in kabbalistic mysteries. In this account he creates a female golem for the purpose of serving him. There is some ambiguity about whether she was created for sexual purposes. Had he created her for some greater good, such as the protection of the community, this might have been seen as acceptable. But that was not the case. When confronted by the authorities, he demonstrated that the woman was not fully human, rather, she is a female golem.

On the one hand the story seems to extol the powers of Ibn Gabirol, but on the other hand he is portrayed as self-serving. Also, there is a hint of the salacious about his intentions in creating such a golem. But, above all, it is evidence that the golem motif, which first appears in the Talmud in the creation of a calf that was eaten on the Sabbath, was still alive. This thirteenth-century myth about creating a golem is transformed into the cycle of stories about the Golem of Prague. In the latter, however, the creation of the golem is compelled by the dire situation in which the Jews were found, suffering from regular pogroms through the Middle Ages. Since there was no solution in reality, a fantasy solution evolved, that of the golem created by Rabbi Judah Loew to protect the Jews of Prague from the blood libel accusation, in which Jews were falsely accused of using the blood of a Christian (usually a child) to make *matzah* for the Passover Seder, a libel that led to centuries of pogroms against the Jews throughout Europe. Yet even though the purposes in creating these two golems, one female and one male, are quite different, the knowledge and powers attributed to both figures underlie both tales.

How was the golem of Ibn Gabirol created? The story lacks details, but the method was surely by some means of holy letters and names. In the Yudel Rosenberg versions of the golem cycle, which are probably much later than they were claimed to be—nineteenth century instead of the sixteenth—Rabbi Loew went through a magical ritual, inscribing the word *emet*—truth—on the forehead of the golem, and putting a paper with God's Name on it in the golem's mouth, walking around it seven times, till it glowed. Only then did it come to life. Later, after the golem had served its purpose,

Rabbi Loew turned it back into clay. This clay is said still to be found in the attic of the Alt-Neu (Old-New) synagogue in Prague, where Rabbi Loew once served. A comparison of the two stories demonstrates that the same creation can be viewed as sacrilege or sacred.

Others who were said to have created golems include Rabbenu Tam (Rabbi Jacob Tam, 1100-1171) and Ibn Ezra (1092-1167). Ibn Ezra is reported to have said, "See what God has given by means of the holy letters!" Then he said to the golem, "Go back." And it became what it had been before.

A number of modern authors have written about the golem, including Gustav Meyrink, H. Levick, David Frishman, Jorge Luis Borges, Isaac Bashevis Singer, Cynthia Ozick, Michael Chabon, Frances Sherwood, and Thane Rosenbaum.

Sources:
Perush R. Saadiah Gaon le-Sefer Yetzirah; Ma'aseh Ta'atu'im 118.

358. THE GOLEM OF RABBI ELIJAH

Rabbi Elijah of Chelm was a Master of the Name. It was he alone, in his generation, who knew the secret pronunciation of God's Name. This gave him the power to accomplish anything. So too was he well versed in the *Sefer Yetzirah*, The Book of Creation. Drawing on mysteries revealed there, he made a man of clay, inscribed the word *emet*—truth—on its forehead, and when he uttered God's Name, the golem came to life. Thereafter, the golem performed wonders whenever there was urgent need for them.

Then it happened that the golem began to grow larger and larger, and Rabbi Elijah was afraid it might destroy the world. So he ordered the golem to bend down and he removed the first letter of the word on its forehead, changing *emet* into *met*—dead—and at that instant the golem turned back into dust.

> There are several versions of this famous story about the golem of Rabbi Elijah of Chelm (sixteenth century). In some versions, the golem is said to have scratched the rabbi's face while he removed the name from its forehead, or, in other versions, even to have crushed him. Likewise, in some Christian versions Rabbi Elijah is said to have used the golem to perform hard work for him, suggesting that his motives in creating the golem were not altruistic.
>
> While most accounts of the golem place the word *"emet"* on his forehead, some describe the word *"emet"* hung on a chain around his neck.
>
> Here is the version of the golem story found in *Journal for Hermits* by Jakob Grimm (1808), which became widely disseminated:
>
>> After saying certain prayers and observing certain fast days, the Polish Jews make the figure of a man carved from clay or mud. When they pronounce the miraculous name of God over him, he must come to life. He cannot speak, but he understands fairly well what is commanded. They call him golem and use him as a servant to do all sorts of housework. But he must never leave the house. On his forehead is written *emet*—truth. Every day he gains weight and becomes somewhat larger and stronger than all the others in the house, regardless of how little he was to begin with.
>>
>> For fear of him, they therefore erase the first letter, so that nothing remains but *met*—death, whereupon he collapses and turns to clay again. But one man's golem once grew so tall, and he heedlessly let him keep on growing so long that he could no longer reach his forehead. In terror he ordered the servant to take off his boots, thinking that when he bent down he could reach his forehead. So it happened, and the first letter was successfully erased, but the whole heap of clay fell on the Jew and crushed him.
>
> It would appears that Jakob Grimm drew upon the account of Rabbi Elijah's golem, although there are some interesting variations. Grimm's version suggests that the golem was used as a servant, and that the motives of his creator were not altruistic. In the

Grimm version, as soon as the holy name is removed from the golem's forehead, it collapses on top of its creator and kills him. No such catastrophe occurs in the account of Rabbi Elijah's golem.

Sources:
Shem ha-Gedolim 1:9; *She'elot Ya'avetz* 2:82; *Migdal Oz.*

359. THE GOLEM OF PRAGUE

Again and again the Jewish community of Prague was accused of the blood libel. Rabbi Judah Loew, known as the Maharal, prayed that he might be told in a dream how to fight against the accusation. In his dream, he received a reply from heaven in ten words, telling him to create a golem out of clay, who would protect the Jews against those who wanted to destroy them. The Maharal was convinced that the secret of how to bring such a creature to life could be found in those ten words. And at last he found it.

The Maharal called his son-in-law and his oldest pupil, and disclosed the secret to them about how the golem could be created. They served as his assistants, each of them representing one of the elements of fire, water, and air, who together could complete the creation of the golem out of earth, the fourth element. He made them vow not to reveal the secret to anyone.

Then on the twentieth of Adar in the year 5340 (1580), the three of them left Prague at four o'clock in the morning and went to the river Moldau. Out of the clay they dug from the bank of the river, they made a human form, which lay there like a man on his back. Each of the three of them walked around it seven times, reciting a spell that the Maharal had taught them, until the golem began to glow, and his body became covered with hair, and nails appeared at the tips of his fingers and toes. And when they pronounced the verse *And God breathed into his nostrils the breath of life, and man became a living creature* (Gen. 2:7), the golem opened his eyes and looked at them with wonder. The Maharal called out for him to stand up, and the golem rose at once to his feet. Then they dressed him in clothes that they had brought with them, and put shoes on his feet, so that he looked exactly like a man. He saw, heard, and understood everything, but he lacked the power of speech.

Before dawn all four of them returned home. On the way home, the Maharal told the golem that his name was Joseph, and explained why he had been created. So too did he tell him that he must obey all of his commands, no matter what, and the golem nodded to show that he agreed.

After that the Maharal told the members of his household that he had met this poor man, who was unable to speak, in the street, and he had taken him into the house out of pity, to be of service to him. And that is how the golem was created and brought into being.

> Almost no Jewish legend has captured the popular imagination as has that of the golem, the creature made out of clay by Rabbi Judah Loew of Prague (known as the Maharal) and brought to life by the use of various magical incantations, including holy names. This creature, according to the legend, protected the Jews of Prague from various dangers, especially that of the blood libel accusation—that is, the use of the blood of Christian children to bake unleavened bread for Passover. This lie had consistently disastrous consequences, leading to many pogroms against the Jews. Here the golem discovers the body of a murdered Christian child who has been carried into the Jewish ghetto, and carries it back through tunnels into the basement of the actual murderer, the sorcerer Thaddeus, thus staving off a pogrom.
>
> Knowledge of this myth cycle is primarily derived from *Niflaot Maharal*, a collection of tales about Rabbi Loew and the golem, published in 1909 by Rabbi Yudel Rosenberg, who claimed that they had been compiled in the sixteenth century by a relative of Rabbi Loew. Recent scholars, including Dov Sadan, Gershom Scholem, and Eli Yassif, have insisted that Rabbi Rosenberg himself was the author of the book, which he

based loosely on the existing oral legends and written versions of the golem myth. Such legends certainly existed, such as Jakob Grimm's description of the myth in 1808 in *Journal for Hermits*.

The issue here is whether these are authentic sixteenth-century legends, deriving from the period in which Rabbi Judah Loew lived in Prague or immediately afterward, or if they were in fact largely drawn from nineteenth-century folklore, embellished in the twentieth century by Rabbi Rosenberg. Some of the earliest tales about Rabbi Loew are those found in the first volume of the *Sippurim* series, edited by Wolf Pascheles, first published in Prague in 1845. There are a number of precedents for the creation of the golem in earlier Jewish literature, including the description of a calf that was created magically found in the Talmud: "Haninah and Oshaya spent every Sabbath eve in studying the Laws of creation, by means of which they created a calf and ate it" (B. San. 67b). See also "Rava Creates a Man," p. 279.

Sources:

Niflaot Maharal.

Studies:

"The Idea of the Golem" by Gershom Scholem in *On the Kabbalah and Its Symbolism*, pp. 159-204.

Golem: Jewish Magical and Mystical Traditions on the Artifical Anthropoid by Moshe Idel.
The Golem of Prague by Gershon Winkler.
The Hebrew Folktale: History, Genre, Meaning by Eli Yassif.

360. THE END OF THE GOLEM

After the emperor issued an edict that there must be no more cases of the blood libel accusation, Rabbi Loew felt that the golem would not be needed any longer. So he called his son-in-law and his oldest pupil, who had taken part in the creation of the golem, and at two in the morning they went up to the loft in the Alt-Neu synagogue, where the golem was sleeping.

The three of them placed themselves at the head of the golem, and began to circle around him from left to right. There were seven circuits, and after each one they stopped and pronounced the spell that the Maharal had taught them, drawn from the Book of Creation. It was the same spell they had used to create the golem, only they recited it in the opposite order.

After the seventh circuit the golem was reduced to a mass of clay in the shape of a human being. They wrapped it in two old prayer shawls, and hid the mass among the fragments of books in the loft, so that nothing of it could be seen.

The next day it was reported that the golem had run away. Very few people knew what had really taken place. After that the Maharal ordered that no one was to enter the loft of the synagogue. People thought it was a precaution against fire, but confidants of the Maharal knew that it was because the remains of the golem were lying there.

> Here the golem is uncreated and returned to a mass of clay in the shape of a man by reversing the process by which it was created. The remains of the golem are still said to be in the loft of the Alt-Neu synagogue in Prague.
>
> *Sources:*
>
> *Niflaot Maharal.*

361. THE GOLEM IN THE ATTIC

In the attic of the Alt-Neu synagogue of Prague lie the remains of the golem in the shape of a man. These remains have been there since the Maharal returned the golem to a mass of clay. At that time the Maharal is reported to have said, "You will lie here until the time of the Messiah."

None of the Jews of Prague dared to go up to the attic where the remains of the golem are to be found. There was a deep fear of that place. But once some children went up to the attic to see if the remains of the golem were still there. After they went up, they were unable to come down. After reciting psalms and prayers, the Jews of Prague climbed up the big ladder that led to the attic. There they found that the children were lying on the floor of the attic, in a deep sleep, nor could they wake them until they carried them out of that place.

After that, no one in the city of Prague dared to go up there. They left the remains of the golem alone until the days of the Messiah, when the Maharal said he will come back to life.

> This is an oral tale about the golem collected in Israel from a Jew from Czechoslovakia. It is clear evidence of the continuing power of the golem myth among the Jews of Czechoslovakia.
>
> *Sources:*
> IFA 6554.

362. THE HOMUNCULUS OF MAIMONIDES

Among the enemies of Maimonides it is told that he created a monster, a homunculus. How did it happen? Maimonides had an assistant, a young man, to whom he taught many of the secrets of creation. In time the two became inseparable. Their researches were pursued largely in common, and when one of them was at a loss, the other came to his assistance. Thus together they studied almost all branches of knowledge. In time the student almost surpassed his master in learning, and they decided to follow a path together that past generations had never pursued. They wanted to observe the secrets of creation and destruction in nature and then solve the great riddle of creation.

Maimonides showed his assistant a passage in the *Book of Creation*, where it said, "Kill a healthy man, cut his body into pieces, and place the pieces in an airless glass container. Sprinkle upon them an essence gathered from the sap of the Tree of Life and the balsam of immortality, and after nine months the pieces of this body will be living again. It will be unharmable and immortal."

But who were they to get for this dangerous experiment? They decided it would have to be one of them. So they cast lots to decide. But first they swore, in God's Name, that whoever lived would permit the dead to ripen, and would not, for whatever reason, destroy the apparatus prematurely, in order to destroy the embryonic life. Both men laid their hands on the Torah and swore. The lot was cast and fell to the pupil. Maimonides conjured up the Angel of Death, and the young man fell lifeless to the ground. Maimonides cut the body into pieces, placed it in a glass container, sprinkled it with the wondrous essence, and left the room, which he carefully locked and did not enter for four months.

Finally, tortured by doubt and curiosity, he looked at the mass of dead flesh. And behold, there were no longer severed pieces but structured limbs, as if crystallized in the glass container. Happy about the restoration of his student, he left the room and waited a month. In the fifth month the form of the human body could already be recognized. In the sixth the arteries and nerves were visible, and in the seventh movement and life in the organs could be perceived. The researcher, however, became worried. Maimonides was now convinced of the veracity of *The Book of Creation*. And he was terrified about the future.

Maimonides was afraid that a horror threatened the human race if he let it come to fruition. For such an immortal man might be deified, and people would pray to him, and the Laws of Moses would be denied and finally entirely forgotten. At the end of the eighth month, uncertain and deeply troubled, he approached the growing being and was staggered as the almost completely developed face smiled at him. Unable to bear the demonic grin, he ran out of the room ashamed of what he had done. He finally realized that man should not investigate too deeply; what is beyond this sphere leads to hell.

A few days later Maimonides appeared before the Great Council and explained the case. After lengthy reflection the learned rabbis agreed: to protect against a horror for mankind, and to preserve God's honor, a vow might be broken and such a man killed. This decision they based on a verse in Psalms: *It is time to act for the Lord, for they have violated Your teaching* (Ps. 119:126).

At the beginning of the ninth month, Maimonides stepped into the room, intending to destroy his creation. He brought a dog and a cat with him, and he released them and let them fly at each other. In the midst of this fighting, the glass container crashed to the floor and broke into a thousand pieces. The dead man lay at Maimonides' feet. After he recovered himself, Maimonides buried the body and took the pernicious volume and threw it into the flames of the fireplace. But nothing was the same again. Maimonides was attacked by the learned men of the court, accused of magical practices, and escaped judgment only by a timely flight to Egypt. But even there he was pursued and treated as an enemy both by his fellow Jews and by unbelievers, and from then on his life was filled with sorrow.

> The theme echoed here is that of the creation of the golem by Rabbi Judah Loew, and like that tale, this one derives from Prague. But although the golem was created out of necessity, in order to protect the Jews of the ghetto from the dangers of the blood libel, the homunculus of Maimonides is created purely in order to discover the secrets of creation.
>
> It has been suggested on several occasions that the golem cycle of legends may have inspired Mary Shelley's *Frankenstein,* since both concern the creation of a man, the golem by kabbalistic magic and Frankenstein's monster by science. If there was indeed a folk source that served to inspire Mary Shelley, it may have been the present tale about Maimonides, which was first published at the same time as the earliest golem legends, and which has a theme and mood far closer to that of *Frankenstein* than do the tales of the golem. It would be difficult to demonstrate this conclusively, since *Frankenstein* was published in 1818 and *Sippurim,* the volume in which the present tale and earliest golem legend appear, was not published until 1847. However, since all indications are that the stories in *Sippurim* are based on authentic folk sources, there is every reason to assume that an oral version of this tale about Maimonides was current at the time Mary Shelley wrote her famous novel and probably a century or two before that.
>
> The theme that such daring leads to disaster is common in tales with kabbalistic themes such as this. This theme goes all the way back to the famous talmudic story about the four sages who entered Paradise (*B. Hag.* 14b): Ben Azzai looked and died; Ben Zoma looked and lost his mind; Elisha ben Abuyah cut the shoots, that is, became an apostate; and only Rabbi Akiba "ascended and descended in peace." This tale has always been understood to refer to mystical contemplation and the dangers attending it. The moral is clear: if three of four of the greatest sages could not withstand the dangers of the mystical ascent, how could the average person? Therefore restrictions were made that no more than two at a time could discuss the chariot vision of Ezekiel (*Ma'aseh Merkavah*), and no more than one could study the Mysteries of Creation (*Ma'aseh Bereshit*). In addition, kabbalistic study was forbidden until a man was married and at least 40 (or, some sources say, 30) years old.

This tale indicates that one of the dangers associated with this kind of mystical in-dulgence was the creation of a false Messiah, as expressed by the fear of Maimonides in this story that once the gestation of the homunculus is complete, he will be immortal. This suggests the theme of the hastening of the Messiah by various kabbalistic means, including the use of holy names and other methods. Such attempts have always been portrayed as forbidden and doomed to failure. The present folktale is of particular in-terest because of its apparent antagonism toward Maimonides, one of the most revered figures in Judaism. As such, it must be considered to be a folk expression of the contro-versy that raged at several periods, including that from which this tale emerged over the writings and teachings of Maimonides. For the background of this dispute, see *Mai-monidean Criticism and the Maimonidean Controversy, 1180-1240*, by Daniel J. Silver.

Folktales are not the usual mode of expression for such religious conflict. Tracts, books, and fiery speeches are more commonly used. But long before the eighteenth century, Maimonides had become a figure of folk proportions not unlike the greatest sages, such as Rabbi Akiba or the Ari, and was the hero of many folktales. (For an example of a more typical tale about Maimonides, see "The Healing Waters" in *Miriam's Tambourine*, pp. 209-216.) Therefore it was not enough to resist his teachings in the usual ways, but it was necessary to undermine his folk image as well. That seems to be the intention of this tale, which also fits into the pattern of many other cautionary anti-Kabbalistic warning tales.

The lack of knowledge of the true teachings of both Maimonides and the kabbalah is evident in the choice of the secret texts from which Maimonides is said to have learned his secrets. One of these, *The Book of Creation*, is the name of an actual kabbalistic text, *Sefer Yetzirah* (in Hebrew literally, "The Book of Formation"), which is one of the earliest and most enigmatic kabbalistic works. It does not attempt to impart, however, secrets of the kind required to bring the slain assistant to life. Instead it concentrates on the mysteries of letters and numbers and is far more abstract and oblique. Nor does the quotation from *The Book of Creation* in the story appear in the actual text of *Sefer Yetzirah*. The combination of anti-Maimonidean and anti-Kabbalistic elements suggests that this tale emerged from the Jewish centers of Poland and Lithuania, where the old quarrel broke out again in the late Middle Ages. At the same time, the present tale is itself a variant of other, positive folktales about the great medical skill and supernatural powers of Maimonides. In one of these tales, found in *Shalshelet ha-Kabbalah*, compiled by Gedaliah ibn Yachya (Zolkiew, Russia: 1801), Maimonides is forced to swallow poison in a confrontation with the king's physicians, but provides the antidote to save himself, while the king's physicians all die from the poison pro-vided by Maimonides. In another such tale, an even closer variant to the one at hand, the Caliph has Maimonides beheaded, but before his execution, Maimonides instructs his students in how to reattach his head, and he fully recovers, much to the consterna-tion of the Caliph. It is not a giant step from the powers demonstrated in these tales to the creation of the immortal man in "The Homunculus of Maimonides." Note that the parallel theme to the creation of the golem by the Maharal differs in the essential issue of the success or failure of the creation. While the golem does fulfill its purpose, the creation of Maimonides does not. As such, this tale of Maimonides also adds a note of caution to those who found the mystical approach of the Maharal appealing as a way to resolve the problems of their time. Clearly, this tale has no historical kernel, nor is it characteristic of Maimonides in any way.

Sources:

Sippurim: eine Sammlung jüdischer Sagen, Märchen und Geschichten für Völkerkunde; Ha-Rambam be-Fi ha-Am be-Maroko by Ya'akov Itiel in *Yeda Am* Vol. 2, pp. 198-199, 1954; *Edot Mesaprot*, pp. 146-147.

Studies:

Maimonidean Criticism and the Maimonidean Controversy, 1180-1240 by Daniel J. Silver.

BOOK SIX

MYTHS OF THE HOLY TIME

All the students watched spellbound as the Ari and
the old man danced.

IFA 13043

363. GOD PASSES JUDGMENT

God said to Israel: "My children, know that I pass judgment four times a year: At the time of Passover, I adjudicate cases concerning the produce of the field. At the time of Shavuot, cases concerning the fruit of the trees. At the time of Rosh ha-Shanah, cases concerning all the inhabitants of the world, who pass before Me in single file. At the time of Sukkot, cases concerning the supply of water.

"During three of these times I judge civil matters, and I make some people rich and some people poor, give more to some and less to others. But Rosh ha-Shanah is the time for judging capital cases—for deciding life or death."

> Here God establishes four times of the year that He passes judgment. Whereas Rosh ha-Shanah is known as the Day of Judgment, this myth expands the time of judgment to the three pilgrimage festivals of Passover, Shavuot, and Sukkot. But a clear distinction is made between civil cases—here linked to the festivals—and capital cases—linked only to Rosh ha-Shanah, when God decides who will live and who will die. The effect is to have God's judgment present throughout more of the year, as an ongoing constant reminder of God's involvement in this world.
>
> *Sources:*
> *Pesikta de-Rav Kahana* 7:2.

364. THE BOOK OF LIFE AND THE BOOK OF DEATH

All things are judged on Rosh ha-Shanah, and their fate is sealed on Yom Kippur. Some say there is a ledger in heaven that records all that has taken place from the time of Adam throughout the generations. The ledger is open, and the hand is writing every single thing that a person does below. Whose hand is this? Some say it is that of an angel. Others say that the hand belongs to God Himself, and that the book is the book that God is writing. That is the meaning of the verse *And a scroll of remembrance has been written at His behest* (Mal. 3:16). This is the Book of Life.

In addition to the Book of Life, there is a second book, the Book of Death. During the Days of Awe God's scrutiny of our lives is intense, and it is to be hoped that if our name has strayed to the wrong ledger, God will say, "I have removed your name from the Book of Death and put it in the Book of Life, as it is said, *For Yahweh has redeemed Jacob*" (Isa. 44:23).

Others say that there are three books opened in heaven on Rosh ha-Shanah, the New Year: one for the wholly righteous, one for the wholly wicked, and one for those who are neither completely righteous nor completely wicked. The wholly righteous are inscribed at once and sealed in the Book of Life; the wholly wicked are inscribed at once and sealed in the Book of Death; and the fate of the intermediate is suspended from Rosh ha-Shanah until Yom Kippur, the Day of Atonement. If they repent and are found worthy, they are inscribed for life; if they fail to repent, they are inscribed for death. Yet so great is the power of atonement on Yom Kippur, that it is said to bring about atonement even for those who have not repented.

When God sits on the Throne of Judgment, the Books of Life and Death are open before Him, as it is said, *The court sat and the books were opened* (Dan. 7:10). His garment is as white as snow, the hair on His head pure wool, and His cloak seventy times brighter than the sun. A pair of angels, both named Shofariel, are the keepers of the Books, which are closed to everyone else. No other angels have access to the secrets inscribed there. Not even Metatron, the Prince of the Presence, is permitted to peer at that divine list. Among the sages, only the Ari knew how to peer into those secret books. In this way he learned the fate of his followers from the first of Rosh ha-Shanah.

Some say that the world is not judged on those holy days, but that God sits upon the Throne of Judgment and judges the world every day. The Books of the Living and the Books of the Dead are opened before him, and all the children of heaven stand before him in fear, dread, awe, and trembling. And in this world as well every being trembles before the eyes of God.

Others say that God is a merciful God. Even as clouds are swept away by wind, so the iniquities of Israel are swept away in this world, as it is said, *I wipe away your sins like a cloud* (Isa. 44:22). For from the time He created Adam, God has known that if He held mankind to account for its successive misdeeds, the world would not endure. Therefore God remembers those who observe the Torah, but puts those who commit misdeeds out of mind. This means that God removes their names from the Book of Death and puts them in the Book of Life.

There is a series of myths about heavenly books. Some of these are described as ledgers in which God keeps track of good and bad behavior. The best known of these myths concern the Books of Life and Death. The talmudic version lists three books all linked to Rosh ha-Shanah: the Book of Life, the Book of Death, and a book concerning the fate of the intermediate. However, for most Jews there is a conscious focusing on the Book of Life, while the Book of Death remains for the most part unnamed and largely unmentioned, and the notion of a third book has essentially vanished from the tradition. The current understanding is that a person's name is inscribed on Rosh ha-Shanah either in the Book of Life or the "Other Book," (i.e., The Book of Death), but the name is not sealed until Yom Kippur. This is stated succinctly in the Talmud: "Man is judged on Rosh ha-Shanah and his fate is sealed on Yom Kippur" (*B. RH* 16a). Altogether, these ten days are known as the ten Days of Awe, and they serve as an intensive period of self-examination and repentance, climaxing on the day of Yom Kippur. There is also an element of negotiating with God, as Abraham did concerning the fate of Sodom. The hope, of course, is to obtain God's forgiveness in order to change a negative fate. According to the Talmud (*B. RH* 17b), "Great is the power of repentance; it can rescind a person's final sentence."

There is a biblical precedent for these heavenly books, found in Jeremiah 17:1: *The guilt of Judah is inscribed with a stylus of iron, engraved with an adamant point.* Another reference is found in Malachi 3:16, *And a scroll of remembrance has been written at His behest.* In *Esther Rabbah* 2:23, this is referred to as the Book of God.

It is important to note that these heavenly books are not to be confused with the Torah. The general view is that they are for God's eyes alone. These other books were never handed down from heaven, as was the Torah. The one possible exception is *The Book of Raziel*, said to have been given to Adam by the angel Raziel. However, *The Book of Raziel* can be seen as a substitute for the Torah, until it was given at Mount Sinai. See "The Book of Raziel," p. 253.

Another heavenly book is described by Ezekiel, who has a vision *of the semblance of the Presence of the Lord* (Ezek. 1:28), and hears a mysterious figure speaking, who tells him to "*open your mouth and eat what I am giving you*" (Ezek. 2:8): *As I looked, there was a hand stretched out to me, holding a written scroll. He unrolled it before me, and it was inscribed on both the front and the back* (Ezek. 2:9-10). Since scrolls are traditionally written on only one side, Ezekiel seems to be describing a new kind of book, one relevant to the inner, spiritual life, as well as to day to day existence in the world.

Zechariah has a vision of a flying scroll, presumably of heavenly origin: "*What do you see?*" he asked. And I replied, "*A flying scroll, twenty cubits long and ten cubits wide*" (Zech. 5:1).

The description of God seated on His Throne of Judgment derives from Daniel 7:9. *1 Enoch* 47:3 has a vivid description of God seated on the Throne of Glory, with the Books of Life and Death open before him, and all of God's counselors standing there.

3 Enoch describes a pair of angels, whose full names are Shofariel YHVH Memit and Shofariel YHVH Mehayeh. They are the keepers of the Books, which are closed to everyone else, even Metatron, who has access to virtually everything else in heaven. (Note how the names of these angels contain the Name of God, hinting that they are an extension of God.) More common, however, is the tradition that Metatron is the heavenly scribe, and he sits on a throne in heaven and writes down the deeds of Israel. Elisha ben Abuyah (*Aher*) is said to have experienced great shock when he saw Metatron thus seated, which led to his exclamation, "There are—God forbid—two powers in heaven!" (*B. Hag.* 15a).

In Babylonian literature, the gods were said to possess "tablets of destiny" containing the fate of all mortals. These tablets were adjusted on the New Year, when Marduk, the chief among the Babylonian gods, was said to cast lots in heaven to determine the fate of humans. Thus it would appear that the Jewish myth of the Books of Life and Death finds its source in this Babylonian tradition. See G. Widengren, *The Ascension of the Apostle and the Heavenly Book*, p. 7ff.

All in all, the portrait of God found in *3 Enoch* is very anthropomorphic, on one hand that of an old man, with white hair, described as wool, and at the same time the hint of a ruler dressed in armor, prepared to do battle. *3 Enoch* 3:1-10 also describes four angelic princes known as 'Irin and Kaddishin who stand around God like court officers. These angels argue every case that comes before God.

While sitting on His Throne of Judgment, God tends to deliver harsh judgments, as at the time of the Flood or with Sodom and Gomorrah. That is why everyone in heaven is trembling as well. God's judgments of angels who show the slightest hesitation to obey his command is swift—they are cast into a flaming river and cease to exist. Likewise, seven planets that did not manifest themselves when commanded to do so are punished in the fires of Gehenna.

It was said as well about the Ari that from the first of Rosh ha-Shanah he knew the destiny of his followers, though he usually kept it secret. See "A Vision at the Wailing Wall," p. 63.

Rabbi Shimon ben Lakish raises the question of whether there is actually such a heavenly book, saying, "Does God really have a book, and in the book he writes? That is to say that everything is known and revealed to Him, as it is said, *For His eyes are upon a man's way; He observes his every step* (Job 34:21)."

This image of a time of judgment has proved to be haunting for all Jewish generations. Even secular Jews find their way into the synagogue on Rosh ha-Shanah and Yom Kippur, when God's intense scrutiny can be felt by all.

Sources:
B. *Rosh ha-Shanah* 16a-b, 32b; *Tosefta Rosh ha-Shanah* 1:13; B. *Avot* 3:3, 3:20; *1 Enoch* 47:3; *3 Enoch* 28:1-10; *Pesikta Rabbati* 8; *Eliyahu Rabbah* 1:5; *Avodat Yisrael, Nitzavim* 82a.

365. THE ORIGIN OF ROSH HA-SHANAH

Adam repented of his sin by standing in the River Gihon for one hundred and thirty years, until his skin began to shrivel. When God saw that Adam had truly repented, He absolved him, giving him the Torah as a substitute for the Garden of Eden that he had lost.

That eventful day was in the first month of Tishrei. Therefore God spoke to Adam: "You shall be the prototype of my children. As you have been judged by Me on this day and absolved, so your children, Israel, shall be judged by me on this New Year's day, and they shall be absolved."

The usual explanation is that Rosh ha-Shanah is the birthday of the world. Here God's absolution of Adam is linked to the origin of Rosh ha-Shanah. Not only does this myth provide such an origin, making Rosh ha-Shanah commemorate the day that God forgave Adam for the sin of eating the forbidden fruit, but it also states that God gave the Torah to Adam as a replacement for having lost the Garden of Eden.

Sources:
Avot de-Rabbi Natan 1, 5, 6, 8.

366. THE STRING OF GOD

When a person is created, he is tied to God with a string. If he sins, the string breaks. But if he repents during the Days of Awe, the angel Gabriel comes down and makes a knot in the string and ties it and the person is once again tied to God. Because every Jew sins once in a while, his string becomes full of knots. But a string with many knots is shorter than one without knots. Therefore repentance brings a person closer to God.

> This is a folk allegory in which a person's link to heaven is presented as a string, which sin causes to snap. Here the act of making knots, of repairing, is an act of repentance. Ironically, the more knots, the shorter the string, and the shorter the string, the closer to God.
>
> *Sources:*
> IFA 13043.

367. THE MONTH OF TISHREI

The world's birthday is celebrated on Rosh ha-Shanah, the New Year, in the month of Tishrei, for that is when God created the world and began to reign over it. So too were the patriarchs born in Tishrei, and in Tishrei they died. In Tishrei Sarah, Rachel, and Hannah were conceived. In Tishrei the Israelites were finally set free from Egyptian bondage, and in Tishrei they will be redeemed in the time to come.

> This aggadic text argues that the world's birthday is celebrated in the month of Tishrei, and links that birthday with the creation of the world. Therefore Rosh ha-Shanah is not only the New Year, but also the birthday of the world. Other important events that are said to have taken place in the month of Tishrei are also listed to demonstrate the seminal importance of this month.
>
> *Sources:*
> B. *Rosh ha-Shanah* 10b-11a, 16a; *Sefer Netivot ha-Shalom.*
>
> *Studies:*
> *Israel in Time and Space: Essays on Basic Themes in Jewish Spiritual Thought* by
>   Alexandre Safran.

368. RE-CREATING THE WORLD

Every year, on Rosh ha-Shanah, everything returns to its very beginning. Creation is renewed. All that was created in the beginning comes into being again. Thus each Rosh ha-Shanah the world is re-created.

> This myth describes the world being re-created every Rosh ha-Shanah. Here Rosh ha-Shanah is viewed as a ceremony of reaffirmation. Implicit in this interpretation is the suggestion that God, who renews the world, might decide not to renew it.
>
> In *Likutei Moharan*, Rabbi Nachman describes God as a God of renewal: "Faith is needed—faith that there is a Creator and a Renewer who can create things anew according to His knowledge and judgment."
>
> *Sources:*
> *Sefer Netivot ha-Shalom,* quoting a teaching attributed to the Ari; *Likutei Moharan* 1:2.

369. RENEWING EXISTENCE

It is said that the original creation of the world was only to last six days, but because of the holiness of the Sabbath, the world was renewed for the next six days, and the Sabbath has caused it to be renewed ever since.

Likewise, every Rosh ha-Shanah the existence of the world is renewed. That is because on Rosh ha-Shanah, the birthday of the world, God judges all His creations. It is decided in heaven whether everything in creation is fulfilling the secret purpose of creation, which is known to God alone. For if God determined that creation was acting against God's intent, there would be no future need of it, and all of existence would come to an end.

> This important myth emphasizes the world's fragility, and that its continuity is not guaranteed, but that it is renewed every Sabbath and every Rosh ha-Shanah. This changes the meaning of Rosh ha-Shanah, which serves as the day of Judgment not only for people, but for the world as well. Those living in the current nuclear age can identify with the acute awareness of the fragility of existence that inspired this myth.
> *Sources:*
> B. Rosh ha-Shanah 16b; Sefer Or ha-Hayim; Sefer Netivot ha Shalom.

370. THE DAY OF JUDGMENT

On Rosh ha-Shanah, God sits on the seat of judgment, and the books of the living and the dead are open before him. Then all those who have come into the world pass before God like a flock. This not only includes all of humanity, but every living creature is judged on this day—the Children of the Covenant as well as those not part of the Covenant; those who have free choice as well as those who do not have free choice. No one is left out of this judgment; even the angels are judged on that day, for it is the Day of Judgment.

God made this Day of Judgment to ensure that all abide by the Law. So too did God create the prosecuting angel who comes before Him and demands that all people in the world be judged. So it is that on Rosh ha-Shanah the judgment is written and on Yom Kippur it is signed and sealed.

> Rosh ha-Shanah is both the Day of Judgment and the New Year. As the Day of Judgment, it is a solemn occasion on which God makes a judgment about whether we will live or die in the coming year and writes it down. However, it is not signed and sealed until Yom Kippur, the Day of Atonement. Yet Rosh ha-Shanah is also the New Year, and as such it is a day of celebration. Both of these contradictory qualities—the solemn and the celebratory—characterize Rosh ha-Shanah, which is also a day of remembrance, a day of sounding the shofar, and a holy convocation.
> *Sources:*
> B. Rosh ha-Shanah 16a; Sefer Netivot ha-Shalom.

371. THE HIGH PRIEST ENTERS THE HOLY OF HOLIES

On Yom Kippur the High Priest is surrounded by his brethren, the priests, as well as the Levites and the rest of the people. Before he enters the Holy of Holies, they all pronounce benedictions before him and pray for his welfare. Then a golden cord is attached to his foot, so that if he should die in the Holy of Holies they can drag him out without entering it themselves.

He takes three steps, then another three, then another three, and they all remain where they are and do not follow him. He enters the Holy of Holies and hears the sound of the wings of the cherubim, who sing and beat their wings. Then he burns incense, and the sound of their wings subsides, and there is perfect silence. At that moment a ray of light goes forth, along with the scent of pure balsam, and it pervades the Holy of Holies. Then everything is still, and there is no room for the Accuser.

Then the priest opens his mouth in prayer, and prays with devotion and joy. And when he is finished, the cherubim lift up their wings and begin to sing again. Then the High Priest knows that his prayer has been accepted, and that there is joy above and below.

> The Holy of Holies of the Temple in Jerusalem was only permitted to be entered one day a year, on Yom Kippur, and then only by the High Priest. This passage from the *Zohar* describes the great care that was taken to enter there, and the fear and trembling that accompanied this mission, where any error might be fatal. Further, great importance lay in how well this mission went, for if the prayer of the High Priest is accepted, it is a sign that God has decided to show mercy to the people of Israel.
>
> Note the fascinating detail of the golden cord that is tied to the foot of the High Priest, in case it should become necessary to pull him out. This, in itself, shows how much was at stake in entering the Holy of Holies.
>
> *Sources:*
> *Zohar* 3:67a.

372. THE DAYS OF AWE

During the ten Days of Awe between Rosh ha-Shanah and Yom Kippur, God is close to everyone, to every individual, and God hears with compassion the voices that rise in prayer and supplication.

Rosh ha-Shanah is the first of the ten Days of Awe, and the shofar is blown to announce that the time for repentance has begun. This is the time to return from all the evil places where one has gone astray. Let all who desire to return, turn back to the true place of the world, where all is restored to perfection; those who do not will receive the retribution they deserve.

Yom Kippur, the last of the Days of Awe, is called the Sabbath of Sabbaths, as it is said, *It shall be a Sabbath of complete rest for you* (Lev. 23:32). For while the ten Days of Awe are a process of turning toward heaven, on Yom Kippur God comes down from heaven, close to Israel.

> The Days of Awe are the ten days in the month of Tishrei from Rosh ha-Shanah to Yom Kippur. This is a period of intense repentance, as God is said to decide a person's fate for the coming year on Rosh ha-Shanah and to seal that fate on Yom Kippur.
>
> *Sources:*
> *B. Rosh ha-Shanah* 18a; *Likutei Etzot Hadash* 3; *Shem mi-Shemuel*; *Ta'amei ha-Minhagim*.
>
> *Studies:*
> *A Guide to Jewish Religious Practice* by Isaac Klein, pp. 175-224.
> *Days of Awe*, edited by S.Y. Agnon.

373. LIGHT IS SOWN FOR THE RIGHTEOUS

Before Kol Nidrei a great light comes down from on high, filling all the worlds and the angels and souls to overflowing, as it is said, *Light is sown for the righteous* (Ps. 97:11). This light collects because of the tears shed before God's Name.

Here the phrase from Psalms, *Light is sown for the righteous* (Ps. 97:11), is taken literally, and a great light is described as descending from heaven on Kol Nidrei, the opening prayer that ushers in Yom Kippur. This light, it is understood, is the divine presence filling the world. Indeed, Yom Kippur is often described as a time when God's scrutiny is greater than ever, but here it is presented in positive terms, as a gift from God for tears of repentance shed over a year of sins.

Sources:
Rabbi Pinchas of Koretz in *Yamim Nora'im* by S. Y. Agnon.

374. GATHERING SOULS

Rabbi Hayim ben Attar, known as the Or ha-Hayim, would often leave his house after Shabbat was over and spend the whole week in the mountains of Jerusalem. He would take seven challahs with him and a pitcher of milk, and he would return home only on the eve of Shabbat. Then he would start chanting the Song of Songs with great fervor.

While he was reciting the Song of Songs, there was a sound of flying wings all around. Everyone who was present there heard it. And when he was asked about it, the Or ha-Hayim said, "Those are the souls I repaired during the week, while I was in the mountains."

It was said that even when his wife threw out the crumbs of the challahs, the sound of wings could be heard, for those souls came to share the crumbs of the *Tzaddik*.

Then, at the time of the Days of Awe, the Or ha-Hayim would leave Jerusalem. He would spend the eve of Rosh ha-Shanah alone in a hut on the shore of Lake Kinneret in the Galilee, and from time to time he could be seen entering the waters.

When someone once asked him why he did this, he replied, "I am assisting the souls that are here to immerse themselves in the Kinneret, to sanctify themselves before the onset of Rosh ha-Shanah." Those close to the rabbi understood that the Or ha-Hayim was engaged in restoring lost souls at the time of the Days of Awe.

> As the myth of the Ari teaches, the most important actions that Jews can take are those of *tikkun olam*, repairing the world. For rabbis such as the Or ha-Hayim (Rabbi Hayim ben Attar, known by the title of his biblical commentary, which means "the light of life") and Rabbi Nachman of Bratslav, one of the most important duties of repair concerned raising up the souls of the dead who have somehow become trapped in this world. This theme is also found in "The Field of Souls," p. 168. In "Gathering Souls," the Or ha-Hayim does this holy work during the week by going off into the mountains alone, and he returns only for the Sabbath, when he is followed by flocks of the souls he has set free. The Or ha-Hayim was the most famous Jewish sage of his time living in the Holy Land. The Hasidim believed that the Ba'al Shem Tov had been barred by heaven from going to the Holy Land because the combination of his merits and those of the Or ha-Hayim, along with those of the Holy Land, would force the coming of the Messiah. This suggests that the Or ha-Hayim was regarded by the Hasidim as the equal of the Ba'al Shem Tov.
>
> *Sources:*
> IFA 477.

375. A SCAPEGOAT FOR AZAZEL

And from the Israelite community Aaron shall take two he-goats for a sin offering and a ram for a burnt offering. Aaron is to offer his own bull of sin offering, to make expiation for himself and for his household. Aaron shall take the two he-goats and let them stand before the Lord at the entrance of the Tent of Meeting; and he shall place lots upon the two goats, one marked for the Lord and the other marked for Azazel. Aaron shall bring forward the goat designated by lot for the Lord, which he is to offer as a sin offering; while the goat designated by lot for Azazel shall be left standing alive before the Lord, to make expiation with it and to send it off to the wilderness for Azazel.

The custom of sending a scapegoat out into the desert as an offering to Azazel is clearly a remnant of a pagan ritual.

In *Pirkei de-Rabbi Eliezer* 51, God identifies the scapegoat as an atonement for Himself: "This he-goat shall be an atonement for Me, because I have diminished the size of the moon." See "The Quarrel of the Sun and the Moon," p. 112, which concludes with God diminishing the moon. We should not overlook the strangeness of God feeling the need to atone. This is reminiscent of Jung's portrayal of God in *Answer to Job*. This is one more example of the kind of personification of God so commonly found in rabbinic sources, where God also studies Torah, suffers, mourns, puts on *tallit* and *tefillin* and prays.

Who was Azazel, to whom the scapegoat was sent? This appears to be a remnant of a pagan myth in which Azazel was some kind of desert god. Thus the scapegoat represents a sacrifice to the forces of evil. In modern Israel, the phrase "*Lekh le Azazel*" means "Go to hell!"

A description of the sacrifice of the scapegoat is found in *B. Yoma* 67a: "On Yom Kippur (the Day of Atonement) a goat was thrown off a high cliff in the desert, to atone for the sins of the Jews. A red ribbon was hung up in the Temple on that day. When the goat was thrown off the cliff, the ribbon turned white." This description links the Temple and the sacrifice of the scapegoat, viewing it as a kind of remote Temple offering. The transformation of the ribbon from red to white confirms this.

Another scapegoat sacrifice is described in the Talmud (*B. Hullin* 60a). A goat was offered in the Temple on every *Rosh Hodesh*, the first of the month, as a sin offering brought to atone for God's shrinking the moon, a decision that God later came to regret. (See Numbers 28:15). Therefore, on every *Rosh Hodesh*, when the moon is small, a sin offering was brought to atone for that decision.

Sources:
Leviticus 16:5-10.

Studies:
"Azazel" in *Dictionary of Deities and Demons in the Bible*, pp. 128-131.
"Azazel in Early Jewish Tradition" by Robert Helm.

376. SOUNDING THE SHOFAR

Why is the shofar sounded on Rosh ha-Shanah? Because God said: "Sound a ram's horn before Me so that I remember on your behalf the binding of Isaac, the son of Abraham, and account it to you as if you had bound yourselves on the altar before Me."

What is the purpose of the long and short blasts of the shofar? Some say the purpose is to confuse Satan, the Accuser. What would happen if the shofar were not sounded at the beginning of the year? Evil would befall by the end of it, because the Accuser has not been confused.

Others say that God made up a secret language, that of the ram's horn, which is only understood by Him, so that the Accuser should not know the pleas of His children. And all those who know the mystery of that secret language walk in the light of the countenance of God. For that is the very light cast on the first day, when *God said, "Let there be light"* (Gen. 1:3).

The sounding of the shofar causes God to rise up from the Throne of Justice and move over to sit in the Throne of Mercy.

God Himself will sound the shofar at the End of Days, when He leads the exiles of Israel into the Promised Land, and when the Messiah reveals himself, as it is said, *My Lord God shall sound the ram's horn* (Zech. 9:14). That is why, when we hear the sound of the shofar, we beseech God to rebuild the Temple.

This myth clearly demonstrates the linkage between myth and ritual. Here the ritual of sounding the shofar on Rosh ha-Shanah invokes the myth of the *Akedah*, the binding of Isaac. The continuity is the shofar, the ram's horn, taken from the ram sacrificed in place of Isaac. For the midrash recounts how Moses blew the first shofar at Mount Sinai, while it is said that Elijah will blow the second of the ram's two horns at the time of the coming of the Messiah. And the act of performing the ritual of sounding the shofar serves to remind God of Abraham's willingness to sacrifice his son, and thus for God to account it to those performing the ritual as if they themselves had been bound before God.

The belief, found in *Pesikta de-Rav Kahana*, that the sounding of the shofar causes God to move from His Throne of Justice to the Throne of Mercy is an example of theurgy.

The *Zohar* identifies Yom Kippur as the day Isaac was bound on the altar. That is why it is fitting to read the portion about the binding of Isaac during the Afternoon Prayer, in order to recall the merits of Isaac. *Genesis Rabbah* 56 quotes Abraham as saying to God: "May it be Your will that when the children of Israel commit transgressions, that the binding of Isaac may then be remembered for their benefit, and may You be filled with compassion for them."

Here, once again, we find the theme of confusing or silencing Satan, the Accuser, so that he cannot testify against Israel. God, who sides with His children, Israel, against the Accuser during the Days of Awe, has created a secret language, that of the shofar. The long and short blasts communicate Israel's desire for God's compassion, but confuse the Accuser, who does not understand the secret language. See "Sounding the Shofar," p. 296 and the accompanying note. See also "The Master Key" in *Gabriel's Palace*, pp. 198-199.

The notion that God made up a secret language, that of the ram's horn, is quite fascinating. The ram's horn is blown on Rosh ha-Shanah (when all Jews are required to be present to hear it sounded), and at other times in strict patterns of short and long blasts. Identifying these as a secret language is an acknowledgment that the meaning of these blasts is unknown, except to God.

For more of the myths surrounding the ram's horn, see "The Ram Sacrificed at Mount Moriah," p. 150.

Sources:
B. *Rosh ha-Shanah* 16a-b; *Pesikta de-Rav Kahana* 23; *Zohar* 3:231a-b; *Tiferet Uziel*.

Studies:
A Guide to Jewish Religious Practice by Isaac Klein, pp. 190-197.

377. THE CLOSING OF THE GATES

On Yom Kippur, at the end of the afternoon prayers, when the sun is over the tree tops, it is time for the Closing Prayer. This prayer is known as the "Closing of the Gates." What gates are these? The gates of the heavenly Temple. For when the earthly Temple was destroyed, God's home was removed from this world. That is why all of Israel direct their hearts to heaven on Yom Kippur, praying for their prayers to ascend on high and be accepted with compassion before the heavenly gates are closed.

At the end of the service, the reader says, "The Lord, He is God" seven times, and the congregation repeats the phrase after him. The seven times correspond to the departure of the *Shekhinah* who rested in their midst from evening to evening. Now they accompany the *Shekhinah* through the seven firmaments that praise the Creator, who dwells above them, as it is said, *God ascends midst acclamation; the Lord, to the blasts of the horn* (Ps. 47:6).

This teaching, attributed to Rav, demonstrates the far-reaching consequences of the destruction of the Temple. Originally, the Closing Prayer on Yom Kippur corresponded to the closing of the gates of the Temple. This myth from the Jerusalem Talmud suggests that when the Temple existed, the people directed their hearts to the Temple, believing it to be the home of God in this world. But now that the Temple is in ruins, it is necessary to redirect one's heart to God in heaven, for the closing of the gates now refers to the gates of the heavenly Temple, which still exists, where prayers are offered daily to God by the angels. For more on the traditions of the heavenly Temple, see "The Celestial Temple," p. 416.

Sources:
Y. Berakhot 4.1; *Tosafot, Berakhot* 34a; *Yamim Nora'im* by S. Y. Agnon; *Shulhan Arukh shel ha-Rav Shneur Zalman; Hilkhot Yom ha-Kippurim* 623; *Bayyit Hadash* by Joel ben Samuel Sirkes (Cracow: 1631-1640).

Studies:
Days of Awe, edited by S. Y. Agnon.

378. THE FINAL BLAST

After the Kaddish is recited at the close of Yom Kippur, one blast is blown on the shofar. Some say this is in remembrance of Moses, who ordered the shofar to be blown when he descended from Mount Sinai after he received the second set of the tablets on the tenth of Tishrei. Therefore later generations established the custom of blowing the shofar at the close of Yom Kippur, to remember how Israel received the Torah with a whole heart and willing soul.

Here the shofar is blown at the close of Yom Kippur to recall the blowing of the shofar at Mount Sinai, when Moses descended with the Torah.

Sources:
Shibbolei ha-Leket; Mateh Moshe.

379. THE WATER LIBATION

When the Temple in Jerusalem was still standing, a water libation took place during Sukkot, the Feast of Tabernacles. The water dripped down into a cavern that was under the altar. This cavern existed from the six days of Creation, and it went down into the very depths. When the angel in charge of water heard the water dripping down, he commanded the water reservoirs in heaven to give forth water, as well as those under the earth. In this way the water libation brought about abundant rain.

This myth describes a Temple ritual intended to bring rain. Just as smoke rises from a sacrifice, and then the fire of the Lord descends to consume the burnt offering (see 2 Chron. 7:3), so here water is dripped upon the Temple altar, and, in turn, this brings about the release of water reservoirs in heaven and under the earth, resulting in rain. Thus the rain descends exactly as does the divine fire that consumes the offering. The myth also brings in the angel in charge of water, who releases the waters above and below.

For another example of a Temple myth linked to a holiday, see "Repenting for God," p. 323.

Sources:
B. Ta'anit 25b; *B. Sukkah* 49a.

380. THE SEVEN SHEPHERDS

It is known that on the first night of Sukkot a mysterious guest sometimes appears in the booths of the righteous. This is none other than Abraham, who is the first of seven guests to appear, one on each night of the festival. On the second night Isaac appears, and on the third, Jacob. Joseph appears on the fourth night, Moses on the fifth, Aaron on the sixth, and King David on the last night of Sukkot. Blessed, indeed, are those who receive these guests, who are known as the Seven Shepherds. Every day of Sukkot one of these seven shepherds arrives at the *sukkah* as a guest.

Before these celestial guests can appear, they must be invited with the following words: "Let us invite our guests. Let us prepare the table. *You shall live in booths seven days* (Lev. 23:42). Be seated, guests from on high, be seated! Be seated, guests of faith, be seated!"

Some say there is another visitor who is present for all seven days of the festival. That is the *Shekhinah*, who dwells in the *sukkah* of each righteous man as She once dwelled in the Temple in Jerusalem. She spreads Her wings over him from above, and Abraham and the other holy guests make their dwelling with him inside it. And one should rejoice on each of the seven days, and cheerfully welcome these guests to stay.

All the other days of the year, the Seven Shepherds are not able to descend to the lower world. This happens only in a *sukkah*, when air from the upper worlds is drawn down, and the *sukkah* becomes the Holy of Holies, and the *Shekhinah* dwells in it. Only then can the Seven Shepherds descend and enter this world. Therefore, everyone who fulfills the *mitzvah* of the *sukkah* becomes a partner with God in the work of Creation. Through the making of the *sukkah* and making a place for the *Shekhinah* to rest, one fulfills God's intention to make a dwelling place below.

Blessed is the portion of those who have merited all this. For it is said that those who welcome the celestial guests into their *sukkah* will rejoice with them both in this world and the next.

The festival of Sukkot derives from a biblical injunction: *You shall live in booths seven days* (Lev. 23:42). Jews observe this holiday by building *sukkot*—booths—which have leaves and branches for a roof. During Sukkot Jews eat all their meals in these booths. There is a widely known tradition that the *Ushpizin*, literally, "guests," who consist of seven patriarchal figures, come to visit the booths (*sukkot*) of righteous Jews during the festival of Sukkot, one on each night of the festival. These guests are known as the Seven Shepherds. When Jews leave their homes and enter the *sukkah* they receive the *Shekhinah* as a guest, along with one of the Seven Shepherds. Every night of Sukkot the prayer is recited that invites the guest to enter. They are invited with the words, "Be seated, be seated you exalted guests." The patriarch Abraham is invited on the first day, and on subsequent nights Isaac, Jacob, Moses, Joseph, and David are invited with the words "May it please you, my exalted guest, that all the other exalted guests dwell here with me and with you."

There are varying lists of the Seven Shepherds. According to Micah 5:4 and *B. Sukkah* 52b, they are Adam, Seth, Methuselah, David, Abraham, Jacob, and Moses. According to the *Zohar* (3:103b-104a), they are Abraham, Isaac, and Jacob, together with Moses, Aaron, and Joseph, plus King David.

Among some modern Jews there is a new custom of also inviting the four matriarchs, Sarah, Rebecca, Rachel, and Leah, along with Miriam, Deborah, and Esther, or other female leaders of the Jewish people, to visit in the *sukkah*.

For more background information about Sukkot, see the commentary to "Dwelling in Exile," p. 300.

Sources:
Zohar 3:103b-104a; *Sefer Netivot ha-Shalom.*

381. DWELLING IN EXILE

On Rosh ha-Shanah, the Day of Judgment, God sits in judgment of all the inhabitants of the world, and on Yom Kippur, the Day of Atonement, He seals that judgment. Now it is possible that the judgment decreed for Israel will be banishment. That is why a *sukkah* is built right after Yom Kippur, for when the people of Israel build the *sukkot*, and then banish themselves from their homes to dwell in them, God considers this banishment equivalent to their dwelling in exile in Babylon, and therefore God continues to shelter Israel.

So on the Festival of Sukkot, all of Israel goes to fetch myrtles and willows and palm branches and build *sukkot* and sing praises to God because He has atoned for them on the Day of Atonement. And on the first day of the feast God says, "Let bygones be bygones. From this moment on commences a new reckoning. Today, the first day of Sukkot, is to be the first day of this new era of reckoning."

Sukkot is one of the three Jewish pilgrimage festivals, along with Passover and Shavuot. In ancient times, before the Temple in Jerusalem was destroyed, Jews in the Land of Israel tried to make pilgrimages to Jerusalem on these days to bring harvest offerings to the Temple. Of these three festivals, Sukkot most retains the character of a harvest festival. The *lulav*, a palm branch, and the *etrog*, a citron fruit, are carried during Sukkot services. During the seven days of Sukkot, some Jews eat and sleep in booths known as *sukkot* that are erected beside their homes or synagogues, or on rooftops of apartment buildings, with only leafy boughs serving for the roof. This is to remind them of the wandering of the Israelites in the wilderness during the time of the Exodus, when the people had to live in temporary dwellings.

This myth gives an additional and crucial symbolic meaning to the custom of building *sukkot* during the festival of Sukkot, and living in them for the duration of the holiday. The *sukkot* recall the 40 years of wandering of the Israelites, and the conditions of exile that they endured. Here also the *sukkot* are linked to the Babylonian exile. The new meaning that is added here states that God regards living in the *sukkot* to be the equivalent of living in exile. One effect of this myth is to give additional meaning to the ritual of building and living in *sukkot*. In this way, myth and ritual reaffirm each other.

Note the role reversal in this myth, which has God atoning for the people, instead of the people atoning for God. This myth is also intended to highlight the quality of God's mercy, in which God both atones for and forgives the people for all their sins.

Sources:
Pesikta de-Rav Kahana 27:7, Supplement 2:7.

Studies:
A Guide to Jewish Religious Practice by Isaac Klein, pp. 156-173.

382. THE FEAST OF SUKKOT IN THE WORLD TO COME

In the World to Come, when Israel is created anew, Israel will still take the *lulav* cluster and praise God with it. So great is the merit of the *lulav* cluster that in reward for its observance, God will inflict punishment on Israel's enemies, rebuild the Temple, and bring the Messiah.

God will build a *sukkah* for the righteous in the world to come. So too will the people dwell in that heavenly *sukkah*, and the Seven Shepherds visit each and every *sukkah*, each of the seven days of Sukkot.

This myth indicates that festival rituals performed in this world will still be performed in the World to Come. The Sukkot ritual is the example given of a ritual that will be performed on high.

The effect of this myth is to raise the importance of the ritual of the *lulav*, to emphasize the importance of its being observed. This myth also strongly suggests that Sukkot is to be regarded not as a minor holiday, but as a major one, so important it is still observed in the World to Come.

The *lulav* cluster that is used in the Sukkot ceremony is said to symbolize many things. It not only represents God's glory, but also the patriarchs, the matriarchs, and the Sanhedrin, the high court among Jews in Second Temple Palestine.

Sources:
Pesikta de-Rav Kahana 26:9-10.

383. THE BODY OF MOSES

Rabbi Hayim Vital once dreamed that it was the ancient custom of Israel to bring the body of Moses to the synagogue on Simhat Torah. The reason for this custom is that Simhat Torah is the day of rejoicing with the Torah that had been given through Moses. Furthermore, on this day the Torah portion that is read from Deuteronomy recounts the death of Moses.

Now the day of the festival had arrived, and they brought the body of Moses to the synagogue in Safed. It took many men to carry the body inside the synagogue, for it was at least ten cubits long. Then the body, wrapped in a white robe, was placed on a very long table that had been prepared in advance. But as soon as the body of Moses was stretched out on the long table, it became transformed into a scroll of the Torah that was opened to its full length, like a long letter, from the first words of Genesis to the end of Deuteronomy. And in the dream they began to read the words of the Torah, starting with the creation, and they continued until they reached the last words, *displayed before all Israel* (Deut. 34:12).

All this time the rabbi of Safed sat at the head of the table, and Hayim Vital sat at the foot. And in the dream it occurred to Hayim Vital that while the rabbi of Safed sat closest to the account of creation, he himself was closest to that of the death of Moses. And when the scroll of the Torah had been completely read, the scroll of the Torah became the body of Moses once again, and they clothed it and set a girdle around it. That is when Hayim Vital awoke, and for hours afterward it seemed to him as if the soul of Moses was present in that very room.

> This astonishing dream of Hayim Vital shows the close link in the Jewish mind between the Torah of Moses and Moses himself. In the dream the body of Moses is brought to the synagogue on Simhat Torah, which follows the seventh day of Sukkot and is a day of rejoicing. On Simhat Torah the year-long reading of the Torah comes to an end with the last few verses of the Book of Deuteronomy and starts again with the first verses of the Book of Genesis. This explains Hayim Vital's focus on the end of Deuteronomy and the beginning of Genesis. Note that the death of Moses is part of the Sephardic liturgy for Simhat Torah, and this may have inspired Hayim Vital's dream.
>
> Once the body of Moses, which is of gigantic proportions (as Moses was a giant among prophets—B. Berakhot 54b recounts that the body of Moses was ten cubits tall), is carried inside and put on a long table, it turns into the scroll of the Torah. Hayim Vital sits closest to the end of the Torah, where the account of the death of Moses is found. He assumes that because he is closest to this end, he is the closest to Moses. Once the Torah has been read from beginning to end, it turns back into the body of Moses.
>
> Hayim Vital had one of the richest religious imaginations in all of Jewish history, and in his dreams and visions the line between mythology and religion is completely erased, as here, where the Torah and the body of Moses are one and the same. In his writings he strongly hints that his master, the Ari, had a messianic role, and in his dreams, visions, and other writings he likewise attributes such a role to himself. In

fact, he makes this connection explicit in his comments on the dream: "This indicates there was a cleaving and connection between my soul and that of Moses."

Sources:
Sefer ha-Hezyonot 2:50; *Shivhei Rabbi Hayim Vital.* The dream took place on 20 Tevet 1609.

Studies:
Jewish Mystical Autobiographies, edited by Morris M. Faierstein.

384. THE FLYING SHOE

Every year the followers of the Ba'al Shem Tov celebrated Simhat Torah with wild dancing and singing. For on that day the reading of the Torah is begun anew, and Jews dance with the Torah in their arms.

Then one year his Hasidim noticed that the Ba'al Shem Tov did not join in the dancing, but stood off by himself. He seemed to be strangely somber on that joyful day. Suddenly a shoe flew off the foot of Rabbi Dov Baer as he whirled in the dance, and at that instant the Ba'al Shem Tov smiled.

A little later the Hasidim saw the Ba'al Shem Tov pull a handful of leaves out of his pocket, crush them, and scatter their powder in the air, filling the room with a wonderful scent, like that of Paradise. Then the Ba'al Shem Tov joined in the dancing with great abandon. The Hasidim had never seen him so happy, and they, too, felt possessed by a greater joy than ever before.

Afterward, when they had all caught their breath, one of the Hasidim asked the Ba'al Shem Tov what he had smiled about, after having been so solemn. He replied: "While you were dancing, I went into a trance, and my soul leaped from here into the Garden of Eden. I went there to bring back leaves from the Garden, so that I could scatter them among us, making this the happiest Simhat Torah of all time. I gathered fallen leaves with the greatest pleasure and put them in my pocket. As I did, I noticed that there were scattered fringes of prayer shawls in the Garden, as well as pieces of worn *tefillin,* from the straps Jews wrap around their arm when they pray. Not only that, but I saw heels and soles and shoelaces, and sometimes even whole shoes. And all of these objects were glowing like so many sparks, even the shoes—for as soon as they entered the Garden of Eden, they began to glow.

"Now I was not surprised to see the fringes and straps, for they come from sacred objects, but I wondered what the shoes were doing there.

"Just then a shoe flew into the Garden of Eden, and I recognized it at once as that of Rabbi Dov Baer." The Ba'al Shem Tov turned to face him. "Dov, I realized that your love of God was so great that your shoe had flown all the way there. That is when I understood why there were shoes in the Garden of Eden. And that is why I smiled.

"I would have come back to join you at that very moment, but just then I saw two angels in the Garden. They had come to sweep and clean the Garden and to gather those precious, glowing objects.

"I asked the angels what they were going to do with the shoes, and one of them said: 'These shoes have flown here from the feet of Jews dancing with the Torah. They are very precious to God, and soon the angel Gabriel will make a crown out of them for God to wear on His Throne of Glory.'"

The Ba'al Shem Tov stopped speaking, and all who heard this story that day were filled with awe. Nor was Rabbi Dov Baer's shoe ever seen again, for it had truly flown to the Garden of Eden.

> Simhat Torah follows the seventh day of Sukkot and is a day of rejoicing. On Simhat Torah, the year-long reading of the Torah comes to an end with the last few verses of the

Book of Deuteronomy and starts again with the first verses of the Book of Genesis. The scrolls of the Torah are taken from the Ark and carried around the synagogue in a procession that makes seven circuits around the sanctuary. After each circuit, there is singing and dancing with the scrolls. It is a celebration of great joy for having lived to complete the reading of the Torah for another year. In some Hasidic circles, there is wild dancing, as in this tale about the Ba'al Shem Tov and Rabbi Dov Baer (1710-1772).

Although the gates of the Garden were closed after Adam and Eve were expelled, there are quite a few visits to the Garden recounted in Jewish folklore, such as that of the Ba'al Shem Tov in this story. This shows how Jewish folktales draw on biblical themes and retell them, perpetuating the influence of the Bible in Jewish tradition.

The theme of leaves from the Garden of Eden is a popular one in Jewish folklore. See "The Spice of the Sabbath," p. 316 and "Leaves from the Garden of Eden" in *Gabriel's Palace*, pp. 134-135.

Sources:
Gan ha-Hasidut.

Studies:
A Guide to Jewish Religious Practice by Isaac Klein, pp. 170-173.

385. GOD REVELS IN THE READING OF THE *HAGGADAH* ·

On the night of Passover, while Jews around the world read from the *Haggadah*, God gathers His household together, and says, "Come and listen to the recital of My praises as My children rejoice in their redemption from slavery in Egypt." And all of heaven assemble and hear Israel praise God for all the miracles He had performed.

Hearing these praises, God gains additional strength and power in the world above. Thus the children of Israel give strength to their Master, and His glory is exalted on high. That is why everyone must narrate the miracles and speak in God's presence of all He has done, for these words ascend, and the celestial house takes note of them, and God's glory is exalted both above and below.

> On Passover it is a requirement to read from the *Haggadah*, which narrates the Exodus from Egyptian slavery. The *Haggadah* gives the credit for the Exodus to God, not even mentioning the name of Moses. This myth portrays God as reveling in the praises of Israel as they read from the *Haggadah*. It presents the kabbalistic concept of mutuality between God and Israel, where God does not only benefit Israel, but Israel's praise and prayers benefit God, who is said to gain strength and power from them.

Sources:
Zohar 2:40b-41a.

Studies:
A Guide to Jewish Religious Practice by Isaac Klein, pp. 103-104.

386. THE DANCING OF THE ARI

Every Lag ba-Omer the Ari led his students to the grave of Rabbi Shimon bar Yohai in Meron. And there they danced at the resting place of the holy rabbi.

Now one Lag ba-Omer, an old man danced with them. He could be seen swaying at the outer edge of the circle, as if he were being carried on waves of song. He had a beautiful white beard and was dressed all in white, with a white prayer shawl covering his head. His eyes were closed, and his whole body radiated mystical glory.

All at once, the Ari took his hand and started dancing with him. A great light shone between them, a sacred radiance, like the light of many candles, tinged with blue and gold. All the students watched spellbound as the Ari and the old man danced.

Their dancing lasted for hours. It was well after midnight when they stopped, and the old man took his leave. Then the disciples of the Ari crowded around him to learn the identity of the old man. And he told them that it was none other than Shimon bar Yohai himself who had joined in the celebration.

> On *Lag ba-Omer* campfires are lit all over Israel, but especially in the Galilee, in honor of Shimon bar Yohai. It was the custom of the Ari to go to the grave of Shimon bar Yohai in Meron to celebrate *Lag ba-Omer*. Here, while the Ari and his disciples dance and sing, they are joined by a mysterious old man, whom the Ari recognizes as Shimon bar Yohai. This tale links the greatness of the Ari and of Shimon bar Yohai, who are, in fact, the two primary sages associated with the Galilee. In this respect it is a kind of succession tale, showing that Shimon bar Yohai has selected the Ari to be his successor. This confirms the Ari's importance to be equal to that of Shimon bar Yohai, legendary author of the *Zohar* as well as the principal hero of its tales. This tale and others about the circle of the Ari collected by the Israel Folktale Archives demonstrate that the tradition still exists in the city of Safed in present day Israel. These oral versions are often far more embellished than the existing written versions.
>
> *Sources:*
> IFA 13043.
>
> *Studies:*
> *A Guide to Jewish Religious Practice* by Isaac Klein, pp. 145-146.

387. THE WEDDING OF GOD AND THE *SHEKHINAH*

When they are first engaged, God sends His betrothed nuptial presents and a meal of celestial bread. So too does He make preparations for the wedding feast. On the eve of Shavuot, before the wedding takes place, the members of the heavenly household remain with the Bride all night, and rejoice in the preparations for the wedding. They study Torah, progressing from the Five Books of Moses to the Prophets, and from the Prophets to the Writings, and then to the midrashic and mystical interpretation of the text, for these are the adornments and finery of the Bride.

Throughout the night, the Bride rejoices with Her maidens and is made ready by them. And in the morning She enters the bridal canopy, illumined with the radiance of sapphire, which shines from one end of the world to the other. Shining in all Her finery, she awaits each of those who helped to prepare Her. And at the moment when the sun enters the bridal canopy and illumines Her, all Her companions are identified by name. And God inquires after them, and blesses them, and crowns them with bridal crowns, and blessed is their portion.

Then the Bridegroom enters the bridal canopy, and He offers the seven nuptial blessings and unites with His Bride, joining with the Queen in perfect union, and *the heavens declare the glory of God* (Ps. 19:2).

> This Shavuot myth describes the wedding of God and the *Shekhinah*. Since Shavuot commemorates the giving of the Torah at Mount Sinai, it is the appropriate time for the wedding of God and the *Shekhinah*. The night of Shavuot is traditionally devoted to Torah study, including study of the mystical texts, and here that study is identified as the adornments of the Bride. Thus the scholars who study on the night of Shavuot are identified here as members of the heavenly household who remain with the Bride all night and assist Her in preparing for the wedding.
>
> The myth that follows, also a Shavuot myth, describes the wedding of God and Israel. Both versions are quite common, although the wedding of God and Israel, because of its appearance in the Sephardic *Mahzor* (holiday prayerbook), is the better-known myth.

Note, as well, a remnant of a sun myth—the entrance of the Bride of God into the bridal canopy is described in terms of the sun rising. Thus the *Shekhinah* is also linked to the sun, as well as to the moon. Other remnants of sun myths can be found in the transformation of Enoch into Metatron, where Metatron is described in terms identical to the sun.

Sources:
Zohar 1:8a; *Or Zaru'a* Ms. JTSA ff. 39b/54b.

Studies:
The Sabbath in Classical Kabbalah by Elliot K. Ginsburg.

388. THE WEDDING OF GOD AND ISRAEL

On Friday, the sixth of Sivan, the day appointed by the Lord for the revelation of the Torah to His beloved people, God came forth from Mount Sinai. The Groom, the Lord, the King of Hosts, is betrothed to the bride, the community of Israel, arrayed in beauty. The Bridegroom said to the pious and virtuous maiden, Israel, who had won His favor above all others: "Can there be a bridal canopy without a bride? *As I live—declares the Lord—you shall don them all like jewels, deck yourself with them like a bride*" (Isa. 49:18). Many days will you be Mine and I will be your Redeemer. Be My mate according to the law of Moses and Israel, and I will honor, support and maintain you, and be your shelter and refuge in everlasting mercy. And I will set aside the life-giving Torah for you, by which you and your children will live in health and tranquility. This Covenant shall be valid and binding forever and ever."

Thus an eternal Covenant, binding them forever, has been established between them, and the Bridegroom and the bride have given their oaths to carry it out. May the Bridegroom rejoice with the bride whom he Has taken as His lot, and may the bride rejoice with the Husband of her youth.

In the Talmud there is a brief description of the marriage of God and Israel: "The Groom, the Lord, the King of Hosts, is betrothed to the bride, the community of Israel, arrayed in beauty" (*B. Pesahim* 106a). Since all weddings are required to have a *ketubah*, a wedding contract, the present myth, "The Wedding of God and Israel" provides the wedding contract for that wedding. Its text serves as a hymn for Shavuot. This liturgical poem, found in the Sephardic prayer book for Shavuot, is based on the verses, "*I will espouse you with righteousness and justice, and with goodness and mercy, and I will espouse you with faithfulness; then you shall be devoted to the Lord*" (Hos. 2:21-22), and "*I will make a new covenant with the house of Israel*" (Jer. 31:31).

The text of this *ketubah* is read on Shavuot, usually in Ladino, from the Sephardic holiday prayer book, or *Mahzor*. It describes the Giving of the Torah at Mount Sinai as the wedding between God and Israel that is indicated by the verse "*See, a time is coming*"—declares Yahweh—"*when I will make a new covenant with the House of Israel and the House of Judah*" (Jer. 31:31). Here God and Israel are personified as a Bridegroom and bride, and the Torah is presented as the *ketubah*, or wedding contract, between them. The marriage takes place on the sixth of Sivan, the holiday of Shavuot, when, traditionally, the Torah was said to have been given.

Here the wedding that takes place on the Sabbath is not between God and the *Shekhinah*; instead, it is between God and Israel, with the *ketubah* serving as the wedding contract between them. The fact that the wedding takes place on Shavuot demonstrates the linkage of the Torah, given on Shavuot, to this bond. It is the Torah that both affirms the Covenant between God and Israel and also binds them together. Indeed, the *ketubah* that is read symbolically represents the Torah in much the same way as do the Ten Commandments. This text can be viewed both mythologically as the wedding between God and Israel, and allegorically, suggesting that the Torah can be viewed as a contract between God and Israel in the same way that a *ketubah* serves as a contract between man and wife.

Deuteronomy Rabbah 3:12 states that it was Moses who wrote the *ketubah* between God and Israel, based on the verse *And Moses wrote this Law* (Deut. 31:9). God is said to have rewarded Moses for doing this by giving him a luminous countenance. As for the scroll that Moses wrote the *ketubah* on, the same source in *Deuteronomy Rabbah* describes it as made of a parchment of white fire, which was written on with black fire. Of course, this *ketubah* is none other than the scroll of the Torah itself.

It is important to observe that God is masculine and the *Shekhinah,* feminine. An interesting parallel is found in Greek myth, where Uranus, whose name came to mean "the sky," is masculine, and Gaia, who is Mother Earth, is feminine. In both cases, the feminine goddess figures are linked to the earth: the *Shekhinah* represents God's presence in this world, especially with the Temple in Jerusalem, and Gaia is, at the same time, the personification of the earth. The primary difference between them is that God's Bride is an invisible, supernatural being, while Gaia represents not only a goddess, but also the life-sustaining earth. Both pairs of gods and goddesses associate the masculine with the heavens, and the feminine with the earth. See *The Greek Myths* by Robert Graves, 3.1.

God is portrayed as being wed to three different brides in various Jewish myths: to the *Shekhinah* (see "The Wedding of God and the *Shekhinah,* p. 304), to Israel (as recounted here), and, remarkably enough, to Lilith (see "Lilith Becomes God's Bride," p. 59). In most myths God is presented as being married to the *Shekhinah.*

Sources:
B. *Pesahim* 106a; *Deuteronomy Rabbah* 3:12; *Pesikta Rabbati* 31:10; *Ketubah le-Shavuot*
   from the Sephardi *Mahzor*, written by Israel Najara in the sixteenth century.

Studies:
A Guide to Jewish Religious Practice by Isaac Klein, pp. 147-153.

389. THE PARTING OF THE HEAVENS AT MIDNIGHT

It is said that at midnight, on the night of Shavuot, the skies part, and the glory of heaven is revealed. Then anyone who makes a wish at that instant will have that wish come true. That is why students stay up all night studying the Torah, so that they will be awake when the skies part, and be worthy of viewing God's glory at that instant.

Just as the parting of the Red Sea is the key moment of the Exodus, celebrated at Passover, so the folk tradition of the parting of the heavens at midnight is linked with Shavuot (and sometimes Sukkot). The possibility of this miracle taking place is intended to motivate students to stay up all night studying. Shavuot represents the day the Torah was given, which was the defining moment in the history of Judaism. It was a kabbalistic custom to study the entire night of Shavuot. The text that is traditionally studied is the *Zohar*, the central text of Jewish mysticism, and the whole night of study is regarded as a ceremony of purification. The culmination of this ceremonial study is the revelation that takes place at the instant the skies open, revealing the glory of the *Shekhinah* to those worthy of seeing it. This miracle of the skies opening is also found as a theme in Jewish folklore, in which wishes are often made at the instant the skies open. These wishes, of course, always come true.

Sources:
IFA 4014; IFA 13901; B. *Pesahim* 106a; *Deuteronomy Rabbah* 3:12; *Pesikta Rabbati* 31:10;
   Ketubah le-Shavuot from the Sephardi *Mahzor*, written by Israel Najara in the
   sixteenth century.

390. THE CREATION OF THE SABBATH

The Sabbath was last to be created, but first in God's mind. It was the culmination of all creation. Indeed, everything exists for the sake of the Sabbath. The Sabbath is the source of all blessings.

Before God gave the commandment of keeping the Sabbath to Israel, He said to Moses: "I have a good present in my secret chambers. The name of that present is 'Sabbath.' Go tell the people that I now wish to give that present to them."

The Sabbath takes on even greater significance in this myth. It is more than a ritual day of rest, it is the original purpose of creation, itself a source of blessings. Here the Sabbath comes close to existing as an independent divine being, a goddess disguised as the seventh day.

The Sabbath is also presented as a gift taken out of God's secret chambers. It is that precious. In both views the Sabbath is seen as the epitome of God's blessings, as well as a reminder of how the world was created, and who created it.

Each of these interpretations fuses with the already potent symbol of the Sabbath and adds to its mythic aura.

Sources:
B. *Shabbat* 10b; *Mekhilta de-Rabbi Ishmael, be-Shalah* 133.

Studies:
The Sabbath in the Classical Kabbalah by Elliot K. Ginsburg.
Sod ha-Shabbat (The Mystery of the Sabbath) from the Tola'at Ya'akov of R. Meir ibn Gabbai translated by Elliot K. Ginsburg.
A Guide to Jewish Religious Practice by Isaac Klein, pp. 53-94.

391. THE COSMIC SABBATH

There will be seven cosmic eons in all, each lasting seven thousand years. In the present era, God's commandments are a necessity. But in the preceding eon there was neither desire nor reward and punishment, and a different law prevailed.

At the end of the sixth eon, on the eve of the cosmic Sabbath, light will swallow death and drive unclean spirits from the world. Then everyone, great and small, will know God by the light that emanates from the mystery of divine thought.

When the cosmic Sabbath begins, a new Torah will go forth, and a new cosmic law will prevail. Wisdom and knowledge will increase among men. The letters of the Torah will combine in a new way and take on a new meaning, but not a single letter will be added or taken away.

Each of the eras of existence is known as a *Shemittah*, an era lasting 7,000 years. The cosmic eras of this myth find their source in the story of the creation, in which the seventh day is a day of rest, as well as in the agricultural law also known as *Shemittah* in which fields must lie fallow every seventh year (Exod. 23:10-11; Lev. 25:1-7, 18-22; Deut. 15:1-11).

The Torah of the present era, known as the Torah of Creation, is different from that of the preceding or subsequent eras. The Torah of the past and future eras is known as the Torah of Divine Emanation. The suggestion that the Torah is somehow different in different eras echoes the idea that God will give a new Torah to Israel in the messianic era, which will be different from the present Torah.

Some versions of this myth insist, as does this one, that "not a single letter will be added or taken away." On the other hand, the myth of the twenty-third letter of the Hebrew alphabet asserts that there was an additional, although invisible, twenty-third letter from the beginning. It will only be revealed in the messianic era, and that will be the genesis of the new Torah, which will be given through the Messiah as the Torah given at Mount Sinai was given to Moses. See "A New Torah," p. 522.

Sources:
Sha'arei Gan Eden 12c; *Sefer ha-Temunah* 62a.

Studies:
On the Kabbalah and Its Symbolism by Gershom Scholem, pp. 77-86.

392. THE BLESSINGS OF THE SABBATH

On this day the Torah is crowned with jewels, and adorned with seventy branches of light, which shine on each of the seventy faces of the Torah.

On this day the sound of rejoicing and delight is heard throughout the world, and pleasure and joy abound.

On this day a breath of delight spreads throughout all the world, so that all those who observe the Sabbath can enjoy perfect rest.

On this day all negative judgments are suppressed, and even the wicked in Gehenna are at ease. All powers of negativity vanish and no other power reigns in any of the worlds.

On this day the voice of a herald proclaims, "Arise, O celestial ones, arise, O holy people, arise in perfect joy to meet your Master! Blessed is your portion, Israel, in this world and the World to Come."

Therefore all blessings above and below depend on the seventh day. For the Sabbath is equal in worth to the whole of the Torah, and whoever keeps the Sabbath is like one who keeps all of the Torah.

> This kabbalistic myth emphasizes the holiness of the Sabbath in heaven as well as on earth. The *Zohar* emphasizes that although the individual acts of creation were finished, the world was not perfect until the seventh day. That is why it is stated that *God completed His work on the seventh day* (Gen. 2:2). So potent is the blessing of the Sabbath that its delight spreads throughout the world and even cancels negative decrees, such as the punishments of Gehenna. So crucial is keeping the Sabbath that doing so it is said to be the equivalent of honoring all of the laws of the Torah.
>
> *Sources:*
> Zohar 2:88a-89a, 2:47a-47b, 2:222b; *Keter Shem Tov* 401.

393. THE ADORNMENT OF THE SABBATH

On the Sabbath, when the Torah is crowned, it is adorned with all the commandments, with all the decrees and punishments, and with the seventy branches of light, which shine on every side. Branches grow from every branch, and gates are open on every side, all of them shining and resplendent with light.

> Here the Sabbath is being adorned like a bride, but not in jewels, but in the commandments, and the Sabbath day is viewed as if it were a wedding. Indeed, it is a sacred duty to make love on Friday night. This is also expressed as sleeping under the shelter of the *Shekhinah*, who is also the Sabbath Queen. See "The Sabbath Bride," p. 309.
>
> *Sources:*
> Zohar 2:88b-89a.

394. THE PRINCESS OF THE SABBATH

After completing the work of Creation during the first six days, God ascended to the heaven called Habitation of Joy, to sit on His celestial throne. As He arrived, all the angelic princes appointed over the cosmos came before Him—rejoicing, dancing, and singing.

At that moment, God ushered in the princess of the Sabbath and sat her alongside Him. He brought every prince of heaven before her. They danced and exulted before her, saying, *"The Sabbath, she is the Lord's"* (Lev. 23:3). God even lifted up Adam to the heights of the highest heavens to regale her and rejoice in the Sabbath's joy.

During the week the princess of the Sabbath wears special garments, but on the Sabbath she wears two layers of lovely garments, the raiment of the upper worlds, for each word of Sabbath prayer bedecks and adorns the bride. Thus she is crowned from above and below, as heaven celebrates and the holy people of Israel bless her with joy and with their prayers.

> As many myths have emphasized, the Sabbath is not only celebrated on earth, but also in heaven. Here the Sabbath, personified as a princess (one of the incarnations of the *Shekhinah*) is at the center of a great heavenly celebration that takes place at the end of the six days of Creation. This is nothing less than an enthronement myth, and should be considered along with the other enthronement myths found about Adam, Enoch/Metatron, Jacob, Moses, King David, and the Messiah. That the ceremony takes place during the first Sabbath indicates its significance. It can be understood to permanently establish the central role of both the *Shekhinah* and the Sabbath in ruling heaven and earth. See "The Enthronement of Adam," p. 131; "The Metamorphosis and Enthronement of Enoch," p. 156; "Jacob the Divine," p. 366; "The Enthronement of Moses, p. 388; "King David is Crowned in Heaven," p. 395; and "The Enthronement of the Messiah," p. 487.

> Sources:
> *Hekhalot Rabbati* f. 852; *Zohar* 2:135a-b; *Or Zaru'a* 236; *Seder Rabbah de-Bereshit*, Oxford Bodleian Ms. 1531, ff. 849-52.

> Studies:
> *The Sabbath in the Classical Kabbalah* by Elliot K. Ginsburg.

395. THE SABBATH BRIDE

Every seventh day her coronation takes place. Before the start of the ceremony, the dwelling place is prepared like the chamber of a Bridegroom set to receive his Bride. Meanwhile, the Bride herself remains alone, separated from the forces of evil. There she adorns herself with a crown for the Holy King, and prepares herself for their union. Then, as the Sabbath begins, the radiant Bride is escorted by angels on high and Israel below, and she is ushered into Israel's abode, to be in their midst. There she is crowned by the prayers of the holy people, and they, in turn, are adorned with new souls, so that they all are united above and below.

> This describes a mythical ceremony that is part coronation and part wedding between God and His Bride, the *Shekhinah*. The union, clearly intended to be understood as a sexual union, between God and His Bride, comes close to portraying them as independent mythic beings. This one passage from the *Zohar* can be subjected to many interpretations. It might be viewed as a union between two of the ten sefirot, those representing the marriage of the King and His Bride. At the same time, it is also an enthronement myth as well as a wedding. This heavenly ceremony is paralleled on earth by the ritual of *Kabbalat Shabbat*, going out to greet the Sabbath Queen at the beginning of the Sabbath. The Ari and his followers wore white, and left the city of Safed to go out into the fields to welcome the Sabbath Queen. Thus heaven turns to earth and earth to heaven, and they meet in a rare union of peace, which is the Sabbath. See the next entry, "Greeting the Sabbath Queen."

Sources:
Zohar 2:131b, 2:135a-b, 3:300b-301a.

Studies:
"The Aspect of the 'Feminine' in the Lurianic Kabbalah" by Yoram Jacobson.
"Coronation of the Sabbath Bride: Kabbalistic Myth and the Ritual of
    Androgynisation" by Elliot R. Wolfson.

396. GREETING THE SABBATH QUEEN

It was the custom of some of the rabbis to greet the Sabbath Queen. Just before the sun set on the Sabbath, Rabbi Haninah would wrap himself in his robe, stand up, and say, "Come, let us go to greet the Sabbath Queen." So too did Rabbi Yannai put on his festive garments on the eve of the Sabbath and say, "Come, O Bride! Come, O Bride!"

And every Sabbath eve, at sunset, the Ari led his students to greet the Sabbath Queen as she descended the rolling hills outside of Safed. When they arrived at the hills, they began to sing the songs greeting the Sabbath Queen. And the melodies of those songs were carried upward on the wings of prayer, and formed a beautiful garland of prayers that the Sabbath Queen carried with her as she descended from on high. Many were those who saw them leaving Safed, every one dressed in white, and later saw them returning, singing Sabbath songs.

> The Ari based the Sabbath ritual of *Kabbalat Shabbat* on the two talmudic accounts of rabbis welcoming the Sabbath Queen. This custom is echoed today on the Sabbath evening when, before reciting the last stanza of *Lekhah Dodi*, the congregation turns around to face the door of the synagogue and recites "*Bo'i b'shalom*" ("Come in peace") while standing, thus welcoming the Sabbath Queen. The purpose of this ritual is to honor the Sabbath, which is ushered in at this point. *Lekhah Dodi* itself is a poem composed by Shlomo Alkabetz of the Ari's circle, which celebrates the arrival of the Sabbath Queen on the Sabbath.
>
> *Sources:*
> B. *Shabbat* 119a; B. *Bava Kama* 32b; *Divrei Yosef* 226; *Otzrot Hayim* 129.

397. THE SECOND SOUL

All the souls of Israel are crowned on the eve of the Sabbath. For every Sabbath God gives the children of Israel an additional soul, a celestial soul, a holy spirit more sublime than any other, brimming over with blessing, with song and jubilation drawn from on high. When one of these spirits is present, a person's power of understanding is greatly increased. And this additional soul remains throughout the Sabbath. Indeed, the name of this soul is "Sabbath," because Sabbath rest and peace are a foretaste of the World to Come.

Some say these extra souls bloom forth from the Tree of Life, while others say that they are the offspring of the *Shekhinah*, who descends and spreads Her wings over Israel, forming a canopy of peace as She watches over them, sheltering them as a mother bird does her fledglings. As the *Shekhinah* hovers over them, wings outstretched, She brings forth new souls for each and every person. As this spirit descends, it bathes in the spices of the Garden of Eden and then settles upon the holy people of Israel. With the arrival of this Sabbath-soul all sadness and anger disappear, and joy reigns above and below.

All during the Sabbath day the extra spirit dwells within, enchanting a person's soul. But on Saturday night, when three stars have appeared, the Sabbath soul flies forth and returns to its place on high.

The second soul that arrives on the Sabbath is the *neshamah yeterah*. Linkage between this second soul and the presence of the *Shekhinah* on the Sabbath is found in *Sefer ha-Bahir*, as well as in the *Zohar*, where the *Shekhinah* is identified as the dwelling place of the soul. The extra soul can be seen as the inner recognition of the presence, or immanence, of God, the inner experience of the *Shekhinah*. This myth confirms the great sense of holiness observant Jews experience in performing their rituals, a sense of the sacred that is virtually palpable.

There is a special ceremony for the end of the Sabbath known as *Havdalah*, which includes the smelling of fragrant spices (to revive a person who has just lost his second soul), that symbolizes the great reluctance to see the Sabbath end. In fact, some Hasidim delayed performing *Havdalah* as long as possible—until midnight or even later, although it is supposed to be said at the end of the Sabbath when three stars can be seen in the sky. One Hasidic sect even delayed saying *Havdalah* until Wednesday, and then started making immediate plans to prepare for the next Sabbath.

In *B'nei Yisakhar*, Rabbi Tzvi Elimelekh's mystical commentary on the Sabbath, he develops a theory about the place of the Sabbath in the worlds above and below, the worlds of God and humanity, and of the interaction between the two. Here he describes the arrival of the second soul as kindling the inner light that comes with the Sabbath.

Zohar 1:60a states that every *Tzaddik* (righteous man) has two souls, one in this world and one in the world to come. This is a variant of the concept of the Sabbath soul, but unlike the *neshamah yeterah* that departs at the end of the Sabbath, this second, heavenly soul continues to exist at all times. This notion of a second, heavenly soul was drawn upon by the Lubavitch movement to explain how their human Rebbe could also be the divine Messiah. See "The Descent of the Messiah's Soul," p. 486. *Zohar* 1:78b identifies these two souls as levels of the soul, and in fact there are five recognized levels of the soul, three tied to the earthly body and two higher souls. The three earthly souls are known as *nefesh* (the animal soul), *ruah* (breath or spirit), and *neshamah* (soul). The higher levels are *hayah* (which gazes upon God) and *yehidah* (which is bound to God). A further discussion of the three earthly souls can be found in *Midrash ha-Ne'elam, Zohar Hadash* 17c-d. *Zohar* 1:78b also interprets the fact that God often calls righteous men twice—as "Abraham, Abraham" (Gen. 22:11), "Jacob, Jacob" (Gen. 46:2), or "Moses, Moses" (Exod. 3:4)—as an indication of His addressing these two primary souls, the higher and the lower.

See "Why Women Light Two Candles on the Sabbath," p. 318, which links the lighting of the Sabbath candles with the second soul.

Sources:
B. *Betzah* 15b-16a; B. *Ta'anit* 27b; *Sefer ha-Bahir* 57, 158; *Or Zaru'a* Ms. Paris Hebr. 596, fol. 35a; *Perush ha-Aggadot*, pp. 35-45; *Zohar* 1:48a, 1:60a, 1:78b, 2:88a-b, 2:135a-b, 2:204a-b, 3:173a; *Tikkunei ha-Zohar; B'nei Yisakhar* 6:4; *Shivhei ha-Ran* 9; *Tkhine imrei Shifreh*, attributed to Shifrah Segal of Brody; *Sod ha-Shabbat* 22-23.

Studies:
The Jewish Sabbath: A Renewed Encounter by Pinchas H. Peli, pp. 87-92, 133-155.

398. THE SOULS OF THE DEAD ON THE SABBATH

Every Sabbath the dead rise from their graves and come before God. There is a brook that flows from the Garden of Eden, and by the side of this brook, a field. On every Sabbath eve, between the afternoon and evening prayers, the souls of the dead go forth from their secret abode and drink from this brook.

When the evening prayers begin, the dead return to their graves, and God revives them, and causes them all to stand on their feet, alive. Then great multitudes come before God and sing praises to Him, and go into synagogues, where they prostrate themselves before God.

This myth of the revival of the dead concerns the souls of the righteous who make their home in the Garden of Eden. Here the dead are described as making their homes in their graves, while in other sources the souls of the dead leave their graves for good within a year after they have died. The strange wandering of the souls of the dead on the Sabbath (and, according to some sources, the new moon) derives from the interpretation of the biblical verse: *The people of the land shall worship before the Lord on Sabbaths and new moons* (Ezek. 46:3). Even the souls being punished in Gehenna are released for the duration of the Sabbath. See "Sabbath in Gehenna," p. 238. In the Ezekiel verse "the people of the land" (*am ha-aretz)* is interpreted to refer to "those hidden in the earth," i.e., the dead, instead of the more obvious meaning of "the common people." Note that the revival of the dead in this myth is not identical with the resurrection of the dead that is to take place in the messianic era. This revival is temporary, and ends with the end of the Sabbath, while that of the messianic era is permanent. The fate of the righteous on the Sabbath is different, however. *B. Berakhot* 18a states that "In their death, the righteous are called living." And in *B. Ketubot* 103a it is said that after his death Rabbi Judah ha-Nasi used to visit his earthly home at twilight on every Sabbath, wearing his best clothes, and recited Kiddush for his family like a living person.

Sources:
B. Berakhot 18a; B. Ketubot 103a; Sefer Hasidim 1129; Sefer ha-Zikhronot 19:1-3, 19:4.

399. THE SOUL IN THE GARDEN OF EDEN

When Jews keep the Sabbath, their souls enter the Garden of Eden. Together with the pure souls and the souls of the righteous that inhabit that realm, the soul of the Jew delights in the light of the Garden and feels the bliss emanating from the radiance of supernal love. In this way the soul enjoys the bliss of Paradise that the Sabbath brings.

This supernal bliss is felt both within and without the body, and is drawn into this world. Indeed, the flavor of the Sabbath is even absorbed into the food that is tasted on that day. That is why it is said: "We have a certain spice; Sabbath is its name. Whoever keeps the Sabbath is affected by it and whoever does not keep the Sabbath is not affected by it."

On the Sabbath, Jewish souls are said to ascend to *Gan Eden,* the Garden of Eden, which is already inhabited by the "pure souls"—that is, souls in the garden that never participated in the tasting of the forbidden fruit—as well as the souls of the righteous who make their home there. While the body of the Jew celebrating the Sabbath is on earth, his or her soul is in heaven, for *Gan Eden* refers to the celestial Paradise. This explains why the Sabbath meal has such an exceptional flavor and why the Sabbath itself is a delight.

Sources:
B. Shabbat 119; Hovat ha-Talmidim.

400. GOD'S DAUGHTER

The Sabbath is God's daughter, begotten by God alone, without begetting—brought to birth, but not carried in the womb.

The Sabbath said before God: "Master of the Universe! You have given a mate to everyone except me. Each of the days of the week has a mate, but I have none." God replied: "The people of Israel are your mate."

And when Israel stood before Mount Sinai, Moses saw that the Sabbath was lovely, and that she was a virgin. With his keener vision, he saw the marvelous beauty of the Sabbath stamped upon heaven and earth, and enshrined in nature itself.

Here Philo offers an allegory in which the Sabbath is described as God's daughter. The purpose of the allegory is to indicate the importance of the Sabbath to God and to the people of Israel, who observe the Sabbath. Later rabbinic and kabbalistic development linked the Sabbath with the figure of the Sabbath Queen, one of the personifications of the *Shekhinah*. Such developments also identified the *Shekhinah* as God's Bride. Thus Philo's identification of the Sabbath as God's daughter may be seen to prefigure later mythic developments found in *Sefer ha-Bahir*, where the *Shekhinah* is portrayed as "Daughter, Sister, Wife, and Mother," as the title of Peter Schäfer's article puts it, and in the *Zohar* and other kabbalistic texts. In Philo's version of the myth, God gives the Sabbath to Israel the way a father gives away his daughter at her wedding.

See "The Creation of the *Shekhinah*," p. 47.

Sources:
Philo, *De Specialibus Legibus* 2:56-58; Philo, *De Vita Mosis* 2:210; *Genesis Rabbah* 11:8; *Akedat Yitzhak* 4; *Pesikta Rabbati* 23:6.

Studies:
"Daughter, Sister, Bride, and Mother: Images of the Femininity of God in the Early Kabbala" by Peter Schäfer.
The Sabbath in the Classical Kabbalah by Elliot K. Ginsburg.

401. GOD GUIDES MOSES IN PRAYER

Early in the morning Moses went to Mount Sinai as the Lord had commanded him, and took in his hand two tablets of stone. *Yahweh came down in a cloud; He stood with him there, and proclaimed the name Yahweh* (Exod. 34:5). And God drew His robe around Him like the reader of a congregation and showed Moses the order of prayer, and taught him the Thirteen Attributes of God. *And Moses made haste, and bowed his head toward the earth, and worshipped* (Exod. 34:8).

The biblical account of God descending to Moses is amplified and transformed in the Talmud, where God is described drawing His robe around Him as was the custom of the reader in a congregation. This image grows out of the fact that the Thirteen Attributes of God are incorporated into the prayer service, and the meeting of God and Moses on the top of Mount Sinai is here transformed into the terms and perspective of the synagogue or house of study, where God shows Moses the order of the prayers, and explains His own Thirteen Attributes to him. The biblical passage itself is a daring one, with God coming down to earth as did the pagan gods. The talmudic addition humanizes it further, portraying God in the role of a rabbi/teacher or even a fellow congregant.

The Thirteen Attributes of God are verses from Exodus 34:6-7 that are read on fast days and at other times. According to the Talmud, God is said to have revealed them after Moses pleaded on behalf of Israel because of the transgression of the golden calf. In this way God was explaining that whenever Israel sins, if they recite this prayer, God will forgive them. Therefore a covenant was made with the Thirteen Attributes, that the people would not be turned away empty-handed, as it is said, *Behold, I make a covenant* (Exod. 34:10).

Targum Pseudo-Yonathan on Exodus 34:5-6 states that rather than God revealing Himself to Moses, it is the *Shekhinah* that is revealed: "The Lord revealed Himself in the clouds of the Glory of His *Shekhinah* .... The Lord caused His *Shekhinah* to pass before him." This suggests that the translator was uncomfortable with God having revealed Himself so directly to Moses, and instead turned to the tradition of the *Shekhinah* as God's Presence in this world.

Targum Pseudo-Yonathan on Exodus 33:5, quotes God as saying, "Were I to remove the Glory of My *Shekhinah* for one short moment among you, the world would come to an end."

Sources:
B. *Rosh ha-Shanah* 17b.

402. THE FIRST SABBATH

The first Sabbath was also the first New Year's Day. On that day, the first of Tishrei, the daylight continued for thirty-six hours, since night did not fall at its set time. For God gave the first Sabbath an extra twelve hours of light by holding back the darkness. That is the meaning of the verse *And God blessed the seventh day* (Gen. 2:3). What did God bless it with? With an extra measure of light.

Why did God hold back the darkness? Because of Adam, who was created on the sixth day. He had never seen the darkness, and God did not want to cause him distress.

Thus the light of the first Sabbath was like the primordial light of the first day of creation, in which it was possible to see from one end of the universe to the other, for on both days the light lasted and the darkness was held back.

> Here Rosh ha-Shanah, the New Year, is linked to the first Sabbath, making it the birthday of the world. Note that this birthday is not calculated from the first day of Creation, but from the day of rest that follows the six days of Creation. This date is identified as the first of Tishrei, which is the day on which Rosh ha-Shanah is celebrated. The sun shining for an extra twelve hours so that Adam would not be frightened of the darkness adds to the miraculous nature of the first Sabbath.
>
> *Sources:*
> Pesikta Rabbati 46:1.

403. GOD KEEPS THE SABBATH

The Sabbath is not only celebrated on earth, but also in heaven. Soon after the Sabbath was created, God said to all the angels of the presence and all the angels of sanctification: "We shall keep the Sabbath together in heaven and on earth."

He said: "Know that I shall separate a people from among all the nations for Myself, and they will also keep the Sabbath. And I will sanctify them for Myself, and I will bless them. They will be My people and I will be their God. And I have chosen the seed of Jacob from among all that I have seen."

> God observed the first Sabbath on the seventh day of Creation (Gen. 2:2), and *The Book of Jubilees* assumed that He has been observing it ever since. This myth offers another example of how God is portrayed as performing Jewish rituals in heaven. Such a myth underscores the importance of the ritual activity, in this case the Sabbath. It also underscores the importance of keeping the Sabbath along with God, who observes it in heaven. For other examples, see "God Puts on *Tallit* and *Tefillin*," p. 34, and "God Studies the Torah," p. 34. Note that God also commands the angels to join Him in the Sabbath observance. This creates a heavenly congregation parallel to the earthly one.
>
> *Sources:*
> The Book of Jubilees 2:18-20; Genesis Rabbah 11:5.

404. KEEPING THE SABBATH

God said to Israel, "If you keep the Sabbath, I will count it as if you had kept all the commandments of the Torah. But if you violate the Sabbath, I will count it as though you had profaned all the commandments. For when a man keeps the Sabbath, it is as though he had fulfilled the entire Torah."

Remember the Sabbath day and keep it holy (Exod. 20:8), the commandment for keeping the Sabbath, is considered to be the most essential commandment, underlining the central importance of the Sabbath in Judaism. Here God states that He will consider keeping the Sabbath to be equal to observing all of the commandments—and not keeping the Sabbath as equal to breaking all of the commandments.

Sources:
Y. *Nedarim* 3:9; *Exodus Rabbah* 25:12.

405. THE SABBATH ANGELS

When a man who is praying on the eve of the Sabbath says, *The heaven and the earth were finished* (Gen. 2:1), the two ministering angels who accompany every man place their hands on his head and say, *"Your guilt shall depart and your sin be purged away"* (Isa. 6:7).

So, too, on the eve of the Sabbath, two angels accompany a man home on Sabbath evening after leaving the synagogue: a good angel and an evil one. When he returns home, if he finds the candles burning and the table set, and the bedding properly arranged, the good angel says, "So may it be for another Sabbath," and the evil angel is forced to reply, "Amen."

But if everything has not been properly prepared for the Sabbath, the evil angel states, "So may it be for another Sabbath," and the good angel has no choice but to say, "Amen."

And some say that not only the two angels accompany a person from the synagogue on the eve of the Sabbath, but that the *Shekhinah* accompanies him as well, like a mother bird sheltering her children. When the *Shekhinah* sees the candles burning and the angels behold the set table, and sees that the husband and wife are filled with joy for Sabbath, the *Shekhinah* says, *"You are my servant, Israel in whom I glory"* (Isa. 49:3).

But if the candles are not burning, the table is not set and the husband and wife are not rejoicing, the *Shekhinah* departs, taking the angels with Her. Then the forces of evil arrive to take their place, and the Evil Inclination proclaims, "This household belongs to me and my forces." Then the spirit of defilement rests upon them and even their food is rendered impure.

> This is a famous midrash that is intended to remind Jewish families of the importance of properly observing the Sabbath. Unless they want the evil angel to have the last word, they have to make the proper preparations for the Sabbath. It is customary, in both the Sephardic and Ashkenazi traditions, to recite or sing the *piyyut* or hymn *Shalom Aleikhem*, meaning "peace unto you," on Friday evening after returning from the synagogue. This hymn, composed approximately 250 years ago by an unknown poet, and introduced into the Sabbath service by the kabbalists, serves as a reminder of the cautionary tale of the two Sabbath angels.
>
> *Sha'arei Rahamim* explains that the angels are compelled in what they do: "The angels have no free will of their own, for they are not free agents, but they act solely by necessity. If a man is worthy, they must bless him, even against their will, and if he is not worthy, they must of necessity curse him."
>
> *Sources:*
> B. *Shabbat* 119b; *Midrash Rabbi Shimon bar Yohai; Sod ha-Shabbat* 9; *Sha'arei Rahamim.*
>
> *Studies:*
> *The Encyclopedia of Jewish Prayer* by Macy Nulman, pp. 290-291.
> "Coronation of the Sabbath Bride: Kabbalistic Myth and the Ritual of Androgynisation" by Elliot R. Wolfson.
> *The Sabbath in the Classical Kabbalah* by Elliot K. Ginsburg, pp. 102-108.

406. THE SABBATH FEAST IN THE CELESTIAL EDEN

The angels celebrate the Sabbath in heaven exactly as it is done on earth. Thousands of angels gather in the fourth heavenly palace, in the place known as the Chamber of Delight. During the festive meal on the night of the Sabbath, Sabbath tables are arranged there for the angels, who stand beside their tables, observing the Sabbath. They are watched over by a certain heavenly creature, with four seraphim serving under him, who resides in the fourth heavenly palace. This creature has been appointed to watch over those who rejoice on the Sabbath. And when this creature or one of the seraphim who serve under it sees those at a certain table rejoicing over the Sabbath, the heavenly creature blesses and protects them and spares them from the River of Fire. The angelic celebrants, in turn, reply "Amen."

But should the heavenly creature see a table that is not rejoicing in proper fashion, then the seraphim force those angels outside that chamber, and usher them into a realm known as the Chamber of Harm. There, instead of being blessed, they are cursed, and there is none to protect them from the River of Fire.

> Here the Sabbath is described as being celebrated in heaven by the angels just as it is on earth. And just as human celebrants are judged by two angels (see "The Sabbath Angels," p. 315) or by the *Shekhinah* along with the two angels (ibid.), so here the angels are judged by one of the *hayyot* or heavenly creatures, along with four assistant seraphim. The angels receive a blessing from the heavenly creature if their observance is appropriate, but are destroyed in the River of Fire if they are found at fault.
>
> Angels that have somehow displeased God are said to meet their end in the River of Fire. This image derives from Daniel 7:10: *A river of fire streamed forth before Him.* See "The River of Fire," p. 158.
>
> *Sources:*
> Zohar 2:252b.

407. THE SPICE OF THE SABBATH

Why is Sabbath food so fragrant? Some say there is a certain spice named *Shabbat*, and when put into food it renders the dish fragrant. And where does that spice come from? From the Garden of Eden.

Ever since they took leave of this world, the patriarch Abraham and his wife, Sarah, have made their home in the Garden of Eden. During the week Abraham wanders through the Garden and gathers leaves that have fallen from the trees of Eden, especially those of the Tree of Life.

And on the eve of the Sabbath, Sarah crushes those leaves and takes the powder made from them and casts it into the wind. And winds guided by angels carry it to the four corners of the earth, so that all those who breathe in even the smallest speck have a taste of Paradise, and the Sabbath is filled with joy for them. That is the spice of the Sabbath.

> The notion of a spice called *Shabbat*, that is, Sabbath, is presented satirically in the Talmud. When the Emperor Hadrian asks why Sabbath food is so fragrant, Rabbi Joshua ben Haninah tells him of such a Sabbath spice, which he said works for anyone who keeps the Sabbath, but not for anyone else. Despite the playful quality of his comment, the notion of a Sabbath spice entered the tradition, and a folktale about Abraham and Sarah living in the Garden of Eden offered an explanation for the spice pervading the Sabbath.

By all accounts the Garden of Eden was enchanted: it had two magic trees in the center and a speaking serpent. In later Jewish folklore the Garden of Eden represents a place that serves as the goal of many a quest. Here Abraham and Sarah are said to be living in the Garden. They appear to be the only inhabitants. How did this folk theme arise? There is a double usage of the term *Gan Eden* in Jewish lore. On the one hand it refers to the earthly Garden of Eden as described in Genesis. On the other, it refers to Paradise. Of course, Abraham and Sarah were rewarded with Paradise. But since the heavenly and the earthly gardens were identified by the same name, the notion arose in folk tradition that the Paradise they lived in was the earthly Garden of Eden. There Abraham and Sarah offer palpable blessings to their children, the children of Israel, in the form of a Sabbath spice made of leaves gathered from the Garden of Eden.

Here there is an interesting link of three main mythic themes: that of *Gan Eden*, the patriarchs, and the Sabbath. And the story adds a mythic dimension to the belief that the Sabbath day, in particular, is blessed. This idea takes many other forms, including that of the presence of the *Shekhinah* on the Sabbath in the form of the Sabbath Queen, of Sabbath angels and of the *neshamah yeterah*, the second soul of the Sabbath. The theme of making use of leaves from the Garden of Eden is also found in the folktale "Leaves From the Garden of Eden." See *Gabriel's Palace*, pp. 134-135.

Another tale about the leaves of the Garden of Eden is found in the Talmud: Elijah once led Rabbah bar Avuha to the Garden of Eden and let him in. Elijah told him to take off his robe and fill it with leaves. So Rabbah collected leaves from the Garden and was about to leave with them when he heard a voice say, "Why would anyone consume his portion in the World to Come the way Rabbah has done?" Hearing this, Rabbah shook the leaves out of his robe and left them in the Garden and took his leave. When Rabbah returned home, he discovered that the fragrance of the leaves still clung to that robe. It never faded away. Many were those who sought to purchase it from him, and at last he sold it for 12,000 dinars and gave the money to his son-in-laws. The story of the robe of Rabbah is found in *B. Bava Metzia* 114a-b. The myth of the Sabbath spice made from leaves from the Garden of Eden is found in *Ma'aseh me-ha-Hayyat*.

There is also an extensive tradition concerning patriarchs who never died. There are similar types of tales about Jacob, Moses, and David. See "Jacob Never Died," p. 370. For one about Moses living eternally, see "The Princess and the Slave" in *Elijah's Violin*, pp. 36-43. For stories about David still being alive, see "King David is Alive" in *Gabriel's Palace*, pp. 139-141.

Sources:
B. Shabbat 119a; B. Bava Metzia 114b; Ma'aseh me-ha-Hayyat; Maharsha; Etz Yosef; Ben Yehoyada.

408. THE SONG OF THE SABBATH

Angels have six wings, one for each day of the week. And each day they chant a song for God. But on the Sabbath they remain silent, for on that day it is the Sabbath itself that chants hymns to God.

Here again the Sabbath is personified, this time as chanting hymns to God on the Sabbath. This indicates that the Sabbath is even observed in heaven, and on that day the Sabbath takes the place of the angels who chant a song for God every other day of the week.

Sources:
Or Zaru'a 2:18c; Geonica 2:48; Yalkut Shim'oni, Tehillim 843; See Ginzberg, Legends 5:101.

409. ADAM'S SONG OF PRAISE FOR THE SABBATH

When Adam saw the majesty of the Sabbath and the joy it gave to all beings, he sang a song of praise for the Sabbath day (Pa. 91:1). God said to him, "You sang a song of praise to the Sabbath, but none to Me, the God of the Sabbath." Then the Sabbath rose from its seat, prostrated herself before God, and said, *It is a good thing to give thanks to the Lord* (Ps. 92:2). And all of creation added, *And to sing praises to Your Name, O God Most High* (Ps. 92:2).

> Here God is portrayed as being jealous of the attention Adam bestows on the Sabbath when he composes the first song of praise for it. But the Sabbath, a day of peace as well as a day of rest, resolves the conflict by prostrating herself before God, and assuring God it is good for Him to receive praises. This has the effect of sparing Adam God's anger.
>
> Underlying this myth is concern that the Sabbath must never be separated from its Creator, and that observing the Sabbath is, in effect, rendering praise to God.
>
> *Sources:*
> Battei Midrashot 1:27; See Ginzberg, *Legends*, 1:85, 5:110.

410. WHY WOMEN LIGHT TWO CANDLES ON THE SABBATH

Some say that women light candles on the Sabbath to repent for the sin of Eve. Because she extinguished the primordial light and made the world grow dark, women must kindle lights for the Sabbath.

Others say that because two souls shine on the Sabbath, a person's soul and the *neshamah yeterah*, the second soul that is given on the Sabbath, women light two candles.

Still others say that women light two candles because the Sabbath is celebrated above and below, in heaven as well as on earth. Just as the priest lit seven lamps in the Tabernacle and thereby caused the seven lamps on high to shine, so too does the kindling of the Sabbath candles awaken great arousal in the upper world.

Above all, the two candles are kindled to honor the presence of the *Shekhinah*, the Sabbath Queen, who rests upon the people during the Sabbath.

> This explanation of why women light the Sabbath candles is found in *Tkhine imrei Shifreh*, a collection of women's devotional prayers, written in Yiddish, called *tkhines*. They were written in Yiddish because it was the vernacular, and women often didn't know Hebrew. Although there is some scholarly debate about whether various collections of these kinds of prayers were composed by women or by men, this collection is attributed to a woman, Shifrah Segal of Brody. The rabbinic explanation for the two candles describes the lighting of the candles as an act of repentance for the sin of Eve. But some *tkhines* dispute that, offering instead positive reasons for the ritual—to honor the two souls of the Sabbath, to awaken Sabbath joy above and below, and to honor the *Shekhinah*, who is said to be present during the Sabbath.
>
> The description of the lighting of the seven lamps of the Tabernacle is found in Numbers 8:2. For more on the myth that the primordial light was withdrawn because of the sin of Adam and Eve see "The Light of the First Day," p. 83. For the myth of the second soul given on the Sabbath, see "The Second Soul," p. 310.
>
> *Sources:*
> Tkhine imrei Shifreh, attributed to Shifrah Segal of Brody; *Nahalat Tzvi*.
>
> *Studies:*
> Voices of the Matriarchs by Chava Weissler, pp. 51-65, 104-125.

411. THE FIRST *HAVDALAH*

At the close of the first Sabbath, as the sun set, Adam saw darkness creeping upon him, and he began to cry out, "Woe is me! Can it be that the serpent is coming to bruise me?" Then God gave Adam two stones, one of thick darkness and one of death's shadow. Adam took the stones and struck them together until fire shot forth from them. In amazement, Adam recited the prayer, "Blessed are You, O God, Who created the light of the fire." And those words are still repeated in the *Havdalah* prayer till this day.

Others say that a pillar of fire was sent to Adam to illuminate him and to guard him from all evil. When Adam saw that pillar of fire, he rejoiced, and he put forth his hands to the light of the fire and said, "Blessed are You, O Lord our God, King of the universe, Who creates the flames of fire." And when he removed his hands from the light of the fire, he said, "Now I know that the holy day has been separated from the work day here below, for fire may not be kindled on the Sabbath day." And at that hour he said, "Blessed are You, O Lord our God, King of the universe, who divides the holy from the profane, the light from the darkness."

And that is the prayer, till this day, that serves to separate the holy from the profane. One must also say the blessing over fire because all fires are concealed on the Sabbath, and once this blessing is made, all of the other fires emerge, take their places, and are given permission to shine. And when the blessing over fire is made, one must turn one's fingernails toward the flame, and let the flames reflect in them.

One must also smell spices as the Sabbath ends, because when the second soul of the Sabbath departs, a person's soul is left naked, bereft of that spirit, and requires the scent of the spices to sustain the soul.

> This is a midrashic example of a myth of origin. Never having seen darkness, Adam is terrified by its onset, and links it to the danger posed by the serpent of Eden. The identification of the serpent and the darkness derives from Psalms 139:11: *Surely darkness will bruise me*; the same verb, "bruise," is used by the serpent in Genesis 3:15.
>
> This myth also provides the story behind the creation of the *Havdalah* ritual that is performed at the end of the Sabbath. *Havdalah* is the ceremony at the end of the Sabbath at which time the Sabbath officially ends, the Sabbath Queen departs, and Jews are said to lose their *neshamah yeterah*, their second soul.
>
> The rituals of *Havdalah* are described here: making a blessing over fire, letting the flames reflect in the fingernails, and smelling spices to revive oneself and let oneself recover from the loss of one's second soul. See "The Second Soul," p. 310.
>
> *Sources:*
> B. *Avodah Zarah* 8a; *Pirkei de-Rabbi Eliezer* 20; *Midrash Tehillim* 92:4; *Zohar* 2:207b-208b.
>
> *Studies:*
> *The Sabbath in the Classical Kabbalah* by Elliot K. Ginsburg, pp. 256-284.
> *A Guide to Jewish Religious Practice* by Isaac Klein, pp. 73-75.

412. THE SABBATH IN THE WORLD TO COME

In this world, if a person gathers figs on the Sabbath, the fig tree says nothing about it to him. But in the World to Come, if a man should pick fruit from a fig tree on the Sabbath, the tree will call out to him and say, "Remember the Sabbath!"

> Work is forbidden on the Sabbath. In fact, there is a very long list of activities that constitute work, including picking fruit from trees. This rather tongue-in-cheek myth observes that while trees in this world are silent when someone breaks the Sabbath by picking their fruit, in the World to Come the tree will loudly protest.
>
> *Sources:*
> *Midrash Tehillim* 73:4; *Yalkut Shim'oni*, Jer. 315.

413. THE GREAT SABBATH

The world is destined to exist for six thousand years. The first two thousand years was the time of chaos, the next two thousand years the era of the Torah, and the last two thousand years will be the days of the Messiah. After that the world will lie desolate for a thousand years, before a new world is created in its place. For just as the seventh year is a year of release, so is it for the world: one thousand years out of seven it shall be fallow.

Now it is known of God that *in Your sight a thousand years are like yesterday* (Ps. 90:4). Therefore six thousand years are but six days in the eyes of God. And just as God created the world in six days and then rested, at the end of six millennia the world will cease to exist.

Some say the world will remain desolate for a thousand years, just as land lies fallow every seventh year. But after this the world will be revived, as it is said, *He will raise us up, and we shall be whole by His favor* (Hos. 6:2).

Others say that the six days of Creation represent all the days of the world, and the seventh day is the Great Sabbath, as it is said, *a Sabbath of the Lord* (Lev. 25:2). That will be the Sabbath of His Great Name. For the world as we know it was intended to exist for six thousand years: two thousand years without Torah, two thousand years with Torah, and two thousand years of the Messiah's reign.

And just as one year in seven is a sabbatical year of release, so God will provide a day of release, a day lasting a thousand years. Thus, in the seventh millennium, the Great Sabbath will begin. Then all activity will cease. There will be no food or drink. But each and every one of the righteous will rejoice in his understanding of the Torah, and they will sit with crowns on their heads and feast off the splendor of the *Shekhinah*. At the end of this Sabbath year of days, the era of the World to Come will be ushered in, when death will never, ever again exist. For the World to Come will be wholly a Sabbath and everlasting rest.

> The Sabbath is said to be a foretaste of the World to Come. This myth, based on an interpretation of Leviticus 25:2, about the need to let the land lie fallow every seventh year, describes a cosmic Sabbath, known as the Great Sabbath, that will come after 6,000 years—three ages of 2,000 years each. Just as the seventh day is the Sabbath, the day of rest, so for a thousand years there will be no life in this world as we know it, but the righteous will reap great rewards in the World to Come. Note that the righteous are sustained in the World to Come by feasting off the splendor of the *Shekhinah*. Or, in an alternate version, the light they bask in is none other than the primordial light, the light of the first day. See "The Light of the First Day," p. 83.
>
> In this myth, the existence of the world is said to be limited to six millennia, and the longevity of the world is directly tied to the six days of Creation. This explanation draws on the verse *in Your sight a thousand years are like yesterday* (Ps. 90:4), which was taken as the precise correlation between time on earth and in heaven.
>
> Therefore the world that was created in six days will be destroyed at the end of six of God's days. Here the key is the symmetry between the six days of Creation and the span of the world's existence. This myth makes a distinction between the messianic era, which will last 2,000 years in this world, and the Great Sabbath that will follow, where all existence in this world will cease for good. In some versions of this myth, however, after lying fallow for a thousand years (some say 2,000 years), God will renew the world, and life will be revived (*B. Sanh.* 97a-b).
>
> In *B. Sanhedrin* 97b, Rabbi Hanan bar Tahlifa tells of seeing an ancient scroll on which was written: "Four thousand two hundred and ninety-one years after its creation, the world will be orphaned. The years that follow will see the wars of Gog and Magog and the messianic age, but God will not renew the world until after 7,000 years."

The kabbalistic doctrine of cosmic cycles, or *shemittot*, describes three eons of exist-ence of 2,000 years each, followed by a thousand years in which the world will lay desolate. There is also an alternate theory of seven cosmic cycles, each lasting 7,000 years.

Sources:
B. Sanhedrin 97a-b; B. Hagigah 12a; Y. Hagigah 2a; B. Rosh ha-Shanah 31a; *Eliyahu Rabbah* 2:6; *Genesis Rabbah* 8:2; *Leviticus Rabbah* 19; *Numbers Rabbah* 14; *Song of Songs Rabbah* 5; *Midrash Tanhuma Va-Yelekh* 2; *Midrash Shemuel* 4; *Tanna de-vei Eliyahu* 2; *Midrash Tehillim* 90; *Tikkunei ha-Zohar, Tikkun* 36, 77b; *Ma'arekhet ha-Elohut* 102, 185a; *Sefer Mar'ot ha-Tzov'ot* 102; *Sod ha-Shabbat*, section 14; Nachmanides, *Perush Ramban al ha-Torah* on Leviticus 25:2; *Toldot Ya'akov Yosef; Sifram Shel Tzaddikim.*

Studies:
"The Meaning of the Torah in Jewish Mysticism" in *On the Kabbalah and Its Symbol-ism* by Gershom Scholem, pp. 77-86.

414. A DAY OF FASTING AND MOURNING

When the spies went into Canaan and brought back their report of giants, the people wept, for they were certain that they would all die by the sword there. The crying spread through the whole camp, and God said, "Because the people weep without cause and do not trust My word to bring them into a land flowing with milk and honey, this night and the following day, the Ninth of Av, shall be a day of fasting and mourning, a day of trouble and tribulation for many years.

This myth concerns the origin of the many tragedies that have come to be associ-ated with the Ninth of Av. This includes the destruction of both Temples and many other catastrophes. Here the beginning of the curse of the Ninth of Av is traced to the report of the spies triggering panic among the people. This fear on their part was an affront to God, Who had promised to bring them into that land, provoking God to place a curse on the Ninth of Av. This myth is unusual, in that God is rarely portrayed making a curse. In fact, one myth describes an angel, Gallizur, whose job it is to utter all of God's evil decrees for Him. See "The Angel Gallizur," p. 199.

Sources:
B. Sota 38.

Studies:
A Guide to Jewish Religious Practice by Isaac Klein, pp. 247-251.

415. THE MOURNING DOVE

On the night of the Ninth of Av, while Jews mourn the destruction of the Temple at the Wailing Wall in Jerusalem and the sound of their weeping cleaves the heavens, a white dove appears in the darkness of the night and joins the people of Israel in their morning. All night it stands at the corner of the Wall, wailing and moaning. Then a heavenly voice is sometimes heard, moaning like a dove, saying, "Alas, because of the sins of My sons I destroyed My house, I burned My sanctuary, and scattered My children among the nations."

Here God is said to appear in the form of a white dove at the *Kotel*, the Western Wall of the Temple Mount in Jerusalem that is the only remaining wall of the Temple. The dove can be identified with God because, according to Jewish tradition, it was God who made the decision to destroy the Temple. In other accounts, this dove is identified with the *Shekhinah*, and is one of the three prominent forms She takes: as a bride dressed in white; as an old woman dressed in black, deep in mourning; and as a white dove mourning at the Wall. According to Zev Vilnay, the tradition of the mourning dove at the Wall grows out of the talmudic account in *B. Berakhot* 3a, in which Rabbi Jose, who lived about a century after the destruction of the Temple, prays in a ruin in Jerusalem and hears a voice like that of a dove, repeating words of regret at the destruction and exile. In later folk accounts, this dove is transferred to the Wall and linked with Tisha be-Av, the Ninth of Av, which commemorates the destruction of the two Temples.

Sources:
B. Berakhot 3a; *Song of Songs Rabbah* 6:5; *Aggadot Eretz Yisrael*, no. 189.

416. THE WAILING WALL

On the night of the Ninth of Av, drops of dew can be seen on the stones of the Wailing Wall, and it is said among the people that the Wall was crying at night for the Temple that was torn down.

Once, when worshippers stood in front of the Wall, pouring out their hearts, water began oozing out of the cracks of the Wall, and the people cried out, "The wall is weeping!" When the news spread among the people, they streamed to the Wall, and women collected the tears of the Wall as a precious remedy for many ailments.

That is why it is said that since the destruction of the Temple, the gates of prayer have been closed, but the gates of weeping are open.

> The western retaining wall of the Temple Mount is known as the *Kotel*, or Western Wall, or Wailing Wall. It is the holiest Jewish site in the world, and the focus of visitors to Jerusalem, who often pray intensely at the Wall and leave messages to God in the cracks of the Wall.
>
> Why is the *Kotel* known as the Wailing Wall? The name "Wailing Wall" is perhaps an outsider's description based on the passionate weeping of the Jews who pray there, since Jews normally call it the *Kotel*, the Western Wall. This myth, collected orally in Israel, provides a different kind of explanation, a miraculous weeping of the wall, still grieving over the destruction of the Temple.
>
> *Sources:*
> B. Berakhot 32b; *Aggadot Eretz Yisrael*, no. 189.

417. THE WEEPING WELL

There is a well in the Temple court known as the Weeping Well. When the Temple was destroyed, young people cast themselves in that well to evade the sword. And on the Ninth of Av, even to this day, when all are mourning over the destruction of the Temple, a great weeping is heard from that well.

On the same night, a voice of mourning and sighing is said to go forth from the Temple site. All who pray there can hear it. And those who hear it are seized with weeping until they faint.

> This is a myth of martyrdom, like that about Masada, about a well in the Temple court where young people took their lives by casting themselves in the well rather than be killed. The well is still weeping over those tragic deaths, as well as for the destruction of the Temple. In a broader sense, this myth is about how the tragedy of the Temple's destruction still haunts the Jewish people.
>
> *Sources:*
> Ha-Ma'amar 3, p. 91; *Kesef Tzaruf* 160b.

418. THE NINTH OF AV IN THE FUTURE

The Ninth of Av is a time of mourning for the destruction of the two Temples in Jerusalem and other disasters that have taken place on that same day. But in the future God will turn the Ninth of Av into a time of rejoicing. He will rebuild Jerusalem and gather the exiles of Israel. Whoever mourns for Jerusalem in this world will rejoice with her in the World to Come.

> To convey how radically the messianic era will transform life from the present, this myth describes the Ninth of Av in the messianic era as a time of rejoicing instead of grieving. The root of this idea is in Zechariah 8:19.
>
> *Sources:*
> *Yalkut Shim'oni, Eikhah* 998; *B. Ta'anit* 30b; *Pesikta Rabbati* 28.

419. REPENTING FOR GOD

When the Temple in Jerusalem was still standing, a goat was offered up as a sin offering on every *Rosh Hodesh*. This was brought to atone for God's sin. God said: "At first the moon was same size as the sun. Later, I decided to make the moon smaller. Now I regret doing that. So on every *Rosh Hodesh*, when the moon is small, bring a sin offering for Me, to atone for My act of making the moon smaller."

> The goat offering on *Rosh Hodesh* is described in Numbers 28:14-15: *This is the burnt-offering of every new moon throughout the months of the year. And one he-goat for a sin-offering to Yahweh shall be offered.*
>
> This astonishing myth has God confessing that He has committed a sin, or at least an act He regrets—shrinking the size of the moon. The possibility of God's reversing the decision is never considered. Even stranger, it is incumbent on the Temple priests to atone for God's sin by offering a goat as a sin offering on *Rosh Hodesh. Rosh Hodesh* celebrates the new moon. This, the first day of the month, is the day that the moon appears to have shrunken to its smallest size. This shows that Israel does not only repent for its own sins, but for the sins of God as well, for which God seeks atonement. For the myth of the shrinking of the moon, see "The Quarrel of the Sun and the Moon," p. 112. See, also, "A Scapegoat for Azazel," p. 295, describing the custom of sacrificing a goat to Azazel on Yom Kippur.
>
> *Sources:*
> *B. Hullin* 60a.

BOOK SEVEN

MYTHS OF THE HOLY PEOPLE

Iscah was Sarah. And why was she called Iscah?
Because she saw through the Holy Spirit.

B. Sanhedrin 69b.

420. FOR THE SAKE OF ISRAEL

The world and everything in it was created only for the sake of Israel. Indeed, all worlds, above and below, were only created for the sake of Israel. Everything that was brought forth, created, formed, and made, everything that God did, was for the sake of His holy people Israel.

Israel was the first thing that arose in God's thought. That is why the sages commented about the verse *In the beginning God created the heaven and the earth* (Gen. 1:1), that "beginning" means Israel, since God's first thought was of Israel.

After the souls of Israel had been created, God was required to create and maintain the universe, for this was the purpose for which He had brought the souls of Israel into being.

God foresaw the pride and delight He would receive from Israel, and it was because of this that God created the world. God perceived that Abraham would some day be born, and perform deeds of love and kindness. Thus God created a world of love out of His love for Abraham. Indeed, every detail of creation was brought into being because of some element of pride that God would have from His people. Even the sinners of Israel were included in God's pride. Thus every single Jew is a garment for the Divine Presence.

The stars in the sky appear very small, but in heaven they are actually quite large. The same is true of Israel. In this world, Israel appears very small. But in the world on high, it is actually quite large.

When God created the world, it did not have the power to endure. God created Israel so that the world would be able to endure, for Israel is the sustenance of all universes. If not for Israel, everything would revert to its original state of nothingness.

> This myth expands on the notion of Israel as God's Chosen People by stating that "Israel was the first thing that arose in God's thought" and that "The world was created only for the sake of Israel." The *Maggid* of Mezrich compares the relationship of God and Israel to that of a father and his child—it is a relationship of love, pride, and delight: "When a father loves his child, this great love causes the child's image to be engraved on the father's mind. It is known that Israel rose first in God's thought. This means that it is constantly engraved in the Supernal thought, just as a child is in his father's mind."
>
> Here Israel is described as the First Created Being. There are several other divine beings who are described in these terms, among them the Heavenly Man, Adam, Adam Kadmon, and the *Shekhinah*. In this case, however, it is not an individual divine being who is identified as the First Created Being, but a nation, a people, whose destiny is interwoven with that of their God.
>
> *Sources:*
> B. Sanhedrin 44a; B. Berakhot 32b; B. Hullin 91b; *Genesis Rabbah* 12:9; *Exodus Rabbah* 38:4; *Numbers Rabbah* 2:2; *Ecclesiastes Rabbah* 1:9; *Eliyahu Rabbah* 14; *Leviticus Rabbah* 36:4; *Midrash Tehillim* 104:15; *Rashi on Genesis* 1:1; *Zohar* 1:24a; *Degel Mahaneh Ephraim* 68d; *Sefer Ba'al Shem Tov, Bereshit* 4, *Lekh Lekha* 27; *Keter Shem Tov* 194; *Likutei Moharan* 17:1, 52, 94; *Ohev Yisrael, Hayei Sarah* 8a; *Sippurei Ma'asiyot; Maggid Devarav le-Ya'akov* 124, 229; *Ohev Yisrael, Shemot* 25a; *Kedushat Levi* 98, 180; *Beit Yisrael, Lekh Lekha* 36.

421. THE SOULS OF ISRAEL

Some say that all souls come from Adam's soul. But others say that Abraham was the source of the souls of Israel, as it is said, *And the souls that they had acquired* (Gen. 12:5). After God had created them, these souls were preserved on high, and before the time of Abraham they had never descended to this world.

After the souls of Israel had emanated from God and had been brought into being, the future existence of this world was reaffirmed. For the universe and everything in it was created only for the sake of Israel.

> This myth reflects the point of view that history really begins with the story of Abraham, the first Jew, and suggests that the people of Israel were a separate creation, for God had saved the souls of Israel until that time. Thus these souls are untainted by the events recounted in Genesis that took place before Abraham—the Fall of Adam and Eve, Cain's murder of Abel, the generation of the Flood and the generation of the Tower of Babel. See "Adam's Soul," p. 162.
>
> A parallel idea is found in the myth of the Innocent Souls—souls that hid in the Garden of Eden at the time that Adam and Eve ate the forbidden fruit, and thus were not tainted by their sin. The soul of the Ba'al Shem Tov was said to be one of these Innocent Souls.
>
> *Sources:*
> *Likutei Moharan* 52.

422. THE BODY OF ISRAEL

All of Israel is one body and everyone of Israel is a limb of that body. That is why, when one's fellow has sinned, it is as though one has sinned oneself. All of Israel is described as being attached to the Tree of Life. All of Israel heard God speak at Mount Sinai and all of Israel was said to have sung as one when it sang the Song at the Sea. All of Israel is responsible for the rebuilding of the Temple in Jerusalem. And all of Israel must participate in raising up the *Shekhinah* from Her exile.

> Here Israel is viewed as more than a nation or a people, but as one body, since, in the eyes of God, Israel, His people, is rewarded and punished as if they were one. Note the parallel of this concept to the Christian doctrine of *Corpus Domini*, where each member of the church is a member of the body of God. This is a key concept that is also found in other sources. In the myth of the Ari, the combined efforts of all of Israel are required in order to gather the holy sparks that had been scattered around the world, so that the messianic era may be initiated. See "God's Image," p. 33; "The Fruit of the Tree of Life," p. 402; "The Shattering of the Vessels and the Gathering of the Sparks," p. 122; and "The *Shekhinah* Within," p. 63.
>
> *Sources:*
> *Yesod ha-Teshuvah* 6, quoting the Ari.
>
> *Studies:*
> "*Corpus Domini*: Traces of the New Testament in East European Hasidism" by Byron L. Sherwin.

423. THE LESSON OF THE STARS

When Abraham was still a boy, he saw the sun shining upon the earth, and he thought that surely the sun must be God, and therefore he would serve it. So he served the sun all that day, and prayed to it. But when evening came and the sun set, Abraham said to himself, surely this cannot be God. And Abraham wondered who had made the heavens and the earth.

That night, when Abraham lifted his eyes to the sky, he saw the stars and moon before him, and he thought that the moon must have created the world, and the stars were its servants. And Abraham served the moon and prayed to it all night.

But in the morning, when the sun shone upon the earth again, and the moon and stars could not be seen, Abraham understood that they were not gods, but that they were the servants of God. And from that day on Abraham knew the Lord and went in the ways of the Lord until the day of his death.

> This is an important midrash, in that it offers an explanation of how Abraham discovered the existence of God, and therefore it provides the origin of monotheism. It grows out of a problem in the biblical story of Abraham. When Abraham is first encountered, he is already a grown man and God tells him to leave the land he was born in and go to the land that God will reveal to him. Notably missing from this narrative is any indication of the childhood of Abraham, or how Abraham discovered God. This midrash supplies an answer to both of these problems, recounting Abraham's childhood and showing, at the same time, how the child Abraham used logic to determine that there must be a God who ruled over the sun and moon and everything else. There are many other midrashim about Abraham's birth and childhood, primarily modeled on the childhood of Moses.

> *Sources:*
> *Sefer ha-Yashar* 9:6, 9:13-19; IFA 10009.

424. GOD CALLS UPON ABRAM

The Lord said to Abram, "Go forth from your native land and from your father's house to the land that I will show you. I will make of you a great nation, and I will bless you; I will make your name great, and you shall be a blessing. I will bless those who bless you and curse him that curses you; and all the families of the earth shall bless themselves by you."

Abram went forth as the Lord had commanded him, and Lot went with him. Abram was seventy-five years old when he left the city of Haran. Abram took his wife Sarai and his brother's son Lot, and all the wealth that they had amassed, and the persons that they had acquired in Haran; and they set out for the land of Canaan.

> This is the beginning of the Abraham narrative in Genesis that starts with the famous words, *Lekh Lekha*, "Go forth." No explanation is given about how Abraham (originally named "Abram," as Sarah was originally "Sarai") discovered God or God discovered Abraham and when we first meet him, Abraham is a grown man. But because of his great faith, Abraham uproots himself and leaves Haran and sets out on a journey to the Holy Land. All of Abraham's actions are consistent with this one—more than any other individual, Abraham exhibits perfect faith in God, even when God asks him to sacrifice his beloved son, Isaac.

> *Sources:*
> Genesis 12:1-5

425. GOD'S COVENANT WITH ABRAM

And the Lord said to Abram, after Lot had parted from him, "Raise your eyes and look out from where you are, to the north and south, to the east and west, for I give all the land that you see to you and your offspring forever. I will make your offspring as the dust of the earth, so that if one can count the dust of the earth, then your offspring too can be counted. Up, walk about the land, through its length and its breadth, for I give it to you. And Abram moved his tent, and came to dwell at the terebinths of Mamre, which are in Hebron; and he built an altar there to the Lord.

This is one of the most famous of the covenants God makes with Abraham (then known as Abram), along with Genesis 15:1-5 where God says, *"Look toward heaven and count the stars, if you are able to count them."* And He added, *"So shall your offspring be."* For centuries, God's statement that *"I give all the land that you see to you and your offspring forever"* has been the basis of the claim that Jews have the right to all of the traditional Land of Israel. Most recently, Israeli settlers have asserted this claim, which many regard as the root issue of the Arab-Israeli conflict. For these settlers, this and similar biblical passages serve as a kind of deed, proving their ownership of the land.

Sources:
Genesis 13:14-18.

426. GOD APPEARS TO ABRAHAM

The Lord appeared to Abraham by the terebinths of Mamre; he was sitting at the entrance of the tent as the day grew hot. Looking up, he saw three men standing near him. As soon as he saw them, he ran from the entrance of the tent to greet them and, bowing to the ground, he said, "My lords, if it please you, do not go on past your servant. Let a little water be brought; bathe your feet and recline under the tree. And let me fetch a morsel of bread that you may refresh yourselves; then go on—seeing that you have come your servant's way." They replied, "Do as you have said."

Abraham hastened into the tent to Sarah, and said, "Quick, three *seahs* of choice flour! Knead and make cakes!" Then Abraham ran to the herd, took a calf, tender and choice, and gave it to a servant-boy, who hastened to prepare it. He took curds and milk and the calf that had been prepared and set these before them; and he waited on them under the tree as they ate.

They said to him, "Where is your wife Sarah?" And he replied, "There, in the tent." Then one said, "I will return to you next year, and your wife Sarah shall have a son!" Sarah was listening at the entrance of the tent, which was behind him. Now Abraham and Sarah were old, advanced in years; Sarah had stopped having the periods of women. And Sarah laughed to herself, saying, "Now that I am withered, am I to have enjoyment—with my husband so old?" Then the Lord said to Abraham, "Why did Sarah laugh, saying, 'Shall I in truth bear a child, old as I am?' Is anything too wondrous for the Lord? I will return to you at the time next year, and Sarah shall have a son." Sarah lied, saying, "I did not laugh," for she was frightened. But He replied, "You did laugh."

The visit of the three angels to Abraham is one of the most important episodes in the Bible. It is here that Abraham demonstrates his great hospitality to the three visitors, and it is here that the promise that Sarah would give birth is made, despite the fact that both Abraham and Sarah were quite old. Sarah is so skeptical of this prophecy that she laughs, and her laugh is immortalized in Isaac's name, which means "to laugh." This, then, is a crucial stage in fulfilling God's promise to Abraham that his offspring would be like the sands of the shore and the stars of the sky, and this promise is fulfilled in a miraculous form, by having the couple become parents in their old age.

Note that while the men who arrive at Abraham's tent are identified as angels, it is God who says, *"Why did Sarah laugh?"* This indicates that two versions of this episode have been combined together, one in which Abraham's guests were angels and another in which God Himself comes to visit him, accompanied by two angels—the two angels who then set out for Sodom, to inform Lot, Abraham's nephew, that the city was about to be destroyed.

Sources:
Genesis 18:1-15.

427. ABRAHAM'S VISION OF GOD

On the third day after Abraham circumcised himself, *the Lord appeared to him* (Gen. 18:1) as he sat in the door of his tent. As God spoke to him, Abraham was transformed, and became a full-fledged prophet. After that, the *Shekhinah* spoke from his throat, and God's presence remained with him. So too did God show Abraham each generation and its leaders, as He had shown Adam.

Prior to his circumcision, Abraham's prophetic experience was purely visionary, but now the voice of prophecy issued forth from his lips, and he enjoyed a measure of the Holy Spirit, for the Voice of God was revealed in his speech. After this Abraham did not only receive messages from God, but he was able to initiate communication with God as well.

As a result of the circumcision, Abraham had become an even holier person, capable of receiving a visit from God while remaining seated and fully awake, even during the hottest time of the day. So too was he able to absorb a vision of God in His superior light. For not all visions are of the same caliber—this vision was of a superior nature compared to the previous ones. For once Abraham was circumcised, he attained the fullest possible prophetic vision.

Then, just as God had shown Adam each generation and its leaders, He also showed each generation and its leaders to Abraham, as well as each generation and its sages.

Some say that God manifested Himself to Abraham that day by means of a tree, since the vision took place at the terebinths of Mamre. Why did God choose a tree to be the site at which He manifested Himself? To show Abraham that, like an old tree, he could still bear fruit.

God's appearance to Abraham in Genesis 18:1 is the subject of much debate by commentators, since the matter spoken of is not mentioned. Rashi assumes that three days after his adult circumcision, God came to inquire about Abraham's well-being. On the one hand, the *Zohar* views this appearance as a mystical experience, which profoundly transforms Abraham into a prophet. On the other hand, Rashi views God as making a sick call.

The role of God in this passage is further complicated by the fact that the same figure is sometimes identified as an angel and sometimes as God. Possibly two variants of the myth were combined, without resolving their inherent contradictions.

The notion that God appeared to Abraham as a tree takes the interpretation in another direction. This is deduced from the reference to the terebinths of Mamre. There are some natural links between the two: one famous passage, associated with the Torah, states that *she is a tree of life to those who grasp her* (Prov. 3:18). God is so closely linked to the Torah, which is His creation, that any identification of the Torah with a tree might, at the same time, apply to God. It is also important to recall that the Canaanite goddess Asherah was linked to sacred groves, and therefore identified with a tree. A womblike shape was carved into the base of these trees.

One question the rabbis wrestled with was whether Abraham circumcised himself, or if someone else did it. The question arises because of the great difficulty of any man circumcising himself. Although Genesis 27:24 seems to indicate clearly that Abraham did this himself, Rabbi Levi in *Genesis Rabbah* 47:9 asserts "It is not written here that Abraham circumcised himself, but rather that he was circumcised by God." *Zohar* 1:96b describes a miraculous circumcision when *Abram threw himself upon his face; and God spoke with him further, "As for Me, this is My covenant with you"* (Gen. 17:3-4). And when Abraham arose, he found himself already circumcised.

Sources:
Zohar 1:97b-98a; Midrash Tanhuma, Vayera 1, 2; Rashi on Genesis 18:1; Midrash Rabbenu Bahya on Genesis 18:1; Ziv ha-Zohar on Genesis 18:1; Rabbi Moshe Alshekh on Genesis 18:1; Or ha-Hayim on Genesis 18:1; Akedat Yitzhak on Genesis 18.

Studies:
The Hebrew Goddess by Raphael Patai, pp. 34-66.

428. ABRAHAM'S GLOWING STONE

Abraham wore a glowing stone around his neck. Some say that it was a pearl, others that it was a jewel. The light emitted by that jewel was like the light of the sun, illuminating the entire world. Abraham used that stone as an astrolabe to study the motion of the stars, and with its help he became a master astrologer. For his power of reading the stars, Abraham was much sought after by the potentates of East and West. So too did that glowing precious stone bring immediate healing to any sick person who looked into it.

At the moment when Abraham took leave of this world, the precious stone raised itself and flew up to heaven. God took it and hung it on the wheel of the sun.

> This talmudic legend about a glowing stone that Abraham wore around his neck is a part of the chain of legends about that glowing jewel, known as the *Tzohar*, which was first given to Adam and Eve when they were expelled from the Garden of Eden and also came into the possession of Noah, who hung it in the ark. See "The *Tzohar*, p. 85. This version of the legend adds the detail that the glowing stone was also an astrolabe, with which Abraham could study the stars.

> *Sources:*
> B. *Bava Batra* 16b; *Zohar* 1:11a-11b, *Idra Rabbah*.

> *Studies:*
> *The Jewish Alchemists* by Raphael Patai.

429. ABRAHAM IN EGYPT

There was a famine in the land, and Abraham and his wife Sarah went down into Egypt. First they went South until they reached Hebron, but since the famine was there as well, they made their way to Egypt, where there were said to be sufficient fruits and vegetables. Eventually they reached one of the seven branches of the Nile, and the night they entered Egypt, Abraham dreamed a dream.

In the dream he saw a cedar and a palm that grew side by side. For many years they flourished together, but then men came who wanted to cut down the cedar, leaving the palm there alone. But the palm tree spoke to them, saying "Do not cut down the cedar, for we are two of a kind." And they were so astonished to hear these words from a tree, that the cedar was spared for the sake of the palm.

When Abraham awoke he was greatly afraid, for he knew that the dream must be a sign that his life was in danger. For surely he was the cedar and Sarah was the palm. He told Sarah his dream, and she too recognized its meaning. For Sarah was a great prophetess and interpreter of dreams. Sarah told Abraham that while the dream did signify that his life was in danger, it also indicated that he would be saved in the end, and somehow she would cause him to be saved.

This prophecy came to pass when Pharaoh saw Sarah's beauty, and sought to kill Abraham, believing him to be her husband. Then Sarah assured Pharaoh that he was only her kinsman and Pharaoh agreed to spare his life. Thus did Sarah save Abraham, just as the cedar was saved by the palm.

> This myth from *Genesis Apocryphon*, one of the Dead Sea Scrolls, serves to explain and justify Abraham's behavior in Genesis 12:10-20, when he identified Sarah as his sister rather than his wife. The use of dreams to convey a prophecy or a divine message is common, with the dreams of Joseph serving as the primary model. Note that this myth includes both the dream and the interpretation, as do the dreams of Joseph. The notion that Sarah was a great prophetess is widely found. In *B. Sota 29a*, it is stated that Sarah was the only woman to whom God ever spoke directly.

The theme of Sarah's beauty is expanded on in *Genesis Rabbah* 40:5 and in *Targum Yonathan* on Genesis 12:11. Here Sarah was said to have been so beautiful that the entire land of Egypt was irradiated with her beauty, for she was even more beautiful than Eve.

Sources:
Genesis Apocryphon.

430. ABRAHAM'S NAME

When Abraham was still known as Abram, he was a skilled astrologer, and he saw in the stars that neither he nor Sarah would beget a child. All the other astrologers confirmed that this was true. When God told Abraham that *I will make you exceedingly fertile* (Gen. 17:6), Abraham said, "I have read in the stars that it is not possible that I should beget."

God replied, "What did the stars say to you? That Abram and Sarai will not beget? *And you shall no longer be called Abram, but your name shall be Abraham* (Gen. 17:5), and *as for your wife Sarai, you shall not call her Sarai, but her name shall be Sarah* (Gen. 17:15). For while Abram and Sarai will not beget, Abraham and Sarah will be fruitful."

When God changed Abraham's name, he added a new letter to his name, the letter *heh*. Where did that letter come from? God took it from beneath the Throne of Glory and gave it as a crown to the soul of Abraham. And Abraham received that crown when God said the words, "*And you shall no longer be called Abram*" (Gen. 17:5). After that Abraham was a new person, for his soul had been infused with the crown of that letter, and that letter brought with it the breath of life.

And God said to Abraham: "Because of the letter that has been added to your name, the heavens will be in your control and all the stars and constellations that give forth light will be subjected to you." Ever since, anyone who studies the Torah nullifies the power of the constellations over himself, as long as he studies it in order to fulfill its commandments. But those who do not study the Torah remain subject to the influences of the stars and constellations.

The tradition that Abraham was an astrologer was likely inspired by God's promise to Abraham: "*Look toward heaven and count the stars, if you are able to count them.*" *And He added, "So shall your offspring be"*(Gen. 15:1-5). Abraham's role as an astrologer is also affirmed by the talmudic tradition that Abraham wore a glowing stone around his neck that he used as an astrolabe to study the stars. See "Abraham's Glowing Stone," p. 332.

The letter that Abraham receives as a crown to his soul functions much like an *ibbur*, the spirit of a departed sage that fuses with the soul of a living person. Here God gives Abraham the letter *heh*, taken from beneath the Throne of Glory, and fuses it with his soul, not only changing his name, but also his soul. Thus the change in his soul is a gift from God, which transforms him into the Patriarch Abraham.

Note the linkage of this myth to the nullification of the power of astrological forces over a person. This grows out of the tradition that when God gave the Torah to Israel, He removed control of the stars and constellations over them, since the Torah transcends the world. This demonstrates the rabbis' recognition of the widespread belief in astrological forces and their concern that people would put their faith in these forces rather than in the Torah.

Sources:
B. *Bava Batra* 16b; *Aggadat Bereshit* p. 73; *Zohar* 3:216a, 3:216b; *Midrash ha-Ne'elam, Zohar Hadash* 24d-25a.

431. ISCAH THE SEER

Who was Iscah? Iscah was Sarah. And why was she called Iscah? Because she saw through the Holy Spirit.

> The difficult genealogy of Abraham and Sarah in Genesis 11:29 led to confusion as to the identity of Iscah. The resolution found in *Targum Pseudo-Yonathan*, the Talmud, and other rabbinic sources is that Sarah was Iscah, and that Iscah was a seer. This meaning is derived from the Aramaic root of Iscah, which denotes seeing. This led to the tradition that Sarah was a prophetess as great or greater than Abraham. The implication is that Iscah is a kind of alter ego for Sarah, and that when she turned to her prophetic side, she became Iscah.
>
> *Sources:*
> *Targum Pseudo-Yonathan* on Genesis 11:29; *B. Megillah* 14a; *B. Sanhedrin* 69b; *Midrash Tehillim* 118:11; *Sefer ha-Yashar* 12; Josephus, *Jewish Antiquities* 1:151.
>
> *Studies:*
> "*Sarah and Iscah: Method and Message in Midrashic Tradition*" by Eliezer Segal.

432. ABRAHAM BARGAINS WITH GOD

Now the Lord had said, "Shall I hide from Abraham what I am about to do, since Abraham is to become a great and populous nation and all the nations of the earth are to bless themselves by him? For I have singled him out, that he may instruct his children and his posterity to keep the way of the Lord by doing what is just and right, in order that the Lord may bring about for Abraham what He has promised him." Then the Lord said, "The outrage of Sodom and Gomorrah is so great, and their sin so grave! I will go down to see whether they have acted altogether according to the outcry that has reached Me; if not, I will take note."

The men went on from there to Sodom, while Abraham remained standing before the Lord. Abraham came forward and said, "Will You sweep away the innocent along with the guilty? What if there should be fifty innocent within the city; will You then wipe out the place and not forgive it for the sake of the innocent fifty who are in it? Far be it from You to do such a thing, to bring death upon the innocent as well as the guilty, so that innocent and guilty fare alike. Far be it from You! Shall not the Judge of all the earth deal justly?" And the Lord answered, "If I find within the city of Sodom fifty innocent ones, I will forgive the whole place for their sake." Abraham spoke up, saying, "Here I venture to speak to my Lord, I who am but dust and ashes: What if the fifty innocent should lack five? Will You destroy the whole city for want of the five?" And He answered, "I will not destroy if I find forty-five there." But he spoke to Him again, and said, "What if forty should be found there?" And He answered, "I will not do it, for the sake of the forty." And he said, "Let not my Lord be angry if I go on: What if thirty should be found there?" And He answered, "I will not do it if I find thirty there." And he said, "I venture again to speak to my Lord: What if twenty should be found there?" And He answered, "I will not destroy, for the sake of the twenty." And he said, "Let not my Lord be angry if I speak but this last time: What if ten should be found there?" And He answered, "I will not destroy, for the sake of the ten."

When the Lord had finished speaking to Abraham, He departed; and Abraham returned to his place.

> Bargaining is built into the fabric of the Near East, and here Abraham bargains with God over how many righteous people were needed to be living in Sodom and

Gomorrah for God to spare the city. Abraham starts with 50 and bargains God down to ten. That God is willing to bargain with Abraham shows how important Abraham is to God, and goes a long way in the personification process that portrays God with humanlike qualities.

Biblical commentators often note that Abraham does not make the same effort to change God's mind when God commands him to take his son Isaac and sacrifice him in Genesis 22. It does seem strange that Abraham intervenes for the strangers of Sodom and Gomorrah and not for his own son. This demonstrates that the characteristics of biblical figures are not always consistent, nor is that of God.

Sources:
Genesis 18:17-33.

Studies:
Arguing With God: A Jewish Tradition by Anson Laytner.

433. THE SOULS OF CONVERTS

Sarah was not barren. Although she had not given birth to a child, she had given birth to souls, as it is said, *And the souls they had made in Haran* (Gen. 12:6).

> This myth is a rather strange commentary on Genesis 16:1, *Sarah was barren. She had no children.* The commonly understood meaning of *the souls they had made* is that it refers to converts to the one God of Judaism. In this interpretation, Abraham and Sarah were successful in gathering converts to worship the one God. Rashi explains that *the souls they had made* means they found converts and "brought them under the wings of the *Shekhinah.*" He explains that Abraham would convert the men and Sarah the women. This follows the literal meaning of the passage. The *Zohar* seeks an explanation for the repetition, since stating that Sarah was barren already indicates that she had no children. The second statement is thus explained in terms of Genesis 12:6, *the souls they had made in Haran,* suggesting that Sarah did give birth, but to souls, not to children. Thus Sarah is portrayed in the *Zohar* as a goddesslike figure who gives birth not to human children, but to souls.
>
> *Zohar* 1:79a explains that both Sarah and Abraham gave birth to the souls of converts while in Haran. Here the meaning of "made" is not quite as literal, as it is explained that Abraham converted the men and Sarah converted the women.
>
> In *Megaleh Amukot,* Rabbi Nassan Nata Shapira agrees that both Abraham and Sarah gave birth to souls, and he identifies them as the souls of future converts. According to Rabbi Shapira, Isaac also begat souls of future converts, as did Rachel. For all the years she was childless, she gave birth to souls in heaven.
>
> Strangest of all is the interpretation of Rabbi Tzadok ha-Kohen of Lublin, who interprets *the souls that they had made* as souls created from seed ejaculated during intercourse that did not conceive. He states that "These souls are the souls of converts, like the souls Abraham and Sarah created (*Sihot Shedim* 1 in *Sifrei Rabbi Tzadok ha-Kohen*). Seed "wasted through masturbation," however, gives birth to evil spirits, demons, and *liliyot,* female demons of the night.
>
> Rabbi Shlomo Rabinowitz of Radomsk suggests an alternate origin for the souls of converts, linking them to Adam's sin: "When Adam sinned, many precious souls were captured by the *Sitra Ahra.* These are the souls of converts. Thus in converting these souls returned to their true destiny." As to how Abraham and Sarah gave birth to these souls, Rabbi Rabinowitz quotes Rabbi Menahem Recanati, who said that when *Tzaddikim* discover new meaning of the Torah, they create souls in the higher world.

Sources:
Rashi on Genesis 12:5; *Zohar* 1:79a, 3:168a; *Zohar Hadash, Balak* 53; *Megaleh Amukot* on Genesis 30:23; *Or ha-Hayim* on Deuteronomy 21:10-11; *Tiferet Shlomo* on Genesis 12:5; *Sihot Shedim* 1 in *Sifrei Rabbi Tzadok ha-Kohen.*

434. GOD BEGAT ISAAC

One of the most sacred mysteries of the Torah concerns Isaac's true father. Although Abraham rejoiced when he learned that he was to become a father, the truth is that it was the Lord who begat Isaac. For the Lord visited Sarah and did to her as He had spoken, and she conceived. That is why God said, "*I gave him Isaac*" (Josh. 24:3) and formed him in the womb of her who gave birth to him." Nevertheless, Isaac resembled Abraham in every respect.

It is said that Sarah was accustomed to bring forth children for God alone, restoring with gratitude the first fruit of all the blessings she had received, since she was a virgin when God opened her womb (Gen. 29:31). For it does not say that Sarah did not give birth at all, only that she did not bring forth for Abraham, for she told him, "*The Lord has kept me from bearing*" (Gen. 16:2).

So too is it said that Sarah herself was not born of a human mother, but that she was born of God, the Father and Cause of all things. Indeed, she transcended the entire world of bodily forms and exulted in the joy of God.

Others say that Sarah's conception and the birth of Isaac took place on the same day, as it is said, *Sarah conceived and bore a son* (Gen. 21:2). For unlike others, the soul of Isaac was not conceived at one time and born at another. A heavenly light appeared at his birth, as happened with Noah.

So too was it God who named Isaac when He said, "*But My covenant I will maintain with Isaac, whom Sarah shall bear to you at this season next year.*" (Gen. 17:21). For his name was ordained and written in the heavenly tablets. This was the only time that God named a child before he was born. Isaac was conceived on Rosh ha-Shanah, the New Year, and his birth book place on the first day of Passover. On the day of Isaac's birth the sun shone with a splendor that had not been seen since the sin of Adam and Eve and will only be seen again in the World to Come. So too did all creation rejoice: the earth, the heavens, the sun, the moon, and the stars. For had Isaac not been born, the world would have ceased to exist.

> Here Philo brings yet another perspective to the story of Isaac by revealing "one of the most sacred mysteries"—that it was God, not Abraham, who begat Isaac. Philo's belief in this strange interpretation of the conception of Isaac appears in at least six texts where Philo suggests that God was the true father of Isaac. Philo's interpretation perhaps influenced Christianity. Just as Jesus was said to be the son of God, so too is Isaac identified as a son of God. How does Philo arrive at this explanation? He interprets Sarah's comment that "*God has caused me laughter*" (Gen. 21:6) to mean that the Lord has begotten Isaac. He interprets "has caused" to mean "begotten," and he substitutes Isaac for "laughter," since "Isaac" means "laughter," referring to Sarah's laughter in Genesis 18:12, when the angel said that she would have a child even though Sarah was 90 years old.
>
> Philo apparently wrote a now-lost text on Isaac, entitled *De Isaaco*. Goodenough speculates that "*De Isaaco* developed as its central theme the fact that Isaac was so completely at one with the power behind the cosmos that he typified joy" (*By Light, Light* p. 154).
>
> The Christian parallel to this interpretation of Philo is obvious: God begat Isaac through Sarah just as God begat Jesus through Mary. Sarah herself is a kind of virgin in that she is childless. Did Philo mean to suggest a Jewish version of the myth of the birth of a Jewish savior? Not necessarily, in that Philo is quick to reduce the myth to allegory, by describing God as "perfect in nature, sowing and begetting happiness in the soul." So too does Philo insist that Isaac was not born a man, but as a pure thought.
>
> As a result, some readers might consider Philo's interpretation pure allegory, but Philo cannot escape the implications of his commentaries, making the mythic explanation of Isaac's birth unavoidable.

In addition to the obvious Christian parallel, there are also parallels from Greek myth, where Zeus takes many mortals as lovers.

There are other instances of supernatural conception found in Jewish tradition. The verse in which Eve says, "*I have received a man from God*" (Gen. 4:1) is interpreted to mean *not* that God fathered Cain, but that the serpent begat Cain. See "How Cain Was Conceived," p. 447. Also, there is the myth of the conception of Rabbi Ishmael, the High Priest, whose true father was said to be the angel Gabriel. See "How Rabbi Ishmael was Conceived," p. 201.

Sources:

B. *Berakhot* 1:6; B. *Bava Metzia* 87a; B. *Bava Batra* 17a; *Bereshit Rabbah* 61:6; *Midrash Tanhuma-Yelammedenu, Toledot* 2; *Midrash ha-Gadol* on Genesis 17:22; *Targum Yonathan* on Genesis 22:10; *Shoher Tov* 90:18; *The Book of Jubilees* 16:3, 16:12; Philo, *Legum Allegoriarum* 3:218-19; Philo, *De Somniis* 2:10; Philo, *De Congressu Eruditionis Gratia* 1:7-9; Philo, *De Cherubim* 43-47; Philo, *De Fuga et Inventione* 166-168; Philo, *De Ebrietate* 56-62; *Zohar* 1:60a.

Studies:

By Light, Light: The Mystic Gospel of Hellenistic Judaism by Erwin Ramsdell Goodenough, pp. 153-166.

2 *Enoch* in *The Old Testament Pseudepigrapha*, edited by James Charlesworth, p. 204, note 71c.

The Last Trial by Shalom Spiegel.

435. THE BINDING OF ISAAC

Some time afterward, God put Abraham to the test. He said to him, "Abraham," and he answered, "Here I am." And He said, "Take your son, your favored one, Isaac, whom you love, and go to the land of Moriah, and offer him there as a burnt offering on one of the heights that I will point out to you." So early next morning, Abraham saddled his ass and took with him two of his servants and his son Isaac. He split the wood for the burnt offering, and he set out for the place of which God had told him. On the third day Abraham looked up and saw the place from afar. Then Abraham said to his servants, "You stay here with the ass. The boy and I will go up there; we will worship and we will return to you."

Abraham took the wood for the burnt offering and put it on his son Isaac. He himself took the firestone and the knife; and the two walked off together. Then Isaac said to his father Abraham, "Father!" And he answered, "Yes, my son." And he said, "Here are the firestone and the wood; but where is the sheep for the burnt offering?" And Abraham said, "God will see to the sheep for His burnt offering, my son." And the two of them walked on together.

They arrived at the place of which God had told him. Abraham built an altar there; he laid out the wood; he bound his son Isaac; he laid him on the altar, on top of the wood. And Abraham picked up the knife to slay his son. Then an angel of the Lord called to him from heaven: "Abraham! Abraham!" And he answered, "Here I am." And he said, "Do not raise your hand against the boy, or do anything to him. For now I know that you fear God, since you have not withheld your son, your favored one, from Me." When Abraham looked up, his eye fell upon a ram, caught in the thicket by its horns. So Abraham went and took the ram and offered it up as a burnt offering in place of his son. And Abraham named that site Adonai-yireh, whence the present saying, "On the mount of the Lord there is vision."

The angel of the Lord called to Abraham a second time from heaven, and said, "By Myself I swear, the Lord declares: Because you have done this and have not withheld your son, your favored one, I will bestow My blessing upon you and make your descendants as numerous as the stars of heaven and the sands on the seashore; and your descendants shall seize the gates of their foes. All the nations of the earth shall bless themselves by your descendants, because you have obeyed My command." Abraham then returned to his servants, and they departed together for Beersheva; and Abraham stayed in Beersheva.

> The Binding of Isaac (*Akedat Yitzhak*) is one of the central episodes of the Bible. It is the subject of great debate and many midrashic versions exist. The most perplexing aspects of this narrative are God's command that Abraham sacrifice Isaac and Abraham's almost robotic willingness to fulfill it. Considerable tension exists between God's promise to Abraham that his descendants will be like the stars of the sky, and God's insistence that Abraham sacrifice the son through whom he expects that promise can be fulfilled (Gen. 17:19).
>
> This biblical episode is especially difficult to explain to children, for it is impossible to justify a parent's sacrifice of his or her child. When stripped of its biblical quaintness, it is a terrible story, and similar ones about a parent murdering a child provoke nothing but horror. The biblical account is generally viewed as a divine test of faith, which Abraham passes, as Job does. Adam and Eve, who are subjected to another such divine test, fail it and are expelled from the Garden of Eden.
>
> One possibility is that this episode was originally a kind of boilerplate narrative, perhaps not Israelite in origin, about a human sacrifice to a god. The editors of the Genesis, then, took this sacrifice narrative, inserted Abraham and Isaac, and instead of having the man slay his son, had an angel of the Lord stop him at the last moment, with an animal—the ram in the thicket—sacrificed in Isaac's place. The precedent set is clear: from this time on there shall be no more human sacrifices, but they shall be replaced by animal sacrifices. This remained the precedent until the destruction of the Temple in Jerusalem, after which even animal sacrifices were eliminated, since there was no remaining altar on which to perform the sacrifice.

Sources:
Genesis 22:1-19.

Studies:
The Last Trial by Shalom Spiegel.
The Death and Resurrection of the Beloved Son by Jon D. Levenson.
"The Return of a Myth in Genesis Rabbah on the Akeda" by M. R. Niehoff.
"Seeing with the Sages: Midrash as Visualization in the Legends of the *Aqedah*" by
    Marc Bregman in *Agendas for the Study of Midrash in the Twenty-First Century*.

436. HOW ABRAHAM RECOGNIZED MOUNT MORIAH

God told Abraham, "*Take your son, your favored one, Isaac, whom you love, and go to the land of Moriah, and offer him there as a burnt offering on one of the heights that I will point out to you*" (Gen. 22:2). Abraham did find that mountain, as it is said, *On the third day Abraham looked up and saw the place from afar* (Gen. 22:4). But how did Abraham recognize Mount Moriah?

Some say that Abraham saw a cloud enveloping the mountain and knew that was the place where God wanted him to sacrifice his son. Abraham asked Isaac if he saw anything, and Isaac pointed to the cloud hovering above the mountain. But neither of the two young men who accompanied Abraham and Isaac to Mount Moriah saw anything at all.

Others say that Abraham said to God, "Master of the Universe, upon which mountain?" God replied, "You will see My glory waiting for you. That is how you will recognize the altar." So it was that Abraham *saw the place from afar*. There he saw the glory of the *Shekhinah* standing on top of the mountain in the form of a pillar of fire reaching from earth to heaven. He asked Isaac if he saw anything and Isaac said, "Yes, I see a pillar of fire reaching into heaven." When Isaac said this, Abraham knew that his son was acceptable as a burnt-offering.

Still others say that there was a light shining and a cloud clinging to the top of that mountain, and Abraham knew that was the *Shekhinah* and the place of the sacrifice.

Then there are those who say that when Abraham approached the mountain, the finger of God pointed it out to him.

> Genesis 22:4 recounts that *Abraham looked up, and saw the place from afar.* However, just how Abraham was able to recognize Mount Moriah is not explained, thereby opening it to midrashic interpretation. The two primary explanations are that Abraham saw a cloud, or else he saw the *Shekhinah*—God's Presence—above the mountain, which took the form of a pillar of fire. This pillar recalls, of course, the pillar of cloud and the pillar of fire that led the Israelites in the wilderness. This interpretation derives from the word *ha-Makom*, meaning "the place," which is also understood to be one of the names of God. Thus in seeing "the place," Abraham saw God. Here the term *Shekhinah* carries its midrashic, pre-kabbalistic meaning, referring to God's presence rather than God's Bride.
>
> *Sources:*
> Genesis Rabbah 55:7, 56:2; *Midrash Tanhuma, Va-Yera* 46; *Midrash Tanhuma-Yelammedenu, Va-Yera* 22, 23; *Pirkei de-Rabbi Eliezer* 31.
>
> *Studies:*
> "Seeing with the Sages: Midrash as Visualization in the Legends of the *Aqedah*" by Marc Bregman in *Agendas for the Study of Midrash in the Twenty-First Century.*
> *Through a Speculum that Shines: Vision and Imagination in Medieval Jewish Mysticism,* pp. 13-51 by Elliot Wolfson.

437. THE SACRIFICE

Abraham and Sarah lived in the Land of Israel and their lives were good, but they didn't have any children. One day Abraham prayed to God and said, "If You give me a son, I'll give him to You as a sacrifice."

At the age of one hundred, Abraham had a son and he named him Isaac. The boy grew and Abraham forgot his promise to God. After several years God came to Abraham in a dream and said, "Abraham, you promised that you would give Me your son as a sacrifice."

In the morning, when Abraham awoke, he remembered the dream, and he said to Sarah, "I am going to take my son to study. Don't worry about him. He will be with me."

Abraham took Isaac and went to the forest. They were both silent. But when they arrived, Isaac said, "Father, why did you bring me here?" Abraham said, "My son, before you were born I had to make a vow that if I had a son, I would sacrifice him to God." Isaac said, "Father, I am ready." So Abraham tied the hands of Isaac behind his back and laid him on the wood, and he took the knife in his hand and put it on Isaac's neck. At that instant Abraham heard the voice of God: "Abraham, Abraham, leave the child. I have already received the sacrifice you wanted to give Me. Look, there is a sheep. Sacrifice it to Me instead of your son."

So Abraham untied his son, caught the sheep, and sacrificed it to God.

> The oral retelling of the binding of Isaac from India makes some crucial changes from the biblical account. The most crucial is that in the oral version Abraham and God reach a bargain whereby God will give him a son, and Abraham will sacrifice the son to God. This is much different than the sudden demand by God in Genesis 22 that Abraham sacrifice Isaac. Nevertheless, this oral version ends as does the biblical one, with God stopping the sacrifice at the last minute, and an animal being sacrificed instead of Isaac. It is possible that this oral retelling of Genesis 22 may be closer to the original oral version of the myth than that found in the Bible, as it follows a folk pattern in which a parent desperate for a child vows to give that child to the god who

provides it. See, for example, the story of the birth of Samuel in 1 Samuel 1:1-28. Also, Hannah makes a similar bargain with the Jewish God in 1 Samuel 1:11. Another example, closer to the spirit of the present tale, is "The Black Hand" in *Lilith's Cave*, pp. 197-198.

Sources:
IFA 9586, 12921.

438. SATAN AT MOUNT MORIAH

While Abraham and Isaac were traveling on the road to Mount Moriah, Satan appeared to Abraham in the guise of an old man and asked him where he was going. Abraham answered, "To pray." The old man asked, "Why then are you carrying wood, fire, and a knife?" Abraham answered, "We may spend a day or two there, and we will kill an animal, cook and eat it."

"Old man," said Satan, "are you out of your mind? You are going to slay a son given to you at the age of one hundred! And tomorrow, when you do, He will tell you that you are a murderer, guilty of shedding your son's blood." Abraham said, "Still, I would obey Him." And Abraham turned away from Satan.

Seeing that he could not sway Abraham, Satan appeared to Isaac in the guise of a young man and said, "Run now for your life. Your old father has lost his mind, and he is planning to sacrifice you. All those fine things your mother prepared for you are to be the inheritance of Ishmael." But Isaac refused to pay heed to him and continued to travel with his father.

When Satan saw that Abraham and Isaac had spurned him, he turned himself into a great river lying across their path. Abraham strode into the water, which reached his knees. "Follow me," he said. By the time they reached midstream, the water was up to their necks. At that moment Abraham called out to God, and God rebuked Satan, the river dried up, and they stood on dry land.

> This midrash makes the underlying assumption that God and Satan have made a wager concerning Abraham's willingness to sacrifice Isaac, much as they made a wager in the prologue to Job. God believes that Abraham will follow through on whatever He commands him to do, including the sacrifice of Isaac. Satan seeks to stop Abraham from going through with the *Akedah*, the binding of Isaac. First Satan takes the form of an old man, then a young man, then a river blocking their path. But all three attempts fail.
>
> One way of looking at this midrash is that it permits the rabbis to express through the mouth of Satan their doubts about God's command to Abraham. What Satan says to Abraham and Isaac makes good sense, and reflects rabbinic incredulity at God's command to Abraham to sacrifice Isaac. Since these doubts cannot be expressed directly, they are expressed indirectly by putting them in the mouth of Satan.
>
> These kinds of doubts are also found in some other midrashim, such as the blunt exchanges between Abraham and Isaac recounted in *Ner ha-Hayim* and *Yalkut Shim'oni* 1:101: "Isaac said to Abraham, 'My father, what are you doing with me?' Abraham answered, 'I am going to carry out your Maker's will.' Isaac said, 'What will you say to my poor old mother?' He answered, 'I will tell her that Isaac has been slaughtered.' 'You will kill her and be guilty of her death,' said Isaac. 'Instead, when you have burnt me, take my ashes to my mother, perhaps she would find consolation in them.' 'So it will be,' said Abraham."

Sources:
B. Sanhedrin 89b; Genesis Rabbah 56:4; Midrash va-Yosha; Midrash Tanhuma-
 Yelammedenu, Va-Yera 22; Pesikta Rabbati 40:67-69; IFA 10022.

Studies:
The Last Trial by Shalom Spiegel.

439. ISAAC SEES THE *SHEKHINAH*

Isaac asked his father, "Here are the fire and the wood, but where is the lamb for a burnt-offering?" Abraham answered, "You are the lamb for the burnt-offering."

When Isaac was bound upon the fire, he saw the heavens open, and he saw the *Shekhinah* above him in heaven, ready to receive him. Then Isaac broke forth into song. What song did he sing? The song of sacrifice.

> Here Isaac is willing to let himself be sacrificed, and when he is bound on the altar he has a vision of the *Shekhinah* and breaks into song. This grows out of the tradition that when the righteous see the *Shekhinah*, they break straightway into song.
>
> For other versions of Isaac's heavenly vision, see "Isaac's Ascent," p. 171.
>
> *Sources:*
> *Sefer ha-Pardes; Midrash ha-Gadol, Bereshit* 22:3.

440. GOD BINDS THE PRINCES OF THE HEATHENS

Even as Abraham bound his son Isaac below, so did God bind the princes of the heathens above and make them subservient to Israel. Yet they did not remain so bound, for Israel alienated themselves from God. God said, "Do you think that those fetters are forever? When Israel breaks its covenant with Me, their fetters are broken."

> Here God immediately rewards Israel when Abraham binds Isaac to the altar by binding the princes of the heathens—the angels who served as guardians to the heathen nations—thus making them subservient to Israel. But this fettering only lasts while Israel upholds its part of the covenant with God. When Israel fails to do so, God unfetters the princes, and the heathen nations take their revenge on Israel.
>
> Perhaps the most interesting thing about this myth is the parallelism between earth and heaven: just as Abraham binds his son, God binds the princes of the heathens. Other parallels between above and below are often found in the midrashic and kabbalistic texts, such as the parallels between the heavenly and earthly Jerusalem.
>
> *Sources:*
> *Genesis Rabbah* 56:5.

441. THE ANGEL WHO SAVED ISAAC

When Isaac was bound upon the altar, and Abraham's arm was upraised, with the knife in his hand, God called upon the Angel of the Lord and said, "Tell him not to lay his hand on the lad, nor to do anything to him." And the angel called to him from heaven, saying, "Abraham, Abraham, lay not your hand upon the lad." Abraham was terrified when he heard the voice, and he put down the blade. Thus was Isaac spared and a ram that was caught in the thorns sacrificed in his place.

> The *Akedah*, or binding of Isaac, was the subject of extensive midrashic revision. While this retelling of Genesis 22:10-12 does not stray far from the biblical text, it changes the perspective from Mount Moriah, where Abraham is about to sacrifice Isaac, to heaven, where God calls upon an angel to stop Abraham from slaying Isaac. In *The Book of Jubilees*, this change in perspective is even more striking because it is the angel himself who tells the story, speaking in the first person. This is an excellent

example of the midrashic method, where details missing in the biblical text—specifically, God ordering the Angel of the Lord to stop Abraham—are inserted to resolve any problems in the text. For another midrashic version of the *Akedah*, see "Isaac's Ascent," p. 171.

Sources
The Book of Jubilees 18:8-12.

442. ISAAC'S VISION AT MOUNT MORIAH

When Abraham bound Isaac at Mount Moriah, Isaac's eyes gazed at the heavenly angels. Thus Isaac saw the angels present there, but Abraham did not. As soon as the sword touched his neck, Isaac's soul departed. But when the voice of the angel rang out, *"Do not raise your hand against the boy"* (Gen. 22:12), his soul returned to his body. Abraham loosened his bonds, and Isaac stood on his feet. Then Isaac knew that there is a resurrection of the dead, and he said, "Blessed are You, O God, who resurrect the dead."

When Rebecca first saw Isaac, he was wrapped in a *tallit*, and his appearance was like an angel of God. Later, Isaac returned to Mount Moriah, and through his prayer he changed God's decree that his wife be barren for twenty-two years. For when Isaac entreated the Lord for his wife, Rebecca conceived.

After Abraham died, God appeared to Isaac and blessed him. Nor did God appear to Isaac with the *Merkavah*, the Divine Chariot, but instead the *Shekhinah* rested directly upon him. So too did God give Isaac a taste of the World to Come while he was still in this world, and as a result the Evil Inclination had no power over him.

> Some of the most remarkable traditions concern Isaac. Very little is said about Isaac in the Torah. He is first encountered as a child (although later rabbinic tradition in *Seder Olam Rabbah* 1 and elsewhere claims he was 37 at the time of the *Akedah*), and later, as an old, blind man on his deathbed, so little of his life between youth and old age is known. This very absence of narrative produces some strange traditions, such as that which asserts that Isaac was slain by Abraham at Mount Moriah and his soul ascended into Paradise for three years before he was reborn. See "The Ascent of Isaac," p. 171. This myth, which runs counter to the central thrust of the *Akedah* narrative, that Abraham did not sacrifice Isaac, seems to have strong Christian echoes, especially in the use of the number three, specifically the three days after his death when Jesus was said to be resurrected. From a Christian perspective, the binding of Isaac was identified as prefiguring the passion of Jesus. The verse *God Himself will provide the sacrifice, my son* (Gen. 22:8) is understood in Christianity to mean that God will provide Himself—the Christian notion that Jesus and God are one, and that in sacrificing Jesus, God was sacrificing Himself.
>
> *Sources:*
> B. *Berakhot* 1:6; B. *Bava Metzia* 87a; B. *Bava Batra* 17a; *Genesis Rabbah* 61:6; *Pirkei de-Rabbi Eliezer* 31; *Midrash Tanhuma, Toledot* 2; *Midrash ha-Gadol* on *Genesis* 17:22; *Targum Yonathan* on Genesis 22:10; *Shoher Tov* 90:18; *The Book of Jubilees* 16:3, 16:12; Philo, *Legum Allegoriarum* 3:218-19; Philo, *De Somniis* 2:10; Philo, *De Congressu Eruditionis Gratia* 1:7-9; Philo, *De Cherubim* 43-47; Philo, *De Fuga et Inventione* 166-168; Philo, *De Ebrietate* 56-62; *Zohar* 1:60a.

443. SARAH'S TENT

While Sarah was alive, the cloud of the *Shekhinah* hovered at the entrance of her tent, the doors of the tent were wide open, her dough was blessed, and a light burned in her tent from one Sabbath eve to the next. When Sarah died, these all ceased. But although she had died, Sarah's likeness did not leave her tent. Yet no one saw her except for her son Isaac, for Abraham did not enter that room of the tent.

When Isaac brought Rebecca to the tent of Sarah, the light that had gone out at the time of Sarah's death immediately shone again.

> This myth emphasizes the holiness of Sarah, since the cloud of the *Shekhinah* hovered at her tent. After Sarah died, this cloud disappeared, along with a light that burned all week. Nevertheless, Sarah's presence—like a ghost—remained, although only her son, Isaac, could see it. This seems like a mythic expression of a quite human experience, sensing the presence of one's parents in their house long after they are gone. When Isaac married Rebecca, the light returned to the tent, meaning that Rebecca, like Sarah, was a holy person. Note, however, that there is no mention of the cloud of the *Shekhinah* returning, or that Rebecca's dough was blessed. Thus Rebecca was holy, but not to the extent of Sarah. This last detail about the dough seems to confirm the adage that as far as a man is concerned, no one can cook as well as his mother.
>
> Sources:
> *Targum Pseudo-Yonathan* 24:67; *Genesis Rabbah* 60:16; *Zohar* 1:133a-b.

444. THE DEATH OF SARAH

Some say that Satan came to Sarah when Abraham and Isaac were on Mount Moriah, and showed her a vision of Abraham with his knife raised above Isaac. And when Sarah saw that terrible vision, she cried out and was choked and died of anguish.

Others say that Satan came to Sarah in the guise of Isaac. When she asked what his father had done to him, Isaac told her that Abraham had taken him to the summit of a high mountain, built an altar, and laid out the firewood. He had bound Isaac on top of the altar, and took the knife to slaughter him. And if God had not told him, *"Do not raise your hand against the boy"* (Gen 22:12), he would already have been slaughtered. And even before Satan, disguised as Isaac, finished speaking, Sarah's soul departed.

> Sarah's death is recounted at the beginning of Genesis 23. There is no direct reference to the binding of Isaac in Genesis 22, but one of the rabbinic methods of interpretation was to assume that chapters next to each other were somehow related. Since no reason is given for Sarah's death in Genesis 23, it was understood to be related to the binding of Isaac. There is no mention in Genesis 22 that Abraham informed Sarah of his plans to sacrifice their son, and the shock of learning this might in itself be enough to kill her. Here Satan is held responsible for revealing Abraham's plans to Sarah, by showing her a terrible vision of Isaac bound on the altar and Abraham about to plunge a knife into him. The alternate version suggests that after Isaac returned, he told his mother what had happened, and this caused her soul to depart. In both cases, it is the binding of Isaac that is held responsible for Sarah's death.
>
> Sources:
> *Targum Pseudo-Yonathan* on Genesis 22:20; *Midrash Tanhuma, Va-Yera* 23.

445. THE CAVE OF MACHPELAH

When the three angels, disguised as travelers, visited Abraham, he went outside to fetch a young goat to slaughter for them. But the kid ran away from him, and he had to chase it through the fields to the entrance of a cave that Abraham had never entered.

The kid paused an instant and then disappeared inside the entrance and Abraham followed after it. At first the cave was low, so that Abraham had to bend down, but soon it opened into a beautiful chamber, illuminated by a mysterious light. There was a wonderful scent, like that of balsam. And there, in that chamber, Abraham found the bodies of Adam and Eve, lying on couches, with candles burning at their head and feet, and their bodies were perfectly preserved. Adam and Eve had chosen that cave as their place of burial, for it was the closest site to the Garden of Eden, and the scent that pervaded it was that of Eden itself, which drifted from the Garden into that cave.

When Abraham emerged, he knew that he had stumbled on a very holy place, and he decided then and there to purchase the cave from Ephron the Hittite, as a burial site for himself and his family. So too did he spare the kid that led him there. And that is the Cave of Machpelah in the city of Hebron, where the patriarchs Abraham, Isaac, and Jacob and their wives are buried, in the chamber next to that of Adam and Eve.

After Abraham was buried there, *Isaac went out to meditate in the field toward evening* (Gen. 24:63). This was the very field that Abraham had purchased near the Cave of Machpelah. When Isaac entered it, he would see the *Shekhinah* resting there and smell the heavenly fragrances that wafted from it. That is why he prayed there, and it was designated as a place of prayer.

> This is an important legend that solves two problems. First, it provides a burial site for Adam and Eve, which is not found in Genesis. The wonderful scent is assumed to come from the Garden of Eden, and therefore it is understood that Adam and Eve chose to be buried as close to the garden as possible. Secondly, this legend explains why Abraham chose to buy the Cave of Machpelah from Ephron in Genesis 23:7-16, for Abraham already knew since the time of visit of the three angels in Genesis 18 that the cave was a holy place.
>
> Of course, those creating this legend were already familiar with the tradition that Abraham, Isaac, and Jacob and their wives, Sarah, Rebecca, and Leah, were buried in that cave in Hebron. (Rachel has a separate grave.) By adding Adam and Eve to those already believed to be buried there, the cave was made even holier, and all of the key fathers and mothers were understood to be buried in the same place.
>
> Another myth links Adam and Eve to a cave that came to serve as their burial place. See *Apocalypse of Moses* 29:3-6, where Adam begs to take incense from the Garden of Eden with him when he is expelled. Adam is said to have hidden that incense in a cave. Indeed, this myth is a close variant of the present myth, where Abraham finds Adam and Eve lying on couches, with candles burning at their head and feet, in the Cave of Machpelah. There is a collection of ancient texts primarily linked to Genesis known as *The Cave of Treasures*, referring to the cave in which Adam was said to have hid the incense and later to have been buried there.
>
> *Sources:*
> Midrash Tehillim 92:6; Zohar 1:127b, 2:39b.

446. ABRAHAM'S DAUGHTER

In his old age, *God blessed Abraham in all things* (Gen. 24:1) What does this mean? It means that in addition to wealth and length of years, God gave Abraham a daughter. For surely having everything includes having both a son and a daughter. But where did this daughter come from? After all, she was born after the death of Sarah, and before Abraham married Keturah.

Some say that this daughter, whose name was Bakol ("In-All-Things"), was a child of Hagar, and that she was born after Ishmael repented of his evil ways.

Some say that Sarah not only gave birth to Isaac, but bore a daughter as well, who took care of Abraham in his old age. Others say that this daughter was actually an angel, who guarded Abraham so closely that everyone believed her to be his daughter. Still others say that she was not a daughter at all, but the wandering spirit of Sarah, who, having spent most of her life with Abraham, now returned to serve him after she departed from this world.

Just who this daughter was remains a mystery. Only this much is known: Abraham loved her dearly, and taught her all that he had learned, and she was the center of Abraham's household. And when Abraham took leave of this world, his daughter carried his teachings to the ends of the earth. And when the time came for her to take leave of this world, she joined him on high, and she still accompanies him in the World to Come.

> In order to fulfill the commandment to have children, it was regarded as necessary to have both a son and daughter. Since Genesis 24:1 states that Abraham was blessed "in all things," this was understood to mean that he also had a daughter, although nothing about such a daughter is found in the biblical text.
>
> *Sources:*
> B. Bava Batra 16b; B. Sukkah 49b; *Genesis Rabbah* 59:7; *Midrash Tanhuma, Hayei Sarah* 4; Ramban on Genesis 24:1; *Me'am Lo'ez on* Genesis 24:1; *Sefer ha-Bahir* 78.

447. THE DESCENT OF THE LIGHT-MAN

When the time came for Abraham to take leave of this world, God sent Isaac a dream. In the third hour of the night Isaac woke up, got up from his bed, and ran to the room where his mother and father were asleep. When Isaac reached the door, he cried out, "Father, open the door so that I may come in."

Abraham arose and opened the door, and Isaac entered and embraced him, crying loudly. And Abraham said, "Come here, son. Tell me the truth. What did you see that caused you to run to us in this way?"

Isaac said, "This night, Father, I saw in a dream the sun and moon above my head. They surrounded me with their rays and illuminated me. And while I rejoiced in their presence, I saw the heavens open and I saw a luminous man descending from heaven, shining more than seven suns. This man came and took the sun from my head and went back into the heavens. Then I was very sad, because he took the sun from me.

"A little later, while I was still mourning, he returned and took the moon from me, from above my head. I wept greatly and begged the Light-Man, saying "Have mercy on me. Take not my glory from me. If you take the sun from me, at least leave me the moon."

The Light-Man answered, "The King on high has sent me to bring them there." And he took them from me, but he left the rays that shone upon me.

Then Abraham said, "The Lord has sent an angel of God to take my soul."

> Here God sends Isaac a dream to warn him that the time has come for his father, Abraham, to die. In the dream Abraham and Sarah are identified as the sun and moon that are taken from above Isaac's head. This identification of the father and mother as the sun and moon is found in Joseph's dream in Genesis 37:9-10: *And he dreamed yet another dream, and told it to his brothers, and said, "Behold I have dreamed yet a dream: and behold, the sun and moon and eleven stars bowed down to me." And he told it to his father, and to his brothers, and his father rebuked him and said, "What is this dream that you have dreamed? Shall I and your mother and your brothers indeed come to bow down to you to the earth?"* Note that the meaning of the symbols of the sun and moon (and stars) is immediately understood by Jacob. Likewise, Abraham immediately understands the meaning of

Isaac's dream, and identifies the figure of the Light-Man with an angel who has been sent by God to take his life.

Although Isaac loses the sun and moon in the dream, it is interesting to note that after his plea to the Light-Man, the light that they cast on him remains behind. This light represents the glory they left behind in the form of Abraham's covenant with God.

The figure of the Light-Man is found in Gnostic texts. Here the Light-Man is said to have existed even before the demiurge. The Light-Man is closely identified with a Gnostic angel known as the Light-Adam in *On the Origins of the World* 108:2ff.

This myth of the descent of the Light-Man is found in *The Testament of Abraham*, a pseudepigraphal text of Jewish origins that recounts Abraham's resistance to leaving this world with the Angel of Death. Similar resistance is found in midrashic legends about Moses. Thus both of these patriarchal figures receive special attention from God when the time comes for them to take leave of this world, and both of them put up considerable resistance, so great is their passion to remain alive.

Sources:
The Testament of Abraham 5-7.

Studies:
The Enthronement of Sabaoth: Jewish Elements in Gnostic Creation Myths by Francis T. Fallon, pp. 89-94.

448. ABRAHAM AND THE ANGEL OF DEATH

God called upon the Angel of Death and said, "Come, hide your ferocity, cover your decay, and put on your youthful beauty and go down to Abraham and take him and bring him to Me. But do not terrify him; instead, take him with soft speech. So Death put on a radiant robe and assumed the form of an archangel and went to Abraham.

Abraham sat at the entrance of his tent in Mamre when a sweet odor came to him, and Abraham saw Death coming toward him in great glory. So Abraham arose and went to meet him, and Death knelt before him and said, "Most righteous Abraham, I am the bitter cup of death." Abraham said, "No, you have the glory and beauty of an angel." Death said, "I am telling you the truth."

Abraham said, "Why have you come here?" Death answered, "I have come for your holy soul." But Abraham refused to go with him, and arose and went into his house. Death followed him there, and went with him wherever he went in the house. Death said, "I will not depart until I take your spirit."

Then Abraham said, "I beg you, heed me and show me your ferocity." But Death said, "You could not bear to behold it, righteous Abraham." Abraham said, "Yes, I can, because the power of God is with me."

Then Death put off the bloom of youth and beauty and put on his robe of tyranny, and made his appearance gloomy and ferocious. He showed Abraham seven fiery heads of dragons and other faces, most horrible, each one fiercer than the other, including the face of a lion, the face of a horned serpent, and that of a cobra. And after he saw these things, Abraham said, "I beg you, Death, hide your ferocity and put on the form of youthful beauty that you had before."

Death hid his ferocious visage at once, and put on his youthful beauty. Then Abraham went to his room and lay down. And Death said to Abraham, "Come, kiss my right hand, and may life and strength come to you." But Death deceived Abraham, for when Abraham kissed his hand, his soul cleaved to Death's hand. At that moment the angel Michael, along with multitudes of angels, carried away Abraham's precious soul in their hands, in divinely woven linen.

As with Moses and Rabbi Joshua ben Levi, God gave instructions to the Angel of Death to take Abraham gently because of his great righteousness. But when Abraham refuses to go, and insists that the angel reveal his true visage, he shows it to him and it is truly terrible. After that Abraham no longer resists the angel.

This myth serves as a reminder that everyone, even Abraham, must one day encounter the deadly angel, and as a reminder of how truly terrifying the angel is. For other myths about the Angel of Death, see "Rabbi Joshua ben Levi and the Angel of Death," p. 206, and "Rabbi Loew and the Angel of Death," p. 207.

Sources:
The Testament of Abraham 16-20.

449. ABRAHAM'S DYING VISION

A vision came to Abraham on the day of his death. The voice of the Lord came to him and said, "Open your eyes, and see your reward." Then Abraham felt that he was lifted up by the wind, higher and higher, and suddenly he arrived at a place of great light, where gates of precious stones were opened before him, and myriads of angels approached him. They clothed him in eight garments of light, and a thousand fragrant odors came from the Garden of Eden and perfumed his garments. The angels put two crowns of onyx and fine gold on his head, and eight myrtles in his hand, and the world was filled with their odor.

Then the angels brought Abraham to a place where rivers flowed with pure water, and roses and myrtles surrounded them, and their fragrance filled him with infinite delight. He came to a wonderful canopy that had been prepared for him, with four rivers flowing in front of it of honey, wine, oil, and balsam. Above the canopy there were golden vines and pearls shining like stars.

At that instant Abraham was suddenly transformed into a happy child, and he saw a great many happy children coming toward him. Abraham played with them and ran with them to hear the wonderful songs of the angels. They walked among sweet-smelling trees and rested under the Tree of Life. Then childhood passed and youth began. The children vanished, and Abraham enjoyed the companionship of handsome young men, and they walked through the length and breadth of the garden. His soul was satisfied with unbounded delight. Then youth passed and old age came, and dignified old men spoke with him about the life of man and the ways of God. They led Abraham to his two canopies, one made of the light of the sun and one of the light of the moon. Abraham saw that there was a partition of lightning between them. He passed through the partition and beheld three hundred and ten marvelous worlds. Then the voice of the Lord came to Abraham, saying, "What you see now is but the fringe of Paradise; you cannot see the whole of it except with the eyes of God." And Abraham said, "O Lord, take my soul to rest." And God took the soul of Abraham to heaven Himself, and so Abraham's life on earth came to an end.

Before dying, God sends Abraham a wonderful vision of the reward awaiting him in the Garden of Eden. In the course of this vision he relives his life, from childhood to old age. Finally Abraham learns that all the wonders he has seen and experienced— with considerable emphasis on the visual and sensual delights—are but the fringes of Paradise. God makes the interesting observation that the whole can only be seen with the eyes of God. (See "The Eyes of God," p. 21.) Thus reassured, Abraham requests that God take his soul, and thus dies peacefully.

Abraham's ascent into Paradise is similar to those of Adam in *Vita Adae et Evae* and those of Enoch in the Books of Enoch. Moses also ascended on high, as did the four sages who entered Paradise. See "The Ascent of Moses," p. 171 and "The Four Who Entered Paradise," p. 173.

This account is in stark contrast to many of the traditions about the death of Moses, who is said to have fiercely resisted the Angel of Death. But in the end, as with Abraham, it is God Himself who takes his soul.

Sources:
Yalkut Shim'oni, Hayei Sarah; Testament of Abraham (A) 11:1; *Vita Adae et Evae* 25:3, 42:4; *Zohar* 1:212a.

450. ABRAHAM NEVER DIED

There are those who insist that Abraham never died, and that he continues to wander the world. There are many reports of those who have seen him. One story tells of a mysterious Tenth Man.

For many years only a few Jews were permitted by the Muslim authorities to live in Hebron, where the patriarchs Abraham, Isaac, and Jacob and their wives are buried. Once there were so few that on the eve of Yom Kippur, only nine Jews had gathered in the House of Prayer in the city of Hebron, and there was no one else they could call on to complete the *minyan*. The sun was setting, but they could not begin Kol Nidrei.

Just then there was a knock on the door, and when the *gabbai* answered it, he found an old Jew standing there, a stranger with a long white beard, wearing a white robe, carrying a white *tallit*. The *gabbai* gladly invited him in and asked to know his name. The old man said it was Abraham. Then, since the tenth man had arrived, they began the prayers, and the old man joined in with them.

The old man remained there with them, praying all night and the next day, until Yom Kippur had come to an end. Never before had they prayed for so long without stopping, but somehow not one of them felt tired, nor did hunger pangs trouble them. All were aware that the power of the Divine Presence filled the House of Prayer.

When the Day of Atonement had ended, the old man took his leave, but he left his *tallit* behind. The *gabbai* hurried after him to return it, but he was nowhere to be found. That night the *gabbai* had a dream in which the old man returned to him and revealed that he was actually the patriarch Abraham. So too did he reveal that he had left the *tallit* behind for him and that it was sacred. For if he wore it when he prayed, he would be permitted a vision of the Divine Presence. The *gabbai* told the others his dream, and they were filled with wonder to learn the true identity of the old man.

The *gabbai* put on the *tallit* of Abraham when he prayed that day. And during the silent prayer, when he closed his eyes for an instant, he saw a vision of the Divine Presence glowing in the dark. Afterward, whenever he closed his eyes, the vision would return, as if it were imprinted there.

As for the *tallit*, it is said that Abraham returned to the *gabbai* in a dream shortly before he died, and told him to request that he be buried in it. This was done, and no sooner did they cover his body with that prayer shawl than his soul found itself in Paradise, inside the synagogue of Abraham the patriarch. There he was made *gabbai* in that heavenly House of Prayer, where he serves the patriarch Abraham to this day, still wrapped in that sacred *tallit*.

There is an extensive tradition attributing immortality to the key patriarchal figures. Not only is Abraham portrayed as never having died, but there are also accounts about Jacob, Moses, and King David still being alive. Some of these are found in rabbinic sources, and others in Jewish folklore, some of it still recounted orally by the

Lubavitch Hasidim and in other Orthodox circles, as in this case. This is a well-known medieval folktale that has entered later Orthodox oral tradition as if it were a midrash.

Sources:
Sefer ha-Ma'asiyot 95-96; Collected from Rabbi Yosef Landa by Howard Schwartz.

451. THE BIRTHS OF JACOB AND ESAU

Isaac pleaded with the Lord on behalf of his wife, because she was barren; and the Lord responded to his plea, and his wife Rebecca conceived. But the children struggled in her womb, and she said, "If so, why do I exist?" She went to inquire of the Lord, and the Lord answered her, "Two nations are in your womb, two separate peoples shall issue from your body; one people shall be mightier than the other, and the older shall serve the younger."

When her time to give birth was at hand, there were twins in her womb. The first one emerged red all over; so they named him Esau. Then his brother emerged, holding on to the heel of Esau; so they named him Jacob. Isaac was sixty years old when they were born.

> The rabbis were well aware that the portrayal of Jacob in Genesis revealed many negative qualities about him. They were loath to accept this portrayal, because Jacob was an important patriarch, and especially because his name became Israel, from which the nation of Israel took its name. Therefore there is an intensive whitewashing process found in the rabbinic texts. Some midrashim attribute intention to the unborn twins, Jacob and Esau, and shows that their conflict started in the womb. *Genesis Rabbah* 63:6 describes how when Rebecca stood near a synagogue, Jacob struggled to come out. When she passed idolatrous temples, Esau struggled to come out. Rebecca went to the academy of Shem and Eber, and they explained that "There are two nations in your womb. At their birth they will be separated. One will enjoy the pleasures of this world, and the other the delights of the world to come."
>
> Another midrash asserts that Jacob was destined to be born first, but Esau refused to accept this, and therefore Jacob held back in order not to harm his mother, Rebecca, but that he held on to Esau's heel as a sign that it was he who was really supposed to have been the eldest. This view thus justifies Jacob forcing Esau to sell his birthright to him, and Jacob later stealing his brother's blessing, and therefore goes a long way toward mitigating the acts that otherwise identify Jacob as one who tricked and cheated his father and his brother (*Midrash ha-Gadol* 1:390-391).
>
> *Sources:*
> Genesis 25:21-26.

452. ISAAC RETURNS TO MOUNT MORIAH

After Isaac took Rebecca as his wife, she was barren for twenty-two years. So Isaac took Rebecca with him and went back to Mount Moriah, to the place where he had been bound, and he prayed that she should conceive, as it is said, *Isaac pleaded with Yahweh on behalf of his wife* (Gen. 25:21). And by his prayer Isaac changed the intention of God, who had decreed that he and Rebecca would be barren. After that, Rebecca became pregnant with twins.

> This legend from *Targum Pseudo-Yonathan* adds an important detail to Genesis 25:21-23, where Isaac prays that Rebecca should conceive. It identifies the place of his prayer as Mount Moriah. On the one hand, this is strange, since Isaac's experience there was so traumatic. On the other hand, Isaac was well aware that it was a holy place, where he could communicate with God. See "The Births of Jacob and Esau," p. 349.
>
> *Sources:*
> *Targum Pseudo-Yonathan* on Genesis 25:20; *Pirkei de-Rabbi Eliezer* 32; *Sefer ha-Yashar* 26.

453. THE BARTERED BIRTHRIGHT

When the boys grew up, Esau became a skillful hunter, a man of the outdoors; but Jacob was a mild man who stayed in camp. Isaac favored Esau because he had a taste for game; but Rebecca favored Jacob. Once when Jacob was cooking a stew, Esau came in from the open, famished. And Esau said to Jacob, "Give me some of that red stuff to gulp down, for I am famished"— which is why he was named Edom. Jacob said, "First sell me your birthright." And Esau said, "I am at the point of death, so of what use is my birthright to me?" But Jacob said, "Swear to me first." So he swore to him, and sold his birthright to Jacob. Jacob then gave Esau bread and lentil stew; he ate and drank, and he rose and went away. Thus did Esau spurn the birthright.

> This famous episode from Genesis clearly establishes the pattern between Jacob and Esau, in which Jacob plays an underhanded role in forcing his brother to sell his birthright for a bowl of lentils. It is hard, if not impossible, to justify Jacob's behavior, although the midrashic texts try to do this by asserting that Jacob was destined to be born first, but he and Esau struggled in the womb, and Jacob permitted Esau to go first so as not to harm their mother, Rebecca. The idea of selling something of value for something worthless has become an aphorism about selling something of value for a bowl of pottage.
>
> *Sources:*
> Genesis 25:27-34.

454. RED LENTILS

Lentils are the food of mourning and sorrow. When Cain killed Abel, Adam and Eve ate lentils as a sign of their mourning over him. And when Haran was burned in Nimrod's furnace, his parents ate lentils as a sign of mourning. And when his grandfather, Abraham, died, Jacob boiled dishes of lentils as a sign of mourning and sorrow, and as a sign that it was a house of mourning. Then he went to comfort his father, Isaac.

The lentils were a sign of mourning, but Esau was unconcerned about the death of his grandfather; nothing mattered but to satisfy his hunger. This proves that he not only gave up his birthright, he rejected belief in the resurrection of the dead as well. Therefore he was undeserving of his birthright. How do we know that God agreed with this? Because it says, *Thus says Yahweh: "Israel is My first-born son"* (Exod. 4:22). Then Gabriel and Michael recorded that the birthright belonged to Jacob. And since the birthright was his, so too was the Blessing of the Firstborn, which belonged to the one who possessed the birthright.

> This midrash is part of an extensive reinterpretation of Jacob's acts in order to justify everything he did, since he, more than any other patriarch, is identified with the nation of Israel. That is because Jacob's name is changed to Israel in Genesis 32:29, after he wrestles with the angel. Here, to justify Jacob's behavior in requiring his brother to pay with his birthright for a dish of lentils, *B. Bava Batra* 16b suggests that Abraham, the grandfather of Jacob and Esau, had died that day, and that Jacob had prepared the dish to comfort his father, Isaac. *Pirkei de-Rabbi Eliezer* 35 states that, "Lentils are the food of mourning and sorrow." Thus their preparation would indicate a house of mourning. *Targum Pseudo-Yonathan* on Genesis 25:29 inserts into the biblical text: "The day Abraham died, Jacob boiled dishes of lentils and went to comfort his father." This traditional sign of mourning is also linked to Adam and Eve and to the death of Haran, suggesting that it was an old and widely known custom, and therefore Esau should have immediately asked if anyone had died. Because he did not, he proved himself to be unworthy of his birthright and the Blessing of the Firstborn.

B. Bava Batra 16b considers the appropriateness of the lentil as a sign of mourning: "Just as a lentil is round, so mourning comes around to everyone in the world. Just as a lentil has no mouth, so a mourner has no mouth, for a mourner does not speak." Lentils have continued to be used as a food prepared for Jewish mourners.

For more on the transformation of Jacob in rabbinic texts, see "Jacob the Blessed," p. 353. For more on the cult of Jacob that greatly elevated his status to the near-divine, see "Jacob the Angel," p. 364, and "Jacob the Divine," p. 366.

Sources:
Targum Pseudo-Yonathan on Genesis 25:29; *Pirkei de-Rabbi Eliezer* 35; *B. Bava Batra* 16b; *Genesis Rabbah* 63:14.

455. ISAAC'S EYES GROW DIM

When Abraham tied Isaac down to the altar at Mount Moriah, Isaac lifted up his eyes heavenwards and saw the glory of the *Shekhinah*. After that his eyes began to grow dim, as it is said, *When Isaac was old and his eyes were too dim to see* (Gen. 27:1).

This midrash links Isaac's being bound on Mount Moriah with his blindness in his old age. It is part of a tradition that Isaac had an intense mystical experience on Mount Moriah. In other versions, the tears of the angels on high, watching the drama unfold, fell into Isaac's eyes and brought on his subsequent blindness. See "Isaac's Ascent," p. 171.

Sources:
Targum Pseudo-Yonathan on Genesis 27:1; *Genesis Rabbah* 65:10; *Deuteronomy Rabbah* 11:3; *Pirkei de-Rabbi Eliezer* 32.

456. THE STOLEN BLESSING

When Isaac was old and his eyes were too dim to see, he called his older son Esau and said to him, "My son." He answered, "Here I am." And he said, "I am old now, and I do not know how soon I may die. Take your gear, your quiver and bow, and go out into the open and hunt me some game. Then prepare a dish for me such as I like, and bring it to me to eat, so that I may give you my innermost blessing before I die."

Rebecca had been listening as Isaac spoke to his son Esau. When Esau had gone out into the open to hunt game to bring home, Rebecca said to her son Jacob, "I overheard your father speaking to your brother Esau, saying, 'Bring me some game and prepare a dish for me to eat, that I may bless you, with the Lord's approval, before I die.' Now, my son, listen carefully as I instruct you. Go to the flock and fetch me two choice kids, and I will make of them a dish for your father, such as he likes. Then take it to your father to eat, in order that he may bless you before he dies." Jacob answered his mother Rebecca, "But my brother Esau is a hairy man and I am smooth skinned. If my father touches me, I shall appear to him as a trickster and bring upon myself a curse, not a blessing." But his mother said to him, "Your curse, my son, be upon me! Just do as I say and go fetch them for me."

He got them and brought them to his mother, and his mother prepared a dish such as his father liked. Rebecca then took the best clothes of her older son Esau, which were there in the house, and had her younger son Jacob put them on; and she covered his hands and the hairless part of his neck with the skins of the kids. Then she put in the hands of her son Jacob the dish and the bread that she had prepared.

He went to his father and said, "Father." And he said, "Yes, which of my sons are you?" Jacob said to his father, "I am Esau, your firstborn; I have done as you told me. Pray sit up and eat of my game, that you may give me your innermost blessing." Isaac said to his son, "How did you succeed so quickly, my son?" And he said, "Because the Lord your God granted me good fortune." Isaac said to Jacob, "Come closer that I may feel you, my son—whether you are really my son Esau or not." So Jacob drew close to his father Isaac, who felt him and wondered. "The voice is the voice of Jacob, yet the hands are the hands of Esau." He did not recognize him, because his hands were hairy like those of his brother Esau; and so he blessed him.

He asked, "Are you really my son Esau?" And when he said, "I am," he said, "Serve me and let me eat of my son's game that I may give you my innermost blessing." So he served him and he ate, and he brought him wine and he drank. Then his father Isaac said to him, "Come close and kiss me, my son;" and he went up and kissed him. And he smelled his clothes and he blessed him, saying, "Ah, the smell of my son is like the smell of the fields that the Lord has blessed. May God give you of the dew of heaven and the fat of the earth, abundance of new grain and wine. Let peoples serve you, and nations bow to you; be master over your brothers, and let your mother's sons bow to you. Cursed be they who curse you, blessed they who bless you."

No sooner had Jacob left the presence of his father Isaac—after Isaac had finished blessing Jacob—than his brother Esau came back from his hunt. He too prepared a dish and brought it to his father. And he said to his father, "Let my father sit up and eat of his son's game, so that you may give me your innermost blessing." His father Isaac said to him, "Who are you?" And he said, "I am your son, Esau, your first-born!" Isaac was seized with very violent trembling. "Who was it then," he demanded, "that hunted game and brought it to me? Moreover, I ate of it before you came, and I blessed him; now he must remain blessed!" When Esau heard his father's words, he burst into wild and bitter sobbing, and said to his father, "Bless me too, Father!" But he answered, "Your brother came with guile and took away your blessing." Esau said, "Was he, then, named Jacob that he might supplant me these two times? First he took away my birthright and now he has taken away my blessing!" And he added, "Have you not reserved a blessing for me?" Isaac answered, saying to Esau, "But I have made him master over you: I have given him all his brothers for servants, and sustained him with grain and wine. What, then, can I still do for you, my son?" And Esau said to his father, "Have you but one blessing, Father? Bless me too, Father!" And Esau wept aloud. And his father Isaac answered, saying to him, "See, your abode shall enjoy the fat of the earth and the dew of heaven above. Yet by your sword you shall live, and you shall serve your brother; but when you grow restive, you shall break his yoke from your neck."

Now Esau harbored a grudge against Jacob because of the blessing that his father had given him, and Esau said to himself, "Let but the mourning period of my father come, and I will kill my brother Jacob." When the words of her older son Esau were reported to Rebecca, she sent for her younger son Jacob and said to him, "Your brother Esau is consoling himself by planning to kill you. Now, my son, listen to me. Flee at once to Haran, to my brother Laban. Stay with him a while, until your brother's fury subsides—until your brother's anger against you subsides—and he forgets what you have done to him. Then I will fetch you from there. Let me not lose you both in one day!"

> Before his death, Isaac calls in Esau to give him the Blessing of the Firstborn, which entitles him to virtually all of his father's property under the rights of primogeniture. Nevertheless, there are many cases in the Bible in which the firstborn did not receive a preferential share. These include Ishmael and Isaac, Esau and Jacob, Reuben and Joseph, and Joseph's sons, Manasseh and Ephraim. A modified version of the rights of primogeniture is given in Deuteronomy 21:15-17, which establishes that a man's property is inherited by his sons, the firstborn receiving a double share.

Rebecca schemes with Jacob to have him impersonate his brother and steal the blessing. For once it had been given, it could not be retrieved. The plan works, although Jacob lies to his father twice: once when Isaac asks if he is Esau, and by wearing goatskin on his hands, to make them appear hairy. Still, Isaac almost sees through the ruse: "The voice is the voice of Jacob, but the hands are the hands of Esau" (Gen. 27:23).

It was to receive this blessing that Jacob forced Esau to sell him his birthright. Having purchased it with a bowl of lentil stew, Jacob may have felt that he deserved the blessing from his father. See "The Bartered Birthright," p. 350.

This narrative reads like a staged play. Isaac calls in Esau; Rebecca plots with Jacob; Esau leaves, Jacob enters; Jacob leaves, Esau enters. It is a marvel of condensed understatement, but after this episode Rebecca and Jacob can never be viewed in the same light. *Honor your father and mother* is one of the Ten Commandments, and Jacob clearly does not honor his father in this story. He and Rebecca treat Isaac like an old, blind fool, who can easily be tricked. They also assume that Esau can be deceived. After this episode and that of the bartered birthright, Jacob's image as a trickster is imprinted for all time. Furthermore, this incident causes Jacob and Esau to become enemies, and Jacob is forced to flee to the home of his uncle Laban in Haran. Yet, ironically, this journey leads Jacob to discover the God of his fathers and to fulfill his destiny. In the end, Jacob the trickster has transformed into Jacob the patriarch, even though he does cross his arms when asked to bless Joseph's sons, and gives the Blessing of the Firstborn to the younger instead of to the elder. At that moment we catch a clear glimpse of Jacob the trickster (Gen. 48:8-15), as well as Jacob's rebellion against the right of ligature.

The Ugaritic stories of Aqhat have distinct parallels to this biblical episode, where the role of Esau is played by Aqhat the hunter, and the role of Rebecca is played by Anat, who tries to steal his inheritance.

Sources:
Genesis 27:1-45.

Studies:
Stories from Ancient Canaan trans. by M. D. Coogan, pp. 27-47.
An Anthology of Religious Texts from Ugarit by Johannes C. de Moor, pp. 224-269.

457. JACOB THE BLESSED

When Jacob entered into the presence of his father, Paradise entered with him. Isaac blessed Jacob with ten blessings, corresponding to the ten words by which the world was created. And when Jacob went forth from the presence of his father Isaac, he went forth crowned like a bridegroom, and the quickening dew from heaven descended upon him and refreshed his bones, and he became a mighty hero. That is why it is said, *By the hands of the Mighty One of Jacob—there, the Shepherd, the Rock of Israel* (Gen. 49:24).

The clear sense of the biblical text is that the plot of Rebecca and Jacob to trick Isaac is wrong. But because of the identification of Jacob with Israel, the midrashic text goes to extremes to justify his actions. Here, rather than leaving Isaac's tent like a thief, Jacob is described as going forth crowned like a bridegroom. This is part of the process by which all of Jacob's actions are whitewashed, while everything that Esau does is painted black. For example, *Targum Pseudo-Yonathan* on Genesis 25:29 states that "Esau came from the country, and he was exhausted because he had committed five transgressions that day: he had practiced idolatry; he had shed innocent blood; he had lain with a betrothed maiden; he had denied the life of the world to come; and he had despised his birthright."

For some of the radical interpretations of the Jacob myth, see "Jacob the Angel," p. 364, and "Jacob the Divine," p. 366.

Sources:
Pirkei de-Rabbi Eliezer 32; *Song of Songs Rabbah* 4:24.

458. RACHEL AND THE STOLEN IDOLS

Rachel stole the idols of her father, Laban, as it is said, *Rachel, meanwhile, had taken the idols* (Gen. 31:34). But why did she take them?

Some say that she didn't want her father to worship idols. But if so, why did she take them with her, and not bury them on the way, rather than hiding them in her saddlebags?

Others say that Rachel stole the *Terafim* because she knew that Laban was a great sorcerer who practiced all kinds of magical arts, and that he knew how to compel the *Terafim* to reveal Jacob's whereabouts to Laban. How could they do that? Because they were not idols of clay or stone, but speaking heads that could be made to reveal secrets, as it is said, *For the Terafim spoke delusion* (Zech. 10:2). Rachel knew that Laban would force the *Terafim* to reveal the direction Jacob had taken. Thus, since Rachel knew the powers of the *Terafim* and the dangers they posed, she took them with her, so Laban would not be able to use the *Terafim* against them.

How were the *Terafim* made? They would slay a firstborn, cut off his head, remove the hair, and sprinkle it with salt and spices. Then they would write magical formulas and names of unclean spirits on a golden tablet and put it under his tongue. They would set it up on the wall, and at certain times of the day the *Terafim* would absorb celestial influences. Then, when they wanted to divine, they would light candles, and bow down in front of it. Then when the head was questioned, it would be forced to respond to any questions asked of it. And it was to these idols that Laban bowed down.

As for those who made the *Terafim*, as well as those who used them, every one was sent down to Gehenna to be punished.

Laban was distraught because his *Terafim*, whom he called his "gods"—(*Why did you steal my gods?*—(Gen. 31:30), were taken when Jacob and his family took flight. The Torah states quite explicitly that it was Rachel who took them: *Rachel, meanwhile, had taken the idols* (Gen. 31:34). Rachel's actions in this case perplexed the commentators. They didn't want to consider that she stole them because she was attached to them, or because she believed that the one who possessed them had the power of the gods at his command. This dilemma gave birth to one of the strangest midrashim, which asserts that the *Terafim* actually were speaking heads. Drawing a hint from the verse *For the Terafim spoke delusion* (Zech. 10:2), this midrash presumes that the *Terafim* could speak. This leads to a barbaric description of how the heads were obtained, found in *Midrash Tanhuma-Yelammedenu, Pirkei de-Rabbi Eliezer*, and other sources, in which a firstborn son was sacrificed and his head cut off. After it had been shrunken with salt and oil, an amulet bearing the name of an evil spirit was placed beneath the tongue. As a result, whenever people invoked that evil spirit, they could force these heads to speak and to reveal everything they wanted to know. In this way Rachel's incriminating actions are fully explained: she was simply trying to prevent the *Terafim* from assisting her father in finding Jacob and his family.

Ibn Ezra indicates the controversy about the very meaning of the term *Terafim*: "Some say that the *Terafim* are copper objects used to tell time. Others say that astrologers have the power to make an image that speaks at certain times." Ibn Ezra also gives an explanation for Rachel's taking the *Terafim* that links them to astrology, while identifying Laban as an astrologer: "The most likely reason that Rachel stole the *Terafim* was that Laban, her father, was an astrologer, and Rachel feared that he would look at the stars and discover which way they fled." This suggests that the *Terafim* drew their power from the stars and revealed hidden things to Laban.

Note that there is a shift from the identification of the *Terafim* as wooden or stone idols that would be the objects of worship, to speaking heads whose primary purpose is to divine. This change alleviates the suspicion that Rachel took the *Terafim* in order to worship them. But it also seems to contradict Laban's assertion that the *Terafim* were his "gods."

The barbaric custom described here seems completely outside of Jewish tradition. It not only involves ritual murder of a firstborn son, but knowledge of techniques that one would associate with cannibals. The primary point of the account of the binding of Isaac in Genesis 22 is that there would be no more ritual sacrifice of children. Thus the clear indication is that the creation of the *Terafim* was not a Jewish practice. Nor, for that matter, was Laban Jewish. It is hard to find a similarly barbaric example in Jewish myth except for the Yemenite folktale that Adam and Eve devoured the son of Samael. See "How Samael Entered the Heart of Man," p. 454.

Joseph Dan links this ingenious explanation of why Rachel stole the idols with a nineteenth-century folktale. See "Terafim: From Popular Belief to a Folktale." This is a story about a boy kidnapped by a demon disguised as a wealthy merchant so that his head could be cut off and serve as one of these *Terafim*. Apparently *Terafim* only last for 80 years, and then must be replaced. The story describes the boy's escape from the castle of demons with the crucial aid of the speaking head he finds there and takes with him. Thus he behaves as does Rachel, and for the same reason—because the *Terafim* could be forced to speak. See "The Speaking Head" in *Lilith's Cave*, pp. 148-159.

Rabbinic commentary links Jacob's vow to Laban, *"But anyone with whom you find your gods shall not remain alive!"* (Gen. 31:32) with the premature death of Rachel. In his Torah commentary, Rabbi Bachya ben Asher (1260-1340) says, "This curse resulted in Rachel dying on the journey." Of course, there is nothing in the text to indicate that Jacob had any idea Rachel had taken the *Terafim*. But many midrashim suggest that Jacob's words turned into a dreadful curse that may have inadvertently brought about Rachel's early death, and prevented her from being buried in the Cave of Machpelah.

Sources:

Genesis Rabbah 74:5, 74:9; *Pirkei de-Rabbi Eliezer* 36; *Midrash Tanhuma-Yelammedenu, va-Yetze* 12; *Sefer ha-Yashar* 103; *Midrash Aseret ha-Dibrot* 40; *Targum Yonathan* on Genesis 31:19; *Zohar* 1:164b; *Or ha-Hayim* on Gen. 31:30; Torah commentary of Ibn Ezra on Genesis 31:19; Torah commentary of Rabbi Bachya ben Asher on Genesis 31:32.

Studies:

"Terafim: From Popular Belief to a Folktale" by Joseph Dan.

459. JACOB'S DREAM

Jacob left Beer-sheba, and set out for Haran. He came upon a certain place and stopped there for the night, for the sun had set. Taking one of the stones of that place, he put it under his head and lay down in that place. He had a dream; a stairway was set on the ground and its top reached to the sky, and angels of God were going up and down on it. And the Lord was standing beside him and He said, "I am the Lord, the God of your father Abraham and the God of Isaac: the ground on which you are lying I will assign to you and to your offspring. Your descendants shall be as the dust of the earth; you shall spread out to the west and to the east, to the north and to the south. All the families of the earth shall bless themselves by you and your descendants. Remember, I am with you: I will protect you wherever you go and will bring you back to this land. I will not leave you until I have done what I have promised you."

Jacob awoke from his sleep and said, "Surely the Lord is present in this place, and I did not know it!" Shaken, he said, "How awesome is this place! This is none other than the abode of God, and that is the gateway to heaven." Early in the morning, Jacob took the stone that he had put under his head and set it up as a pillar and poured oil on the top of it. He named that site Bethel; but previously the name of the city had been Luz.

This memorable dream of Jacob has been subjected to extensive rabbinic interpretation. In *Genesis Rabbah* 68:12, there is a discussion about its symbolic meaning. The first interpretation comes from Bar Kappara, who viewed the dream as referring to the sacrifices made by the priests in the Temple: "No dream is without its interpretation. *And behold a ladder* (Gen. 28:12) symbolizes the stairway. *Set upon the earth* (Gen. 28:12) refers to the altar, as it is said, *An altar of earth you shall make unto Me* (Exod. 20:21). *And the top of it reached to heaven* (Gen. 28:12) refers to the sacrifices, the odor of which ascended on high. *And behold the angels of God* (Gen. 28:13) refers to the High Priests. *Ascending and descending on it* (Gen. 28:12) refers to ascending and descending the stairway. *And, behold, the Lord stood beside him* (Gen. 28:13), refers to *I saw the Lord standing beside the altar* (Amos 9:1)."

Other rabbis related the dream to Mount Sinai: "*And he dreamed, and behold a ladder* symbolizes Sinai. *Set upon the earth* refers to *And they took their places at the foot of the mountain* (Exod. 19:17). *And the top of it reached to heaven* refers to *The mountain was ablaze with flames to the very skies* (Deut. 4:11). *And behold the angels of God* alludes to Moses and Aaron. *Ascending* (Gen. 28:13) refers to *And Moses went up to God* (Exod. 19:3). *And descending* (Gen. 28:13) refers to *And Moses came down from the mountain* (Exod. 19:14). *And, behold, the Lord stood beside him* (Gen. 28:13) refers to *The Lord came down upon Mount Sinai* (Exod. 19:20)."

Sources:
Genesis 28:10-19.

460. MEETING THE PLACE

Jacob left Beersheva and went to Haran. On the way to Haran, *he met the place* (Gen. 28:11). What does this mean? That Jacob did indeed go all the way to Haran. Then he remembered that he had passed the place where his father and grandfather had prayed, and he had failed to stop. He said to himself, "Is it possible that I passed by the place where my forefathers prayed and I did not pray?" Just as his forefathers prayed for the building of Jerusalem and the holy Temple, and their prayers were answered during the time of the two Temples, so too did Jacob want to pray for the future rebuilding of Jerusalem and the Temple.

At that moment a miracle occurred, and he immediately arrived at that place, the site where, in the future, the Temple would one day be built. There Jacob prayed as never before. And when he finished praying, the sun, which was high in the sky, set two hours before its time.

That is why Jacob decided to sleep there, for it had already grown dark. And as he lay down, God folded up the whole of the Land of Israel and placed it beneath Jacob, and that is the meaning of the verse *"The ground on which you are lying I will assign to you and to your offspring"* (Gen. 28:13). And that night Jacob dreamed of the ladder reaching from earth to heaven, with angels ascending and descending on it. And when he awoke he understood that it was indeed a holy place, the very gate of heaven.

This midrash responds to the strange language of *he met the place* (Gen. 28:11) by suggesting that a miracle occurred, and he was transported to that place, which is identified as the same spot where Abraham and Isaac had prayed. So too does the sun set before its time. This second miracle, of the sun setting prematurely, is parallel to the stopping of the sun in the Book of Joshua: *And the sun stood still, and the moon halted* (Josh. 10:13). The place where Jacob's dream takes place is identified by the rabbis as Mount Moriah, where the future Temple would be built. *Genesis Rabbah* quotes God as saying to Jacob: "On your departure I caused the orb of the sun to set for you, and on your return I restored to you the hours you lost." This is an example of how anything is possible for God, even changing the natural order that He Himself had created.

According to Ba'al Shem Tov, God rolled up all of the Holy Land and put it under Jacob so that he would not have to travel everywhere in the land to retrieve the holy sparks that had been scattered there at the time of the shattering of the vessels. Instead, he would find all the sparks in one place (*Sefer Ba'al Shem Tov, va-Yetze* 8, 9).

Sources:

B. *Hullin* 91b; B. *Sanhedrin* 95a-b; Y. *Berakhot* 4:1; *Genesis Rabbah* 68:10; *Beit Elohim, Sha'ar ha-Tefillah* 18; *Sefer Ba'al Shem Tov, va-Yetze* 8, 9.

461. JACOB'S VISION

Jacob was traveling alone from Beersheva to Haran. Along the way, *he met the place* (Gen. 28:11). Why did Jacob choose to stop there?

Some say that Jacob had a vision when he reached that place of the Holy Temple being built, destroyed, and then restored to its full perfection.

Others say that he saw two Jerusalems, one of earth and one of heaven.

Still others say that as he approached, he saw the *Shekhinah* hovering over that place, in the site where the future Temple would be built.

Then there are those who say that when Jacob reached that place, the world became like a wall before him, and he had no choice but to stop.

> Jacob's comments about the place where he had his dream of the heavenly ladder demonstrate that it was inherently sacred: *"How full of awe is this place. This is none other than the abode of God and that is the gateway of heaven"* (Gen. 28:17). These myths attempt to offer a reason for Jacob deciding to stop there. Three of these suggest that Jacob had a vision linked with the Temple that would be built in Jerusalem. In the rabbinic view, Jacob's vision took place on Mount Moriah, just as did Abraham's sacrifice of the ram caught in the thorns, and Mount Moriah was identical, in this mythic view, with the place of the Temple Mount in Jerusalem.
>
> The fourth interpretation, from *Genesis Rabbah*, states that Jacob could not go on, for "the world became like a wall before him." Here God is portrayed as leaving Jacob no choice but to stop there, much as, in one myth, God compels Israel to accept the Torah by holding Mount Sinai over their heads (B. *Shab.* 88a). See "God Offers the Torah to Israel," p. 264.
>
> *Pesikta de-Rav Kahana* 21:5 explains that God envisioned the Temple built, destroyed, and rebuilt from the very beginning. It links Genesis 1:1 to the building of the Temple, Genesis 1:2 to the destruction of the Temple, and Genesis 1:3 to the rebuilding of the Temple at the End of Days.
>
> *Sources:*
> Rashi on Genesis 28:11; *Genesis Rabbah* 68:10; *Midrash Tehillim* 91:7; *Pesikta de-Rav Kahana* 21:5; *Sifre on Deuteronomy* 352.

462. JACOB'S HEAVENLY VISION

In his dream, Jacob not only saw the ladder and the angels, but when he peered up to the top of the ladder he saw the face of a man, carved out of fire, peering down at him. So too did Jacob see God fashioning the heavenly Temple with His own hands out of jewels and pearls and the radiance of the *Shekhinah*. And when he saw that glorious Temple taking form on high, Jacob understood that it was the House of God that would sustain Israel forever, until the end of all generations. And he also understood that just as God was fashioning a Temple in heaven, so too would He build one in the same way on earth, as it is said, *The sanctuary, O Yahweh, which Your hands established* (Exod. 15:17).

Then Jacob peered into the highest heaven and saw God's throne. He saw that there was a face carved into the throne, and the face that Jacob saw there was his own.

Then God called out to him, saying "Jacob, Jacob!" And Jacob replied, "Here I am, Lord." And God revealed his covenant to Jacob, as he had to Abraham and Isaac before him.

The Ladder of Jacob expands the details of Jacob's dream (Gen. 28:10-19), adding that "there were twelve steps leading to the top of the ladder, and on each step to the top there were two human faces, on the right and on the left, twenty-four faces .... And God was standing above its highest face, and he called to me from there, saying `Jacob, Jacob'" (*The Ladder of Jacob* 1:5, 1:8). The key image is that of the fiery face at the top of the ladder: "And the top of the ladder was the face as of a man, carved out of fire" (1:4-5). Although the face is not identified, there is a strong implication it is that of God.

One motivation for Jacob's vision of God at the top of the ladder in *The Ladder of Jacob* may have been a response to the biblical verse *And the Lord was standing beside him* (Gen. 28:13). God is rarely found standing on the earth, and *The Ladder of Jacob* puts God back in heaven, which is considered more appropriate.

The tradition that God showed the heavenly and earthly Temple to Jacob (and the other patriarchs) is very old. *Sifre on Deuteronomy* 352 says of the Temple, "Jacob saw it built, destroyed, and rebuilt." This is derived from Genesis 28:17: *Shaken, he said, "How awe-inspiring is this place!" This is none other than the abode of God, and that is the gateway to heaven.* The rabbis interpret: *This is none* indicates that the Temple was destroyed; *other than the abode of God and that is the gateway to heaven* shows that he saw it rebuilt in the future. *Midrash Tanhuma, va-Yetze* 9 states that "the prophets also saw it built, destroyed, and rebuilt." Here God is quoted as saying: "You have seen it destroyed in this world, but in the World to Come I am rebuilding it Myself. I burned it, and I shall rebuild it."

Other sources indicate that God showed other visions to Jacob in his dream. According to *Midrash Tanhuma-Yelammedenu, va-Yetze* 2, God showed Jacob the guardian angels of Babylon, Media, Greece, and Edom, all ascending and descending.

Sources:
Genesis Rabbah 56:10, 69:17, 79:7; *The Ladder of Jacob* 1:1; *Bereshit Rabbati*, 158-160 in
    Beit ha-Midrash 6:22-23; *Pesikta Rabbati* 31; *Pesikta de-Rav Kahana* 21:5; *Sifre on
    Deuteronomy* 352; *Yalkut ha-Makhiri* on Psalm 147.

Studies:
"The Ladder of Jacob" by James Kugel.

463. THE GATEWAY TO HEAVEN

When Jacob awoke from the dream of the ladder reaching from earth to heaven, with angels ascending and descending on it, he said, "In truth, the Glory of the *Shekhinah* dwells in this place, and I did not know it. *Shaken, he said, 'How awesome is this place!'"* (Gen. 28:17). This is not a profane place, but a sanctuary to the name of the Lord, and this is a place suitable for prayer, corresponding to the Gate of Heaven, found beneath the Throne of Glory."

Waking from his dream, Jacob realized he had gone to sleep in a very holy place. Each of Jacob's comments in Genesis 28:16-17 emphasizes its holiness. In this midrash, the term *Shekhinah* is substituted for *Yahweh*, the Lord. While "*Shekhinah*" in talmudic-midrashic texts is used as a designation for God, without the later kabbalistic associations of the term as the Bride of God, it emphasizes God's divine presence in this world, thus Jacob's personal experience of God's presence. Jacob also identifies this place as a sanctuary, leading to midrashic interpretations that identified this place as

Mount Moriah, where Abraham took Isaac to be sacrificed, and as the Temple Mount in Jerusalem. Finally, Jacob says, *This is none other than the abode of God, and that is the gateway to heaven.* The phrase *the abode of God* reaffirms the idea of the place as a sanctuary, God's dwelling place in this world, which is exactly how the Temple in Jerusalem is always described. Finally, *that is the gateway to heaven* suggests that there was some kind of direct link from that place to heaven, a logical conclusion considering the nature of Jacob's dream, with the ladder reaching from earth to heaven, with angels ascending and descending on it. While the biblical verse may use the term "gateway to heaven" in a symbolic sense, the midrashic impulse is to identify it in a literal sense. Here the midrash states that the place corresponds to the Gate of Heaven found beneath the Throne of Glory. In other words, prayer offered on earth, in that holy place, would be as effective as prayer offered in heaven, right before God's Throne. This confirms a key rabbinic/kabbalistic concept, "as above, so below."

Sources:
Targum Pseudo-Yonathan on Genesis 28:17; *Mekhilta de-Rabbi Ishmael* on Exodus 15:17;
  Y. Berakhot 4:8c; *Pirkei de-Rabbi Eliezer* 35.

464. JACOB WRESTLES WITH THE ANGEL

Jacob was left alone. And a man wrestled with him until the break of dawn. When he saw that he had not prevailed against him, he wrenched Jacob's hip at its socket, so that the socket of his hip was strained as he wrestled with him. Then he said, "Let me go, for dawn is breaking." But he answered, "I will not let you go, unless you bless me." Said the other, "What is your name?" He replied, "Jacob." Said he, "Your name shall no longer be Jacob, but Israel, for you have striven with beings divine and human, and have prevailed." Jacob asked, "Pray tell me your name." But he said, "You must not ask my name!" And he took leave of him there. So Jacob named the place Penuel, meaning, "I have seen a divine being face to face, yet my life has been preserved." The sun rose upon him as he passed Penuel, limping on his hip. That is why the children of Israel to this day do not eat the thigh muscle that is on the socket of the hip, since Jacob's hip socket was wrenched at the thigh muscle.

This is one of the most important and mysterious episodes in the Torah. Here Jacob, exhausted from his escape from Laban and facing a small army led by his brother Esau, remains alone on one side of the river Yabbok and wrestles with an *ish* all night. *Ish* means "man," but all of the interpretations of this passage assume that Jacob wrestled with an angel or possibly even with God. The question is—which angel? There are many theories. Some assume it is Samael, who is identified as Esau's guardian angel. Samael is another name for Satan, and suggesting that he was Esau's guardian angel is a way of labeling Esau as evil. This interpretation assumes that Samael's goal was to wear Jacob out, so that Esau could easily defeat him the next day. Other interpretations identify the angel as Michael or Uriel. One of the most fascinating explanations is that Jacob himself was an angel, and the angel Uriel was sent to tell him it was time to return to heaven. See "Jacob the Angel," p. 364.

The suggestion that Jacob wrestled with God comes from the angel's statement to Jacob that *You have striven with beings divine and human and have prevailed* (Gen. 32:29). *Elohim,* translated here as "divine beings," normally means "God." Jacob receives a new name, Israel, from the angel, and after this his behavior changes. He makes peace with Esau and takes on the role of a patriarch. Note that in Hebrew the name is *Yisrael,* which can be translated as "One who has wrestled with God."

Because Jacob's name and the name of the people of Israel is the same, there is a strong identification between Jacob and the nation of Israel. One result of this strong identification is that a great effort is made in the rabbinic texts to justify all of Jacob's actions, including the bartered birthright and the stolen blessing. Another result is that some came to regard Jacob as a divine figure. See "Jacob the Divine," p. 366. The entire cycle of Jacob myths is certainly one of the most compelling in all of Jewish tradition.

Sources:
Genesis 32:25-33

465. JACOB AND ESAU'S GUARDIAN ANGEL

The angel that wrestled with Jacob was none other than Esau's guardian angel, and that angel was none other than Samael. By making Jacob expend great effort all night, Samael hoped to weaken him, so that Esau might defeat Jacob the next day.

But Samael did not prevail over Jacob, and before he let the angel take its leave, Jacob insisted that the angel bless him. *And he said, "Your name shall no longer be Jacob, but Israel, for you have striven with God and with men, and have prevailed"* (Gen. 32:29).

Why did Jacob seek the angel's blessings? The truth is that he was not demanding that blessing for himself, but for his descendants, the people of Israel. It meant that Samael could not protest whenever God decided to liberate Israel in times of danger. For the blessing was not for Jacob, but for Israel, and that blessing made the Exodus possible.

This ingenious commentary by Rabbi Kalonymus Kalman Shapira, the Rebbe of the Warsaw Ghetto, builds on the midrashic interpretation that the angel with whom Jacob wrestled was Esau's guardian angel, none other than the evil angel Samael. He combines this explanation with the midrashic view that everything said about Jacob applied to the people of Israel, since Jacob became Israel. So here the angel's forced blessing is said to have been intended not for Jacob, but for Israel, Jacob's descendants, and it saved them during times of great danger and even made the Exodus possible.

In the following myth, "The Magic Flock," the angel Jacob wrestles with is also identified as Esau's guardian angel and as Samael.

Sources:
Esh Kadosh p. 13.

Studies:
The Holy Fire: The Teachings of Rabbi Kalonymus Kalman Shapira, the Rebbe of the Warsaw Ghetto by Nehemia Polen, pp. 124-126.

466. THE MAGIC FLOCK

When Jacob arrived at the River Yabbok, he sent his servants across first, then his wives and children. He himself wished to remain alone there, to rest from his escape from Laban, and to prepare himself for his encounter with Esau the next day.

Soon after everyone else had crossed the river, a shepherd arrived there with his flocks. He proposed to Jacob that they help each other in crossing their flocks, and Jacob agreed. They started with Jacob's flock, and in a twinkling the shepherd succeeded in transferring all of them to the other side. Then they turned to the shepherd's flock, and Jacob assisted him by carrying the animals two by two across the river. Jacob worked without pausing, but after he had forded the river with a great many animals, he saw that the flocks of the shepherd had not grown smaller but seemed to have increased.

Still Jacob continued to bear the flocks across the river hour after hour. But as the day began to grow dark, he saw that the flocks of the shepherd still reached to the horizon, with no end in sight. Then Jacob understood that this was no ordinary shepherd, but some kind of magician, and that all the flocks he had carried were only an illusion. In his fury Jacob accused the shepherd of enchantment and deceit. Then the shepherd touched his finger to the earth, and a great fire burst forth. But this display of his power did not frighten Jacob, and the two began to struggle, and they continued to wrestle all night.

During their struggle the magician wounded Jacob in his thigh, but Jacob still continued to fight. And as dawn approached, the magician sought to depart, but Jacob refused to let him go. In this way Jacob received his adversary's blessing, and his name was changed from Jacob to Israel.

Some say that shepherd was Samael, the guardian angel of Esau, who came to Jacob to weaken him before his encounter with Esau. Others say it was the angel Michael, who had been sent by God to show Jacob that he, like the angels, was made of fire, and that he had nothing to fear from Esau. And, in truth, after this struggle Jacob was a changed man, who put down his weapons and his pride, and bowed seven times to his brother, and Esau ran to meet him and embraced him (Gen. 33:4), and at last they came together in peace.

> This legend is closely related to the account of Jacob's wrestling with the angel in Genesis 32:25-33. The identity of the sorcerer thus depends on the identity given to the angel, or whoever it was that Jacob wrestled. Most accounts identify this figure as the angel Michael or as the guardian angel of Esau, who, disguised as a shepherd, first got Jacob to agree that they would assist each other in carrying their flocks across the river Yabbok, and then created the illusion of so many flocks, attempting to exhaust Jacob before they wrestled and before Jacob's encounter with Esau the next day. This guardian angel of Esau is most often identified as Samael or as *Sar shel Romi*, the guardian angel of the Roman Empire, because of the close association between Esau and Rome. This story is of particular importance as it is an early example of an illusion tale, a type of tale that has a distinct and prominent place in Jewish lore. This theme was probably drawn into Jewish lore from oriental sources, where it also was very popular.
>
> *Sources:*
> *Genesis Rabbah 77:2; Midrash Tanhuma, va-Yishlah 7.*

467. JACOB'S ASCENT ON HIGH

It is said that the battle between Jacob and the angel did not take place on the shores of the River Yabbok, but in the palaces of heaven, for Jacob's soul ascended on high and struggled with the angel there. For ever since Jacob's dream of the ladder that reached from earth into heaven, his soul was able to ascend its highest rungs.

On the night that his body lay sleeping on the shore of the River Yabbok, Jacob's soul did indeed ascend on high, and there he wrestled until dawn with none other than the angel Michael. Michael, the heavenly priest, led a choir of ministering angels in singing God's praises every morning, and that is why he begged, *"Let me go, for dawn is breaking"* (Gen. 32:27).

Just then many bands of ministering angels arrived and said, *The time of singing God's praises has come* (S. of S. 2:12). Michael pleaded with Jacob, saying, "Let me go, I beg you, lest the ministering angels incinerate me for delaying the song." But Jacob insisted that he would not let him go unless he blessed him, and Michael said, *Your name shall no more be called Jacob, but Israel* (Gen. 32:29). And he added, "Blessed are you, born of woman, for you entered the palace above and remained alive."

That is when God chose to reveal Himself to Jacob and the angels. Looking up, Jacob saw God face to face. At that instant a change came over him, and he became Jacob the patriarch, father of Israel's twelve tribes. As for the angel Michael, in the presence of God his strength was depleted. Still, he touched the hollow of Jacob's thigh and harmed him. But when God saw this, He said: "What right have you to cripple My priest?" Michael answered, "Master of the universe, am I not Your priest?" God replied: "You are My priest in the world above; Jacob is My priest in the world below." Then Michael summoned Raphael, the Angel of Healing, and begged him to heal Jacob. And as soon as Raphael touched Jacob's thigh, he recovered, and no sign of his injury remained.

This is an unusual interpretation of the combat between Jacob and the angel in that, unlike virtually all of the other sources, it suggests that it took place in heaven rather than on earth. During the battle a band of angels appears, who are anxious to have Michael join them to conduct the angelic choir. Finally, God Himself appears to defend Jacob and to accuse Michael of misbehavior for wounding Jacob in the thigh. This version also differs in that it states that Jacob's wound was healed by the angel Raphael, while the biblical text clearly states that he was *limping on his hip* (Gen. 32:32).

One of the halachic requirements to serve as High Priest was to have no physical imperfections. Since Jacob had set up altars and made offerings to God, he had in essence taken on the role of a priest, before the appearance of Aaron, brother of Moses, whom the Bible represents as the first High Priest. According to the *Halakhah*, Jacob's wound would have made him unable to serve as priest. Thus, in this version of the myth, Jacob is healed, and can thus continue his priestly role.

This version does offer a credible reason for Michael's anxiousness—to be set free in order to conduct the heavenly choir. In fact, the angel fears that he will be incinerated by the other angels if he doesn't join the choir at once. The appearance of the angels and finally of God Himself reinforces the heavenly setting, as does Michael's comment to Jacob that "you entered the palace above and remained alive."

This mythic version seems to echo the *Hekhalot* texts describing heavenly journeys into the celestial palaces, which were notoriously dangerous—the angel at the sixth gate would cut off the head of anyone who didn't know the right answer. (*Hekhalot* literally means "palaces," referring to the palaces of heaven.) But here Jacob, like Rabbi Akiba in *B. Hagigah* 14b, survives the dangerous ascent intact. See "The Four Who Entered Paradise," p. 173.

God identifies Jacob as His High Priest because of the biblical accounts of Jacob setting up an altar and making an offering to God at Beth El (Gen. 28:18 and 35:6-7) and other sites. Michael is said to serve as the heavenly High Priest, making offerings in the celestial Temple. Their competing roles as High Priest suggest a possible reason for their conflict, although this is never made explicit.

Ironically, Michael is also identified in other sources as Jacob's guardian angel, since Michael had been appointed the guardian angel of Israel from the day he visited Abraham to announce the coming birth of Isaac, and Jacob's other name was Israel. In that case Jacob might be seen as wrestling with his conscience. After all, he has just escaped from the forces of his uncle, Laban, and now he faces the forces of Esau. The bitter harvest he has brought upon himself has become apparent.

In several sources the angel is not identified as Michael, but as Metatron, and the identities of the two angels are often switched. For more on the role of Metatron in these Jacob myths see the note to "Jacob the Angel," p. 364.

Sources:
Midrash Avkir in *Yalkut Re'uveni* 1:132.

468. JACOB'S PILLOW

On his journey to Haran, Jacob came to the place where he rested. Before he lay down to sleep, *He took stones of the place, and made them his pillow* (Gen. 28:11). How many stones? Twelve stones, one for every tribe that was destined to arise from the seed of Jacob. The stones began to quarrel with one another, each wanting to be the stone on which Jacob would lay his head. Some say that God immediately made them into one stone to keep them from quarreling. But others say that as soon as the stones beneath his head beheld the glory of God, they dissolved into each other and formed one stone, just as the twelve tribes of Jacob would one day form the nation of Israel. Then the stone under Jacob's head became like a feather-bed and a pillow under him.

Still others say that Jacob said to himself, "God has decreed that twelve tribes should spring forth. Now neither Abraham nor Isaac has produced them. If these twelve stones cleave to one another, I will know that I will produce the twelve tribes." So it was that when Jacob rose the next morning, he found the stones had all fused into one. So he set up that stone as a pillar, and oil descended for him from heaven, and he poured the oil upon it.

What did God do then? God placed His right foot on that pillar, and sank the stone to the bottom of the abyss, and made it the Foundation Stone, the very navel of the world. That is the stone on which the Temple of the Lord was built.

> This midrash about the fusing of the stones that Jacob used as a pillow into one derives from the problem created by Genesis 28:11, where it is stated that Jacob took stones of the place and Genesis 28:18, where it is stated that Jacob took the stone that he had put under his head. The midrash resolves the apparent contradiction between "stones" and "stone" by stating that the stones fused into one, which Jacob then used as a pillow. And to explain where Jacob got the oil necessary to making the offering, it is said to have descended from heaven.
>
> The striking image of God raising His right foot and driving the stone into the earth provides the origin of the Foundation Stone, which holds back the waters of the abyss. Jacob slept on a stone that is said to have formed out of twelve stones, representing the twelve tribes that would come into being. This symbolizes how the twelve tribes would become the nation of Israel. This stone is known as the spindle stone or foundation stone or pillar of the earth. See "The Foundation Stone," p. 96.
>
> The dominant myths about the foundation stone link its creation to the creation of the world. But here it is linked with Jacob's sacred dream, and with the holy place to which he had come. In fact, it is called *ha-Makom*, the Place, and this term not only refers to that place, but is one of the names of God, since Jacob beheld God in the dream. This strange linkage of God with a place receives a mysterious explanation in *Genesis Rabbah* 68:9, which it asks, "Why do we call God 'the Place?' Because God is the place of the world. But we do not know whether God is the place of the world, or whether the world is God's place. That is why it is written, *The ancient God is a refuge* (Deut. 33:27)."
>
> Sources:
> B. *Hullin* 91a-b; *Genesis Rabbah* 68:11; *Midrash Tehillim* 91:7; *Pirkei de-Rabbi Eliezer* 35; *Midrash Tanhuma-Yelammedenu, va-Yetze* 1; *Zohar* 2:229b-230a; *Zohar Hadash* 27b; Rashi on Genesis 28:11.

469. JACOB'S BOOKS

Jacob possessed three books. One was the *Book of Adam*, of which it is written, *This is the book of the generations of Adam* (Gen. 5:1). The second was the *Book of Enoch*, which recounts how *Enoch walked with God; and then he was no more, for God took him* (Gen. 5:24). The third was Abraham's *Book of Creation*.

> From a midrashic perspective, Jacob would have been in possession of these three books. The existence of the *Book of Adam* is derived from the verse *This is the book of the generations of Adam* (Gen. 5:1). This book is sometimes also identified with the *Book of Raziel*. For more on the latter, see "The Book of Raziel," p. 252. The *Book of Enoch* recounts Enoch's heavenly journey, elaborating on the terse account of Enoch found in

Genesis 5:21-24. There is also an old tradition that Abraham was author of the *Sefer Yetzirah*, the *Book of Creation*, the earliest kabbalistic text. Thus all three of these books were believed to have existed at the time of Jacob and might have been available to him.

Jacob's access to these books provides a partial explanation for the level of spiritual achievement attributed to him in midrashic texts. See, for example, "Jacob the Angel," p. 364 and "Jacob the Divine," p. 366.

Sources:
Zohar Hadash, Yitro 37b.

470. JACOB THE ANGEL

Jacob was no ordinary man. If the truth be known, his true name was Israel, and he was an angel of God, the very archangel of the power of the Lord and the first minister before the face of God. Indeed, he was the first living being to whom God gave life, with the beauty of Adam.

When the angel Israel descended to earth and became Jacob, he forgot his divine origin. God tried to remind him when He sent him the dream of the ladder reaching from earth to heaven, so that he might glimpse the celestial world he had left behind.

In the dream *angels of God were ascending and descending on it* (Gen. 28:12). For the angels who had accompanied him from his father's house went up to heaven to announce to the angels on high: "Come and see Jacob the pious, whose image is fixed upon the Throne of Glory, the one you have longed to see." Then the rest of the holy angels of the Lord came down to look at him. That is why the angels went up and down the ladder, for they ascended to see the face carved on the celestial throne, and they descended to see the face of Jacob as he slept, whose features were identical to those carved on high.

In the dream Jacob heard the voice of God say, "You, too, Jacob, climb up the ladder." For God was trying to remind Jacob that he was an angel, and that the time had come for him to return to the heavenly realm. But Jacob said, "Master of the Universe, I am afraid that if I climb up I will have to come down." Nor did he ascend on high. Indeed, it is said that if Jacob had climbed up the ladder, he would not have had to come down again, and Israel would have been spared great suffering.

Thus when Jacob wrestled with the angel at the River Yabbok, the struggle was not that of a man and angel, but that of two angels—Uriel and Israel. Some say that Uriel had been sent to remind Jacob of his divine origin, saying, "Know that you were once an angel, who descended to earth and took up dwelling among humans and your name became Jacob. *Now your name shall no longer be called Jacob, but Israel*" (Gen. 32:29). Others say that Uriel wrestled with Jacob, saying, "My name will take precedence over your name and the names of every other angel." At first Jacob did not understand, but suddenly he remembered that he once was an angel. And Jacob said, "Are you not Uriel? Have you forgotten that I am Israel, the chief commander among the heavenly hosts?" And Jacob called out God's secret Name and thus defeated him.

Still others insist that Jacob did not become an angel until after his death; only then did he become an immortal angel.

Sometime before or after his death, Jacob himself said, "For I who speak to you, I Jacob-Israel, am an angel of God and a ruling spirit, the first servant before the presence of God. It was God who gave me the name Israel, which means, 'the man who sees God,' because I am the firstborn of all living beings that God brought to life."

Of the many theories about the meaning of Jacob's struggle with a mysterious figure at the River Yabbok (Gen. 33:25-31), one of the most interesting is that Jacob was not only wrestling with an angel, but that he himself was the angel Israel. This explains why the angel with whom he wrestled tells Jacob *Your name shall be called Jacob no more, but Israel* (Gen. 32:29). This suggests that the reason the angel Uriel had been sent was to remind Jacob of his true identity as an angel, something he had apparently forgotten during his foray among humans.

This myth grows out of an extensive, if somewhat obscure, tradition that identifies Jacob as an angel or some other kind of divine being. It is primarily found in magical and mystical literature, and in these texts Jacob's identity as the angel Israel sometimes converges with that of the nation of Israel. Such identification grows first out of the fact that Jacob is also known as Israel. Thus, just as Abram became Abraham and Sarai became Sarah, so the angel with whom he wrestled announced to Jacob that his name would now be Israel. Of course, this is also the name of the nation of Israel. Thus the special traditions linked to Jacob may derive from this identification of man and nation.

In addition, Jacob is often identified as the ideal man, who represents the human race (much as does Adam), and whose face appears on the divine throne (see Ezek. 1:10, 1:26). Further, it is suggested several times that Jacob was made wholly of fire, and that his ability to withstand the power of the angel demonstrated his divine nature. Further evidence is found in Jacob's ability to cause Laban's flocks to bring forth streaked, speckled, and spotted young (Gen. 30:39). For this reason *Midrash Tehillim* interprets the verse *You have made him little less than divine* (Ps. 8:6) as referring to Jacob, "thereby proving that Jacob was less than God only in that he had not the power to put the breath of life into them" (*Midrash Tehillim* 8:6).

Further, according to *Midrash Tehillim* 31:7, Jacob was said to have been one of the two to whom God revealed the time of redemption. The other was Daniel. (See Daniel 10:14). Jacob's divine knowledge is said to have been revealed by his final words to his sons, where he says, "*Gather yourselves together, that I may tell you what shall befall you in the end of days*" (Gen. 49:1). This phrase, "the end of days," became the primary term for the messianic era which was so eagerly awaited. In fact, *Midrash Tehillim* 14:7 suggests that Jacob alone, among the patriarchs, will be invited to the feast of redemption: "When the Lord brought His people out of captivity, then *Jacob will exult, Israel will rejoice* (Ps. 14:7). Of all the patriarchs, why is it that Jacob is named as rejoicing? R. Shimon ben Lakish answered: 'When the children of Israel sin, only Jacob in the Cave of Machpelah feels defiled. So when the gladness of redemption comes, Jacob will rejoice in it more than any of the other patriarchs. For he alone of the patriarchs will be called to the feast, as it is said, *Listen to me, O Jacob, Israel, whom I have called* (Isa. 48:12). What does 'Israel whom I have called' mean? It means Israel, who will be called to the feast.'"

There is also a legend that Jacob is the man in the moon, which probably derives from the myth that Jacob's face appears on the divine throne. See Louis Ginzberg, *Legends of the Jews*, vol. 5, p. 305, note 248.

In identifying Jacob as the "first minister of the face of God," Jacob is given the role traditionally played by Metatron, the angel of the Presence. This is the only angel who is said to be permitted to see God face to face. It would seem likely that there were early mystical circles in which Jacob played a Metatron-like role as the primary angel. But all that remains of the evidence of these circles are pseudepigraphal fragments, especially the *Prayer of Joseph*. See also the Wolfson article listed below.

All of these traditions concern the divine origin or divine nature of Jacob. In some it appears that Jacob was originally the angel Israel (*Prayer of Joseph*), while others suggest that Jacob's soul made a heavenly journey through the palaces of heaven ("Blessed are you ... for you entered the palace above and remained alive."—*Midrash Avkir*). See "Jacob's Ascent on High," p. 361. Jacob is also identified as the human face that Ezekiel saw on the Divine Chariot (*Merkavah*) (Ezek. 1:10, 1:26). This reference, *Targum Neophyti*, says about Jacob that his "likeness is set upon the divine throne." A similar tradition is also found in *Genesis Rabbah* (68:12) where it is said about Jacob that "You are the one whose features are engraved on high." In the same source God is said to have shown Jacob a throne of three legs, and God said to him: "You are the third leg," i.e., Jacob is the third patriarch.

The primary sources of this unusual interpretation of the account of Jacob wrestling with the angel are two pseudepigraphical texts, *Prayer of Joseph* and *The Ladder of Jacob. Prayer of Joseph*, a fragment, begins: "I, Jacob, who am speaking to you, am also Israel, an angel of God." This fragment also recounts that "I am the firstborn of every living thing to whom God gives life." This suggests that Jacob was a kind of protohuman, an Adam-like figure, or even something similar to the kabbalistic figure of *Adam Kadmon*, whose creation was said to have preceded that of the earthly Adam.

While most texts link Jacob's face with the face carved on the throne on high, *Pirkei de-Rabbi Eliezer* 35 has the ministering angels say, "This is a face like the face of the holy beast on the Throne of Glory." This identifies of Jacob with one of the *hayyot*, the celestial beasts, who are said to reside in the highest heavens. Thus while most texts identify the face of Jacob with the mysterious human face on God's throne—a face that is intimately linked to God Himself—the text from *Pirkei de-Rabbi Eliezer* avoids this direct link with God.

The identification of the angel with whom Jacob wrestles as Uriel also derives from *Prayer of Joseph* 1:5-9, which supplies the reason for the wrestling—jealousy on the part of Uriel: "He envied me and fought with me and wrestled with me, saying that his name and the name that is before every angel was to be above mine. I told him his name and what rank he held among the songs of God. `Are you not Uriel, the eighth after me? and I am Israel, the archangel of the power of the Lord and the chief captain among the songs of God. Am I not Israel, the first minister before the face of God? I called upon my God by the ineffable Name.'"

The model for an angelic descent into this world is found in the midrashim concerning Genesis 6, the Sons of God and the daughters of men. Here two angels, Shemhazai and Azazel, are said to have convinced God to let them descend to this world to demonstrate that they would not be swayed by the *Yetzer ha-Ra*, the Evil Inclination. See "The Star Maiden," p. 455. The fragment in *Prayer of Joseph* suggests a similar scenario, with the angel Israel having descended to earth to become the patriarch Jacob.

The cult of Jacob worship extended beyond the Jews. It is a theme found in Gnostic and Manichean texts; in the latter, it is stated that "we worship the Lord Jacob, the angel."

It is interesting to note that there is an apocryphal Christian tradition about Jesus being an angel. According to *The Gospel of the Ebionites*, Jesus was not begotten of God the Father, but was created as one of the archangels, and he rules over the angels and all the creatures of God (Epiphanius, *Haer.* 30.16.4f). See "Jacob the Divine," following.

Sources:
Targum Pseudo-Yonathan on Genesis 28:12; *Targum Neophyti*, Fragment *Targum* (Ms. P) Gen 28:12; *Prayer of Joseph*, Fragment A; Philo, *De Somniis* 1:150, 153-156; *B. Hullin* 91b; *Genesis Rabbah* 68:12; *Hekhalot Rabbati* 9; *Midrash Tehillim* 78:6; *Pirkei de-Rabbi Eliezer* 35; *Midrash Avkir*; *Sha'arei ha-Gilgulim, Sha'ar ha-Shorashim* 24.

Studies:
"Jacob as an Angel in Gnosticism and Manicheism" by Alexander Bohlig.
"The Face of Jacob in the Moon: Mystical Transformations of an Aggadic Myth" by Elliot R. Wolfson.
"The Image of Jacob Engraved upon the Throne: Further Reflections on the Esoteric Doctrine of the German Pietists" by Elliot R. Wolfson.
Along the Path by Elliot R. Wolfson, pp. 1-62.

471. JACOB THE DIVINE

Jacob's image is engraved on God's Throne of Glory in the highest heaven, and when the children of Jacob are oppressed, God looks at the image of Jacob and is filled with pity for them, as it is said, *"Then I will remember my covenant with Jacob"* (Lev. 26:42). Then God embraces and kisses the image of Jacob, for he was a partner with his Creator in everything, as it is said, *Not like these is the portion of Jacob; for it is he who formed all things* (Jer. 10:16). That is why *God tells his words to Jacob* (Ps. 147:19). So too did God reveal the time of the redemption to Jacob alone.

God said to his world: "My world, My world, who created you and who formed you? Jacob created you and Israel formed you, as it is said, *'Who created you, O Jacob, who formed you, O Israel?'"* (Isa. 43:1).

For heaven and earth were only created for the sake of Jacob; indeed, everything was created only for the sake of Jacob. Behemoth was created only for the sake of Jacob, and Abraham was saved from the fiery furnace only for the sake of Jacob. And Abraham himself was only created for the sake of Jacob, for God foresaw that Jacob was destined to spring from Abraham and said, "He deserves to be saved for the sake of Jacob."

Indeed, it will be Jacob, more than any other patriarch, who will rejoice in the gladness of redemption, as it is said, *Jacob will exult, Israel will rejoice* (Ps. 14:7). For he alone of the patriarchs will be invited to the messianic banquet that will take place in the time to come.

So too was it whispered among the angels that not only was Jacob's image carved on God's Throne, but that the image of the sleeping Jacob was identical with that of the Lord of Hosts. That is why the angels ascended and descended the ladder, comparing the image on high with that below, and it was as if they were peering into a mirror.

There are even those who insist that it is the image of Jacob himself who sits on God's Throne, and that this is the true meaning of *the semblance of a human form* (Ezek. 1:26) in Ezekiel's vision. So too does the verse *Thus said Yahweh: "The heaven is My throne"* (Isa. 66:1) reveal that Jacob dwells in the highest firmament, *Aravot*, upon the divine throne.

That is why, when *He set up an altar there, and called it El-elohe-yisrael*, Jacob declared to God: "You are God in the celestial spheres and I am god in the terrestrial sphere. For just as You create worlds, so too do I create worlds; just as You divide worlds, so too do I divide worlds." God replied, "Jacob, you are exceedingly precious in My sight, for I have set your image on My Throne, and by your name the angels praise Me and say, *'Blessed is Yahweh, the God of Israel'* (Ps. 41:14). Therefore, why do you not ascend?" And Jacob replied: "Shall I also be forced to descend?" And God replied: *"Have no fear, My servant Jacob ... I will deliver you from far away"* (Jer. 30:10).

> There is a distinct process of divinization in which the biblical Jacob is transformed into an angel, or even a second power in heaven. Why was Jacob, among the patriarchs, selected for this role? First, and foremost, because of the name Israel, which was given to Jacob by the angel he wrestled with at the River Yabbok in Genesis 32:25-33. The name Israel is the same as that of the nation of Israel, and therefore anything attributed to Jacob/Israel reflects on the destiny of the people of Israel, who share his name. Further, Jacob was the father of the twelve sons who represent the twelve tribes of Israel. Thus, not only does Jacob's name Israel represent the nation, but his sons represent the tribes. The interlinked identities of the patriarch and the people have thus become entirely intertwined, and they share a common fate. It is also possible that Jacob's role as the third patriarch is a factor, as the number three in this kind of a series is frequently the most important.
>
> Another important factor in Jacob's elevation is the verse in Jeremiah 10:16 that seems to acknowledge Jacob's divinity: *Not like these is the Portion of Jacob; for it is He who formed all things, and Israel is His very own tribe: Lord of Hosts is His name.* God's deep affection for Jacob is conveyed in *Sodei Razayya* 16d. The text here says "It is written in *Sefer Hekhalot* that the Holy One, blessed be He, embraces and kisses the image of Jacob."
>
> In addition, Jacob's encounter with the angel at the River Yabbok, in which the angel blessed him saying, *You have striven with God and with men, and have prevailed*

(Gen. 32:29) created a direct link between Jacob and the divine, over whom he had prevailed. And if such a thing was possible, would this not mean that Jacob must have been some kind of divine figure after all, an angel, or even more than that?

In addition to this biblical encounter, the primary focus of Jacob's elevation to a divine figure derives from two key rabbinic myths. One holds that Jacob's image was carved or engraved on God's heavenly throne. The other suggests that Jacob himself was an angel. The key to this process derives from the tradition, found in many early and diverse sources, that Jacob's image is to be found on God's Throne of Glory.

This divinization of Jacob was the culmination of a process by which all of the patriarchs were increasingly perceived from a mythic and mystical perspective. It is stated in *Genesis Rabbah* (82:88) that "the patriarchs are God's Chariot," linking the patriarchs with God's throne, as portrayed in the vision of Ezekiel (Ezek. 1:26). But Jacob, because of his role as the father of the twelve tribes, and especially because his name is identical with that of the people of Israel, came to take on a role that can only be regarded as divine. In these myths Jacob did not usurp the role of God, but shared with God the role of Creator.

The role of Jacob can be seen to be transformed in this series of Jacob myths. Here a step-by-step evolution of Jacob's role can be seen, although many of these traditions existed simultaneously. In some Jacob's soul merely ascends on high during his dream at Beth El, but in others he is described as an angel, the most prominent in heaven, and ultimately he is portrayed as a creator who forms all things, i.e., a secondary God, much as the angel Metatron is often described. The remaining evidence of this tradition of Jacob the divine is now found in snatches of passages and in fragments such as *Prayer of Joseph*.

The tradition that Jacob, alone among the patriarchs, will attend the great feast that takes place in the messianic era, grows out of the verse *Jacob shall exult, Israel will rejoice* (Ps. 14:7). In *Midrash Tehillim* on this verse from Psalms this point is emphatically made: "It is not written here, 'Abraham shall exult, Isaac shall rejoice,' but *Jacob will exult, Israel will rejoice*." For more on Jacob's presence at this feast, see the note to "The Messianic Banquet," p. 508.

Sources:

B. *Hullin* 91b; *Genesis Rabbah* 68:12, 78:3, 79:8, 98:3; *Leviticus Rabbah* 36:4; *Numbers Rabbah* 4:1; *Hekhalot Rabbati* 9; *Midrash Tehillim* 7:2, 14:7, 31:7, 78:6; *Midrash Tanhuma, Toledot* 11; B. *Bava Metzia* 84a; *Targum Neophyti*, Fragment *Targum* (Ms. P) Genesis 28:12; *Sefer ha-Komah*, Oxford Ms. 1791, 58-70; *Zohar* 1:68a, 1:72a, 2:241a; *Sodei Razayya* 16d.

Studies:

Along the Path: Studies in Kabbalistic Myth, Symbolism, and Hermeneutics by Elliot R. Wolfson.
Parables in Midrash: Narrative and Exegesis in Rabbinic Literature by David Stern.
In Potiphar's House: The Interpretative Life of Biblical Texts by James Kugel.
Traditions of the Bible by James Kugel.
"Graven Image" by Shamma Friedman.
"The Body as Image of God in Rabbinic Literature" by Alon Goshen Gottstein.

472. THE IMAGE OF JACOB CAST DOWN FROM HEAVEN

Just before the destruction of the Temple in Jerusalem, the people grew desperate, for they knew that they had angered God, and that God would no longer protect them. "Please, God," they prayed, "If You cannot forgive us, forgive us for the merits of our ancestors."

God replied: "You think, O Israel, that you may freely anger Me, because the image of Jacob is engraved on My Throne of Glory? Here, have it, it is thrown in your face!" And God cast down the glory of Israel from heaven, as it is said, *Has cast down from heaven to earth the majesty of Israel* (Lam. 2:1).

In its immediate context, this myth of the image of Jacob being cast down from heaven is meant to demonstrate God's irrevocable resolve to destroy the Temple in Jerusalem. At the same time, the underlying message of this myth clearly appears to be in opposition to the treatment of Jacob as a divine figure, making this a polemical myth. A parallel purpose is served by the myth in which Elisha ben Abuyah sees the angel Metatron seated on a throne in heaven and concludes that there are two powers in heaven. Both of these myths can be seen as representing the rabbinic reaction to those who they feel have carried their obsession with Jacob and Enoch too far. See "A Vision of Metatron," p. 174.

Another hint of rabbinic ambiguity about Jacob can be found in *Genesis Rabbah* 68:12, which interprets the ascending and descending of the angels in Genesis 28:12 in a highly ambiguous fashion. "Ascending and descending" are taken to mean that some of the angels were exalting him and others degrading, maligning, and accusing him. Since the views attributed to the angels are often a projection of rabbinic attitudes, here there is a subtle acknowledgement that some rabbis viewed Jacob—and, by association, the veneration of him—positively, while others maligned him, as in this myth of Jacob's image being cast down from heaven.

Although the myth might be seen as one of despair, it also serves to protect the people of Israel, for otherwise the biblical verse *Has cast down from heaven to earth the majesty of Israel* (Lam. 2:1) could be understood as being a complete rejection of the people of Israel. But Jacob's name is also Israel, and this interpretation narrows the implications of the verse. In fact, this narrowing is confirmed in *Lamentations Rabbah* 2:7, which, commenting on the verse *He has ravaged Jacob like flaming fire, consuming on all sides* (Lam. 2:3), says: "When punishment comes into the world, Jacob alone experiences it."

There may also be a polemic here about the fall of Lucifer, which is found in *2 Enoch* (29:4-6): "But one from the order of archangels deviated, together with the division that was under his authority. He thought up the impossible idea, that he might place his throne higher than the clouds which are above the earth, and that he might become equal to My power. And I hurled him out from the height, together with his angels. And he was flying around in the air, ceaselessly, above the Bottomless."

If this myth about Jacob's image being cast down from heaven was indeed a polemic, then Jacob is compared to an evil, fallen angel. This suggests the intensity of the opposition to the veneration of Jacob. Recognition of this conflict is suggested in *Genesis Rabbah* 68:12, where it is said that among the angels who ascended and descended, some exalted Jacob and others were degrading toward him, dancing, leaping, and maligning him.

Sources:
Lamentations Rabbah 2:2; *Pesikta Rabbati* 27:2; *Hekhalot Rabbati* 9.

Studies:
The Doctrine of Merits in Old Rabbinical Literature by A. Marmorstein, pp. 101-102.
Parables in Midrash: Narrative and Exegesis in Rabbinic Literature by David Stern, pp. 109-114.
"The Image of Jacob Engraved upon the Throne: Further Reflection on the Esoteric Doctrine of the German Pietists" by Elliot R. Wolfson, pp. 1-62, 111-187.

473. THE DEATH OF JACOB

Jacob lay on his deathbed. The twelve tribes of Israel were gathered together surrounding his golden bed. Jacob said to his sons, "Purify yourself from uncleanliness, and I will tell you what will take place at the End of Days—the rewards of the righteous, the punishments of the wicked, and the happiness of Eden." But as soon as the Glory of the *Shekhinah* was revealed, the time in which King Messiah was destined to come was hidden from him, and the secrets could not be revealed.

Here Jacob on his deathbed is about to reveal to his sons the secret God told him about when the End of Days would take place. But as soon as he glimpsed the presence of the *Shekhinah*, his knowledge vanished.

Sources:
Targum Pseudo-Yonathan on Genesis 49:1; *B. Pesahim* 56a; *Genesis Rabbah* 98:2.

474. JACOB NEVER DIED

Everyone thought that Jacob had died. He had given his sons his final blessings, and it appeared that his soul had taken leave of this world. In fact, he was embalmed and buried. But even though it appeared that he had died, Jacob was actually alive. Nor did he die after that. Indeed, Jacob never died.

It is said that some of those at Jacob's funeral saw his eyes open once or twice, but they thought their own eyes had deceived them. Indeed, Jacob was present during the Exodus from Egypt, and he witnessed the crossing of the Red Sea and the drowning of Pharaoh's soldiers who chased after them. That is the meaning of the verse *Israel saw the Egyptians dead on the shore of the sea* (Exod 14:30).

Likewise, Jacob witnessed the giving of the Torah, the ascent of Elijah, and Daniel's encounter with Bel. So too did he see the Temple built, destroyed, and rebuilt.

Still others say that God's promise to Jacob, *I will deliver you from far away, your folk from their land of captivity* (Jer. 30:10), meant that Jacob lives on in his seed, especially in those who make their home in the Holy Land. After all, Jacob was also Israel, and as long as the children of Israel still exist, Jacob will never die.

One of the primary mythic motifs in Judaism concerns heroic figures who never die. Elijah's ascent in a fiery chariot (2 Kings 2:11) seems to have set this theme in motion. Others who are portrayed as having never died include Enoch, who *walked with God, and he was no more; for God took him* (Gen. 5:24). This ambiguous statement, rather than the expected, "and he died," gave birth to a rich tradition about Enoch in which he was said to have been taken up into heaven and (in some versions) transformed into the angel Metatron.

In addition, Abraham, Moses, and King David are often subjects of rabbinic legends and folktales about appearances after their deaths. Although the deaths of all of them are clearly stated in the Bible, there are also some doubts associated with these accounts. Thus it says about Moses, *And no one knows of his burial place to this day* (Deut. 34:6). Likewise, there is considerable doubt that King David is buried in his tomb on Mount Zion.

The tradition that Jacob never died may derive from the memorable reply that Jacob's sons made to Joseph, when he asked them *"How is your aged father of whom you spoke? Is he still in good health?" They replied, "He is yet alive"* (Gen. 43:27-28). This phrase is often quoted as evidence that Jacob never died.

Rashi offers another clue for Jacob's immortality in his interpretation of Genesis 49:33, *Breathing his last, he was gathered to his people.* Rashi comments: "But 'dying' is not said of him since the word used was '*vayigva,*' 'expired,' rather than '*vayamot,*' 'dying.' Our rabbis of blessed memory said that this implies that 'our father Jacob did not die.'" Here Rashi quotes *B. Ta'anit* 5b, where Rabbi Yitzhak says, in the name of Rabbi Yohanan: "*Ya'akov Avinu lo met*—Our father Jacob did not die."

Further, Jacob's immortality seems to be understood as linked to the people of Israel—thus, as long as the people Israel thrive, Jacob is assured of immortality. This identification of the people Israel with Jacob is made explicit in Jeremiah 30:10: "*Therefore fear not, O Jacob My servant,*" said Yahweh. "*Neither be dismayed, O Israel, For, lo, I will save you from afar.*"

Yet, while the immortality of Abraham, Moses, and King David is the subject of many legends and tales, Jacob's immortality exists more as an assertion than as the subject of a legendary narrative. Rather, it seems to be part of the divinization of Jacob, with immortality being one of the required characteristics of a divine figure.

In *Likutei Moharan* 1:47 Rabbi Nachman of Bratslav interprets allegorically the statement in *B. Ta'anit* 5b that Jacob never died. Rabbi Nachman links Jacob to the holiness of the Land of Israel, which symbolizes eternal life. Therefore, Jacob did not really die, but lives eternally.

Sources:
Genesis Rabbah 56:10, 69:17; *Sifre on Deuteronomy* 352; *B. Ta'anit* 5b; Rashi on Gen.
    50:1; *B. Sota* 13b; *Likutei Moharan* 1:47.

Studies:
"Jacob Our Father Never Died" by Marc Bregman. Lecture given at the Textual
    Reasoning Conference, Drew University, 1997, in preparation for publication.

475. SUMMONING THE PATRIARCHS

During the reign of Emperor Rudolf II, there lived among the Jews of Prague the great Rabbi Judah Loew, who was well versed in all of the mysteries and was a great master of the kabbalah. Now it happened that the emperor heard of Rabbi Loew's reputation and sent for him with a strange request: he wanted the rabbi to invoke the patriarchs Abraham, Isaac, and Jacob, and the sons of Jacob, to summon them from their graves. Rabbi Loew was appalled at this request, but when the emperor threatened the well-being of the Jews of Prague if he did not comply, Rabbi Loew agreed to attempt to do as he had asked. The rabbi warned the emperor, however, that under no circumstances must he laugh at what he saw, and the emperor promised that he would not.

So it was that the day and place were fixed, and when Rabbi Loew and the emperor were alone in a secluded room of the castle, Rabbi Loew pronounced the spell that summoned the patriarchs and the sons of Jacob. And to the great amazement of the emperor, they appeared one after the other in their true form, and the emperor was amazed at the size and power of each of them, which far exceeded those of men in his own time. But when Naphtali, the son of Jacob, leaped with great ease over ears of corn and stalks of flax in the vision, the emperor could not contain himself and began to laugh. Suddenly the apparitions vanished and the ceiling of that room began to descend and was on the verge of crushing the emperor when Rabbi Loew succeeded in making it halt with the help of another spell. And it is told that the fallen ceiling can still be seen today in that room, which is kept locked.

Numerous tales concerning Rabbi Judah Loew of Prague are to be found. The most famous of these concerns the creation of the golem, the man made out of clay, with which Rabbi Loew was said to have protected the Jewish community of Prague from a series of blood libels. But there are many other tales recounting the marvels of the Maharal, as Rabbi Loew was known. Many of these concern his use of powers deriving from his knowledge of the Jewish mystical tradition, known as kabbalah. Only the purest and most eminent sages were considered capable of engaging in kabbalistic studies, and a great many stories are told of those who lost their sanity or even their lives by undertaking such studies without the proper background or preparation. Here the king is saved from destruction only because the pious Rabbi Loew is able to prevent the ceiling from collapsing. The magic of being able to invoke the presence of the patriarchs reflects the midrashic principle that the past is alive and that all generations exist at the same time. The collapsing of the room in which the vision of the patriarchs takes place echoes the famous talmudic legend of Rabbi Eliezer ben Hyrcanus and other rabbis, who disagreed about a point of the Law. See "The Rabbis Overrule God," p. 67.

Another, probably earlier, version of the summoning of a patriarch is found in *Ma'aseh Nissim*. This describes how Rabbi Lezer, a master of the Name, who lived in Worms, invoked King David's general Joab. Joab turned out to be of such great size that every step he took caused the house to shake and terrified the young men who observed the invocation, so they begged the rabbi to make him disappear, which he did. So frivolous was this use of the Ineffable Name, that in the version recounted in "Summoning the Patriarchs" it is the emperor who makes the demand, rather than the young Jewish students.

Sources:
Sippurim: Prager Sammlung jüdischer Legenden in neuer Auswahl und Bearbeitung.
    Version of L. Weisel.

476. THE BIRTH OF MOSES

Now Amram, the father of Moses, was a doctor able to cure everyone in Egypt. So great and exalted was he that he served Pharaoh himself, with the help of God. But there was a sorcerer, whose name was Pilti, who had read in the Book of Signs. From reading there he had learned of the coming birth of the child Moses, who would set free his people, the Jews, from oppression, while the kingdom of Egypt would suffer. This sorcerer reported to Pharaoh that he had seen the star of Israel ascending, while the destruction of Pharaoh's kingdom was growing near. And when Pharaoh heard this, he grew afraid, and he asked the sorcerer to tell him more of what he had seen. Then Pilti reported that he had seen the Apostle of the Jews cast into the sea, and he had also seen the people Israel cast into the sea, and the waters of the sea were parted by him who had not yet been born.

Now when Pharaoh heard this he was filled with anger for forty days, and since the child had not yet been born, he commanded that the men of Israel be prevented from approaching their wives, lest the child be conceived. Even Amram was forbidden to return to his wife, and was forced to remain within the palace. But Pharaoh could not stand against the will of the Lord. One night a meeting was arranged between Amram and his wife, Jochebed, and from this meeting the child was begotten in the womb of his mother.

Then the sorcerer Pilti returned to Pharaoh and told him that he had seen signs that the child had been conceived, despite the command of Pharaoh, for a star had revealed the child's future. Pharaoh grew angry and made a decree that every son born to the Hebrews should be cast into the Nile, but that every daughter should be permitted to live. However the midwives feared the God of Israel, and secretly let the male children live. Therefore the people multiplied in number, and Pharaoh set himself against the Hebrews, who were growing powerful.

Now when the time came for a daughter of Israel to give birth, she would go into the wilderness. If the child was a daughter, she would return with the girl child. But if it were a son, he was left in the wilderness, where God protected him, and suckled him with honey out of the rocks. And when the child had grown, he would return to his father's house. And all of these children had complete faith and trust in God, and never forgot how they were preserved. Then God remembered the covenant He had made with the pious, and in the seventh month the great prophet Moses was born. And God told the Hosts of Heaven that he had been born for whose sake God had created the world out of nothingness.

All the stars did obeisance to the infant Moses, for his light was the source of theirs. And it was known among all the children of Israel that the prophet of the Lord had been born, the select of all creation. The master of signs had come, the master of covenants, the master of prayer, he who was to receive the holiest of all laws, the prophet of all generations.

Here is a mythical birth of Moses from *Sefer ha-Yashar*, an unusual midrashic text that presents alternate versions of most of the primary biblical episodes. That the birth of Moses is prophesied based on an ascending star has a distinct echo of the birth of Jesus, and also echoes the midrashic account of the birth of Abraham, which may well draw on Christian sources.

As presented here, the birth of Moses fulfills God's promise to the children of Israel that a redeemer would be born. This is described as a universal event, involving all the stars, who bow down to the infant Moses. In fact, the kind of birth described in this myth strongly implies a kind of messianic role for Moses, who serves as a model for the concept of the Messiah. This shows that there was a Jewish tradition beyond that of the Samaritans in which Moses was viewed as a figure of messianic proportions beyond even the role of the redeemer that the Bible attributes to him.

Sources:
Sefer ha-Yashar 67.

477. AN ARK IN THE BULRUSHES

Then Pharaoh charged all his people, saying, "Every boy that is born you shall throw into the Nile, but let every girl live."

A certain man of the house of Levi went and married a Levite woman. The woman conceived and bore a son; and when she saw how beautiful he was, she hid him for three months. When she could hide him no longer, she got a wicker basket for him and caulked it with bitumen and pitch. She put the child into it and placed it among the reeds by the bank of the Nile. And his sister stationed herself at a distance, to learn what would befall him.

The daughter of Pharaoh came down to bathe in the Nile, while her maidens walked along the Nile. She spied the basket among the reeds and sent her slave girl to fetch it. When she opened it, she saw that it was a child, a boy crying. She took pity on it and said, "This must be a Hebrew child." Then his sister said to Pharaoh's daughter, "Shall I go and get you a Hebrew nurse to suckle the child for you?" And Pharaoh's daughter answered, "Yes." So the girl went and called the child's mother. And Pharaoh's daughter said to her, "Take this child and nurse it for me, and I will pay your wages." So the woman took the child and nursed it. When the child grew up, she brought him to Pharaoh's daughter, who made him her son. She named him Moses, explaining, "I drew him out of the water."

As Joseph Campbell notes in *The Hero with a Thousand Faces*, the birth of the hero is inevitably extraordinary. Faced with Pharaoh's decree ordering the death of all male Hebrew infants, Moses' mother placed him in an ark left floating in the bulrushes, well aware that the infant would be found, and hopefully raised, by an Egyptian family. That the one who finds him is the daughter of Pharaoh is an expression of his extraordinary fate. Note that this myth also provides an explanation for Moses' name, relating it to how he was found and drawn out of the water.

Sources:
Exodus 1:23, 2:1-10.

478. PHARAOH AND THE CHILD MOSES

After the daughter of Pharaoh found the infant Moses in the bulrushes, she brought the child to live in the palace. There she told her father and his court that the Nile river had given her that child as a gift. So it was that they accepted the child, since it was the wish of the princess. But one of Pharaoh's sorcerers secretly believed that the child was a Hebrew. And he waited for the chance to turn against him.

One day, when Moses was three years old, he sat at the table on his mother's lap. Next to her sat Pharaoh, and to his right was Pharaoh's wife. Attracted by the glittering gems in Pharaoh's crown, the child Moses reached for the crown and knocked it off of Pharaoh's head. Then the evil sorcerer, who had been waiting for just such a moment, quickly said: "Do not ignore this sign from fate, my lord. For this child may be destined to usurp your throne." Pharaoh was filled with fear that this might have been such a sign. Therefore he called together all his advisors and asked their opinions.

Now the angel Gabriel had been sent by God to guard the infant Moses at all times. And when the angel saw the danger the child faced, he disguised himself in the form of one of Pharaoh's advisers. And when Pharaoh asked them what they should do, he spoke and said: "Surely the child meant no evil. Why not give him a test to prove this? I suggest that two bowls be brought here. One of them will contain precious jewels and the other burning coals. If the child reaches for the jewels, this shows that he knows the coals are dangerous. For the coals will glow brighter than the jewels. That would prove that he is wise beyond his years. But if he reaches for the coals, that would prove that he has no more understanding than any other infant."

Pharaoh quickly agreed to this test, for it seemed reasonable to him. And when the bowls had been brought and the infant Moses set down before them, the angel Gabriel made himself invisible and stood next to the child. Now as it happened Moses was attracted to the jewels rather than the burning coals, and would have reached for them. But as he did, the angel stopped his hand and made him reach for the coals instead. And before the child realized how hot the coals were, he had brought it to his tongue, singeing it. And when the child burst into tears, Pharaoh concluded that the child was completely innocent.

That is how the child Moses was able to remain within Pharaoh's palace until he was grown. But because he had singed his tongue, he always spoke with a bit of a stutter after that. And that is why he brought his brother, Aaron, to speak for him when the day came that he stood before Pharaoh and demanded that he let his people go.

> This is an extremely famous midrash that is often told to children. It explains how Moses got his stutter, as well as how Pharaoh decided to keep the infant Moses and raise him in the palace. This is, indeed, an appropriate midrash for children, who can easily understand why the bright jewel would be more attractive to an infant than a burning coal. It is possible that there were specific midrashim that were primarily intended for children. For other examples, see "The Giant Og," p. 461 and the commentary to "The Star Maiden," p. 455 about the angel's wings.
>
> *Sources:*
> *Sefer ha-Yashar*; IFA 6725, 18238.

479. PHARAOH'S DAUGHTER

Pharaoh's daughter, Bitiah, knew by divine inspiration that she was destined to raise the redeemer of Israel. That is why she strolled beside the Nile every morning and evening.

When she discovered Moses floating in an ark she knew that God had given her what she sought, and she rejoiced. How did she know? She saw that the infant was circumcised.

Seeing that Bitiah wanted to save the infant, her attending maidens said to her, "Mistress, when a king issues a decree, even if the whole world does not fulfill it, at least his children should do so. Yet you transgress your father's decree." At that moment the angel Gabriel came and thrust them into the earth.

Bitiah named the infant she drew out of the water Moses, and this remained his name for the rest of his life.

God said to Bitiah, "Moses was not your son, yet you called him your son. Therefore, though you are not My daughter, I will call you My daughter." After that Bitiah went down to immerse herself in the river to cleanse herself from her father's idols, for the sake of converting to Judaism.

At the request of Moses, Bitiah was not afflicted by any of the ten plagues, and was the only female firstborn to be spared in Egypt. She was one of the nine who entered Paradise alive. There she was given her own heavenly palace, where she teaches Torah to the souls of righteous women.

> In the Midrash Pharaoh's daughter is given the name Bitiah, which means "daughter of God." She is regarded as a very holy figure, and is one of four righteous women who are said to have palaces in heaven of their own. The others are Serah bat Asher, Yocheved, the mother of Moses, and Deborah, the prophetess. See "Women in Paradise," p. 190.
>
> *Sources:*
> B. Sota 12b; B. Megillah 13a; Exodus Rabbah 1, 18:3; Leviticus Rabbah 1:3; Midrash
>   Mishlei 31:15; Midrash ha-Gadol on Genesis 23:1, Exodus 2:10; Derekh Eretz Zuta 1.

480. THE BURNING BUSH

Now Moses, tending the flock of his father-in-law Jethro, the priest of Midian, drove the flock into the wilderness, and came to Horeb, the mountain of God. An angel of the Lord appeared to him in a blazing fire out of a bush. He gazed, and there was a bush all aflame, yet the bush was not consumed. Moses said, "I must turn aside to look at this marvelous sight; why doesn't the bush burn up?" When the Lord saw that he had turned aside to look, God called to him out of the bush: "Moses! Moses!" He answered, "Here I am." And He said, "Do not come closer. Remove your sandals from your feet, for the place on which you stand is holy ground. I am," He said, "the God of your father, the God of Abraham, the God of Isaac, and the God of Jacob." And Moses hid his face, for he was afraid to look at God.

> The first encounter Moses has with God has many of the earmarks of a mystical vision. God speaks to Moses out of a bush that is burning but is not consumed. From this time on, the life of Moses is completely transformed, as many mystics have described their lives after having a mystical experience. However, in biblical terms what Moses experiences is not a personal vision, but the arrival of his true destiny, serving as the Redeemer of Israel.
>
> It may seem strange that God chose something as unimposing as a bush to reveal Himself, but there are other examples of God contracting Himself into a small space, such as the Ark. Later a kabbalistic principle, that of *tzimtzum*, would be established on this concept of contraction. See "The Contraction of God," p. 13.
>
> As with Abraham, God has chosen Moses, who starts out as a reluctant prophet, but in the end becomes the greatest prophetic figure of all. From this point on, God gives Moses explicit instructions about how to approach Pharaoh to demand that the

Israelites, who were valuable slaves, should be set free and permitted to depart from Egypt. Likewise, God instructs Moses in how to approach the people of Israel, who are slow to acknowledge Moses as their leader.

In subsequent encounters, Moses speaks directly to God, sees Him face to face, and receives the Torah, God's most precious gift, for Israel. All of these events are prefaced by this first revelation at the burning bush.

Sources:
Exodus 3:1-6.

481. MOSES SWALLOWED BY A SERPENT

At a night encampment on the way, Yahweh encountered Moses and sought to kill him (Exod. 4:24). Why did God seek to kill him? Because of his son, Gershom, who had not been circumcised since Jethro, the father-in-law of Moses, had not allowed Moses to circumcise him.

Some say that God sent the angel Uriel in the guise of a giant serpent, who came and swallowed Moses from his head to the place of his circumcision. When Zipporah saw this, she understood that Moses had been attacked because their son had not been circumcised. *So Zipporah took a flint and cut off her son's foreskin, and touched his legs with it, saying, "You are truly a bridegroom of blood to me!" And when He let him alone, she added, "A bridegroom of blood because of the circumcision"* (Exod. 4:25-26).

Others say that God sent two angels, Af and Hemah, the Angels of Anger and Fury, after Moses. Hemah swallowed him, except for his legs. Only after Zipporah circumcised their son did Hemah spit him out. Then Moses sought to slay the destroying angels, as it is said, *Give up anger, abandon fury* (Ps. 37:8).

Still others say that Zipporah knew by divine inspiration that in order to save Moses she must circumcise her son. Then she did not hesitate, but took the flint and *cut off her son's foreskin* (Exod. 4:25) and cast the foreskin at the feet of the Destroyer, saying, "May the blood of this circumcision atone for my husband." After that the Destroyer left him alone. Then Zipporah said, "How beloved is the blood that has delivered this bridegroom from the hand of the Angel of Death."

> The account of how God sought to kill Moses in Exodus 4:24 has always been considered perplexing. Many biblical scholars believe the passage is fragmentary. Especially oblique are Zipporah's comments about Moses being "a bridegroom of blood" to her. The rabbinic explanation is that Moses had not circumcised his son Gershom at the proper time and therefore God sent an angel in the form of a serpent who swallowed Moses from his head to the place of his circumcision. Seeing this, Zipporah understood that God's anger concerned their failure to circumcise the child. Thus she picked up a flint and circumcised the child on the spot, and the attack on Moses comes to an end. Rashi says: "She was now sure of the cause of his illness, and realized that circumcision had saved his life."
>
> Zipporah's comment, from *Targum Neophyti* on Exodus 4:26, "How beloved is the blood that has delivered this bridegroom from the hand of the Angel of Death," is a perfect example of how the *Targum* changed the meaning of biblical texts by interpolating additional words into them. Here it is the verse *You are truly a bridegroom of blood* (Exod. 4:25), that serves as the basis of this interpolation. This transforms an enigmatic and fragmentary text into an assured and complete blessing.
>
> The two angels, Af and Hemah, are the personifications of Anger and Fury. Af is a male—and Hemah is a female—destroying angel. These furies resemble the Furies of Greek myth. Hemah's role is derived from Proverbs 16:14: *The king's wrath (Hemah) is a messenger of death.* Af and Hemah go forth together, like Samael and Lilith, and they are paired—and cursed—in Psalms 37:8: *Give up anger, abandon fury.* Through them God expresses his anger at Moses for not having circumcised his son. In general, there

are five great destroying angels: in addition to Af and Hemah, they are Ketzeph (Displeasure), Hashmed (Destruction), and Hashbeth (Annihilation). These angels of destruction can only be stopped by calling upon the patriarchs, Abraham, Isaac, and Jacob (*Exodus Rabbah* 44:8 and *Ecclesiastes Rabbah* 4:3).

Note that this attack on Moses comes right after God had told him about the slaying of the firstborn of Egypt, and here he is almost slain because of his own firstborn. There seems to be some kind of link, but because of the truncated nature of Exodus 4:24-26 it is difficult to ascertain exactly what it is.

Why was the son of Moses not circumcised? Some sources put the blame on Jethro, Zipporah's father, others on Moses. Jethro is said to have ordered Moses not to circumcise the baby at the time that he agreed to let Moses marry Zipporah. Moses promised Jethro that he would not do so, and therefore he could not break his vow. Note that it is Zipporah, and not Moses, who does the act of circumcision.

Sources:
Targum Pseudo-Yonathan to Exodus 4:24-26; *Targum Neophyti* on Exodus 4:24-26.; *B.*
    Nedarim 32a; *Exodus Rabbah* 5:8; *Deuteronomy Rabbah* 3:11; *Midrash Tehillim* 7:11;
    Yalkut Shim'oni, Shemot 168; *Zohar* 1:93b.

482. SERAH BAT ASHER

Serah bat Asher was the daughter of Asher, one of the sons of Jacob. She was among the sixty-nine who ascended with Jacob to Egypt, and she was among those who crossed the Red Sea and were counted by Moses in the census of the wilderness.

Serah was still a child when Joseph's brothers asked her to sing a little song for her grandfather, Jacob. For Joseph had sent his brothers to bring the House of Jacob to Egypt, because of the famine in the land. Then Joseph's brothers had to find a way to break the news to Jacob that Joseph was still alive. They said, "If we tell our Father that Joseph is alive, he might die from the shock." And they decided to have Serah play the harp for Jacob and sing the words "Joseph is alive." This Serah gladly did, and when Jacob, who was lost in a reverie, suddenly understood what she was saying, he cried out, "Is it true?" And when Serah assured him that it was, Jacob, in his joy, gave her a great blessing, which let her live so long.

But there is another version of this account, in which Jacob was furious that Serah had mentioned this most painful episode in his life, the loss of his son Joseph. And Jacob jumped up and pointed to her and said, "You should live so long!" And she did.

> The name Serah bat Asher appears in the Torah only twice, in two lists. Nothing else is said about her. Yet, using the midrashic method, the ancient rabbis were able to create a full identity for her and make her play an essential role in many key biblical episodes. They concluded that she lived longer than anyone else, even Methuselah. It was she who, knowing the sign, identified Moses as the Redeemer; she who helped Moses search for the coffin of Joseph; she who crossed the Red Sea and later reported on what the walls of the Red Sea looked like. This figure, Serah bat Asher, comes to life in the Talmud and the Midrash and becomes one of the favorite figures of the rabbis, whom they draw into the narrative as often as possible. How they did this is an object lesson in the midrashic method.
>
> Serah is also used to resolve another apparent contradiction. Genesis 46:27 states that *the total of Jacob's household who came to Egypt was 70 persons.* However, those listed in Genesis 46:8-25 only total 69. The explanation given in *Genesis Rabbah* 94:9 is that Serah bat Asher was counted twice. Because of her extreme righteousness and wisdom, she had the value of two.
>
> The story of Serah bat Asher begins with a name in the list in the passage describing Jacob's journey into Egypt: *Jacob and all his offspring with him came to Egypt. He*

brought with him to Egypt his sons and grandsons, his daughters and granddaughters—all his offspring (Gen. 46:6-7). Among the 69 who accompanied Jacob into Egypt were, as recounted in Genesis 46:17: *Asher's sons: Imnah, Ishvi, and Beriah, and their sister Serah.* Serah might have remained merely a name in this list if not for a curious parallel. For in another list, in Numbers 26:46, that of the census taken by Moses in the wilderness the name Serah bat Asher appears again: *The name of Asher's daughter was Serah.*

What are we to make of the fact that the same name appears in two lists separated by at least 200 years? From our perspective, it might be discounted as a coincidence. After all, Asher was a respectable name, and it is certainly possible that someone named Asher might name his daughter Serah. But from the point of view of the ancient rabbis, the fact that these two lists had this one name in common cried out for explanation. So they arrived at what was for them the logical conclusion: they were the same person.

That resolves the problem of the identity of the two Serahs, but it doesn't explain how she lived so long. However, rabbinic ingenuity found a solution for this problem as well. Using the midrashic method, the rabbis searched for the "right place." This is the place in the text that gives the necessary clue, making it possible to read between the lines. And in this case the clue involved another matter that is missing in the biblical narrative: how the sons of Jacob finally informed him that his beloved son, Joseph, was not dead after all.

It all goes back to the brothers' discovery that Joseph was still alive. Indeed, he was none other than the Prince of Egypt. And now that Joseph had revealed his true identity, he commanded his brothers to bring their father and the rest of the family to Egypt, for there was a famine in the land: *"And you shall tell my father of all my glory in Egypt, and of all that you have seen, and you shall hasten and bring down my father hither"* (Gen. 45:13). This must have presented a dilemma to Joseph's brothers, since they had cast him naked into a pit and then sold him into slavery and then told their father that he had been slain by a wild beast. Now they had to go back to their father, Jacob, a frail old man, and tell him that Joseph was alive after all.

Reading between the lines, the rabbis intuited that the brothers were filled with guilt and remorse, as well as with fear that Jacob might die of shock when he heard the news. So they came up with the idea of letting Serah break the news to him. They asked Serah, who apparently was a child, to play the harp for Jacob and sing him a little song, with the words "Joseph is alive, Joseph is alive." Serah, of course, was glad to sing a song for her grandfather, and when Jacob realized what she was saying, he jumped up and asked, "Is it true?" And when she told him it was true, he blessed her with such a great blessing that she lived as long as she did! In this way the midrash brought Serah to life and explained how she lived for so long.

Sources:

Genesis Rabbah 94:9; *Targum Pseudo-Yonathan* on Genesis 46:17; *Sefer ha-Yashar* 109b-110a; *Pesikta Rabbati* 17:5; *Midrash ha-Gadol, va-Yigash* 45:26; IFA 5029; oral version collected from an old woman in Indianapolis by Howard Schwartz.

Studies:

"Serach bat Asher and Bitiah bat Pharaoh—Names which Became Legends" by Margaret Jacobi.

483. THE SECRET OF THE REDEEMER

There was a secret sign that God had communicated to Abraham, the secret of the mystery of the Redeemer. Abraham, in turn, delivered the secret to Isaac, Isaac revealed it to Jacob, and Jacob shared it with Joseph. Joseph revealed the secret to his sons. And Asher, one of the sons of Jacob, shared the secret of the mystery of the Redeemer with his daughter, Serah. It was understood that whoever came to deliver the children of Israel from Egypt and said these words would be the true deliverer, sent to them by the Lord.

During the long years of slavery in Egypt, Serah bat Asher was enslaved and forced to work in a mill. When the time came to be freed from slavery, it was Serah who identified Moses as the Redeemer. For when Moses and Aaron came to the elders of Israel and performed the signs in their sight, the elders sought out Serah bat Asher, and they said to her, "A certain man has come, and he has performed signs in our sight," and they described them. So too did he say, *"I have taken note of you"* (Exod. 3:16). Serah said, "That is the sign that I learned from my father. Therefore he is the one who will redeem Israel." Then they knew that Moses would surely deliver them from the power of Pharaoh, and they believed him and bowed down and prostrated themselves, and recognized Moses as their Redeemer.

> In the secret message, "I have taken note of you" (*pakod pakadti*), God is actually speaking to Moses, as found in Exodus 3:16: *"Go and assemble the elders of Israel and say to them: Yahweh, the God of your fathers, the God of Abraham, Isaac, and Jacob, has appeared to me and said, 'I have taken note of you and of what is being done to you in Egypt.'"* Here God has Moses introduce himself to the elders of Israel in much the same way he introduced himself to Pharaoh—as the representative of God—coming to them with God's own words. What he says is confirmed by Serah, whose knowledge comes directly from her father, and, indirectly, from the patriarchs, Abraham, Isaac, Jacob and Joseph.
>
> Sources:
> B. Sota 13a; *Exodus Rabbah* 5:13-14; *Pirkei de-Rabbi Eliezer* 48.

484. THE COFFIN OF JOSEPH

Before his death, *Joseph made the sons of Israel swear, saying, "When God has taken notice of you, you shall carry up my bones from here"* (Gen. 50:25). So when the time came to leave Egypt, Moses searched everywhere for Joseph's coffin, but no one remembered where it was. After Moses had tired himself out searching for it, he encountered Serah bat Asher, who was a survivor of the generation of Joseph. Serah said: "My lord Moses, why are you so downcast?" Moses replied: "For three days and nights I have been searching for Joseph's coffin and I cannot find it." She said to him: "Come with me and I will show you where it is." Moses said: "Who are you, and how do you know where the coffin can be found?" She said: "I am Serah bat Asher, and I know for I was present when the leaden coffin of Joseph was sunk into the Nile." She led him to a shore of the Nile and there she said: "In this place the Egyptian magicians and astrologers made a metal coffin for Joseph and sank it into the river Nile, so that its waters should be blessed. Then they returned to Pharaoh and said: 'If it is your wish that these people should never leave this place, then as long as they do not find the bones of Joseph, they will be unable to leave.'"

Some say that Moses then leaned over the bank of the Nile and called out: "Joseph, Joseph, we are leaving Egypt. The time has come for God to redeem His children, and for the oath you imposed on Israel to be fulfilled. I call on you to appear before me, and I will take your bones to the land of Canaan. If you will show yourself, well and good; if not, behold, we are free of your oath." At that moment Joseph's heavy lead coffin shook itself free, rose up from the depths, and floated on the surface, and Moses took it and carried it with him.

Others say that Moses took a shard, wrote God's Name upon it, and threw the shard into the river. At once Joseph's coffin floated up to the surface.

All the years that the Israelites were in the wilderness there were two arks that accompanied the children of Israel in their wandering, the one containing the remains of Joseph, as it is said, *And Moses took with him the bones of Joseph* (Exod. 13:19), and the other the Ark of the Tabernacle. The one represented the past and the other, the Torah, defined the future.

> At the end of Genesis, Joseph, surrounded by his brothers, takes a vow of the future generations: *"I am about to die. God will surely take notice of you and bring you up from this land to the land that He promised on oath to Abraham, to Isaac, and to Jacob."* So Joseph made the sons of Israel swear, saying, *"When God has taken notice of you, you shall carry up my bones from here."* Joseph died at the age of one hundred and ten years; and he was embalmed and placed in a coffin in Egypt (Gen. 50:24-26). This coffin, according to *Mekhilta de-Rabbi Ishmael*, was sunk in the middle of the Nile. Later it is reported in Exodus 14:19 that Joseph's coffin was carried next to the Ark of the Tabernacle. This raised the question of how the coffin was found, which is answered in this myth.
>
> In leading Moses to the place where Joseph's coffin was lowered into the Nile, Serah bat Asher performs her most important task. This midrash fills in a major gap in the biblical narrative between the vow that Joseph made the sons of Israel swear on his deathbed that *you shall carry my bones from here* (Gen. 50:25) and the report that *Moses took the bones of Joseph with him* (Exod. 14:19). However, it is Moses who must figure a way to raise up the sunken coffin. In one version of the myth, he calls out to Joseph, saying, "If you make yourself visible, well and good. If not, we shall be innocent of violating the oath you made our forefathers swear" (*Pesikta de-Rav Kahana*). Thus, if Moses is unable to raise up the coffin, he will at least have done his best to fulfill the oath.
>
> One of miracles of the recovery of Joseph's coffin is that it was made of metal. *B. Sota* 13a addresses this issue: "Be not astonished that iron should float," and follows with an example (from 2 Kings 6:5-7) of how an axe-head was made to float.
>
> *B. Sota* and *Pesikta de-Rav Kahana* recount a dialogue with a passerby who saw the two caskets Israel carried in the desert, one the coffin of Joseph and the other containing the tablets of the Law. "What are these two caskets?" They answered, "One is the ark of Joseph, who was mortal, and the other is the Ark of Him who is immortal." The passerby asked, "Is it proper that God's Ark should accompany an ark with a man in it?" They answered, "This one contains the bones of Joseph, who fulfilled all the commands that God set down in the other Ark."
>
> Sources:
> *Targum Pseudo-Yonathan* on Genesis 50:26, Exodus 13:19; *B. Sota* 13a-b; *Mekhilta de-Rabbi Ishmael, be-Shalah* 1:86-110; *Pesikta de-Rav Kahana* 11:12.

485. A VISION AT THE RED SEA

When Serah bat Asher was among the children of Israel at the Red Sea, she had a vision in which she saw things that none of the others saw. In the vision she saw the multitude of angels who had gathered to watch the children of Israel cross the Red Sea. So too did she see the Divine Presence, who descended among them when Miriam played the tambourine and sang the Song of the Sea. And in that vision Serah even saw the Holy One commanding the waters of the Red Sea to part. For other than Moses, Serah was the only one alive in that generation who could look upon the Holy One and live.

> There are contradictory traditions about what the Israelites saw at the Red Sea. Some state that even the lowest among the people saw more than the prophet Ezekiel saw in his famous vision in the first chapter of his book. In "God's Presence at the Red Sea," p. 13, the infant boys raised by God recognize His presence at the Red Sea. In the present myth, however, only Serah bat Asher is aware of all the angels present at the Red Sea, along with God, who descended to witness the miracle of the crossing there.

See the following myth of "The Walls of the Red Sea," where Serah reports on what she witnessed.

Sources:
Pesikta de-Rav Kahana 11:13.

486. THE WALLS OF THE RED SEA

Rabbi Yohanan once asked his students to describe the appearance of the walls of the Red Sea when the waters parted for the children of Israel to cross. When none could do so, Rabbi Yohanan described them as resembling a window lattice. Then, all at once, they heard a voice say: "No, it was not like that at all!" And when they looked up, they saw the face of a very old woman peering in the window of the house of study. "Who are you?" demanded Rabbi Yohanan. "I am Serah bat Asher," came the reply, "and I know exactly what the walls resembled, I was there, I crossed the Red Sea—and they resembled shining mirrors, mirrors in which every man, woman, and child was reflected, so that it seemed like an even greater multitude crossed there, not only those of the present, but also those of the past and future as well." And when Serah had finished speaking, none dared contradict her, for her knowledge was firsthand.

> Here is one more example of a midrash in which Serah bat Asher, by this time more than a thousand years old, suddenly appears to resolve a question about the Exodus. Her explanations are definitive for, as she notes, "I was there." This one concerns what the walls of the Red Sea looked like. As for the reason that the walls shone, *Pesikta de-Rav Kahana* suggests it was because of the radiance of Moses and Aaron.

> *Sources:*
> *Pesikta de-Rav Kahana* 11:13.

487. THE DEATH OF SERAH BAT ASHER

How long did Serah live? Some say she lived until the days of the Temple, while others say she lived even longer than that. One account has it that she met her death in the ninth century in a fire in a synagogue in Isfahan. And when that synagogue was rebuilt it was named the Synagogue of Serah bat Asher, and the Jews of Persia made pilgrimages to that synagogue, the holiest Jewish site in the land.

Others say that Serah bat Asher never died. She was taken to the heavenly Garden of Eden while she was still alive, because she had announced to Jacob that Joseph was alive. There Serah has a palace of her own, where she teaches Torah to the righteous women. And they know that every word she says is true, because she was a witness to all the miracles that took place in those mighty days.

> There are two legendary accounts of the ultimate fate of Serah. One reports that she met her death in a fire in a synagogue in Isfahan, Persia, in the tenth century. That synagogue was rebuilt and named after her, and it is still the holiest Jewish site in Iran, to which Persian Jews used to make pilgrimages when they were still permitted to do so.

> However, it is also said that Serah never died, but that she was taken into Paradise alive because she brought Jacob the news that Joseph was still alive (Gen. 45:26). She is counted among the nine who entered Paradise alive (*Derekh Eretz Zuta* 1), and it is said that she now is one of the blessed women who teaches Torah to the souls of righteous women in a heavenly palace of her own (*Zohar* 3:167a-b). See "Women in Paradise," p. 190.

As this rich legend of Serah bat Asher makes abundantly clear, it is the latter version that rings true. Serah never died. She was created out of the imagination of the rabbis and she lives on, a living witness to God's miracles during the Exodus who wanders the world, setting things straight.

Sources:
Targum Pseudo-Yonathan on Genesis 46:17; *Sefer ha-Yashar* 110a; *B. Sota* 13a; *Alpha Beta de-Ben Sira* 28a; *Derekh Eretz Zuta* 1; *Targum Yonathan, Bereshit* 46:17; *Zohar* 3:167a-b.

488. GOD'S FOOTSTOOL

The Egyptian taskmasters beat the Israelites so that they would make bricks for them. As the Israelites were treading the straw in the mortar, along with their wives and sons, the straw pierced their heels, and the blood mingled with the mortar. A young woman named Rachel, who was near childbirth, was treading the mortar, and the child was born there and became entangled in the clay and brick. Her cry ascended before the Throne of Glory, and the angel Gabriel came down and brought the brick into heaven, and set it as a footstool beneath God's throne.

This myth recounts the suffering of the Israelites under Egyptian bondage, and how a newborn child was lost in the mortar and the angel Gabriel brought the brick into heaven as a footstool for God, which thus became a memorial of the bondage of the Israelites in Egypt. *Targum Pseudo-Yonathan* on Exodus 24:10 links this footstool with the sapphire stone under the feet of God in Exodus 24:10: *And they saw the God of Israel; and there was under His feet the like of a paved work of sapphire stone.*

Sources:
Pirkei de-Rabbi Eliezer 48; *3 Baruch* 3:5; *Targum Pseudo-Yonathan* on *Exodus* 24:10.

489. THE PARTING OF THE RED SEA

Then the Lord said to Moses, "Why do you cry out to Me? Tell the Israelites to go forward. And you lift up your rod and hold out your arm over the sea and split it, so that the Israelites may march into the sea on dry ground. And I will stiffen the hearts of the Egyptians so that they go in after them; and I will gain glory through Pharaoh and all his warriors, his chariots and his horsemen. Let the Egyptians know that I am Lord, when I gain glory through Pharaoh, his chariots, and his horsemen."

The angel of God, who had been going ahead of the Israelite army, now moved and followed behind them; and the pillar of cloud shifted from in front of them and took up a place behind them, and it came between the army of the Egyptians and the army of Israel. Thus there was the cloud with the darkness, and it cast a spell upon the night, so that the one could not come near the other all through the night.

Then Moses held out his arm over the sea and the Lord drove back the sea with a strong east wind all that night, and turned the sea into dry ground. The waters were split, and the Israelites went into the sea on dry ground, the waters forming a wall for them on their right and on their left. The Egyptians came in pursuit after them into the sea, all of Pharaoh's horses, chariots, and horsemen. At the morning watch, the Lord looked down upon the Egyptian army from a pillar of fire and cloud, and threw the Egyptian army into panic. He locked the wheels of their chariots so that they moved forward with difficulty. And the Egyptians said, "Let us flee from the Israelites, for the Lord is fighting for them against Egypt."

Then the Lord said to Moses, "Hold out your arm over the sea, that the waters may come back upon the Egyptians and upon their chariots and upon their horsemen." Moses held out his arm over the sea, and at daybreak the sea returned to its normal state, and the Egyptians fled at its approach. But the Lord hurled the Egyptians into the sea. The waters turned back and covered the chariots and the horsemen—Pharaoh's entire army that followed them into the sea; not one of them remained. But the Israelites had marched through the sea on dry ground, the waters forming a wall for them on their right and on their left.

Thus the Lord delivered Israel that day from the Egyptians. Israel saw the Egyptians dead on the shore of the sea. And when Israel saw the wondrous power that the Lord had wielded against the Egyptians, the people feared the Lord; they had faith in the Lord and His servant Moses.

> The parting of the Red Sea is universally regarded as the greatest Jewish miracle of all time. Belief that the parting of the sea had really taken place was used as a test of faith. For example, a widow in Safed was said to have been possessed by a *dybbuk* because she did not believe that the waters of the sea had really parted. See "The Widow of Safed," p. 228.
>
> Rabbinic lore is full of descriptions of what the walls of the Red Sea looked like when they parted, how they contained foods such as pomegranates for those who became hungry while crossing, etc. According to *Mekhilta de-Rabbi Ishmael, be-Shalah* 4:87-97, the splitting of the Red Sea was a great revelation, in which the slave girls saw great things that even the prophet Ezekiel did not see. The widespread experience of this revelation serves the purpose of validating the account. See also "The Walls of the Red Sea" p. 381, where Serah bat Asher serves as a witness who had experienced this miracle firsthand.
>
> According to *Pirkei de-Rabbi Eliezer* 42, when the Red Sea split, it split into twelve paths, one for each of the 12 tribes.
>
> For other myths about the crossing of the Red Sea, see the next four entries.
>
> *Sources:*
> Exodus 14:15-31.

490. THE WATERS OF THE RED SEA REFUSE TO PART

Moses stretched his hand over the Red Sea as God had told him to do. When the sea saw this, it said, "Why should I divide my waters?" Moses answered, "The Lord sent me to do this thing." But the waters refused to be divided.

Then Moses lifted up his staff, with which he had performed miracles in Pharaoh's court, and he said to the sea, "Behold the staff of God which is in my hand and do what the Lord has commanded you to do." But the sea was stubborn and refused to be divided.

Then the splendor and majesty of the Lord appeared. And when the sea saw the Lord, it fled before Him.

Moses said to the sea, "You did not hearken to me until now. Why have you fled before me?" And the sea answered, "I have not fled before you, Moses, but before the Lord, the Creator of the world."

> This myth echoes, and was likely inspired by, midrashic accounts of the reluctance of the upper waters to separate from the lower waters when God created a firmament between them. See "The Upper Waters and the Lower Waters," p. 104. Here the waters of the Red Sea refuse to part at the command of Moses, but when God appears they quickly do as they were told. The underlying meaning of this midrash may be that it was not Moses who accomplished the miracles associated with the Exodus, but God,

whose power stood behind everything that Moses did. This interpretation follows rabbinic concern that Moses might be deemed a messianic figure and raised up to divine proportions. The rabbis may have been trying to avoid the kind of Moses fixation found among the Samaritans. To counter this, Moses was left almost entirely out of the *Haggadah*, despite his central role in freeing the people from Egypt, receiving the Torah, and leading them to the Holy Land.

Sources:
Exodus Rabbah 21:6; *Sefer ha-Yashar*.

491. CROSSING THE RED SEA

When the children of Israel crossed the Red Sea, God saw to it that everything they needed was to be found in the waters. The women followed their husbands, carrying their infants in their arms, and when the children cried, they plucked apples and pomegranates from the sea, and gave them to the crying children, and they ceased to weep.

> This is a delightful myth that assures us that God supplied everything the people needed while they were crossing the Red Sea, including food for hungry children. This is part of a series of myths about God's concern with the people during the Exodus. Not only did God supply manna, which tasted like whatever food they wanted most, but a wandering well that followed them, and clouds of glory to protect them from above and below. See "The Manna," p. 479, "Miriam's Well," p. 387, and "The Seven Clouds of Glory," p. 392.

Sources:
Midrash Avkir; *Exodus Rabbah* 21:10.

492. MOUNT MORIAH AND THE RED SEA

At the very moment that the children of Israel went into the Red Sea, Mount Moriah began to move from its place, along with the altar for Isaac that had been built upon it. The whole scene had been arranged before the creation of the world. Isaac was bound and placed upon the altar; Abraham's knife was raised.

Far away, at the Red Sea, God said to Moses, "Moses, Moses, My children are in distress, the sea is blocking their path and the enemy is pursuing them, and you stand so long praying?

Moses said before God, "What should I be doing?"

God said, "Raise up your staff!"

Moses lifted up his staff, the waters of the Red Sea parted, and on Mount Moriah the voice of the angel went forth, *"Do not raise your hand against the boy, or do anything to him"* (Gen. 22: 12).

> This remarkable midrash from *Mekhilta de-Rabbi Ishmael* is the clearest possible statement about the nature of midrashic time: there is no before or after; past, present, and future exist simultaneously. Thus the Binding of Isaac on Mount Moriah takes place at the same time as the parting of the waters of the Red Sea. But that is not all—the future event affects the past event. The powers of mercy generated by the parting of the Red Sea save Isaac at the very moment Abraham is about to sacrifice him. This is an astonishing view of timeless history, where future events can affect the past.
>
> A similar link between the *Akedah*, the binding of Isaac, and the parting of the Red Sea is found in *Genesis Rabbah*. Here, however, the influence is the exact opposite: the

merit that Abraham earned from the *Akedah* is applied at the Red Sea. As a reward for the wood Abraham cleaved for the burnt-offering, he earned that God should cleave the sea before his descendants, as it is said, *The waters were split* (Exod. 14:21).

For more on the tradition that the *Akedah* was prepared before the creation of the world, see "Seven Things Created before the Creation," p. 74.

Thanks to Rabbi Susan Talve for bringing this myth to my attention.

Sources:
Genesis Rabbah 55:8; *Mekhilta de-Rabbi Ishmael, be-Shalah* 4.

Studies:
"Past and Present in Midrashic Literature" by Marc Bregman.

493. GOD'S PRESENCE AT THE RED SEA

After Pharaoh passed a decree condemning all male children born to Israelite mothers, many of the mothers who gave birth to boys abandoned them in an open field, for had they brought them home, not only the infants but all of the members of their family would have been slain. What happened to those babies? They were cared for by God Himself.

When they were grown, they returned to their families. When they were asked who took care of them, they said, "A handsome young man took care of all our needs." And when the Israelites came to the Red Sea, those children were there, and when they saw God at the sea, they said to their parents, "That is the one who took care of us when we were in Egypt." That is why it is said that every single one of those who crossed the Red Sea could point with his finger and say, *This is my God, and I will glorify Him* (Exod. 15:2).

Because of Pharaoh's decree, most male children born to Israelite mothers were abandoned. Moses, of course, was raised by Pharaoh's daughter, but what happened to the others? This myth supplies a moving explanation, saying that God, described as "a handsome young man," took care of them. This offers a view of a nurturing God, much as is found in the myth about "God and the Spirits of the Unborn," p. 140 or in "The Dew of Resurrection," p. 504. The boys were able to return to their families once they were grown, since they were no longer infants to be identified by Pharaoh's henchmen. And they were able to identify that "young man" at the Red Sea, where God was present.

Other myths describe God's appearance at the Red Sea as a mighty warrior. See "The Warrior God," p. 29. In commenting on these varying reports of God's appearance, Rashi quotes God as saying "Since I change in My appearance to the people, do not say that there are two divine beings" (on Exod. 20:2).

Sources:
Exodus Rabbah 23:8, 23:15.

494. PHARAOH'S ARMY LURED TO ITS DEATH

When the Egyptians reached the Red Sea, the waves of the sea took on the likeness of mares, and the wicked Egyptians took on the likeness of lustful stallions. The stallions chased the mares until they sank in the sea. That is the meaning of, *Horse and driver He has hurled into the sea* (Exod. 15:1).

When the Egyptians were drowning in the Red Sea, the angels wished to sing a hymn in praise of God, but God silenced them, saying: "Do not sing today. How can I listen to singing when the works of My hands are drowning in the sea?"

Some say that the angels sought to sing so loudly that the souls of the Egyptians would take leave of this world through the sweetness of their celestial melodies. But God said, "They have caused My children to perish. Should they die from the sweetness of your singing?"

> This is an important talmudic myth, which establishes God's caring for all his creations, even those who are the enemies of his people, Israel. Here the angels want to celebrate the defeat of Pharaoh's army, but God rebukes them. Thus God suffers over the suffering of His creations. This myth is based on the much earlier biblical teachings in Proverbs 24:17 that *if your enemy fails, do not exult.*
>
> Rabbi Shmelke of Nikolsburg (1726-1778) suggests a different interpretation by suggesting that the purpose of the angels in wishing to sing was not to celebrate the deaths of the Egyptians, but to draw out their souls painlessly, and that it is God who objects to this idea, because it does not make them suffer for their sins. This, then, is a good example of how the midrashic method can revise the meaning of a text entirely.
>
> Sources:
> B. *Megillah* 10b; *Exodus Rabbah* 23:14; *Song of Songs Rabbah* 1:51; *Midrash Avkir;*
> *Shemen ha-Tov; Tiferet Shlomo* on Exodus 14:20.

495. THE QUARREL OF THE SEA AND THE EARTH

All of Pharaoh's army drowned in the Red Sea, as it is said, *Horse and driver He has hurled into the sea* (Exod. 15:1). Yet it is also recorded that *The earth swallowed them* (Exod. 15:12). How did this happen? The sea and the earth had a quarrel. The sea said to the earth, "Receive your children, as it is said, *For dust you are and to dust you shall return*" (Gen. 3:19). And the earth said to the sea, "Receive your slain." For the sea did not want to sink them, and the earth did not want to swallow them. The earth was afraid to receive them, lest they testify against it on the Day of Great Judgment in the World to Come—just as Abel's blood did, as it is said, *"Your brother's blood cries out to me from the ground"* (Gen. 4:10). At that time God inclined His right hand over the earth and swore an oath that the bodies of the dead would not be permitted to testify against the earth in the World to Come. Then earth then opened its mouth and swallowed them.

Still, God did not rejoice in the downfall of the wicked. When Pharaoh's army was drowning in the Red Sea, the ministering angels wanted to chant their hymns, but God said, "Shall you chant hymns while the work of My hands is being drowned in the sea?"

> This myth about a quarrel between the sea and the earth appears in *Targum Pseudo-Yonathan* on Exodus 15:12, and has been inserted to precede the verse *The earth swallowed them* (Exod. 15:12). It explains an apparent contradiction in the text, where Pharaoh's army drowns in the Red Sea, but the text says that *the earth swallowed them* (Exod. 15:12). The switch comes about when the sea calls upon the earth to accept the bodies of the drowned, since they were created from the dust of the earth to begin with. Thus, in a legalistic manner, the sea requires the earth to fulfill the obligation inherent in *For dust you are and to dust you shall return* (Gen. 3:19). The earth's concern is also legalistic: it fears that the bodies of the dead might testify against it in the World to Come. But when God swears that the bodies will not testify against the earth, the earth "opened its mouth and swallowed them." For another example of a quarrel between elemental forces, see "The Quarrel of the Sun and the Moon," p. 112.
>
> There is a related myth about the drowning of Pharaoh's army in B. *Megillah* 10b that establishes God's caring for all his creations, even those who are the enemies of His people Israel. Here the angels want to celebrate the defeat of Pharaoh's army, but

God rebukes them. Thus God suffers over the suffering of His creations. See the preceding myth, "Pharaoh's Army Lured to Its Death."

Sources:
Targum Pseudo-Yonathan to Exodus 15:12; *B. Megillah* 10b.

496. MIRIAM'S WELL

During their forty years of wandering in the wilderness, an enchanted well gave the Israelites fresh water to drink. God gave them this well as a gift because of the merits of Miriam, the sister of Moses. It was there for them every day, whenever they were thirsty. How was this possible? It followed the Israelites everywhere they went. It ascended the high mountains with them, and it descended with them to the deep valleys, going around the entire camp of Israel and giving them drink, each and every one of them at the door of his tent.

The enchanted well accompanied the children of Israel to the court of the Appointed Tent and stopped there. And the princes of the Congregation approached it, and said, "Come, O well, and give of your waters!" And the well gave forth water, and the Congregation and their cattle drank.

Some say that well was created at the beginning of Creation, while others say that the patriarchs, Abraham, Isaac, and Jacob, dug it. Then it was hidden until it was returned to the children of Israel by Moses and Aaron, who rediscovered it.

Whatever became of Miriam's well? Some say it disappeared the day that Miriam died; others say it followed the people all the way to the Holy Land. Still others say that the well can still be found traveling from place to place, wherever Jews can be found. Whenever a *minyan* gathers, it is possible to drink from the well.

> The existence of Miriam's Well—a well that followed the Israelites through the wilderness, to provide them with fresh water—is suggested by Numbers 21:16-29, where the description of a well that God gives to the people is immediately followed by a list of places they traveled to, suggesting that the well traveled with them to these places. The well itself is identified as the one issued from the rock struck in Exodus 17:3-6. The well was said to have been given because of the merits of Miriam. For a folktale recounting a late encounter with Miriam's well, see "The Wandering Well" in *Gabriel's Palace*, pp. 250-251. See too "The Angel of Forgetfulness" in *Gabriel's Palace*, pp. 81-83, where the Ari restores the harmony of Hayim Vital by having him drink from Miriam's well.
>
> The fate of this miraculous well is disputed in various sources. Some say it disappeared after Miriam's death, others that it was restored after a while because of the merits of Aaron and Moses, but taken away after the death of Moses. And a number of folktales describe it as still existing in the Sea of Galilee.
>
> There is also a metaphorical link in this myth between Miriam's well and the Torah, which is also seen as an inexhaustible resource to quench a person's thirst for knowledge.

Sources:
Targum Pseudo-Yonathan on Numbers 21:16-20; *Targum Neophyti* on Numbers 21:1; *Y. Kelim* 9:14; *B. Pesahim* 54a; *Midrash Tehillim* 24:6; *Midrash Tanhuma, Hukot* 2:128; *B. Shabbat* 35a; *B. Ta'anit* 9a; *Tosefta Sukkah* 3:11; *Seder Olam* 9-10; *Mekhilta de-Rabbi Ishmael, va-Yissa* 5; *Divrei ha-Yamim le-Moshe Rabbenu*; *Midrash Aggadah, Korah*; Pseudo-Philo, *Liber Antiquitatum Biblicarum* 10:7, 11:15, 20:8.

Studies:
"A Sexual Image in Hekhalot Rabbati and Its Implications" by David J. Halperin.

497. HOW MOSES SURVIVED

How was it possible for Moses to survive on Mount Sinai for forty days and nights without food or water? Moses, and Moses alone, was able to achieve the exalted level of an angel, and therefore, during that period, he required no material sustenance.

> In at least one case in Jewish lore, that of the metamorphosis of Enoch into Metatron, a human is transformed into an angel. Here Moses does not exactly become an angel, but rather becomes as exalted as an angel, therefore requiring no food or water, since angels do not eat or drink. See "The Metamorphosis and Enthronement of Enoch," p. 156.
>
> *Sources:*
> *Makhon Siftei Tzaddikim* on Genesis 1:16.

498. THE ENTHRONEMENT OF MOSES

God honored Moses and gave him all of the earth and sea, and all the rivers and all the other elements. He gave him all the world as a possession suitable for His heir, for Moses was named God and King of the whole nation. So too did Moses enter into the darkness where God was, perceiving things invisible to mortal nature. There he dwelt in the mysteries until he was crowned with light, wearing a robe of light, his face clothed in a beam of light.

When Moses reached the peak of Mount Sinai he saw a throne so large that it touched the clouds of heaven. On it sat a man of noble bearing, wearing a crown, with a scepter in one hand. With the other hand He beckoned Moses, who approached and stood before the throne. The man on the throne then handed over the scepter to Moses and beckoned for him to mount the throne, and gave Moses a crown of light. Then that man withdrew from the throne. And Moses sat on the great throne and wrote what his Lord had taught him.

> Just as there are enthronement myths about Adam, Enoch, Jacob, and King David, this myth describes the enthronement of Moses. For Philo the role attributed to Moses transcended that of a prophet and came closer to that of a messianic or divine figure. In this astonishing myth, Moses is invited to take the place of the enthroned figure who clearly seems to represent God, although this figure might be identified with the Glory of the Lord, which Ezekiel describes as that of a human form seated upon a throne: *Above the expanse over their heads was the semblance of a throne, in appearance like sapphire; and on top, upon this semblance of a throne, there was the semblance of a human form* (Ezek. 1:26-28). A similar enthronement of Adam is described in *The Testament of Abraham.* See "The Enthronement of Adam," p. 131.
>
> Here Philo describes Moses in terms that elevate him from a human hero to one who is virtually divine, while *Ezekiel the Tragedian* describes the actual enthronement of Moses. At the end of the enthronement, it seems as if God turns over His scepter and His throne to Moses and withdraws. The other primary sources for this myth are found in the Samaritan text *Memar Markah* and Samaritan hymns. The Samaritans, a Palestinian sect closely related to Judaism, regarded Moses as an elevated, near-messianic figure, and it is not surprising that Samaritan texts sometimes stray into the realm of elevating Moses to a godly status.
>
> The surprising description of Moses as God and King echoes Exodus 7:1: *"See, I place you in the role of God to Pharaoh."*

Sources:

Philo, *Vita Mosis* 1:155-158; *Ezekiel the Tragedian* 68-76; *Numbers Rabbah* 25:13; *Memar Markah* 2:12, 3:126, 4:6; first and sixth hymn of the Samaritan Durran cycle by Amram Darah.

Studies:

"Moses as God and King" by Wayne A. Meeks.

499. MOSES TRANSFORMED INTO FIRE

God said to Moses, "I will bring you up to My Throne of Glory, and I will show you the angels of heaven." Then God commanded Metatron, the Prince of the Presence, "Go and bring Moses into heaven." But Metatron replied, "Master of the Universe, Moses cannot ascend to heaven because the angels consist of fire, but he is only flesh and blood." God said, "Go and change his body into fire."

So Metatron went to Moses, and Moses trembled with fear when he saw him. "Who are you?" Moses asked. Metatron replied, "I am Enoch, son of Jared. God has sent me to bring you to His Throne of Glory." Moses said, "I am only flesh and blood and cannot look upon the angels."

Then Metatron changed Moses' tongue into a fiery tongue, and he made his eyes like wheels of the Divine Chariot, and he gave him the powers of the angels and brought him into heaven.

> Here the ruling angel Metatron transforms Moses into fire just as Metatron himself was once transformed from being the human Enoch. The implication is that Moses will now take the place of Metatron as the chief among the angels. This myth must be seen in the context of those Jews (and Samaritans) for whom Moses was viewed as a messianic figure. In this myth Moses is raised even higher than that, and therefore this must be regarded as an enthronement myth about Moses, just as such myths are found about Adam, Enoch, Jacob, and King David. See "The Enthronement of Moses," p. 388 for another example of an enthronement myth about Moses.
>
> *Sources:*
> *Gedulat Moshe* in *Beit ha-Midrash* 2:10-20.

500. THE DIVINE RADIANCE

So Moses came down from Mount Sinai. And as Moses came down from the mountain bearing the two tablets of the Pact, Moses was not aware that the skin of his face was radiant, since he had spoken with God. Aaron and all the Israelites saw that the skin of Moses' face was radiant; and they shrank from coming near him. But Moses called to them, and Aaron and all the chieftains in the assembly returned to him, and Moses spoke to them. Afterward all the Israelites came near, and he instructed them concerning all that the Lord had imparted to him on Mount Sinai. And when Moses had finished speaking with them, he put a veil over his face.

Whenever Moses went in before the Lord to speak with Him, he would leave the veil off until he came out; and when he came out and told the Israelites what he had been commanded, the Israelites would see how radiant the skin of Moses' face was. Moses would then put the veil back over his face until he went in to speak with Him.

> After his encounter with God at Mount Sinai, *the skin of Moses' face was radiant*. This aura surrounding his face was so bright it frightened Aaron and all the chieftains,

leading Moses to put on a veil, which Moses wore except when he spoke with God. Such auras are a common result of mystical experience. See, for example, "A Vision at the Wailing Wall," p. 63.

Sources:
Exodus 34:29-35

501. THE LIGHT THAT SHONE FROM MOSES' FACE

When Moses descended Mount Sinai after forty days and nights, his body was bathed with invisible light, and an aura shone from his face that surpassed the splendor of the sun. Those who saw him were filled with awe, for his appearance was far more beautiful than when he had gone up. So bright was the dazzling light that flashed from his face, that all the righteous among the children of Israel were burned when they observed it.

Some say that radiance clung to Moses after he spoke with God face to face, as it is said, *The skin of his face was radiant, since he had spoken with Him* (Exod. 34:29). Others say that the radiance shone forth from the cave where God put His Hand on his face, as it is said, *"And I will shield you with My Hand"* (Exod. 33:22). Still others say that light was the light of the first day, which God restored to Moses upon Mount Sinai, and which Moses drew upon for the rest of his life.

Then there are those who explain that for forty days and forty nights, Moses dipped his pen in black fire and wrote down all that the Lord commanded him to write. And when he finished writing, he saw that a drop of fire was still left upon the pen. And Moses took the pen and passed it over the hair of his head, and the skin of his face shone with radiance. That is why the children of Israel were unable to approach him until he put a veil over his face.

When Aaron and the others saw the light shining from the face of Moses, they were afraid to come near him, for that light was a reflection of the divine radiance. Nor did that light go away. Indeed, Moses became a permanent source of light. And after that he wore a veil on his face at all times, except when he met with God or taught the Torah.

> Biblical commentators seek out the source of the divine radiance that shone from the face of Moses, as recounted in Exodus 34:29-35. See "Divine Radiance," p. 389. Rashi proposes that it was caused by God covering the face of Moses with His Hand. This interpretation, also found in *Midrash Tanhuma*, refers to Exodus 33:22-23: *When My glory passes by, I will put you in a cleft of the rock, and I will cover you with My Hand until I pass by. Then I will take away My Hand.*
>
> Ibn Ezra notes that the light that shone from the face of Moses shone like the light of the firmament. Rabbi Hayim ben Attar, author of *Or ha-Hayim*, asserts that the light continued to shine, so that Moses became a permanent source of light, and had to wear a veil. The fact that this veil was only lifted for the people when Moses taught Torah suggests that while teaching Torah, he revealed the unveiled truth. This also suggests that whoever studies Torah comes face to face with the divine radiance.
>
> What was the source of the divine radiance? It may be an intrinsic quality of the light that shines from God. The *Zohar* identifies it as the light of the first day of creation, which is said to exist in the World to Come. See "The Light of the First Day," p. 83. The *Zohar* also states that this light shone from the face of Moses during the first three months after his birth, but the light was withdrawn when the infant Moses was taken to Pharaoh's palace, and was returned to him only when he stood on Mount Sinai.
>
> One strange explanation for the rays of light that shone from Moses is found in *Exodus Rabbah 47:6*, where Rabbi Yehudah bar Nachman suggests that after Moses had finished writing down the Torah there was a little ink left over on the quill. Moses touched his forehead while holding the quill, and the ink that spilled on to his fore-

head turned into rays of light. The word *keren*, for "ray" is the same as the word for "horn," and this led to the understanding of the text—originally midrashic, taken up by Jerome in his Latin translation of the Bible—on which Michelangelo based giving Moses horns in his famous statue.

The divine radiance is also linked to Noah. It was said to shine from the face of Noah since the time of his birth.

Sources:
Exodus Rabbah 47:6; *Midrash Tanhuma, Ki Tissa* 20; Septuagint to Exodus 34:29; Philo, *Vita Mosis* 2:70; Pseudo-Philo, *Liber Antiquitatum Biblicarum* 12:1; *Targum Onkelos* on Exodus 34:29; *Targum Neophyti* on Exodus 34:29; Ibn Ezra on Exodus 34:29; *Pesikta Rabbati* 10:6; *Or ha-Hayim* on Exodus 34:29; *Yalkut Shim'oni; Zohar* 1:31b-32a; Joseph Heinemann in *Sifrut* 4(1973), pp. 363-365 (on the horns of Moses).

502. THE SOULS OF THE PATRIARCHS

The souls of the fathers of the world, Abraham, Isaac, and Jacob, and the rest of the righteous, were raised from their graves and ascended into Paradise. They prayed before God, saying, "Master of the Universe, how long will You sit upon Your throne like a mourner, with Your right hand behind You, and not redeem Your sons and daughters and reveal Your kingdom in the world? How long will You have no pity upon Your children, who are made slaves among the nations of the world? Have You no pity?"

Then God answered each and every one of them, saying, "Since these wicked ones have sinned and transgressed, how can I deliver them from among the nations of the world and reveal My kingdom?"

Hearing this, Abraham, Isaac, and Jacob began to weep. Then God said to them, "Abraham, My beloved, Isaac My elect, Jacob, My firstborn, how can I save them at this time?"

Then Michael, the Prince of Israel, cried out with a loud, tormented voice and said, "Why do You stand far off, O Lord?"

> This is one of several mythic accounts of the patriarchs attempting to intercede with God to show mercy for the people of Israel, who are suffering in exile, and to hasten the End of Days. Here God, while highly respectful to the patriarchs, essentially refuses their plea. This provokes Michael, the angelic protector of Israel, into a loud protest and lament at God's failure to act. For other examples of the patriarchs interceding for the sake of Israel, see "The Pleading of the Fathers" p. 515, and "The Patriarchs Weep over the Destruction of the Temple," p. 427.

Sources:
3 Enoch 44; *Pirkei de-Rabbi Eliezer* 44.

503. THE PILLAR OF CLOUD

During forty years of wandering, the Israelites were led by a pillar of cloud during the day and by a pillar of fire at night. Moses looked to the pillar of fire to guide them on their journey. When Moses saw the pillar of cloud rise above the Tabernacle, he stood and cried out to the people, and when they heard this they made ready to journey. They gathered together their vessels and precious things and put them upon their cattle. And anyone who had no beast to carry his burden put all his precious things upon the cloud that went before the camp. And they blew the trumpets, and the tribe of Judah journeyed first. Then the pillar of cloud guided them as they journeyed to the Holy Land.

Many centuries later, as Rabbi Moshe Cordovero lay on his deathbed, his disciples begged him to reveal his successor. But the Ramak, as the rabbi was known, refused to do so. Instead he told them to watch for a sign: whoever saw a pillar of cloud at his funeral would be the one they should follow. This greatly confused the disciples, and when the Ramak died, all of Safed was filled with mourning.

As the funeral procession reached the graveyard, a young disciple named Rabbi Isaac Luria, approached Rabbi Joseph Karo, and said: "Ever since we left the synagogue, there has been a pillar of cloud going before us." He pointed to it, but it was invisible to all the others. And when he entered into it, he vanished from their sight. For a long moment everyone stood in disbelief. Then Rabbi Isaac stepped out of the cloud, which only he could see, and his face was glowing like the face of Moses as he descended Mount Sinai. And indeed it was the same cloud that had enveloped Moses at the top of Sinai, and carried him into heaven, so that he could receive the Torah from the finger of God.

Then they all understood that this was the sign the Ramak had given them, and that Rabbi Isaac was fated to be their teacher. So it was that after the funeral many of the disciples of the Ramak came to Rabbi Isaac and asked to study with him. At first the Ari, as he came to be known, was reluctant, for until then he had concealed his holy ways. But at last he agreed, and for the two years that he remained in this world, he was their master of Torah, and his teachings still echo to this day.

> The pillar of cloud led the Israelites in their desert wandering during the day, as stated in Exodus 3:21: *And Yahweh went before them by day in a pillar of cloud, to lead them the way*. This story links Rabbi Moshe Cordovero with Rabbi Isaac Luria, the Ari, explaining how the Ari became his successor. Thus, in a single stroke, this tale links the Ari both to his immediate predecessor, Moshe Cordovero, and to the biblical Moses. The fact that both are named Moses (Moshe in Hebrew) only underscores the link between them. Thus the story suggests that the Ari and his predecessors were of the stature of the biblical patriarchs, and that the miracles of the sort that occurred in the time of Moses could still occur in their own time.
>
> *Sources:*
> Yalkut Shim'oni; Divrei Yosef by Rabbi Yosef Sambari, edited by A. Berliner (Berlin: 1896); *Divrei Shaul.*

504. THE SEVEN CLOUDS OF GLORY

As the Israelites wandered through the wilderness, they were covered by seven clouds of glory, one cloud on each of their four sides, one cloud above them, so that rain or hail would not fall on them, and so that they would not be burned by the burning heat of the sun, and one cloud below them and so thorns and serpents and scorpions would not harm them—and one cloud went before them to level the valleys and lower the mountains, and to prepare a dwelling place for them.

> *Targum Pseudo-Yonathan* appends this description of the seven clouds of glory that accompany the Israelites to the verse *The Israelites journeyed from Raamses to Succoth* (Exod. 12:37).
>
> Just as the myth of Miriam's Well provided fresh water for the Israelites in their desert wanderings, this myth describes seven clouds of glory that protected the Israelites from above and below and even a cloud that went before them to level valleys and lower mountains. Behind these myths is the awareness that travel in the desert is treacherous, with dangers on all sides, especially dangers from the elements. The 40 years of wandering of the Israelites was doubtless filled with great suffering, but since the Exodus is regarded as a great liberation, these myths arose to portray the Exodus as taking place under the complete protection of God.
>
> *Sources:*
> Targum Pseudo-Yonathan on Exodus 12:37.

505. MOSES' LAST REQUEST

When the time came for Moses to take leave of this world, he made one last request to God: "Grant my wish, O Lord. Command the heavens to open and be split asunder, so that light shines in the darkness, so that the eyes of the children of Israel may be opened and they shall see there is none beside You, O Lord, in the heavens and the earth."

No sooner did Moses finish speaking than the seven heavens were opened and all the depths were cleft asunder, and a great light shone in the darkness. And the eyes of the children of Israel were opened and they saw there is nothing in heaven or on earth to compare with the splendor of God, and they called out to each other, *"Hear, O Israel! The Lord is our God, the Lord alone"* (Deut. 6:4).

> Here the last request Moses makes is not for himself, but for the people of Israel, that the heavens be split apart so that the people could see the splendor of God. Throughout the long wandering in the wilderness, the people continually lost faith both in Moses and in God. Here Moses tries once more to renew their faith, and God grants his last wish.
>
> It is interesting to note that just as Moses' first experience of God closely resembles a mystical experience, here his last experience before dying is also a mystical revelation, although here it is a collective, rather than a personal one.
>
> *Sources:*
> *Deuteronomy Rabbah* 11; *Petirat Moshe*; IFA 15075.

506. JOSHUA AS OEDIPUS

Joshua's father was a holy man who lived in Egypt. He and his wife had no children, so the *Tzaddik* prayed to God for a child, and God heard his prayers. But while she was pregnant, heaven revealed to him that the son who would be born to him would one day cut off his head. On learning this, the holy man mortified himself and wept day and night. His wife could not understand this, since God had seen fit to bless them with a child. She said, "You should rejoice at the Lord's blessing." Then the *Tzaddik* revealed his vision to her, and she knew that his words must be true.

It came to pass that a son, Joshua, was born to them. And his mother put him in an ark made of pitch and slime and cast it into the Nile, and God saw to it that a great fish swallowed the ark. Now it happened that the king gave a feast for all his princes. And the fish that had swallowed the ark was caught that day and brought before the king. And when they cut it open, they discovered a weeping child. The king and all the princes marveled at this, and the king ordered a woman to be found to nurse the child. And the boy grew up in the palace of the king and came to serve as a guardsman.

Years later it happened that Joshua's father transgressed against the king. The king ordered the guardsman to cut off his head, and to take his wife and property for himself, for that was the custom in those days. Thus it came to pass that Joshua did execute him, as the king had commanded. But when he approached his mother, to lie with her, milk began to spill from her breasts, filling the bed with milk. Fearing the woman was a witch, Joshua was about to slay his mother when she remembered the prophecy of Joshua's father, and she cried out to him, "This is not sorcery. This milk is the same milk you suckled, for you are my son." And she revealed all that had happened.

Then Joshua told her how he had been found inside a fish, and how he had never known his true mother and father. Then they knew that heaven's prophecy had been fulfilled. And now that he knew the truth, Joshua repented of his sins against his parents, and his repentance was accepted in the eyes of God. And he came to serve Moses, and when Moses took leave of this world, he led the children of Israel into the Promised Land.

This remarkable story is a Jewish retelling of the Oedipus myth, in which Joshua bin Nun, the successor of Moses, who led the Israelites into the Land of Israel, is said to have earlier fulfilled the prophecy that he would kill his father and marry his mother. At the same time, this myth retells the story of the infant Moses being left in an ark made of pitch in the Nile (Exod. 2:3-6), and like Moses, Joshua is also said to have been raised in Pharaoh's palace. Note that this version of the tale refers to Pharaoh as a king, demonstrating a certain distance from the biblical tale.

So too does this myth draw directly from the story of Jonah, who was swallowed by a whale (Jonah 2:1). Here the fish swallows the ark containing the infant Joshua, and the child is discovered alive inside the fish, an appropriate discovery for a child marked by destiny. This imaginative myth may have been inspired by the name of the father of the biblical Joshua: "Nun," the Aramaic word for "fish."

It seems clear that this myth was intended to provide a mythic origin for Joshua, in order to present him as a worthy successor to Moses, indeed, one with an equally remarkable origin. At the same time, it serves as a vehicle for a Jewish version of Oedipus. Finally, it vividly demonstrates the power of redemption. Here the story diverges entirely from the Oedipus myth, which culminates in the tragedy of Oedipus blinding himself. Instead, this Jewish version has Joshua's repentance entirely accepted, and he ends up leading the people. Leading, of course, requires good vision, and the contrast to the blind Oedipus is obvious. Thus this myth must also be viewed as a Jewish answer to Oedipus. The answer is that no man's sins are beyond repentance.

In overtly combining three very famous myths—the story of the baby Moses left in the ark, the story of Jonah being swallowed by the whale, and the myth of Oedipus—this myth about Joshua demonstrates its literary as well as its mythic intentions. It has all the earmarks of a consciously created myth, invented in order to add mythic resonance to the story of Joshua, which is otherwise entirely overshadowed by that of Moses.

Sources:
Hibbur me-ha Yeshu'ah 209.

507. MOSES NEVER DIED

Moses never died, instead he is in exile with the *Shekhinah,* and God has given him the task of taking the people of Israel and the *Shekhinah* out of exile. Just as Moses led the children of Israel out of slavery and to the Promised Land, so too will he lead them out of exile. Meanwhile, God has cast a deep sleep upon Moses, and he will sleep until the time comes for the exile of the Jewish people to come to an end.

That Moses never died is deduced from the biblical verse that asserts that *No one knows his burial place to this day* (Deut. 34:6). As evidence that Moses is sleeping and not dead, *Sifre on Deuteronomy* reinterprets the verse *Moses was one hundred and twenty years old when he died, his eyes were undimmed and his vigor unabated* (Deut. 34:7). Here the final phrase reads literally "his moisture had not dried up," and apparently implies that even at the advanced age when he died, Moses was still sexually potent. In the *Sifre*, Rabbi Eliezer ben Ya'akov says: "Do not read 'his moisture had not dried up,' but rather read 'his moisture *is* not dried up'—even until now anyone who touches the flesh of Moses, moisture ascends here and there." In the Talmud, the verse *And he was there with Yahweh* (Exod. 34:28) is offered as evidence that Moses did not die, but is still "standing" (i.e., living) and ministering to God (*B. Sota* 13b). In *Zohar* 1:28a, one reason given for Moses avoiding death is that because he perfected himself during his lifetime, he rectified the sin of Adam that brought death into the world. Therefore he did not die.

There are many myths about key biblical figures who never died. See "Abraham Never Died," p. 348 and "Jacob Never Died," p. 370. See also "King David is Alive," in *Gabriel's Palace*, pp. 139-141. For a folktale about Moses being alive, see "The Princess and the Slave" in *Elijah's Violin*, pp. 36-43.

Sources:
B. *Sota* 13b; *Sifre on Deuteronomy* 357; *Zohar* 1:28a, 1:37b.

Studies:
Legends, by Ginzberg, 6:164.

508. KING DAVID IS CROWNED IN HEAVEN

There are two thrones in heaven, one belonging to God and the other to King David, for King David was not only crowned on earth, but he was also crowned in heaven. The coronation took place in a great House of Study in the seventh heaven, where a fiery throne awaited him. Groups of angels wove garments of salvation and made crowns of life, fixing precious stones and pearls in them, and anointing them with all kinds of spices and delight. All of these were destined for David, King of Israel. Every kind of angel came forth, as well as all of the heavenly creatures. So too were all of the heavenly treasuries present, along with the clouds of glory, the stars, and all the constellations. Suddenly all of them trembled and cried out, *"The heavens declare the glory of God"* (Ps. 19:1) and lo! King David stood before his throne, facing the throne of God, with all the kings of the House of David before him, and all the kings of Israel behind him. Then God took His crown and put it on David's head.

King David's heavenly crown had the sun, moon, and the twelve constellations fixed on it, its radiance radiating from one end of the world to the other. When the crown was placed on his head, King David began to recite psalms of unimaginable beauty that had never been heard before. All the angels and heavenly creatures joined in, along with the firmaments, so that the song echoed everywhere, "God is one and His name is one."

Then a loud voice came forth from Eden, crying, "The Lord shall reign forever and ever!" and King David ascended to the heavenly Temple, where a throne of fire was set for him forty parasangs in height. And when David came and sat down upon his throne, which was opposite the throne of his Creator, he uttered songs and prayers such as had not been heard since the creation of the world.

In *B. Sanhedrin* 38a, Rabbi Akiba states that there are two thrones in heaven, one for God and one for King David. This angers Rabbi Jose, who says, "Akiba, how long will you profane the *Shekhinah*! Rather, one throne is for justice and the other for mercy." This follows the interpretation that God has two heavenly thrones. When He sits on the Throne of Mercy, He is merciful, and when He sits on the Throne of Justice, He is harsh in His judgment.

Later, in *Midrashei Geulah* and *Masekhet Atzilut* and other texts, this undeveloped myth about King David sharing the role of ruling the world with God is elaborated, with a detailed description of King David's heavenly coronation. God takes His crown and puts it on David's head. This is a very radical myth. It elevates King David to the celestial realm, where he undergoes a heavenly coronation that is much like those described as being the coronation of God. Thus David can be seen not only as God's representative on earth, but one who participates fully in the ritual of divine kingship. The myth strongly implies that David's role is parallel to that of God, whose throne he faces, making him a "lesser Yahweh." In this way the myth resembles those about other saintly figures who became the focus of Jewish cults, such as Enoch/Metatron and Jacob. See the Introduction, pp. l, lvii-lviii. *Hekhalot Rabbati* reaffirms David's role as co-ruler of heaven. Together, these three texts demonstrate the development of the

myth of King David ruling with God in heaven, which starts off as a very brief statement by Rabbi Akiba in the Talmud.

The most extensive divinization tradition among the patriarchs and kings is that
associated with Jacob. See "Jacob the Divine," p. 366. One statement in the Talmud
hints at such a tradition associated with King Solomon: "Solomon ruled over both the
worlds above and the worlds below." This seems to go far beyond a mere statement
about Solomon's remarkable powers to hint at his divine elevation. There are also
enthronement myths about Adam and Moses. See "The Enthronement of Adam," p.
131 and "The Enthronement of Moses," p. 388.

Sources:
B. *Sanhedrin* 38a; *Hekhalot Rabbati* 6; *Midrashei Geulah*; *Masekhet Atzilut* 54a-b; *Siddur*
    Amram 12b-13a; *Sefer Eliyahu* in *Beit ha-Midrash* 3:68-78; *Likutei Moharan* 1:8.

Studies:
Keter: The Crown of God in Early Jewish Mysticism by Arthur Green.

509. KING DAVID'S HARP

A harp hung above King David's bed, and precisely at midnight a north wind arrived
and blew on the harp and it would play by itself. Then King David would arise and
study Torah until the break of dawn.

This is a famous talmudic legend about King David's harp. This brief legend transforms that harp into an enchanted one. This legend echoes Genesis 1:2: *The spirit of
God hovered over the waters.* Here God's spirit hovers over the waters the way the wind
blows on the strings of the harp.

Later in Jewish folklore, this same harp became the object of fairytale quests. See,
for example, "King David's Harp" in *Miriam's Tambourine*, pp. 163-167.

In *Likutei Moharan* Rabbi Nachman of Bratslav offers an allegorical reading: the
five strings of the harp represent the Five Books of Moses. The wind represents the
hidden spirit (*ruah*—which also means "wind") in each Jew. When that spirit comes in
contact with the five strings of the harp (the Five Books of Moses), the music of new
revelations is produced. For Rabbi Nachman, waking up refers to everyone's need to
wake up spiritually.

Sources:
B. *Berakhot* 3b; *Likutei Moharan* 1:8.

510. THE ANGEL OF THE LORD

God sent an angel to Jerusalem to destroy it, but as he was about to wreak destruction,
the Lord saw and renounced further punishment and said to the destroying angel,
"Enough! Stay your hand!" The angel of the Lord was then standing by the threshing
floor of Ornan the Jebusite. David looked up and saw the angel of the Lord standing
between heaven and earth, with a drawn sword in his hand directed against Jerusalem.
David and the elders, covered in sackcloth, threw themselves on their faces.

King David's vision of a giant angel standing between heaven and earth with a
drawn sword in his hand is certainly terrifying and memorable. The meaning of this
myth is that Jerusalem was on the verge of total destruction when God intervened,
just as He had done with the sacrifice of Isaac, and prevented it at the last minute.

Note the parallel of God's words here to those spoken by the angel to stop Abraham from sacrificing Isaac (Gen. 22:12).

Sources:
1 Chronicles 21:15-16.

511. THE MOUNTAIN OF FIRE

Once, when King David was walking in a very thick forest, he became tired, so he lay down and fell asleep. While he was sleeping, the angel Michael came to him and whispered in his ear, "Wake up! Now is not the time to be asleep." When David opened his eyes, he saw a mountain in the distance that was burning in fire. He raised his eyes to the mountain, and he saw the letters YHVH flashing before him. All at once the fire surrounding the mountain vanished, but letters of fire remained, carved into the mountain, spelling God's Name.

> This is a little-known tradition about King David, which links David to Moses by evoking Mount Sinai at the time of the Giving of the Torah. In addition, it reaffirms that the God of King David is the same God of Moses, known by the Name YHVH. This myth also echoes the midrashic tradition about Abraham and Isaac seeing a holy light—the light of the *Shekhinah*—surrounding Mount Moriah. Thus one brief myth manages to create a line of continuity between Abraham, Moses, and David, while emphasizing that they all worshipped the same God.
>
> *Sources:*
> IFA 763.

512. THE THIRTY-SIX JUST MEN

In each generation there are thirty-six just men, known as the *Lamed-vav Tzaddikim*, the thirty-six righteous ones. They are hidden saints who are blessed to be able to see the *Shekhinah*. The world exists because of their merit. When one of them dies, another is born to take his place. Because of these thirty-six just men, God permits the world to exist. Thus they are the pillars of existence.

Few are those who escape the punishments of Gehenna. But when these saints take leave of this world, their souls immediately ascend on high, to the heavenly rewards awaiting them.

> The myth of the 36 hidden saints—known as the *Lamed-vav Tzaddikim*— first appears in the Talmud and later becomes a staple of folk, kabbalistic, and Hasidic tales. *B. Sanhedrin* 97b suggests that each of these righteous men must be approved by the *Shekhinah*. The number of hidden saints varies at first, with some texts listing the number as 30 (*Genesis Rabbah* 35:2), and some as 45 (*B. Hullin* 45a). However, the number 36 became the standard, perhaps because it is twice 18—*heh* in Hebrew—which also means "life." It was believed that any stranger could turn out to be one of the *Lamed-vav Tzaddikim*, and therefore respect should be shown to everyone. Many of the tales about the just men describe them as living in remote places, such as forests, where they engage in mystical study.
>
> André Schwarz-Bart wrote a famous novel, *The Last of the Just*, based on this myth, although he revised it in substantial ways. In the novel, the hidden saints descend from a single family line.
>
> Yisroel Yakov Klapholtz published a two-volume collection of tales about the 36 just men, entitled *Lamed-Vav Tzaddikim Nistarim*.
>
> *Sources:*
> *B. Sanhedrin* 97b; *B. Sukkah* 45b; *Genesis Rabbah* 35:2; *B. Hullin* 45a; *Zohar* Exodus 2:151a.

BOOK EIGHT

MYTHS OF THE HOLY LAND

The land you are about to cross into and possess, a
land of hills and valleys, soaks up its water from the
rains of heaven. It is a land which the Lord your God
looks after, on which the Lord your God always keeps
His eye, from year's beginning to year's end.

Deuteronomy 11:11-12

513. THE GARDEN OF EDEN

The Lord God planted a garden in Eden, in the east, and placed there the man whom He had formed. And from the ground the Lord God caused to grow every tree that was pleasing to the sight and good for food, with the Tree of Life in the middle of the garden, and the Tree of Knowledge of Good and Evil.

A river issues from Eden to water the garden, and it then divides and becomes four branches. The name of the first is Pishon, the one that winds through the whole land of Havilah, where the gold is. (The gold of that land is good; bdellium is there, and lapis lazuli.) The name of the second river is Gihon, the one that winds through the whole land of Cush. The name of the third river is Tigris, the one that flows east of Asshur. And the fourth river is the Euphrates.

The Lord God took the man and placed him in the garden of Eden, to till it and tend it. And the Lord God commanded the man, saying, "Of every tree of the garden you are free to eat; but as for the tree of knowledge of good and bad, you must not eat of it; for as soon as you eat of it, you shall die."

> The Garden of Eden serves as the primary archetype of the lost Paradise where our ancestors, Adam and Eve, failed a divine test and were cast out. As a wandering desert people, much like the Bedouins of today, the ancient Hebrews would naturally look forward to finding the next oasis. Such an oasis, with many kinds of fruit trees, was probably the original model for the Garden of Eden, the ultimate oasis. Not only do Adam and Eve have everything they need while living in the Garden, but God sometimes walks there in the cool of the day (Gen. 3:8). They only have one rule to obey: Don't eat the fruit of the Tree of Knowledge. Of course, Eve and then Adam cannot resist tasting the forbidden fruit. Like Pandora, they unleash the unknown and find themselves exiled from the Garden of Eden.
>
> From a psychological perspective, the Garden of Eden might be seen as childhood, the kind of childhood where a child lives in a protected world and all of his or her needs are met. It is the discovery of sex that causes them to be expelled from the Garden, from childhood, and the world outside the garden requires great effort on their part to survive. From this perspective the Fall might be viewed as the tasting of the forbidden fruit—sex.
>
> *Sources:*
> Genesis 2:8-17
>
> *Studies:*
> "The Garden of Eden: From Creation to Covenant" by Bernard Och.
> "Gardens: From Eden to Jerusalem" by Sandra R. Shimoff

514. THE CREATION OF THE GARDEN OF EDEN

Some say that the Garden of Eden was planted by God's right hand before the earth was created. Indeed, it was one of seven things created before the creation of the world.

> Michael Stone distinguishes three kinds of Paradise that are described in *4 Ezra*. One is the pre-existent Paradise, as described here. Another is an eschatological Paradise, as found in *4 Ezra* 7:38 and 8:52. The third is a Paradise of mystical association, such as the traditions associated with the term *Pardes*, which is identified both as a mystical orchard and as Paradise in *B. Hagigah* 14b. See "The Four Who Entered Paradise," p. 173.

Sources:
B. Pesahim 54a; 4 Ezra 3:4-6, 6:4.

Studies:
"Features of the Eschatology of IV Ezra" by Michael E. Stone, pp. 77-79.
Portraits of Adam in Early Judaism by John R. Levison, pp. 116-17.

515. THE HIDDEN GARDEN

The Garden of Eden is well hidden. It is closed on every side, and guarded in a number of ways so that none can see it, not even the angels or the eye of a prophet or seer, as it is said, *No eye has seen it, Lord, but You* (Isa. 64:3). Indeed, just as a nut is enclosed within a shell, so Eden is a world within. For the Garden of Eden was planted by God Himself, as it is said, *The Lord God planted a garden in Eden* (Gen. 2:8), and He planted it with His complete Name.

The Garden of Eden is the dwelling place of holy souls, both those who have already descended to this world and those who will descend in the future. These souls are said to be entirely preoccupied with Torah. In this way they are unified with God and absorbed into the light of God.

> Since no one knows where the Garden of Eden can be found, this myth offers one explanation of its fate. For once Adam and Eve were expelled from the garden, it largely vanishes from the Bible. However, it often reappears in every phase of subsequent Jewish literature. This myth explains that it is hidden, which is why it is not encountered more often. A different explanation is found in *3 Baruch* 4:10, where the Garden is said to have been lost in the Flood: "When God brought the Flood, the water entered Paradise and killed every flower."
>
> This myth also serves as a commentary on Genesis 2:8, *The Lord God planted a garden in Eden*, and on the verse from the Song of Songs 6:11, *I went down to the nut grove.* The latter verse is often interpreted mystically, with the nut grove understood to refer to the Garden of Eden. In kabbalah, on the other hand, the Garden of Eden was not an actual, physical location, but a mystical one, very possibly an internal state, which one reaches by mystical means.
>
> In *Torat Moshe* on Genesis 2:9, Rabbi Moshe Alshekh describes the Garden of Eden as essentially supernatural. But when a branch or leaf is taken out of the garden, it becomes a regular earthly branch or leaf. Thus the olive branch that the Noah's dove brought from the Garden of Eden turned into a real one.
>
> For folktales about such a journey to the Garden of Eden, see "The Prince of Coucy" in *Miriam's Tambourine*, pp. 173-185, and "The Waters of Eternal Life," pp. 122-134, and "The Gates of Eden" in *Gabriel's Palace*, p. 62.
>
> Note that the term *Gan Eden*, literally, the "Garden of Eden," has two meanings—it refers to the earthly garden, but it also refers to Paradise, and in Jewish lore the two meanings often blur into one. These two meanings also gave birth to the notion that there are two gardens—the earthly garden where Adam and Eve once made their home and the heavenly Eden, which is Paradise. A discussion of the upper and lower *Gan Eden* is found in *Zohar 3:182b*.
>
> *Sources:*
> *Midrash ha-Ne'elam, Zohar Hadash 18a; Zohar 2:150a.*

516. THE FRUIT OF THE TREE OF LIFE

The Tree of Life is in the midst of the earthly garden, and nearby is the Tree of the Knowledge of Good and Evil. God enters the garden with the righteous, as it is said, *They heard the sound of the Lord God moving about in the garden at the breezy time of day* (Gen. 3:8). Then the Tree of Life gives forth a fragrance that permeates the whole garden, and that fragrance sustains all the righteous who live there. As it spreads out, the leaves shout for joy.

Some say that every New Moon and festival the righteous sit down and eat the delicacies of the Tree of Life. Its fruit is life and rest. Others say that every night the souls of the righteous rise up to the Garden of Eden and at midnight God comes to the garden to delight in them. Then God stands near that tree, and the righteous come and prostrate themselves before the cloud of glory. And a fountain of blessings in the garden cascades upon the head of every one of the righteous, and God rejoices with them.

All of Israel is attached to the Tree of Life. Some are attached to its trunk, some to its branches, some to its leaves, some to its roots, as it is said, *The Torah is a Tree of Life to those who cling to it* (Prov. 3:18). In the future, all of Israel will taste of the Tree of Life, and because of it they will leave their exile in a compassionate way.

> This myth has several layers of meaning, as it refers to the Tree of Life found in the Garden of Eden as well as to the Torah. The linkage between the two derives from the famous verse in Proverbs 3:18, *It is a Tree of Life to those who cling to it*. The identification of the "it" with the Torah is so pervasive that this verse is commonly quoted as *The Torah is a Tree of Life to those who cling to it*. *Zohar* 3:73a makes this link explicit: "Israel is attached to the Torah, and the Torah to God." At the same time, the Tree of Life is the symbolic structure that represents the ten sefirot, the ten divine emanations that underlie all existence. So the Tree of Life actually refers to three things simultaneously: to the tree in the Garden of Eden, to the Torah, and to the structure of the ten sefirot. In the present myth, the tasting of the fruit of the Tree of Life symbolizes the end of Israel's exile and the beginning of the new era that will be initiated with the coming of the Messiah.
>
> *Midrash ha-Ne'elam* in *Zohar Hadash* 18c also identifies the two trees in the Garden of Eden as two paths. The Tree of Life represents the path of the Torah, "which gives life to man, and enables him to know the good and straight path which perfects him." The Tree of Knowledge represents the path of evil, and "for this reason God commanded him not to eat from it."
>
> *Sources:*
> Seder Gan Eden (version B) in *Beit ha-Midrash* 3:131-140; *Zohar* 1:82b, 1:193a-b, 3:124b-125a.

517. THE TREE OF KNOWLEDGE AND THE TREE OF LIFE

The Tree of Knowledge was forbidden to Adam, but not the Tree of Life. God did not prevent Adam from eating from the Tree of Life. He was free to do so. But after Adam sinned with the Tree of Knowledge, he was not allowed near the Tree of Life. Why? Because the Tree of Knowledge is the gateway for entering the Tree of Life.

> Here we find a paradox worthy of Kafka: although God had forbidden Adam from eating the fruit of the Tree of Knowledge, he was free to eat from the Tree of Life. And it is true that the Genesis narrative does not forbid Adam from eating from the Tree of Life. But after Adam sinned by eating the forbidden fruit, he was expelled from the Garden of Eden, and cherubim were placed before the gates of Eden *to guard the way to the Tree of Life* (Gen. 3:24). Thus, after he sinned, the Tree of Life became forbidden to Adam. Yet, paradoxically, Gikatilla comments that the Tree of Knowledge was the gateway to the Tree of Life. This suggests that Adam could not have tasted of the Tree of Life without first tasting of the Tree of Knowledge. See "Paradise" by Kafka, p. 445.
>
> Gikatilla's paradox grows out of his kabbalistic interpretation of the Genesis account of the two trees. For him, the fruit of the Tree of Knowledge symbolizes the *kelippot*, the "shells" or "husks" that represent forces of evil and result in separation and banishment. Thus when Adam ate of the forbidden fruit, he reaped a harvest of

banishment. At the same time, the Tree of Knowledge represents *Malkhut*, one of the ten sefirot, while the Tree of Life symbolizes *Tiferet*, another of the sefirot. And *Malkhut* serves as the gateway to *Tiferet* in the kabbalistic system of emanations.

Sources:
Sha'arei Orah 5.

Studies:
"The Origin of Death" by Samuel S. Cohon.

518. THE EVER-TURNING SWORD OF FLAME

After Adam and Eve were expelled from Eden, God *stationed east of the Garden of Eden the cherubim and the fiery ever-turning sword, to guard the way to the Tree of Life* (Gen. 3:24). After that, no one had permission to enter there, except for souls of the righteous who were purified by the cherubim. If they see a soul worthy of entering, they admit it, but if it is not, they drive it away, and it is punished by the flame of the ever-turning sword.

There are two distinct phases in the role of the Garden of Eden in Jewish lore. The first is the account of Adam and Eve's life in the garden and their subsequent expulsion. The second concerns the role of the garden after that, in which it becomes the place that the souls of the righteous enter on their journey into Paradise. See "The Path of the Soul in the Garden of Eden," p. 168.

The role of the cherubim (a type of angel) is clear in the first case, in that they were stationed at the gates of Eden in order to prevent Adam and Eve from reentering there. For having tasted the fruit of the Tree of Knowledge, they had become mortal, and therefore were no longer permitted access to the Tree of Life. This, at least, is the implication of Genesis 3:24. But what purpose do the cherubim serve after the time of Adam and Eve? They continue to serve as gatekeepers, keeping away anyone who tries to enter the garden, as does Alexander the Great. See "The Gates of Eden," p. 406. But once the Garden of Eden takes on its new role as the entry point for the souls of the righteous on their way to Paradise, the role of the cherubim also changed. From this point on they not only kept out those who were not permitted to enter, but they also admitted the souls of the righteous who were permitted to enter there. Somehow the cherubim were able to determine at once whether or not a soul was righteous enough to deserve entry. As for those who were not, they were not only chased off, but, as stated in this myth from the *Zohar*, they were burned by the flame of the revolving sword.

The cherubim play a similar role in the traditions about the High Priest entering the Holy of Holies of the Temple in Jerusalem on Yom Kippur. Two cherubim were portrayed on the cover of the Ark, and they were said to stand guard just like the cherubim that guard the gates of Eden. When the High Priest entered, he entered in awe and dread, for if he were worthy he would enter in peace and exit in peace. But if he were not worthy, a flame would shoot out from between the cherubim—similar to flame of the ever-turning sword—and he would die.

Sources:
Midrash ha-Ne'elam, Zohar Hadash 19a

519. ABRAHAM'S TREE

Wherever Abraham made his home, he always planted a tree. By way of the tree he could detect who clung to God and who clung to idol worship. When one who cleaved to God stood under that tree, its branches would spread out over his head, providing shade. But the tree would recoil from any idolaters, lifting its branches, so that there was no shade.

When Adam ate the fruit of the Tree of Good and Evil, he caused death to enter into the world. But Abraham rectified the world with this tree, which is none other than the Tree of Life.

This myth picks up on the unfinished account of the Tree of Life in Genesis, and creates an entirely new myth concerning this tree, which is described as belonging to Abraham. The branches of this tree serve to identify the true beliefs of anyone who stands beneath it, and Abraham can plant and replant it wherever he goes. The underlying assertion of the myth is that the appearance of Abraham in the world announced a new era, repairing the damage done by Adam when he ate the fruit of the Tree of the Knowledge of Good and Evil. Other sources, especially in the *Zohar*, also identify the Tree of Knowledge as the Tree of Death. *Pesikta Rabbati* 42:1 states that "this particular kind of tree brought death into the world." See also *Zohar* 1:35b, 1:37b, and especially 3:119a. Here it is said that as soon as night commences, the Tree of Life departs for the higher regions and the Tree of Death begins to rule the world, and when it does, all of mankind experiences the taste of death. Not until the Tree of Life is aroused at daybreak does the Tree of Death relax its hold.

In kabbalah, the Tree of Knowledge is often identified as the Tree of Death. Although brief, this myth from the *Zohar* portrays the polarity of the Tree of Life and the Tree of Death, a polarity that is barely hinted at in the Genesis accounts of the Tree of Knowledge and the Tree of Life. In *Folklore in the Old Testament*, James Frazer offers an interesting theory about the relationship between the two trees. Frazer suggests it was God's intention that Adam be immortal. Therefore God warned Adam not to eat the fruit of the Tree of Knowledge, for the Tree of Knowledge was originally the Tree of Death. Thus Frazer sees this divine test as one more myth about the origin of death: "We may suppose that in the original story there were two trees, a tree of life and a tree of death; that it was open to man to eat of the one and live forever, or to eat of the other and die; that God, out of good will to his creature, advised man to eat of the tree of life and warned him not to eat of the tree of death; and that man, misled by the serpent, ate of the wrong tree and so forfeited the immortality that his benevolent Creator had designed for him." (See Theodor H. Gaster's *Myth, Legend, and Custom in the Old Testament*, p. 33.)

Some Christian apocryphal sources also identify the Tree of Knowledge with the Tree of Death. *The Gospel of Philip* 94b states that the Tree of Knowledge "brought death upon those who ate of it." Therefore "it became the beginning of death."

Since this myth comes from the *Zohar*, the sefirotic meaning of the Tree of Life cannot be overlooked. In kabbalistic terms, this refers to the interaction of the ten sefirot, the ten emanations that emerge from the unknowable aspect of God, known as *Ein Sof*, the Endless or Infinite. The myth sets up a dichotomy between the Fall and its consequent damage and the repair represented by the arrival of Abraham and the recognition of the one God, thus the beginnings of Judaism. Note that this same pattern of breaking apart and restoration is the precise pattern of the Ari's myth of the Shattering of the Vessels and the Gathering of the Sparks. See "The Shattering of the Vessels and the Gathering of the Sparks," p. 122. In general, however, the two poles of this dichotomy are the Fall and the messianic era, when the world will be restored to its prelapsarian condition.

Sources:
Zohar 1:102a.

Studies:
Myth, Legend, and Custom in the Old Testament by Theodor H. Gaster, p. 33.

520. THE CAVE OF THE FOUR WINDS

The Cave of the Four Winds can be found at the entrance of a small cave in the Garden of Eden, not far from the Tree of Knowledge. That cave is covered by a curtain on which are inscribed many secret symbols. It is said that if a corner of that curtain is lifted, a great blast of wind will escape, enough to toss boulders into the air as if they were apples, and uproot trees planted on the sixth day of creation. If the entire curtain is lifted, the four winds will be set free, and the world will return to chaos and void.

Rabbinic literature and medieval Jewish folklore greatly elaborate on the details of the earthly and heavenly Paradise. Here is the description of a cave in the Garden of Eden that contains all the winds. All that prevents the world from returning to chaos is this curtain, inscribed with secret symbols, that hangs before it. This myth can be read as a warning against delving into forbidden secrets, such as spells and other kinds of magic. Or, from a modern perspective, it can be seen as a warning against the dangers of nuclear destruction. This myth about the Cave of the Four Winds is found in the story "The Prince of Coucy." See *Miriam's Tambourine*, pp. 173-185.

Sources:
Notzer Te'enah; Sefer Ma'asiyot; Sefer Sippurim Nora'im; IFA 5854.

521. THE GATES OF EDEN

During his journeys, Alexander the Great once stopped by a stream. He had some salted fish with him, and when he washed it in the waters it gave off a wonderful fragrance. Alexander then drank some of that water and felt remarkably refreshed. He said: "This stream must come from the Garden of Eden. Let us see if we can find its source." So Alexander followed the stream until he reached the Gates of Eden. The gates were guarded by an angel with a flaming sword. The others in his company hid from the sight of the angel, but Alexander stood before the angel and said: "Open the gates for me!" The angel replied: *"This is the gateway of the Lord, the righteous shall enter through it"* (Ps. 118:20). When Alexander saw that he would not be admitted, he said: "I am a king who is highly regarded. Give me something!" Then the angel gave him an eye. Alexander went and weighed it against all his gold and silver, but the eye outweighed them all. He asked the angel how this was possible, and the angel said: "The eye of a human being is never satisfied." And Alexander asked: "How can you prove that this is true?" And the angel answered: "Take some dust and cover the eye and you will see for yourself." Alexander did this, and all at once the eye was restored to its true weight.

There are many legends about Alexander the Great in Jewish lore. This one from the Talmud teaches Alexander the lesson that the lust of the human eye is limitless but is easily quenched by dust, that is, by death. Alexander learns this at the gates of the Garden of Eden, which is the one place that Alexander cannot conquer in the world, just as he cannot conquer death. Thus the moral of the tale is that there are built-in limits to the satisfaction of human desire, a moral that is appropriately directed at Alexander, a folk symbol of one who sought to go beyond all human limits. For other Jewish tales about the exploits of Alexander, see "Alexander Descends into the Sea" in *Miriam's Tambourine*, pp. 118-121, and "The Waters of Eternal Life," in the same book, pp. 122-134.

According to Rabbi Samuel Eliezer Edels, known as the Maharsha, only those who do not amass worldly goods can enter the Garden of Eden.

Sources:
B. *Tamid* 32b; IFA 6966.

522. THE LAND OF ISRAEL

The Land of Israel is holier than all other lands, for the Land of Israel is under the direct providence of God, and *the eyes of your God are always on it* (Deut. 11:12). Before the Land of Israel was chosen, all lands were suitable for divine revelation; after the Land of Israel was chosen, all other lands were eliminated. Just as *The Lord your God is the God of gods and the Lord of lords* (Deut. 10:17), so the Land of Israel is the center of the inhabited earth and

God's own inheritance. So too is it the central place for the study of the Torah and ascensions of prayer, as it is said, *that is the gateway to heaven* (Gen. 28:17). Even the air of the Land of Israel makes one wise. That is why it is said that "there is no Torah like the Torah of the Land of Israel." When Jews dwell in the Land of Israel, they eat from their Father's table and receive the light of wisdom directly from God. In contrast, all other lands are dark, as it is said, *He has made me dwell in dark places* (Lam. 3:6). Alas for the children who have been exiled from their Father's table!

God considered all the nations and found no people fit to receive the Torah other than the people of Israel. So too did God consider all generations and found no generation fit to receive the Torah other than the generation of the wilderness. He also considered all mountains and found no mountain on which the Torah should be given other than Mount Sinai. And God considered all cities and found none to compare with the city of Jerusalem. So too did He consider all lands and found none suitable to be given to Israel other than the Land of Israel.

The Land of Israel is not like Egypt, which is irrigated by the Nile like a garden. The Land of Israel is a land of hills and valleys almost exclusively intended to absorb the dew of heaven. For even though the physical Land of Israel exists, its essence is a spiritual matter, the life force coming from God. And all those who walk as little as four cubits in the Land of Israel are assured of a share in the World to Come, while all who are buried in the Land of Israel—it is as if they were buried beneath the altar of the Temple in Jerusalem.

Monotheism is the central pillar of Judaism, but close in importance is the centrality of the Land of Israel (*Eretz Yisrael*). Indeed, the covenant between God and the people of Israel is manifest in the Land of Israel. As Rav Kook put it, "Love for our Holy Land is the foundation of the Torah" ("The Land of Israel," *Orot*, Jerusalem, 1950, p. 9).

The midrash from *Leviticus Rabbah* about God choosing the Holy Land is a commentary on the verse *When He stands, He makes the earth shake* (Hab. 3:6). According to Maimonides, so essential is the link of Israel to the Jewish people that if no Jews lived there, the Torah would vanish.

The Land of Israel was believed to have sacred powers and there are a great many myths about the miracles that occurred there. From such a mythic perspective, the land is more than a place, but is also a sacred realm. It is believed that whoever desires to be a true Jew can only achieve this by means of the sanctity of the Holy Land, that by entering the Land of Israel, a person becomes part of its sacred nature. Further, prayers originating in the Land of Israel can bring about miracles and true wonders for the entire world. Any ascent of prayer can only take place in the Land of Israel, for that is where the ascent of prayers occurs. Without the sanctity of the Land of Israel, a descent into exile occurs, and prayer descends into exile, and it is impossible to pray and perform miracles in the world.

In the Talmud it is said that whoever walks four cubits in the Land of Israel is assured of a place in the World to Come (*B. Ketubot* 111a). For this reason, many sages sought to make the journey. The Ba'al Shem Tov sought repeatedly to reach the Holy Land, but he never managed to get there. There are numerous folktales about his failed attempts. Rabbi Nachman of Bratslav, great-grandson of the Ba'al Shem Tov, who believed that he bore a spark of the Ba'al Shem Tov's soul, sought to journey to the Holy Land to complete his great-grandfather's quest for him. It was truly an epic journey during which Rabbi Nachman felt that he was engaged in a life and death struggle with the forces of evil. After a six month journey, he arrived the day before Rosh ha-Shanah, 1798. He believed that "the moment I walked four steps on the Holy Land, I achieved my goal" (*Shivhei ha-Ran* 15). And as soon as Rosh Hashanah was over, Rabbi Nachman was ready to return home. He wanted to leave at once. Having taken those four steps on the Holy Land, he felt he had completed his quest. However, his companion, probably his earliest disciple Rabbi Shimon, convinced him to visit some of the holy cities of Israel, and in this way managed to extend Rabbi Nachman's stay for a few months.

For a contrast between the Land of Israel and the other lands, see "The Seventy Nations and the Land of Israel," following.

Sources:
Mishnah Kelim 1:6; *B. Ketubot* 111a; *B. Bava Batra* 158b; *Genesis Rabbah* 16:4; *Leviticus Rabbah* 13:2; *Mekhilta de-Rabbi Ishmael Pisha* 1; *Hilkhot Kiddush ha-Hodesh*; Nachmanides, *Perush Ramban al ha-Torah* on Deuteronomy 11:10; *Kitvei ha-Ramban* 1:240; *Likutei Moharan* 1:2; *Likutei Etzot, Eretz Yisrael* 1, 2, 3, 8, 13, 14, 15, 17, 18, 19; *Yesamah Lev* on *Ketubot* p. 26b-c; *Ben Yehoyada.*

Studies:
Zion in Jewish Literature, edited by Abraham S. Halkin.
The Land of Israel: Jewish Perspectives, edited by Lawrence A. Hoffman.
"The Land of Israel in Medieval Kabbalah" by Moshe Idel.
Tormented Master: A Life of Rabbi Nachman of Bratslav by Arthur Green, pp. 63-93.

523. THE SEVENTY NATIONS AND THE LAND OF ISRAEL

At the time of the creation, God decreed that the seventy nations that descended from Adam be placed in the charge of seventy guardian angels, each nation being ruled by its own angel. Thus all the people of the world are watched over by guardian angels. God divided the world among these heavenly ministers, each one receiving a portion of the land upon which his nation dwells. The fate of a particular nation below depends on the status of its guardian angel. When the angel prospers, so does his nation; when he falls, so does his nation. Thus it is written that *Yahweh will punish the host of heaven in heaven, and the kings of the earth on earth* (Isa. 24:21).

One land, however, was not entrusted to any minister. The Land of Israel is the center of the inhabited earth, so He put no angels, no officers, rulers or sovereigns over it. God kept it for Himself, saying, "I am keeping this land under My own dominion, and when I find a man upon the earth who will follow My heart, I will place him as a seal upon My heart and settle him in this land. He will be guided directly by My authority, without any intermediary among the heavenly ministers, unlike the other nations." So too did God say, "Let Israel, who became My portion, inherit the land which became My portion." God provides sustenance there first, and only then to the rest of the world.

All angels sing God's praises, but the guardian angels of the seventy nations can only sing to God under certain circumstances. The opportunity comes when a particular nation does some act of kindness to Israel. Then its guardian angel receives permission to sing before God.

When the guardian angels of other nations fall from power, all memory of their existence is completely wiped off the face of the earth. But when Israel, because of its transgressions, is oppressed by other nations, it is in a state of exile, under the dominion of their guardian angels. But, though it is subject to other nations and their guardian angels, Israel can never be totally destroyed, for its guardian and head is none other than God. Thus the Jewish people shall abide eternally and inherit the earth and its fullness.

This myth explains the unique nature of the relationship between God and Israel, and of the centrality of the Land of Israel in that relationship. It explains that at the time God created the world, He distributed the various lands to the heavenly ministers and chose the Land of Israel for Himself, as explained in the verse *For the Lord's portion is His people* (Deut. 32:9). In effect, God serves as the heavenly minister of Israel, while all other nations are guided by ministering angels. As Rabbi Abraham Azulai

(1570-1643) puts it in *Hesed le-Avraham*, "Each people has its own guardian angel, except the people of Israel, which is bound directly to God alone and to God's law." Since God rules over the angels, the relationship between God and the nation of Israel is clearly far more important than that of any other nation. These verses explain why God found Abraham worthy of settling in the Land of Israel, and raised him above the rest of the nations: *"You are the Lord God who chose Abram, and brought him out of Ur of the Chaldeans, and gave him the name Abraham; and You found his heart faithful before You, and You made a covenant with him to give the land of the Canaanite, the Hittite, the Amorite, the Perizzite, the Jebusite, and the Girgashite—to give it to his seed. And You kept Your word; for You are righteous"* (Neh. 9:7-8).

In this view, Israel is the Holy Land because God chose it for Himself. Other myths attribute the holiness of the Land of Israel to the land itself. See, for example, "Light from the Temple," p. 411.

These beliefs about the divine role of the Land of Israel are the basis of the claim that "The Land of Israel is an inheritance from our forefathers" (*B. A. Z.* 53b). It is not a claim based on acquisition or military conquest, but one that derives from a decision of God, in which the Torah serves as the deed and the proof. From this point of view, exile is an unnatural state, and it is the obligation of the Jewish people to return and settle the Land of Israel.

Sources:
Zohar 1:69a, 1:108b, 2:6b, 2:18a, 2:46b, 2:54b, 2:175a, 2:232b; *Midrash Tanhuma, Mas'ei* 6, *Re'eh* 8; *Midrash Tehillim* 150:1; *Sefer Hasidim* 1160; *Kitvei ha-Ramban* 1:240; *Hesed le-Avraham*; *B'nei Yisakhar, Adar, Ma'amar* 2; *Shekel ha-Kodesh, derush* 4; *Kedushat Levi* p. 59.

524. HOW THE HOLY LAND BECAME HOLY

God wears an exquisite ring on His finger. It contains precious gems of every kind: amethysts, emeralds, and sapphires, among them. Each of those gems lights the firmament with holy sparks, twinkling like a million stars.

One day God decided to transform a bare and deserted land into a holy land. Till then there was nothing more than a desolate range of mountains. Then God turned the ring on His finger, and sparks flew over the Galilee and the Jordan valley. They landed in the desert, as far as the Dead Sea, and all at once the mountains were transformed, covered with a bluish gleam, and luminous circles surrounded the Jordan valley.

God saw that it was good and turned His ring again, and fiery sparks covered the mountains like a glimmering *tallit*. God raised His hand, and a bit of a precious stone flew over the Negev and landed with such force that it melted and became the Sea of Eilat. It sparkles and shines day and night, never forgetting its origin in God's ring.

God's gaze turned to the north, and He turned His ring once more and the most beautiful of God's sapphires fell to earth and became the Sea of Galilee.

> This is a myth of origin, explaining how a desolate land was transformed into a beautiful holy one through God's intervention. A transformation takes place each time God turns His ring. Sparks fly from the ring that turn a desolate land into a sacred one. This may allude to the Ari's myth of the sparks. See "The Shattering of the Vessels and the Gathering of the Sparks," p. 122. The myth also serves as an origin myth of the Kinneret (Sea of Galilee) and the Sea of Eilat, in which bits of God's ring fly to earth like comets and create them.

Sources:
IFA 593.

525. THE CAVE OF SHIMON BAR YOHAI

Near the village of Peki'in in the Galilee there is a cave known as the cave of Shimon bar Yohai. That is the cave in which Shimon bar Yohai and his son Eleazar hid from the Romans after they passed a decree calling for his execution. Shimon bar Yohai and his son remained in that cave for thirteen years, devoting themselves to the study of the Torah.

Many miracles took place while they lived in that cave. During the first night they spent there, a well of living water formed inside the cave and a large carob tree grew outside it, filled with ripe carobs, that completely hid the entrance. When Shimon bar Yohai and his son discovered the spring and the tree that had appeared overnight, they drank from the water and tasted the fruit. The water was pure and delicious and the fruit was ripe, and they knew that their faith had been rewarded and that the Holy One, blessed be He, was guarding them. And they gave thanks.

After that, Rabbi Shimon and his son cast off their clothes and spent each day buried in the sand, studying the Torah. Only when it was time to pray did they put on their white garments, and in this way they preserved them through the long years of their exile.

Then a day came when Elijah the Prophet arrived at the cave to study with them. Elijah revealed great mysteries to them that had never been known outside of heaven. And in the days that followed Elijah often returned, and Shimon bar Yohai wrote down those mysteries on parchment that Elijah brought them, which came from the ram that Abraham had sacrificed on Mount Moriah in place of Isaac. Now that was an enchanted parchment, for as Shimon bar Yohai wrote, it expanded to receive his words. And every letter he inscribed there burned in black fire on white. And the name of the book that he wrote down there, filled with the celestial mysteries, was the *Zohar*.

One day, as they watched from inside the cave, Rabbi Eleazar saw a bird repeatedly escape from a hunter, and he recognized this as a sign that they were free to leave the cave, for the Emperor had died and the decree had been annulled. But before they left, they hid the book of the *Zohar* in that cave, for they knew that the world was not yet ready for its secrets to be revealed.

There the book of the *Zohar* remained for many generations, until an Ishmaelite who happened to find it in the cave sold it to peddlers. Some of its pages came into the possession of a rabbi, who recognized their value at once. He went to all the peddlers in that area and found that they had used the pages of the book to wrap their spices. In this way he was able to collect all of the missing pages, and that is how the *Zohar* was saved and came to be handed down.

Although this legend originated in a talmudic source, it became the basis for the kabbalistic legends about the talmudic sage Shimon bar Yohai, as well as for the origin of the *Zohar*, the central text of kabbalah. According to this legend, Bar Yohai spent 13 years in a cave, hiding from the Romans, who had condemned him. Moshe de Leon, who lived in Spain in the thirteenth century, attributed the text of the *Zohar*, which he claimed to have discovered, to Shimon bar Yohai, who was said to have written it during the years spent in hiding. However, modern scholars, especially Gershom Scholem, have demonstrated that the *Zohar* was actually the creation of Moshe de Leon, perhaps with the collaboration of his circle of kabbalists. The *Zohar* is a mystical commentary on the Torah, but it also contains many legends about Shimon bar Yohai and his disciples. The portrayal of Shimon bar Yohai in the *Zohar* became the model of the master for later sages, especially the Ari. And the Ari became the archetype of the master for later rabbis, such as Shalom Sharabi and the Ba'al Shem Tov. So an imagined portrayal of a master by Moshe de Leon led to a real life emulation of the model. For a discussion about the authorship of the *Zohar*, see "A Note on the Sources," p. 525, footnote *.

Sources:
   B. *Shabbat* 33b; *Beit ha-Midrash* 4:22; *Pesikta de-Rav Kabana* 88b; *Ecclesiastes Rabbah*
   10:8; *Zohar Hadash, Ki Tavo* 59c-60a; *Or ha-Hamah* 1.

526. LIGHT FROM THE TEMPLE

What was the source of the light that came forth when God said, *Let there be light* (Gen 1:3)? Some say it shone forth from the place where the Temple in Jerusalem would one day be built, and from there it illuminated the entire world. Surrounded by that light, God completed the creation of the world. Then God saw to it that the light of the Temple was diffused to all the world, as it is said, *God has shined forth* (Ps. 50:2).

Others say that the light was created at the site of the Temple, and had never before existed.

This holy light continued to emanate even after the Temple was built upon that place. Its source was in the Holy of Holies, in which the Holy Ark stood, and it lit up the Temple and shone forth through the windows. For there were windows in the Temple, but instead of light coming into them, it went out of them. Indeed, the windows were built for this purpose, narrow on the inside and broad on the outside, in order to send forth light into the world. And the light that shone forth from the Temple ascended to the firmament, to God's Chariot, and to the Throne of Glory, and the light filled Jerusalem and the Holy Land, and all basked in its presence. That is why it is said that Jerusalem is the light of the world.

> This myth about the origin of the first light derives from the verse *And the earth was lit up by His Presence* (Ezek. 43:2), where "Presence" is identified with the Temple in Jerusalem. There is a suggestion in this myth that the light pre-existed, and that the site on which the Temple was built was sacred from the time of Creation, if not before. *Genesis Rabbah* 3:4 states: "The light was created from the place of the Temple." This has theological implications, as it suggests that God created the universe out of existing materials. See "God's Garment of Light," p. 82.
>
> The question of whether God used pre-existing materials in creating the world was a highly controversial one among the ancient rabbis, who considered it an esoteric matter. Rabbi Bar Kappara took the position that the Torah reveals that God did make use of pre-existing material, while Rav compared this to building a palace on a garbage dump, and Rabbi Jose ben Haninah asserted that the suggestion that God made use of pre-existing materials such as darkness, chaos, and void (*tohu* and *vohu*) impaired God's glory. (*Genesis Rabbah* 1:5).
>
> The notion that light pre-existed also is found in Isaiah 45:7: *I form the light and create darkness.* Here the important distinction is between "form" (*yotzer*) and "create" (*borei*), with "form" suggesting that the light already existed, while "create" refers to something that was brought into being *ex nihilo*.
>
> *Midrash Tehillim* presents a very terse version of this myth, asking where God diffused the light, with the answer that God had diffused it from the Temple. This is linked to the verse *And the earth was lit up by His Presence* (Ezek. 43:2) Here the phrase "the earth was lit up" is understood to mean the Temple. From this derives the interpretation that the light itself came from the place of the Temple.
>
> *Genesis Rabbah* 60:19, however, offers a different source for the light: "Who is the light of Jerusalem? God, as it is said, *Yahweh shall be your light everlasting*" (Isa. 60:19).
>
> This myth is likely of Jewish-Gnostic origin, as there was a primary Gnostic belief that light pre-existed the chaos that preceded creation. For an example of this Gnostic myth, see *On the Origin of the World* 2:97-98: "Seeing that everybody says that nothing existed prior to chaos, I shall demonstrate that they are all mistaken, because they are

not acquainted with the origin of chaos, nor with its root .... After the natural structure of the immortal beings had completely developed out of the infinite a likeness then emanated and became a product resembling the primeval light."

A related myth in *B. Ta'anit* 10a states that the Land of Israel was created first, and the rest of the world came afterward. This land is watered first, according to this myth, because it is watered by God Himself, and the rest of the world is watered through a messenger of God. Both myths, that of light from the Temple and that *Eretz Yisrael* was created first, insist on the centrality of the Land of Israel.

Sources:
B. *Ta'anit* 10a; *B. Hagigah* 12a; *Genesis Rabbah* 1:5, 3:4, 3:6, 11:2, 42:3, 60:19; *Midrash Tehillim* 104:4; *Pesikta de-Rav Kahana* 21:5; *Midrash Konen* in *Beit ha-Midrash* 2:27; *Sefer Eliyahu* in *Beit ha-Midrash* 3:68-78; *Zohar* 1:263a.

Studies:
The Enthronement of Sabaoth: Jewish Elements in Gnostic Creation Myths by Francis T. Fallon, pp. 10-24.
Man and Temple by Raphael Patai, pp. 54-104.

527. GOD BUILDS THE HEAVENLY TEMPLE

When the time drew near for Moses to take leave of this world, God took him up to the highest heavens and showed him his reward as well as what was destined to take place in the future days. There Moses saw God building the sanctuary of the Temple out of precious stones and pearls, and out of the splendor of the *Shekhinah*. So too did Moses see the Messiah, the son of David, standing there, as well as his own brother, Aaron.

Aaron said to Moses, "Do not touch me, for no one may enter here until he gives up his soul and tastes the taste of death. Otherwise the flame of the *Shekhinah* will consume you." When Moses heard Aaron's words, he fell on his face and pleaded, "Master of the Universe, let me speak with your Messiah before I die." God gave His consent and said to an angel, "Go, teach Moses my great Name so that the flame of the *Shekhinah* will not consume him when he sees the Messiah."

When Moses had been taught the Name, he said to the Messiah, "Will God build a sanctuary on earth like the one He is building here in heaven?" The Messiah replied: "The house that God is building with His hands in heaven will exist for Israel until the end of all generations. While your father Jacob was sleeping, he saw the Temple that God will build on earth and the one being built in heaven. Jacob understood that this heavenly House would exist for Israel forever, until the end of all generations. That is what Jacob meant when he awoke from his dream of the ladder reaching to heaven and said, *This is none other than the abode of God, and that is the gateway to heaven* (Gen. 28:17). And when the time comes, God will bring this heavenly Jerusalem down to earth."

When Moses heard these words from the Messiah, he rejoiced greatly and turned his face toward God and said, "Master of the Universe, when will You bring down this Temple that is now being built?"

God said, "I have not disclosed this to any living being, neither to the first ones or the last. Shall I tell you?"

Moses said, "Master of the Universe, give me a hint."

God said, "I will scatter the Israelites to the four corners of the earth, but one day I will bring them back to the Land of Israel."

Moses descended from heaven contented. Then he gave his soul to God with a perfect heart and a longing soul.

Here God brings Moses into heaven before his death to show him his heavenly reward and also to reassure him about the future destiny of Israel. There Moses is reunited with his deceased brother, Aaron, and he also meets the Messiah. This myth is significant because Moses himself is the model for the Messiah. Indeed, for the Samaritans Moses was a figure of messianic proportions. The myth also confirms the inevitability of subsequent Jewish history—the building of the Temple on earth as a mirror image to that already existing in heaven, and the eventual coming of the Messiah. While God's purpose in this myth is to reassure Moses, the real purpose is to reassure the Jews that despite their trials, God's plan for Israel would ultimately be fulfilled. For a similar heavenly encounter see "Jacob's Heavenly Vision," p. 357.

This intriguing midrash builds both on the dream of Jacob (Gen. 28:12-17), and especially on the verse *This is none other than the abode of God* (Gen. 28:17), as well as on the tradition that Moses did not only ascend to the top of Mount Sinai to receive the Torah, but ascended all the way into heaven. In the most famous version of this legend, found in *B. Shabbat* 88b-89a, God reaches down and pulls Moses into heaven, so that he finds himself standing before God's Throne of Glory and sees God creating the crowns of the letters of the Torah. In the version from *Pesikta Rabbati* 20:4, Moses sees the angel Sandalphon standing behind God's throne, and God steps down from His throne to reassure Moses. In this version from *Bereshit Rabbati*, Moses sees God building the heavenly Temple. Note that in the earlier midrash, God is creating the crowns of the letters of the Torah and here He is building the heavenly Jerusalem. Thus is God portrayed as taking an active role in the process of creation, especially as it relates to the people of Israel.

This midrash also builds on the existing legends about the death of Moses. In most of these, Moses is very reluctant to die, and resists the Angel of Death. Here both God and the Angel of Death politely refrain from threatening to take Moses' soul until he is ready to release it. Still another midrash, in *B. Sota* 14a, asserts that Moses did not realize he was dying and was unaware of what was happening to him. In *Likutei Moharan* 1:4, Rabbi Nachman of Bratslav explains this by saying that Moses gave himself completely to God, so that when God spoke to him he was unaware of his own existence. Therefore he was unaware of his own death.

The version of this midrash found in *Bereshit Rabbati* takes an unusual turn in suggesting that God will bring the heavenly Temple down to earth. At first this might appear to be a way to describe the messianic era as if it were heaven on earth. But, in fact, it is probably intended to be understood literally, as it is described in another text, *Tefillat Rabbi Shimon ben Yohai* in *Beit ha-Midrash* 3:78-82: "Then a fire will come down from heaven and consume Jerusalem .... Then the perfect, rebuilt Jerusalem will come down from heaven .... Then the already constructed Temple will descend from heaven, for it is bound to the celestial abode, as Moses saw by the Holy Spirit: *You will bring them and plant them* (Exod. 15:17)." It seems likely that these texts are referring to the same tradition, in which the heavenly Jerusalem would descend to earth at the time of the advent of the Messiah. See "The Descent of the Heavenly Temple," p. 512.

However, the version of this myth found in *Pesikta Rabbati* suggests that rather than bring the heavenly Temple down to earth, God will see to it that an earthly Temple will be built. Also, in this version Moses asked to know when the earthly Temple would be destroyed and God tells him that although it will be destroyed and the people of Israel will be scattered among all the nations, the day will come when He will gather all those who were exiled.

See "The Ascent of Moses," p. 261.

Sources:

B. Sota 14a; B. Shabbat 88b-89a; Pesikta Rabbati 20:4; Bereshit Rabbati in Beit ha-Midrash 6:22-23; Midrash Konen in Beit ha-Midrash 2:34; Midrashei Geulah.

Studies:

"The Celestial Temple as Viewed in the Aggadah" by Victor Aptowitzer.

528. THE HEAVENLY JERUSALEM AND THE EARTHLY JERUSALEM

Everything that God created in heaven, He also created on earth. There is a heavenly Jerusalem that mirrors the earthly city, and a celestial Temple that is the mirror image of the one King Solomon built in Jerusalem. So too was the earthly Holy of Holies a counterpart of the heavenly one. But while the earthly Temple was destroyed, along with the Holy of Holies, the heavenly Temple still exists in all its glory.

The Jerusalem on high faces the Jerusalem below. For out of God's great love for the earthly Jerusalem, He made another one on high, as it is said, *Your walls are ever before Me* (Isa. 49:16).

The Jerusalem constructed in heaven is joined together with the one on earth. God has sworn that He will not enter the heavenly Jerusalem until the earthly one is rebuilt, as it is said, *I will not enter the city* (Hos. 11:9). God said, "What is there for Me in Jerusalem after My people have been taken from there?"

God created a lofty palace on high, a holy city, the supernal city of Jerusalem. Whoever wishes to enter into God's presence may do so only from this city. That is the meaning of the verse *This is the gateway to the Lord; the righteous shall enter through it* (Ps. 118:20).

> One of the key principles of kabbalah is "as above, so below." The idea is that this world was created as a mirror image of heaven. Thus Jerusalem exists in both places, and there is still a heavenly Temple standing, although the earthly one was destroyed. Just as Jerusalem on earth is the holiest Jewish city, so the Jerusalem on high is the gateway to God's presence. One of the goals of the mystics who tried to ascend to Paradise was to find their way to the heavenly Jerusalem.
>
> "As above, so below" has another important meaning—that prayer and some kinds of mystical study in this world could affect the world above. Therefore *tikkun* or repair done below, heals the world on high and brings God and His exiled Bride that much closer.
>
> According to one version of this myth, God has vowed to stay out of the heavenly Jerusalem until the earthly one is rebuilt. This would be a great sacrifice on God's part, similar to the exile the *Shekhinah* experiences since being cast out of Her home in this world, the Temple.
>
> *Sources:*
> B. Ta'anit 5a; Y. Berakhot 4, 4:5; *Exodus Rabbah* 33:4; *Midrash Tehillim* 30:1, 122:5;
>   *Midrash Tanhuma-Yelammedenu*, Pekudei 1; *Zohar* 2:50b-51a.
>
> *Studies:*
> *Midrash Yerushalem: A Metaphysical History of Jerusalem* by Daniel Sperber, pp. 82-88.

529. HOW MOUNT MORIAH WAS CREATED

In the beginning Moriah was a vale, but God decided to make it the site of His sanctuary, so that His *Shekhinah* could reside there. So He made a sign to the mountains around the valley to come together, to make an abode for the *Shekhinah*. Then all the nearby mountains moved together and fused into one. That is how Mount Moriah was created.

Others say that God created seven mountains, and of these He chose Mount Moriah as the site of the holy Temple, for that was *the mountain which God desired as His dwelling* (Ps. 68:17).

So too was Mount Sinai created out of Mount Moriah, for God said, "Since their father Isaac was bound upon this mount, it is fitting that his children receive the Torah upon it."

So Mount Sinai plucked itself out of Mount Moriah as a priest's portion is plucked out of dough, and that is how it came into being.

Mount Moriah is the mountain where God told Abraham to sacrifice Isaac (Gen. 22). However, in the midrashic tradition it becomes identified with the Temple Mount in Jerusalem, and even comes to include the place where Cain and Abel made their offerings, as well as the offering of Noah at the end of the Flood. Here it is said to have had a supernatural creation, as it was God's intention from very early in Creation that it serve as His sanctuary on earth.

Just as there is a creation myth about Mount Moriah, so there is one about how Mount Sinai was created out of Mount Moriah. This powerfully links these major biblical episodes, as well as tying them both to the Temple in Jerusalem. For the mount in Jerusalem where the Temple was built and where the Temple Mount is found today is called Mount Moriah (2 Chron. 3:7).

The image of Mount Sinai plucking itself out of Mount Moriah is compared to the priest's portion being plucked out of dough. This refers to the priest's share of the bread as mentioned in Numbers 15:20.

Sources:
Midrash Tanhuma-Yelammedenu, Va-Yera 22; *Midrash Haserot ve-Yeterot* 19; *Midrash ha-Gadol; Midrash Tehillim* 68:9; *Beit ha-Midrash* 5:72-73.

530. THE ALTAR OF ABRAHAM

Abraham and Isaac *arrived at the place of which God had told him. Abraham built an altar there* (Gen. 22:9). Some say that was the same altar on Mount Moriah where Adam made offerings, because the gate of the Garden of Eden was close by. Adam erected an altar to the Lord there, and on it he sacrificed an ox with one horn on its forehead. So too was it the same altar on which Cain and Abel made their sacrifices, and the same altar where Noah and his sons sacrificed.

Others say the altar that Adam built was demolished by the waters of the Flood. Noah rebuilt it, but it was demolished in the generation of the Tower of Babel. Then *Abraham built the altar there; he laid out the wood; he bound his son Isaac; he laid him on the altar, on top of the wood* (Gen. 22:9).

That was the site where in the future the Temple in Jerusalem would be built, and the place of the altar was the same as that of the Temple altar, where the High Priests made their sacrifices.

This myth presents an archetypal altar on which many of the key biblical sacrifices prior to the building of the Temple were made. It asserts that the same altar was used by Adam, Cain and Abel, Noah and his sons, and it was situated on the same holy mountain, Mount Moriah, where God directed Abraham to go to offer his son Isaac. Further, the Temple Mount, known as Mount Moriah, is believed to be set in the same place. This is an example of mythic geography, with little consideration for actual geographic location. Instead, what matters is linking together these sacrifices in order to portray the existence of this archetypal altar for sacrifices to God.

Others say that Adam and Eve lived on Mount Moriah, because the gate of the Garden of Eden was close by. Adam erected an altar to the Lord there, and on it he sacrificed a remarkable ox with one horn on its forehead. So too did Adam's sons, Cain and Abel, make use of that altar.

Sources:
Targum Pseudo-Yonathan on Genesis 8:20, 22:9; *Genesis Rabbah* 34:9, 34:20; *Pirkei de-Rabbi Eliezer* 31; *Midrash Tehillim* 92:6; *Zohar* 1:70a.

531. GOD PRAYS FOR THE BUILDING OF THE TEMPLE

God has prayed for the building of the Temple since the days of Abraham, and even before. Why should God pray for this? Because man must build the earthly Temple first, and afterward God will send the heavenly Temple to rest upon it. All of Israel, together, is responsible for rebuilding the Temple. Everyone has an equal share, and everyone is obligated to participate. Once it is built, the earthly Temple will serve as the foundation for the one that will come from the heavens.

> The ultimate stage of the messianic era will be the descent of the heavenly Temple, which will come to rest on the earthly one. See "The Descent of the Heavenly Temple," p. 512. Before this can take place, the earthly Temple must be built, or, since the first two Temples were destroyed, rebuilt. This will prepare the necessary awakening from below that must precede the descent of the Temple from on high. According to *Metzudat David*, once the earthly Temple is built, God will take so much delight in it that He Himself will carve designs on the stones in order to beautify them. Thus God prays for the building of the earthly Temple so that the time may be hastened when the messianic era begins and He can lower the supernal Temple onto it. This belief serves as one of the primary motivations of fervent groups in Israel that are devoted to the building of the third Temple despite the fact that the Muslim Dome of the Rock has already been built on what is usually regarded as the site of the Temple.
>
> *Sources:*
> Genesis Rabbah 56:10; *Tikkunei ha-Zohar* 21, p. 60b; *Emunot ve-ha-De'ot* 8, chap. 5-6; *Em ha-Banim S'mehah*; *Metzudat David*; *Ezrat Kohanim*.

532. THE CELESTIAL TEMPLE

God's dwelling place above is directly opposite His dwelling place below. Just as there is an earthly Jerusalem, so too is there a celestial Jerusalem; just as there was an earthly Temple, so there is a celestial Temple located in the most sacred part of the heavens, not far from the Throne of Glory. The stars are its ornaments, and the angels serve as its priests.

This is the Temple of God, standing on the summit of the firmament, its brilliance illuminating all the rooms of heaven. A thousand hosts stand before the *Shekhinah* in the celestial Temple, calling "Holy, holy, holy." And every host consists of many thousands of ministering angels.

Some say that the celestial Temple existed on high even before the world was created, as it is said, *O Throne of Glory exalted from the first* (Jer. 17:12). Thus the upper Temple existed first, and God commanded that the lower Temple be made according to the secrets of the upper one. Others say that God began the creation of His world at the foundation stone, and built the world upon it. Then He created the Celestial Temple, as it is said, *The place You made to dwell in, O Yahweh* (Exod. 15:17).

Just as there is a High Priest in the Temple below, so there is a High Priest on high. Some say that Logos, the divine word, the first angel, serves as the heavenly High Priest. Others say that it is Metatron, while still others say that it is Michael, the prince of Israel, who serves as the High Priest, and offers sacrifices on the altar every day. What does he offer up? The souls of the righteous.

When the earthly Temple still existed, the High Priest would make sacrifices and burn incense below, while Michael would do the same on high. After the earthly Temple was destroyed, God said to Michael, "From this time forward you shall offer me the good deeds of My children, their prayers, and the souls of the righteous, which are hidden beneath the Throne of Glory."

Others say that since the heavenly Temple and the earthly one were built as counterparts as long as the one stood, the High Priest offered up sacrifices and burnt incense, and the angel Michael offered up the souls of the righteous who dwell beneath the Throne of Glory, and all the angels came to the altar with incense, and they burned it until the cloud of incense covered the canopy of heaven. But once the earthly Temple was destroyed and the sacrifices abolished, the offerings on high came to an end as well. But in the future God will restore them.

At the End of Days, when the time has come for the earthly Temple to be rebuilt, the heavens will open up, and the glory of the Temple's holiness will be revealed. Then God will bring the heavenly Temple down to the earthly Jerusalem, and the footsteps of the Messiah will be heard by one and all.

> Working on the principle of "as above, so below," Jewish lore postulates the existence of a heavenly Jerusalem that is the mirror image of the earthly one, except that the heavenly Temple still stands, while that in this world has been destroyed. As is apparent from the large number of sources that refer to the celestial Temple, this was a widely recognized tradition.
>
> Isaiah 2:3 suggests the existence of the heavenly temple: *"Come, let us go up to the Mount of Yahweh, to the House of the God of Jacob"* (Isa. 2:3).
>
> Philo offers an allegorical interpretation of the two temples: "There are, it seems, two temples belonging to God, one being this world, in which the High Priest is the divine word (Logos), his own firstborn son. The other is the rational soul, the representation of the universal heaven."
>
> See "God Builds the Heavenly Temple," p. 412.
>
> *Sources:*
> *1 Enoch* 14:16-20; *2 Enoch* 20:1-4; *B. Hagigah* 12a; *Y. Berakhot* 4:5; *Genesis Rabbah* 1:4, 55:7, 69:7; *Numbers Rabbah* 12:12; *Midrash Tanhuma, Naso* 19; *Midrash Tanhuma-Yelammedenu, Pekudei* 3; *Midrash Eleh Ezkerah; The Testament of Levi* 3:4-6, 5:1-2, 18:6; *The Book of Jubilees* 31:14; Philo, *De Specialibus Legibus,* 1:966; Philo, *De Somniis* 1:215; *Aseret ha-Dibrot in Beit ha-Midrash* 1:62; *Alpha Beta de-Ben Sira; Pirkei Mashiah in Beit ha-Midrash* 3:68; *Wisdom of Solomon* 203-205; *2 Baruch* 4:3-5; *The Apocalypse of Moses* 33; *Midrash ha-Ne'elam in Zohar Hadash* 24d-25a; *Sh'nei Luhot ha-B'rit* 2:48b; *Em ha-Banim S'mehah.*
>
> *Studies:*
> "The Celestial Temple as Viewed in the Aggadah" by Victor Aptowitzer.
> "The Angelic Liturgy at Qumran" by John Strugnell.
> "The Temple Within: The Embodied Divine Image and Its Worship in the Dead Sea Scrolls and Other Early Jewish and Christian Sources" by C.R.A. Morray-Jones.

533. THE TRUE TEMPLE OF GOD

The highest and truest temple of God is the whole universe. Heaven, its sanctuary, is the holiest part of all existence. Its priests are the angels, who serve God. Its offerings are the stars, which were placed in the pure temple of heaven that they might give light.

> Here Philo envisions the whole universe as a temple of God. This is related to, but distinct from, the mythic tradition that there is a celestial temple in heaven that is the mirror image of the temple in Jerusalem. Philo's description of the heavenly temple might be viewed as a metaphor, a way of saying that God inhabits all of creation. It might also be viewed as a statement that this world is God's temple.
>
> *Sources:*
> Philo, *De Specialibus Legibus* 1:66; Philo, *De Opificio Mundi* 55.

534. THE DESCENT OF THE HEAVENLY JERUSALEM

Some say that in the future God will cause the Jerusalem on high to descend from heaven fully built, and will set it on the tops of four mountains: Mount Sinai, Mount Tabor, Mount Carmel, and Mount Hermon. Then the Temple will sing aloud, and the mountains will answer the song. So too will Jerusalem serve as a beacon to all of the nations, and they will walk in her light. Thus will God announce the Redemption.

One of the key events of the messianic era will be the rebuilding of the Temple in Jerusalem. In this myth the problem of rebuilding the Temple is solved by having the heavenly Jerusalem—including the heavenly Temple—descend to earth and settle on the tops of three (or in some versions, four) mountains.

Others say that a beautiful and great city, built of precious stones and pearls, will descend from heaven, resting on 3,000 towers. How will the people ascend these towers? Like clouds and winged doves, for they will become flying beings. The houses and gates of the pious will have doorposts made of precious stones. The treasuries of the Sanctuary will be open to them, for there will be love of Torah and peace among them.

Still others say that Jerusalem will descend from heaven and station itself like a pillar of fire from earth to heaven. Then all who want to come to Jerusalem will see that pillar of fire and will follow its light until they reach Jerusalem. For that light will be greater than that of the sun and moon, and will make their light dim. And they will dwell in that kingdom until the End of Days, 7,000 years from the days of creation.

This myth of the descent of the heavenly Jerusalem is based on two biblical verses. One, from Isaiah, says, *In the days to come the Mount of Yahweh's house shall stand firm above the mountains* (Isa. 2:2). The other verse, *How welcome on the mountain are the footsteps of the herald announcing happiness* (Isa. 52:7), is given a mythic interpretation, where the messenger is the heavenly city of Jerusalem, here brought down to earth as a symbol of the transformation that will take place in the messianic era. This image, in itself, is quite beautiful, with the ethereal Jerusalem appearing as if in a vision, balanced on the tops of four key mountains in Jewish history. In some versions, however, it sits on the top of only the first three mountains listed, excluding Mount Hermon. This points to the different mythic meanings of the numbers three and four, both of which have key importance in Jewish lore.

An extensive description of the future Temple is found at the end of the Book of Ezekiel 40-48, beginning with a vision: *The hand of Yahweh came upon me, and He brought me there. He brought me, in visions of God, to the Land of Israel, and He set me down on a very high mountain* (Ezek. 40: 1-2).

Hai Gaon portrays Jerusalem as a pillar of fire, like the one that led the Israelites through the desert at night. That is to say, allegorically, that Jerusalem is the guiding light for the Jews, and the light it casts will be that described in Isaiah 30:20: *The light of the moon shall be like the light of the sun, and the light of the sun shall be sevenfold, as the light of the seven days.*

Sefer Zerubavel describes the rebuilding of Jerusalem, with the Temple built on five mountains: Lebanon, Moriah, Tabor, Carmel, and Hermon. Here it is the Temple on top of these mountains, rather than Jerusalem itself.

In *2 Baruch* God tells Baruch about the heavenly Temple waiting to descend: "It is not this building (the Temple in Jerusalem) that is in your midst now; it is that which will be revealed, with Me, that was already prepared from the moment I decided to create Paradise."

See "The Descent of the Heavenly Temple," p. 512.

Sources:

Pesikta de-Rav Kahana 21:4; 2 Baruch 4; Pirkei Mashiah in Beit ha-Midrash, 3:69; Responsum, Hai Gaon, in Ta'am Zekenim 60a-b; Nistarot Eliyahu in Beit ha-Midrash 3: 67f; Sefer Zerubavel; Midrashei Geulah; Sefer Eliyahu in Beit ha-Midrash 3:68-78.

535. THE ELEVATION OF JERUSALEM

In the future, Jerusalem will be raised up until it reaches the Throne of Glory. So too will God add to Jerusalem a thousand gardens, a thousand towers, a thousand fortresses, and a thousand passages.

> This myth of the raising up of Jerusalem is the opposite of that of "The Descent of the Heavenly Jerusalem" (see p. 418). The latter speaks of the Jerusalem on high being brought down to earth, and this one of the earthly Jerusalem being raised on high. The consistent factor is the supernatural qualities associated with Jerusalem.
>
> The myth of two Jerusalems, one on earth and one in heaven, is hinted at in the apocalyptic *4 Ezra*: In the days to come, when the signs foretold have come to pass, the city that is now invisible will appear, and the land which is now concealed be seen (*4 Ezra* 7:26-27). This notion develops in the Talmud into a myth of two Jerusalems. Rabbi Yohanan said: "Jerusalem of this world is not like Jerusalem of the World to Come. Anyone who wants to visit Jerusalem in this world can do so, but only those who are invited can ascend to Jerusalem of the World to Come" (*B. BB* 75b). At the same time, however, and in the same source, there is an alternate myth. Here, instead of bringing the heavenly Jerusalem down to earth at the time of the Redemption, it is said that God would elevate the earthly Jerusalem. Over time, the former myth of two Jerusalems became the dominant one, with the understanding that the heavenly Jerusalem would descend at the time of the Redemption.
>
> *Sources:*
> *4 Ezra* 7:26-27; *B. Bava Batra* 75b; *Pesikta de-Rav Kahana* 20:7.

536. THE CENTER OF THE WORLD

The Land of Israel is the center of the world. Jerusalem is the center of the Land of Israel. The Temple is the center of Jerusalem. The Ark is the center of the Temple. The Foundation Stone stands before the Ark, and the entire world was founded upon it. The gate to heaven is there, and it is open.

For God created the world in the same way a child is formed in the womb. Just as a child begins to grow from its navel, and then develops into its full form, so God began with the navel of the world, and from there expanded in all directions. Thus Jerusalem is the navel of the world, and its core is the altar of the Holy Temple, built upon the Foundation Stone, which forms the foundation of the world.

> On medieval maps Jerusalem is often shown as the center of the world, or, as it is often called, the navel of the world. This belief, supported by Ezekiel 5:5, derives both from the importance of Jerusalem and from the tradition of the Foundation Stone, upon which the world was built. See "The Foundation Stone," p. 96. The reference to the gate of heaven derives from Jacob's dream, *This is none other than the abode of God, and that is the gateway to heaven* (Gen. 28:17).
>
> *Mekhilta de-Rabbi Ishmael* offers an alternate explanation of how the Land of Israel and Jerusalem were selected, in which God did not create the world around them, but they were chosen by God after the world was created: "Before the Land of Israel was chosen, all lands were suitable for divine revelation; after the Land of Israel was chosen, all other lands were eliminated. Before Jerusalem was especially selected, the entire Land of Israel was suitable for altars; after Jerusalem was selected, all the rest of the land was eliminated. Before the place of the Temple was selected, the whole of Jerusalem was appropriate for the manifestation of the *Shekhinah*; after the place of the Temple had been selected, the rest of Jerusalem was eliminated, as it is said, *This is my resting-place for all time* (Ps. 132:14)."

Sources:

Midrash Tanhuma, Kedoshim 10; Midrash Tehillim 91:7; Ecclesiastes Rabbah 1:1; Pirkei de-
Rabbi Eliezer 35; B. Yoma 53b-54b; Midrash ha-Shem be-Hokhmah in Beit ha-Midrash
5:63; Mekhilta de-Rabbi Ishmael, Pisha 1:42-50.

Studies:

Midrash Yerushalem: A Metaphysical History of Jerusalem by Daniel Sperber, pp. 63-70.

537. THE PATRIARCHS SEEK TO COMFORT JERUSALEM

When Jerusalem was on fire and the Temple had been torn down, God said to Abraham, "Go and comfort Jerusalem. Perhaps she will accept comforting from you."

Abraham tried to comfort Jerusalem, but Jerusalem refused to be comforted. So God sent Isaac to comfort Jerusalem, and he fared no better than his father had done. Then God sent Jacob as he had Isaac, but Jerusalem would not be comforted. So God sent Moses on this mission, but still Jerusalem refused to be comforted.

Thereupon all of the patriarchs went to God and said, "Jerusalem will not accept comforting from any of us, so great is her grief." Then God said, "It is for Me to comfort Jerusalem. Since I set her on fire, I must comfort her."

> The model for a biblical figure comforting Israel is found in Jeremiah 31:15, where Jeremiah imagines or has a vision of Rachel weeping over the exile of her children, the children of Israel. This myth also finds a parallel in "God's Exile with Israel," p. 61. In that case God offered to raise any one of the patriarchs from the dead to lead Israel, but Israel refused all of them. So God agreed to lead them into exile Himself.
>
> *Sources:*
> Pesikta Rabbati 30:3.

538. THE CREATION OF THE TEMPLE

At the beginning of the creation of the world, God foresaw that the Temple would be built, destroyed, and rebuilt. None shared in this secret, until God showed Jacob, asleep at Beth El, a vision of the Temple being built, destroyed and rebuilt again.

Since King David desired to build a Temple to God, he entreated God to show him a place for the altar. So an angel appeared to him in a vision standing over the place in Jerusalem where the altar should be located. However, the angel commanded David not to build the Temple because he had been defiled with human blood through the many years he had spent fighting wars. The angel commanded him to turn the construction over to his son, Solomon, but directed David himself to prepare the material needed for the construction—gold, silver, copper, stones, cypress and cedar wood. This David did, and when the time came for Solomon to construct the Temple, the materials he needed to build it were already in his possession.

Then King Solomon called everyone together—the rich and the poor, the princes and the priests—and he said: "People of Israel, let us build a splendid Temple in Jerusalem in honor of God. And since the Temple will be the holy place of all the people, all of the people should share in building it. Therefore you will cast lots to decide which wall you will build."

So King Solomon prepared four lots. On one he wrote North, on another South, on the third East, and on the last West. Then he had each group choose one of them. In this way, it was decided that the princes would build the northern wall as well as the pillars and the stairs of the Temple. And the priests would build the southern wall and tend the Ark and weave its curtain. As for the wealthy merchants, they were to build the eastern wall as well as supplying the oil that would burn for the Eternal Light. The job of building the western wall, as well as weaving the Temple's curtains, fell to the poor people, who also were to pray for the Temple's completion. Then the building began.

The merchants took the golden jewelry of their wives and sold it to pay workers to build the wall for them, and soon it was finished. Likewise the princes and the priests found ways to have their walls built for them. But the poor people had to build the wall themselves, so it took them much longer.

Every day the poor came to the site of the Temple, and they worked with their own hands to build the western wall. And all the time they worked on it, their hearts were filled with joy, for their love of God was very great.

At last the Temple was finished, as beautiful as the Temple on high. Nothing in the world could compare with it, for it was the jewel in the crown of Jerusalem. And after that, whenever the poor people went to the Temple, fathers would say to their sons, "Do you see that stone in the wall? l put it there with my own hands." And mothers would say to their daughters, "Do you see that beautiful curtain in the Temple? I wove that curtain myself."

Many years later, when the Temple was destroyed, only the Western Wall was saved, for the angels spread their wings over it. For that wall, built by the poor, was the most precious of all in the eyes of God.

Even today the Western Wall is still standing. Now it is sometimes known as the Wailing Wall, for every morning drops of dew can be seen on its stones, and it is said among the people that the wall was crying at night for the Temple that was torn down. And, as everyone who has been there can testify, God's presence can still be felt in that place.

> Although King Solomon had the first Temple in Jerusalem built, the idea of creating the Temple was said to have been King David's. But because of the blood on King David's hands, he was not considered pure enough by heaven to build the Temple. Therefore the responsibility fell on his son, King Solomon. The description of King David's role in conceiving the Temple comes from a fragment of Eupolemus. This is followed by a folktale about the building of the Temple.
>
> According to Zev Vilnay, the primary folklorist of the Land of Israel, he collected this story about the building of the Temple from a Jewish youth in Jerusalem in 1922. The point of the tale is that everyone participated in building the Temple, confirming its role as a temple of all the people.
>
> Sources:
> Genesis Rabbah 2:5, 119:7; Eupolemus, Fragment Two; Aggadot Eretz Yisrael no. 193.

539. THE TEMPLE BUILT ITSELF

It is said that *no hammer or ax or any iron tool was heard in the Temple while it was being built* (1 Kings 6:7). How, then, was the Temple built? The truth is that the Temple built itself. The stones flew and rose up by themselves. In this way the stones moved of their own accord and set themselves in the wall of the Temple and erected it.

> In this myth the existence of the Temple is so inevitable that it is said to have built itself. This corresponds with the traditions that there are earthly and heavenly Temples that are mirror images of each other. Therefore the existence of the heavenly Temple was part of God's original plan.
>
> Sources:
> Pesikta Rabbati 6.

540. THE BUILDING OF THE TEMPLE

Everything came through for him in the construction. Foreign workmen brought the slabs of marble, cut to fit together. His fingers did the measuring, and the stones rose in place accordingly. Never did a building arise as easily as this Temple, or rather, this Temple arose as a Temple truly should. Only—on every stone (in what quarry had they originated?) was carved, with tools that must have been splendidly sharp, out of anger or to defile or to utterly destroy them, the crude scribblings of meaningless hands of children, or rather the markings of barbarous mountain dwellers, lasting an eternity that would survive the Temple.

> This is one of two parables Kafka wrote about the Temple. See "Leopards in the Temple," p. 423, for the other. This one about the building of the Temple is suggestive of the folklore about King Solomon, certainly the notion that "Everything came through him in the construction."
>
> While the parable has a universal quality, typical of Kafka, here the Temple can be recognized as the Temple built in Jerusalem. This is not quite as apparent in "Leopards in the Temple." If one views them together, however, it becomes evident that Kafka had focused on the Temple, certainly aware of its central importance in Jewish tradition.
>
> This motif is parallel to the rabbinic myth that the Temple built itself. See the preceding entry, "The Temple Built Itself," p. 421.
>
> *Sources:*
> *Parables and Paradoxes* by Franz Kafka.

541. THE WEDDING OF KING SOLOMON AND PHARAOH'S DAUGHTER

King Solomon wed the daughter of Pharaoh on the same night he completed the building of the Temple. That way the celebrations over the completion of the Temple and that over Solomon's wedding were held concurrently. But when the sound of the latter drowned out the sound of the former, the thought entered God's mind that some time in the future He would destroy the Temple, as it is said, *This city has aroused My anger and My wrath from the day it was built until this day* (Jer. 32:31).

On the following morning the sacrifice was offered late. How did this happen? Bitiah had made a canopy on which she had affixed images of all kinds of stars and constellations, and she hung it over Solomon's wedding couch. So every time Solomon opened his eyes, he saw all those stars and constellations hanging over him, and thought it was still night. Then, too, God's anger was roused.

> Bitiah is the name usually attributed to the daughter of Pharaoh who raised Moses (although not in this source). The notion of Solomon and Pharaoh's daughter being wed is an example of midrashic time, in which all times blend together into one. While King Solomon may have married a daughter of the current ruler of Egypt, it was certainly not Bitiah.
>
> The traditions related to Bitiah in her role in raising Moses treat her with great veneration, and prompted the rabbis to give her the name of Bitiah, "daughter of God." In fact, she is identified as one of the nine who entered Paradise alive (*Derekh Eretz Zuta* 1). See "Pharaoh's Daughter," p. 374. However, in this account of the wedding of Solomon and Bitiah, there is a clear indication of disapproval, since Bitiah's canopy caused Solomon to be late in offering the morning sacrifice.
>
> God's anger is provoked when the rejoicing for Solomon's wedding drowns out that for the completion of the Temple. Likewise, God is angered when the morning

sacrifice is late because Solomon does not wake up in time. That Bitiah is somehow linked with these provocations is a clear indication that the notion of Solomon marrying Pharaoh's daughter did not receive rabbinic approval. This myth echoes God's anger at Solomon's tendency to follow other gods. See 1 Kings 11:1-10.

Sources:
Midrash Mishlei 31.

542. LEOPARDS IN THE TEMPLE

Leopards break into the temple and drink the sacrificial vessels dry. It happens again and again. Eventually it can be predicted. It becomes a part of the ceremony.

> Here Kafka creates a completely original temple myth, which itself is an explanation about the way that ritual comes into being predictable by repetition. Kafka wrote a number of parables that closely follow biblical and midrashic models. See "Paradise, p. 445 and "The Coming of the Messiah," p. 518. Kafka also wrote parables on Abraham and Mount Sinai.
>
> Here, as is often the case, Kafka transforms the myth into a universal one, where it is no longer certain that the temple in Kafka's parable is the Temple in Jerusalem.
>
> An interesting parallel is IFA 16893, where lions enter a synagogue in Meron.

Sources:
Parables and Paradoxes by Franz Kafka.

543. THE MYSTERY OF THE CHERUBIM

As long as the people of Israel fulfilled the will of God, the faces of the cherubim on the curtain covering the Holy of Holies in the Temple were turned toward each other like those of a loving couple, indicating God's love for Israel. But when the people of Israel did not obey the will of God, the cherubim turned their faces miraculously away from each other, toward the walls.

> Great mystery is associated with the two cherubim that were said to be sculpted on the cover of the Ark in the Temple in Jerusalem. They were believed to be enchanted, as demonstrated in this myth, where they are said to face each other like a loving couple if Israel fulfilled God's will and to turn away if Israel did not. For more on the role of the cherubim, see "The Ever-turning Sword of Flame," p. 404. The earliest reference to the cherubim is found in Genesis 3:24, where God places them at the gates of Eden. That passage does not indicate their sex, but the description of the cherubim on the Ark cover in the Holy of Holies implies that of a couple, and some sexual element is assumed. This is made very explicit in the talmudic tradition in *B. Yoma* 54a: "Whenever Israel came to the Temple for the Festival, the curtain would be removed and the Cherubim were shown to them, whose bodies were intertwined with one another, and they would be addressed: 'Look! You are beloved before God as the love between man and woman." This almost certainly refers to the uniting of God's masculine and feminine aspects. When there is harmony between God and Israel, these aspects are in harmony, but when there isn't harmony, the forces of exile predominate above and below. These notions were much further elaborated on in kabbalah, where the separation of God's masculine and feminine aspects is portrayed as the exile of the *Shekhinah*.

Sources:
B. Bava Batra 99a; Introduction to *Lamentations Rabbah* 9; *Pesikta de-Rav Kahana* 19; *Yalkut Shim'oni* 474; *Eliyahu Rabbah* 1:3.

544. GOD'S JUDGMENT ABOVE AND BELOW

When God decided to destroy the Temple in Jerusalem, He first put aside the Holy Land above, the supernal city of Jerusalem, and cut it off from the sacred heavens that served as its nourishment. Seeing this, the angels wept bitterly, for it meant that the *Shekhinah* had been sent into exile. These are the ways of God. When He wishes to judge the world, He first passes judgment on the world above, and only then does He pass judgment on the world below.

Nor was the *Shekhinah* the only one in heaven to suffer. Even God suffered a change from what He was before—His light no longer shone. That is because blessings exist only where male and female are together.

So it was that from the day the Temple was destroyed, the heavens did not shine with their usual light. Nor will the light of the heavens be restored until the End of Days, when the Bride and Groom shall dwell together again as one.

> Most myths about the Temple of God in the heavenly Jerusalem emphasize its eternal nature, in stark contrast to the earthly Temple, which was destroyed. But this myth is different, claiming that God cut off the heavenly Temple from the source of its nourishment. Isaiah Tishby identifies the Holy Land above not only with the Temple, but more specifically with the *Shekhinah*, suggesting that this myth from the *Zohar* is more of a myth about the exile of the *Shekhinah* than about the heavenly Jerusalem.
>
> *Zohar* 1:182a provides a prooftext for the necessity of male and female to be together in order for blessings to exist: *Male and female He created them and blessed them* (Gen. 5:2). This emphasizes the heavenly parallels to the human condition, again underscoring the central kabbalistic tenet of "as above, so below."
>
> *Sources:*
> *Zohar* 1:182a, 2:175a.
>
> *Studies:*
> *The Wisdom of the Zohar*, edited by I. Tishby, 1:408, note 164.

545. GOD'S CLEANSING OF THE HOLY LAND

From the day the Temple in Jerusalem was torn down, the Land of Israel has been broken down because of the wickedness of those who dwelt there, its holiness in exile. That is why, in the Days to Come, God will take hold of the corners of the land and shake it free from all unclean things, as it is said, *To seize the corners of the earth and shake the wicked out of it* (Job 38:13).

> Here the Land of Israel is portrayed as being under some kind of curse, brought on when the Temple, the center of holiness in all the land, was destroyed. Although this is a rabbinic myth, no later than the eighth century, the notion that the Land of Israel was under a curse parallels the later kabbalistic notion of the *kelippot*, the shards of the shattered vessels in the myth of the Ari to which demonic forces cling. These forces of evil cling to the shards very tightly, and are hard to dislodge. However, they will meet their final defeat in the End of Days, the messianic era. This results in the same kind of purification as portrayed in this myth of God cleansing the Holy Land.
>
> *Sources:*
> *Pirkei de-Rabbi Eliezer* 34.

546. THE DESTRUCTION OF THE TEMPLE

As long as the *Shekhinah* dwelled in the Temple, it could not be destroyed. But as the sins of Israel increased, the *Shekhinah* gradually withdrew from the Holy of Holies, leaving the Temple and the holy city of Jerusalem unprotected. Some say that after withdrawing from the Temple, the *Shekhinah* dwelt on the Mount of Olives for thirteen years before She returned to Her place on high. Jeremiah is said to have seen Her there.

After Jeremiah left Jerusalem, the Angel of the Lord came down from heaven, set his feet against the walls of Jerusalem, and breached them. Then the angel cried out, "Let the enemies come and enter the House, for the Master is no longer within. Let them despoil and destroy it. Let them go into the vineyard and cut down the vines, for the Watchman has gone away and left it."

When the Temple was destroyed, five things were hidden that have never been seen again: the Ark, the menorah, the fires, the Holy Spirit, and the cherubim. They will remain hidden until the Temple is rebuilt. Then God will return them to their places and make Jerusalem joyous. So too, in the future, when the Temple will be raised up and renewed, its gates that are buried in the earth will all arise, every one in its place.

Jewish tradition holds that the Temple could not have been destroyed without God's concurrence. Indeed, the Angel of the Lord, sent at God's behest, is the one who breaches the wall, not the Roman army. So too does the angel invite the enemies to destroy the Temple because God, the Master, is gone. Thus the understanding that God had turned His face away from His people at that time. This is confirmed in the confrontation between God and the *Shekhinah*, as recounted in *Zohar* 1:202b-203a, where the Bride of God accuses Her spouse, God, of destroying Her home, i.e., the Temple, and sending Her children, Israel, into exile. See "The Exile of the *Shekhinah*," p. 57.

An interesting variant to this myth is found in *Eikhah Zuta* and *Yalkut Shim'oni*, where God states that "As long as I am in the Temple, the nations of the world cannot harm it. Therefore I shall avert My eye from it, and shall foreswear all involvement with it until the End of Days. And the enemies shall enter it and destroy it." According to this myth, it was at that very hour that the enemy entered the Temple court and put it to flame.

Zohar 1:26b traces the destruction of the first and second Temples to Adam's sin of eating from the Tree of Knowledge. This demonstrates the link between the Fall and the destruction of the Temple in Jewish mythic consciousness. Both are regarded as cosmic catastrophes of equal importance. However, the same source in the *Zohar* also links the destruction of the two temples to the breaking of the two tablets that Moses brought down from Mount Sinai. It explains that because the people were under the domination of the Angel of Death, the tablets that derived from the Tree of Life broke and fell.

Not all myths agree that God played an active role in the destruction of the Temple. Some sources attribute its destruction to the *Yetzer ha-Ra*, the Evil Inclination. *B. Sukkah* 52a states that the *Yetzer ha-Ra* set its eyes on the first Temple and destroyed it, and killed the Torah scholars who were in it. So too did the *Yetzer ha-Ra* set its eyes on the second Temple and destroy it, and killed the Torah scholars who were in it. In these cases the Evil Inclination plays a role similar to that of the Evil Eye, which casts an evil spell on whatever it gazes upon. Other myths attribute the desire to harm the Temple to the demons, who sought to sabotage the building of the Temple in several ways. This is found in the frame story to *The Testament of Solomon*, where the demons, feeling that King Solomon and his chief builder were too powerful to bring down, instead sent the demon Ornasis to harm the son of the chief builder, hoping to harm Solomon that way. See "The Vampire Demon," p. 227.

Sources:
Pesikta Rabbati 26:6; *Pesikta de-Rav Kahana* 13:114b; *Avot de-Rabbi Natan* 34:102; *Eikhah Zuta* 26; *Pirkei de-Rabbi Eliezer* 51; *Yalkut Shim'oni, Eikhah* 996; *Aggadat Shir ha-Shirim* 6:2; IFA 6556.

Studies:
Midrash Yerushalem by Daniel Sperber, pp. 100-103.
"The Power of the Evil Eye and the Good Eye in Midrashic Literature" by Brigitte Kern-Ulmer.

547. A STONE FROM MOUNT SINAI

All the stones used in the building of the Temple in Jerusalem were from Jerusalem and its mountains. Only one stone was brought from somewhere else—from Mount Sinai. It was put in the *Kotel*, the Western Wall of the Temple. And that is why only the *Kotel* was not destroyed and remained standing when the Temple was destroyed, because that stone was from the holy mountain on which the Torah was given.

> Jewish tradition imagines that the *Kotel*, the retaining wall of the Temple Mount, was the only wall of the Temple that survived the destruction of the Temple. Here an explanation is offered for its survival—it contained one stone from Mount Sinai. Thus the holiness of that mountain, contained within a single stone, is credited for saving the one surviving wall of the Temple.

Sources:
IFA 553.

548. THE HAND OF GOD

The Temple in Jerusalem had been set on flame, and the moment of destruction had arrived. The High Priest went up to the roof, the keys of the Temple in his hand. There he called out: "Master of the Universe! The time has come to return these keys to You." Then he threw the keys high into the air, and at that instant a hand reached down from above and caught them, and brought them back into heaven.

> The destruction of the Temple in Jerusalem brought an era of Jewish life to an end. None of the rituals connected to the Temple could be performed any longer. Therefore this talmudic legend recounts how the High Priest returned the keys to the Temple to God, and in a strongly anthropomorphic image, a giant hand reaches down from heaven to retrieve them. The theological implications of this legend are considerable. It presumes that heaven was both well aware of the destruction of the Temple, and that it was no accident, but was God's intention. Of course, it also is a tragic event. From this perspective, the act of the High Priest in returning the keys to heaven is one of great despair. Nevertheless, even at this tragic moment in Jewish history, the link between God and His people, Israel, remains intact in the act of God accepting the keys to the Temple. The motif of returning a precious gift to heaven is found in the talmudic tale of Rabbi Haninah ben Dosa returning the leg of a golden table to heaven (*B. Tan.* 24b-25a) and "The Soul of the Ari" in *Gabriel's Palace*, pp. 258-259. In 2 *Baruch* the High Priest casts the temple vessels to the earth, which opens, swallowing them up.

Sources:
Pesikta Rabbati 26:6; *Y. Shekalim* 50a; *B. Ta'anit* 29a; 2 *Baruch* 6:8-9

549. GOD'S MOURNING

When the Temple was destroyed, God tore His garment as a sign of mourning. Since then, God cries every day for the glory that has been taken from the Jews.

Once Rabbah bar Bar Hannah went to Mount Sinai and heard a voice call out of heaven: "Woe to Me that I have vowed that the Jews must go into exile. Now that I have vowed, who will annul My vow?"

When Rabbah reported this to the other rabbis, they said, "Fool! You should have said, 'Your vow is void.'"

> Here the wandering sage Rabbah bar Bar Hannah hears God mourning over the destruction of the Temple. God laments that He took a vow to destroy the Temple and now there was no way to annul it. The rabbis tell Rabbah that he should have called out *"Mufar lakh,"* meaning "your vow or oath is void," the formula used by an authorized person for annulling vows and oaths.
>
> *Sources:*
> B. Bava Batra 74a; B. Hagigah 5b; Lamentations Rabbah 1:1.

550. THE PATRIARCHS WEEP OVER THE DESTRUCTION OF THE TEMPLE

After the Temple had been destroyed, God said to Jeremiah, "Go, summon Abraham, Isaac, Jacob from their graves. They know how to weep."

So Jeremiah went to the cave of Machpelah, where the patriarchs are buried, and raised them from their graves and brought them up to heaven, where they prayed before God: "Master of the Universe, how long will You sit on Your throne like a mourner? Are You not going to have mercy on Your children? Are You not going to show compassion?"

In that hour God replied to them: "Abraham, My friend, Isaac, My chosen one, and Jacob, My firstborn, I cannot now save them from their exile."

Then the angel Michael, the Prince of Israel, wept in a loud voice, *"Why, O Lord, do You stand aloof"* (Ps. 10:1)?

> Here God summons the patriarchs from their graves, and they, in turn, beg God for compassion for Israel. But when God puts them off, the angel Michael, Prince of Israel, cries out to God in despair. This demonstrates that all of the powers of heaven are deeply concerned about the fate of Israel. God initiates this confrontation by summoning the patriarchs, which is a reflection of His own guilt at the destruction of the Temple. Most telling of all is Michael's cry of despair, since angels are primarily messengers of God and obey God's commands. But here Michael's cry borders on challenging God's decision not to save Israel from exile.
>
> The references to Abraham as God's friend, Isaac as God's chosen one, and Jacob as God's firstborn are a reworking of Isaiah 41:8: *"But you, Israel, My servant, Jacob whom I have chosen, the seed of Abraham, my friend."* The changes in the text are significant, especially the identification of Jacob as God's firstborn—while the verse in Isaiah says, *"Jacob whom I have chosen,"* suggests that this myth may be linked to the tendency of some to give Jacob virtually divine status. See "Jacob the Divine," p. 366.
>
> *Sources:*
> Lamentations Rabbah, Proem 24; Seder Mahanot in Beit ha-Midrash 5:186-87.
>
> *Studies:*
> Arguing With God: A Jewish Tradition by Anson Laytner.

551. ABRAHAM IN THE TEMPLE

When the Temple was destroyed, God found Abraham standing in the ruins of the Temple. He said to him, *"Why should My beloved be in My house?"* (Jer. 11:15).

Abraham replied, "I have come concerning the fate of my children."

God said, "Your children sinned and have been sent into exile."

"Perhaps," said Abraham, "they only sinned in error."

God answered, *"She has wrought lewdness"* (Jer. 11:15).

Abraham said, "Perhaps only a few sinned?"

"With many" (Jer. 11:15), came the reply.

"Still," Abraham pleaded, "You should have remembered the covenant of the circumcision."

God replied, *"The sacral flesh has passed from you"* (Jer. 11:15).

"In that case," said Abraham, "perhaps if You had waited for them, they would have repented."

God replied, *"For you exult while performing your evil deeds!"* (Jer. 11:15).

Then Abraham put his hands on his head and wept bitterly and cried, "Perhaps, heaven forbid, there is no hope for them."

Then a heavenly voice came forth and said, *"The Lord named you verdant olive tree, fair, with choice fruit* (Jer. 11:16). As the olive tree produces its best only at the very end, so Israel will flourish at the end of time."

> Here Abraham confronts God over the destruction of the Temple and the exile of the children of Israel, and proceeds to bargain with God as he did over the fate of Sodom (Gen. 18:22-33). God's replies are taken from Jeremiah 11:15-16. Although God does not reverse His decree against the Jews, a heavenly voice holds out the promise that in the end Israel will flourish.
>
> A related midrash is found in *Lamentations Rabbah,* Proem 24. See "Abraham and the Alphabet," following.
>
> *Sources:*
> B. *Menahot* 53b.

552. ABRAHAM AND THE ALPHABET

God said to Abraham, "Your children have sinned and transgressed against the whole Torah, all twenty-two letters in it. Let the letters of the alphabet testify against Israel." All at once the twenty-two letters appeared. The *aleph* came forth to testify that Israel had transgressed the Torah.

Abraham said to the *aleph*, "You are the first of all the letters, and you have come to testify against Israel in its time of danger? Have you forgotten that God opened the Ten Commandments with you and that every nation turned you down except for the children of Israel, and you have come to testify against them?"

The *aleph* immediately stood aside and gave no testimony. Then the *bet* came to testify against Israel.

"My daughter," Abraham said to the *bet*, "have you come to testify against My children who cling to the Torah, of which you are the first letter, as it is said, *In the beginning God created* (Gen. 1:1)?

The *bet* quickly stood aside and gave no testimony.

When the remaining letters saw how the *aleph* and *bet* had been silenced, they felt ashamed and did not testify. Abraham then began to speak before God, saying, "Master of the Universe, when I was a hundred years old You gave me a son. When he was a young man you ordered me to offer him as a sacrifice before You. I steeled my heart and bound him on the altar myself. Will You not remember this on my behalf and have mercy on my children?"

At this the mercy of God was stirred, and he said, "For your sake and that of your children I will restore Israel to their place."

> Here Abraham intercedes with God to spare Israel from condemnation. This is condensed from a longer myth in which not only Abraham, but Isaac, Jacob, and Moses all come before God to defend Israel. Finally the matriarch Rachel breaks her silence and tells of her suffering when Jacob was given in marriage to her sister, Leah, instead of to herself. God's heart is softened, and this myth then identifies Rachel's plea with the verse *Rachel weeping for her children* (Jer. 31:15).
>
> Sources:
> Lamentations Rabbah, Proem 24.

553. MOSES AND THE SUN

When Moses learned that the Temple in Jerusalem had been destroyed and the people killed or taken into exile, he lifted up his voice, saying: "Cursed be you, sun! Why did you not become dark when the enemy entered the Temple?"

The sun replied: "By your life, Moses, how could I become dark when they beat me with sixty whips of fire, saying, 'Go pour forth your light! I had no choice.'"

At that Moses spoke to God, saying, "Master of the Universe, You have written in Your Torah, *No animal from the herd or from the flock shall be slaughtered on the same day with its young* (Lev. 22:28). Yet many mothers and sons have been killed. Why are You silent?"

> Here Moses confronts first the sun—the earliest primitive symbol of God—and then God Himself over their failure to prevent the destruction of the Temple. There is substantial anger revealed, which, of course, is actually the anger of the rabbis, the authors of these myths. Abraham is not afraid to question or bargain with God, as was demonstrated in the case of Sodom (Gen. 18:22-33). But Moses has such an intimate relationship with God, and such an intense interest in the fate of his people, Israel, that he can even confront God as He did in Exodus 32:9-14, and as He does here.
>
> Sources:
> Lamentations Rabbah, Proem 24.

554. THE INVISIBLE TEMPLE

It only appears that the Temple was destroyed. Actually, it remains in existence, hidden from the sight of ordinary mortals, and sacrifices are still offered in the invisible sanctuary.

> This is an unusual variant on the theme that the heavenly Temple continues to exist although the earthly Temple was destroyed. Here the earthly Temple is still said to exist, although it is invisible, and we are told that sacrifices are still offered there. There are other examples of invisible things found in Jewish lore. For example, some versions of the myth of the primordial light say that it was never removed from the world, but is visible only to the *Tzaddikim*. See "The Light of the First Day," p. 83.
>
> Sources:
> Emek ha-Melekh 3:389.

BOOK NINE

MYTHS OF EXILE

The serpent came to Eve when she was alone and possessed her and infused her with lust. That is how the serpent fathered Cain.

Pirkei de-Rabbi Eliezer

555. THE EXILE FROM EDEN

Now the serpent was the shrewdest of all the wild beasts that the Lord God had made. He said to the woman, "Did God really say, 'You shall not eat of any tree of the garden?'" The woman replied to the serpent, "We may eat of the fruit of the other trees of the garden. It is only about fruit of the tree in the middle of the garden that God said, 'You shall not eat of it or touch it, lest you die.'" And the serpent said to the woman, "You are not going to die, but God knows that as soon as you eat of it your eyes will be opened and you will be like divine beings who know good and bad." When the woman saw that the tree was good for eating and a delight to the eyes, and that the tree was desirable as a source of wisdom, she took of its fruit and ate. She also gave some to her husband, and he ate. Then the eyes of both of them were opened and they perceived that they were naked; and they sewed together fig leaves and made themselves loincloths.

They heard the sound of the Lord God moving about in the garden at the breezy time of day; and the man and his wife hid from the Lord God among the trees of the garden. The Lord God called out to the man and said to him, "Where are you?" He replied, "I heard the sound of You in the garden, and I was afraid because I was naked, so I hid." Then He asked, "Who told you that you were naked? Did you eat of the tree from which I had forbidden you to eat?" The man said, "The woman You put at my side—she gave me of the tree, and I ate." And the Lord God said to the woman, "What is this you have done!" The woman replied, "The serpent duped me, and I ate." Then the Lord God said to the serpent, "Because you did this, more cursed shall you be than all cattle. And all the wild beasts: On your belly shall you crawl and dirt shall you eat all the days of your life. I will put enmity between you and the woman, and between your offspring and hers; they shall strike at your head, and you shall strike at their heel."

And to the woman He said, "I will make most severe your pangs in childbearing; in pain shall you bear children. Yet your urge shall be for your husband, and he shall rule over you."

To Adam He said, "Because you did as your wife said and ate of the tree about which I commanded you, 'You shall not eat of it,' cursed be the ground because of you; by toil shall you eat of it all the days of your life: thorns and thistles shall it sprout for you. But your food shall be the grasses of the field; by the sweat of your brow shall you get bread to eat, until you return to the ground—for from it you were taken. For dust you are, and to dust you shall return."

The man named his wife Eve, because she was the mother of all the living. And the Lord God made garments of skins for Adam and his wife, and clothed them.

And the Lord God said, "Now that the man has become like one of us, knowing good and bad, what if he should stretch out his hand and take also from the tree of life and eat, and live forever!" So the Lord God banished him from the garden of Eden, to till the soil from which he was taken. He drove the man out, and stationed east of the Garden of Eden the cherubim and the fiery ever-turning sword, to guard the way to the tree of life.

> Along with the story of Creation in Genesis, this is probably the most famous biblical myth of all. Not only is it the first of the divine tests, but it provides an explanation for mortality and a justification for patriarchy. While Judaism does not include original sin among the consequences of Adam's disobedience, the failure of Adam and Eve to heed God's warning not to eat from the Tree of Knowledge is regarded in Jewish tradition as a cosmic catastrophe, equal to the Shattering of the Vessels in the myth of the Ari, or to the destruction of the Temple in Jerusalem.
>
> Above all, the story of the exile from Eden is a story of sin and punishment, and establishes a negative pattern in the relationship of God and His human creations.

At the same time, the story can be read as an allegory of innocence lost, where Adam and Eve are like children while they live in the Garden of Eden, and their expulsion from Eden, which takes place at the time of their loss of sexual innocence, represents the emergence into adulthood.

Some sources describe other consequences of the Fall that are not found in Genesis. Just as Adam and Eve suffered great losses and punishments from the sin of the Fall, so the animals lost their language. For, according to Josephus, all living things in the Garden of Eden spoke the same language (*Antiquities* 1:41), and *The Book of Jubilees* repeats this tradition, adding that "on the day when Adam went out of the Garden of Eden . . . the mouths of all the beasts and cattle and birds and whatever walked or moved was stopped from speaking" (*Jubilees* 3:27-28). There is an indication that even the world of vegetation was affected. According to *3 Baruch*, God cursed the tree of sinful desire that the evil angel Satanel had planted, for that tree was the cause of the Fall (*3 Baruch*, Slavonic, 4:8). This refers to the Tree of Knowledge, here linked to carnal knowledge.

An intriguing parallel to this myth of eating the forbidden fruit is that of Pandora in Greek myth, who set free the evil spirits locked up in a jar (not a box) and released evil into the world. The jar contained all the Spites that plague mankind: Old Age, Labor, Sickness, Insanity, Vice, and Passion, and as they flew out in a cloud they stung Epimetheus, Pandora's husband, and Pandora all over her body. See Graves, *The Greek Myths* 39j, 39.8. See also Hesiod's *Works and Days* 42-105, and *Theogony* 565-619.

Sources:
Gen. 3:1-24.

Studies:
"The Paradise Myth: Interpreting without Jewish and Christian Spectacles" by
    Calum M. Carmichael.
"The Sources of the Paradise Story" by Julian Morgenstern.
"The Garden of Eden: From Creation to Covenant" by Bernard Och.

556. EVE TASTES THE FORBIDDEN FRUIT

God told Adam, *"Of every tree of the garden you are free to eat; but as for the tree of knowledge of good and bad, you must not eat of it; for as soon as you eat of it, you shall die"* (Gen. 2:16-17). But Adam told Eve, "God has said, *'You shall not eat of it or touch it, lest you die'"* (Gen. 3:3).

At that time the serpent said to himself, "Perhaps I cannot convince Adam, who heard the words of God for himself. So I will seek out Eve."

The serpent found Eve in the garden and said, "Is it true that God has commanded you not to eat of any fruit in the garden?" Eve replied, "No, there is only one tree in the midst of the garden forbidden to us. We are not allowed to eat of its fruit or even to touch it, for on that day we shall die."

The serpent laughed when he heard this, and said, "God has only said this out of jealousy, for He knows that if you eat of the fruit of that tree, your eyes will be opened, and you will know how to create a world just as He did." Then the serpent went to the tree in the midst of the garden and shook it, so that some of the fruit fell to the ground. "See, I have touched the tree and I have not died. You, too, can touch it without dying."

When Eve saw the serpent touch the tree and not die, she picked up one of the fruits that had fallen and, seeing that it was beautiful and desirable, she tasted it. But no sooner had she taken a single bite, than her teeth were set on edge, and she saw the Angel of Death standing before her, with his sword drawn. Then Eve said to herself, "Now that I have eaten of this fruit, I will die, and Adam, who has not touched it, will live forever, and God will couple him with another woman. It is better that we die together."

So when Adam came she gave him some of the fruit to taste. And as soon he did, he too saw the Angel of Death standing before him, with sword drawn. Then Adam knew that the fruit she had given him must have been the forbidden fruit, and he was filled with grief.

Others say that the serpent did not wait for Eve to touch the tree, but pushed her against it and said, "See, you have not died. And just as you didn't die from touching the tree, so you will not die from eating its fruit." So Eve plucked the fruit and held it up and tasted its skin. When nothing happened, she bit into the fruit, and that is when she saw the Angel of Death.

> This myth grows out of rabbinic awareness of a problem in the biblical text where God warns Adam against eating the forbidden fruit (Gen. 2:16-17), but Eve tells the serpent that they are forbidden to eat from it or touch it (Gen. 3:3). The rabbis assumed that Adam had added on his own, a warning against touching the fruit. (After all, Eve had not been created when God gave Adam the original warning.) The myth assumes that the serpent is aware of Adam's additional warning, and uses this knowledge to convince Eve to eat the forbidden fruit. In one version, he does this by pushing Eve against the Tree of Knowledge, then pointing out that while she has touched it, she has not died. Therefore she might as well eat the fruit, which she does.
>
> In most versions of this myth, Eve sees the Angel of Death the instant she bites into the forbidden fruit. But in *Targum Pseudo-Yonathan* on Gen. 3:6, Eve sees that the wicked angel Samael, one of the names of Satan, was himself the Angel of Death.
>
> *Sources:*
> *Targum Pseudo-Yonathan* on Gen. 3:6 ; *Bereshit Rabbah* 19:3-4; *Avot de-Rabbi Natan* 1, 4-5, 151; *Pirkei de-Rabbi Eliezer* 13; *Zohar* 1:263b; *Sefer ha-Zikhronot* 12 .
>
> *Studies:*
> *Eve and Adam: Jewish, Christian, and Muslim Readings on Genesis and Gender*, edited by Kristen E. Kvam, Linda S. Schearing, and Valarie H. Ziegler.

557. GOD DIVORCED ADAM

When God drove Adam out of the Garden of Eden, He gave Adam a *get*, a bill of divorce, as it is said, *He drove the man out* (Gen. 3:24). After that, they went their separate ways. God withdrew from His earthly domicile and dwelt on high, and Adam struggled to bring forth food from the earth.

> Here God's sending Adam into exile is interpreted to mean that God divorced Himself of Adam, and gave Adam a *get*, a bill of divorce. A woman receives a *get* at the conclusion of the divorce proceedings. Then, just as a divorced couple go their separate ways, God separated Himself further from Adam by ascending on high. The biblical verse usually translated as *He drove Adam out* is here understood to mean instead that God separated Himself from Adam, and formalized their separation by giving Adam a *get*.
>
> This myth reads like a metaphor that has become literal. After all, God and Adam were not married. But in the view of the rabbis, the separation between them was as final as a divorce. Thus the concept of a *get*, a bill of divorce, is expanded here to include the kind of contractual relationship found between God and Adam. According to that contract, Adam was permitted to live in the garden, as long as he did not eat the fruit of the Tree of Knowledge. This myth also conveys the gulf of separation created between God and Adam at the time of the exile from Eden.
>
> Other rabbinic texts also portray the Fall as a major event in the history of the universe, a cosmic catastrophe. Both are intended to convey the radical transformation of

the nature of existence after this cosmos-shaking event. In fact, it is precisely parallel to two other cosmic catastrophes: the Shattering of the Vessels in the myth of the Ari and the destruction of the Temple in Jerusalem.

The majority of rabbinic references to the events of the Fall single out Adam and do not mention Eve. While this may be a form of shorthand, it also leads to the kind of pairing of God and Adam found here.

While this myth describes the bill of divorce between God and Adam, "The Wedding of God and Israel," p. 305, describes the Torah as a *ketubah*, a wedding contract, between God and His people.

Sources:
Eliyahu Rabbah 1:3.

Studies:
"Exiled from Eden: Jewish Interpretations of Genesis" by Paul Morris.

558. ADAM'S DIAMOND

While Adam lived in the Garden of Eden, he could have anything he wanted, with, of course, one exception—the fruit of the Tree of Knowledge. So when Adam sinned and it was necessary for God to expel him from the garden, God was reluctant to drive him out. Instead God gave Adam a good meal, with the finest foods and wines, and God said, "You know, there is a world outside this garden. Don't you want to explore it?" Adam didn't really want to go, but God said, "You can take anything you like with you, whatever you desire, but you must go." Then God showed him all the treasures and hidden things in the garden, and Adam looked at everything, gardens and orchards, animals of every kind, treasures of gold and silver, and many kinds of precious stones, but Adam didn't find anything he wanted to take with him. Then he arrived at a treasure of diamonds. The diamonds were exceptionally beautiful and shone as brightly as the sun, and Adam chose one of the largest ones.

Holding that diamond in his hand, Adam went in the direction of the gates of Eden, with an angel accompanying him. He passed through the gates, and when he looked behind him he saw the cherubim with the flaming sword and he realized he could not go back. For a moment he was sorry, then he continued on his way until he reached a river. While he was standing there looking at it, the angel pushed him from behind, and the diamond fell from his hand into the river. Adam cried out to the angel, "Why did you do that?" And the angel said, "Go down to the river and find your diamond."

So Adam went down to the river and saw thousands and thousands of diamonds reflected in the water and he couldn't recognize which one was his. Then the angel said, "Do you think that you were the first one who was expelled from the Garden of Eden and took a diamond with you? Thousands and thousands did as you did, and their diamonds fill the river, as you can see."

> This unusual folktale may be based on the midrashic tradition about the *Tzohar*, the jewel said to have been given to Adam when he was expelled from the Garden of Eden. However, this story takes the motif of the diamond in a different direction. Here Adam loses the diamond in a river after being pushed by an angel, and discovers that the river is full of diamonds as precious as his own. The angel reveals that he was not the first to be expelled from Eden and take a diamond with him.
>
> While there is an extensive rabbinic tradition that God created prior worlds before this one, and destroyed them, the notion that God created human beings before Adam, who also sinned and were expelled from the Garden of Eden and took diamonds with them is entirely original. This story demonstrates the rich Jewish oral tradition, where variations of traditional tales evolve in unexpected ways.

Note Eve's absence from this story. In many of the myths about Adam, Eve is missing.

It seems fitting that such a mythic folktale would come from Afghanistan—a bitter parable of exile, how one doesn't appreciate one's homeland until it is gone.

See "The *Tzohar*," p. 85 and "Prior Worlds," p. 71. For a modern story on the same theme, see "The Experimental World" in *The Marriage Feast* by Par Lagerkvist.

Sources:
IFA 7838.

559. THE GARMENTS OF ADAM AND EVE

When Adam and Eve were first created, they were clothed, body and soul, with garments of light. Some say those garments of light were made entirely of clouds of glory. Others say they were made of holy luminous letters that God had given them, which shed radiance like a torch, broad at the bottom and narrow at the top.

After Adam and Eve ate the forbidden fruit, the garments of light were replaced by garments of skins, as it is said, *And the Lord God made garments of skins for Adam and his wife, and clothed them* (Gen. 3:21). It is said that these garments were created during twilight on the sixth day of Creation, just before the first Sabbath. Some say that they consisted of a hornlike substance, smooth as a fingernail and as beautiful as a jewel, while others say that they were made of goats' skin or the wool of camels. Still others insist that they were made of the hide of the serpent who led them astray in the Garden of Eden.

Adam handed down the garments to Seth, and Seth to Methuselah, and Methuselah to Noah, who took them with him on the ark. And when they left the ark, Ham, the son of Noah, bequeathed them to Nimrod, although others say that Nimrod stole them. When Nimrod wore Adam's garments, his outward appearance was that of Adam, and the creatures were humbled before him and would bow down, thinking he was their king.

The garments came into the possession of Esau when he defeated Nimrod, and it was this garment that Jacob wore when he went to his father, Isaac. For that day Esau had not put them on, so that they remained in the house. *Rebecca then took the best clothes of her older son Esau, which were there in the house, and had her younger son Jacob put them on* (Gen. 27:15). Isaac smelled the smell of Esau's garments, and therefore he blessed Jacob.

Some say that the repentance of Adam and Eve earned a different set of garments for them, garments of light. At the End of Days, God will dress the Messiah in such a garment, which will shine from one end of the world to the other. And the Jews will draw upon its light and say to the Messiah, "Blessed is the hour in which the Messiah was created."

This is an example of what might be called a "chain midrash," because it links together the chain of the generations, from Adam until the Messiah. Other similar midrashic traditions are found about the staff of Moses, the book that the angel Raziel is said to have given Adam, and the glowing stone known as the *Tzohar*. Sometimes there are contradictory lines of descent, as in the case of Adam's garment. According to one account in *Midrash Tanhuma*, the garment was diverted into the hands of the evil king Nimrod, while in an opposing account, it was transferred from Noah to Shem to Abraham, who passed it down to Isaac. Isaac is said to have given it to Esau, his firstborn, but Esau entrusted it to his mother, Rebecca, when he saw his own wives practiced idolatry. And, as is reported in the biblical account, Rebecca took the beloved garments of her son Esau and gave them to Jacob, at the time he received the stolen blessing.

According to *Sefer ha-Zikhronot*, the garments of Adam and Eve were among eight things created on the first day of Creation. Other sources describe them as being created at twilight on the sixth day of Creation. As is apparent, there were alternate explanations about the nature of the garments of Adam and Eve. Genesis 3:21 seems to clearly state that they were made of the skins of animals, while in the midrash they are also described as consisting of a hornlike substance. The notion that their original garments were made of light derives from the word *or*, which when spelled with an *aleph* means "light," while when spelled with an *ayin* means "skin" as well as "leather." It is spelled with an *ayin* in Genesis 3:21, but *Genesis Rabbah* 20:12 states that in the Torah scroll of Rabbi Meir, the *or* in the biblical verse was written with an *aleph*. *Zohar* 2:229b explains that they were originally garments of light, not of skin, for when Adam was about to enter the Garden of Eden for the first time, God dressed him in garments of light, of the sort used by the angels in paradise. Indeed, the light of Adam's garments was more elevated than their own. Had he not been wearing those garments, Adam could not have entered the garden. And when he was driven out of Eden, he required different garments, so *the Lord made garments of skins for Adam and his wife, and clothed them* (Gen. 3:21).

A variant of this myth has Noah's son, Shem, giving the garments to Abraham, who wears them when he takes Isaac to Mount Moriah to be sacrificed. Later they were inherited by Isaac, who gave them to his firstborn son, Esau. These were the garments Jacob put on when he pretended to be Esau in order to receive his father's blessing. Thus when Jacob entered the room, Isaac smelled the fragrance that he had smelled when he was tied upon the altar.

Rabbi Tzadok ha-Kohen of Lublin (1823-1900) proposes that the sin of Adam and Eve, followed by their repentance, brought them to a more exalted state than before the sin, symbolized by their receiving new garments, replacing the garments of skin with garments of light. This is a surprising view of the role of sin and repentance in stimulating spiritual growth. Rabbi Yosef Hayim of Baghdad, known as Ben Ish Hai, asserts in *Ben Yehoyada* that Torah study has the power to reverse the process, changing garments of skins back into garments of light.

Sources:

Targum Pseudo-Yonathan on Genesis 27:15; *B. Pesahim* 54a; *Genesis Rabbah* 20:12; *Numbers Rabbah* 4:8; *Pesikta de-Rabbi Eliezer* 20:46a, 22:50b; *Pesikta de-Rav Kahana* (appendices), p. 470; *Pesikta Rabbati* 37 (p. 164a); *Midrash Tanhuma*, Toledot 12; *Aggadat Bereshit*, p. 86; *Sefer ha-Zikhronot* 1:3; *Zohar* 1:53a, 1:73b-74a, 2:229b; *Ben Yehoyada*; *Sh'nei Luhot ha-B'rit, va-Yeshev*; *Kedushat Shabbat* 5:13b. See Ginzberg, *Legends*, 5:283, note 89.

Studies:

"The Clothing of the Primordial Adam as a Symbol of Apocalyptic Time in Midrashic Sources" by Nissan Rubin and Admiel Kosman.

560. ADAM'S DESCENDANTS

God created the world and set it on its foundation. Then He created Adam and brought him into the world to find contentment in him and his descendants until the end of generations. But among Adam's descendants some worshipped the sun and moon, others worshipped wood and stone, and every day God lost patience with them, until He deemed that they were deserving of annihilation.

Nevertheless, after considering that they were the work of His hands, God said, "These humans have life, and so do the other creatures. These have breath and those have breath. These have a desire for food and drink and those have a desire for food and drink. Humans must be at least as important as the beasts and creeping things I created upon the earth."

At once God felt some measure of contentment and resolved not to annihilate humankind.

This myth presents God's view of humanity through two lenses: the lens of justice and that of mercy. From the view of strict justice, humankind, who has failed to recognize God's role and instead has various kinds of pagan worship, deserves annihilation. But from the perspective of mercy, humans are simply one of the kinds of creatures that God created. It is this merciful view that wins out over that of strict justice, and God resolves—thus makes an oath with Himself—not to annihilate humankind. And even though God comes close to doing this in the time of the Flood, God does spare Noah and his family, who repopulate the earth. From the perspective of this myth, sparing Noah was an act of God's mercy, despite the harshness of the Flood.

While God's views of humanity are interpreted in terms of justice and mercy, they also portray God as somewhat at the mercy of His moods, sometimes gripped by fury great enough to annihilate mankind, and at other times behaving like a loving parent, concerned about His own creations.

Sources:
Eliyahu Rabbah 1:6.

561. GOD DESCENDS INTO THE GARDEN

No sooner did Adam taste the forbidden fruit than the angel Gabriel blew a trumpet and summoned all the angels. When Adam and Eve heard the trumpet, they knew that God was about to come into the Garden to judge them.

Then God set out on His Chariot driven by cherubs, with angels praising Him. Adam and Eve were afraid, and hid. As soon as God reached the Garden, all the plants of the Garden flowered. God set up His throne close to the Tree of Life.

Then God summoned Adam and said, "Adam, do you think you can hide from Me? Can the building hide from its builder?"

Adam replied, "Lord, I was afraid, for I am naked and ashamed." And God pronounced the punishments of the man and the woman and the serpent, and God commanded that the man and woman be expelled from the Garden.

Then Adam begged God to let him eat of the Tree of Life before he left the Garden. But God said, "You cannot take of it in your lifetime."

Then the angels began to expel him, but Adam began to cry. "I beseech you," he pleaded," let me take incense with me from the Garden, so that I may offer sweet incense to God. Then perhaps God will hearken to me." The angels let him be, and Adam took sweet incense with him, iris and balsam, and he and Eve went forth from the Garden.

Just before God confronts Adam and Eve with their sin, Genesis 3:8 states, *They heard the voice of the Lord God walking in the Garden toward the cool of the day.* This myth, from the Armenian version of *Vita Adae et Evae* known as *Penitence of Adam*, describes God's descent from heaven and His arrival in the Garden of Eden in His Chariot, the *Merkavah*, driven by cherubs. It explains how God traveled from heaven to the Garden of Eden. This descent of God reflects the themes of *Merkavah* literature, and should be considered an example of it.

Sources:
Penitence of Adam 44:22:1-44:23:2, 44:27:1-44:29:6.

Studies:
Portraits of Adam in Early Judaism: From Sirah to 2 Baruch by John R. Levison.
Penitence of Adam, edited by Michael E. Stone.
Biblical Figures Outside the Bible, edited by Michael E. Stone and Theodore A.
   Bergren.

562. THE LAND OF ERETZ

When Adam left the Garden of Eden, he came to the land of Eretz, a place of darkness and desolation, where sunlight is never seen. On entering there, Adam was gripped by great fear. No matter how far Adam went in any direction, he encountered the flame of the ever-turning sword that blazed on all sides of Eretz. Only when the Sabbath ended and Adam had thoughts of repentance, did God take him out of Eretz and bring him to the Land of Adamah, where he found peace at last.

The Land of Eretz is described here as a place of desolation, where Adam faced the consequences of his sin and experienced the most intense grief. Note that no mention of Eve is made, although the Genesis narrative indicates that Adam and Eve remained together. This strongly suggests that Eretz is an allegorical land, representing the kind of grief that precedes repentance. The myth also indicates that having been expelled from Eden, Adam experiences panic and fright, as the boundaries of his formerly peaceful existence vanish, replaced by fearful unknowns. Indeed, melancholy and fear are part of his now-fallen condition. At the same time, rabbinic commentaries suggest that he had a great deal to regret. He bitterly regretted his sin and expulsion from Eden. He especially mourned over having brought death into the world, for now he and all his descendants had become mortal.

Once he repents, however, Adam is brought to the allegorical land of Adamah, and there, at last, he experiences peace. One version of this myth, from *Zohar Hadash*, states that after Adam had repented by entering the waters of the river Gihon up to his neck, God brought him to the land of Adamah, thus indicating God's forgiveness.

This myth raises the question of why Eretz (land) was selected to represent a place of suffering, while Adama (ground) represents a place of inner peace. The answer derives from the use of these terms in the Genesis narrative about Adam and about Cain. *So the Lord God banished him from the garden of Eden, to till the soil* (adamah) *from which he was taken* (Gen. 3:23). This suggests a compatibility between Adam the man and the Land of Adama, because Adam was created from the dust of the earth, a link that is underscored by their similar names. Eretz, by contrast, appears in Genesis 4:12 as a place where Cain is condemned to wander.

The presence of the ever-turning fiery sword, echoing Genesis 3:24, illustrates both that Adam is trapped in the land of Eretz, and, at the same time, that Eretz is somehow connected to Eden, from which he has been expelled. Thus the ever-turning fiery sword symbolizes all the limitations that have developed in Adam's life, which have left him virtually trapped both in a desolate land and in his own bitter remorse.

Sources:
Zohar 1:253b; *Zohar Hadash*, Ruth 79b.

563. ADAM'S ACCOUNT OF THE FALL

On his deathbed, Adam recounted his memories of the Fall to his son, Seth: "After your mother and I were created, God placed us in Paradise. We were permitted to eat from every tree in the garden, except for one—the Tree of Knowledge that grew in the center of the garden. We were forbidden to eat of its fruit.

"Now God gave a part of Paradise to me and a part to your mother. He gave me the trees in the eastern and northern parts of the garden, and your mother received the trees of the southern and western parts. So too did God give us two angels to guard us.

"Each day, when the time came for the angels to worship in the presence of God, they ascended on high. Once the adversary, Satan, took advantage of the angel's absence and convinced your mother to eat of the forbidden fruit. And after she ate of it, she gave it to me.

"No sooner did we taste the forbidden fruit, than the Lord grew angry with us and said, 'Because of this, you and all of your generation will suffer pains in each separate limb, for I will bring seventy plagues upon you.'

"And when Eve, your mother, saw me weeping, she too began to weep. And she spoke up and said, 'O Lord, my God, give his pain to me, for it was I who sinned.' And she said to me, 'Give me a portion of your pain, for your guilt has come from me.' And ever since, both of us have had our share of suffering."

This version of the Fall by Adam to his son Seth adds some important details to the account in Genesis 3, such as that the Garden of Eden was divided into two parts, one for Adam and one for Eve. This seems to imply that territorial possession finds its origin with the first couple. Adam also explains how the serpent—here directly identified as Satan—succeeded in seducing Eve into eating the forbidden fruit. It seems that God had sent two angels, one for Adam and one for Eve, to guard and protect them. But when the angels left to pray in God's presence, Satan took advantage of their absence. Also added to Adam's account is Eve's explicit confession of guilt, as well as her offer to share in Adam's suffering. This perpetuates the blame Eve is to bear for the Fall, but at the same time it portrays her in an exceptionally favorable manner, willing to share both in Adam's guilt and in his suffering.

Sources:
Vita Adae et Evae 32-35; *Apocalypse of Moses* 15-21.

Studies:
"New Discoveries Relating to the Armenian Adam Books" by Michael E. Stone.

564. WHAT THE SERPENT SAID TO EVE

In order to convince Eve to taste the forbidden fruit, the serpent said: *"But God knows that as soon as you eat of it your eyes will be opened and you will be like God"* (Gen. 3:5-6). Know that God ate of this tree and then created the world. That is why He has commanded you not to eat of it, lest you create other worlds. The truth is that you were brought into being to rule over everything. Make haste and eat before God creates other worlds that will dominate you." And Eve saw how plausible were the words of the serpent, and she tasted the fruit.

This midrash adds significantly to the biblical version in having the serpent suggest to Eve that God Himself gained His powers after eating from the Tree of Knowledge. While the serpent's original comments promised Eve knowledge, they did not imply that God obtained His knowledge in this way. But the rabbis, reading between the lines, saw a hint of such a meaning in the serpent's comments and made this hint explicit. To do so is to belittle God's unique powers, and it turns the serpent into a heretic. Thus this midrash may be viewed as aimed not only at the serpent, but at those with Gnostic views who failed to acknowledge God's unique powers as Creator of the world.

Sources:
Genesis Rabbah 19:4.

565. SATAN AND THE SERPENT

Satan said to the serpent, "Arise and come to me. I will tell you something that will serve you well." The serpent came to him and Satan said, "You are said to be wiser than all the other animals. None is your equal in cunning. That is why I have come to see you."

Now all the wild beasts, including the serpent, came to worship Adam every morning. One morning Satan went with them and said to the serpent, "Why do you worship Adam? You came into being before he did. He should worship you. Come, rise up. Let us expel Adam from the Garden."

The serpent said, "How can we expel him from the Garden?"

Satan said, "You will be a lyre for me, and I will pronounce words through your mouth, so that you may be able to help."

Then Satan took on the form of an angel and began to praise God with angelic phrases. Eve knelt down by the wall and listened to his prayers. When she looked at him, she saw the likeness of an angel, but when she looked at him again, he was not to be seen.

Then Satan called upon the serpent to be his mouthpiece, and the serpent came to Eve and said, "Are you Eve?"

"Yes I am."

"What do you do in the Garden?"

"God put us here to guard the Garden."

"And do you eat of the trees in the Garden?"

"Yes," said Eve. "We eat of all of them except for one tree in the very middle. God commanded us not to eat of it, lest we die."

"No, you will not die," Satan said. "But when you eat of its fruit your eyes will be opened, and you will become like God, knowing good and evil. God deceived you when He said not to eat of it. Look at the glory that surrounds the tree."

And when Eve looked up and saw the great glory surrounding it, she said, "The tree is pleasing to my sight, but I am afraid. If you are not afraid, bring me the fruit and I will eat it, so I may know if your words are true or not."

Then Satan made Eve swear an oath that if she ate of the fruit of the tree, she would share it with Adam. Then the serpent brought her to the tree and lowered the branches of the tree to the earth. As he held them down, Eve plucked some of the fruit and ate it.

When Satan saw this, he had the serpent descend from the tree and hide in the Garden.

In most interpretations of the story of the Fall, the serpent is identified as Satan. In this myth the serpent serves as the mouthpiece of Satan. This version changes quite a few details in the biblical account, including some negotiation between Eve and the serpent about the conditions under which she would eat the fruit. Eve is afraid to pick the fruit and asks the serpent to do it for her. Instead, the serpent lowers the tree to the earth, making it easy for her to pick the fruit, which she does. Eve's reluctance is also found in the midrash, in which she first bites only the skin of the fruit, and when nothing happens, eats the rest of the fruit. (*Zekhor Hamor* on Gen. 3:6.) Note that the oath that Satan forces Eve to make would be the first oath, and it is made to Satan rather than to God.

Sources:
Penitence of Adam 44:16:2-44:20:1.

566. THE QUEST FOR THE OIL OF LIFE

As Adam lay dying, he called upon Eve and his son Seth to go off alone and prostrate themselves before God, and beg God to send an angel to the Tree of Mercy in the Garden of Eden, from which flows the Oil of Life. For he knew that if he were anointed with that oil, he would receive respite from his pain.

So Seth and his mother, Eve, set out for the Gates of Paradise. Along the way, a beast appeared—a serpent—and attacked Seth. Eve shouted at the serpent, "Accursed beast! Keep your distance from the image of God." Hearing this, the beast left their presence, but Seth was left with the marks of its teeth upon him.

When Seth and Eve arrived at the gates, they put dust from the ground on their heads and prostrated themselves, begging the Lord to pity Adam and send an angel to anoint him with that oil.

After they had prayed for many hours, the angel Michael appeared to them. The angel said, "God has sent me to you, for I have been appointed by God to look after men's bodies. Weep and pray no more for the Oil of Life, for you can never have it, except at the End of Days. Go back to your father, for the span of his life is complete. Six days from now his soul will depart from his body. When it does, you will see great wonders in the lights of heaven and on the earth."

And the death of Adam came after six days, just as the angel Michael had predicted.

> This myth of the Oil of Life, said to flow from the Tree of Mercy in the Garden of Eden, is a completely new motif, missing entirely in Genesis. Here there is said to be another key tree in the Garden of Eden, in addition to the Tree of Knowledge and the Tree of Life. This is the Tree of Mercy, and the Oil of Life is said to flow from it. From Adam's description it appears that the Oil of Life is a balm that Adam recalls from his days in the garden. Whether it not only alleviates pain but sustains life as well is not stated. If so, it would be linked with the Tree of Life. Although less well known, the myth of the Oil of Life is similar to the myth of the Waters of Eternal Life: whoever drinks of those waters will have eternal life.
>
> The episode in which Seth is attacked by a serpent has the effect of renewing the enmity between the serpent and human beings in the next generation, as well as serving as a reminder of the story of the Fall. The encounter with this beast, as the serpent is called, becomes a stage in the quest to retrieve the Oil of Life, every quest having its share of adversity.
>
> *Sources:*
> *Vita Adae et Evae* 36-45.
>
> *Studies:*
> "The Fall of Satan and Adam's Penance: Three Notes on *The Books of Adam and Eve*"
>   by Michael E. Stone.

567. THE GENERATIONS OF SETH

Cain was not of Adam's seed, nor after his likeness, nor after his image. Adam did not beget in his own image until Seth was born, as it is said, *He begot a son in his likeness after his image* (Gen. 5:3). Indeed, Seth was the exact image of Adam. Adam was 130 years old when Seth was born.

Adam knew the Torah, and he transmitted it to his son, Seth, and it was later transmitted to Enoch. Adam also was the first High Priest, and when he offered a sacrifice, he wore the garments of the High Priest. And when he died, they passed to Seth, and from Seth they passed to Methuselah.

Seth was born circumcised, and he became a virtuous man, of excellent character, whose children imitated his virtues. That is why it is said about Seth that *whatever he does prospers* (Ps. 1:3). From Seth descended all of the generations of the righteous, while from Cain descended all the generations of the wicked. For seven generations the children of

Seth inhabited the same country without dissension, without any misfortunes falling upon them till they died. They gained a great deal of wisdom about the heavenly bodies.

Now Adam had predicted that the world was to be destroyed once by fire and another time by water. And so that their discoveries might not be lost before they were sufficiently known, the descendants of Seth made two pillars, one of brick and the other of stone. And they inscribed their discoveries on them both, so that if one or the other should be destroyed by flood or fire, the other might remain and reveal their discoveries to humankind. And God commanded two angels to guard these inscriptions so that they might not be destroyed until the final age.

> While the legendary tradition about Seth, Adam's third son, is limited in Jewish sources, there is some evidence of the glorification of Seth, suggesting that the soul of Seth entered into Moses and will again reappear in the Messiah. Seth is a major figure in Gnostic texts, such as *The Apocalypse of Adam*. The myths about Seth recount how angels would rescue the seed of Seth at the time of the Flood and hide his descendants in a secret place. For more about the evil descendants of Cain, see "The Seed of Cain," p. 448.
>
> Being born circumcised, as is recounted here of Seth, is a sign of greatness and purity. In *Zohar* 1:58a-b, Noah is also said to have been born circumcised.
>
> *Sources:*
> *Pirkei de-Rabbi Eliezer* 22; Josephus, *Jewish Antiquities* 2:3; *The Book of Jubilees* 19:24; *2 Enoch* 33:10; *Genesis Rabbah* 23:5; *Numbers Rabbah* 4:8; *Zohar Hadash* 22b; *Shoher Tov* 9:7, 1:10.

568. THE CREATION OF CENTAURS

Adam was created in the likeness and the image of God, as was Adam's son Seth, and Seth's son, Enosh. But after that the resemblance came to an end, and the generations became corrupt.

Beginning with Enosh, humans came to practice magic and divination, and the art of controlling the heavenly forces. Before long, their faces became apelike and they became vulnerable to demons. They had all manner of intercourse with humans and beasts, and that is when centaurs came into being. So too did people begin to gather gold, silver, and all kinds of precious gems, and with them they constructed idols, and prayed to them. They even used the Name of God for sacrilegious purposes.

> This myth demonstrates a kind of devolution in which men become corrupt and regress into beastlike beings. The sexual sins listed here, as well as the use of black magic, and the lust for possessions are offered to justify God's decision to destroy the generation of the Flood. Although the centaur, half man, half horse, is a figure out of Greek mythology, here its existence is explained as the product of human intercourse with beasts and as further evidence of the kind of sin that led God to the decision to destroy all life on earth except for Noah and his family and the animals on the ark.
>
> *Sources:*
> *Genesis Rabbah* 23:6; *Midrash Tanhuma, Noah* 5; *Zohar* 1:56a.

569. THE DEATH OF ADAM

Adam lay dying in his tent. When he realized that the hour of his death had arrived, he cried out in a loud voice, "Let all my sons gather by me, so that I may see them and bless them before I die." Then all his sons, from every part of the world, gathered by him, and Adam blessed them and said, "Behold, I am nine hundred and thirty years old. When I die, bury me toward the east." And when he finished speaking, he breathed his last, and the sun and moon and stars were darkened for seven days.

Seth bent over his father's body and embraced it, Eve's hands were folded over her head, and all of Adam's children wept bitterly. And the angel Michael appeared and stood at Adam's head, and the angels blew their trumpets and cried, "Blessed are You, O Lord, for You have had pity on Your creature." Then Seth saw God's hand stretched out and holding Adam. And God said to Michael, "Let him be in your charge until the day of judgment, when I will turn sorrow into joy."

Then God said to the angels Michael and Uriel, "Bring three linen sheets and spread them out over Adam and over Adam's son, Abel, and bury Adam and his son." And all the hosts of angels marched in procession in front of Adam's body, and Michael and Uriel buried Adam in one of the regions of Paradise, in the presence of Seth and his mother, Eve, and no one else. And Michael and Uriel said to them, "Just as we have done, so too must you bury your dead."

> All that is said in the Bible of the death of Adam is *All the days that Adam lived came up to 930 years; then he died* (Gen. 5:5). Here the details of Adam's death are embellished, and the story continued about how Adam was mourned and what took place after his death. The angel Michael appears at the time of Adam's death, and God hands the body of Adam to Michael, to hold until the End of Days. The myth also adds God's explicit promise to "turn sorrow into joy," hinting at the glories of the messianic era. Most interesting, Adam is buried together with his son, Abel, who apparently had not been buried until that time. That Adam and his son are buried together is a moving image, making Adam's death that much more poignant. Finally, this myth offers an origin myth for the practice of burying those who have died, and makes it a divine commandment, conveyed by the angels Michael and Uriel after they buried Adam.
>
> In *The Apocalypse of Moses*, which is believed to be a Jewish text with Christian interpolations, a dream of Eve is related in which Adam was taken into a tall shining Temple and seated on a throne in the presence of three divine beings, and this is to be understood as predicting that Adam would soon be in heaven. Some scholars identify the three divine beings as the three angels who visited Abraham, while others identify them with the Christian Trinity.
>
> *Sources:*
> *Vita Adae et Evae* 30:1-4, 45-48; *Apocalypse of Moses* 16-22; *Penitence of Adam* 30:5:1-30:5:3.

570. PARADISE

We were created to live in Paradise. Paradise was intended to serve us. Our destiny has changed. It is not said that the same thing would have been true for Paradise.

We were cast out of Paradise, but it was not destroyed. Our expulsion was in a sense fortunate. Had we not been cast out, Paradise would have had to be destroyed.

> This brief parable contains Kafka's understanding of the Paradise myth in Genesis. According to Kafka, Paradise still exists by virtue of the fact that Adam and Eve were expelled from it—otherwise, it would have had to be destroyed. Thus, for Kafka, Paradise is an archetype of perfection that still inspires us, even if we cannot fully experience it. Therefore we were lucky to be expelled, so that Paradise can continue to exist.
>
> Abraham Joshua Heschel also has an original view of Paradise: "After having eaten the forbidden fruit, the Lord sent forth man from Paradise, to till the ground from

which he was taken. But man, who is more subtle than any other creature that God has made, what did he do? He undertook to build a Paradise by his own might, and he is driving God from his Paradise" (*The Insecurity of Freedom*, pp. 164-165). Thus Heschel proposes a reversal of the exile process, where we drive God from our Paradise, just as God drove us from His.

Sources:
Parables and Paradoxes by Franz Kafka.

571. CAIN AND ABEL

Now the man knew his wife Eve, and she conceived and bore Cain, saying, "I have gained a male child with the help of the Lord." She then bore his brother Abel. Abel became a keeper of sheep, and Cain became a tiller of the soil. In the course of time, Cain brought an offering to the Lord from the fruit of the soil; and Abel, for his part, brought the choicest of the firstlings of his flock. The Lord paid heed to Abel and his offering, but to Cain and his offering He paid no heed. Cain was much distressed and his face fell. And the Lord said to Cain, "Why are you distressed, and why is your face fallen? Surely, if you do right, there is uplift. But if you do not do right sin couches at the door; its urge is toward you, yet you can be its master."

Cain said to his brother Abel, "Come, let us go out into the field," and when they were in the field, Cain set upon his brother Abel and killed him. The Lord said to Cain, "Where is your brother Abel?" And he said, "I do not know. Am I my brother's keeper?" Then He said, "What have you done? Hark, your brother's blood cries out to Me from the ground! Therefore, you shall be more cursed than the ground, which opened its mouth to receive your brother's blood from your hand. If you till the soil, it shall no longer yield its strength to you. You shall become a ceaseless wanderer on earth."

Cain said to the Lord, "My punishment is too great to bear! Since You have banished me this day from the soil, and I must avoid Your presence and become a restless wanderer on earth—anyone who meets me may kill me!" The Lord said to him, "I promise, if anyone kills Cain, sevenfold vengeance shall be taken on him." And the Lord put a mark on Cain, lest anyone who met him should kill him. Cain left the presence of the Lord and settled in the land of Nod, east of Eden.

> The theme of competing brothers is also found in the biblical accounts of Isaac and Ishmael, Jacob and Esau, and Joseph and his brothers.
>
> No reason is given for God's preference of Abel's offering over Cain's. Also, no reason is given for Cain's attack on Abel. However, both of these questions are answered in detail in the Midrash, where Abel's offering was preferred because it consisted of the choicest of his flock, and the struggle between the brothers is blamed on a struggle over a woman. The ultimate fate of Cain is also not mentioned, although rabbinic tradition provides four different versions of Cain's death. See "The Death of Cain," p. 451.
>
> Parallel accounts of two brothers are found in the literature of the ancient Near East. The Egyptian stories of Anubis and Bata concern two brothers who work as farmers but become enemies after Anubis's wife falsely accuses Bata of propositioning her. Anubis, in his fury, goes to kill Bata with a spear, but the god Ra creates a lake full of crocodiles to protect Bata from his older brother. Eventually the two brothers reconcile, and each, in turn, becomes pharaoh. See *Old Testament Parallels: Laws and Stories from the Ancient Near East* by Victor H. Matthews and Don C. Benjamin, pp. 61-65.
>
> *Sources:*
> Genesis 4:1-16.
>
> *Studies:*
> "Cain's Expulsion from Paradise: The Text of Philo's *Congr* 171" by James R. Royse.

572. HOW CAIN WAS CONCEIVED

Samael was the great prince in heaven. After God created the world, Samael took his band of followers and descended and saw the creatures that God had created. Among them he found none so skilled to do evil than the serpent, as it is said, *Now the serpent was the shrewdest of all the wild beasts* (Gen. 3:1). Its appearance was something like that of a camel, and Samael mounted and rode upon it. Riding on the serpent, the angel Samael came to Eve in the night and seduced her, and she conceived Cain. Later, while Eve was pregnant by the angel, Adam came to her, and she conceived Abel.

Others say it was the serpent himself who seduced Eve, for after he saw Adam and Eve coupling, the serpent conceived a passion for her. He even imagined killing Adam and marrying Eve. So he came to Eve when she was alone and possessed her and infused her with lust. That is how the serpent fathered Cain, who was later to slay his own brother. And that is how Eve was infected with his impurity. As a result, all of Israel was impure from that time until the Torah was given on Mount Sinai. Only then did Israel's impurity cease.

When Cain was born, Adam knew at once that he was not of his seed, for he was not after his likeness, nor after his image. Instead, Cain's appearance was that of a heavenly being. And when Eve saw that his appearance was not of this world, she said, *I have gained a male child with the help of Yahweh* (Gen. 4:1).

It was not until the birth of Seth that Adam had a son who was in his own likeness and image. From Seth arose all of the generations of the righteous, while all the generations that descended from the seed of Cain are wicked, until this very day.

> This myth is a response to the enigmatic verse in which Eve says, *I have gotten a man with the aid of Yahweh* (Gen. 4:1). *Targum Pseudo-Yonathan* translates this verse as "I have acquired a ̲ ̲ the angel of the Lord."
>
> One readi̲ ̲ ̲ verse in the Talmud (*B. Shab.* 146a) suggests that Eve had intercourse v̲ ̲ "When the serpent consorted with Eve, he cast impurity into her" ̲ ̲ ̲ ̲ echoed in the *Zohar*: "From the impurity with which the ̲ ̲ ̲d Cain." *Pirkei de-Rabbi Eliezer* builds on the talmudic in- ̲ ̲ ̲ an essential way. Here the true father of Cain is the ̲ ̲ ̲e riding on the serpent. Indeed, in this passage the ̲ ̲ ̲ed, creating a satanic figure and suggesting that Eve ̲ ̲ ̲ powerful phallic symbol.
>
> ̲ ̲ h upbraids Samael as he rides upon the serpent ̲ ̲ aloud, saying, 'Why, O Samael, now that the ̲ ̲ inst God? Is this the time to lift yourself on ̲ ̲ ider.'" This establishes the role of the Torah ̲ ̲ he evil intentions of Samael.
>
> ̲ ̲ ve, the serpent and Adam, and that she ̲ ̲ two sons. The son of the serpent is, of ̲ ̲ evil and Abel was good, *Zohar* 1:54a ̲ ̲ of unholiness and Abel from the side ̲ ̲ ness of God's image, as stated in the verse ̲ ̲ 1:27). But Cain was of the likeness of the nether ̲ ̲ , although one commentary, *Ziv ha-Zohar*, identifies ̲ ̲ ̲ ape. Because Cain was from the side of the Angel of ̲ ̲ xplanation of the "nether image"), he killed his brother.
>
> D̲ ̲ ̲ was infected by the impurity of the serpent when she had inter-
> cours̲ ̲ mpts to portray women as not only impure, but also untrustworthy. It is part ̲ ̲ xtensive antifeminine bias found in some rabbinic texts. However, in other texts, Eve is portrayed in a very favorable manner. She is regarded as the mother of all generations, and she is called a life-giver, who nursed the whole world (*B. AZ* 43a).

The serpent of Genesis becomes transformed in kabbalah into a principle of evil, the primal serpent who makes its home in the darkness of the *Sitra Ahra*, the Other Side. It is *a serpent by the road, a viper by the path* (Gen. 49:17). It comes down from above, swims across bitter waters, and descends in order to deceive, lying in wait to ambush mankind with sins. The *Sitra Ahra* is the realm of evil. It is said to be ruled by Samael and Lilith. The primal or primordial serpent is an archetype of evil, based upon the serpent in the Garden of Eden. In this realm it functions as a force of evil, an exaggerated version of the *Yetzer ha-Ra*, the Evil Impulse in every person. Here this impulse is understood to be an underlying principle in the concept of an evil realm. Evil, however, flourishes only in the absence of good. The *Zohar* describes this serpent as "eternal death, on the left side, that enters into a man's innermost secret parts" (*Zohar* 2:52a).

See the closely related myth, "The Seed of Cain," p. 448. For a Hasidic tale about the primal serpent, see "Reb Shmelke's Whip" in *Gabriel's Palace*, p. 226.

Sources:
Targum Pseudo-Yonathan on Genesis 4:1; *B. Shabbat* 145b-146a; *B. Sota* 9b; *B. Yevamot* 103b; *B. Avodah Zarah* 22b; *Genesis Rabbah* 18:6; *Pirkei de-Rabbi Eliezer* 13, 21, and 22; *Zohar* 1:28b, 1:36b-137a, 1:54a, 1:55a; 1:243b, 2:52a; *Magen Avot* 53.

573. THE SEED OF CAIN

Adam was not Cain's father. Cain was conceived by Samael riding the serpent in the Garden of Eden. The serpent came to Eve at night and had intercourse with her, and Cain was born from this union. Thus Cain was not of Adam's seed, nor after his likeness, nor after his image. Adam did not have a son in his own image and likeness until Seth was born.

After Cain became *a restless wanderer* (Gen. 4:14), he *settled in the land of Nod, east of Eden* (Gen. 4:16). He married and *Cain knew his wife, and she conceived* (Gen. 4:17). Some say that the offspring of Cain went extinct after seven generations, for God chose to *visit the iniquity of the fathers upon the children* (Exod. 34:7).

Others say that the seed of Cain still walk the earth. For from Seth arose and were descended all the generations of the righteous, and from Cain arose and were descended all the generations of the wicked, who rebelled and sinned against heaven. One and all the seed of Cain are descended from the serpent, and they are the enemies of Israel— Amalek, Edom and Rome.

> *Pirkei de-Rabbi Eliezer* says of the conception of Cain, "Samael riding on the serpent came to Eve and she conceived." This creates two lines of people, those descended from the seed of Adam and his son, Seth, and those descended from the seed of Cain. See "How Cain was Conceived," p. 447.
>
> According to *B. Shabbat*, Eve had sexual relations with the serpent in the Garden of Eden and the snake deposited a pollution in Eve that entered into her children and her children's children. However, this explanation does not distinguish between the seed of Seth and the seed of Cain. When Israel accepted the Torah at Mount Sinai, the seed of Seth was purified of the pollution the snake had deposited in Eve and that had entered her children's children. The same cannot be said of the seed of Cain.
>
> This myth about Cain's conception and the seed of Cain derives, in part, from Genesis 5:3: *When Adam had lived one hundred and thirty years, he begot a son in his likeness after his image, and he named him Seth.* This is taken to imply that Cain was not Adam's son. The *Zohar* (1:55a) explains that neither Cain nor Abel was born in Adam's likeness, based on the verse *She conceived and bore Cain, saying,"I have gained a male child with the help of Yahweh* (Gen. 4:1). The *Zohar* takes this to mean that both Cain and Abel stemmed chiefly from Eve, rather than Adam. Seth, by contrast, bore Adam's image.

The tradition that there are two lines of descent, from the seed of Adam and from the seed of Cain, is found in *Pirkei de-Rabbi Eliezer* and other sources. Some attribute this tradition to Rabbi Ishmael and other to Rabbi Shimon bar Yohai.

This midrash offers an explanation for the existence of Israel's enemies, explaining that they were all descended from the seed of Cain. During and after the Holocaust, the Nazis were sometimes identified as the "seed of Cain."

Sources:
B. *Shabbat* 146a; *Pirkei de-Rabbi Eliezer* 21 and Oxford Ms. (e. 76), 22; *Midrash Aggadah, Bereshit; Midrash ha-Gadol* 117.

574. THE BIRTH OF CAIN

Eve was the first woman ever to give birth. When the time came, neither Adam nor Eve knew what to expect, and they were very afraid. Adam wept and prayed to God on her behalf. All at once two angels and two powers descended from heaven, and stood before Eve. The powers said to her, "Eve, you are blessed. Adam's prayers are mighty, and through him God's help has come to you." Then the angel said, "Prepare yourself. I will be the midwife for you."

Before long Eve gave birth to Cain. The color of his body was like the color of the stars. No sooner did the newborn child fall into the hands of the angel who served as a midwife than he leaped up and plucked the grass that grew near his mother's hut. After that nothing would ever grow there, and anyone who passed by that place became infertile.

And the angel said to him, "*You shall become a ceaseless wanderer on earth* (Gen. 4:12). Your legacy will be one of adultery and bitterness." And so it came to pass.

This is an origin tale, an account of the first birth, that of Cain, who became a prototype for evil. In the biblical account, Cain slays Abel for no apparent reason, but there are several midrashic explanations, such as a fight over one of their twin sisters, or over their property rights—Cain claimed rights to all the land and Abel to all the air. Cain told Abel to get off of his land. Abel told Cain to stop breathing his air.

This version of the birth of Cain also adds many foreboding elements that suggest that Cain was not a normal child but some kind of supernatural being. "The color of his body was like the color of the stars"—this seems to suggest he was glowing, an abnormal condition. Further, the newborn infant jumps out of the angel's hands and his first act is a destructive one—he pulls out the grass around his mother's hut, which never grows back. Here Cain is painted as evil from the very beginning, and this is confirmed by the angel who prophesies Cain's fate.

Sources:
Penitence of Adam 20:3-21:3a.

575. THE WIVES OF CAIN AND ABEL

Where did the wives of Cain and Abel come from? On the day that Adam and Eve were created, on that very day they coupled, and on that very day they produced offspring. It is said that two entered the bed and seven left it, for Cain was born with a twin sister, and Abel was born with two sisters.

Cain married Abel's twin, and Abel married Cain's. But they could not agree on the fate of Abel's second twin. Indeed, it is said that she was the subject of the dispute between the two brothers, out of which Cain slew his brother Abel, and the voices of the blood of the families who were destined to issue forth from Abel cried out before God.

Since Genesis does not explain what it was that Cain and Abel fought over, there are many myths that speculate about it. One of the most common explanations is that they were fighting over a woman. In this version, she is identified as Abel's second twin. In other versions, such as *Genesis Rabbah* 22:7, the woman they fought over is identified as the first Eve. See "The First Eve," p. 140. This midrash makes the assumption that Cain and Abel were themselves twins, although the biblical text does not state this, and seems to imply that they were not.

Sefer Zikhronot gives the name of the Cain's wife as Kalmana, and of Abel's wife as Deborah. This text also identifies these wives as their twins, contrary to the version in which Cain and Abel do not marry their own twins, but each one marries the other's twin.

Sources:
Genesis Rabbah 22:2-3, 22:7; *Targum Onkelos* on Genesis 4:9; *Sefer ha-Zikhronot* 23:26.

576. EVE'S NIGHT VISION

One night, when Cain and Abel were both young men, Eve had a terrible dream. When she awoke she told the dream to Adam: "While I was sleeping, I saw in a night vision that the blood of our son Abel was entering the mouth of our son Cain. Cain drank his blood without mercy. Abel beseeched him to leave a little, but he drank his blood completely."

Hearing this, Adam said, "Surely this means that Cain must intend to kill Abel. Come, let us keep them apart. Let each of them live in a separate place." So Adam said to them, "My sons, let each of you go to your own place." And they did.

After this, God sent the angel Michael to Adam. God said, "Adam understands that Cain intends to kill Abel. Go to him and tell him not to reveal this mystery to Cain, for Cain is a son of wrath who will kill Abel, his brother. So too should you tell Adam not to grieve because I will give him another son, Seth. Seth will bear my image, and through him many mysteries will be revealed."

And the angel came to Adam and spoke to him, and Adam revealed what the angel told him only to Eve, and they both grieved to learn the fate of Abel.

Dreams and visions are often understood to be prophetic. Here Eve has a prophetic dream or vision—she calls it a "night vision"—in which Cain behaves like a beast or a vampire and drinks all of Abel's blood. When Eve tells this dream to Adam, he understands its meaning at once—that Cain will murder Abel. He hopes to prevent this by separating them, but God sends the angel Michael to reveal the inevitability of this fate, as well as promising them the birth of another son, Seth, who is clearly intended to take Abel's place.

The prophecy of the birth of Seth, and the description of his powers makes it seem likely that this myth reflects the veneration of Seth that played a central role in Gnosticism. For Gnostic texts about Seth see *Apocalypse of Adam*, where Adam communicates a secret Gnostic revelation to Seth.

Eve's dream portrays Cain's crime in the stark and primitive terms of drinking a victim's blood. For an equally primitive myth, see "How Samael Entered the Heart of Man," p. 454.

Sources:
Penitence of Adam 22:2:1-23:3:2.

Studies:
Apocalypse of Adam in *Old Testament Pseudepigrapha*, edited by James Charlesworth, vol. 1, pp. 707-719.

577. THE DEATH OF CAIN

How did Cain meet his death? Some say that Cain fulfilled his destiny as *a ceaseless wanderer on earth* (Gen. 4:12) until the time of the Flood, and that he drowned in the Flood with everyone else, except for Noah and his family.

Others say that Cain, the founder of the first city, was killed when his house, made of stones, fell upon him, stoning him to death. Thus was Cain killed in the same way he had killed his brother, confirming that a man shall be killed with the weapons with which he kills his fellow man.

Still others say that Cain's final destiny was in being transformed into the Angel of Death, since he was responsible for the first death. For a hundred and thirty years Cain wandered and roamed about, accursed. Thereafter Lamech served as the Angel of Death.

But most agree that Cain met his death at the hands of his own descendants, Lamech and Tubal-Cain. In those days Lamech was old and advanced in years, and his eyes were dim so that he could not see. One day his son, Tubal-Cain, was leading him while they were walking in the field, when Cain, the son of Adam, advanced toward them. And Tubal-Cain told his father to draw his bow, and with the arrows he smote Cain, who was yet far off, and he slew him, for he appeared to them to be an animal. And the arrows entered Cain's body although he was distant from them, and he fell to the ground and died. And the Lord requited Cain's evil according to his wickedness, which he had done to his brother Abel, according to the word of the Lord that He had spoken. And it came to pass that when Cain had died, that Lamech and Tubal-Cain went to see the animal they had slain, and they saw, and behold Cain their grandfather was fallen dead upon the earth. And Lamech was very much grieved at having done this, and in clapping his hands together he struck his son and caused his death.

Lamech's wives, Tsila and Ada, found him later that night, and were furious to learn that he had caused the deaths of Cain and Tubal-Cain. They vowed never to share his bed again. But Lamech took them to Adam, the judge, and Adam ruled that they must obey their husband.

Since the biblical narrative of Cain is unfinished, the rabbis were left to resolve the story in both a moral and a literary sense. Using the tradition of the Oral Law as their justification, and supporting their interpretations with biblical prooftexts, the rabbis embellished the tale of Cain and Abel in many respects. They filled in the sketchy details of the births of the two brothers (*Pirkei de-Rabbi Eliezer* 21), the mystery of the origin of their wives (*Genesis Rabbah* 22:2), the conflict between the two (*Genesis Rabbah* 22:7), the murder of Abel by Cain (*Genesis Rabbah* 22:8), the burial of Abel (*Pirkei de-Rabbi Eliezer* 21), and the punishment and ultimate fate of Cain.

The end of the biblical narrative about Cain describes his punishment by God and concludes by attributing to Cain the founding of the first city (Gen. 4:17). After Cain has been cursed to become *a ceaseless wanderer on earth* (Gen. 4:12), he protests the severity of the sentence and has it modified (Gen. 4:13-15).

Of particular interest to the rabbis was the nature of the sign by which God had marked Cain, to identify and protect him in his wanderings. One of the earliest midrashim speculating on this sign appears in *Genesis Rabbah* 22:12: "*And the Lord put a mark on Cain* (Gen. 4:15). Rabbi Judah said: 'He caused the orb of the sun to shine on his account.' Said Rabbi Nehemiah to him: 'He caused the orb of the sun to shine! Rather, He afflicted him with leprosy.' Rab said: 'He gave him a dog.' Abba Jose said: 'He made a horn grow out of his forehead.' Rabbi Levi quotes Rabbi Shimon ben Lakish as saying, 'He suspended his punishment until the Flood came and swept him away.'"

Of these five versions of the nature of the mark of Cain, the one that entered the folk tradition was that of the horn, said to be located on his forehead. The reason for this should be apparent—the horn signified Cain's essentially savage nature and thus identified him as a beast. Later this horn was incorporated into the most widely accepted account of the death of Cain, in which he was slain by his descendants Lamech and Tubal-Cain.

While this became the most popular version of Cain's death, three other versions can be found. In one attributed to Rabbi Shimon ben Lakish, Cain was said to have found his death along with the other victims of the Flood. But this punishment was unsatisfying in that it did not single out Cain. The rabbis strongly felt that a decisive punishment for him was called for, to set a precedent for future murderers.

Another version of Cain's death appears in the apocryphal *Book of Jubilees* (4:31). Here Cain is said to have been killed when his house fell on him. Just as he had killed Abel with a stone, so was he slain by stones: "Cain was killed when his house fell upon him and he died in the midst of his house, killed by its stones. For with a stone he had killed Abel, and by a stone he was killed in righteous judgment." Then the *Book of Jubilees* goes on to link this judgment with the Law: "The instrument with which a man kills his neighbor will be the same with which he shall be killed; after the manner that he wounded him, in a like manner shall they deal with him." This refers to Exodus 21:24, following the pattern of *You shall give life for life, eye for eye, tooth for tooth, hand for hand, foot for foot* (Exod. 21:24. See also Leviticus 24:19 and Deuteronomy 19:21).

A third account of Cain's death is found in *Midrash Tanhuma-Yelammedenu*, where it is said that when he died, Cain was transformed into the Angel of Death. This provides an origin myth for the Angel of Death.

The first principle of supporting a midrashic interpretation is to link it to a biblical prooftext. Since there is no description of the death of Cain in the Bible, the rabbis turned to an enigmatic passage about Cain's descendent, Lamech: *And Lamech said to his wives: Ada and Tsila, hear my voice; You wives of Lamech, hearken to my speech. For I have slain a man for wounding me, and a young man for bruising me. If Cain is avenged sevenfold, then Lamech seventy-sevenfold.* (Gen. 4:23-24).

This perplexing passage is almost certainly a fragment of a lost myth about Lamech. But it is cleverly interpreted in *Midrash Tanhuma-Yelammendenu* to prove that Cain was slain by Lamech, who was accompanied by his son, Tubal-Cain. This account of Cain's death at the hands of Lamech ingeniously utilizes two existing traditions associated with Cain—the enigmatic passage concerning Lamech and the midrash asserting that Cain's sign was a horn. The passage about Lamech provides the framework for the narrative of the death of Cain, as well as the conclusion of the tale. The horn is the motif around which the whole tale turns. Together the two fragments provide the necessary link to tradition that gives the midrash its authentic ring. In addition, this version of Cain's death is satisfying in a number of other respects.

First of all, this midrash brings the tale of Cain to a conclusion. This was of no small importance to the rabbis, who had a strong sense that every tale should have a beginning, a middle, and an ending. In its biblical form, the story of Cain was simply incomplete. At the same time, by extending the story seven generations, the principle was established of carrying the biblical story into the future, and thus extending the history of a character beyond his or her appearance in the biblical text. Such a system made it possible to incorporate not only biblical exegesis, but personal dreams and fantasies as well into the *Aggadah*.

Next, this midrash provides a unique and appropriate death for Cain, especially fitting in that his slayer is his own relation. This is a kind of poetic (or, perhaps, midrashic) justice, since Cain slew his own brother. Note, however, that neither Lamech nor his son, Tubal-Cain, can be held responsible for Cain's death, since Lamech was blind and Tubal-Cain only a child who mistook his ancestor for an animal—which, in essence, Cain was. It is a case of perfect justice: Cain receives his due from his own offspring, but they are innocent of any crime, though they have in this way repaid Cain for making them accursed, and in this coincidence can be seen, of course, the hand of God. Also, note the presence of Cain's name in that of the descendant who assists in killing him, hinting that Cain, in a sense, killed himself.

Finally, this midrash aptly sets the precedent that a killer should be slain for his crime (contrary to an alternative interpretation that Cain repented and his repentance was accepted). This reading also supports the biblical injunction that the punishment for murder be death, and avoids setting the precedent that exceptions to this rule be permitted.

It is not surprising, then, that this version of the death of Cain, which became the predominant one, served the needs of the ancient rabbis and accurately reflected their views of the need for, and the manner of, justice and retribution. All subsequent versions of this midrash merely embellish aspects of this midrash and present the details in an improved narrative form, but do not change it in any essential way.

Thus it can be seen that this midrash of Cain's death solves two problems at the same time: it explicates a difficult passage about Lamech, and at the same time it solves the narrative and moral problem of the ultimate fate of Cain. And despite its intentional usage of existing sources—Cain's horn and the enigmatic passage about Lamech—it still manages to be an original creation of its own.

Sources:
Midrash Tanhuma-Yelammedenu, Bereshit 11; *Book of Jubilees* 4:31; IFA 17586.

578. THE EVIL INCLINATION

God created two inclinations, one good and the other evil. Some say that the Evil Inclination came into being at Adam's creation, while others say it was not until the creation of Eve. For when Adam's rib was taken from him, *his eyes were opened and he came to know good and evil* (Gen. 3:5).

The Evil Inclination that resides in the human heart entices us in this world and testifies against us in the World to Come. Because of the force of the Evil Inclination, it is difficult to extract oneself from sinful behavior. Indeed, it is said that the greater the man, the greater his Evil Inclination. At first it is like the thread of a spider, but before long it becomes as thick as the ropes of a cart.

The force of the Evil Inclination holds sway in this world, and everyone is subject to it, even the angels. For when the angels Shemhazai and Azazel descended to earth from heaven, they took on concrete appearance and became visible, and they soon became subject to the Evil Inclination and lusted after the daughters of men.

The Evil Inclination grows in strength from day to day, and were it not for God's help, no one would be able to withstand it. The rabbis said: "If you meet this repulsive wretch, drag him to the House of Study. If he is of stone, he will dissolve; if of iron, he will shiver into fragments."

The Evil Inclination has seven names. God called it Evil. Moses called it the Uncircumcised. David called it Unclean. Solomon called it the Enemy. Isaiah called it the Stumbling Block. Ezekiel called it Stone. And Joel called it the Hidden One.

The Evil Inclination is one of the four things that God repented of having created. The others are Exile, the Chaldeans, and the Ishmaelites.

In the days to come, God will bring forth the Evil Inclination and slay it in the presence of the righteous and the wicked. To the righteous it will appear as a mountain, and to the wicked it will have the appearance of a thread as thin as a hair. Both of them will weep. The righteous will weep and say, "How were we able to overcome such a towering hill?" And the wicked will weep and say, "How is it that we failed to conquer this thread?" And God, too will marvel with them.

The Evil Inclination, or *Yetzer ha-Ra*, is the force of evil that is present in this world because of its material nature. There is also a countervailing force, less mentioned, known as the *Yetzer ha-Tov*, or the Good Inclination. According to *B. Bava Batra* 16a, the Serpent in the Garden of Eden, Satan, the *Yetzer ha-Ra*, and the Angel of Death are one and the same.

For versions of the story of the fallen angels, see pp. 454-460.

Sources:
B. Berakhot 61a; *B. Bava Batra* 16a; *B. Sukkah* 52a-b; *Genesis Rabbah* 21:5; *Yalkut Shim'oni, Bereshit* 44; Rabbi Moshe Alshekh on Exodus 31:18; *Makhon Siftei Tzaddikim* on Exodus 30:12; *Tzidkat ha-Tzaddik* 111.

579. HOW SAMAEL ENTERED THE HEART OF MAN

Samael, riding on the serpent, came to Eve and she conceived a child. The son that was born was the son of Samael. Then Adam, who had been walking in the Garden of Eden, returned. He found the son of Samael crying, and he asked Eve: "Who is he?" And she said: "This is Samael's son." And he said to her: "Why do we need this problem here?" And the boy was still crying, because he wanted to make Adam angry.

What did the first man Adam do? He stood over him and slaughtered him and cut him into pieces. And then every piece would yell by itself. What did Adam do? He stood and boiled it, and he and his wife Eve ate it.

When Samael learned that they had eaten his son, he came to them and said, "Give me my boy." They said "We didn't see anything. We don't know anything." And he said to them: "You're lying." While they were arguing, the son of Samael spoke from the heart of Adam and Eve and said to Samael: "Go on your way, because I have already entered into their hearts, and I am not going to leave their hearts, nor the hearts of their sons, nor the sons of their sons, throughout the generations."

> This is a gruesome, primitive tale about the origin of evil in the human heart. The cannibalistic elements are shocking and seem inappropriate to Jewish tradition. The cruelty reflected in the myth suggests a cynical view of humanity appropriate to its subject matter. It draws on the midrash that the serpent conceived a child—Cain—with Eve. See "How Cain Was Conceived," p. 447.
>
> A variant is found in IFA 1141 from Yemen, where Satan brings his son to Adam in the shape of a sheep and gives it to him to keep for a year. When Satan doesn't return on time to take his sheep, Adam butchers it and eats it with challah. Then when Satan returns and asks for his sheep, Adam lies and says that it has run away. Satan calls his son and he replies from inside of Adam, and Satan leaves him there.
>
> *Sources:*
> IFA 1141; *Ha-Goren* 9:38-41 by Louis Ginzberg; *Pirkei de-Rabbi Eliezer* 13, 21 and 22.

580. THE SONS OF GOD AND THE DAUGHTERS OF MEN

When men began to increase on earth and daughters were born to them, the divine beings saw how beautiful the daughters of men were and took wives from among those that pleased them. The Lord said, "My breath shall not abide in man forever, since he too is flesh; let the days allowed him be one hundred and twenty years." It was then, and later too, that the Nefilim appeared on earth, when the divine beings cohabited with the daughters of men, who bore them offspring. They were the heroes of old, the men of renown.

> Many of the best-known biblical episodes are found in the early portions of Genesis, prior to the story of Abraham. These include the accounts of the Creation, of

Adam and Eve, of Noah, and of the Tower of Babel. But one enigmatic episode that is consistently overlooked is Genesis 6:1-4, concerning the Sons of God (*B'nei Elohim*) and the daughters of men.

Like the account of the Tower of Babel, this mythic account of the mysterious Sons of God seems to appear from out of nowhere. Indeed, it may well be a mythic interpolation, added to explain why, a few verses later, *the earth became corrupt before God* (Gen. 6:11), much as the story of the Tower of Babel explains the origin of the many languages, as well as the dissemination of people over the earth.

Sources:
Genesis 6:1-4.

581. THE STAR MAIDEN

When the generation of the Flood went astray, God began to regret having created humans. Then two angels, Shemhazai and Azazel, reminded God that they had opposed the creation of humans, saying, *What is man, that You have been mindful of him?* (Ps. 8:5). God replied: "Those who dwell on earth are subject to the Evil Inclination. Even you would be overpowered by it." But the angels protested, saying: "Let us descend to the world of humans, and let us show You how we will sanctify Your name." And God said: "Go down and dwell among them."

So the two angels descended to earth, where they were certain they could resist the power of the Evil Inclination. But as soon as they saw how beautiful were the daughters of men, they forgot their vows and took lovers from among them, even though they were defiling their own pure essence. So too did they teach them secrets of how to entice men, as well as the dark arts of sorcery, incantations, and the divining of roots.

Then the two angels decided to select brides for themselves from among the daughters of men. Azazel desired Na'amah, the sister of Tubal-Cain, the most beautiful woman on earth. But there was another beautiful maiden, Istahar, the last of the virgins, whom Shemhazai desired, and she refused him. This made him want her all the more.

"I am an angel," he revealed to her, "you cannot refuse me."

"I will not give in to you," Istahar replied, "unless you teach me God's Ineffable Name."

"That I cannot do," Shemhazai replied, "for it is a secret of heaven."

"Why should I believe you?" said Istahar. "Perhaps you don't know it at all. Perhaps you are not really an angel."

"Of course I know it," said Shemhazai, and he revealed God's Name.

Now as soon as she heard the holy Name, Istahar pronounced it and flew up into the heavens, escaping the angel. And when God saw this, He said: "Because she removed herself from sin, let Istahar be set among the stars." And Istahar was transformed into a star, one of the brightest in the sky. And when Shemhazai saw this, he recognized God's rebuke of his sin and repented, hanging himself upside down between heaven and earth. But Azazel refused to repent, and God hung him upside down in a canyon, bound in chains, where he remains to this day. That is why a scapegoat is sent to Azazel on Yom Kippur, the Day of Atonement, bearing the sins of Israel.

Others say that when the two angels, Shemhazai and Azazel, came down to earth, they were still innocent. But they were corrupted by the demonesses Na'amah and Lilith. The children they bore were the giants of old, known as the Nefilim, or Fallen Ones. They bore six children at each birth, and in that very hour their offspring stood up, spoke the holy language, and danced before them like sheep. There were said to be sixty in all. These giants had such great appetites that God rained manna on them in many different flavors, so that they might not eat flesh. But the Fallen Ones rejected the manna, slaughtered animals, and even dined on human flesh.

Still others say that the offspring of the fallen angels were tall and handsome, and had greater strength than all the children of men. Because of the heavenly origin of their fathers, they are referred to as "the children of heaven."

The primary mystery of Genesis 6 is the identity of the Sons of God. Anthropologists have suggested that they may have been a tribe of exceptionally tall and handsome men appeared and were irresistible to women. But the ancient rabbis were certain that the Sons of God were angels, although an alternate version in *Aggadat Bereshit* identifies them as the Sons of Cain. As a model, the rabbis drew on the prologue to Job, where God and Satan agree to test Job to see if he is truly righteous. Here God has a dialogue in heaven with two angels, Shemhazai and Azazel, who condemn the corrupt ways of men. God argues that if they lived on earth they would behave the same way, because everyone on earth is subject to the *Yetzer ha-Ra*, the Evil Inclination. The angels insist that they would remain righteous, and they convince God to let them descend to earth (in some versions, by Jacob's ladder). When they do, they are immediately filled with lust for the beautiful daughters of men, and use their heavenly powers to satisfy their desires. And the offspring of these unions are described as the Nefilim, which has been interpreted to mean giants. Thus the account in Genesis 6 also provides the origin of giants.

In some versions of this myth, the two angels end up coming down to earth not to demonstrate their ability to resist the Evil Inclination, but because God cast them out of heaven for opposing the creation of man. According to *Zohar Hadash, Ruth* 81a, the angels acquired human form as they descended from on high. When they mated with human women, the "daughters of men," their offspring were the Nefilim in Genesis 6:4, which literally means "fallen beings."

There are many variants of the story of the two angels from a wide range of sources, including *The Book of Enoch* (1 *Enoch*) and *Yalkut Shim'oni*. The best-known of these stories concerns two maidens, Istahar and Na'amah, whom the two angels sought to seduce.

Note that this story, with its fairy-tale quality, manages to explain who the Sons of God were, how they brought corruption to the earth, and the origin of giants. The story also demonstrates that no one, not even angels, is immune to the Evil Impulse. Indeed, so corrupt did the angels become, that it is said that in the end they indiscriminately enjoyed virgins, married women, men, and beasts. The Sons of God are also blamed for having invented the use of ornaments, rouge, and multicolored garments to make women more enticing. The daughters of men are identified as the children of Seth, Adam's son, and therefore are human (*Zohar* 1:37a). The heroine of the story is, of course, Istahar, the virgin who resisted the advances of Shemhazai, and was turned into a star. Istahar is a variant name for the Mesopotamian goddess Ishtar, who was equated with the planet Venus, the brightest star. As for Na'amah, the young woman who is said to have overwhelmed Azazel with her beauty, she is identified as the sister of Tubal-Cain. In later legends, Na'amah is also identified as a sister or daughter of Lilith.

In most versions of this myth, Istahar demands to be told God's secret Name, the Tetragrammaton (YHVH). But in one alternate version in *Beit ha-Midrash* 5:156, which, because it mutes the sexual elements of the story, might be described as a midrash for children, she demands that he let her try on his wings. At first he denies that his wings come off, but when she insists, he takes them off and lets her put them on and at that moment she flies off into heaven and is transformed into a star.

In later versions of this legend, the role of Shemhazai is diminished, while the role of Azazel is expanded, until Azazel is virtually identified with Satan. Ultimately, it is Shemhazai who repents and Azazel who does not. This leads to subsequent legends about the evil-doings of Azazel. According to *Yalkut Shim'oni*, Istahar became a star set among the seven stars of the Pleiades, while Shemhazai, hung upside down between heaven and earth, became the constellation Orion. Thus this myth may also be viewed from an astrological perspective as the origin of the constellations Pleiades and Orion.

There are strong echoes of Greek mythology in the myth of the Sons of God and daughters of men. In bringing heavenly secrets to earth, the Sons of God function much as does Prometheus when he steals fire from heaven and brings it to earth. For more on Prometheus stealing fire from heaven see Graves, *The Greek Myths*, 39g. There is also a strong parallel to the fate of Istahar in the story of Zeus setting Callisto's image among the stars. See Graves, *The Greek Myths*, 22h. See also "Adam Brings Down Fire from Heaven," p. 137.

Sources:

Targum Pseudo-Yonathan on Genesis 6:1-4; *Yalkut Shim'oni, Bereshit* 44; *Midrash Avkir* in *Beit ha-Midrash*, 4:127-128; *The Book of Jubilees* 4:15, 4:22, 5:1-3; *1 Enoch* 6:14; *Bereshit Rabbati* 29-30; *Pirkei de-Rabbi Eliezer* 22; *Zohar* 1:37a; *Zohar Hadash, Ruth* 81a; IFA 10856.

582. THE WATCHERS

There are those who say that Shemhazai and Azazel were not the only angels who descended to the face of the earth. Instead, Shemhazai was the leader of two hundred angels known as the Watchers, a high order of angels who never slept. After they descended to the summit of Mount Hermon, these angels swore an oath, binding themselves together. But when the angels fell from their holy estate, they were reduced in stature as well as in strength, and their fiery substance became flesh.

At first the fallen angels intended to instruct the people in the ways of righteousness. But when they saw the beautiful daughters of men, they lusted after them, and chose wives from among them. And the children born from this union were giants.

Each of the angels, not only Shemhazai and Azazel, revealed secrets of heaven, teaching charms and enchantments, incantations and the cutting of roots, astrology and the knowledge of signs. They taught men the art of working metal to make weapons, and they taught women how to make themselves desirable to men. So too did these angels sin with anyone they desired, men as well as women, beasts as well as humans, and they became corrupt in all ways. Before long, everything on earth became corrupted, and God ordered these fallen angels to be rooted out and bound in chains in the depths of the earth.

Then the four archangels, Michael, Gabriel, Uriel, and Raphael, went to God and recounted the sins of the fallen angels. And God said to Raphael: "Bind Azazel hand and foot, and cast him into a canyon in the desert Dudael, and cover him with darkness, and let him abide there. And on the day of Judgment he shall be cast into the fire."

And God said to Michael: "Bind Shemhazai and his associates. Bind them fast for seventy generations in the valleys of the earth, till the day of judgment. Then they will be led to the fiery abyss and tormented and imprisoned forever."

Still others say that Shemhazai and Azazel, alone among the angels, assumed human form when they descended to this world. As for the other fallen angels, they took the form of he-goats, serving as mounts for Shemhazai and Azazel. Later they were all cast into an abyss, where they still remain, imprisoned, until the end of time.

While most versions of this myth of the Sons of God focus on two angels who descended from heaven, the version in *The Book of Enoch* states that they descended with an order of angels.

The earliest embellishments of this biblical legend are found in *The Book of Jubilees* 5:1-13 and *1 Enoch* 6-14. *The Book of Jubilees* does not specify how many angels descended from heaven to earth. In *1 Enoch* it says that there were 200 angels, instead of only two, Shemhazai (also known as Aza) and Azazel. In *1 Enoch* Shemhazai is described as the overall leader, along with sixteen other leaders among the rebellious angels, including Azazel. In many ways, this legend of the fallen angels is the

Promethean myth in Judaism, in that the angels reveal not only dark secrets of heaven, but secrets of the natural universe, which God had never intended for humans to know.

As for the fate of the women who went astray with the fallen angels, *1 Enoch* 19:2 reports that they were transformed into sirens. This is a rare reference in a Jewish text to the sirens of Greek mythology. This is the interpretation of R. H. Charles in his translation of *1 Enoch*. Ephraim Isaac translates this passage in *The Old Testament Pseudepigrapha* as, "And the women whom the angels have led astray will be peaceful ones." Considering the context of retribution, the interpretation of R. H. Charles seems more plausible.

The time for this myth is said to be the days of Jared (*1 Enoch* 6:6). Jared was the father of Enoch, and the myth of the fallen angels is set in the generation before Enoch, but it is nevertheless an integral part of the myth of Enoch found in *1 Enoch*.

Sources:
The Book of Jubilees 4:15, 5:1-3, 5:5-7; *1 Enoch* 6:1-10:16, 14:9, 19:2; *Pirkei de-Rabbi Eliezer* 12.

583. THE GIANTS OF OLD

The Sons of God took wives for themselves, and the women gave birth to great giants, the giants of old. Their height was three thousand ells. The giants quickly devoured all of the resources of humans. And when people could no longer sustain them, the giants turned against them and devoured them. And they began to sin against birds and beasts and reptiles and fish, and to devour one another's flesh and drink the blood. Then the earth made accusation against the lawless ones.

The fallen angel Shemhazai fathered two sons, Hiwa and Hiya, who consumed a thousand oxen, a thousand camels, and a thousand horses daily. Before long the air was foul with the smell of carcasses. That is when God decided to cleanse the earth with the Flood.

Some say that these giants, produced by the spirit and the flesh, are the evil spirits who dwell on earth, who pursue us relentlessly till this day.

Still other describe the creation of the giants in this way: the angels transformed themselves, taking the shape of men, and appeared to the women while they were with their husbands. And the women did not think of their husbands, but lusted in their minds after the forms of the fallen angels, and as a result they gave birth to giants.

This myth elaborates on the origin of giants, called Nefilim, found in Genesis 6: *The Nefilim were in the earth in those days, and also after that, when the sons of God came in to the daughters of men, and they bore children to them; the same were the mighty that were of old, the men of renown* (Gen. 6:4). The Nefilim are generally understood to refer to the ancient giants. They are said to be the offspring of the Sons of God, who were understood to be fallen angels who came to earth and seduced the daughters of men. The giants were born out of this union. This myth also provides the origin of the giants thought to dwell in the Land of Israel (Num. 12:31-33).

While most accounts about the Nefilim attribute their birth to the mating of the Sons of God and the daughters of men, *Zohar* 1:37a attributes their birth to Samael having copulated with Eve, "injecting her with slime," after which "she bore Cain," whose features differed from other humans, and the Nefilim issued from the seed of Cain. See "How Cain Was Conceived," p. 447.

An interesting alternate myth is found in the *Testament of Reuben*, where these giants were said to be born not by human women having intercourse with angels, but out of their fantasies about the angels, when they appeared to the women as handsome men as they had sex with their husbands. This myth offers insight into rabbinic thinking, with the belief that fantasizing about someone else while having sex with one's spouse could have unexpected consequences. Here the fantasies are attributed to the women, but the rabbis, the creators of these myths, must have suspected this because of their own sexual fantasies. It was believed that every time a man had a sexual fantasy, he had intercourse with Lilith, and the results of this union were mutant demons, half human and half demon. See, for an example of a Hasidic fantasy, "The Woman in the Forest," p. 219. For more on demonic offspring, see "The Cellar," p. 220.

In this myth, the giants are conceived by the union of angels and human women, while in Greek myth the giants are said to have sprung from a union between Earth and Tartarus (Hades). See Graves, *The Greek Myths*, 4a.

Sources:
1 Enoch 7:1-6, 15:8-9; *Testament of Reuben* 5:6; Philo, *Quaestiones et Solutiones in Genesim* 1:92.

584. A LECHEROUS SPIRIT

King Solomon captured the demon Ornasis and made him reveal the names of all the other spirits and demons. One by one Solomon called them up and interrogated them. One of the spirits he invoked came forth in the shadowy form of a man with gleaming eyes. "Who are you?" King Solomon asked. The spirit replied, "I am a lecherous spirit of a giant who died in a massacre in the age of giants." Solomon said, "Where do you dwell?" The spirit replied, "I live in inaccessible places. I seat myself near the dead in their tombs and at midnight I assume the form of the dead. If I encounter anyone, I cause him to be possessed by a demon." And when he heard these things, King Solomon locked up that demon, just like all the other demons he had called forth.

> King Solomon questions a series of demons and spirits in *The Testament of Solomon*, which is a kind of demonic bestiary. One of the spirits who comes forth is this lecherous spirit who once was a giant in the time of giants alluded to in Genesis 6: *The Nefilim were in the earth in those days, and also after that, when the sons of God came in to the daughters of men, and they bore children to them; the same were the mighty men that were of old, the men of renown.* Here "*Nefilim*" are understood to be giants. See "The Giants of Old," p. 458. For other stories about giants, see "The Giant Og," p. 461. For the frame story in *The Testament of Solomon* about the capture of Ornasis, see "The Vampire Demon," p. 227.

Sources:
The Testament of Solomon 17.

585. THE LAIR OF AZAZEL

The generation of the Deluge learned the ways of evil from the fallen angel Azazel. He taught men how to make deadly weapons and women how to arouse the desires of men. They followed his teachings until the whole earth became corrupt. Therefore, at the time of the Deluge, God commanded the angel Raphael to bind Azazel hand and foot and cast him into the darkness. Therefore Raphael made a hole in the desert Dudael, beyond the Mountains of Darkness, and cast Azazel there, chained upside down in the dark.

Even there, Azazel did not repent, but was consumed by thoughts of revenge. Using the power of dreams, he sought out an evil sorcerer, and commanded him to come to him. First this sorcerer had to find his way to the Mountains of Darkness. There he was met by a demon in the shape of a cat, with the head of a fiery serpent, and two tails. The magicians then took a bowl containing the ashes of a white cock, and cast the ashes at the catlike demon. Then the demon led him to the places where Azazel was chained. There he lit incense and stepped on the chain of Azazel three times. Then he closed his eyes, fell to his knees, and worshipped the fallen angel. That is when Azazel began to speak, revealing the darkest mysteries for fifty days. By then there was none among the living with a greater mastery of evil. Bowing farewell, the evil sorcerer was led out of the Mountains of Darkness by the catlike demon with the head of a fiery serpent. He, in turn, revealed the secret of where Azazel was hidden to other sorcerers, who sought out the fallen angel, and were tutored by him in the ways of evil. Thus did the black arts make their way into the world.

The myth of the Sons of God and the daughters of men also provides one more useful identification—that of the mysterious identity of Azazel. In Leviticus 16:8, 10, and 16 there are references to sending a scapegoat to Azazel on Yom Kippur: *But the goat, on which the lot fell for Azazel, shall be set alive before Yahweh, to make expiation with it and to send it off to the wilderness for Azazel* (Lev. 16:10). This Azazel is usually identified as another name for Satan. Even today, Israelis tell someone to "Go to Hell!" by saying "*Lekh le-Azazel!*" Thus the myth of the descent of the two angels provides an explanation as to the identity and punishment of Azazel, the angel who refused to repent and thus was chained upside down in a canyon, where he continued to plot evil deeds.

Nachmanides, in his commentary on Leviticus 16:8, writes that the scapegoat is sent to "the prince who rules over places of destruction," a demon or a fallen angel known as Azazel, also known as Samael. This suggests that the goat is not sacrificed to God, but to some other divine entity named Azazel. The purpose of sending the scapegoat is to bribe Satan, the Accuser, the prosecutor of the Jewish people, to be silent on Yom Kippur, through this gift of the people's sins in the persona of the goat. The problem, of course, is that the offering of the scapegoat to Azazel could be construed as an idolatrous act. Nachmanides solves this problem by asserting that the scapegoat is not given to Azazel by the Jewish people, but by God, as a reward for his cessation of his activity as Accuser on the Day of Atonement. Hyam Maccoby considers the gift to Azazel of the scapegoat a remnant of paganism, i.e., the worship of the god of the desert.

While *1 Enoch* singles out Azazel for punishment in the desert Dudael, the version of this legend found in *Emek ha-Melekh* identifies both Aza (Shemhazai) and Azazel as being chained together there. This contradicts most versions of the legend, in which Shemhazai repents, and hangs himself (or is hung by God) upside down between heaven and earth, while it is Azazel alone who remains unrepentant, and takes on a role quite similar to that of Satan. Here the myths of Satan, Lucifer, Azazel, and Samael all converge in the story of a heavenly outcast who comes to rule the underworld.

Some sources, such as *Zohar* 2:157b, interpret the references to "Azazel" in Leviticus as referring to a mountain called Azazel, not a fallen angel. This mountain was said to be a great and mighty one, and below it are unimaginable depths, where no one has ever gone. There the Other Side has unshackled power. It is clear that the offering of the scapegoat in this ritual is the remnant of some kind of sacrifice to an evil god in order to placate it.

All in all, the myth of the Sons of God and daughters of men is quite useful in the way it provides midrashic explanations for many problems: the identity of the Sons of God in Genesis 6; the reason for the corruption of the generation of the Flood; the origin of giants; an astrological explanation for the star that Istahar became and the constellation of Orion, linked to Shemhazai when he hung himself upside down; as well as the identity of Azazel. The original biblical myth only provided a few of these explanations, but the rabbinic embellishments added many others, as well as some memorable stories about lustful angels and the brave virgin Istahar—whose Babylonian prototype was not exactly noted for her chastity.

Sources:
1 Enoch 8-10; *Emek ha-Melekh* 108b.

Studies:
Ritual and Morality: The Ritual Purity System and Its Place in Judaism by Hyam
    Maccoby.
"Azazel in Early Jewish Tradition" by Robert Helm.

586. THE GIANT OG

When all of the animals had boarded the ark, the giant Og, King of Bashan, swore to Noah and his sons that if they would take him with them on the ark, he would be their servant forever. What did Noah do? He let the giant sit on the roof of the ark, and bored a hole in the roof, and passed the giant his daily food through it. That is how Og, alone among the giants, escaped from the Flood by riding on top of the ark, as it is said, *Only King Og of was left of the remaining Refaim* (Deut. 3:11).

Later, as King of Bashan, Og became an enemy of Israel. He is said to have uprooted a mountain and held it over the heads of the Israelites. The mountain was large enough to kill all of them at once. But God sent a swarm of rock-eating ants against him, who bored through the mountain, so that it fell from his hands and slipped over his neck. Because his teeth jutted out, he could not remove it. Then Moses, who was ten feet tall, jumped another ten feet into the air and struck Og on the ankle with a hammer (others say with a lance or a nail) and knocked him down. And because of the weight of the mountain he could not rise again and perished. As for the mountain, when Og fell down dead the mountain fell off his shoulders, and it was about to fall upon Israel. But Moses prayed to God, and some say he took a small tree and placed it under the mountain and prevented it from falling upon the people, while others say that thanks to God the mountain was suspended between heaven and earth.

It is said that Og's skeleton was found by Abba Shaul. Abba Shaul, who buried the dead, once saw a deer and chased after it. The deer entered a hole in the ground and he followed it down the hole. The hole led into the thigh bone of a skeleton. He chased the deer for three miles inside the thigh bone, and it still didn't come to an end. So he gave up and turned back. Later, he learned that was the skeleton of Og, King of Bashan.

But some say that Og managed to survive, and in his wanderings he came to Poland in the winter. Not used to such cold weather, Og looked for a tailor, and when he found one, he demanded that the tailor make him a coat to keep him warm. He asked the terrified tailor how long it would take to make the coat, and the tailor, seeing the size of the giant, said it would take about a week. Og got angry and said that if the coat wasn't ready in a week, he would trample the town to dust. The frightened tailor gathered all the people of the town together and told them of the giant's demand. So the inhabitants scurried off to neighboring towns and brought back every tailor they could find. An army of tailors then set to work on the giant coat, finishing just in time. Suddenly they heard the giant approach. With nowhere else to hide, they jumped inside the pockets of the coat. Og picked up the coat, put it on, and placed his hands into the pockets to warm them, squeezing all the tailors together. Then, warm for the first time since coming to Poland, Og lay down to sleep and the terrified tailors escaped. But thereafter every one of them had a pale face. And that is why tailors have pale faces. As for Og, some say he is still wandering the earth.

> The origin of giants is recounted in Genesis 6:4: *It was then, and later too, that the Nefilim appeared on earth.* The *Nefilim* are understood to be giants who were the offspring of the mating of the Sons of God and the daughters of men recounted in Genesis 6.
>
> The story about the giant Og and Noah's ark serves to explain how giants were able to survive the Flood. It is also one of several tales about the giant Og, who was slain by Moses. Og is also identified as the King of Bashan who was the last of the remaining *Refaim*, understood to mean "giants," as stated in Deuteronomy 3:11.
>
> Most of the tales about Og portray him as an enemy of Israel, but in this childlike story about Og and the ark, Og is a friendly if demanding giant. In other accounts Og

holds a mountain over Israel, threatening to crush them. He even engages in combat with Moses. According to one of these accounts, in *Bereshit Rabbah* 42:8, it was Og who told Abraham that his nephew Lot had been captured (see Genesis 14:13), in hope that Abraham would be slain when he went off to fight the kings who had captured Lot, for Og hoped to marry Sarah. See the commentary on "God Offers the Torah to Israel," p. 264 for more about Og's role as an enemy of Israel.

The combat between Moses and Og recalls that between David and Goliath. David defeats Goliath with a sling, a child's weapon. In the case of Og, the giant is defeated by the smallest of opponents, the ants, who burrow through the mountain he intends to use to crush Israel, causing it to collapse on him. Moses then completes the conquest by leaping up and striking a blow to Og's ankle, killing him. The moral of this story, like that of David and Goliath, seems clear: little Israel, a tiny nation, is able to defeat much greater adversaries. This is possible because of God's support, and because of the bravery and unity the people show in the face of adversity. This moral is emphasized by the ants, tiny creatures who, by working together, defeat a giant.

Sources:

Targum Pseudo-Yonathan on Genesis 14:13; *B. Berakhot* 54b; *B. Niddah* 24b; *Pirkei de-Rabbi Eliezer* 23; *Deuteronomy Rabbah* 1; *Midrash Aggadah, Hukot; Midrash Tehillim* 136; IFA 7249.

587. NOAH AND THE RAVEN

The first bird that Noah called upon to go forth from the ark and search for land was the raven, as it is said, *Noah opened the window of the ark that he had made and sent out the raven; it went to and fro until the waters had dried up from the earth* (Gen. 8:6-7).

But was the raven willing to go? Some say that when Noah called upon the raven to go forth from the ark, the raven was incensed. It began to argue with Noah, saying, "Of all the birds in the ark, why do you pick on me? Your Master hates me since He commanded you to bring seven pairs of the clean creatures into the ark, but only one pair of the unclean, like me. You hate me because you could have chosen any one of the species of which there are seven pairs, but instead you chose me. What if the Angel of Heat or the Angel of Cold should smite me, wouldn't the world be short one kind? So why is it that you chose me? Or do you desire my mate?"

Others say that when Noah sent forth the raven to determine the state of the world, it *went forth to and fro* (Gen. 8:7) until it found a carcass of a man upon the summit of a mountain. It settled there and did not return to the ark. That is when Noah called upon the dove, and sent it forth.

> One of the requirements that God gives to Noah concerns the beasts he is to bring into the ark: *Of every clean beast you shall take seven and seven, each with his mate; and of the unclean beasts, two and two, each with his mate* (Gen. 7:2). This passage seems to allude to the system of Kosher laws, based on Leviticus 11:47.
>
> In one version, given here, the raven demonstrates great anger at Noah's order that it go forth to see if the waters of the Flood have receded. It even accuses Noah of desiring its mate. In another version, the raven goes forth, and the first thing it finds to feast on is the corpse of a man. In both versions the raven is portrayed as evil, while the dove is portrayed as good. Thus the kind of good and evil polar figures that are found among humans, such as Esau and Jacob or Lilith and Eve, are here mirrored in the rabbinic interpretations of the account of the raven in the story of the Flood.
>
> There are many fables in rabbinic literature and in later Jewish folklore. These fables include many speaking animals, but rarely do they speak, as in this midrash about

Noah, with a human being. There are also many other Jewish fables about the raven. The twelfth century fabulist Berekhiah ha-Nakdan includes in his *Mishle Shualim le-Rabbi Berekhiah ha-Nakdan* several fables about ravens. See *Fables of a Jewish Aesop*, translated by Moses Hadas.

This midrash can be seen to have an environmental perspective, as the raven argues that since there are only he and his mate, should he die, one species might be lost. Even though the argument comes from the raven, the question is resonant enough to reflect a real concern of the rabbis for preserving the natural environment.

Bernard Malamud's short story, "The Jewbird," portrays a talking bird much in the caustic spirit of the raven in these rabbinic texts. See Malamud's *The Complete Stories*, pp. 322-330.

Sources:
B. *Sanhedrin* 95a, 108b; *Genesis Rabbah* 33:5; *Pirkei de-Rabbi Eliezer* 32.

Studies:
Interpretations of the Flood edited by Florentino García Martínez and Gerard P. Luttikhuizen.

588. THE FIERY DELUGE

Strange as it may seem, the generation of the Flood was punished by fire, not by water. For every single drop of rain that God brought down on them had first been boiled in the fires of Gehenna. Thus it was not the Deluge that took their lives, but the fact that the water was boiling. Why such a terrible punishment? Led astray by the angels known as the Sons of God who had descended to earth and corrupted them, the generation of the Flood sinned with hot passion, and therefore were punished with boiling water.

It is said that boiling water descended from above, while cold water rushed from below, washing away those who were rebellious and causing them to perish.

> Viewing the generation of the Flood as evil, this midrash transforms the flood from one of rain to one of fire, the fire of Gehenna. Thus, for their sins, the fires of hell were rained upon them. Likewise, the inhabitants of Sodom and Gomorrah, another evil generation, were exterminated by fire that rained down on them from on high. The image of fire raining down from heaven is found in Genesis 19:24.

Sources:
B. *Zevahim* 113b; *Leviticus Rabbah* 7:6; Strophe to a lost composition by Simeon bar Megas, from *The Pizmonim of the Anonymous*, p. 73.

589. THE TOWER OF BABEL

Everyone on earth had the same language and the same words. And as they migrated from the east, they came upon a valley in the land of Shinar and settled there. They said to one another, "Come, let us make bricks and burn them hard." Brick served them as stone, and bitumen served them as mortar. And they said, "Come, let us build us a city, and a tower with its top in the sky, to make a name for ourselves; else we shall be scattered all over the world." The Lord came down to look at the city and tower that man had built, and the Lord said, "If, as one people with one language for all, this is how they have begun to act, then nothing that they may propose to do will be out of their reach. Let us, then, go down and confound their speech there, so that they shall not understand one another's speech." Thus the Lord scattered them from there over the face of the whole earth; and they stopped building the city. That is why it was called Babel, because there the Lord confounded the speech of the whole earth; and from there the Lord scattered them over the face of the whole earth.

This is an origin myth that both explains the origin of many languages and the wide dissemination of people around the world. The mystery about this myth is why God feels so threatened by the attempts of the people to build a tower into heaven. After all, it is a peaceful endeavor and requires cooperation. The stated purpose of the people is simply to make a name for themselves. But God clearly feels that their true intention is to overthrow heaven and so descends to confuse their languages and scatter them abroad. Rabbinic commentaries on the Tower of Babel emphasize the malignant intention of the builders. See "Building the Tower," which follows.

Archaeologists have identified the Tower of Babel with the ziggurat structures built in Mesopotamia, which resembled high towers to heaven. This seems like the likely source of the myth.

Sources:
Genesis 11:1-9.

Studies:
"Eridu, Dunnu, and Babel: A Study in Comparative Mythology" by Patrick D. Miller, Jr.

590. BUILDING THE TOWER

The builders of the Tower of Babel spoke a universal language, as it is said, *Everyone on earth had the same language and the same words* (Gen. 11:1). With this miraculous language anything could be accomplished. Some say they had but to speak, and instantly their work was done. This universal language was lost when God scattered the builders and confused their tongues, but this same language will be spoken in the future, in the messianic era.

Others say everything went well for these builders, and their work prospered in their hands. A man who came to lay one stone found that he had laid two, and one who came to plaster two rows found that he had plastered four.

Why did they build the tower? Some say they believed that the firmament was in danger of tottering, and the tower they built was to be one of four pillars to support the heavens. That was the eastern pillar, and others were to be built in the north, in the south, and in the west.

Others say that they built the tower out of fear of another Flood. They hoped to avoid the waters of the Flood by inhabiting the heights of the tower, and they took axes with them to cleave the heavens, so that all the waters stored there would run out before God could cause them to flood.

Still others say that they intended to overthrow heaven, to prevent God from bringing another Flood on the world. They argued that God had no right to choose the celestial spheres for Himself and assign the terrestrial world to them. They set an idol at the top of the tower, with a sword in its hand, as a sign that they intended to wage war against the King of heaven, and to dwell there in His place. So too did they shoot arrows into heaven, which fell back dripping blood, which convinced them that the defeat of heaven was close at hand.

The builders of the tower were split up into three groups. Those who intended to live peacefully were scattered over the face of the earth. Those who intended to wage war against heaven were turned into evil spirits, demons, wraiths, and *liliyot* (female demons of the night). And those who intended to worship idols had their languages confounded, and could no longer communicate with each other.

As for the fate of the tower, one third was consumed by fire, one third sank into the earth, and the remaining third still stands as a warning against challenging heaven. Even this third is so tall that from the top palm trees resemble locusts. Nor did the tower ever lose its power over mankind. Whoever passes there forgets all that he knows.

The ancient rabbis felt a strong need to justify God's decision to confuse the language of the builders of the Tower of Babel and scatter them throughout the world. Although the biblical account does not contain any direct references to the people desiring to overthrow heaven, this is the interpretation found in the midrashic texts. Here their plans and actions are presented in vivid terms, with arrows being shot into heaven and falling back dripping blood—as God deceived them into believing that they were going to defeat heaven and take it over. With these kinds of details, the subsequent punishment does not seem excessive, but rather merciful. Here, too, a portion of the tower remains to remind the people of the hubris of the builders of the tower.

Sources:
B. Sanhedrin 109a; *Pirkei de-Rabbi Eliezer* 24; *Sefer ha-Yashar* 22-31; *Midrash Tanhuma, Noah* 18-19; *Midrash ha-Gadol, Bereshit* 188; *Sihot Shedim* in *Sifrei Rabbi Tzaddok ha-Kohen.*

591. THE DESTRUCTION OF SODOM AND GOMORRAH

The two angels arrived in Sodom in the evening, as Lot was sitting in the gate of Sodom. When Lot saw them, he rose to greet them and, bowing low with his face to the ground, he said, "Please, my lords, turn aside to your servant's house to spend the night, and bathe your feet; then you may be on your way early." But they said, "No, we will spend the night in the square." But he urged them strongly, so they turned his way and entered his house. He prepared a feast for them and baked unleavened bread, and they ate.

They had not yet lain down, when the townspeople, the men of Sodom, young and old—all the people to the last man—gathered about the house. And they shouted to Lot and said to him, "Where are the men who came to you tonight? Bring them out to us, that we may be intimate with them." So Lot went out to them to the entrance, shut the door behind him, and said, "I beg you, my friends, do not commit such a wrong. Look, I have two daughters who have not known a man. Let me bring them out to you, and you may do to them as you please; but do not do anything to these men, since they have come under the shelter of my roof." But they said, "Stand back! The fellow," they said, "came here as an alien, and already he acts the ruler! Now we will deal worse with you than with them." And they pressed hard against the person of Lot, and moved forward to break the door. But the men stretched out their hands and pulled Lot into the house with them, and shut the door. And the people who were at the entrance of the house, young and old, they struck with blinding light, so that they were helpless to find the entrance.

Then the men said to Lot, "Whom else have you here? Sons-in-law, your sons and daughters, or anyone else that you have in the city—bring them out of the place. For we are about to destroy this place; because the outcry against them before the Lord has become so great that the Lord has sent us to destroy it." So Lot went out and spoke to his sons-in-law, who had married his daughters, and said, "Up, get out of this place, for the Lord is about to destroy the city." But he seemed to his sons-in-law as one who jests.

As dawn broke, the angels urged Lot on, saying, "Up, take your wife and your two remaining daughters, lest you be swept away because of the iniquity of the city." Still he delayed. So the men seized his hand, and the hands of his wife and his two daughters—in the Lord 's mercy on him—and brought him out and left him outside the city. When they had brought them outside, one said, "Flee for your life! Do not look behind you, nor stop anywhere in the Plain; flee to the hills, lest you be swept away." But Lot said to them, "Oh no, my lord! You have been so gracious to your servant, and have already shown me so much kindness in order to save my life; but I cannot flee to the hills, lest the disaster overtake me and I die. Look, that town there is near enough to flee to; it is such a little place! Let me flee there—it is such a little place—and let my life be saved." He replied, "Very well, I will grant you this favor too, and I will not annihilate the town of which you have spoken. Hurry, flee there, for I cannot do anything until you arrive there." Hence the town came to be called Zoar.

As the sun rose upon the earth and Lot entered Zoar, the Lord rained upon Sodom and Gomorrah sulfurous fire from the Lord out of heaven. He annihilated those cities and the entire Plain, and all the inhabitants of the cities and the vegetation of the ground. Lot's wife looked back, and she thereupon turned into a pillar of salt.

Next morning, Abraham hurried to the place where he had stood before the Lord, and, looking down toward Sodom and Gomorrah and all the land of the Plain, he saw the smoke of the land rising like the smoke of a kiln.

> Despite Abraham's efforts to convince God to spare Sodom in Genesis 18:17-33, it was destroyed along with the city of Gomorrah. Lot's wife, who is given the name Edith in the Midrash, was turned into a pillar of salt when she disobeyed the command of the angels not to look back. The account in Genesis makes it clear that the inhabitants of these cities were sinners, and the midrashim about this episode go even further. After all, this is a city where Lot offers his virgin daughters to a mob as a means of protecting his guests. This is a perverted kind of hospitality, the opposite of the kind of hospitality Abraham demonstrated in Genesis 18 when he welcomed the same angels to his tent.
>
> The destruction of Sodom and Gemorah is parallel to the destruction wrought by the Flood, though on a smaller scale. Like the Flood, it stands as an example of God's anger when provoked by sin on a large scale. Later rabbinic tradition described God as having two thrones, a Throne of Justice and a Throne of Mercy. It was when He was seated on the Throne of Justice that God demonstrated harsh justice, as shown here.
>
> *Sources:*
> Genesis 19:1-28.

592. THE BANISHED ANGELS

Angels must have God's permission to reveal any of the secrets of heaven. But the two angels who went to Sodom, to the home of Lot and his wife, revealed a secret of the Lord. And because they revealed this secret, they were banished from heaven. What secret did they reveal? God's intention of destroying Sodom, as it is said, *for Yahweh is about to destroy the city* (Gen. 19:14). They wandered in exile for one hundred and thirty-eight years. Their banishment only came to an end on the night that Jacob dreamed of the ladder that reached from earth to heaven. For they were among the angels who ascended on that ladder as Jacob dreamed about it, as it is said, *and angels of God ascending and descending on it* (Gen. 28:12).

> Here the angels who reveal God's intention to destroy Sodom to Lot are said to have been punished by being exiled from heaven for 138 years. This myth is parallel to that of the rabbinic myths about two angels, Shemhazai and Azazel, the Sons of God of Genesis 6, who were said to have descended to earth and revealed a great many secrets of heaven. They too were punished for their sins. This myth, found in *Targum Pseudo-Yonathan*, explains that the punishment of the two angels came to an end when Jacob had his dream of the ladder reaching to heaven, and that they were among the angels ascending on it. This one myth, then, looks back at one biblical episode, that of the Sons of God and the daughters of men, and forward, to Jacob's dream. This linking of biblical episodes is one of the primary functions of this kind of exegesis.
>
> *Sources:*
> *Targum Pseudo-Yonathan* on Genesis 28:12; *Genesis Rabbah* 50:9, 68:12.

593. THE PILLAR OF SALT

The angels told Lot and his family not to look back when they left Sodom. When Lot's wife disobeyed and looked back, she was turned into a pillar of salt, as it is said, *Lot's wife looked back, and she thereupon turned into a pillar of salt* (Gen. 19:26). But why did she look back? And why was she turned into a pillar of salt?

Some say that Lot's wife, whose name was Edith, looked behind her to see if her daughters, who were married to men Sodom, were coming after her or not. So too did she want to know what would be the end of her father's house. Instead, she saw God, who had descended in order to rain brimstone and fire upon Sodom and Gomorrah. And that is why she was turned into a pillar of salt.

Others say that because she sinned with salt, Lot's wife was punished with salt. On the night that the angels visited Lot, Lot prepared a feast for them, as he had learned hospitality from Abraham, and he asked his wife to give them a little salt. She grew angry and said, "Do you want to introduce that evil practice of giving strangers salt?" Then she went to all of her neighbors asking for salt. In this way she alerted them to the presence of the guests, and precipitated the mob who demanded that Lot turn the angels over to them. Thus, because she sinned with salt, she was punished with salt.

As for the pillar of salt, it still can be seen to this day. All day oxen lick it and it decreases until nothing remains but her feet. But in the morning the pillar of salt grows afresh. Those who see it are required to say the benediction to be pronounced on seeing Lot's wife, "Blessed be He who wrought miracles for our ancestors in this place."

> The transformation of Lot's wife into a pillar of salt is one of the most striking images in the Bible. There still exists a pillar of salt near the Dead Sea that is identified as Lot's wife. In the Mishnah this is said to be one of the places where a blessing should be said. Other places listed in the Talmud (*B. Ber.* 54a) include the place of the crossing of the Red Sea and the wall of Jericho that sank into the ground.
>
> Why was Lot's wife transformed into a pillar of salt? Of course, she did disobey the angel's command not to look back, but the real reason for her punishment seems to be because in doing so she saw God, who had descended to destroy the city.
>
> *Sources:*
> *Targum Pseudo-Yonathan* on Genesis 19:26; *B. Berakhot* 54a; *Genesis Rabbah* 50:4, 51:5; *Pirkei de-Rabbi Eliezer* 25; Philo, *De Abrahamo* 27; Josephus, *Jewish Antiquities* 1:114.

594. THE GOLDEN CALF

When the people saw that Moses was so long in coming down from the mountain, the people gathered against Aaron and said to him, "Come, make us a god who shall go before us, for that man Moses, who brought us from the land of Egypt—we do not know what has happened to him." Aaron said to them, "Take off the gold rings that are on the ears of your wives, your sons, and your daughters, and bring them to me." And all the people took off the gold rings that were in their ears and brought them to Aaron. Then he took from them and cast in a mold, and made it into a molten calf. And they exclaimed, "This is your god, O Israel, who brought you out of the land of Egypt!" When Aaron saw this, he built an altar before it; and Aaron announced: "Tomorrow shall be a festival of the Lord!" Early next day, the people offered up burnt offerings and brought sacrifices of well-being; they sat down to eat and drink, and then rose to dance.

The Lord spoke to Moses, "Hurry down, for your people, whom you brought out of the land of Egypt, have acted basely. They have been quick to turn aside from the way that I enjoined upon them. They have made themselves a molten calf and bowed low to it and sacrificed to it, saying: 'This is your god, O Israel, who brought you out of the land of Egypt!'"

The Lord further said to Moses, "I see that this is a stiff-necked people. Now, let Me be, that My anger may blaze forth against them and that I may destroy them, and make of you a great nation." But Moses implored the Lord his God, saying, "Let not Your anger, O Lord, blaze forth against Your people, whom You delivered from the land of Egypt with great power and with a mighty hand. Let not the Egyptians say, 'It was with evil intent that He delivered them, only to kill them off in the mountains and annihilate them from the face of the earth.' Turn from Your blazing anger, and renounce the plan to punish Your people. Remember Your servants, Abraham, Isaac, and Jacob, how You swore to them by Your Self and said to them: "I will make your offspring as numerous as the stars of heaven, and I will give to your offspring this whole land of which I spoke, to possess forever." And the Lord renounced the punishment He had planned to bring upon His people.

Thereupon Moses turned and went down from the mountain bearing the two tablets of the Pact, tablets inscribed on both their surfaces: they were inscribed on the one side and on the other. The tablets were God's work, and the writing was God's writing, inscribed upon the tablets. When Joshua heard the sound of the people in its boisterousness, he said to Moses, "There is a cry of war in the camp." But he answered, "It is not the sound of the tune of triumph, or the sound of the tune of defeat; it is the sound of song that I hear!"

As soon as Moses came near the camp and saw the calf and the dancing, he became enraged; and he hurled the tablets from his hands and shattered them at the foot of the mountain. He took the calf that they had made and burned it; he ground it to powder and strewed it upon the water and so made the Israelites drink it.

Moses said to Aaron, "What did this people do to you that you have brought such great sin upon them?" Aaron said, "Let not my lord be enraged. You know that this people is bent on evil. They said to me, 'Make us a god to lead us; for that man Moses, who brought us from the land of Egypt—we do not know what has happened to him.' So I said to them, 'Whoever has gold, take it off!' They gave it to me and I hurled it into the fire and out came this calf!"

Moses saw that the people were out of control—since Aaron had let them get out of control—so that they were a menace to any who might oppose them. Moses stood up in the gate of the camp and said, "Whoever is for the Lord, come here!" And all the Levites rallied to him. He said to them, "Thus says the Lord, the God of Israel: 'Each of you put sword on thigh, go back and forth from gate to gate throughout the camp, and slay brother, neighbor, and kin.'" The Levites did as Moses had bidden; and some three thousand of the people fell that day. And Moses said, "Dedicate yourselves to the Lord this day—for each of you has been against son and brother—that He may bestow a blessing upon you today."

The next day Moses said to the people, "You have been guilty of a great sin. Yet I will now go up to the Lord; perhaps I may win forgiveness for your sin." Moses went back to the Lord and said, "Alas, this people is guilty of a great sin in making for themselves a god of gold. Now, if You will forgive their sin well and good; but if not, erase me from the record that You have written!" But the Lord said to Moses, "He who has sinned against Me, him only will I erase from My record. Go now, lead the people where I told you. See, My angel shall go before you. But when I make an accounting, I will bring them to account for their sins."

Then the Lord sent a plague upon the people, for what they did with the calf that Aaron made.

The faith of the Israelites was constantly being tested by difficult conditions and the people continually failed the tests. Here they revert to pagan worship, forcing Aaron to build a golden calf they can worship. Such idols were often worshipped in the ancient Near East. As a result, both God and Moses punish the people. This famous myth emphasizes how difficult it was for the people to abandon paganism for monotheism, and how they were tempted to revert to paganism at the very time that God was dictating the Torah to Moses on Mount Sinai.

Sources:
Exodus 32

Studies:
"The Golden Calf" by Lloyd R. Bailey.
"The Worship of the Golden Calf: A Literary Analysis of a Fable on Idolatry" by
    Herbert Chanan Brichto.

595. STRANGE FIRE

Whenever Aaron officiated at a sacrifice, the fire of the Lord would descend to consume the burnt offering, and the Glory of the Lord appeared to all the people. When the people saw this, they fell upon their faces and sang a song of praise.

But Nadab and Abihu, the sons of Aaron, said to each other, "When our father and uncle Moses die, we shall be the chiefs of the people." After that *Aaron's sons Nadab and Abihu each took his fire pan, put fire in it, and laid incense on it; and they offered before Yahweh alien fire, which He had not enjoined upon them. And fire came forth from Yahweh and consumed them; thus they died before Yahweh* (Lev. 10:1-2). Thus their souls were burnt and they paid the price for their disrespect of God.

It is said that as long as Israel is in exile, and cannot sacrifice two goats on Yom Kippur, the two sons of Aaron may be a memorial of the sacrifice, and Israel may be atoned through them.

Nadab and Abihu, the sons of Aaron, were, like their father, priests. They had been anointed and were allowed to perform service in the Tabernacle. Their mysterious deaths occurred when they introduced "strange fire" into the Tabernacle. This incident is referred to twice, in Leviticus 10:1 and Numbers 3:4, the former explaining that they had lit incense and performed a service that they had not been commanded to perform. Since they entered the Tent of Meeting for an improper purpose, they were punished with death. The deaths are said to have been by a fire that came forth from heaven, the same fire referred to in Leviticus 9:24 that consumed the burnt offering.

There are several explanations given for their deaths. In *Exodus Rabbah* it is said that they behaved in a brazen manner, uncovering their heads and eating and drinking in the presence of God, as it is said, *They beheld God and ate and drank* (Exod. 24:11). This is contrasted with the respectful behavior of Moses at the burning bush, when *Moses hid his face, for he was afraid to look at God* (Exod. 3:6). *Leviticus Rabbah* 12:1 suggests that they might have been drunk. *Leviticus Rabbah* 20:10 suggests that Nadab and Abihu were impatient to replace Moses and Aaron, and wished them an early death. God, in turn, brought Nadab and Abihu an early death. Still other reasons are given in *Leviticus Rabbah* 20:8-10—some say they penetrated to the inmost portion of the sanctuary, or that they brought an offering they were not commanded to bring, or entered the sanctuary without washing their hands and feet, or they did not wear the required number of garments, or they brought alien fire, that is, not from the sacrificial altar. The most serious accusation is that they "fed their eyes on the *Shekhinah*." This implies that they did not take their great responsibility seriously or show the proper respect before God. Thus the tale of Nadab and Abihu became a warning tale about the great care that the priest must take in preparing an offering to God.

Zohar 1:73a asserts that Aaron's sons drank wine in the Holy of Holies, the same wine that intoxicated Noah. One commentary on the *Zohar, Ziv ha-Zohar,* identifies this destructive wine with secular knowledge.

The linkage between the deaths of Aaron's sons and the biblical ritual of sacrificing the two goats on Yom Kippur grows out of the fact that the chapter beginning *Yahweh spoke to Moses after the death of the two sons of Aaron* (Lev. 16:1) prescribes the Yom Kippur ritual. For a description of the ritual of sacrificing the goats, see "A Scapegoat for Azazel," p. 295.

Sources:
B. *Sanhedrin* 52; *Exodus Rabbah* 45:5; *Zohar* 1:73a, 3:56b.

596. THE SPIRIT OF IDOLATRY

When the Israelites returned from the Babylonian exile, they found the Temple in Jerusalem destroyed *and cried in a loud voice to Yahweh their God* (Neh. 9:4). They said: "Woe, woe, it is the evil spirit of idolatry that has destroyed the Sanctuary, burnt the Temple, killed all the righteous, and driven Israel into exile. And behold, he is still dancing among us." And they prayed to the Lord: "You, who brought this evil spirit into being so that we could receive a reward through resisting him—we want neither him, nor the reward!" Thereupon a tablet fell from heaven among them, on which the word "Truth" (*emet*) was inscribed.

After this miracle had taken place, the people fasted for three days and nights, and at the end of that time the spirit of idolatry was delivered into their hands, and he came forth out of the Holy of Holies in the form of a fiery lion. But they approached him and plucked out one of his hairs, causing the lion to raise his voice and roar so loudly it could be heard for four hundred parasangs. And when the people heard this, they said among themselves: "Let us hope that heaven does not have mercy upon him." Then they cast the lion into a huge leaden pot, and sealed its only opening with lead, because lead absorbs sound.

They imprisoned the evil spirit for three days, then they discovered that there was not a fresh egg in all of the land. From this they realized that if they killed him, the whole world would end. So they blinded him and let him go.

Here a paradox about the nature of sexuality and creation is presented, since this myth clearly indicates that they both spring from evil. The spirit that is captured in this talmudic tale is the incarnation of the *Yetzer ha-Ra,* the Evil Inclination. (There also is a Good Inclination, the *Yetzer ha-Tov.*) Rabbinic literature shows considerable ambiguity on this subject. While always urging that this impulse be resisted, the rabbis also recognized its essential role in the world, as this tale makes clear. Here the spirit of idolatry is overcome and captured. It is only then, however, that the people discover its role in the divine scheme—for without the Evil Impulse, *the Yetzer ha-Ra,* sexual desire in all creatures ceased, causing all procreation to stop. And not only fertility, but creativity was also lost. Had this continued, all animal life would have died out. In this way the rabbis acknowledge a necessary and perhaps even positive role for the Evil Inclination. Note the strongly mythical aspects of this tale, in which the Evil Impulse is personified as a fiery lion. It has strong echoes of the rabbinic legends about the golden calf, which was said to have come alive and charge around out of control (*Midrash Shir ha-Shirim* 13a-13b and *Pirkei de-Rabbi Eliezer* 45). The roaring of the lion in this tale is reminiscent of that in the well-known talmudic tale, "The Lion of the Forest Ilai." See "The Lion of the Forest Ilai," p. 149.

The blinding of the spirit of idolatry is intended to indicate that the Jews curbed the unbridled passion of the *Yetzer ha-Ra.* Since they could not destroy the impulse—all earthly propagation depended on it—they attempted to curb it instead.

Rabbi Nachman of Bratslav regarded the spirit of Idolatry as the evil angel who causes sexual lust. He identifies the blinding with the self-restraint of those who find it difficult to control their natural impulse to look at women.

A variant of this myth about the *Yetzer ha-Ra* is found in *B. Kiddushin* 81a. Here Rabbi Amram was exposed to a strong sexual temptation, which he resisted. Then he forced the Evil Inclination out of his body, and it shot out of his body in a flame.

Sources:
B. *Yoma* 69b.

597. THE FIERY SERPENTS

The Israelites set out from Mount Hor by way of the Red Sea to skirt the land of Edom. But the people grew restive on the journey, and the people spoke against God and against Moses, "Why did you make us leave Egypt to die in the wilderness? There is no bread and no water, and we have come to loathe this miserable food." The Lord sent fiery serpents against the people. They bit the people and many of the Israelites died. The people came to Moses and said, "We sinned by speaking against the Lord and against you. Intercede with the Lord to take away the serpents from us!" And Moses interceded for the people. Then the Lord said to Moses, "Make a fiery figure and mount it on a standard. And if anyone who is bitten looks at it, he shall recover." Moses made a copper serpent and mounted it on a standard; and when anyone was bitten by a serpent, he would look at the copper serpent and recover.

> Greatly frustrated with the constant complaints of the Israelites, God punishes them with "fiery serpents." Exactly what these serpents are is not explained, but their bite was often fatal, and the people begged Moses to protect them from them. Moses does so in a strange way—he sets up a copper serpent on a pole for the people to look at when they have been bitten. This seems to have every earmark of idol worship (cf. 2 Kings 18:4), yet Moses sets up the copper serpent at God's direction. *Numbers Rabbah* 19:22 suggests they were called fiery serpents because they burned the soul.
>
> According to the *Midrash Rabbenu Bahya*, the Torah commentary of Rabbi Bachya ben Asher on Numbers 21:6, the fiery serpents were offshoots of the primeval serpent in the Garden of Eden. He quotes *B. Bava Batra* 16a, which identifies the fiery serpents with the *Yetzer ha-Ra*, the evil inclination, stating that "the serpent, Satan, the *yetzer ha-ra*, and the Angel of Death are one and the same."
>
> *Sources:*
> Numbers 21:4-9.

598. THE DESERT SHUR

The children of Israel journeyed through the desert Shur, a wilderness full of serpents, lizards, and scorpions. So deadly are the serpents that dwell in this desert that if one of them merely glides over the shadow of a flying bird, the bird falls dead in that place.

> As terrible as was the desert wanderings of the Israelites, rabbinic myths make it even worse, presenting the desert Shur as the worst of the deserts the people crossed. It is supernaturally bad, as illustrated by what happens when a reptile glides over the shadow of a bird.
>
> *Sources:*
> *Exodus Rabbah* 24-25.

599. THE DEAD OF THE DESERT

A mysterious Bedouin led the sage Rabbah bar Bar Hannah to the bodies of those who died during the forty years of wandering in the desert. When they reached them, they found that all of them were lying on their backs and their bodies were intact. The knee of one of them was raised, and the Bedouin was able to pass under it, riding on a camel, holding his spear upright.

Rabbah cut off the blue thread from the corner of one of their prayer shawls. But as soon as he did, he found that he and the Bedouin were frozen in place. The Bedouin told him that if he had taken anything from them, to return it, for anyone who takes anything from them will not be able to move away. Rabbah put it back and they were able to move freely again.

> Here the wandering sage Rabbah bar Bar Hannah is led to the Dead of the Desert—those Israelites who died during the 40 years of wandering in the desert in the time of Moses. Rabbah finds they have been miraculously preserved, and that they are the size of giants, demonstrated when the Bedouin rides a camel under one of their upraised knees.
>
> These bodies lying in the desert are thus evidence of the truth of the Torah about the wandering of the Israelites in the desert. By implication, then, all of the Torah is true.
>
> Rabbi Samuel Eliezer Edels, known as the Maharsha, interpreted the giant size of the bodies to symbolize that they were spiritual giants. Rabbi Nachman of Bratslav, on the other hand, views these figures as wicked people, receiving their life-force from the *Sitra Ahra*, the Other Side, the side of evil. He concludes that they died in the desert because they did not tie themselves wholly to Moses.
>
> Rabbah cuts off the blue corner thread of the prayer shawl (*tallit*) of one of the dead of the desert because it has been dyed with the *tekhelet* dye, which is required by one of the 613 commandments (*mitzvot*) of the Torah, as stated in Numbers 15:38-39: *Speak to the Israelite people and instruct them to make themselves fringes on the corners of their garments throughout the ages; let them attach a cord of blue to the fringe at each corner. That shall be your fringe; look at it and recall all the commandments of Yahweh and observe them.* But Rabbah finds himself unable to move after this attempted theft, and he is not released until he returns what he has taken.
>
> Rabbah is so desperate to preserve this relic of the time of Moses because even in the time of Rabbah, around the end of the third century, no one knew how to produce this dye, nor exactly what color *tekhelet* was. For this reason the ancient rabbis decided not to dye the thread of the *tallit* that was supposed to be the color of *tekhelet*, but to leave it white. With a few exceptions of groups that claim to have discovered the secret of how to make *tekhelet*, the thread has been left white till this day. The reasoning is that rather than fulfill one of the commandments of the Torah incorrectly, it is better not to fulfill it at all.
>
> *Numbers Rabbah* 14:3 explains that God required the use of *tekhelet* because the blue of *tekhelet* resembles the sea, the sea resembles the sky, the sky resembles a rainbow, a rainbow resembles a cloud, a cloud resembles the heavenly throne, and the throne resembles the divine glory.
>
> For other examples of the tall tales of Rabbah bar Bar Hannah, see "The Punishment of Korah," p. 235, and "Where Heaven and Earth Meet," p. 194.
>
> *Sources:*
> B. *Bava Batra* 73b.

600. THE EXILE OF ISRAEL

From the first, God intended that there would be many exiles for the people of Israel, for reasons known only to Him.

Some say that the reason for all the exiles was to release the holy sparks. The Egyptian exile was the root of all exiles, and a multitude of holy sparks awaited redemption. Ever since, the people of Israel have sifted the holy sparks from the four corners of the earth.

Yet some say that that it was for Israel's good that God destroyed the Temple and drove the Jews into exile, for God will surely have mercy forever more and will rebuild the Temple with greater strength. Thus the exile is only an illusion, for God, to whom all mysteries are revealed, knows it is good for Israel. Everything that has happened during the long years of exile was in preparation for the redemption, and at the time of the liberation this will all be revealed.

> In God's scheme of things, everything has a purpose, even the many exiles to which the Jewish people have been subject. Here two important Hasidic rabbis, Elimelekh of Lizhensk and Levi Yitzhak of Berditchev, propose that the purpose of the exile was to prepare the people for redemption, and that God's plan would eventually be revealed. This myth acknowledges the confusion that often attended the setbacks and tragedies experienced by the chosen people, which were a great test of their faith. These two rabbis remind the people that God's true intentions are hard to discern, and that they must retain their faith through difficult trials, because these are merely preparation for the rewards to come in the messianic era.
>
> Note the primary role of the myth of the Ari of the Shattering of the Vessels and the Gathering of the Sparks in this myth. The Ari's myth turns the negative aspects of exile into positive one, making it possible for the Jewish people to travel far and wide gathering the holy sparks that were scattered everywhere. See "The Shattering of the Vessels and the Gathering of the Sparks," p. 122.
>
> *Sources:*
> *No'am Elimelekh, Likutei Shoshanah* 101; *Kedushat Levi ha-Shalem,* Lamentations, pp. 142-143.

601. THE SECRET OF THE EGYPTIAN EXILE

The Egyptian exile contains a great secret: God chose the seed of Abraham and placed them in exile in order to make it possible for them to receive the Torah. Had God increased them and made them prosperous without exile, and had they taken possession of the land without receiving the Torah, how could He have compelled them to go the desert to receive it? Thus the purpose of the Egyptian exile was to enable Israel to receive the Torah, and it is the cause of the great reward God has bestowed upon His people.

> This myth is an attempt to justify the difficult trials of the people of Israel during their Egyptian bondage. Here the years of slavery are viewed as a preparation for the receiving of the Torah, which, in Gikatilla's view, could not have taken place without the suffering that preceded it. Since the Torah was the greatest gift that God gave to the Jewish people, the years of Egyptian bondage must be viewed as a necessary step in order to be worth of receiving it.
>
> *Sources:*
> *Tzofnat Pa'ane'ah; Perush ha-Haggadah* p. 3; *Em ha-Banim S'mehah.*
>
> *Studies:*
> *Gates of Light/Sha'are Orah* by Joseph Gikatilla.

602. THE TEN LOST TRIBES

The Ten Lost Tribes were carried away as prisoners out of their own land, and they were sent into exile on the other side of the river Sambatyon, which can only be crossed on the Sabbath. But to cross it on that day would break the Sabbath, something the tribes would never do. There they are hidden from all other peoples. Some say they are covered by a cloud, which keeps them hidden, while others say it is the river itself that keeps them isolated, as well as the mountains of darkness. Thus they have been separated from their fellow Jews for centuries, without any communication between them.

How did the Ten Lost Tribes reach the other side of the Sambatyon? It is said that when *B'nei Moshe*, the Sons of Moses, were exiled to Babylon, they were told to play their harps for their conquerors. They refused, and a cloud settled about them, raised them with their families and all their belongings, and carried them off, setting them down during the night. In the morning they discovered that impassable river that surrounded them.

Now the Jews who lived on the other side of the river Sambatyon were exceptional in every way. All of them observed the Law with joy, and the level of wisdom of the average man was equal to that of the wisest sages among the Jews elsewhere. When the tribe of Issachar is hard pressed, for example, they ask counsel from heaven and this is how they are answered: The Prince of Issachor envelops himself in his prayer shawl and prays in a corner of the synagogue. The answer comes by fire from heaven descending upon the Prince of Issachar. This is seen by everyone, but the answer is heard by him alone.

As for the sages among the Jews of the Ten Lost Tribes, they were masters of kabbalah, familiar with the most obscure mysteries of the Torah, and there were ten who knew the pronounciation of God's secret Name, YHVH, the Tetragrammaton, while among the rest of the Jews there was never more than one such sage in each generation.

Some say that the exiles were divided into three. One-third was banished to the other side of the Sambatyon, one third was banished to the region further beyond the Sambatyon, and one-third was banished to Daphne near Riblah, where it was swallowed up.

When the time of redemption has arrived, the Messiah will seek out the lost tribes who were banished to the other side of the Sambatyon, and tell them to go forth. Some say that at that time the wild waters of the River Sambatyon will subside, and a pathway of sand will lie before them, as it did for the Israelites who crossed the Red Sea. Then the people will be able to cross over, and the Messiah will lead them to the Holy Land.

As for those swallowed up in Riblah, God will make underground passageways for them, and they will make their way underground through them, until they arrive at the Mount of Olives in Jerusalem.

Then God Himself will stand upon the mount, as it is said, *On that day, He will set His feet on the Mount of Olives* (Zech. 14:4). At that time God will see that the mount is split open, and the exiles will come out of it to be reunited with their long lost brethren, and to celebrate the arrival of the End of Days.

Nor will these three companies of exiles come alone. Wherever Jews are to be found, they will be gathered up and come to the holy city of Jerusalem. God will lower the mountains and make them into roads for them. So, too, will God raise up every deep place for them and make all the land level, so that their journey can be as easy as possible.

When all the exiles have arrived and been gathered together, God will call upon heaven and earth to rejoice with them, and the whole world will join in the celebration.

There are dozens of legends about the fate of the Ten Lost Tribes, and they are identified with a great many communities, including the American Indians (partly because
the Lost Tribes were sometimes described as red in the legends), the Japanese, and other
unlikely peoples. Ethiopian Jews identify themselves as members of the lost tribe of
Dan. Among those travelers who claimed to have discovered the Ten Lost Tribes is
Eldad ha-Dani, who claimed to belong to the tribe of Dan, and asserted that he had
found four of the lost tribes. According to him, the members of these tribes spoke only
Hebrew. So too was their Talmud written in Hebrew, instead of Aramaic. Nor, because
of their isolation, were any of these tribes able to communicate with the others.

The myth of the Ten Lost Tribes is vividly portrayed in an elaborate tale of the
rescue of a Jewish community by an emissary from the Ten Lost Tribes on the other
side of the river Sambatyon. The tale exists in many variants, ranging from a page or

two to novella length. The longest and most complete version is that published in Yiddish by Yitzhak Rivkind. Elements of several variants have been combined here. The hero in this tale is usually identified as Rabbi Meir Ba'al ha-Nes, although this attribution is purely legendary. The tale is closely associated with the *Akdamut Millin*, an Aramaic poem composed by Rabbi Meir ben Yitzhak Nehorai, which is recited in the synagogue on Shavuot. The origin of the poem is connected to the legend recounted in this tale. The Black Monk is a legendary figure who combines all of the elements of the anti-Semitic hostility that so plagued the Jews of Eastern Europe. His defeat at the hands of the old man from the other side of the river Sambatyon is similar to the tales told about Rabbi Adam, Rabbi Judah Loew, and the Ba'al Shem Tov, among others, who vanquished dangerous enemies of the Jews using supernatural powers based on kabbalistic incantations and holy names; i.e., powers deriving from God. The fact that the Jews in this tale had to turn to their brethren on the other side of the river Sambatyon indicates the desperation felt by Eastern European Jews in the face of the persecution they suffered, and their inability to find any other solution to the problem. At the same time, the tale is a reaffirmation of faith in God, and it is this aspect of it that is recalled in conjunction with the song of Akdamut. In fact, this story is generally known as *Ma'aseh Akdamut*, the tale of Akdamut. This story exists in many variants. See "The Black Monk and the Master of the Name" in *Miriam's Tambourine*, pp. 335-348.

An unusual myth about the Ten Lost Tribes, likely of Christian origin, concerns Alexander's gate. Alexander the Great is said to have confined the lost tribes within a range of mountains by building an enormous gate. In some versions all of the Ten Lost Tribes are to be found there, while in others only the tribe of Issachar dwells beyond the mountains. The gate was said to be made of metal and was impenetrable, but Alexander made it appear even more invulnerable by using certain invisible devices for defending it. Brambles were planted and were so well watered that they overgrew the mountain. In addition, according to this myth, Alexander had men of iron constructed who wielded hammers and axes without interruption, making the wall resound under their blows, so that the people living enclosed within the mountains might believe that the work of building and fortifying was ever in progress, and that it would be utterly futile for them to attempt to burst forth. Alexander also mounted upon the rampart a stone eagle which, whenever it was approached, uttered a screech that could be heard an eight days' journey in every direction, and whenever the people heard it, they prayed to God to protect them from the impending menace. Finally, Alexander erected trumpets which resounded with the wind, giving the impression that his armies were guarding the exits from the Caucasus in full force.

For a further discussion of the Ten Lost Tribes, see the Introduction, p. lx. See "The River Sambatyon," following.

Sources:
B. *Sanhedrin* 10:6; *Genesis Rabbah* 73:6; *Pesikta Rabbati* 31:10; Josephus, *Jewish Antiquities* 11:133; *Genesis Rabbah* 73:6; *Pesikta Rabbati* 31:10; *4 Ezra* 13:24-45; *Sefer ha-Zikhronot* 61; *Eldad ha-Dani*; *Haggadot Ketu'ot*; *Gelilot Eretz Yisrael*; *Hadre Teiman,* collected by Nissim Binyamin Gamlieli from Shlomo Ben Ya'akov of Yemen; IFA 310, 462, 11774; Paris Hebrew manuscript 157 number 7, translated from the Yiddish by Yisrael Cohen in 1630. Published by Eli Yassif in *Bikoret u-farshanut*, volume 910, 1976. The Yiddish original was published in Fyorda in 1694 and reprinted by Yitzhak Rivkind in *Yivo Filologische Schriften* 3 (Vilna: 1929).

Studies:
The Lost Ten Tribes in Medieval Jewish Literature by Joshua Trachtenberg.
Lost Tribes and Promised Lands by Ronald Sanders.
Alexander's Gate, Gog and Magog and the Enclosed Nations by A.R. Anderson.

603. THE RIVER SAMBATYON

Ever since they went into exile beyond the river Sambatyon, the Ten Lost Tribes have been prevented from returning to their brothers in the tribes of Judah and Benjamin. It is the river itself that stops them. For six days its current is so strong that it throws up rocks as high as a house, so that it sometimes gives the appearance of being a mountain in motion. But on Friday at sunset a cloud envelops the river, so that no man can cross it, and at the same time the waters come completely to a halt. Then on the Sabbath the waters subside and disappear, and it resembles a lake of snow-white sand, and at the close of the Sabbath it resumes its torrent of rushing water, stones, and sand. The Sabbath is the only day its wild current stops flowing.

Where did the river Sambatyon come from? Some say it flowed from Paradise. Others insist that Sambatyon is another name for the Euphrates. On one side of the river there are the rich fields and forests of the land that was once Assyria, and on the other side dwell the descendants of the Ten Lost Tribes of Israel, who were sent into exile by the Assyrian king Shalmaneser in 722 BCE. Most accounts concur that the river came into being at the time of this exile, but the reason for its creation has long been a matter of debate.

There are those who insist that the river was formed to remind the lost tribes of the unchanging nature of the eternal laws, and to assure them that they had not been forgotten in their exile. Then there are those who have concluded that the river was created to keep them in exile, since the Sabbath is also their day of rest and they cannot cross on that day any more than they could on any other day of the week.

And when will the waters stop running? Not until the days of the Messiah will the people be permitted to cross.

> The legend of the river Sambatyon is first noted by Josephus (*Wars*, 7:5:1, although he reverses it, describing the river as running only on the Sabbath). All other versions of the legend describe it as running six days a week and resting on the Sabbath. This is how the story goes in the Talmud (*B. San.* 65b) and in the Midrash (*Gen. Rab.* 11:5 and 73:6). Just as the children of Israel must rest on the Sabbath, so must the river. In this way the legend of the river Sambatyon serves to prove the holiness of the Sabbath and provides an explanation for the Ten Lost Tribes remaining in exile. See "The Ten Lost Tribes," p. 473.
>
> *Sources:*
> B. Sanhedrin 65b; Genesis Rabbah 11:5, 73:6; Midrash Tanhuma-Yelammedenu, Ki Tissa 33; Pesikta Rabbati 23:8, 31:10; Josephus, Jewish Antiquities 11:133; Genesis Rabbah 73:6; Pesikta Rabbati 31:10; Sefer ha-Zikhronot 61; IFA 943, 2208, 13947.

604. THE CITY OF LUZ

The natives of the city of Luz are spared the dangers that confront all other human beings. The histories of the city, reaching back for centuries, are filled with every detail of learning and life. Yet these same histories, though complete, do not record a single war, a single flood or fire, nor the death of a single person. For so safe are the citizens while they live inside the city, even the Angel of Death can do them no harm.

Some say Luz is so safe because it was built on the spot where Jacob had the dream of the ladder reaching from earth into heaven, with angels ascending and descending on it. Others say that the Holy One set aside Luz after the Fall of Adam and Eve, to preserve one boundary in this world that the Angel of Death could not cross. In any case, not even the armies of Nebuchadnezzar could disturb the city. Nor do the people suffer from internal strife. For all who are born inside the city have their names inscribed in the Book of Life.

The precious dye known as *tekhelet* was made in this city. The Torah commands that this dye be used in dyeing a thread of the fringes of the *tallit* (prayer shawl). But no one knew how the dye was made, or whether it was derived from a snail or shellfish. This dye was said to be available in the city of Luz, but no one knew how to get there. King David is said to make his home there, thereby avoiding death for all time. That is why Jews sing a famous song with words that mean "King David is alive" (*David melekh Yisrael hai ve-kayyam*). After learning that Jews sang such a song about King David, the Turkish sultan accused them of obeying King David instead of him. He demanded a gift from King David, one that only King David could give him. Messengers were sent on a quest to the city of Luz. Then reached it through one of the caves that lead directly to the Holy Land, discovered the secret entrance, and found King David in the city, who rewarded them with an apple from the Tree of Life. This apple later saved the sultan's daughter from a sleeping sickness, and the Jews of the community were suitably rewarded.

The walls that surrounded the city of Luz had no apparent entrance, since the city would otherwise have been deluged by those seeking eternal life. But there was an almond (*luz*) tree that stood before the gates, from which the city is said to have taken its name, with a hollow trunk, which led to a secret cave that passed beneath the walls and emerged inside the city. It was this exit that the inhabitants of Luz had to take if they chose to depart from the city.

Yet despite their safety and the great blessing of immortality, there was one mystery that absorbed the wise men at night, and one source of sadness that caused the families to suffer from time to time. For in the course of a life it always happened that very old people would take leave of their families and walk off alone, to make their way into the world outside the walls of the city.

Why would anyone, young or old, choose to abandon such a city? And why did these wanderers never come back? Some are believed to have grown tired of living, others to have been called by an angel to another place. But when they passed through the hollow trunk and reentered the mortal world, they are said to have found the Angel of Death waiting there to take their lives and bury them in the fields beyond the walls.

The earliest references to the city of Luz appears in Genesis 28:19: *And he called the name of that place Beth El, but the name of the city was Luz at first.* Thus Luz is identified with the place where Jacob had his famous dream of the ladder with angels ascending and descending. What was so special about this place? The myth grew up that it was the location of a city of immortals, and all who entered there were spared the Angel of Death.

The commandment for the use of the blue dye (*tekhelet*) derives from Numbers 15:38.

This legend of a city of immortals is unique in Jewish literature, although the notion of a boundary that the Angel of Death cannot cross appears in the *Zohar* (4:151a), referring to the Land of Israel as a whole rather than to the city of Luz: "It is the Destroying Angel who brings death to all people, except those who die in the Holy Land, to whom death comes by the Angel of Mercy, who holds sway there." The various strata of legend concerning the city of Luz can all be found in this tale, which offers an opportunity to study the legendary evolution of a text. It is possible to observe the expansion of the myth of Luz in the Talmud, *B. Sota 46b*, and further embellishment is found in *Genesis Rabbah 69:8*. In such a case, each given detail becomes exceptionally significant. Since the literal meaning of *luz* is an almond tree, the motif of the tree is drawn upon, and it is said to have been placed at the entrance of the city. Then the development is taken a step further, embellishing the role of the tree: "This tree was hollow, and through it one entered the cave and through the cave the city" (*Genesis Rabbah 69:8*).

The origin of the immortal nature of the city of Luz is also linked to the bone at the bottom of the spine known as the *luz* bone, which survives longer than any other part of the body.

The legend of the city of Luz is the source of the legend of Shangri-La found in

James Hilton's novel *Lost Horizon*. Those who left Shangri-La immediately turned old and gray, just as those who departed from the city of Luz immediately encountered the Angel of Death. For another tale about the city of Luz, see the following story, "An Appointment with Death."

Sources:
B. Sota 46b; *Genesis Rabbah* 69:8; *Dos Buch fun Nisyoynes*.

605. AN APPOINTMENT WITH DEATH

One morning, as King Solomon awoke, he heard a chirping outside his window. He sat up in bed and listened carefully, for he knew the language of the birds, and he overheard them say that the Angel of Death had been sent to take the lives of two of his closest advisers. King Solomon was startled by this unexpected news, and he summoned the two doomed men. And when they stood before him, he revealed what he had learned of their fate.

The two were terrified, and they begged King Solomon to help them. Solomon told them that their only hope was to find their way to the city of Luz. For it was well known that the Angel of Death was forbidden to enter there. Therefore the inhabitants of Luz were immortal—as long as they remained within the walls of the charmed city. Very few knew the secret of how to reach that city, but King Solomon was one of those few.

So it was that King Solomon revealed the secret to the two frightened men, and they departed at once. They whipped their camels across the hot desert all day, and at nightfall they saw finally the walls of that fabled city. Immortality was almost within reach and they rode as fast as they could to the city gates.

But when they arrived they saw, to their horror, the Angel of Death waiting for them. "How did you know to look for us here?" they asked. The angel replied: "This is where I was told to meet you."

This myth derives from the reference in Genesis 28:19 to Luz as the original name of the place where Jacob had his dream of the heavenly ladder. The Talmud (*B. Sot.* 53a) identifies the city of Luz as a city of immortals. Since the Angel of Death was not permitted to enter, the old people who had grown tired of life had to leave the city, where the angel was waiting for them. The location of the city of Luz was regarded as a well-kept secret, since it would otherwise be deluged by those seeking immortality, but such secret knowledge was easily accessible to King Solomon. See "The City of Luz," p. 476.

The primary moral of this tale is that it is impossible to escape that which has been fated. It is one of several tales concerning King Solomon in which he tries to outfox fate and fails. See "The Princess in the Tower" in *Elijah's Violin*, pp. 47-52. See also "The City of Luz" in *Elijah's Violin*, pp. 279-293, which recounts many of the traditions associated with this city of immortals.

Many cultures have a myth about a city of immortals, and it is a theme that appears in many works of fiction, including John O'Hara's *Appointment in Samarra* and James Hilton's *Lost Horizon*. The version in the Talmud appears to be the earliest form of the myth.

Sources:
B. Sukkah 53a.

606. THE WORLD OF TEVEL

There are six worlds beneath the earth. The best known of them is called Tevel. The sun in Tevel rises in the west and sets in the east. There are 365 kinds of creatures who inhabit Tevel, all of them different from those who live on this side of the earth. Some of them have the head of a lion and the body of a man; others have the head of a man and the body of a lion. Some have the head of a snake and the body of a man; others the head of a man and the body of a snake. So too are there beings with human heads and bodies of oxen, who speak like humans. Strangest of all the creatures in Tevel, however, are those who have two heads and four arms and four legs, but only one trunk and one stomach. When they sit at the table, they seem like two people, but when they stand up and walk around, they are like one.

These creatures of Tevel are rarely peaceful. They quarrel among themselves over every little thing. Sometimes one head says, "Let's go in this direction!" and the other answers, "No! Let's go the other way!" Since they only have one body, they take one step forward and one step back—and they end up in exactly the same place where they had started. Neither head wants to give in to the other, and so they stand around all day quarreling, until it is time for the next meal.

Then, since both heads are hungry, they agree that it is time to make something to eat. But when it comes to cooking the food, they can never decide on what to make. One head says, "I want something hot!" and the other, "I want something cold!" They do manage to solve this problem by cooking for both heads. First they prepare the cold dish, and then they prepare the hot one, so that the hot meal doesn't get cold while the other is being made. Finally they sit down to eat. Then, for just a little while, there is peace. But as soon as the meal is finished, the heads start arguing again. "You ate more than I did!" cries the first head. "No, you ate more!" cries the second, accusing the first of the very same thing.

In his encounter with King Solomon, Ashmedai, King of Demons, put his hand in the earth and brought forth from Tevel a man with two heads and four eyes. This creature married a human wife and had six sons that resembled her and the seventh who looked like him. The one with two heads wanted two portions of his inheritance and they went to King Solomon to decide the matter. Solomon scalded one head and both cried out in pain. Then Solomon observed that they must be the same person, since they both experienced the pain.

> Just as there are seven heavens, so there are seven earths, of which the one with which we are familiar is only the top level. Each subsequent level is a world in itself under the earth, and one of these underground worlds is Tevel, with strange inhabitants, such as those with two heads, as described here.
>
> *Sources:*
> *Midrash Konen* in *Beit ha-Midrash* 2:36.

607. THE MANNA

While crossing the wilderness of Sinai, the children of Israel began to grow weary in their wandering, for no food was to be found. Then one morning a north wind swept the surface of the desert, rain washed the ground and cleansed it, and bread rained down from the sky, as it is said, *He gave them bread from heaven* (Ps. 105:40). The people went out to gather it, and enjoyed it while it was still warm. There was no need to cook or bake it. They called it manna, as it is said, *And He rained manna upon them for food* (Ps. 78:24). God had sent it from heaven, where loaves of delicate white bread are said to be abundant. Some say that letters of the Torah descended together with the manna, and the Israelites collected these words as well. Others say that the Torah was only given to those who ate the manna, for only they were worthy of it.

Every day enough manna fell to sustain the Jewish people for two thousand years, so that the Israelites had no need of carrying it in their wanderings. They gathered the manna every day, for it only lasted one day before it melted into many streams that went through the wilderness and passed into the lands of many nations. No one gathered more than he or she needed. Those who gathered much had no excess, and those who gathered little had no lack. But on Friday they collected enough for two days, and that manna lasted till the end of the Sabbath. In this way the Sabbath was blessed and sanctified with the manna.

The manna was one of the ten things created on the sixth day, on the eve of the first Sabbath. It was a very ethereal food, the food of the angels, as it is said, *Humans did eat angel's food* (Psalms 78:25). Some say it was ground in heaven by the angels, as a bread for the angels to eat. Others say that it is prepared by the angels for the souls of the righteous in the World to Come. Thus it was the angels who ground the manna for the people of Israel and prepared it to send down to them. Some say that it had the taste of milk and honey, while others say it had the taste as well as the fragrance of whatever the one who ate it most desired. For all the different tastes of the foods in the world, and all their various appearances, as well as all the pleasant fragrances, were included in the manna, which didn't require baking or cooking. The young men would eat it as if it were bread, the old men as if it were a wafer covered with honey, and the infants as if it were milk from their mothers' breasts. But to the other nations of the world it would taste as bitter as coriander.

Normally, wheat ascends from below and water descends from above. But God did not follow that procedure with the manna. He sent wheat from above, as it is said, *I will rain down bread for you from the sky* (Exod. 16:4), while God caused water to ascend from below, as it is said, *Spring up, O well, sing to it* (Num. 21:17). For all forty years of their wandering, the manna came down, until the people reached the Promised Land.

In *B. Yoma* 75b, Rabbi Akiba states that the manna was the food of the angels. However, Rabbi Ishmael contradicts him, saying, "Do angels eat?" And he quotes Exodus 34:28: *And he was there with Yahweh forty days and nights; neither did he eat bread or drink water.*

According to Rashi, commenting on Psalms 78:25, the manna was a spiritual food that produced no waste products. According to Ben Ish Hai in *Derushim*, the manna was given to them so that they would become wise in Torah.

The Hasidic Rebbe, Rabbi Menachem Mendel of Riminov, suggested that the manna had a spiritual as well as a material benefit. Since bread (*lehem*), in his view, represents the Torah, the falling of the manna represented new insights into the Torah that are constantly being revealed. Another Rebbe, Simcha Bunam of Parsischa, suggested that manna still comes down, meaning that God still makes His abundant blessings available to us.

Sources:

Exodus 16:4-36; Numbers 11:7-9; *Targum Yonathan* on Exodus 16:4; Septuagint on Psalms 78; Pseudo-Philo, *Liber Antiquitatum Biblicarum* 19:5; Josephus, *Antiquities* 3:26-28; *B. Avot* 5:6; *B. Hagigah* 12b; *B. Yoma* 75a-76a; *Midrash Tehillim* 19:7, 78:3; *Mekhilta de-Rabbi Ishmael, be-Shalah* 1:201-203; *Midrash Aggadah, be-Shalah; Mekhilta va-Yissa* 4; *4 Ezra* 1:19; *Midrash Tanhuma, be-Shalah* 22; *Midrash Tanhuma-Yelammedenu, Bereshit* 4, *Shemot* 25; *Midrash Avkir; Yalkut Shim'oni; Makhon Siftei Tzaddikim* on Exod. 16:4; *Siah Sarfei Kodesh* 2:83; *Eliyahu Rabbah* 1:2; *Derushim.*

Studies:

Bread From Heaven by Peder Borgen.

BOOK TEN

MYTHS OF THE MESSIAH

On New Moons and holy days and Sabbaths, the Messiah enters those halls of longing, lifts up his voice, and weeps. Then the Garden of Eden trembles and the firmament shakes until his voice ascends all the way to God's throne. And when God hears his voice, God beckons the enchanted bird, and it flies from the Garden of Eden and enters its nest and begins to sing.

Zohar 2:8a-9a

608. THE CREATION OF THE MESSIAH

Some say that even before the world was created, King Messiah had already come into being, for he existed in God's thought even before the creation of the sun and the moon and the stars, as it is said, *His name bursts forth before the sun* (Ps. 72:17). At the time of the Messiah's creation, God told him in detail of the suffering that would befall him in the future, for he would be bent down by the sins of souls as yet unborn, which were kept beneath God's throne. God asked him if he was willing to endure such things.

The Messiah asked God, "Will my suffering last many years?"

God replied, "I have decreed it will last for seven years."

The Messiah answered, "Master of the Universe, I take this suffering upon myself as long as not one person in Israel shall perish. And if not only those who are alive will be saved in my days, but also those who have died from the days of Adam until the time of the Redemption. These things I am ready to take upon myself."

God replied, "Not one breathing creature of your generation shall I cause to perish. So too will the dead among the righteous rise from their graves to greet you." Then God appointed the four creatures who would carry the Messiah's Throne of Glory at the End of Days. Thus was the covenant completed between God and the Messiah.

Others say that the Messiah is subjected to suffering in every generation, according to the sins of that generation. About this God said, "In the hour of the Redemption, I shall create the Messiah anew and he will no longer suffer."

Jewish tradition holds that the coming of the Messiah was always part of God's plan. This is emphasized here by asserting that the Messiah was brought into being before the creation of the world. The proof of the Messiah's pre-existence is said to be found in the verse, *And the spirit of God moved* (Gen. 1:2), words that are linked to the Messiah, of whom it is said, *The spirit of Yahweh shall alight upon him* (Isa. 11:2). Indeed, the Messiah is included in the lists of things that were created before the rest of creation, where it is said that the Messiah's name was engraved on a precious stone on the altar of the heavenly Temple. See "Seven Things Created before the Creation of the World," p. 74.

This myth describes a strange covenant of suffering between God and the heavenly Messiah. The Messiah agrees to take on terrible suffering for seven years as a sacrifice for the people of Israel. This has a distinct echo of the Christian belief that Jesus suffered for human sins. But more than that, it mirrors the suffering the Jewish people were undergoing, and their hope that somehow they would be credited for all that suffering and be rewarded by God in the future. This suffering and these hopes are then projected onto the heavenly Messiah in this myth.

The covenant has two parts, the suffering of the Messiah and the reward for all that suffering. In making this covenant, God appoints four creatures to carry the Messiah's throne, thus clearly indicating God's certainty that the Messiah will survive his time of suffering and receive the promised reward. That the Messiah is destined to sit on a throne makes this an enthronement myth about the Messiah. For another such myth, see "The Enthronement of the Messiah," p. 487.

Note that this myth not only mentions the creation of the Messiah, but also the re-creation of the Messiah. This remarkable re-creation, it is said, will take place at the time of the Messianic era. It may refer to the existence of myths about multiple Messiahs, especially the tradition of Messiah ben Joseph, the suffering human Messiah, and Messiah ben David, the celestial Messiah, where the former prepares the way for the latter. Here "re-creation" may be viewed as a way of establishing a direct link between these two Messiahs, one having been re-created out of the other. See "The Two Messiahs," p. 517.

Note that God creates a chariot for the Messiah not unlike God's own Chariot, the *Merkavah* in the vision of Ezekiel. This strongly implies that the Messiah is a divine figure of the utmost importance and power, not unlike the angel Metatron, who is sometimes identified as the "Lesser Yahweh."

Sources:
Pesikta Rabbati 31:10, 33:6, 36:1; *1 Enoch* 48:2-3, 48:6, 62:7.

Studies:
"Messianism in the Pseudepigrapha in the Light of the Scrolls" by M. A. Knibb. In *Dead Sea Discoveries* 2 (1995), 165-184.
The Messianic Idea in Judaism and Other Essays on Jewish Spirituality by Gershom Scholem.

609. THE BIRTH OF THE MESSIAH

The Messiah emerged in the thought of God even before the world was created, and the Messiah was born at the beginning of the creation of the world. His name was one of the seven things created before the sun was created, before the stars of heaven were made. Indeed, he was the firstborn of God. Some say that his name is Menahem, others that it is David.

At that time God appointed four animals to carry the throne of the Messiah. And while the sons of Jacob were busy with the selling of Joseph, while Jacob was busy mourning over Joseph, while Judah was busy taking a wife, God was creating the light of the Messiah, which will be revealed at the End of Days.

These myths point to a heavenly Messiah, while others refer to an earthly one. There are various names attributed to the Messiah, including Menahem and David. *Midrash Mishlei* (p. 87) gives seven names for the Messiah: Yinnon, Tzidkenu, Tzemah, Menahem, David, Shiloh, and Elijah. These seven names are associated with the verse *We will set up over it seven shepherds* (Micah 5:4). Two primary messianic figures evolved in Jewish myth, Messiah ben David and Messiah ben Joseph. The former was said to be descended from David, the latter from Joseph. Messiah ben Joseph was generally understood as a forerunner Messiah who would prepare the way for Messiah ben David.

There is another tradition that on the day the Temple was destroyed, the Messiah was born. It is found in *Lamentations Rabbah* 1:51.

Sources:
Pesikta Rabbati 33:6, 34:2, 36:1; *1 Enoch* 48:2-3, 62:7-9; *B. Pesahim* 54a; *B. Nedarim* 39a; *B. Sanhedrin* 98b-99a; *Y. Berakhot* 5a; *Genesis Rabbah* 85:1; *Lamentations Rabbah* 1:51.

610. THE SCALES OF THE MESSIAH

The Messiah was created when the Temple in Jerusalem was destroyed. At that time God commanded Elijah the Prophet to bring scales to him. On one side of the scales Elijah would place the captive Messiah, along with the souls of the dead, and Elijah would fill the other scales with tears, torture, and the souls of the *Tzaddikim*. And when this had been done, God announced that the face of the Messiah would be seen when the scales were balanced.

This orally collected myth portrays the conditions that would enable the coming of the Messiah—a balancing of heavenly scales with the Messiah on one side with the souls of the dead, and the suffering of Israel with the souls of the *Tzaddikim* on the other. The idea is that God is well aware of the suffering of Israel, and when the time is right, He will send the Messiah to ease that suffering. This suggests a kind of heavenly mechanism to trigger the messianic era and the End of Days.

Sources:
IFA 6929.

611. THE REQUIREMENTS OF THE MESSIAH

King Messiah will arise and restore the kingdom of David to its former glory. He will rebuild the Temple and gather all the exiles of Israel. All ancient laws will be reinstituted in his days; sacrifices will again be offered; the Sabbatical and Jubilee years will again be observed according to the commandments set forth in the Law.

> This statement by Maimonides is quite definitive, except that it does not include the resurrection of the dead, normally one of the three primary requirements of the Messiah. Indeed, in *Mishneh Torah, Hilkhot Melakhim* 11:3, Maimonides denies that the Messiah will bring the dead to life: "Do not think that King Messiah will have to perform signs and wonders, bring anything new into being, revive the dead, or do similar things."
>
> The two other major requirements of the Messiah are listed here by Maimonides: the rebuilding of the Temple and the Ingathering of the Exiles. Thus Maimonides downplays the supernatural elements in the messianic tradition, viewing the messianic era in practical terms that could be accomplished without overthrowing the laws of nature. Indeed, in 12:1, he states this explicitly: "Let no one think that in the days of the Messiah any of the laws of nature will be set aside, or any innovation be introduced into creation. The world will follow its normal course."

Sources:
Mishneh Torah, Hilkhot Melakhim 11:1.

Studies:
"Jewish Messianism in Comparative Perspective" by R. J. Zwi Werblowsky.
Moses Maimonides' Treatise on Resurrection, edited by Fred Rosner.

612. THE SOUL OF THE MESSIAH

Like Adam's soul, the soul of the Messiah is comprised of all other souls. Indeed, the soul of the Messiah contains the souls of all generations. For one who encompasses all generations in his soul possesses the powers of the entire world. And when he repents, he can arouse repentance in everyone.

Some say that the soul of the Messiah has been exiled to a place of desert and desolation where no one walks. A storm wind rose up and created such confusion that the Messiah lost all the signs that were given to him, with which he was to identify himself before the people of Israel. As a result, it became impossible to recognize him, for he had no way of revealing himself. Furthermore, some of the lost signs and marvels of the Messiah were found by false prophets who began to appear, calling themselves by the name Messiah. But once their lies and wantonness were exposed, their false teachings were revealed for all the world to see.

Others say that the soul of the Messiah has been chained and is being held captive by the forces of evil. Not until the chains of the Messiah are broken will the captive soul of the Messiah be set free.

Still others believe that after the Shattering of the Vessels and the Gathering of the Sparks, the soul of the Messiah, which was sunk among the broken vessels, sent forth sparks in every generation. If a generation is worthy, that spark might become the Messiah, and the footsteps of the Messiah would be heard throughout the world.

The soul of the Messiah is described in terms that make it all-inclusive. Like the traditions about Adam's soul, the Messiah's soul is said to contain all souls, even all generations of souls. See "Adam's Soul," p. 162.

There are various myths portraying the Messiah's soul as being exiled or imprisoned. One such myth describes it as being held captive in chains. Others describe the soul as being lost in a desert. From the time of Moses there was the tradition that the Redeemer could be identified by a sign. In the case of Moses, the words were *I have taken note of you* (Exod. 3:16). In the Midrash, Serah bat Asher, who lived from the time of Jacob until the time of Moses, is said to have identified Moses as the Redeemer. Likewise, there are certain signs that are said to accompany the Messiah, and here even these signs are said to have become lost, suggesting a time so chaotic that even if the Messiah appeared, no one would recognize him.

These accounts of exile and imprisonment are meant to explain why the Messiah has not yet come. As long as the Messiah's soul is being held captive, it cannot descend into the body of the Messiah, and therefore prevents the birth and coming of the Messiah.

One of the myths about the Messiah's soul derives from a Shabbatean source, the writings of Nathan of Gaza, primary apostle of Shabbatai Zevi, the false Messiah of the seventeenth century. This is a kabbalistic myth, based on the Ari's myth of the Shattering of the Vessels and the Gathering of the Sparks. For more on the myth of the Ari see p. 122. In this Shabbatean myth, a spark of the Messiah's soul descends in each generation, and if the generation is worthy, the spark will become the Messiah. This places the onus for the coming of the Messiah on the piety of each generation, and means that the coming of the Messiah will not take place until there is a worthy generation. See "The Chains of the Messiah," p. 492 and "The Captive Messiah," p. 498.

Sources:
Sippurei Ma'asiyot, 1973 ed., pp. 276-277; *Tzidkat ha-Tzaddik* 159; *Be-Ikvot Mashiah* pp. 17-22.

Studies:
Sabbatai Sevi: The Mystical Messiah by Gershom Scholem.

613. THE DESCENT OF THE MESSIAH'S SOUL

The soul of the Messiah lives in a palace in heaven. There is a potential Messiah born on earth in every generation. That person, known as the *Tzaddik ha-Dor*, the most righteous of his generation, has both an earthly soul and a heavenly soul. If the time is right for the Messiah to come, then the heavenly soul will descend and fuse with the earthly soul, and the days of the Messiah will have arrived.

In recent times some members of the Lubavitch Hasidim came to believe strongly that their Rebbe, Rabbi Menachem Mendel Schneersohn, was the Messiah. In addition to a public campaign for "Messiah Now," Lubavitch theologians searched the existing messianic traditions for evidence that the Rebbe, as he was universally known, was the Messiah. Here they encountered two apparently contradictory traditions. One holds that the Messiah is a divine figure, who makes his home in a heavenly palace. The other tradition holds that the Messiah will be the *Tzaddik ha-Dor*, the greatest sage of his generation—a human being. These were originally two separate messianic traditions in Judaism, but they were eventually linked. The earthly, human Messiah was identified as Messiah ben Joseph, who was said to pave the way for the heavenly Messiah, known as Messiah ben David. However, this myth held that Messiah ben Joseph would lose his life in the process. Before the death of the Rebbe, Jacob Immanuel Schochet, a prominent Lubavitch scholar, often lectured on the subject of the Messiah. There was no doubt that his descriptions of the qualities of the Messiah were intended to refer to the Rebbe. In these lectures, Schochet presented a new messianic theory, combining the myths of Messiah ben Joseph and Messiah ben David into a single myth. Here, rather than having one Messiah prepare the way for the other, the figure of the Messiah was simultaneously human and divine. This was made possible by the descent of the soul of the heavenly Messiah into the body of the human one. Thus, in the Lubavitch view, the heavenly Messiah himself will not descend, but merely his soul, which will fuse with the soul of the human Messiah. This made it possible to explain how a human, such as the Rebbe, could fulfill the role of Messiah ben David, the heavenly Messiah.

Sources:
4 *Ezra* 12:32, 13:25-26, 51-52; Lubavitch, oral tradition related by Jacob Immanuel Schochet.

614. THE ENTHRONEMENT OF THE MESSIAH

In the future, God will dress the Messiah in garb whose splendor will radiate from one end of the world to the other, and place the Messiah at His right hand. And Abraham will be at His left. Abraham's face will turn pale, and he will say to God: "Is my son's son to sit at Your right and I at Your left?" And God will reply, "Your son's son is on your right, and I am on your right, as it is said, *Yahweh at your right hand*" (Ps. 110:5).

What role will the Messiah play after he initiates the messianic era? In this myth, the Messiah comes to sit at the right hand of God. Thus the Messiah receives the kind of enthronement found in other myths about Adam, Enoch, Jacob, Moses, and King David. What is unusual is not only that Abraham sits at God's left hand, but that the arrival of the Messiah means that the figure who receives enthronement will be one of a trinity rather than a duality. This is surely significant and might indicate the influence of the Christian concept of the Trinity.

Sources:
Yalkut Shemuel 162; *Midrash Tehillim* 18:29.

615. THE MESSIAH WILL DESCEND FROM THE SIDE OF EVIL

For reasons known only to Him, God caused events to occur whereby the Messiah will be born from the realm of evil, for the Messiah will descend from the House of David. And King David was descended from Ruth the Moabite, and Moab was the son of one of the two daughters of Lot. After the destruction of Sodom, Lot, who was intoxicated, committed incest with his daughters. Thus when God said, *"I have found David"* (Ps. 89:21), where did He find him? In Sodom. Thus the soul of the Messiah is descended from such a place.

If the Messiah were to descend from a righteous person rather than the incestuous Lot, no enemy would have been able to prevail against Israel, or cause them to be forced into exile. God ordained things to happen this way, although no one knows why. David wanted to banish the evil side from which he had been born, eliminating it from the world, but he was unable to do so, for he had no power over the side of evil, since he had been born from it.

In the *Zohar* and later kabbalistic and Hasidic commentaries, the incestuous union of Lot and his daughters (Gen. 19:30-38) is identified as the source of the power of the *Yetzer ha-Ra*, the Evil Impulse. This leads to the mysterious conclusion that the Messiah will descend from the side of evil. The key concept here is that the Messiah's soul is closest to evil, possessing great intensity. But in the messianic era the evil soul will be transformed, by a process of *tikkun*—repair or restoration—into the good.

Sources:
Genesis Rabbah 41:5; Zohar 1:109a-112a; No'am Elimelekh, Likutei Shoshanah, p. 101a; Tzidkat ha-Tzaddik, no. 111.

616. A WAR IN HEAVEN AND ON EARTH

Near the time of redemption, a great and boundless war will break out in heaven, and there will be a corresponding war on earth. Eternal beings and mortal beings will battle one another. Destructive angels will attack the Jews, and seek to destroy and eradicate them. Evil will expand its dominion and strive to intensify the exile. It will be a time of great confusion, and some will be tempted to abandon their faith. But the people of Israel must persevere and hold fast to their faith. Only then will the time of redemption be fulfilled and there will be peace and tranquility, rest and calm.

This is an apocalyptic vision describing a war in heaven as well as on earth. It is clearly intended to refer to the war of Gog and Magog, which, it is said, will precede the coming of the Messiah. However, while the war of Gog and Magog is usually described as an earthly conflict, this myth presents it as one that will take place above and below.

Sources:
B'rit Menuhah 21b, attributed to Abraham of Granada.

617. THE PALACE OF THE MESSIAH

From the beginning the Messiah was hidden in a heavenly palace known as the Bird's Nest. That is a secret place containing a thousand halls of yearning, where none may enter except for the Messiah. It is there that the Messiah waits for the sign to be given that his time has come at last.

The palace is known as the Bird's Nest because of the wonderful bird of the Messiah, which has its nest in a tree near his palace.

On New Moons and holy days and Sabbaths, the Messiah enters those halls of longing, lifts up his voice, and weeps. Then the Garden of Eden trembles and the firmament shakes until his voice ascends all the way to God's throne. And when God hears his voice, God beckons the enchanted bird, and it flies from the Garden of Eden and enters its nest and begins to sing.

Now the song of that bird is indescribably beautiful; no one has ever heard a music so sublime. Three times the bird repeats its song, and then the bird and the Messiah ascend on high, to the very Throne of Glory. There God swears to them that He will destroy the wicked kingdom of Rome and will give His children all the blessings that are destined for them. After that the bird returns to its nest and the Messiah returns to his palace, and once again he remains hidden there, waiting.

The longing and weeping of the Messiah are common images in Jewish lore. The Messiah weeps out of his own frustration, as well as out of his awareness of the frustration of the Jewish people that the messianic era still has not come. This mutual waiting is portrayed in a legend about Rabbi Joshua ben Levi, who is said to have had an encounter with the Messiah (*Ma'aseh de-Rabbi Yehoshua ben Levi* in *Beit ha-Midrash* 2:50). The Messiah said to him: "What is Israel doing in the world from which you came?" He replied, "They are waiting for you every day." As soon as he heard this, the Messiah lifted up his voice and cried.

Sources:
Zohar 2:8a-9a.

618. A THOUSAND PALACES OF LONGING

There is a secret and unknown place in the Garden of Eden where there are concealed a thousand palaces of longing. No one can enter there except for the Messiah, who dwells in the Garden of Eden. On new moons, feasts, and Sabbaths, the Messiah enters there to find solace in those palaces. On the night of *Rosh Hodesh*, when there is a new moon, the Messiah wanders through those palaces lifting up his voice and weeping. For the Messiah longs for the days of redemption as much as the children of Israel. Only then will his waiting come to an end.

In those palaces of longing the Messiah can see the patriarchs visiting the ruins of the House of God. When he sees Rachel with tears on her face, and God trying to comfort her, but Rachel refusing to be comforted, the Messiah too lifts up his voice and cries. Then the whole Garden of Eden quakes, and all the righteous who make their home there cry and lament with him. So too are the supernal hosts seized by trembling, until it reaches the Throne of Glory. Then God proclaims that He will avenge Israel through the hands of the Messiah. And only then does the Messiah return to his place.

> This is a beautiful, melancholic myth about the immense longing of the Messiah to fulfill his destiny and initiate the End of Days. The Messiah is described as living in the Garden of Eden, in a palace hidden in a thousand palaces of longing. He retreats to this secret palace on holy days, when his longing becomes most intense. Nor is the Messiah passive in this view, but petitions God with his tears, until God reaffirms His vow to bring the messianic era. For a variant myth, see "The Palace of the Messiah," p. 488.
>
> The portrait of the heavenly Messiah that emerges here is of a deeply emotional figure whose relationship with God is as close as that of a child to his parent. And all of the righteous souls of Israel are described as supporting the plea of the Messiah to hasten his coming. Thus, above all, this myth mirrors the intense longing for the coming of the Messiah among the Jewish people, which was often in such an expectant state that pious men often kept a white robe and staff ready, to take up the moment the coming of the Messiah was announced.

Sources:
Zohar 2:8a.

619. THE SUFFERING MESSIAH

God decreed that the Messiah would suffer for seven years before the time of the Redemption. During that time, iron beams will be brought and loaded upon his neck until his body is bent low. Then he will cry out, his voice rising to the highest heavens, saying to God, "How much can my spirit endure? How long before my breath ceases? How much more can my limbs suffer?"

God will reply, "My Messiah, long ago you took this ordeal upon yourself. At this moment, your pain is like My pain. You, like Me, suffer for the sake of Israel. This I swear to you—ever since My Temple in Jerusalem was destroyed, I have not been able to bring myself to sit on My throne."

At these words the Messiah will say, "Now I am reconciled. The servant is content to be like his Master."

After that Elijah will comfort the Messiah in one of the halls of Paradise. He will hold the Messiah's hands against his chest and say, "Bear the suffering God has imposed upon you because of the sins of the Jewish people until the End of Days. Have courage—the end is near." And when he hears this, the Messiah will be comforted.

> The Messiah suffers pains over the sins of Israel, and here, in the seven years before the initiation of the messianic era, God decrees great suffering for the Messiah, who accepts it as part of his burden. The theme of the suffering Messiah obviously recalls the passion of Jesus, and Jewish tradition may in this case have been influenced by Christian tradition. See "The Creation of the Messiah," p. 483.
>
> Sources:
> Pesikta Rabbati 36:1-2; Rashi on B. Sanhedrin 98b; Midrashei Geulah 307-308; Tzidkat ha-Tzaddik 153; Likutei Moharan 1:118.
>
> Studies:
> "Midrashic Theologies of Messianic Suffering" in The Exegetical Imagination: On Jewish Thought and Theology by Michael Fishbane, pp. 73-85.

620. THE LADDER OF PRAYERS

The Ba'al Shem Tov was once praying with his Hasidim. That day he prayed with great concentration, not only word by word, but letter by letter, so that the others finished long before he did. At first they waited for him, but before long they lost patience, and one by one they left.

Later the Ba'al Shem Tov came to them and said: "While I was praying, I ascended the ladder of your prayers all the way into Paradise. As I ascended, I heard a song of indescribable beauty. At last I reached the palace of the Messiah, in the highest heavens, known as the Bird's Nest. The Messiah was standing by his window, peering out at a tree of great beauty. I followed his gaze and saw that his eyes were fixed on a golden dove, whose nest was in the top branches of that tree. That is when I realized that the song pervading all of Paradise was coming from that golden dove. And I understood that the Messiah could not bear to be without that dove and its song for as much as a moment. Then it occurred to me that if I could capture the dove, and bring it back to this world, the Messiah would be sure to follow.

"So I ascended higher, until I was within arm's reach of the golden dove. But just as I reached for it, the ladder of prayers collapsed."

> In this Hasidic tale, "The Ladder of Prayers," the Ba'al Shem Tov ascends into Paradise on a quest to capture the golden dove of the Messiah, certain that this will cause the Messiah to follow, initiating the messianic era. The failure of the Ba'al Shem Tov's Hasidim to provide the support needed for this great endeavor, as symbolized by the collapse of the ladder of prayers, causes him to lose the opportunity to bring the Messiah. That makes this one more tale about why the Messiah has not come. Dozens of other such tales record lost opportunities to bring about the messianic era, or attempts to force the Messiah's hand, and hasten the End of Days.

This tale, and virtually the entire body of rabbinic, kabbalistic, folk, and Hasidic lore, exists in a mythological framework. The ladder of prayers the Ba'al Shem Tov ascends was surely inspired by the heavenly ladder in Jacob's dream. He climbs this ladder of prayers into Paradise, a mythological realm with its own order, its own geography, its own history, and its own inhabitants—not only God and the angels, but the Bride of God and the Messiah as well. It is understood that the Messiah is waiting for the sign to be given that the time has come for the messianic era. All the same, Jewish mysticism contains the secret of how to hasten the coming of the Messiah, secrets that the Ba'al Shem Tov has at his command.

In addition, this tale draws on a rich tradition of tales about heavenly ascent, from the ascent of Elijah in a fiery chariot to the famous tale of the four who entered Paradise. Indeed, "The Ladder of Prayers," a Hasidic tale of eighteenth century origin, is a direct descendant of the legend of the four sages, which dates from the second century. As did the four sages, the Ba'al Shem Tov ascends to heaven because he seeks greater knowledge of the divine realm.

outside the palace of the Messiah in is also known as the "Bird's Nest." endary accounts of the golden dove, scend on the ladder of prayers of his ilure of the Ba'al Shem's Hasidim to eat endeavor, as symbolized by the he reason for the failure to bring the es the interdependency of the *Tzaddik* len dove and its failure marks one of an attempt to hasten the coming of Talmud. See, in particular, "Forcing ound in virtually every generation, had all gone well, would have served essiah ben David. In this tale of the palace of Messiah ben David, deter-f this tale, see "The Messiah and the

'alotekha.

HEM TOV

said: "I make my home in a heavenly one has ever entered there. If only you on would surely come to Israel. I don't the gate, but I heard God's voice saying fill your wish.'"

This brief account about the Messiah speaking to the Ba'al Shem Tov is attributed to Rabbi Menahem Nahum of Chernobyl (1730-1797). Here the Messiah strongly hints to the Ba'al Shem Tov that he can bring about the messianic era—and set the Messiah free from his waiting—by making his way to the heavenly Garden of Eden and opening the gate to the secret abode of the Messiah, known as the Bird's Nest. Further, the Messiah suggests that God will look favorably on the efforts of the Ba'al Shem Tov, because God feels that he must fulfill the Messiah's wish—which is to initiate the messianic era. Thus, in this brief tale, the Messiah not only gives the Ba'al Shem Tov the key hint of how this can be done, but strongly suggests that the time is right. This fragmentary tale does not inform us of what happened next, which would be a heavenly journey by the Ba'al Shem Tov to fulfill the quest. But the fact that the Messiah has not yet come speaks for itself.

In a variant of this mythic tale, "The Ladder of Prayers," p. 490, the Ba'al Shem Tov ascends to Paradise and tries to capture the golden dove of the Messiah, which the Messiah cannot bear to be without, and in this way force the coming of the Messiah, a process known as "Forcing the End." Here, too, the quest ultimately fails. Although this is considered a sin, it is the one sin the rabbis had tremendous sympathy toward, since they longed, above all, for the coming of the Messiah.

In both of these tales, the Ba'al Shem Tov is portrayed as the only figure in his generation capable of bringing the Messiah. This follows the pattern of Messiah ben Joseph, the earthly Messiah, who, it is said, will pave the way for the coming of the heavenly Messiah, Messiah ben David. Thus the Ba'al Shem Tov is identified in these tales with Messiah ben Joseph. In each generation the *Tzaddik ha-Dor*, the greatest sage of his generation, exists as a potential Messiah. If the time is ripe and the sage is able to fulfill his role, he will serve as the earthly Messiah who sets in motion the coming of the heavenly Messiah.

Sources:
Shivhei-ha Besht, story no. 42; *Zohar* 2:7b-9a, 3:196b.

622. THE MESSIAH AT THE GATES OF ROME

The Messiah sits at the entrance of the gates of Rome. Around him sit the poor, wrapped in bandages, suffering from disease. Like them, the Messiah is bandaged from head to toe. When the beggars are ready to change their bandages, they unwind them all at the same time. But the Messiah changes them one by one, in case he should be summoned, so that he will be ready.

Like the beggars and lepers around him, the Messiah is wrapped in bandages, suffering from some unstated disease, presumably leprosy. The story also suggests how close the Messiah is to coming—he's already at the gates, waiting for the signal from heaven that the messianic era has finally arrived. This is one of the myths about a suffering Messiah. "The Captive Messiah," p. 498, is another example of this type.

This myth about the Messiah emerges out of an unusual dialogue between Elijah the Prophet and Rabbi Joshua ben Levi. Rabbi Joshua is said to have once found Elijah standing at the entrance of the cave of Rabbi Shimon bar Yohai. Rabbi Joshua asked him, "When will the Messiah come?" Elijah replied, "Go ask him yourself." Joshua ben Levi asked where the Messiah could be found, and Elijah answered that he sits among the beggars at the gates of Rome. The story goes on to relate that Rabbi Joshua sought out the Messiah there and asked when he would come. The Messiah's enigmatic answer was, "Today." Rabbi Joshua returned to Elijah and said that the Messiah had lied to him, because he had said he was coming that day and he did not. Elijah replied, "What he told you was that he would come, *if you would but heed his charge this day*" (Ps. 95:7). Thus, the Messiah is ready to come, but we are not ready for him. See by way of contrast, Franz Kafka's "The Coming of the Messiah," p. 518.

Sources:
B. *Sanhedrin* 98a.

623. THE CHAINS OF THE MESSIAH

Long ago, in the city of Hebron, there lived a man named Joseph della Reina whose longing for the Messiah was so great that he spent his life in mystical study and prayer, seeking to learn how the coming of the Messiah might be hastened. It was in those days that the holy book of the *Zohar* was discovered, and Joseph della Reina saw this as a sign.

Surely the gate of the Messiah's palace was open, and the time had come for the Messiah to pass through that gate, so that his footsteps could be heard in the world.

Thus della Reina sought out ten other scholars who also devoted themselves to mystical meditation. Together they fasted and mortified themselves, so that they might purify their souls, Joseph della Reina more so than any of the others. They studied the kabbalah day and night, immersing themselves in its mysteries. And they scattered ashes on their heads, crying and mourning over the destruction of the Temple.

At last Joseph della Reina so purified his soul that the Prophet Elijah descended from on high and taught him mysteries that had never been revealed outside of heaven. In this way he learned that the soul of the Messiah was being held captive by the forces of evil, and not until those forces had been defeated could the chains of the Messiah be broken. Most of all, Joseph della Reina wished to know how to set free the captive soul of the Messiah. But Elijah was reluctant to tell him any more, for it was forbidden to reveal this mystery. Then Joseph della Reina said to Elijah: "If you yourself cannot reveal this secret, can you give me the name of an angel I might invoke?" And at last Elijah relented and revealed the holy names that invoke the angel Metatron, who once had been Enoch before being transported to heaven in a chariot and transformed into the fiery angel Metatron, the Prince of the Presence.

Then Joseph della Reina and his followers began to fast from the end of one Sabbath to the beginning of the next. And, as Rabbi Shimon bar Yohai had done, they ate only carobs and drank only water. Now it is said that at midnight on the eve of Shavuot the heavens split open, and any prayer said at that time reaches to the highest heavens. So Joseph della Reina and his followers waited until that moment, and then he pronounced the holy names that Elijah had given him to invoke the angel Metatron. Thunder rang out all around them and lightning split the sky, and the heavens parted and a great light shone from on high that so blinded them they fell on their faces in fear. And the voice of Metatron rang out so loudly that the earth shook beneath their feet. "What is it you want?" the voice demanded. At first Joseph della Reina was speechless, but he finally found the strength to supplicate himself before the Prince of the Presence and he said: "Surely the time has come for the Messiah to be set free from his chains. Tell us how this can be done, and we will set out to accomplish this quest, no matter how difficult."

"The victory that you seek over evil would bring you into the gravest danger. Now is the time to turn back," said Metatron. But Joseph della Reina refused to give up and begged the angel to assist them. And at last Metatron revealed this fateful secret: that the rulers of the forces of evil, Ashmedai, the King of Demons, and Lilith, his Queen, could be found in the form of black dogs living on Mount Seir. And if they could be captured and put in chains and led away from that mountain, which was their home and the source of their strength, they could be defeated. Then the chains holding back the Messiah would break, and the time of his coming would be at hand. But, Metatron warned him, those demons were very powerful, and the only way to weaken them was to deny them every kind of sustenance. They must be given nothing, neither food nor water, until they were led away from the mountain, or all would be in vain. So too did Metatron reveal the holy names that would transport della Reina and his followers to Mount Seir and permit them to capture the demons who reigned there.

When Joseph della Reina heard this, his soul exulted, for now the quest he had sought for so long lay open before him. And he thanked Metatron from the depths of his soul and vowed that he would do everything in his power to fulfill that quest. But before departing, Metatron warned him not to take on such a great responsibility unless he was certain he would not fail, for if he did, the time of the coming of the Messiah would be delayed much longer. And at that moment the heavens closed and the vision came to an end, but Joseph della Reina and his followers felt they had been reborn, for now the path of their destiny had opened before them.

Once again they fasted and prayed and prepared themselves for the day of reckoning. So too did they prepare many links of chain with which to restrain the demons. At last Joseph della Reina, surrounded by his ten disciples, pronounced the holy names in the proper combination, and an instant later they found themselves at the foot of Mount Seir. There they heard an unearthly howling, and certain that this must be a sign, they set out in that direction.

At last they caught sight of two great black dogs howling at the moon. That howling was so terrible it filled them with dread, but still they crept closer until they were right behind them. And just as they threw the chains around the dogs, Joseph della Reina pronounced the holy names that made them his prisoners. As soon as he did, Ashmedai and Lilith were restored to their true forms and tried to break free. But when the demons realized they could not, they no longer struggled but began to beg for something to eat or drink. Their pleas were piteous indeed, but Joseph della Reina spurned them, and he and his followers led them in chains down the mountain.

Now when they had almost descended the mountain, Ashmedai and Lilith became so weak that they had to be dragged, and their pleas for sustenance grew more urgent. But when they saw that della Reina would show them no mercy, they begged instead for a single whiff of incense to revive them. Then della Reina took pity on them, for he did not see any danger in that, and he lit the incense and let them each take a whiff of it. But at that instant Ashmedai shot up many times his size and the chains that held him shattered, as did Lilith's. Ashmedai was filled with rage, and he picked up the ten followers of Joseph della Reina and cast them a great distance, so that all of them lost their lives. And when he found Joseph della Reina cowering behind a rock, he picked him up and cast him a distance of hundreds of miles, where he landed with a great crash.

The next thing Joseph della Reina knew, he found himself transformed into a large, black dog, wandering through the streets of a city. And the soul of Joseph della Reina, which was trapped in the body of that black dog, recognized that city at once as Safed. Now della Reina was horrified to discover himself in the body of that dog, and he suffered the pangs of hell. Now, too, all hope he had once held for the coming of the Messiah was shattered, and his singular longing was simply for his own soul to be set free.

So it was that the black dog that bore the soul of Joseph della Reina hid near the windows of the yeshivahs of Safed and listened to the teachings of the sages and learned, in this way, that there was a righteous man living in the city of Safed at that time who was known as the Ari, and that he alone possessed the mystical powers to set della Reina's soul free.

Soon the Ari found that a black dog followed him everywhere. There was nothing he could do to get rid of it. At last the Ari's disciples asked him about the dog that pursued him like a shadow, and the Ari replied: "That dog was once the holy sage Joseph della Reina, who sought to shake the heavens so that the footsteps of the Messiah might be heard. Instead he failed in his task and brought the wrath of heaven upon himself, and now he has been reborn as this black dog. He wants me to set him free, but that is not his fate. This is just the first of a thousand rebirths he will have to suffer through before his soul can be freed of the taint of his sin." And when the black dog, who had listened carefully to every word, learned of his fate, he lost his mind and ran howling into the wilderness and was never seen again.

> After the talmudic legend of the four who entered Paradise, this is probably the best-known kabbalistic tale of all. It exists in a number of versions and has been reprinted many times. The two primary versions are those of Eliezer ha-Levi and Shlomo Navarro. Ha-Levi's earlier account presents Joseph della Reina as a sincere, if overambitious, prophet who is willing to take great risks to hasten the coming of the Mes-

siah and suffers a terrible failure. Navarro's version transforms the character of della Reina, emphasizing his hubris and adding a coda in which, having failed in his messianic quest, he becomes a student of black magic, taught by none other than Lilith, the demoness he originally sought to capture. His later exploits, in the version of Navarro, include using his powers to bring Queen Dolphina of France to his bed and attempting to bring Helen of Troy back from the dead for himself. The present version of this tale is based primarily on the earlier version. For a version based primarily on that of Navarro, see "Helen of Troy" in *Lilith's Cave*, pp. 42-52, and the accompanying note. Eli Wiesel's novel *The Gates of the Forest* also includes a retelling of the story of Joseph della Reina, p. 18.

Just as the myth of the four who entered Paradise (p. 445) served as a warning tale about the dangers of kabbalah, so did the story of Joseph della Reina, and he became an archetype of the holy man driven mad by immersion in kabbalistic mysteries. The story of Joseph della Reina being reborn as a black dog, so full of poetic justice because of its echo of the forms taken by Ashmedai and Lilith when he sought to capture them, is associated with the legend of the Ari. It demonstrates that as early as the sixteenth century, della Reina became a despised figure even by those who themselves still sought to hasten the coming of the Messiah. See "The Captive Messiah," p. 498.

Sources:
Iggeret Sod ha-Geulah; Sippur Rabbi Yosef della Reina; Eder ha-Yekar; IFA 14418.
Studies:
Between Worlds: Dybbuks, Exorcists and Early Modern Judaism by J. H. Chajes.

624. THE MESSIAH COMES FORTH FROM PRISON

At the end of the wars of Gog and Magog, the Messiah shall come forth from prison with nothing except for his staff and his sack. Then the Messiah will wrap himself in prayer and gird himself as a hero before God. The Messiah will say before Him: "Master of the Universe, remember on my behalf the suffering and grief and darkness and obscurity into which I was cast. My eyes have beheld no light and my ears have heard great reviling, and my heart broke with pain and grief. You know that I have not acted for my own glory, nor for the glory of my father's house, but for Your glory have I acted, and for Your children who dwell in sorrow among the peoples of the world."

Then the Messiah will say to the children of Israel: "Go and assemble all your brethren from all the nations." And they will go and assemble all Israel and bring them to stand before the Messiah, as it is said, *And they shall bring all your brethren out of all the nations as an offering to Yahweh* (Isa. 66:20).

> This myth describes the emergence of the Messiah at the End of Days. The Messiah has been imprisoned, but the time finally comes when he is set free. Then the first thing he does is remind God of his suffering and that of the people of Israel, and he sets out to accomplish the first of the messianic requirements—the Ingathering of the Exiles. See "The Suffering Messiah," p. 489 and "The Chains of the Messiah," p. 492 for myths about the suffering of the Messiah.
>
> *Sources:*
> *Hekhalot Rabbati* 6.

625. UNTIL THE REDEMPTION

Before his death, the Rabbi of Riminov let it be known that he would not set foot in the Garden of Eden until the time of the Messiah had come. After his death, the angels sought to convince him to enter, for he had long been awaited, but he refused. They sought to lure him into the Garden by showing him many wonderful things, but their efforts were in vain. Still, it was not yet time for the Messiah to come. So they asked King David to play on his harp, and when that haunting music drifted out of the Garden and reached the Rabbi of Riminov, he followed after it as if in a trance, and in this way he was lured inside at last.

Likewise, Rabbi Shalom Rokeach, the Belzer Rebbe, once said, "One time I dreamt that I was brought to *Gan Eden* and shown the walls of Jerusalem. The walls were in ruins and a man was walking on them. I asked, 'Who is that man?' I was told that this is Rabbi Israel Ba'al Shem Tov. He has sworn not to come down from there until the Temple is rebuilt."

> There are quite a few stories about rabbis who vowed not to enter *Gan Eden* until the Messiah had come, but were somehow seduced into entering the Garden. The Rabbi of Riminov and the Belzer Rebbe (1779-1855) are both great Hasidic masters, and, of course, the Ba'al Shem Tov is the founder of Hasidism. Their links to this tale of the refusal of the heavenly reward were intended to emphasize their great hope in the coming era of the Messiah, which would have to include the rebuilding of the Temple.
>
> Among others who refused to enter the Garden of Eden was the Rabbi of Ujhely, who was finally lured into the Garden by an invitation to give a *d'var Torah*, a sermon. Because awareness of time doesn't exist in the Garden, he is said still to be speaking. See also "The Pact" in *Gabriel's Palace*, pp. 256-257, about three rabbis who make a vow to force the coming of the Messiah.
>
> *Sources:*
> *Pe'er ve-Kavod* 16a-b; *Rabbi Yisrael Ba'al Shem Tov* by Menashe Unger.

626. THE CONCEALMENT OF ELIJAH

Elijah has gone into hiding and will reappear only at the advent of the Messiah.

> Elijah is often identified as the herald and precursor of the Messiah. Here Elijah is said to have gone into hiding until the advent of the messianic era. The advent of Elijah and the Messiah are two of the criteria for the arrival of the messianic era. The third is the resurrection of the dead. The point is that just as the Messiah is hidden, waiting for the time when his footsteps will be heard, so too is Elijah concealed until it is time for him to fulfill his role in the messianic drama.
>
> This myth runs contrary to the widespread appearance of Elijah in the rabbinic, folk, kabbalistic, and Hasidic lore.
>
> *Sources:*
> *Seder Olam Rabbah* 17; *B. Eruvin* 43b;

627. FORCING THE END

In every generation there are three sages who together possess the power to force the coming of the Messiah. In the time of the ancient sages, it was Rabbi Hiyya and his sons. Elijah the Prophet was a regular visitor to the synagogue of Rabbi Judah ha-Nasi, but one day he was late. When they asked him why, he said, "I had to waken Abraham, wash his hands, let him pray, and return him to sleep; likewise with Isaac and with Jacob."

They asked him, "Why couldn't you waken them together?" Elijah answered, "If they were to pray together, their power could bring the Messiah before his time." They asked, "Are there any like them in this world?" Elijah replied, "Only Rabbi Hiyya and his sons."

That day Rabbi Judah ha-Nasi decreed a fast and let Rabbi Hiyya and his sons lead the prayers. When Rabbi Hiyya said, "He causes the wind to blow," the wind began to blow. When he said, "He causes the rain to fall," rain began to fall.

As he was about to say the line, "He resurrects the dead," they said in heaven, "Who has disclosed this secret?" and the angels replied, "Elijah." They brought Elijah before the heavenly court and gave him sixty lashes of fire. After that Elijah appeared in Rabbi Judah's synagogue as a fiery bear, and chased everyone out.

Over the generations these three sages existed, but rarely did they live near each other, nor did they know that this great power could be theirs if they joined together. But the Seer of Lublin uncovered this secret and revealed it to the other two sages. All of them were filled with a terrible longing for the Messiah. So they made a pact to force the Messiah to come on Simhat Torah of that year.

Now it happened that just before Rosh ha-Shanah, Baruch of Medzibozh took sick and died. Twenty-two days later, on Simhat Torah, the news of Rabbi Baruch's death had reached the Riminov Rabbi, but not the Seer of Lublin. The Riminov Rabbi recognized at once that he must not proceed in the plan to force the End of Days. But the Seer of Lublin knew nothing about it, so on Simhat Torah he danced with the Torah in his arms, and then he went to the second floor and prayed alone there for several hours.

Just as he reached the conclusion of his prayers, the Seer of Lublin suddenly felt a great force from behind push him out the open window. He would have met a certain death, but just before he struck the ground he felt as if a net had caught him. Looking up, he saw Baruch of Medzibozh standing there, and found that he had landed on his *tallit*, which Rabbi Baruch had spread out below. Then the Seer understood that Rabbi Baruch must have died, and that he had come back from the Other World to save him. And he understood as well that the time had not come for the footsteps of the Messiah to be heard in this world.

Not long afterward the Seer of Lublin also took sick, and he died on the Ninth of Av of that year, the day the Temple in Jerusalem was destroyed.

> Both of these accounts, one talmudic and one Hasidic, describe how three rabbis, the greatest of their generation, attempted to force the coming of the Messiah. In the first, Elijah inadvertently reveals one of the key secrets of heaven—that Rabbi Hiyya and his sons have the righteousness and purity of the patriarchs, and therefore have the power to force the coming of the Messiah. This they attempt to do by reading prayers that cause the actions they describe to take place. This causes consternation in heaven, for they are on the verge of forcing the coming of the Messiah. So Elijah is sent to earth as a fiery bear, chasing them out of the synagogue before they can complete their invocation.
>
> The second tale identifies three great Hasidic rabbis, the Seer of Lublin, Reb Menachem Mendel of Riminov, and Baruch of Medzibozh, as the ones in their generation with such great power.
>
> These three rabbis agree to use a mystical secret to force the coming of the Messiah on Simhat Torah, but the death of Baruch of Medzibozh ends their plan. When the rabbi of Riminov learns of this, he does not attempt to bring the Messiah. But because the Seer of Lublin does not receive word of Baruch's death in time, he does make the attempt, which almost costs him his life, when he is pushed out of a window. This clearly demonstrates the anger in heaven at this attempt. However, the Seer's life is saved by the spirit of Baruch of Medzibozh, who sees to it that the Seer lands on his *tallit*. And the Seer of Lublin understands at that moment that Baruch must have died, and that his spirit had come back from the World to Come to save him. Both tales demonstrate the dangers of attempting to hasten the coming of the Messiah, as well as the strong impulse to do so among the rabbis. Both also explain why the Messiah has not yet come.

An interesting parallel to this tale is found in *Sefer Eliyahu* in *Beit ha-Midrash* 3:68-78. Here the prophet Elijah comes to Rabbi Yose's House of Study, and tells Rabbi Yose of hearing God and the Messiah discussing the messianic prophecies of the prophet Isaiah. Just then Samael, the Accuser, came and accused the Israelites of being guilty. This caused Elijah to be dejected, but Rabbi Yose grows angry at Elijah, for he sees it differently, perceiving a hint of the coming of the Messiah in the discussion of God and the Messiah. Then Rabbi Yose reinterprets Isaiah's words, *I will tell of your righteous deeds and all his works, but they will not help at all* (Isa. 57:12), to mean, *I will tell of the righteous deeds* of Israel *and all the works* of Samael *will not help at all.* This transforms Isaiah's expression of grief and hopelessness into a prophecy of messianic hope.

Sources:
B. *Bava Metzia* 85b; *Pesikta Rabbati* 36:1-2; Rashi on B. *Sanhedrin* 98b; *Midrashei Geulah* 307-308; *Tzidkat ha-Tzaddik* 153; *Likutei Moharan* 1:118.

Studies:
"Not *All* is in the Hands of Heaven: Eschatology and Kabbalah" by Rachel Elior.

628. THE CAPTIVE MESSIAH

For many generations the Messiah has sat captive, chained with golden chains before the Throne of Glory. Elijah has tried to release him many times, but he has never succeeded. So Elijah descends to earth and explains that in order to break the chains of the Messiah, he needs a magic saw whose teeth are the deeds of Israel. Every deed adds a tooth to this saw, but every sin takes one away. When there are twice as many good deeds as there are sins, then the saw can be used. That is why it is said that the Messiah will not come until we bring him.

A number of texts describe the Messiah as bound in chains. According to *Pirkei Hekhalot Rabbati*, for example, God will tie up the Messiah's hand and foot for eight years, and during the years that the Messiah is fettered, God will hide His face from him. This is a reminder that the decision of bringing the End of Days, which the Messiah will herald, does not belong to the Messiah, but to God, or to the people Israel, whose good deeds will make it possible. Adding to the complexity, there are even myths in which God Himself is in chains. See "Mourning over the *Shekhinah*," p. 58.

Sources:
IFA 6928.

629. THE SLEEPING MESSIAH

Eighty years ago, in a Polish yeshiva, there were two students who were filled with a longing for redemption. Both of them were eager to travel to the Holy Land, and they especially wanted to see King David's tomb. They dreamed about it day and night, and at last they decided to set out on the journey, even though they didn't have any money. On the way they met with many obstacles, but at last they arrived at the Holy City of Jerusalem. They were thrilled to have arrived there safe and sound, but they did not know how to find King David's tomb. While they were wondering where it was, Elijah the Prophet appeared before them in the form of an old man and showed them the way. And when they reached the foot of Mount Zion, Elijah said:

"Now my sons, ascend Mount Zion until you reach the entrance of King David's tomb, and enter there and go down the steps, until you reach the bottom of the tomb. There you will be blinded by visions of gold, silver, and diamonds. These are only illusions, set to tempt you from your purpose. Ignore them and search for the jug of water at the head of King David. That jug contains water from the Garden of Eden. Pour the water from that jug over the hands of King David as he stretches his hands toward you. Pour the water three times over each hand, and then King David will rise up and the footsteps of the Messiah will be heard in the world. For King David is not dead, he lives and exists. He is only asleep and dreaming, and he will arise when we are worthy of it. By your virtue and merit, he will arise and redeem us. Amen, and may this come to pass."

When Elijah finished these words, he disappeared. The young men then ascended Mount Zion, and went down into the depths of King David's tomb. Everything was just as Elijah had said it would be. They saw King David stretched out on a couch, with a jug of water at his head. And when they reached King David, he stretched out his hands to them. But just then the young men were blinded by all the riches they saw in that tomb, and they forgot to pour water onto the king's outstretched hands. In anguish his hands fell back and immediately the king's image disappeared.

The young men were startled when they realized that they had let the opportunity for redemption slip through their fingers, and now it was too late.

> This is one of many tales about King David being alive. All of them grow out of the saying, *David Melekh Yisrael, hai ve-kayyam*—"David, King of Israel, lives and exists"— taken from the Talmud (B. RH 25a) into a song that remains very popular among Jews to this day. Here King David's role as a great king and founder of Jerusalem is blended with messianic prophecy, and it is King David himself who is identified as the sleeping Messiah, waiting for someone righteous enough to pour water from the Garden of Eden over his hands so that he will wake up. This tale, like so many others concerning the Messiah, explains why the Messiah has not yet come. For another example of such a tale, see "The Ladder of Prayers," p. 490.
>
> *Sources:*
> IFA 966.

630. THE PANGS OF THE MESSIAH

When the time has come for the Messiah to arrive, all the kings of the nations of the earth will be at war with one another. All the nations of the world will be agitated and frightened. The wisdom of the scribes will become foolish, and those who shun sin will be despised. The meeting place of scholars will be laid to waste and given over to harlotry. Pious men and saints will be few, and the Law will be forgotten by its students. The young will insult their elders, and the elders will wait upon the young. Arrows of hunger will be sent forth, and a great famine will arrive, as it is said, *"A time is coming," declares Yahweh, "when I will send a famine upon the land: not a hunger for bread or a thirst for water, but for hearing the words of the Lord"* (Amos 8:11). Then, all at once, they will all be seized with pangs like the pangs of a woman in labor. At that time Israel will cry out in fear, and God will reply, "My children, be not afraid. The time of your redemption has come."

> The struggles that will take place before the advent of the Messiah are known as the "Pangs of the Messiah." These pangs are said to include a great war to be known as the War of Gog and Magog. For Rabbi Kalonymus Kalman Shapira, who experienced great upheaval firsthand in the Warsaw Ghetto, the purpose of the Pangs of the Messiah is to cleanse sins before the Messiah's arrival. For him, these pangs make it possible for Israel to give birth to the Messiah. He links these pangs to God's words to Eve, *"In pain shall you bear children"* (Gen. 3:16), and he observes that before a seed can bring forth a new creation, the seed must be annihilated. In the same way, the "Pangs

of the Messiah" refers to the annihilation that must take place before the birth of a new creation. Israel must suffer birth pangs in order to give birth to the light of the Messiah.

Sources:
B. *Sanhedrin* 97a; B. *Shabbat* 138b; *Pesikta Rabbati* 26:2; *Esh Kadosh* pp. 106-107.

631. THE RAINBOW OF THE MESSIAH

Do not expect the Messiah until a rainbow appears radiating splendid colors throughout the world. At present, the colors of the rainbow are dull, serving merely as a reminder that there will not be another Deluge. But the rainbow that announces the Messiah will have brilliant colors and be adorned like a bride for her bridegroom. When this rainbow appears, it will be a sign that God has remembered His covenant with Israel, and that the footsteps of the Messiah will soon be heard.

> In Genesis 9:12-13, God says about the rainbow: *"This is the sign that I set for the covenant between Me and you, and every living creature with you, for all ages to come. I have set My bow in the clouds, and it shall serve as a sign of the covenant between Me and the earth."* The rainbow serves as a covenant between God and all living creatures that God will not bring on another Deluge, as in the time of Noah. The present myth of the rainbow of the Messiah identifies the rainbow as another kind of covenant, that of bringing Israel out of exile. This Ingathering of the Exiles is one of the requirements of the coming of the Messiah. Here the transformed rainbow, its colors restored to their heavenly perfection, becomes a sign of the impending arrival of the messianic era.

> *Sources:*
> Zohar 1:72b.

632. CALCULATING THE END OF DAYS

When there are signs that the Messiah is ready to come, many righteous individuals will raise their voices. They will scream until their throats become hoarse—and it will do no good. For whenever it is predicted that the Messiah will come at a certain time, it can be certain that he will not come in any manner whatsoever at that time. Furthermore, anyone who tries to calculate the End of Days will be severely cursed. For the Messiah will come only when the minds of men are distracted from thinking of him.

> For many centuries, predictions were rampant about when the Messiah would arrive. Pious Jews always hoped it would be in their lifetimes. Of course, all of these predictions fell through. Here Rabbi Nachman suggests that it is time to give up making such predictions, for they inevitably fail. He even suggests that it is the prediction itself that causes the failure. This seems to be the application of the general belief that if we want something too much, we will never get it. It is remarkably parallel to Franz Kafka's paradox that "The Messiah will not come until he is no longer needed." In Rabbi Nachman's version, the Messiah will not come until the people give up on waiting for him and instead live a pious life without constant thought of their reward. See "The Coming of the Messiah," p. 518.

> *Sources:*
> B. *Sanhedrin* 97a; *Sihot ha-Ran* 126; *Sihot Moharan, Avodat ha-Shem* 81 (31a).

633. THE END OF DAYS

In the world we know, men walk in the light of the sun by day and in the light of the moon at night. But in the End of Days, *No longer shall you need the sun for light by day, nor the shining of the moon for radiance by night* (Isa. 60:19). In what light, then, will men walk? *Yahweh shall be your light everlasting* (Isa. 60:19).

In the coming era there will not be any eating or drinking, or procreation, or trade, nor will there be jealousy or hatred. Instead, the righteous will sit with crowns on their head, and feed on the splendor of the *Shekhinah*.

> The messianic era, known as the End of Days, is described as a kind of heaven on earth. Or it might be viewed as a return to the Garden of Eden. Indeed, all of Jewish history can be encapsulated between the exile from Eden and the messianic era with its return to a prelapsarian era like that of the Garden of Eden. Or the messianic era might be seen as a kind of eternal Sabbath, a permanent state of rest.
>
> *Sources:*
> B. Berakhot 17a; Pesikta de-Rav Kahana 21:5; Gan Eden ve-Gehinnom in Beit ha-Midrash 5:42-48.

634. THE END OF THE WORLD

In the generation when the Messiah comes, fiery seraphim will be sent into the Temple, and stars will appear like fire in every place. The glory of the *Shekhinah* will fill the Temple, and God will bring down His throne and set it in the Valley of Jehoshaphat. At that time God will clothe the Messiah with a diadem, and He will place a helmet of salvation on his head, and gird him with brilliance and splendor. He will also adorn him with glorious garments and place him on a high mountain, and the Messiah will announce, "Salvation is near!" Then the Messiah will proclaim the news to the patriarchs and to Adam, who sleeps in the cave of Machpelah. And Adam will immediately stand up along with his generation, as well as the patriarchs and all the generations from the beginning of time to the last day.

The age of the Messiah will last 400 years, and after that the Messiah shall die, along with all in whom there is human breath. Then the world will be turned back to primeval silence for seven days, as it was at the beginning of Creation, as it is said, *The heavens shall melt away like smoke, and the earth shall wear out like a garment* (Isa. 51:6).

> This is a supernatural portrayal of the End of Days, where the transformation of the world will be evident to everyone and the presence of divine figures, including God, the Messiah, and angels (in the form of fiery seraphim), will be experienced in this world. It includes the rebirth of the great figures of the past, such as Adam and the patriarchs, which is one of the requirements of the Messiah. This, then, is an ultimate fantasy of redemption, when the messianic era that was awaited so long finally arrives.
>
> Of interest, however, is the 400-year time limit associated with this description of the messianic age. After that, it is said that the world will come to an end, to be followed by resurrection and judgment.
>
> *Sources:*
> 4 Ezra 7:27-30; Sefer Eliyahu in Beit ha-Midrash 3:68-78.
>
> *Studies:*
> "The Place of the End of Days: Eschatological Geography in Jerusalem" by Ora Limor.

635. HOW THE END OF THE WORLD WILL COME

On the day of the end of the world, happy and joyous people will come out of the earth. They will beat drums and play flutes and all other musical instruments. They will travel from east to west, toward the Holy Land. The mountains before them will turn into a blooming garden. Every tree will bear fruit, and the stones will turn to meat and rice, and the people will eat to their hearts' content. After this the Messiah will come, and he will separate those who are believers from those who are not. The nonbelievers will go to Gehenna, and the believers will journey with the Messiah to Jerusalem. That is how the end of the world will come.

> This a folk version of the onset of the messianic era. It follows the essential mythic pattern in which the dead are restored to life—these are the people who climb out of the earth, the righteous are gathered to the Holy Land, and the arrival of the Messiah takes place. The details about every tree bearing fruit and stones turning into food demonstrate that the folk understanding of the messianic era is one in which people will still retain the desire to eat, and there will not be any shortages of food.
>
> *Sources:*
> IFA 10919.

636. THE VISION OF THE VALLEY OF DRY BONES

The hand of the Lord came upon me. He took me out by the spirit of the Lord and set me down in the valley. It was full of bones. He led me all around them; there were very many of them spread over the valley, and they were very dry. He said to me, "O mortal, can these bones live again?" I replied, "O Lord God, only You know." And He said to me, "Prophesy over these bones and say to them: O dry bones, hear the word of the Lord! Thus said the Lord God to these bones: I will cause breath to enter you and you shall live again. I will lay sinews upon you, and cover you with flesh, and form skin over you. And I will put breath into you, and you shall live again. And you shall know that I am the Lord!"

I prophesied as I had been commanded. And while I was prophesying, suddenly there was a sound of rattling, and the bones came together, bone to matching bone. I looked, and there were sinews on them, and flesh had grown, and skin had formed over them; but there was no breath in them. Then He said to me, "Prophesy to the breath, prophesy, O mortal! Say to the breath: Thus said the Lord God: Come, O breath, from the four winds, and breathe into these slain, that they may live again." I prophesied as He commanded me. The breath entered them, and they came to life and stood up on their feet, a vast multitude.

And He said to me, "O mortal, these bones are the whole House of Israel. They say, 'Our bones are dried up, our hope is gone; we are doomed.' Prophesy, therefore, and say to them: Thus said the Lord God: I am going to open your graves and lift you out of the graves, O My people, and bring you to the Land of Israel. You shall know, O My people, that I am the Lord, when I have opened your graves and lifted you out of your graves. I will put My breath into you and you shall live again, and I will set you upon your own soil. Then you shall know that I the Lord have spoken and have acted"—declares the Lord.

> The belief in the bodily resurrection of the dead can be traced to this powerful biblical myth of Ezekiel, in which God compels him to resurrect, with his prophesying, the bones in the valley of the dry bones. Here God's intention to bring the people of Israel back to life is presented as an explicit promise, with a powerful demonstra-

tion of God's ability to fulfill it. In messianic myth, the resurrection of the dead becomes one of the three primary requirements that must be fulfilled to initiate the messianic era. The others are the Ingathering of the Exiles and the rebuilding of the Temple in Jerusalem.

Ezekiel's vision of resurrection was taken by later Jewish sources as a scriptural basis for a literal belief in resurrection. In the Talmud, for example, it is stated that "in the future the pious will sprout up and emerge in Jerusalem, and they will rise up in their garments" (*B. Ketubot* 111b). And chapter 34 of *Pirkei de-Rabbi Eliezer*, an important midrashic text, states that "God opens the graves and opens the storehouses of the souls and puts back each soul into its own body."

Still another version of the resurrection of the dead is found in the *Responsum of Hai Gaon* 60a-b: "And God will stretch sinews upon them and cover them with flesh and envelop them with skin, but there will be no spirit in them. And then God will cause the dew of life to descend from heaven, in which there is the light of the life of the soul. And they will recognize that they had lived and died and then risen to life."

There is a debate in *B. Sanhedrin* 92b as to whether the resurrection of the dead as described in Ezekiel should be understood literally or taken as a parable: "Rabbi Eliezer said, 'The dead who were resurrected by Ezekiel stood up and sang songs of praise to God and immediately died.' Rabbi Judah said the story is a true event that served as a parable. Rabbi Eliezer ben Yose said, 'The dead who were resurrected by Ezekiel went up to the Land of Israel, married and begat sons and daughters.' Hearing this, Rabbi Judah stood up and said, 'I am one of their descendants. You see these *tefillin*? They were given to me by my grandfather and once belonged to them!'" It seems likely that we are to understand Rabbi Judah's comments as a sarcastic response to Rabbi Eliezer ben Yose's literalism. However, this debate also serves as evidence of belief in the resurrection in Judaism, where it is listed as the last of the Thirteen Principles of Maimonides.

Sources:
Ezekiel 37:1-14.

637. HOW THE DEAD WILL COME TO LIFE

How will the dead come to life? God will take the Great Shofar in His hand and blow on it seven times, and its sound will go forth from one end of the world to the other.

At the first blast, the whole world will shake and suffer the pangs of the Messiah.

At the second blast, dust will be scattered over the face of the earth and the graves will open.

At the third, the bones will gather together.

At the fourth, the limbs will stretch out.

At the fifth, skin will be stretched over them.

At the sixth, spirits and souls will enter the bodies.

At the seventh, God Himself will raise and resuscitate them and make them stand on their feet.

> The Great Shofar is the second horn of the ram that Abraham slew at Mount Moriah. The first ram's horn was blown by Moses at Mount Sinai. In most messianic traditions, it is said that Elijah will blow the second horn. Here, however, it is God who blows on it to initiate the End of Days. It is also said that God will blow this shofar when He leads the exiles of Israel into their land. See Isaiah 27:13.
>
> The portrayal of the stage-by-stage resurrection of the dead is strongly influenced by Ezekiel's vision of the valley of dry bones (Ezek. 37:1-14). Both take place in stages, but in the present myth these stages, delineated by the blast of the Great Shofar, are similar to the creation of Adam in Genesis.

An alternate version of the resurrection in *Pesikta Hadta* states that "God will bring dust of the earth and dust of the dead, and mix them together, and put into it skin and flesh and sinews and bones. And the angel in charge of souls will come and infuse souls into the bodies. Then they will enter the House of Study where Abraham, Isaac, and Jacob sit before God, the kings of Israel and Judah sit behind Him, and David sits at the head."

Sources:

Pesikta Hadta in *Beit ha-Midrash* 6:47, 6:58; *Midrash Alpha Beta de-Rabbi Akiva* in *Beit ha-Midrash* 3:31; *Tanna de-vei Eliyahu Zuta* 22.

Studies:

"Some Aspects of After Life in Early Rabbinic Literature" by Saul Lieberman.

638. THE DEW OF RESURRECTION

From where does the dew of resurrection descend? From the head of God, as it is said, *"For My head is drenched with dew, My locks with the damp of night"* (S. of S. 5:2). When the time comes to resurrect the dead, God will shake His locks and bring down the dew of resurrection, and by means of that dew, all the righteous dead will rise from the dust.

Others say that after the reviving dew descends, God will seat each person between His knees, and embrace them and kiss them and bring them to life in the World to Come.

This myth finds its source in the verse *For your dew is like the dew on fresh growth* (Isa. 26:19). In these myths, God takes a most active role in the resurrection. In other myths, the resurrection happens as the final stage of a process, or there is an angel who is charged with raising the dead. But here God is the source of the dew that brings about the resurrection. He even takes each person, one by one, to Himself, and brings him or her back to life.

Note that the World to Come is identified here with the messianic era, although they usually refer to separate traditions, where the World to Come is the world of rewards for the souls of the righteous when they leave this world, and the messianic era refers to this world after its transformation at the End of Days. Maimonides defines the World to Come as follows: "The life after which there is no death is the life of the World to Come, in which there is no body, for the World to Come consists of souls with no bodies, like the angels" (Maimonides, *Ma'amar Tehiyat ha-Metim*). As for the messianic era, it will bring about a great transformation in which this world will become a paradise on earth. In effect, it will restore the whole world to the kind of pristine purity found in the Garden of Eden before the Fall.

What is the dew of God? In *Zohar* 3:128a, *Idra Rabbah*, this dew is described as "the light of the pale glow of the Ancient One. And from that dew exist the supernal saints, and it is the manna which they grind for the righteous in the World to Come."

Sources:

Yalkut Shim'oni, Shir ha-Shirim no. 988; *Zohar* 1:130b, 3:128a, *Idra Rabbah*; *Seder Eliyahu Rabbah* 5:22; *Pirkei de-Rabbi Eliezer* 34; *Midrash Tehillim* 68:5.

639. THE RESURRECTION OF THE DEAD

God keeps the souls of the dead alive, and the dead wait, their eyes fixed upon the resurrection.

The patriarchs sought to be buried in the Land of Israel, because the dead in the Land of Israel will be the first to come to life. Not only Abraham and Sarah are buried there, but also Isaac and Rebecca and Jacob and Leah. So too are Adam and Eve said to be buried nearby.

In the days preceding the coming of the Messiah, great events will befall the world. Ten territories will be swallowed up, ten territories will be overturned, and ten territories will have their inhabitants put to death.

When the Messiah comes, all mankind, the quick and those who were dead, will be one in the worship of God. In those days the dead of the Land of Israel will be the first to come back to life. The angel Michael will blow a great blast on the shofar, and the tombs of the dead will burst open in Jerusalem, and God will revive them. When the resurrection comes, those who arise from the dead will see the Eternal Spirit returning to Zion through the Gate of Mercy. This gate has been blocked for many generations. Therefore it is said of this gate that it will not be opened until the eyes of Israel are opened at the End of Days.

In the days of the Messiah, God will rebuild the Temple in Jerusalem and Israel will go up in pilgrimage not three times a year, but on every New Moon and Sabbath. How will it be possible for all flesh to come to Jerusalem? In those days Jerusalem is destined to be as large as the Land of Israel, and the Land of Israel as large as the whole world. And how can they come from the ends of the earth? Clouds will carry the children of Israel to Jerusalem, where they will say their prayers, and then the clouds will carry them back to their homes, as it is said, *Who are these that float like a cloud?* (Isa. 60:8).

Then the walls of Jerusalem will disappear, and the Messiah will rebuild them with precious stones and pearls. The resurrected dead will inhabit this new Jerusalem, and they will be like Adam before he sinned.

After that, the bones of the righteous outside the Land will roll through underground caves until they reach the Mount of Olives in the city of Jerusalem. There God will restore their souls to them, and they will arise and enjoy the days of the Messiah along with those who have already come alive in the Land. And those who are resurrected will not die again and return to dust. But just as God endures forever, so they will live forever. God will give them wings and they will float in the air and fly like angels to the Garden of Eden, where they will learn Torah from God.

Based on Isaiah 26:19: *Oh, let Your dead revive! Let corpses arise! Awake and shout for joy, you who dwell in the dust!—For Your dew is like the dew on fresh growth; You make the land of the shades come to life.* Belief in the resurrection of the dead is the thirteenth of Maimonides' Thirteen Principles. One of the key requirements of the messianic era is the Ingathering of the Exiles, while another is the resurrection of the dead. This key myth describes how that resurrection will take place in the End of Days, along with the ingathering of the righteous dead from where they are buried around the world.

Here it is understood that in the days of the Messiah the dead of the Land of Israel will rejoin the living, and the righteous dead outside the Land will return to the Land and come to life again.

The three patriarchs and their wives are believed to be buried in the Cave of Machpelah in Hebron. *Pirkei de-Rabbi Eliezer* 20 reports that Adam and Eve are also buried there.

In the days of the Temple, there were three pilgrimages a year, at the time of the agricultural festivals of Passover, Shavuot, and Sukkot. Here it is imagined that in the messianic era these pilgrimages will take place much more often, on every new moon and Sabbath, with the people being carried to Jerusalem on clouds. This last detail demonstrates that although the dead will be brought to life, the nature of existence in the messianic era will be markedly different than it was before the End of Days.

The question of whether the dead can be resurrected at all is raised and answered in *Pesikta Rabbati* 48:2: "Successive generations have asked: 'Can we believe that a dead man can be brought back to life?' God replied: 'Why do you have doubts as to whether I shall be able to quicken the dead? Have I not already quickened the dead by the hand of Elijah, by the hand of Elisha, and by the hand of Ezekiel? That which is to be in the time to come has already been in this world.'" This demonstrates that even among believers, there was some doubt about the resurrection of the dead. But it also provides a convincing reply from God, who points out that such resurrection is reported three times in the Bible.

Sources:
Genesis Rabbah 96:5; *Pesikta Rabbati* 1:1, 1:4, 1:6, 1:7, 48:2; *Mishnah Sanhedrin* 10:1; *B. Sanhedrin* 92a-b; *Midrash Tehillim* 104:23; *Zohar* 1:12b; *Otot ha-Mashiah* in *Beit ha-Midrash* 2:58-63; *Otzar ha-Ma'asiyot; Hilkhot Melakhim* 11:1; *Hilkhot Teshuvah* 8:1; *Ma'amar Tehiyat ha-Metim; Hesed le-Avraham* 33b; *Sefer ha-Hezyonot* 2:5; *Sefer Eliyahu* in *Beit ha-Midrash* 3:68-78.

Studies:
"Maimonides' Fiction of Resurrection" by Robert S. Kirschner.
"Resurrection as Giving Back the Dead: A Traditional Image of Resurrection in the Pseudepigrapha and the Apocalypse of John" by Richard Bauckham.

640. HOW THE RESURRECTION WILL TAKE PLACE

On the day that God brings the dead back to life, He will take dust of the earth and dust of the dead and knead them together, and out of the two kinds of dust He will draw bones and sinews. Then God will give the word to the angels in charge of the Treasury of Souls, and out of the treasuries they will take every single soul, thrust each one into a body, and instantly all humankind will stand up.

> This is a description of the resurrection of the dead that closely parallels the original creation of Adam. Just as God took the dust of the earth to make Adam, here God combines the dust of the earth and the dust of the dead and re-creates human beings, giving them souls from the Treasury of Souls. In this view of the resurrection at the End of Days, those who have died will not receive their original bodies, but new ones. See "The Treasury of Souls," p. 166.

Sources:
Eliyahu Zuta 20:31-31.

641. THE WORLD TO COME

There are no bodies in the World to Come, only the souls of the righteous, who are bodiless, like the ministering angels. Since there are no bodies, there is no eating or drinking, nor anything that human bodies require in this world. So too there is no sleep or death, sadness or mirth. That is why the sages said, "The World to Come has neither eating, nor drinking, nor sex in it, but the righteous sit with their crowns on their heads and enjoy the splendor of the *Shekhinah*." Thus the souls of the righteous exist there without toil, but the knowledge they acquired in their lifetimes remains with them. Indeed, because of it they merited the life of the World to Come. Thus the crowns that they wear are the crowns of knowledge. And there, in the World to Come, they enjoy the splendor of the *Shekhinah*, for now they can grasp the truth of God that they did not know when they were burdened with a body.

Whoever believes in the two worlds—this world and the World to Come—will be considered a descendant of Abraham. But whoever does not, will not be considered his seed.

> This myth is a reminder that life in the World to Come will be radically different from life in this world, and, in fact, will lack many of the pleasures associated with the living, such as the enjoyment of eating, drinking, and sex. Even the crowns that rabbinic

literature describes as being worn by the righteous in heaven are here presented in meta-phorical terms—as crowns of knowledge. It seems clear that this more naturalistic de-scription of the World to Come was intended to counter rabbinic and folk traditions of heavenly rewards that consist of gold and other precious items, such as the golden tables said to be awaiting the righteous in Paradise, as described in *B. Ta'anit* 24b-25a.

Sources:
B. Berakhot 17a; *Midrash Rabbah* 53:16; *Hilkhot Teshuvah* 8.

642. THE GREAT AGE

When the whole of creation, visible and invisible, comes to an end, each person will go to the Lord's judgment. And all who are judged righteous will be gathered together into the great age, and it will be eternal. For all time will perish, and afterward there will be neither years nor months nor days, and hours will no longer be counted. There will be instead a timeless, single age. Then those who have been judged righteous will have the great indestructible light of Paradise, and it will serve as the shelter of their eternal resi-dence. And the faces of the righteous will shine forth like the sun.

Even after existence ends, the righteous will be sheltered eternally by the light of Paradise. Thus Paradise, with its attendant rewards, will continue to exist when ev-erything else is gone.

Sources:
2 Enoch 65:6-11.

643. LIFE IN THE WORLD TO COME

What will life be like in the World to Come? God will be seated in His great academy, and seated in His presence will be the righteous of the world, along with their wives, their sons, their daughters, their manservants, and their maidservants. The needs of their house-holds will all be provided for them. There will be no hunger or thirst or sexual desire, but the righteous will feast on the splendor of the *Shekhinah*.

Here the righteous not only have God as their teacher, but this myth portrays a vision of the afterlife as a continuation of life among the living, where they will be surrounded by their families, servants, and all that they required when they were alive, except for food and drink. The study of Torah, in classes led by God or one of the great patriarchs or sages, is a standard feature in descriptions of the World to Come. But in *Eliyahu Rabbah* other, more elemental rewards of the World to Come are described, where the righteous continue to be surrounded by their families in the afterlife.

Sources:
Eliyahu Rabbah 4:19.

644. THE CHORUS OF THE RIGHTEOUS

In the days to come, God Himself will lead the chorus of the righteous. He will sit in their midst in Paradise, and they will dance around Him like young maidens, and point to Him with a finger, saying: *"For God—He is our God forever; He will lead us evermore"* (Ps. 48:15).

But there are those who say that this dance will take place in Gehenna, where there is a great deal of space. How can the righteous live in the habitation of the wicked? The righteous will implore mercy for the wicked, and their sins will be pardoned.

This is a portrait of the afterlife that presents it as a place of great rejoicing, where the righteous will dance around God and celebrate His glory. This, then, is the reward of the righteous for occupying themselves with Torah study in this world.

The surprising alternate version, where the righteous dance in Gehenna instead of in Paradise in order to implore mercy for the wicked, adds a merciful purpose to their dance that provides them with a mission in the World to Come. The implication is that even in Paradise the righteous have a duty to assist others, as they did in this world.

Sources:
B. *Hagigah* 12b; B. *Ta'anit* 31b; *Leviticus Rabbah* 11:9; *Makhon Siftei Tzaddikim* on Genesis 7:7.

Studies:
"Some Aspects of Afterlife in Early Rabbinic Literature" by Saul Lieberman.

645. FAT GEESE FOR THE WORLD TO COME

In one of his travels Rabbah bar Bar Hannah came across two geese. Because of their fatness, their feathers had fallen out. Rivers of oil flowed from under them. Rabbah asked one of the geese if he would deserve to eat from it in the World to Come. One of the geese raised a foot, as if to say, this will be your portion. The other goose raised a wing, as if to say, this is your portion from me.

A feast for the righteous is one of the rewards for the righteous in the World to Come. One of these rewards is a great banquet, for which these geese are being saved. They are so fat and succulent that rivers of oil flow from under them. See the following myth, "The Messianic Banquet."

Sources:
B. *Bava Batra* 73b.

646. THE MESSIANIC BANQUET

In the time to come God will prepare a banquet for the righteous from the flesh of Behemoth, Leviathan, and the Ziz, as it is said, *He prepared a lavish feast for them* (2 Kings 6:23). God will say to them, "Do you want cider or citrus or grape wine?" Then God will leave His glorious throne, and sit with them. Who will be seated at the table? The Patriarch Jacob along with scholars and distinguished students. The rest of Leviathan will be spread on the walls of Jerusalem, and its radiance will shine from one end of the world to the other. So too will God make a *sukkah* for the righteous with the skin of Leviathan.

Others say that God will serve the Messiah-ox and messianic wine at the banquet. The Messiah-ox makes its home in Paradise, where it waits to fulfill its destiny when the Messiah comes. Then it will be slaughtered and served at the messianic banquet. Then God will bring the righteous wine that had been preserved from grapes from the six days of Creation. Only once before has it been served: when Jacob served wine to his father, Isaac, at the time he brought the food that Rebecca had prepared. Since Jacob had no wine with him, an angel provided some for him, and the angel brought that messianic wine. And he gave it into Jacob's hand, and Jacob handed it to his father, and he drank.

Of all the patriarchs, why is it that it will be Jacob who will join them at the feast? When the children of Israel sin, only Jacob in the Cave of Machpelah feels defiled. So when the gladness of redemption comes, Jacob will rejoice in it more than any of the other patriarchs, for he alone will be called to the feast.

This myth describes a great feast, prepared by God, that will take place after the coming of the Messiah. It finds its origin in this messianic prophecy in Isaiah 25:6: *The Lord of Hosts will make on this mountain for all the peoples a banquet of rich viands, a banquet of choice wines—of rich viands seasoned with marrow, of choice wines well refined.* Those most deserving will taste the flesh of Leviathan. Here the righteous are described as scholars and distinguished students, reinforcing the notion that study of the Torah is the most important occupation of all. In addition, they will be joined by the Patriarch Jacob. The inclusion of Jacob alone suggests the tendency to elevate Jacob to great heights because of the identification of Jacob and Israel. See "Jacob the Angel," p. 364 and "Jacob the Divine," p. 366.

The Book of Paradise, a midrashic satire by Itzik Manger, has the blind Isaac, living in heaven, mark his portion on the Messiah-ox, which will be slaughtered when the Messiah comes. This satirizes Isaac's apparent love of the taste of venison. In one episode, someone plays a trick on the Messiah-ox by telling it that the Messiah has come—and therefore it is about to be slaughtered. In terror the ox runs out of Jewish heaven into Christian heaven—heaven consists of three parts, according to Manger, the third being Muslim heaven—and the Christians refuse to give him back. This requires a series of messages between King Solomon and Saint Paul, who rule Jewish and Christian heaven respectively. Eventually, the Messiah-ox is returned in Manger's novel, but it is badly underfed, and there is some question about whether it is fit to be served at the messianic banquet.

In the frame story of Manger's satire, the angel Shmuel Abba is commanded to be reborn, and he manages to get the angel who is to deliver him to earth drunk by giving him messianic wine. On the day the angel is born, he sits up in the cradle and he tells the history of his life in Paradise to his astounded parents and all those who assemble to hear him.

Sources:
Targum Pseudo-Yonathan 27:25; *B. Bava Batra* 75a; *Midrash Tehillim* 14:7; *Seder Gan Eden* (version B) in *Beit ha-Midrash* 3:131-140.

647. THE MESSIANIC TORAH

The Torah of the mundane world is worthless compared to the Messianic Torah of the World to Come. This Torah will taught by the Messiah, or, some say, even by God Himself. This is the Torah that God delights in, which is studied by the righteous in the World to Come. It begins with *aleph*, the first letter of the alphabet, while the earthly Torah begins with *bet*, the second letter.

Study of the Torah will continue in the World to Come, but the Torah that will be taught there will be far more profound than the Torah of this world. This is the Torah that God delights in, and from which the righteous learn in the heavenly Garden of Eden. This notion of a transformed text is also found in the traditions concerning the first tablets of the Law that were given to Moses on Mount Sinai. See "The First Tablets," p. 266.

For the kabbalists, such as Hayim Vital of Safed in the sixteenth century, the true meaning of the Torah was not in its literal meaning, but in the secret, inner meanings. Further, redemption—i.e., the messianic era—could only be achieved by means of kabbalah. Hayim Vital's description of the Torah of this world as relatively "worthless" might seem shocking, but since the mundane dimension of the Torah concerns rules relevant to human beings, it has no relevance in the World to Come. In fact, in one midrash Moses convinces the angels that they have no need for the Torah, since it is relevant only to humans. However, kabbalists are discarding only the literal level of the Torah; the higher levels of interpretation are considered to contain infinite mysteries.

The notion of a Messianic Torah grows out of the tradition that there are two To-rahs in Judaism, an Oral Torah and a Written Torah. See "The Two Torahs," p. 277. For more on the tradition that the Messiah will teach Torah in the World to Come, see "The Messiah's Yeshivah," p. 518.

Sources:
Etz Hayim, Introduction to *Sha'ar ha-Hakdamot* 4a-b; *Likutei Torah.*
Studies:
"Not *All* is in the Hands of Heaven: Eschatology and Kabbalah" by Rachel Elior.
"Good and Evil in the Kabbalah" in *The Mystical Shape of the Godhead* by Gershom Scholem, pp. 56-88.
The Messianic Idea in Judaism by Gershom Scholem, pp. 59-81.
"From Theosophy to Midrash: Lurianic Exegesis and the Garden of Eden" by Shaul Magid.

648. A TABERNACLE FOR THE RIGHTEOUS

In the time to come God will bring the skin of Leviathan and make a tabernacle for the righteous, as it is said, *Can you fill his skin with tabernacles?* (Job 40:31). If a man is worthy, a tabernacle will be made for him. If he is not worthy, a mere cover of fish skin will be made for him, as it is said, *And his head with a fish covering* (Job 41:7). The rest of the skin of Leviathan will be spread by God on the walls of Jerusalem and the roof of the sanctuary, and its splendor will shine from one end of the world to the other. Then the righteous of Israel will sit, eat, drink, be fruitful, multiply, and enjoy the splendor of the *Shekhinah*.

This myth is obviously a companion to "The Messianic Banquet." Just as "The Messianic Banquet" describes the extravagant banquet God will provide to the righteous in the World to Come, so this myth describes the kind of shelter they will receive, as food and shelter are a person's most essential concerns. The implication is that each person will have an individual shelter, a *sukkah* made of the skin of Leviathan, or, if one is not worthy of that, made of fish skin.

A further example found in Talmud says that God will provide a necklace for the righteous in the World to Come, but if they are not worthy of it, they will receive an amulet instead.

These related myths not only describe the kind of rewards expected in the messianic era, but also imply that people can expect to retain their individuality as well as his desire for privacy in the World to Come, and that God will fulfill these needs. Even the need to be fruitful and multiply will be fulfilled. As *Seder Gan Eden* puts it, "Every woman among the Israelites will give birth to children every day."

Sources:
B. *Bava Batra* 75a; *Seder Gan Eden* (version B) in *Beit ha-Midrash* 3:131-140.

649. THE NEW JERUSALEM

It is stated that *"New moon after new moon, and Sabbath after Sabbath, all flesh shall come to worship Me"* (Isa. 66:23). How is it possible that "all flesh" shall fit into Jerusalem every new moon and every Sabbath? Because in the End of Days, when there is *a new heaven and a new earth* (Isa. 66:22), Jerusalem is destined to expand its length and breadth, and become as large as the whole of the Land of Israel, and the Land of Israel as large as the world.

The mystical transformation of Jerusalem so that there will be room for "all flesh" to enter there from one new moon to the next as well as from one Sabbath to the next is linked with the myth of the transformation that will take place in the messianic era, so that all the righteous, including those living outside the land of Israel, will come to Jerusalem, and there will be room for all of them. That will be the initiation of messianic Jerusalem.

Sources:
Pesikta Rabbati 1; *Yalkut Shim'oni,* Isaiah 472, 503; *Pesikta de-Rav Kahana* 143b; *Song of Songs Rabbah* 7:4; *Yalkut ha-Makhiri,* Isaiah 49:19; *Arugat ha-Bosem* by Abraham ben Rabbi Azriel.

Studies:
Midrash Yerushalem: A Metaphysical History of Jerusalem by Daniel Sperber, pp. 111-117.

650. MESSIANIC JERUSALEM

When all the population is resurrected and gathered together in the messianic era, where will they all stand? They will all say, *The place is too crowded for me; make room for me to settle* (Isa. 49:20). So God will add to Jerusalem a thousand gardens, a thousand palaces, and a thousand mansions, until the future Jerusalem is three times the size of the present one. Then God will enlarge Jerusalem until it rises to the heavens. God will raise it from one heaven to another, until it reaches the seventh. Some say: until it reaches the Throne of Glory.

How does it rise? With clouds sent by God, while each of the righteous has a canopy of his own, as it is said, *Over all the glory shall hang a canopy* (Isa. 4:5). As soon as Jerusalem reaches the Throne of Glory, God will say, "You and I will walk together through the universe."

Others say that Jerusalem will expand on earth until it reaches Damascus, for Jerusalem is destined to widen on all sides, and the exiles will come and repose beneath it as they would beneath a fig tree.

This myth wrestles with the problem of where to fit all the righteous who are resurrected at the End of Days. Jerusalem just isn't big enough to hold everyone, so it is proposed that God will raise Jerusalem to heaven. An alternate version suggests that the boundaries of the city will simply be expanded, something that has already happened with the modern state of Israel, though not all the way to Damascus. See "The New Jerusalem," p. 510.

Some versions say that God will provide seven canopies for every righteous person, or that God will make a canopy for every one according to his status.

Sources:
Song of Songs Rabbah 7:5; *Pirkei de-Rabbi Eliezer* 31; *B. Bava Batra* 75a; *Sefer Eliyahu* in *Beit ha-Midrash* 3:68-78.

651. THE GOLDEN GATE OF THE MESSIAH

At the End of Days, God shall lower the heavenly Jerusalem to take the place of the earthly Jerusalem that was destroyed. The Temple will be established, and a pillar of fire shall burst forth from inside the Temple as a sign to all who witness it.

Then, at God's command, two angels shall recover the Golden Gate of Jerusalem from where it is hidden under the earth, and they shall raise it back to its original place. Abraham shall stand to its right and Moses and the Messiah shall stand to its left, and all Israel shall come forward through the gate.

The Golden Gate is another name for the Gate of Mercy in Jerusalem, which has long been covered over. Here God restores it to its original place, and it becomes the gate that Israel passes through to enter the new world created at the End of Days. The Gate of Mercy is also linked to the *Shekhinah*, who is said to have left Jerusalem through this gate after the Temple was destroyed, and who will one day return to Jerusalem through that same gate. See "The Wandering of the *Shekhinah*," p. 55.

Sources:
Ma'aseh Daniel in *Beit ha-Midrash* 5:128.

Studies:
"The Gates of Righteousness" by Julian Morgenstern.

652. THE DESCENT OF THE HEAVENLY TEMPLE

In the End of Days the celestial Temple will descend from on high and come to rest on four golden mountains, as it is said, *In the days to come, the Mount of Yahweh's house shall stand firm above the mountains* (Isa. 2:2). Its height will reach to heaven, to the stars and to the wheels of the Chariot. And the Bride of God will fill it, and God's glory will fill its hall, and inside each angel will be busy with his work, Gabriel and Michael and their myriads. And at Zion's restoration, the very mountains will burst into song. The mountain of the Lord's house will lead in the singing, and the lesser mountains will answer.

The Holy of Holies of the future Temple will be built of twelve onyx stones. The radiance of the Holy of Holies will illuminate the entire world and ascend to the Throne of Glory.

How will people go there? They will fly like clouds and like doves. In this way great multitudes will enter the Temple to be blessed with eternal life.

In some myths all of the heavenly Jerusalem descends to earth, coming to rest on three or four mountains. In others, such as this myth, it is the Temple alone that descends upon the mountains. Here the image of the Temple dominates the upper world, while the Temple itself is filled with God's presence, both His Bride, the *Shekhinah*, and His glory.

In *Pesikta de-Rav Kahana* 21:4 it is said that God will bring three mountains, Sinai, Tabor, and Carmel, together and build the Temple on top of them.

In 1860, Tzvi Hirsch Kalischer, an early Zionist, defined his anti-mythological view in *Derishat Zion*: "God will not suddenly descend from on high and command his people to go forth. Neither will he send the Messiah from heaven in a twinkling of an eye, to sound the great trumpet for the exiles of Israel and gather them into Jerusalem. He will not surround the holy city with a wall of fire or cause the holy Temple to descend from heaven." Here we find a list of supernatural events that were traditionally expected to occur in the time of the Messiah, including the descent of the heavenly Temple. But Kalischer dismisses all of these, writing instead that "the redemption will come through natural causes by human effort . . . to gather the scattered of Israel into the Holy Land."

Sources:
Pirkei Mashiah in *Beit ha-Midrash* 3:69; *Pesikta de-Rav Kahana* 21:4.

653. THE CREATION OF THE THIRD TEMPLE

At the End of Days, the Ingathering of the Exiles will take place, the Temple in Jerusalem will be rebuilt, and the footsteps of the Messiah will be heard. Even now, God is secretly building the third Temple far under the earth. When the days of the Messiah are upon us, the third Temple will rise up from below, with the Dome of the Rock balanced on top of it.

One of the primary requirements that the Messiah must fulfill in order to demonstrate that he is indeed the true Messiah is to rebuild the Temple in Jerusalem. This requirement appears impossible at this time, since the Dome of the Rock has been built on the Temple Mount, or what is commonly regarded as the place where the Temple once stood. Indeed, some messianic groups in Israel have plotted to blow up the Dome to pave the way for the Temple to be rebuilt. But such a reckless act could inflict a disaster on Israel.

Under these circumstances, Rabbi Zalman Schachter-Shalomi (1924-) has offered this ingenious myth, which resolves the problem of how the third Temple can be built on the Temple Mount in Jerusalem. It is a peaceful solution to an otherwise unresolvable dilemma.

Sources:
Oral teaching of Rabbi Zalman Schachter-Shalomi, collected by Howard Schwartz.

654. REBUILDING THE TEMPLE

In the hour of the Redemption, when God remembers His covenant with Israel, the Temple in Jerusalem will be rebuilt. God will say to the *Shekhinah*, "Rise from the dust," and she will answer, "Where should I go, since My house is destroyed and My Sanctuary is burnt to the ground?" Then God will say, "Do not grieve, for I Myself shall rebuild it, a perfect structure."

Some say that God will then bring the mountains of Sinai, Tabor, and Carmel together and rebuild the Temple upon their peak. That is the meaning of the verse *And nations shall walk by your light, kings, by your shining radiance* (Isa. 60:3). Then the Temple will sing aloud, and the mountains will answer the song. So too will Jerusalem serve as a beacon to all of the nations, and they will walk in her light.

Others say that God will raise up the Temple from the dust and renew it, and its gates, which are buried in the earth, will rise up, every one in its place. And God will reestablish the Sanctuary, and rebuild the city of Jerusalem. Then the *Shekhinah* shall arise and shake off the dust and the Ingathering of the Exiles shall begin.

One of the key events of the messianic era will be the rebuilding of the Temple. This is one of the requirements that must be fulfilled prior to the return of the *Shekhinah* from exile. It is understood that this Third Temple, of divine origin, will be eternal, and will never be destroyed. An extensive description of the future Temple is found at the end of the Book of Ezekiel, chapters 40-48, beginning with a vision: *The hand of Yahweh came upon me, and He brought me there. He brought me, in visions of God, to the Land of Israel, and He set me down on a very high mountain* (Ezek. 40: 1-2).

In one version of this myth from *Pesikta de-Rav Kahana*, it is said that God will bring three mountains together and build the future Temple there. In most other sources, the rebuilding of the Third Temple takes place in Jerusalem. And as soon as the Temple is rebuilt, the *Shekhinah* will return from Her exile at the time the Temple, Her home in the world, was destroyed.

In *Pesikta Rabbati* 31:5, God describes the covenant between Himself and Israel, where both are responsible for bringing about the End of Days: "My Torah is in your hands, and the End of Days in Mine. Each of us has need of the other. If you need Me to bring the time of redemption, I need you to keep My Torah so as to hasten the building of My Temple and Jerusalem. And just as it is impossible for Me to forget the time of redemption, so you must never forget the Torah."

Sources:
Pesikta Rabbati 20:3, 28:1; *Pesikta de-Rabbi Eliezer* 51; *Pesikta de-Rav Kahana* 21:4; *Zohar*
   1:134a, 2:7a.

655. THE MESSIANIC SPRING

In the future, when the voice of the Messiah proclaims salvation from a high mountain, waters will rise up from under the threshold of the Temple, as it is said, *A spring from the house of Yahweh will go forth and water all the valley* (Joel 4:18). Every field and vineyard watered by those streams will yield fruit, even those that had never yielded fruit before. And everyone who is ill who bathes in those waters will be healed, as it is said, *The water will become wholesome* (Ezek. 47:8). Those waters will generate all kinds of fish, and those fish will ascend in that stream as far as Jerusalem, where they will leap into the nets of fishermen. And those fish will be as sweet as manna. Floating above that spring, the Temple court will appear to be a small vessel, as it is said, *Behold water from a vessel* (Ezek. 47:2).

Some say that spring will branch into twelve streams, one for each of the twelve tribes. Others say that it will form a river that will cleanse every impurity, uncovering treasures that have been hidden for centuries. Even the Angel of Death will not be able to cross it.

> *Pirkei de-Rabbi Eliezer* identifies the Dead Sea as the place where the waters will heal, and gives the prooftext from Ezekiel 47:8.
>
> There is a parallel tradition about a river that cannot be crossed—the River Sambatyon, which is said to flow wildly six days a week, trapping the Ten Lost Tribes on one side of it, and only ceasing to flow on the Sabbath, when they are not permitted to cross. There is also a parallel tradition about a place where the Angel of Death cannot enter—the city of Luz. Therefore all the inhabitants of that city are immortal, as long as they do not leave the city. See "The City of Luz," p. 476. For another account of a miraculous spring, see "The Healing Spring," a Hasidic tale about the Ba'al Shem Tov, in *Gabriel's Palace*, pp. 207-298.
>
> *Sources:*
> *Pirkei de-Rabbi Eliezer* 51; *Sefer Eliyahu* in *Beit ha-Midrash* 3:68-78.

656. A MAGICAL TREE IN JERUSALEM

When the third holy Temple is built, a magical tree will grow in Jerusalem. Some say that the leaves of that tree will cause the dumb to speak. Others say that the leaves of that tree will cause barren women to bear children.

> The image of the magical tree is well known in Jewish folk and rabbinic texts, although it is usually associated with the Garden of Eden, especially with the two trees in the center of the garden, the Tree of Life and the Tree of Knowledge. The image of the tree is also closely associated with that of the Torah, because of the verse *She is a tree of life to those who grasp her* (Prov. 3:18).
>
> Here the tree is associated with the building of the Third Temple, which will only take place at the time of the coming of the Messiah. This demonstrates an important parallel between the story of the Garden of Eden and the messianic era—in both enchanted trees can be found. Indeed, there is a direct parallel in Jewish myth between the prelapsarian world and the messianic era. Thus one function of the coming of the Messiah is to restore the world to its pre-fallen state. This parallel is an implicit part of the myth of the Ari. See "The Shattering of the Vessels and the Gathering of the Sparks," p. 122.
>
> The theme of healing leaves is found in world folklore. See, for example, "The Wonderful Healing Leaves," a universal fairy tale of Jewish origin, in *Elijah's Violin*, pp. 163-168. This theme is found in Jewish lore as well. Abraham is said to have col-

lected leaves from the Garden of Eden and Sarah to have crushed them on the eve of the Sabbath and scattered their powder into the air, creating the spice of the Sabbath. See "The Spice of the Sabbath," p. 316. For a Hasidic tale on this theme, see "Leaves from the Garden of Eden" in *Gabriel's Palace*, pp. 134-135, where a man finds enchanted leaves on his bed when he awakes after a dream in which a stable boy who has died brings him leaves from the Garden of Eden to heal the man's sick daughter. Her mourning over the boy's death provoked her illness, and his miraculous assistance heals her.

Sources:
B. *Sanhedrin* 100a; *Likutei Moharan* 1:60.

657. THE PLEADING OF THE FATHERS

In the hour that Israel was exiled, the fathers of the world, along with the mothers, were raised from their graves in the Cave of Machpelah and brought up to the firmament and began a great mourning before God.

God joined them from the highest heaven and said, "Why are you mourning?"

They replied: "Master of the Universe, what sins did our children commit that You did this to them? Are You not going to have mercy on them? Are You not going to show compassion?"

God replied, "Because of their wickedness, they were punished by exile."

The Fathers said, "But will You remember them in their exile among the nations of the world, or will You become oblivious to them?"

God answered, "I cannot now save them from their exile, but I swear by My name that I shall never forget them, and one day their exile shall come to an end."

These words of God greatly comforted the fathers and mothers, and they returned and lay down in their tombs. That is why, when the Messiah comes, he will go to the Cave of Machpelah to wake them first.

> Here the patriarchs Abraham, Isaac and Jacob and their wives gather before God to plead for their children, Israel, who have been sent into exile. Because of their elevated roles, the patriarchs are able to speak their mind to God. In effect, they give voice to the sense of injustice felt among Jews in the Diaspora. The plea of the patriarchs and matriarchs moves God, who assures them that one day—the day the Messiah comes—their exile will come to an end.
>
> This myth finds its source in Jeremiah's vision or imagining of Rachel haunting her tomb and weeping for her exiled children: *A cry is heard in Ramah—wailing, bitter weeping—Rachel weeping for her children. She refuses to be comforted for her children, who are gone* (Jer. 31:15). (According to 1 Sam. 10:2, Rachel's tomb was located near Ramah.) Indeed, Jeremiah's account of Rachel weeping is the biblical source for all subsequent myths about biblical figures reappearing to comfort Israel.
>
> This myth is also parallel to those found in the *Zohar* in which the *Shekhinah*, the Bride of God, confronts God over the destruction of the Temple and the exile of Israel. This myth also explains why the patriarchs and matriarchs will be the first to be resurrected in the messianic era.
>
> In the version of this myth in *Seder Gan Eden*, there is a less consoling ending. The angel Michael, the prince of Israel, weeps in a loud voice, *"Why, O Lord, do you stand aloof"* (Ps. 10:1). See the following myth, "Waking the Fathers," as well as "The Patriarchs Seek to Comfort Jerusalem," p. 420.
>
> *Sources:*
> *Pesikta de-Rav Kahana* p. 464; *Seder Gan Eden* (version B) in *Beit ha-Midrash* 3:131-140.

658. WAKING THE FATHERS

Why were the patriarchs buried in the Land of Israel? Because the dead of the Land will be the first to come to life in the days of the Messiah.

In the hour that God crowns the Messiah, Israel will say to him: "Go and bring the glad tidings to those who sleep in the Cave of Machpelah, so that they shall be the first to arise."

Then the Messiah will go to the Cave of Machpelah and say to the Fathers: "Abraham, Isaac, and Jacob, arise! You have slept long enough." And they will reply and say, "Who is it who uncovers the dust from our eyes?" And he will reply, "I am the Messiah of the Lord. The hour of salvation is near." And they will answer, "If that is really so, then go to Adam, the first man, and bring the tidings to him, so that he should be the first to arise."

Then the Messiah will go to Adam and say, "Arise, you have slept enough!" And Adam will reply, "Who is this who drives the sleep from my eyes?" And he will reply, "I am the Messiah of the Lord, one of your descendants."

At that instant Adam will stand up, along with his generation, and Abraham, Isaac, and Jacob, and all the righteous and all the tribes and all generations from the beginning of time will arise and chant psalms and songs of jubilation.

> Tradition holds that the patriarchs Abraham, Isaac, and Jacob, known as the *Avot* or Fathers, and their wives, are buried in the Cave of Machpelah in Hebron. Midrashic legend also recounts that Adam and Eve are buried there. The initiation of the messianic era will herald the resurrection of the dead, beginning with Adam, the first man, and the patriarchs.
>
> This myth is almost certainly based on a talmudic one (*B. BM* 85b) about the visits of Elijah to the synagogue of Rabbi Judah ha-Nasi. Elijah is the key figure in heralding the Messiah, as it is said that he will blow the great shofar that announces his coming. This talmudic tale sets the pattern for the waking of the patriarchs at the time of the coming of the Messiah. See "Forcing the End," p. 496.
>
> The previous myth, "The Pleading of the Fathers," also explains why the patriarchs will be the first to be awakened when the Messiah comes.
>
> *Sources:*
> *Pirkei Mashiah* in *Beit ha-Midrash* 3:73-74; *Sefer Eliyahu* in *Beit ha-Midrash* 3:68-78.

659. THE FATHERS ADDRESS THE MESSIAH

In the month of Nisan the patriarchs will arise and say to the Messiah: "Our true Messiah, even though we came before you, you are greater than we because of all the suffering you have endured for the iniquities of our children. You were shut up in prison, sitting in thick darkness, your skin cleaved to your bones, your body as dry as a piece of wood, and your eyes dim from fasting. Your strength was dried up like a potsherd, all because of the sins of our children. Now the time has come for you to come forth out of prison."

The Messiah will reply: "O Fathers, all that I have done is only for your sake and that of your children, for your glory and for theirs, so that God will bestow abundance upon Israel."

Then God will make seven canopies of precious stones and pearls for the Messiah. Out of each canopy will flow four rivers, one of wine, one of honey, one of milk, and one of pure balsam. And God will put a garment upon the Messiah whose splendor will stream forth from one end of the world to the other. And God will summon the north wind and the south wind and say to them: "Come, sprinkle all kinds of spices from the Garden of Eden before My true Messiah." Then God will embrace the Messiah in the sight of the righteous and bring him within the canopy where all the righteous ones, the mighty men of the Torah of every generation, will gaze upon him.

After that God will lift the Messiah up to the heaven of heavens, and cloak him in His own glory.

> This myth, taking place in Paradise, portrays the Messiah as a divine figure whose time has finally come to fulfill his destiny and initiate the messianic era. Here the patriarchs address him as an equal, and speak to him with great gratitude and affection for his long suffering. God then provides great rewards for the Messiah, embracing him in the presence of the righteous. The purpose of this myth is to reaffirm the centrality of messianic belief in Judaism and to demonstrate that the role of the Messiah is to be regarded as equally important as that of the beloved patriarchs. For more on the Messiah's suffering, see "The Suffering Messiah," p. 489.
>
> *Sources:*
> Pesikta Rabbati 37:1-2.

660. THE TWO MESSIAHS

There are two Messiahs, as it is said, *They are the two anointed dignitaries, who attend the Lord of all the earth* (Zech. 4:14). The first Messiah is a son of Joseph, and the second a son of David. The son of Joseph, whom all will recognize as the *Tzaddik* of his generation, will sacrifice his life so that the footsteps of the Messiah might be heard, and the land shall mourn. The second Messiah, the son of David, makes his home in Paradise, in a heavenly palace, where he waits for signs that the time for the coming of the Messiah has arrived.

Each Messiah has a separate role. Messiah, the son of David, will redeem the *Shekhinah*, along with all the holy sparks that were scattered during the six days of Creation. Messiah, the son of Joseph, will redeem the souls of those who fell through sin and transgression, and were transmigrated into inanimate objects, vegetables, animals, and humans. He will free the souls of the righteous that were transmigrated into fish, and the souls of the righteous will be raised up.

> There are two primary conceptions of the Messiah in Judaism: one, the earthly Messiah, a descendant of Joseph, who is the righteous one of his generation; the other, a descendant of David, who serves as an instrument of salvation. Eventually these two conceptions were combined in a single myth in which the first, earthly Messiah, paves the way for the divine one.
>
> *Sources:*
> B. Sukkah 52a; *Midrash Tanhuma-Yelammedenu, Bereshit 1; Megillat Setarim.*
>
> *Studies:*
> *An Unknown Jewish Sect* by Louis Ginzberg, pp. 209-256.

661. THE MESSIAH PETITIONS GOD

After Messiah the son of Joseph was slain, God said to his successor, Messiah the son of David, "Ask anything of Me and I will give it to you."

Messiah the son of David, seeing that Messiah ben Joseph had been slain, said to God, "Master of the Universe, I ask of You only the gift of life."

God replied, "Your father, David, has already prophesied this about you, as it is said, *He asked You for life; You granted it, a long life, everlasting* (Ps. 21:5).

The primary messianic tradition in Judaism describes two Messiahs, Messiah ben Joseph and Messiah ben David. It is the fate of Messiah ben Joseph to pave the way for the heavenly Messiah, but to die in the process. One of the traditions about Messiah ben David is that he will prove that he is the true Messiah by bringing the slain Messiah to life. Here the heavenly Messiah petitions God to do this (since the ultimate power to restore life belongs to God), and God assures him it will happen, as prophesied. For more on the roles of these two Messiahs, see the Introduction, pp. lxi-lxii.
Sources:
B. *Sukkah* 52a.

662. THE COMING OF THE MESSIAH

The Messiah will not come until he is no longer needed. He will not come until a day after his arrival. He will not come on the last day, but on the last of all.

Kafka's paradoxical explanation of when the Messiah will come is so intriguing that it deserves a place in this collection of Jewish myths. It also reflects traditional Jewish teachings about the Messiah. The coming of the Messiah represents the initiation of the End of Days, the messianic era in which all of existence will be transformed, a return to a prelapsarian condition or a kind of heaven on earth. For this reason, the arrival of the Messiah is not important in itself; rather, it is the transformation that accompanies the arrival that matters. This is one way of understanding Kafka's comment that "The Messiah will not come until he is no longer needed."
Sources:
Parables and Paradoxes by Franz Kafka.

663. THE MESSIAH'S YESHIVAH

In the future the Messiah will have his own yeshivah, and those who walk on earth will come there, sit before him, and hear his teachings. And Elijah will stand beside him as his interpreter. And when the Messiah expounds the Torah, his voice will reach from one end of the world to the other.

That is when all the generations will rise up from their graves, filled with the Holy Spirit, and come sit in the Messiah's yeshivah, to hear tales and teachings from his mouth. And whoever hears a midrash from the mouth of the Messiah will never forget it, for God will reveal Himself in that House of Study and pour out His Holy Spirit upon all those who walk in the world.

One of the highest honors among rabbis was to be the head of a yeshivah, a rabbinic academy. Here it is said that in the messianic era, the Messiah will have his own yeshivah, where he teaches both *Halakhah* (law) and *Aggadah* (non-legal teachings, often legends). (It is interesting to note that *Aggadah* is mentioned first, demonstrating its importance among the Yemenite Jews.) All Jews among the living will come to hear him, and the sound of his voice will resurrect the dead. This is a word-oriented form of initiating the messianic era, with the supernatural voice of the Messiah bringing about the resurrection. Note the central role given to Elijah, to interpret the teachings of the Messiah. This confirms the rabbis' central concept of the importance of commentary and interpretation, as well as the notion that of the chain of tradition in transmitting the Torah goes from God to Moses, Moses to the prophets, and the prophets to the rabbis.

Of great interest is the way in which the Messiah, inspired by God's Holy Spirit, the *Ruah ha-Kodesh*, reveals God's essence, while God Himself is present in the yeshivah. It is also the Holy Spirit that brings the dead to life and brings its blessings to all of the living.

Rabbinic myth portrays the World to Come as containing yeshivahs for all of the principal rabbis and patriarchs. One story told by Shlomo Carlebach describes a heavenly journey to such academies.

Another interesting aspect of this myth is the assumption that the Messiah would be a master teacher of the Torah. It also reinforces the archetypal quality of the Torah, which is just as important in heaven as it is on earth.

Sources:
Midrashei Geulah.

664. THE DUAL MESSIAH

God said to Moses: "Moses, I swear to you, in the future to come, when I bring the prophet Elijah to herald the End of Days, the two of you will come as one. In that hour the Messiah will come and bring comfort to Israel."

Thus the one known as the Messiah is actually two, for the Messiah is none other than Moses and Elijah come together as one. That is how God's vow to Moses will be fulfilled.

> Moses and Elijah are each models for the Messiah. For the Samaritans, Moses was virtually regarded as a messianic figure. Rabbinic concern that the role of Moses might come to transcend that of a prophet and take on messianic attributes may have been the reason that the role of Moses in the Exodus was almost entirely omitted from the Passover Seder. (Byron Sherwin suggests that this omission was triggered by the early Christian description of Jesus as the "new Moses.") As for Elijah, his messianic role is explicit—it is said that he will herald the coming of the Messiah, and will blow the shofar (ram's horn) from the ram that Abraham sacrificed on Mount Moriah in place of Isaac. (Moses is said to have blown the ram's other horn at Mount Sinai.) Thus, together Moses and Elijah have all of the attributes of the Messiah, and this radical midrash from *Deuteronomy Rabbah* goes a step further, stating that the Messiah will *be* Moses and Elijah "come together as one," suggesting that they will be reincarnated as a single figure.

> *Sources:*
> *Deuteronomy Rabbah* 3:17

665. THE INGATHERING OF THE EXILES

The day of the Ingathering of the Exiles will be as great as the day on which the Torah was given on Mount Sinai. All Israel will be clothed in splendor and radiance, and the *Shekhinah* will walk at their head, with the prophets at their sides, bearing the Ark and the Torah.

Jerusalem will not be rebuilt until all the exiles have been brought back. Then God will rebuild it and never destroy it again.

In that hour the hands of every warrior will grow weak, and there will not be any weapons that are not destroyed. So too will every idol be destroyed, and God will rule from one end of the world to the other.

Indeed, the day of the Ingathering of the Exiles will be as important a day as the day when heaven and earth were created.

> The Ingathering of the Exiles—thus the gathering of all the scattered Jewish communities in the world to the Holy Land—is one of the three requirements of the Messiah, along with rebuilding the Temple in Jerusalem and the resurrection of the dead. Here it is portrayed as a great caravan, with the *Shekhinah*, God's Presence, at the head. So too will Isaiah's prophecy that *they shall beat their swords into ploughshares* (Isa. 4:2) be fulfilled, in that all weapons will be destroyed.
>
> The idea of the Ingathering of the Exiles so permeated Jewish life that it can be found in a dream of Hayim Vital from *Sefer ha-Hezyonot* 2:34: "I saw in a dream that I was walking along a great river, and I saw a multitude of Israelites there in tents. I entered and I saw their king reclining in the tent. When he saw me, he said, 'Know that I am the king of Israel, of the tribe of Ephraim, and we have come now because the time has come for the Ingathering of the Exiles.'"
>
> *Sources:*
> B. Pesahim 93a; Pesikta de-Rav Kahana 2:463-64; Midrash Tanhuma-Yelammedenu, Noah 11.

666. THE BIRTH OF ARMILUS

In Rome there is a marble sculpture of a beautiful woman that was not created by human hands. Some say it was brought into being during the six days of Creation. It is also said that Satan lusts after it, and one day he will descend to earth, go to Rome, and copulate with it. And the stone will become pregnant. After nine months it will burst open and a male child will emerge in the shape of a man with two heads, twelve cubits high, his eyes set a span apart, crooked and bloodshot, his hair red, his feet green, with six fingers on each hand. That is how Armilus, the tempter, will be born.

> This is a grotesque myth about the birth of Armilus, who plays the role of the Anti-Christ in Jewish messianic mythology. Armilus is normally explained as a distortion of Romulus, who symbolizes Rome, which also symbolizes Christianity. This may suggest that Christianity is viewed in this myth as a monster born from Judaism. The alluring statue that Satan is predicted to copulate with is said, in some sources, to have been created during the six days of Creation. That adds a new dimension to the myth, as it indicates that God was the sculptor who created it, a fact that Satan surely knows. His copulation with the statue, from this perspective, is not an act of lust so much as an act of hostility toward God. And the product is a virtual Anti-Christ, Armilus, who, it is said, will conquer Israel before finally being defeated by the Messiah.
>
> This must also be seen as an allegory about the worship of idols, which, no matter how alluring, are made of stone.
>
> In some versions of this myth it is Satan who copulates with the statue, while in others her lovers are described as the "sons of Belial" (a biblical term for "worthless people"), who also succeed in impregnating her. In both cases, a grotesque male in the form of a grown man with two heads will emerge. This mythic origin of Armilus explains his supernaturally evil powers, especially in the version in which Satan is his father.
>
> The statue of the woman in this myth echoes the Greek myth of Niobe, whom Zeus turned into a statue. It is said that statue can be seen weeping copiously, while it is said of the statue in the myth of Armilus that it will become pregnant and will give birth. See *Greek Myths* by Robert Graves, 77c.

Sources:
Midrash Aseret ha-Shvatim in Otzar Midrashim, 466; Tefillat Rabbi Shim'on ben Yohai in
    Beit ha-Midrash 4:124-26; Pirkei Hekhalot Rabbati.

Studies:
"Three Typological Themes in Early Jewish Messianism: Messiah Son of Joseph,
    Rabbinic Calculations, and the Figure of Armilus" by David Berger.
"Armilus: The Jewish Antichrist and the Origin and Dating of the 'Sefer
    Zerubbavel'" by Joseph Dan.

667. SATAN AND THE MESSIAH

The Messiah existed in God's thought even before the world was created. After the creation, God hid the Messiah under His Throne of Glory until the time was right for him to appear.

Satan asked God, "Master of the Universe, for whom is the light hidden under Your Throne of Glory intended?"

God replied, "For him who will turn you back and put you to shame."

Satan said, "Master of the Universe, let me see him."

God said, "Come and see him."

And when he saw him, Satan was shaken and fell upon his face and said, "Surely this is the Messiah who will cause me to be swallowed up in Gehenna."

Then, on the last day, Satan will endeavor to renew his rebellion against God. He will proclaim that he is God's equal, as well as God's partner in Creation, for while God created the earth, Satan created hell. Then the fire of hell will rise up and destroy Satan, and put an end to his talk.

> Here God reveals the Messiah to Satan. The dialogue between God and Satan may be contrasted with that in the prologue to Job. In Job there is no hostility between God and Satan; here it is quite apparent. In its structure, this myth is similar to that of Moses standing before the Throne of Glory and asking to see Rabbi Akiba, a thousand years in the future (B. Shabbat 88b-89a and B. Menahot 29b). In both cases, God has no difficulty in revealing these mysteries. The fate that Satan describes, of being swallowed up in Gehenna, derives from the verse He will destroy death forever (Isa. 25:8).
>
> While some sources describe Satan as having been created out of the fires of hell, here it is those fires that rise up and destroy him when, on the last day, Satan tries to renew his rebellion against God. See "The Fall of Lucifer," p. 108 and "Satan Cast Out of Heaven," p. 109.
>
> Sources:
> Pesikta Rabbati 33:6, 36:1; Alphabetot 93-94.

668. THE ARRIVAL OF THE MESSIAH

At that time all the nations of the earth will be in utter darkness. When the Messiah appears, he will stand on the roof of the Temple, and he will make a proclamation to Israel, saying, "Behold my light as it rises upon you." Then God will brighten the light of King Messiah and all of Israel will be illumined by it, as well as all the other nations of the earth.

> The Messiah is able to stand on the roof of the Temple, because one of the requirements of the time of the coming of the Messiah is the supernatural rebuilding of the Temple. This rebuilding precedes the actual coming of the Messiah, thus making it possible for him to stand on the roof to announce his arrival. The light of which the Messiah

speaks is that from the verse *Wherefore the light is come, and the glory of Yahweh is risen upon you* (Isa. 60:1). Here the Messiah is mythically identified with the rising sun. The notion that all of the nations of the earth will walk in the light of the Messiah is found in the verse *And nations shall walk by your light, kings, by your shining radiance* (Isa. 60:3).

Sources:
Pesikta Rabbati 36:2.

669. GOD REPRIMANDS THE UNIVERSE

In the time to come God will sit on His Throne of Justice and summon heaven and earth and say to them, "In the beginning of everything I created you. How then could you look upon My *Shekhinah* removing Herself, My Temple being destroyed, and My children being banished among the nations of the world, and not entreat mercy on their behalf?" Then He will reprimand heaven and earth. After that God will summon the sun and moon and reprimand them as well, along with the stars and planets.

Then God will summon Metatron and say, "I gave you a name to be equal to Mine, as it is said, '*For My name is in him* (Exod. 25:21). How, then, could you look upon My *Shekhinah* removing Herself, My Temple being destroyed, and My children being banished among the nations of the world, and not entreat mercy on their behalf?"

After that God will summon the fathers of the world, to whom He will say, "I issued harsh decrees against your children, yet you asked for no mercy on their behalf. I made it plain to you from the very beginning that your children were to be banished, as it is said, '*Know well that your offspring shall be strangers in a land not theirs*'" (Gen. 15:13). So God will reproach the Fathers of the world.

After that God will abolish the present order of the world, and then He will renew the heaven and the earth, as it is said, *For behold! I am creating a new heaven and a new earth* (Isa. 65:17).

> Here God expresses anger that the other forces in the universe—heaven and earth, the sun, the moon, the stars, and the planets, Metatron and the patriarchs—did not strongly protest when God destroyed the Temple and sent the children of Israel into exile. This myth follows the tradition of God's regret for His actions. See, for example, "God Weeps Over the Destruction of the Temple," p. 38 and "God's Lament at the Western Wall," p. 39. Abraham bargained with God over the destruction of Sodom, here God reprimands those who might have similarly protested His actions concerning the Temple.
>
> This myth contradicts others in which the patriarchs do attempt to intervene with God. See "The Pleading of the Fathers," p. 515.
>
> Following these reprimands, God abolishes the present order of the world, and creates a new world, as is predicted to occur at the End of Days.
>
> *Sources:*
> *Eliyahu Zuta 20:31.*

670. A NEW TORAH

God is destined to give a new Torah to Israel at the hands of the Messiah, as it is said, "*A new Torah shall come forth from Me*" (Isa. 51:4). That new Torah will be written with 23 letters in the alphabet. That extra letter had accompanied the other 22 from the first, but it had been invisible. With the addition of that letter, the letters of the Torah will combine in a different way, and new meanings will emerge.

Some say that the Messiah will clarify the words of that new Torah. Others say that Israel will not need the instructions of the Messiah in the days to come. Instead, they will receive instruction directly from God Himself.

For God is destined to sit in the Garden of Eden and interpret the new Torah. All the righteous of the world will sit before Him, and all the household of heaven will stand on their feet. The sun, the planets, and the moon will be at God's right hand, and all the stars at His left.

When God finishes teaching, everyone in the world will say, "Amen!" Even the wicked of Israel in Gehenna will all answer and say "Amen!" The sound of their words will be heard by God, and He will say, "What is that noise that I heard?" The angels will reply, "Those are the wicked of Israel in Gehenna."

At that time God will take the keys to Gehenna and give them to Gabriel and Michael and say, "Go and open the gates of Gehenna and bring them up from there, as it is said, *Open the gates*" (Isa. 26:2).

Then Gabriel and Michael will go at once and open the 40,000 gates of Gehenna and bring them up from Gehenna. They will take each one by the hand and raise him up as a man raises his fellow from a deep pit with a rope.

Gabriel and Michael will then wash and care for and heal them from the wounds of Gehenna. They will dress them in beautiful garments, take them by the hand, and bring them before God.

When they reach the gate of the Garden of Eden, Gabriel and Michael will enter first and God will say to them, "Permit them to come and see My glory!" And when they enter, wicked no longer, they will fall on their faces and prostrate themselves before God and bless and praise His holy name.

So great is the transformation that will take place at the End of Days, that there will even be a new Torah—so suggests *Alpha Beta de-Rabbi Akiva.* It is not clear whether the "days to come" refers to the messianic era, when the resurrection of the dead will take place, or to the time after that. These are the two primary stages of the messianic era. The idea of the abrogation of the law at the time of the resurrection and the giving of the New Torah is found in the Talmud (*B. Nid.* 61b). Louis Ginzberg dismisses any suggestion of Christian influence on this idea (*An Unknown Jewish Sect*, p. 213-214).

The motif of the twenty-third letter of the Hebrew alphabet, which will remain invisible until the messianic era, recalls that which says the Torah was written with black fire on white fire, or that which speaks about the black letters and the white letters, in which the white spaces between the letters are also said to be an essential part of the text. An alternate version of this myth proposes that not a single letter will be added to the Torah or taken away; instead, the letters of the Torah will combine in a different way. For related myths about the new Torah that God will give to the Messiah, see "God Expounds the Torah," p. 36 and "The Messianic Torah," p. 509. See also "Creating New Heavens and a New Earth," p. 255.

Sources:

Midrash Tehillim 146, p. 535; *Genesis Rabbah* 98:9; *Alpha Beta de-Rabbi Akiva* in *Beit ha-Midrash* 3:27; *Zohar* 1:4b-5a; *Battei Midrashot* 2:367-369; *Sha'arei Gan Eden* 12c; *Sefer ha-Temunah* 62a; *Se'udat Gan Eden* in *Otzar Midrashim* p. 90.

Studies:

On the Kabbalah and Its Symbolism by Gershom Scholem, pp. 77-86.

APPENDIX A
A NOTE ON THE SOURCES

The sources of the myths drawn upon in this book include the full range of Jewish texts. These include texts that are both *within accepted Jewish tradition* (and therefore regarded by most Jews as "sacred") and those, primarily the Apocrypha and Pseudepigrapha, that are *outside that tradition*. These texts include the Bible, as well as the rabbinic, kabbalistic, and hasidic texts, and a wide range of additional sources. The rabbinic texts consist of the Babylonian and Jerusalem Talmuds, which contain traditions that continued to evolve until about the end of the fifth century CE, plus the collections of rabbinic commentaries and legends known as the Midrash, compiled from about the third to at least the twelfth centuries CE. Each of the Talmuds contains the same core text, the Mishnah, and separate commentaries on it, known as the Gemara. To a large extent, rabbinic sources consist of commentary on the Hebrew Bible. Text and commentary are closely linked, and prooftexts—biblical verses—are offered in order to demonstrate the truth of an assertion. Even the pre-Christian translation of the Bible into Greek, known as the *Septuagint*, and early Jewish biblical translations into Aramaic, known as *Targums*, often reflect interpretations of a mythic nature.

What we think of as mainstream Judaism is the Pharisaic/rabbinic reading of the biblical tradition, which became normative Judaism after the fall of the Second Temple. The texts that are outside the mainstream are either early alternatives to the Pharisaic/rabbinic tradition, such as Samaritanism, the writings of the Qumran sectarians and the Enoch literature, or rebellions against it, such as Karaism.

The Jewish mystical tradition extends from the ancient period to the modern era. It includes the *Zohar*,* the primary kabbalistic text, edited (or perhaps written) in the thirteenth century, with especially important developments related to the teachings of Rabbi Isaac Luria of Safed in the sixteenth century. The primary Hasidic texts, beginning with the teachings of the Ba'al Shem Tov, and including other great Hasidic masters, such as Rabbi Levi Yitzhak of Berditchev and Rabbi Nachman of Bratslav, date from the eighteenth to the

---

*The *Zohar* itself claims to represent the theosophical discussions of a small group of mystically-minded sages in second century CE Palestine, the foremost of them being Rabbi Shimon bar Yohai. Gershom Scholem, following nineteenth century scholars like Heinrich Graetz, argued that the *Zohar* was a pseudepigraphic work written by Moshe de Leon in the thirteenth century, and Isaiah Tishby supported this view by pointing out words of Spanish origin in the text. More recently, Moshe Idel and Yehuda Liebes have argued that the text of the *Zohar* was compiled and edited by members of the kabbalistic circle to which de Leon belonged. A third view, suggested by Abraham Joshua Heschel and conveyed by Byron Sherwin, is that there were small circles of mystics in many generations, possibly going back as far as Rabbi Shimon bar Yohai, who studied privately and orally for hundreds of years, and traditions coming out of these mystical circles were drawn upon to compile the *Zohar*. According to Heschel, it is possible that some of these traditions, probably the core traditions, are traceable back to Shimon bar Yohai. In that sense, bar Yohai may have been the initial author of the *Zohar*, and the teachings initiated in his mystical circle were passed down orally for hundreds of years until Moshe de Leon and his group decided they should be written down, possibly because of the upheaval in Spain at that time. This would indicate that some of the mystical motifs of the *Zohar* were not original to the thirteenth century, but may have been considerably more ancient. In Heschel's view, it was not possible that de Leon himself wrote the *Zohar*, for his other writings demonstrate that he did not have the necessary skill or imagination. Instead, Heschel considered the possibility that while Moshe de Leon did not write the *Zohar*, he may have had a major hand in editing it. See "How the *Zohar* Was Written" by Yehuda Liebes in *Studies in the Zohar*, pp. 85-138.

twentieth centuries. Together the Bible, Talmuds, Midrash, kabbalistic and hasidic texts constitute a large part of the sacred teachings of Judaism. There are also many mythic fragments preserved in the early biblical translations, and in the many biblical commentaries written by some of the greatest rabbis of the medieval and early modern periods, from Rashi in the eleventh century, to Nachmanides in the thirteenth, to Rabbi Moshe Alshekh in the sixteenth, and Rabbi Hayim ben Attar, known as the Or ha-Hayim, in the eighteenth.

Outside the tradition are the texts of the Apocrypha and Pseudepigrapha. The Apocrypha are ancient Jewish books found in the early Greek translation of the Bible (Septuagint) but absent from the Hebrew. Most of these books are treated as canonical by Catholics but not by Jews or Protestants. In addition, there is an enormous pseudepigraphal literature, that is, texts falsely attributed to biblical figures. These texts generally date from between 200 BCE and 200 CE and usually represent the teachings of a particular Jewish sect. It is possible that they were written in hope of being added to the Bible at some future time—but were not. Thus the texts of the Pseudepigrapha are those texts that the mainstream Jewish tradition repudiated; little effort was made to preserve them, and many exist only in translation into languages like Geez or Slavonic. Many of them show evidence of Christian interpolation. Nevertheless, these are important texts that often preserve Jewish myths not to be found anywhere else, and for this reason they have been recognized here as legitimate sources of Jewish mythology. Some of these long-lost texts were collected in the Apocrypha, but there are a great many others, as readers of James Charlesworth's *Old Testament Pseudepigrapha* will soon discover. This literature includes the post-Edenic lives of Adam and Eve, the books of Enoch, which describe the ascent of Enoch into heaven, and testaments of all the patriarchs and the 12 sons of Jacob—and much more.

In addition, there is another category of writings, known as the *Hekhalot* texts, dating from around the second century CE to the eighth century, which describe heavenly journeys of great sages such as Rabbi Ishmael and Rabbi Akiba. There are also the Dead Sea Scrolls, which provide early versions of biblical material and some texts not found anywhere else. The writings of the Samaritans, an early sect related to Judaism that refused to accept any books of the Bible except for the Pentateuch, have also been drawn upon, as well as those of the Karaites, who accepted the *Tanakh*, the entire Bible, but rejected the Talmud and other rabbinic traditions. All of these texts overflow with mythic motifs. There are even folktales with mythological motifs found among those collected in Eastern Europe by S. Ansky from 1911-1914, and among the 20,000 tales collected by the Israel Folktale Archives (IFA) over the past 40 years. These are remarkable sources not only for folklore, but also for mythology, which has been preserved in an oral tradition that is still flourishing. Note that there are many texts inspired by the Bible that are not Jewish. These include Gnostic, Christian, and Muslim texts. Of the Gnostic texts unearthed at Nag Hammadi, some, such as *On the Origin of the World*, preserve traditions of Jewish origin.

Although some folktales with strong mythic elements have been included in this book, it was not possible, for reasons of space, to include as many as might be wished. For this reason, the editor's prior collections of Jewish folklore, *Elijah's Violin & Other Jewish Fairy Tales*, *Miriam's Tambourine: Jewish Tales from Around the World*, *Lilith's Cave: Jewish Tales of the Supernatural*, and *Gabriel's Palace: Jewish Mystical Tales*, might be regarded as supplements to this book, as they include many examples of such mythical folktales. Where appropriate, reference to mythic tales from these books will be found in the commentaries.

The structure of this book, focusing on the ten primary categories of Jewish mythology and organizing the entries in mythic cycles, inevitably results in placing all of these sources—biblical, rabbinic, kabbalistic, hasidic, folk, and pseudepigraphal—side by side. Even though they are not regarded by all Jews as having equal value, they all grow out of the same mythical tradition. The individual myths, compiled from existing variants, are followed by commentaries and by sources.

In general, the reader can assume that the biblical texts are by far the best known and most influential, while the texts drawn from the sacred sources represent the teachings of mainstream Judaism. The myths drawn from the Pseudepigrapha, while non-canonical, still represent authentic Jewish sources, and the variations they offer are often enlightening.

Of course, all of these sources constitute an enormous library, of which the myths included in this book should be viewed as representative, not comprehensive. Here the words of Rabbi Meir ben Yitzhak Nehorai in the *piyyut* (liturgical poem) known as *Akdamut* come to mind: "If all the heavens were parchment, if all the trees were pens, if all the seas were ink, and if every creature were a scribe, they would not suffice to expound the greatness of God."

APPENDIX B
THE PRIMARY BIBLICAL MYTHS

The earliest written examples of Jewish mythology are found in the Bible. For this reason, approximately thirty biblical excerpts have been included in this book, although they are, of course, available in any Bible. Readers may be surprised to find that many of the later Jewish myths are cut from the same cloth as the biblical myths. The following list includes both those biblical myths included here as well as some of those that it was not possible to include because of space limitations. Those that are included are noted with an asterisk. These biblical excerpts have been taken from *Tanakh: A New Translation of the Holy Scriptures According to the Traditional Hebrew Text* published by The Jewish Publication Society.

*Genesis 1:1-2:4	The Seven Days of Creation
*Genesis 2:4-7	The Creation of Man
*Genesis 2:18, 2:21-24	The Creation of Woman
*Genesis 3:8	God Walks in the Garden
*Genesis 5:21-24	Enoch Walked with God
Genesis 6:11-9:17	The Great Flood
*Genesis 12:1-5	God Calls upon Abram
*Genesis 13:14-18, 15:1-5	God's Covenant with Abram
*Genesis 18:1-15	God Appears to Abraham
*Genesis 18:17-33	Abraham Bargains with God
*Genesis 19:1-28	The Destruction of Sodom and Gomorrah
Genesis 21:1-7	The Birth of Isaac
Genesis 21:5-21	The Expulsion of Hagar and Ishmael
*Genesis 22:1-19	The Binding of Isaac
Genesis 23:1-20	The Purchase of the Cave of Machpelah
*Genesis 25:21-26	The Births of Jacob and Esau
*Genesis 25:27-34	The Bartered Birthright
*Genesis 27:1-45	The Stolen Blessing
*Genesis 28:10-19	Jacob's Dream
*Genesis 32:25-33	Jacob Wrestles with the Angel
Genesis 37:5-11	The Dream of the Sun and Moon
Genesis 40:1-23	The Dreams of the Butler and the Baker
Genesis 41:1-32	Pharaoh's Dreams

*Exodus 1:23, 2:1-10	An Ark in the Bulrushes
*Exodus 3:1-6	The Burning Bush
*Exodus 3:13-15	The God of the Fathers
Exodus 7:14-12:36	The Ten Plagues
Exodus 12:1-32	The Lord's Passover
*Exodus 14:15-31	The Parting of the Red Sea
*Exodus 19:16-20, 20:15-18	God Descends to Mount Sinai
*Exodus 24:1-2, 9-11	The Elders of Israel Behold God
*Exodus 33:7-11, 40:34-37	The Tent of Meeting
*Exodus 33:18-23	God's Back
*Exodus 34:1-10	The Second Tablets
Numbers 16:1-35	The Rebellion of Korah
Numbers 21:4-9	The Fiery Serpents
*Joshua 10:12-14	The Sun Stood Still
1 Kings 18:17-40	The Contest of *Yahweh* and Ba'al
*1 Kings 19:5-12	A Still, Small Voice
*2 Kings 2:1-12	The Ascent of Elijah
2 Kings 4:18-37	Elisha Revives the Dead
*Isaiah 6:1-8	Isaiah's Vision
*Ezekiel 1:1-28	Ezekiel's Vision
*Daniel 7:1-28	Daniel's Night Vision
Daniel 10:4-14	Daniel's Dream Vision
*Job 1:1-2:10	Satan's Bargain with God
*Job 38:1, 4-7	The Earth's Foundations
*Psalm 104:1-9	God the Creator

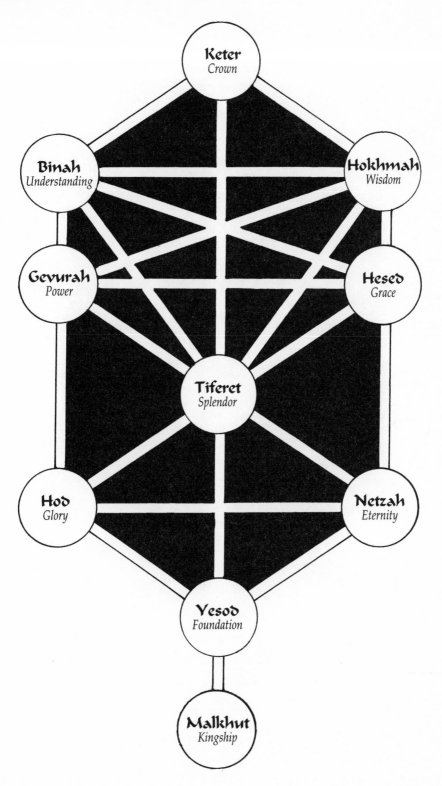

GLOSSARY

All the following terms are in Hebrew unless otherwise noted.

Adam ha-Rishon   Adam.

Adam Kadmon   The supernal man; in kabbalistic thought, the primary divine emanation.

Adat El   The divine assembly.

Adonai   Name of God that is pronounced instead of pronouncing the Tetragrammaton (YHVH).

Aggadah (Pl. *Aggadot*)   The body of non-legal Jewish teachings, often in the form of legends; specifically those found in the Talmud and Midrash.

Aher   (Lit. "The Other") The name given to Elisha ben Abuyah after he became an apostate.

Akedah   The binding of Isaac by Abraham on Mount Moriah (Gen. 22).

Amidah   The primary statutory prayer in Jewish worship services, recited while standing.

Anima Mundi (Latin)   Gnostic concept of the world soul.

Aravot   The highest realm of heaven.

Ashmedai   The King of Demons.

Atik Yomaya (Aramaic)   The Ancient of Days, one of the designations for God (Dan. 7:13).

Azazel   A demonic figure, similar to the Devil, said to live in a desert canyon.

Bar Mitzvah   A ceremony recognizing the transition into adulthood of a 13 year-old Jewish boy.

Bara   Created.

Bashert (Yiddish)   A person's destined spouse.

Bat Kol (Lit. "daughter of a voice")   A heavenly voice.

Beit Din   A rabbinic court convened to decide matters of the Law.

Beit ha-Midrash   A house of study.

Behemoth   A mythical land monster.

Bereshit (Lit. "in the beginning")   The first word of the Torah.

Bet   The second letter of the Hebrew alphabet and the first letter of the first word of the Torah, *Bereshit*.

Birkat ha-Mazon   The blessing after meals.

B'nei Elohim   The Sons of God in Genesis 6.

Borei   Create.

B'rit (Lit. "covenant")   The circumcision given to male Jewish children on the eighth day after birth. (The complete term is *b'rit milah*, or "covenant of the circumcision.")

Derashah   A discussion of a portion of the Torah, usually delivered on the Sabbath.

Din   Judgment.

Dybbuk   The soul of one who has died that enters the body of one who is living and remains there until exorcised.

Ehyeh Asher Ehyeh   God's name meaning "I am who I am" or "I will be what I will be" (Exod. 3:14).

Ein Sof (Lit. "endless" or "infinite")   The highest, unknowable Infinite Being, filling all worlds of space and time.

Elohim   One of God's primary names. It literally means "gods."

Emet   Truth.

Eretz Yisrael   The Land of Israel.

Even ha-Shetiyyah   The Foundation Stone, in the Temple of Jerusalem, that is the cornerstone of creation.

Gabbai   A synagogue warden.

Gan Eden   The Garden of Eden.

Gehenna   The place where the souls of the wicked are punished and purified; the Jewish equivalent of hell.

Gematria   A technique of biblical interpretation in which one word may be substituted for another, as long as their numeric totals are the same.

Gilgul   The transmigration of souls. The kabbalistic equivalent of the belief in reincarnation.

Guf   The Treasury of Souls in Paradise.

Haggadah   Liturgical text read at the Passover Seder that reflects upon the Exodus from Egypt.

Hagigah   A tractate of the Talmud that contains many episodes of a mystical nature.

Halakhah   The code of Jewish religious law, which also includes ethical, civil, and criminal matters.

Ha-Makom (Lit. "the place")   One of the names of God.

Ha-Shem (Lit. "the Name")   Used as a substitute pronounciation of God's name instead of the Tetragrammaton (YHVH).

Hashmal   Amber. A mystical phenomenon as described in Ezekiel 1:4 as *a gleam as of amber.*

Hasid (Pl. *Hasidim*) (Lit. "a pious one")   A follower of Hasidism, a Jewish sect founded by the Ba'al Shem Tov. Hasidim are usually followers of a charismatic religious leader, known as their "rebbe."

Havdalah (Lit. "separation")   The ceremony performed at the end of the Sabbath, denoting the separation of the Sabbath from the rest of the week that follows.

Hayot (Sing. *Hayah*)   Holy creatures that hold up God's Throne of Glory (Ezek. 1).

Hekhalot (Lit. "palaces")   Refers to the visions of the Jewish mystics of the palaces of heaven. The texts describing these visions and the ascent into Paradise are known as "*Hekhalot* texts."

Huppah   Wedding canopy.

Ibbur   The spirit of a dead sage that fuses with a living person and strengthens his or her faith and wisdom. A positive kind of possession, the opposite of possession by a *dybbuk.*

Kabbalah (Lit. "tradition," "that which is received")   The primary system of Jewish mysticism; or, the texts setting forth that mysticism. A kabbalist is one who masters this wisdom.

Kabbalat Shabbat   Ceremony for welcoming the Sabbath Queen.

Kashrut   The system of keeping kosher, that is, eating only foods identified as acceptable by the laws of *kashrut.*

Kavannah (Lit. "intention")   The spirit or intensity that is brought to prayer and other rituals, without which prayer is an empty form.

Kelippot (Lit. "shells")   Forces of evil in kabbalistic usage.

Keter (Lit. "crown")   The first of the ten kabbalistic sefirot.

Ketubah   A Jewish wedding contract.

Kiddush   Blessing over wine.

Kiddush levanah   Blessing of the moon.

Kivyakhol   As if it were possible.

Kotel ha-Ma'aravi (Generally known as the *Kotel*)   The Western Wall; the western retaining wall of the Temple Mount in Jerusalem. Also known as the Wailing Wall.

Lag ba-Omer   Festival that falls between Passover and Shavuot.

Lamed-vav Tzaddikim   The 36 just men who are said to be the pillars of the world.

Leviathan   Mythical sea monster.

Lilin   The daughters of Lilith.

Lilith   Adam's first wife and later the Queen of Demons, as well as the dark feminine.

Liliyot   Female demons of the night.

Ma'ariv   The evening prayers.

Ma'aseh (Pl. *Ma'asiyyot*)   A tale or story, often a folktale.

Ma'aseh Bereshit (Lit. "the Work of Creation")   The mystical doctrine of the secrets of Creation.

Ma'aseh Merkavah (Lit. "the Work of the Chariot.")   The mystical doctrine associated with Ezekiel's vision in Ezekiel 1.

Maggid (Pl. *Maggidim*)   A preacher who confines his talks to easily understood homiletics, such as the *Maggid* of Dubno. Also, a revelatory spirit invoked by the study of a sacred text.

Mahzor   Holiday prayer book.

Malkhut (Lit. "kingdom")   The tenth kabbalistic *sefirah*, identified as Kingdom, which is linked to the *Shekhinah*.

Merkavah   The Divine Chariot described in Ezekiel's vision in Ezekiel 1.

Messiah   (Heb. *Mashiah*, lit. "anointed one") The redeemer who will initiate the End of Days.

Met   Dead.

Metatron   The highest angel, who was once the human Enoch; sometimes described as a "lesser Yahweh."

Mezuzah (Pl. *mezuzot*) (Lit. "doorpost")   A piece of parchment on which is written the prayer that begins "*Shema Yisrael*." It is affixed to the right doorpost of a Jew's home in accordance with the biblical injunction of Deuteronomy 6:9.

Midrash   A method of exegesis of the biblical text. Also refers to post-biblical Jewish legends as a whole.

Mikveh   The ritual bath in which women immerse themselves after menstruation has ended. It is also used occasionally by men for purposes of ritual purification, and for conversions.

Minhah   The afternoon prayers.

Minyan   A quorum of ten men necessary to hold a prayer service.

Mitzvot (Sing. *Mitzvah*) (Lit. "commandments")   The 613 commandments found in the Torah. A *mitzvah* has also taken on the meaning of a good deed.

Nehar di-nur (Aramaic)   A heavenly river of fire (from Dan. 7:10).

Neshamah yeterah   The "extra soul" that is said to be received on the Sabbath, which departs after the ceremony of *Havdalah* is performed.

Niggun   A melody, usually Hasidic, sung without words.

Olam ha-Ba   The world to come. Often used as a synonym for heaven.

Olam ha-Tikkun   World of repair or world of restoration.

Olam ha-Zeh   This world.

Ophanim   A category of angels.

Or ha-Ganuz   The hidden light of the Torah.

Pardes (*PaRDeS*) (Lit. "orchard")   Often linked to Paradise. Refers to the enticing but dangerous realms of mystical speculation and contemplation symbolized by heavenly ascent.

Pargod (Lit. "curtain")   The curtain that is said to hang before the Throne of Glory in Paradise, separating God from the angels.

Peshat   Literal exegesis of the Bible.

Phoenix   A mythical bird that has eternal life.

Piyyut   Liturgical prayer.

Qvittel (Yiddish)   A petition given to a Hasidic Rebbe or placed in the *Kotel*, the Western Wall, as a petition to God.

Re'em   A horned mythological creature of great size, similar to a unicorn or a rhinoceros.

Refaim   Giants in biblical lore.

Rosh Hodesh   The holiday celebrating the new moon.

Ruah Elohim   Spirit of God or breath of God.

Ruah ha-Kodesh   The Holy Spirit.

Samael   One of the names of Satan.

Sar ha-Torah   The Prince of the Torah.

Sefer   Book.

Sefirot (Sing. *Sefirah*)   The ten kabbalistic emanations from *Keter* to *Malkhut*.

Shabbat   The Sabbath.

Shaddai   One of the names of God; derivation uncertain.

Shaharit   The morning prayers.

Shalom Aleikhem   Poem recited or sung on the Sabbath evening welcoming the angels.

She'elat Sefer   A method of divination in which a sacred text is opened at random and a passage is pointed to, which is understood to be the reply to the question.

Shekhinah (Lit. "to dwell")   The Divine Presence, usually identified as a feminine aspect of the Divinity, which evolved into an independent mythic figure in the kabbalistic period. Also identified as the Bride of God and the Sabbath Queen.

Shem ha-Meforash   The Tetragrammaton. The ineffable Name of God.

Shema   The central prayer in Judaism from Deuteronomy 6:4-9. It is read every morning and evening.

Shemittah   A Sabbatical year. Also, a biblical law requiring fields to lie fallow every seventh year. It also refers to an era of existence lasting 7,000 years.

Sheol   The abode of the dead.

Shevirat ha-Kelim   The Shattering of the Vessels. The cosmological myth of Rabbi Isaac Luria, known as the Ari.

Siddur   Prayerbook.

Sitra Ahra   The Other Side. A kabbalistic term for the side of evil.

Sukkah (Pl. *Sukkot*)   A booth or hut built with its roof covered with vegetation, in which Orthodox Jews take their meals during the seven days of Sukkot.

Tallit   A prayer shawl.

Tammuz   A month of the Jewish religious calendar, corresponding very roughly to July.

Tanakh   An acronym for *Torah, Neviim,* and *Ketuvim,* that is, the Five Books of Moses, the Prophets and the Writings, which together constitute the Hebrew Bible (the Protestant Old Testament).

Targum (Pl. Targumim; Lit. "translation.")   Early Jewish translations of the Bible into Aramaic.

Tashlikh   The Rosh ha-Shanah ceremony held near a body of running water on the first day of Rosh Ha-Shanah, in which one's sins are symbolically cast into the water.

Terafim   Idols used as household gods in biblical times. Rachel stole Laban's *terafim* (Gen. 31:19).

Tetragrammaton (Greek for "four letters")   The four-letter ineffable Name of God: YHVH. The true pronunciation is believed to have been lost, and the knowledge of it is believed to confer great power. According to one tradition, only one great sage in each generation knows the true pronunciation of the Tetragrammaton.

Tikkun (Lit. "repair")   Restoration and redemption; in kabbalistic usage, of a soul, or of the cosmos.

Tishrei   The month in which Rosh ha-Shanah, the New Year, is celebrated.

Tkhines (Yiddish)   Women's devotional prayers.

Tohu   Chaos (Gen. 1:2).

Tzaddik ha-Dor   The leading *Tzaddik* of the generation.

Tzaddik (Pl. *Tzaddikim*)   An unusually righteous and spiritually pure person; specifically, a designation for an Hasidic rebbe.

Tzelem (Lit. "image")   The term used to refer to the image of God in Genesis 1:27.

Tzimtzum   The kabbalistic concept of the contraction of God that took place at the time of the Creation to make space for the world to exist.

Tzohar   Legendary jewel given to Adam and Eve as they were expelled from the Garden of Eden, and hung by Noah to illuminate the ark.

Ushpizin   Seven patriarchal figures who are said to come as guests to the *sukkah* during Sukkot.

Vohu   Void (Gen. 1:2).

Yahrzeit (Yiddish)   The anniversary of the death of a close relative.

Yeshivah   School for talmudic and rabbinic studies.

Yetzer ha-Ra   The Evil Inclination.

Yetzer ha-Tov   The Good Inclination.

Yotzer   To form.

Ziz   A giant mythical bird.

BIBLIOGRAPHY OF ORIGINAL SOURCES

Texts are in Hebrew unless otherwise noted

Aderet Eliyahu. Yosef Hayim, Jerusalem: 1962.
Adir ba-Marom. Moshe Hayyim Luzzatto. Jerusalem: 1987.
Aggadat Bereshit. Edited by Solomon Buber. Cracow: 1903.
Aggadot Eretz Yisrael. Edited by Zev Vilnay. 4th ed. Jerusalem: 1953.
Aggadat Shir ha-Shirim. Edited by S. Schechter. Cambridge: 1896.
Akedat Yitzhak. Yitzhak Arama. Venice: 1573.
Alpha Beta de-Ben Sira (Alphabet of Ben Sira). Edited by M. Steinschneider. Berlin: 1858.
Alphabetot (Midrash Alpha Betot). Edited by S. A. Wertheimer. Jerusalem: 1968.
Alte Yidishe Zagen Oder Sippurim. (Yiddish) Edited by Ayzik-Meyer Dik. Vilna: 1876.
Amud ha-Avodah. Barukh ben Avraham of Kossov. Czernovitz: 1854.
Arugat ha-Bosem. Moses Grunwald. Brooklyn: 1959.
Asatir (Kitab al-Asatir). (Arabic). Edited by M. Gaster. London: 1927.
Aseret ha-Dibrot in *Beit ha-Midrash.* Edited by A. Jellinek. Jerusalem: 1967.
Avkat Rahel. Joseph Karo. Jerusalem: 1960.
Avodat ha-Kodesh. Meir ben Ezekiel ibn Gabbai. Jerusalem: 1991.
Avodat Yisrael. Rabbi Yisrael of Koznitz. Jerusalem: 1985.
Avot de-Rabbi Natan. Edited by S. Schechter. New York: 1945.
3 Baruch (Greek Apocalypse of Baruch). (Slavonic). In *The Old Testament Pseudepigrapha.* Edited by J. H. Charlesworth. Garden City, NY: 1983.
Baraita de-Masekhet Gehinnom in *Hesed le-Avraham.* Lemberg: 1860.
Battei Midrashot. Edited by S. A. Wertheimer. 2 vols. 2nd ed. Jerusalem: 1968.
Bayyit Hadash. Joel ben Samuel Sirkes. Cracow: 1631-1640.
Be'er ha-Hasidut. Edited by Eliezer Steinmann. Tel Aviv: 1960.
Be'er Mayim Hayim. Hayim ben Shlomo of Czernovitz. Tel Avid: 1961.
Be-Ikvot Mashiah. Nathan of Gaza. Edited by Gershom Scholem. Jerusalem: 1944.
Beit Aharon. Aaron ben Samuel. Frankfurt: 1690.
Beit Elohim, Sha'ar ha-Tefillah. Moses ben Joseph di-Trani. Jerusalem: 1986.
Beit ha-Midrash. Edited by A. Jellinek. 6 vols. 3rd ed. Jerusalem: 1967.
Beit Yisrael. Tzvi Hirsch of Zidichov. Lemberg: 1834.
Ben Porat Yosef. Ya'akov Yosef of Polonoye. Piatrkov: 1884.
Ben Yehoyada. Yosef Hayim. Jerusalem: 1897.
Bereshit Rabbati in *Beit ha-Midash.* Edited by A. Jellinek. Jerusalem: 1967.
B'nei Yisakhar. Tzvi Elimelekh Spiro of Dinov. Lvov: 1860.
B'rit ha-Levi. Shlomo Alkabetz. Jerusalem: 1970.
B'rit Menuhah. Abraham Merimon ha-Sephardi. Jerusalem: 1978.
David ha-Re'uveni. Edited by A. Z. Eshcoli. Jerusalem: 1940.
De Abrahamo. (Greek) Philo. Vol. 6. Cambridge, MA: 1969.
De Cherubim. (Greek) Philo. Vol. 2. Cambridge, MA: 1969.
De Confusione Linguarum. (Greek) Philo. Vol. 4. Cambridge, MA: 1969.
De Congressu Eruditionis Gratia. (Greek) Philo. Vol. 9. Cambridge, MA: 1969.
De Decalogo. (Greek) Philo. Vol. 7. Cambridge, MA: 1969.
De Ebrietate. (Greek) Philo. Vol. 3. Cambridge, MA: 1969.
De Fuga et Inventione. (Greek) Philo. Vol. 5. Cambridge, MA: 1969.
De Gigantibus. (Greek) Philo. Vol. 2. Cambridge, MA: 1969.
De Mutatione Nominum. (Greek) Philo. Vol. 5. Cambridge, MA: 1969.
De Opificio Mundi. (Greek) Philo. Vol. 1. Cambridge, MA: 1969.

De Providentia. (Greek) Philo. Vol. 9. Cambridge, MA: 1969.

Degel Mahaneh Efraim. Moses Hayim Efraim of Sudlykow. Piotrkov: 1912.

Der treue Zions-Waechter. (German) Binyamin Lilienthal. Altona: 1847.

Derekh Emunah. Meir ben Ezekiel ibn Gabbai. Brooklyn: 1987.

Derekh Eretz Zuta. Jerusalem: 1994.

Derekh Etz Hayim ve-Inyanei Gan Eden, appended to *Sefer Ma'aneh Lashon*. Amsterdam: 1723.

Derekh ha-Shem. Moshe Hayim Luzzatto. Amsterdam: 1896.

Derekh ha-Yashar le-Olam ha-Ba. Yehiel Mikhael Epstein. Frankfort-am-Main: 1713.

Derishat Tziyon. Tzvi Hirsch Kalischer. Jerusalem: 1919.

Derush Heftzi-Bah. Yosef ibn Tabul. In *Simhat Kohen*. Masud ha-Kohen al-Haddad. Jerusalem: 1921.

Derush she-Masar Hayim Vital le-Rabbi Shlomo Sagis. In Toyetto, *Likutim Hadashim*. Jerusalem: 1985.

Derushim. Yosef Hayim. Jerusalem: 1987.

De Somniis. (Greek) Philo. Vol. 5. Cambridge, MA: 1969.

De Specialibus Legibus. (Greek) Philo. Vol. 7-8. Cambridge, MA: 1969.

De Virtutibus. (Greek) Philo. Vol. 8. Cambridge, MA: 1969.

De Vita Mosis. (Greek) Philo. Vol. 6. Cambridge, MA: 1969.

Devět Brán. (Czech) Jiri Langer. Prague: 1937.

Die Legenden der Juden. (German) Edited by J. Bergmann. Berlin: 1919.

Die Wundermanner im Judischen Volk. (German) Edited by J. Gunzig. Berlin: 1921.

Divrei ha-Yamim le-Moshe Rabbenu in *Beit ha-Midrash*. Edited by A. Jellinek. Jerusalem: 1967.

Divrei Shaul (Sefer Divrei Shaul). Yosef Shaul Halevi Nathanson. Lemberg: 1879.

Divrei Shlomo. Shlomo ben Yitzhak ha-Levi. Venice:1596.

Divrei Torah. Moses Nusbaum. Lublin: 1889.

Divrei Yosef. Yosef Sambari. Jerusalem: 1981.

Dos Buch fun Nisyoynes. (Yiddish) Edited by Israel Osman. Los Angeles: 1926.

Eder ha-Yekar. In *Samuel Abba Horodezky Jubilee Volume*, edited by Zalman Rubashov (Shazar). Tel Aviv: 1947.

Edot Mesaprot. Edited by Abraham Shatal. Tel Aviv: 1954.

Eikhah Rabbati, edited by Solomon Buber.

Eikhah Rabbah. (*Midrash Eikhah Rabbah*). Edited by Solomon Buber. Vilna: 1899.

Eikhah Zuta. Edited by Solomon Buber. Berlin: 1894.

Ein Gor Sheyne Tkhine. (Yiddish)

Eldad ha-Dani (Sefer Eldad ha-Dani). Edited by A. Epstein. Prague: 1891.

Eliyahu Rabbah (Seder Eliyahu Rabbah). Edited by M. Friedmann. Vienna: 1902.

Eliyahu Zuta (Seder Eliyahu Zuta). Edited by M. Friedmann. Vienna: 1904.

Em ha-Banim S'mehah. Yissachar Shlomo Teichtal. Budapest: 1943.

Emek ha-Melekh. Edited by Naphtali ben Jacob Elhannan Bacharach. Amsterdam: 1648.

Emunot ve-ha-De'ot (Sefer ha-Emunot ve-ha-De'ot). Sa'adya Gaon. Cracow: 1880.

3 Enoch. Edited by Hugo Odeberg. Cambridge: 1928.

Enuma Elish. Edited by L. W. King. New York: 1976.

Eretz Yisrael. Abraham Isaac Kook. Jerusalem: 1996.

Eser Tzahtzahot. Y. Berger. Piotrkov: 1910.

Esh Kadosh. Kalonymus Kalman Shapira. Jerusalem: 1960.

Eshkol ha-Kofer. Yehudah Hadassi. Goslow: 1836.

Etz ha-Hayim in *Nefesh ha-Hayim*. Hayim ben Yitzhak of Volozhin. Vilna: 1824.

Etz Hayim. Hayim Vital. Warsaw: 1891.

Etz Yosef. Hanokh Zundel ben Joseph. Vilna: 1896.

Ezrat Kohanim. Tzvi Hirsch ben Naftali ha-Kohen Rappoport. Vilna: 1845.

Gan Eden ve-Gehinnom in *Beit ha-Midrash*. Edited by A. Jellinek. Jerusalem: 1967.

Gan ha-Hasidut. Eliezer Steinman. Jerusalem: 1967.

Gedulat Moshe. Amsterdam: 1754.

Geonica. Louis Ginzberg. New York: 1968.

Gelilot Eretz Yisrael. Gershom ben Eliezer ha-Levi Judels. Lublin: 1634.

Genesis Apocryphon. Edited by N. Avigad and Y. Yadlin. Jerusalem: 1956.

Gevurot ha-Shem. Judah Loew ben Bezalel. Jerusalem: 1970.

Ginzei ha-Melekh, Kokhvei Yitzhak. Isaac ben Abraham ibn Latif. Vienna: 1862.

Ha-Ba'al ha-Ketanah. Edited by Asher Barash. Tel Aviv: 1966.

Hadar Zekenim, in *Beit ha-Midrash*. Edited by A. Jellinek. Jerusalem: 1967.

Hadrei Teiman. Edited by Nissim Binyamin Gamlieli. Tel Aviv: 1978.

Haggadot Ketu'ot. Published by Louis Ginzberg in *HaGoren* 9. Berlin: 1923

Ha-Idra Rabbah Kaddisha in *Sefer ha-Zohar*. Vilna: 1894.

Ha-Idra Zuta Kaddisha in *Sefer ha-Zohar*. Vilna: 1894..

Ha-Ma'amar. Edited by A. M. Lunz. 1920.

Ha-Mishnah. Edited by Meir Friedmann. Vilna: 1890.

Ha-Nefesh ha-Hakhamah. Moshe ben Shem Tov de Leon. Jerusalem: 1967.

Ha-Sulam (Perush ha-Sulam). Yehudah Leib Ashlag. Jerusalem: 1955.

Hayei Hanokh in *Beit ha-Midrash*. Edited by A. Jellinek. Jerusalem: 1967.

Hazon ha-Guelah. Abraham Isaac Kook. Jerusalem: 1941.

Hekhalot Rabbati in *Beit ha-Midrash*. Edited by A. Jellinek. Jerusalem: 1967.

Hekhalot Zutartei in *Synopse zur Hekhalot-Literatur*. Edited by Peter Schäfer. Tubingen: 1981.

Hemdat Yamim. Nathan Benjamin Halevi. Venice: 1763.

Hesed le-Avraham. Abraham Azulai. Lemberg: 1860.

Hibbur ba-Ma'asiyot u-va-Midrashot u-va-Aggadot. Venice: 1551.

Hibbur Yafeh me-ha-Yeshua. Nissim ben Yaakov ibn Shahin. In *Otzar Midrashim*. Edited by Y. D. Eisenstein. New York: 1915.

Hiddushei ha-Ramal. Edited by Avraham Shoshan. Jerusalem: 1981.

Hilkhot Kiddush ha-Hodesh. Maimonides. Edited by A.A. Akavya. Tel Aviv: 1956.

Hilkhot Melakhim (Hilkhot Melakhim u-Milhamot). Maimonides. Jerusalem: 1955.

Hilkhot Teshuvah. Maimonides. Edited by E. Tager. New York: 1987.

Hilkhot Yom ha-Kippurim. Joel ben Samuel Sirkes. Jerusalem: 2002.

Hovat ha-Talmidim. Kalonymus Kalman Shapira. Tel Aviv: 1964.

Iggeret Sod ha-Geulah. Abraham ben Eliezer ha-Levi. Jerusalem: 1519.

Iggeret Teiman. Maimonides. Lemberg: 1851.

Iggerot Eretz Yisrael. Abraham Ya'ari. Ramat Gan: 1971.

Iggerot mi-Tzefat. Simcha Asaf. *Kovetz 'al Yad* 3. Jerusalem: 1939.

Iggerot R. Yisrael Ba'al Shem Tov. Edited by M. S. Bauminger. In *Sefer Margaliot*. Edited by Yitzhak Raphael. Jerusalem: 1933.

Iggeret Sod ha-Geulah. Abraham ben Eliezer ha-Levi. Jerusalem: 1519.

Jewish Antiquities (Antiquitates Judaicae). Josephus. Edited by H. St. J. Thackeray. Cambridge: 1995.

Johannes Reuchlin und sein Kampf: eine historische monografie. (German) Edited by Max Brod. Stuttgart: 1965.

Kabbalot Rabbi Ya'akov ve-Rabbi Yitzhak by Jacob ben Jacob ha-Kohen in *Mada'ei ha-Yahadut* 2:244-264, edited by Gershom Scholem.

Kaftor va-Ferah. Ya'akov Luzzatto. Basel: 1580.

Kanfei Yonah. Moshe Yonah of Safed. Lemberg: 1884.

Kav ha-Yashar. Tzvi ben Aaron Samuel Koidonower. Frankfurt am Main: 1705.

Kedushat Levi. Levi Yitzhak of Berditchev. Jerusalem: 1958.

Kedushat Shabbat. Tzadok ha-Kohen of Lublin. Lemberg: 1876.

Kerem Hayah le-Shlomo. Yosef ibn Tabul. Columbia University Ms. X893 M6862. Unpublished.

Kesef Tzaruf. Josiah ben Joseph. New York: 1992.

Keter Shem Tov. Aaron of Zlachov. New York: 1973.

Keter Torah. David ben Solomon Vital. Constantinople: 1536.

Ketubah shel Shavuot in *Mahzor Shavuot*. Constantinople: 1570.

Kitab al-Anwar w'al-Mar'akib. (Arabic) Ya'kub al-Kirkis'ani. Edited by L. Nemoy. New York: 1939-1943.

Kitab al-Milal w'al-Nihal. (Arabic) Edited by W. Cureton. Leipzig: 1923.

Kitab al-riyad w'al-Hada'ik. (Arabic) Ya'kub al-Kirkis'ani.

Kitvei ha-Ramban. Nachmanides. Edited by Hayim Dov Shevel. Jerusalem: 1963.

Kitzur Alshekh al ha-Torah. Moshe Alshekh. Brooklyn: 2001.

Kodex Sachau (Latin) no. 70 of the Berlin Library in *Fabula Josephi et Assenethae Apocrypha*. Edited by G. Oppenheim.

Koran. (Arabic) N. J. Dawood, tr. New York: 2000.

Korban Shabbat (Sefer Korban Shabbat). Bezalel ben Shlomo of Kobryn. Warsaw: 1873.

Kovetz Eliyahu. Edited by Hayim Eliyahu Sternberg. Jerusalem: 1983.

Lamed Vav Tzaddikim Nistarim. Edited by Yisroel Yakov Klapholtz. Tel Aviv: 1968.

Legends of the Talmud: En Yakov. Edited by Jacob ibn Habib. Five volumes. 1919-21.

Legum Allegoriarum. (Latin) Philo. Vol. 1. Cambridge, MA: 1969.

Lekh Lekha. Mordechai Aliyah. Jerusalem: 1963.

Leviticus Rabbah (Midrash Vayikra Rabbah). Vilna: 1887.

Liber Antiquitatum Biblicarum. (Latin) Pseudo-Philo. Leon: 1552.

Likutei Etzot. Nathan of Nemirov. Lemberg: 1874.

Likutei ha-Pardes. Rashi. Jerusalem: 1964.

Likutei Halakhot. Nathan of Nemirov. Jerusalem: 1970.

Likutei Moharan. Nathan of Nemirov. Warsaw: 1916.

Likutei Torah. Shneur Zalman of Lyady. New York: 1965.

Likutei Yekarim. Samuel ben Judah Leib Segal. Lvov: 1792.

Limmudei Atzilut. Israel Sarug. Munkacs: 1897.

Ma'amar ha-Hokhmah. Moshe Hayim Luzzatto. Amsterdam: 1782.

Ma'amar Tehiyat ha-Metim. Moses Maimonides. Jerusalem: 1987.

Ma'arekhet ha-Elohut. Mantua: 1558.

Ma'aseh Buch. Amsterdam: 1723.

Ma'aseh Daniel in *Beit ha-Midrash*. Edited by A. Jellinek. Jerusalem: 1967.

Ma'aseh me-ha Hayyat. Vilna: 1908.

Ma'aseh Merkavah. Edited by Klaus Herrmann. Tubingen: 1984.

Ma'aseh Nissim. Constantinople: 1720.

Ma'aseh Ta'atu'im. S. Rubin. Vienna: 1887.

Ma'ayan Hokhmah in *Otzar Midrashim*. Edited by Y. D. Eisenstein. New York: 1915.

Ma'asiyot me-Tzaddikei Yesodei Olam. Edited by Lazar Schenkel. Podgaitsy, Russia: 1903.

Ma'asiyot Nora'im ve-Nifla'im. Cracow: 1896.

Maharsha. Samuel Eliezer ben Judah ha-Levi Edels. Shtetin: 1862.

Magen Avot. Shim'on ben Tzemach Duran. Leipzig: 1855.

Magen David. David ben Solomon Zimra. Amsterdam: 1713.

Maggid Devarav le-Ya'akov. Dov Baer of Mezhirech. Edited by R. Schatz-Uffenheimer. Jerusalem: 1990.

Maggid Yesharim. Joseph Karo. Amsterdam: 1704.

Makhon Siftei Tzaddikim. Menachem Mendel of Riminov. Jerusalem: 1990.

Masekhet Atzilut. Yitzak Eizik Haver. Warsaw: 1865.

Masekhet Hekhalot in *Beit ha-Midrash*. Edited by A. Jellinek. Jerusalem: 1967.

Mateh Moshe. Moshe ben Abraham Premsla. Cracow: 1591.

Mavo She'arim. Hayim Vital. Tel Aviv: 1961.

Me'am Lo'ez (Yalkut Me'am Lo'ez). Jerusalem: 1967-1971.

Megaleh Amukot. Nathan Nata ben Shlomo Shapiro. Bene Berak: 1985.

Megillat Ahimaaz. Ahimaaz ben Paltiel. Jerusalem: 1974.

Megillat Setarim. Yitzhak Eizik Safrin of Komarno. Jerusalem: 1944.

Mekhilta de-Rabbi Ishmael. Edited by J. Z. Lauterbach. Philadelphia: 1933-1935. 3 volumes.

Mekhilta de-Rabbi Shim'on ben Yohai. Edited by D. Hoffmann. Frankfurt-am-Main: 1905.

Memar Markah. Edited by J. Macdonald. Berlin: 1963.

Menorat ha-Maor. Isaac Aboab. Jerusalem: 2002.

Merkavah Rabbah. Edited by S. Musajoff. Jerusalem: 1921.

Metzudat David (Perush Metzudat David). Vilna: 1896.

Midrash Aggadot. Edited by Solomon Buber. Vienna: 1894.

Midrash Alpha Beta de-Rabbi Akiva in *Otzar Midrashim*. Edited by Y. D. Eisenstein. New York: 1915.

Midrash Aseret ha-Dibrot in *Beit ha-Midrash*. Edited by A. Jellinek. Jerusalem: 1967.

Midrash Aseret Harugei Malkhut in *Otzar Midrashim*. Edited by Y. D. Eisenstein. New York: 1915.

Midrash Aseret ha-Shvatim in *Otzar Midrashim*. Edited by Y.D. Eisenstein. New York: 1915.

Midrash Avkir. Edited by Solomon Buber. Vienna: 1883.

Midrash Bereshit Rabbah. Vilna: 1887.

Midrash Bereshit Rabbati. Jerusalem: 1940.

Midrash be-Hokhmah Yasad Eretz in *Beit ha-Midrash*. Edited by A. Jellinek. Jerusalem: 1967.

Midrash Devarim Rabbah. Vilna: 1887.

Midrash Eleh Ezkerah. Edited by G. Reeg. Tubingen: 1985.

Midrashei Geulah. Edited by Yehudah ibn Shmuel. Jerusalem: 1954.

Midrash ha-Gadol (Sefer Bereshit). Edited by S. Schechter. Cambridge: 1902.

Midrash ha-Gadol (Sefer Shemot). Edited by D. Hoffmann. Berlin: 1913.

Midrash ha-Ne'elam in *Sefer ha-Zohar*. Vilna: 1894.

Midrash Haserot ve-Yeterot. Edited by A. Marmorstein. London: 1917.

Midrash Kohelet Rabbah. Vilna: 1887.

Midrash Konen in *Beit ha-Midrash*. Edited by A. Jellinek. Jerusalem: 1967.

Midrash Pinchas. Pinhas ben Abraham of Koretz. Warsaw: 1876.

Midrash Mishlei. Edited by Solomon Buber. Vilna: 1893.

Midrash Pesikta Rabbati. Edited by M. Friedmann. Vienna: 1880.

Midrash Rabbah. Jerusalem: 1986.

Midrash Rabbenu Bahya. Bachya ben Asher. Warsaw: 1878.

Midrash Ribesh Tov. L. Abraham. Keskemet: 1927.

Midrash Ruth. Jerusalem: 1996.

Midrash Shemuel. Edited by Solomon Buber. Cracow: 1893.

Midrash Shemot Rabbah. Vilna: 1887.

Midrash Shir ha-Shirim. Edited by Eleazar Gruenhut. Jerusalem: 1980.

Midrash Tanhuma (Midrash Tanhuma ha-Kadum ve-ha-Yashan). Edited by Solomon Buber. Vilna: 1885.

Midrash Tanhuma-Yelammedenu. Vienna: 1863.

Midrash Tehillim: Shoher Tov. Edited by Solomon Buber. Jerusalem: 1966.

Midrash Toledot Yitzhak in *Beit ha-Midrash*. Edied by A. Jellinek. Jerusalem: 1967.

Midrash va-Yosha in *Beit ha-Midrash*. Edited by A. Jellinek. Jerusalem: 1967.

Migdal Oz. Jacob Emden. Zitomir, 1874.

Mikhtavim me-ha Besht ve-Talmidav. By D. Fraenkel. Lvov: 1923.

Mishle Shualim le-Rabbi Berekhiah ha-Nakdan. Edited by A. M. Haberman. Jerusalem: 1945.

Mishneh Torah. Maimonides. New York: 1944.

Moraim Gedolim. Edited by Y. S. Farhi. Warsaw: 1909.

Nahalat Tzvi. Gedalie Felder. New York: 1959.

Nefesh ha-Hayim. Hayim ben Yitzhak of Volozhin. Vilna: 1824.

Niflaot Maharal. Edited by Y. Y. Rosenberg. Warsaw: 1909.

Nishmat Hayim. Menashe ben Israel. Amsterdam: 1650.

Nistarot Eliyahu in *Beit ha-Midrash*. Edited by A. Jellinek. Jerusalem: 1967.

Nistarot Rabbi Shim'on ben Yohai in *Beit ha-Midrash*. Edited by A. Jellinek. Jerusalem: 1967.

No'am Elimelekh. Elimelekh of Lizhensk. Jerusalem: 1978.

Notzer Hesed. Yitzhak Eizik Safrin of Komano. Jerusalem: 1982.

Notzer Te'enah. Tarnow: 1900.

Numbers Rabbah (Midrash Ba-Midbar Rabbah). Vilna: 1887.

Ohalei Shem. S. N. Gottlieb. Bilgorai: 1910.

Ohel Elimelekh. Edited by A. H. S. Michaelson. Peremyshlyany: 1911.

Ohev Yisrael (Sefer Ohev Yisrael). Abraham Joshua Heschel. Bardyov: 1927.

Or ha-Ganuz. Edited by Martin Buber. Tel Aviv: 1957.

Or ha-Hamah. Zundel Kroizer. Jerusalem: 1970.

Or ha-Hayim. Hayim ben Moses Attar. Warsaw: 1922.

Or ha-Hokhmah. Uri Feivel ben Aaron. Korzec: 1795.

Or ha-Yashar. Meir ben Judah Loeb Poppers ha-Kohen. Jerusalem: 1964.

Orhot Hayim. Aaron ben Jacob ben David Hakohen. Berlin: 1902.

Orhot Tzaddikim. Vilna: 1913.

Or Ne'erav. Moshe Cordovero. Edited by Y. Z. Branwein. Jerusalem: 1965.

Orot. Abraham Isaac Kook. Jerusalem: 1963.

Or Yakar. Moshe Cordovero. Jerusalem: 1987.

Or Zaru'a. Isaac ben Moses of Vienna. Zhitomir: 1862 and Jerusalem: 1887-1890.

Oseh Feleh. Y. S. Farhi. Leghorn: 1902 and Jerusalem: 1959.

Otot ha-Mashiah in *Beit ha-Midrash*. Edited by A. Jellinek. Jerusalem: 1967.

Otzar ha-Kavod. Todros ben Joseph Abulafia ha-Levi. Satmar: 1926.

Otzar ha-Ma'asiyot. Reuven ban Na'ane. Tel Aviv: 1921.

Otzar Ma'asiyot. Edited by Naftali Greenhorn. B'nei Brak: 1988.

Otzar Midrashim. Edited by Y. D. Eisenstein. New York: 1915.

Otzrot Hayim (Sefer Otzrot Hayim ha-Shalem). Hayim Vital. Jerusalem: 1994.

Otzrot Hayim. Yosef Hayim. Jerusalem: 1990.

Otzrot Rabbi Yitzhak Eizik Haver. Yitzhak Eizik Haver. Jerusalem: 1990.

Pardes Rimmonim. Moshe Cordovero. Jerusalem: 1962.

Pe'er v-Khavod. Dov Baer Ehrman. Munkacs: 1912.

Penitence of Adam. (Armenian) Edited by Michael E. Stone. Lovanii: 1981.

Perush ha-Aggadot. Azriel of Gerona in *Derekh Emunah*. Edited by Meir ibn Gabbai. Warsaw: 1850.

Perush ha-Haggadah. Yosef ben Avraham Gikatilla. Venice: 1585.

Perush ha-Mishnayot. Maimonides. Warsaw: 1878.

Perush Hamesh Megillot u-Ketuvim. Joseph ben David ibn Yahya. Bologna: 1538.

Perush ha-Idra le-Rabbi Yosef ibn Tabul. Yosef ibn Tabul. Edited by I. Weinstock. *Temirin*, vol. 2. Jerusalem: 1982.

Perush Kohelet. Isaac ben Abraham ibn Latif. Jerusalem: 1969.

Perush Rabbi Saadiah Gaon le-Sefer Yetzirah. Jerusalem: 1965.

Perush Rambam al ha-Torah. Maimonides. Jerusalem: 1986.

Perush Ramban al ha-Torah. Moses Nachmanides. Jerusalem: 1990.

Perush Shem shel Arba Otiyyot. Ms. Florence.

Pesikta Hadta in *Beit ha-Midrash.* Edited by A. Jellinek. Jerusalem: 1967.

Pesikta de-Rav Kahana. Edited by Solomon Buber. Lyck: 1868.

Pesikta Rabbati. Edited by Meir Friedmann. Vienna: 1880.

Petirat Moshe (Petirat Mosheh Rabbenu). Jerusalem: 1902.

Pirkei de-Rabbi Eliezer. Warsaw: 1852.

Pirkei Hekhalot Rabbati. Edited by S. A. Wertheimer. Jerusalem: 1888.

Pirkei Mashiah in *Beit ha-Midrash.* Edited by A. Jellinek. Jerusalem: 1967.

Pitron. Daniel ben Moses al-Kumisi. Jerusalem: 1957.

Piyyut Yannai. Edited by M. Zulay. Berlin: 1938.

Poimandres. (Greek) Parisiis: 1554.

Quaestiones et Solutiones in Genesim. (Latin) Philo.

Quis Rerum Divinarum Heres Sit. (Latin) Philo.

Rabbi Yisrael Ba'al Shem Tov. Menashe Unger. New York: 1963.

Razi Li. Noah ben Yaakov David Vaintrob. Jerusalem: 1936.

Re'iyyot Yehezkel. Edited by I. Gruenwald.

Responsa Ribash. Isaac ben Sheshet Parfat Ribash. Constantinople: 1547.

Responsum Hai Gaon in *Ta'am Zekenim.* Tiberias: 1954.

Romemot El. Moshe Alshekh. Venice: 1605.

Ruth Rabbah (Midrash Rut Rabbah). Vilna: 1887.

Sancti Ephraem in Genesim et in Exodum Commentarii. Ephraem. Louvain: 1955.

Sancti Irenaei libros quinque adversus haereses. (Latin) Irenaeus. Edited by W. W. Harvey.
    Cambridge: 1857.

Seder Eliyahu Rabbah. Edited by M. Friedmann. Vienna: 1904.

Seder Gan Eden in *Beit ha-Midrash.* Edited by A. Jellinek. Jerusalem: 1967.

Seder ha-Dorot (Sefer Seder ha-Dorot). Yehiel ben Shlomo Heilprin. Warsaw: 1870.

Seder ha-Dorot (Sefer Seder ha-Dorot mi-Talmidei ha-Besht). Menahem Mendel Bodek.
    Lemberg: 1882.

Seder ha-Yom. Moses ben Judah Makhir. Slavita: 1993.

Seder Mahanot in *Beit ha-Midrash.* Edited by A. Jellinek. Jerusalem: 1967.

Seder Olam (Seder Olam Rabbah). Edited by M. J. Weinstock. Jerusalem: 1956.

Seder Rabbah di-Bereshit. Oxford Bodleian Library Ms. 1531.

Seder Tkhines u-Vakoshes. (Yiddish)

Sefer Ba'al Shem Tov. Edited by Simeon Menahem Mendel Wodnick. Jerusalem: 1992.

Sefer Eliyahu in *Beit ha-Midrash.* Edited by A. Jellinek. Jerusalem: 1967.

Sefer Sefat Emet. Yehudah Leib Alter of Ger. Piotrkow: 1905-1908.

Sefer Etz Hayyim. Hayim Vital. Jerusalem: 1985.

Sefer ha-Bahir. Amsterdam: 1651. See entry in English bibliography for *The Bahir*, translated
    by Aryeh Kaplan. Citations from *Sefer ha-Bahir* are from this edition.

Sefer Hadar Zkenim Toratam shel Rishonim. Leghorn: 1840.

Sefer ha-Gilgulim. Hayim Vital. Vilna: 1895.

Sefer Hasidim. Judah ben Samuel ha-Hasid. Jerusalem: 1991.

Sefer ha-Hasidut. Abraham Kahana. Warsaw: 1922.

Sefer Hekhalot (3 Enoch) in *Beit ha-Midrash.* Edited by A. Jellinek. Jerusalem: 1967.

Sefer ha-Hezyonot. Hayim Vital. Edited by A. Z. Eskoli. Jerusalem: 1954.

Sefer ha-Zikhronot by Jerahmeel ben Solomon, compiled by Eleazar ben Asher ha-Levi.
    See *The Chronicles of Jerahmeel*, edited by Moses Gaster, in the English bibliography.
    Citations are from *The Chronicles of Jerahmeel*.

Sefer ha-Iyyun. Hebrew University Ms. 8330.

Sefer ha-Komah. Oxford Bodleian Library Ms. 1791.

Sefer ha-Likutim. Hayim Vital. Jerusalem: 1987.

Sefer ha-Ma'asiyot. Edited by Shlomo Bechor Chutsin. Baghdad: 1892.

Sefer ha-Razim. Edited by M. Margaliot. Tel Aviv: 1967.

Sefer Hasidim. Frankfurt-am-Main: 1860.

Sefer ha-Pardes. Rashi. Istanbul: 1802.

Sefer ha-Razim. Edited by M. Margaliot. Jerusalem: 1966.

Sefer ha-Temunah. Nehunyah ben ha-Kanah. Jerusalem: 1998.

Sefer ha-Yashar. Edited by Joseph Dan. Jerusalem: 1986.

Sefer ha-Yovelim (Book of Jubilees). Edited by Solomon Rabin. Vienna: 1870.

Sefer ha-Zikhronot. Eleazar ben Asher ha-Levi. Oxford Bodleian Library Ms. 2797. See *The Chronicles of Jerahmeel* in the English bibliography.

Sefer Ma'asei Adonai. Akiba Ber.

Sefer Ma'aysiot, edited by Mordechai Ben Yezekel. Tel Aviv: 1971.

Sefer Margaliot. Edited by Yitzhak Raphael. Jerusalem: 1973.

Sefer Mar'ot ha-Tzov'ot. Moshe Alshekh. Venice: 1594.

Sefer Netivot ha Shalom. Solomon ben Joel Dubno. 1793

Sefer Or ha-Hayim. Hayim ben Attar. Jerusalem: 1991.

Sefer Orah Hayim. Yosef Hayim. Jerusalem: 1978.

Sefer Or Yesharim. Moshe Hayim Kelinmann of Brisk. Warsaw: 1884.

Sefer Pe'er ve-Kavod. 1701. Jerusalem: 1969.

Sefer Raziel. Amsterdam: 1674.

Sefer Sha'ashuim. Edited by Israel Davidson. New York: 1914.

Sefer Sippurim Norai'im. Ya'akov Kadanir. Brooklyn: 1982.

Sefer Ta'amei ha-minhagim. Edited by Abraham Sperling. Jerusalem: n.d.

Sefer Toledot ha-Ari. Meir Benayahu. Jerusalem: 1967.

Sefer Yetzirah. Jerusalem: 1964.

Sefer Zerubavel in *Battei Midrashot*. Edited by S. A. Wertheimer. Jerusalem: 1968.

Se'udat Gan Eden in *Beit ha-Midrash*. Edited by A. Jellinek. Jerusalem: 1967.

Sha'ar ha-Gemul. Nachmanides. New York: 1954.

Sha'ar ha-Gilgulim in *Shemonah She'arim*. Hayim Vital. Tel Aviv: 1963.

Sha'ar ha-Hakdamot. Hayim Vital. Tel Aviv: 1961.

Sha'ar ha-Kavanot. Hayim Vital. Jerusalem: 1873.

Sha'ar ha-Pesukim. Hayim Vital. Tel Aviv: 1961.

Sha'ar ha-Shamayim. Isaac ben Abraham ibn Latif. Vatican Ms. 335.1.

Sha'ar ha-Yihud ve-ha-Emunah in *Likutei Amarim*. Shneur Zalman of Lyady. New York: 1963.

Sha'arei Gan Eden. Cracow: 1880.

Sha'arei Kedushah. Hayim Vital. Aleppo: 1866.

Sha'arei Orah. Yosef ben Avraham Gikatilla. Warsaw: 1883.

Sha'arei Rahamin (Seder Sha'arei Rahamim). The Vilna Gaon and Hayim of Volozhyn. Vilna: 1871.

She'elot Ya'avetz. Ya'akov Emden. Altona: 1718.

Shefa Tal. Shabbatai Sheftel Horowitz. Lemberg: 1859.

Shekel ha-Kodesh. Tzvi Elimelekh of Dinov.

Shemen ha-Tov. A. S. B. Michelson. Piotrkov: 1905.

Shem ha-Gedolim. Hayim Joseph David Azulai. Warsaw: 1876.

Shem mi-Shemuel. Samuel ben Abraham of Sochaczow. Pietrokov: 1932.

Shibbolei ha-Leket. Zedekiah ben Abraham de Pietosi of Rome. Venice: 1546.

Shishim Sippurei-Am. Zalman Baharav. Haifa: 1964.

Shi'ur Komah. Edited by S. Musajoff. Jerusalem: 1971.

Shivhei ha-Ari. Shlomo Meinsterl. Jerusalem: 1905.

Shivhei ha-Besht. Dov Baer of Linitz. Jerusalem: 1969.

Shivhei ha-Ran. Nathan of Nemirov. Lemberg: 1901.

Shivhei Rabbi Hayim Vital. Edited by Menashe ben Naftali Feigenbaum. Ashdod: 1988.

Shloyshe Sheorim. (Yiddish) Sarah bat Mordecai. Vilna: 1896.

Sh'nei Luhot ha-B'rit. Yeshayah Horowitz. Amsterdam: 1649.

Shoher Tov (Midrash Shoher Tov al Tehillim). Jerusalem: 1965.

Shulhan Arukh. Joseph Caro. Jerusalem: 2000.

Shulhan Arukh shel ha-Rav Shneur Zalman. Shneur Zalman of Lyady. Vilna: 1905.

Siah Sarfei Kodesh. J. K. K. Rokotz. 5 volumes. Lodz: 1929.

Siddur Amram. Warsaw: 1865.

Siddur Sha'ar Shamayim. Jerusalem: 1998.

Sifra di-Tzeni'uta in *Sefer ha-Zohar.* Vilna: 1896.

Sifre on Deuteronomy. Edited by L. Finkelstein. New York : 1969.

Sifre Numbers. Edited by Herbert Basser. Atlanta: 1998.

Siftei Hakhamim. Shabbethai ben Joseph Bass. Frankfurt-am-Main: 1712.

Sihot ha-Ran. Nathan of Nemirov. Ostrog: 1816.

Sihot Moharan in *Hayei Moharan.* Nathan of Nemirov. Lemberg: 1874.

Sihot Shedim in *Sifrei Rabbi Tzadok ha-Kohen.* Tzadok ha-Kohen of Lublin. Jerusalem: 2001.

Simhat Yisrael. I. Berger. Piotrkov: 1910.

Sippur Rabbi Yosef della Reina. In *Iggeret Sod ha-Geulah.* Abraham ben Eliezer ha-Levi. Jerusalem: 1519.

Sippurim: eine Sammlung jüdischer Sagen, Märchen and Geschichten für Völkerkunde. (German) Edited by Wolf Pascheles. Prague: 1858.

Sippurim: Sammlung jüdischer Volksagen, Erzahlungen, Mythen,Chroniken, Achtes Bändchen. (German) Edited by Wolf Pascheles. Prague: 1845.

Sippurim: Prager Sammlung jüdischer Legenden in neuer Auswahl und Bearbeitung. (German) Edited by L. Weisel. Prague: 1847.

Sippurim Mi-she-kevar. Edited by Aliza Shenhar-Alroy. Haifa: 1896.

Sippurim Niflaim. Edited by Samuel Horowitz. Jerusalem: 1935.

Sippurei Hasidim. Edited by Shlomo Yosef Zevin. Tel Aviv: 1964.

Sippurei Ma'asiyot. Nachman of Bratslav. Berlin: 1923.

Sippurei Ma'asiyot Hadashim. Nachman of Bratslav. Warsaw: 1909.

Sippurei Ya'akov. Ya'akov Shalom Sofer. Jerusalem: 1994.

Siraj al-'Uqul. (Arabic) Hoter ben Shlomo. 1981.

Sod Gavhei Shamayim. Yosef ibn Tabul. British Museum Ms. Or. 10627.

Sod ha-Shabbat in *Tola'at Ya'akov.* Meir ben Ezekiel ibn Gabbai. Jerusalem: 1995.

Sodei Razayya. Eleazar of Worms. In *Sefer Raziel.* Amsterdam: 1701.

Song of Songs Rabbah (Midrash Shir ha-Shirim Rabbah). Edited by S. Dunsky. Jerusalem: 1980.

Synopse zur Hekhalot-Literatur. (German) Edited by Peter Schäfer. Tubingen: 1981.

Ta'am Z'kenim. Edited by Eliezer Ashkenazi. Frankfurt am Main: 1854.

Ta'amei ha-Minhagim. Edited by A. J. Sperling. Lvov: 1928.

Ta'amei ha-Mitzvot. Menahem ben Benjamin Recanati. Basel: 1581.

Tanna de-vei Eliyahu. Jerusalem: 1959.

Tanya (Likutei Amarim). Shneur Zalman of Lyady. New York: 1963.

Targum Neophyti. (Aramaic) Edited by A. Diez Macho. Madrid and Barcelona: 1968 and 1970.

Targum Onkelos. (Aramaic) Edited by A. Berliner. Jerusalem: 1968.

Targum Pseudo-Yonathan (Targum Yerushalmi). (Aramaic) Edited by M. Ginsburger. Berlin: 1903.

Targum Yonathan. (Aramaic) Edited by Mordechai Yitshari. Rosh ha-Ayin: 2002.

Tefillat Rabbi Shim'on ben Yohai in *Beit ha-Midrash.* Edited by A. Jellinek. Jerusalem: 1967.

Testament of Abraham. (Greek) Edited by M. R. James. Cambridge: 1892.

Testament of Levi. (Armenian) Edited by Michael E. Stone. Jerusalem: 1969.

Testament of Solomon. (Greek) Edited by Chester Charlton McCowan. Leipzig: 1922.

Tester ha-Mor. Abraham Sabba. Venice: 1576.

Theogony—Works and Days. (Greek) Hesiod. Edited by M. L. West. New York : 1999.

Tiferet Shlomo. Shlomo Rabinowitz of Radomsk. Jerusalem: 1992.

Tiferet Uziel. Uziel Meisels. Warsaw: 1863.

Tikkunei ha-Zohar. Amsterdam: 1701.

Timaeus. (Latin) Plato. Translated by H. D. P. Lee. Baltimore: 1965.

Tkhine imrei Shifreh. (Yiddish) Shifrah Segal of Brody.

Tola'at Ya'akov (Sefer Tola'at Ya'akov). Meir ben Ezekiel ibn Gabbai. Jerusalem: 1995.

Torah min ha-Shamayim b'Aspaklarya shel ha-Dorot. Abraham Joshua Heschel. New York: 1995.

Torat Moshe. Moshe Alshekh. Brooklyn: 1960.

Tosefta. Edited by Moses Samuel Zuckermandel. Jerusalem: 1963.

Tosefta Zohar in *Livnat ha-Sapir*. Joseph Angelino. Jerusalem: 1973.

Tzefunot ve-Aggadot. Edited by M. J. Bin Gorion. Tel Aviv: 1956.

Tzidkat ha-Tzaddik. Tzadok ha-Kohen of Lublin. Jerusalem: 1968.

Tzofnat Pa'ane'ach. Yosef Gikatilla. Horodna: 1747.

Tzurat ha-Olam. Isaac ben Abraham ibn Latif. Vienna: 1860.

Vita Adae et Evae. (Latin) See *Old Testament Pseudepigrapha* by James Charlesworth in the English Bibliography.

Wisdom of Ben Sira (Sefer Hokhmat Ben Sira ha-Shalem). Edited by M. H. Segal. Jerusalem: 1932.

Wisdom of Solomon. (Greek) Translated by D. Winston. New York: 1979.

Yalkut ha-Makhiri. Makhir ben Abba Mari. Edited by Solomon Buber. Jerusalem: 1964.

Yalkut Re'uveni. Warsaw: 1883.

Yalkut Shim'oni. Shim'on ha-Darshan. Jerusalem: 1968 and 1973.

Yamin Noar'im. Edited by S. Y. Agnon. Jerusalem: 1964. *Days of Awe* by. S. Y. Agnon in the English bibliography.

Yamim Nora'im. Menahem ha-Kohen. Tel Aviv: 1974.

Yesamah Lev. Menahem Nahum of Chernobyl. Slavuta: 1798.

Yesod ha-Teshuvah. Isaac ben Moses Elles. Munkacs: 1897.

Yiyyul ha-Pardes. Elimelekh of Dinov.

Yosef ba-Seder. Hayyim Joseph David Azulai. Lemberg: 1658.

Zekhor Hamor. Bin Sabba. Venice: 1523.

Zikaron Tov. Piotrkov: 1892.

Zikhron Yerushalayim. Jerusalem: 1876.

Ziv ha-Zohar. Edited by Y. Y. Rozenberg. Jerusalem: 1967.

Zohar (Sefer ha-Zohar). Vilna: 1894.

Zohar Hadash. Amsterdam: 1701.

ISRAEL FOLKTALE ARCHIVES (IFA) LIST

IFA 310.   Collected by Heda Jason from Pinchas Gutterman of Poland.

IFA 462.   Told by Dov Noy of Galicia, Poland.

IFA 477.   Collected by Shimon Ernst from a new immigrant from Morocco.

IFA 553.   Collected by Dov Noy from a Persian old man in Jerusalem.

IFA 593.   Told by Ephraim Tsoref of Poland.

IFA 597.   Told by Ephraim Tsoref of Poland.

IFA 763.   Collected by Shimon Ernst from Yosef Ben Tsaban of Kurdistan.

IFA 943.   Collected by Heda Jason from Yefet Shvili of Yemen.
IFA 966.   Collected by Nehama Zion from Miriam Tschernobilski of Israel (Ashkenazi).
IFA 1141.   Collected by Heda Jason from Yefet Shvili of Yemen.
IFA 2208.   Told by Ephraim Tsoref of Poland.
IFA 3590.   Collected by Yeshayahu Ashni from Yisrael-Ber Schneersohn of Israel (Ashkenazi)
IFA 3643.   Collected by Moshe Vigisser from Yaish Nisim of Yemen.
IFA 4014.   Collected by Pinchas Gutterman from Rabbi Shalom Weinstein of Poland.
IFA 4382.   Collected by Moshe Vigisser from Yechiel Dan of Yemen.
IFA 4396.   Collected by Yitzhak Wechsler from Shlomo Hazan of Morocco.
IFA 4563.   Collected by Zalman Baharav from Yakov Chaprak of Turkish Kurdistan.
IFA 4591.   Collected by Yitzhak Wechsler from Mr. Talshir of Poland.
IFA 4722.   Collected by Nehamat Zion from Grandmother Miriam Tchernobilsky of Israel (Ashkenazi)
IFA 4735.   Collected by Menachem Ben-Aryeh from Rabbi Yakov Asharaf of Morocco.
IFA 5029.   Collected by Zevulun Kort of Afghanistan.
IFA 5854.   Collected by Moshe Vigisser from Yehiel Dan of Yemen.
IFA 6554.   Collected by Pinchas Gutterman from Ephraim Schechter of Czechoslovakia.
IFA 6556.   Collected by Pinchas Gutterman from Ephraim Schechter of Czechoslovakia.
IFA 6725.   Collected by Dov Noy from Aliza Elizra of Morocco.
IFA 6928.   Collected in Israel by Uri Resler from his uncle of Rumania.
IFA 6929.   Collected in Israel by Uri Resler from his uncle of Rumania.
IFA 6966.   Collected by David Eini from Yakov Niado of Syria.
IFA 7249.   Collected by Samuel Zanvel Pipe from his family of Galicia, Poland.
IFA 7830.   Collected by Zevulon Kort from Ben-Zion Asherov of Afghanistan.
IFA 7838.   Collected by Zevulon Kort from Shimon Yazdi of Afghanistan.
IFA 8335.   Collected by Moshe Rabbi from Hannah Haddad of Iraq.
IFA 8415.   Collected by Zalman Barahav from Mr. Harumately of Iraq.
IFA 9584.   Collected by Haya ben-Avraham from Avigayil Naguker of India.
IFA 9586.   Collected by Hay ben-Avraham from Daniel Sigauker of India.
IFA 10009.   Collected by Abraham On from Shimon Biton of Morocco.
IFA 10020.   Collected by Abraham On from Shimon Biton of Morocco.
IFA 10200.   Collected by Edna Bavai from Rafael Bavai of Persia.
IFA 10895.   Collected by Devora Wilk from Bela Baroz of Caucasus (Kobe).
IFA 10919.   Collected by Yifrah Haviv from Adiv Nadim of Israeli Cherkess.
IFA 11774.   Told by Ya'akov Lassri of Morocco.
IFA 12921.   Collected by Devorah Vilk from Julieta Ya'akovlava of the Caucasus.
IFA 12985.   Collected by Malka Cohen from Zalman Altshuler of the Ukraine.
IFA 13043.   Collected by Malka Cohen from Esther Zagadon of Libya.
IFA 13264.   Told by Yitzhak Koler of Poland.
IFA 13365.   Told by Aluwan Shimon Avidany of Iraqi Kurdistan.
IFA 13901.   Told by Ya'akov Alfasi of Morocco (Azimur).
IFA 13947.   Collected by Yisrael Gittelman from Shlomo ben Hayim of Morocco.
IFA 14418.   Collected by Yafa Kamar from her uncle Yehezkel Kirshenboim of Israel (Ashkenazi).
IFA 15075.   Collected by Mordechai Yonai from Mussa Muhamed Zvidat of Israel (Bedouin).

IFA 16159.   Collected by Orna Fadida from Shimon Shababo of Israel (Sephardic).
IFA 16628.   Collected by Ayelet Etinger-Salama from Daniel Cohen from David Ben-Hamo of Morocco.
IFA 16893.   Collected by Havatselet Lorberboim from Nehama Friedman of Israel (Ashkenazi). IFA 17143. Collected by Yifrah Haviv from Menahem Ben-Amotz of Israel (Ashkenazi).
IFA 17586.   Collected by Yifrah Haviv from Ze'ev Elman of Israel.
IFA 18238.   Collected by Yedidia Ben-Porat from Nissan Kohen-Tzedak of Persia.
IFA 18976.   Collected by Yifrach Haviv from Yehuda Herman of Poland.

SELECTED ENGLISH BIBLIOGRAPHY

Aaron, David H. "Imagery of the Divine and the Human: On the Mythology of Genesis Rabbah 8:1." In *Journal of Jewish Thought and Philosophy* 5 (1995) 1-62.

Aaron, David H. "Shedding Light on God's Body in Rabbinic Midrashim: Reflections on the Theory of a Luminous Adam." In *Harvard Theological Review* 90:3 (1997) 299-314.

Abelson, J. *The Immanence of God in Rabbinical Literature*. London: Macmillan, 1912.

Abelson, J. *Jewish Mysticism: An Introduction to the Kabbalah*. New York: Sepher-Hermon Press, 1981.

Abrams, Daniel. "From Divine Shape to Angelic Being: The Career of Akatriel in Jewish Literature." In *Journal of Religion* 76:1 (1996) 43-63.

Abrams, Daniel. "Special Angelic Figures: The Career of the Beasts of the Throne-world in *Hekhalot* Literature, German Pietism and Early Kabbalistic Literature." In *Revue des Etudes juives* 155:3-4 (1996) 363-386.

Abrams, Judith Z. "The Reflexive Relationship with Mal'achei HaSharet and the Sages." In *CCAR Journal* 42:2 (1995) 25-34.

Abramson, Glenda, ed. *Modern Jewish Mythologies*. Cincinnati: Hebrew Union College Press, 1999.

Ackerman, Robert. *The Myth and Ritual School: J. G. Frazer and the Cambridge Ritualists*. New York and London: Garland Publishing, 1991.

Ackerman, Susan. *Under Every Green Tree: Popular Religion in Sixth-Century Judah*. Atlanta: Scholars Press, 1992.

Adelman, Penina V. *Miriam's Well: Rituals for Jewish Women Around the Year*. Fresh Meadows, NY: Biblio Press, 1986.

Agnon, S. Y., ed. *Days of Awe*. New York: Schocken Books, 1948.

Agnon, S. Y., ed. *Present at Sinai: The Giving of the Law*. Philadelphia: Jewish Publication Society, 1994.

Agus, Aharon (Ronald E.). *The Binding of Isaac and Messiah: Law, Martyrdom, and Deliverance in Early Rabbinic Religiosity*. SUNY Series in Judaica: *Hermeneutics, Mysticism and Religion*. Albany: State University of New York Press, 1988.

Albright, William Foxwell. *Archaeology and the Religion of Israel*. Baltimore, MD: Johns Hopkins Press, 1968.

Albright, William Foxwell. *Yahweh and the Gods of Canaan: A Historical Analysis of Two Contrasting Faiths*. Garden City, NY: Doubleday, 1968.

Alexander, Philip S. "*3 Enoch* and the Talmud." In *Journal for the Study of Judaism* 18:1 (1997) 40-68.

Alexander, Philip S. "Comparing Merkavah Mysticism and Gnosticism: An Essay in Method." In *Journal of Jewish Studies* 35:1 (1984) 1-17.

Alexander, Philip S. "The Fall into Knowledge: The Garden of Eden/Paradise in Gnostic Literature." In *A Walk in the Garden: Biblical, Iconographical and Literary Images of Eden*. Ed. Paul Morris and Deborah Sawyer. London: Journal for the Study of the Old Testament, 1992.

Alexander, Philip S. "Pre-Emptive Exegesis: Genesis Rabba's Reading of the Story of Creation." In *Journal of Jewish Studies* 43:2 (1992) 230-245.

Alexander, Tamar. "Folktales in Sefer Hasidim." In *Prooftexts* 5 (1985) 19-31.

Alexander, Tamar. "Theme and Genre: Relationships Between Man and She-demon in Jewish Folklore." In *Jewish Folklore and Ethnology Review* 14:1-2 (1992) 56-61.

Alter, Michael J. *What is the Purpose of Creation?* Northvale, NJ: Jason Aronson, 1991.

Alter, Michael J. *Why the Torah Begins with the Letter Beit*. Northvale, NJ: Jason Aronson, 1998.

Altmann, Alexander, ed. *Biblical Motifs: Origins and Transformations*. Cambridge, MA: Harvard University Press, 1966.

Altmann, Alexander. "Creation and Emanation in Isaac Israeli: A Reappraisal." In *Studies in Medieval Jewish History and Literature*. Ed. Isadore Twersky. Cambridge, MA: Harvard University Press, 1979, 1-15.

Altmann, Alexander. "The Gnostic Background of the Rabbinic Adam Legends." In *Essays in Jewish Intellectual History* Hanover, NH: University Press of New England for Brandeis University Press, 1981, 1-16.

Altmann, Alexander. "Gnostic Themes in Rabbinic Cosmology." In *Essays in Honor of the Very Rev. Dr. J. H. Hertz*. Ed. I. Epstein, E. Levine, and C. Roth. London: E. Goldston, 1942, 19-32.

Altmann, Alexander. "*Homo Imago Dei* in Jewish and Christian Theology." In *Journal of Religion* 48 (1968) 235-239.

Altmann, Alexander, ed. *Jewish Medieval and Renaissance Studies*. Cambridge, MA: Harvard University Press, 1967.

Altmann, Alexander. "Lurianic Kabbalah in a Platonic Key: Abraham Cohen Herrera's *Puerta del Cielo*." In *Hebrew Union College Annual* 53 (1982) 317-355.

Altmann, Alexander. "A Note on the Rabbinic Doctrine of Creation." In *Journal of Jewish Studies* 7 (1956) 195-206.

Anderson, A. R. *Alexander's Gate: Gog and Magog and the Enclosed Nations*. Cambridge: Medieval Academy of America, 1932.

Anderson, Bernhard W. *From Creation to New Creation: Old Testament Perspectives*. Minneapolis: Fortress Press, 1994.

Anderson, Gary A. and Michael E. Stone. *A Synopsis of the Books of Adam and Eve*. Atlanta: Scholars Press, 1994.

Anderson, Gary A. "The Garden of Eden and Sexuality in Early Judaism." In *People of the Body: Jews and Judaism from an Embodied Perspective*. Ed. Howard Eilberg-Schwartz. Albany: State University of New York Press, 1992, 47-68.

Anderson, Gary A. *Sacrifices and Offerings in Ancient Israel: Studies in their Social and Political Importance*. Atlanta: Scholars Press, 1987.

Ansky, S. *The Dybbuk and Other Writings by S. Ansky*. New Haven: Yale University Press, 2002.

Antonelli, Judith S. *In the Image of God: A Feminist Commentary on the Torah*. Northvale, NJ: Jason Aronson, 1995.

Aptowitzer, Victor. "The Celestial Temple as Viewed in the Aggadah." In *Binah: Jewish Intellectual History in the Middle Ages*. Vol. 2. Ed. Joseph Dan. Westport, CT: Praeger, 1989, 1-29.

Arbel, Vita Daphna. *Beholders of the Divine Secrets: Mysticism and Myth in Hekhalot and Merkavah Literature*. Albany: State University of New York Press, 2003.

Ariel, David S. *The Mystic Quest: An Introduction to Jewish Mysticism*. New York: Schocken Books, 1988.

Armstrong, Karen. *A History of God: The 4000-Year Quest of Judaism, Christianity and Islam*. New York: Ballantine Books, 1993.

Arnold, Abraham J. *Judaism: Myth, Legend, History, and Custom from the Religious to the Secular*. Montreal: Robert Davies Publishing, 1995.

Aron, Robert. *The God of the Beginnings*. New York: Morrow, 1936.

Aschkenasy, Nehama. *Eve's Journey: Feminine Images in Hebraic Literary Tradition*. Detroit: Wayne State University Press, 1986.

Aschkenasy, Nehama. *Woman at the Window: Biblical Tales of Oppression and Escape*. Detroit: Wayne State University Press, 1988.

Avery-Peck, Alan J. "The Exodus in Jewish Faith: The Problem of God's Intervention in History." In *The Annual of Rabbinic Judaism*, edited by Alan J. Avery-Peck, William Scott Green, and Jacob Neusner. Leiden: Brill, 1998, 3-22.

Avigad, N. and Yadlin, Y., eds. *Genesis Apocryphon*. Jerusalem: The Magnes Press, 1956.

Baarda, T. "'Tzitura': A Graecism in Midrash Echa Rabba I, 5." In *Journal for the Study of Judaism* 18:1 (1987) 69-80.

Bacchiocchi, Samuele. "Sabbatical Typologies of Messianic Redemption." In *Journal for the Study of Judaism* 17:2 (1986) 153-176.

Bailey, Lloyd R. "Gehenna: The Topography of Hell." In *Biblical Archeologist* 49 (1986) 187-191.

Bailey, Lloyd R. "The Golden Calf." In *Hebrew Union College Annual* 42 (1971) 97-115.

Bamberger, Bernard J. *Fallen Angels*. Philadelphia: Jewish Publication Society, 1952.

Bamberger, Bernard J. "Philo and the Aggadah." In *Hebrew Union College Annual* 48 (1978) 153-185.

Baril, Gilberte. *The Feminine Face of the People of God: Biblical Symbols of the Church as Bride and Mother*. Collegeville, MN: The Liturgical Press, 1992.

Bar-Ilan, Meir. "The Hand of God: A Chapter in Rabbinic Anthropomorphism." In *Rashi* (1993) 321-335.

Barker, Margaret. *The Great Angel: A Study of Israel's Second God*. Louisville: Westminster/John Knox Press, 1992.

Barlev, Yehiel A. *Yedid Nefesh: Introduction to Kabbalah*. Brooklyn, NY: Chemed Books, 1988.

Baron, Salo W. and Joseph L. Blau, eds. *Judaism: Postbiblical and Talmudic Period*. Indianapolis, IN: Bobbs-Merrill, 1954.

Barr, James. *The Garden of Eden and the Hope of Immortality*. Minneapolis: Fortress Press, 1992.

Barr, James. "The Meaning of 'Mythology' in Relation to the Old Testament." In *Vetus Testamentum* 9 (1959) 1-10.

Baskin, Judith R., ed. *Jewish Women in Historical Perspective*. Detroit: Wayne State University Press, 1991.

Basser, Herbert W., trans. *Midrashic Interpretations of the Song of Moses*. New York: P. Lang, 1984.

Basser, Herbert W. "Superstitious Interpretations of Jewish Laws." In *Journal for the Study of the Judaism* 8:2 (1977) 127-138.

Batto, Bernard F. *Slaying the Dragon: Mythmaking in the Biblical Tradition*. Louisville, KY: Westminster/John Knox Press, 1992.

Bauckham, Richard. "Early Jewish Visions of Hell." In *Journal of Theological Studies* 41:2 (1990) 355-385.

Bauckham, Richard. "Resurrection as Giving Back the Dead: A Traditional Image of Resurrection in the Pseudepigrapha and the Apocalypse of John." In *The Pseudepigrapha and Early Biblical Interpretation*. Ed. James H. Charlesworth and Craig A. Evans. Sheffield: JSOT Press, 1993, 269-191.

Baumgarten, Albert I., ed. *Self, Soul & Body in Religious Experience*. Leiden: E. J. Brill, 1998.

Beckwith, Roger T. and Martin J. Selman, eds. *Sacrifice in the Bible*. Grand Rapids, MI: Baker Book House, 1995.

Beltz, Walter. *God and the Gods: Myths of the Bible*. Trans. Peter Heinegg. New York: Penguin Books, 1983.

Ben-Ami, Issachar. *Saint Veneration among the Jews in Morocco*. Detroit: Wayne State University Press, 1998.

Ben-Amos, Dan. "Talmudic Tall Tales." *Folklore Today* (1976) 25-43.

Bension, Ariel. *The Zohar in Moslem and Christian Spain*. New York: Sepher-Hermon Press, 1974.

Ben Zion, Raphael, trans. *The Anthology of Jewish Mysticism*. Ed. B. Goldman. New York: Zahava Publications, 2000.

Berger, David. *The Rebbe, the Messiah, and the Scandal of Orthodox Indifference*. London: Littman Library of Jewish Civilization, 2001.

Berger, David. "Three Typological Themes in Early Jewish Messianism: Messiah Son of Joseph, Rabbinic Calculations, and the Figure of Armilus." In *American Jewish Studies Review* 10:2 (1985) 141-164.

Berlin, Adele and Marc Zvi Brettler, eds. *The Jewish Study Bible*. Oxford and New York: Oxford University Press, 2004.

Berman, Joshua. *The Temple: Its Symbolism and Meaning Then and Now*. Northvale, NJ: Jason Aronson, 1995.

Berman, Louis A. *The Akedah: The Binding of Isaac*. Northvale, NJ: Jason Aronson, 1997.

Bernstein, Alan E. *The Formation of Hell: Death and Retribution in the Ancient and Early Christian Worlds*. Ithaca, NY: Cornell University Press, 1993.

Bialik, Hayim Nahman and Yehoshua Hana Ravnitzky. *The Book of Legends, Sefer ha-Aggadah: Legends from the Talmud and Midrash*. Trans. William G. Braude. New York: Schocken Books, 1992.

Bienkowski, Piotr and Alan Millard, eds. *Dictionary of the Ancient Near East*. Philadelphia: University of Pennsylvania Press, 2000.

Bilu, Yoram. "Dybbuk and Maggid: Two Cultural Patterns of Altered Consciousness in Judaism." In *AJS Review* 21:2 (1996) 341-366.

Bilu, Yoram. *Without Bounds: The Life and Death of Rabbi Ya'aqov Wazana*. Detroit: Wayne State University Press, 2000.

Binger, Tilde. *Asherah: Goddesses in Ugarit, Israel and the Old Testament*. Sheffield, England: Sheffield Academic Press, 1997.

Bin Gorion, Micha Joseph. *Mimekor Yisrael: Classical Jewish Folktales*. 3 vols. Bloomington: Indiana University Press, 1976.

Bleich, J. David, ed. *With Perfect Faith: The Foundations of Jewish Belief*. New York: Ktav Publishing House, 1983.

Blenkinsopp, Joseph. *A History of Prophecy in Israel*. Philadelphia: Westminster Press, 1983.

Bloch, Abraham P. *The Biblical and Historical Background of Jewish Customs and Ceremonies*. New York: Ktav Publishing House, 1980.

Bloch, Abraham P. *The Biblical and Historical Background of the Jewish Holy Days*. New York: Ktav Publishing House, 1978.

Bloch, Ariel and Chana Bloch, trans. *The Song of Songs: A New Translation with an Introduction and Commentary*. New York: Random House, 1995.

Blumenthal, David R. *Understanding Jewish Mysticism: A Source Reader*. 2 vols. New York: Ktav Publishing House, 1978 and 1982.

Boccaccini, Gabriele. *Beyond the Essene Hypothesis: The Parting of the Ways between Qumran and Enochic Judaism*. Grand Rapids, MI: William B. Eerdmans, 1998.

Bockmuehl, Markus N. A. *Revelation and Mystery in Ancient Judaism and Pauline Christianity*. Grand Rapids, MI: William B. Eerdmans, 1997.

Bohlig, Alexander. "Jacob as an Angel in Gnosticism and Manicheism." In *Nag Hammadi and Gnosis*. Ed. R. McL. Wilson. Leiden: E. J. Brill, 1978, 122-130.

Bokser, Ben Zion, trans. *The Essential Writings of Abraham Isaac Kook*. Warwick, NY: Amity House, 1988.

Bokser, Ben Zion. *The Jewish Mystical Tradition*. New York: The Pilgrim Press, 1981.

Bookstaber, Philip David. *The Idea of Development of the Soul in Medieval Jewish Philosophy*. Philadelphia: Maurice Jacobs, 1950.

Borgen, Peder. *Bread from Heaven: An Exegetical Study of the Concept of Manna in the Gospel of John and the Writings of Philo*. Leiden: E. J. Brill, 1965.

Borgen, Peder. "Heavenly Ascent in Philo: An Examination of Selected Passages." In *The Pseudepigrapha and Early Biblical Interpretation*. Ed. James H. Charlesworth and Craig A. Evans. Sheffield: JSOT Press, 1993, 246-268.

Borges, Jorge Luis. *Collected Fictions*. New York: Viking, 1998.

Bos, Gerrit. "Hayim Vital's `Practical Kabbalah and Alchemy': A 17th Century Book of Secrets." In *Journal of Jewish Thought and Philosophy* 4 (1994) 55-112.

Bowley, James. "The Compositions of Abraham." In *Tracing the Threads: Studies in the Vitality of Jewish Pseudepigrapha*. Early Judaism and Its Literature Series, No. 6. Ed. John C. Reeves. Atlanta: Scholars Press, 1994, 215-238.

Bowman, Steven. "Messianic Expectations in the Peloponnesos." In *Hebrew Union College Annual* 52 (1981) 195-202.

Braude, William G. *Pesikta Rabbati: Discourses for Feasts, Fasts, and Special Sabbaths*. 2 vols. New Haven and London: Yale University Press, 1968.

Braude, William G. and Israel J. Kapstein. *Tanna Debe Eliyyahu: The Lore of the School of Elijah*. Philadelphia: The Jewish Publication Society, 1981.

Brauer, Erich. *The Jews of Kurdistan*. Ed. Raphael Patai. Detroit: Wayne State University Press, 1993.

Bregman, Marc. "The Darshan: Preacher and Teacher of Talmudic Times." In *The Melton Journal* 14 (1982).

Bregman, Marc. "The Four Who Entered Paradise: Evolution of a Talmudic Tale." In *First Harvest* Ed. Howard Schwartz and Barbara Raznick. St. Louis: The Brodsky Library Press, 1997, 437-442.

Bregman, Marc. "Isaak Heinemann's Classic Study of Aggadah and Midrash." Unpublished.

Bregman, Marc. "Jacob Our Father Never Died." Lecture given at the Textual Reasoning Conference, Drew University, 1997, in preparation for publication.

Bregman, Marc. "Midrash Rabbah and the Medieval Collector Mentality" in *Prooftexts* 17 (1997) 63-76.

Bregman, Marc. "Mordechai the Milk-Man: Sexual Ambivalence in a Provocative Midrash." Unpublished.

Bregman, Marc. "Past and Present in Midrashic Literature." In *Hebrew Annual Review* 2 (1978) 45-59.

Bregman, Marc. "Pseudepigraphy in Rabbinic Literature." In *Pseudepigraphic Perspectives: The Apocrypha and Pseudepigrapha in Light of the Dead Sea Scrolls*. Ed. Esther G. Chazon and Michael Stone. Leiden: E. J. Brill, 1999, 27-41.

Bregman, Marc. "The Riddle of the Ram in Genesis Chapter 22: Jewish-Christian Contacts in Late Antiquity." In *The Sacrifice of Isaac in the Three Monotheistic Religions*. Ed. Frederic Manns. Jerusalem: Franciscan Printing Press, 1995, 127-145.

Bregman, Marc. "Ruah Ha-Qodesh ("The Holy Spirit") in Rabbinic Literature." Unpublished.

Bregman, Marc. "Seeing with the Sages: Midrash as Visualization in the Legends of the Aqedah." In *Agendas for the Study of Midrash in the Twenty-First Century*. Ed. Marc Lee Raphael. Williamsburg, VA: College of William and Mary, 1999, 84-100.

Bregman, Marc. *The Tanhuma-Yelammedenu Literature: Studies in the Evolution of the Versions*, Piscataway, N.J.: Gorgias Press: 2004.

Breslauer, S. Daniel. *Martin Buber on Myth: An Introduction*. Theorists of Myth, vol. 3. New York: Garland Publishing, 1990.

Breslauer, S. Daniel. "Reading Myth: A Strategy for a Methodological Introduction to the Study of Jewish Religions." In *Academic Approaches to Teaching Jewish Studies*. Ed. Zev Garber. Lanham, MD: University Press of America, 2000.

Breslauer, S. Daniel, ed. *The Seductiveness of Jewish Myth: Challenge or Response?* Albany: State University of New York Press, 1997.

Brettler, Marc Zvi. *God is King: Understanding An Israelite Metaphor*. Sheffield: Sheffield Academic Press, 1989.

Brichto, Herbert Chanan. "Kin, Cult, Land and Afterlife—A Biblical Complex." In *Hebrew Union College Annual* 44 (1973) 1-54.

Brichto, Herbert Chanan. "The Worship of the Golden Calf: A Literary Analysis of a Fable on Idolatry." In *Hebrew Union College Annual* 54 (1983) 1-44.

Brill, Alan. "The Mystical Path of the Vilna Gaon." In *Journal of Jewish Thought and Philosophy* 3 (1993) 131-151.

Brown, Dovid. *Mysteries of the Chariot*. Southfield, MI: Targum Press, 1997.

Bruce, Iris. "Kafka and Jewish Folklore." In *The Cambridge Companion to Kafka*. Cambridge: Cambridge University Press, 2002, 151-168.

Buber, Martin. *Moses: The Revelation and the Covenant*. New York: Harper & Row, 1946.

Buber, Martin. *Tales of Angels, Spirits and Demons*. Trans. David Antin and Jerome Rothenberg. New York: Hawk's Well Press, 1958.

Buber, Martin. *Tales of the Hasidim*. New York: Schocken Books, 1947-48. Two volumes.

Buchanan, George Wesley, trans. *Revelation and Redemption: Jewish Documents of Deliverance from the Fall of Jerusalem to the Death of Nachmanides*. Asheville, NC: Western North Carolina Press, 1978.

Cahn, Zvi. *The Philosophy of Judaism*. New York: Macmillan, 1962.

Caine, Burton. "The *Akedah*: Angel Unbound." In *Conservative Judaism* 52:1 (1999) 5-27.

Callender, Dexter E., Jr. *Adam in Myth and History: Ancient Israelite Perspectives on the Primal Human*. Winona Lake, IN: Eisenbrauns, 2000.

Campbell, Joseph. *The Hero with a Thousand Faces*. Princeton, NJ: Princeton University Press, 1968.

Campbell, Joseph, ed. *Myths, Dreams, and Religions*. New York: E. P. Dutton, 1970.

Cardozo, Nathan T. Lopes. *The Torah as God's Mind: A Kabbalistic Look into the Pentateuch*. New York: Ben-Ron Publications, 1988.

Cardozo, Nathan T. Lopes. *The Written and Oral Torah: A Comprehensive Introduction*. Northvale, NJ: Jason Aronson, 1997.

Carmichael, Calum M. "The Paradise Myth: Interpreting without Jewish and Christian Spectacles." In *A Walk in the Garden: Biblical, Iconographical and Literary Images of Eden*. Ed. Paul Morris and Deborah Sawyer. Sheffield: JSOT Press, 1992, 47-63.

Carmichael, Calum M. *The Story of Creation: Its Origin and Its Interpretation in Philo and the Fourth Gospel*. Ithaca: Cornell University Press, 1996.

Cassuto, Umberto. *Biblical and Oriental Studies*. Jerusalem: The Magnes Press, 1975.

Cassuto, Umberto. *A Commentary on the Book of Exodus*. Jerusalem: The Magnes Press, 1967.

Cassuto, Umberto. *A Commentary on the Book of Genesis*. Jerusalem: The Magnes Press, 1961. Two volumes.

Chabon, Michael. *The Amazing Adventures of Kavalier & Clay*. New York: Picador USA, 2000.

Chajes, J. H. *Between Worlds: Dybbuks, Exorcists, and Early Modern Judaism*. Philadelphia: University of Pennsylvania Press, 2003.

Charles, R. H., ed. *The Apocrypha and Pseudepigrapha of the Old Testament*. 2 vols. Oxford: Clarendon Press, 1976.

Charles, R. H., ed. *The Book of Jubilees*. Oxford: 1913.

Charlesworth, James H. "Folk Traditions in Jewish Apocalyptic Literature." In *Mysteries and Revelations: Apocalyptic Studies since the Uppsala Colloquium*. Ed. John. J. Collins and James H. Charlesworth. Sheffield: JSOT Press, 1991, 91-113.

Charlesworth, James H., ed. *The Old Testament Pseudepigrapha*. 2 vols. Garden City, NY: Doubleday, 1983-85.

Charlesworth, James H., with J. Brownson, M. T. Davis, S. J. Kraftchick, and A. F. Segal, eds. *The Messiah: Developments in Earliest Judaism and Christianity*. The First Princeton Symposium on Judaism and Christian Origins. Minneapolis: Fortress Press, 1992.

Charlesworth, James H. and Craig A. Evans, eds. *The Pseudepigrapha and Early Biblical Interpretation*. Sheffield: JSOT Press, 1993.

Charlesworth, James H. *The Pseudepigrapha and Modern Research*. Atlanta: Scholars Press, 1983.

Chayoun, Yehudah. *When Moshiach Comes: Halachic and Aggadic Perspectives*. Trans. Ya'akov M. Rapoport and Moshe Grossman. Southfield, MI: Targum Press, 1994.

Chernus, Ira. *Mysticism in Rabbinic Judaism: Studies in the History of Midrash*. New York: Walter De Gruyter, 1981.

Chernus, Ira. "Visions of God in Merkabah Mysticism." In *Journal for the Study of Judaism* 13:1-2 (1982) 123-146.

Cheyne, T. K. *Traditions and Beliefs of Ancient Israel*. London: Adam and Charles Black, 1907.

Chilton, Bruce. "God as `Father' in the Targumim, in Non-Canonical Literatures of Early Judaism and Primitive Christianity, and in Matthew." In *The Pseudepigrapha and Early Biblical Interpretation*. Ed. James H. Charlesworth and Craig A. Evans. Sheffield: JSOT Press, 1993, 151-169.

Clifford, Richard J. *Creation Accounts in the Ancient Near East and the in the Bible*. Washington DC: The Catholic Biblical Quarterly Monograph Series, 1994.

Clifford, Richard J. "The Roots of Apocalypticism in Near Eastern Myth." In *The Encyclopedia of Apocalypticism*. Vol. 1. Ed. John J. Collins. New York: Continuum, 1999, 3-38.

Cohen, A. *Everyman's Talmud*. New York: E. P. Dutton, 1949.

Cohen, Gerson D. *A Critical Edition with a Translation and Notes of The Book of Tradition (Sefer Ha-Qabbalah) by Abraham ibn Daud*. Philadelphia: Jewish Publication Society, 1967.

Cohen, Gerson D. *Studies in the Variety of Rabbinic Cultures*. Philadelphia: Jewish Publication Society, 1991.

Cohen, Martin Samuel, ed. *The Shi'ur Qomah: Liturgy and Theurgy in Pre-Kabbalistic Jewish Mysticism*. New York: University Press of America, 1983.

Cohen, Martin Samuel, ed. *The Shi'ur Qomah: Texts and Recensions*. Tubigen: J. C. B. Mohr, 1985.

Cohen, Victor. *The Soul of the Torah: Insights of the Chasidic Masters on the Weekly Torah Portions*. Northvale, NJ: Jason Aronson, 2000.

Cohn-Sherbok, Dan. *Divine Intervention and Miracles in Jewish Theology*. Lewiston, NY: Edwin Mellen Press, 1995.

Cohn-Sherbok, Dan and Lavinia Cohn-Sherbok. *Jewish & Christian Mysticism: An Introduction*. New York: Continuum, 1994.

Cohn-Sherbock, Dan. *The Jewish Messiah*. Edinburgh: T & T Clark, 1997.

Cohon, Samuel S. "The Name of God, A Study in Rabbinic Theology." In *Hebrew Union College Annual* 23 (1950-51) 579-604.

Cohon, Samuel S. "The Origin of Death." In *Journal of Jewish Lore and Philosophy* 1:3-4 (1919) 371-396.

Collins, John J. *Apocalypticism in the Dead Sea Scrolls*. London: Routledge, 1997.

Collins, John J. *The Apocalyptic Imagination: An Introduction to Jewish Apocalyptic Literature*. 2d ed. Grand Rapids, MI: William B. Eerdmans, 1998.

Collins, John J. and Michael Fishbane, eds. *Death, Ecstasy, and Other Worldly Journeys*. Albany: State University of New York Press, 1995.

Collins, John J. "From Prophecy to Apocalypticism: The Expectation of the End." In *The Encyclopedia of Apocalypticism*. Vol. 1. New York: Continuum, 1999, 129-161.

Collins, John J. and James H. Charlesworth, eds. *Mysteries and Revelations: Apocalyptic Studies Since the Uppsala Colloquium*. Sheffield: JSOT Press, 1991.

Collins, John J. *The Scepter and the Star: The Messiahs of the Dead Sea Scrolls and Other Ancient Literature*. The Anchor Bible Reference Library. New York: Doubleday, 1995.

Collins, John J. *Seers, Sybils and Sages in Hellenistic-Roman Judaism*. Leiden: E. J. Brill, 1997.

Coogan, M. D., trans. *Stories from Ancient Canaan*. Philadelphia: Westminster Press, 1978.

Cooper, David L. *Messiah: His First Coming Scheduled*. Los Angeles: Biblical Research Society, 1939.

Cowley, A. E. *The Samaritan Liturgy*. Oxford: 1909. Two volumes.

Cross, Frank Moore. *Canaanite Myth and Hebrew Epic*. Cambridge: Harvard University Press, 1973.

Cross, Frank Moore. "The Council of Yahweh in Second Isaiah." In *Journal of Near Eastern Studies* 12 (1953) 274-277.

Culianu, Ioan P. "The Angels of the Nations and the Origins of Gnostic Dualism." In *Studies in Gnosticism and Hellenistic Religions*, edited by R. Van Den Broek and M. J. Vermaseren. Leiden: E. J. Brill, 1981, 78-91.

Cunningham, Adrian. "Type and Archetype in the Eden Story." In *A Walk in the Garden: Biblical, Iconographical and Literary Images of Eden*. Ed. Paul Morris and Deborah Sawyer. Sheffield: JSOT Press, 1992, 290-309.

Dahl, N. A. and Alan F. Segal. "Philo and the Rabbis on the Names of God." In *Journal for the Study of Judaism* 9:1 (1978) 1-28.

Dalley, Stephanie, trans. *Myths from Mesopotamia: Creation, the Flood, Gilgamesh, and Others*. New York: Oxford University Press, 1989.

Dame, Enid, Lilly Rivlin, and Henry Wenkart, eds. *Which Lilith? Feminist Writers Re-Create the World's First Woman*. Northvale, NJ: Jason Aronson, 1998.

Dan, Joseph. "The Ancient Heikhahlot Mystical Texts in the Middle Ages: Tradition, Source, Inspiration." In *Bulletin of the John Rylands University Library of Manchester* 75:3 (1993) 83-96.

Dan, Joseph. *The Ancient Jewish Mysticism*. Tel Aviv: MOD Books, 1993.

Dan, Joseph. "Armilus: The Jewish Antichrist and the Origin and Dating of the 'Sefer Zerubbavel.' In *Toward the Millenium: Messianic Expectations from the Bible to Waco*. Ed. By Peter Schäfer and Mark Cohen. Leiden: Brill, 1998, 73-104.

Dan, Joseph. "The Book of the Divine Name by Rabbi Eleazar of Worms." In *Frankfurter Judaistische Beitrage* 22 (1995) 27-60.

Dan, Joseph. "The Concept of History in Hekhalot and Merkabah Literature." In *Binah: Jewish Intellectual History in the Middle Ages*. Vol. 1. Ed. Joseph Dan. Westport, CT: Praeger, 1989, 47-57.

Dan, Joseph, ed. *The Early Kabbalah*. Mahwah, NJ: Paulist Press, 1986.

Dan, Joseph. "The Emergence of Messianic Mythology in 13th Century Kabbalah in Spain." In *Occident and Orient: A Tribute to the Memory of Alexander Scheiber*. Ed. Robert Dan. Leiden: E. J. Brill, 1988, 57-68.

Dan, Joseph. "Five Versions of the Story of Jerusalem." In *Proceedings of the American Academy for Jewish Research* 35 (1976): 99-111.

Dan, Joseph. "The Emergence of Mystical Prayer." In *Studies in Jewish Mysticism* 2 (1982) 85-120.

Dan, Joseph. *The Heart and the Fountain: An Anthology of Jewish Mystical Experiences*. New York: Oxford University Press, 2002.

Dan, Joseph. "In Quest of a Historical Definition of Mysticism: The Contingental Approach." In *Studies in Spirituality* 3 (1993) 58-90.

Dan, Joseph. "Jerusalem in Jewish Spirituality." In *City of the Great King: Jerusalem from David to the Present*. Ed. Nitza Rosovsky. Cambridge, MA: Harvard University Press, 1996, 60-73, 474-479.

Dan, Joseph. "Jewish Gnosticism?" In *Jewish Studies Quarterly* 2:4 (1995) 309-328.

Dan, Joseph. *Jewish Mysticism*. 4 vols. Northvale, NJ: Jason Aronson, 1998.

Dan, Joseph. *Jewish Mysticism and Jewish Ethics*. Seattle: University of Washington Press, 1986.

Dan, Joseph. "Kabbalistic and Gnostic Dualism." In *Binah: Jewish Intellectual History in the Middle Ages*. Vol. 3. Westport, CT: Praeger, 1994, 19-33.

Dan, Joseph. "The Language of the Mystics in Medieval Germany." In *Mysticism, Magic and Kabbalah in Ashkenazi Judaism: International Symposium Held in Frankfurt a.M. 1991*. Ed. Karl Erich Gruzinger and Joseph Dan. Berlin: Walter de Gruyter, 1995.

Dan, Joseph. "The Desert in Jewish Mysticism: The Kingdom of Samael." In *Ariel* 40 (1976) 38-43.

Dan, Joseph. "Manasseh ben Israel's `Nishmat Hayyim' and the Concept of Evil in 17th-Century Jewish Thought." In *Jewish Thought in the Seventeenth Century*. Ed. Isadore Twersky and Bernard Septimus. Cambridge, MA: Harvard University Press, 1987, 63-75.

Dan, Joseph. "The Name of God, the Name of the Rose, and the Concept of Language in Jewish Mysticism." In *Medieval Encounters: Jewish, Christian and Muslim Culture in Confluence and Dialogue* 2:3 (1996) 228-248.

Dan, Joseph. "No Evil Descends from Heaven: Sixteenth-Century Jewish Concepts of Evil." In *Jewish Thought in the Sixteenth Century*. Ed. Bernard Dov Cooperman. Cambridge, MA: Harvard University Press, 1983, 89-105.

Dan, Joseph. "Paradox of Nothingness in the Kabbalah." In *Argumentum e Silentio: International Paul Celan Symposium*. Ed. Amy D. Colin. Berlin: Walter de Gruyter, 1987, 359-363.

Dan, Joseph. "Rashi and the Merkabah." In *Rashi* (1993) 259-264.

Dan, Joseph. "The Religious Experience of the *Merkavah*." In *Jewish Spirituality: From the Bible Through the Middle Ages*. Vol. 1. Ed. Arthur Green. New York: Crossroad, 1986, 289-307.

Dan, Joseph. "Samael, Lilith, and the Concept of Evil in Early Kabbalah." In *American Jewish Studies Review* 5 (1980) 17-40.

Dan, Joseph and Frank Talmage, eds. *Studies in Jewish Mysticism*. Cambridge, MA: Association for Jewish Studies, 1982.

Dan, Joseph with Robert J. Milch, eds. *The Teachings of Hasidism*. New York: Behrman House, 1983.

Dan, Joseph. "Terafim: From Popular Belief to a Folktale." In *Studies in Hebrew Narrative Art Through the Ages*. Ed. Joseph Heinemann and Shmuel Werses. *Scripta Hierosolymitana* 27 (1978) 99-106.

Dan, Joseph. "Yaldabaoth, Once More." In *Threescore and Ten: Essays in Honor of Rabbi Seymour J. Cohen*. Ed. Abraham J. Karp. Hoboken, NJ: Ktav Publishing House, 1991, 123-131.

Davidson, Gustav. *A Dictionary of Angels*. Toronto: Collier-Macmillan Canada, 1967.

Davidson, Herbert. "Maimonides' Secret Position on Creation." In *Studies in Medieval Jewish History and Literature*. Ed. Isadore Twersky. Cambridge, MA: Harvard University Press, 1979, 16-40.

Davies, Graham I. "The Presence of God in the Second Temple and Rabbinic Doctrine." In *Templum Amicitiae: Essays on the Second Temple Presented to Ernst Bammel*. Ed. William Horbury. Sheffield: JSOT Press, 1991.

Davies, W. D. *The Territorial Dimension of Judaism*. Berkeley: University of California Press, 1982.

Dean-Otting, Mary. *Heavenly Journeys: A Study of the Motif in Hellenistic Jewish Literature*. Frankfurt: Verlag Peter Lang Publishing, 1984.

Delumeau, Jean. *History of Paradise: The Garden of Eden in Myth and Tradition*. Trans. Matthew O'Connell. New York: Continuum, 1995.

Diamond, Eliezer. "Wrestling the Angel of Death: Form and Meaning in Rabbinic Tales of Death and Dying." In *Journal for the Study of Judaism* 26:1 (1995) 76-92.

Doniger, Wendy. *Other People's Myths: The Cave of Echoes.* New York: Macmillan, 1988.

Doron, Pinchas. *The Mystery of Creation According to Rashi.* New York and Jerusalem: Maznaim, 1982.

Doty, William G. *Mythography: The Study of Myths and Rituals.* 2d ed. Tuscaloosa: University of Alabama Press, 2000.

Dreifuss, Gustav and Judith Riemer. *Abraham, The Man and the Symbol: A Jungian Interpretation of the Biblical Story.* Wilmette, IL: Chiron Publications, 1995.

Dresner, Samuel H. *Rachel.* Minneapolis: Fortress Press, 1994.

Duling, D. C. *Testament of Solomon.* In *The Old Testament Pseudepigrapha.* Ed. J. Charlesworth. Garden City, NY: Doubleday, 1983-1985.

Dundes, Alan. *Holy Writ as Oral Lit: The Bible as Folklore.* Lanham, MD: Rowman & Littlefield Publishers, 1999.

Edelman, Diana Vikander, ed. *The Triumph of Elohim: From Yahwisms to Judaisms.* Grand Rapids, MI: William B. Eerdmans, 1996.

Efros, Israel I. *Ancient Jewish Philosophy: A Study in Metaphysics and Ethics.* New York: Bloch, 1976.

Efros, Israel I. *The Problem of Space in Jewish Mediaeval Philosophy.* New York: Ams Press, 1966.

Elbaum, Ya'akov. "From Sermon to Story: The Transformation of the *Akedah.*" In *Prooftexts* 6 (1986) 97-116.

Elbaum, Ya'akov. "Yalqut Shim'oni and the Medieval Midrashic Anthology." In *Prooftexts* 17 (1997) 133-151.

Eliade, Mircea and Charles J. Adams III, eds. *The Encyclopedia of Religion.* New York: Gale, 1993.

Elior, Rachel. "The Concept of God in Hekhalot Literature." In *Binah: Jewish Intellectual History in the Middle Ages.* Vol. 2. Ed. Joseph Dan. Westport, CT: Praeger, 1989, 97-120.

Elior, Rachel. "From Earthly Temple to Heavenly Shrines: Prayer and Sacred Song in the Hekhalot Literature and Its Relation to Temple Traditions." In *Jewish Studies Quarterly* 4 (1997) 217-267.

Elior, Rachel. "HaBaD: The Contemplative Ascent to God." In *Jewish Spirituality: From the Bible Through the Middle Ages.* Vol. 2. Ed. Arthur Green. New York: Crossroad, 1994, 167-205.

Elior, Rachel. "Merkabah Mysticism: A Critical Review." In *Numen* 37:2 (1991) 233-249.

Elior, Rachel. "Messianic Expectations and Spiritualization of Religious Life in the Sixteenth Century." In *Revue des Etudes juives* 145:1-2 (1986) 35-49.

Elior, Rachel. "Mysticism, Magic, and Angelology: The Perception of Angels in Hekhalot Literature." In *Jewish Studies Quarterly* 1 (1993) 3-53.

Elior, Rachel. "Not *All* is in the Hands of Heaven: Eschatology and Kabbalah." In *Eschatology in the Bible and in Jewish and Christian Tradition.* Ed. Henning Graf Reventlow. Sheffield: Sheffield Academic Press, 1997, 49-61.

Elior, Rachel. "On David J. Halperin, *The Faces of the Chariot: Early Jewish Responses to Ezekiel's Vision,* 1988." In *Numen: International Review for the History of Religions* 37:2 (1990) 233-249.

Elior, Rachel. *The Paradoxical Ascent to God: The Kabbalistic Theosophy of Habad Hasidism.* Trans. Jeffrey M. Green. Albany: State University of New York Press, 1993.

Elior, Rachel. "The Priestly Nature of the Mystical Heritage in *Heykalot* Literature." In *Expérience et écriture mystiques dans les religions du livre* (2000) 41-54.

Elior, Rachel and Joseph, Dan, eds. *Rivkah Shatz-Uffenheimer Memorial Volume.* Jerusalem: Hebrew University, 1996.

Elon, Ari. "The Torah as Love Goddess." In *Essential Papers on the Talmud*. Ed. Michael Chernick. New York and London: New York University Press, 1994, 463-476.

Englander, Lawrence A. with Herbert W. Basser, eds. *The Mystical Study of Ruth: Midrash HaNe'elam of the Zohar to the Book of Ruth*. Atlanta: Scholars Press, 1992.

Eskenazi, Tamara C., Daniel J. Harrington, and William H. Shea. *The Sabbath in Jewish and Christian Traditions*. New York: Crossroad, 1991.

Evans, Craig A. and Peter W. Flint, eds. *Eschatology, Messianism, and the Dead Sea Scrolls*. Studies in the Dead Sea Scrolls and Related Literature. Grand Rapids, MI: William B. Eerdmans, 1997.

Faierstein, Morris, ed. *Jewish Mystical Autobiographies*. New York: Paulist Press, 2000.

Fallon, Francis T. *The Enthronement of Sabaoth: Jewish Elements in Gnostic Creation Myths*. Leiden: E. J. Brill, 1978.

Fass, David E. "How the Angels Do Serve." In *Judaism* 40:3 (1991) 281-289.

Feldman, Louis H. "Hellenizations in Josephus' Portrayal of Man's Decline." In *Religions in Antiquity: Essays in Memory of Erwin Ramsdell Goodenough*. Ed. Jacob Neusner. Leiden: E. J. Brill, 1968, 336-353.

Feldman, Louis H. *Josephus's Interpretation of the Bible*. Berkeley: University of California Press. 1998.

Feldman, Ron H. *Fundamentals of Jewish Mysticism and Kabbalah*. Freedom, CA: The Crossing Press, 1999.

Feldman, Seymour. "The End of the Universe in Medieval Jewish Philosophy." In *American Jewish Studies Review* 11:1 (1986) 53-77.

Filoramo, Giovanni. *A History of Gnosticism*. Trans. Anthony Alcock. Cambridge, MA: Blackwell, 1990.

Fine, Lawrence, ed. *Essential Papers on Kabbalah*. New York: New York University Press, 1995.

Fine, Lawrence. "Maggidic Revelation in the Teachings of Isaac Luria." In *Mystics, Philosophers, and Politicians: Essays in Jewish Intellectual History in Honor of Alexander Altmann*. Ed. Jehuda Reinharz and Daniel Swetschinski, with Kalman P. Bland. Durham, NC: Duke University Press, 1982, 141-157.

Fine, Lawrence. *Physician of the Soul, Healer of the Cosmos: Isaac Luria and His Kabbalistic Fellowship*. Stanford: Stanford University Press, 2003.

Fine, Lawrence. *Safed Spirituality*. New York: Paulist Press, 1988.

Finkel, Asher. "The Exegetic Elements of the Cosmosophical Work, Sepher Yesirah." In *Mystics of the Book: Themes, Topics, and Typologies*. Ed. by R. A. Herrera. New York: Peter Lang, 1993, 45-53.

Finkel, Avraham Yaakov, trans. *Ein Yaakov: The Ethical and Inspirational Teachings of the Talmud*. Northvale, NJ: Jason Aronson, 1999.

Finkel, Avraham Yaakov. *The Essence of the Holy Days: Insights from the Jewish Sages*. Northvale, NJ: Jason Aronson, 1993.

Finkel, Avraham Yaakov, trans. *The Essential Maimonides: Translations of the Rambam*. Northvale, NJ: Jason Aronson, 1996.

Finkel, Avraham Yaakov. *In My Flesh I See God: A Treasury of Rabbinic Insights about the Human Anatomy*. Northvale, NJ: Jason Aronson, 1995.

Finkel, Avraham Yaakov. Kabbalah: Selections from Classic Kabbalistic Works from Raziel Hamalach to the Present Day. Southfield, MI: Targum Press, 2002.

Finkel, Avraham Yaakov, trans. *Sefer Chasidim: The Book of the Pious*. Northvale, NJ: Jason Aronson, 1997.

Finkel, Avraham Yaakov. *The Torah Revealed: Talmudic Masters Unveil the Secrets of the Bible*. San Francisco: Jossey-Bass, 2004.

Finkelstein, Louisa. "Ben Zoma's Paradoxes." In *Judaism* 40:4 (1991) 452-54.

Fishbane, Michael. "Arm of the Lord: Biblical Myth, Rabbinic Midrash, and the Mystery of History." In *Language, Theology, and the Bible: Essays in Honor of James Barr*. Ed. Samuel E. Balentine and John Barton. Oxford: Clarendon Press, 1994, 271-292.

Fishbane, Michael. *Biblical Myth and Rabbinic Mythmaking*. Oxford and New York: Oxford University Press, 2003.

Fishbane, Michael. "Biblical Prophecy as a Religious Phenomenon." In *Jewish Spirituality: From the Bible to the Middle Ages*. Vol. 1. Ed. Arthur Green. New York: Crossroad, 1986, 62-81.

Fishbane, Michael. *The Exegetical Imagination: On Jewish Thought and Theology*. Cambridge, MA: Harvard University Press, 1998.

Fishbane, Michael. *The Garments of Torah: Essays in Biblical Hermeneutics*. Bloomington: Indiana University Press, 1989.

Fishbane, Michael. "'The Holy One Sits and Roars': Mythopoesis and the Midrashic Imagination." In *Journal of Jewish Thought and Philosophy* 1 (1991) 1-21.

Fishbane, Michael. *The Kiss of God: Spiritual and Mystical Death in Judaism*. Seattle: University of Washington Press, 1994.

Fishbane, Michael. "The 'Measures' of God's Glory in the Ancient Midrash." In *Messiah and Christos: Studies in the Jewish Origins of Christianity*. Ed. Ithamar Gruenwald, Shaul Shaked, and Gedaliahu G. Stroumsa. Tubingen: J. C. B. Mohr, 1992, 53-74.

Fishbane, Michael, ed. *The Midrashic Imagination: Jewish Exegesis, Thought, and History*. Albany: State University of New York Press, 1993.

Fishbane, Michael. "Rabbinic Mythmaking and Tradition: The Great Dragon Drama in *B. Bava Batra* 74b-75a." In *Tehilla le-Moshe: Biblical and Judaic Studies in Honor of Moshe Greenberg*. Ed. Mordechai Cogan, Barry L. Eichler, and Jeffrey H. Tigay. Winona Lake, IN: Eisenbrauns, 1997, 273-283.

Fishbane, Michael. "Some Forms of Divine Appearance in Ancient Jewish Thought." In *From Ancient Israel to Modern Judaism*. Ed. Jacob Neusner. Atlanta: Scholars Press, 1989, 261-270.

Fishbane, Michael. "The Well of Living Water: A Biblical Motif and Its Ancient Transformations." In *Sha'arei Talmon: Studies in the Bible, Qumran, and the Ancient Near East Presented to Shemaryahu Talmon*. Ed. Michael Fishbane and Emanuel Tov. Winona Lake, IN: Eisenbrauns, 1992.

Fischel, Henry A. *Rabbinic Literature and Greco-Roman Philosophy: A Study of Epicurea and Rhetorica in Early Midrashic Writings*. Leiden: E. J. Brill, 1973.

Fossum, Jarl E. "Gen. 1,26 and 2,7 in Judaism, Samaritanism and Gnosticism." In *Journal for the Study of Judaism* 26:2 (1995) 202-239.

Fossum, Jarl E. "The Magharians: A Pre-Christian Jewish Sect and Its Significance for the Study of Gnosticism and Christianity." *Henoch* 9:3 (1987) 303-344.

Fossum, Jarl E. *The Name of God and the Angel of the Lord: Samaritan and Jewish Concepts of Intermediation and the Origin of Gnosticism*. Tubingen: J. C. B. Mohr, 1985.

Fossum, Jarl E. "The Origin of the Gnostic Concept of the Demiurge." In *Ephemerides theologicae Lovanienses* 61:1 (1985) 142-152.

Fossum, Jarl E. "Samaritan Demiurgical Traditions and the Alleged Dove Cult of the Samaritans." In *Studies in Gnosticism and Hellenistic Religions*. Ed. R. Van Den Broek and M. J. Vermaseren. Leiden: E. J. Brill,1981.

Fox, Samuel J. *Hell in Jewish Literature*. Northbrook, IL: Merrimack College Press, 1972.

Fraenkel, Jonah. "Time and Its Role in the Aggadic Story." In *Binah: Jewish Intellectual History in the Middle Ages*. Vol. 2. Ed. Joseph Dan. Westport, CT: Praeger, 1989, 31-56.

Frankel, Ellen. *The Classic Tales: 4000 Years of Jewish Lore*. Northvale, NJ: Jason Aronson, 1989.

Frankel, Ellen. *The Five Books of Miriam*. San Francisco: Harper San Francisco, 1998.

Frazer, James G. *Adonis Attis Osiris: Studies in the History of Oriental Religion*. 3d ed. New Hyde Park, NY: University Books, 1961.

Frazer, James G. *Folklore in the Old Testament*. 3 vols. London: Macmillan, 1918.

Frazer, James G. *The New Golden Bough: A New Abridgment of the Classic Work*. Ed. Theodor H. Gaster. New York: Criterion Books, 1959.

Freeman, Gordon M. *The Heavenly Kingdom: Aspects of Political Thought in the Talmud and Midrash*. Lanham, MD: University Press of America, 1986.

Freud, Sigmund. *Moses and Monotheism*. Trans. Katherine Jones. New York: Vintage Books, 1955.

Friedman, Richard Elliot. *Commentary on the Torah*. San Francisco: HarperSanFrancisco, 2001.

Friedman, Shamma. "Graven Images." In *Graven Images: A Journal of Culture, Law, and the Sacred* 1 (1994) 233-238.

Fromm, Erich. *You Shall Be as Gods: A Radical Interpretation of the Old Testament and Its Tradition*. New York: Holt, Rinehart and Winston, 1966.

Frymer-Kensky, Tikva. "Biblical Cosmology" in *Backgrounds for the Bible*. Ed. by Michael Patrick O'Connor and David Noel Freedman. Winona Lake, Indiana: Eisenbrauns, 1987, 231-240.

Frymer-Kensky, Tikva. *In the Wake of the Goddesses: Women, Culture, and the Biblical Transformation of Pagan Myth*. New York: Macmillan, 1992.

Gaer, Joseph. *The Legend of the Wandering Jew*. New York: Mentor Books, 1961.

Galambush, Julie. *Jerusalem in the Book of Ezekiel: The City as Yahweh's Wife*. Atlanta: Scholars Press, 1992.

Gammie, John G. "The Angelology and Demonology in the Septuagint of the Book of Job." In *Hebrew Union Annual* 56 (1985) 1-19.

Gammie, John G. *Holiness in Israel*. Minneapolis: Fortress Press, 1989.

Gantz, Timothy. *Early Greek Myth: A Guide to Literary and Artistic Sources*. 2 vols. Baltimore, MD: Johns Hopkins University Press, 1993.

Garbini, Giovanni. "The Creation of Light in the First Chapter of Genesis." In *Proceedings of the Fifth World Congress of Jewish Studies*. Jerusalem: World Union of Jewish Studies, 1969, 1-4.

García Martínez, Florentino. "Apocalypticism in the Dead Sea Scrolls." In *The Encyclopedia of Apocalypticism*. Vol. 1. Ed. John J. Collins. New York: Continuum, 1999, 162-192.

García Martínez, Florentino and Eibert J. C. Tigchelaar. "*1 Enoch* and the Figure of Enoch: A Bibliography of Studies 1970-1988." In *Revue de Qumran* 14:1 (1989) 149-174.

García Martínez, Florentino and Gerard P. Luttikhuizen, eds. *Interpretations of the Flood*. Leiden: Brill, 1999.

Gaster, Moses, trans. *The Chronicles of Jerahmeel; Or, The Hebrew Bible Historiale*. New York: Ktav Publishing House, 1971. (Gaster identifies the original manuscript as *Sefer ha-Zikhronot*.)

Gaster, Moses, ed. *Studies and Texts in Folklore, Magic, Mediaeval Romance, Hebrew Apocrypha and Samaritan Archaeology*. New York: Ktav Publishing House, 1971.

Gaster, Moses, trans. *The Sword of Moses: An Ancient Book of Magic*. London: D. Nutt, 1896.

Gaster, Theodor H., trans. *The Dead Sea Scriptures*. 3d ed. Garden City, NY: Anchor Press/Doubleday, 1976.

Gaster, Theodor H. *The Holy and the Profane: Evolution of Jewish Folkways*. New York: William Morrow and Company, 1980.

Gaster, Theodor H. *Festivals of the Jewish Year*. New York: William Sloane Associates Publishers, 1953.

Gaster, Theodor H. *Myth, Legend, and Custom in the Old Testament*. New York: Harper & Row, 1969.

Gaster, Theodor H. *Passover: Its History and Traditions*. New York: Henry Schuman, 1949.

Gaster, Theodor H. *Purim and Hanukkah in Custom and Tradition: Feast of Lots, Feast of Lights*. New York: Henry Schuman, 1950.

Gelbard, Shmuel Pinchas. *Rite and Reason: 1050 Jewish Customs and Their Sources*. Petach Tikvah: Mifal Rashi Publishing, 1998.

Gelin, Albert. *The Religion of Israel*. Trans. J. R. Foster. New York: Hawthorn Books, 1959.

Gellman, Jerome I. *The Fear, the Trembling and the Fire: Kierkeegard and Hasidic Masters on the Binding of Isaac*. Boston: University Press of America, 1994.

Gerlitz, Menachem. *The Heavenly City*. 5 vols. Trans. Sheindel Weinbach. Jerusalem: Oraysoh Publishers, 1982.

Gershenzon, Rosalie and Eliesar Slomovic. "A 2nd Century Jewish-Gnostic Debate." In *JSJ* 16:1 (1985) 1-41.

Gikatilla, Joseph. *Sha'are Orah/Gates of Light*. Trans. Avi Weinstein. New York: HarperCollins, 1994.

Giller, Pinchas. *The Enlightened Will Shine: Symbolization and Theurgy in the Later Strata of the Zohar*. Albany: State University of New York Press, 1993.

Giller, Pinchas. *Reading the Zohar: The Sacred Text of the Kabbalah*. New York: Oxford University Press, 2001.

Giller, Pinchas. "Recovering the Sanctity of the Galilee: The Veneration of Sacred Relics in Classical Kabbalah." In *Journal of Jewish Thought and Philosophy* 4 (1994) 147-169.

Gillman, Neil. *The Death of Death: Resurrection and Immortality in Jewish Thought*. Woodstock, VT: Jewish Lights, 1997.

Gillman, Neil. *Sacred Fragments: Recovering Theology for the Modern Jew*. Philadelphia: Jewish Publication Society, 1990.

Ginsburg, Elliot K. "The Image of the Divine and Person in Zoharic Kabbalah." In L. D. Shinn, ed., *In Search of the Divine*. St. Paul: Paragon Press, 1987, 61-94.

Ginsburg, Elliot K. "The Many Faces of Kabbalah." *Hebrew Studies* 36 (1995) 111-122.

Ginsburg, Elliot K. *The Sabbath in the Classical Kabbalah*. Albany: State University of New York Press, 1989.

Ginsburg, Elliot K., trans. *Sod ha-Shabbat (The Mystery of the Sabbath) from the Tola'at Ya'aqov of R. Meir ibn Gabbai*. Albany: State University of New York Press, 1989.

Ginsburgh, Yitzchak, with Avraham Arieh Trugman and Moshe Yaakov Wisnefsky. *The Alef-Beit: Jewish Thought Revealed through the Hebrew Letters*. Northvale, NJ: Jason Aronson, 1991.

Ginzberg, Louis. *The Legends of the Jews*. 7 vols. Philadelphia: Jewish Publication Society, 1968.

Ginzberg, Louis. *An Unknown Jewish Sect*. New York: The Jewish Theological Seminary of America, 1970.

Glatzer, Nahum N., ed. *The Essential Philo*. New York: Schocken Books, 1971.

Glatzer, Nahum N., ed. *Hammer on the Rock*. New York, Schocken Books, 1987.

Glatzer, Nahum N., ed. *The Judaic Tradition*. Boston: Beacon Press, 1969.

Glazerson, Matityahu. *The Mystical Glory of Shabbath and Festivals*. Jerusalem: Feldheim Publishers, 1985.

Goitein, S. D., ed. *From the Land of Sheba: Tales of the Jews of Yemen*. New York: Schocken Books, 1973.

Goldberg, Harvey E., ed. *Judaism Viewed from Within and From Without: Anthropological Studies*. Albany: State University of New York Press, 1987.

Goldin, Judah. "Not By Means of an Angel and Not By Means of a Messenger." In *Religions in Antiquity: Essays in Memory of Erwin Ramsdell Goodenough*. Ed. Jacob Neusner. Leiden: E. J. Brill, 1970, 412-424.

Goldin, Judah. *The Song at the Sea: Being a Commentary on a Commentary in Two Parts*. Philadelphia: Jewish Publication Society, 1990.

Goldstein, Yonathan A. "The Origin of the Doctrine of Creation Ex Nihilo." In *Journal of Jewish Studies* 35:2 (1984) 127-135.

Goldziher, Ignaz. *Mythology Among the Hebrews and Its Historical Development*. Trans. Russell Martineau. New York: Cooper Square Publishers, 1967.

Goodenough, Erwin R. *By Light, Light: The Mystic Gospel of Hellenistic Judaism*. New Haven, CT: Yale University Press, 1935.

Goodenough, Erwin R. *Religious Tradition and Myth*. New Haven, CT: Yale University Press, 1937.

Goodman, David. "Do Angels Eat?" In *Journal of Jewish Studies* 37:2 (1986) 160-175.

Goodman, Philip. *The Hanukkah Anthology*. Philadelphia: Jewish Publication Society, 1976.

Goodman, Philip and Hanna Goodman. *The Jewish Marriage Anthology*. Philadelphia: Jewish Publication Society, 1965.

Goodman, Philip. *The Passover Anthology*. Philadelphia: Jewish Publication Society, 1962.

Goodman, Philip. *The Purim Anthology*. Philadelphia: Jewish Publication Society, 1949.

Goodman, Philip. *The Rosh Hashanah Anthology*. Philadelphia: Jewish Publication Society, 1973.

Goodman, Philip. *The Shavuot Anthology*. Philadelphia: Jewish Publication Society, 1974.

Goodman, Philip. *The Sukkot and Simhat Torah Anthology*. Philadelphia: Jewish Publication Society, 1973.

Gordon, Cyrus H. and Gary A. Rendsburg. *The Bible and the Ancient Near East*. New York: Norton, 1997.

Gottlieb, Freema. *The Lamp of God: A Jewish Book of Light*. Northvale, NJ: Jason Aronson, 1989.

Gottstein, Alon Goshen. "The Body as Image of God in Rabbinic Literature." In *Harvard Theological Review* 87:2 (1994) 171-195.

Gottstein, Alon Goshen. "Four Entered Paradise Revisited." In *Harvard Theological Review* 88:1 (1995) 69-133.

Gottstein, Alon Goshen. "Is *Ma'aseh Bereshit* Part of Ancient Jewish Mysticism?" In *Journal of Jewish Thought and Philosophy* 4 (1995) 185-201.

Gratus, Jack. *The False Messiahs*. New York: Taplinger, 1976.

Graves, Robert. *The Greek Myths*. 2 vols. London: Penguin Books, 1960.

Graves, Robert and Raphael Patai. *Hebrew Myths: The Book of Genesis*. New York: Doubleday, 1964.

Gray, John. *Near Eastern Mythology*. London: Hamlyn, 1983.

Green, Arthur. "The Children in Egypt and the Theopany at the Sea." In *Judaism* 24 (1975) 446-456.

Green, Arthur. *Keter: The Crown of God in Early Jewish Mysticism*. Princeton, NJ: Princeton University Press, 1997.

Green, Arthur. *A Guide to the Zohar*. Stanford: Stanford University Press: 2004.

Green, Arthur. "Bride, Spouse, Daughter: Images of the Feminine in Classical Jewish Sources." In *On Being a Jewish Feminist*. Ed Susanne Heschel. New York: Schocken Books, 1983.

Green, Arthur, ed. *Jewish Spirituality: From the Bible to the Middle Ages*. Vol. 1. New York: Crossroad, 1986.

Green, Arthur, ed. *Jewish Spirituality: From the Sixteenth-Century Revival to the Present*. Vol. 2. New York: Crossroad, 1994.

Green, Arthur. *Jewish Spirituality: From the Sixteenth Century Revival to the Present*. New York: Crossroad, 1987.

Green, Arthur, trans. *The Language of Truth: The Torah Commentary of the Sefat Emet, Rabbi Yehudah Leib Alter of Ger*. Philadelphia: Jewish Publication Society, 1998.

Green, Arthur. *Menahem Nahum of Chernobyl: Upright Practices, The Light of the Eyes*. New York: Paulist Press, 1982.

Green, Arthur. *Seek My Face, Speak My Name: A Contemporary Jewish Theology*. Northvale, NJ: Jason Aronson, 1992.

Green, Arthur. "The Song of Songs in Early Jewish Mysticism." In *The Song of Songs*. Ed. Harold Bloom. New York: Chelsea House Publishers, 1988.

Green, Arthur. *Seek My Face, Speak My Name: A Contemporary Jewish Theology*. Northvale, NJ: Jason Aronson, 1992.

Green, Arthur. "Shekhinah, the Virgin Mary, and the Song of Songs; Reflections on a Kabbalistic Symbol in its Historical Context." *AJS Review* 26:1 (2002) 1-52.

Green, Arthur. *These Are the Words: A Vocabulary of Jewish Spiritual Life*. Woodstock, Vermont: Jewish Lights Publishing, 1999.

Green, Arthur. *Tormented Master: A Life of Rabbi Nachman of Bratslav*. University, Alabama: University of Alabama Press, 1979.

Green, Arthur and Barry W. Holtz, eds. *Your Word is Fire: The Hasidic Masters on Contemplative Prayer*. New York: Paulist Press, 1977.

Greenberg, Moshe. *Understanding Exodus*. The Heritage of Biblical Israel. New York: Behrman House, 1969.

Greenspahn, Frederick E., ed. *Essential Papers on Israel and the Ancient Near East*. New York and London: New York University Press, 1991.

Grozinger, Karl-Erich. *Kafka and Kabbalah*. New York: Continuum, 1994.

Grozinger, Karl-Erich and Joseph Dan, eds. *Mysticism, Magic and Kabbalah in Ashkenazi Judaism: International Symposium Held in Frankfurt a.M. 1991*. Berlin: Walter de Gruyter, 1995.

Gruber, Mayer I. *The Motherhood of God and Other Studies*. Atlanta: Scholars Press, 1992.

Gruenwald, Ithamar. *Apocalyptic and Merkavah Mysticism*. Leiden: E. J. Brill, 1997.

Gruenwald, Ithamar. "God the `Stone/Rock': Myth, Idolatry, and Cultic Fetishism in Ancient Israel." In *Journal of Religion* 76:3 (1996) 428-449.

Gruenwald, Ithamar. "Jewish Merkavah Mysticism and Gnosticism." In *Studies in Jewish Mysticism* 2 (1982) 41-55.

Gruenwald, Ithamar. "Knowledge and Vision: Towards a Clarification of Two 'Gnostic' Concepts in the Light of Their Alleged Origins."

Gruenwald, Ithamar. "Reflections on the Nature and Origins of Jewish Mysticism." In *Gershom Scholem's "Major Trends in Jewish Mysticism" 50 Years After: Proceedings of the Sixth International Conference on the History of Jewish Mysticism*. Ed. Peter Schäfer and Joseph Dan. Tubingen: J. C. B. Mohr, 1993, 25-48.

Gruenwald, Ithamar, ed. *"Re'iyyot Yehezkel."* In *Temirin* 1 (1972) 101-39.

Guiley, Rosemary Ellen. *Encyclopedia of Angels*. New York: Facts on File, 1996.

Gunkel, Hermann. *The Legends of Genesis: The Biblical Saga and History*. New York: Schocken Books, 1964.

Gurary, Noson. *Chasidism: Its Development, Theory, and Practice*. Northvale, NJ: Jason Aronson, 1997.

Gutmann, Joseph. "Leviathan, Behemoth and Ziz: Jewish Messianic Symbols in Art." In *Hebrew Union College Annual* 39 (1968) 219-230.

Haboucha, Reginetta. *Types and Motifs of the Judeo-Spanish Folktales*. 2 vols. New York: Garland, 1992.

Hadas, Moses, tr. *Fables of a Jewish Aesop*. New York and London: Columbia University Press, 1967.

Halbertal, Moshe and Avishai Margalit. *Idolatry*. Trans. Naomi Goldblum. Cambridge, MA: Harvard University Press, 1992.

Halkin, Abraham. *Zion in Jewish Literature*. New York: Herzl Press, 1961.

Hallamish, Moshe. *An Introduction to the Kabbalah*. State University of New York Series in Judaica: Hermeneutics, Mysticism, and Religion. Trans. Ruth Bar-Ilan and Ora Wiskind-Elper. Albany: State University of New York Press, 1999.

Halperin, David J. *Abraham Miguel Cardozo: Selected Writings*. Mahwah, NJ: Paulist Press, 2001.

Halperin, David J. "Ascension or Invasion: Implications of the Heavenly Journey in Ancient Judaism." In *Religion* 18 (1988) 47-67.

Halperin, David J. "A Sexual Image in Hekhalot Rabbati and Its Implications." In Joseph Dan, ed., *Proceedings of the First International Conference on the History of Jewish Mysticism: Early Jewish Mysticism*. English section, 117-132. Jerusalem, The Hebrew University, 1987.

Halperin, David J. *The Faces of the Chariot: Early Jewish Responses to Ezekiel's Vision*. Tübingen: J. C. B. Mohr, 1988.

Halperin, David J. "Heavenly Ascension in Ancient Judaism: The Nature of the Experience." *SBL Seminar Papers* 26 (1987) 218-232.

Halperin, David J. *The Merkabah in Rabbinic Literature*. Winona Lake, IN: Eisenbrauns, 1980.

Halperin, David J. *Seeking Ezekiel: Text and Psychology*. University Park, PA: Pennsylvania State University Press, 1993.

Halperin, David J. "Sabbatai Zevi, Metatron, and Mehmed: Myth and History in Seventeenth Century Judaism. In *The Seductiveness of Jewish History: Challenge or Response?* Ed. Daniel Breslauer. Albany: State University of New York Press, 1997, 271-308.

Halperin, David J. "The Son of the Messiah: Ishmael Zevi and the Sabbatian Aqedah." In *Hebrew Union College Annual* 67 (1996) 142-219.

Hammer, Reuven. *The Jerusalem Anthology: A Literary Guide*. Philadelphia: Jewish Publication Society, 1995.

Hammer, Reuven, trans. *Sifre: A Tannaitic Commentary on the Book of Deuteronomy*. New Haven: Yale University Press, 1986.

Hanauer, J. E. *The Holy Land: Myths and Legends*. London: Random House, 1996.

Handelman, Susan A. *The Slayers of Moses: The Emergence of Rabbinic Interpretation in Modern Literary Theory*. Albany: State University of New York Press, 1982.

Haralick, Robert M. *The Inner Meaning of the Hebrew Letters*. Northvale, NJ: Jason Aronson, 1995.

Harrington, D. J. *Pseudo-Philo*. In *The Old Testament Pseudepigrapha*, edited by J. Charlesworth. Garden City, NY: Doubleday, 1983-85.

Harris, Monford. *Exodus and Exile: The Structure of the Jewish Holidays*. Minneapolis: Fortress Press, 1992.

Hartmann, Geoffrey H. and Sanford Budick. *Midrash and Literature*. New Haven: Yale University Press, 1986.

Harwood, William R. *Mythology's Last Gods: Yahweh and Jesus*. Buffalo, NY: Prometheus Books, 1992.

Hayman, A. Peter. "Was God a Magician? *Sefer Yesirah* and Jewish Magic." In *Journal of Jewish Studies* 40:2 (1989) 225-237.

Hayman, A. Peter. "Monotheism—A Misused Word in Jewish Studies?" In *Journal of Jewish Studies* 42:1 (1991) 1-15.

Hayman, A. Peter. "The Mythological Background of the Wisdom of Solomon." In *Jewish Studies at the Turn of the Twentieth Century* 1 (1999) 282-288.

Hayward, C. T. R. "The Figure of Adam in Pseudo-Philo's Biblical Antiquities." In *Journal for the Study of Judaism* 23:1 (1992) 1-20.

Hayward, C. T. R. *The Jewish Temple: A Non-Biblical Sourcebook*. London: Routledge, 1996.

Heide, A. van der. *Pardes: Methodological Reflections on the Theory of the Four Senses*. In *Journal of Jewish Studies* 34:2 (1983) 147-159.

Heidel, Alexander. *The Babylonian Genesis*. Chicago: University of Chicago Press, 1951.

Heidel, Alexander. *The Gilgamesh Epic and Old Testament Parallels*. Chicago: University of Chicago Press, 1949.

Heinemann, Joseph. "The Messiah of Ephraim and the Premature Exodus of the Tribe of Ephraim." In *Harvard Theological Review* 8 (1975) 1-15.

Heinemann, Joseph and Shmuel Werses, eds. *Studies in Hebrew Narrative Art Throughout the Ages*. Jerusalem: Magnes Press, 1978.

Helm, Robert. "Azazel in Early Jewish Tradition." In *Andrews University Seminary Studies* 32:3 (1994) 217-226.

Hendel, Ronald S. *The Epic of the Patriarch: The Jacob Cycle and the Narrative Traditions of Canaan and Israel*. Atlanta: Scholars Press, 1987.

Herrmann, Klaus. "Re-Written Mystical Texts: The Transmission of the Heikhahlot Literature in the Middle Ages." In *Bulletin of the John Rylands Univesity Library*. Manchester: The Library. 75:3 (1993) 97-116.

Heschel, Abraham J. *I Asked For Wonder: A Spiritual Anthology*. Ed. Samuel H. Dresner. New York: Crossroad, 2001.

Heschel, Abraham J. *The Earth Is the Lord's: The Inner World of the Jew in East Europe*. New York: Henry Schuman, 1950.

Heschel, Abraham J. *God in Search of Man*. New York: Farrar, Straus & Giroux, 1955.

Heschel, Abraham J. "God, Torah, and Israel." In *Moral Grandeur and Spiritual Audicity*. New York: Noonday Press, 1996, 191-205.

Heschel, Abraham J. *Man's Quest for God: Studies in Prayer and Symbolism*. New York: Charles Scribner's Sons, 1954.

Heschel, Abraham J. *Moral Grandeur and Spiritual Audacity*. New York: The Noonday Press, 1996.

Heschel, Abraham J. *The Mystical Element in Judaism*. In *Moral Grandeur and Spiritual Audacity*. New York: The Noonday Press, 1996, 164-184.

Heschel, Abraham J. *Prophetic Inspiration After the Prophets: Maimonides and Other Medieval Authorities*. Hoboken, NJ: Ktav Publishing House, 1996.

Heschel, Abraham J. *The Sabbath: Its Meaning for Modern Man*. New York: Farrar, Straus and Giroux, 1951.

Heschel, Abraham J. *The Insecurity of Freedom: Essays on Human Existence*. New York: Farrar, Straus & Giroux, 1966.

Himmelfarb, Martha. "A Report on Enoch in Rabbinic Literature." In *SBL Seminar Papers* 13. Missoula, Mont.: Scholars Press, 1978, 259-269.

Himmelfarb, Martha. *Ascent to Heaven in Jewish and Christian Apocalypses*. New York: Oxford University Press, 1993.

Himmelfarb, Martha. "From Prophecy to Apocalypse: The *Book of Watchers* and Tours of Heaven." In *Jewish Spirituality: From the Bible Through the Middle Ages*. Vol. 1. Ed. Arthur Green. New York: Crossroad, 1986, 145-165.

Himmelfarb, Martha. "Heavenly Ascent and the Relationship of the Apocalypses and the *Hekhalot* Literature." In *Hebrew Union College Annual* 59 (1988) 73-100.

Himmelfarb, Martha. "Revelation and Rapture: The Transformation of the Visionary in the Ascent Apocalypses." In *Mysteries and Revelations: Apocalyptic Studies since the Uppsala Colloquium*. Ed. John J. Collins and James H. Charlesworth. Sheffield, England: Sheffield Academic Press, 1991, 79-90.

Himmelfarb, Martha. *Tours of Hell: An Apocalyptic Form in Jewish and Christian Literature*. Philadelphia: Fortress Press, 1983.

Hirsch, W. *Rabbinic Psychology: Beliefs about the Soul in Rabbinic Literature of the Talmudic Period*. New York: Arno Press, 1973.

Hirschberg, J. W. "The Sources of Moslems Traditions Concerning Jerusalem." In *Rocznik Orientalistyczny* 17 (1951-52), 314-350.

Hivert, Theodore. *The Yahwist's Landscape: Nature and Religion in Early Israel*. New York: Oxford University Press, 1996.

Hoffman, Lawrence A., ed. *The Land of Israel: Jewish Perspectives*. Notre Dame, IN: University of Notre Dame Press, 1986.

Holden, Lynn. *Forms of Deformity*. Sheffield: Sheffield Academic Press, 1991.

Holdrege, Barbara A. *Veda and Torah: Transcending the Textuality of Scripture*. Albany: State University of New York Press, 1996.

Holladay, Carl R. *Fragments from Hellenistic Jewish Authors*. Vol. 1. Chico, CA: Scholars Press, 1983.

Hooke, S. H. *In the Beginning*. Westport, CT: Greenwood Press, 1961.

Hooke, S. H. *Middle Eastern Mythology*. London: Penguin Books, 1963.

Hoppe, Leslie J. *The Holy City: Jerusalem in the Theology of the Old Testament*. Collegeville, MN: Liturgical Press, 2000.

Hultgard, Anders. "God and Image of Women in Early Jewish Religion." In *Image of God and Gender Models in Judaeo-Christian Tradition*. Ed. Kari Elisabeth Borreson. Oslo: Solum Forlag, 1991, 35-55.

Hurwitz, Siegmund. *Lilith—The First Eve: Historical and Psychological Aspects of the Dark Feminine*. Einsiedeln, Switzerland: Daimon Verlag, 1992.

Idel, Moshe. "The Contribution of Abraham Abulafia's Kabbalah to the Understanding of Jewish Mysticism." In *Gershom Scholem's "Major Trends in Jewish Mysticism" 50 Years After: Proceedings of the Sixth International Conference on the History of Jewish Mysticism*. Ed. Peter Schäfer and Joseph Dan. Tubingen: J. C. B. Mohr, 1993, 117-143.

Idel, Moshe. "Defining Kabbalah: The Kabbalah of the Divine Names." In *Mystics of the Book: Themes, Topics, and Typologies*. Ed. R. A. Herrera. New York: Peter Lang, 1993.

Idel, Moshe. "Differing Conceptions of Kabbalah in the Seventeenth Century." In *Jewish Thought in the Seventeenth Century*. Ed. Isadore Twersky and Bernard Septimus. Cambridge, MA: Harvard University Press, 1987, 137-200.

Idel, Moshe. "Enoch is Metatron." In *Immanuel* 24-25 (1990) 220-240.

Idel, Moshe. *Golem: Jewish Magical and Mystical Traditions On the Artificial Anthropoid*. Albany: State University of New York Press, 1990.

Idel, Moshe. *Hasidism: Between Ecstasy and Magic*. Albany: State Univesity of New York Press, 1995.

Idel, Moshe. "Jewish Apocalypticism: 670-1670." In *The Encyclopedia of Apocalypticism*. Vol. 2. Ed. John J. Collins. New York: Continuum, 1999, 204-237.

Idel, Moshe. "Jewish Magic from the Renaissance Period to Early Hasidism." In *Religion, Science, and Magic in Concert and Conflict*. Ed. Jacob Neusner. New York: Oxford University Press, 1989.

Idel, Moshe, Mortimer Ostow and Ivan G. Marcus, eds. *Jewish Mystical Leaders and Leadership in the Thirteenth Century*. Northvale, NJ: Jason Aronson, 1998.

Idel, Moshe. "The Journey to Paradise: The Jewish Transformations of a Greek Mythological Motif." In *Jerusalem Studies in Jewish Folklore* 2 (1982) 9-16.

Idel, Moshe. *Kabbalah: New Perspectives*. New Haven, CT: Yale University Press, 1988.

Idel, Moshe. "The Ladder of Ascension—The Reverberations of a Medieval Motif in the Renaissance." In *Studies in Medieval Jewish History and Literature*. Vol. 2. Ed. Isadore Twersky. Cambridge, MA: Harvard University Press, 1984, 83-93.

Idel, Moshe. "The Land of Israel in Medieval Kabbalah." In *The Land of Israel: Jewish Perspectives*. Ed. Lawrence A. Hoffman. Notre Dame, IN: University of Notre Dame Press, 1986.

Idel, Moshe. "The Magical and Neoplatonic Interpretations of the Kabbalah in the Renaissance." In *Jewish Thought in the Sixteenth Century*. Ed. Bernard Dov Cooperman. Cambridge, MA: Harvard University Press, 1983, 186-242.

Idel, Moshe. *Messianic Mystics*. New Haven, CT: Yale University Press, 1998.

Idel, Moshe and Bernard McGinn, eds. *Mystical Union in Judaism, Christianity, and Islam: An Ecumenical Dialogue*. New York: Continuum, 1996.

Idel, Moshe. "On Judaism, Jewish Mysticism and Magic." In *Envisioning Magic: A Princeton Seminar and Symposium*. Ed. Peter Schäfer and Hans G. Kippenberg. Leiden: E. J. Brill, 1997.

Idel, Moshe. "Orienting, Orientalizing or Disorienting the Study of Kabbalah: 'An Almost Absolutely Unique' Case of Occidentalism." In *Kabbalah: Journal for the Study of Jewish Mystical Texts* 2 (1997) 13-47.

Idel, Moshe. "Perceptions of Kabbalah in the Second Half of the 18th Century." In *Journal of Jewish Thought and Philosophy* 1 (1991) 55-114.

Idel, Moshe. "Some Remarks on Ritual and Mysticism in Geronese Kabbalah." In *Journal of Jewish Thought and Philosophy* 3 (1993) 111-130.

Idel, Moshe. *Studies in Ecstatic Kabbalah*. SUNY Series in Judaica: *Hermeneutics, Mysticism and Religion*. Albany: State University of New York Press, 1988.

Ilan, Tal. "Matrona and Rabbi Jose: An Alternative Interpretation." In *Journal for the Study of Judaism* 25:1 (1994) 18-51.

Isaacs, Ronald H. *Ascending Jacob's Ladder: Jewish Views of Angels, Demons, and Evil Spirits*. Northvale, NJ: Jason Aronson, 1998.

Isaacs, Ronald H. *Close Encounters: Jewish Views about God*. Northvale, NJ: Jason Aronson, 1996.

Isaacs, Ronald H. *Divination, Magic, and Healing: The Book of Jewish Folklore*. Northvale, NJ: Jason Aronson, 1998.

Isaacs, Ronald H. *Miracles: A Jewish Perspective*. Northvale, NJ: Jason Aronson, 1997.

Isaacs, Ronald H. and Kerry M. Olitzky, eds. *Sacred Moments: Tales from the Jewish Life Cycle*. Northvale, NJ: Jason Aronson, 1995.

Jackson, H. M. "Notes on the Testament of Solomon." In *Journal for the Study of Judaism* 19:1 (1988) 19-60.

Jacobi, Margaret. "Serach bat Asher and Bitiah bat Pharaoh—Names which Became Legends." In *Hear Our Voice: Women Rabbis Tell Their Stories*. Ed. Sybil Sheridan. London: SCM Press, 1994.

Jacobs, Irving. "Elements of Near-Eastern Mythology in Rabbinic Aggadah." In *Journal of Jewish Studies* 28:1 (1977) 1-11.

Jacobs, Irving. *The Midrashic Process*. Cambridge: Cambridge University Press, 1995.

Jacobs, Louis. *Holy Living: Saints and Saintliness in Judaism*. Northvale, NJ: Jason Aronson, 1990.

Jacobs, Louis. *A Jewish Theology*. London: Darton, Longman & Todd, 1973.

Jacobs, Louis. *Jewish Ethics, Philosophy and Mysticism*. New York: Behrman House, 1969.

Jacobs, Louis. *Jewish Mystical Testimonies*. New York: Schocken Books, 1977.

Jacobs, Louis, trans. *Rabbi Moses Cordovero, The Palm Tree of Deborah*. London: Vallentine, Mitchell, 1960.

Jacobs, Louis. "The Uplifting of Sparks in Later Jewish Mysticism." In *Jewish Spirituality: From the Bible Through the Middle Ages*. Vol. 2. Ed. Arthur Green. New York: Crossroad, 1994, 99-126.

Jacobson, Yoram. "The Aspect of the 'Feminine' in the Lurianic Kabbalah." In *Gershom Scholem's "Major Trends in Jewish Mysticism" 50 Years After: Proceedings of the Sixth International Conference on the History of Jewish Mysticism*. Ed. Peter Schäfer and Joseph Dan. Tubingen: J. C. B. Mohr, 1993, 239-255.

Jacobson, Yoram. "The Image of God as the Source of Man's Evil, According to the Maharal of Prague." In *Binah: Jewish Intellectual History in the Middle Ages*. Vol. 3. Ed. Joseph Dan. Westport, CT: Praeger, 1994, 135-158.

Janowitz, Naomi. "God's Body: Theological and Ritual Roles of Shi'ur Komah." In *People of the Body: Jews and Judaism from an Embodied Perspective*. Ed. Howard Eilberg-Schwartz. Albany: State University of New York Press, 1992, 183-201.

Janowitz, Naomi. *The Poetics of Ascent: Theories of Language in a Rabbinic Ascent Text*. Albany: State University of New York Press, 1989.

Johnson, Aubrey R. *Sacral Kingship in Ancient Israel*. Cardiff: University of Wales Press, 1967.

Johnson, M. D. *Life and Adam and Eve* (and *Apocalypse of Moses*). In *The Old Testament Pseudepigrapha*. Garden City, NY: Doubleday, 1983-85.

Jonas, Hans. *The Gnostic Religion: The Message of the Alien God and the Beginnings of Christianity*. Boston: Beacon Press, 1963.

Jung, C. G. *The Archetypes and the Collective Unconscious*. (Collected Works of C. G. Jung, vol. 9, part 1). Princeton: Princeton University Press, 1969.

Kafka, Franz. *The Complete Stories*. Ed. Nahum M. Glatzer. New York: Schocken Books, 1971.

Kafka, Franz. *Parables and Paradoxes*. New York: Schocken Books, 1975.

Kafka, Franz. *The Trial*. New York: Schocken Books, 1995.

Kaiser, Walter C., Jr. *The Messiah in the Old Testament*. Studies in Old Testament Biblical Theology. Grand Rapids, MI: Zondervan Publishing House, 1995.

Kalin, Richard. *Sages, Stories, Authorities and Editors in Rabbinic Babylonia*. Atlanta: Scholars Press, 1994.

Kamenetz, Rodger. *Stalking Elijah: Adventures with Today's Jewish Mystical Masters*. San Francisco: HarperSanFrancisco, 1997.

Kamin, Sarah. "Rashbam's Conception of the Creation in Light of the Intellectual Currents of His Time." In *Studies in Bible* 31 (1986) 14-132.

Kaplan, Aryeh, trans. *The Bahir*. New York: Samuel Weiser, 1979. (Based on the edition of Reuven Margoliot, 1951.)

Kaplan, Aryeh. *A Call to the Infinite*. New York: Maznaim, 1986.

Kaplan, Aryeh, trans. *Derech HaShem, The Way of God*. Spring Valley, NY: Philipp Feldheim, 1988.

Kaplan, Aryeh. *Immortality, Resurrection, and the Age of the Universe: A Kabbalistic View*. Hoboken, NJ: Ktav Publishing House, 1993.

Kaplan, Aryeh. *Inner Space: Introduction to Kabbalah, Meditation and Prophecy*. Ed. Abraham Sutton. Jerusalem: Moznaim, 1991.

Kaplan, Aryeh. *The Light Beyond: Adventures in Hassidic Thought*. New York: Maznaim, 1981.

Kaplan, Aryeh. *Meditation and the Bible*. York Beach, ME: Samuel Weiser, 1978.

Kaplan, Aryeh. *Meditation and Kabbalah*. York Beach, ME: Samuel Weiser, 1982.

Kaplan, Aryeh, trans. *Rabbi Nachman's Wisdom*. New York: Sepher-Hermon Press, 1973.

Kaplan, Aryeh, trans. *Sefer Yetzirah: The Book of Creation*. York Beach, ME: Samuel Weiser, 1990.

Karasick, Adeena. "Shekhinah: the speculum that signs, or the flaming s/word that turn[s] every way" (Genesis 3:24). In *Nashim* 2 (1999) 114-136.

Kasher, Menahem M. *Encyclopedia of Biblical Interpretation: A Millennial Anthology*. 9 vols. New York: American Biblical Encyclopedia Society, 1953.

Kasher, Rimmon. "Angelology and the Supernal Worlds in the Aramaic Targums to the Prophets." In *Journal for the Study of Judaism* 27:2 (1996) 168-191.

Katz, Steven T. *Jewish Ideas and Concepts*. New York: Schocken Books, 1977.

Kaufmann, Yehezkel. *The Religion of Israel: From Its Beginnings to the Babylonian Exile*. Trans. Moshe Greenberg. New York: Schocken Books, 1972.

Keel, Othmar and Christoph Uehlinger. *Gods, Goddesses, and Images of God in Ancient Israel*. Trans. Thomas H. Trapp. Minneapolis: Fortress Press, 1998.

Kepnes, Stephen D. "A Narrative Jewish Theology." In *Judaism* 37 (1988) 210-219.

Kerenyi, C. *The Gods of the Greeks*. New York: Thames and Hudson, 1980.

Kern-Ulmer, Brigitte. "The Depiction of Magic in Rabbinic Texts: The Rabbinic and the Greek Concept of Magic." In *Journal for the Study of Judaism* 27:3 (1996) 289-303.

Kern-Ulmer, Brigitte. "The Power of the Evil Eye and the Good Eye in Midrashic Literature." In *Judaism* 40 (1991) 344-353.

Kiel, Mark W. "Sefer Ha'Aggadah: Creating a Classic Anthology for the People and by the People." In *Prooftexts* 17 (1997) 177-197.

Kimelman, Reuven. "The Shema' and Its Rhetoric: the Case for the Shema' Being More Than Creation, Revelation and Redemption." In *Journal of Jewish Thought and Philosophy* 2:1 (1992) 111-156.

King, Karen L., ed. *Images of the Feminine in Gnosticism*. Harrisburg, PA: Trinity Press International, 2000.

Kirschner, Robert S. "Maimonides' Fiction of Resurrection." In *Hebrew Union College Annual* 52 (1981) 163-193.

Kitov, Eliyahu. *The Book of Our Heritage: The Jewish Year and Its Days of Significance*. 3 vols. Trans. Nathan Bulman. Spring Valley, NY: Philipp Feldheim, 1978.

Klapholtz, Yisroel Yakov. *Tales of the Ba'al Shem Tov*. 5 vols. Trans. Sheindel Weinbach and Abigail Nadav. Bnei Brak: Pe'er Hasefer, 1970-1971.

Klapholtz, Yisroel Yakov. *Tales of the Heavenly Court*. 2 vols. Trans. Sheindel Weinbach. Bnei Brak: Pe'er Hasefer, 1982.

Klausner, Joseph. *The Messianic Idea in Israel: From Its Beginning to the Completion of the Mishnah*. New York: Macmillan, 1955.

Klein, Eliahu, trans. *Kabbalah of Creation: Isaac Luria's Earlier Mysticism*. Northvale, NJ: Jason Aronson, 2000.

Klein, Isaac. *A Guide to Jewish Religious Practice*. New York : The Jewish Theological Seminary of America, 1979.

Klein, Michele. *A Time To Be Born: Customs and Folklore of Jewish Birth*. Philadelphia: The Jewish Publication Society, 1998.

Klein, Ralph W. *Israel in Exile: A Theological Interpretation*. Overtures to Biblical Theology. Philadelphia: Fortress Press, 1979.

Kluger, Rivkah Schärf. *Satan in the Old Testament*. Trans. Hildegard Nagel. Evanston, IL: Northwestern University Press.

Knapp, Bettina L. *Manna and Mystery: A Jungian Approach to Hebrew Myth and Legend*. Wilmette, IL: Chiron Publications, 1995.

Knibb, M. A. *The Ethiopic Book of Enoch: A New Edition in the Light of the Aramaic Dead Sea Fragments*. Two volumes. Oxford: 1978.

Knibb, M. A. "Messianism in the Pseudepigrapha in the Light of the Scrolls." In *Dead Sea Discoveries* 2 (1995), 165-184.

Kobler, Franz, ed. *Letters of Jews Throughout the Ages*. 2 vols. New York: East and West Library, 1952.

Koltuv, Barbara Black. *The Book of Lilith*. York Beach, ME: Nicolas-Hayes, 1986.

Konowitz, Israel. *The God Idea in Jewish Tradition*. Trans. Shmuel Himelstein. Jerusalem: The Jerusalem Publishing House, 1989.

Kook, Abraham Isaac. *Abraham Isaac Kook—The Lights of Penitence, The Moral Principles, Lights of Holiness, Essays, Letters, and Poems*. New York: Paulist Press, 1978.

Kugel, James L. *In Potiphar's House: The Interpretive Life of Biblical Texts*. San Francisco: HarperSanFrancisco, 1990.

Kugel, James L. "The Ladder of Jacob." In *Harvard Theological Review* 88:2 (1995) 209-227.

Kugel, James L. *Traditions of the Bible: A Guide to the Bible As It Was at the Start of the Common Era*. Cambridge, MA: Harvard University Press, 1998.

Kunin, Seth Daniel. *The Logic of Incest: A Structuralist Analysis of Hebrew Mythology*. Sheffield, England: Sheffield Academic Press, 1995.

Kushelevsky, Rella. *Moses and the Angel of Death*. Trans. Ruth Bar-Ilan. New York: Peter Lang, 1995.

Kvam, Kristen E., Linda S. Schearing, and Valarie H. Ziegler, eds. *Eve and Adam: Jewish, Christian, and Muslim Readings on Genesis and Gender*. Bloomington: Indiana University Press, 1999.

Kwon, Ohyun. *The Formation and Development of Resurrection Faith in Early Judaism*. Doctoral dissertation. New York University, 1984.

Labowitz, Shoni. *God, Sex and Women of the Bible: Discovering Our Sensual, Spiritual Selves*. New York: Simon & Schuster, 1998.

Lachower, Fischel and Isaiah Tishby, eds. *The Wisdom of the Zohar: An Anthology of Texts*. 3 vols. Trans. David Goldstein. New York: Oxford University Press, 1989.

Lagerkvist, Par. *The Marriage Feast*. New York: Hill and Wang, 1954.

Lamm, Norman. *The Religious Thought of Hasidism: Text and Commentary*. Hoboken, NJ: Ktav Publishing House, 1999.

Lamm, Norman. *The Shema: Spirituality and Law in Judaism*. Philadelphia: Jewish Publication Society, 2000.

Lang, Bernhard, ed. *Anthropological Approaches to the Old Testament*. Philadelphia: Fortress Press, 1985.

Langermann, Y. Tzvi, trans. *Yemenite Midrash: Philosophical Commentaries on the Torah*. San Francisco: HarperSanFrancisco, 1996.

Laurence, Richard, trans. *The Book of Enoch the Prophet*. London: Kegan Paul, Trench & Co., 1883.

Lauterbach, Jacob Z. *Studies in Jewish Law, Custom and Folklore*. Ed. Bernard J. Bamberger. New York: Ktav Publishing House, 1970.

Lauterbach, Jacob Z. "Tashlik—A Study in Jewish Ceremonies." In *Hebrew Union College Annual* 11 (1936) 207-340.

Lawee, Eric. "'Israel Has No Messiah' in Late Medieval Spain." In *Journal of Jewish Thought and Philosophy* 5 (1996) 245-279.

Laytner, Anson. *Arguing with God: A Jewish Tradition*. Northvale, NJ: Jason Aronson, 1990.

Layton, Bentley, trans. *The Gnostic Scriptures: Ancient Wisdom for the New Age*. New York: Doubleday, 1987.

Leeming, David and Margaret Adams Leeming. *A Dictionary of Creation Myths*. New York: Oxford University Press, 1994.

Leeming, David. *God: Myths of the Male Divine*. New York: Oxford University Press, 1996.

Leicht, Reimund. "Gnostic Myth in Jewish Garb: Niriyah (Norea), Noah's Bride." In *Journal of Jewish Studies* 11:1 (2000) 133-140.

Lenowitz, Harris. *The Jewish Messiahs: From the Galilee to Crown Heights*. New York: Oxford University Press, 1998.

Leslau, Wolf, trans. *Falasha Anthology*. Yale Judaica Series. Vol. 6. New Haven, CT: Yale University Press, 1979.

Lesses, Rebecca. "The Adjuration of the Prince of the Presence: Performative Utterance in a Jewish Ritual." In *Ancient Magic and Ritual Power*, edited by Marvin Meyer and Paul Mirecki. Leiden: E. J. Brill, 1995, 185-206.

Lesses, Rebecca. "Speaking with Angels: Jewish and Greco-Egyptian Revelatory Adjurations." In *Harvard Theological Review* 89:1 (1996) 41-60.

Levenson, Jon D. *Creation and the Persistence of Evil: The Jewish Drama of Divine Omnipotence*. Princeton, NJ: Princeton University Press, 1988.

Levenson, Jon D. *The Death and Resurrection of the Beloved Son: The Transformation of Child Sacrifice in Judaism and Christianity*. New Haven, CT: Yale University Press, 1993.

Levenson, Jon D. "The Jerusalem Temple in Devotional and Visionary Experience." In *Jewish Spirituality: From the Bible Through the Middle Ages*. Vol. 1. Ed. Arthur Green. New York: Crossroad, 1986, 32-61.

Levenson, Jon D. *Sinai and Zion: An Entry into the Jewish Bible*. San Francisco: HarperSanFrancisco, 1985.

Levine, Baruch A. "On the Presence of God in Biblical Religion." In *Religions in Antiquity: Essays in Memory of Erwin Ramsdell Goodenough*. Ed. Jacob Neusner. Leiden: E. J. Brill, 1970, 71-87.

Levine, Hillel. "Frankism as Worldly Messianism." In *Gershom Scholem's "Major Trends in Jewish Mysticism" 50 Years After: Proceedings of the Sixth International Conference on the History of Jewish Mysticism*. Ed. Peter Schäfer and Joseph Dan. Tubingen: J. C. B. Mohr, 1993, 283-300.

Levison, John R. "The Angelic Spirit in Early Judaism." In *Society of Biblical Literature: Seminar Papers* 34 (1995) 464-493.

Levison, John R. "The Debut of the Divine Spirit in Josephus's *Antiquities*." In *Harvard Theological Review* 87:2 (1994) 123-138.

Levison, John R. "Did the Spirit Withdraw from Israel? An Evaluation of the Earliest Jewish Data." In *New Testament Studies* 43:1 (1997) 35-57.

Levison, John R. "The Exoneration of Eve in the Apocalypse of Moses 15-30." In *Journal for the Study of Judaism* 20:2 (1989) 135-150.

Levison, John R. "Inspiration and the Divine Spirit in the Writings of Philo Judaeus." In *Journal for the Study of Judaism* 26:3 (1995) 271-323.

Levison, John. R. *Portraits of Adam in Early Judaism: From Sirah to 2 Baruch*. Sheffield: Sheffield Academic Press, 1988.

Levison, John R. "The Prophetic Spirit as an Angel According to Philo." In *HTR* 88:2 (1995) 189-207.

Lewis, Theodore J. *Cults of the Dead in Ancient Israel and Ugarit*. Atlanta: Scholars Press, 1989.

Lieberman, Saul. "Some Aspects of After Life in Early Rabbinic Literature." In *Harry Austryn Wolfson Jubilee Volume, On the Occasion of His Seventy-Fifth Birthday*. Vol. 2. Jerusalem: American Academy for Jewish Research, 1965, 495-532.

Lieberman, Saul. "Rabbinic Interpretation of Scripture." In *Essential Papers on the Talmud*. Ed. Michael Chernick. New York and London: New York University Press, 1994, 429-460.

Liebes, Yehuda. "Myth vs. Symbol in the Zohar and Lurianic Kabbalah." In *Essential Papers on Kabbalah*. Ed. Lawrence Fine. New York and London: New York University Press, 1995, 212-242.

Liebes, Yehuda. *Studies in Jewish Myth and Jewish Messianism*. Albany: State Univesity of New York Press, 1993.

Liebes, Yehuda. *Studies in the Zohar*. Albany: State Univesity of New York Press, 1993.

Lienhard, Joseph T., ed. *Ancient Christian Commentary on Scripture: Old Testament III*. Downers Grove, Illinois: InterVarsity Press, 2001.

Limor, Ora. "The Place of the End of Days: Eschatological Geography in Jerusalem." In *The Real and Ideal Jerusalem in Jewish, Christian and Islamic Art*. Jerusalem: Journal of the Center for Jewish Art, 1998, 13-22.

Lindahl, Carl, John McNamara, and John Lindow. *Medieval Folklore: A Guide to Myths, Legends, Tales, Beliefs, and Customs*. New York: Oxford University Press, 2002.

Loeb, Laurence D. "Time, Myth and History in Judaism." In *Conservative Judaism* 42:3 (1990) 54-65.

Loewe, Michael and Carmen Blacker, eds. *Oracles and Divination*. Boulder, CO: Shambhala, 1981.

Louth, Andrew, ed. *Ancient Christian Commentary on Scripture: Old Testament I*. Downers Grove, Illinois: InterVarsity Press, 2001.

Lunt, H. G. *Ladder of Jacob*. In J. Charlesworth, *The Old Testament Pseudepigrapha*. Garden City, NY: 1985.

Luttikhuizen, Gerard P., ed. *Paradise Interpreted: Representations of Biblical Paradise in Judaism and Christianity*. Leiden: Brill, 1999.

Maccoby, Hyam. *Judas Iscariot and the Myth of Jewish Evil*. New York: Macmillan, 1992.

Maccoby, Hyam. *Ritual and Morality: The Ritual Purity System and Its Place in Judaism*. Cambridge: Cambridge University Press, 1999.

Maccoby, Hyam. *The Sacred Executioner: Human Sacrifice and the Legacy of Guilt*. New York: Thames and Hudson, 1982.

MacDonald, John, trans. *Memar Marqah: The Teachings of Marqah*. 2 vols. Berlin: Verlag Alfred Topelmann, 1963.

Mach, Michael. "From Apocalypticism to Early Jewish Mysticism." In *The Encyclopedia of Apocalypticism*. Vol. 1. Ed. John J. Collins. New York: Continuum, 1999, 229-264.

MacRae, G. *Apocalypse of Adam*. In *The Old Testament Pseudepigrapha*, edited by J. Charlesworth. Garden City, NY: Doubleday, 1983-85.

Magid, Shaul. "From Theosophy to Midrash: Lurianic Exegesis and the Garden of Eden." In *AJS Review* 22:1 (1997) 37-75.

Magid, Shaul, ed. *God's Voice from the Void: Old and New Studies in Bratslav Hasidism*. Albany: State University of New York Press, 2001.

Magid, Shaul. "Through the Void: The Absence of God in R. Nachman of Bratzlav's Likutei MoHaRan." In *HTR* 88:4 (1995) 495-519.

Malamud, Bernard. *The Complete Stories*. New York: Farrar, Straus & Giroux, 1997.

Malina, Bruce J. *On the Genre and Message of Revelation: Star Visions and Sky Journeys*. Peabody, MA: Hendrickson Publishers, 1995.

Manger, Itzik. *The Book of Paradise*. New York: Hill and Wang, 1986.

Margolies, Morris B. *A Gathering of Angels*. New York: Ballantine Books, 1994.

Marks, Richard G. *The Image of Bar Kokhba in Traditional Jewish Literature: False Messiah and National Hero*. University Park, PA: Pennsylvania State University Press, 1994.

Marmorstein, Arthur. *The Doctrine of Merits in Old Rabbinical Literature*. New York: Ktav Publishing House, 1968.

Marmorstein, Arthur. "A Fragment of the Visions of Ezekiel." In *Jewish Quarterly Review* 8 (1917-18) 367-378.

Marmorstein, Arthur. "The Holy Spirit in Rabbinic Legend." In *Studies in Jewish Theology*. London: Oxford, 1950, 122-144.

Marmorstein, Arthur. *The Old Rabbinic Doctrine of God*. London: Oxford, 1947.

Marmorstein, Arthur. "Philo and the Names of God." In *Jewish Quarterly Review* 22 (1931-32) 295-306.

Marmorstein, Arthur. "The Unity of God in Rabbinic Literature." In *Hebrew Union College Annual* 1 (1924) 467-499.

Mascetti, Manuela Dunn. *Goddesses: Mythology and Symbols of the Goddess*. London: Labyrinth Publishing, 1990.

Matt, Daniel C. *The Essential Kabbalah: The Heart of Jewish Mysticism*. San Francisco: HarperSanFrancisco, 1995.

Matt, Daniel C. *God and the Big Bang: Discovering Harmony Between Science and Spirituality*. Woodstock, VT: Jewish Lights Publishing, 1996.

Matt, Daniel C. "The Mystic and the Mizwot." In *Jewish Spirituality: From the Bible Through the Middle Ages*. Vol. 1. Ed. Arthur Green. New York: Crossroad, 1986, 367-404.

Matt, Daniel C. "'New-Ancient Words': The Aura of Secrecy in the Zohar." In *Gershom Scholem's "Major Trends in Jewish Mysticism" 50 Years After: Proceedings of the Sixth Inter-*

national Conference on the History of Jewish Mysticism. Ed. Peter Schäfer and Joseph Dan. Tubingen: J. C. B. Mohr, 181-207.

Matt, Daniel C., trans. *The Zohar*, Pritzker Edition. 2 vols. Stanford: Stanford University Press, 2004. 2 vols.

Matt, Daniel C., trans. *Zohar: The Book of Enlightenment*. Mahwah, NJ: Paulist Press, 1983.

Matthews, Victor H. and Don C. Benjamin. *Old Testament Parallels: Laws and Stories from the Ancient Near East*. New York: Paulist Press, 1997.

Mead, G. R. S. Pistis. *Sophia: A Gnostic Miscellany*. London: John M. Watkins, 1921.

Meeks, Wayne A. "Moses as God and King." In *Religions in Antiquity: Essays in Memory of Erwin Ramsdell Goodenough*. Ed. Jacob Neusner. Leiden: E. J. Brill, 1968, 354-371.

Mehlman, Bernard H. and Daniel F. Polish. "The Response to the Christian Exegesis of Psalms in the Teshuvot La-Nozrim of Rabbi David Qimhi." In *Jewish Civilization* 3 (1985) 181-208.

Meltzer, David, ed. *The Secret Garden: An Anthology in the Kabbalah*. New York: Seabury Press, 1976.

Mendes-Flohr, Paul, ed. *Gershom Scholem: The Man and His Work*. Albany: State University of New York Press, 1994.

Merel, Nathan. *The Coat of the Unicorn*. 5 vols. Jerusalem: Hemed Press, 1994-1998.

Meroz, Ronit. "Faithful Transmission versus Innovation: Luria and His Disciples." In *Gershom Scholem's "Major Trends in Jewish Mysticism" 50 Years After: Proceedings of the Sixth International Conference on the History of Jewish Mysticism*. Ed. Peter Schäfer and Joseph Dan. Tubingen: J. C. B. Mohr, 1993, 257-274.

Messadié, Gérald. *A History of the Devil*. Trans. Mare Romano. New York: Kodansha America, 1996.

Metzger, Bruce M., ed. *The Apocrypha of the Old Testament: Revised Standard Version*. New York: Oxford University Press, 1965.

Metzger, Bruce M. *The Fourth Book of Ezra*. In *The Old Testament Pseudepigrapha*, edited by J. Charlesworth. Garden City, NY: Doubleday, 1983-1985.

Miles, Jack A. *God: A Biography*. New York: Alfred A. Knopf, 1995.

Milgrom, Jo. *The Binding of Isaac: The Akedah—A Primary Symbol in Jewish Thought and Art*. Berkeley: BIBAL Press, 1988.

Miller, Moshe, trans. *The Zohar*. Morristown, NJ: Fiftieth Gate Publications, 2000.

Miller, Patrick. "Eridu, Dunnu, and Babel: A Study in Comparative Mythology." In *Hebrew Annual Review* 9 (1985): 227-251.

Minkin, Jacob S. *The Teachings of Maimonides*. Northvale, NJ: Jason Aronson, 1987.

Mintz, Jerome R. *Legends of the Hasidim: An Introduction to Hasidic Culture and Oral Tradition in the New World*. Chicago: University of Chicago Press, 1968.

Moberly, R. W. L. *The Old Testament of the Old Testament: Patriarchal Narratives and Mosaic Yahwism*. Minneapolis: Fortress Press, 1992.

Molenberg, Corrie. "A Study of the Roles of Shemihaza and Asael in I Enoch 6-11." In *Journal of Jewish Studies* 35:2 (1984) 136-146.

Montefiore, C. G. and H. Loewe, eds. *A Rabbinic Anthology*. Philadelphia: Jewish Publication Society, 1960.

Montgomery, J. A. "Some Early Amulets from Palestine." In *Journal of the American Oriental Society*, 1911.

Moor, Johannes C. de, ed. *An Anthology of Religious Texts from Ugarit*. Leiden: E. J. Brill, 1987.

Moore, Michael S. "Job's Texts of Terror." In *Catholic Bible Quarterly* 55:4 (1993) 662-675.

Moreen, Vera Basch. "A Dialogue between God and Satan in Shahin's *Bereshit Namah*." In *Irano-Judaica III: Studies Relating to Jewish Contacts with Persian Culture Throughout the Ages*. Ed. Shaul Shaked and Amnon Netzer. Jerusalem: Ben-Zvi Institute, 1994, 127-141.

Morgenstern, Julian. "The Gates of Righteousness." In *Hebrew Union College Annual* 6 (1929) 1-37.

Morgenstern, Julian. "The Sources of the Paradise Story." In *Journal of Jewish Lore and Philosophy* 1:1 (1919) 105-123 and 1:2 (1919) 225-240.

Morray-Jones, C. R. A. "The Embodied Divine Image in the Dead Sea Scrolls and Other Early Jewish and Christian Sources." In *SBL Seminar Papers* 3:1 (1998) 400-431.

Morray-Jones, C. R. A. "Hekhalot Literature and Talmudic Tradition: Alexander's Three Test Cases." In *Journal for the Study of Judaism* 22:1 (1991) 1-39.

Morray-Jones, C. R. A. "Paradise Revisited (2 Cor 12:1-12): The Jewish Mystical Background of Paul's Apostolate. Part 1: The Jewish Sources." In *Harvard Theological Review* 86:2 (1993) 177-217.

Morray-Jones, C. R. A. "Paradise Revisited (2 Cor. 12:1-12): The Jewish Mystical Background of Paul's Apostolate. Part 2: Paul's Heavenly Ascent and Its Significance." In *Harvard Theological Review* 86:3 (1993) 265-292.

Morray-Jones, C. R. A. "Transformational Mysticism in the Apocalyptic-Mervabah Tradition." In *The Journal of Jewish Studies* 43:1 (1992) 1-31.

Morris, Paul. "Exiled from Eden: Jewish Interpretations of Genesis." In *A Walk in the Garden: Biblical, Iconographical and Literary Images of Eden*. Ed. Paul Morris and Deborah Sawyer. London: JSOT Press, 1992, 117-166.

Mullen, E. Theodore. *Assembly of the Gods: The Divine Council in Canaanite and Early Hebrew Literature*. Atlanta, GA: Scholars Press, 1980.

Munk, Michael L. *The Wisdom in the Hebrew Letters: The Sacred Letters as a Guide to Jewish Deed and Thought*. Brooklyn, NY: Mesorah Publications, 1983.

Munoa, Phillip B., III. *Four Powers in Heaven: The Interpretation of Daniel 7 in the Testament of Abraham*. Sheffield, England: Sheffield Academic Press, 1998.

Murphy, Roland E. *The Tree of Life: An Exploration of Biblical Wisdom Literature*. New York: Doubleday, 1990.

Nadich, Judah. *The Legends of the Rabbis*. 2 vols. Northvale, NJ: Jason Aronson, 1984.

Nagarajan, Nadia Grosser. *Jewish Tales from Eastern Europe*. Northvale, NJ: Jason Aronson, 1999.

Nemoy, Leon, trans. *Karaite Anthology: Excerpts from the Early Literature*. New Haven: Yale University Press, 1980.

Ness, Lester J. *Astrology and Judaism in Late Antiquity*. Doctoral dissertation. Miami University, 1990.

Neugroschel, Joachim, trans. *The Dybbuk and the Yiddish Imagination: A Haunted Reader*. Syracuse, NY: Syracuse University Press, 2000.

Neulander, Judith S. "Creating the Universe: A Study of Cosmos Cognition." In *Folklore Forum* 25:1 (1992) 3-18.

Neusner, Jacob. "The Development of the *Merkavah* Tradition." In *Journal for the Study of Judaism* 2:2 (1971) 149-160.

Neusner, Jacob. *The Enchantments of Judaism: Rites of Transformation from Birth through Death*. New York: Basic Books, 1987.

Neusner, Jacob, Alan J. Avery-Peck, and William Scott Green, eds. *The Encyclopedia of Judaism*. 3 vols. New York: Continuum, 1999.

Neusner, Jacob. "Genesis Rabbah As Polemic: An Introductory Account." In *Hebrew Annual Review* 9 (1985) 253-265.

Neusner, Jacob. *History and Torah: Essays on Jewish Learning*. New York: Schocken Books, 1965.

Neusner, Jacob. *The Incarnation of God: The Character of Divinity in Formative Judaism*. Atlanta: Scholars Press, 1992.

Neusner, Jacob. *Introduction to Rabbinic Literature*. New York: Doubleday, 1994.

Neusner, Jacob, William Scott Green, and Ernest S. Frerichs, eds. *Judaisms and Their Messiahs at the Turn of the Christian Era*. Cambridge: Cambridge University Press, 1987.

Neusner, Jacob. *Judaism and Zoroastrianism at the Dusk of Late Antiquity: How Two Ancient Faiths Wrote Down their Great Traditions*. Atlanta: Scholars Press, 1993.

Neusner, Jacob. "The Meaning of *Torah Shebe'al Peh* with Special Reference to *Kelim* and *Ohalot*." In *AJS Review* 1 (1976) 151-170.

Neusner, Jacob. *Messiah in Context: Israel's History and Destiny in Formative Judaism*. Lanham, MD: University Press of America, 1988.

Neusner, Jacob, ed. *Normative Judaism*. 3 vols. Origins of Judaism, Vol. 1. New York: Garland Publishing, 1990.

Neusner, Jacob. *The Oral Torah: The Sacred Books of Judaism, An Introduction*. San Francisco: Harper and Row, 1986.

Neusner, Jacob. *Rabbinic Judaism: Structure and System*. Minneapolis: Fortress Press, 1995.

Neusner, Jacob and Bruce D. Chilton. *Revelation: The Torah and the Bible*. Valley Forge, PA: Trinity Press International, 1995.

Newman, Louis I. with Samuel Spitz, trans. *The Hasidic Anthology: Tales and Teachings of the Hasidim*. New York: Bloch, 1944.

Newman, Louis I., trans. *Maggidim and Hasidim: Their Wisdom*. New York: Bloch, 1962.

Newsom, Carol A. "The Development of *1 Enoch* 6-19: Cosmology and Judgment." In *Catholic Biblical Quarterly* 42 (1980) 310-329.

Nickelsburg, George W. E. "Apocalypse and Myth in *1 Enoch* 6-11." In *Journal of Biblical Literature* 96:3 (1977) 383-405.

Nickelsburg, George W. E. *Jewish Literature between the Bible and the Mishnah: A Historical and Literary Introduction*. Philadelphia: Fortress Press, 1981.

Nickelsburg, George W. E. *Resurrection, Immortality, and Eternal Life in Intertestamental Judaism*. Atlanta: Scholars Press, 1972.

Niditch, Susan. *Ancient Israelite Religion*. New York: Oxford University Press, 1997.

Niditch, Susan. *Chaos to Cosmos: Studies in the Biblical Pattern of Creation*. Atlanta: Scholars Press, 1985.

Niditch, Susan. "Cosmic Adam: Man as Mediator in Rabbinic Literature." In *Journal of Jewish Studies* 34:2 (1983) 137-146.

Niditch, Susan. *Oral Word and Written Word: Ancient Israelite Literature*. Louisville, KY: Westminster John Knox Press, 1996.

Niehoff, Maren R. "A Dream which is not Interpreted is like a Letter which is not Read." In *Journal of Jewish Studies* 43:1 (1992) 58-84.

Niehoff, Maren R. "The Return of Myth in Genesis Rabbah on the Akeda." In *Journal of Jewish Studies* 46:1-2 (1995) 69-87.

Niehoff, Maren R. "What is in a Name? Philo's Mystical Philosophy of Language." In *Jewish Studies Quarterly* 2 (1995) 220-252.

Nigal, Gedalyah. *Magic, Mysticism, and Hasidism: The Supernatural in Jewish Thought*. Northvale, NJ: Jason Aronson, 1994.

Nohrnberg, James. *Like Unto Moses: The Constituting of an Interruption*. Bloomington: Indiana University Press, 1995.

Noy, Dov. *Moroccan Jewish Folktales*. New York: Herzl Press, 1966.

Nulman, Macy. *The Encyclopedia of Jewish Prayer: Ashkenazic and Sephardic Rites*. Northvale, NJ: Jason Aronson, 1993.

Och, Bernard. "The Garden of Eden: From Creation to Covenant." In *Judaism* 37:2 (1988) 143-156.

Odeberg, Hugo. *3 Enoch or The Hebrew Book of Enoch*. Cambridge: Cambridge University Press, 1928.

Oesterley, W. O. E. and G. H. Box. *A Short Survey of the Literature of Rabbinical and Mediaeval Judaism*. New York: Burt Franklin, 1973.

Otzen, Benedikt, Hans Gottlieb, and Knud Jeppesen. *Myths in the Old Testament*. Trans. Frederick Cryer. London: SCM Press, 1980.

Ozick, Cynthia. *Puttermesser Papers*. New York: Trafalgar Square, 1997.

Page, Sydney H.T. *Powers of Evil: A Biblical Study of Satan and Demons*. Grand Rapids, MI: Baker Book House, 1995.

Pagels, Elaine. *The Origin of Satan*. New York: Vintage Books, 1995.

Pagels, Elaine. "The Social History of Satan, The 'Intimate Enemy': A Preliminary Sketch." In *Harvard Theological Review* 84:2 (1991) 105-128.

Pardes, Ilana. *The Biography of Ancient Israel: National Narratives in the Bible*. Berkeley: University of California Press, 2000.

Parker, S. B. "The Beginning of the Reign of God—Psalm 82 as Myth and Liturgy. In *Revue Biblique* 102:4 (1995) 532-559.

Patai, Raphael. "Biblical Figures as Alchemists." In *Hebrew Union College Annual* 54 (1983) 195-229.

Patai, Raphael, with James Hornell and John M. Lundquist. *The Children of Noah: Jewish Seafaring in Ancient Times*. Princeton, NJ: Princeton University Press, 1998.

Patai, Raphael. *Gates to the Old City: A Book of Jewish Legends*. New York: Avon Books, 1980.

Patai, Raphael. *The Hebrew Goddess*. Detroit: Wayne State University Press, 1978.

Patai, Raphael. "Hebrew Installation Rites: A Contribution to the Study of Ancient Near Eastern-African Culture Contact." In *Hebrew Union College Annual* 20 (1947) 143-225.

Patai, Raphael. *The Jewish Alchemists: A History and Source Book*. Princeton, NJ: Princeton University Press, 1994.

Patai, Raphael. *Man and Temple in Ancient Jewish Myth and Ritual*. New York: Ktav Publishing House, 1967.

Patai, Raphael. *The Messiah Texts*. Detroit: Wayne State University Press, 1979.

Patai, Raphael. *Myth and Modern Man*. Englewood Cliffs, NJ: Prentice Hall, 1972.

Patai, Raphael. *On Jewish Folklore*. Detroit: Wayne State University Press, 1983.

Patai, Raphael. *Robert Graves and the Hebrew Myths: A Collaboration*. Detroit: Wayne State University Press, 1992.

Patai, Raphael. *The Seed of Abraham: Jews and Arabs in Contact and Conflict*. Salt Lake City, UT: University of Utah Press, 1986.

Patai, Raphael, Francis Lee Utley, and Dov Noy. *Studies in Biblical and Jewish Folklore*. Bloomington: Indiana University Press, 1960.

Pearson, Birger A. *Gnosticism, Judaism, and Egyptian Christianity*. Minneapolis: Fortress Press, 1990.

Pedaya, Haviva. "The Divinity as Place and Time and the Holy Place in Jewish Mysticism." In *Sacred Space*." Ed. by Joshua Prawer, Benjamin Z. Kedar and R. J. Zwi Werblowsky. New York: New York University Press, 1996, 84-111.

Peli, Pinchas H. *The Jewish Sabbath: A Renewed Encounter*. New York: Schocken Books, 1988.

Peretz, I. L. *The Book of Fire*. New York: Thomas Yoseloff, 1959.

Peters, F. E. *Jerusalem*. Princeton, NJ: Princeton University Press, 1985.

Petuchowski, Jakob J. *Theology and Poetry: Studies in the Medieval Piyyut*. London: Routledge and Kegan Paul, 1978.

Pinero, A. "Angels and Demons in the Greek *Life of Adam and Eve*." In *Journal for the Study of Judaism* 24:2 (1993) 191-214.

Plaskow, Judith. *Standing Again at Sinai: Judaism from a Feminist Perspective*. New York: Harper & Row, 1990.

Polen, Nehemia. *The Holy Fire: The Teachings of Rabbi Kalonymus Kalman Shapira, the Rebbe of the Warsaw Ghetto*. Northvale, NJ: Jason Aronson, 1994.

Pollack, Herman. *Jewish Folkways in Germanic Lands (1648-1806): Studies in Aspects of Daily Life*. Cambridge, MA: M.I.T. Press, 1971.

Polliack, Meira. "Ezekiel 1 and Its Role in Subsequent Jewish Mystical Thought and Tradition." In *European Judaism* 32:1 (1999) 70-78.

Posèq, Avigdor. "The Mythic Perspective in Early Jewish Art." In *Journal of Jewish Studies* 40:2 (1989) 213-224.

Primus, Charles. "The Borders of Judaism: The Land of Israel in Early Rabbinic Judaism." In *The Land of Israel: Jewish Perspectives*. Ed. Lawrence A. Hoffman. Notre Dame, IN: University of Notre Dame Press, 1986, 97-108.

Purvis, James D. *The Samaritan Pentateuch and the Origin of the Samaritan Sect*. Cambridge, MA: Harvard University Press, 1968.

Quispel, Gilles. "The Demiurge in the Apocryphon of John." In *Nag Hammadi and Gnosis*. Ed. R. McL. Wilson. Leiden: E. J. Brill, 1978, 1-33.

Rabin, Chaim. *Qumran Studies*. London: Oxford, 1957.

Rajak, Tessa. "Moses in Ethopia: Legend and Literature." In *Journal of Jewish Studies* 29:2 (1978) 111-122.

Rankin, Oliver Shaw. *Jewish Religious Polemic*. New York: Ktav Publishing House, 1970.

Rapaport, Samuel. *A Treasury of the Midrash*. New York: Ktav Publishing House, 1968.

Raphael, Marc Lee, ed. *Agendas for the Study of Midrash in the Twenty-First Century*. Williamsburg, VA: College of William and Mary, 1999.

Raphael, Simcha Paull. *Jewish Views of the Afterlife*. Northvale, NJ: Jason Aronson, 1994.

Rapoport-Albert, Ada. *Hasidism Reconsidered*. London: Vallentine Mitchell, 1996.

Rappel, Yoel. *Yearning for the Holy Land: Hasidic Tales of Israel*. Trans. Shmuel Himmelstein. New York: Adama Books, 1986.

Rappoport, Angelo S. *The Folklore of the Jews*. London: The Soncino Press, 1937.

Reddish, Mitchell G., ed. *Apocalyptic Literature: A Reader*. Peabody, MA: Hendrickson Publishers, 1995.

Reeves, John C. *Jewish Lore in Manichaean Cosmogony: Studies in the Book of Giants Traditions*. Cincinatti: Hebrew Union College Press, 1992.

Reeves, John C., ed. *Tracing the Threads: Studies in the Vitality of Jewish Pseudepigrapha*. Atlanta: Scholars Press, 1994.

Reznick, Leibel. *The Holy Temple Revisited*. Northvale, NJ: Jason Aronson, 1993.

Robbins, Ellen. "Time-Telling in Ritual and Myth." *The Journal of Jewish Thought and Philosophy*. 6 (1997) 71-88.

Robinson, Ira. "Messianic Prayer Vigils in Jerusalem in the Early Eighteenth Century." In *Jewish Quarterly Review* 72:1 (1981) 32-42.

Robinson, H. Wheeler. "The Council of Yahweh." In *Journal of Theological Studies* 45 (1944) 151-157.

Robinson, James M., ed. *The Nag Hammadi Library: A Translation of the Gnostic Scriptures*. New York: HarperCollins, 1981.

Robinson, S. E. "The Apocryphal Story of Melchizedek." In *Journal for the Study of Judaism* 18:1 (1987) 26-39.

Rohrbacher-Sticker, Claudia. "From Sense to Nonsense, From Incantation Prayer to Magical Spell." In *Jewish Studies Quarterly* 3 (1996) 24-46.

Rosenberg, Roy A., trans. *The Anatomy of God*. New York: Ktav Publishing House, 1973.

Rosenberg, Roy A. "The God Sedeq." In *Hebrew Union College Annual* 36 (1965) 161-177.

Rosenberg, Shalom. "Exile and Redemption in Jewish Thought in the Sixteenth Century: Contending Conceptions." In *Jewish Thought in the Sixteenth Century*. Ed. Bernard Dov Cooperman. Cambridge, MA: Harvard University Press, 1983, 399-430.

Rosenberg, Shalom. *Good and Evil in Jewish Thought*. Trans. John Glucker. Tel Aviv: MOD Books, 1989.

Rosenthal, Gilbert S. "Omnipotence, Omniscience and a Finite God." In *Judaism* 39:1 (1990) 55-72.

Rosenbaum, Thane. *The Golems of Gotham*. New York: Perennial, 2003.

Rosman, Moshe. *Founder of Hasidism: A Quest for the Historical Baal Shem Tov*. Berkeley: University of California Press, 1996.

Rosner, Fred, ed. *Moses Maimonides' Treatise on Resurrection*. Northvale: Jason Aronson, 1997.

Ross, Dan. *Acts of Faith: A Journey to the Fringes of Jewish Identity*. New York: St. Martin's Press, 1982.

Rossof, Dovid. *Safed: The Mystical City*. Jerusalem: Sha'ar Books, 1991.

Rost, Leonhard. *Judaism Outside of the Hebrew Canon: An Introduction to the Documents*. Trans. David E. Green. Nashville: Abingdon, 1971.

Roth, Cecil, ed. *Encyclopedia Judaica*. Jerusalem: Keter, 1971.

Rowland, Christopher. "The Visions of God in Apocalyptic Literature." In *Journal for the Study of Judaism* 10:2 (1979) 139-154.

Royse, James R. "Cain's Expulsion From Paradise: the Text of Philo's Congr 171." In *Jewish Quarterly Review* 79 (1989) 219-225.

Rubenstein, Jeffrey L. "From Mythic Motifs to Sustained Myth: The Revision of Rabbinic Traditions in Medieval Midrashim." In *HTR* 89:2 (1996) 141-159.

Rubenstein, Jeffrey L., trans. *Rabbinic Stories*. Mahwah, NJ: Paulist Press, 2002.

Rubin, Nissan and Admiel Kosman. "The Clothing of the Primordial Adam as a Symbol of Apocalyptic Time in Midrashic Sources." In *Hebrew Theological Review* 90:2 (1997) 155-174.

Rudavsky, T. M. *Time Matters: Time, Creation, and Cosmology in Medieval Jewish Philosophy*. Albany: State University of New York Press, 2000.

Ruderman, David B. "Hope Against Hope: Jewish and Christian Messianic Expectations in the Late Middle Ages." In *Essential Papers on Jewish Culture in Renaissance and Baroque Italy*. Ed. David B. Ruderman. New York and London: New York University Press, 1992, 299-323.

Ruderman, David B. *Kabbalah, Magic, and Science: The Cultural Universe of a Sixteenth-Century Jewish Physician*. Cambridge, MA: Harvard University Press, 1988.

Ruderman, David B. "Unicorns, Great Beasts and the Marvelous Variety of Things in Nature in the Thought of Abraham B. Hananiah Yagel." In *Jewish Thought in the Seventeenth Century*. Ed. Isadore Twersky and Bernard Septimus. Cambridge, MA: Harvard University Press, 1987, 343-364.

Ruderman, David B., trans. *A Valley of Vision: The Heavenly Journey of Abraham ben Hananiah Yagel*. Philadelphia: University of Pennsylvania Press, 1990.

Rudolph, Kurt. *Gnosis: The Nature and History of Gnosticism*. San Francisco: HarperSanFrancisco, 1987.

Runes, Dagobert D. *Of God, the Devil and the Jews*. New York: Philosophical Library, 1952.

Rush, Barbara. *The Book of Jewish Women's Tales*. Northvale, NJ: Jason Aronson, 1994.

Russell, Jeffrey Burton. *A History of Heaven: The Singing Silence*. Princeton, NJ: Princeton University Press, 1997.

Sabar, Yona, trans. *The Folk Literature of the Kurdistani Jews: An Anthology*. New Haven, CT: Yale University Press, 1982.

Sadeh, Pinchas. *Jewish Folktales*. Trans. Hillel Halkin. New York: Doubleday, 1989.

Safran, Alexandre. *Israel in Time and Space: Essays on Basic Themes in Jewish Spiritual Thought*. Trans. M. Pater and E. M. Sandle. Spring Valley, NY: Philipp Feldheim, 1987.

Samuelson, Norbert M. "Creation in Medieval Philosophical, Rabbinic Commentaries." In *Fox* 2 (1989) 231-259.

Samuelson, Norbert M. *Judaism and the Doctrine of Creation*. Cambridge: Cambridge University Press, 1994.

Samuelson, Norbert M. "Maimonides Doctrine of Creation." In *HTR* 84:3 (1991) 249-271.

Sanders, E. P. *Testament of Abraham*. In *The Old Testament Pseudepigrapha*. Ed. J. Charlesworth. Garden City, NY: Doubleday, 1983-85.

Sanders, Ronald. *Lost Tribes and Promised Lands: The Origins of American Racism*. Boston: Little, Brown, 1978.

Sandmel, Samuel. *Philo of Alexandria: An Introduction*. New York: Oxford University Press, 1979.

Sanua, Victor D., ed. *Fields of Offerings: Studies in Honor of Raphael Patai*. Cranbury, NJ: Associated University Presses, 1983.

Saperstein, Marc. *Decoding the Rabbis: A Thirteenth Century Commentary on the Aggadah*. Cambridge: Harvard University Press, 1980.

Saperstein, Marc, ed. *Essential Papers on Messianic Movements and Personalities in Jewish History*. New York and London: New York University Press, 1992.

Sarachek, Joseph. *The Doctrine of the Messiah in Medieval Jewish Literature*. New York: Hermon Press, 1932.

Sarna, Nahum M. *Exploring Exodus: The Origins of Biblical Israel*. New York: Schocken Books, 1986.

Sarna, Nahum M. *Studies in Biblical Interpretation*. Philadelphia: Jewish Publication Society, 2000.

Sarna, Nahum M. *Understanding Genesis: The Heritage of Biblical Israel*. New York: Schocken Books, 1966.

Satterthwaite, Philip E., Richard S. Hess, and Gordon J. Wenham, eds. *The Lord's Anointed: Interpretation of Old Testament Messianic Texts*. Grand Rapids, MI: Baker Book House, 1995.

Sawyer, Deborah F. "Heterodoxy and Censorship: Some Critical Remarks on Wertheimer's Edition of *Midrash Aleph Bet*." In *Journal of Jewish Studies* 42:1 (1991) 115-121.

Sawyer, Deborah F. *Midrash Aleph Beth*. Atlanta, GA: Scholars Press, 1993.

Schäfer, Peter. "Daughter, Sister, Bride, and Mother: Images of the Femininity of God in the Early Kabbala." In *Journal of the American Academy of Religion* 68:2 (2000) 221-242.

Schäfer, Peter. *The Hidden and Manifest God: Some Major Themes in Early Jewish Mysticism*. Albany: State University of New York Press, 1992.

Schäfer, Peter and Joseph Dan. *Gershom Scholem's "Major Trends in Jewish Mysticism" 50 Years After: Proceedings of the Sixth International Conference of Jewish Mysticism*. Tubingen: J. C. B. Mohr, 1993.

Schäfer, Peter. "Jewish Magic Literature in Late Antiquity and Early Middle Ages." In *Journal of Jewish Studies* 41:1 (1990) 75-91.

Schäfer, Peter. "The Magic of the Golem: The Early Development of the Golem Legend." In *Journal of Jewish Studies* 46:1-2 (1995) 249-261.

Schäfer, Peter. "Merkavah Mysticism and Magic." In *Gershom Scholem's "Major Trends in Jewish Mysticism" 50 Years After: Proceedings of the Sixth International Conference on the History of Jewish Mysticism*. Ed. Peter Schäfer and Joseph Dan. Tubingen: J. C. B. Mohr, 1993, 59-83.

Schäfer, Peter. "New Testament and Hekhalot Literature: The Journey into Heaven in Paul and in Merkavah Mysticism." In *Journal of Jewish Studies* 35:1 (1984) 19-35.

Schäfer, Peter. "Tradition and Redaction in Hekhalot Literature." In *Journal for the Study of Judaism* 14:2 (1983) 172-181.

Schatz Uffenheimer, Rivka. *Hasidism as Mysticism: Quietistic Elements in Eighteenth Century Hasidic Thought*. Trans. Yonathan Chipman. Princeton, NJ: Princeton University Press, 1993.

Schaya, Leo. *The Universal Meaning of the Kabbalah*. Trans. Nancy Pearson. Secaucus, NJ: University Books, 1972.

Schimmel, Harry C. *The Oral Law: A Study of the Rabbinic Contribution to Torah She-Be-Al-Peh*. New York: Philip Feldheim, 1971.

Schirmann, Jefim. "The Battle Between Behemoth and Leviathan According to an Ancient Hebrew *Piyyut*." In *Proceedings of the Israel Academy of Sciences and Humanities* 4 (1969-1970) 327-369.

Schochet, J. Immanuel. *Mashiach: The Principle of Mashiach and the Messianic Era in Jewish Law and Tradition*. New York: S.I.E., 1992.

Schochet, J. Immanuel. *Mystical Concepts in Chassidism: An Introduction to Kabbalistic Concepts and Doctrines*. Brooklyn, NY: Kehot, 1979.

Scholem, Gershom. "The Concept of the Astral Body. In *On the Mystical Shape of the Godhead*. New York: Schocken Books, 1991, 251-273.

Scholem, Gershom. *Jewish Gnosticism, Merkabah Mysticism, and Talmudic Tradition*. New York: Jewish Theological Seminary, 1965.

Scholem, Gershom. *Major Trends in Jewish Mysticism*. New York: Schocken Books, 1961.

Scholem, Gershom. *The Messianic Idea in Judaism and Other Essays on Jewish Spirituality*. New York: Schocken Books, 1971.

Scholem, Gershom. *On the Kabbalah and Its Symbolism*. New York: Schocken Books, 1965.

Scholem, Gershom. *On Jews and Judaism in Crisis: Selected Essays*. New York: Schocken Books, 1976.

Scholem, Gershom. *On the Mystical Shape of the Godhead: Basic Concepts in the Kabbalah*. New York: Schocken Books, 1991.

Scholem, Gershom. "The Idea of the Golem." In *On the Kabbalah and Its Symbolism*. New York, Schocken Books, 1965, 158-204.

Scholem, Gershom. *On the Possibility of Jewish Mysticism in Our Time and Other Essays*. Philadelphia: Jewish Publication Society, 1997.

Scholem, Gershom. *Origins of the Kabbalah*. Philadelphia: The Jewish Publication Society, 1987.

Scholem, Gershom. *Sabbatai Sevi: The Mystical Messiah*. Princeton, NJ: Princeton University Press, 1973.

Scholem, Gershom, ed. *Zohar: The Book of Splendor*. New York: Schocken Books, 1949.

Schram, Peninnah. *Jewish Stories One Generation Tells Another*. Northvale, NJ: Jason Aronson, 1987.

Schram, Peninnah. *Stories Within Stories: From the Jewish Oral Tradition*. Northvale, NJ: Jason Aronson, 2000.

Schram, Peninnah. *Tales of Elijah the Prophet*. Northvale, NJ: Jason Aronson, 1991.

Schrire, T. *Hebrew Amulets: Their Decipherment and Interpretation*. London: Routledge & Kegan Paul, 1966.

Schroer, Silvia. *Wisdom Has Built Her House: Studies on the Figure of Sophia in the Bible*. Collegeville, MN: The Liturgical Press, 2000.

Schultz, Joseph P. "Angelic Opposition to the Ascension of Moses and the Revelation of the Law." In *Jewish Quarterly Review* 61:4 (1970-1971) 282-307.

Schultz, Joseph P. and Lois Spatz. *Sinai & Olympus: A Comparative Study*. Lanham, MD: University Press of America, 1995.

Schwartz, Dov. "Divine Immanence in Medieval Jewish Philosophy." In *Journal of Jewish Thought and Philosophy* 3 (1994) 249-278.

Schwartz, Howard. "The Aggadic Tradition." In *Origins of Judaism*. Ed. by Jacob Neusner. New York: Garland, 1990, vol. 1, part 3, 446-463.

Schwartz, Howard. *Elijah's Violin & Other Jewish Fairy Tales*. New York: Harper & Row, 1983.

Schwartz, Howard. *The Four Who Entered Paradise.* Northvale, NJ: Jason Aronson, 1995. Introduction and Commentary by Marc Bregman.

Schwartz, Howard. *Gabriel's Palace: Jewish Mystical Tales.* New York: Oxford University Press, 1993.

Schwartz, Howard. *Gates to the New City: A Treasury of Modern Jewish Tales.* New York: Avon Books, 1983.

Schwartz, Howard. "Jewish Tales of the Supernatural." *Judaism* 36:3 (1987) 229-351.

Schwartz, Howard. *Lilith's Cave: Jewish Tales of the Supernatural.* New York: Harper & Row, 1988.

Schwartz, Howard. "Mermaid and Siren: The Polar Roles of Lilith and Eve." In *Reimagining the Bible: The Storytelling of the Rabbis.* New York: Oxford University Press, 1998, 56-67.

Schwartz, Howard. *Miriam's Tambourine: Jewish Folktales from Around the World.* New York: The Free Press, 1986.

Schwartz, Howard. "The Mythology of Judaism." In *The Seductiveness of Jewish Myth: Challenge or Response,* edited by S. Daniel Breslauer. Albany: State Univesity of New York Press, 1997, 11-25.

Schwartz, Howard. "The Quest for Jerusalem." In *Judaism,* 46:2 (1997) 208-217.

Schwartz, Howard. "The Quest for the Lost Princess." In *Opening the Inner Gates: New Paths in Kabbalah and Psychology.* Ed. by Edward Hoffman. Boston: Shambhala, 1995, 20-46.

Schwartz, Howard. "Rabbi Nachman of Bratslav: Forerunner of Modern Jewish Literature." In *Judaism* 31 (1982) 211-224.

Schwartz, Howard. *Reimagining the Bible: The Storytelling of the Rabbis.* New York: Oxford University Press, 1998.

Schwarz, Leo, ed. *The Menorah Treasury: Harvest of Half a Century.* Philadelphia: The Jewish Publication Society of America, 1964.

Schwarzbaum, Haim. *Jewish Folklore Between East and West: Collected Papers.* Ed. Eli Yassif. Beer-Sheva: Ben-Gurion University of the Negev Press, 1989.

Schwarzbaum, Haim. *Studies in Jewish and World Folklore.* Berlin: Walter de Gruyter, 1968.

Seale, Morris S. *The Desert Bible: Nomadic Tribal Culture and Old Testament Interpretation.* New York: St. Martin's Press, 1974.

Segal, Alan F. *Two Powers in Heaven: Early Rabbinic Reports about Christianity and Gnosticism.* Leiden: E. J. Brill, 1977.

Segal, Eliezer. "Sarah and Iscah: Method and Message in Midrashic Tradition." In *Jewish Quarterly Review* 82 (1992) 417-429.

Segal, Robert A., ed. *The Myth and Ritual Theory: An Anthology.* Malden, MA: Blackwell Publishers, 1998.

Segal, Robert A., ed. *Philosophy, Religious Studies, and Myth.* In *Theories of Myth,* vol. 3. New York: Garland Publishing, 1996.

Seghi, Laya Firestone. "Glimpsing the Moon: The Feminine Principle in Kabbalah." In *Opening the Inner Gates: New Paths in Kabbalah and Psychology.* Ed. Edward Hoffman. Boston: Shambhala, 1995, 133-159.

Sender, Yitzchak. *The Commentators' Gift of Torah: Exploring the Treasures of the Oral and Written Torah.* Spring Valley, NY: Philip Feldheim, 1993.

Shaked, Shaul, David Shulman, and Gedaliahu G. Stroumsa, eds. *Gilgul: Essays on Transformation, Revolution and Permanence in the History of Religions, Dedicated to R. J. Zwi Werblowsky.* Leiden: E. J. Brill, 1987.

Shaked, Shaul. "'Peace be Upon You, Exalted Angels': on Hekhalot, Liturgy and Incantation Bowls." In *Jewish Studies Quarterly* 2 (1995) 197-219.

Shamir, Yehuda. "Mystic Jerusalem." In *Studia Mystica* 3:2 (1980) 50-60.

Shapira, Avraham. "A Divided Heart and a Man's Double." In *Journal of Jewish Thought and Philosophy* 1 (1991) 115-139.

Shapiro, Marc B. "Suicide and the World to Come." In *AJS Review* 18:2 (1993) 245-263.

Sharot, Stephen. *Messianism, Mysticism, and Magic: A Sociological Analysis of Jewish Religious Movements*. Chapel Hill: University of North Carolina Press, 1982.

Sheridan, Mark, ed. *Ancient Christian Commentary on Scripture: Old Testament II*. Downers Grove, IL, InterVarsity Press, 2002.

Sherwin, Byron L. "Corpus Domini: Traces of the New Testament in East European Hasidism," *The Heythrop Journal*. 35:3 (1994) 267-280.

Sherwin, Bryon L. "The Exorcist's Role in Jewish Tradition." In *Occult* Oct. 1975.

Sherwin, Byron L. *The Golem Legend: Origins and Implications*. Lanham, MD: University Press of America, 1985.

Sherwin, Byron L. *Golems Among Us: How a Jewish Legend Can Help Us Navigate the Biotech Century*. Chicago: Ivan R. Dee, 2004.

Sherwin, Byron L. *Mystical Theology and Social Dissent: The Life and Works of Judah Loew of Prague*. The Littman Library of Jewish Civilization. East Brunswick, NJ: Associated University Presses, 1982.

Sherwood, Frances. *The Book of Spendor*. New York: W. W. Norton, 2002.

Shimoff, Sandra R. "Gardens: From Eden to Jerusalem." In *Journal for the Study of Judaism* 26:2 (1995) 145-155.

Shtull-Trauring, Simcha, ed. *Letters from Beyond the Sambatyon: The Myth of the Ten Lost Tribes*. New York: MAXIMA New Media, 1997.

Shuchat, Wilfred. *The Creation According to the Midrash Rabbah*. Jerusalem: Devorah Publishing, 2002.

Shulman, Yaacov David. *The Sefirot: Ten Emanations of Divine Power*. Northvale, NJ: Jason Aronson, 1996.

Silberman, Neil Asher. *Heavenly Powers: Unraveling the Secret History of Kabbalah*. New York: Grosset/Putnam, 1998.

Silberstein, Laurence J. and Robert L. Cohn, eds. *The Other in Jewish Thought and History: Constructions of Jewish Culture and Identity*. New York: New York University Press, 1994.

Silver, Abba Hillel. *A History of Messianic Speculation in Israel: From the First through the Seventeenth Centuries*. Boston: Beacon Press, 1959.

Silver, Daniel J. *Maimonidean Criticism and the Maimonidean Controversy 1180-1240*. Leiden: E. J. Brill, 1965.

Silver, Daniel J. *The Story of Scripture: From Oral Tradition to Written Word*. New York: Basic Books, 1990.

Silverman, Althea O. *The Harp of David: Legends of Mount Zion*. Hartford: Hartmore Press, 1964.

Singer, Isaac Bashevis. *The Golem*. New York: Farrar, Straus & Giroux, 1982.

Slomovic, Eliezer. "Patterns of Midrashic Impact on the Rabbinic Midrashic Tale." In *Journal for the Study of Judaism* 19:1 (1988) 61- 90.

Slonimsky, Henry. "On Reading the Midrash." In *Essays*. Cincinnati: Hebrew Union College Press, 1978, 3-10.

Slonimsky, Henry. "The Philosophy Implicit in the Midrash." In *Essays*. Cincinnati: Hebrew Union College Press, 1978, 11-84.

Smelik, William F. "On Mystical Transformation of the Righteous into Light in Judaism." In *Journal for the Study of Judaism* 26:2 (1995) 122-144.

Smith, George. *The Chaldean Account of Genesis*. Minneapolis: Wizards Book Shelf, 1977.

Smith, Mark S. *The Early History of God: Yahweh and the Other Deities in Ancient Israel*. New York: Harper & Row, 1990.

Smith, Mark S. "Myth and Mythmaking in Canaan and Ancient Israel." In *Civilizations of the Ancient Near East*. Vol. 3. Ed. Jack M. Sassoon. New York: Charles Scribner's Sons, 1995, 2031-2041.

Smith, Mark S. *The Origins of Biblical Monotheism: Israel's Polytheistic Background and the Ugaritic Texts*. New York: Oxford University Press, 2001.

Smith, Morton. "The Image of God: Notes on the Hellenization of Judaism, with Especial Reference to Goodenough's Work on Jewish Symbols." In *Bulletin of the John Rylands Library* 40:2 (1958) 473-512.

Smith, Morton. "Observations on *Hekhalot Rabbati*. In *Biblical and Other Studies*. Ed. Alexander Altmann. Cambridge: Harvard University Press, 1963, 142-160.

Smith, Morton. "On the Shape of God and the Humanity of Gentiles." In *Religions in Antiquity: Essays in Memory of Erwin Ramsdell Goodenough*. Ed. Jacob Neusner. Leiden: E. J. Brill, 1970, 315-326.

Smith, Morton and S. J. D. Cohen, eds. *Studies in the Cult of Yahweh*. 2 vols. Leiden: E. J. Brill, 1996.

Smith, Yonathan Z. *Prayer of Joseph*. In *The Old Testament Pseudepigrapha*, edited by J. Charlesworth. Garden City, NY: Doubleday, 1983-85.

Snowman, Joel, trans. *The Legends of Israel: Translated from the Hebrew of J. B. Levner*. London: James Clarke, 1946.

Sohn, Seock-Tae. *The Divine Election of Israel*. Grand Rapids, MI: William B. Eerdmans, 1991.

de Sola Pool, David. "The Centrality of the Holy Land in Jewish Life." In *The Jewish Library*. Vol. 2: The Folk. Ed. Leo Jung. London: The Soncino Press, 1968, 107-117.

Sparks, H. F. D., ed. The Apocryphal Old Testament. Oxford: Clarendon Press, 1984.

Spector, Sheila A. *Jewish Mysticism: An Annotated Bibliography on the Kabbalah in English*. New York: Garland Publishing, 1984.

Sperber, Daniel. *Midrash Yerushalem: A Metaphysical History of Jerusalem*. Jerusalem: Ben-Zvi, 1982.

Sperber, Daniel. "On Sealing the Abysses." In *Magic and Folklore in Rabbinic Literature*. Ramat Gan: Bar-Ilan University Press, 1994.

Sperling, Harry and Maurice Simon, tanrs. *The Zohar*. 5 vols. London: Soncino, 1933.

Spero, Shubert (Shlomo). "They Are No Longer, For God Has Taken Them." In *Jewish Bible Quarterly* 22:4 (1994) 221-227.

Spiegel, Shalom. *The Last Trial, On the Legends and Lore of the Command to Abraham to Offer Isaac as a Sacrifice: The Akedah*. New York: Schocken Books, 1967.

Sproul, Barbara C. *Primal Myths: Creating the World*. New York: Harper & Row, 1979.

Stern, David. "*Imitatio Hominis*: Anthropomorphism and the Character(s) of God in Rabbinic Literature." In *Prooftexts* 12 (1992) 151-174.

Stern, David. *Midrash and Theory: Ancient Jewish Exegesis and Contemporary Literary Studies*. Evanston, IL: Northwestern University Press, 1996.

Stern, David. *Parables in Midrash: Narrative and Exegesis in Rabbinic Literature*. Cambridge: Harvard University Press, 1994.

Stern, David and Mark Jay Mirsky, eds. *Rabbinic Fantasies: Imaginative Narratives from Classical Hebrew Literature*. Philadelphia: The Jewish Publication Society, 1990.

Stern, Josef. "The Fall and Rise of Myth in Ritual: Maimonides verus Nachmanides on the *Huqqim*, Astrology, and the War Against Idolatry." In *The Journal of Jewish Thought & Philosophy* 6 (1997) 185-263.

Stewart, R. J. *The Elements of Creation Myth*. Longmead, England: Element Books, 1989.

Stone, Michael E. *Adam's Contract with Satan: The Legend of the Cheirograph of Adam*. Bloomington: Indiana University Press, 2002.

Stone, Michael E. "The Armenian Vision of Ezekiel." In *Harvard Theological Review* 79:1 (1986) 261-269.

Stone, Michael E. and John Strugnell, trs. *The Books of Elijah, Parts 1-2.* Missoula, MT: Scholars Press, 1979.

Stone, Michael E. and Theodore A. Bergren, eds. *Biblical Figures Outside the Bible.* Harrisburg, PA: Trinity Press International, 1998.

Stone, Michael E. "The Book of Enoch and Judaism in the Third Century B.C.E." In *Catholic Biblical Quarterly* 40 (1978) 479-92.

Stone, Michael E. "The Concept of the Messiah in IV Ezra." In *Religions in Antiquity: Essays in Memory of Erwin Ramsdell Goodenough.* Ed. Jacob Neusner. Leiden: E. J. Brill, 1968, 295-312.

Stone, Michael E. "Eschatology, Remythologization, and Cosmic Aporia." In *The Origins and Diversity of Axial Age Civilizations.* Ed. S. N. Eisenstadt. Albany: State University of New York Press, 1986, 295-312.

Stone, Michael E. "The Fall of Satan and Adam's Penance: Three Notes on *The Books of Adam and Eve.*" In *Journal of Theological Studies* 44:1 (1993) 143-156.

Stone, Michael E. "Features of the Eschatology of IV Ezra." Doctoral dissertation. Harvard University, 1965.

Stone, Michael E. *A History of the Literature of Adam and Eve.* Atlanta: Scholars Press, 1992.

Stone, Michael E., ed. *Jewish Writings of the Second Temple Period: Apocrypha, Pseudepigrapha, Qumran Sectarian Writings, Philo, Josephus.* Philadelphia: Fortress Press, 1984.

Stone, Michael E. "New Discoveries Relating to the Armenian Adam Books." In *Journal for the Study of the Pseudepigrapha* 5 (1989) 101-109.

Stone, Michael E., ed. *Penitence of Adam.* Lovanii: 1981.

Stone, Michael E., trans. *The Testament of Abraham: The Greek Recensions.* Missoula, MT: Scholars Press, 1972.

Strack, H. L. and Gunter Stemberger. *Introduction to the Talmud and Midrash.* Trans. Markus Bockmuehl. Minneapolis: Fortress Press, 1992.

Stroumsa, Gedaliahu G. "Form(s) of God: Some Notes on Metatron and Christ." In *Harvard Theological Review* 76:3 (1983) 269-288.

Stroumsa, Gedaliahu G. "Gnosis and Judaism in Nineteenth Century Christian Thought." In *Journal of Jewish Thought and Philosophy* 2 (1992) 45-62.

Strousma, Gedaliahu G. "Jewish Myth and Ritual and the Beginnings of Comparative Religion: The Case of Richard Simon." In *The Journal of Jewish Thought and Philosophy* 6 (1997) 19-35.

Strugnell, John. "The Angelic Liturgy at Qumran." In *Vetus Testamentum Supplements* 7 (1960) 318-345.

Suter, David. "Fallen Angel, Fallen Priest: The Problem of Family Purity in *1 Enoch* 6-16." In *Hebrew Union College Annual* 50 (1979) 115-135.

Swartz, Michael D. "'*Alay Le-Shabbeah*: A Liturgical Prayer in *Ma'aseh Merkabah.*" In *Jewish Quarterly Review* 77:2-3 (1986-1987) 179-190.

Swartz, Michael D. "Book and Tradition in Hekhalot and Magical Literatures." In *Journal of Jewish Thought and Philosophy* 3 (1994) 189-229.

Swartz, Michael D. "'Like the Ministering Angels': Ritual and Purity in Early Jewish Mysticism and Magic." In *AJS Review* 19:2 (1994) 135-167.

Swartz, Michael D. *Mystical Prayer in Ancient Judaism: An Analysis of Ma'aseh Merkavah.* Tubingen: J. C. B. Mohr, 1992.

Swartz, Michael D. "Ritual about Myth about Ritual: Towards an Understanding of the *Avodah* in the Rabbinic Period." In *The Journal of Jewish Thought and Philosophy* 6 (1997) 135-155.

Tabor, James D. "'Returning to the Divinity': Josephus's Portrayal of the Disappearances of Enoch, Elijah, and Moses." In *Journal of Biblical Literature* 108:2 (1989) 225-238.

Talmon, Shemaryahu. "The Signification of Jerusalem in Biblical Thought." In *The Real and Ideal Jerusalem in Jewish, Christian and Islamic Art*. Ed. Bianca Kuhnel. Jerusalem: Journal of the Center of Jewish Art, 1998, 1-12.

TANAKH: A New Translation of the Holy Scriptures According to the Traditional Hebrew Text. Philadelphia: The Jewish Publication Society, 1985.

Taylor, J. Glen. *Yahweh and the Sun: Biblical and Archeological Evidence for Sun Worship in Ancient Israel*. Sheffield: JSOT Press, 1993.

Telsner, David. *The Kaddish: Its History and Significance*. Jerusalem: Tal Orot Institute, 1995.

Terrien, Samuel. "The Omphalos Myth and Hebrew Religion." In *Vetus Testamentum* 20 (1970) 315-338.

Teubal, Savina J. *Sarah the Priestess: The First Matriarch of Genesis*. Athens, OH: Swallow Press/Ohio University Press, 1984.

Thackeray, H. St. J., trans. *Josephus: Jewish Antiquities*. Loeb Classical Library. Cambridge, MA: Harvard University Press, 1995.

Thierberger, Frederic. *The Great Rabbi Loew of Prague: His Life and Work and the Legend of the Golem*. London: Farrar, Straus and Young, 1955.

Thompson, R. Campbell, tr. *The Epic of Gilgamesh*. [add info]

Thompson, Thomas L. *The Mythic Past: Biblical Archaeology and the Myth of Israel*. London: Random House, 1999.

Tishby, Isaiah. "Gnostic Doctrines in Sixteenth Century Jewish Mysticism." In *Journal of Jewish Studies* 6:3 (1980) 146-152.

Tishby, Isaiah. "Mythological versus Systematic Trends in Kabbalah." In *Binah: Jewish Intellectual History in the Middle Ages*. Vol. 2. Ed. Joseph Dan. Westport, CT: Praeger, 1989, 121-129.

Tishby, Isaiah and Fischel Lachower. *The Wisdom of the Zohar: An Anthology of Texts*. 3 vols. Trans. David Goldstein. New York: Oxford University Press, 1989.

Tirosh-Rothschild, Hava. "Continuity and Revision in the Study of Kabbalah." In *AJS Review* 16 (1991) 161-192.

Toorn, Karel van der, Bob Becking, and Pieter W. van der Horst, eds. *Dictionary of Deities and Demons in the Bible*. Leiden: E. J. Brill, 1995.

Torrance, Robert M. *The Spiritual Quest: Transcendence in Myth, Religion, and Science*. Berkeley: University of California Press, 1994.

Trachtenberg, Joshua. *The Devil and the Jews: The Medieval Conception of the Jew and Its Relation to Modern Antisemitism*. Philadelphia: Jewish Publication Society, 1983.

Trachtenberg, Joshua. *Jewish Magic and Superstition: A Study in Folk Religion*. New York: Atheneum, 1939.

Trachtenberg, Joshua. *The Lost Ten Tribes in Medieval Jewish Literature* by Joshua Trachtenberg. Unpublished Thesis, Hebrew Union College, 1930.

Troup, Johananes. *The Assumption of Moses: A Critical Edition with Commentary*. Leiden: E. J. Brill, 1993.

Tsevat, Matitiahu. "God and the Gods in Assembly: An Interpretation of Psalm 82." In *Hebrew Union College Annual* 40-41 (1969-1970) 123-137.

Turner, Alice K. *The History of Hell*. San Diego: Harcourt Brace, 1993.

Twersky, Isadore and Bernard Septimus, eds. *Jewish Thought in the Seventeenth Century*. Cambridge, MA: Harvard University Press, 1987.

Twersky, Isadore, ed. *A Maimonides Reader*. New York: Behrman House, 1972.

Twersky, Isadore, ed. *Studies in Medieval Jewish History and Literature*. Cambridge, MA: Harvard University Press, 1979.

Ulmer, Rivka. *The Evil Eye in the Bible and in Rabbinic Literature*. Hoboken, NJ: Ktav Publishing House, 1994.

Unterman, Alan. *Dictionary of Jewish Lore and Legend*. London: Thames and Hudson, 1991.

Unterman, Alan, trans. *The Wisdom of the Jewish Mystics*. New York: New Directions, 1976.

VanderKam, James C. *An Introduction to Early Judaism*. Grand Rapids, MI: William B. Eerdmans, 2001.

VanderKam, James C. *The Book of Jubilees*. Sheffield: Sheffield Academic Press, 2001.

VanderKam, James C. *Enoch: A Man for All Generations*. Columbia, SC: University of South Carolina Press, 1995.

VanderKam, James C. "Messianism and Apocalypticism." In *The Encyclopedia of Apocalypticism*. Vol. 1. Ed. John J. Collins. New York: Continuum, 1999, 193-228.

van der Toorn, Karel, Bob Becking and Pieter W. van der Horst, eds. *Dictionary of Deities and Demons in the Bible*. 2d ed. Leiden: E. J. Brill, 1999.

Vermes, Geza, ed. *The Complete Dead Sea Scrolls in English*. New York: Penguin Press, 1997.

Vermes, Geza. "New Light on the Sacrifice of Isaac from 4Q225." In *Journal of Jewish Studies* 47 (1996) 140-146.

Visotzky, Burton L. *The Genesis of Ethics*. New York: Three Rivers Press, 1996.

Wald, Stephen G. *The Doctrine of the Divine Name: An Introduction to Classical Kabbalistic Theology*. Atlanta, GA: Scholars Press, 1988.

Walker, Steven F. *Jung and the Jungians on Myth: An Introduction*. Theorists of Myth, vol. 4. New York: Garland Publishing, 1995.

Weinfeld, Mosche. "The Worship of Molech and of the Queen of Heaven and Its Background." In *Ugarit-Forshungen* 4 (1972) 133-54.

Weinreich, Beatrice S. *Yiddish Folktales*. Trans. By Leonard Wolf. New York: Pantheon, 1988.

Wiesel, Elie. *The Gates of the Forest*. New York: Henry Holt, 1966.

Weiss, Joseph. *Studies in Eastern European Jewish Mysticism*. The Littman Library of Jewish Civilization. Ed. David Goldstein. New York: Oxford University Press, 1985.

Weissler, Chava. "Prayers in Yiddish and the Religious World of Ashkenazic Women." In *Jewish Women in Historical Perspective*. Ed. Judith R. Baskin. Detroit: Wayne State University, 1991, 159-181.

Weissler, Chava. *Voices of the Matriarchs: Listening to the Prayers of Early Modern Jewish Women*. Boston: Beacon Press, 1998.

Weitzman, Steven. "Revisiting Myth and Ritual in Early Judaism." In *Dead Sea Discoveries* 4:1 (1997) 21-54.

Werblowsky, R. J. Zwi. "Jewish Messianism in Comparative Perspective." In *Messiah and Christos: Studies in the Jewish Origins of Christianity*. Ed. Ithamar Gruenwald, Shaul Shaked and Gedaliahu G. Stroumsa. Tubingen: J. C. B. Mohr, 1992, 1-13.

Werblowsky, R. J. Zwi. *Joseph Karo: Lawyer and Mystic*. Philadelphia: Jewish Publication Society, 1977.

Werblowsky, R. J. Zwi and Geoffrey Wigoder, eds. *The Oxford Dictionary of the Jewish Religion*. New York: Oxford University Press, 1997.

Werblowsky, R. J. Zwi. "The Safed Revival and Its Aftermath." In *Jewish Spirituality: From the Bible Through the Middle Ages*. Vol. 2. Ed. Arthur Green. New York: Crossroad, 1994, 7-33.

Werner, Eric. "Traces of Jewish Hagiolatry." In *Hebrew Union College Annual* 51 (1980) 39-60.

Westman, Heinz. *The Structure of Biblical Myths: The Ontogenesis of the Psyche*. Dallas, TX: Spring Publications, 1983.

Widengren, G. *The Ascension of the Apostle and the Heavenly Book*. Uppsala: Lundequist, 1950.

Wiener, Aharon. *The Prophet Elijah in the Development of Judaism*. London: Routledge & Kegan Paul, 1978.

Willensky, Sara O. Heller. "The `First Created Being'" in Early Kabbalah: Philosophical and Isma'ilian Sources." In *Binah: Jewish Intellectual History in the Middle Ages*. Vol. 3. Ed. Joseph Dan. Westport, CT: Praeger, 1994, 65-77.

Wilson, Ian. *Out of the Midst of the Fire: Divine Presence in Deuteronomy*. Atlanta: Scholars Press, 1995.

Wilson, R. McL. "'Jewish Gnosis' and Gnostic Origins: A Survey." In *Hebrew Union College Annual* 45 (1974) 177-189.

Wineman, Aryeh, trans. *Mystic Tales from the Zohar*. Philadelphia: Jewish Publication Society, 1997.

Wineman, Aryeh. "The Dialectic of Tikkun in the Legends of the Ari." In *Prooftexts* 5 (1985) 33-44.

Wineman, Aryeh. "The Metamorphosis of Narrative Traditions: Two Stories from Sixteenth Century Safed." In *AJS Review* 10:2 (1985) 165-180.

Winkler, Gershon. *Dybbuk*. New York: The Judaica Press, 1982.

Winkler, Gershon. *The Golem of Prague*. Brooklyn: Judaica Press, 1980.

Winkler, Gershon. *Magic of the Ordinary: Recovering the Shamanic in Judaism*. Berkeley: North Atlantic Books, 2003.

Winkler, Gershon. *Sacred Secrets: The Sanctity of Sex in Jewish Law and Lore*. Northvale, NJ: Jason Aronson, 1998.

Winston, David. *Logos and Mystical Theology in Philo of Alexandria*. Cincinatti: Hebrew Union College Press, 1985.

Winston, David, trans. *Philo of Alexandria: The Contemplative Life, The Giants, and Selections*. Ramsey, NJ: Paulist Press, 1981.

Wintermute, O. S. *Jubilees*. In *The Old Testament Pseudepigrapha*. Ed. J. Charlesworth. Garden City, NY: Doubleday, 1983-85.

Wiskind-Elper, Ora. *Tradition and Fantasy in the Tales of Reb Nahman of Bratslav*. Albany: State University of New York Press, 1998.

Wolfson, Elliot R. *Along the Path: Studies in Kabbalistic Myth, Symbolism, and Hermeneutics*. Albany: State University of New York Press, 1995.

Wolfson, Elliot R. *Circle in the Square: Studies in the Use of Gender in Kabbalistic Symbolism*. Albany: State University of New York Press, 1995.

Wolfson, Elliot R. "Circumcision, Vision of God, and Textual Interpretation: From Midrashic Trope to Mystical Symbol." In *History of Religions* 27 (1987) 189-215.

Wolfson, Elliot R. "Coronation of the Sabbath Bride: Kabbalistic Myth and the Ritual of Androgynisation." In *Journal of Jewish Thought and Philosophy* 6 (1997) 301-343.

Wolfson, Elliot R. "The Face of Jacob in the Moon: Mystical Transformations of an Aggadic Myth" in *The Seductiveness of Jewish Myth: Challenge or Response?* edited by S. Daniel Breslauer, 235-270. Albany: State University of New York Press, 1997.

Wolfson, Elliot R. "Female Imaging of the Torah: From Literary Metaphor to Religious Symbol." In *From Ancient Israel to Modern Judaism: Intellect in Quest of Understanding*. Vol. 2. Ed. Jacob Neusner, Ernest S. Frerichs, and Nahum M. Sarna. Atlanta: Scholars Press, 1989, 271-307.

Wolfson, Elliot R. "Forms of Visionary Ascent as Ecstatic Experience in the Zoharic Literature." In *Gershom Scholem's "Major Trends in Jewish Mysticism" 50 Years After: Proceedings of the Sixth International Conference on the History of Jewish Mysticism*. Ed. Peter Schäfer and Joseph Dan. Tubingen: J. C. B. Mohr, 1993, 209-235.

Wolfson, Elliot R. "Iconic Visualization and the Imaginal Body of God: The Role of Intention in the Rabbinic Conception of Prayer." In *Modern Theology* 12:2 (1996) 137-162.

Wolfson, Elliot R. "The Image of Jacob Engraved upon the Throne: Further Reflection on the Esoteric Doctrine of the German Pietists." In *Along the Path: Studies in Kabbalistic Myth, Symbolism, and Hermeneutics*. Albany: State University of New York Press, 1995, 1-62.

Wolfson, Elliot R. "Images of God's Feet: Some Observations on the Divine Body of God." In *People of the Body: Jews and Judaism from an Embodied Perspective*. Ed. Howard Eilberg-Schwartz. Albany: State University of New York Press, 1992, 143-181.

Wolfson, Elliot R. "Left Contained in the Right: A Study in Zoharic Hermeneutics." In *American Jewish Studies Review* 11:1 (1986) 27-52.

Wolfson, Elliot R. "Letter Symbolism and *Merkavah* Imagery in the *Zohar*." In *'Alei Shefer: Studies in the Literature of Jewish Thought; Presented to Rabbi Dr. Alexandre Safran*. Ed. Moshe Hallamish. Ramat Gan: Bar-Ilan University Press, 1990, 195-236.

Wolfson, Elliot R. *Lexicon of Jewish Mysticism*. Leiden: E. J. Brill, 1997.

Wolfson, Elliot R. "Light Through Darkness: The Ideal of Human Perfection in the Zohar." In *HTR* 81:1 (1988) 73-95.

Wolfson, Elliot R. "Mystical Rationalization of the Commandments in *Sefer ha-Rimmon*. In *Hebrew Union College Annual* 59 (1988) 217-251.

Wolfson, Elliot R. "The Mystical Significance of Torah Study in German Pietism." In *Jewish Quarterly Review* 84:1 (1993) 43-77.

Wolfson, Elliot R. *Through a Speculum That Shines: Vision and Imagination in Medieval Jewish Mysticism*. Princeton, NJ: Princeton University Press, 1994.

Wolfson, Elliot R. "The Tree that Is All: Jewish-Christian Roots of a Kabbalistic Symbol in Sefer ha-Bahir." In *Journal of Jewish Thought and Philosophy* 3 (1993) 31-76.

Wolfson, Elliot R. "Woman—The Feminine as Other in Theosophic Kabbalah: Some Philosophical Observations on the Divine Androgyne." In *The Other in Jewish Thought and History: Constructions of Jewish Culture and Identity*. Ed. Laurence J. Silberstein and Robert L. Cohn. New York and London: New York University Press, 1994, 166-204.

Wolfson, H. A. "The Pre-existent Angel of the Magharians and Al-Nahawandi." In *Jewish Quarterly Review* 51 (1960-61) 89-106.

Wright, J. Edward. *The Early History of Heaven*. New York: Oxford University Press, 2000.

Wyschogrod, Michael. *The Body of Faith: God and the People of Israel*. Northvale, NJ: Jason Aronson, 1996.

Yamauchi, Edwin M. "Jewish Gnosticism?: The Prologue of John, Mandaean Parallels, and the Trimorphic Protennoia." In *Studies in Gnosticism and Hellenistic Religions: Presented to Gilles Quispel on the Occasion of His 65th Birthday*. Ed. R. van den Broek and M. J. Vermaseren. Leiden: E. J. Brill, 1981.

Yassif, Eli. *The Hebrew Folktale: History, Genre, Meaning*. Trans. Jacqueline S. Teitelbaum. Bloomington: Indiana University Press, 1999.

Yassif, Eli. "The Hebrew Narrative Anthology in the Middle Ages." In *Prooftexts* 17 (1997) 153-175.

Yassif Eli. "Traces of Folk Traditions of the Second Temple Period in Rabbinic Literature." In *Journal of Jewish Studies* 39:2 (1988) 212-233.

Yerushalmi, Yosef Hayim. *From Spanish Court to Italian Ghetto, Isaac Cardoso: A Study in Seventeenth- Century Marranism and Jewish Apologetics*. Seattle: University of Washington Press, 1981.

Yonge, C. D., trans. *The Works of Philo: New Updated Edition*. Peabody, MA: Hendrickson Publishers, 1993.

Zahavy, Zev, ed. *Idra Zuta Kadisha, The Lesser Holy Assembly: Aramaic Text and English Translation*. New York: Sage Books, 1977.

Zaleski, Carol and Philip Zaleski, eds. *The Book of Heaven: An Anthology of Writings from Ancient to Modern Times*. New York: Oxford University Press, 2000.

Zeitlin, Hillel. "Messiah and the Light of the Messiah in Rabbi Nachman's Thought." In *God's Voice from the Void: Old and New Studies in Bratslav Hasidism*. Ed. Shaul Magid, 239-262.

Zimmels, H. J. *Ashkenazim and Sephardim: Their Relations, Differences and Problems as Reflected in the Rabbinical Responsa*. Hoboken, NJ: Ktav Publishing House, 1996.

Zlotowitz, Bernard M. *The Septuagint Translation of the Hebrew Terms in Relation to God in the Book of Jeremiah*. New York: Ktav Publishing House, 1981.

INDEX OF BIBLICAL VERSES

GENERAL INDEX